WAR AND

REMEMBRANCE

a novel by

Herman Wouk

Little, Brown and Company

NEW YORK BOSTON

Back Bay Books / Little, Brown and Company
Time Warner Book Group
1271 Avenue of the Americas, New York, NY 10020
Visit our Web site at www.twbookmark.com

Originally published in hardcover by Little, Brown, October 1978
First Back Bay paperback edition, February 2002

The characters and events in this book are fictitious. Any similarity
to real persons, living or dead, is coincidental and not intended
by the author.

ACKNOWLEDGMENTS

The author is grateful to the following publishers for permission to reprint excerpts from selected
material as noted below: Chappell Music Company for "Hut-Sut Song" by Leo V. Killion, Ted
McMichael, and Jack Owens. Copyright 1941 by Schumann Music Co. Copyright renewed, assigned
to Unichappell Music, Inc. (Belinda Music, publisher). International copyright secured. All rights
reserved. Used by permission; Edward B. Marks Music Corporation and Chappell Music Company
for "Lili Marlene" by Norbert Schultze. All rights for the United States copyright © by Edward B.
Marks Music Corporation. Used by permission. All rights for Canada copyright © by Chappell Music
Co., Inc. International copyright secured. All rights reserved. Used by permission. All rights for the
Philippines reproduced by permission of EMI Music Publishing Ltd. 138–140 Charing Cross Road,
London WC2N OLD; Southern Music Publishing Company, Inc. for "Der Fuehrer's Face" by Oliver
Wallace. Copyright 1942 by Southern Music Publishing Company, Inc. Copyright renewed. Used by
permission; United Artists Music Publishing Group, Inc. and West's Ltd. for "Three O'Clock in the
Morning" by Dorothy Terriss and Julian Robledo. Copyright 1921, 1922, renewed 1949, 1950 by
West's Ltd. All rights for North America administered by Leo Feist, Inc. All rights reserved. Used by
permission. All rights for the Philippines administered by West's Ltd. 138–140 Charing Cross Road,
London WC2N OLD.

LIBRARY OF CONGRESS CATALOGING-IN-PUBLICATION DATA

Wouk, Herman.
    War and remembrance.

    The winds of war, Prologue.
    I. World War, 1939–1945 — Fiction.   I. Title.
PZ3. W923War   [PS3445.098]   813'.5'4   78-17746
ISBN 0-316-95501-9 (hc)/0-316-95499-3 (pb)

10 9 8 7 6 5

Q-MART

PRINTED IN THE UNITED STATES OF AMERICA

In Remembrance

Abraham Isaac Wouk
"Abe"
firstborn son of
Betty Sarah and Herman Wouk
September 2, 1946–July 27, 1951

בלע המות לנצח

He will destroy death forever.

Isaiah 25

WRITE THIS FOR A REMEMBRANCE IN A BOOK . . . THAT THE LORD HAS A WAR WITH AMALEK FROM GENERATION TO GENERATION.

Exodus 17

The Author to the Reader

Little, Brown and Company, the publisher of *The Winds of War* and *War and Remembrance*, has requested a special author's introduction to this new edition of the novels in a changed format. The two books tell one overarching story — how the American people rose to the challenges of World War II, the first global war, after fearsome setbacks forgotten today in the shining memory of final victory.

As I write these words late in October 2001, a new war is just beginning, global again in scope but totally different in character. In the last global war, before VE day and VJ day came, there befell the collapse of France, the Bataan death march, the fall of Singapore, the siege of Stalingrad, bloody Tarawa, and bloodier Guadalcanal; and at the hidden heart of that global war, concealed by the smoke of battle, there burned the Holocaust. That eternal benchmark of barbarism, let us remember, was set not by a Third World country, not by Orientals, not by the Muslims, but by the Germans, an advanced European nation. The evil in human hearts knows no boundary, except the deeper, stronger human will to freedom, order, and justice. In the very long run, that will so far has prevailed.

Now it is the destiny of America — for all its faults and weaknesses, the greatest free society in history — to lead the world against a new grim outbreak of evil, a savage stab at the core of freedom on earth, a dark, shocking start to a new millennium. May the Father of all men prosper our arms in the new fight, as He prospered — in the end — the cause of men of good will in World War II, the great and terrible global battle that these two novels portray.

— Herman Wouk

Preface to the First Edition

War and Remembrance is a historical romance. The subject is World War II, the viewpoint American.

A prologue, *The Winds of War*, published in 1971, set the historical frame for this work by picturing the events leading up to Pearl Harbor. This is a novel of America at war, from Pearl Harbor to Hiroshima.

It is the main tale I had to tell. While I naturally hope that some readers, even in this rushed age, will find the time for both novels, *War and Remembrance* is a story in itself, and can be read without the prologue.

The theme of both novels is single. The last words of Victor Henry's commentary on the Battle of Leyte Gulf give it plainly enough:

"Either war is finished, or we are."

I have put this theme in the colors and motion of the fiction art, so that "he who runs may read," and remember what happened in the worst world catastrophe. As to the history in both tales, I trust that knowing readers will find it has been presented responsibly and with care.

These two linked novels tend to one conclusion: that war is an old habit of thought, an old frame of mind, an old political technique, that must now pass as human sacrifice and human slavery have passed. I have faith that the human spirit will prove equal to the long heavy task of ending war. Against the pessimistic mood of our time, I think that the human spirit — for all its dark side that I here portray — is in essence heroic. The adventures narrated in this romance aim to show that essence in action.

The beginning of the end of War lies in Remembrance.

Washington
23 March 1978
Purim, 5738

Herman Wouk

PART ONE

"Where is Natalie?"

1

A LIBERTY boat full of sleepy hung-over sailors came clanging alongside the U.S.S. *Northampton*, and a stocky captain in dress whites jumped out to the accommodation ladder. The heavy cruiser, its gray hull and long guns dusted pink by the rising sun, swung to a buoy in Pearl Harbor on the incoming tide. As the boat thrummed off toward the destroyer nests in West Loch, the captain trotted up the steep ladder and saluted the colors and the quarterdeck.

"I request permission to come aboard."

"Permission granted, sir."

"My name is Victor Henry."

The OOD's eyes rounded. In his starched whites with lacquered gold buttons and his white gloves, with the ritual long glass tucked under an arm, this fresh-faced ensign was stiff enough, but he stiffened more. "Oh! Yes, *sir*. I'll notify Captain Hickman, sir — messenger!"

"Don't disturb him yet. He isn't expecting me. I'll just mosey around topside for a bit."

"Sir, I know he's awake."

"Very well."

Henry walked forward on a forecastle already astir with working parties in dungarees, who were dodging the hose-down by barefoot deckhands. The iron deck underfoot felt good. The pungent harbor breeze smelled good. This was Pug Henry's world, the clean square world of big warships, powerful machinery, brisk young sailors, heavy guns, and the sea. After long exile, he was home. But his pleasure dimmed at the tragic sight off the starboard bow. Bulging out of the black oil coating the harbor waters, the streaked red underside of the capsized *Utah* proclaimed the shame of the whole Pacific Fleet in one obscene symbol. Out of view in the shambles of Battleship Row, the ship he had come to Hawaii to command, the U.S.S. *California*, sat on the mud under water to its guns, still wisping smoke ten days after the catastrophe.

The *Northampton* was no *California*; a treaty cruiser almost as long, six hundred feet, but with half the beam, a quarter the tonnage, smaller main battery, and light hull far too vulnerable to torpedoes. Yet after his protracted shore duty it looked decidedly big to Captain Henry. Standing by the flapping blue jack and the anchor chain, glancing back at the turrets and the tripod mast, with bridge upon bridge jutting up into the sunlight, he had a qualm of self-doubt. This ship was many times as massive as a destroyer, his last command. Battleship command had been a dream; getting the *California* had never seemed quite real, and after all, it had been snatched from him by disaster. He had served in heavy cruisers, but command was something else.

The roly-poly gangway messenger, who looked about thirteen, trotted up and saluted. Altogether the crew appeared peculiarly young. Pug had at first glance taken for junior lieutenants a couple of young men sporting the gilt collar leaves of lieutenant commanders. Surely they had not served the grinding fifteen years that two and a half stripes had cost him! Fast advancement was a sugar-coating of wartime.

"Captain Henry, sir, Captain Hickman presents his compliments, sir. He's taking a shower, is all. He says there's mail for you in his quarters, forwarded from the *California*'s shore office. He invites you for breakfast, sir, and please to follow me."

"What's your name and rating?"

"Tilton, sir! Cox'un's mate third, sir!" Crisp eager responses to the incoming captain.

"How old are you, Tilton?"

"Twenty, sir."

Ravages of age; everybody else starting to seem too damned young.

The captain's quarters enjoyed the monarchical touch of a Filipino steward: snowy white coat, round olive face, dark eyes, thick black hair. "I'm Alemon, sir." The smiling astute glance and dignified head bob, as he handed Captain Henry the letters, showed pride of place more than subservience. "Captain Hickman will be right out. Coffee, sir? Orange juice?"

The spacious outer cabin, the steward, the handsome blue leather furnishings, the kingly desk, elated Pug Henry. Capital ship command would soon be his, and these perquisites tickled his vanity. He couldn't help it. A long, long climb! Many new burdens and no more money, he told himself, glancing at the batch of official envelopes. Among them was a letter from Rhoda. The sight of his wife's handwriting, once such a joy, punctured his moment of pride, as the overturned *Utah* had gloomed his pleasure at walking a deck again. In a wave of desolate sickness, he ripped open the pink envelope and read the letter, sipping coffee served on a silver tray with a Navy-monogrammed silver creamer.

December 7th

Pug darling —

I just this minute sent off my cable to you, taking back that *idiotic* letter. The radio's still jabbering the horrible news about Pearl Harbor. Never in my *life* have I been more at sixes and sevens. Those horrible little yellow monkeys!

I know we'll blow them off the face of the earth, but meanwhile I have one son in a submarine, and another in a dive-bomber, and you're God knows where at this point. I just pray the *California* wasn't hit. And to cap it all I wrote you that perfectly *ghastly, unforgivable* letter six short days ago! I would give the world to get that letter back unread. Why did I ever write it? My head was off in some silly cloudland.

I am *not* demanding a divorce anymore, not if you really still want me after my scatterbrained conduct. Whatever you do, don't blame or hate Palmer Kirby. He's a very decent sort, as I think you know.

Pug, I've been so damned lonesome, and — I don't know, maybe I'm going through the change or something — but I've been having the *wildest* shifts of moods for months, up and down and up and down again. I've been very unstable. I really think I'm not quite well. Now I feel like a criminal awaiting sentence, and I don't expect to get much sleep until your next letter arrives.

One thing is true, I love you and I've never stopped loving you. That's something to go on, isn't it? I'm *utterly* confused. I just can't write any more until I hear from you.

Except — Natalie's mother telephoned me not half an hour ago, all frantic. Strange that we've never met or spoken before! She hasn't heard from her daughter in weeks. The last word was that Natalie and the baby were flying back from Rome on the 15th. Now what? The schedules must be all disrupted, and suppose we go to war with Germany and Italy? Byron must be wild with worry. I have never held it against him, I mean, marrying a Jewish girl, but the dangers, the complications, are all so magnified! Let's pray she gets out, one way or another.

Mrs. Jastrow sounds perfectly pleasant, no foreign accent or anything, except that she's so *obviously* a New Yorker! If you get news of Natalie, do send the poor woman a telegram, it'll be a kindness.

Oh, Pug, we've plunged into the war, after all! Our whole world is coming apart. You're a rock. I'm not. Try to forgive me, and maybe we can still pick up the pieces.

> All my love
> Rho

Not a reassuring letter, he thought, if wholly Rhoda-like. The passage about his daughter-in-law deepened Pug's sickness of heart. He had been burying awareness of her plight from his mind, laden with his own calamities and, as he thought, helpless to do anything about her. He was in a world crash, and in a private crash. He could only take things day by day as they came.

"Well! Is Alemon treating you right? Welcome aboard!" A tall officer with thick straight blond hair, a froglike pouch under his chin, and a belly strained into two bulges by his belt burst from the inner cabin, buttoning a beautifully ironed khaki shirt. They shook hands. "Ready for some chow?"

Alemon's breakfast, served on white linen with gleaming cutlery, was better than anything Victor Henry had eaten in months: half a fresh pineapple, hot rolls, steaming coffee, and a rich egg dish with ham, spinach, and melted cheese. Pug said, by way of breaking the ice, that he had short-circuited protocol and come aboard this way because he had heard the *Northampton* might be leaving soon with a carrier task force to relieve Wake Island. If Hickman wanted the change of command before the ship left, he was at his service.

"Christ, yes. I'm mighty glad you've showed up. I hate to go ashore with a war starting, but I've been putting off minor surgery and I'm overdue for relief." Hickman's big genial face settled into lines of misery. "And to be frank, Henry, I have wife trouble back home. It just happened in October. Some deskbound Army son of a bitch in Washington —" the thick shoulders sagged in misery. "Oh, hell. After twenty-nine years, and her a grandmother three times over! But Ruth is still gorgeous, you know? I swear, Ruth has got the figure of a chorus girl. And left to herself half the time — well, that's been the problem right along. You know how that is."

So often, Pug thought, he had heard such plaints before; the commonest of Navy misfortunes, yet not till it had struck him had he remotely imagined the searing pain of it. How could Hickman, or any man, discuss it so freely? He himself could not force words about it from his throat; not to a minister, not to a psychiatrist, not to God in prayer, let alone to a stranger. He was grateful when Hickman turned prominent eyes at him, ruefully grinned, and said, "Well, the hell with that. I understand you've had duty in Berlin and in Moscow, eh? Damned unusual."

"I went to Moscow with the first Lend-Lease mission. That was a short special assignment. I did serve in Berlin as naval attaché."

"Must have been fascinating, what with all hell breaking loose over there."

"I'll take the *Northampton*."

At Victor Henry's harsh tone of disenchantment with his years ashore, Hickman cannily winked. "Well, if I do say so, Henry, she's a good ship with a smart crew. Except this big fleet expansion's bleeding us white. We're running a goddamn training ship here these days." Hickman pulled the ringing telephone from its bracket on the bulkhead. "Christ, Halsey's barge is coming alongside." Gulping coffee, he rose, put on his gold-crusted cap, and snatched a black tie.

Pug was astonished. The *Northampton* was the flagship of Rear Admiral Spruance, who commanded Halsey's screening vessels. It was Spruance's place to call on Halsey, not the other way around. Straightening the tie and cap, Hickman said, "Make yourself at home. Finish your breakfast. We can get started on the relief this morning. My chief yeoman's got the logs and other records all lined up, and luckily we just did a Title B inventory. The registered pubs are up-to-date and the transfer report is ready. You can sight the books anytime."

"Does Halsey come aboard often?"

"First time ever." His eyes popping, Hickman handed Pug a clipboard of messages. "Something's afoot, all right. You might want to look over these dispatches. There's a long intercept from Wake."

Through the porthole Pug could hear Halsey piped aboard. As he glanced through the flimsy sheets, his pain over Rhoda faded. The mere look and feel of fleet communications, the charge of war electricity in the carbon-blurred dispatches, stirred life in him. Hickman soon came back. "It was the Old Man, all right. He looks madder than hell about something. Let's go to the ship's office."

Impeccable inventories, account books, and engineering records were spread for Victor Henry's inspection by young yeomen in spotless whites, under the glaring eye of a grizzled chief. The two captains were deep in the records when the flag lieutenant telephoned. The presence of Captain Victor Henry, he said, was desired in Admiral Spruance's quarters. Hickman looked nonplussed, relaying this to his visitor. "Shall I take you there, Henry?"

"I know the way."

"Any idea what it's about?"

"Not the foggiest."

Hickman scratched his head. "Do you know Spruance?"

"Slightly, from the War College."

"Think you can relieve me before we sortie? We're on seventy-two hours' notice."

"I intend to."

"Splendid." Hickman clasped his hand. "We've got to talk some about the ship's stability. There are problems."

"Hello, Pug," Halsey said.

It was the old tough wily look from under thick eyebrows; but the brows were gray, the eyes sunken. This was not Billy Halsey, the feisty skipper of the destroyer *Chauncey*. This was Vice Admiral William F. Halsey, ComAir-BatForPac, with three silver stars on his collar pin. Halsey's stomach sagged, his once-thick brown hair was a gray straggle, his face was flecked and creased with age. But the square-set jaw, the thin wide crafty smile, the curving way he stuck out his hand, the hard grip, were the same. "How's that pretty wife of yours?"

"Thank you, Admiral. Rhoda's fine."

Halsey turned to Raymond Spruance, who stood beside him, hands on hips, studying a Pacific chart on the desk. Spruance was a little younger, but far less marked by time, possibly because of his austere habits. His color was fresh, his skin clear, his plentiful hair only touched with gray; he seemed not to have changed at all since Pug's tour under him at the War College. It was a Halsey byword that he wouldn't trust a man who didn't drink or smoke. Spruance did neither, but they were old fast friends. In Halsey's destroyer division, during Pug's first duty at sea, Spruance had been a junior skipper.

"You know, Ray, this rascal had the sassiest bride of any ensign in the old division." As Halsey chain-lit a cigarette, his hand slightly trembled. "Ever meet her?"

Spruance shook his head, the large eyes serious and remote. "Captain Henry, you worked on the Wake Island battle problem at the College, didn't you?"

"I did, sir."

"Come to think of it, Ray, why were you running a Wake problem in thirty-six?" said Halsey. "Wake was nothing but scrub and booby birds then."

Spruance looked to Victor Henry, who spoke up, "Admiral, the purpose was to test tactical doctrine in a problem involving Orange dominated waters, very long distances, and enemy land-based air."

"Sound familiar?" Spruance said to Halsey.

"Oh, hell, what does a game-board exercise away back then prove?"

"Same distances. Same ship and aircraft performance characteristics."

"Same doctrines, too — like *seek out enemy and destroy him.*" Halsey's jaw jutted. Pug knew that look well. "Have you heard the joke that's going around in Australia? They're saying that pretty soon the two yellow races may really come to blows in the Pacific — the Japanese and the Americans."

"Not a bad quip." Spruance gestured with dividers at the chart. "But it's over two thousand miles to Wake, Bill. Let's even say we sortie tomorrow, which isn't very feasible, but —"

"Let me interrupt you right there. If we have to, we will!"

"Even so, look at what happens."

The two admirals bent over the chart. The operation to relieve Wake Island, Pug quickly gathered, was on. The aircraft carriers *Lexington* and *Saratoga* with their support ships were already steaming westward, one to knock out the land-based air in the Marshalls south of Wake, the other to deliver reinforcements to the Marines, and attack any Japanese sea forces it encountered. But Halsey's *Enterprise* was being ordered to a station less than halfway to Wake, where it could cover the Hawaiian Islands. He wanted to go all the way. He was arguing that the Jap fleet would not dare another sneak attack on Hawaii, with the Army Air Corps on combat alert; that carriers operating together vastly increased their punch; and that if the

Japs did try an end run for Hawaii, he could double back and intercept them in time.

The 1936 game-board exercise, Pug realized, had been prophetic. In the game, the Marines had been beleaguered on Wake after a sneak Japanese attack on Manila. The Pacific Fleet had sailed to relieve them and bring the Jap main body to action. The mission had failed. "Orange" air had clobbered "Blue" into turning back. "Blue" carrier attacks had not knocked out the enemy's island airfields, the umpires had ruled, due to bad weather, pilot inexperience, and unexpected Jap strength in AA and aircraft.

Spruance ticked off distances, times, and hazards until Halsey exploded, "Jesus Christ and General Jackson, Ray, I know all that. I want some arguments to throw at Cincpac so I can shake myself loose!"

Dropping the dividers on the chart, Spruance shrugged. "I suspect the whole operation may be cancelled."

"Cancelled, hell! Why? Those marines are holding out splendidly!"

His sympathies all with Halsey, Pug Henry put in that while flying from Manila to Hawaii on the Pan Am Clipper, he had been under bombardment at Wake Island.

"Hey? What's that? You were there?" Halsey turned angrily glinting eyes on him. "What did you see? How are their chances?"

Pug described the Marine defenses, and said he thought they could resist for weeks. He mentioned the letter he had brought from the Marine commander to Cincpac, and quoted the colonel's parting words in the coral dugout: *"We'll probably end up eating fish and rice behind barbed wire anyway, but at least we can make the bastards work to take the place."*

"You hear *that,* Ray?" Halsey struck the desk with a bony gray-haired fist. "And you don't think we're honor bound to reinforce and support them? Why, the papers back home are full of nothing but the heroes on Wake. *'Send us more Japs!'* I've never heard anything more inspiring."

"I rather doubt that message ever came from Wake. Newspaper stuff," said Spruance. "Henry, were you stationed in Manila?"

"I was coming via Manila, Admiral, from the Soviet Union. I was naval adviser on the Lend-Lease mission."

"What? Rooshia?" Halsey gave Victor Henry a jocular prod with two fingers. "Say, that's right! I've heard about you, Pug. Hobnobbing with the President and I don't know who all! Why, old Moose Benton told me you went for a joyride over Berlin in a Limey bomber. Hey? Did you really do that?"

"Admiral, I was an observer. Mostly I observed how frightened I could get."

Halsey rubbed his chin, looking roguish. "You're aboard to relieve Sam Hickman, aren't you?"

"Yes, Admiral."

"Like to come with me and handle operations instead?"

Victor Henry sparred. "I've got my orders, Admiral."

"They can be modified."

Pug knew this man well enough from the destroyer days. Lieutenant Commander Halsey had given him his first "outstanding" fitness report for duty at sea. Once Bill Halsey went charging into a fleet action — he was bound to do that sooner or later, he had always been hot for fame and a fight — his operations officer might decide the course of a big battle, for Halsey leaned heavily on subordinates. It was a temptation of a sort; much more so than the Cincpac staff assignment Pug had dodged.

But Victor Henry was tired of being a flunky to mighty men, tired of anonymous responsibility for major problems. The *Northampton* meant a return to the old straight career ladder: sea duty, shore interludes, more sea duty; and at last battle-line command, and the bright hope of flag rank. The *Northampton* was that all-important last rung of major sea command. He would be firing eight-inch guns in battle. He was a gunnery man to the bone.

Yet rejecting Vice Admiral Halsey to his face was an unhealthy undertaking. Pug was hesitating, wondering how to handle this, when Raymond Spruance, leaning over the chart with the dividers, remarked, "Bill, isn't that a three-striper slot?"

Halsey turned on him. "It damned well shouldn't be. Not the way operations are expanding! I can get that changed mighty fast."

With Spruance's casual words, Pug Henry was off the hook. He did not even have to speak. Halsey gave Pug a calculating glance and picked up his cap. "Well, I'm going back to Cincpac, Ray, and I mean to win this argument. Stand by to get under way tomorrow. Good seeing you, Pug. You've kept very well." Out swept the gnarled hand. "Still play tennis?"

"Every chance I get, Admiral."

"And read your Bible every morning, and Shakespeare at night?"

"Well, sort of. At least I still try."

"You clean-living types depress me."

"Well, I smoke and drink like anything now."

"Honor bright?" Halsey grinned. "That's progress."

Spruance said, "I'm going ashore, Bill."

"Well, come along. How about you, Pug? Like a ride to the beach?"

"Yes, thank you, Admiral, if I may."

At the quarterdeck, he gave the OOD a message for Hickman, then descended the ladder to the sumptuous black barge, and sat apart from the admirals. The boat cruised like a ferry through the malodorous oil and flotsam that since the Jap attack was fouling the harbor. On the fleet landing stood a gray Navy Chevrolet with three-star flags fluttering on the front fenders. A stiff marine in dress uniform opened the door. "Well, gentlemen," said Halsey, "can I give anybody a lift?"

Spruance shook his head.

"Thank you, Admiral," Victor Henry said. "I'm going up to my son's house."

"Where does your son live?" Admiral Spruance asked as the Chevrolet drove off.

"Up in the hills over Pearl City, sir."

"Shall we walk it?"

"It's five miles, Admiral."

"Are you pressed for time?"

"Well, no, sir."

Spruance strode off through the clangorous Navy Yard. After a week of heavy drinking to blot out night thoughts of Rhoda, Pug had trouble keeping up with him. They began climbing an asphalt road through green hills. Though Spruance's khaki shirt blackened with sweat his pace did not slow. He did not speak, but it was not for lack of wind. Pug was embarrassed by his own puffing compared to the even deep breaths of the older man. Rounding a turn of the uphill road, they looked out on a broad panorama of the base: docks, cranes, nests of destroyers and of submarines — and the terrible smashed half-sunk battleships, burned-out aircraft, and blackened skeletal hangars.

Spruance spoke. "Good view."

"Too good, Admiral." The admiral's face turned. The big sober eyes flashed agreement. "I planned to spend the day aboard the *Northampton,* sir," Pug panted, now that they were talking, "but when Admiral Halsey thinks of getting under way tomorrow, I figure I better fetch my gear."

"Well, I doubt the urgency exists." Spruance patted a folded white handkerchief on his wet brow.

Wake Island's remote exposed location and the Navy's present weakness, he said, all but precluded a fight. Admiral Kimmel, no doubt wanting to recover face after December 7th, had ordered the rescue just before the President had fired him. But the Fleet was awaiting a new Cincpac, and its temporary commander, Vice Admiral Pye, was having second thoughts. Abandoning the relief mission would cause great controversy, and there were good arguments on both sides, but Spruance suspected that these marines, like the phantoms in the War College exercise, were fated to spend the war in prison camps.

Talking in a calm War College vein, marching at a pace that made Victor Henry's heart gallop, Spruance said that December 7th had changed the Pacific balance of forces. The United States had been half-disarmed. The odds were now ten or eleven carriers to three, ten combat-ready battleships to none, and nobody knew where those heavy enemy forces were. The Japanese had shown prime combat and logistical ability. They had unveiled ships, planes, and fighting men as good as any on earth. The Philippines, Southeast Asia, and the East Indies might be theirs for the taking, stretched thin as the British were. Right now the Navy could do little but hit-and-run raids to gain battle skill and keep the Japanese off balance. But it had to hold a line from Hawaii to Australia at all costs, through the arc of islands outside Japanese aircraft range. New carriers and battleships would in time join the fleet. Jumping off from Hawaii and Australia, they would start battering back Japan from the east and the south. But that was a year or more away. Meantime Australia had to be held, for it was a white man's continent. Its overrunning by nonwhites might trigger a world revolution that could sweep away civilization. With this arresting remark Raymond Spruance fell silent.

They trudged uphill through tall sweet-smelling green walls of sugarcane under an ever-hotter sun, amid peaceful bird song.

"Pessimistic picture, Admiral," Victor Henry ventured.

"Not necessarily. I don't think Japan can cut the mustard. Weak industrial base, not enough supplies for a long struggle. She'll have a hot run for a while, but we'll win the war if the spirit at home holds up. We've got a strong President, so it ought to. But our country's in a two-front war, and the German front is the decisive one, so we're second in line out here. And we've started with a big defeat. Therefore the realities are against any early heroics in the Pacific, such as an all-out battle to relieve Wake."

Set back from the road amid lawns and gardens, its verandas roomy and sprawling, Warren's home looked more suited to an admiral than to a naval aviator. Spruance said when they halted, pouring sweat, "Your son lives here?"

"His father-in-law bought it for them. She's an only child. He's Senator Lacouture of Florida. Actually, it's not that large inside."

Patting his red face with a handkerchief, Spruance said, "Senator Lacouture! I see. Rather changed his mind about the war, hasn't he?"

"Admiral, a lot of good people honestly thought we ought to stay out of it."

Lacouture had been a leading and noisy isolationist until the eighth of December.

"To be sure."

Spruance declined to come in and rest. He asked for a glass of water, and drank it in the doorway. Handing back the glass, he said, "So, you'll be bringing your gear aboard today?"

"Yes, sir. I'd better expedite the change of command," Pug said, "all things considered."

Amusement brightened Spruance's grave eyes. "Oh, yes. Always execute orders promptly." Neither of them had to mention Halsey's notion of recruiting Pug for his staff. "Join me for dinner, then. I'd like to hear about your flight over Berlin."

"I'll be honored, Admiral."

Janice crouched in a broad brown dug-up patch of the back lawn, wearing a damp lilac halter, soiled gray shorts, and sandals. Her wheat-colored hair was tumbled, and her long bare legs and arms were burned brown. Because of the special controls being imposed on Japanese truck farmers, fresh vegetables were already becoming scarce. She had started a victory garden and seemed the merrier for it.

She straightened up, laughing, wiping her brow with an arm. "My stars, look at you! Been gardening or something?"

"Admiral Spruance walked me up from the Navy Yard."

"Oh, *him!* I hear that all the junior officers hide when he comes on deck. Commanding the *Northampton* will put you in shape, if it doesn't kill you. Warren telephoned. He's coming home for lunch."

"Good. He can run me down to the fleet landing with my gear."

"You're going already?" Her smile faded. "We'll miss you."

"Dad?" Warren's voice sounded some time later through the bedroom door. Pug opened it, pushing aside two half-packed footlockers. Uniforms and books were piled on the bed. "Hi. I stopped by the *California* shore office. They're sending your mail to the *Northampton*, but these just came in."

The sight of British stamps jolted Pug. Alistair Tudsbury's office address was on the envelope. First he opened the cable, and without a word passed it to Warren.

> WHERE IS NATALIE URGE REPEAT URGE YOU INQUIRE STATE DEPARTMENT
> CABLE ME DEVILFISH SUB BASE MARIVELES   BYRON

Warren wrinkled his sunburned forehead over the cable. In his flying suit, the everlasting cigarette dangling from his compressed mouth, he looked weary and grim. "Who do you know at State, Dad?"

"Well, a few people."

"Why don't you try phoning? Briny's pretty cut off out there in Manila."

"I will. I should have done it sooner."

Warren shook his head. "She may be in one hell of a fix." He gestured at the letter from London. "Alistair Tudsbury. Is that the British broadcaster?"

"That's him. Your mother and I met him on the boat to Germany."

"Great gift of gab. Lunch in half an hour, Dad."

Pug opened the letter after Warren went out. On arriving in Pearl Harbor, he had sadly mailed off a short dry letter to Pamela Tudsbury, finally breaking with her. She could not have received it and answered; the letters had crossed. In fact, he saw, hers was dated a month ago.

November 17th, 1941

My love:

I hope this will somehow reach you. There's news. The BBC has asked my father to make a sort of Phileas Fogg broadcasting tour clear around this tortured planet, touching the main military bases: Alexandria, Ceylon, Singapore, Australia, Pearl Harbor, the Panama Canal, and so on. Theme: the sun never sets on the Union Jack, and there's another possible foe besides Hitler — to wit, Japan — and the English-speaking peoples (including the reluctant Americans) must stand to their guns. Talky has stipulated that I go along again. More and more nowadays when he's fatigued or under the weather — his eyes are getting very bad — daughter writes up the broadcasts and even the articles. By now the product, though ersatz, is usable.

When he broached the thing to me, I heard only two words — *Pearl Harbor!* If the whole proposal doesn't blow up, and if we can maintain our dicey plane-and-boat schedule, we should reach Hawaii in a month or so. Where you will be with your blessed *California,* I don't know, but I'll find you.

Well, there you have it! I know you were supposed to write to me before I broke silence. Sorry I violated your rule, but for all I know your letter or cable will come next week and I'll be gone. Perhaps there's a screed for me already in the mail from Vladivostok, or Tokyo, or Manila. If so, I hope it was a love letter, not a prudent dismissal, which was what I feared and expected. Whatever it was, Pug, I never got it.

Dearest, you can love your wife and also love me. Do I shock you? Well, the fact is you already do. You know you do. You've even told me so. You have only to act realistically about it. To be blunt, it's just as possible for your wife to love you, and also love another man. Maybe that shocks you even more. But this sort of thing happens all the time, my sweet, I swear it does, especially in wartime, to perfectly good and decent people. You and Mrs. Henry have somehow spent a quarter of a century shut off in a very special church-and-Navy shell. Oh, dear! I haven't time to type this over, or I'd cut this last stupid paragraph. I know it's hopeless to argue.

I hate to stop writing to you now that I'm doing it at last. It's like the breaking of a dam. But I must stop. With any luck you won't hear from me again, you'll see me.

The weather in London is unspeakable, and so is the war news. It really looks as though we got out of Moscow none too soon; it actually may fall, as it did to Napoleon! What a prospect! But for me, to be quite honest, the only news that counts — and it's glorious — is that suddenly there's a chance to see you again. I had a horrible feeling in Moscow, for all your kindness and sweetness, that I was looking my last on you. Now (crossed fingers) here I come!

Love,
Pam

He could see the young face, hear the young warm elegantly accented voice pouring out these hurried words. The wistful, hopeless little romance with Tudsbury's daughter which had briefly flared in Moscow was best snuffed out. Pug knew that. He had tried. Moreover, until now he thought he had succeeded. The residue of the strange frail wartime relationship — a little more than a flirtation, pathetically less than an affair — had been a better understanding of what had happened to Rhoda, and a long start on forgiving her. He only wanted his wife back. He had already written her that in strong terms. There was no conceivable future with this young woman, twenty-nine or thirty, drifting in her celebrated father's wake.

Best snuffed out; yet his mind raced through calculations of where they might be now. Could they have made it to Singapore before December 7th? Tudsbury was a hard-driving traveller, a human bulldozer. If he could hitch rides on warships or bombers, he would keep going. Supposing by a freak the Tudsburys did show up in Honolulu? What a rich irony Pam's unwitting defense of Rhoda was! Pug tore up the letter.

Eating lunch on the back porch, Warren and Janice looked at each other as Pug came out humming in his blue service uniform.

"We're mighty formal," said Janice.

"Crease the uniform less if I walk it aboard."

"Mighty cheerful," remarked Warren.

"Prospect of sea pay." Pug dropped in a chair at the iron-and-glass table. He consumed a large plateful of the very savory stew, asking for more onions and potatoes; more food than they had seen him put away at midday since his arrival in Pearl Harbor.

"Mighty good appetite," observed Warren, watching his father eat. He and Janice knew nothing of Rhoda's divorce letter; they had ascribed Pug's boozing and his depression, which now seemed to be lifting, to his loss of the *California*.

"Admiral Spruance hustled me five miles uphill."

"Dad, Jan has an idea about Natalie."

"Yes, why don't you just call or cable my father?" Pug shot a sharp glance at his daughter-in-law. "He'll get some quick action from the State Department, if anyone can."

"Hm! What time is it in Washington? Is he there now?"

"There's five hours' difference. He's probably just leaving his Senate office. Try him at home a little later."

"That's a good notion, Janice."

When Warren helped Pug carry out the footlockers, Janice was bathing the baby. Little Victor was gurgling and splashing at her; she was a flushed, happy, sexy young wife, unabashed at the show of her breasts through the soaked halter. Recollection flashed upon Pug of Rhoda bathing Warren in just this way, in their bungalow on the San Diego base. A quarter of a century and more, gone like a breath! And an infant the image of this one had metamorphosed into the tall hard-faced young man in the flying suit, smiling down at his own baby son. Pug shook off an awed sad sense of passing time, made a joke about having drunk all of Janice's liquor, and kissed her wet smooth cheek.

"Come back whenever you're in port, Dad. Your room will be ready, and the bar will be stocked."

He held up a flat palm. "I'm back on the wagon while I've got a sea command."

Warren drove the pool jeep downhill with one hand. Cigarette bobbing in his mouth, he said after a silence, "Is the *Enterprise* going all the way to Wake Island, Dad?"

"What makes you think so?"

"You're in a big hurry to take over the screen flagship."

"And you're spoiling for a fight, are you?"

"I didn't say that." Warren looked sidelong at him through cigarette smoke. "I have my doubts about barrelling off with our last flattop. I don't trust the Army Air Corps all that much to protect this base, and my wife and kid. Well? Not talking?"

"I just don't know, Warren."

"It's all over the *Enterprise* that Halsey's screaming bloody murder up at Cincpac so we can get to go."

"Could be. How are your new pilots checking out?"

"Dad, they're green. *Green.* They haven't put in the hours. The squadron needs them, so they'll break their necks on the barriers, or drown, or learn. While we're in port, I'll drill the ass off them."

"You're an instructor now? That happened fast."

"My CO gave me the detail. I didn't argue. He's recommended me for instructor duty in the States, too, but I'm yelling plenty about *that*. This is no time to leave the Pacific."

Warren dropped his father at the telephone exchange, saying he would take the footlockers to the fleet landing. Their parting was almost as casual as if they expected to dine together, but they shook hands, which they seldom did, and stared for a moment in each other's eyes, smiling.

The small smoky telephone exchange was crowded with waiting sailors and officers. The chief operator, a buxom lady of forty or so with a heavy Southern accent, brightened when Pug mentioned Lacouture. "Now *thah*'s a great man! If he'd been President, we wouldn't be in this mess, would we, Captain? Ah'll do mah best to put you through."

Within a half hour Senator Lacouture was on the line, in his Georgetown home. Astounded to hear from Pug, quickly grasping the situation, he put a few terse questions. "Right. Right. Okay. Got it. I remember her from the wedding party. Maiden name again? Right. Jastrow, like that famous uncle of hers. Natalie Jastrow Henry. Dark girl, very pretty, quick tongue. Being Jewish may create problems. Still, Italy isn't bad in that regard, and travelling with a famous writer ought to be a help. Why, even I've heard of Aaron Jastrow!" Lacouture hoarsely chuckled. "She's probably all right, but it's best to be sure. How do I get back to you?"

"Just call Captain Dudley Brown at BuPers, Senator. He'll put the word on a Navy circuit. Make Byron an addressee on the *Devilfish*."

"Got that. And you're commanding the *California*, right?"

"The *Northampton*, CA–26, Senator."

A pause. "What happened to the *California*?"

Pug paused too. "I'm commanding the *Northampton*."

The senator, low and grave: "Pug, can we handle them out there?"

"It'll be a long pull."

"Say, I may resign from the Senate and go into uniform. What do you think? The Army's getting gouged on lumber and paper. I can save the war effort several million a year. They've offered me colonel, but I'm holding out for brigadier general."

"I certainly hope you get it."

"Well, give my love to the kids. You'll hear from me about the Jewish girl."

After twenty-four hours, Victor Henry felt as though he had been aboard the *Northampton* a week. He had visited the ship's spaces from the bilges to the gun directors, met the officers, watched the crew at work, inspected the engine rooms, fire rooms, magazines, and turrets, and talked at length with the executive officer, Jim Grigg; a laconic bullet-headed commander from Idaho, with the dark-ringed eyes, weary pallor, and faint air of desperation appropriate to a perfectionist exec. Pug saw no reason not to relieve Hickman straight off. Grigg was running the ship. Any fool could take it over; his incompetence would be shielded. Pug didn't consider himself a fool, only rusty and nervous.

He relieved the next day, in a ceremony pared of peacetime pomp and flourish. The officers and crew, their white sunlit uniforms flapping in a warm breeze, lined up in facing ranks aft of the number three turret. Standing apart with Hickman and Grigg, Victor Henry read at a microphone his orders to assume command. As his eyes lifted from the fluttering dispatch, he could see beyond the ranks of the crew the oil-streaked crimson bottom of the *Utah*.

Turning to Hickman, he saluted. "I relieve you, sir."

"Very well, sir."

That was all. Victor Henry was captain. "Commander Grigg, all ship's standing orders remain in force. Dismiss the crew from quarters."

"Aye aye, sir." Grigg saluted like a marine sergeant, wheeled, and gave the order. The ranks broke. Pug saw his predecessor piped over the side. Hickman was acting as though it were his birthday. A new letter from his wife, hinting that all might not be lost, had made him impatient as a boy to get back to her. He ran down the ladder to the gig without a backward glance.

All afternoon Pug read dispatches and ship's documents piled on his desk by Commander Grigg. Alemon served him in lone majesty a dinner of turtle soup, filet mignon, salad, and ice cream. A marine messenger brought him a handwritten note as he was drinking coffee in an armchair. The envelope and the sheet inside were stamped with two blue stars. The handwriting was upright, clear, and plain:

Dec. 19, 1941

Captain Henry,
    Glad you've taken over. We sortie tomorrow. You'll have the operation order by midnight. The new Cincpac will be Nimitz. The relief of Wake is looking more dubious. Good luck and good hunting —

R. A. Spruance

Next morning, in calm sunny weather, the cruiser got under way. The deck force unmoored with veteran ease. On the swing of the tide the bow was pointed down-channel. With assumed calm that seemed to deceive the bridge personnel, Victor Henry said, "All ahead one third." The quartermaster rang up the order on the engine room telegraph. The deck vibrated — an inexpressibly heartwarming sensation for Pug — and the *Northampton* moved out to war under its new captain. He had not yet heard from Senator Lacouture about Natalie Jastrow Henry.

2

SHE was embarked in a very different vessel, a rusty, patch-painted, roach-ridden Turkish coastal tramp called the *Redeemer*, undergoing repairs alongside a pier in Naples harbor; supposedly bound for Turkey, actually for Palestine. In the stormy week since she had come aboard, the old tub had yet to move. It listed by the stone wharf, straining at its lines with the rise and fall of the tide, wallowing when waves rolled in past the mole.

On the narrow afterdeck, under a flapping crimson flag with badly soiled yellow star and crescent, Natalie sat with her baby. For once the sky had cleared, and she had brought him out into the afternoon sunshine. Bearded men and shawled women gathered around, admiring. There were some thin, sad-eyed children aboard the *Redeemer,* but Louis was the only babe in arms. Perched on her lap, he looked about with lively blue eyes that blinked in the chilly wind.

"Why, it's the Adoration," said Aaron Jastrow, his breath smoking. "The Adoration, to the life. And Louis makes an enchanting Christ child."

Natalie muttered, "I'm one hell of a miscast Madonna."

"Miscast? Hardly, my dear." Wrapped in his dark blue travelling cloak, gray hat pulled low on his head, Jastrow calmly stroked his neat beard. "Typecast, I'd say, for face, figure, and racial origin."

Elsewhere on the slanting deck, Jews crowded the walkways, swarming out of the fetid holds to stroll in the sun. They squeezed past lifeboats, crates, barrels, and deck structures, or they gathered on hatches, talking in a babel of tongues, with Yiddish predominating. Only Jastrow and Natalie sat blanketed in deck chairs. The Palestinian organizer of the voyage, Avram Rabinovitz, had dug the chairs out of the bilges, mildewy and rat-chewed but serviceable. The baby worshippers thinned away, leaving a respectful patch of vacant rusty iron plate around the Americans, though the strollers kept glancing at them. Since arriving aboard, Jastrow, known as *der groiser Amerikaner shriftshteller,* "the great American author," had scarcely spoken to anyone, which had only magnified his stature.

Natalie waved a hand at the blue double hump of mountain, far across the bay. "Will you look at Vesuvius! So sharp and clear, for the first time!"

"A fine day for visiting Pompeii," Jastrow said.

"Pompeii!" Natalie pointed at the fat policeman in a green greatcoat patrolling the wharf. "We'd be scooped up as we stepped off the gangplank."

"I'm acutely aware of that."

"Anyway, Pompeii's so depressing! Don't you think so? A thousand roof-less haunted houses. A city of sudden mass death. Ugh! I can do without Pompeii, obscene frescoes and all."

Herbert Rose came shouldering along the deck, a head taller than most of the crowd, his California sports jacket bright as a neon sign in the shabby mass. Natalie and Jastrow had been seeing little of him, though it was he who had arranged their flight from Rome and their coming aboard the *Redeemer*. He was berthing below with the refugees. The smart-aleck film distributor, who had booked most American movies in Italy until the declaration of war, was uncovering a Zionist streak, declining to share the organizer's cabin because — so he said — he was now just one more Jew on the run. Also, he wanted to practice speaking Hebrew.

"Natalie, Avram Rabinovitz wants to talk to you."

"Just Natalie?" asked Jastrow.

"Just Natalie."

She tucked Louis into his basket under the thick brown blanket. Rabin-ovitz had obtained the basket in Naples, together with other baby supplies, and a few things for Natalie and her uncle, who, with Rose, had fled Rome in the clothes in which they stood. The Palestinian had also brought aboard the tinned milk on which Louis was living. In Rome, even at the United States embassy, canned milk had long since run out. To her amazed inquiry, "Where on earth did you get it?" Rabinovitz had winked and changed the subject.

"Aaron, will you watch him? If he cries, shove the pacifier in his face."

"Is it about our departure?" Jastrow asked Rose as she left.

Dropping into the vacant deck chair, Rose put up his lean long legs. "He'll tell her what it's about." He was smooth-shaven, bald, lean, with a cartoonlike Semitic nose. His air and manner were wholly American, as-sured, easy, unselfconsciously on top of the world. "Solid comfort," he said, snuggling in the chair. "You Yankee-Doodles know how to live."

"Any second thoughts at this point, Herb?"

"About what?"

"About sailing in this wretched scow."

"I don't think it's a wretched scow."

"It's not the *Queen Mary*."

"The *Queen Mary* isn't running Jews to Palestine. Tough! It could run twenty thousand at a crack, and clear a million bucks on every run."

"Why have we been idle for a week?"

"It took two days to install the armature. Then came this three-day gale. We'll leave, don't worry."

A cold gust flapped the blanket off Louis. Rose tucked it back in.

"Herb, didn't we simply panic in Rome, the three of us? That mob around the American embassy was just a lot of loafers, I'm sure, hoping for a little excitement after the declaration of war."

"Look, the police were arresting people who tried to go in, right and left. We both saw that. God knows what happened to them. And at that, they probably weren't Jews."

"I'll bet," said Jastrow, "that if their passports were in order, Jews or not, they're now quartered in some pleasant hotel, awaiting exchange for Italians caught in the States."

Rose snapped, "I wouldn't go back to Rome if I could. I'm happy."

Jastrow said in perfect Hebrew, "And how are you progressing with your new language?"

"Jesus Christ!" Rose stared at him. "You could teach it, couldn't you?"

"There's no substitute," Jastrow smiled, stroking his beard and resuming his Bostonian English, "for a Polish yeshiva education."

"Why the devil did you ever drop it? I wasn't even bar mitzvahed. I can't forgive my parents."

"Ah, the greener grass," said Jastrow. "I couldn't wait to escape from the yeshiva. It was like a jail."

Natalie meantime made her way to Rabinovitz's cabin under the bridge. She had not visited it before. He offered her his chair at a desk piled with papers, dirty clothes, and oily tools, and sat on an unmade bunk, hunching against the bulkhead adorned with sepia nudes torn from magazines. The single electric bulb was so dim, and the tobacco smoke so thick, that Natalie could just make these out. At her embarrassed grin, Rabinovitz shrugged. He wore bulky grease-streaked coveralls, and his round face was mud-gray with fatigue.

"It's the chief engineer's art collection. I took his room. Mrs. Henry, I need three hundred American dollars. Can you and your uncle help out?" Taken aback, she said nothing. He went on, "Herb Rose offered the whole amount, but he's already shelled out too much. We wouldn't have gotten this far if not for him. I'm hoping you and your uncle will give a hundred each. That would be fairer. Old men tend to be pikers, so I thought I'd put it to you." Rabinovitz's English was clear but heavily accented, and his slang was dated, as though it came from reading old novels.

"What's the money for?"

"*Fetchi-metchi.*" He slid a thick thumb back and forth over two fingers, and wearily smiled. "Bribery. The harbor master won't clear us to depart. I don't know why. He started out friendly, but he changed."

"You think you can bribe him?"

"Oh, not him. Our captain. You've seen him, that drunken bearded old scalawag in the blue jacket. If we leave illegally, he forfeits his ship's papers. The harbor master's office is holding them. I'm sure he's done it often, he's a smuggler by trade. But it's an extra."

"Won't that be very dangerous?"

"I don't think so. If the coast guard stops us, we'll say we're test-running our repaired engine, and head back. We'll be no worse off than we are."

"If we're stopped, will he return the money?"

"Good question, and the answer is that he gets paid when we pass the three-mile limit."

All week long, with too much time to think, Natalie had been imagining calamitous reasons for the failure to depart, and wondering whether she had done the right thing in fleeing from Rome. The prospect of a trip across the Mediterranean in this hulk was growing uglier by the day. Still, she had clung to the thought that it would at least get her baby away from the Germans. But to start by breaking the Fascist law, and trying to outrun the coast guard's gunboats!

Rabinovitz said in a hard though not hostile tone as she sat silent, "Well, never mind. I'll get it all from Rose."

"No, I'll chip in," Natalie said. "Aaron will, too, I'm sure. I just don't like it."

"Neither do I, Mrs. Henry, but we can't sit here. We have to try something."

On a hatch cover near Dr. Jastrow, who was writing in a notebook, two young men were arguing over an open battered Talmud volume. Rose was gone. Jastrow paused in his work to listen to their dispute about a point in *Gittin,* the treatise on divorce. In the Polish yeshiva, Jastrow had earned many a kiss from his teachers for unravelling problems in *Gittin.* The sensation of those damp hairy accolades came to mind, and he smiled. The two arguers saw this and shyly smiled back. One touched his ragged cap, and said in Yiddish, *"Der groiser shriftshteller* understands the little black points?"

Jastrow benignly nodded.

The other young man — gaunt, yellow-faced, with a straggling little beard and bright sunken eyes, a pure yeshiva type — spoke up excitedly. "Would you join us, and perhaps teach us?"

"As a boy, I did once study the Talmud," Jastrow said in cool precise Polish, "but that was long, long ago, I fear. I'm rather busy."

Subdued, the pair resumed their study. Soon, to Jastrow's relief, they moved away. It might have been amusing, he thought as he resumed writing, to join the lads and astound them with memory feats. After fifty years, he remembered the very passage in dispute. The retentiveness of a boy's mind! But a long voyage lay ahead. Keeping one's distance in these crowded conditions, especially amid these tribally intimate Jews, was the only way.

Jastrow was starting a new book, to pass the time and make some use of his disagreeable predicament. In a deliberate echo of his big success, *A Jew's Jesus*, he was calling it *A Jew's Journey*. But what he had in mind was not a travel diary. As Marcus Aurelius had written classic meditations on the battlefield by candlelight, so Jastrow proposed to coin his wartime flight into luminous thoughts on faith, war, the human condition, and his own life. He guessed the idea would charm his publisher; and that if he brought it off, it might even be another book club selection. In any case, at his age, it would be a salutary reckoning of the soul. On this notion, characteristically combining the thoughtful, the imaginative, and the catchpenny, Aaron Jastrow was well into the first notebook borrowed from Rabinovitz. He knew the book could never be a success like *A Jew's Jesus*, which had hit the book club jackpot and the best-seller lists, with its novel portrayal of Christ in his homely reality as a Talmud prodigy and itinerant Palestinian preacher; but it would be something to do.

After the yeshiva boys had moved off, the little scene struck him as worth writing down. He detailed the subtle point in *Gittin* which, so long ago, he had disputed in much the same terms with his clever young cousin, Berel Jastrow, in the noisy study hall of the Oswiecim yeshiva. He described that distant scene. He made gentle fun of his own gradual change into a cool Westernized agnostic. If Berel were still alive, he wrote, and if he had been invited into this dispute over page 27A of *Gittin*, he would have picked up the thread with zest, and argued rings around the yeshiva lads. Berel had remained true to the old orthodoxy. Who could now say which of them had chosen more wisely?

But what has become of Berel? Does he yet live? In my last glimpse of him, through the eyes of my venturesome and well-travelled niece, he stands amid the smoky wreckage of the Warsaw Jewish quarter in 1939 under German bombardment — erect, busy, aged but sturdy as a peasant, with the full gray beard of the orthodox, a paterfamilias, a community leader, a prosperous merchant; and beneath that conventional surface a steely survivor, an Ahasuerus of Christian legend, the indestructible Wandering Jew. Seven or eight years younger than I am, Berel served four years on the battlefronts in the First World War. He was a soldier; he was a prisoner; he escaped; he fought on several fronts, in three different armies. In all that time, through all those perils (so he once wrote me, and so I believe) not only did he emerge unharmed; not a particle of forbidden food ever passed his lips. A man who could care so much about our old God and our ancient Law puts to shame, in point of gallantry, his assimilated cousin who writes about Jesus. And yet the voice of enlightened humanism, speaking with all respect, might well ask whether living in a dream, however comforting and powerful —

"Damn it, Aaron! How long has he been uncovered like this?" Crouched over the basket, Natalie was angrily pulling the flapping blanket back over Louis, who began to cry.

"Oh, has it come undone?" Jastrow said with a start. "Sorry. He's been quiet as a mouse."

"Well, it's time to feed him." She picked up the basket, giving him an exasperated glare. "If he's not too frozen to eat, that is."

"What did Rabinovitz want?"

She bluntly told him.

"Really, Natalie! That much money! An illegal departure! That's terribly upsetting. We must be careful with our money, you know. It's our only salvation."

"We've got to get out of here. That's our salvation."

"But perhaps Rabinovitz is just squeezing the rich Americans a bit — now Natalie, don't scowl so! I only mean —"

"Look, if you don't trust him, go ashore and give yourself up. I'll split the three hundred with Rose."

"Good heavens, why do you snap at me so? I'll do it."

Heavy vibration woke her. Sitting up, clutching over her nightgown the sweater in which she slept, she looked through the open porthole. Cold foggy fishy-smelling air came drifting in. The pier was sliding backward in the misty night. She could hear the slosh of the propellers. Aaron snored in the upper bunk. On the deck beside her, the baby rustled and wheezed in his basket.

She snuggled down again beneath the coarse blankets, for it was very cold. Under way! A departure was always exhilarating; this risky clandestine slip from the trap of Nazi Europe, doubly so. Her mind sleepily groped ahead to Palestine, to getting word to Byron, to making her way home. The geography of the Middle East was blurry to her. Could she perhaps find passage at Suez to Australia, and from there go on to Hawaii? To wait out the war in Palestine was impossible. At best it was a disease-ridden barren country. The Germans in North Africa were a menace. So were the Arabs.

At each change in engine sound she grew more wakeful. The rolling and pitching were bad right here in the harbor; what would they be like on the open sea? The extra oil tanks welded on the main deck clearly made the vessel very unstable. How long to reach the three-mile limit? Dawn was making a violet circle at the porthole. The captain would have to go slow in this fog, and daylight would increase the chance of being caught. What a business, what a predicament! So Natalie lay tense and worrying, braced against the unsteady bunk through a long, long half hour, while the porthole brightened to whitish-gray.

WHUMP!

On the instant she was out of her bunk, bare feet on the icy iron deck, pulling on a coarse bathrobe. Natalie had heard a lot of gunfire in Warsaw.

She knew that noise. Cold wet wind through the porthole tumbled her hair. The fog had lifted a little off the rough sea, and she saw far ahead a gray ship with a white number on its bow. From this bow came a smoky yellow flash.

WHUMP!

The engines pounded, the deck shivered and tilted, the vessel swerved. She hastily dressed, shuddering in the raw air. So small was the room that she barked elbows and knees on the cold-water basin, the bunk, and the doorknob. Aaron slept on. She would not wake him yet, she thought. He would only dither.

At the porthole an enormous white 22 appeared, blocking off the black waves and the gray sky. The gun slowly moved forward into view — not very big, painted gray, manned by boyish sailors in black short raincoats. Both vessels were slowing. The gunners were looking at the *Redeemer* and laughing. She could imagine why: the motley paint job, patches of red primer, of white coat, of old unscraped rust; the extra fuel tanks, spread along the deck like bad teeth in an old man's jaw. Outside harsh voices bawled back and forth in Italian.

The deck trembled. The coast guard vessel fell away. Through the porthole Natalie saw the green crags of Capri and Ischia; then, swinging into view dead ahead, the hills of Naples, lined with white houses in wan sunlight. Through all this Aaron Jastrow slept. Turning back! She fell on the bunk, face down in the pillow. The trip she had been dreading now seemed a passage to lost bliss. The hunted feeling rose in her breast again.

"My goodness, what a commotion!" Aaron poked his frowsy head out of the bunk. Sunshine was streaming through the porthole, and the crewmen were cheerily shouting and cursing outside. The *Redeemer* was tying up to the same wharf, with the same potbellied policeman in green patrolling it. "Why, it's broad daylight. You're all dressed. What's happening? Are we leaving?"

"We've left and returned. The coast guard stopped us."

Jastrow looked grave. "Oh dear. Two hundred dollars!"

Rabinovitz came to their door, freshly shaved, in a stained dark suit, a gray shirt, a red tie. His face was set in hard angry lines, and he was holding out some American money. "I can only refund half, sorry. He wouldn't leave the pier unless I advanced half. I had to gamble."

"You may need the rest," Natalie said. "Keep it."

"If I need it, I'll ask again."

Jastrow spoke from the upper bunk. "We've never discussed paying for our passage, you know, and —"

Rabinovitz slapped the money into Natalie's hand. "Excuse me. I'm going to bust in on that damned harbor master. We're a neutral vessel. We just put in here for emergency repairs. Holding us up like this is a damned outrage!"

They were having their noonday tea when Rabinovitz reappeared at their cabin door. "I was short-tempered this morning. Sorry."

"Come in," Natalie said amiably. "Tea?"

"Thanks. Yes. What's the matter with your baby?" Louis was whimpering in his basket.

"He caught a chill. Is there any news?"

Rabinovitz squatted with his back to the door, holding the glass in two hands and sipping. "Dr. Jastrow, when we left Rome so suddenly, you seemed very upset about the manuscript you had to leave behind."

"I'm still upset. Four years of my life!"

"What was the title of your book?"

"The Arch of Constantine. Why?"

"In Rome, did you know anybody at the German embassy?"

"The German embassy? Obviously not."

"You're sure?"

"I had nothing to do with the German embassy."

"You've never heard of a guy named Werner Beck?"

"Werner Beck?" Jastrow repeated, half to himself. "Why, yes, I did know a Werner Beck, years ago. What about him?"

"There's a Dr. Werner Beck at the gangway. He's one of the two Germans I saw in your hotel suite in Rome, when Rose and I went looking for you. He just drove up in a Mercedes. He says he's from the German embassy in Rome, and he's an old friend of yours. And he says he's brought your manuscript of *The Arch of Constantine.*"

In sober silence, broken only by the baby's snorts and snuffles, Natalie and her uncle looked at each other. "Describe him," said Jastrow.

"Middle height. Sort of fat. Pale, a lot of blond hair, a high voice. Pleasant manners."

"Glasses?"

"Thick rimless glasses."

"It's probably Werner Beck, though he wasn't fat then."

Natalie had to clear her throat to talk. "Who is he, Aaron?"

"Why, Werner was a student in my last graduate seminar at Yale. One of the good German students, a demon for work. He had language difficulties, and I helped him over some hurdles. I haven't seen or heard from him since then."

"He says he took the manuscript from your suite," said Rabinovitz. "He was there, that I can assure you. He was the polite one. The other one was damned ugly."

"How did he track me here?" Jastrow seemed dazed. "This is very ominous, isn't it?"

"Well, I can't say. If we deny you're here, the OVRA will come on board to search. They do anything the Gestapo wants."

Shakily Natalie put in, "What about the Turkish flag?"

"Up to a point, the Turkish flag is fine."

Jastrow took a decisive tone. "There's really no alternative, is there? Shall I go to the gangway?"

"I'll bring him to you."

It was some comfort to Natalie that the Palestinian was showing so little alarm. To her this was a devastating, hideous development. She was frightened to the core for her baby. Rabinovitz left. Jastrow said meditatively, "Werner Beck! Dear me. Hitler wasn't even in power when I knew Werner."

"Was he for Hitler?"

"Oh, no. A conservative, gentle, studious sort. Rather religious, if memory serves. From a good family. He was aiming for the Foreign Office, I remember that."

The baby sneezed. Natalie busied herself trying to clean out his clogged tiny nose. She was too shocked to think clearly.

"Professor Jastrow, here's Dr. Werner Beck." Rabinovitz stepped into the cabin. A man in a gray overcoat and gray hat bowed in the doorway, lifting the hat and bringing together his heels. Under his left arm he carried a very thick yellow envelope wrapped in string.

"You do remember me, Professor Jastrow?" His voice was prim and high. He smiled in an awkward, almost apologetic way, half-shutting his eyes. "It's been twelve and a half years."

"Yes, Werner." Jastrow proffered a gingerly handshake. "You've put on weight, that's all."

"Yes, far too much. Well, here is *The Arch of Constantine*."

Jastrow set the package on the bunk beside the restless baby, undid the string with shaking fingers, and riffled through the mass of onionskin sheets. "Natalie, it's all here!" His eyes glistened at the man in the doorway. "What can I say, Werner, but thank you? *Thank you!*"

"It wasn't easy, Professor. But I knew what it would mean to you." Dr. Beck turned to Rabinovitz. "It was my Gestapo confrere, you see, who got it away from the OVRA. I don't think I could have. I regret you and he had words, but you returned him some very short answers, you know." Rabinovitz shrugged, his expression blank. Beck looked back to Jastrow, who was fondling his papers. "I took the liberty of reading the work, Professor. What an advance over *A Jew's Jesus!* You demonstrate a very special grasp of early Byzantium, and of the eastern church. You bring that whole lost world to life. The book will seal your popular fame, and this time the academics will praise your scholarship as well. It's your finest achievement."

"Why, how kind of you, Werner." Jastrow assumed his simpering way with admirers. "And as for you, your English has amazingly improved. Remember the trouble at your orals?"

"Indeed I do. You saved my career."

"Oh, hardly so."

"I've since served seven years in Washington. My boys — I have three — are bilingual in English and German. Now I'm first secretary in Rome. And it's all thanks to you."

"Three boys. Well, fancy that."

Natalie found it hard to believe that this small talk was going on. It was like dialogue in a dream. There the man stood in the cabin doorway, an official of Nazi Germany, a stoutish harmless-looking person, with glasses that gave him a bookish look. His hands holding the hat were folded before him in a peaceful, almost priestly way. Talking about his boys, praising Aaron's work, he made a benign appearance; if anything — especially with the alto voice and proper manners — a bit soft and academic. The baby coughed, and Werner Beck looked at him. "Is your child well, Mrs. Henry?"

Harshly she burst out, "How do you know my name? How did you know that we were at the Excelsior? And how did you find out we'd come here?"

She could see that Aaron was pained by her manner. Rabinovitz's face remained wooden. Dr. Beck replied in a patient tone, "The Gestapo keeps a current list, of course, of foreign nationals at Rome hotels. And the OVRA reported to the Gestapo that you had boarded this vessel."

"Then you're in the Gestapo?"

"No, Mrs. Henry. As I said, I'm a Foreign Ministry officer. Now, would you and your uncle care to lunch with me at the Grand Hotel? They say it has the best dining room in Naples."

Lips parted in silent stupefaction, Natalie looked to Jastrow, who said, "Surely you're not serious, Werner."

"Why not? You might enjoy some good food and wine. You'll be starting tomorrow on a long hard voyage."

"Tomorrow? That's more than I know," Rabinovitz spoke up, "and I've just come from the harbor master."

"Well, that is my information."

Natalie almost barked, "As soon as we set foot ashore we'll be arrested and interned. You know that. So do we."

"I have police passes for both of you." She shook her head violently at Jastrow. Dr. Beck quietly went on, "Suppose I withdraw so you can talk it over? If you're hesitant, let's just chat at the gangway before I leave. But it's quite safe for you to come ashore with me, and there really is much to discuss."

Jastrow struck in severely. "What were you doing in my hotel room, Werner?"

"Professor, when Mussolini declared war, I thought I'd better offer you my help. I brought the Gestapo man to handle the Italian police."

"Why didn't you call on me long before that?"

With a sudden hangdog look at Natalie, Beck answered, "Shall I be candid? So as not to inflict an odious presence on you." He lifted his hat, bowed, and left.

Jastrow glanced doubtfully from the Palestinian to his niece.

"Aaron, I'm not getting separated from Louis. Not for one minute!" Natalie turned strident. "I'm not even going out there to the gangway!"

"What do you think?" Jastrow said to Rabinovitz, who turned up his hands. "Well, d'you suppose it's all an elaborate scheme to collar me? Now that he's found me, can't he just get the OVRA to drag me off your ship, if that's what he's after?"

"This way he'd avoid a fuss."

"How much of a fuss?"

Rabinovitz bitterly grinned. "Not much of a fuss."

Jastrow pulled at his beard, eyes on his glowering niece. Then he reached for his hat and cloak. "Well, Natalie, I've been a confounded dunderhead right along. I may as well follow my nature. I shall go ashore with Werner Beck."

"Oh, by all means!" The baby was wailing now, and Natalie was beside herself. "Enjoy your lunch! Maybe his Gestapo pals will join you, to make things jollier."

Rabinovitz helped Jastrow with his cloak. "Find out all you can about our departure."

"I shall. If I don't return," said Jastrow to Natalie, as she rocked the screaming infant in her arms, "you'll simply be rid of a millstone, won't you?"

Two hours passed. Hard rain cleared the deck of strollers. Natalie waited alone at the gangway under an umbrella, watching the dripping policeman pace the wharf. A small black Mercedes at last appeared through the rain. Dr. Beck got out to open the door for Dr. Jastrow, waved to her, and drove off. Mounting the gangplank, Jastrow spread his arms under the blue cloak. "Well, my dear! I have returned, you see."

"Thank God for that."

"Yes. Now let's have a talk with Rabinovitz."

"Sure you don't want your nap first?"

"I'm not sleepy."

The Palestinian, in his greasy coveralls, opened the cabin door to their knock. The little room smelled strongly of sweat, grease, and cigarette ashes. Jastrow blinked at the pinups of naked women. "Please sit down," Rabinovitz said. "I'll have to get rid of those pretty ladies. I don't notice them, but everybody else does. So. I'm very glad you're back. You have guts. Was it an interesting lunch?"

"Rather." Jastrow sat stiffly in the desk chair, Natalie on a stool beside him. "To begin with, your Turkish captain betrayed you. He told the coast guard that you would try a clandestine departure. That's why you were caught. So Werner says."

Rabinovitz nodded, his face sour. "I thought as much. We can't charter another vessel, so I have to forget it — for the time being."

"The Turk also reported our arrival aboard last week. The harbor master decided to notify the OVRA in Rome, and clear up this matter of fugitive Americans, before letting you go. Hence the week's delay."

"Well. So it all fits together." Rabinovitz was clenching and unclenching clasped fingers in his lap. "What about our leaving tomorrow?"

"Yes, he says you will. Now, about that." Jastrow's tone sharpened. "Was this vessel formerly called the *Izmir*?"

"It's the *Izmir*."

"Were you recently checked for seaworthiness?"

"A port inspector came to verify our certificate, yes."

"Werner says he appended a page of comment. You're overcrowded and overloaded. The added tanks topside have dangerously decreased your stability. In a panic, if the passengers all rush to one side, this vessel may actually capsize. Is that correct?"

"They're a disciplined group," Rabinovitz said very tiredly. "They won't panic."

"Your food, water, and sanitary facilities are acutely substandard," Jastrow went on. "Of course, Natalie and I have already observed that. Medical facilities are poor. The engine is thirty-five years old. Its log shows several recent breakdowns. You're certified only for coastal waters, not for the open sea."

Rabinovitz's tone turned acid. "Did you mention that we Jews have to accept such risks so as to escape German persecution?"

"Almost in those words. He didn't like it. But he said that if Palestine had been under a German mandate, most of Europe's Jews would have been sent there long since in seaworthy vessels. Your use of a floating death trap like this is due to Allied, not German, policy. England's closed Palestine off so as to win over the Arabs — a silly gesture, since they're heart and soul for Hitler. America has shut its gates. So your organization, which he knows all about, must try to smuggle refugees into Palestine, in derelicts like the *Izmir*."

"Yes, the Nazis are ardent Zionists," said Rabinovitz. "We know that."

Jastrow took an envelope from an inside breast pocket. "Now, here are the Italian police regulations for American internees. They're being sent to Siena to await exchange. As it happens, my home is in Siena. My staff is still living there."

Rabinovitz glanced through the mimeographed sheets, his eyes sad and dull.

"Those regulations could be faked," Natalie exclaimed.

"They're real." Rabinovitz handed the sheets to her. "So, does that settle it? Are you two getting off and going to Siena?"

"I told Werner," Jastrow replied, "that it's up to Natalie. If she sails with you, I'll sail. If she elects to return to Siena, I'll do that."

"I see. Very nice." With a brief shift of his eyes to Natalie, who sat pale and still, Rabinovitz asked, "What did Dr. Beck say to that?"

"Well, as a mother, he says, she'll no doubt decide wisely. The risks of the voyage for her infant are pointless and intolerable. She's not a stateless refugee. That's what he wanted to tell her."

"You haven't seen this man in twelve years, Aaron." Natalie's voice almost broke in mid-sentence. Her hands were crumpling the mimeographed sheets. "He's trying to keep you here. Why?"

"Well, why indeed? Do you suppose he wants to murder me?" Jastrow said, with tremulous facetiousness. "Why should he? I gave him straight A's in my seminar."

Rabinovitz said, "He doesn't want to murder you."

"No. I believe he wants to help his old teacher."

"God in heaven," Natalie all but shouted, "will you ever show a trace of common sense? This man is a high-placed Nazi. What makes you willing to accept a word he says?"

"He's not a Nazi." Jastrow spoke with calm pedantry. "He's a professional diplomat. He regards the Party as a pack of gross ill-educated opportunists. He does admire Hitler for unifying Germany, but he has grave misgivings about the way the war is going. The Jewish policy appalls him. Werner once studied for the ministry. I don't think there's an anti-Semitic bone in his body. Unlike some American consuls we've been dealing with."

There was a double knock at the door. The rough-looking man who was Rabinovitz's assistant looked in to hand him an envelope sealed with red wax. Rabinovitz read the letter and stood up, peeling the coveralls off a clean white shirt and dark trousers. "Well, all right. We'll talk some more later."

"What is it?" Natalie blurted.

"We're cleared to leave. I'm to pick up the ship's papers at once from the harbor master."

3

BEREL JASTROW, in a tattered Soviet army greatcoat, shuffles up to his ankles in snow along a road in southwest Poland. The long column of Russian prisoners is winding through flat white fields of the area historians call Upper Silesia. Green-clad SS men guard the column, clubs or machine guns in hand. Leading and trailing the column, two large clanking army vehicles full of more SS men ride. This labor draft, culled from the sturdiest prisoners in the Lamsdorf Stalag, has been walking the whole way. Death has shrunken it en route by about a third. The daily meal at 10 A.M. has been a slice of blackish woody stuff resembling bread, lukewarm soup made of nettles, spoiled potatoes, rotten roots, and the like. Even this ration has often failed, and the men have been turned loose in the fields to forage like goats under the SS guns. For twelve to fourteen hours each day, they have had to foot it at the pace of the stout healthy guards, who march and ride in two-hour shifts.

Berel Jastrow's oaken constitution is nearing collapse. All around him, men have been dropping in their tracks right along; often silently, sometimes with a groan or a cry. When kicking or clubbing does not rouse a man who falls, he gets a bullet through the head. This is a routine precaution, for partisans might otherwise revive and recruit him. Calmly but punctiliously the Germans blow each skull to pieces, leaving a red mass on the snow by the neck of the huddled Russian greatcoat.

The column is walking now from Cracow to Katowice; fresh signposts in heavy German lettering call it KATTOWITZ. Berel Jastrow numbly surmises that the trek may soon be ending, for Katowice is a center of industry and mining. He is too low in vital energy, too shrunken by cold, hunger, and crushing weariness, to wonder at the chance that brings him to familiar scenes. All his waning attention is focussed on keeping his eyes on the man ahead, his legs moving, and his knees stiff, for he fears if he relaxes the joints they will buckle, and he will go down and get his head blown off.

In forty years the old road has not changed much. Berel can predict each turn. He knows when the next peasant home or wooden church will loom through the fine dry blowing snow. Is the draft going to the Katowice coal mines? Not a bad fate! Mines are warmer in winter than the open air. Miners have to be well-fed to produce.

For all the suffering on this march, Berel is grateful to God that he is in the labor column and out of the Stalag. Nothing in his experience of the last war, nothing in the Warsaw ghetto, equals what he has seen at Lamsdorf. The Stalag is not really a prison camp, for there are no barracks, no buildings, no roll calls, no administration; no means of order, except fear of the manned machine guns on the watchtowers, and of the blazing searchlights at night. The installation is just a barbed-wire enclosure open to the sky, stretching farther than the eye can see, penning in two hundred thousand starving men. On the eastern front the Geneva Convention does not exist. The Soviet Union never signed it.

The Germans are not prepared, anyway, to support such a vast bag of captives. The supply of food and water is scanty. The rule of life at Lamsdorf is self-preservation, in filth, stench, snarling dogfights over edible scraps, and untended sickness. Dead bodies lie about in the muck and the snow. Daily the dead are cremated in heaps, fueled by wood and waste oil, outside the barbed wire. The pyres flame far into the night. The camp stinks as though a huge meat-packing plant were nearby, where animals are rendered and the hair or bristles scorched off their hides.

Prisoners captured in the Germans' November drive on Moscow make up this labor draft. Those who are dying in Lamsdorf were caught in the summer campaign. Reduced by now to walking skeletons, they collapse randomly, all over the place, day and night. Of the varied Lamsdorf horrors, one still scars Jastrow's soul. He himself has glimpsed, in the night gloom beyond the searchlights, the small packs of prisoners, insane with hunger, who rove the frozen wastes of the camp, eating the soft inner parts of new-fallen corpses. He has seen the mutilated corpses by day. The watchtower guards shoot the cannibals, when they spot them. Prisoners who catch them kick or beat them to death. But the instinct to live outlasts human nature in these creatures, and cancels fear. The cannibals are crazy somnambulists, idiot mouths seeking to be filled, with enough cunning left in their blasted brains to feed at night, skulking in shadow like coyotes. Whatever lies ahead in Katowice, Berel Jastrow knows that nothing can be worse than Lamsdorf.

Yet it seems the column is not going to Katowice. The ranks ahead are making a left turn. That will take the draft south to Oswiecim, Berel knows; but what is there for such a large labor force to do in Oswiecim? The place of his boyhood yeshiva is a town of small manufactures, isolated in the marshy land where the Sola meets the Vistula. Mainly, it is a railroad junction. No heavy labor there. At the turn in the road, he sees a new Gothic-lettered arrow, nailed above the faded Oswiecim signpost. The Germans are using the old name, which Berel remembers from his youth when Oswiecim was Austrian. Not only is it harsher, as German names tend to be; AUSCHWITZ hardly even sounds like Oswiecim.

4

RABINOVITZ returned in a rusty van loaded with supplies, followed by two tank trucks carrying fresh water and diesel fuel. This touched off a frenzy of work through the twilight and into the night. Shouting, laughing, singing Jews passed the stores hand to hand up the gangway, across the deck, and down the hatches: sacks of flour and potatoes, net bags of wormy cabbages and other stunted, gnarled vegetables, bundles of dried fish, and boxes of tinned food. The ragged Turkish crewmen brought aboard the fuel and water hoses to throb and thump and groan; they fastened down hatches, tinkered at the anchor windlass, coiled ropes, blasphemed, hammered, and bustled about. The old vessel itself, as though infected with the excitement of imminent departure, creaked, rolled, and strained at its mooring lines. Frigid gusts were driving swells in past the mole, but despite the wind, happily babbling passengers thronged the unsteady deck watching the preparations. When they went below to eat, the wind was working up to a near-gale under a glittering half-moon.

In a purple crepe dress, her face touched with rouge and lipstick, Natalie stood hesitating on the wobbly deck outside Rabinovitz's cabin door. Close-wrapped around her shoulders was Aaron's gray shawl. She sighed, and knocked.

"Well, hello there, Mrs. Henry."

On the grimy bulkheads in place of the pinups were pallid yellow rectangles. Otherwise the rank disorder was as before: unmade bunk, piled papers, swirling tobacco smoke, workman's smells from clothes dangling on hooks. He said as he closed the door, "Isn't that Sarah Elowsky's dress?"

"I bought it from her." Natalie steadied herself against the doorway. "That everlasting brown wool dress of mine I've come to loathe, truly loathe."

"Sarah would wear that when we talked to the authorities at Nice. She has a way with Frenchmen."

"I hardly know her. I know so little about all you people!"

"How's your baby?"

"Cranky. He keeps pawing at his right ear, and he's feverish."

"You've had him to the infirmary?"

"Yes. They gave me pills for him."

"Well? And are you coming with us?"

"I'm trying to make up my mind."

"That shouldn't be hard." He offered her his desk chair, and squatted on the iron deck. "Decide what's best for yourself, and do it."

"Why did you ever bring us aboard, anyway? You only created trouble for yourself."

"Impulse, Mrs. Henry." He drew hard on a cigarette. "When we sailed from Nice we had no plan to stop here. The generator burned out. I had to get an armature and some more money in Rome. I contacted Herb Rose. He told me your uncle was there. I'm an admirer of his. So —"

"Are your passengers all from Nice?"

"No. None of them. They're Zionist pioneers, refugees now, mostly Polish and Hungarian. They'd have left from Constanta on the Black Sea — that's the usual route — but their Rumanian fixer ran off with their money. They got shunted around by the Jewish agencies for months, and ended up in Italian-occupied France. It's not a bad place for Jews, but they wanted to go on to Palestine, no matter what. That's what I do, get Jews to Palestine. So, that's the story."

"Are you going straight to Palestine, or via Turkey? I've heard both rumors."

"I'm not sure. I'll receive radio signals at sea about that."

"If it's via Turkey, you'll have to take your people through the Syrian mountains illegally, won't you? Hostile Arab country?"

"I've done that before. If we can go straight home, of course we will."

"Are your engines going to break down at sea?"

"No. I'm a marine engineer. The ship is old, but it's French. The French build good ships."

"What about the overcrowding? Those stacks of bunks down below — those long open latrine troughs! Suppose another three-day storm comes along? Won't you have an outbreak of disease?"

"Mrs. Henry, these people are trained for rough conditions."

"Hasn't it occurred to you" — she twisted the shawl in her hands — "that you may not sail? That the clearance could just be a trick to lure my uncle quietly away? It's quite a coincidence that you got your papers right after Werner Beck showed up." Rabinovitz made a skeptical face. She went on quickly. "Now I've thought of something. If we do leave the *Redeemer* — I'm not saying we will — but if we do, Aaron could insist on going straight to the Turkish consulate. There we'd wait for a signal from you, relayed through the coast guard, that you're past the three-mile limit. If no signal comes, we'd claim Turkish sanctuary, and — what are you smiling at?"

"There's no Turkish consulate here."

"You said there was."

"He's an honorary consul, an Italian banker. A converted Jew, as it happens, and he's been a help. The nearest consulate is in Bari, on the Adriatic."

"Oh, hell."

"Anyway, a consulate doesn't give territorial sanctuary, like an embassy." His smile broadened. "But you've been thinking hard, haven't you?"

"Oh, I even had the signal."

"Really? What was it?"

"Well —" with a certain embarrassment she brought it out — " *'Next year in Jerusalem.'* Just the last line of the Passover seder."

"I know what it is." His smile faded to a stern businesslike look. "Listen, Mrs. Henry, the Italians have no use for a lot of hungry stateless Jews. We'll go. You ought to come, too."

"Oh, I should? And why?" The swaying of the smoky little room, with the bumping against the wharf, was making Natalie queazy.

"Let's say because your baby's Jewish, and should go to the Jewish homeland."

"He's only half-Jewish."

"Yes? Ask the Germans."

"Look, don't you understand that I feel no emotion about Palestine? None! I'm an American, completely irreligious, married to a Christian naval officer."

"Tell me about your husband."

The question took her aback. She awkwardly replied, "I haven't seen him for ages. He's on a submarine somewhere in the Pacific."

He took out a worn wallet and showed her a snap of a big-bosomed dark girl with heavy hair. "That was my wife. She was killed in a bus that the Arabs blew up."

"That's frightful."

"It happened eight years ago."

"And you want me to take my baby there?"

"Jews live in danger everywhere."

"Not in America."

"You're strangers there, too. In Palestine you're home."

Natalie took from her purse a small colored photograph of Byron in uniform. "Here's my husband."

Byron came alive in her memory as Rabinovitz knotted his brows over the picture. "He looks young. When did you get married?"

For months she had been shutting her marriage from her thoughts — that hazy tangle of imbecile decisions, leading to delirious labor pains alone in a foreign hospital, surrounded by strange faces and half-understood medi-

cal babble in Italian. For all the delicious love flooding her at seeing the tiny
wrinkled red baby, she had felt then that her life was wrecked. More or less,
she still did. But as she sketched the story to the Palestinian, Byron Henry's
charm and dash, his ingenuity, his boyish appeal, all came back to her; also
the terrific sweetness, however harebrained the thing had been, of the fleeting honeymoon in Lisbon. She thought — though she did not say this to
Rabinovitz — that a crippled lifetime might be fair pay for such joy. Besides,
she had Louis.

Rabinovitz chain-lit a cigarette as he listened. "You never met any Jewish young men like him?"

"No. The ones I went out with were all determined to be doctors, lawyers, writers, accountants, or college professors."

"Bourgeois types."

"Yes."

"Bring your son to Palestine. He'll grow up a man of action like his father."

"What about the hazards?" Natalie feared she might be getting seasick,
here beside the wharf. The motion was really nauseating. She got out of the
chair and leaned against the bulkhead. "I hope this ship makes it across the
Mediterranean, but then what? End up in a British prison camp? Or take an
infant through Arab mountains, to be shot at or captured and butchered?"

"Mrs. Henry, it's risky to take him to Siena."

"I don't know about that. My uncle talked by telephone to our chargé
d'affaires in Rome, during his lunch with Beck. The chargé advised Aaron to
go to Siena. He called this trip an unnecessary hazard for us."

"Your chargé d'affaires told him to trust a Hitler bureaucrat?"

"He said that he knows Beck well. He's not a Nazi. Our own Foreign
Service respects him. Beck has offered to drive us back to Rome tomorrow,
straight to the embassy. I don't know what to believe, and frankly — *Oh!*"
The deck of the small cabin sharply pitched and bumped. Natalie staggered,
he jumped up to steady her, and she fell against him, crushing her breasts
on his chest. He caught her upper arms in a hard grip, and held her gently
away.

"Steady."

"Sorry."

"Okay."

He let her go. She forced a smile, her arms and breasts tingling.

"The wind keeps backing around. The weather reports aren't good.
Still, we sail at first light."

"That may solve my problem. Maybe Beck won't come that early."

"He will. You'd better decide. It's a tough one for you, at that. I can see
it is."

Aaron Jastrow in a blue bathrobe, his thin gray hair blown about, knocked and opened the door. "Sorry to interrupt. The baby's acting strange, Natalie." Her face distorted with alarm. "Now don't be frightened. Just come and see."

Rabinovitz seized her arm and they went out together. In their scurry down the moonlit windswept deck, Natalie's hair blew wildly. Louis lay in his basket on the bunk, his eyes shut, thrashing clenched fists this way and that.

"Louis!" She bent over him, putting both hands on the writhing little body. "Baby! Baby! Wake up — oh, he won't open his eyes! What is it? He's wriggling so!"

Rabinovitz took the child up in a blanket. "It's a convulsion from the fever. Don't worry, infants come out of convulsions." Louis's head was jerking above the blanket, eyes still shut. "Let's get him to the infirmary."

Natalie ran after him, down into the fetid gloom of the lower decks, into the miasma of latrines, of crowded unwashed bodies and clothes, of stale overbreathed air. Rabinovitz pushed past the queue jamming the passageway outside the infirmary. In the narrow white-painted cabin he thrust the baby on the doctor, a haggard graybeard in a soiled white coat. With a harassed air the doctor unwrapped Louis, looked at the jerking body, and agreed that it was a convulsion. He had no medicine to give. He reassured Natalie in a hoarse weak voice, speaking a Germanic Yiddish, "It's that inflamed right ear, you know. It's a febrile episode, I'm sure, nothing involving the brain. You can expect he'll come out of it soon with no harm done." He did not look as cheerful as his words.

"What about a warm bath?" Rabinovitz said.

"Yes, that could help. But there's no hot water on this boat, only cold showers."

Picking up Louis, Rabinovitz said to Natalie, "Come."

They hurried down the passageway to the ship's galley. Even when the galley was cleaned up and shut for the night, as now, it was malodorous and greasy. One piece of equipment, however, a tremendous vat, shone in the flickering electric light. Soup was the mainstay of the refugees' diet. Rabinovitz had somewhere procured this restaurant boiler and installed it. Briskly he opened a faucet and a valve. Water poured into the vat, and from a nozzle at the bottom live steam bubbled up.

"Feel that," he said after a few seconds. "Too hot?"

She dipped in a hand. "No."

Stripping the writhing infant, she pushed back her purple sleeves and immersed the little body in the tepid water to the chin. "Get some on his head, too." She obeyed. The stiff arch of Louis's back soon loosened. Rabinovitz let in more cool water. The spasms weakened, her son went limp in her hands, and she glanced at Rabinovitz with nervous hope.

"When my baby brother went into a convulsion," he said, "that's what my mother always did."

The blue eyes opened, the baby's gaze focussed on Natalie, and he gave her a tired little smile that wrung her heart. She said to Rabinovitz, "God bless you."

"Take him back up and keep him warm," Rabinovitz said. "My brother used to sleep for hours afterward. Let me know if you have more trouble. There's a clinic on shore we can go to, if we must."

Later he came and looked into her cabin, which was lit by two candles. His face and hands were black with grease. Aaron was asleep in the upper bunk. Natalie sat by the baby, in a bathrobe, her hair pinned up, one hand resting on the blanketed basket.

"How's he doing?"

"He's in a deep sleep, but even so, he keeps rubbing his ear."

Rabinovitz produced a small flat bottle, and filled a small glass. "Drink this," he said to Natalie. "Slivovitz, if you know what that is."

"I've drunk slivovitz. Lots of it." She drained the glass. "Thank you. What's the matter with the electricity?"

"The dumb generator again. I'm trying to fix it. You have enough candles?"

"Yes. Can you sail if it isn't working?"

"It will be working, and we will sail. More slivovitz?"

"No. That was fine."

"See you later."

When the lamps flickered on about 2 A.M., Natalie began to pack a cardboard suitcase she had bought from a passenger. That took only a few minutes, and she resumed her vigil. It was a long bad night, a sterile churning of regrets and afterthoughts stretching back to her girlhood, interspersed with nightmarish dozes. The baby slept restlessly, turning and turning. She kept feeling his forehead, and to her it seemed cool; yet when the porthole began to pale he broke out in a flooding sweat. She had to change him into dry swaddlings.

Herb Rose met her on the breezy deck as she carried the suitcase to the gangway. The dawn was breaking, a clear pleasant day. The deck was full of jubilant passengers. On one hatch cover some were singing around a concertina player, their arms thrown over each other's shoulders. The Turkish crewmen were bawling back and forth from the wharf to the deck, and there was much noisy slinging around of tackle.

"Good God," Rose said. "You're not really doing it, Natalie? You're not putting yourself in the hands of that German?"

"My baby's sick as hell."

"Listen, honey, babies' fevers are scary, but it's amazing how they can recover. Just a few days at sea and you'll be safe, once for all. Safe, and free!"

"You may be at sea for weeks. You may have to cross mountains."

"We'll get there. Your baby will be fine. Look at the weather, it's a good omen."

What he said about the weather was true. The harbor had calmed down, the breeze was almost balmy, and Vesuvius seemed inked on the apple-green horizon. Happiness diffused all over the crowded deck like a flower fragrance. But when Natalie had changed Louis he had been trembling, pawing at his ear again, and whimpering. Her memories of the convulsion, the infirmary, the ghastly night, the pestilential air below decks, were overpowering. She set the suitcase down at the gangway. "I don't suppose anybody will steal this. Still, please keep an eye on it, for a minute."

"Natalie, you're doing the wrong thing."

Soon she returned, bearing the bundled-up baby in his basket, with Jastrow pacing behind her in cloak and hat. Beck's Mercedes, with its large diplomatic medallion on the radiator — crimson shield, white circle, heavy black swastika — drove up the wharf and stopped. Rabinovitz stood beside Rose at the gangway now, his hands, face, and coveralls black-smeared. He was wiping his hands on a rag.

The jocund chorus of passenger noise on deck cut off with the arrival of the Mercedes. Unmoving, the passengers stared at the car and at the Americans. The raucous cursing of the crewmen, the slosh of water, the cries of sea birds, were the only sounds. Rabinovitz picked up the suitcase, and took the basket from Natalie. "Okay, let me help you."

"You're very kind."

As she set foot on the gangplank, Herb Rose darted at her and clutched her arm. "*Natalie!* For God's sake, let your uncle get off if he insists. He's had his life. Not you and your kid."

Jostling the American aside, Rabinovitz grated at him, "Don't be a goddamned fool."

Sporty in a tweed overcoat and corduroy cap, Dr. Werner Beck hopped out of the Mercedes, opened the front and back doors, and bowed and smiled. The scene was swimming around Natalie. Jastrow got in at the front door as Beck loaded the two suitcases in the trunk. Carefully, Avram Rabinovitz bestowed the basket in the back seat. "Well, good-bye, Dr. Jastrow," he said. "Good-bye, Mrs. Henry."

Beck got into the driver's seat.

She choked to Rabinovitz, "Am I doing the right thing?"

"It's done." He touched a rough hand to her cheek. "Next year in Jerusalem."

Tears sprang to her eyes. She kissed his bristly, greasy face, and stumbled into the car. He shut the door on her. "Let's go!" he called in Italian at the crewmen. "Get the plank in!"

The Mercedes drove down the wharf, with Jastrow and Beck blithely chatting. Natalie bent over the baby's basket, dry suppressed sobs convulsing her throat. As the car headed north out of Naples on a deserted macadam highway, the sun rose in a white blaze. Its slanted afternoon rays were lighting the Via Veneto when Werner Beck halted his car at the American embassy, and helped Natalie alight. Louis had a high fever.

The Red Cross was handling mail for the internees. Before Natalie left for Siena, she wrote Byron what had happened, summing it up so:

> Now that I'm back in civilization — if you call Mussolini's Italy that — I can see that I did the prudent thing. We're safe and comfortable, an American doctor's been treating Louis, and he's on the mend. That boat was a horror. God knows what will become of those people. Still, I wish I didn't feel so lousy about it. I'll not rest easy until I learn what happened to the *Redeemer*.

5

EXCEPT for the haunting uncertainty about his wife and baby, Byron Henry was enjoying the new war with Japan. It had freed him for a while from the *Devilfish* and its exacting captain, for salvage duty in the ruins of the Cavite naval base. Under the bombed-out rubble and broken burned timbers lay great mounds of precious supplies in charred boxes or crates — electronic gear, clothing, food, machinery, mines, ammunition, the thousand things needed to keep a fleet going; above all, spare parts now desired above diamonds. With a sizable work gang, Byron was digging out the stuff day by day, and trucking it westward to Bataan.

His feat of retrieving torpedoes under fire during the Cavite raid had brought him this assignment direct from Admiral Hart's headquarters. He had *carte blanche* in the burned ruins, so long as he produced the goods at the peninsula enclosing the bay to the west, where American forces were digging into the mountains for a possible long siege. This freedom of action enchanted Byron. His contempt for paperwork and regulations, which had gotten him into such hot water aboard the *Devilfish,* was a prime scavenger virtue. To get things moving he signed any paper, told any lie. He commandeered idle men and vehicles as though he were the admiral himself. For overcoming resistance and settling arguments, he used fire-blackened cases of beer and cartons of cigarettes — which worked like gold coin — from a vast cache he had come upon in the ruins. His drivers and loaders got plenty of these, too, and he made sure they were well fed. If he had to, he brought them into officers' messes, brassily pleading emergency.

Once during an air raid he marched his seventeen men into the grill of the Manila Hotel. The dirty, sweaty crew ate a sumptuous lunch on white napery to string music, while on the waterfront bombs exploded. He paid the enormous check with a Navy voucher full of fine print, adding a five-dollar tip from his own pocket; and he walked out fast, leaving the head waiter staring dubiously at the flimsy blue paper. Thus Byron got his raggle-taggle pickup gang of sailors, longshoremen, marines, and truck drivers — Filipino, American, Chinese, he didn't care — to drudge cheerily from dawn to nightfall. They stuck to him because he kept them on the move, rewarded them as a trainer throws fish to his seals, and turned a blind eye to their own pilferings in the rubble.

The stinking smashed-up Cavite base reminded him of battered Warsaw, where he had been caught with Natalie by Hitler's invasion. But this was a different war: sporadic bombings from the azure tropic sky setting ships ablaze and raising pretty bursts of flame among the waterfront palm trees; nothing like the storm of German bombs and shells that had wrecked the Polish capital. Nor was there yet the fear of an enemy closing in. Cavite had been a hot show, a thorough rubbing-out of a military target, but the base was just a smudge on the untouched hundred-mile coast of Manila Bay. The city itself kept its peacetime look: shimmering heat, glaring sunshine, heavy automobile traffic and crawling oxcarts, a few white men and hordes of Filipinos strolling the sidewalks. Sirens, fires, sandbags, tiny Japanese bombers glinting over green palm-feathered hills far above the thudding black AA puffs, made a war of it — a war slightly movie-ish in feel.

Byron knew things would get rougher. Pessimistic rumors abounded: as, that the entire Pacific Fleet had been sunk at Pearl Harbor, carriers and all, but that the guilty President was suppressing the catastrophic news. Or, that MacArthur's announcements of "small-scale" enemy landings on Luzon were lies; that the Japs were already ashore in force, thundering toward Manila with thousands of tanks. And so forth. Most people believed what General MacArthur told them: that the Jap landings in the north were light feints, well-contained, and that massive help was on the way. There were also optimistic rumors of a huge relief convoy, already en route from San Francisco with a Marine division and three mechanized Army divisions, plus two aircraft carriers crammed with fighters and bombers.

Byron wasn't much concerned either way. A submarine could leave Luzon at a half hour's notice. As for his father and brother at Pearl Harbor, Victor Henry seemed indestructible to Byron, and he doubted the *Enterprise* had been sunk. That would have come out. He would have been quite happy, had he only been sure that Natalie and the baby were homeward bound. The work was a godsend. It kept him too busy by day and too worn out by night to worry overmuch.

This pleasant time abruptly ended. Stopping his truck convoy in downtown Manila to report on his progress, he met Branch Hoban coming out of the Marsman building with a thick envelope in hand, blinking in the sunshine.

"Well, well, Briny Henry himself, loose as a goose!" The captain of the *Devilfish* caught at his arm. "This simplifies matters."

Hoban's handsome face had a hard set to it; the jaw was thrust far forward; the neat Clark Gable mustache seemed to bristle. He squinted at the four heavily laden trucks, and at Byron's work gang, all bare-chested or in dirty undershirts, drinking warm beer from cans. "Heading for Mariveles, were you?"

"Yes, sir, after making my report."

"I'll ride along. You're securing from this duty."

"Sir, Commander Percifield expects me, and —"

"I know all about Commander Percifield. Go ahead in. I'll wait."

Percifield told Byron that the admiral wanted to see him, and added, "You've done a 4.0 job, Ensign Henry. We'll miss you. Turn over your men and vehicles to Captain Tully at Mariveles."

Byron was led by a yeoman into the presence of the Commander-in-Chief of the Asiatic Fleet, a dried-up small old man in whites at an oversize desk, facing out on a spectacular panorama of the blue palm-lined bay.

"You're Pug Henry's boy, aren't you? Warren's brother?" Hart twanged with no other greeting. His round face, weathered in red-brown streaks and patches, wore a harried embittered look. His neck was all sunburned cords and strings. He held himself straight and stiff in the swivel chair.

"Yes, Admiral."

"I thought as much. When I was Academy Superintendent, Warren was a battalion commander. A real comer, Warren. And your father's an outstanding gent. Have a look at this." He tossed Byron a dispatch.

FROM: THE CHIEF OF PERSONNEL
TO: CAPTAIN VICTOR (NONE) HENRY
DETACHED CO CALIFORNIA (BB–44) X RELIEVE CO
NORTHAMPTON (CA-26)

So the *California* was out of action, and his father had a cruiser instead! This was news. But why was Thomas Hart, who bore naval responsibility for the whole Asian theatre, taking notice of an ensign?

"Thank you, Admiral."

"Not a bad consolation prize, the *Northampton*," Hart said in brusque gravelly tones. "The *California*'s sitting on the mud in Pearl, with a hell of a big torpedo hole in her hull. That's confidential. Now then. You seem to be an original, hey, Ensign?" The admiral picked up two papers clipped together. "Seems you've been put up for a letter of commendation, for pulling a quantity of torpedoes out of Cavite under fire. As a submariner, I deeply appreciate that exploit. We're very low on fish. And you've since been recovering other valuable stores, I understand, including mines. Well done! On the other hand, young fellow —" he turned over a sheet, and his face soured, "you've gone and applied for transfer to Atlantic duty!" Leaning back, Hart clasped his hands under his chin and glared. "I wanted a look at the Henry boy who would put in such a request at a time like this."

"Sir, my wife —"

Hart's hostile look softened, and his tone too. "Yes, I'm told that your wife is Jewish, and that she may be caught in Italy with a baby. That's a very bad business and I sympathize, but what can you do about it?"

"Sir, I'll be ten thousand miles closer, if by chance there is something to do."

"But we need submarine officers here. I'm combing them from the tender and the beach. For all you know, your wife's back home by now. Isn't that the real truth?"

"It's not likely, but even so, I've never seen my son, Admiral."

Hart stared at Byron and shook his head in a tired way. "Dismissed."

It was a long glum run to Bataan with Branch Hoban on the driver's seat beside Byron, in an Army truck groaning with crated mines. At the Mariveles Navy headquarters he said good-bye to his work gang. They responded with offhand waves and grunts as they began unloading. He doubted that they would stay together long.

"Now then," Hoban jovially remarked, as the dinghy puttered out past the green rocky island of Corregidor into the breezy bay, "the next question is, where's the *Devilfish?*" He stared around at empty waters stretching everywhere. Manila lay beyond the horizon thirty miles off. Smoke from an air raid marked its location. Not a ship was in sight; not a tug, not a garbage lighter. Fear of the bombers had cleared the bay. "The squadron's lying doggo on the bottom out around here, Byron. We'll just wait." For about an hour periscopes briefly rose from the waves, looked about, and vanished, while the dinghy lay to, tossing. Finally one scope popped up, turned, fixed a stare at the dinghy like the wet head of a sea serpent, and made for it. The dark hull broke the surface, streaming white water; and soon Byron was back aboard the cramped *Devilfish*, which, much as he disliked it, felt and smelled like home.

The executive officer staggered him by saying that his relief had reported aboard. At his hoot of disbelief Lieutenant Aster insisted, "He's here, I tell you. It's Ensign Quayne. You know him, that long drink of water off the poor old *Sealion*. They're reassigning her officers. You were up for a letter of commendation, my boy, but the admiral instead is transferring you to the Atlantic."

Byron said with false nonchalance, "Then when can I leave, Lady?"

"Hold your horses. Quayne's had only four months at sea. He has to qualify first. Wardroom meeting, incidentally, in a couple of minutes."

Ensign Quayne, a pale nail-biter, fresh off a submarine sunk at Cavite, was the one new face at the small green-covered table. Captain Hoban showed up clean-shaven. He looked not only younger, Byron thought, but less obnoxious; the dashing peacetime hotshot and lady's man giving way to an officer meaning business.

"If any of you are wondering about the soup strainer," Hoban grinned, unfolding the old scuffed H.O. chart of the northern Pacific on the table, "it's a war casualty. Not much chance of keeping it properly trimmed at sea, so — the word from headquarters, gentlemen, is to stand by for war patrol number one. Button up all maintenance work in three days, or scrub it. We top off, take on provisions and torpedoes, and go. The intelligence is that a mess of big transports have already left the Jap home islands, escorted by battleships, carriers, cruisers, and Christ knows what else, for an invasion of Luzon in force. Destination, probably Lingayen Gulf. Looks like Christmas on patrol for the *Devilfish* and most of the squadron. Our orders are simple. Targets, in order of priority: first, loaded troop transports. Second, major combat vessels. Third, any combat vessels. Fourth, any Jap ship."

A thrill rippled down Byron's spine. Around the table he saw tightened lips, widened eyes, sobered expressions; on Carter Aster's long face, a peculiar fleeting grin.

The captain tapped the blue and yellow chart. "Okay. First, to review the basics. We're eighteen hundred miles from Tokyo here. Five hundred from the Formosa bomber base that's been slugging at us. *Seven thousand miles from San Francisco, lads.* More than four thousand miles from Pearl Harbor.

"As you know, Guam and Wake look to be goners. They'll probably be operational Jap air bases in a week." Hoban's finger jumped from point to point on the worn creased chart. "So our line is cut. We're in the Japs' back yard, surrounded and trapped. That's how it is. How we got into this mess, you can ask the politicians some time. Meantime help can reach the Philippines only by sea, by the long route via Samoa and Australia outside Jap air range. Ten thousand miles, *each* way." His meaningful look went round the table.

"Incidentally, that story about the big convoy from San Francisco is horse manure to bolster civilian morale. Forget it. We'll patrol in waters totally controlled by the enemy. The rest of the Asiatic Fleet will be heading south to Java. They can't take the bomber raids. Only the submarines will stay. Our mission is to harass the landing of the main Japanese expeditionary force — where, it goes without saying, destroyers will be thick as fleas on a dog's back." Another glance around; a tough, exhilarated smile. "Questions?"

Sitting in an easy slouch, Aster held up a hand. "What was that fourth priority, sir? Any Jap ship?"

"Affirmative."

"Unarmed merchantmen and tankers, too?"

"I said any Jap ship."

"We follow Geneva Convention procedures, of course — warning, search, putting the crew into boats, et cetera?"

Hoban slid coarse gray mimeographed sheets from a manila envelope. "Okay, here's orders on *that* point." He flipped pages. His voice became monotonous and declamatory. "Here we are. 'On December 8, this force received the following fleet order from the Commander-in-Chief, Pacific Fleet:

EXECUTE UNRESTRICTED REPEAT UNRESTRICTED SUBMARINE WARFARE AGAINST JAPAN.' " Hoban paused to give his officers a meaningful look. " '*Devilfish* will govern itself accordingly.' "

"Captain," Byron said, "didn't we declare war on the Germans in 1917 for doing just that?"

"Glad you brought it up. Negative. The Germans sank neutral ships. We'll attack only enemy ships. 'Unrestricted' here means warship or merchant vessel, no difference."

"Sir, what about Article Twenty-two?" Ensign Quayne said, holding up a bony finger with a chewed nail.

Sans mustache, Hoban's smile looked boyish. "Right. You just memorized the articles for the qualification course. Repeat it."

In a dull flat voice, Quayne self-consciously recited:

"Except in the case of persistent refusal to stop on being duly summoned, a submarine may not sink or render incapable of navigation a merchant vessel, without having first placed passengers, crew, and ship's papers in a place of safety. For this purpose, the ship's boats are not regarded as a place of safety, unless the safety of the passengers and crew is assured, in the existing sea and weather conditions, by the proximity of land, or the presence of another vessel which is in a position to take them on board."

"Outstanding," said Hoban. "Unlearn it." Quayne looked like a startled fowl. "Gentlemen, the Japs attacked Pearl Harbor without warning in the middle of peace talks. We didn't throw away the rule book of civilized war. They did. This isn't the war we trained for, but it's sure as hell the war we've got. And it's just as well. By the time we'd go through that rigmarole, our target would shoot off an SOS and Jap planes would be swarming on us."

"Captain, let me understand you." Aster touched a match to a thick gray cigar. "Does this mean if we see them, we sink them?"

"We see them, Lady, we *identify* them, and we sink them." A jocularly ferocious grin lit his face. "When in doubt, of course, we give them the benefit of the doubt. We shoot. Any further questions? Then that's all, gentlemen."

As the officers left the wardroom the captain said, "Briny?"

"Yes, sir?"

Byron turned. Hoban was extending a hand and smiling. The wordless gesture, the youthful smile, seemed to wipe out six months of hostile tension. This was leadership, Byron thought. He grasped the captain's hand. Hoban said, "Glad you'll have at least one war patrol with us."

"I'm looking forward to it, Captain."

He had been up since dawn, working hard; and he worked late into the night in the torpedo rooms with his chiefs and crewmen, getting ready for a combat patrol. Falling asleep was seldom a problem for Byron Henry, but this night his thoughts kept drifting to his wife and son. In the cabin he now shared with Quayne were all his mementos: her picture taped on the bulkhead, her letters worn and wrinkled with rereading, the scarf he had filched from her in Lisbon, a single cracking snapshot of the infant. Lying wide-awake in the dark, he found himself reliving the best moments of the helter-skelter romance — their first meeting, their adventures in Poland, her declaration of love in the pink boudoir of Jastrow's villa, the rendezvous in Miami, the wild lovemaking of the three-day honeymoon in Lisbon, and their dockside farewell in a foggy dawn. He could call up these scenes in detail, her own words and his, her littlest gestures, the look in her eyes; but the memories were dulling, like old phonograph records played too often. He tried to picture where she was now, and what his baby might look like. He gave way to fantasies of a passionate reunion. Like a jewel in his possession was the knowledge that his relief was aboard; that this first war patrol would be his last voyage on the *Devilfish;* that if he survived it, he would be going to the Atlantic.

6

THE day Pamela Tudsbury wrote her letter to Captain Henry — three weeks before the Pearl Harbor attack — a chill November fog had been darkening London for a week, seeping through windows and keyholes and past closed doors, penetrating every cranny. Doorknobs and banisters were sticky to the touch. Indoors or out one breathed fog; there was no escaping the damp. Bronchitis had her feverish, shivering, and coughing up phlegm as she sorted out her things for tropic travel.

The six o'clock news droning out of her bedside radio chilled like the fog. The threat of the Japanese to enter the war was becoming acute. Rejecting Roosevelt's latest peace formula, they were massing troops and ships on the French Indo-China coast, a clear menace to Malaya and Singapore. Radio Moscow was denying that Rostov, the key to the Caucasus and its great oil fields, had fallen to the Germans, but every Nazi victory claim these days was lamely conceded by the Soviets within a week; by now they had confirmed that Leningrad was cut off and under siege, and that the Wehrmacht was surging toward Moscow. Moreover, a German submarine had in fact — as Radio Berlin had been claiming for days — sunk the carrier *Ark Royal* off Gibraltar. The announcer read out this budget of disaster with that BBC calm which was becoming so threadbare. She packed cheerfully, all the same, because she might see Victor Henry on the other side of the world. As for the news, she was numb to it. For months there had been only bad news.

The telephone rang. She turned off the radio to answer it.

"Pamela? It's Philip Rule."

A voice from the past; a deep, self-assured, unwelcome voice. Arresting an impulse to hang up, she said, "Yes?"

"That's a dim 'yes,' Pam. How are you?"

"I have a filthy cold."

"You do sound it. Sorry. What are you doing?"

"At the moment? Packing."

"Oh? For that round-the-world thing Talky's announced?"

"Yes."

"Is Singapore on the itinerary?"

"Yes. Why?"

"I'm going there myself next week for the *Express*. Getting a ride direct in a Blenheim bomber."

Pamela allowed a silence to lengthen.

"Pam, Leslie Slote's in town from Moscow. He's asking after you. I thought you might join us for dinner. He's told me quite a bit about your friend, Captain Henry."

"Oh? Is there any news about him?"

"Well, Pam, I don't know how up-to-date you are on Captain Henry."

"What's Leslie doing here?"

"He's on his way to the U.S. legation in Bern. That's his new post."

"Strange. He'd only been in Moscow a few months."

"He got into trouble there."

"Of what sort?"

"Something about the Jews, I gather. It's a sore point. Don't bring it up with him."

"Where are you dining?"

"At the Savoy."

"I can't get to the Savoy in this blackout and fog."

"I'll come for you, darling. Seven o'clock?"

At the attempted airy intimacy Pamela said, "How's your wife?"

"God knows. Last I heard, she was working in a factory outside Moscow. Seven o'clock, then?"

Pamela hesitated. She was resolved to steer clear of Philip Rule, but she did want to find out what Slote knew about Pug Henry's movements. Leslie Slote was an arid ambitious Foreign Service man, who had jilted Natalie Jastrow back in the old Paris days, after the four of them had had merry times together for about a year. He and Phil had seemed equally heartless then. She felt a bit more kindly to Slote now, because he regretted what he had done. It seemed extremely odd that he had had anything to do with Jewish matters; for he had dropped Natalie mainly to avoid the career problem of a Jewish wife.

"Are you there, Pamela?"

"Oh, all right. Seven o'clock."

At first glance the crowded Savoy Grill appeared to be riding out the war well. But tarnished sconces, dusty draperies, tablecloths washed threadbare, elderly waiters moving slowly in black uniforms gone green at the cuffs and elbows, showed the pinch. The diners too, the most prosperous of Londoners, had a peaked and shabby look. Slote took a spoonful of gummy Scotch broth, for which he had waited twenty-five minutes. With a grimace, he dropped the spoon. "The Savoy's gone downhill."

"What hasn't?" Pamela fingered the pearl choker around her thin throat. Slote guessed she must have a fever: red spots in her cheeks, glittering eyes, intermittent cough, gray cardigan buttoned up tight.

"Singapore hasn't," said Philip Rule. "Today I interviewed a general back on medical leave. They've got the place bristling with big guns and aircraft, and they're quite ready for the Japanese. Their peckers are up, the stengahs are flowing free at the clubs, and even the old Raffles Hotel is very jammed and gay. So he said. He found London shockingly run down."

Pamela said, coughing, "Like the inhabitants."

Rule pulled at his thick red mustache, grinning. "You, darling? You've seldom looked more desirable."

Long ago this crooked grin had affected her like alcohol. Rule's squarish face was fatter, his once-heavy hair was going, but his intent blue eyes still stirred her. She had thought herself cured of him. Not quite!

Their Paris affair had never run smooth. She had made trouble about his waitresses and whores, low tastes which he had seen no reason to alter for her sake. She had turned seriously nasty over a handsome Yale boy, an Antinous out of Bridgeport, with whom he had gone off for three blissful weeks in Majorca. At public school Rule had acquired a taste for this sort of thing, though by and large he preferred women. On his return she had forced a wild scene, and he had knocked her flat on her face; whereupon, half-insane with humiliated fury, she had drunk a bottle of iodine, and he had driven her at three in the morning, writhing and retching, to a hospital. The episode had finished them. Rule had gone on with his life as though nothing had happened, and from his viewpoint very little had.

Like Slote he had been studying Russian in Paris; this was how they had come to room together. Once settled in the Soviet Union as a correspondent, he had met a Bolshoi ensemble girl, so beautiful that he had married her — so he had written Pamela — simply in order to have her, because she was extremely prim and would hear of nothing else. The ceremony in a communist "wedding palace" he had described as comical bosh: a fat stern lady in a tailored suit, briefly lecturing them on communist marriage, while Valentina's parents, relatives, and Bolshoi chums stood about smirking, and the bride, all blushes, clung with one arm to her handsome British catch, and with the other to a bunch of wilting yellow roses. So it was that Rule had a Russian wife. When he was out of Russia he paid no attention to the circumstance.

Avoiding his intimate stare, Pamela spoke hoarsely. "You believe all that about Singapore?"

"Why not? Our monopoly capitalists built themselves the hell of a strong air force and defense system right here in Blighty under our noses, through several pacifist ministries. Surprised our own people, as well as Jerry! The Empire pivots on Singapore, Pam. If we want to go on oppressing and sweating half a billion Asiatics, and stealing the wealth of Australia and New Zealand from the silly aborigines, Singapore has to be impregnable. So no doubt it is."

"Oh, the Empire's finished, no matter what," said Slote.

"Don't be too sure, Les. Winnie's raised another alliance after all, to keep it gasping along. The Russians will beat the Germans for us. Sooner or later your sleepy countrymen will come in and thrash the Japanese. The whole monopoly capital system with its colonies is rotten, and has to go, but not just yet. The white exploiter is a tenacious world master. It will take a global revolution to get rid of him. At a guess that's half a century off."

"What on earth makes you think the Russians will beat the Germans?" Pamela put in. "Didn't you hear the evening news?"

Again the lopsided grin, the old lazy shift of the big body in the chair, the broad gesture with two hairy hands. "Darling, you don't know the Soviet Union."

"I do," Slote said. "I was in Moscow until last Thursday. I've never seen such a collapse of nerve. Everybody who could get wheels or a horse ske-daddled."

"They're only human. They'll recover." Rule's voice dropped to a mellifluous rumble. "Isn't it disconcerting, dear boy, to have the main body of Hitler's army coming at you, fifty miles away?"

"I've been through it twice. It's hell. But I'm a damned coward. I expected more of the Russians."

Pamela and Rule laughed. Pamela liked Slote the better for his honesty, though nothing could make him seem attractive. The skinny pale ex–Rhodes Scholar with his rimless glasses, well-gnawed tobacco pipe, and nervous ways had always struck her as a physical neuter. He had made passes at her in Moscow, which she had yawned off. She had never comprehended Natalie Jastrow's old passion for him.

A shiver racked her. "Leslie, how long did Captain Henry stay on in Moscow?" To put this question she had come to the Savoy, ill as she was.

"Well, let's see. You and Talky went on the sixteenth, didn't you? At the height of the scare?"

"Yes."

"He stayed another week, trying to nail down train tickets beyond Kuibyshev. I thought it would be impossible in that panic but finally he did, and he headed eastward, across Siberia, Hawaii bound."

"Then he'll have gotten there by now."

"Should think so."

"Wonderful."

Rule said to Pamela, in the pleasantest way, "Were you lovers?"

Her tone was just as pleasant. "None of your bloody business."

"Leslie says," Rule persisted with a blink at the rebuff, "that la Jas-trow has gone and married this same chap's son, a submarine officer much younger than she is. He also confides, in great secrecy, that his own heart still bleeds over Natalie. Why ever did she do such a grotesque thing? Did the lad get her pregnant?"

Pamela shrugged. "Ask Leslie."

"They were isolated in a villa outside Siena," Slote said gloomily. "I told you that. Month after month, before he joined the Navy. He was working for Aaron Jastrow as a researcher. I think they were the only two Americans under sixty left in Tuscany. No doubt nature took its course. I spent a whole night in Washington arguing with her about this mismatch. She was irrational. Turned to stone."

"You mean she was in love with him," Pamela said, "and out of love with you."

"Actually, I do mean that," Slote replied with a sudden sad grin that charmed Pamela. "She used to be damned sensible, but she's gone harebrained. Married this youth, stayed on in Italy with Jastrow, and she's still there, last I heard, with an infant on her hands."

Rule chuckled in his chest. "You shouldn't have spent that night in Washington arguing."

"Anything else would have gotten me a black eye."

"Well, if it's any consolation," Pamela said, "Captain Henry also tried to break it up and couldn't. It's a very passionate business."

"That's the man I'd like to meet," Rule said. "Captain Henry."

"Nothing easier. Get yourself an assignment to interview the commanding officer of the U.S.S. *California* in Hawaii," Pamela snapped.

"What do you like about him, Pam?"

"He's decent to the bone."

"I see. The charm of novelty."

The meal went by. Their desserts stood uneaten, gelatinous puddings of tasteless pink goo. The waiter had been paid. Slote wished that Rule would leave. He meant to have another try at Pamela, fever or no; he had not had a woman in months, and unlike Rule he did not enjoy whores. Rule called himself a man of pleasure; Slote thought him rather an animal. He himself had mistreated Natalie, but never in the harsh ways that had driven Pamela to try suicide. Slote had muffed with Pamela in Moscow, he believed, because of Captain Henry. Henry was far away now. Pam was likable and pretty; also easygoing and free-spirited, or so Slote hoped.

"Well! Les is just in from Stockholm today, Pam," Rule said. Obviously he nursed similar notions. "Probably we shouldn't keep him up. Let me drive you to your flat."

"As a matter of fact, I hear music," Pam said. "I'd like to dance."

"Dearest, since when? You haven't danced a step since I've known you."

"My American friends have been working on me. Pity you don't dance. What about it, Leslie?"

"I'd be delighted."

Rule stood up, grinning in defeat. "My best to Talky, then. I'm off to Singapore Monday. See you there, no doubt."

Pamela stared at his departing back, the spots crimson on her gray cheeks.

Slote said, "Are you sure you want to dance?"

"What? Of course not. I feel horrible. I just wanted to get rid of that sod."

"Come up to my room and have a drink." The invitation was plain, but not leering.

A quick smile — knowing, amused, faintly giddy — illumined her face, lovely even in its sickliness. She put a clammy hand to his cheek. "Bless my soul, Leslie, you're still harboring indecent thoughts about me, aren't you? How sweet of you. Sorry, I'm in hopeless shape. I'm burning with fever, and anyway, no."

Slote said, "Okay," with a resigned shrug.

"You really should have married Natalie in Paris, dear. She was so insistent!"

"Oh, Pamela, go screw yourself."

She burst out laughing, took his hand and placed it on her damp hot forehead. "Feel that? Honestly, I'd better find a cab and get on home, don't you think? Good luck in Switzerland. Thanks for the news about Captain Henry."

She wrote the ebullient letter when she got back to her flat.

In a flying boat circling over Singapore, Alistair Tudsbury pulled off his tie, threw open the white linen jacket strained over his paunch, and fanned his wet jowls with a straw hat. "This will be worse than Ceylon, Pam. We're dropping into a bloody inferno."

"Peaceful little inferno," said Pamela, looking down through the tilting window. "Where are the vast fortress walls, the masses of cannon, the swarms of Spitfires and Hurricanes?"

"Nothing shows, naturally. But that small green scorpion down there packs the hell of a sting. I say, there's the *Prince of Wales!* Can't miss those turrets."

Seen from the air Singapore was a broken-off tip of the craggy Malayan mountains; a green triangle in the wrinkled open sea, hanging to the mainland by a thread of causeway. Two gray warts blotched its jungle beauty: to the southeast a modern city sprinkled with red roofs, and up north, near the causeway, an expanse of sheds, cranes, barracks, streets, houses, and broad green playing fields: the Singapore naval base. The base looked oddly quiet. In its docks and wide anchorage not one vessel lay. On the other side of the island, warships and merchant vessels clustered by the city's waterfront.

"Hello there!"

In the immigration shed, Philip Rule pushed through the crowd and plunged past the wooden rail. He wore army shorts and shirt, his face and arms were burned red-brown, and he held a purple orchid in a swollen bandaged hand. "Barely in time. You're both invited to Admiral Phillips's reception aboard the *Prince of Wales*."

"Admiral's reception!" Tudsbury limped up and shook hands. "Smashing."

Rule handed Pamela the orchid. "Welcome to the bastion of Empire, love. These things grow by the roadside here. Come, I'll whisk you through the formalities."

"What's wrong with your hand, Phil?"

"Oh, out on jungle maneuvers with the Argyll and Sutherland Highlanders, I got bitten by a centipede. Nasty brute, a foot long. I hardly knew whether to step on him or shoot him! Charms of the tropics." Rule spoke cheerily over his shoulder, leading them to a small office. Here a perspiring red-faced little man in a brass-buttoned coat stamped the passports.

"Well, well! Mr. Alistair Tudsbury! What an honor. Correspondents are fairly pouring in now, but you're the most famous one yet."

"Why, thank you."

"Let me say, sir, that we've had these Jap scares before. They always blow over. The vultures are gathering in vain, so to speak. No offense, sir. Have a pleasant stay, sir."

Rule collected their luggage, piled it in his car, and raced them to town, where he drove slowly through narrow stifling hot streets, thronged with Asiatics of all ages and skin shades: some in native dress, some dressed Western style, some rich-looking and fat, some bony and naked but for rags. Sweet, spicy, and disgusting smells drifted turn by turn into the car windows. Brightly colored shop signs in strange alphabets lined the streets.

When the car emerged on a boulevard, the scene metamorphosed: broad avenues, green palm-lined parks, signs in English, tall buildings; glimpses of a waterfront, and gusts of refreshing sea breeze; dark-faced, white-gloved Bobbies directing traffic; a British seaport city, burning in un-British heat, its pavements crowded with colored faces. At the big ramshackle Raffles Hotel Rule dropped their bags. A navy launch took them from a steel and concrete pier, roofed with high arches, out to a gaudily camouflaged battleship moored to a buoy. Helped by Rule, clutching her flimsy skirt, Pamela climbed the accommodation ladder. Behind her Tudsbury painfully grunted.

"Oho!" she said as she set foot on deck. "The British! I wondered where they were."

"Everybody's here that matters," said Rule.

Under a brown awning the laughing, chattering guests were standing around drinking cocktails, or waiting in a reception line that stretched to the sunlit forecastle. The men wore white linen suits or bright-hued blazers, the women, flowery print dresses fluttering in the breeze. All the faces were white, unless the owner of the face carried a tray. Four long guns painted in garish patches like snakeskin projected beyond the awning.

"Mr. Tudsbury?" said a young officer at the gangway. "The admiral's compliments, sir. Please follow me."

They went to the head of the line. The admiral, a surprisingly small man with crusted gold shoulder marks on his white uniform, held out a small scrubbed hand. "Frightfully pleased. Very keen on your broadcasts."

He presented them to several stiff old men lined up beside him. Their sharply tailored tropical uniforms showed knobby gray-haired knees and elbows; their military titles were majestic, the highest brass in Singapore. The roar of airplanes interrupted the pleasantries; wave upon wave coming in low from seaward, scarcely clearing the *Prince of Wales*'s masts, then zooming over the waterfront. Distant guns boomed. Beyond the city, clouds of white smoke puffed up against the blue sky. Tudsbury shouted to the admiral, "Would those be our famous coastal guns?"

"Just so. Heaviest calibre in the world. Jolly good marksmanship, my target-towing ships report. Approaching Singapore in anger from the sea *not* advisable!"

"I'd like to visit those guns."

"It will be arranged."

All this was a series of yells through the racket of the air show. Tudsbury gestured upward. "And these planes?"

A tall grayhead in RAF uniform, standing next to the admiral, flashed pride from filmy wrinkled eyes. "Vildebeest and Blenheim bombers leading the pack. The fighters are American Buffaloes. Can't touch our Spitfires, but dashed good, better than what the Japs have got."

"How do you know that, sir?"

"Oh, Jap planes have fallen in China, you know." The gray eyebrows arched in cunning. "We have the book on them. Second-rate, rather."

Rule and Pamela stood at the rail amid a crowd of beaming British, watching the planes. He picked drinks off a tray passed by a Chinese boy. "God, Pam, your father does have a way with the brass. That's Air Chief Marshal Brooke-Popham talking to him. Boss of the whole theatre, Commander-in-Chief, Far East. They're chatting like old school chums."

"Well, everyone wants a good press."

"Yes, and they know he's got the popular touch, don't they? All acid and disenchanted in tone, yet in the end it comes out straight Rudyard Kipling, every time. For God and for Empire, eh, Pam?"

"Anything wrong with that?"

"Why, it's pure gold. False as hell to the future, but why should he care, since he believes it?"

The planes were dwindling in the distance. Pamela sipped her drink, peering fore and aft along the gigantic deck. "You know, Phil, Captain Henry visited this ship when it brought Churchill to Newfoundland. Now we walk its deck off Malaya, and he's commanding a monster like this in Hawaii. Unreal."

"Rather on your mind still, your Yankee captain?"

"That's why I'm here. Pearl Harbor's my destination. Talky knows that."

Rule grimaced and pulled at his mustache. "Look, I'm staying at the home of Jeff McMahon, the head of the Malayan Broadcasting System. Let's all go to dinner at Raffles tonight, shall we? Jeff wants to meet your father and put him on the air. Talky will like Elsa. She's the most beautiful woman in Singapore."

"Then her husband's a fool to have you in the house."

"Why, darling, I don't abuse a man's hospitality." Pamela's response was an arched eyebrow and a contemptuously wrinkled mouth. "You'll come to dinner, then?"

"I don't mind. I can't speak for Talky."

Later the fat old correspondent, in the highest spirits, readily agreed to dine with Singapore's most beautiful woman. "Of course, dear boy. Smashing. I say, the air chief marshal's a brick. I'm to visit the most secret military installations here. Not one door closed. And I'm to write what I bloody well please."

Elsa McMahon wore clinging ivory silk jersey, the only modish dress Pamela had yet seen in the colony. Her heavy glossy black hair might have been done in Paris. Four children milled and clattered about the rambling house, pursued by scolding servants; but the woman had a willowy figure, a cameo face, and the clear smooth skin of a girl, tanned to a rosy amber by tennis. She showed Pamela her house, her books, a whole wall of phonograph records, and before the sunset failed, her tennis court and the garden: a big disorderly expanse of lawn, high palms, flowering bushes and trees — gardenias, hibiscus, jasmine, and jacaranda —in air almost chokingly perfumed. Her easy English had a Scandinavian lilt, for her father had been a Norwegian sea captain. Her husband kept eyeing her as though they had been married a month.

They were killing time over drinks, waiting for Tudsbury to get away from an interview with the governor, when he rang up. The governor had just asked him to dine at the Tanglin Club. He was at the club now. Would Pamela and her friends forgive him, and join them, at the governor's invitation, for a drink?

Rule said testily, as Pam still held the phone, "Pamela, that's damned rude of him. Our dinner was all set. Tell him and that pompous-ass governor they can both go to hell."

"Nonsense, he can't turn down the governor," said Jeff McMahon amiably. "The Tanglin Club's on our way. Let's go."

It was a short drive from the McMahon house. Pulling to a stop at the club entrance, the director of the Malayan Broadcasting System turned to Pamela. "Here you are. Elsa and I will buzz on to the Raffles bar. Don't hurry for dinner. The music goes on till midnight."

"Nonsense. Park the car and come on in. The governor invited all of us."

"I resigned from the Tanglin, Pam, when I married Elsa."

"I beg your pardon?"

Elsa McMahon in the front seat turned her head. The dark eyes were solemn, the lovely mouth taut with irony. "My mother was Burmese, dear. See you at the Raffles."

The Tanglin was spacious, sprawling, and stuffy. Full-length court portraits of the king and queen dominated the foyer; London magazines and newspapers were scattered about; and under the slow-turning fans, the everlasting white-coated colored boys hustled with drinks. A bibulous and strident noise filled the club, for the evening was well along. Tudsbury sat at the bar amid the same people Pamela had seen aboard the *Prince of Wales.* The men were getting quite drunk. The women's evening dresses were as dowdy as their daytime getups. The governor was a placid, unbelievably dull person. Pamela and Rule downed one drink and left.

"Well, the McMahons didn't miss much!" she said, as they came out into a moonlit night heavy with flower scent. British clear through, Pamela believed in the happy breed's superiority, though she never spoke of it. She knew such clubs had such rules; all the same, the exclusion of Elsa McMahon had enraged her.

"Come along, you're surely not just discovering the hard facts of imperialism." Rule beckoned to a waiting taxicab. "How do you suppose twenty thousand whites, most of them frail ninnies, manage to rule four and a half million Malayans? Not by hobnobbing with them."

"She's as much a native as I am."

"One can't allow exceptions, love. The dikes of imperial snobbery hold back a raging sea of color. One pinhole, and they crumble. That's doctrine. Elsa's a wog." He put on a nasal aristocratic voice. "Dashed pity, and all that — so in you go, and let's join our wog lady friend."

In the open palm-lined courtyard of the Raffles, a five-piece band of old white men played listless out-of-date jazz. It was very hot and damp here. The McMahons sat at a table, watching three gray-haired couples sweatily shuffling on the floor. Their greeting to Pamela and Rule was untainted by rancor. They gossiped about the governor with tolerant amusement as they ate.

He was a harmless sort, they said, the son of a vicar. The heat, the bureaucracy, the confusion and complications of his job, had reduced him in seven years to a blob of benign jelly. Nothing could shake, change, or ruffle him. The Malay States were an administrative madhouse, with eleven separate local governments — including some touchy sultans — to deal with. Somehow half of the tin and a third of the rubber that the democracies used came out of this mess. There was money to be made, and it was made. Dollars had been steadily flooding into the British war chest. The people who did the work — two million Moslem Malays, two million Buddhist Chinese, about half a million Indians — all disliked each other, and united in loathing the white handful who ran things, headed by this serene white invertebrate living in Government House, on a high hill inside a big park, far from the congestion and smells of native Singapore. He had had seven years of continuous commendation from London, for keeping the wheels turning. He had done absolutely nothing except let it happen. In the British Colonial Service, said Jeff McMahon, that approached genius.

"Perspectives differ," Rule observed. "I heard a three-hour tirade today against him. The Associated Press man, Tim Boyle, says he's a tough bully with a censorship mania. Tim wrote a piece about the night life here. The censor killed it dead. Tim demanded a meeting with this governor, who bawled him out like a coolie. The governor's first words were, 'I read that story. If you were an Asiatic, I'd put you behind bars.' "

"Ah, that's different," said Elsa. "The British Colonial Office has a long memory. America started as a colony. Once a native, always a native."

The McMahons ate little. After the coffee they got up and danced sinuously to the thin music. Rule held out his hand. "Pamela?"

"Don't be an ass. I break out in a sweat here, with every move I make. Anyway, you know you can't dance. Neither can I."

"You asked Slote to dance with you in London."

"Oh, I was cutting you."

"Sweetie, you can't still be angry with me." The red mustache spread in an unoffended grin. "It all happened in another age."

"Granted, Phil. You're a yellowing diploma on the wall. Just hang there."

"Crushed again! Well, I like your indignation over Elsa. But she's a popular woman, and the Tanglin Club is a bore she can do without. What about the Chinese and Indians you saw uptown, swarming like rats in a garbage dump? That's Singapore's real color problem."

Pamela was slow to answer. She had no political, social, or religious certainties. Life was a colorful painful pageant to her, in which right and wrong were wobbly yardsticks. Values and morals varied with time and place. Sweeping righteous views, like Victor Henry's Christian morality and Rule's militant socialism, tended to cause much hell and to cramp what little happiness there was to be had. So she thought.

"I'm a duffer on those matters, Phil. You know that. Hasn't Asia always been more or less like this — a few rajahs and sultans eating off gold plate, building temples and Taj Mahals, while the masses multiply in cow dung and mud?"

"We came to change all that, love. So says Kipling. And Alistair Tudsbury."

"Haven't we made things better?"

"In a way. Railroads, civil service, a modern language. But Pam, there's just been the hell of a flap here at the Tanglin Club. They barred from their swimming pool the Indian officers — the *officers*, I repeat — of the Fifth Indian Regiment! Educated military men, stationed here to lead soldiers to fight and die for the Tanglin Club! The decision stuck, too. It undid fifty years of Kipling."

The McMahons left early to get back to their children; polite as they were about it, Talky's defection had made the evening pointless. Philip Rule walked with Pamela through the hotel lobby. "Tuck your mosquito netting in firmly, darling," he said at the stairway. "Check every edge. A few of those creatures can drain you like Dracula."

Pamela looked around at the Chinese boys in white coats, crisscrossing through the broad lobby with trays. "The boozing, the boozing! Does it ever stop?"

"I was told, the first day I came," said Rule, "and I've since heard it forty times in the white man's clubs — that Singapore is a place of 'drinks, Chinks, and stinks.' " He kissed her cheek. "Good-night. I shall now hang myself back on the wall."

The first bombs fell on Singapore at four in the morning. Pamela was half-awake, sweating under the mosquito net, when she heard thrumming overhead. Vaguely she thought it was a night fighter exercise. At the first distant thumps she sat up, swept aside the netting, and ran into the sitting room. Tudsbury lumbered out of his room blindly blinking, clutching pajamas over his hairy belly. "That's bombing, Pam!"

"I know it is."

"Well, the yellow bastards! They're really trying it on, are they? By Christ, they'll regret this!"

Airplane roars came and went overhead. Bombs were bursting closer and louder. Pulling off his pajama top, Tudsbury stumbled back into his room. Pamela called from the french windows, "Talky, we haven't even blacked out!" The streets were brilliantly lit. Clouds overhead reflected the glow. She saw no searchlights or tracer bullets, heard no sirens or ack-ack. It was nothing like a London raid. The one difference from other warm odorous Singapore nights, in fact, was that invisible planes overhead were dropping bombs, which the city was serenely ignoring.

His muffled answer came, "Well, nobody was expecting this. There are no land-based Jap bombers with the range to hit Singapore. Brooke-Popham told me that himself."

"Then what on earth is going on?"

"Carrier raid, maybe. Of course, the *Prince of Wales* will intercept and sink any flattop around, if the RAF doesn't get them first. One can't reckon on suicidal madness in the enemy."

Soon he hurried out of his room, untidily dressed. The bombing had moved farther off, but planes still drummed in the sky. She was at the desk, half-nude in her brief nightgown, dully leafing a typescript, hair falling around her face. "This broadcast is obsolete now, Talky."

"Why? My military summary stands. That's the meat of it. It's twice as timely now! I need a new opening about this onslaught, and a resounding wind-up. Have a go at those, won't you? I'll redictate your draft when I return."

"Where the devil do you think you're going, during an air raid?"

"Army Public Relations. I rang Major Fisher. He's holding a press conference right now, and — what's the matter?"

Her head was sinking on the desk in her naked arms. "Oh, it just depresses me so! The whole thing, starting up again out here."

"Courage, girl. These aren't Germans. The planes up there are made of bamboo shoots and rice paper. We'll smash these bastards. Ye gods, look at the lights, will you? This town's really ablaze like a Christmas tree. *Somebody* will catch hell for being asleep on watch! I'm off. You'll draft that new stuff?"

"Yes, yes. Go along," she muttered into her arms.

Pamela was thinking that Clipper flights would certainly stop at once; that the sea lanes to Hawaii would become infested with Japanese submarines; that in fact she was cut off from Victor Henry for years or for good. To have come so far in vain! Would she even be able to get out of Singapore?

Dawn was breaking, and a faint cool breeze through the open french windows was freshening the room with garden scents, when her father burst in, trumpeting like a mad elephant, "Pam! Pam, have you heard?" Still in her nightgown, she looked up blearily from the typewriter. "Have I heard what?"

"Why, you silly frippet, we've WON THE WAR!" Tudsbury's eyes were bulging from his head, and his hands were shaking. "Those yellow sods have gone and attacked *Pearl Harbor!*"

"What!"

"You heard me. Huge carrier raid! All kinds of enormous damage. The Yanks are in it, Pam! In it up to their necks this time! What else matters? We've won the damned war, I tell you! I must have a drink on it or I'll die."

He splashed whiskey into a tumbler, gulped it, and coughed. "Whew. We've *won it*. Won it! What a close-run thing. We've really won this damned war. I'll have to rewrite that piece from page one, but by God, what a glorious moment to live in! These are the days of the giants, Pam. Their footsteps are shaking the earth —"

"What ships were hit?"

"Oh, the Yanks aren't talking, naturally. But the damage is immense. That much comes straight from the wire services in Honolulu. *We* weren't caught short *here*, thank the Christ! They tried to come ashore at Khota Baru airfield, but we shoved them back into the sea. They did gain a beachhead in Thailand. We'll be marching up there this morning to knock them all on the head. Two crack divisions are on the border, ready to jump off. The Japs have really run their heads into a noose this time, and — *now* what's wrong?"

The back of her hand to her eyes, Pamela was striding to her bedroom. "Nothing, nothing, nothing!" She gestured at the desk. "There's your damned draft."

Tudsbury's broadcast brought telephone calls and cables of congratulations from London, Sydney, and New York. He spoke of vast secret stockpiles and fortifications that he had seen with his own eyes; of heavy reinforcements on the way, as he knew from the highest military sources; of the striking calm of Europeans and Asiatics alike under the bombing. His draft script had cited the street lamps burning during the raid, as a humorous instance of Singapore's sangfroid. Hesitantly, apologetically, the censor had asked him to cut this. He had amiably agreed.

Reeling off the statistics of America's giant industrial resources, Tudsbury closed with this peroration: *"Wars are not fought by cold statistics, true, but by warm-blooded suffering men. Yet statistics foreshadow outcomes. This war, though it must yet cause grisly tragedy to mankind, will be won. We know that now.*

"For the grim closing struggle, I can report, Fortress Singapore is ready. Fortress Singapore does not expect a tea party. But it is well prepared for its uninvited guests. Of one thing, let the outside world rest assured. The Japanese will not enjoy — if they ever get close enough to taste it — the bitter brew that awaits them at Fortress Singapore."

When he walked into the bar of the Tanglin Club after the broadcast, the people there rose to a man and clapped, bringing tears trickling on his fat face.

The bombers did not come again to Singapore. There was little word of fighting up-country, either. For Pamela it was a queerly evocative tropical replay of the "phony war" in 1939: the same lift of excitement, the same odd unreality, the same "back to business-as-usual." The blackout was regarded as awkward novel fun, though the shortage of dark cloth gave the club ladies a cause for anxious twittering as they sat rolling bandages in sultry flowery gardens. Air raid wardens in tin hats self-importantly stalked the streets. However, there were no air raid shelters.

This lack bothered Tudsbury. He quizzed the governor. "Watery subsoil, dear fellow," said the governor. Tudsbury pointed out that at the naval base he had seen giant concrete bunkers deep in the earth endlessly stacked with cannon shells, food, and fuel. What about the watery subsoil? The governor smiled at his sharpness. Yes, those caverns had been sunk in the swampy ground at great cost, for the security of the Empire. But in the city such a drastic measure, quite aside from the expense, would alarm the Asiatic populace. Adequate instructions existed for taking shelter in cellars and stone buildings. If required, an elaborate evacuation plan was ready. Tudsbury reluctantly accepted all this. He was the lion of the Tanglin Club, Singapore's reassuring radio voice to the world.

But he had trouble filling his broadcast time. In the first army communiqués the Jap invasion vessels were reported retiring, leaving a few troops behind on surrounded beachheads, and these stranded invaders were being wiped out according to plan. Since then the information had been getting sparser. The place names had been sliding strangely southward. One day the communiqué in its entirety read, *"Nothing new to report."* A theory began circulating at the white men's clubs. Like the Russians fighting Hitler, the military command was cleverly trading space for time, wearing the Japs out in the equatorial jungle, which was as hard on troops as the Russian winter.

Then there was the "monsoon" theory. Army experts had long held that after October, Singapore could rest easy for half a year, since the enemy could not land during the northeast monsoon. But the Japs had in fact landed. The experts now were explaining that any rash military plan could be tried, but the Japanese invasion, fatally weakened by losses in monsoon surf, was bound to peter out in the jungle. Though Tudsbury broadcast these theories, the absence of hard news gnawed at him. The way he had been welcomed, and the impact of his first broadcast, had pushed upon him the role of optimist, but he felt he was getting out on a limb.

Then came the sinking of the *Prince of Wales* and the *Repulse*. Here was hard news! Disaster at the outset, with a strong odor of blundering; sickening, yet familiar in British war-making. Two correspondents returned alive from the *Repulse*, shaken and ill, with historic scoops. Tudsbury had to compete. He burst in on his high military friends, demanded the truth, and got it. The brave little admiral had steamed north, intending to surprise the invasion force, smash it up fast, and escape from the Jap land-based bombers. He had had no air cover. The nearest British carrier was in India. The local RAF command had lacked the planes or had missed the signals; that part was vague. Japanese torpedo planes and dive bombers had roared in and sunk both capital ships. The admiral had drowned. The Empire lay open now to a Japanese navy that included ten battleships and six major aircraft carriers, with only a much-weakened American navy at its back to worry about.

Tudsbury rushed to the Raffles and dictated this hot story to Pamela, centering it on one theme: air power. His broadcast was half an editorial. England had just bought with blood the knowledge that warships could not stand up against land-based air. He pleaded: turn the lesson against the enemy! The Royal Air Force was the world's greatest air arm. Quick massive air reinforcements of Malaya could cut off and doom the Jap invaders. Here was an opportunity worth any sacrifice on other fronts; a turnabout that would redeem the disaster and preserve the Empire.

He sent the draft to the censor's office by runner. Three hours before broadcast time, the censor telephoned him; the broadcast was fine, except that he could not say the ships had lacked air cover. Not accustomed to such interference, Alistair Tudsbury sped to the censor's office in a taxi, sweating and muttering. The censor, a frail blond man with a pursed little smile, shook with terror at Tudsbury's roars, staring at him with round moist little eyes. His military adviser was a navy captain, plump, white-haired, pink-skinned, clad in faultless tropic whites, who gave no reason for his ruling except a reiterated, "Frightfully sorry, old chap, but we can't have it."

After long arguing Tudsbury thrust quivering grape-colored jowls right in his face, bellowing, "All right, before I go directly to Air Chief Marshal Brooke-Popham, WHY can't you have it?"

"It's vital military information. We must deny it to the enemy."

"The *enemy*? Why, who do you suppose *sank* those ships? My broadcast can bring Singapore such a cloud of fighter planes that nothing like that will happen again!"

"Yes, sir, that part is splendidly written, I grant you."

"But unless I *say* there was no air cover, the story is pointless! Can't you see that? Incomprehensible! Idiotic!"

"Frightfully sorry, sir, but we can't have it."

Tudsbury catapulted out to the nearest telephone. The air chief marshal was unavailable. The governor was out inspecting defenses. The time before his broadcast shrank. Arriving at the broadcasting studios in a rage, he proposed to Jeff McMahon that he go on the air, read his uncut script, and take the consequences.

"Good Lord, we're at war, Tudsbury!" McMahon protested. "Do you want us all to go to prison? We'll have to switch you off."

The fat old correspondent was running out of indignation and energy. "I broadcast for four years from Berlin, McMahon," he grated. "Goebbels himself never dared to tamper with my scripts like this. Not once! The British administration of Singapore does dare. How is that?"

"My dear fellow, the Germans only talk about being the master race," Elsa McMahon's husband said drily. "You're on in ten minutes."

7

In a heavy sea, in the early darkness of the morning watch, the U.S.S. *Devilfish* pounded along the west coast of Luzon toward Lingayen Gulf. Byron stood wedged by the gyroscope repeater on the tiny bridge in sticky foul weather clothes, and with every plunge of the forecastle, warm black spray struck his face. The lookouts were silent shadows. They wouldn't doze tonight, Byron thought. Except for this sense of heading toward trouble, and for running darkened, Byron's first OOD watch under way in wartime was like any other night watch: uneventful peering into the gloom on a windy wet rolling bridge, through long empty hours.

About the trouble ahead, he knew more than the crewmen. This was less a patrol than a suicide mission; Aster had showed him on the Lingayen Gulf chart the shallow depth figures, and the reefs that nearly blocked the mouth of the gulf. The clear entrance to the east would be crawling with Jap antisubmarine vessels. If an American sub did by some fluke slip past them to torpedo a troop transport, thereby alerting the whole invasion force — well, as Aster put it, from then on life aboard might be disagreeable and short.

Byron accepted all this. Yet Prien's penetration of Scapa Flow to sink the *Royal Oak* had been as dangerous a venture. The U-boat captain had brought it off, and come home safe to a hero's welcome and a medal from Hitler's hands. Advancing through the dark in a lone submarine, toward a huge enemy force that commanded the air and sea, filled Byron with high-strung zest; possibly a stupid feeling, he knew, but a real one. The exec obviously felt the same way. Carter Aster was smoking a long brown Havana tonight. That meant his spirits were high; otherwise he consumed vile gray Philippine ropes. As for Captain Hoban, he was almost fizzing with combat verve.

Byron's resentment of his commanding officer was gone. The captain had ridden him hard, but that contest of wills now seemed his own fault; his persistence in sloth had been childish. Branch Hoban was a superb ship-handler. He had proved it again, threading out through the tricky new mine fields laid in Manila Bay to block Jap I-boats. He was a skilled submarine engineer, ready and quick to get his hands dirty on a diesel engine, or to sting them with battery acid. His failings were only those of any Academy eager beaver; anxiety to make a record, tough punctiliousness about paperwork, a tendency to grease four-stripers and admirals. So what? He had won E's in engineering and torpedo shooting. Those were the things that mattered in combat. Heading toward the enemy, Hoban was a reassuring boss man.

When the east showed a faint graying, the captain came up on the bridge for a look at the lowering sky. "Lady wants to submerge at 0600. Why the devil should we, with this visibility? We're a long way from Lingayen. I'm not crawling there at three knots, and let the *Salmon* and the *Porpoise* beat me to the attack. Put on four extra lookouts. Conduct continuous quadrant searches of the sky, and go to full speed."

"Aye aye, sir."

The day brightened. The *Devilfish* nauseatingly corkscrewed and jarred through gray wind-streaked swells at twenty knots. Hoban drank mug after mug of coffee, and smoked cigarette after cigarette in a cupped. hand, ignoring the spray that drenched him. Coming off watch, Byron found Aster bent over the navigator's chart in the conning tower, gloomily chewing a dead cigar. To Byron's "Good morning," he barely grunted a response.

"What's the matter, Lady?"

With a side glance at the helmsman, Aster growled, "How do we know the Jap planes don't have radar? They're full of surprises, those yellow monkeys. And what about Jap subs? In daylight we're a sitting tin duck. I want to get to Lingayen fast, too. But I want to *get* there."

Over Aster's shoulder, Byron glanced at the chart. The peninsula projected northwestward of Luzon's land mass like the thumb of a yellow mitten; the U-shaped blue space between thumb and hand was Lingayen Gulf. The course line showed the submarine halfway up the thumb. Beyond the tip, the projected course was a turn east along the reefs and shoals, then a turn south, back down the whole length of the thumb to the assumed landing beach, the point nearest Manila.

"Say, Lady, did you ever hear of Gunther Prien?"

"Sure. The kraut that sank the *Royal Oak* at Scapa Flow. What about him?"

"He gave a lecture in Berlin. I was there." Byron ran a finger along the line of reefs. "He penetrated Scapa Flow through stuff like this. Found a hole and slipped through on the surface."

Aster turned his long-jawed face to Byron, forehead knotted, mouth corners curled in his strange cold smile. "Why, Briny Henry, you getting eager to polish medals? *You?*"

"Well, we'd get there faster if we cut through the reefs, wouldn't we? And we'd duck the destroyers up at the entrance."

Aster's satiric look faded. He reached for the coastal pilot book.

A-OOGHA! A-OOGHA! A-OOGHA!

"Dive, dive, dive." Branch Hoban's voice, urgent but calm, boomed through the boat. The deck pitched forward. Lookouts dropped trampling through the dripping hatch, followed by the OOD, the captain, and last the quartermaster, slamming the hatch and dogging it shut. Byron heard the old hiss and sigh, as though the boat were a live monster taking a deep breath, and felt in his ears the sudden airtightness, before the chief below called, *"Pressure in the boat!"* The *Devilfish* slowed, plowing sluggishly downward with loud gurglings and sloshings.

Hoban wiped his streaming face. "Whitey Pringle spotted a low-flying plane. Or maybe it was a seagull. Pringle has good eyes. *I* didn't argue. The sun's starting to break through, anyhow, Lady. Level off at three hundred."

"Aye aye, sir," Aster said.

Byron slithered down to the control room, and walked forward on the downslanted deck. The Christmas tree of small lights on the port bulkhead, flashing the condition of every opening in the hull, showed solid green. The planesmen at their big wheels had calm eyes fixed on the depth gauges; no trace of combat anxiety here.

"Blow negative to the mark!"

The routine procedure scarcely registered on Byron. In the forward torpedo room he found Chief Hansen and his crewmen affixing warheads to two torpedoes newly loaded aboard. Byron's eyes smarted; he had had no sleep since the departure from Manila, but he wanted to confirm torpedo readiness for himself. Hansen reported all six bow tubes loaded; all fish checked out in working order; the new secret exploders ready for insertion in the warheads. Racked along the bulkheads were yellow dummy warheads, which in peacetime had been filled with water for practice shots; compressed air would empty them, and the torpedoes would float for recovery. Unpainted iron warheads full of TNT now tipped the torpedoes; impossible to detonate without exploders, yet Byron had seen the crew handle these gray warheads with gingerly respect for the havoc and murder in them.

As Byron drank coffee with the torpedomen, crouched on a bunk slung over a torpedo, Lieutenant Aster appeared. "By the Christ, Briny, he's going to try it."

"Try what?"

"Why, that notion of yours. He's been studying the chart and the sailing directions. We're going to surface and look for a break in the reefs. He wants to talk to you about that U-boat skipper's lecture."

In a sparkling noonday, the black snout of the submarine broke the surface. Byron stepped unsteadily out into brilliant hot sunshine on the pitching slippery forecastle, still aslosh with foaming seawater. Lookouts and leadsmen in bulky life jackets stumbled and slipped after him. He could not help a swift glance up at the cloudless blue sky. After the stale air below, the fresh wind was delicious as always, and the pleasure was sharper today because of the danger. Dead ahead, where the dark ocean merged into green shallows, foaming breakers roared against tiny palm islands and jagged brown rocks. White gulls came cawing and screeching over the submarine.

"All ahead one-third! Heave your leads!" Hoban's shout from the bridge was muffled by the heavy wash on the hull and the grinding sound of the breakers. Coral heads were showing, far down in the deep — pink spires, rounded gray domes. The *Devilfish* was heading for a notch between two rocky little islands.

"Mark! Four fathoms, starboard!"

Byron perceived yellow coral sand slanting up, full of immense waving sea fans. Blown dry of ballast, the *Devilfish* was drawing about thirteen feet.

"Mark! Three fathoms, port!"

Eighteen feet. Five clear feet under the keel. With each swell the boat was rising and falling, staggering Byron's party and drenching them with spray. The smaller island was drifting so close that he could count the coconuts on the trees. On the bridge, at the bullnose, and on the fantail, lookouts were combing the sky with binoculars. But in this sunlit waste of air, water, palms, and rocks, the only sign of man was the grotesque black vessel risen from the deep.

"All engines stop!"

From the bridge, Aster yelled through cupped hands, "Fathometer's showing fifteen feet, Briny! What do you see?"

Slipping about, wet to the skin, Byron flailed both arms forward. "Okay! Keep coming!" he bawled, for the water shaded toward blue again beyond the notch. On either side of the submarine, ugly breakers were smashing and creaming on pitted brown rocks. The propellers thrashed; a heavy swell lifted and dropped the vessel. With a crunching *clang, clang!* the *Devilfish* shuddered and jolted forward. Byron caught a fragrant whiff of palm fronds as the islands slid by, near enough to hit with a thrown hat.

"Four fathoms, port!"

"Four fathoms, starboard!

Coral heads drifted below the hull like anchored mines, deeper and deeper. The bow was heading into blue water now. Over the crash and slosh of the breakers came the captain's exultant bellow. "Secure leadsmen and lookouts! Prepare to dive!"

Byron stood in his cabin naked amid sodden clothes piled on the deck, drying himself with a rough grimy towel. Grinning from ear to ear, Aster looked in, green eyes brilliant as emeralds. "How about this? Well done."

"You found the hole," Byron said.

"Lucked into it. That chart is goddamn vague. Glad the patrol plane pilots were having their noon sukiyaki, or whatever."

"What happened there? Did we ground?"

"Starboard screw struck a coral head. The shaft's not sprung. The captain's pleased as hell, Briny. Get some rest."

Yawning and yawning, Byron slipped into the mildewy hot bunk. The *Devilfish* had sneaked itself into a tight predicament, he thought, with no easy way out. However, that was the captain's problem. He turned off his mind like a light — Byron could do that, and it contributed much to his health, though it had often infuriated his father and his naval superiors — and fell asleep.

A shake and a husky whisper woke him. He smelled the tobacco-chewer's breath of Derringer, the chief of the boat. "Battle stations, Mr. Henry."

"Huh? What?" Byron slid aside the curtain, and confronted the jowly smelly face in the dim light from the passageway. "*Battle* stations?"

"Screw noises."

"Oh ho."

Now through the thin hull Byron heard the underwater commotion, and a high faint shuddery *ping* — a very familiar sound from exercises at sea and from the attack teacher. This echo-ranging was different: shriller, more vibrating, with a peculiar timbre.

The enemy.

They were running silent, he realized. The ventilators were off. The air was stifling. Chief Derringer's heavy face was tightly lined with worry and excitement. Byron impulsively put out his hand. The chief grasped it with a horny paw, and left. Byron's watch showed he had been asleep for an hour.

At general quarters he was the diving officer. Hurrying to his battle station, he was reassured by the cool working demeanor of every man in the control room — the bow and stern planesmen at their big wheels watching the depth gauges, Derringer and his plotting team huddled around the dead reckoning tracer, Whitey Pringle on the trim manifold, just as in peacetime exercises off Pearl Harbor. They had been through this a thousand times. Here was the payoff, Byron thought, of Hoban's stiff monotonous drill schedule. Aster, smoking a long rich Havana, stood with the chief of the boat, watching the plot take form. The echo-ranging was getting louder; so was the confused noise of propellers. Ensign Quayne was at the diving officer's post. Of all the men in the control room, only he had the wide-open eyes and shaky lips of fear. Quayne wasn't yet part of the team; he had just survived a sinking; he was not long out of sub school. With these forgiving thoughts, Byron relieved him.

"Lady, when did all this break?"

"We picked up these clowns on sonar at about nine thousand yards. All of a sudden. We must have come out from under a thermal layer."

"Sounds like a mess of them," Byron said.

"Sounds like the whole goddamn landing force. This stuff is spread across a hundred degrees. We can't sort it out yet." Aster lightly mounted the ladder to the conning tower, gripping Byron's shoulder as he passed.

Byron strained to hear the low conversation of Aster and the captain in the tower. A command down the voice tube, Hoban's confident voice, quiet and tense: "Briny, come up to seventy feet. No higher, hear? *Seventy feet.*"

"Seventy feet. Aye aye, sir."

The planesmen turned their wheels. The *Devilfish* tilted up. The gauges reeled off the ascent. The outside noises grew louder still: pings and propeller thrums, now plainly ahead.

"Seventy feet, Captain."

"Very well. Now, Briny, listen carefully. I'm going to raise number two periscope all the way." The captain's voice was firm and subdued. "Then I want you to come up exactly a foot, and level off — another foot, and level off — just the way we did it in that last run on the *Litchfield*. Nice and easy, you know?"

"Aye aye, sir."

The narrow shaft of the attack scope slid softly upward behind Byron, and stopped.

"Coming to sixty-*nine* feet, sir."

"Very well."

A level-off. A pause. "Coming to sixty-*eight* feet, sir."

The planesmen were the best on the boat, an ill-sorted pair: Spiller, the freckled Texan who said "fuck" at every third word, and Marino, the solemn Italian from Chicago, never without the crucifix around his neck, never uttering so much as a "damn"; but they worked like twins, inching the submarine upward.

"Okay! Hold it! That does it!" Hoban's voice went high, loud, almost frantic. "Wow! *Jesus Christ! Mark!* Target angle on the bow forty starboard. Down scope!"

A silence. A crackling in the loudspeaker.

P-i-i-i-ing . . . P-i-i-i-ng . . .

The captain's voice through the quiet submarine, controlled but with a fighting thrill in it: "Now all hands, listen to me. I've got three large transports in column, screened by two destroyers, one point on the port bow. The Rising Sun is flapping plain as day on all of them. It's brightly sunny up there. This is it! I'm coming to normal approach course. Prepare the bow tubes."

Hot pins and needles ran along Byron's shoulders and arms. He could hear Aster and the captain arguing about the range. The periscope bobbed up behind him, and straightway down again. There was rapid talk in the conning tower about masthead heights, and the captain harried the quarter-master for recognition manuals. The echo-ranging grew sharper and stronger, the propeller noises louder. Byron had done enough work on the torpedo data computer to picture the trigonometry in his head. On the dead reckoning tracer, the problem showed clearly: the *Devilfish* as a moving spot of light, the enemy course and its own course as two converging pencil lines. But the target's line was jagged. The transports were zigzagging. They were still beyond torpedo range, according to Aster; or, in the captain's judgment, barely within range. The two men were equally adept at guessing distance by masthead heights. On a submarine there was no more precise range-finder. The transports were on a zig away, and they moved faster than the crawling sub.

Utter silence fell in the conning tower. Silence throughout the boat. All the noise now was outside, a cacophony of machinery sounds and the plangent searching probes of the Japanese sonar.

Piiiing! Piiiiing! P-i-i-i-ing! Pi-i-i-i-ing!

"Up scope. *Okay, here they come! They've turned back!* Mark! Range forty-five hundred. Mark! Bearing zero two zero. Mark! Target angle on the bow seventy starboard. Down scope!"

A pause. The captain's voice, hushed and urgent on the PA system: *"Now all hands, I intend to shoot. Open outside doors on bow tubes."*

His natural voice, in the conning tower: "Damn! An absolute setup, Lady, but an outside range. We're not going to close them much with that angle on the bow. What stinking luck!"

"Captain, why don't we hold our fire and track them? It's a fantastic chance. That zigzag plan will slow their advance. Maybe we can pull ahead and close the range."

"No, no, no. *Now's* our chance, Lady. They're making fifteen knots on a radical plan. If they zig away again we may lose the bastards. I've got a setup and a solution, and I'm going to shoot."

"Aye aye, sir."

"Outside doors are open, sir!"

"Very well. Slow setting!"

Concentrating on holding depth, Byron could scarcely grasp that at last this was the real thing; not the launch of a yellow-headed dummy, but a TNT warhead attack on ships filled with Japanese soldiers. Except for the different sonar sound and the choking tension, it was so much like an attack school drill, or an exercise at sea! It was going very fast now, along old familiar lines. Hoban had even used this slow setting for the hit on the *Litchfield* that had clinched the E.

"Up scope! Mark! Bearing zero two five. Range four thousand. Down scope!"

The aiming was harder on a slow setting, the chance for missing greater, detection of torpedo wakes by the enemy more likely. In this decision to make his first wartime shot on slow setting, Hoban was accepting marginal conditions. Fifteen years as a naval officer, ten years as a brilliant peacetime submariner, lay in back of that decision. . . . Byron's heart thudded, his mouth was dry as dust . . .

"*Fire one!* . . . *Fire two!* . . . *Fire three!* . . . *Fire four!*"

With the usual jolts and rushing water noises, the torpedoes left the *Devilfish*.

"Up scope. Oh, wow. Four wakes! Four beautiful wakes, running hot, straight, and normal. Down scope!"

Heart-stopping expectant silence again, all through the *Devilfish*. Byron watched the second hand of the control room clock. It was easy to calculate the time to target, at slow setting, on the last called range.

"Up scope!"

A long, long silence. Time passed for all four torpedoes to hit. Byron stiffened with alarm. No impacts; and the periscope had been up for ten seconds, and was staying up! Maximum safe exposure was six seconds.

"Down scope. Four misses, Lady. Goddamn." The captain sounded sick. "At least two wakes had to go under the lead transport. I *saw* them heading there. I don't know what went wrong. Now they've spotted the wakes, and turned away. The near destroyer's coming at us, with a hell of a bone in its teeth. Let's go to ten knots." He called through the tube, "Byron! Take her down to two hundred fifty feet."

On the loudspeaker his voice turned dull and cranky. "Now all hands, rig for depth charge on the double."

Two hundred fifty feet? Lingayen Gulf was nowhere deeper than a hundred seventy feet. The captain's impossible order shocked and baffled Byron. He was grateful for Aster's lively interposition. "You mean a hundred fifty, Captain. That's about down to the mud here."

"Right. Thanks, Lady — a hundred fifty, Byron."

With a silent jar of acceleration, the submarine tilted and dove. Aster spoke again. "What course, Captain?"

It was almost a silly question, but Hoban was giving no order for the all-important evasive turn. Overhead on the surface of the sea, four slick white bubbly torpedo wakes certainly led straight to the *Devilfish*. The destroyer must be charging up those visible tracks at forty knots. The pitch of the echo-ranging was rising to a scream, and the probes were coming thick and fast on short scale: *ping, ping, ping, ping!*

"Course? Oh, yes, yes, left full rudder! Come to — oh, make it two seven oh."

"Left to two seven oh, sir," called the helmsman.

The diving vessel tilted sideways. The oncoming Japanese ship sounded much like the *Litchfield* in practice runs, but noisier and angrier, though that very likely was Byron's imagination; like a train approaching on loose old tracks, *ker-da-trum, ker-da-trum, KER-DA-TRUM!*

Throughout the *Devilfish*, shouts, slams, clangs of maximum watertight rigging.

The destroyer came closer, passed right overhead — *ker-da-TRAMM-TRAMM-TRAMM-TRAMM* — and moved away.

The pitch of the sonar dropped. White faces in the control room turned to each other.

Byron heard one clear *click,* as though a ball bearing had bounced off the submarine's hull. Another quiet second, and the depth charge exploded.

8

CHRISTMAS carols filtered scratchily over the loud drunken talk and the clack-clack of iron wheels. Palmer Kirby disliked club cars, and Christmas carols depressed him, but he needed to drink. This express train howling toward Washington through the snowy night carried no gloomier passenger.

Rhoda Henry would be waiting at Union Station. He was hungrily glad of that, yet ashamed of his yearnings. She was the wife of another man, a battleship captain out fighting the Japanese. After stumbling into this affair, he had tried to right himself by proposing marriage to her. She had considered it, but backed off. Resuming the sex relationship after that had been ignominious; so he now thought, in his low mood. Dr. Kirby had no religious or moral scruples; he was a dour decent atheist, a widower of old-fashioned habits. This constrained and messy adultery was a damned poor substitute for having a wife. He had to limit his attentions to avoid scandal, yet his sense of honor tied him down like a husband. In his travels he now was ignoring attractive secretaries and receptionists, whose eyes sometimes glinted at this tall ugly bony-faced man with thick grizzled hair. He had been telephoning Rhoda regularly. Pug's cable from Pearl Harbor that she had read him, AM FINE HAVE JUST BEGUN TO FIGHT, had both gladdened and humiliated Kirby. He liked and admired the man he was cuckolding. It was a wretched business.

The root of Dr. Kirby's dark mood, however, was the war. He had been touring a land legally a belligerent, yet paralyzed by frivolity, indecision, lack of leadership — and above all, by Christmas, Christmas, Christmas! This whoop-dee-do of buying, selling, decorating, gorging, and guzzling, to the endless crooning of Bing Crosby's inescapable gooey voice, this annual solstice jamboree faking honor to the Christ child, this annual midwinter madness was possessing the country as though Hitler did not exist, as though Pearl Harbor were untouched, as though Wake Island were not falling. The Lucky Strike ads showed jolly red-cheeked old Santa Claus wearing a tin soldier hat, cutely tilted. In one sickening image, that was the national attitude.

Kirby had found some sense of war on the West Coast: hysterical air raid alarms, brief panics, spotty blackouts, confused and contradictory orders from the Army and from Civil Defense, rumors of submarines shelling San Francisco, fear of the Japanese mixed with inexplicable cocksureness that America would win the war. Eastward even this shallow awareness dimmed. By Chicago the war had faded to a topic for talk over drinks, or a new angle for making money. The thought of defeat entered few people's minds. Who could beat America? As for the Armageddon swirling before Moscow, the terrific counterstrokes of the Red Army against the Wehrmacht hordes — to most Americans Santa Claus in a tin hat was considerably more real.

Perhaps in the muddled turmoil of Franklin Roosevelt's management agencies, production boards, and emergency committees, now multiplying in Washington like amoebas, something was being accomplished. Perhaps in army camps, naval bases, shipyards, and airplane factories, a capacity for war was growing. Kirby didn't know. He knew he was returning in despair from a tour of the country's resources for producing actino-uranium. He had seen a national industrial plant so disorganized and swamped by war orders that even if the scientists solved the theory of nuclear explosives, the factories could never produce the weapons. Everywhere the wail was not enough copper, not enough steel, lack of labor, lack of parts, lack of machine tools, skyrocketing prices, ignorant government officials, favoritism, corruption, and confusion. He had travelled with good credentials from Washington, but men with such credentials were swarming over the land. He had been unable to reveal what he was after. If he could have — and he had tried some hints — it would not have helped. To the harassed factory managers, atom bombs belonged in science fiction tales with spaceships and time machines. Warning articles had long since appeared in scientific journals, and even in *Time* and *Life*. But people could not grasp that this futuristic horror was upon them.

Yet it was.

Uranium had been disintegrating harmlessly through aeons. Human awareness of radioactivity was not fifty years old. For about forty years it had seemed a minor freak of nature. Then in 1932, the year before Franklin Roosevelt and Adolf Hitler had simultaneously come to power, an Englishman had discovered the neutron, the uncharged particle in atoms, and after only seven years of further unsettling discoveries in Italy, France, Germany, and America — seven years, a micro-second of historical time — the Germans had shown that neutron bombardment could split uranium atoms and release vast primordial energies.

In 1939, Kirby had attended a physicists' convention where chilling news had started as a whisper and swelled to an uproar. Columbia University scientists, following up on the German experiments, had proved that a splitting uranium atom emitted, on the average, more than one neutron. This answered the key theoretical question: was a chain reaction in uranium possible? Ominous answer: *yes*. A new golden age of available power was thus opening. There was, however, another, and very horrible, aspect. An isotope discovered only four years earlier, called U-235 or actino-uranium, could conceivably fire off in a self-sustaining explosion of incalculable magnitude. But could any country produce enough pure U-235 to make bombs for use in this war? Or would some blessed fact of nature crop up, in dealing with large lumps instead of tiny laboratory quantities, that would render the whole doomsday project a harmless failure, a physical impossibility? Nobody on earth yet knew these things for sure.

So the race was on to isolate enough of the fearsome isotope to try to make bombs. On all the evidence of Palmer Kirby's senses, and of the information available to him, Adolf Hitler's scientists were going to win this race hands down. They had a formidable lead. British science and industry were already too strained for an all-out atomic bomb effort. Unless the United States could overtake the Germans, the superb Nazi war plants were likely to furnish the lunatic Führer with enough U-235 bombs to wipe out the world's capitals one by one, until all governments grovelled to him.

Such was Palmer Kirby's view of the actino-uranium picture. If the future really held that shape, what other military plans or operations mattered? What human relationships mattered?

In a black cloth coat with a silver fox collar, a tilted little gray hat, and gray gloves, Rhoda Henry was pacing back and forth at the train gate well before its arrival time. She was taking a chance on being seen meeting him; but he had been away almost a month, and this reunion was bound to be pivotal. Kirby did not yet know that she had written Pug to ask for a divorce, that the Pearl Harbor attack had intervened, and that she was now vaguely craw-fishing. All these disclosures now lay before her.

The letter to Pug had been a desperate thing. Several bad developments had made Rhoda spring like a frightened cat. For one thing, his letter from Moscow about the *California* had arrived; and though that was fine news, she had feared that next he might ask her to come to Hawaii. Palmer Kirby, a much less inhibited man than Pug, had wakened late-blooming lusts in her. She dreaded giving him up. She loved Washington, and detested life on Navy bases overseas. Kirby was right here in Washington, doing his hush-hush work, whatever it was. She had never asked; his presence was what mattered.

But at the time Pug's letter came, her relationship with Kirby had been getting shaky. His work had taken him off on long trips. The anniversary of his wife's death had dejected him. He had once again begun muttering about feeling guilty, and about breaking off. Thoroughly scared by a long lugubrious talk over dinner in a restaurant, she had gone with him one evening to his apartment, instead of bringing him to her house. By rotten luck they had run straight into Madge and Jerry Knudsen in the lobby. Madge had a big mouth, and the Navy wives' grapevine was the fastest communication network in the world. A nasty story might well be winging to Pug in Hawaii!

Pushed into this corner, in a spell of three straight days of sleet and rain, alone in the twelve-room Foxhall Road house, with Kirby off on another trip, and not telephoning her, Rhoda had sprung. Now that the children were grown, she had decided, only five or eight tolerable years were left to her before she shrivelled into an old dry crone. Life with Pug had run down. Kirby was a vigorous lover, a self-made wealthy man. He was mad about her, as Pug had not seemed for many years. Perhaps the collapse of the marriage was her own fault and she was not a very good person (some of this had crept into what she wrote to her husband), but it was now or never. Divorces among four-stripers were common, after all, as Navy families grew up and apart, and the long separations took their toll. Come to that, she knew a tangy tale or two about Madge Knudsen!

So off the letter had gone. Hard upon it, by the most appalling mischance, the Japanese had attacked, and blown all Rhoda's little calculations to smithereens. Rhoda's reactions to the bombing of Pearl Harbor had been not admirable, perhaps, but human. After the shock, her first thought had been that the start of a war spelled a quick sharp rise in the prospects of naval officers. Commanding a battleship in the Pacific, Pug Henry was poised now for a brilliant recovery to — who could say? Certainly to flag rank; perhaps to Chief of Naval Operations! In asking for the divorce just now, had she blundered like the Wall Street man who held an oil stock for twenty years, and then sold out a week before the corporation struck a new field?

With this practical concern went genuine regret at having hit her husband at a bad time. She still loved him, somewhat as she loved her grown children. He was part of her life. So she had fired off the repentant cable, and the short agitated letter which he read aboard the *Northampton*, withdrawing her divorce request. His reply to the request had filled her with remorse, pride, and relief; remorse at the pain traced in each sentence, pride and relief that Pug could still want her.

So Pug knew the worst, and she still had him. But what about Kirby? One look at him, hurrying up the train platform with those long legs, coatless and hatless in the billowing vapor, told Rhoda that she still had this man too. Her risky spring was turning out well. You never knew! She stood there waiting, gray-gloved hands outstretched, eyes wide and shining. They did not kiss; they never did in public.

"Palmer, no coat? It's ARCTIC outside."

"I put on long johns in Chicago."

She darted him a mischievous intimate glance. "Long johns! Shades of President McKinley, dear."

Side by side they left the thronged terminal, clamorous with train announcements and with Bing Crosby blare. Dr. Kirby peered through whirling snow as they walked out into the lamplit night. "Well, well! The Capitol dome's dark. There must be a war on."

"Oh, there's all kinds of a war on. The shortages are starting already. And the prices!" She hugged his arm, her motions elastic and happy. "I'm one of these awful unpatriotic hoarders, dear. Do you LOATHE me? I bought two dozen pairs of silk stockings yesterday. Paid double what they cost three weeks ago. Cleaned out two stores of my size! Silk's all going into parachutes, they say, and soon we'll be lucky to get even nylon stockings. Ugh! Nylon! It bags around the ankles, and it's so CLAMMY."

"Heard again from Pug?"

"Nary another word."

"Rhoda, on the West Coast they're saying we lost all the battleships at Pearl Harbor, the *California* included."

"I've heard that, too. Pug's letter sort of did sound like it. Real low. But if it's true, he'll get some other big job. It's inevitable now."

Kirby slung his suitcase into Rhoda's car in the dark parking area. Once inside the car they kissed, whispering endearments, his hands straying under her coat. But not for long. Rhoda sat up, switched on the lights, and started the motor. "Oh, say, Madeline's here, dear."

"Madeline? Really? Since when?"

"She fell in on me this afternoon."

"Staying long?"

"Who knows? She's muttering about becoming a Navy nurse's aide."

"What about her broadcasting job?"

"I guess she's quitting — oh, BLAST you, you IMBECILE!" A red Buick pulled out from the curb ahead of her, forcing her to brake, skid, and wrestle with the wheel. "I swear, the MORONS who have the money to buy cars nowadays! It's so AGGRAVATING."

This kind of irascible snap was normal for Rhoda. Her husband would not even have noticed. But it was new to Palmer Kirby, and it grated on him. "Well, in wartime prosperity does seep down, Rhoda. That's one of the few good things that happens."

"Possibly. All I know is, Washington's becoming UNLIVABLE." Her tone stayed shrill and hard. "Just BOILING with dirty pushy strangers."

Kirby let it pass, weighing the news of Madeline's presence in the house. Would Rhoda consent to come to his apartment? She didn't like doing that, she knew too many people in the building. So the reunion looked to be a fiasco, at least for tonight. His inamorata had a family, and he had to put up with it.

In point of fact, Rhoda was counting on Madeline's surprise visit to help her through a difficult evening. Madeline's presence luckily postponed certain tactical and moral questions; such as, whether she should sleep with Palmer, after having written to Pug that she wanted to preserve their marriage. In a quandary Rhoda's rule was "If possible, do nothing." With her daughter in the house, doing nothing would be simple. Her casual announcement of Madeline's presence had masked great tension about how Kirby would take the news, and this lay under her little outburst at the Buick. Her natural crabbiness had hitherto been unthinkable with Kirby; in irritated moments she had bitten her tongue, choked down her bile, and kept her face smiling and her voice honeyed. It amused and relieved her to note that he reacted like Pug; after one admonishing remark, he did not speak again. He too was manageable.

They were driving past the darkened White House, on the side where the Christmas tree stood on the lawn, amid crowds of gawkers. "I suppose you know that Churchill's in there," she said gaily, sensing that the silence was getting long. "Churchill himself. What a time we're living in, love!"

"What a time, indeed," he replied with deep moroseness.

Like most pretty girls, Madeline Henry had a doormat suitor. She had briefly fallen in love with Midshipman Simon Anderson at her first Academy dance because his white uniform fitted so well and he could rhumba so smoothly. He too had fallen in love, mooning and carrying on about the beautiful Henry girl, and sending her atrocious poems; and upon graduation he had fecklessly proposed to her. She was barely seventeen. Enchanted with this very early bloody scalp on her belt, Madeline of course had turned him down.

Scalped or not, Simon Anderson was a dogged customer. Five years later he still pursued Madeline Henry. He was with her tonight. On her telephoning him from New York that afternoon, he had made himself free for her. A prize-winning physics student at the Academy, Lieutenant Anderson was now working at the Bureau of Ordnance, on a secret radical advance in antiaircraft fuses. But to Madeline Sime remained the doormat: good for filling an evening on short notice, and for pumping up her ego when it lost pressure. Anderson accepted this status, tolerated her treading on him, and bided his time.

Rhoda and Dr. Kirby found them drinking by a log fire in the spacious living room of the Foxhall Road house. Rhoda went off to the kitchen. Kirby accepted a highball and stretched his legs, chilled despite the long johns, before the blaze. He was struck by Madeline's almost blatant allure. Her red wool dress was cut low, her crossed silk-clad legs showed to the knee, and she had a roguish buoyant sparkle to her. "Oh, Dr. Kirby. The very man I want to talk to."

"Delighted. What about?"

Madeline did not dream, of course, that there was anything between her mother and Kirby but elderly friendship. Rhoda's church activities and her prim manners and speech had in no way changed. Kirby seemed a nice old gentleman, with a hint in his eye of relish for women, which decades ago might have been beguiling.

"Well, we've been having the maddest conversation! My head's spinning. Sime says that it's become possible to make radioactive bombs that may blow up the world."

Anderson spoke crisply. "I said conceivable."

Kirby gave Anderson a cautious glance. This blond middle-sized lieutenant looked like any other junior naval officer: young, clean-cut, commonplace. "Are you a physicist, Lieutenant?"

"That was my major, sir. I did postgrad work at Cal Tech. I'm a regular officer of the line."

"Where are you stationed?"

Erect on his chair, Anderson rapped out his words like answers to an oral examination. "BuOrd Proving Ground, sir."

"I have an E.E. from Cal Tech. How would you go about making this frightful bomb?"

"Well, sir —" he glanced at Madeline — "it requires a new technology. You of course know that. All I said was that Germany might be well along toward it. Their technology is outstanding. They made the first discoveries, and they have high military motivation."

"Why, I'd be *petrified*," Madeline exclaimed, "if I could believe any of that. Imagine! Hitler drops one of those things on the north pole, just to show his power, and it melts half the polar cap and lights up the night sky, clear to the equator. Then what happens?"

"Good question," Kirby replied mournfully. "I wouldn't know. How long will you be in Washington, Madeline?"

"I may just stay here."

Kirby saw surprised gladness on Anderson's face. "Oh? You're giving up your radio work?" As he said this, Rhoda came in wearing a frilly apron over her gray silk dress.

"I'm not sure. It's getting hard to take — same idiotic cheerfulness, same grubby commercials, war or no war. Just phony patriotic stuff. Why, we had a songwriter on the show last night, singing his brand-new war ditty, 'I'm Going to Find a Fellow Who's Yellow, and Beat Him Red, White, and Blue.' What a creep!"

Anderson's sober face cracked in a boyish laugh. "You're kidding, Mad."

Her mother asked, "Now what is this, dear? Have you quit your job or not?"

"I'm trying to decide. As for Hugh Cleveland, that egomaniac I work for, what do you suppose *he's* contributing to the war effort, Mom? Why, he's bought his wife a sable coat, that's what. And he's taken her off to Palm Springs. Just left the show on my hands, with a dumb comedian named Lester O'Shea to interview the amateurs. Christ, what a coat, Mama! Huge collar and cuffs, solid sables down to mid-calf. I mean it's *vulgar* to own and wear such a coat in wartime. I plain got disgusted and came home. I need a vacation myself."

Madeline had told Rhoda with great indignation of Mrs. Cleveland's unjust suspicions about her and Cleveland. The mother now had a clue to Madeline's conduct. "Madeline, dear, was that quite responsible?"

"Why not? Didn't *he* just up and leave?" She jumped to her feet. "Come on, Sime, feed me."

"Won't you two eat here, dear? There's plenty."

Madeline's ironic glance at Kirby made him feel his years, it declared so plainly her lack of interest in the idea.

"We're just snatching a bite, Mom, before the movie. Thanks."

Rhoda treated her lover, in the matter of creature comforts, as she had her husband. She served him excellent lamb and rice, and a good wine. She had a hot mince pie for him, and the heavy Italian coffee he preferred. They brought the coffee into the living room by the fire. Kirby lolled his great legs on the sofa, mildly smiling at her in warm well-being over the coffee cup.

This was the moment, Rhoda thought, and she walked out on the tight-rope. "Palmer, I have something to tell you. I wrote Pug about a month ago, asking for a divorce."

His smile faded. His heavy brows knotted. He put down his coffee and sat straighter. Rhoda was not surprised, though this was a letdown; he might have showed gladness. In good balance, she ran lightly along the rope. "Now, darling, listen, you're free as air. Just remember that! I'm not sure I ever want to marry again. I'm in a terrible turmoil. You see, I thought he might ask me to come and set up house in Honolulu. I simply couldn't face leaving you. So I did it, and now it's done."

"What reason did you give him, Rhoda?"

"I simply said that we'd been seeing each other, and that I'd fallen so hopelessly in love that it was wrong not to tell him."

Slowly, heavily, he shook his head. "Gruesome timing."

"I agree. I'm not clairvoyant, my darling. I couldn't know that the Japs were about to bomb Pearl Harbor."

"Has he answered yet?"

"Yes. A lovely, heartbreaking letter."

"Let me see it."

She went to her bedroom to get it.

Kirby clasped his hands between his knees, staring at the fire. He at once thought of repeating his proposal. In the circumstances, it seemed mandatory. But marrying Rhoda Henry now wore a different aspect than it had in his hotel room fantasies. He was on the spot. This development struck Kirby as a maneuver. He was a hard-grained man, he knew maneuvering, and on principle resisted being outmaneuvered.

The war rose again in his mind. How much better was he, after all, than the Christmas celebrants he despised? Stuffed with lamb, rice, mince pie, and wine, hoping to sleep with another man's wife, and perhaps to steal her for good while the man fought the war; could self-indulgent pettiness sink any lower? Right now his place was back in the apartment, writing a report for the meeting tomorrow with Vannevar Bush . . .

In the bedroom, meantime, Rhoda read over her husband's letter, as it were with the engineer's eyes. For an instant, she saw herself as shallow, tawdry, and unworthy of either man. She weighed making some excuse to withhold it from Kirby. But she had observed in his eyes all evening that he desired her. That was the main thing. Let the rest go as it would. She brought him the letter where he sat hunched, poking the fire. He read it, studied the scuffed snapshot of Natalie and Louis, then without a word handed the envelope to her. He rested his head on the back of the sofa, rubbing his eyes.

"What's the matter, dear?"

"Oh, nothing. I've still got a report to write tonight."

"It is awkward, isn't it — I mean, Madeline being here and all?"

With a grimace and a shrug of one shoulder Palmer Kirby said, "It really doesn't matter."

So chilly were those words, all of Rhoda's recently gained security was blasted away. "Palmer," she said in a charged voice, "take me to your apartment."

This startled life into his drooping eyes. "What? Is that what you want?"

"What do you think, you fool?" They looked at each other. Rhoda's expression smouldered and a little half-smile curved her thin pretty lips. "Don't you?"

She returned to the house around one. The living room was dark, and Madeline was not in her bedroom. Having already bathed in Kirby's apartment, Rhoda changed into a housecoat and went downstairs. She felt a bit silly about all this rapid-fire dressing and undressing. Otherwise she felt very good indeed — an afterglow in her body, a new peace in her mind. Kirby had proposed, as expected, after the lovemaking. She had firmly put him off. She could not consider, she had told him, a proposal made under pressure. Brilliant response! He had wonderfully cheered up, his dutiful manner vanishing in a great grin and a strong hug.

"Well, meantime, Rhoda, will we — well, go on seeing each other?"

"Dear, if 'seeing' is what you choose to call this, why yes, by all means. I loved being seen by you tonight. Very penetrating vision." Rhoda enjoyed such wheezy ribaldry with Kirby; a taste that somehow, with Victor Henry, she seldom indulged. Her remark brought Kirby's sudden vulgar smile, showing teeth and gums. Then when she left, some time later, his unreflecting remark, "When will I see you again?" made them both whoop with laughter.

She threw logs on the red embers, mixed herself a drink, and reread Pug's letter. With Kirby's proposal in hand, it affected her differently. She was a grandmother twice over, and here she was loved and wanted by two fine men! Not since her adolescent days, when the phone had jangled with dance invitations, and she had turned down two boys in the gamble that a preferred third one would call, had she felt quite this pleasure in her own power to attract.

With such thoughts running through her mind, she jumped when the telephone rang. It was the long-distance operator, calling from Palm Springs for Madeline Henry.

"She's not here. I'm her mother."

Rhoda heard Cleveland's unmistakable voice: "Operator! Operator! I'll talk to this party . . . Hello, Mrs. Henry? Sorry to disturb you." The celebrated rich rumble charmed and soothed the ear. "Is Maddy really in Washington?"

"Yes, but she's out for the evening."

"Look, how serious is she about becoming a nurse's aide? I mean, I'm all for patriotism, Mrs. Henry, but that's a ridiculous notion. Any nigger girl can become a nurse's aide."

"Frankly, Mr. Cleveland, I admire her. There's a war on."

"I realize that." Cleveland heavily sighed. "But the morale effect of *The Happy Hour* is a great war service, I assure you. You should see the letters from admirals and generals framed in my office!" The voice grew warmer and more intimate. "Rhoda — if I may call you that — with two sons and a hubby in the armed forces, aren't you making enough of a sacrifice? Suppose they send her overseas? You'd be alone all through the war."

"Madeline didn't like your going off on a vacation at this time, Mr. Cleveland. She feels you're indifferent to the war. And she said something about sables."

"Oh, Jesus! What did she say about the sables?"

"Sables for your wife, I believe."

With a low groan, Cleveland said, "Christ, if it isn't one thing it's another. She manages the show backstage, Rhoda. I can step out for a week, but she can't. We have to train a replacement for her. Please tell her to call me when she gets in."

"I'll probably be asleep. I can leave her a message."

"Thanks. Write it in lipstick on her mirror." That made Rhoda laugh. "I'm not kidding. I must talk to her tonight."

Rhoda was finishing her drink by the fire when she heard Madeline in the hallway saying good-bye to Sime Anderson. The daughter marched in perkily. "Hi, Mom. Nightcap? Think I'll join you."

"Dear, Hugh Cleveland called."

The daughter halted, frowning. "When?"

"Not long ago. His number in Palm Springs is on the telephone table."

Tossing her nose in the air like a little girl, Madeline sat down by the waning fire, and picked up the snapshot beside her father's letter. "Wow, Briny's baby, hey? Poor Natalie! She looks fat as a cow here. Mom, can't you find out what's happened to them?"

"Her mother wrote to the State Department. I haven't heard from her since."

"That's a weird marriage anyway. Most marriages seem to be. Take Claire Cleveland. She hasn't grown with Hugh, and that makes her insanely jealous. Did Dad write anything about that stupid letter I sent him?"

"Only in passing."

"What did he say?"

Rhoda looked through the three sheets. "Here we are. It's short. 'I don't know what went wrong with Madeline. I'm kind of sick about that, and don't propose to dwell on it. If the fellow wants to marry her, that may clean the mess up as much as anything can. If not, he'll be hearing from me.' "

"Oh, dear. Poor, poor Dad!" Madeline struck a little fist on the sofa. "She'd no more have divorced Hugh! I should never have written. I just panicked, because I was so astounded at her accusations."

"Write him again, dear. Tell him that it was all nonsense."

"I intend to." With a huge yawn, Madeline stood up. "Sime is sort of sweet, you know? So crushed, so obliging! If I asked him to cut off his own head, he'd fetch an axe and do it. Boring, actually."

"Do go and call Mr. Cleveland, Madeline."

The daughter went out. Later Hugh Cleveland called again. The phone rang and rang until Rhoda answered. She went to her daughter's room and shouted at her through the bath door, over the sound of gushing water, to take the call.

"What the Christ does he want?" Madeline yelled. "I can't be bothered. Tell him I'm covered with soap."

Cleveland said he would wait until Madeline dried herself.

"Oh, Jesus! Tell him I like to soak myself for half an hour before I go to bed. This is outrageous, pestering me at half past two in the morning!"

"Madeline, I'll NOT go on with this idiotic bellowing through a door. Dry yourself and come out."

I *WON'T*. And if he doesn't like it, tell him I quit, and to kindly go and hang himself."

"Hello? Mr. Cleveland? Better wait until morning. She's truly in a very bad mood."

"He'll call *you* in the morning," she carolled, her teasing singsong conveying Madeline's victory.

"I couldn't care less," Madeline sang back.

Rhoda tossed in the darkness for almost an hour, then got up, fetched a writing pad and pen, and sat up in bed.

Dearest Pug —

I could write forty pages, expressing how I feel about you, and our life together, and the wonderful letter you've written me, but I'll keep this short. Of one thing I'm sure. You're mighty busy now!

First of all, Madeline. It's a long story, but the nub of it is she was frightened by an utterly false accusation and an utterly scurrilous threat. I'm sure she's innocent of any wrong-doing. She's come to stay with me for Christmas, so I don't feel totally alone, and I must say she's turned into quite the spiffy New York gal. Believe it or not, Sime Anderson still dances attendance! He took her out tonight. She's in excellent control of her situation, and you can put that problem out of your mind.

If you can do it, please put me out of your mind, too, for the next few months, except as the little old lady back home. You have a war to fight. What I said in my last letter still goes, but there's this *horrible* time lag in our correspondence, and we just can't thrash anything out this way. I've been around a long time, and I'm not going to do anything drastic. When you get back, I'll be right here in Foxhall Road, waiting like a good Navy wife in my best bib and tucker, with a full martini jug.

I cried when I read your offer to forget my letter and go on as before. That's like you. It's almost too generous to accept, and we both ought to take time to think about it. It may well be that I'm "not a schoolgirl," and that I've actually been going through a sort of middle-aged "hot flash." I'm doing my best to "sort myself out," right down to the bottom. That you would be willing to forgive me is almost inconceivable — to anyone who doesn't know you as I do. Believe me, I have never respected and loved you more or been more proud than when I read your letter.

There's no news yet about Natalie and her baby, is there? None here. Please send any news of Byron. Love to Warren, Janice, and little Vic —

And of course, and forever to you —

Rho

Having written this, and meant every word of it, Rhoda turned out the light and slept the sleep of the just.

9

POUNDING at the door.

The floor of the old Raffles Hotel bedroom shook as Pamela went running out, fumbling a negligee around her. "Who is it?"

"Phil Rule."

She opened the door and got a shock.

She had last seen him on the morning after the Japanese attack, all nervy and dashing in jungle war rig, about to fly a rented private plane to the front. Rule was a sport flyer, and in pursuing a combat story he could be foolhardy. He had first fascinated Pamela during the Spanish Civil War with tales of his wild plane flights; his romantic yarns salted with Marxist rhetoric had put her in mind of Malraux. Now he was sodden wet, his hair hung in strings, his unshaven face was gaunt and hollow-eyed, and his bandaged hand was horribly swollen. Beside him, just as drenched, a short hard-faced army officer with iron-gray hair slapped a dripping swagger stick on a palm.

"My God, Phil! Come in."

"This is Major Denton Shairpe."

Tudsbury limped out of his bedroom in droopy yellow silk pajamas. "Bless me, Philip, you're drowned," he yawned.

"There's a cloudburst outside. Can you give us some brandy? Penang has fallen. We've just come from there."

"Good Christ, *Penang?* No."

"Gone, I tell you. Gone."

"Are they *that* far south? Why, that island's a fortress!"

"It was. All Malaya's falling. It's an utter rout, and your broadcasts are criminal lies. Why in Christ's name are you sucking up to the mendacious incompetent bastards who've botched this show and probably lost the Empire — not that it was worth saving?"

"I've told the truth, Phil." Tudsbury's face flushed as he handed the two men glasses of brandy. "Such as I could find out."

"Bollocks. It's been a lot of *Rule Britannia* gooseberry jam. Malaya's gone, gone!"

"I say, jolly good brandy!" The major's voice was astonishingly high and sweet, almost like a girl's. "Don't mind Phil, he's got the wind up. He's never been through a retreat like this. Malaya isn't gone. We can still defeat these little bastards."

"Denton was on General Dobbie's staff," Rule said hoarsely to Tudsbury. "I don't agree with him, but listen to him! He'll give you something to broadcast."

Pamela went into her room for a bathrobe because Philip Rule kept staring at the thin silk over her breasts and thighs.

"Do you have a map of Malaya about?" Shairpe piped, as Tudsbury refilled his glass.

"Right here." Tudsbury went and lit a hanging lamp over a wicker table in mid-room.

Using his swagger stick as a pointer on the map, Shairpe explained that this campaign had all been foreseen. He had himself helped to plan General Dobbie's staff exercises. Years ago they had predicted where the Japs would probably land for an invasion, and how they would advance. Dobbie had even staged a mock invasion during the monsoon, to prove its feasibility. But nobody in the present Malaya Command seemed aware of the Dobbie studies. Indian and British troops in the north, caught off guard in a wild night storm, had retreated pell-mell from the Japanese beachhead. The Japs had come on fast. Fixed fall-back positions around Jitra, built and stocked to hold out for a month, had fallen in hours. Since then the army had been stumbling backward without a plan.

Moreover, the troops were weakly dispersed over the peninsula — Shairpe flicked the stick here and there — to protect airfields foolishly sited by the RAF without consulting the army. Their defense could not be coordinated, and several fields had already fallen. So the Japs had taken control of the air. Furthermore, they had tanks. There was not one British tank in Malaya. The War Office in London had decided that tanks would be useless in jungle warfare. Unfortunately, Shairpe said in dry high nasal tones, the Japanese had not been informed of this piece of wisdom. Though their tanks were poor stuff, they were punching along unopposed, panicking the Asiatic troops. Antitank obstacles were piled in Singapore, but nobody was putting them in place.

With all this the defenders still had the edge, Shairpe insisted. Three Jap divisions had landed. The British could muster five, with plenty of air and ground reinforcements on the way. The Japs were well trained for jungle war — lightly dressed, able to live on fruits and roots, equipped with thousands of bicycles for fast movement down captured roads — but Japan was attacking all over the Pacific; and most likely this landing force had to live and fight on whatever supplies it had brought or could seize. If the defenders would scorch the earth, and force the invaders with delaying actions to use up their food, fuel, and bullets on the long march south, the attrition in time would halt them. They could then be destroyed.

Shairpe showed on the map where strong fall-back defenses ought to exist. General Dobbie's report had called for building these in peacetime. It hadn't been done — a major folly — but there was still time. The material lay ready in warehouses. A labor pool of two million Chinese and Malayans, who all hated and dreaded the Japs, was available. They could do the work in a week or ten days. Two very strong lines were needed, close in: one in Johore on the other side of the strait, the other along the north shore of Singapore Island itself, with underwater obstacles, petroleum pipes, searchlights, pillboxes, barbed wire, machine gun nests —

"But that's been done," Tudsbury interrupted him. "The north shore's already impregnable."

"You're wrong," Shairpe replied, his oddly girlish voice roughened by brandy. "There's nothing on the north shore of this island but marsh."

After a pop-eyed pause, Alistair Tudsbury said, "I saw massive fortifications there myself."

"You saw the outer walls of the base. They're to keep out busybodies. The base is not a defensible strong point."

"Are you telling me that the BBC has been lied to, by the highest officials in Singapore?"

"Oh, my dear fellow, the BBC's a propaganda channel. One uses you. That's all I'm here for. I hope you can somehow get the Malaya Command cracking." Shairpe thinly smiled and slapped the stick on his palm. "Phil says you've a heart of oak, and all that sort of thing. The Empire's teetering in the balance, Tudsbury. That's not journalism. That's a military fact."

Tudsbury stared at this calm, wet, powerfully convincing officer. "All right. Can you come back about nine this morning?" He was limping about the room in agitation. "I'll stay up all night to draft this story. Then I want you to vet it."

"Really? Nine o'clock? Jolly good! Keen to help."

"But you've got to shield Denton," Rule put in, "even if they twist your balls in red-hot clamps."

Shairpe left. Rule asked if he might stay and doze in an armchair. He meant to go to a hospital at first light.

"Look, get off those wet clothes. Hang them up and have a bath," Tudsbury said. "Then use the extra bed in my room."

"Thanks awfully. I do stink all over. At Jitra we went wading through bogs. I had to pick forty leeches off myself. Filthy little horrors!"

"What's happened to your hand?" Pamela said. "It looks awful."

"Oh, an imbecile army medico lanced it at Jitra." Rule gave the hand a miserable, worried glance. "I hope I don't lose it. I may have a touch of blood poisoning, Pam. I'm shaking from head to foot."

Pamela smiled. With all his daredeviling, Rule had always been a hypochondriac. Tudsbury asked, "Where's your plane, Phil?"

"The Malacca airfield. We caught an army lorry from there. They wouldn't refuel me. Denton and I flew there from Penang. We had to beat people off the plane at Penang, Talky, and I mean white people. Army officers, in fact!"

Pamela drew a bath and laid out fresh towels, but then she found him asleep in his clothes. She took off his boots and outer uniform, which had a foul swampy odor, and tucked the mosquito netting about him. As she rolled him about, he muttered in his sleep.

Memories assailed her. Up till now, here in Singapore, he had been the ex-lover: older, sleekly flirtatious, repellent. But this big worn-out dishevelled blond man, lying asleep in his dank underwear with everything showing, seemed much more the Phil Rule of Paris days. Russian wife and all, at least he was not ordinary! In Paris he had always been — in his jagged and tormenting fashion — fun.

"What the devil, Pamela?" Tudsbury called. "Get at the typewriter and let's go."

Stumping here and there, waving his arms, he dictated a broadcast called "Conversation with a Defeatist." At the Golf Club, he recounted, he had talked with a crusty old retired army colonel, full of alarmist opinions. Denton Shairpe's views came out as this old carper's words. Defeatism tended to conjure up such nightmares, Tudsbury pointed out, and the story showed a human side of the Singapore defenders. He himself was sure that the fixed defense lines existed, that the fighting retreat was going wholly according to plan, and that the north shore of Singapore Island was a bristling death trap. This episode merely proved that free speech still prevailed in Fortress Singapore, that democracy in Malaya remained self-confident.

When he finished, Pamela opened the blackout curtain. The sky was gray. Rain was still coming down hard.

"Adroit, what?" her father asked, when she failed to comment. "Tells the story, yet they can't fault me."

She said, rubbing her eyes, "You'll never get away with it."

"We'll see. I'm going to catch an hour's sleep."

Major Shairpe, much spruced up and wearing a pith helmet, arrived on the dot of nine. Making a few small rapid corrections on the script in pencil, he piped, "I say, you've got the hell of a retentive memory, Tudsbury."

"Long practice."

"Well, it's a smasher. Most ingenious. Congratulations! Hope it has some effect. I shall be listening for it up-country. Jolly glad Phil got me to come."

Pamela dropped the script at the censor's office and went shopping.

Buyers were crowding in and out of the stores, mostly run by Chinese, and still crammed with peacetime goods at far cheaper prices than in London — silk lingerie, jewelry, gourmet food and wines, kid gloves, elegant shoes and purses. But in nearly every store there now hung a copy of the same sign, newly printed in vaguely Oriental red lettering: *Cash Only Please — No More Charge Accounts or Chits.*

"Is that you, Pam?" Tudsbury called as she dropped her bundles on the map table.

"Yes. Any news?"

"Rather. I've been summoned to Government House." He emerged from his room freshly shaved and ruddy, in a white linen suit and a rakishly tilted hat, with a pugnacious gleam in his eye. "Berlin all over again!"

"Did Phil ever wake up?"

"Long since. He left a note in your bedroom. Cheerio!"

Rule had written in childish block letters: *"Excuse left hand printing luv. Appreciate thoughtfulness mosquito netting. Sorry you had to put on bathrobe due my sudden attack of memory and desire. My hand's killing me. A toi, Malraux."*

She threw the note into a wastebasket, and fell fast asleep on a couch. The telephone woke her. An hour had passed.

"Hello, Pam?" Tudsbury sounded excited and gay. "Throw together a bag for me. I'll be travelling for about a week."

"Travelling? Where to?"

"Can't talk now."

"Shall I also pack?"

"No."

He soon arrived, his suit dark-patched with sweat at the armpits. "Where's the bag?"

"On your bed, all ready."

"Let me have a stiff gin and bitters. The fat's in the fire, Pamela. My destination's Australia."

"Australia!"

"I am in very, very hot water, my dear." He threw off his jacket, opened his tie, and fell into an armchair with a creak. "It's *worse* than Berlin. By God, that script raked raw nerves! The governor and Brooke-Popham were fairly jigging with rage. I got the unruly native treatment, Pam. These two lords of creation actually tried to bully me. Bloody fools, they're the ones who are in trouble. But they're determined to throttle anybody who wants to shake them out of their dream world. It was an hour of revelation, Pam, bitter and ominous revelation. What I saw was dry rot, pervasive and terrible, at the very top. Ah, thank you." He gulped the drink.

"What am I to do? Follow you?"

"No. Brooke-Popham's about to be relieved. Find out what you can. Keep notes. I'll hurry back and cover this battle, but that script must go on the air."

"Talky, there's censorship in Australia."

"Nothing like this. It can't be. The unreality, the unreality! The self-contradiction! Do you know, they first said they had the fixed defense lines. Then no, they admitted they hadn't, because the labor wasn't available! As for Shairpe's native labor pool idea, they called it ignorant poppycock. Malaya's mission is to earn dollars. Every native taken from the gum trees or the tin mines hurts the war effort — this, mind you, with mines and plantations falling day by day to the Japs! Also, the government can't compete with the pay scale of the planters and mine companies. To commandeer the labor at government rates would take three months of correspondence with the War Office. That's how their minds are working, Pamela, with Penang gone and the Japs roaring south."

"Singapore will fall," Pam said, wildly wondering how she could get out of this place.

"Not if Shairpe's view prevails. I've lent myself to this government's suicidal sham. Now I must make amends. Thank God Phil brought Shairpe here — hullo, here we go!" He sprang at the ringing telephone. "Yes? Yes? — Ah, beautiful! Superb. Thank you — Pam, they did it! They bumped a poor American merchant off the flying boat. I'm on my way."

"You'll be in Australia for Christmas, then. And I'll be here."

"Pam, what's to be done? It's the war. This should be a historic broadcast. The BBC can sack me afterward. I don't really care. Once the deed's done, and the dust settles, I'll come back, or you'll fly to Australia." Tudsbury babbled all this as he combed his hair, straightened his tie, and ran to get his bag. "Sorry to bolt like this. It's only for a few days."

"But will the Japanese come in those few days? That's what I'm wondering."

"Do you think I'd abandon you to face that? They're three hundred miles away, and advancing only a few miles a day."

"Well, good. Given the choice, I'd rather not be raped by platoons of slavering Orientals."

"See here, do you feel I'm treating you badly?"

"Oh, Talky, on your way! Merry Christmas."

"That's my girl. Cheerio."

Major Shairpe had told the plain truth. Fortress Singapore was a phantom. What the Tudsburys had seen from the arriving aircraft was the simple fact. It wasn't there.

When an empire dies, it dies like a cloudy day, without a visible moment of sunset. The demise is not announced on the radio, nor does one read of it in the morning paper. The British Empire had fatally depleted itself in the great if laggard repulse of Hitler, and the British people had long since willed the end of the Empire, by electing pacifist leaders to gut the military budgets. Still when the end was upon them, it was hard to face. Illusion is an anodyne, bred by the gap between wish and reality. Such an illusion was Fortress Singapore.

It was not a bluff. Nothing is clearer from Churchill's memoirs than that he himself believed that there was a fortress at Singapore. Of all the people on the spot — army officers, naval officers, colonial administrators, all the way up the grand chain of command — there was not one man to tell the Prime Minister that Fortress Singapore did not exist. And the British belief in the "bastion of Empire" was infectious, at least for Europeans. Hermann Göring warned a visiting Japanese general, months before Japan struck, that Fortress Singapore would hold out for a year and a half. This same general later captured Singapore in seventy days.

Nor was the illusion generated out of thin air. Singapore did command the main eastern trade routes, at the water passage between the Indian Ocean and the South China Sea. In the lean pacifist years, many millions in military funds had been poured into it, for the Japanese threat had been anticipated. Early in the century the English had themselves built Japan's modern navy, with great profit to British shipyards. The quaint feudal Japanese had caught on fast, defeating Czarist Russia's navy to the warm applause of the British press. But when the smoke of the First World War cleared away, the shift in world forces made it conceivable that those same quaint Nipponese might one day try to vex the Empire. Accordingly, the gigantic naval base at Singapore, capable of servicing the whole Royal Navy, had been constructed. The plan was that if ever trouble from Japan threatened, the main fleet would steam to Singapore, to end the trouble by awe or by force. That the Germans might make trouble at the same time, requiring the main fleet to stay at home, seems to have been overlooked.

So Singapore was stocked with food, fuel, and ammunition for a siege of seventy days. That was the time the fleet would need to muster up and get there. Great fixed cannon pointed seaward, to hold off any attempted assault by the Japanese fleet before help came. All this did give the feeling of a fortress.

Yet the sea did not entirely moat Singapore. An attack could come by land from the north, down the wild Malayan peninsula and across the narrow Johore strait. But the planners judged that four hundred miles of jungle made a stouter barrier than fortress walls. Moreover, actual walls on the island's north side, they felt, would suggest a fear that the Japanese might come from the north one day, and that the British army might not be able to stop them. The British ruled in Asia by an aura of invincibility. With the main fleet seventy days away, what pressing need was there for such a mortifying precaution? The walls were not built. Instead, to make assurance doubly sure, Singapore Island's stockpile was doubled to last one hundred forty days.

Thus the "Fortress Singapore" image arose. The years of planning, the outpouring of treasure, the rivers of ink in newspapers and journals, the resounding political and military debates, fostered an all but universal fantasy, reaching to Britain's highest leaders, and all over the Western world, that a fortress was there. The lifeblood of the British working class went into a naval base twenty miles square, with the largest docks in the world, with cranes, repair shops, every conceivable spare part and machine, elaborate housing and recreation facilities; and with enough ammunition, food, and oil to supply the whole fleet for many months, squirrelled away in the giant concrete caverns sunk in the swamps. In its way it was as striking an engineering feat as the Maginot Line.

But to the last, to the moment when the last retreating Scots brigade crossed the causeway in February with bagpipes playing, and demolition charges blew a hole in the one link to the mainland swarming with oncoming Japanese soldiers, the north side of Singapore remained without defenses: defenses that Churchill always assumed were there, as — in his own words — he assumed that "a battleship could not be launched without a bottom."

In the event, the fleet never came. It was too busy fighting the Germans in the Atlantic, in the Mediterranean, and in home waters. The vast facilities stood empty until, with the Japanese army a mile away, the British did their best to blow up or burn the base. But it fell in usable condition, a staggering military haul. Churchill's insistence on trying a ragged remnant of the seventy-day plan, by dispatching the *Prince of Wales* and the *Repulse*, only doomed them.

Airfields had also been laid out in Malaya and heavily stocked up — except with planes. The RAF never came in force. It had lost too many planes saving England from the Luftwaffe, and had shipped hundreds more to the Soviet Union; though of those a large number never flew, sunk in the sea by German torpedoes. The few aircraft on hand in Malaya were shot from the sky fast. The Japanese planes "made of bamboo shoots and rice paper" turned out to be Zeroes, the most advanced fighter aircraft then on the planet. The Japanese seized the splendid airstrips, which they called "Churchill aerodromes"; and from these richly supplied fields their planes helped batter Singapore into surrender.

So the confused Singapore record now reads. Congress investigated Pearl Harbor, but Parliament did not investigate Singapore. Churchill shouldered the blame, stooped an inch or two lower, and went on with the fight.

The confusion still extends to the very name. What was "Singapore"? Singapore was the city; Singapore was the island; Singapore was the naval base; Singapore was "the bastion of Empire." But at bottom "Singapore" was a narcotic myth, which dulled the pain while the gripping hand of white Europe on Asia was amputated.

The unused strategy of General Dobbie — so it turned out after the war — had been absolutely sound, for the invaders did arrive at Singapore at their last gasp, greatly outnumbered by the defenders, their fuel and bullets almost spent. In one final assault, they daringly burned up and shot off everything they had left. The Singapore command caved in, and the colored Malayans had new masters with colored skins.

Alistair Tudsbury made his broadcast from Australia. Pamela heard him in the McMahons' guest cottage, where Philip Rule, arm in a sling, was bedridden. The hand had been lanced again, and he had to rest for a week. The McMahons and their dinner guests down at the main house had shown little interest in listening to her father. After a copious *pahit* and a big meal with several wines, they were singing carols around a piano. Through the darkness, over the drumming of the rain and the bass croaking of bullfrogs from nearby mangroves, their voices dimly floated to the cottage, where Pamela sat under a large slowly turning fan that stirred her hair and fluttered her thin long skirt. Perhaps half as bright as a candle, the radio dial diffused a faint orange glow in the room. Through the open window came sprays of rain and wisps of frangipani scent.

The reception was good, the script almost intact. The fictitious colonel no longer asserted that the island's north shore was undefended; it needed "some dashed double-quick stiffening." The charge that the RAF had put down airfields without regard for their defensibility was gone; and Tudsbury's closing disclaimer was more strongly phrased.

"Was it worth it, Phil?" Pamela asked, turning down the sound but leaving the dial to glow.

He drew on a cigarette, his face shadowed with deep lines of bitter irony. He was looking better. Rule was very strong, and a few days of rest pulled him out of most distempers. "A wee bit too clever. The dotty old crank came off quite lifelike. It won't be taken seriously, not by anybody who counts."

"How else could Talky have done it?"

"I don't know. I'm amazed it got by, even so."

"Phil, will Singapore fall?"

Rule harshly laughed. "Darling, I fear so. But blaming the governor, or Brooke-Popham, or Duff Cooper, or even Churchill is pointless. There's just a general collapse. Nothing's working. The system's just rotten-ripe to fall apart. Up-country there's simply no leadership. The men want to fight. They *try* to fight, even the Indian troops do. But again and again come these pusillanimous orders from Singapore — fall back, pull out, retreat. I've seen the men crying over their orders. These Tanglin Club overlords down here have bad consciences, Pam. They're played-out funks. They fear the Japs, and they fear our own Asiatics. When you think about it, this domination of Asia by white Europeans has always been damned silly. It was bound to be temporary. Why grieve at its passing?"

"How do I get out of Singapore?"

"Oh, you'll get out. The Japs are still far off. There are vessels waiting to evacuate the white women and children. That's what they did at Penang, you know. They got out the Europeans — soldiers and all — and left the Asiatics with their women and children to face the Japs. Do you know that? And then Duff Cooper went on the air and announced that *all the inhabitants of Penang had been rescued!* He really meant it, Pamela. To Duff Cooper, the Asiatics were part of the animal life of Penang. It's causing an uproar now — what happened, and what he said. I don't think the Asiatics care anymore who's top dog here. Maybe we're gentler than the Japanese, but at least they're colored. The Asian endures brutality better than contempt."

"You don't believe in the American rescue expedition everyone's talking about?"

"Wishful fantasy. The Americans have no fleet. It was all sunk at Pearl Harbor."

"Nobody knows what happened at Pearl Harbor."

"Denton Shairpe does. They lost all eight of their battleships. The Americans are finished for two years in the Pacific, if not forever. A rescue expedition for Singapore is as likely to come from Switzerland, but — what the hell's the matter with you?" Pamela Tudsbury was burying her face in an arm on the back of the chair. "Pamela! What is it?" She did not answer. "Oh, Christ, you're thinking of your Yank! Sorry, old girl. When Denton first told me, I thought of him myself. Pam, I know nothing about the casualties. There's every chance your man's all right. They were sunk inside a harbor, in shallow water."

Still she said nothing and did not move. Outside, the rain, the bullfrogs, and a distant chorus —

> *God rest ye merry, gentlemen,*
> *Let nothing you dismay —*

Suddenly a wild gibbering and giggling just outside the window, as by a frightened lunatic, made Pamela sit up with a shriek. "Oh! My God! What's *that?*"

"Easy now. That's our apricot monkey. He comes and goes in the trees. Sounds dreadful, but he's harmless."

"God Almighty, I hate Singapore! I would have hated it in peacetime." Pamela stumbled to her feet, wiping her moist brow. "Let the Japanese have it, and good riddance! I'm going back to the house. Are you all right? Do you want anything?"

"I'll be lonely, but that's no reason for you to miss the fun. Run along."

"Fun! I just don't want to be rude to my hosts. They'll be thinking I've gotten into bed with a sick man."

"Well, why don't you, Pam?" She stared at him. "Truly, wouldn't it be charming? Christmas Eve and all that? Remember Christmas Eve in Montmartre? When Slote and Natalie had that monumental fight at dawn, and we went sneaking off to Les Halles for onion soup?" The mustache twisted in a slow beguiling well-remembered smile, shadowy in the orange radio glow. He held out his good arm. "Come, Tudsbury."

"You're a swine, Philip, an unchanging swine" — Pam's voice trembled — "and everything else I called you in our little Bastille Day chat."

"Darling, I was born in a rotting system, and so perhaps I'm a rotter, if the word has any meaning. Let's not have that old quarrel again, but aren't you the inconsistent one? When everything's breaking up, there's nothing but pleasure. You believe that yourself. I take my pleasures lightly, you insist on drama. That won't change, I grant you. I do love you."

"And your wife? I'm just curious. In Paris you had no wife, at least."

"Sweetie, I don't know if she's alive. If she is, I hope she's screwing the brains out of some nice deserving Russian fighting man on leave. Though I doubt it, she's a worse prig than most Englishwomen are nowadays."

Pamela plunged out the door.

"You'll need the umbrella," he called after her.

She returned, snatched the umbrella, and darted outside. She had not gone ten steps in the blackness, when, almost at her ear, the monkey set up its blood-freezing cry. With a little scream Pamela sprinted forward and ran into a tree. The bark scratched her face. The branches swept the umbrella from her hand and showered her. She caught it up and stood paralyzed, soaking wet. Almost straight ahead she could hear the singing —

> *There'll always be an England,*
> *While there's a country lane —*

but the night was pitch-black. She had come by starlight, in an interval between showers. She had no clear idea of how to proceed. The path twisted steeply through the banks of oleanders and bougainvillea.

It was a bad moment for Pamela. Her father's broadcast had sunk her spirits. The familiar voice, coming from so far away, had intensified her nervous sense of being alone and unprotected. In recent days, threatening Japanese broadcasts in broken English had scared her. The guttural alien voices had sounded so close, so horrible! She had almost felt callused hands with tough nails ripping at her underwear and forcing her thighs apart. More than most threatened females she knew how weak Singapore was.

And now Rule had Shairpe's word that Victor Henry's ship had been sunk! Even if Henry had survived, he would be reassigned. Even if she got out of Singapore, she would probably never see him again. And if she should, by some bizarre chance, then what? Did he not have a wife? She had set out on a wild goose chase around the world, and here she was, wet and lost in the hot black night, under an umbrella in the garden of strangers in a downpour, on Christmas Eve, perhaps her last.

> *There'll always be an England,*
> *And England shall be free —*

She did not want to join these drunken Singapore British in their songs. This cheap ditty unbearably brought back the first days of the war, the brilliant summer of the Battle of Britain, and the best moment of her life, when Commander Henry had come back from the flight over Berlin and she had flung herself into his arms. All that glory was crumbled now. She liked the McMahons, but their friends were dullards from the club crowd and the army. Two young staff lieutenants had been paying court to her, from the *pahit* drinking onward; both crashing bores but handsome animals, especially a long-faced blond lieutenant with a languid Leslie Howard air. They would be after her again, as soon as she returned to the house — if she could find her way without falling on her face in muck. Obviously they both were intent on sleeping with her; if not tonight, another night.

How wrong were they? What did it matter? What was her spell of continence, vaguely for Victor Henry's sake, but a stupid out-of-character joke, after all the damned screwing she had done in her life?

Behind her, the open window of the guest cottage was a faint orange oblong in the dark. To someone who did not know it was really there, it would have seemed an optical illusion. In the all-encompassing blackness and rain, it was the only hint of light, the only way to go.

10

B YRON had never heard a depth charge detonate under water; nor had anybody else on the *Devilfish*.

A hideous ear-splitting *BONG* shuddered through the whole vessel, like the blow of a sledgehammer on a giant bell. The control room tumbled in nauseating earthquake motions; glass smashed, loose objects flew, and the lights blinked scarily, all in the roaring reverberation of a thunderclap. While the planesmen managed to cling to their control wheels, the plotting party went staggering, Chief Derringer falling to his hands and knees, the others toppling against bulkheads. Byron felt such sharp stabbing pains in his ankles that he feared they were broken. An instrument box sprang off the overhead and dangled on an electric cable, emitting blue sparks and the stinking smoke of burning rubber. Confused yells echoed through the vessel.

BONG!

This second metallic thunderbolt blacked out the lights and flung the deck bow-upward. In the darkness the blue sparks kept flaring, terrified groans and shouts arose over the thunderous roaring outside the hull, and a heavy body with flailing arms fetched up against Byron, crushing his back agonizingly against the ladder to the conning tower.

This time it truly felt like the end, with the submarine on a horrible up-slant, sounds of breakage all around, Derringer weighing him down like a warm corpse — he could smell the tobacco breath — and the Japanese sonar baying loud, fast, and triumphant on short scale: *peeng-peeng-peeng-peeng!* Another explosion made the tortured hull scream and ring. A squirt of cold water struck Byron's face.

Except for the lancing death in its torpedoes, the *Devilfish* was very weak and very slow. Even on the surface it could go only half as fast as the destroyer overhead. Underwater its sprint was eleven knots, its usual crawl three knots. The destroyer could run circles around it, probing for it with sonar; and the tumbling depth charges did not even have to hit. Water transmits an explosion in a shock wave. A miss thirty feet off could finish the *Devilfish*. It was just a tube of nine long narrow cylinders joined together, a habitable section of sewer pipe. Its pressure hull was less than an inch thick.

It had only one military advantage to balance its feeble sluggishness —

surprise; and it had blown its surprise. Now it was a creeping scorpion in a flashlight beam. Its only resort was to dive; the deeper it dove, the less the chance of being found and pinned by sound echoes. But in Lingayen that refuge was denied. The test depth of a fleet submarine, then a guarded secret, was four hundred twenty feet, and the safety margin was close to a hundred percent. *In extremis* the submarine captain could as a rule burrow down as far as six hundred feet, with some hope that his poor tube might survive the leaks springing at the fittings. Deeper, the heavy black fist of the sea would crumple the steel hull like tinfoil. Hoban would gladly have risked the *Devilfish* beyond test depth now; but the end of the line for him in most of Lingayen was shallow muck at about a hundred feet.

There were other hazards. A surface ship had a natural balance, but a submerged submarine was a waterlogged object. Trapped air bubbles in its tanks held it suspended, a wobbly thing hard to control. Water and fuel oil, pumped here and there through pipe mazes, made the long tube tilt one way or another, and the submarine unfolded planes much like an aircraft's to steady it. But the vessel had to keep moving or the planes would not work.

Stopped for long, a submarine like the *Devilfish* was done for. It would slowly sink below its test depth — or in this case, into the muck — or it would pop to the surface to face the destroyer's five-inch guns. And it could not keep moving underwater for more than a few hours, at any speed. For underwater there is no air for a combustion engine to consume. As it had only so much bottled air for its crew to breathe in a dive, so it had only so much stored power to use. Then it had to stop, lie on the bottom, or come up for air to burn fuel and get itself going again.

On the surface, the submarine wound itself up for moving underwater. The diesels not only drove the boat but also charged two huge banks of batteries with energy to their chemical brim. Submerged, the *Devilfish* would draw on these batteries. The faster it moved underwater, the quicker the batteries would go flat. At three or four knots it could stay down for about twenty-four hours. Doing radical escape maneuvers at ten knots, it would be finished in an hour or so. In extreme hazard, the captain could try to outwait his pursuer, lying on the bottom while the crew used up its air. That was the final limit: forty-eight to seventy-two hours of lying doggo, and a submarine had to choose between asphyxiation below and destroyer guns above.

The lights flickered yellowly on. Byron wiped the salt water off his face — from some fitting strained by the explosion but holding, thank God! The chief pushed himself off Byron, his mouth forming apologetic words the ensign was too deafened to hear. However, as through cotton wool he did hear Aster directly overhead bawling, "Captain, he's got our depth cranked in. We're getting creamed. Why don't we go to fifty feet and give him a knuckle?"

The captain's voice blared in the tube, "Briny, come up to fifty feet! *Fifty feet!* Acknowledge!"

"Fifty feet! Aye aye, sir!"

The planesmen steadied the vessel to climb. Their response was calm and expert, though both of them looked over their shoulders at Byron with round eyes in livid faces. As it climbed through the depth charge turbulence, the *Devilfish* made a sharp turn to create the "knuckle," more turbulence to baffle the echo-ranging. The sailors clung to anything handy. Locking an elbow on the ladder, Byron noted on the depth gauges that the power plant must still be working, for at this angle and rate of climb they were making ten knots. Four more explosions shook the deck; hideous sounds, but farther off. This time nothing broke in the control room, though the sailors swayed and staggered, and particles of loose debris rattled in Byron's face.

"Levelling off at fifty feet, Captain!"

"Very well. Everything okay down there?"

"Seems to be, sir." Derringer was yanking at the broken sparking cable. The other sailors, shakily cursing, were picking instruments and rubbish off the deck.

Several more charges rumbled and grumbled below, each one duller and farther away. Then Byron's heart jumped, as the pings of the Jap destroyer shifted to long scale: *p-i-i-i-ng! pi-i-i-i-ng!* In the Pearl Harbor drills that had been the moment of triumph, the hunter's mournful wailing confession that he had lost the scent, and was forced back to routine search; and the down Doppler — the lowered pitch of the sound — betrayed that the destroyer had turned away from the *Devilfish.*

A joy as intense as his previous fear, a wave of warm physical delight, swept over Byron. They had shaken loose, and he rode in a blooded submarine! The *Devilfish* had survived a depth charging! It had taken hard punishment, and it had eluded its pursuer. All the submarine action narratives he had ever read paled once for all into gray words. All the peacetime drills seemed child's play. Nobody could describe a depth charging, you had to live through it. By comparison, the bombings he had experienced in Warsaw and Cavite had been mild scares. This was the real thing, the cold skull-grin of the Angel of Death, frightful enough to test any man at war. Such thoughts shot through Byron Henry's mind with the joyous relief, when he heard the destroyer pinging again on long scale with down Doppler.

Things became quieter. The plotting team gathered again around the dead reckoning tracer. Aster and Captain Hoban descended from the conning tower to watch the picture form. The plot soon coalesced into two course lines; the destroyer heading toward the beachhead at Lingayen, the *Devilfish* moving the opposite way.

Aster said, grinning with relief, "I guess he figures we'd still try for the landing area."

"I don't know what he's figuring, but this is just great!" Hoban turned to Byron. "All right. Tour the compartments, Briny, and let me have a survey of the damage."

"Aye aye, sir."

"And talk to the crew. See how they're doing. We got some crazy screaming about water in the after torpedo room. Maybe a valve came unseated for a minute, or something."

The captain spoke in collected tones, and seemed in every way himself, yet something about him was changed. Was it the vanished mustache? No, not that. It was the look of his eyes, Byron thought; they seemed bigger and brighter, yet dark-ringed as though with fatigue. Hoban's brown eyes now dominated his face, alert, concerned, and shiny. The boss man had tasted his full responsibility. That would sober anybody. As Byron left the control room, Lady Aster, moistening the end of a Havana, gave him a contorted wink.

Every compartment had some minor breakage or malfunction to report — dangling bunks, shattered lamp bulbs, overturned tables, jammed water lines — but under the pounding the *Devilfish* had proved remarkably resilient; that was the sum of what Byron saw. Nothing essential to operations was down. The crew was another matter. Their condition ranged from pallid shock to profane defiance, but the note all through the submarine was dispirited; not so much because of the depth charging, though there was much obscene comment on its terrors — and in one compartment a strong smell of befouled trousers — but because the torpedoes had missed. They had taken the beating for nothing. It was a sour outcome after all the E's in drills. This crew was used to success. Some sailors ventured mutters to Byron about the captain's hasty shot on slow setting.

When Byron brought back his report to the wardroom, Aster and Hoban had their heads bent over a sketch for the battle account. The captain was diagramming his attack in orange ink for the enemy track, blue for the *Devilfish,* and red for the torpedoes. Hoban's diagrams were always textbook models. "I *saw* those wakes, goddamn it, Lady," he said wistfully, inking ruled lines. "Those new magnetic exploders are defective. I'm going to say so, by God, in the war diary and in the action report both. I don't care if I hang for it. I know our range was long, but we had an excellent solution. The wakes went directly under the first and third ships. Those ships should have had their backs broken. The torpedoes never exploded."

"Better check in with plot before you take the watch," Aster said casually to Byron. "We're heading for the entrance."

"The entrance?"

The captain's dark-ringed eyes gleamed at the puzzled note. "Of course. The whole landing area is on submarine alert now, Briny. We can't accomplish anything there. Up at the entrance we might find some fat pickings."

"Yes, Captain."

Over Hoban's head, as he bent over the diagram, Aster grotesquely winked again. The implication was clear and jarring to Byron. The mission of the *Devilfish*, the only way it could now justify twenty years of maintenance and training, was to oppose the Japanese landing at the beachhead, no matter what the risk. They were being paid for extra-hazardous duty! Byron had assumed that, once out of the attack area, Hoban would unquestionably circle and make for the troop transports. This was the submarine's moment, the reason it had been built and manned. Giving prudent arguments, Branch Hoban was abandoning the mission with an intact submarine, still loaded with twenty torpedoes.

They had evaded but not shaken off the destroyer. Its long-scale pings still shivered sadly and faintly in the *Devilfish*'s sonar receiver.

On Derringer's plot the Japanese search plan soon became clear: a pattern of widening squares, much as in American antisubmarine doctrine. Off Pearl Harbor, in the peacetime exercises, a submarine that had gotten clear of its pursuer would send a sonar signal, and the destroyer would speed over for another attack run; the search phase being a tedious boring process that wasted time and fuel. But now the process was far from boring; it was the real thing, ugly, tense, and perilous. The searcher above intended to find and sink the *Devilfish*. His chances still were good.

For though the scorpion was out of the flashlight beam now, and crawling away in the dark, there was no satisfactory place to hide. Hoban had heavily depleted his batteries. The pursuer, fresh from Japan with full oil bunkers, could steam at eight or ten times Hoban's normal underwater speed. In another few hours the *Devilfish* would have a "flat can" — no battery juice left. Much now depended on brute luck. Hoban was making a beeline away from the point where the destroyer had lost him. That was doctrine, though Byron (and obviously Aster, too) thought he should not be heading for the entrance. The destroyer captain, having completed two tight squares, was heading out on a wider sweep. If he happened to choose the right turns, he might pick up the unseen crawler again. But the night sea was a gloomy tossing blank, the choices were infinite, and failure was discouraging. Also, he might be called off to other duty. These were the hopeful factors in the problem; except that "problem" was a peacetime word, somewhat too bland for the dogged pursuit by this anonymous menace.

Standing watch in the conning tower, Byron heard the captain and the exec discuss tactics. The time of sunset had passed, and Aster wanted to surface. Running on the diesels, they could race out of the destroyer's search pattern at flank speed, and charge up the can for more underwater action; perhaps for an attack on this very pursuer. Hoban roundly vetoed the idea. "Goddamn it, Lady, surface? How can we gamble on unknowns? What's the weather like up there? Suppose it's a calm crystal-clear night? We might be up-moon from him — ever think of that? A black tin duck in the moonlight! Even the periscope could show up in binoculars. How reliable are our sonar ranges? Plus or minus a mile, we figure, but with five-inch guns waiting for us up there, maybe we'd better make that *two* miles, hey? All right. Plot has him at what now — seven thousand?"

"Seventy-five hundred and opening, sir, with strong down Doppler."

"All right. Even so! At three or four thousand yards a lookout can pick us up with binoculars. It's all poppycock that Japs can't see in the dark. If that destroyer spots us surfaced with a flat can, we've had the course. Now if *we* could open the range to twelve or fourteen thousand, surfacing might make some sense. In fact, that's the thing to try for. Byron! Go to seven knots."

"Seven knots, sir?"

"Are you deaf? Seven knots."

"Seven knots. Aye aye, sir."

The decision baffled Byron. Aster's face went dead blank. At seven knots the *Devilfish* had little more than an hour of underwater propulsion left. Captain Hoban, in an attempt to be cautious, seemed to be invading the last margin of safety.

Plot reported the Japanese destroyer making a turn; and after a short interval, another turn. Sonar announced, "Up Doppler." The destroyer was now closing the *Devilfish*. The power-consuming time dragged on, while in the conning tower Aster and the captain speculated on the pursuer's last action. Had the Jap picked up a stray sonar echo? Had he by bad luck gotten an echo from a school of fish, in the submarine's direction? Should they change course? Hoban elected to bear on toward the entrance. The sonar range gradually dropped to seven thousand yards; twenty minutes later, to six thousand — three miles. If the night was dark or rainy, Byron thought, they still might surface and flee at twenty-one knots. Why didn't the skipper at least chance a periscope glimpse of the weather? As the range dropped to four thousand, the option to surface was dimming. Sonar pings now began reverberating faintly through the hull itself. Byron's remaining hope was that the destroyer would pass without picking up an echo; but this faded too, when he heard Derringer announce below, in a sepulchral voice, that the destroyer was turning to a collision course.

Aster came scrambling up the ladder, eyes narrowed, dead gray cigar clenched in his teeth. "Battle stations, Briny."

"What now?"

"Well, he's found us, all right. The captain's going to the bottom."

"Will that work?"

"Depends."

"On what?"

"For one thing, on how good his sonar is. Maybe he can't screen out bottom return."

Byron remembered this tactic from submarine school exercises off New London. Echo-ranging on a vessel on the bottom was inexact; the random return diffused the readings. Hurrying down the ladder to his post as diving officer, he saw Captain Hoban staring at the plot, where the destroyer's pencilled course was curving in, dot by dot, toward the white moving point of the *Devilfish*.

"Flood negative! Retract sonar head!" Hoban plunged for the ladder, shouting up through the hatch. "Lady, give me a fathometer reading and pass the word for all hands to stand by to ground! Hard right rudder!"

The submarine mushed downward, slowing and turning. Byron levelled off, well above fathometer depth. Shortly there came a jolt, another jolt, and the *Devilfish* settled, rocking and grinding, on the mud; according to the depth gauges, at the exact figure of the fathometer reading — eighty-seven feet.

Silence, dead waiting silence, in the *Devilfish*; outside, loud long-scale pings, and the mutter of propellers. On the dead reckoning tracer, the destroyer track moved closer and closer to the halted point of light. The propeller noise intensified. Derringer was getting no sonar ranges now, the attacker was too close; he was projecting the destroyer's track by using his ears and his judgment. As Byron's breath all but failed him, the pencil line passed the point of light, and slowly moved away. A sharp fall of pitch of the long-scale pings to down Doppler confirmed Derringer's guesswork plot. All the men in the control room heard it — the young sailors, the young officer, the old chief — and all looked around at each other with wan hope.

How totally a submariner depended on the captain, Byron thought, how crucial was confidence in him! Though he had once hated Hoban, he had never until now doubted his skill; he had in fact resented his crushing superiority. Now the rat of panic was gnawing at Byron's spirit. Was he in shaky or amateurish hands, after all, a hundred feet down in the sea in a long vulnerable metal tube, waiting for a ship on the surface to dynamite him to a vile death by drowning? Black seawater under terrible pressure gripped the thin hull; one opened seam, one blown valve, and his life would be choked out by flooding salt water. He would never again see Natalie, nor even once lay eyes on the baby he had fathered. He would rot on the floor of Lingayen Gulf, and fish would swim in and out of his bones.

This awareness of being in peril under water, which submariners suppress but never for a moment wholly forget, was clamping a cold hold on Byron Henry. Not forty-eight hours ago, just before reporting to the Marsman building, he had been jolting down a Manila boulevard in hot sunshine, perched in the back of a truck on a crated mine, jocularly drinking beer with his working party. And now —

Derringer said huskily, "Mr. Henry, I think he's turning back."

The pinging outside shifted to short scale.

Now fear stabbed Byron's very bowels. This time the submarine was caught; caught dead on the bottom and almost out of power, and he was caught in it, and all this was no dream, dreamlike though the horror seemed. Death under the sea was now coming at him, screaming through the short-scale pings in malevolent rising glee, *"Found you! Found you! Found you!"*

The faces in the control room took on one expression — stark terror. Chief Derringer was not looking at the plot, but staring vacantly upward, his heavy mouth wide open, his big fat face a Greek mask of fright; the man had five children and two grandchildren. The propellers came drumming and thrashing directly overhead once again — *KER-DA-TRAMM! TRAMM! TRAMM!* Morelli at the bow planes clutched his crucifix, crossed himself, and muttered a prayer.

Click, click, click, like little pebbles or balls bouncing on the hull; it was the arming of the depth charges at their preset depth, though Byron did not know that this caused the noise. He too was praying; nothing complicated, just, "God, let me live. God, let me live."

11

THE block leader's yells and curses rouse the Russian prisoners at 4:30 A.M. from their uneasy dozing. It is the only sleep they can get, jammed three in a bunk in the cold and stench of the quarantine camp blockhouses, on straw pallets crawling with vermin. Getting down from his upper bunk for roll call, Berel Jastrow murmurs the obligatory *Hear O Israel* morning devotion. He should wash first, but that can't be done, water is a hundred yards away and forbidden at this hour. He adds the Talmud's brisk summary prayer for times of danger, and concludes, "*Yehi ratzon she-ekhye* — Let me live." Next will come an hour or more of standing at attention in ranks, in the icy wind and darkness of the Polish midwinter, clad in a thin prison suit of striped ticking.

"Let me live" is a practical heartfelt plea. What with the heavy beatings at any provocation or none, and the physical drills that go on till the weakest drop, and the starvation, and the long roll calls of nearly naked men, in sub-zero frost, and the hard work — digging drainage ditches, hauling lumber, dragging rocks, demolishing peasant houses in the evacuated villages, and carrying the materials, sometimes several kilometers, to the new blockhouse sites — and what with the guards shooting on the spot men who falter or fall, or finishing them off with the butt-ends of their rifles, the roster of Russians in the quarantine camp at Oswiecim is rapidly shrinking.

The Soviet prisoners of war are in fact proving a major disappointment to the Commandant.

Draft after draft they arrive sick, emaciated, all but prostrate with exhaustion, in half the promised numbers, the rest having died on the way. With this deteriorated rubbish as a labor force he is supposed to execute not one but several urgent construction projects: to double the size of the base camp, located in the tobacco monopoly buildings and the old Polish army barracks; to lay out and man the ambitious experimental farms and fisheries that Reichsführer SS Himmler plans as the real showpieces of the Auschwitz establishment; to erect a whole new camp of unprecedented magnitude out at Birchwoods, three kilometers to the west, accommodating *one hundred thousand prisoners of war* for labor in armament factories; and to commence surveying and preparing the factory sites! No German concentration camp until now has held much more than ten thousand prisoners. It is a breath-taking job, an assignment to be proud of, a great chance for advancement. The Commandant realizes that well.

But he is not being given the tools. The whole thing would be impossible, if he did not have a solid base of Polish and Czech political prisoners who can still put in a good day's work, and a steady supply of fresh ones. Only the strongest Russians, maybe ten percent of each draft, are of any use in the labor gangs. Given any feeding at all, these can still revive and do a job. Hardy fellows! But right there is the big problem: confusion from the top down about the true mission of the Auschwitz Interest Area, these forty square kilometers of marshy farmland allotted to the Commandant's rule. Conscious of the responsibility entrusted to a mere SS major, he is eager to do a job. For a year and a half he has put heart and soul into Oswiecim. It was just a dismal swamp with a straggle of buildings and a few scattered villages when he came here in 1940 to start the camp up. Now it is looking like something! But what is really wanted of him? Maximum production for war, or maximum elimination of the nation's enemies? He is still not clear.

The Commandant considers himself a soldier. He will do either job. He cannot do both at the same time! Yet contradictory orders come down in a steady stream. Take the very matter of these Russian POWs! In retaliation for the inhuman treatment of German prisoners in the Soviet Union, they are to be used "without pity." For those with any trace of political responsibility, execution at once; for the rest, swift working to death, at slave labor on rations below what dogs need to survive.

. . . *Very fine, Reichsführer Himmler; but how about the hundreds and hundreds of barracks, just by the way, that you've ordered me to build out in Birchwoods (Brzezinka, in the uncivilized Polish spelling; adapted into smooth German as Birkenau). Oh yes, the barracks; and oh yes, the experimental farms; and oh yes, the factories! Well, well, let Sturmbannführer Hoess worry about all that. Hoess is a chap who delivers. He complains, sends long pessimistic reports, declares assignments are impossible. But in the end Hoess carries out orders. There's a chap you can rely on* . . .

The Commandant values this reputation of his. Even in these heart-breaking conditions he means to maintain it, or kill himself trying. Like the next fellow, he wants to rise in the service, do well by his family, and all that. But Reichsführer SS Himmler is taking advantage of his outstanding conscientiousness, and this sinks him in depression. It just is not fair.

In a cloudy noonday, shielded from the knifelike wind by a heavy great-coat, the Commandant waits in the snow outside the crematorium for the arrival of the three hundred Russians. Combed out of several drafts as political officers or ratings, they have been sentenced to death by the military circuit court from Kattowitz. The Commandant has no quarrel with the sentence. The life-and-death struggle with Bolshevism is what this war is about. If European culture is to be saved, no mercy can be shown to the barbaric eastern foe. It is just too bad that some of the condemned appear so ablebodied.

At least their deaths will not be a total waste. They will yield important information. Major Hoess accepts no optimistic reports of subordinates. He learned the hard way, as Rapportführer in Sachsenhausen, to see things for himself. The tendency in a concentration camp chain of command is to lie, to cover up, to pretend that things are more efficient than they are. Reports on a previous gassing with the camp's strongest insecticide of some condemned Russians in the cellar of Block 11, while the Commandant was off reporting to Reichsführer SS Himmler in Berlin, have been contradictory. One subordinate, whose idea it was, claims they all died almost at once. Others say that it took forever for the Russians to croak; that they rushed one door of the cellar and almost broke it down, even as they were being gassed. What a hell of a mess, if they had actually forced their way out and released a cloud of that smelly poisonous blue stuff all over the main camp!

Just the usual thing, inattention to detail. The door wasn't reinforced enough, and the supposed airtight sealing of the cellar was done with clay; what stupidity! This experiment in the morgue room of the crematorium is being run under the Commandant's personal supervision. Airtightness has been tested with chlorine under pressure; satisfactory, just a faint sort of swimming-pool odor near the door, which has since had its rubber gaskets doubled up. The crematorium is off in the grassy area beyond the camp, not smack in the middle of the main buildings like Block 11. Just a little common sense!

The Russians approach — drawn, ghastly, with white-rimmed sunken eyes, in their ragged uniforms marked *SU* in huge black letters. They are flanked by guards with tommy guns. Their faces show awareness that they are going to their deaths. Yet their formation is good. Their wooden clogs squeak in the snow with a ghostly echo of military precision. Strange people! He has seen them in their work area, fighting like wolves over a dump of garbage from the SS kitchen, grasping each other by the throats for a rotten potato, snarling and cursing; he has seen them wandering like sleepwalkers, skin and bones, dead on their feet, impervious to the blows and threats of guards, crumpling and falling bloody to the ground without complaining. But put them in a formation, give them an order, a sense that they are in a group; and feeble and terrorized though they are, these Russians come to life and work and march like men.

The prisoners disappear single file into the gray flat-roofed building. Guards wait on the roof with canisters, by pipe apertures recently pierced. Three hundred men can be packed into the wide low cement room. That detail has been tested. The aperture flaps seal tight; that too has been tested. The Commandant walks up and down in the snow, swinging his arms to keep warm, three aides at his heels, all in well-fitted green uniforms. He is a martinet about uniforms. Sloppy appearance in guards is the beginning of a breakdown in camp morale. He saw that in his early service at Dachau . . .

Activity on the roof!

In due course he enters the building with his aides. The gas-masked SS men on duty inside give the Commandant a momentary remembrance of his service in the last war. Accepting and donning a mask, he observes that the process in the mortuary is not a silent one. That is for sure. Muffled yells, screams, shouts sound through the door, although this noise did not carry outside. He glances at his wristwatch. Seven minutes since activity on the roof began. He steps up to the thick glass peephole in the door.

The harsh mortuary lights are blazing, but this damned glass will have to be replaced; poor quality, it makes everything yellow and wavering, distorts details. Most of the prisoners are already down, piled all over each other, some not moving, others rolling or writhing. Perhaps fifty or so are still on their feet, stumbling and jumping about. Several right here at the door are pounding and clawing, with open yelling mouths in crazy faces. An ugly sight! But even as he watches, they are one by one dropping away like flies in a spray of pyrethrum. The Commandant has seen many and many a flogging, hanging, and shooting, having been himself eight years an unjustly sentenced political prisoner under Weimar, and eight more years a concentration camp officer. One learns to take this sort of thing; one gets hard. Yet he feels rather sick to see this process. It is something different. Still, what can one do? One is carrying out orders.

The stuff works, no doubt of that. With decent airtightness it really seems to do the job. For an instant the Commandant lifts his mask. No odor out here in the corridor, none whatever. That is important; no danger to personnel. Perhaps masks can be dispensed with in time.

It is getting quiet in there now. The mass of bodies is quiescent but for a hump here and there still heaving and flopping. No reason to linger. He leaves, handing his mask to the guard at the door. Outside he fills his lungs with the cold air of snowy Auschwitz, sweet and delicious after the nasty, rubbery, chemical smell of air filtered through a mask.

He closely questions the lieutenant in charge of ventilating the chamber. Until it is safe, he wants no show-off personnel going in there, even with masks. The ventilation is poor, the lieutenant admits. Big portable fans will be used. They should do the job in an hour. The Commandant issues a flat order: for three hours after ventilation begins, nobody inside the mortuary! Safety factor of two hundred percent; that's how to run a hazardous operation.

His personal aide drives him in his staff car to the Residence, where his wife and children await him for Christmas dinner. The Commandant is in no mood for festivity. He has kept a hard calm face all through this business. It is up to him to set the example! But he is human, though nobody in the Interest Area especially thinks so. That is how it must be, with the orders that he has to carry out. He takes a hot shower, scrubbing himself vigorously, and puts on a fresh uniform, though the other is fresh, too, and carries no smell. He cannot relax on the base, he is always in uniform when he is not asleep; and there is something unseemly in eating Christmas dinner in the same uniform he wore before.

As he showers and dresses, trying to be cold and businesslike in his thoughts, he has to be pleased with the results. Reichsführer Himmler already told him back in July — honoring him with a long private interview in his inner office — about the big Jewish project. It is something so secret that he half-suppresses it, even in his thoughts. The orders come direct from the Führer, so there can be no argument. Several other camps will take some of the load, but Auschwitz is to be a main disposal center.

Hoping all the while that it may be an exaggerated scheme — a lot of Himmler's ideas are mostly talk — the Commandant has nevertheless been compelled to look into the problem. Visits to camps where such actions on a small scale are already under way have convinced him that no existing means will serve to do what Himmler forecasts. The asphyxiation by carbon monoxide at Treblinka is a drawn-out, messy affair, very wasteful of fuel and of time, and not one hundred percent effective. Shooting on the projected scale is also out of the question. The psychological effect on the execution squads would be unendurable, setting aside the serious ammunition problem.

No, the poison gas in rooms of large capacity has always been an idea worth trying; but which gas? Today's experiment shows that Zyklon B, the powerful insecticide they have been using right along at the camp to fumigate the barracks, may be the surprisingly simple solution. Seeing is believing. In a confined airtight space, with a plentiful dose of the blue-green crystals, those three hundred fellows didn't last long! Much larger rooms, carefully built, with a humane and orderly procedure to pack large numbers in at a time, will give satisfactory results. The problem of disposing of the bodies remains. That tough one is just being dumped in his lap, as usual. No bright suggestions from above; leave it to Hoess. But the present small crematorium can barely handle the prisoners who die a natural death and the various offenders who are shot or hanged.

Well, time for Christmas dinner. The Commandant joins his family. But it is not a gay occasion, though the handsomely furnished Residence is full of fine decorations, and a nice tree twinkles its ornaments in the foyer. His wife keeps filling his wineglass with Moselle, an apprehensive look on her face.

The kids are all dressed up and shiny-faced, but they too have scared expressions. The Commandant would like to create a warm home atmosphere, but his burdens are too heavy. He can't be the good German husband and father he'd like to be. He is morose. His brief conversation has a growling note. He can't help it. The roast goose is excellent, the brisk services of the Polish girls can't be faulted, but the Commandant has had a rotten day, Christmas or no Christmas, and that's that.

He does feel sorry for the kids. When he goes off with the brandy bottle, to smoke a cigar and drink by himself, he ponders again about sending them back to Germany to school. His wife objects. Life is lonely enough on the base as it is, she keeps saying. Of course, she knows nothing about what goes on across the road, beyond the barbed wire. She can't understand that the atmosphere of Oswiecim is just not the best for growing kids. He will have to look into it again. The private tutoring they are getting from young educated SS officers is no way for German children to grow up. They need friends their own age, merry games, athletics, a normal life.

As the Commandant methodically empties the brandy bottle, worrying despite the welcome numbing of alcohol about his kids and about a dozen pressing camp problems, and getting unpleasant intermittent mental pictures of the heaving flopping pile of Russians seen through the yellow peephole, dusk is falling over the long rows of blockhouses in the quarantine camp. The Russian POWs are marching in from their day's work at the Birkenau site. Some stagger under the weight of limp bodies in striped ticking. All the corpses must be brought back from the work site for the evening roll call, since the count of living and dead has to match the number of men who left in the morning, to establish that nobody has escaped Auschwitz except by dying. The prisoners' band is thumping out a march, for the workers always leave and return to merry, brassy music.

Berel Jastrow bows beneath a very light corpse. The head swings like a stone on a rope. It is a man unknown to him who, just before work stopped, fell and died before his eyes in the lumberyard. He lays the body down in the row of corpses on the parade ground, and hurries to his place in ranks. When roll call ends it is dark. Returning to his block, Berel finds it less crowded than before. Some of the gassed men came from this house.

"Yuri Gorachov!" the block captain yells. That is the false name Berel used to join the Red Army in Moscow. He stiffens, pulling off his striped cap and dropping his arms rigidly to his sides. The block captain, a Ukrainian kapo and a very ugly customer, approaches him in the gloom, holding a piece of paper.

"Get your belongings!"

Carrying his ragged little sack, Jastrow marches after him out on the snow, and far down the line of floodlit buildings. Berel is too weary, starved, and numbed by cold and constant terror to be overconcerned about what may well be his imminent death. Let come what God wills.

They enter a block near the gate. The light is brighter in this block. The crowded prisoners look cleaner and better fed. Nor are they Russians, for Berel sees nowhere the big black *SU* that is painted on his own back.

The Ukrainian hands over the gray paper to a big man in a kapo armband, with a tremendous red beard and tiny wrinkled blue eyes; he gestures at Berel, mutters in garbled German, and goes. Taking the prisoner roughly by an elbow, the red-bearded man hustles him down the wooden tiers of bunks to the far end of the block. There, Jastrow sees Sammy Mutterperl, leaning his back on a tier, talking to another prisoner.

This is as stunning and gladsome a surprise as a reprieve from execution.

For, recognizing Mutterperl in the lumberyard that afternoon, just before picking up the light corpse, Berel took his life in his hands to whisper to him. Talking between prisoners is punishable with instant death by clubbing, whipping, or shooting. But Mutterperl was obviously a privileged prisoner — not a kapo, but some sort of foreman — for he was shouting orders at a squad of big Poles stacking lumber. There was no mistaking Mutterperl, an Oswiecim building contractor, formerly a fellow yeshiva student; a very pious, very burly man with a mashed nose from an accident on a construction job. So Berel risked brushing past him and whispering his name and his block number. Mutterperl, fat and powerful-looking as ever in the striped prison garb, his matted hair and whiskers still almost all brown, made no sign of recognition or even of hearing him.

The red-bearded kapo gestures to Berel that he will sleep in the topmost bunk of the tier Mutterperl leans against; and off he goes. Not looking at Jastrow, Mutterperl drops into his Polish chatter with the other prisoner a brief, *"Sholem aleichem, Reb Berel."*

It is Jastrow's first hint that God may let him live.

12

THIS time the *Devilfish* caught a barrage. The thunderous clangs, the jolting shocks, the sharp pain in the ears, the blackout, the agonizing bouncing and grinding of the darkened submarine on the sea floor, the sounds of breakage, the panicky yells, the unseen things hitting Byron's face — one of them felt jagged and cut his cheek — all seemed weirdly natural, all part of one simple experience, one sudden catastrophe, his death in the *Devilfish*. Even the previous depth charging had been nothing to this black bombinating ringing bedlam, this chaos of life bursting apart.

"*I'm taking her up. Blow tanks! Surface! Surface!*" He could barely hear the captain's strained bellow in the voice tube, but before he could issue orders to the planesmen, there came another hoarse howl. "*Belay that, Byron. I'm taking her up to fifty feet! Blow negative! Maximum up angle! All ahead full!*"

The lights came on, showing the planesmen clinging for dear life to their control wheels. The other sailors clutched stanchions, valve heads, anything that would keep them from breaking their limbs or their skulls in this tossing quaking space with its hundreds of iron projections. The depth charges boomed and crashed in a hell without letup. Books, cups, measuring instruments, were clattering and flying about; cork fragments rained in the air. Nevertheless, the planesmen obeyed orders, frantically twisting their wheels, and the submarine with a grind and a bound went forward, wallowing, shuddering, bucking in the roiled water. It was proving a tough vessel. Whatever the havoc so far, the hull was holding, there was some charge left in the can, and the engines were turning; but the control room had a wrecked look, two of the sailors were bleeding — Byron too put his hand to a wet spot on his cheek, and brought it away red — and Chief Derringer was horribly gagging and vomiting behind the dead reckoning tracer. Death still seemed very close at hand.

However, the submarine had gained a shade of advantage from the attack. Even in the deep ocean, the heavy explosions would have created a screen of turbulence opaque to sonar, and therefore a new chance to sneak away. With the *Devilfish* on the bottom, the rain of depth charges had raised a broad cloud of mud. Through this cloud it moved off, momentarily hidden from the enemy's sonar. Astern the depth charges blasted and rumbled. Obviously the destroyer captain, his charges set by fathometer, was plastering the area to bring up debris as proof of his victory.

But Byron's awareness of this tactical situation was nil. Somehow they were under way again; that was all he knew. As he stanched the cut on his face with a handkerchief, Carter Aster's voice on the loudspeaker startled him. *"Now pharmacist's mate to the conning tower on the double."* The quartermaster came trampling down from conn to tell Byron in a low voice that the captain had been thrown off his feet by one of the explosions, fallen in the darkness, and struck his head. When the lights came on Aster had found him on the deck, eyes closed, bleeding from his forehead. So far he had not revived. The exec didn't want to alarm the crew; he had sent the quartermaster to let Byron know why he would be giving the voice tube orders for a while.

Aster did not alter Hoban's tactics. The *Devilfish* ran on, just above the bottom, squandering its last reserve voltage at ten knots while the pharmacist's mate worked on the captain. The depth charging astern ceased. The pinging continued on short scale with up Doppler. So the destroyer was once more on the move and closing the range. In search, or in direct pursuit? No telling.

And now sonar reported propeller sounds of two other vessels, approaching at high speed from the direction of the entrance. Derringer began plotting them on the tracer at a range of five miles. "There're two more goddamn destroyers, Mr. Henry," the chief said, rolling his eyes at Byron. "Speed thirty knots." He repeated the news by telephone to the conning tower.

Aster's voice in the speaking tube, choked and tense: "Periscope depth, Briny!"

"Aye aye, sir. Periscope depth."

The planesmen turned their wheels. The polished oily shaft of the attack periscope slid noiselessly upward behind Byron. The submarine climbed.

"Sir, levelling at sixty-one —"

An exultant yell cut Byron off. "Why, it's raining! Pouring! It's a goddamn squall, black as a black cow's inside!" Aster shifted to the loudspeaker. "Surface, surface, surface! *STAND BY TO MAKE TWENTY-ONE KNOTS!*"

Seldom had Byron Henry heard more welcome words, or more welcome sounds than the roar and swash of the blowing tanks. Swiftly the *Devilfish* rose. He could feel the motion of the sea, the steep pitching, the levelling off, and he knew that the submarine was breaking into the rainy night. His ears recorded the change of pressure. Sweet damp air poured in through the vent. The diesels coughed and roared into life. The *Devilfish* smashed forward, once more a surface vessel breathing and burning the open air!

Rude cheers, happy blasphemies, roistering obscenities rang through the long vessel in every compartment. Temporarily, anyway, praying time was over.

They were still at battle stations. Red-stained handkerchief to his face, Byron mounted the ladder on his way to his post on the bridge. Aster, at the chart desk, said, "Stand by, Briny." The pharmacist's mate was bent over the captain, who sat with his back to the torpedo data computer, eyes open, complexion bluish, head bandaged, khaki shirt splashed with blood. Hoban gave Byron a sickly smile. "Well, I see you caught it, too." His voice was hoarse and weak.

"It's just a cut, sir."

"You were luckier than me."

Aster said, "Captain, do you want to try walking?"

"In a minute. You're heading south, you say? Why south?" It was a tired, petulant query. "The entrance is the other way."

"That's it, sir. He's tracked us, he knows where we were heading. A line between the two contact points shows him. With two more tin cans coming for us, I figure we better do a wide end run. Ten miles south, ten miles east, and then up the east coast to the entrance."

"Very well. Help me up." Aster and the pharmacist's mate lifted him by his elbows. On his feet, Hoban weaved and grasped a stanchion. "Whew! Dizzy. That's not a bad plan, Lady. But keep the men at battle stations. I'd better take a half hour or so in my bunk."

"Aye aye, sir."

Aided by the pharmacist's mate, the captain tottered to the ladder, and the bloody bandaged head sank through the hatch. Aster took up rulers and divider. "Briny, better have Doc Hviesten fix you up."

"I'm all right, Lady. I'll just go to my station." Byron wanted to climb outside, see the waves, breathe fresh air.

Aster gave him a hard penetrating look. "Do as you're told. And put on foul weather gear."

"Aye aye, sir."

When he did get to the bridge, he found blackness, spray, wind, rough swells. These were beautiful to him. The fire control officer had the deck; a blond lieutenant from Virginia, Wilson Turkell II, nicknamed Foof in some forgotten Annapolis episode. But only the captain and Aster called him Foof. He was an accomplished officer with two marked habits: total silence except on ship's business, and a way of drinking himself insensible on the beach. Turkell said nothing when Byron arrived, and nothing thereafter.

The bridge was the captain's battle station. Half an hour passed and he did not come. Aster shouted an order through the open hatch to turn east. From the dark form of Turkell, surprising Byron almost like speech from a tree, issued five words: "This is a bad business."

"What? Why, Wilson?"

But the tree had spoken its wooden piece. Except for orders Turkell said nothing more.

Half an hour passed in rainy, pitching, tossing silence, and the dark. Sonar lost the three destroyers. The *Devilfish* turned again to run along the coast. The loudspeaker grated, "Now secure from battle stations. Meeting of officers in the wardroom."

The captain was not at the meeting. In his place sat Aster, looking grim, smoking a gray cigar. When all the officers were seated, he pulled the green curtain. "Okay, I'll make this short," he said in low troubled tones. "I've been with the captain for the past hour. His concussion seems serious. Doc Hviesten says his pulse is elevated, so's his blood pressure, and his vision is impaired. He may have a fractured skull. The *Devilfish* has to return to base."

Aster paused, looking around at the officers' set faces. Nobody said a word or made a gesture. He took a long puff at his rank cigar. "Now I guess you all feel as badly about this as I do. We came here to do a job. But there's no alternative. We can't break radio silence. If we could, ComSubRon 26 would just order us in. Captain Hoban isn't up to conducting attacks, and he can't delegate command. The safety of the boat and crew becomes paramount. The thing to do is get the hell out of here. Let's hope the *Salmon*, the *Porpoise*, and those other guys get some scores down at the landing beach."

"How do we get out, Lady?" Turkell asked in an offhand way. "And when?"

"On the surface, Foof, straight through the entrance at twenty-one knots" — Aster glanced at his watch — "approximately forty minutes from now."

Turkell's reaction was a marked downcurving of his mouth and a single nod. "Any comments?" Aster inquired, after a silence. "We're all in this together."

The engineering officer lifted a hand, an awkward formality among *Devilfish* officers. He was a peppery little lieutenant j.g. from Philadelphia named Samtow, a humorless fanatic about machinery maintenance, but otherwise rather a joker. "The captain's conscious? He's aware of what's going on?"

"Of course. He's ill and dizzy. He doesn't feel up to conducting attacks, and there's no point in wasting torpedoes."

"Does he know we'll transit the entrance on the surface?"

"Yes."

Turkell's lips barely moved. "That's his desire?"

"Well, Foof, we tossed it back and forth." Aster slouched, puffing on his cigar, shedding some of his forced dignity. "It's a tough one. Destroyers and sub chasers will be thick up there as whores on Market Street. We know that. These monkeys may even have mined the entrance. For all we know they have radar, too, though our intelligence says no." Aster swept both his arms wide, and shrugged. "On the other hand we've got zero visibility topside, haven't we? With the diesels we can run through and get away in a quarter of an hour. This hole is twelve miles wide, and that's one hell of a big expanse to bottle up solid with patrol vessels on a rainy night. But if we pull the plug it'll take us four times as long to transit the hot zone, with all those tin cans pinging for us. I grant you, two hundred feet of water overhead is a nice margin of safety. The captain finally said I'd have the conn, and to do it my way. So I say again, any comments?"

The officers looked at each other.

"That's the way to go," Turkell said.

Aster let several wordless seconds go by. He nodded. "Okay then. One more thing. Captain Hoban told me to express his regret at aborting the patrol. He says the boat, the crew, and the officers all performed admirably. If not for malfunctioning torpedoes we'd be heading home with a couple of major sinkings chalked up. We've learned that the *Devilfish* can catch a lot of hell and still go on fighting. The patrol hasn't been a dead loss, and he says well done." Aster spoke all this in a dry monotone. In his natural tone he added, "And that's that. Back to battle stations. I just secured for a while to give the crew a chance to grab a sandwich and a piss."

"You mean," said Samtow, "there's somebody left in this boat who hasn't pissed in his pants?"

The meeting broke up in coarse relieving laughter. The escape through the entrance was an anticlimax. Aster, Byron, and Turkell stood on the bridge in rubber clothes, peering into driving black rain. The sonar operator, stammering with excitement, reported more and more screw noises and pinging; far ahead at first, then getting closer, then sounding all around the *Devilfish*. Apparently in the sonar receiver terrifying pandemonium was echoing, through 360 degrees, but on the bridge all was wet, dark and peaceful. They went cruising straight through the heavy Japanese patrol line and saw no sign of it as they plunged and wallowed uneventfully through the night out of the gulf and into the open ocean.

"Just goes to show you, Briny," Aster remarked while the sonar operator was chattering alarm after alarm, "that ignorance is bliss. Here we are absolutely ringed by these yellow rascals, and it's like a pleasure cruise. Let's just hope we don't ram one."

He kept the submarine at General Quarters until the pinging had faded from the sonar, far astern; then he stationed the watch. "Briny, when you're relieved, see me in my cabin."

"Aye aye, sir."

He was lying on his bunk in jockey shorts, smoking a cigar, when Byron came. "Hi. Draw the curtain and sit down." Aster raised himself on an elbow. "How do you like submarine duty?"

Byron took a moment to answer, then spoke the truth. "It's for me."

Aster's green eyes flashed, and his mouth corners curved in his highly individual, cold, almost mirthless smile. "Now listen carefully." Aster leaned toward him — their heads were only a foot or so apart — and spoke almost in a whisper, *"There's nothing wrong with Captain Hoban except that he's scared absolutely shitless."*

"What? No concussion?"

"Nah! He confessed to Doc Hviesten. Doc told me. Then the three of us had it out. He did fall, but he wasn't knocked cold, he simulated it. It isn't malingering or cowardice, he just can't hack it, Briny. He got the message when the first depth charge went off. You know, I guessed it, watching him. It was pitiful. He crumpled up in a ball like a girl caught naked. I guess he's doing the right thing, because he sure as hell can't conduct an attack. He's broken. He's in terror. Doc had to put him to sleep with a strong sedative. As soon as we reach Manila, he's going to transfer out of submarines."

This was staggering news to Byron. "Oh, he'll think better of that. His whole career —"

"No, he won't. He's through. He told me that, Briny."

"Ten years in submarines, Lady —"

"Look, he was in the wrong business. There was just no way he could find out. I'll never blame any man who decides he can't hack this, and I feel sorry for him. Actually he did well in his condition. He kept his self-control, and he maneuvered properly under fire."

"Who else knows about him?"

"Well, Foof was right there. You can't deceive Foof. But he's no blabbermouth. Doc Hviesten won't talk, he's very ethical. I think the sailors were too scared to notice. I'm backing Hoban's story. When he's transferred the truth will get out. Meantime we have to run this submarine. We're returning to base with our tail between our legs, and that's poison for the crew. So if we make a fat contact on the way back, I'm going to ask Hoban's permission to shoot. We've still got twenty torpedoes left. If we do run an attack, Foof will be my kibitzer, he'll punch the Is-Was, and you'll man the TDC. Got that? You're the best diving officer I've ever seen, except maybe me, but Quayne will have to do that."

"Jesus Christ."

"What's your problem?"

"I can't run that TDC."

"You did all right in the attack trainer. Better than Samtow. There's nobody else."

"Dive, dive, dive." Through the mists of sleep Byron heard the loudspeaker and the clamorous flooding of the ballast tanks. On the instant he was out of his bunk naked. Sitting at the tiny desk writing a report, his roommate, Samtow, yawned. "Easy. It's almost dawn, so Lady's pulling the plug."

"Dawn? It is? How could I sleep five hours?"

"It's a talent."

"What's happening?"

"We're about fifty miles out of Manila."

"What about the captain?"

Samtow shrugged. "Haven't seen hair nor hide of him."

Byron dressed, drank coffee, and went to check on the torpedo rooms, bow and stern. The submarine stank. Listless cleanup and repair went on here and there, but the mood of defeat was as pervasive as the odor of malfunctions and decay. Most of the sailors were taciturn, but their feeling was plain — stunned humiliation that the red-hot *Devilfish* crew should be skulking home empty-handed from their first patrol, mauled by Japs, barely saving their skins.

Then the sonar operator reported the faint beating of a propeller. The plotting party came on duty. The count of propeller turns per minute gave the vessel's approximate speed. Its very slow movement relative to the submarine showed it some forty miles away. The distance was astonishing, but depending on sea conditions, the equipment could sometimes pick up screw noises at great ranges. Several times the contact faded out and returned, still on the same closing course at the same speed.

A rumor flashed through the compartments that Lieutenant Aster was going after it; and, as by a blast of compressed air, the sickly atmosphere in the vessel blew away. The torpedomen came to life, feverishly checking their weapons. The engineering gang fell earnestly to work on jammed valves, malfunctioning pumps, and broken fuel and water lines. The crew began an intensive cleanup. A cheerful fragrance of frying chicken soon obliterated the stench of leaking drains and filthy men. About midday curiosity overcame Byron. Pulling the curtain behind him, he stepped into Aster's cabin, where the exec, quite naked, sat correcting typed logs. "What's the dope, Lady?"

"About what?"

"Will we attack this target?"

"Oh, you require a special briefing, do you?"

"Sorry if I'm off base."

"Well, since you ask, I have the captain's permission to close him and take a look." Aster was distant and uncordial.

The propeller sounds slowly grew stronger, hour by hour. Derringer's plot showed that with this submerged approach, the *Devilfish* would not sight the ship much before evening, but a daylight run on the surface in these waters was far too risky.

Byron had the afternoon watch. At five o'clock Aster appeared in the conning tower in clean khakis, freshly shaved, smoking a long Havana, and humming the "Washington Post March," his habit when in the highest spirits. "Well, now, gentlemen, just let's see if this rascal is in view yet, hey? Plot says he ought to be. Up periscope! — Well, well, well! By the Christ, there's our friend. Bearing. Mark! Two one zero. Range. Mark! Fourteen thousand yards. Down scope!"

He shouted in the tube, "Chief, right on the money! He's there over the hill, hull down." Happy laughter resounded from the control room. Aster turned to Byron, his face glowing. "Briny, let's go to General Quarters."

At the alarm the usual racket ensued: loud scurrying and shouting, clanging of watertight doors, barked reports by telephone talkers. Turkell arrived and slung around his neck the Is-Was, a convoluted plastic instrument that gave bearings for a torpedo shot if the TDC failed. Byron nervously took his place at the computer. He had worked the black-faced instrument and its constantly turning dials in sub school and the simulator on shore, but had never before manned one at sea. The device put together the three moving elements of the attack problem — torpedo, submarine, victim — boiling down all the evolving data to one crucial number: the final bearing on which to launch the torpedo. The information coming in was of varying reliability. Course and speed of the *Devilfish* were precise; but the data on the target ship consisted of sonar readings and periscope glimpses, inexact and fleeting. The officer on the TDC had to guess which readings were fluky, which more or less accurate, in feeding new numbers into the machine. Wilson Turkell had rare insight for this. The responsibility weighed on Byron but excited him, too.

On the plot and on the computer, submarine and target continued to draw together. Aster paced and smoked, waiting for the time of sunset to put up the periscope again. "I'm not scaring off our plump little friend up there," he observed to Turkell. His usually pale face was bright pink, and his lithe nervous pacing and finger-snapping were working up tension in the attack party which Byron could see on the sailors' faces.

"All right," Aster said at last, crouching at the periscope well, "up scope!" He caught the handles and snapped them in place. Rising with the scope as stylishly as Hoban had done, he was looking through the eyepiece as it went up. "Range. Mark! Six thousand. Bearing. Mark! Two two four." The periscope had scarcely stopped when he ordered it down again. "Okay. Angle on the bow, twenty port. It's a medium-sized tanker, Foof. About five thousand tons."

"Jap silhouette?"

"Hell, tanker silhouette! What other nationality is chugging around in the South China Sea?"

"That's what we don't know, Lady," said a melancholy voice.

Like a ghost's, the bristly face of Branch Hoban rose through the hatchway. He climbed into the conning tower, his eyes haunted and sickly bright, his head bloodily bandaged, his lean frame stooped in his old tiger-pattern bathrobe, which dragged on the deck. "Maybe some fool Dutchman hasn't got the word. Maybe it's one of our own ships out to rendezvous with a fleet unit. We just don't know."

"Sir, it sure as hell doesn't look American."

"Lady, we've got to *know*."

"Okay. Identification manual, Jap merchants, tankers," Aster snapped at the quartermaster. Again he raised the periscope to call range, bearings, and angle on the bow. "Come on, come on, Baudin. Where's the manual?"

"Here, sir!" Hurriedly the sailor spread the open book on the navigator's desk. "Tanker silhouettes."

"I see them." Aster stared at the book, seized a red pencil, heavily ringed a silhouette, and showed it to Hoban. "That's the type, forty-five hundred tons. You can't mistake the broken line of that bridge house. It even looks like a goddamn pagoda. Take a look, sir. He's like a cardboard cutout in the sunset."

"Up scope," said Hoban. His movements were slow and slack. He called no data as he peered through the eyepiece. "All right, down scope. . . . Well, it's a setup, Lady. My vision's very fuzzy. You've identified him, so go ahead."

"Attack, Captain?"

"Yes, if you want to, go ahead and shoot him."

"Byron! Normal approach course?"

"Normal approach course one six zero, sir," Byron rapped out.

"Helmsman, come to one six zero."

"Coming to one six zero, sir!"

"Make ten knots!"

Aster took the loudspeaker microphone. "All hands. The *Devilfish* is commencing an attack on a tanker."

Hoban said rapidly and hoarsely, "One piece of advice. Those new magnetic exploders are lousy. I fought this fight in BuOrd years ago. I know. They cost me two hits yesterday. Set your torpedoes to strike the hull, otherwise you'll miss the way I did."

"We have orders to shoot ten feet under the keel, sir."

"True, but I hear the Japs are building flat-bottom tankers, Lady." Hoban winked. In his sad chalk-white face the effect was peculiarly clownish. "Don't you know about that? Drafts of six inches and less."

With a keen glance at the captain, Lieutenant Aster ordered a shallow setting for the torpedoes.

From the start, this second attack was so like the drills in the Cavite attack trainer that Byron's sense of reality became numbed. Aster had conducted dozens of mock torpedo runs, with Turkell as kibitzer, and Byron on the computer. This situation seemed exactly like a school problem, complete with a rapid fire of reports, orders, questions, and course changes to keep the TDC officer frantically at work. The conning tower in the trainer on the beach had looked the same, even smelled the same — mainly of sailors' sweating bodies, Aster's cigar, and the acrid odor of the electric equipment. Byron became utterly absorbed. He wanted to do well at this game and to earn praise. He knew that they were underwater and that a real target ship was generating the data, but that was a foggy awareness compared to his sharp hot focus on the numbers, the trigonometry, the turning dials, and the oncoming moment for his solution — that all-important final bearing, which would fix the gyro angle of the torpedo.

The whole thing seemed to race. Aster approached even closer than he had in the school drills. The computer showed the target at nine hundred yards before he said in brisk tight tones, "*Final bearing and shoot.* Up scope. Mark! Bearing one nine eight. Down scope!"

"Bearings on," Byron called. "Gyro angle one seven port!"

"Shoot!"

"Fire one!" The torpedoman pressed the firing key. "Fire two!"

The jolts of the launch shook Byron into realizing that two TNT-loaded weapons were now lancing through the water to destroy a ship and its unsuspecting crew, guided by his mathematics of death. The tanker had not once changed course or speed. This was unrestricted warfare, all right, he thought: a shotgun to the head of a pigeon. If only the torpedoes worked this time! The seconds ticked away —

BRAMM!

BRAMM!

Another surprise! Exploding torpedoes at nine hundred yards knocked the *Devilfish* about almost like depth charges. The deck jerked, the hull rumbled, the attack party staggered. Yells echoed through the submarine, and Lady Aster shouted, "Oh, WOW! Oh Jesus! Oh my *God,* what a sight! Captain, Captain!"

Hoban hurried to the periscope, his robe flapping around his bare shanks, and bent to the eyepiece. "Oh, beautiful! By Christ, Lady, it's a successful patrol! This does it! It just takes one! Oh, that's just beautiful! Magnificent!"

Byron snatched the ship's camera from a drawer, and as the captain stepped away, he fitted it to the eyepiece. Slapping his back, Aster chortled,

"Goddamn, Briny, well done! Just get a couple of shots, then take a look, baby, take a look. He'll burn for a good while. It's the sight of a lifetime! Foof! You look next. Let *everybody* take a look. Everybody in the attack party!"

As Byron stooped to the eyepiece, a spectacular night scene leaped into view, framed in the black circle of the scope. Against a starry sky a flame shaped like a candle flare hundreds of feet high was rising from a black tanker shape half-enveloped in a red ball of darker fire. Pouring from the top of the candle flame, billows of black smoke blotted out many stars. The sea was a bath of gold. Lady Aster slapped his bent back. "How about that? A perfect solution, you young sack rat. Perfect! Two out of two! Well done! Have you ever seen anything more beautiful in your life?"

Byron was trying to grasp that all this was true, that this was a kill, that the depth charging was avenged, that Japs were dying horribly in that gorgeous holocaust, but a sense of reality still eluded him. His honest sensations were above all heart-pounding triumph at the good shot, admiration of the wild thrilling fire spectacle, and a trace of theatrical sadness, as at the end of a drama or a bullfight. He searched his spirit — all in these few seconds at the periscope — for compassion for the frying Japanese sailors, and could find none. They were abstractions, enemies, stepped-on ants.

"I never have seen anything half as beautiful," said Byron Henry, yielding the scope to Turkell. "I swear to God I never have, sir."

"You bet you haven't!" Aster threw long arms around the ensign and squeezed him like a gorilla. "Merry Christmas! Now you've got a story to tell Natalie!"

13

LESLIE SLOTE tended to see Natalie Henry in any lithe tall girl with heavy dark hair pulled back in soft waves. When he spied one at an eggnog party in Bern, the usual slight shock ran along his nerves. False alarm, of course. Natalie was capable of showing up almost any place, but he knew where she was.

This pseudo-Natalie was chatting with the host of the Christmas party, the British chargé d'affaires, under a bright painting of King George VI in a much-bemedalled uniform. Slote maneuvered in the noisy polyglot crowd for a better look at the oval face, the big slanted dark eyes set far apart, the high cheekbones with slight hollows underneath, even the too-orange lipstick — remarkable resemblance! She was certainly Jewish. Her figure was slighter and therefore more seductive than Natalie's, which to Slote's taste had always been a bit large-boned. He kept watching the girl as she moved through the smoky reception room. She began to return his glances. He followed her into a panelled library, where she halted, sipping a tall drink, by a globe on a bronze stand.

"Hello."

"Hello." The intense eyes turned up to him were clear and innocent, like the eyes of a clever teenager, though she looked to be in her twenties.

"I'm Leslie Slote, first secretary at the American legation."

"Yes, I know."

"Oh, have we met?"

"I asked someone about you, because you kept staring at me." She spoke in a mild sweet voice with a British accent, faintly Germanic in intonation.

"My apologies. You look amazingly like a girl I'm in love with. She's happily married, so it's rather idiotic of me, but anyway, that's why I stared."

"Really? Now I already know too much about you, while you don't even know my name. It's Selma Ascher." She held out a thin hand with a grip less firm, more girlish than Natalie's. She wore no rings. "My friend said you were transferred from Moscow for being too partial toward Jews."

This irritated Slote. The story was all over Bern. Who in the legation was spreading it? "I wish I could claim such martyrdom. My transfer was routine. I'm glad to find myself where food is good, lights go on at night, and guns don't go off."

She shook a schoolteacherish finger at him. "Don't! Don't be ashamed of it. Can't you realize how that distinguishes you in your Foreign Service?" She turned the creaky globe with a pale hand. "A big world, isn't it? And yet there is not one place left on it for Jews to go. Always before, down all the centuries, there's been at least one open gate. Now all are barred."

Slote had not thought to run into such heavy weather. Could this girl, with her smartly tailored suit, her assured manner, her laughing demeanor with other men, be a refugee? He had long since become callous to the woes of the driven unfortunates who haunted the legation. There was no other way to keep one's sanity.

"Are you in difficulties?"

"I myself? No. My family left Germany when I was a child. We're Swiss citizens. People thought Hitler was a joke then, but Papa was not amused." She tossed her head, and her tone changed. "Well! Tell me about the girl I resemble. But first, please, get me more soda water with lemon peel."

At the bar he paused to throw down a hooker of gin. When he returned, Selma Ascher stood at the globe, arms crossed, one hip and leg thrust to a side, outlining a delicious thigh under the slim blue skirt; an old Natalie pose. "Well, about this girl," he said, "she's the niece of Aaron Jastrow, the author — if that means anything to you."

"Oh? *A Jew's Jesus,* and *A Jew Named Paul?* Of course. I didn't much care for the books. They're brightly written, but rather shallow and atheistical. So she's Jewish! How did you meet, and where is she now?"

She avidly took in his story about Natalie. Selma Ascher could focus her pellucid brown eyes like a light beam. Slote's eyes kept going to the strong pulse beating in her white throat above a lacy blue blouse. High nervous energy here.

"But what a strange business! Why didn't she abandon this leech of an uncle, famous or not?"

"She was gradually sucked in. When it was too late she frantically tried to get herself and the baby out. The Pearl Harbor attack trapped her."

"And where is this young Gentile naval officer now, the father of her baby?"

"On a submarine in the Pacific."

"Most peculiar! I feel sorry for her, but her judgment must be very bad. How do you know she's in Siena?"

"I'm working on the exchange of interned nationals. That's where Italy's housing our journalists. She's on the list with Dr. Jastrow."

"Does she know you're trying to effect her release?"

"I hope so. The Swiss legation in Rome transmits our messages, and I've written to her."

"Will you get her out?"

"I don't know why not. Her uncle's published magazine articles, and she's been his researcher. A lot of Italian journalists are caught in my country. It'll take time, but there shouldn't be too much trouble."

"Perfectly fascinating." Selma Ascher offered her hand. "You must write her about the girl you met in Bern who resembled her."

"Let me take you home."

"I have my car, thank you."

"But I'd very much like to see you again."

"Oh, no, no." Her eyes rounded in ironical amusement. "I'd only depress you, reminding you of your lost love."

With a swing of hips as pleasant as waltz music, she left the library.

"Then you think the Soviet Union will hold out?" said Dr. Ascher, a plump man with heavy gray hair and a big hooked nose. He sat at the head of the table, his deathly tired face sagging on his chest.

Slote was disconcerted by the bald question, much as he had been by the unlooked-for dinner bid, and by the wealth of the Ascher home. They were dining off heavy gold-trimmed china. On the panelled walls two Monets glowed in pencil-beams of light from ceiling apertures. Selma smiled across the table at Slote. "Papa, you'll never get such a flat commitment from a diplomat."

She sat between a red-faced priest in clerical garb, who was eating and drinking with lusty appetite, and a tall stringy old Englishman with an ugly wart on his nose, who accepted only vegetables and left them almost untasted. There were ten at the table, all strangers to Slote but Selma. The father and Selma's brother, a prematurely bald little man, wore black skullcaps. In all his travels, Leslie Slote had never before dined with Jews who wore caps at table.

Selma's mother touched Slote's hand. On her slim fingers red and blue fire danced in two large diamonds. "But you're fresh from Moscow. Do tell us your impressions."

"Well, things were at their worst when I left in November. They've somewhat improved since."

Slote slipped smoothly into his monologue on the winter counterattack: generals' photographs in *Pravda* over victory headlines, sheepish officials streaming back to Moscow from Kuibyshev, improved food supply, fading air raids, columns of unshaven gaunt Germans marching down Gorki Boulevard in the snow under Red Army tommy guns, wiping snotty noses on their ragged sleeves. " 'Winter Fritz,' the Russians call these fellows," Slote said, and his hearers laughed and looked happy. "But here it is mid-January. The Germans gave some ground, but Hitler still holds western Russia. The counterattack looks to be petering out. One can't be too optimistic. Except that the Russian people do impress me with their stamina, patriotism, and sheer numbers."

Dr. Ascher wearily nodded. "Yes, yes. But without ninety percent of her heavy industry, how can the Soviet Union go on with the war?"

"They moved factories behind the Urals all during their 1941 defeats. It was a superhuman job."

"Mr. Slote, Hitler's factories didn't have to be moved. They're the best in the world, and they have steadily been grinding out mountains of arms. He'll start a big new offensive as soon as the mud dries from the spring thaw. Can those transplanted factories give the Russians enough arms?"

"They're also getting Lend-Lease supplies."

"Not enough," snapped the old Englishman. "Not for them, and not for Britain."

"What I fear," said Ascher sadly, "is that if he takes the Caucasus in 1942, and Leningrad and Moscow are still cut off, one can't exclude a separate peace."

"Precisely what Lenin did in 1917," said the Englishman. "Communists will sell out their allies at the drop of a hat. They're total realists."

Selma's mother said, "That would be the end for the Russian Jews."

The priest, his small eyes darting at Slote, paused in his vigorous attack on half a duck. "What's the condition of those Jews in Russia now?"

"Behind the German lines? Probably fearful. Elsewhere, tolerable. The regime shunts them about like cattle, but that's how Russia more or less handles everyone."

"Are the stories coming out of Russia and Poland true?" said Dr. Ascher. Slote did not answer. "I mean about the big massacres."

Hard stares at him, from all around the table.

"Such things are difficult to prove." He spoke hesitantly. "It's wartime. The world press is shut out of those areas. Even the German press is. Massacre victims can't talk, and of course the murderers wouldn't."

"Drunkards talk, and Germans drink," Selma said.

Mrs. Ascher touched his hand again. The strands of gray in her hair, the pretty bone structure of her wrinkled face, the long-sleeved black dress buttoned to the throat, all gave this woman of sixty or so a stately charm. "Why did you say conditions behind the German lines are fearful?"

"I saw some documentary evidence before I left Moscow."

"What kind of documentary evidence?" The question came sharp and fast from the priest.

Less and less comfortable, Slote evaded. "Pretty much the sort of thing one hears about."

The Englishman cleared his throat, rapped the table with a knuckle, and spoke in a rheumy voice. "Bern is such a gossipy small town, d'you know, Mr. Slote? One's told you were sent from Moscow to Switzerland by your State Department for being too concerned about the Jews."

"There's no truth in it. My country's State Department itself is very concerned about the Jews."

"One's told, in fact," persisted the Englishman, "that you disclosed your documentary evidence to American newspapermen, and so incurred the displeasure of your superiors."

Slote could not handle this probe smoothly. "Gossip is seldom worth discussing," was all he said.

In the long silence that fell, a maid put small prayer books by each diner's place. Dr. Ascher and his son solemnly intoned a grace in Hebrew, while Slote, feeling awkward, turned pages of German translation. When the men and women went to different sitting rooms for coffee, Selma cut Leslie Slote off in a hallway, putting both her arms on his. Her black velvet bodice half-revealed pretty breasts smaller than Natalie's. Glancing around and seeing nobody else, she leaned to him, and gave him a little cool kiss on the mouth.

"What's that for?"

"You are so skinny. We must feed you up." She rushed away.

An entire floor of the house was Dr. Ascher's library: a long dark room with floor-to-ceiling rows of volumes, most of them leather-bound. The smell was heavy, bookish, musty. On the wall behind a broad cluttered desk hung signed pictures of politicians and opera stars. A wooden stand nearby displayed a war map of the world full of colored pins.

"You've been listening to Radio Berlin again, Jacob!" At the map, the Englishman rapped shaky fingers on the Malay peninsula. "The Jap has been stopped much farther north than this."

Ascher said to Slote, "You see, I am fool enough to bring the war into my spiritual retreat."

"You've a better picture here than we do at the legation. We tend to forget the Pacific entirely."

"But, Herr Slote, it's the key, isn't it? If Singapore should fall, that starts a slide" — he raked spread fingers down across India to Australia — "which may not end short of world chaos." He swept the fingers up to the German front in Russia, a wavy north-south row of red pins from the Arctic Ocean to the Black Sea. "Look at what Hitler holds! The Soviet Union is a cripple without arms or legs."

"Singapore won't fall," said the Englishman.

"And a sovereign nation can grow new limbs," Slote said. "It's a rude tough form of life, like a crab."

Ascher's whey-pale face wanly lit up at the comparison. "Ah, but Germany is so strong. If only she could be struck from behind!" The fingers jumped to the Atlantic coast. "But now the slide in East Asia will drag America and England in the other direction." Ascher heavily sighed, and dropped on the brown leather sofa beside Slote.

"That jolly well mustn't happen!" The Englishman, perching himself in a high-backed chair, began to needle Leslie Slote about the U-boat sinkings off the Atlantic shore. Couldn't Slote's countrymen exert enough self-discipline, even in wartime, to black out their coastal cities? Radio Berlin was openly boasting that the glow set up for the U-boats their easiest hunting of the war. The BBC had just confirmed appalling German figures for December sinkings off the American coast. At this rate the Allies were lost.

Furthermore — the old man was almost jumping from his chair, in worked-up indignation — why were the Japanese advancing so rapidly on Luzon? The British army was stretched all over the earth, and it had been at war for over two years; small wonder Singapore was threatened. But American forces in the Philippines had had two precious extra years of peace to prepare, and the United States wasn't fighting anywhere else in the world. Why weren't the invaders being thrown into the sea? If America could not pull even *that* much weight in this war, well, then England would save civilization alone, and then confront the Russian bear afterward. But it would be a damned long haul. America had the resources, but it wanted the will to fight.

The tirade did not much anger Slote, for the manner and the cracking voice were senile. A peaceful nation needed time, he calmly returned, to get into the war mood. England under Chamberlain had showed that. But he had a question or two also. How did it help the British war effort to shut out of Palestine the Jewish refugees fleeing Hitler? How could a supposedly civilized democracy force women and children to keep sailing hopelessly around the Mediterranean in dangerous old hulks?

"There are reasons — reasons of regional policy, reasons of state —" the Englishman's eyes watered, and he dashed a hand across them. "Empire brings responsibilities and dilemmas, you know — one's sometimes between the devil and the deep — excuse me." He got up and bolted from the room. In a moment his unpainted and unattractive daughter appeared and said, "We must be leaving." With a reproachful look at Slote, she turned on her heel and went out.

"I'm sorry," Slote said to Ascher.

"When Treville was on duty here in the legation," Ascher said firmly, "he was our good friend. He's unwell, he loves his country, and he's old."

So the party broke up. Slote and the priest went out together into a freezing windy starlit night. Putting up his collar, Slote said he would walk to his flat. The priest proposed to accompany him for the exercise. Slote thought the fat small cleric might hold him back, but it was he who had to hurry, as they strode under bare-limbed trees and past dry fountains. In the quiet night Slote could hear the priest's hard even breathing. Vapor jetted from the broad nose as from a little steam engine. They did not exchange a word, walking about a mile.

"Well, here we are," Slote said, halting outside his apartment house. "Thanks for the company."

The priest looked straight in his face. "Would further documentary evidence about what is happening to the Jews interest you?" This was said abruptly in crisp German.

"What? Ah — certainly my government, as I said at dinner, is concerned to alleviate the sufferings of the Jews."

The priest's hand waved toward a gloomy little children's park across the street, where swings and seesaws stood amid empty benches. They crossed the street and walked once around the park in silence.

"Frightful. Frightful. Frightful." The words burst from the priest in a tone so different, so grief-stricken and intense, that Slote halted, shaken. The priest looked up at him, his face distorted in the light of a distant street lamp. "Herr Slote, I am Bavarian by birth. I watched this pile of filth, Adolf Hitler, make speeches on street corners to twenty people in Munich in 1923. I saw him make insolent speeches at his trial in 1924 after the putsch. At the 1936 *Parteitag*, I saw him speak to a million people. He has always been the same pile of filth. He has never changed. He hasn't to this day. The same hand on the hip, the same shaking fist, the same vulgar voice, and dirty language, and stupid primitive ideas. And yet he is Master of Germany. He is the evil genius of my people. He is a scourge sent by God."

Suddenly the priest resumed walking. Slote had to run a few steps to get beside him. "You must understand Germany, Herr Slote." The tone was calmer. "It is another world. We are a politically inexperienced people, we know only to follow orders from above. That is a product of our history, a protracted feudalism. We have been wavering for a century and a half between our dreamy socialist optimists, and our romantic materialistic pessimists. Between sweet visions of utopia, and brutal power theories. Basically, today, we are still caught between the liberal epicureanism of the western democracies, and the radical atheism of the eastern Bolsheviki." The priest stretched his arms wide, as the abstract phrases rolled in a practiced way from his tongue. "And between them, a hideous gap, what a vacuum, what a void! Both these modernist humanisms propose to ignore God. We Germans know in our hearts that both these theses are equally oversimple and false. There we are right. There we are not deceived. We have been groping to put love and faith and, yes, Christ back into modern life. But we are naïve, and we have been humbugged. An Antichrist has beguiled us, and with his brutish pseudoreligious nationalism he is leading us on the path to hell. Our capacity for religious fervor and for unthinking energetic obedience is unfortunately bottomless. Hitler and National Socialism are a ghastly perversion of an honest German thirst for faith, for hope, for a sound modern metaphysics. We are drinking salt water to quench our thirst. If he is not stopped, the end will be an immeasurable cataclysm."

Deeply stirred, as much by the ever-tightening grip of the priest's heavy hand as by this passionate outburst, Slote said, "I believe all that, and it is well said."

The bullet head nodded. The priest said with a simper, in a ridiculous change to a casual tone, "Do you like the cinema? I'm very partial to the films myself. It's a frivolous misuse of time, I confess."

"Yes, I go to films."

"How nice. Perhaps we could go together, some day."

Foreign Service officers were approached from time to time with offers of intelligence, and movie houses were a commonplace rendezvous. It had never before happened to Slote. Nonplussed, he sparred, "What is your name again? I'm very sorry, I should have caught it, but I didn't."

"I am Father Martin. Shall we count on taking in a film together, one of these days? Let me give you a call."

After a considerable pause, Slote nodded.

What went into that small gesture? Often thereafter Leslie Slote wondered, because it shaped the rest of his days. The sense of representing America, and the feeling that America was at bottom — whatever the surface cross-currents and prejudices — compassionate; his own haunting belief that he had been a short-sighted ass in rejecting a splendid Jewish girl; an itch to conquer his own timidity, which was beginning to disgust him; an awareness that his revelation of the Minsk documents to the Associated Press, however it had harmed his career, remained a source of perverse pride; finally, as much as anything else, curiosity; these things impelled him into a new life.

Three weeks went by. This strange talk in the night faded from Slote's mind. Then out of the blue Father Martin called. "Mr. Slote, do you like Bing Crosby? I find him so amusing. The latest Bing Crosby film is playing at the Bijou cinema, you know."

The priest was waiting with tickets already bought. For the seven o'clock showing the house was less than full. Father Martin took an aisle seat and Slote slipped in beside him. For a half hour or so they watched Bing Crosby, dressed as a collegian, caper and swap jokes with pretty girls in very short skirts. Without a word the priest left his seat to move farther down front. Shortly a thin man in glasses came and sat down, juggling a hat, an umbrella, and a thick envelope. The hat dropped to the floor. "*Bitte,*" he said, laying the envelope on Slote's lap as he groped under the seat. On the other side of Slote, a pimply girl, watching Bing Crosby open-mouthed, observed none of this. The man retrieved the hat and settled down. Slote kept the envelope. When the picture ended he tucked it under his arm and left, his heart beating fast. In the twilight outside, nobody in the departing audience gave Slote a glance.

He strolled back to his flat, resisting the impulse to hurry, in fact to run. Behind locked doors and drawn shades, he pulled out of the envelope a sheaf of photostat pages, white on black; a copy of an official German document, stained on some pages with a brown slop that blurred the words. An acrid chemical smell rose from the dark sheets as he riffled them.

A rubber stamping on the top page stood out clearly, white on black — *Geheime Reichssache (National Secret)*. The title of the documents was

CONFERENCE PROTOCOL
Meeting of Under Secretaries of State
Held in Gross-Wannsee, 20 January 1942

The first pages listed fifteen high government officials with orotund titles. Reinhard Heydrich, the deputy chief of the SS, had chaired their meeting in the Berlin suburb of Wannsee. Slote was just starting to sight-translate the text when his telephone rang.

"Hello. It's Selma Ascher. Will you take me dinner?"

"Selma! God, yes!" She burst into rich laughter at his enthusiasm. "When? Where?"

Before dressing, he skimmed the document. The main topic was a transfer by railroad of large numbers of European Jews to the conquered eastern territories, for forced labor on highways. This was neither novel nor very shocking. Russian and French war prisoners were being used as slave labor. The Germans were pressing even Italians into their factories. They were harsh overlords, and harshest to the Jews, hence the road-building project. Slote wondered why the priest had been at such pains to get the material to him. He tucked the envelope under his mattress for a close reading later.

Selma picked him up in her gray Fiat two-seater. Half-hidden by a white fox collar, her face was solemn as she greeted him, her eyes bright and shy. She drove to a tiny restaurant in a side street.

"Since meeting you I've done two bad things for the first time in my life." Selma clasped and unclasped her small hands on the checked tablecloth. "One of them is to ask a man to take me to dinner."

"That's not so bad, and I'm happy you did. What's the other thing?"

"Far worse." She suddenly, heartily laughed, touched her hand on his, and jerkily withdrew it.

"Selma, your hand's cold."

"No wonder. I'm awfully nervous."

"But why?"

"Well — to get one thing out of the way, it wasn't my idea to ask you to dinner last month. Papa took me by surprise. You seem not to mind a forward girl — from what you've said about your friend in Siena — but that's the last thing I am. I did tell my parents I'd met you. They'd heard about you. Papa's headed the Jewish Council here for years. It's been an education for me," Selma exclaimed, talking rapidly after her first halting sentences, "a real education in cynicism, to see our friendships here in Bern dwindle down with every German victory. Papa has supported the hospital, the opera, the repertory theatre, everything! We used to be a popular family. Now — well —"

"Selma, who was the priest I met at your house?"

"Father Martin? A good German. Oh, they exist. There are many, but unfortunately not enough to make a difference. Father Martin has helped Papa get many South American visas."

"He offered me secret information on German mistreatment of the Jews."

"He *did?*"

"Would his information be reliable?"

"I can't really judge anything about a priest, even a friendly one. I'm sorry." She made an agitated negative gesture with both hands, as though waving the topic away. "Things are in such a turmoil at home! I had to get out tonight. Papa's moving his business to America. He's just exhausted, and Mother doesn't want him to die of grief and worry. It's a very complicated deal, it involves trading off factories in Turkey and Brazil, and I don't know what else, and — I'm talking my head off."

"I'm glad you're confiding in me. I never repeat anything."

"Does Natalie talk so much?"

"Much more. She's quite opinionated, and very argumentative."

"I think we're not really much alike."

"I'm rapidly forgetting the resemblance."

"Truly? Poor me. That's the only reason you were interested in me."

"Not once you spoke half a dozen words."

Selma Ascher colored and turned away her head, then faced him, bridling. "The other reason, the real one, that my father is moving is that I'm going to marry an American, a lawyer in Baltimore, quite orthodox."

"Are you — well, are you yourself actually religious? Or do you conform to your parents' wishes?"

"I have a fine Hebrew education. I even know some Talmud, which girls aren't supposed to learn. I've always been a serious student. It makes my father happy. He and I are studying Isaiah together right now, and it's really glorious. But as to God"— again she made the nervous negative gesture — "I grow more skeptical all the time. Where is He nowadays? How can He allow the things that are happening? I may yet become a lost soul."

"Then what about marrying that devout young man?"

"Oh, I couldn't possibly marry any other kind." She chuckled at his puzzled frown. "You don't understand that? Well, you don't have to."

It was now perfectly evident to Slote that there was nothing doing with this girl. They talked aimlessly until the food came. He began to look for her unattractive points, an old trick of his when trying to back off. All girls had flaws. Selma's long drippy earrings were badly chosen. Her sense of style was deficient: prudishness and femininity were awkwardly at odds in the high-necked dress, which concealed her throat but made provocative mounds of her small breasts. Her eyebrows were heavy and unplucked. What had seemed at first remarkable freshness and innocence apparently was nothing but overprotected narrowness. He was dining with — of all things — a pious virgin! He began to feel taken in. What was the point of this dinner?

"Do you like to dance?" Selma was picking idly at her steamed fish.

"So-so," said Slote with faint ungraciousness. "And you?"

"I dance abominably. I've done it so little. I would like to dance tonight."

"By all means." It was a way, if no very satisfying one, of taking the pious virgin in his arms.

"You're angry at me."

"Not in the least."

"Can't you guess the other bad thing that I've done for the first time in my life?"

"I'm afraid not."

"All right. Then I'll tell you. It was kissing a Gentile. I've not kissed many Jews, either."

They went to a casino where two bands spelled each other. She kept stepping on his feet, turning the wrong way, holding herself a foot away from him, seeming at once confused, distraught, and delighted. Holding this slim clodhopping girl in his arms at whatever distance, and with whatever punishment to his toes, brought back wistful memories of high school proms. She kept watching a large wall clock, and precisely at a quarter past eleven, she said, "We must go now. That was very nice."

She let him out of the Fiat at his flat without a handshake and roared off. He plodded upstairs, knowing that Selma Ascher's image, and the remembered sensations of embracing her body and smelling her hair, would keep him awake for hours. Mixing himself a dark whiskey and water, he dropped in an armchair. His eye fell on the bed. With a sigh he got up and went for the Wannsee Protocol, thinking that translating official German prose might make him sleepy. Settling down with a yellow pad, a pencil, and the black sheets, he began to read and write.

After an hour or so, he let the sheet he was reading fall to the floor. "Jesus . . . Christ!" he exclaimed, more wide awake than ever, staring with horror-stricken eyes at his own dead-white face in a mirror on the wall. "Jesus . . . CHRIST!"

*　　*　　*

World Holocaust

by General Armin von Roon

(adapted from his *Land, Sea, and Air Operations of World War II*)

English Translation by

VICTOR HENRY

14

𝕿ranslator's 𝕱oreword

(with a note on "The Wannsee Protocol")

Time usually hangs heavy on the hands of a retired naval officer, but in recent years I have been well occupied translating General Armin von Roon's *World Empire Lost* and its sequel, *World Holocaust.*

These strategic summaries are extracted from Roon's massive two-volume operational analysis of World War II, written in prison while serving a sentence for war crimes. Without the battle analyses that documented these summaries, Roon's judgments may seem sweeping. But his whole work is for military specialists, and they can read German. Other people must get Roon's views in this short form, first compiled by a German publisher as a two-part popular history of the war.

Though much colored by Roon's nationalism, the strategic overview in these two volumes should interest readers who want a clear and readable account of the whole war as it looked "from the other side of the hill." Roon's penetrating analyses of the sea battles in the Pacific, a theatre so remote from his own field, show German military professionalism at its soundest. Where I have felt compelled to dissent from Roon's views, my comments are plainly set off in italics.

I have prefaced this book with an essay Roon wrote for a military journal shortly before his death, entitled "The Wannsee Protocol." I believe this essay should be required reading for first-year students in all military academies.

Since the publication of *World Empire Lost* I have received a number of letters, some from old friends and comrades-in-arms (including a Soviet general), wondering at my willingness to spread the views of a convicted German war criminal. I hold no brief for the Germans. They started the worst war in mankind's history and came too close to winning it, and under the cloak of wartime secrecy they committed unheard-of crimes. I believe we must study the German state of mind that generated their huge (and militarily remarkable) assault, and their persisting fealty to an insane tyrant. Without the Armin von Roons who followed him and fought for him to the last, Adolf Hitler would have lived and died an impotent fanatical loud-mouth, instead of becoming the most powerful monster of history, who all but brought down the civilized world. That is why I have translated Armin von Roon; and why I think "The Wannsee Protocol" should be required reading for military men.

Victor Henry

Oakton, Virginia
12 September 1970

Note to the Third Edition

Readers continue to write and argue with me as though I shared Armin von Roon's views; whereas I translated his books just because his views appall me.

As a professsional military analyst, Roon is often sound, sometimes brilliant. His facts are seldom wrong. Where they are, I have said so in my notes. But his interpretations of the facts tend to be twisted by the German nationalism that led to Hitler; and if I had noted all my disagreements, the books would have been twice as long. In these pages, therefore, one peers into an able but distorted mind. Readers who find themselves agreeing with Armin von Roon had better take a good hard look at themselves and their ideas; readers who disagree with him are probably in my camp.

Victor Henry

Oakton, Virginia
17 October 1973

The Wannsee Protocol

BY GENERAL ARMIN VON ROON

Military writers tend to shun the topic of this paper, but the Jewish question affected the conduct of the Second World War and its outcome. The question cannot be forever ignored. Nor need one fear a frank probing of the problem, for the honor of the German soldier emerges intact.

Long before the war, the National Socialist policy on Jewry had created a military perplexity. Eleven million dispersed inhabitants of Europe had been designated as our nation's blood enemies. In Germany the Nuremberg decrees had expelled them from civic, business, and professional life. The Third Reich, once it began its armed drive to normalize Europe, therefore had to reckon at the outset with this closely knit community branching all over the continent, with powerful connections and substantial resources overseas. The army could not dig back into the origins of the problem. It had to deal with the security situation as it existed.

The Jews had to be classed as a potential underground, formidable in numbers, cleverness, and means. The worst enemy is always the desperate one who has nothing to lose. Partisans of other nationalities could change their allegiance and side with us. This option was not open to Jews. The army had no choice but to cooperate with the regime's special Jewish measures.

The nature of the measures was not a responsibility of the army. Various federal police agencies shared in this task: RSHA, Gestapo, SD, regular SS, and so on, a multiple façade for the various Nazi bigwigs contending for power. These all added up to a single iron instrument of Adolf Hitler's will, for from Adolf Hitler alone proceeded the policy regarding the Jews. The essence of this policy was the elimination of the Jewish race in Europe. It should be noted that this policy failed. Despite the regime's grip on the continent for almost four years, approximately half of the European Jews survived. Bureaucratic botching, thoroughly unmilitary, characterized the execution of the policy from start to finish.

Indeed, of Hitler's actual aim, the German army, from the lowest foot soldier to the highest general in Supreme Headquarters, had no knowledge whatever until the war ended and the so-called death camps were uncovered by the victorious armies.

The surviving documentation of this secret policy is naturally tenuous. The policy was carried out with circumspection. Crucial orders were given verbally, "under four eyes." So thin is the paper record, in fact, that some authorities soberly contend that the so-called extermination never took place. In this view, all the Jews except a few hundred thousand really escaped to the Soviet Union, to the West, or to Palestine; the so-called death camps were concentration camps of undesirables, where conditions were understandably harsh; and the crematoriums were routine hygienic installations for the disposal of those who died in confinement.

Unhappily the written record, slender though it is, suggests the contrary. For instance, the camp rosters that have survived show few entries of death by execution; but several thousand prisoners often died on the same day of "heart failure." Obviously such mass simultaneous heart failures had to be induced. To distinguish these demises from executions is to split legalistic hairs.

There are, moreover, SS documents which discuss the merits of Zyklon B gas for euthanasia purposes versus shooting and carbon monoxide asphyxiation, etc., etc., also detailed correspondence between German industrial firms and SS officials on the design and building of very large-scale crematoriums, etc., etc. All these undeniably authentic papers suggest a plan to produce and dispose of great numbers of human corpses on a systematic basis. Thus, one is forced to grant that the elimination process took place.

Of these surviving German documents, none is more instructive than the Protocol of the Wannsee Conference of January 20, 1942.

The Wannsee Protocol

The Protocol came to light because of the sudden collapse of our fronts. Many tons of our nation's most secret papers, which by standard security practice should have been burned, fell intact into American, British, or Russian hands. Among these papers was the Wannsee Protocol.

Had Moscow suddenly fallen to our Army Group Center in December 1941, documents equally compromising would have come into our hands. Stalin was fully as ruthless a personage as Hitler. He ordered many vast secret slaughters of his own Russian people, which his minions obediently carried out. The figure has been put as high as sixty million! But no official records have been exposed to horrify the world. Consequently, nobody brands the Russian people as a nation of murderers.

Or supposing that we had taken London, in the swift cross-Channel attack which I vainly advocated in June 1940? What shameful Whitehall records might we not have uncovered of hideous episodes in India, in Egypt, in Malaya, in South Africa, in fact wherever British imperialism carried the Union Jack, and British arms brutally suppressed native populations which resisted being bled dry for Anglo-Saxon enrichment? But these things remain shrouded secrets.

Only Germany suffered the ignominy of having her records unveiled. Only Germany was stripped naked. Even the defeated Japanese were allowed to keep their emperor and their government structure, which ensured suppression of their papers on the sack of Nanking and the Bataan Death March.

"Wannsee Protocols" exist in the secret papers of every nation. Human nature is everywhere alike. Let America uncover its files about its extermination of the Red Indian, its robbery of Texas from Mexico, its oppression of the Nisei after Pearl Harbor. Then let us see how the facts compare with the disclosures in the Wannsee Protocol.

The Wannsee Conference

The Protocol, a fifteen-page mimeographed secret document, was found by American investigators digging through the vast captured files of our Foreign Ministry. A notation shows that thirty copies originally existed. Only number 16, the Foreign Ministry's copy, survived. On such a slender thread hung world history's insight into Hitler's Jewish policy. The secret was almost kept!

The document describes a conference held at the International Police Building in the Gross-Wannsee section of Berlin on January 20, 1942, shortly after America entered the war. The chairman was Heydrich, a shady cashiered naval officer, who in the topsy-turvy Nazi era became chief of the Security Police and head of the Reich Security Main Office.* This Heydrich person was number two man under the unsavory Himmler in the SS. Already early in 1942 the SS had gained control over our federal security and police departments. So when Heyrdrich called this conference, undersecretaries of state came scurrying. They met for about an hour and a half with seven SS men, one of whom, Lieutenant Colonel Adolf Eichmann, kept the minutes. These minutes, edited by Heydrich, constitute the Wannsee Protocol.

The eight high officials came from the Ministry of Justice, the Ministry for the Interior, the Foreign Ministry, the Ministry for the Occupied Eastern Territories, the Government General in Poland, the Reich Chancellery, and the Plenipotentiary for the Four-year Plan — in fact, from every major government department except the armed forces. *No evidence exists that any member of the armed forces ever knew the conference took place.*

This is the crucial fact that emerges from the Wannsee Protocol. The honor of the German nation was entrusted to our armed forces, and the armed forces were innocent. It was a joint meeting of the secret police and the federal bureaucracy. The Eichmann-Heydrich document proves this.

*In German this is *Reichs-sicherheits-haupt-amt,* run together as one word; acronym RSHA. — V.H.

TRANSLATOR'S NOTE: *General von Roon does not usually resort to such fudging of the facts in his writings. He is not being a military historian here, however, but a special pleader. In fact, though no Wehrmacht representative attended the Wannsee Conference, the documentation of the German army's involvement in the Jewish policy is all too real and depressing. — V.H.*

Heydrich seems to have called the conference to impress his superiors. Six months earlier, on July 31, 1941, when our invasion of the Soviet Union was rolling, Reichsmarschall Hermann Göring had ordered him in a top-secret letter to organize a disposition of the Jewish problem; to bring in other government departments as needed; and to submit to Göring, "as soon as possible," a draft showing what action had been taken, and what the further plans were. Despite the usual SS practice of not putting such things on paper, the Wannsee Protocol evidently came into existence to impress Göring with Heydrich's diligence.

Göring's letter used the words, "a final solution to the Jewish question." Since the exposure of the Protocol, this expression, "The Final Solution,"* has come to take on unpleasant overtones in anti-German literature. Heydrich often used a more precise term, "the territorial solution." This term will be used here.

The Territorial Solution

Three alternative solutions to the Jewish question had emerged in policy analyses over the years: the *emigration* solution, the *expulsion* solution, and the *territorial* solution.

At first the Nazis believed that once they took power, most of the Jews would emigrate. But the German Jews, as it turned out, were reluctant to abandon their homes and businesses, and the graves of their ancestors, even after Hitler's Nuremberg laws made them pariahs. They hoped that the Nazi regime would prove a passing storm. Elsewhere in Europe few Jews seemed to believe that war would come, or that if it did, Germany would win. As a result, far more Jews remained in Germany than left. Outside our borders, Jewish emigration was insignificant.

But even for the few who wanted to leave, the emigration solution hit a snag. If Hebrews were no longer welcome in Germany, it developed that they were not much more welcome anywhere else. Year by year after Hitler took power, western Europe stiffened its restrictions against admitting

*German: *Endlösung.* — V.H.

Jews. The sparsely settled vast lands of the New World, led by the "haven of oppressed mankind," the U.S.A., clanged iron doors shut in the Jews' faces. This was a black chapter in the tale of man's inhumanity to man.

When it became clear to the Hitler regime that the Jews would not emigrate and would find it hard at all events to get in elsewhere, the *expulsion* solution came forward: i.e., forcibly removing them. The awkward question remained: where to?

Of all the expulsion ideas, the one most prominent in the surviving documents is the *Madagascar Plan*. The forcible resettling of Europe's Jews on this French island of South Africa received some study. But in view of the gross difficulties — lack of shipping to transport eleven million people, enemy control of the seas, stupendous cost, offense to Vichy France whose collaboration we were seeking, and nonviability of this wild tropical island for Europeans — it is hard to say how serious this project was. When the navy indicated to Hitler that the British might one day land in Madagascar to protect their Indian Ocean sea lanes, all talk of settling the Jews there ended. The Führer declared that the British would only "let the bacillus loose again on the world."

Thus it developed that the problem would have to be solved on European soil: hence, *territorial solution*. At Wannsee, Heydrich lifted the veil of secrecy, so that the federal bureaucrats would understand plainly, once for all, what the nature of their job was.

The Program

This draconic program should certainly have had no place in the twentieth century. Alas! Cologne, Dresden, Katyn, and Hiroshima showed that this kind of moral failure in wartime was certainly not confined to Germany. The territorial solution of the Jewish question was a harebrained scheme dreamed up by irresponsible and inept Berlin desk officials. Administratively, it was from start to finish a mess. Like most projects dreamed up in the comfortable suites of a government building, it had about it a specious neatness and clarity, but in the field it broke down. All too many Jews did perish in the process, but on the whole it was a monumental fiasco.

The key to the territorial solution lay in our vast 1941 conquests. *The occupied eastern areas were at last the long-sought place where the Jews could be sent.* For here no government had to be consulted, and no local population had to be mollified. It was a thinly settled half-continent under German guns.

Heydrich outlined a most plausible and simple plan. The Jews of Europe would be "cleaned up from west to east," temporarily collected in transit ghettos, and then shipped to the Occupied Territories in huge labor columns, separated by sexes. There they would build roads, of which this backward region stood in great need for military purposes. In the course of this action "a great part of the Jews would undoubtedly be eliminated by natural causes," that is, by poor conditions and debilitating labor. As for the few who survived the ordeal, Heydrich said bluntly that they would have to be "treated accordingly," since as the tough product of natural selection they would otherwise constitute a spore for the rebirth of the Jewish people. Such was the unrelenting ideology of the government of the time.

The unanimous reaction of the cabinet officials was extreme enthusiasm, and a variety of suggestions for improving or speeding up the plan. The conference ended on a note of cordial agreement, and an excellent and convivial luncheon followed in the usual high bureaucratic style.

But the scheme collapsed almost at the outset. The labor columns were never organized. The roads were never built. From 1943 on in our forced-march retreats from Russia, the army felt keenly the impact of this failure. True, the Jews were collected all over Europe and shipped eastward, to transit ghettos of Poland. But there they stayed — a colossal prison population, an immense drain on German resources, and a festering rear-area threat both to health and to security.

No subsequent SS protocol has survived to explain why Heydrich's plan was abandoned. The territorial solution was modified in a haphazard way to become the construction of big factories near the ever-swelling transit ghettos, and the use of Jewish forced labor on the spot. The hoped-for natural diminution was sought through reduced nutrition, drastic work schedules, etc., etc. But the uprooting and resettling of a population of eleven million people proved an almost unimaginable administrative task, quite beyond the Berlin bunglers in charge of the program, with the result that half the Jews, as has been stated, escaped elimination. No more than five and a half, or by the highest estimate six, million were caught by the scheme.

The Mercy Deaths

We still do not know exactly when or how the switch to euthanasia (mercy death) in gas chambers occurred. This difficult aspect has been widely distorted and misunderstood.

Heydrich's plan turned out to be a vast folly, projected by soft-living bureaucrats not experienced, as soldiers are, in large-scale suffering, privation, and death. The resources of the human spirit and body are remarkable. Prisoners of war endure wretched conditions for years. They learn to eat or drink almost anything. The demands of their depleted bodies shrink almost to zero, in the natural urge to live on. All these phenomena occurred in the transit ghettos. The slow rate of attrition became worrisome. Plagues broke out, and plague germs do not distinguish between captors and prisoners.

The weakened Jews therefore became a standing menace to the local populations and to our armed forces.

These developments apparently brought forward the thought: since these people were in any case condemned to death, would not a quick, unexpected, painless end free them from long woes? And would it not simultaneously relieve our forces of a clogging problem, the proportions of which had not been realized in time?

Here, in these essentially humane considerations, lay the reason for the gas chambers. Rescuing the Jews was out of the question. Adolf Hitler had decreed their end, and his will was law. One could only carry it out in the most decent, practical, and civilized fashion. Much has been made of the undeniable fact that a million children were thus gassed to death, and it is an unfortunate episode to recall. Yet starvation would have been a slower, more painful demise for the children, and their parents would have endured the misery of watching them waste away.

As for the spoliation of the arriving Jews, and even of the dead bodies of these unfortunates, such practices cannot be extenuated. The SS amassed several billion marks' worth of gold, jewelry, and goods in this fashion, but whether the German war effort benefitted remains doubtful, for the Himmler-Heydrich agency was a high-handed and corrupt one. The story of soap manufacture from the bodies was, of course, a baseless British fabrication from the First World War.

Military Effects: (1) Manpower

This was not a rear-area matter of no military weight. The territorial solution materially damaged our armed effort.

The worst damage was in manpower. Large numbers of healthy German men were diverted from combat roles to the herding of Jews. Round-up squads, camp guards, etc., were recruited from local populations, but even so enough Germans for several divisions may have been fussing with Jews in bureaus and in camps, instead of fighting.

The manpower shortage was also chronic in our factories. The prisoners of war and the forced laborers from occupied lands gave halfhearted service at best, and they persisted in sabotage no matter how many were shot. But the Jews constituted a vast pool of clever workmen and artisans, or professional men and women quick to learn any skilled labor. They were so used, in fact, until the inexorable round-up squads came to ship them off. They committed very little sabotage. Rather, they displayed a desperate anxiety to preserve their own lives and those of their loved ones by turning in superlative work. We thus lost the labor of several million workers of high reliability, motivation, and productivity.

Finally, it was fashionable under National Socialism to sneer at the fighting capacity of the Jews. Indeed, under SS handling they appeared a docile and vulnerable lot. But that this was a condition capable of startling reversal has been shown by postwar events in Palestine. How well we could have used on the eastern front one or two million fighters of the calibre of the present-day Jewish armies! At the time the idea would have seemed a joke. Today, when it is too late, we can only wonder.

Military Effects: (2) Supplies and Services

The railroading burden was oppressive and continuous. No matter how tightly the trains were packed — and that this was carried to excess is common knowledge — the tying up of rolling stock remained a grave problem. There never were sufficient trains and locomotives for the fighting fronts. Combat divisions sat shivering at rear depots while trains devoted to shuttling the Jews rolled eastward jam-packed and went back empty, cut off from use for any other purpose. This noncombat usage had a secret overriding priority such as in America was given only to making the atomic bomb.

Military Effects: (3) Morale

While the ultimate intent of the policy remained secret, many German army formations did see the process in action. That is a matter of record. Regrettably, some units were also coopted to assist not only in transporting or guarding the Jews, but in the liquidation process.

Local army commanders sometimes supplied and transported the mobile execution squads, since they were on government business. These SS squads, called *Einsatzgruppen* (Special Action Units), had entered Russia close behind our advancing armies. They had orders to shoot political commissars without trial, in order to nip partisan activity in the bud; this was the well-known "Commissar Order" of March 1941. They also were instructed to liquidate forthwith, as a prime menace to German security, all the Jews they could round up. Local populations gladly volunteered to join the *Einsatzgruppen* against their Jews, with episodes of frightfulness resulting, especially in Lithuania, Rumania, and Hungary. By the more orderly German squads themselves, hundreds of thousands of Jews were systematically shot within areas of army cognizance.

German soldiers could not always avert their eyes from these happenings. Isolated instances occurred of misguided local army commanders allowing or even ordering their units to take part. Thus authentic photographs exist of men in Wehrmacht uniform, shooting Jewish women holding babes in their arms. Such occurrences unquestionably spread in our ranks a certain demoralization, and a questioning of our aims in fighting the war. When this happens in an army, its fighting spirit has been injured. Like so many aspects of the territorial solution, one cannot state this morale damage in our army in percentage points, or other meaningful figures. It was, however, a real factor on the eastern front. Like defeatism, self-doubt is an invisible but heavy weight on a war effort.

A soldier is trained to the job of killing. It is his life against the enemy's; that is soldiering at its cleanest. Soldiers sometimes have to do sadder, dirtier jobs. They must shoot spies and partisans who are standing blindfolded and helpless. On orders, they must sometimes hang boys, girls, and women, who make good partisan fighters. But that does not mean that the soldier — especially a German soldier, trained to decency and honor, as much as to hardness in the field — can always stomach such work. What the Nazis did, in this regard, to our German youth is hard to forget or to excuse.

The Nature of the Enemy

We come therefore to the heart of the whole matter: was the solution, with all these drawbacks, nevertheless an imperative wartime security measure? Were the Jews the ultimate security menace to the Reich that Hitler postulated? Within this question lies another question — *"Which Reich?"*

Ever since the French Revolution two irreconcilable Reich concepts had emerged in our philosophy and in our politics:

(a) The *liberal* concept: a peaceful Reich universalist in culture, with freedom for the Jews, the establishment of bourgeois democracy in imitation of France and England, and a subordinate military position for Germany.

(b) The *nationalist* concept: the Reich as a rising world force, the natural successor to the British Empire; a German culture purged of foreign strains; armed forces on the Bonapartist basis of "the nation in arms"; a hard mystical loyalty to king, to soil, and to old Christian virtues.

Cutting across both ideas came *socialism,* with its sentimental and poisonous farrago of world brotherhood, egalitarianism, and the abolition of private property. But nationalism was the truly German essence. Whenever the nationalist Reich prevailed — in 1866, in 1870–71, in 1914, in 1917 — we were strong and victorious. Whenever the liberal and socialist elements surfaced, Germany suffered.

It was Adolf Hitler's political genius to weld the mystique of the nationalist Reich to the rabble-rousing appeal of socialism. *National Socialism* resulted, an explosive mass movement. The modified socialism of Hitler was unobjectionable to the army. It amounted to spartan economic controls, and basic employment, health, and welfare measures for all the people except the Jews.

But the Jews were the backbone of German liberalism. Liberalism had given them the rights and privileges of citizens. Liberalism had turned them loose to use their energy and cleverness in finance, the professions, and the arts. These people who had been kept apart were now to be seen everywhere — prosperous, exotic, holding high places, and indiscreetly displaying their new-won gains. To the Jews, liberalism was their salvation. Therefore, to a dedicated nationalist like Adolf Hitler, the Jews appeared as ultimate enemies.

Tragically, it all depended on the point of view.

The Actual Power of the Jews

Yet all attempts to justify the territorial solution finally fall before one practical historical truth. The Jews proved unable to save themselves, or to influence anybody else to save them; and self-preservation is the test of a nation's true power.

The Jews beyond Hitler's reach looked on helplessly while their European blood brothers were going to an obscure but grim fate. Where then was their political stranglehold on the West, that Hitler took as an article of faith? Where was their boundless wealth, when they could not induce or bribe a single country — not even one small South American republic — to open its doors? In 1944, where was their all-penetrating influence, when the secret began to leak out, and they in vain implored the Anglo-Americans to bomb Auschwitz?

These things speak for themselves. Hitler exaggerated the threat of the Jews, and badly led astray the well-meaning German people. The Jews would have served us well. Their weight in manpower, skill, and international influence, added on our side instead of subtracted from it, would have been most welcome. Perhaps the war might even have ended differently!

For if the Jews outside Europe lacked the power to command deliverance, they did have a strong voice. Their outcries lent credence to Roosevelt's and Churchill's unfair portrayal of our folk as Huns and savages, even while we were fighting the battle of Christendom against the Red hordes. And so arose the two policies fatal to our cause —"Germany First," and "unconditional surrender"— which ranged the two powerful plutocracies irrevocably on the side of Eurasian Bolshevism.

Had the Nazi regime handled the millions of Jews under our rule with wisdom, none of this need have happened. This is the tragic military paradox of the territorial solution. The Jews were not strong enemies; but they might have been strong friends. Seen in this light, the Nazi policy toward the Jews must be called a costly military blunder. But the armed forces were not consulted and cannot be blamed. This is the inescapable conclusion from the prime surviving document of the matter, the Wannsee Protocol.

TRANSLATOR'S NOTE: *When I first submitted this article in translation to the* U.S. Naval Institute Proceedings, *the editor, Vice Admiral Turnbull C. "Buck" Fuller, USN, returned it with a large red-ink scrawl,* "Just what is the purpose of offering to the Proceedings this obtuse, cold-blooded, sickening drivel?" *He was an old salt and a good friend. I wrote under his words,* "To show ourselves what we might be capable of," *and sent the piece back. Six months later the article appeared in the* Proceedings. *I met Buck Fuller on many occasions thereafter. He never once referred to Armin von Roon's essay. He still has not. — V.H.*

*   *   *

15

U.S.S. NORTHAMPTON
Plan of the Day, 1 February 1942

1. Commencing at sunrise, Task Group 8.1 (this vessel with *Salt Lake City* and *Dunlap*) will bombard Wotje atoll in the northern Marshall Islands.
   a. Air strikes from *Enterprise* will neutralize enemy air strength and shore batteries before bombardment commences.
   b. Charts of these enemy waters being old and unreliable, and hazards from coral reefs abounding, condition Zed will be set at 0000 hours.
2. *Northampton* is proud to be flagship of Bombardment Group North, under Vice Admiral Halsey's Task Force 8, as the Pacific Fleet at last hits back at the treacherous Nips throughout the Marshall and Gilbert island groups.
3. "This is It." All hands govern themselves accordingly.

                                                        JAMES C. GRIGG
                                                        EXECUTIVE OFFICER

"*Commence firing!*"

The *Northampton*'s three turrets thundered out white smoke and pale fire. The deck jerked and shuddered. Though plugged with cotton, Victor Henry's ears rang. The flash, the roar, the smell of gunpowder from this first salvo at the enemy that had wrecked Pearl Harbor and the *California*, filled him with exultation. Astern, at the same moment, the *Salt Lake City*'s main battery blasted and flamed, and the two clusters of eight-inch projectiles, plain to see with binoculars, arched off toward the vessels anchored in the lagoon.

Off the port quarter, the rim of the sun was blazing up over a sharp horizon. The two cruisers and the destroyer *Dunlap*, flying huge battle flags, were steaming in column at full speed, broadside to the smoking green lump on the sea that was Wotje Island. The *Enterprise* planes, mere specks in the sky (Warren's no doubt among them), were heading back to the carrier, barely visible to the north. They had struck the island at dawn, on schedule.

Pug was still seething over the messy catapulting of his own four spotter planes. One craft had just missed going into the sea. Another had been twenty minutes loading on the catapult, for the crane had jammed. Damned bad start! Admiral Spruance, standing beside him on the bridge in the brightening dawn, had said not a word, but disappointment at the performance had radiated from him. He was clearly disappointed too at the lack of targets in Wotje. There were no warships, only a scattering of merchantmen. Halsey's first hit-and-run raid against the Japs would not amount to much if the pickings were no better at the other atolls.

But even this minor gunnery action began badly. The enemy ships weighed anchor made smoke, and dodged and twisted in the lagoon, hard to see and harder to hit. Not one visibly sank or even flamed under continuous heavy gunfire. The spotter planes reported splashes as hits, then corrected themselves. A nervy little minesweeper sortied from the lagoon, shooting its popguns and zigzagging. The destroyer *Dunlap* engaged it at point-blank range, with five-inch salvos that kept churning up futile splashes in the sea. Lookouts on all three ships next began sighting periscopes, in a hysterical wave of reports. Neither Pug Henry nor the admiral could see the periscopes, but Spruance had little choice. He ordered an emergency turn. The attack fell apart. The three warships milled about on the quiet sunny sea off the smoking island, preoccupied with dodging reported torpedo tracks and avoiding collisions. At last Pug Henry resolved to ignore periscopes and torpedo wakes he couldn't see. Heading into Wotje on a firing course, he blasted away at the elusive merchant vessels, lavishing the costly shells to give his crew at least the experience of failure, the exposure to the thumping shore batteries, the practice of rushing shells from magazine to gun breech, the smell and the sound and the fear of combat; and to force into the open the humiliating realities of a warship system still clogged with peacetime fat.

Rear Admiral Spruance, issuing order after order on the TBS, finally regained a semblance of control. The *Dunlap* sank the minesweeper. The three ships formed up, moved in close to shore, and set ablaze most of the island's rickety buildings. But the shore batteries found the range, and colored splashes began howling up around the attackers. When Spruance saw the *Salt Lake City* straddled twice, he called a cease-fire. Ordering Captain Henry to lead Task Group 8.1 back to the *Enterprise* screen, the admiral left the bridge frozen-faced. The action had lasted an hour and a half.

"Meeting of all officers not on watch in the wardroom," Pug said to Jim Grigg.

"Aye aye, sir," said the exec, his countenance under the new blue-painted helmet as fallen as Spruance's.

A subdued crowd of young men in khaki got to their feet as the captain came into the long narrow room. He kept them standing for his short talk. They had just taken part in a nuisance raid, he said. They had failed to be much of a nuisance. A long war lay ahead. The *Northampton* would commence improving its combat readiness. Dismissed.

All day, all evening, past midnight, department heads were summoned to the captain's quarters, where, speaking without notes, he ticked off weak points and ordered remedial action. The *Northampton*'s poor showing had not greatly surprised Pug Henry. In his first month or so as captain, sizing up his ship, he had kept his eyes and ears open and his mouth more or less shut. There were too many raw recruits and draftees aboard; the experienced personnel, enlisted and officers alike, were a sparse lot. Ship routine went well, spit-and-polish was adequate, but everything was slack, grooved, comfortable, and faintly civilian. Still, the men looked good to Pug, and he had been waiting for just such a crisis to show his hand.

He startled all the officers from the exec down with his hard manner and precise criticisms, for they had been taking him as a quiet sort, out of touch after all his years on the beach. The conferences went on for fourteen straight hours. Alemon kept brewing and serving fresh coffee, pot after pot, and made hamburgers for dinner, which Grigg and the captain ate as they conferred. When Grigg, having taken hundreds of notes in his "urgent" notebook and drunk a dozen cups of coffee to stay alert, looked ready to faint, Pug quit. "Prepare a dispatch to ComCruPac," he said, "requesting a tug with target upon our return to base."

"We can't break radio silence, sir," said Grigg nervously. "Not for that."

"I know. Send a scout plane with it."

Halsey's task force, a long column of gray warships streaming battle flags, entered Pearl Harbor to a wild welcome: sirens, whistles, bells, cheers, and rainbows of flags decking every ship in port. For journalists and radio commentators the raid had been a mighty shot in the arm. They were hailing Admiral Halsey's gigantic attack on the Marshalls and Gilberts as the resurgence of American power in the Pacific, the turn of the tide, the proof of the resilience of free governments, and so on and so forth. Coded intercepts of battle reports had told Victor Henry a different story. Air attacks at Kwajalein had destroyed some planes and probably sunk a few small ships. The coordinated air strikes by the *Yorktown* in the Gilberts had produced small results. Surface bombardments had nowhere been effective.

The captain summoned his officers to the wardroom as soon as the *Northampton* moored. They had all been out on deck enjoying the tumultuous victory greeting, and they looked fresh and happy. "Let's understand one thing," he said. "The purpose of all the hoopla out there is to boost civilian morale. Hirohito isn't losing any sleep over what this raid did. As for what the *Northampton* did, the less said the better. We sortie at dawn for gunnery runs."

He had some trouble obtaining the target vessel. ComCruPac summoned him by messenger mail to explain his failure to schedule liberty for his crew after their arduous combat cruise. He went ashore and brusquely confronted the chief of staff, an old classmate. The *Northampton* had to be jolted into war, he said. Wives, girl friends, bars, beds, would all be there when the cruiser returned from forty-eight hours of hard drills. He got a promise of a target.

Returning aboard, he found on his desk a pile of personal mail: two letters from Rhoda, a thick one from Madeline, one from his father, who at eighty-one seldom wrote, one from his brother, a soft-drink dealer in Seattle, also one from Senator Lacouture, which he tore open as he settled in the armchair of his inner cabin. The news that Natalie was interned with a group of journalists in Siena upset him, though the attached State Department letter was reassuring about her prospects of getting home. It was better than not knowing where she was; at least, he hoped Byron would take the news that way. Rhoda's letter written at Christmas was long, conciliatory, submissive —"When you get back, I'll be right here in Foxhall Road, waiting like a good Navy wife in my best bib and tucker, with a full martini jug. . . . I have never respected and loved you more . . ." The other, a short note, merely gossiped, as though nothing had ever gone wrong, about a big snowfall on New Year's Eve, and the dinner at the Army and Navy Club.

The thickness of Madeline's letter proved deceptive. It was a single typed yellow sheet, triple-spaced, with a folded page from a theatrical trade paper. Madeline bubbled that she hated publicity and couldn't imagine how this silly story had gotten into print, but here it was.

> . . . Love to Byron and Warren, if you see them. Tell them I'll write them both long letters very soon. To you, too. This one doesn't count. Hugh is screaming at me to start the script conference. Just wanted you to know that your wandering girl is fine and happy, and not exactly unknown anymore.
>
> Love,
> Madeline
>
> P.S. — Look, about that last dopey letter of mine, just pretend you never got it. Mrs. Cleveland is a very sick woman. It's a good thing she didn't go ahead with all those threats, especially about naming *me*. I guess she's not that crazy. I could have sued her to kingdom come.
>
> M.

In the *Variety* page, a marked paragraph was all about Madeline Henry, Hugh Cleveland's assistant. "Maddy" came from a great Navy family. Her father commanded an aircraft carrier, one brother led a squadron of fighter planes, and the other was skipper of a submarine. A publicity agent had used the Henry background, obviously, to puff Cleveland; he was mentioned four times. Aside from the inaccuracies and the wisenheimer slang, the whole thing revolted Pug. His pretty, clever daughter, once his darling, had sunk into a world of crass fools, and was turning into one herself. He could do nothing about it; best to close his mind to that misfortune.

On a tan envelope addressed with green ink in an unfamiliar hand, the postmark was Washington, the posting date blurred. The single sheet was undated and unsigned.

Dear Pug,

    This is from a true and well-meaning friend, who has known you and Rhoda for years. I realize what war can do to marriage, but I can't stand to see it happening to a "model couple" such as you two dear people have always been.

    Write Rhoda and ask her about that *very* tall man (his name begins with K) that she plays tennis with at the St. Albans court. That isn't all she "plays." She has been seen with him in the wrong places and at the wrong times — *if* you know what I mean, and I *think* you do. Everybody in Washington who knows you two is talking about it. Rhoda stands in awe of you, as we all do, and a word from you probably can still make her "straighten up and fly right." Better do it before it's too late. That's a "word to the wise" from a well-wisher.

The letter had come by surface mail. It could be months old, dating back to the time before Rhoda's request for a divorce. Still, it brought back the full pain of the first disclosure, with the bitter new knowledge that his misfortune was on people's tongues.

While the other crews of Halsey's task force celebrated victory on the beach, the *Northampton* went back out to sea. The word was going around the decks that this bastard meant business. After the first mutterings subsided, there was little real dissatisfaction. The crew had tasted the disgrace of bad shooting. They had passed through showers of warm salt water from close misses of enemy salvos. They had seen the *Salt Lake City* straddled, and they had heard that five men in a twin-forty mount had been hit and blown to bloody smears. They were ready to learn how to fight. From the first collision drill, which started with sirens and alarm gongs while they were still in the channel, the sailors responded to the whip. Catapulting and recovering the float planes, a chronic sore of the Hickman days and the prime disgrace at Wotje, smoothed down in a day to a controlled chore. The time for setting condition Zed was halved. Surprise fire drills, air attack drills, abandon ship drills, broke out at all hours. It was hell, but by 2300, when Pug's drastic drill schedule at last ended, the crew was exhilarated as well as exhausted.

Not Pug. The anonymous letter had sapped him. He sat in his cabin well past midnight, leafing through three weeks' accumulation of news magazines. They showed a country still grinning at itself from giggly advertisements, still failing in any way — war production, war training, combat operations — to show awareness that defeat was not only possible, but coming on. The whole country was like the *Northampton* at Wotje. Meantime, the U-boats had wolfishly lunged against American shipping. The figures passed all belief; *over a million tons sunk in one month!* Rommel was sweeping across North Africa, smashing up the British armies. With the Americans falling back on Bataan, and the British retreating to Fortress Singapore, Pug could see little hope anywhere, except in the Russian counterattacks. These, too, seemed mere holding actions, while the tough gigantic Wehrmacht regrouped for the summer knockout.

In his War Plans service, Victor Henry had come to know well the inventory of armed force and natural resources of the planet. The changing picture seemed to him frightening. Java, Sumatra, and Borneo, which looked sure to fall, were immense prizes, greater in area and in warmaking potential than Japan itself. The Japanese advance into Burma threatened the United States, because it shook the British hold on the murmuring hundreds of millions of Indians. The loss of India could close the Persian Gulf, the best Lend-Lease route to the Soviet Union, and the great fountain of petroleum, the propellant of this whole world disaster. All the land masses, all the oceans, were strategically interlocked in this war. Everywhere except on the Russian front the situation was growing catastrophic; and nothing was worse in the whole flaming panorama than the continuing softness, complacency, and ignorance of the American people.

The secret mail he had read during the day reinforced his gloom. The landing craft program was stalled. Production was far behind the schedule he had himself drawn up in the War Plans section. Like a tidal wave a thousand miles off, a crisis was rolling toward President Roosevelt: a shortage that would one day halt major landing operations, or lead to shoestring assaults and bloody defeats. Pug felt he could avert that. He knew the problem to its core. He had grappled with the chief people in design and manufacture. He knew how to get raw material priorities. The Navy decision makers listened to him. Even Ernest King did, on the matter of landing craft. Many four-stripers could command a heavy cruiser. Nobody else had his grip on this key aspect of the war.

The fact he was coming to face was that he had plunged for forgetfulness into a past which he had outgrown. Big ship command was a challenge and an honor, but it was less than the best he could do in the war. Wotje had in any case deepened his doubts about heavy cruisers. The submarine panic had reflected the fear of the *Salt Lake City* skipper — fear he had himself felt — of the vulnerability of these beautiful, heavily armed, thin-skinned monsters. All operations plans now starred the carriers. The battleships were finished; and what was the *Northampton* but a kind of flimsy battleship that one torpedo or bomb could finish off? Wotje had rubbed his nose, too, in the mistake of his career, his choice of big guns over naval air. His son Warren, in a gnatlike dive-bomber, with one enlisted gunner, had perhaps caused more damage at Kwajalein than he had at Wotje, with his ten-thousand-ton cruiser and its crew of twelve hundred officers and men.

Worry about Warren, too, plagued him. Not till his visit to ComCruPac, when he had telephoned Warren's home and heard his son's cheery casual "Hello!" had his heart leaped with relief. Warren crashing, Warren burning, were anxious pictures that rose in his bad nights, and this was one of them. At two in the morning he went and woke the ship's doctor, a paunchy old regular, and asked him for a sleeping pill. The doctor sleepily proposed a good dose of medicinal brandy: it would promote the skipper's slumber better than a pill, he said, and might be a hell of a lot more fun. Victor Henry, standing in the doctor's cabin in an old bathrobe, barked, "Never suggest that again, Doc. Not to me. Not to any other officer or man on this ship. Not for sleeplessness."

The doctor stammered. "Well, ah, Captain, sometimes in the case of excessive nerve fatigue et cetera — you know, Captain Hickman, he —"

"Insomnia and nerves at sea in wartime are not emergencies. They're common nuisances. You prescribe brandy for them, and I'll end up with a wardroom of closet drunks. If they can't have the stuff, I can't. Understood?"

"Ah — understood, Captain."

Next day the concentration was on shooting. ComCruPac sent out a minesweeper with a sled and a plane towing a red sleeve-target. Everything about the cruiser's gunnery — rate of fire, ammunition handling, communications, fire control, score of hits — improved. So did Pug's mood. Recruits or draftees, these sailors were quick learners. When the *Northampton* moored in Pearl Harbor at sunset, the exec announced that, except for a skeleton watch, there would be liberty for all hands. Usually only half the crew went ashore at once. A cheer went up that sealed the status of Captain Henry; he was no longer the new skipper, he was the Old Man.

The flag lieutenant brought Pug a handwritten note:

Captain — Will you be dining ashore with your family? Otherwise, please join me. Armed Forces will rebroadcast your friend Tudsbury from Singapore at eight.

R. A. Spruance

Since the admiral had walked off the bridge at Wotje, Victor Henry had not once seen him. Through several days of fine weather, he had failed to appear topside. Pug showered and was dressing for dinner when the mail orderly came in. There was only one personal letter, another tan envelope addressed in green, this time sent airmail, its postmark clear, January 25; one month after Rhoda's contrite Christmas letter.

Dear Pug,
    You may hate me, "sight unseen," because the truth often hurts. But the whole thing is now getting too *blatant* for words, and unless you do something "p.d.q." you can kiss your marriage good-bye. They go to the theatre together now, and to restaurants and I don't know "what all." *Everybody* who has ever

known you two is talking about it, and I mean *talking*. Write to any "old pal" who is stationed in Washington. Tell him you're getting letters from this "awful person" (me) and ask him on his honor what he knows about Rhoda. "Nuff sed!"

With this black acid eating at his heart, Pug Henry went to dine with the admiral.

He found Spruance neat and erect as ever, but morose and dull of eye. Silence stretched through the meal, but it did not embarrass either of them, for they had come to know each other. Addiction to exercise was their bond. Spruance would stride the main deck for an hour or more in fair weather, and in port he would walk daily five or ten miles. Pug went along when he could, and their walks passed for the most part in such long silences. When Spruance now and then asked him to his quarters for a meal, they sometimes talked about their sons in submarines, and about themselves. The admiral, like Pug, harbored rueful second thoughts about having stayed in surface ships. Halsey's foresight in learning to fly at fifty Spruance considered masterful. He was not happy with a cruiser division, and foresaw a war career pass in obscure drudgery. Pug thought that the Wotje fiasco must be weighing on him as a blight on that career.

Over a dessert of canned peaches, Spruance surprised Pug by telling him to prepare for an award ceremony at morning quarters. He, Spruance, would receive the Navy Commendation Medal from Nimitz's own hands for his distinguished leadership in the Wotje bombardment. Bitter humor glimmered in the admiral's eyes as he said this. "The Navy needs heroes right now. To get decorated, it's enough to have been shot at. All I did at Wotje was lose control of a small task group. Turn on the radio, it's time for your friend. My compliments, incidentally, on what you're doing with the *Northampton*. It's needed."

Tudsbury sounded shaken and grave. Japanese heavy artillery was shelling downtown Singapore across the Johore Strait, the correspondent reported, killing hundreds of civilians each day. The enemy army was in plain sight on the far shore, making large-scale preparations to cross the water barrier. The military authorities now conceded (here Tudsbury's voice sharpened) that Singapore's one hope lay in letting the democratic world know exactly how desperate the situation was, since if help were ever to come, it had to come now.

Spruance and Pug Henry exchanged quizzical looks near the end, when Tudsbury said, "*My American friends will forgive me if I quote one of the many gallows-humor jokes circulating here. It goes so: 'Do you know where the American Navy is? Well, it can't operate because it's still under contract to Metro-Goldwyn-Mayer.'*

"*Still, whether relief comes or not, I still believe that the Europeans and the Asians of Singapore, rallying shoulder to shoulder, can themselves, even at this late hour, turn the tide and destroy the badly worn-down invaders. I will gamble my overstuffed old hide on this belief, but not the person of my daughter, Pamela, a clever and lovely young woman who assists me in my work. So off she goes tomorrow with the other women and children who are being evacuated. She told me a story not two hours ago that I want her to share with you. Here, then, is Pamela."*

With a strong effort of the will, Pug kept his face calm and his attitude relaxed.

"My story is a short one." The remembered husky sweet voice cut into him with a sensation of joy verging on agony. *"For the past two weeks, I have been working at a troop hospital as a volunteer. Today a badly wounded man left his bed, took me aside, and gave me a thing called a Mills bomb. It's a sort of grenade. 'Ma'am, you've been very nice to us. If you think a Jap is about to rape you, ma'am,' he said, in a charming Aussie accent, his face calm and serious, 'just pull the pin and you'll know nothing more.'*

"I have only one thing to add. I leave under protest. Good-night."

"Good-night," came the other voice, *"from Alistair Tudsbury in Singapore."*

"There are interesting parallels, Henry," said Spruance, reaching over and snapping off the radio, "between the battle problems in Malaya and Luzon. White garrisons plus mixed native troops defend water-girt land masses with Asian populations. An Asian invader advances on a north-south axis. The defenders execute a fighting fall-back toward a heavily armed island citadel in the extreme south. We seem to be doing a bit better with the problem than the British. After the war, it'll be instructive to compare the campaigns in detail."

"Yes, sir," said Pug, for once having not the vaguest idea of what an admiral was talking about.

16

LESLIE SLOTE gave the Wannsee photostats to the minister of the American legation in Bern, describing the material as "explosively urgent."

William Tuttle was a retired California railroad millionaire, a West Point graduate. The loss of an eye to German shrapnel in the First World War had cut off his Army career. Instead, he had gotten rich. This tall paunchy Republican grayhead naturally hated the New Deal and had strongly opposed a third term for that socialistic son of a bitch in the White House. With the fall of France in June 1940, however, and the nomination by the Republicans in July of a political amateur named Wendell Willkie, Tuttle had decided that the socialistic son of a bitch had better stay in the White House. He had headed the California branch of "Republicans for Roosevelt," earning the disgust of his friends and family before the election, and the sugar-plum of a diplomatic post afterward. Slote liked this maverick legation head. If the railroad man was short on diplomatic experience he was long on horse sense, and he could make tough decisions without dithering.

Slote did not hear from Tuttle for three days, then the minister telephoned him in mid-morning. "Oh, say, Les, come on up and let's chin a bit."

It was a modest office for the representative of the United States of America in Switzerland: bookshelves stacked with unread-looking official volumes, dark old furniture, and three windows facing out on bare trees in mist, through which on clear days one could see the Alps. The minister puzzled Slote with aimless war talk, leaning back in his swivel chair with thick fingers folded over his belly. The successful escape from Brest of the *Scharnhorst* and the *Gneisenau,* he said, was a worse sign of British decay than the crumbling of Malaya. "Ye gods and little fishes, Les! Malaya's on the other side of the earth. But if the Royal Navy and Air Force between them couldn't stop two damaged German battleships from slipping away up the English Channel, right under their guns, then something's rotten — their intelligence, their combat readiness, or both."

Slote caught a whiff of rum-flavored tobacco, and the third secretary, August Van Winaker, walked in with the portfolio in which Slote had put the Wannsee papers. This appalled Slote. Van Winaker was the legation's stickiest man on Jewish matters; whether because of a consular background — he had shifted over not long ago to the Foreign Service track — or a bone-deep genteel anti-Semitism, Slote could not tell. He knew that Jastrow had had trouble with this same fellow in Florence. Slote thought Van Winaker a pompous nuisance, absurdly preoccupied with his genealogy.

"Les, Augie's had some intelligence background," said Tuttle. "Mind if he sits in?"

"Not at all, sir."

Van Winaker smiled and sat down, crossing short plump legs and laying the portfolio on the desk.

"Okay, then," said the minister, "what's your evaluation of this material, Les? And what action do you recommend?"

"I believe it's an authentic document of grave import. The legation should shoot off an urgent summary cable to the Secretary of State, and send him the document by special air courier."

The minister looked toward Van Winaker, whose smile indulgently broadened. "Augie thinks differently."

"Indeed I do. A kindly description would be 'a compassionately motivated fraud.' "

Slote forced a grin. "Let's hear your reasons, Augie."

Van Winaker puffed blue rum-smelling smoke through his smile. "Okay. Let's start at the point of contact. You meet a pretty girl at a party, Leslie. Some time later her father, one Dr. Jacob Ascher, unexpectedly invites you to dinner. You're a new arrival, not too familiar with Bern, with a reputation for compassion to Jews. Whereupon —"

"Now, stop right there —"

"Just let me finish, laddie." Van Winaker rolled his eyes at the minister, and ran a hand through his close-cropped blond hair. "Whereupon a priest at that dinner party offers to slip you documentary evidence on the Jewish situation. Interesting! Jacob Ascher happens to be president of the Jewish Council of Bern, a rich man who hounds all the legations for refugee visas. Still, he's an honest sort, so let's say some wily fabricator put one over on him and your priest, possibly with this so-called document, perhaps mulcting Ascher of a goodly sum in the process. Of course, he'd jump at it, it's a fine propaganda tool for him."

"Augie, that's just theorizing. If the Germans are committing mass murder under cover of war — and I think they are — President Roosevelt can turn world opinion against them with this document."

"Oh, come on, laddie. The Nazi mistreatment of Jews was wrung dry years ago. People are numb to it. As for mass crime, the document is sheer fantasy."

"Why?"

"Why? Well, for pity's sake, cabinet-level government men meeting and discussing such a gruesome scheme so calmly — and putting it into writing! Not a word of such business would ever appear on paper. Oh, the stilted language, the labored jocularity, the coffee-hour tone! The whole thing is amateur romancing, Leslie, very badly done." Languidly Van Winaker picked up the portfolio and slid out the black sheets, releasing the nasty chemical odor. "And just look at this mess! The Germans have the best copying equipment in the world, and white on black, incidentally, is *not* the way they reproduce documents. They print from a negative film, and it comes out black on white. I mean, I respect your compassion, but —"

"Never mind my compassion," snapped Slote. "I'm well aware who Dr. Ascher is. Now as to the text, I say it's real. It's turgid, boring, like most German official documents we've both waded through. Everybody at the meeting is a droning pedant. Everybody's fawning German-fashion on the chairman, Heydrich. It's all Teutonic government prose to the life. Moreover, as to the reduction of an inhuman plan to writing"— Slote turned to Tuttle —"sir, nothing is more German than that. I took my degree in German political history. Look, Augie, read Treitschke. Read Lueger. Read Lagarde. Christ, read *Mein Kampf!* Hitler's just a self-educated street agitator, but even he uses thick political jargon, and a grandiose pseudo-philosophical moral frame, to justify the most bloodthirsty proposals. I don't want to make a classroom lecture of this, but —"

"I've read *Mein Kampf*," said Tuttle.

Slote struck the desk with a fist. "Well, sir, I say a person from the submerged Germany, the liberal Germany, copied this document. I say he was risking torture, death, and the exposure of his anti-Nazi group. I say he sneaked a portable apparatus into a top-secret file room, his heart in his throat, and did a hurried job. Printing this copy was as risky as taking the pictures. You probably can't even buy black-on-white photocopy paper in Germany today without signing a receipt that can hang you."

"You're a warm advocate, laddie." Van Winaker was smiling again. "But notice that the thing is dated January twentieth. A top-secret report written, approved, mimeographed, filed, surreptitiously copied, and secretly delivered to Bern, all in less than three weeks? No, Les, I sympathize with your compassion, but —"

"Jesus *Christ*, Augie," Slote exploded, "stop using that goddamned word! Of course they'd rush it to the outside world! It describes a crime almost beyond human imagination!"

"Why, I admire compassion, Les," Van Winaker returned softly. "Just let me tell you a little story. A document came to me in Florence, in much the same cloak-and-dagger way, about top-secret Italian war plans. In language and physical appearance, unlike this crude botch, it was flawless. I guessed it was a fraud, all the same. I *said* so. Our embassy in Rome swallowed it, however, and gave it to the British. Well, they analyzed it and laughed it off. It was hogwash, intended to misdirect their entire North Africa strategy. So there you are. These things are an art, and that"— he waved limp fingers at the photostats —"is the work of a low-grade bungler."

"Okay, Augie," Bill Tuttle said. "Many thanks."

With a friendly, even apologetic smile at Slote, and a wave of the pipe, the third secretary got up and left.

Swivelling his chair in a half-turn, Tuttle laced his fingers behind his head. "Sorry, Les, I'm with Augie. That stuff is the pipe dream of an ignoramus, making up a horror story and doing a bum job."

This was a real shock to Slote, though he had anticipated Van Winaker's reaction. "May I ask why you say that?"

Tuttle was lighting a cigar. He rolled it with relish in his mouth, and waved it at the portfolio. "The railroading part. I've been handling intelligence on European railroads since I got here. General Marshall asked me to do that. I've known George forever. I send him periodic summaries. The rolling stock in all of German-held Europe couldn't do it. You're talking here about transporting millions upon millions of civilians, Leslie, with a deteriorating rail system that's already in a bind. Hitler's having trouble just moving his troops, his supplies, and his foreign laborers around. Depots are piling up with vital things like food, fuel, tanks, and shells. Whole divisions are sitting on their duffs on sidings because the trains can't get them to the front, and the British are bombing the hell out of their locomotive factories and railroad yards. It's not going to get better but worse. Okay? Now how does such a broken-down system go shunting eleven million people all over the continent for some crazy massacre scheme?" Tuttle shook his head. "It's stupid nonsense. The faker who did that document didn't know anything about railroading. He should have done a little research."

Slote was chewing on his cold pipe during the minister's tirade, slumped in the armchair, a picture of pale discouragement. "Sir, at the risk of seeming compassionate, may I respond?"

"Go ahead," grinned Tuttle.

"It's just that the job isn't that big. It's a sweep of a dragnet through western Europe, sort of fanwise" — Slote made a half-circle in the air with spread fingers — "Scandinavia, Holland, Belgium, France, then Italy and the Balkans, all spilling into Poland and conquered Russia. Out of reach of the Red Cross and the press. Away from liberal populations. Backward areas, where communication is bad or nonexistent, and anti-Semitism is rife. But, sir, *most of the Jews are there already, in Poland and occupied Russia.* That's the whole point. They don't have to be moved far, if at all. Bringing the Jews from the west shouldn't overtax the rails. There's no fighting in the west."

The minister puffed at his cigar, cocking his good eye at Slote. "How would you go about authenticating this document?"

"What would you consider authentication, sir?"

"That's the problem. I don't believe the damned thing, not one bit. I say the railroading problem's insurmountable. Now, I'm not telling you to forget this thing. Bring in some authentication, if you can, and meantime give the document maximum security storage."

"I will, sir."

"Maximum security storage isn't, for instance, the hands of an Associated Press reporter."

His face hot and tingling, Slote replied, "Nobody will see it unless you release it."

"Okay, then."

Returning to his office with the portfolio, Slote felt drained, defeated, stupid, with no notion of what to do next. He drudged through the lunch hour on official papers, haunted by a sense of defeat which made his lips tremble. About three o'clock a secretary looked in. "Will you see Dr. Jean Hesse?"

"Absolutely."

The Swiss diplomat entered briskly, a decent, sad little man Slote had known since Warsaw, with a red tuft of chin beard. They sometimes played chess, and Hesse gloomed over the board in Spenglerian tones about the collapse of European man. "Well, I have been to Siena, and I have seen Mrs. Natalie Henry," said Hesse, rasping open his briefcase. "A handsome woman. Jewish, isn't she?"

"Yes, she's Jewish."

"Mmmmm!" The sidewise look and a pull at the beard expressed concurrence with a naughty erotic taste. "I gave her your letter. Here's an answer."

"Thank you, Jean. How are the other journalists doing?"

"Desperately bored. Drunk all day. In that respect I could envy them. I'm going to report now to your minister. They'll probably come out in March or April, the way the negotiation is going."

Slote locked his door, ripped open the letter, and read the yellow sheets at the window.

Dear old Slote:

Well, what a marvelous surprise! Your nice Dr. Hesse is having a cup of tea out in the lemon house with Aaron while I hammer this off.

First of all, I'm fine and so is Louis. It's crazy, how comfortable we are here. But I feel sick to the heart whenever I think of the *Izmir*. We almost sailed on that boat, Leslie! A German diplomat who knew Aaron got us off and drove us to Rome. I still don't know what his motives were, but he rescued us from terrible danger, possibly from death. The BBC didn't make much of the story, but apparently the *Izmir* just vanished after the Turks forced it to leave Istanbul. What in God's name became of it? Do you know? The news here is so scanty! I still have nightmares about it. What a world! I saved my baby, and I suppose I should be thankful, but I keep thinking about those people.

We found the house in good shape. Took off the dust covers, put sheets on the beds, lit the fire and there we were! Maria and Tomaso are going on with their work in exactly the old way. The weather is chilly, but lovely once the morning mists lift. Only the internees down at the Excelsior Hotel remind us of the war. They come up here for lunch, one or two at a time. The police are nice about that. Correspondents, wives, a singer, a couple of clergymen — an odd lot, bored to death, mostly staying ossified on Tuscan wine, and full of cranky little complaints, but perfectly okay.

Oh Lord, I can't *begin* to tell you how glad I am to have your letter! When Dr. Hesse left the room just now, I cried. It's been so goddamned lonesome here! And you're in Bern — so close, and working on our release! I still haven't caught my breath.

Well, one thing at a time. I'd better jump to what's most on my mind.

Slote, Aaron is playing with the notion of staying on here, war or no war.

Between the archbishop and the chief of police, both old friends of his, he's being treated like royalty in exile. It's eerily like peacetime, for us. Last Sunday he was even allowed to go and have lunch with Bernard Berenson in his mansion outside Florence — you know, that old American art critic. Well, Berenson told Aaron that he has no intention of leaving. He's too old to move, Italy is his home, etc., etc., and he'll stay and take what comes. Berenson's a Jew too — of sorts, like Aaron. Aaron came back with this bee in his bonnet. If Berenson can do it, why can't he? As for me, I'm free to go home, of course. GRRRR!

Bernard Berenson, I have pointed out, has important, powerful connections. He has authenticated paintings for billionaires, lords, national museums, kings. He may well be under Mussolini's protection. None of this applies to Aaron in the least. He grudgingly admits that. But he says he too is old. His home too is Italy. His rheumatism is worse (that is true). A long rail trip and an Atlantic crossing could knot him all up, maybe disable him. He's started what he considers his most important book, "the last panel," about Martin Luther and the Reformation. The book does begin well, and I must say it's kept us both occupied.

But what he apparently can't picture is his plight once the rest of us leave. His isolation will be frightful. If he becomes ill, he'll be in the hands of hostile strangers. *He's in enemy country!* That's the brute fact he won't face. He says Mussolini's declaration of war on America was a comedy to keep the Germans quiet. He has an answer for everything.

He squirrels and gloats over one sweaty little ace in the hole, Leslie. During some futile little romance in his early twenties, Aaron was once converted to Catholicism. Did you know that? He dropped it fast but he's never de-converted, if there is such a thing. A friend of his in the Vatican obtained copies of the American documents and gave them to him. Aaron now regards these scruffy photographs as his shield and buckler. It's a curse that he ever obtained them!

You see, he's read up on the Nuremberg laws. I'm not sure of the details, but it seems that a conversion before 1933, when Hitler came to power, makes a material difference for German Jews, or maybe it's for half-Jews. Anyhow, Aaron says he can handle the Italians; and as for the Germans, why, between his precious conversion documents and his position as an American journalist, he refuses to worry. In short, he has only a few years to live, the one thing he cares about is his work, and he works best here.

I beg you to get word to Aaron to drop this notion. Possibly he'll listen to you. I have no effect on him any more. He's apologetic toward me, and in every way tries to mollify me. He's made me the heir of all his property and copyrights. Aaron's a prudent man, and quite wealthy. But I remain furious at him, and terribly concerned.

I really don't know why I should be so upset about Aaron. It's his life. I came to work for him simply to be nearer you, in those simple lost days when my only worry was a messed-up romance. (God, how young I was!) I hardly knew him then. Now my destiny's bound up with his. My father's gone. My mother's a million miles away in body and spirit, playing canasta and going to Hadassah meetings in Miami Beach while the world explodes. Next to Louis, my uncle seems almost the only family I have. Byron himself is a disembodied idea, an aureate memory, compared with Aaron. I know even you much better than I do my baby's father.

Omigosh, I hear the voices of Aaron and your Swiss friend, and I have to end this —

Old Slote, my dear, you can't imagine how GOOD it makes me feel, just knowing you're close by. You were a fool not to marry me in Paris, when I proposed. How I loved you! Oh, if one only understood sooner that things happen *once* and then roll away into the past, leaving one marked and changed forever, and — well, this hasty maundering is to no avail. Think of something to do about Aaron, my dear, please!

I'm a lot thinner again in the enclosed, and at least I'm smiling. Isn't Louis cute?

Love,
N

Slote sat at his desk and stared at the snapshot, comparing Selma Ascher in his mind to this young woman in a plain housedress, holding a pretty baby on her arm. How Selma faded! Something was wrong with him, he thought. When one lost a girl, it ought to be like having a tooth out; brief sharp pain, then a rapid healing of the hole. Every man went through it. But Natalie Jastrow, utterly gone, preoccupied him yet like a teasing mistress. The very look of the letter gave him a poignant bittersweet sensation; ah, the passionate outpourings he had received on just such yellow sheets, in this Remington typeface with the crooked *y!* Gone, all gone, that fiery love, that once-in-a-lifetime golden chance!

Though it might be a couple of weeks before a letter could even start back to her through the diplomatic channel, he stopped work and wrote a three-page reply. Pouring out words to Natalie Henry was in itself a real if frustrating pleasure. Then he wrote a short letter to Jastrow, cautioning him against the plan to remain in Italy. He tore up a draft referring to "new documents" about the danger to Jews that he had come upon. He did not want to scare Natalie uselessly. The minister's reproof about security before authentication troubled him, too.

But what would be authentication?

17

STEPPING from an ice-cold shower in a shivery glow, Natalie towelled herself fast and hard at the tall antique mirror framed in pink-and-gilt curlicued wood; turning here and there, feeling thankful for the flat belly she saw. Louis's passage into the world had left, after all, only a few fading purple stretch marks. Even her breasts were not too bad, not too bad. Meager wartime rations helped! She might be twenty.

Her nakedness struck memory sparks of the Lisbon honeymoon. Sometimes she could hardly remember how Byron looked, except in the few old snapshots she still had. At this moment she could picture his mouth curling in the old beguiling grin, feel the thick red-brown hair in her fingers, feel the touch of his hard hands. What a dry death-in-life this was, what a waste of love, of young years! She bent one knee in the female pose common to the Venus de Milo and Rabinovitz's girlie pictures. This fleeting thought of Rabinovitz sobered her. "Vain old bag," she said aloud, wondering how to dress for the unusual dinner guest. The telephone rang. She pulled the damp towel around her and answered it.

"Hello, Mrs. Henry. Dr. Beck here. I've finished my meeting at the bank, so I can still get to Florence for the seven o'clock train to Rome. May I take a cup of tea first with you and Professor Jastrow?"

"Tea? But we're expecting you for dinner."

"You're very kind, but dinner guests in wartime are a trouble. Now tea —"

"Dr. Beck, we've got veal."

"Veal! Amazing."

"The archbishop sent it over for Aaron's birthday. We saved it for you. Do come."

"I'm flattered. And hungry! Ha ha! The morning train's faster, anyway. Veal! I accept."

The black and white cathedral in slant sunset light, rising out of Siena's old walls and ascending red roofs, made a fine view through the tall windows of Jastrow's sitting room. But Italy was full of fine views and virtually empty of Scotch whiskey. The bottle of Haig and Haig which Natalie brought in with glasses, soda, and ice really impressed Dr. Beck. Jastrow explained that

Bernard Berenson had given him the whiskey "out of sheer gratitude at hearing another American voice." She also briefly fetched in the baby. Dr. Beck cooed at Louis, his glasses misting, his face glowing. "Ach, how I miss my kiddies," he said.

The Scotch put Jastrow in his vein of jocose persiflage. The philosopher George Santayana had also lunched with him and Berenson, and Jastrow satirized the foibles of both men at table, such as Santayana's drinking a whole bottle of wine, and Berenson's hogging the conversation and admiring the play of his own shapely little hands. He was waspishly amusing about all this. Dr. Beck roared with laughter, and Natalie yielded up a few giggles.

She found herself warming a bit to the visitor. She never could truly like or trust him, but his admiration of her baby pleased her, and they owed him their present safety. His square face topped with thick lank blond hair was not unhandsome, and he even had a clumsy humor of his own. She asked him when he had last eaten veal. "I'm not sure, Mrs. Henry," he said. "I was served veal two weeks ago in Rome, but I think that particular calf had been well broken to the saddle."

The dinner was a decided success. Happy to be cooking veal again, the housekeeper had made superb scallopini in Marsala. The archbishop had also sent champagne for Aaron's birthday, and they quaffed both bottles. Natalie drank more than she wanted to, mainly so that Aaron would not get her share of the wine. In his isolation, and perhaps in a suppressed state of nerves, he was becoming a toper, and when he had had too much his mood could turn unstable, and his tongue could loosen. At the end of the meal, as they ate raspberry tarts and ice cream, an exquisite aroma drifted in.

"My dear professor, *coffee?*" said Beck.

Jastrow smiled, dancing his fingertips together. "The Swiss chargé d'affaires brings Berenson little gifts. My generous friend shared half a pound with me."

"One begins to understand," said Beck, "why Berenson has decided not to leave."

"Ah, creature comforts aren't everything, Werner. There are shortages at I Tatti. The place is in shocking disrepair. B.B. has spells of depression about it. But he says it's his only home now. As he puts it, he'll 'ride out the storm at anchor.'" With an arch and not exactly sober smile he added, "B.B. thinks it will all end well, meaning that your side will lose. Of course, he's an expert on Italian paintings, not warfare."

"Dr. Freud might call that wishful thinking," Beck replied, pursing his lips. "In view of what's happening in Singapore, and Burma, and the Atlantic, and North Africa. However, whichever side wins, such a prominent person needn't worry."

"A prominent Jew?" It was a measure of Natalie's unbending that she could say this without edginess.

"Mrs. Henry, victory softens harsh wartime policies." Beck's tone was calm. "That's my profound personal hope."

The housekeeper proudly bore in the coffee service. They watched the steaming brew fill the cups, as though a magician were pouring it from an empty pot.

"Ah," Beck exclaimed over his first sip. "Worth the trip to Siena."

"Of course Santayana has no problem, he's neither Jew nor American," Jastrow mused aloud, sipping his coffee. "He's a strange personality, Werner, a true exotic. A fixture at Harvard for twenty years, writing and speaking exquisite English, yet he has retained Spanish nationality. He explained why, but I couldn't follow. Either he or I had had too much wine. He's Gentile to the bone, a bit of a Spanish grandee, and not too fond of the Hebrews himself. One could hear that in his subtle digs at Berenson's opulent surroundings. Santayana holes up in a little cell in a Roman convent, writing his memoirs. He says that a scholar living in one small room near a major library is as close to happiness as a man can come on earth."

"A true philosopher," said Beck.

"Well, I could live like that, too." Jastrow waved a hand around at the walls. "When I bought this place with the book-club money for *A Jew's Jesus*, I was fifty-four. It was my fling. I can leave with a cheerful shrug and never look back."

"You too are a philosopher," said Beck.

"Then again I can always get my niece angry" — Jastrow's glance at her was sly and tipsy — "by suggesting that she and the baby go home while, like Berenson, I ride it out at anchor."

"I'm enjoying my coffee," said Natalie sharply.

"And why should you do that?" said Beck.

"Because a philosopher is above worrying about concentration camps," said Natalie. Jastrow shot her a vexed look. "Is that discourteous? I have trouble making Aaron face realities. Somebody must."

"Perhaps not all Germans, either, are enthusiastic about concentration camps." Beck's voice was kindly and sad. His fat cheeks reddened.

"And what about the stories coming out of eastern Europe, Dr. Beck? Stories that your soldiers have been massacring the Jews?"

Jastrow stood up, raising his voice. "We'll have brandy and more coffee in the sitting room."

That they were unendurably on each other's nerves was all too evident. "I take it, Mrs. Henry," Beck said, settling into a corner of a sofa in the other room, carefully lighting a cigar, and making his voice easy and conciliatory, "that your question was not merely provocative. I have standard replies to standard provocations. I can also give you an honest opinion about your uncle's safety, if he should elect to stay on."

"Can you?" She sat tensed on the edge of the sofa, facing Beck. Jastrow stood at a window, brandy glass in hand, glowering at her. "How much do you really know about what's happening to Jews?"

"In Italy? Nothing is happening."

"And elsewhere?"

"The Foreign Service does not operate in the Occupied Territories, Mrs. Henry. The army governs the combat areas. Drastic measures are imperative there, and life is hard for both occupiers and the occupied."

"Worse for the Jews, no doubt," said Natalie.

"I don't deny it. Anti-Semitism is rife all through eastern Europe, Mrs. Henry. I'm not proud of our own excesses, but the Jews had to be rounded up for their own safety! Of that I assure you. They would otherwise have been plundered and murdered en masse in places like Lithuania, Poland, and the Ukraine. The local hooligans were amazed, when German forces arrived, that they didn't want them to join in straightway to rob and kill the Jews. They expected an 'open season,' as one might say."

Jastrow cut in. "What excesses by your own forces?"

"Professor, our police units are not always the highest types," Beck replied, looking unhappy. "Scarcely the representatives of an advanced culture. There has been rough handling. The Jews have passed a bad winter. There were outbreaks of disease. True, in the snow outside Moscow and Leningrad our soldiers have also suffered terribly. War is a vile business." He faced Natalie and his voice rose. "But when you ask me, Mrs. Henry, whether the German army is massacring Jews, I respond that this is a lie. My brother is an army officer. He has spent much time in Rumania and in Poland. He assures me that the army has not only refrained from atrocities, but has at times interfered to protect the Jews from the local population. That is God's truth, as I know it."

Aaron Jastrow said, "I was born and grew up in eastern Europe. I believe you."

"Don't let me gloss things over. Our regime will have much to answer for." Werner Beck spread his pudgy hands, puffed at his cigar, and drank brandy. "Even in victory decent Germans are not going to forget, I promise you. This is excellent brandy, Professor. Your friend Berenson again?"

"No." With a pleased look, Jastrow passed his glass under his nose. "I'm rather a fancier of French brandy. I had enough foresight to lay in several cases of this stuff back in 1938."

"Yes, my brother told me some fantastic things. Strangely enough, one can visit these wretched ghettos. Imagine that! The elegant Polish ladies and our officers sometimes enjoy a night of slumming among the Jews. There are even grotesque little nightclubs. Helmut went several times. He wanted to see conditions for himself. He tried to do something about improving supplies. He's in the quartermaster corps, and he had some success in Lodz. But the whole thing remains bad. Very bad."

"Has your brother visited concentration camps?" Natalie inquired very politely.

"Let's change the subject," said Jastrow.

"Mrs. Henry, those are secret political prisons." Beck gave a miserable shrug.

"But that's where the worst things are happening." The studied patience of his manner was impressing Natalie, for all her rising irritation. She regretted having started this topic, but why had Aaron brought up his fatuous maddening notion of remaining in Italy?

"Mrs. Henry, dictatorships use terror to keep order. That is classic politics. What forced the German people to submit to a dictatorship is a long, complex question, but the outside world — including America — is not guiltless. I have never so much as seen the outside walls of a concentration camp. Have you ever visited an American prison?"

"That's not a reasonable comparison."

"I'm comparing only your ignorance and mine about penal institutions. I'm sure that American prisons are very bad. I imagine our concentration camps are worse. But —" he passed a hand across his forehead and cleared his throat. "We began with the question of your uncle's safety, if he should stay in Italy."

"Never mind!" Jastrow knit his brow fiercely at his niece. "We asked Werner here to give him a good dinner, Natalie. It's not his problem. Bernard Berenson is a very shrewd and worldly man, yet he too —"

"*Damn* Berenson!" Natalie exploded, and she thrust a demanding finger at Beck. "Supposing Germany occupies Italy? Is that so impossible? Or supposing Mussolini decides to ship all Jews to the Polish ghettos? Or just supposing some Fascist bigwig up and decides that he'd like to live in this villa? I mean it's so incredible, so childish, to even *think* of taking such risks —"

"It would be I, only I, taking those risks," Aaron Jastrow burst out, slamming down his glass so that the brandy flew, "and frankly I'm getting sick of this. Werner is our guest. You and your baby are alive because he rescued you. Anyway, I never said I wouldn't leave." Jastrow jerkily, noisily threw open a casement window. Cool air streamed in, and a patch of blue moonlight fell on the Oriental rug. He stood with his back to the window, and picked up his glass in a badly shaking hand. "One crucial difference between you and me, Natalie, is that you're hardly Jewish. You know nothing about our culture and our history, and you're not interested. You married a Christian without turning a hair. I'm a Jew to the core. I'm a *Polish* Jew!" He said this with a proud glare. "A Talmud scholar! I could resume the study tomorrow if I chose. All my writings turn on my identity. My nerve ends are antennae for anti-Semitism, and I detected it in George Santayana before we'd been in the same room five minutes. *You* needn't warn *me* about the hazards of being Jewish!" He turned to Dr. Beck, "You haven't an anti-Semitic bone in you. You serve a detestable regime, and whether you should be doing that is another and a very large question — one you and I should discuss another time — but —"

"Professor, this was for me, and still remains, a radical ethical dilemma."

"I should think so. What your government has done to the Jews is unforgivable. But alas, how far back it all goes! There are anti-Jewish rules in Aquinas's *Summa* that make your Nuremberg laws look mild. The church has yet to repudiate them! We're the eternal strangers, the outsiders in Christian Europe, and in times of breakdown we feel the impact first and hardest. It happened to us during the Crusades, it happened in the plague years, it has happened during most wars and revolutions. The United States is the modern liberal oasis, full of natural wealth and protected by the oceans. We're able and we're hard workers, so we've done well there. But Natalie, if you think we're any less strangers there than in Germany, *you're* the childish one, not I! If the war should take a bad turn, a defeated America will be uglier than Nazi Germany. Louis will be no safer there than here, and perhaps less so, because the Italians at least love children and are not very violent. These are simple truths you can't grasp because your Jewish blood runs so thin."

"Nonsense! Plain nonsense!" Natalie shot back. "Nazi Germany is a freakish monster of history. Not Christian, not Western, not even European. To equate it with America, even in defeat, is just drunken babble. As for my Jewish blood —"

"Why? What's so freakish about Hitler? Why are the Germans more wrong, in trying for world mastery, than the British were two centuries ago when they succeeded? Or than we Americans are, for making our own bid now? What do you suppose this war is about, anyway? Democracy? Freedom? Fiddlesticks! It's about who rules next, who fixes the currencies, who dominates the markets, who gets the raw materials and exploits the vast cheap labor of the primitive continents!" Jastrow was wound up now, and his wine-loosened tongue flew; not at all blurrily, but with the clipped edged classroom accents of an enraged professor. "Mind you, I think we'll win. I'm glad of that, because I'm a liberal humanist. Radical nationalism like Hitler's or Stalin's tends to crush free thought, art, and discourse. But I'm honestly not sure at this late hour of my life, Natalie, whether human nature is happier under tyranny, with its fixed codes, its terrorized quiet, its simple duties, or amid the dilemmas and disorders of freedom. Byzantium lasted a thousand years. It's doubtful whether America will last two hundred. I've lived more than ten years in a Fascist country, and I've been more at peace than I ever was in the money-chasing hurly-burly back home. I really fear an American 1918, Natalie. I fear a sudden falling apart of those unloving elements held together by the common pursuit of money. I foresee horrors in defeat, amid abandoned skyscrapers and grass-grown highways, that will eclipse the Civil War! A blood bath with region against region, race against race, every man's hand against his brother, and all hands against the Jews."

Werner Beck made a gesture and wink at Natalie as though to say, *Don't stir up the old fellow any more.* He took a soothing, almost unctuous tone. "Professor, you surprise me with your penetrating insight about America. Frankly, when I was in Washington I was shocked. Some of the best-connected persons whispered in my ear total approval of the Führer's position on the Jews, never supposing that I might not agree."

"Ah, upper-crust anti-Semitism is epidemic, Werner. Elites always detest gifted and nimble outsiders. Who made the British policy to turn back the refugee ships, but old-school-tie anti-Semites? The upper-crust anti-Semites who run our State Department have closed all the Americas to refugees. Why am I still here? Only because of obscure sabotage of my papers."

Natalie said, striving for a calm note, "You were dilatory, Aaron."

"Granted, my dear. Granted." He sank into an armchair. *"Mea culpa, mea culpa, mea maxima culpa.* But it's done. The question is, what next? I quite understand that those bored newspaper soaks down at the Excelsior Hotel can't wait to get out of Siena, and I know that you want to take Louis home. But I believe there may be a negotiated peace this year, and I for one would welcome it."

"Welcome it!" Natalie's face and Beck's showed almost the same degree of astonishment. "Welcome peace with Hitler?"

"My dear, the best chance for mankind's survival is simply for the war to stop. The sooner the better. The fabric of civilization has been shaken loose already by the industrial and scientific revolutions, the collapse of religion, and two mechanized world wars. It can't stand much more of a pounding. In a bitter way I almost welcome the fall of Singapore —"

"It hasn't fallen —"

"Oh, that's a question of days," put in Beck. "Or for all we know, hours. The British are finished in Asia."

"Let's face it," said Jastrow, "the Japanese belong there and the Europeans don't. The Russian front is at a stalemate. The Atlantic front is at another stalemate. A negotiated peace would be the best thing for the world, for America, and certainly for the Jews. It's much more desirable than a vengeful five-year crusade to destroy the have-nots. I suppose if we marshal all our industrial power we'll crush them, but to what purpose? They've shown their mettle. The hegemony can be shared. The British and the French learned to do that after centuries of bloodletting. It will have to be shared in any case with the Russians. The longer the war goes on, the worse things will get for Jews behind the Nazi lines, my dear, and if we do crush Germany, the end of it will merely be a Soviet Europe. Is that so desirable? Why shouldn't we hope instead that the bloody madness will stop? And if it does stop, how silly I'll look to have uprooted my whole life for nothing! Nevertheless, you won't go without me, so I'll leave. I've never said otherwise. But I'm not a soft-headed old fool to consider remaining, and I'll not have you take that tone with me again, Natalie."

She did not answer him.

"Mrs. Henry, I find your uncle's vision of the war lucid and inspiring," said Werner Beck excitedly. "He gives all this stupid carnage a theme, a direction, and a hope."

"He does? Peace with Hitler? Who can believe a word Hitler says, or have faith in a paper he signs?"

"That is not an insoluble problem," Beck quietly returned.

"Exactly. There are other Germans. There are even other Nazis," said Jastrow. "The skin of the tyrant is not steel plate. So history teaches."

"Professor, I have not had such a conversation, except with my brother, in ages." The eyes of Werner Beck strangely flashed at Jastrow, and his voice quavered. "I will pretend I never had this conversation. Yet I will tell you, my old and trusted teacher, that my brother and I have more than once discussed into the dawn the ethics of tyrannicide."

"My baby gets fed now." Natalie stood up, and Werner Beck jumped to his feet.

"Let me thank you for the best dinner I have had in months, Mrs. Henry."

"Well, we probably owe you our lives. I'm not unaware of that. So if I —" Without looking at her uncle, she broke off and hurried from the room. Jastrow stood at the open casement, his thin hair blowing, his face heavily shadowed by the moonlight.

"Professor, your discussion of the war stunned me," said Dr. Beck. "You spoke with the grasp of a Thucydides."

"Ah, Werner, it was just an angry rush of words. Poor Natalie. Even an animal mother fears for her baby. She's not very good company these days."

"I would urge you, Dr. Jastrow, when you get home, to write a short book developing those thoughts. A book like *The Last Palio*, your exquisite little elegy over the Europe of the Versailles Treaty."

"Oh, did you read that?" Jastrow sounded flattered. "A minor *jeu d'esprit.*"

"But your vision of the war! That a man like yourself, a humanist, a Jew, can speak with such understanding of the Japanese problem, and of the German revolution! Can even suggest that 'sharing the hegemony,' in your brilliant phrase, might be preferable to a grim five-year mutual bloodletting!

It's breathtaking. It restores one's faith in the possible brotherhood of mankind. What a profound tribute to the Jewish spirit!"

"You're too kind, but I shall write nothing about this accursed war. I shall get on with Martin Luther. Well! Shall we have a nightcap?"

"*Bitte*. Let me telephone for my car."

Beck made his call, while Jastrow poured two snifters fuller than usual. They drank standing at the open window, chatting about the view and about the quiet charm of Siena. "I understand your reluctance to leave," Beck said. "What you have here is a private little paradise."

"Well, I've been happy here." Jastrow's mood was much improved. "And brandy has helped me snare many an elusive theme and thought."

"Professor, would you consider coming to Rome and talking to press correspondents of neutral countries? *Only* of neutral countries. None of Goebbels's propagandists or Gayda's hacks."

"To what purpose?"

"Your views on the war would command attention. They are original, magnanimous, and wise. Their impact would be great. I can tell you" — the diplomat's voice sank low — "that better elements in Germany would be encouraged."

Jastrow stroked his beard, his face wrinkling into sharp smiling lines. "Hardly. I'm a very minor writer."

"Not so. You have news value. Only Berenson and Santayana, besides yourself, have lived so long in the Italian dictatorship. I urge you to think about this."

"Out of the question. On my return home, I should be pilloried." A car came rolling into the driveway, the same bank limousine that had brought the diplomat. "Ah, then you must go?" said Jastrow. "Pity. I did want you to see my library."

Beck leaned out of the window and spoke a few crisp words to the driver. Jastrow led him upstairs to the library, where they made a circuit of the room, brandy glasses in hand. "Bless my soul," said Beck, "don't you have as good a private collection on Christianity as one will find anywhere?"

"Oh, no! This is a pathetic scratch of the surface. And yet —" Jastrow's eyes moved along the shelves, and the look on his face was deeply sad. "You know, Werner, I've had no family life. No children. If my love has an object, it's this collection of books. Santayana's right, of course, an institutional library is best. Yet there's something personal and — this will sound mawkish — alive for me in this room. These books speak to me. The authors are all my friends and colleagues, though some of them crumbled to dust fifteen centuries ago. I shall leave the villa with no regret, but it will hurt to leave these books behind, knowing that it may be the end of them."

"Dr. Jastrow, could I not have them crated up for you, after you go, and sent to Switzerland or Sweden? All wars end. Then you could retrieve them."

The mournful aged eyes shone with delight. "*Could* you do that, my dear fellow? Would it work?"

"I will find out details on my return to Rome, and telephone you about it."

"Why, I'll never forget you! And I'm already so much in your debt."

"Please! You pulled me through my doctorate. That shaped my whole career. And now I bid you good-night. I thank you for a grand evening. Dr. Jastrow, I shall be pressing you yet again to share your prophetic insights with a suffering world. Fair warning."

"I am not a prophet, nor the son of a prophet, Werner," said Jastrow archly. "Pleasant journey."

18

LESLIE SLOTE came trudging back to the legation after a too-heavy Swiss lunch with too much Swiss wine, all ingested to comfort himself in his mood of profound futility. Head down to the wind-driven rain, collar turned up, he almost butted Augie Van Winaker, coming out of the legation building. "Steady there, laddie."

"Hi."

"No offense, I hope, about that meeting yesterday."

"No offense."

"Good. You'd have looked very silly — or worse — if the matter had gone further."

In his office Slote threw his wet coat and hat down, seized the telephone, and called Selma Ascher. A heavy weary voice came on. "Ja? Who is that?"

"Ah — it's Leslie Slote, Dr. Ascher."

"So." Pause. "You wish to speak to my daughter? My daughter is not here."

"It's not important. Thank you."

"My daughter will return at six. Shall she telephone you?"

"If she has a moment."

He went to work, and ground through his paper pile at half his usual speed. The telephone rang at the stroke of six. "Hello? This is Selma Ascher speaking."

"Are you free to talk, Selma?"

"Certainly. What is it I can do for you?"

The stiff cool tone was warning enough. "Well, I'd rather like to call the English girl I met at your house."

"You mean Nancy Britten? They live at 19 Tellenstrasse in the Pension Gafen. Would you like Nancy's number?"

"Please. Sorry to trouble you."

"No trouble. One moment — here we are. Nancy's number is 68215."

"I'm much obliged."

"Good-bye then, Mr. Slote."

He was stuffing his briefcase despondently when the phone rang again.

Her voice was breathless and gay. "Yes, Leslie? I'm in a pay telephone down at the corner garage."

"Selma, that priest I met at your house —"

"Father Martin? What about him?"

"I have to talk to him. Your father mustn't know, and I can't telephone his parish house."

"Oh. I see. Is that it?" The girlish tone turned brisk. "I'll have to call you back."

"I'm about to go to my flat. The number —"

"No, stay where you are."

She called again half an hour later. "The corner of Feldstrasse and the Boulevard. You know where that is?"

"Of course."

"Wait there. I'll pick you up."

He had scarcely arrived at the busy boulevard corner when the gray Fiat roadster came zipping up and the door flew open. "Nancy Britten, indeed!" Selma exclaimed with an agitated smile. "Hop in."

"Well, I had to say something." He slammed the door shut. The smell of the leather seats and of her perfume brought back strongly the mood of their one clumsy night out. "Wasn't your father standing beside you?"

"Indeed he was." She shifted gears and went off in a jackrabbit start. "I hardly know Father Martin, but I drove over and saw him. He gave me some strange instructions. I can take you only partway. He said you mustn't involve me again. I've never been in such a situation before. It's like a film." Slote laughed. She added, "No, truly. Is there any danger?"

"No."

"Has this to do with his information about the Jews?"

"Never mind."

"My father found out about our evening together."

"How?"

"He asked me. I can't lie to him. I'm disobeying him by seeing you again."

"What is his objection to me?"

"Oh, Leslie, don't talk rot."

"I'm serious. His attitude puzzles me."

"Don't you find me attractive?" The question shot out at him as she whisked the car into a dark side street.

"Terrifically."

"I find you attractive. I'm engaged to be married. We're a religious family. What puzzles you about my father's attitude?" In these crackling commonsense sentences, Slote could hear Natalie Jastrow, as in old days, pinning him to the wall.

Selma braked the car on a hill lined with town houses, near a street-lamp where two bundled-up children played hopscotch in the pool of light. "Here I leave you. You walk to the top of the hill and turn left. Go along the park until you come to a stone parish house, with a wooden garden door in the stone wall. Knock at that door when nobody else is in sight."

"Selma, won't we see each other again?"

"No."

Round soft eyes glistened under a red shawl. Shawled in much the same way against winter, Natalie had often looked like this — aroused, melancholy, tense from the effort at control. Once again he felt the throb of recognition and regret. She took his hand and pressed it hard in her cold fingers. "Be very careful. Good-bye."

"Ja?" A woman's voice responded to his knock at the heavy wooden garden door.

"Herr Slote."

The door creaked open. A short shapeless person led him toward a bay window glowing orange in the darkness, where he could see the priest at a candlelit table. As Slote came inside, Father Martin rose and waved to a dinner setting beside him. "Welcome! Join me." He lifted the lid of a tureen. "These are tripes *à la mode de Caen.*"

"What a pity," said Slote, glancing down at the steamy pungent-smelling brown mass. He had eaten tripe once in his life, and classed it, like octopus, as a rubbery abomination to be avoided. "I've eaten."

"Well, then," said Father Martin as they sat down, pouring red wine from a clay jug. "Try this."

"Thank you. — I say! It's superb."

"Ah?" The priest looked happy. "It is from my brother's family vineyard near Würzburg."

Father Martin did not speak again while he methodically and placidly devoured a loaf of bread, chunk by chunk, with the tripes, sopping up brown juice from his plate. Each time he broke the bread, his gestures and his shiny red face showed pleasure at the feel and smell of the loaf. He kept refilling his glass and Slote's. The thick-lipped moon face remained almost stupidly serene. The roly-poly housekeeper, a middle-aged woman with a bristling mustache, in a full black skirt down to the floor, brought in a yellow cheese and another bread loaf.

"You will take a bite of cheese," said the priest. "Surely you will."

"I guess so, thanks." By now Slote was ravenous. The cheese, the fresh bread, the wine, were all delicious.

Father Martin happily sighed and wiped his mouth after demolishing most of the cheese. "Now let us have a little air."

A wind was springing up outside, making the tall old trees in the garden creak their leafless boughs. "What is it you want?" The voice turned businesslike and anxious. "I can say nothing within walls, even my own."

"It's about the document I received in the theatre. Have you read it?"

"No."

"I have to establish its authenticity."

"I was told the authenticity was self-evident."

Silence, and the crunching of their steps on the gravel walk.

"Does Jacob Ascher know about it?"

"No."

"Did he arrange our meeting at his house?"

"He did not."

"May I tell you how things stand at my end?"

"*Bitte.*"

Slote recounted his interview with the minister and Van Winaker, and he described the contents of the Protocol. The priest uttered peculiar gasps and grunts. Up and down the garden they paced as the wind gusted heavily and the trees whipped.

"Frightful. Frightful! But as to the authenticity, Herr Slote, are you not butting a stone wall, *the will not to believe?*" He spoke the words slowly, sternly, bitterly, grasping Slote's elbow and thrusting a stubby finger toward his face. "The will not to believe! It's nothing new to me. I meet it on deathbeds. I hear it in the confessional. I hear it from deceived husbands, from parents whose sons are missing in action, from trapped bankrupts. The will not to believe. It is simple human nature. When the mind cannot grasp or face up to a horrible fact it turns away, as though refusing credence will conjure away the reality. That is what you're encountering."

"Father Martin, our minister is an able and tough-minded man. He'll face up to hard facts, if I can provide them."

"What hard facts? What would your minister accept as authentication, Herr Slote? How can one argue with the will not to believe? Supposing I persuaded a certain man in the German legation to meet him face to face? Do you appreciate the risk? The Gestapo net spreads all through Bern. It might mean the man's death. And what would be gained? Your minister suspects he has seen fake papers. Well? Won't he simply suspect he has talked to the faker?"

"I could identify a man from the German legation. You'd better tell your man that all the risk so far has been in vain. Tell him Americans say about the document, 'Incredible contents. Dubious origins.'"

The priest let go of his arm, opened the garden door, and peered out. "Good-night. Straight on beyond the park, outside the Café William Tell, you will find a taxi stand."

"You won't help me any further?"

"Herr Slote, I have asked my Provincial to transfer me from Bern." The priest's voice was shaking badly. "You must not approach me anymore. You Americans really don't comprehend Europe. And in the name of God do not bring in the Aschers again."

August Van Winaker poked his head into Slote's office a few days later. "Hi. I've just been having a long hot session with a friend of yours. He'd like to say hello."

"Certainly. Who is it?"

"Dr. Jacob Ascher."

In a black homburg, and a black suit that hung loose on his bowed shoulders, Dr. Ascher looked like an invalid forced from his bed by an emergency. But his handshake was surprisingly strong.

"Well, I'll leave you two lovebirds together," Van Winaker said with a jolly wink. "I'm sure you have lots to talk about."

"I have only come for a moment," Ascher said, "and I beg you to join us."

Wagging a finger at him Van Winaker replied in sing-song, "Ah-ah. Two's company, thre-e-e's a crow-w-wd, ta-ta," and he danced out, gaily winking.

Dr. Ascher sat down heavily in the chair Slote offered him. "Thank you. We are going to America earlier than planned. In fact, next Thursday. This has involved the hurried execution of some complicated international contracts. That is why I was seeing Mr. Van Winaker."

"Has Augie been helpful?"

"Oh, yes." The look from under Dr. Ascher's heavy gray eyebrows was veiled. "Most helpful. Well!" Ascher looked hard at Slote, with eyes sunk in terrible dark hollows. "I seldom ask a personal favor of any man. Yet I've come to ask such a favor of you, sir, though I hardly know you."

"Please!" Slote returned.

"We leave only eight days from now. If my daughter Selma should happen to telephone you during this time, I ask you not to see her." Slote quailed before the stern face of the old Jew. "Is that a very difficult request?"

"I happen to be hard pressed with work, Dr. Ascher. I couldn't see her anyway."

Painfully, Dr. Ascher rose, holding out his hand.

"I wish you happiness in the United States," Slote said.

Ascher shook his head. "It has taken me sixteen years to feel at home in Bern. Now I'm going to Baltimore, a place I don't know at all, and I'm seventy-three. Still, Selma comes first. She is a brilliant and good girl, though all girls are difficult at times. Since my son is an old bachelor, her future is the only future I have. Good-bye, sir."

Slote went back to work. He had the Vichy France assignment in the legation. A treaty was in the works for continuing three-way trade, despite the war, between Switzerland, the United States, and occupied France. For their own practical reasons, the Germans were allowing this. But it was tricky business, and a mountain of paper had accumulated. Slote was pushing through a draft for a meeting that afternoon when his telephone rang.

"Mr. Leslie Slote?" The aged high voice was very British. "Treville Britten here. We met at the home of the Aschers."

"Of course. How are you?"

"Splendid. We had some interesting talk that evening, didn't we? Ah, Winston Churchill will broadcast tonight, you know, and ah, my daughter Nancy and I thought if you cared to join us for dinner — it's frugal vegetarian fare, but Nancy does it rather well. We might listen to Churchill together. Discuss the new developments."

"I'd be charmed," said Slote, thinking that few invitations could be less attractive, "except that I must work straight through the night, pretty near."

The hemming and hawing ceased. "Mr. Slote, I'm not going to take no for an answer."

Slote caught a professional hardening of the elderly voice that was a signal. This was a British Foreign Service man, after all. "How nice of you to insist."

"Pension Gafen, 19 Tellenstrasse, apartment 3A. About seven."

Perhaps there were two gray Fiat roadsters like Selma Ascher's in Bern, Slote thought that evening, seeing the car parked in front of the pension, a dismal-looking house in a dilapidated part of Bern. Question: did his promise to Selma's father bind him not to go up to the flat and see? Doing rapid mental casuistry, he mounted the stairs two at a time. Selma had not telephoned him. He wasn't sure that she was in the Britten apartment. He had accepted the dinner invitation in good faith. In short, the worried old Jewish father be damned! For all Slote intended to do, Selma Ascher would leave Bern *virgo intacta.*

There she was in a dowdy blue frock, little more than a housedress, with her hair carelessly pinned up. She had a tired unhappy air, and her greeting was anything but flirtatious; offhand, rather, and faintly resentful. She and the English girl worked in the kitchen while, in a small musty study crammed with old books and magazines, Britten poured very stiff whiskeys. "How fortunate that alcohol is a vegetable product, what? If it were distilled from animal corpses, all my principles would have to give way. Hee hee." Slote felt Britten had made this joke and giggled this way a thousand times.

The old man was eager to talk about Singapore. Once the Japanese had landed in Malaya, he explained, the obvious strategy had been to lure them all the way south with a fighting retreat, to within range of Singapore's terrible guns. The news meantime had been depressing, but now the turnabout was surely at hand. Winnie obviously had something exciting to impart to-night about Singapore. *"The will not to believe,"* thought Slote; what an egregious example was here! Even the BBC was broadly hinting that Singapore was falling. Yet Britten's crack-voiced optimism was utterly unfeigned.

It was a strained, impoverished meal. The four people crowded the small table. The peculiar mock-meat puddings and stews that the daughter served were insipid stuff. Selma ate little, scarcely looking up, her face sullen and withdrawn. They were starting on a dessert of very tart stewed rhubarb when Churchill's cadences began to roll out of the shortwave radio. For a long time in his sombre talk he did not mention Singapore. Britten conveyed to Slote, with reassuring winks and gestures, that all this was quite in line with his prediction. The great disclosure was coming.

Churchill paused, and took an audible breath.

And now, I have heavy news. Singapore has fallen. That mighty bastion of Empire, which held out so long against insuperable odds, has honorably surrendered to spare its civilian population from further useless slaughter . . .

The old man's wrinkled face wilted into a pained smile, getting redder and redder, his watery eyes taking on a queer gleam. They listened in silence to the very end of the speech:

. . . and so let us go on, into the storm, and through the storm.

Shakily Britten reached over and turned off the radio. "Well! Bit mistaken on that one, wasn't I?"

"Oh, the Empire's gone," said his daughter with vinegary satisfaction. "High time we all faced that, Father. Especially Winnie. What an obsolete romantic!"

"Just so. Night falls. A new world order cometh." Britten's voice fell into the rhythms of Churchill, a reedy grotesque echo. "The Hun will join hands with the Mongol. The Slav, the born helot, will serve new masters. Christianity and humanism are dead creeds. The thousand-year night of technological barbarism descends. Well, we English fought the good fight. I have lived my life. You young people have my sympathy."

He was so obviously distraught that Slote and Selma left almost at once. On the staircase she said, "Is it really that bad, the fall of Singapore?"

"Well, to him it's the end of the world. It may spell the end of the British Empire. The war will go on."

On the street she seized his hand, twining the fingers in hers. "Come into my car."

She drove to a busy boulevard and parked at the curb with the motor running. "Father Martin gave me a message for you. Here are his exact words. 'It is arranged. Wait for a visitor in your flat at six o'clock Sunday evening.' "

Immensely surprised, Slote said, "I thought he didn't want you involved."

"He was at the house last night. Papa told him we'd be gone by next Thursday. I suppose he decided that I'm a safe messenger, since I'll be gone so soon."

"I'm sorry you had to disobey your father."

"Did you mind Nancy's horrible food?"

"It was worth it."

She stared at him and turned off the motor. "I suppose you had an affair with this Natalie girl?"

"Of course I did. I told you that."

"Not in so many words. You were very diplomatic. Do you imagine you could possibly have had an affair with me?"

"I wouldn't have dreamed of it."

"Why not? I thought I was like her. How am I different? Not sexually exciting?"

"This is a stupid conversation, Selma. Thanks for the message."

"I can't forgive my father for going to you. It's so humiliating!"

"He shouldn't have told you."

"I got it out of him. We had some bitter words. Well, you're quite right, this *is* a stupid conversation. Good-bye." She started the motor, and held out her hand.

"Ye gods, Selma, your circulation must be bad. Your hands are always icy."

"Nobody but you has ever mentioned that. Well — what do the English say? 'In for a penny, in for a pound.' " She leaned to him and kissed him hard on the mouth. The sweetness of it shook Slote deeply. Her voice dropped to a whisper. "There! Since you find me so exciting, remember me a little. I'll remember you always."

"And I you."

She shook her head. "No, you won't. You've had so many adventures! You'll have so many more! I've had my one, my very little one. I hope that you get your Natalie back. She'd be happier with you than with that Navy fellow"— Selma's expression turned darkly mischievous —"as long as she insists on having a Gentile husband."

Slote opened the car door.

"Leslie, I don't know what your business with Father Martin is," Selma exclaimed, "but take care! I have never seen a more frightened person."

Nobody came to Slote's flat on Sunday evening. The front page of the Zurich *Tageblatt*, lying on his desk Monday morning, had a spread of Japanese photographs about the Singapore victory, furnished by the German news service: the surrender ceremony, the hordes of British troops sitting on the earth in a prison compound, the celebration in Tokyo. The story about Father Martin was so short that Slote almost missed it, but there it was at the bottom of the page. The truck driver, who claimed that his brakes had failed, was being held for questioning. The priest was dead, crushed.

19

A Jew's Journey
(excerpt from Aaron Jastrow's manuscript)

APRIL 23, 1942.

American bombers have raided Tokyo!

My pulse races as it once did when, an immigrant in love with everything American, infected with baseball fever, I saw Babe Ruth hit a home run. For me America is the Babe Ruth of the nations. I unashamedly confess it. And the Babe has come out of his slump and "hit one over the fence"!

Strange, how Allied airplane bombs infallibly fall on churches, schools, and hospitals; what a triumph of military imprecision! If Berlin radio speaks the truth — and why should Germans lie, pray? — the RAF has by now flattened nearly all institutions of worship, learning, and healing in Germany, while unerringly missing all other targets. Now we are told that Tokyo was unscathed in the raid except for a great number of schools, hospitals, and temples demolished by the barbarous Americans. Most extraordinary.

My niece calls this "Doolittle raid" (an intrepid Army Air Corps colonel of that name led the attack) just a stunt, a token bombing. It will make no difference to the war; so she *says*. What she *did*, when the news came through on the BBC, was to entrust her baby to the cook, rush down to the Excelsior Hotel where our fellow journalists are housed, and there get joyously drunk with them. They are drunk nearly all the time, but I have not seen Natalie inebriated in years. I must say that when her chief local admirer, a banal-minded Associated Press reporter, brought her back, she was full of amusing raillery, though scarcely able to walk straight.

Her mood was so gay, in fact, that I was tempted to disclose then and there the grave secret I have been harboring for two weeks, not even entrusting it to these pages. But I refrained. She has suffered enough on my account. Time enough to reveal this bombshell when the fuse has burned down to the danger point. This it may never do.

The departure date of the American internees in Siena has been fixed for the first week in May. We are to proceed to Naples or Lisbon, embark in a Swedish luxury liner, and sail for home. On the first of April (I remember noting that it was April Fool's Day!) my old friend, the Siena chief of police, paid me a visit. With many a Tuscan sigh and shrug and circumlocution, he hinted that for us there might be a hitch. He would not elaborate.

Detailed word came within a few days, in a letter from our embassy in Rome. The nub of the matter is this: the Nazis claim that three Italian journalists, interned in Rio de Janeiro and awaiting trial as German agents in disguise, are in fact *bona fide* journalists, barbarously detained by the Brazilian authorities at Allied instigation. In retaliation, since the Germans can lay their hands on few Brazilians, they have asked the Italians to detain three Americans so as to force our State Department to persuade Brazil to set these men free. It is just crude Teutonism, of course, a game to recover clumsy spies who got themselves caught. Unhappily, the three hostages, if it comes to that, may be myself, my niece, and her baby, since our "journalist" credentials are marginal, to say the least. The international dickering has, in fact, already begun, and we are among those marked for possible detention. So the embassy has disclosed.

But that it will happen is unlikely. Brazil will probably bow to the intercession of our State Department. Then again, our friend and rescuer, Dr. Werner Beck, is moving heaven and earth to get us released, or at the very least, to designate three other Americans from the list for the retaliation, if it comes to that. Probably I should not let him do this, but I have learned already to turn feral in wartime. *Sauve qui peut* is the cry.

I have concealed this news from Natalie. Her dread of the Germans and what they may do to her baby borders on the psychotic. As for me, I am not alarmed. I would just as lief work on here to the last, and — when the worst befalls and however it befalls — have my ashes scattered in the garden. For one way or another, my time of ash is not far off. I cannot say how I know this. My health is fair. Nevertheless I do know it. It neither frightens nor saddens me. It strengthens my resolve to wring all the work I can out of the passing days, and finish my *Luther*.

For Natalie's sake, however, I must do all I can to ensure that we will go. Upon completing my morning's work, I shall go and have a word with the archbishop. He is not without influence in the Italian Foreign Ministry. The time has come to pull every string, and turn over every stone.

20

T HE red beard scratched and tickled Janice Henry's cheek. She hugged Byron a shade tighter than family affection called for, thinking that he had been out on that submarine a pretty long time. Too, though incest was as far from her thoughts as parricide, she did feel — she always had — a mild fugitive attraction to Warren's younger brother. She didn't mind the rum reek on his breath, nor the grease streaks on his rumpled khakis, for she knew that he had come straight from the victory celebration of the *Devilfish*. A double frangipani lei, heavily and sweetly odorous, dangled around his sunburned throat.

"Well!" She touched the beard. "Are you going to keep that?"

"Why not?" He took off the lei and hung it around her neck.

Flustered, sniffing at the flowers, she said, "I feel so dumb about your phone call. You and he do sound alike, you know."

Janice had begun blurting a sexy wife-to-husband greeting on hearing his voice. "Look, it's Byron," he had interrupted, and after an embarrassed pause they had both roared with laughter.

Byron shyly grinned. "Expecting Warren, were you?"

"Well, the scuttlebutt is that Halsey's due back with the carriers."

"Minus the *Lex,* I hear."

"Minus the *Lex.*" She shook her head sadly. "Sunk in the Coral Sea. That's definite."

"Where's my nephew?"

"In the nursery. Bathed, fed, sleepy, smelling like a rose."

"More than you can say for me, I guess." Byron did, in fact, smell rather gamy. "We just piled off the boat and started celebrating — hi, Vic. Holy cow, Janice," Byron called from the nursery, "he's gigantic."

"Don't rouse him. He'll give us no peace."

Byron strolled into the kitchen after a while and dropped on a chair. "Marvelous kid," he said, with a faraway look. He sounded doleful.

Janice crouched at the stove in an apron, a shirt, and shorts, the pink lei hanging loose. She pushed heavy yellow hair away from her face. "Sorry I'm such a mess. Seems I never dress up any more. Warren's so seldom home."

"I'd call Washington," Byron said, "but it's midnight there. I'll call in the morning. Natalie and my kid are interned in Italy, I suppose you know that."

"Briny, they're out."

"What! They *are?*" Byron sprang joyfully to his feet. "Jan! How do you know?"

"I talked to my father in Washington — oh, three, four days ago. He's been keeping after the State Department about it."

"But, was he positive?"

"Yes, there's this Swedish liner en route from Lisbon with the interned Americans. She's aboard with her baby."

"Fantastic!" He seized Janice and hugged and kissed her. "Maybe I'll telephone him."

"He's left there. He's a brigadier general, assigned to MacArthur's staff in Australia. You can talk to him when he passes through here, probably Saturday."

"Oh, Lord, how I've waited for this news!"

"I'll bet. Some reunion coming up, eh?" Her grin was sly as he released her. "How much time did you two have on your honeymoon, three days?"

"Less. Dunno about the reunion, though." He dropped in the chair again. "Aster wants me to stick with the *Devilfish.* Most of our squadron's been pulled back off patrol. That's damned unusual. There's a smell around the sub base. Something brewing."

She gave him a worried glance. "Yes? At Cincpac, too."

"Aster heard that the Japs are going to try to take the Hawaiian Islands. Biggest battle of the war coming up. No time for me to leave, that's his argument."

"Don't you have orders to SubLant?"

"He has to detach me. I could stay aboard for the battle, if there's one imminent. Maybe I ought to, I don't know."

"So Aster's got command now?"

"Yes, it's Captain Aster, no more Lady."

"I don't like him."

"Why not?"

"Oh, God's gift to women, isn't he? And he grins like the phantom of the opera."

That made Byron laugh. "Phantom of the opera! Not bad."

He helped her carry food and wine out to a table of wrought iron and glass on the lanai. She lit candles, though the sunset still glowed beyond the trees. They drank California burgundy with the meat loaf she had hastily prepared. Byron emptied glass after glass as he talked about Aster's first patrol. They had sunk two ships before the summons back to base, and Byron thought Carter Aster was going to be one of the great skippers of the war. His eyes began to gleam. "Say, Jan, can you keep a secret?"

"Indeed I can."

"We sank a hospital ship."

"My *God*, Byron!" She stared and gasped. "Why, that's an atrocity, it's —"

"Just let me *tell* this, will you? It was the goddamnedest experience of my life. I spotted the ship myself when I had the deck, about midnight. Unescorted, floodlights on a white hull, brilliant running lights, huge red cross painted on her side. This was in the Makassar Strait off Java. Aster came topside, took one look, and ordered a dive and an approach. Well, I figured it was a practice run. But when he said, 'Open the outer doors,' I cracked. 'Captain,' I said, 'is this an attack?' He ignored me, just kept boring in. I was on the computer. At about fifteen hundred yards I had a perfect solution, but I felt guilty as hell, and the exec was just scratching his head and keeping his mouth shut. 'Captain,' I said, 'this target is a hospital ship. If there's a general court martial I'll have to say so.' 'Yes, you do that, Briny. I'm going to shoot him now,' he says, cool as a popsicle, chewing on his cigar. 'Stand by! Up periscope. Final bearing and shoot!' And off went four fish."

"Byron, he's a maniac!"

"Janice, will you listen? That baby blew up in a fireball you could see for a hundred miles! It was a disguised ammunition ship. Nothing else could have blown like that. We surfaced and watched it burn. It kept whizzing and popping and spraying fire. It took forever to sink. The fireworks just went on and on. And once it did go down, why, the sea was full of strange dark floating shapes. We hove to till dawn, and they turned out to be huge balls of crude rubber, ten or fifteen feet across. Those things were bobbing all the way to the horizon. That ship was transporting rubber from Java, honey, with a big load of ammo. Probably captured Dutch stuff."

"How could he know that? He might have drowned two thousand wounded men."

"He guessed right. Don't ever repeat that story, Jan."

"Horrors, no."

The doorbell rang. She left the table and soon reappeared. "Speak of the devil." Carter Aster followed her in dress whites, clean-shaven, slim and straight, cap under his arm.

"Briny, the base pool ran out of jeeps. Will you give me a lift down the hill about ten? The cabs won't come up at curfew time."

"Where will you be?"

"I'll turn up here again." Aster directed his strange grin — curled corners on a hard mouth — at Janice. "If that's okay with you."

Janice said to Byron, "Won't you be sleeping over?"

"I hadn't thought about it. A hot bath, a real bed? Thanks, I sure will."

"We're on twenty-four hours' notice, Byron," Aster said.

"I'll be back at 0800, Captain."

"Made up your mind yet about staying aboard?"

"Let you know in the morning."

Janice could guess why Byron was saying nothing about Natalie. The news would only intensify Aster's pressure on him to remain with the *Devilfish*.

"The latest poop is that they're coming in force to invade Alaska," Aster said to Janice. "Heard anything like that at Cincpac?"

She shook her head, unsmiling. He grinned at her and left.

"Which lucky lady is he visiting up here?" Janice asked.

Byron's answer was an evasive shrug.

"Now that's mean, Briny. I'll suspect every wife on the hill."

"Can't help your evil mind, Jan."

As they chatted into the evening about the family and the war, moving inside and drawing the blackout curtains, Byron's manner began to strike Janice as odd. He was wandering in his talk, and giving her awkward, sombre glances. Too much wine? Sexual stirrings? In her brother-in-law that seemed inconceivable. Still, he was a young sailor back from the sea. When he went off for a bath she decided to stay dressed, to keep the lights turned up, and to put away the liquor.

"God, that was marvelous." He emerged in Warren's pajamas and robe, towelling his head. "I haven't had a bath since Albany."

"*Albany?*"

"Albany, Australia." He flopped loose-limbed on the rattan couch. "Lovely tiny town, as far away as you can go on God's green earth. Wonderful people. Our tender was berthed there. Got any bourbon, Jan?" His manner was quite matter-of-fact.

Janice felt ashamed of her imaginings. She brought two drinks. Stretching out on the couch, he took a swig, and morosely shook his head. "God, to think of seeing Natalie again! And the baby. Incredible."

"You don't sound all that happy."

"There was a girl in Albany. Maybe I'm feeling guilty."

"Wow." She made a small drama of falling in an armchair.

"I met her in church. She sang in the choir, a small choir, everything's small in Albany. Just three other singers and this girl. She played the organ, too. It's a tiny little toy seaport, Albany — just three streets and a church and a town hall. Clean, charming, lots of lawns, flowerbeds, old nice houses, old oaks, totally British and nineteenth-century. It's another world."

"Who is she?"

"Her name's Ursula Cotton. Her father owns the little town bank. Very sweet, very proper. Her guy is a tank corps officer in North Africa. Our sub had two overhauls, two months apart. Both times we were inseparable, every minute I could get ashore."

"And —?"

Byron made a despairing gesture with both hands. "*And?* And we sailed, and here I am."

"Byron, I'm not clear on one point. Did anything happen?"

"Did anything happen?" He angrily frowned. "You mean did I get into her pants?"

"Well, you put it rather horridly."

"Christ! You, too? Carter Aster, every time I'd come back to the sub, he'd say, '*Well, did you get into her pants?*' I finally said if he'd come ashore, and forget about being captain, I'd straighten him out about Ursula once and for all. That ended that."

"Dear, it makes a difference —"

"Look, I said her guy was fighting in North Africa. What do you take me for? That was a torment, but still it was beautiful. It made life endurable. I'll never write her. It's no use. But by God, I'll never forget Ursula."

Janice got out of her chair, and placed both hands on his shoulders. Leaning over him so that her scented yellow hair cascaded on him, she kissed his lips. With a businesslike rub of a thumb on his mouth she said, "Natalie's lucky. Brothers can sure be different. What Warren has put *me* through!"

"Well, you married a hell-raiser, you knew that."

"I did, indeed."

Byron yawned and shook his head. "Strangely, I only got crazier about Natalie all that time. I kept thinking of her. Ursula was lovely, but compared to Natalie! Natalie's a powerhouse. There's nobody in the world like her."

"Well, I envy Natalie. I envy Little Miss Ursula, too. Natalie would forgive you and her both. That's my guess." A bitter wrinkling smile. "Even if you had gotten into her pants, as Lady Aster would say. It's war, you know. Good-night, Byron. Vic gets me up at five."

Next morning she was feeding the baby in the kitchen when she heard the dying cough of a jeep. In came Warren in fresh khakis. She had not seen him in almost a month. He was strikingly bigger and heavier than Byron, and very tanned and bright-eyed. "Janice, what's another jeep doing out here? Got some guy in a closet, with thirty seconds to live?"

As he swept her into a crushing hug, she put a finger on his mouth. "Byron's asleep in the guest room."

"What, Briny's back? Great!"

Janice stammered, her mouth against his, "Darling, Vic's in his high chair —"

Warren strode to the kitchen. The baby turned an egg-smeared face and large solemn eyes on him, then smiled from ear to ear. Warren kissed him. "He smells good. Grows half a foot every time I go out. Come along, feller."

"Where are you taking him?"

The aviator wiped his son's face, carried him to a crib in the nursery, and handed him his teddy bear.

"Darling, listen," Janice protested in low tones, following him, "Byron will come stumbling out any second, looking for eggs and coffee —"

He circled her waist in a powerful arm, took her into the bedroom, and quietly locked the door.

Prone and naked, half-stuporous, she heard the scratch of a match, opened her eyes, and gave her husband a sad, heavy, mischievous look. He was sitting up in the bed. "Honestly," she said, in an unexpected baritone voice that made them both laugh. The sun fell in golden bars on Warren's bronzed chest, and the smoke from his cigarette made blue coils in the sunlight.

"Well, you're a sailor's wife."

"Jesus. Not one of Magellan's sailors."

"Jan, I hear Byron stirring about."

"Oh dear. Well, the coffee's on. I guess he'll find it."

He said a shade gruffly, "I love you." She reared up on an elbow to look at him. He dragged on the cigarette, and blew out a gray cloud. "Quite an exercise, this last one. In futility, that is. A two-carrier task force, roaring thirty-five hundred miles to the Coral Sea and back, and missing the battle by three days. If we'd got there in time we'd have smashed the Japs, instead of losing the *Lex*. The *Yorktown*'s kaput, too. Seven thousand miles for nothing. Halsey's lucky he doesn't have to pay his oil bill."

Janice said, "What's this thing cooking up now? Do you know?"

"Oh, you hear scuttlebutt. Something big, that's for sure. We sortie again in two days."

"Two days!"

"Yep. Working parties replenishing ship around the clock." Yawning, he put a brown arm around her. "Action will be a novelty. All we did on those seven thousand miles was patrol, baby. Patrol, patrol! Two hundred miles out, two hundred miles back, grinding along over clouds, water, hours on end, days on end. I never saw anything except whales. There was lots of leisure to think. I figured out that time's getting precious, and that I should stop screwing around and hurting you. I've done too much of it. I'm sorry. No more. Okay? Guess I'll shower up and talk to Briny. How does he look?"

"Why, why, sort of haggard and scrawny." Stunned with delight at his contrition, Janice tried to sound just as casual. "Thick red beard, like Dad told us." She touched his face. "I wonder how you'd look in a beard."

"Negative! It comes in half-gray. Balls to that. Well, Dad will sure be glad to see Briny, beard and all. The *Northampton* was following us in."

"Byron says the *Devilfish* got two Jap ships."

"Hey, won't that give Dad a charge!"

On the sunny wing of the *Northampton's* bridge, maneuvering to buoys in a strong ebb tide, Pug Henry could see Spruance pacing the main deck far below. The barge lay to, waiting to take them to the *Enterprise*, where the admiral would pay his respects to Halsey. Then they would walk the five miles to Warren's house. That was their routine. As the drenched sailors down on the pitching buoys wrestled with the shackles of the massive anchor chains, Pug and Commander Grigg were talking about urgent yard repairs that they might get done before going back to sea. The magazines were still loaded from the vain Coral Sea dash, but food and fuel were low. Forty-eight hours for turnabout, after seven thousand miles of high-speed steaming! All hell must be about to break loose in the Pacific; but what it was all about, Pug Henry had no idea.

The *Enterprise* was usually bleak and quiet in port; an abandoned nest, the birds having flown off before dawn from a hundred miles out. But this time the utter lack of life was eerie: no pipings at the approach of Spruance's barge, no loudspeaker calls for sideboys and ceremonies; the gangway deserted, not even the OOD in sight. In the cavernous hangar deck there was a cold, ghost-ship feeling. The flag secretary came toward them on the run, his tread thumping and echoing down the empty steel cavern. Unceremoniously he took Raymond Spruance aside by the elbow, turning a pale unshaven face over his shoulder. "Excuse me, Captain Henry. Had coffee with your son at 0300, incidentally, before he took off."

Pug nodded, showing none of the relief he felt. Off the New Hebrides he had seen a Dauntless dive-bomber cartwheel from the *Enterprise* into the sea; probably not Warren, on the odds, but until this moment he had wondered and worried.

"Okay, Henry. Let's go," said Spruance, after a muttered colloquy. The barge rocked and clanged its way to the sub base. Spruance volunteered nothing, Pug asked no questions. The admiral's face looked almost wooden in its calm. He broke his silence as they stepped ashore. "Henry, I have a little business at Cincpac. I suppose you want to join your family right away?" Plainly, from his tone, he hated to give up the walk.

"I'm at your pleasure, Admiral."

"Come with me. It shouldn't take too long."

In a hard chair outside Nimitz's gold-starred doors, twisting his cap round and round, Pug waited, noting the extraordinary bustle all around him; typewriter clatter, telephones ringing, hurrying foot traffic this way and that of yeomen and junior officers. The Cincpac building was as stirred up as the *Enterprise* was dead. Momentous business was in the air, and no mistake. Pug hoped that it was not another Doolittle-type raid. He was a conservative military thinker, and he had been skeptical of that Doolittle show since the task force had first sailed.

With an irrepressible spine tingle he had read over the *Northampton*'s loudspeakers Halsey's message. *"This force is bound for Tokyo."* But how could two carriers, he had thought at once, venture within range of the land-based Japanese air force? Through the crew's cheers and rebel yells, he had skeptically shaken his head at Spruance. Next day, when the *Hornet* had joined up, its deckload of Army B-25 bombers had of course solved the mystery. Watching the oncoming carrier, Spruance had remarked, "Well, Captain?"

"My hat's off to those Army fliers, Admiral."

"Mine too. They've been training for months. They'll have to go on to China, you realize. That deck can't take them back aboard."

"I know. Brave souls."

"Is this good war-making, Captain?"

"Sir, my inferior understanding prevents my grasping the unquestionable soundness of the mission."

For the first time since Pug had met him, Raymond Spruance had laughed heartily. They had not discussed the raid again until a few days ago. At dinner in Spruance's quarters, Spruance had been bemoaning the way they had missed the Coral Sea battle, the first in history in which the opposed warships had never sighted each other; an all-air duel at ranges of seventy-five miles or more. "That's something new in sea warfare, Henry. A lot of War College thinking goes overboard. Possibly you were right about that Tokyo raid. Maybe we should have been down south all that time, instead of roaring back and forth over the Pacific to make headlines. Still, we don't know to what extent Doolittle upset the Japanese war plans."

Spruance remained in Cincpac's sanctum for about half an hour. He emerged with a strange look on his face. "We're on our way, Henry." When they were out of the Navy Yard, and plugging uphill through weedy dusty sugarcane fields on a tarred road, he abruptly remarked, "Well, I'm leaving the *Northampton*."

"Oh? I'm genuinely sorry, sir."

"I am, too, since I'll be going on the beach. I'm to become Admiral Nimitz's chief of staff."

"Why, that's splendid. Congratulations, Admiral."

"Thanks," Spruance said coldly, "but I don't recall your leaping at staff duty when offered."

That closed the topic. They trudged around a bend. The base came in sight, sprawled out far below, beyond flowering trees and terraced green truck gardens; the wharves, drydocks and anchorages crowded with warships, the channels full of small craft moving about; on the wrecked battleships, workmen swarming over the temporary repair structures, and — the most striking sight — along the capsized hull of the *Oklahoma*, the long row of righting cables stretched to winches on Ford Island.

"Henry, you've read the *Yorktown*'s damage report dispatches. How long would you say repairs will take?"

"Three to five months, sir."

"Captain Harry Warendorf is your classmate, isn't he? The Captain of the Yard?"

"Yes, I know Harry well."

"Can he put her back to sea in seventy-two hours? Because he's going to have to. Admiral Nimitz has ordered it."

"Harry will do it, if any man can," Pug answered, astounded. "It's bound to be a patch job."

"Yes, but three carriers instead of two is a fifty percent increase in striking power. Which we'll soon need."

Over steak and eggs on the back porch, Byron was telling Warren about the torpedoes he had salvaged from Cavite. The brothers, both barefoot, both in shorts and beach-boy shirts, had been talking at a great rate for an hour.

"Twenty-six torpedoes!" Warren exclaimed. "No wonder you got your transfer to the Atlantic."

Byron was enjoying, in fact revelling in, this conversation. Eternal months ago in peacetime, Warren had warned him to kowtow to Branch Hoban if he wanted his dolphins. Now Warren knew of Hoban's cave-in, and dolphins were pinned to the sweaty khaki shirt hanging in the guest room. "Warren, Aster's pressuring me to stay aboard the *Devilfish*."

"Do you have a choice?"

"I've got my orders, but it could be managed."

"Rinkydink administration in submarines."

"Sort of."

Warren had no ready advice to give. His self-confidence was solid and deep; he had overwhelmed Byron from boyhood; yet he had always sensed an original streak in Briny that he lacked. Attracting and marrying a brilliant Jewess, the niece of a famous writer, was a deed outside his range; and given the opportunities of wartime, Byron was fast closing the gap as a naval officer.

"Well, let me tell you a story, Byron. Halsey brought the Doolittle fliers to their takeoff point. I suppose you know that."

"That's the word at the sub base."

"It's true. When those Army bombers took off from the *Hornet*, I stood out on our own flight deck and watched them form up and head west for Tokyo. Tears ran down my face, Byron. I bawled."

"I believe you."

"Okay. It was a hell of a brave deed, yet what did it amount to? A token bombing to pep up the home front. There's only one service really hurting the enemy in the Pacific right now, and that's the submarines. There won't be another moment like this in your lifetime. If you go to SubLant you'll boot it. You asked my opinion, and I'm giving it to you. You know Natalie's okay now, and —"

Janice poked her head out of the kitchen. "Your dad and Admiral Spruance are rounding the Smiths' terrace, men, going full steam."

Byron glanced down at his shirt and shorts, and rubbed his beard. "Spruance?"

Warren yawned, scratching a dirty bare foot. "He just drinks a glass of water and goes back down the hill."

The bell rang. Janice went to answer. The brothers jumped to their feet, as the white-clad admiral, his face streaming sweat, walked out on the porch, followed by their father.

"Byron!" Pug grasped his son's hand and they embraced. "Well, here's my submariner, Admiral. I haven't seen him since Thanksgiving."

"My submariner's out in the *Tambor*." Spruance patted his crimson face with a square-folded handkerchief. "How's the hunting been, Lieutenant?"

"Two confirmed sinkings, Admiral. Eleven thousand tons."

Victor Henry's eyes brightened. Spruance smiled. "Indeed? You're ahead of the *Tambor*. What about the Mark Fourteen torpedo?"

"It stinks, Admiral. It's a disgrace. My skipper got his three kills with contact exploders. Against orders, but they worked."

At the impudent freedom of the response, Pug's pleasure subsided. "Briny, when torpedoes miss it's always a temptation to blame the exploders."

"Sorry, Dad. I know you were involved with that magnetic device." In peacetime, Victor Henry had received a letter of commendation for his work on it. "It's gone sour in production, that's all I can tell you. Even with contact exploders, the Mark Fourteen keeps failing. All of SubPac's skippers are up in arms, but BuOrd won't listen. It's sickening, I tell you, to sail five thousand miles to make a torpedo attack, and then have the fish hit the target with a dull thud."

Spruance relieved Pug by commenting, "My son says much the same thing. Admiral Nimitz has taken the matter up with BuOrd." He accepted a glass of iced tea from Janice, and turned to Warren. "Incidentally, what's the range of the Dauntless, again, Lieutenant?"

"We tend to think in hours, Admiral. Three and a half hours airborne, more or less."

The admiral's expression was abstracted. "Your book range is seven hundred fifty miles."

Warren tartly smiled. "Sir, just forming up burns a lot of gasoline. Then over the target the fuel disappears like there's a hole in the tank. Most of us wouldn't get back from a target at two hundred miles."

"And the fighters and torpedo bombers?" Spruance asked as he sipped the tea. "Same speed and range?"

"Approximately, sir." Warren concealed any puzzlement at the questions, answering briskly. "But the TBD is a lot slower."

"Well!" Spruance emptied his glass and stood up. "Most refreshing, Janice. I'll be going down the hill now."

The others were all on their feet. "Admiral, one of the boys can drive you back," Pug said.

"Why?"

"If you have pressing business, sir."

"Not necessary." As he went out, Spruance beckoned to Pug to follow him. Closing the front door he paused, squinting at Victor Henry in the noon sun. He looked much sterner when he put on the big white cap. "Those boys of yours are different in character, but they're both cut from the same cloth."

"Byron should curb his tongue."

"Submariners are individualists, as I well know. It's good they're both in port. Spend all the time with them you can."

"There's much to do on my ship, Admiral."

Spruance's face took on a sudden hard cast. "Henry, this is for your information only. The Japanese are heading east in great force. They're already at sea. Their objective is to seize Midway Island. A Japanese base a thousand miles from Hawaii is unacceptable, so Admiral Nimitz is sending everything we've got up there. We're about to fight the biggest battle of the war."

Pug groped for a response to these stunning words that would not sound defeatist, alarmed, swaggering, or plain stupid. The *Hornet,* the *Enterprise,* with possibly the patched leaky *Yorktown* and their meager train, against that Japanese armada! At least eight carriers, perhaps ten battleships, only God could know how many cruisers, destroyers, submarines! As a fleet problem, it was too lopsided for any peacetime umpire to propose. His hoarse words came unbidden, "Now I know why you don't want to go on the beach."

"I won't just yet." The calm eyes glowed in a way Victor Henry never forgot. "Admiral Halsey has gone to the Cincpac hospital. Unlucky outbreak of a skin disease. He can't fight this battle. He has recommended to Admiral Nimitz that I assume command of Task Force Sixteen, so I'll transfer my gear to Halsey's flag quarters this afternoon. My new assignment starts after the battle."

This was just as stunning as the first disclosure. Spruance, a nonaviator, taking the *Enterprise* and the *Hornet* into battle! Trying to maintain a level tone, Pug asked, "The intelligence is all that certain, then?"

"We think so. If all goes well, we may achieve surprise. Incidentally, I intend to invite you to the battle conference." He held out his hand. "So as I say, spend some time with your boys while you can."

Returning to the back porch, Pug Henry paused in the shadows of the doorway. His sons were talking on the lawn now, folding chairs pulled close, each clasping a beer can. *Cut from the same cloth!* They looked it. What could they be discussing so earnestly? He was in no hurry to interrupt them. He leaned in the doorway, taking in the picture he might not see again for a long time, trying to digest Spruance's savage news. He was ready himself to sail against those odds in the thin-skinned *Northampton*. He had been paid through thirty years to prepare for such an encounter. But Warren and Byron, in their twenties, were just starting to taste life. Yet on the *Northampton* he would be the safest of the three.

In these two young men in gaudy shirts and tan shorts — one lean and red-bearded, the other big and solid, with gray-sprinkled hair — he could still see ghostly shadows of the boys they had been. Byron had smiled just such a smile at five. Warren's emphatic push of both hands outward had been his main gesture as an Academy debater. Pug remembered Warren's great moment, his graduation from the Academy, a battalion commander with a prize in modern history; and poor Byron's sad Columbia commencement, when he had almost failed to graduate because of an overdue term paper. He remembered the rainy March day in 1939 when he had received his orders to Germany, and Warren had come in all sweaty from tennis to say he had applied for flight training, and Byron's first letter from Siena about Natalie Jastrow had arrived. He would break into their talk soon, Pug thought, to ask about her. Not yet. He just wanted to look at them a little longer.

About Warren, Pug thought, he could have done nothing. Warren had always wanted the Navy. By becoming an aviator, he had outdone the father he was emulating. The aviators who survived would become the Navy's next wave of admirals. That was already clear. As for Byron, Pug knew he had forced him into submarines and parted him from his Jewish wife. This was a sunken rock always to be steered around when they were together. Byron would have been called up anyway, and he might even have chosen submarines. But Pug could not clear himself of muddying Byron's life, and — proud as he was of the *Devilfish*'s sinkings — of pushing him into hazard.

A poignant sense engulfed him of the one-way flow of time, of the offhand decisions, the slight impulsive mistakes, that could swell and become a man's fate. There they sat, the little boys he had stiffly disciplined and silently loved, transformed into naval officers and combat veterans. It seemed the work of a master illusionist who could just as easily, if he chose, reverse the trick and change the red-bearded submariner and the broad-chested aviator back into quarrelling lads on a Manila lawn. But Pug knew those lads were gone. He himself had changed into a grim old dog, and they too would keep changing in one direction. Byron would at last come to the adult form and personality that still eluded him. Warren —

The strange thing was that Victor Henry could not picture Warren changing any further. Warren as he sat there in the sun, holding that beer can, the cigarette slanting from his thin mouth, his body developed, full, and powerful, his face carved in lines of self-confidence and resolution, his blue eyes glinting with suppressed humor, was Warren as he would always be. So the father could not help thinking, and as the thought took root, a stinging cold shiver traversed his body. He shouted, stepping out of the doorway; "Say, is there any beer left, or have you two problem drinkers soaked it all up?"

Byron jumped to his feet and brought his father a tall frosty glass of beer.

"Dad, Natalie's coming home on a Swedish boat! That's what Janice's father has heard, anyway. How about that?"

"Why, that's glorious news, Briny."

"Yes, I'm still trying to call the State Department to confirm it. But Warren thinks I shouldn't transfer, because SubPac's where all the glory is."

"I never mentioned glory," said Warren. "Did I say glory? I don't give a shit about glory — pardon me, Dad — I said the subs are carrying the fight in this ocean, and you've got the chance of a lifetime to take a hand in history."

"What else is glory?" said his father.

Byron said, "What do you think, Dad?"

Here was the sunken rock again, thought Pug. He answered at once, "Take your transfer and go. This Pacific war will be a long one. You'll get back here in time to make all the history you can handle. You've never seen your son and — now, why the wise grin?"

"You surprise me, that's all."

The telephone was ringing and ringing in the house.

"By God," Pug said, "that's something to celebrate, Natalie coming home! When were we last together like this, anyway? Wasn't it at Warren's wedding? Seems to me an anniversary party is overdue here also."

"Right," Warren said. "I remembered the date, but I was flying patrols off Samoa."

The ringing stopped.

"Well, I'm for having a champagne dinner at the Moana Hotel tomorrow night," Pug said. "How about it?"

"Hey! Janice would love that, Dad, getting off this hill, maybe dancing —"

"I'm in," said Byron, getting up and making for the kitchen door. "I buy the wine. Maybe that's my call to Washington."

Janice came running out on the lanai, flushed and wide-eyed. "Dad, it's for you and guess who? Alistair Tudsbury. He's calling from the Moana."

PART TWO

Midway

21

The Road to Midway

(from *World Holocaust* by Armin von Roon)

TRANSLATOR'S NOTE: *The German edition opens with an analysis of the Soviet counterattacks in the winter of 1941–1942. For American readers a better starting point is Roon's fine prologue to the Battle of Midway, which also touches on the Russian picture. The different theatres of war affected each other more than is generally appreciated, and Roon is well aware of the linkages. — V.H.*

―――――――――――

The Japanese Surge

After Pearl Harbor we had to face the United States of America as a full and angry belligerent. We gained a brave but poor comrade-in-arms, a far-off Asiatic island folk with less land surface and natural wealth than just one American state, California; and a fresh enemy in the field wielding the greatest war-making potential on earth. The odds had mounted against us. Yet in our General Staff we could still see in the situation elements of an upset victory.

For the bedrock of war is geography, and geographically our posture remained awesome. With one boot on the Atlantic shore and the other on the snows outside Moscow, the Führer bestrode Europe more completely than Napoleon at his far reach, or Charles V of Spain, or the Antonine emperors. From the Arctic to the Mediterranean, every nation was either our ally, or a friendly neutral, or a conquered subject. Under our submarine onslaught, American Lend-Lease help and Britain's colonial resources were going to the sea bottom. Each month fewer Allied ships were left afloat, for all the feverish work in their shipyards. Churchill himself has confessed in his memoirs, "*The one thing that really frightened me during the war was the U-boat campaign.*"

As for the Soviet Union, its winter counterattack had achieved local gains at bloody costs; but as it petered out, our battle-hardened troops still gripped the rich bulk of Russia west of the Volga. As a nation we had burned our bridges, and had turned with one will to fighting the war. Despite England's air bombings, our war production was still mounting.

And now Japan was debouching on the world battleground with blazing victories!

Adolf Hitler at once embraced these doughty little Asians as comrades. The mystical bunkum of Nordic supremacy was for Nazi fanatics. We Wehrmacht officers despised it, and we observed with relief that Hitler did too. If a people twelve thousand miles away could help us gain world empire, their skins might be yellow, black, or green for all the Führer cared. The Japanese were not disturbed by Nazi theories, because by their Shinto faith they themselves were the "master race." Unlike our General Staff, the Japanese high command seems to have allowed this rubbish to affect their judgment.

Military judgment should never stray far from the basic factors of time, space, and force. The key to an Axis upset victory was *time.* As to space, we had the advantage of operating on strong interior lines in Europe, while our foes were scattered around our rim; but our one effective ally lay on the other side of the globe. The cold arithmetic of force, in the long run, added up much to our disfavor. Yet the Americans at the moment were weak, and their impact in the field was at least a year away. Because of their thirst for revenge on Japan, we could expect a fall in their Lend-Lease aid to the hard-pressed British and Russians. In short, we still had an edge in time in which to snatch a victory, or compel a tolerable peace.

The Spherical Battlefield

In December 1941, with the industrial civilization all around the northern hemisphere leaping into flame, one grand theme loomed through the smoke. *The battleground had become the surface of a sphere.* This posed unprecedented strategic choices. England and Russia had to exert all their strength just to contain Germany, but Japan, the United States, and the Third Reich now had to decide: "Which way to strike?"

Ever since 1918, as is well known, the American armed forces had been planning for simultaneous war against Germany and Japan. Their notorious Rainbow Five doctrine, drawn up years before Adolf Hitler ever marched, provided a ready answer to the question: eastward, or "Germany first," on the Clausewitz rule, *strike for the heart.* Franklin Roosevelt had the willpower and the sense, in the face of the storm in his country against Japan, to hold to this sound military precept. Under his bluff jolly exterior of a Christian humanitarian, President Roosevelt was a devious and frigid conqueror, much more fitted for war on the surface of a sphere than the impulsive, romantic, European-minded Führer.

Japan's problem was more complex. To the north lay rich Siberia, half-denuded of troops for the defense of Moscow; to the west, China, on its knees but still mushily resisting; to the southwest, the treasures of Indo-China, the Indies, and vast India; to the south, New Guinea and white Australia; to the southeast, the valuable island chains athwart the supply line from Australia to the United States. To the east America glowered, distant and enfeebled, yet thrusting into Japan's *Lebensraum* its thorny imperialist outposts of Hawaii and Midway.

Japan's oil stocks were burning down like a candle. Six months earlier, Franklin Roosevelt had embargoed Japan's fuel supply, and this cruel bullying had compelled her to go to war. She lacked steel; she lacked food; she lacked most of the necessities for a long war. A reckoning for her spree of early victories had to come. With her limited strength, in her limited time, Japan had to strike one decisive blow. But — "Which way?"

For the moment Siberia was out. Before attacking the imperialist plutocracies, Japan had prudently signed a neutrality treaty with the Soviet Union. Hitler had fatuously failed to demand, as a quid pro quo for his declaration of war on the United States, that Japan denounce the treaty and come in against Russia. Thus Japan's rear was safe, and we could not combine with her against the Bolsheviks.

Truly Germany's position was bizarre! All the members of a world-girdling alliance were attacking us, while Japan, our strongest ally, stayed at peace with Russia, our strongest foe! Already the German people were paying dearly for the *Führerprinzip,* which placed total reliance on Hitler's politics. Italy had a sizable navy and air force and numerous troops; but with her cardboard dictator and unwarlike people, she was a drain on our fuel and steel, and her long open Mediterranean coastline was our worst weak spot.

These factors all pointed one way. Against the English, all three Axis powers could still combine. Even Italy would be of some use in the Mediterranean and in North Africa. Obviously we had one best course: speedily to unite in smashing the faltering British Empire, while going on the defensive against stronger foes — in our case Russia, in Japan's case America. This could be done, *and this could be done in time.* Like nothing else, the fall of England would signal a turn in world history, multiplying the impact of Japan's triumphs in the Far East.

The Mediterranean Strategy

The way to destroy the British Empire was by closing the Mediterranean and cutting its lifeline to India and Australia.

Admiral Raeder had first suggested the plan in 1940. It called for the seizure of Gibraltar, a landing in Tunis, and a drive across Libya and Egypt to the Suez Canal and the Middle East, where we could count on an open-arms welcome from the Arabs and the Persians. A glance at a map shows the glitter of the concept. Spain, France, and Turkey, the three major soft spots in our hegemony, would drop into our camp. With French North Africa in hand, the Greater German Empire would become a hard pyramid, based in the south on Sahara sands from Dakar through Egypt, Palestine, and Syria to the Persian Gulf; its apex in Norway under the midnight sun; its western slope the Atlantic Ocean and its fortified coasts; its eastern slope (in 1940) the border with the Soviet Union.

Our weak southern ally, Italy, would be safely locked within an Axis lake. The island of Malta, Britain's flinty little bastion in mid-Mediterranean, would starve and fall. The riches of Africa would flow in ships to German Europe. We would gain the oil of the Persian Gulf, and the raw materials of Asia. From the bulge of Dakar we would dominate opulent South America. It was the beckoning of the golden age, the dawn of the German world imperium itself.

As early as 1940, and again for a while in 1941, Hitler had shown serious interest in this farseeing plan. The Arabs of the region loathed their French and British masters, and the Arab Freedom Movement welcomed our propaganda and agents. Hitler had actually explored with Franco the Gibraltar question. But the cautious Spaniard had equivocated, and the Führer's heart had been in the coming assault against Russia, so Barbarossa had temporarily eclipsed the Mediterranean strategy.

But now the hour of this historic idea had surely come. A strong German presence had arisen in Greece, Crete, and Yugoslavia. Rommel was on the march in Africa. The Soviet menace had been rolled back almost one thousand miles, far out of bombing range of the Fatherland. The naval forces of England were stretched paper-thin, and the sinking of the *Prince of Wales* and the *Repulse* had created a seapower vacuum in the Indian Ocean. Australia and New Zealand wanted their troops back from North Africa to defend Singapore and their own homelands. We were, in fact, witnessing the crack-up of the British world system before our eyes.

When the foe is staggering, that is the time to knock him out. At that moment, we had the world's strongest navy allied with the world's strongest army. If Japan would assault the British Empire westward via the Indian Ocean, while we attacked eastward overland along the Mediterranean littoral, would not this antiquated imperium be crushed like a rotten hazel nut in a steel nutcracker?

The Kuroshima Strategy

There emerged in Japanese naval circles at this time a wonderfully conceived secret war plan, the Kuroshima strategy. It showed professional insight and daring worthy of a Manstein. The swift fall of the British plutocracy, and a different end to the Second World War, were real possibilities under this plan.

Captain Kameto Kuroshima was the senior fleet operations officer of the Japanese fleet; an eccentric intellectual of unmilitary habits but flashy strategic genius. It was he who had designed the masterly Pearl Harbor attack. Ever since, the Japanese navy had been studying long-range follow-up plans; thrusts to the east, to the south, to the west. The navy's fighting spirit was high, and Captain Kuroshima's concept of "westward operations" was the counterpart of our Mediterranean strategy. His ideas still stir the soul:

Operations should be timed to synchronize with German offensives in the Near and Middle East.

The objectives would be
   a. destruction of the British fleet
   b. capture of strategic points and elimination of enemy bases
   c. establishment of contact between the Japanese and European Axis forces.

Kuroshima's superior, Rear Admiral Ugaki, put aside his own breathtaking plan for seizing the Hawaiian Islands, and set his entire staff to studying Kuroshima's scheme. At that time a Japanese-German military agreement was actually being negotiated in Berlin. Unhappily, it turned out to be a shallow document. The scant two pages made no provision for joint staff studies or combined strategy. The globe was parted into two "operational zones" by a line through western India. Orotund generalities followed: west of the line Germany and Italy would destroy the enemy, east of the line Japan would do likewise, etc., etc. Empty pleasantries about exchanging information, cooperating in supply, and conducting the "trade war" closed the footling instrument. Discouraged by this diplomatic bungling, the Japanese navy planners gave up "westward operations" as a lost cause.

Alas!

Hitler Berserk

Ironically, Hitler just then had been re-examining Raeder's Mediterranean strategy.

An isolationist American newspaper, the *Chicago Tribune,* had got hold of the top-secret Rainbow Five war program, and had printed the full text under big black anti-Roosevelt headlines.* This strange act of treason was of course a fine intelligence break for us. The document was unmistakably genuine; Hitler referred to it in declaring war on America. It called for a

---

*Roon is in error. The *Tribune* printed excerpts from the top-secret "Victory Program," a resources analysis. — V.H.

gigantic invasion of Europe in 1943 by a newly recruited United States Army of millions, with the British Isles as the main invasion base, and large British supporting forces. Admiral Raeder pounced on this information. Clearly a knockout of England would foil the whole scheme and stun the United States.

Even while Hitler was mulling this over, the Japanese smashed Pearl Harbor. Euphoric days ensued. Hitler heard the navy, the army,* and the Luftwaffe argue in favor of Raeder's plan. He fully grasped the main idea — to crush the weakest foe in speedy joint Axis attacks — and at last he indicated tentative approval, and went off to the eastern front. Our staff speedily worked up Führer Directive Number 39, switching to the defensive in Russia, with the necessary withdrawals and preparations of rear positions; and we forwarded it to him at his headquarters.

Thereupon all the devils came storming out of Hell!

Hitler summoned General von Brauchitsch, the army commander-in-chief, and his chief of staff, General Halder, to a midnight meeting. He screeched insults, called Führer Directive Number 39 "drivelling nonsense," and declared that there would be no withdrawals on the eastern front; that every German soldier would dig in where he stood, there to fight or die. He summarily relieved Brauchitsch and took personal command of the army — a corporal, relieving a field marshal! The new strategy, of course, went glimmering, for the heart of it was the release of forty or fifty divisions from the east to clean up the Mediterranean. No doubt this was why our January agreement with Japan came out so thin and trivial.

What had happened to Hitler's thinking?

Returning to his gloomy snowbound field headquarters, he had had to face some nasty facts. Against staff advice he had driven for Moscow into December. Weather and supply difficulties had halted our cold exhausted troops in exposed positions. Russian counterattacks had begun, and local penetrations were occurring. Most unsettling, for a dictator used to nothing but victories!

Hitler was haunted by the spectre of Napoleon. We all knew that; copies of Caulaincourt's *Memoirs* were actually forbidden at staff headquarters, like pornography in a boys' dormitory. Our shaken Führer undoubtedly pictured the front disintegrating, the Wehrmacht routed, the Germans harried out of the land by the Cossacks. This was mere nightmare. Our broad solid front from Leningrad to the Black Sea was nothing like Napoleon's narrow,

---

*Army advocacy was less than unanimous. My memorandum in support of Raeder survives in my files. Generals on the Russian front tended to scorn the Mediterranean strategy as a "fantasy." It was no more a "fantasy," as it turned out, than the notion of beating the Soviet Union. — A.v.R.

horse-mounted penetration to Moscow on thin supply lines. But the false analogy obsessed Hitler, so he issued his draconic "Hold or Die" order, and took personal command to see that it was obeyed.

Granting that every supreme commander is entitled to his *nuit blanche* fears, there was no need to send to the Japanese such a dispiriting scrap of paper. Had Hitler dispatched even a small military mission to Tokyo — perhaps Admiral Raeder with General Warlimont or myself — it might have sufficed to tip the scales for the Kuroshima strategy. Or if Hitler, after Pearl Harbor, had invited some high Japanese commanders to Berlin to consider joint planning, we might have closed the Mediterranean and forced England to her knees even while the Russian front remained static in the snow, and we tooled up for our summer Caucasus thrust. *But no Japanese liaison officer was ever admitted to Supreme Headquarters.*

"Hold or Die"

Some historians and military analysts still hail the "Hold or Die" order on the eastern front as Hitler's great achievement, a deed of sheer will that "saved" the Wehrmacht. But the truth is that with this order, the Austrian adventurer's star began to wane. The political chief needs detachment in the midst of a war, to keep the big picture in view. Once Hitler took on supreme field command, in which he was merely a headstrong dabbler, he was lost.

The "Hold or Die" order was in point of fact a hysterical military blunder. Defiant toughness in adversity is a sound doctrine; however, elasticity of defense is another. Far outnumbered in Russia, we excelled the Slav hordes in leadership, fighting ability, and maneuvering skill. Hitler's order froze maneuver, paralyzed leadership, and discouraged fighting spirit by commanding meaningless death. Our image of invincibility evaporated. A new German soldier appeared in Russian propaganda: "Winter Fritz," a pathetic helmeted scarecrow with icicles on his pinched nose, "holding and dying" in an untenable post.

And thus Raeder's plan, the last coherent idea for German victory, faded. One can turn one's imagination free for extravagant pictures of what might have been: Japanese battleships and aircraft carriers sailing into the Mediterranean under the Rising Sun flag, through a Suez Canal flying the swastika! The political effect would have shaken the earth. And it was feasible. Our defensive lines in Russia, properly shortened and reinforced under Directive Number 39, would have held toughly and bathed the Russian earth in Bolshevik blood. Japan could easily have shielded her Pacific perimeter against the weak Americans in the spring of 1942, with small holding forces.

But dismiss all this as wistful romance. It remains a sober fact, attested by the Churchill memoirs, that Japan could have taken Madagascar at will, and cut the supply line up the east Africa coast to Egypt. There would then have been no Battle of El Alamein. The starved British African army would have fallen to Rommel in June after his brilliant *coup de main* at Tobruk. Churchill would then probably have fallen too; and the war would have taken a major favorable turn for us.

Instead, the Mediterranean strategy dwindled into a phantom "Great Plan," the global stroke with which Hitler would wind up the war after beating Russia. He liked to talk about it at dinner, and that was what it remained: table talk.

The Forgotten Victory

The great Japanese navy dawdled and dawdled. Not until the end of March was Admiral Nagumo, the conqueror of Pearl Harbor, given a real task. Until then he roamed the blue ocean wastes in minor carrier strikes, "cracking eggshells with a sledgehammer," as the commentator Fuchida says. Japan's fast battleships swung to anchor at their base near Hiroshima as the sands of time trickled away. In March Nagumo finally sailed westward to hit British surface and air forces in the Indian Ocean. The purpose was to support the Japanese army's advance into Burma.

Here at last was a trial run of the Kuroshima strategy, and a huge victory resulted. Nagumo's dive-bombers sank an aircraft carrier, two heavy cruisers, and a destroyer. He demolished two bases in Ceylon, and much merchant shipping. His Zeroes wrought such havoc among the defending Swordfish, Hurricanes, and Spitfires that Winston Churchill in his memoirs confesses the Royal Air Force was never so outfought over Europe. The surviving British battleships fled to British East Africa. British seapower, after two centuries of hegemony, vanished from the Indian Ocean. De facto, it became a Japanese lake. Western historians pass over this stupendous event, except for Churchill, who candidly records his own real shock and fear at the time.

Thus the Kuroshima concept was vindicated. Madagascar, the African coast, the Suez Canal, the Persian Gulf, the Mediterranean itself, lay open to the advance of the Japanese fleet. But by now it was too late. Nagumo was recalled for other operations. The Axis edge in time had run out unused.

The Doolittle Raid

A brave if harebrained Yankee propaganda action at this time, the notorious Doolittle terror raid against Tokyo, stung Imperial Headquarters into making at last the long-deferred decision, "Which way?" In near-panic, they chose the worst possible course.

Underestimating the Americans is a mistake their enemies often make.

They seem frivolous and easygoing; in fact they are highly mechanically minded, and capable of considerable ferocity once aroused. The Yanks were too weak in the Pacific just then for anything but light carrier raids. However, they concocted this savage little stunt, the launching of a few Army Air Force bombers against Tokyo from the decks of a carrier. Since Japanese patrols covered only carrier plane ranges, this achieved total surprise. It had no military effect beyond random murder of civilians, a practice the Americans kept up through Dresden and Hiroshima. The aim was to inspirit the home folks and to jolt the foe.

Technically it was no easy feat. But the Americans modified the bombers and altered carrier routine in their usual clever fashion. A group of volunteer pilots under the able army flier Doolittle made the sneak attack. Out of a clear sky, bombs exploded over Tokyo. America rejoiced, the world was astounded, and Japan was jarred to its foundations. After only four months of war the sacred emperor had been exposed to Yankee bombs!

Yamamoto, the daring supreme admiral who had made the Pearl Harbor decision, now determined that this must not happen again; that the impudent Americans must be taught a lesson, and pushed forever out of carrier range. The answer to "which way" thus came, clear and fatal: *"Eastward!"* Eastward, where there was nothing material to be gained; but eastward, where the American fleet might be forced to come out and be annihilated. And Japan would seize an enemy outpost, from which she could ward off all future Doolittle outrages. So Nagumo was recalled and the die was cast. *Eastward!*

In this way, with such misguided leadership, we and the Japanese turned our backs on each other, sparing the British Empire. We each rode off in the wrong direction on the spherical battlefield. The Wehrmacht set forth on the long march to Stalingrad, and the Japanese navy sailed for Midway.

TRANSLATOR'S NOTE: *This analysis is a study topic at the Naval War College. I have lectured on it. As an army officer, Roon tends to minimize the logistical problems of sea supply lines spanning the whole Indian Ocean, and the flanking threat by sea and air from India. Still, the best course for the Axis in the spring of 1942 may well have been to hold against us and Russia, and hit the British hard from both sides. Losses to U-boats were reaching a peak. A Japanese drive toward Suez, combined with Rommel's advances in North Africa, might have had grim consequences for the Churchill government. If Churchill had fallen, it could have been a long step to a separate peace.*

But Roon throughout ignores the fact that combined operations are not congenial to totalitarian governments. Typically they are founded by extremists and fanatics, who come to power through conspiracy and crime. Once power is seized and the conspiracy becomes a government, these traits persist. As thieves tend to fall out, so totalitarians make poor allies. — V.H.

*   *   *

22

Brigadier General Lacouture had been misinformed about Natalie's whereabouts.

A black cloudburst was drenching Siena at midday. In a bad mood, Jastrow was writing at his study desk by lamplight, beside a streaming window. Rainy weather made his shoulders ache; it stiffened his old fingers; and the words always flowed better when he worked out in the sunshine. Natalie's quiet tap signalled, *"Minor matter; if you're busy, ignore."*

"Yes? Come in."

The passage he was writing demanded a long further look at Martin Luther's views on celibacy. Feeling the weariness of his years and the endlessness of his task, Jastrow welcomed the break. In the shadows cast by the lamplight, her bony face looked pale and sad. She was still not over the blow of their detainment, he thought.

"Aaron, have you ever met Mosé Sacerdote?"

"That Jew who owns the cinema, and half of the real estate on the Banchi di Sopra?" Pettishly he pulled off his glasses. "I may have. I know who he is."

"He's on the telephone. He says you've met at the archbishop's palace."

"What does he want?" Jastrow waved the glasses in annoyance. "If he's the man I remember, he is a walleyed and very glum old gent."

"He'd like you to autograph his copy of *A Jew's Jesus.*"

"What? After I've been here eleven years, he asks that?"

"Shall I say you're busy?"

With a slow calculating little grin, Jastrow breathed on his glasses and polished them. " 'Sacerdote,' you know, means *Cohen* in Italian. 'Priest.' We'd best find out what Mr. Moses Cohen actually wants. Let him come after my nap."

The storm had passed, the sun shone, and raindrops sparkled on the terrace flowers when an ancient car wheezed up to the gate. Natalie picked her way around puddles to greet the pudgy elderly man in black. Jastrow, drinking tea in a lounge chair, waved Sacerdote to a bench beside him.

"Well, well. The Italian edition, *Il Gesù d'un Ebreo,*" Jastrow said, as the old man handed him a plain blue-bound volume, one of two he carried. Donning glasses, Jastrow turned the pages of cheap coarse paper. "I no longer have a copy myself. Isn't this rather a collector's item? The printing was only a thousand or so, back in 1934."

"Oh, yes. Very scarce. Very precious. — Ah, thank you, no milk and no sugar." Natalie was pouring tea at a small portable table. Sacerdote spoke Italian with a pure Tuscan accent, mellifluous and clear. "A prize possession, Dr. Jastrow. A fine book. Your discussion of the Last Supper, for instance, carries such impact for our young people! They see *Last Suppers* on church walls, and they attend Passover seders — not always willingly — but they don't connect the two until you do it for them. Your proof that the Romans executed Jesus as a political radical, and that the Jewish common people really loved him, is most important. If only that were better understood! Our mutual friend the archbishop once mentioned that very passage to me."

Jastrow inclined his head, smiling. He loved praise, however trivial, and these days got little of it. "And the other book?"

Sacerdote extended to Jastrow a scuffed little volume. "Another scarce item. I have been spending much time on it lately."

"Why, I didn't know anything like this existed." He held it out for Natalie to see. "*La Lingua Ebraica Contemporanea.* Imagine!"

"The Zionist organization in Milan brought it out long ago. A small group, but well funded." Sacerdote dropped his voice. "Our family may go to Palestine."

Natalie stopped slicing cake and cleared her throat. "How on earth will you get there?"

"My son-in-law is arranging that. I believe you know him. Doctor Bernardo Castelnuovo, he treats your baby."

"Of course. He's *your* son-in-law?"

With a weary gold-toothed smile at the surprised note, Sacerdote nodded.

"He's Jewish, then?"

"Nowadays one doesn't flaunt it, Mrs. Henry."

"Well, I'm amazed. I had no idea."

Jastrow handed back the primer, unscrewed the cap of his pen, and started to write on the flyleaf of *Il Gesù d'un Ebreo*. "Don't you feel secure here? You're contemplating a very risky journey. We know that from experience."

"You refer to your time aboard the boat *Izmir?* My son-in-law and I partly financed the sailing of the *Izmir.*" Natalie and Jastrow exchanged astonished glances. "This evening is the Sabbath, Dr. Jastrow. Won't you and your niece come and dine with us? Bernardo will be there. How long since you've had a real Sabbath meal?"

"About forty years. You're very kind, but I imagine our cook has already started dinner, so —"

Natalie spoke up curtly. "I'd like to go."

Aaron said, "And Louis?"

"Oh, you must bring the infant!" Sacerdote said. "My granddaughter Miriam will adore him."

Jastrow completed his scrawl on the flyleaf. "Well, then, we will come. Thank you."

Sacerdote clasped the book. "Now we have a family treasure."

Natalie ran a hand over her hair, pulled straight back in a bun. "What happened to the *Izmir?* What happened to Avram Rabinovitz, do you know? Is he alive?"

"Bernardo will tell you everything."

The Sacerdotes and the Castelnuovos lived in the modern part of Siena outside the ancient walls, atop an ugly stucco apartment house which Mosé Sacerdote owned, and which he called a "palazzo." The lift was not working, and they had to climb five flights of musty stairs. Manipulating several keys and locks, he let them into a roomy apartment, full of appetizing dinner fragrances, highly polished heavy furniture, whole walls of books, and elegant silver and china in massive breakfronts.

Dr. Castelnuovo met them in a hallway. Natalie had never thought much of him; a small-town doctor, but the best Siena could offer, and his gallant office manners had rather charmed her. His heavy black hair, liquid brown eyes, and dark long face gave him the wholly Tuscan look one saw in old Siena paintings. It had never crossed Natalie's mind that this man might be a Jew.

In the dining room the doctor presented them to his wife and mother-in-law, who also looked quite Italian: both stout, both dressed in black silk, with heavy-lidded eyes, large chins, and similar sweet unworldly smiles. The mother was gray and unpainted; the daughter had brown hair and wore a touch of lipstick. In sunset light that reddened the tall windows, they were preparing to light Sabbath candles on a lavishly set table. As they donned black lace caps, a sallow little girl in brown velvet ran lightly into the room. Halting by her mother's skirt, she smiled at the baby on Natalie's arm. The candles flared up in four ornate silver candlesticks. The two women covered their eyes and murmured blessings. The girl dropped in a chair, holding out her arms and piping in lucid Italian, "I love him. Let me have him."

Natalie put the infant in Miriam's lap. The thin pale arms closed around the baby in a comically competent way. Louis looked her over and nestled against her, hanging on her neck.

Sacerdote spoke hesitantly. "Would you be interested, Dr. Jastrow, to come to the synagogue with us?"

"Ah, yes. The archbishop did tell me, years ago, that a synagogue did exist, somewhere down near the Piazza del Campo." Jastrow sounded surprised and amused. "Is it architecturally interesting?"

"It's just an old synagogue," Castelnuovo said irritably. "We're not very religious. Father is the president. It's never easy to assemble ten men, so I go. One sometimes hears news there."

"Will you forgive me if I don't go?" Jastrow said, smiling. "It would so startle the Almighty, it might ruin His Sabbath. I shall enjoy looking at your library instead."

While Natalie and the doctor's wife fed the children in the kitchen, Anna Castelnuovo chattered away woman-to-woman. She wasn't a believer at all, she cheerily confessed, but kept up the rituals to please her parents. Her husband's Zionism left her just as cold. Her passion was reading novels, especially by Americans. Having an American author in the house, even though he wasn't a novelist, greatly thrilled her. At Natalie's tale of her marriage to a submarine officer, the doctor's wife was enchanted. "Why, it's like a novel," she said. "A novel by Ernest Hemingway. Romantic." They fell to laughing as Miriam took over the feeding of Louis, both children being ridiculously solemn about it. Then they put the girl and the baby in Miriam's toy-crammed room. "She'll take better care of him than any governess," said Anna. "I hear Father and Bernardo. Come to dinner."

Sacerdote and Dr. Castelnuovo looked gloomy on their return. The older man put on a worn white skullcap to make a blessing over wine, then removed it. Natalie gathered from murmurs among the family that somebody was late. "Well, we will eat," Sacerdote said. "Let us sit down." One place was vacant.

The food was neither Italian nor in the kosher style Natalie half-expected. There was a spicy fish dish, a fruit soup, a chicken dish, saffron-flavored rice, and eggplants cooked with meat. Conversation lagged. Halfway through the meal a son named Arnoldo came in; lean, short, twenty or so, his grimy sweater, long tousled hair, and open shirt in jarring contrast to the family's formality. He ate silently and voraciously. Once he arrived the halting talk died. Sacerdote donned his skullcap to lead a little Hebrew song in which the others joined, but not Arnoldo.

Natalie began to regret that she had pushed Aaron to accept this dinner. He was getting through it by emptying his wineglass as fast as the doctor's wife filled it. Uncomfortable looks kept passing among the family, and a vague dread seemed to compound the gloom. Natalie was dying to ask the doctor about Rabinovitz and the *Izmir*, but his face wore a forbidding aspect that stopped her.

Jewish ceremonies depressed Natalie anyway, and the Sabbath candles still burning on the table were a special sore point. Watching Miriam tonight, she had felt an old deep forgotten ache. Standing beside her mother in the same way twenty years ago, she had asked why mama was lighting candles in the daytime. The reply, that making fire was forbidden after sunset on the Sabbath, had seemed perfectly reasonable, since life to a little girl was full of arbitrary prohibitions. But then after the heavy Friday night dinner, her father had struck a flaring wooden match to his long cigar. She had said in all innocence, "Papa, that's not allowed after sunset." A glance of embarrassment and amusement had passed between her parents. She did not remember what her father had replied as he went on smoking; but the glance she could never forget, for in an instant it had destroyed the Jewish religion for her. Her rowdiness at Sunday school had dated from that night, and soon, though her father was a temple officer, the parents had been unable to make her attend.

Straightening his stained sweater, Arnoldo got up while the others were still eating. In rapid Italian, with a winning white-toothed smile, he said to Jastrow, "Sorry I must leave. I read your book, sir. Quite a book."

His mother said sadly, "On a Sabbath when we have visitors, Arnoldo, can't you stay awhile?"

The smiling face turned sullen. A girl's name whipped out of him in a hostile hiss, *"Francesca* is waiting for me. Ciao."

He left behind a heavy silence. Dr. Castelnuovo broke it by turning to Jastrow and Natalie. "Well! Now I have a good report for you. The boat *Izmir* reached Palestine, and the British didn't catch the passengers as they went ashore."

"Ah, my God!" Natalie exclaimed, in a surge of glad relief. "You're sure?"

"I'm in touch with Avram Rabinovitz. There were bad moments, but on the whole it was a success."

Jastrow put a small damp hand on Natalie's. "Great news!"

"That trip cost us a lot of money." Sacerdote was beaming. "It's satisfying when the results are good. That doesn't always happen."

Natalie said to the doctor, "But the papers and radio said the ship disappeared. I had nightmares that it was the *Struma* all over again."

Castelnuovo bitterly grimaced. "Yes, you do hear about the disasters. The world press is not unsympathetic to Jews, once they're destroyed. It's best to keep the successes quiet."

"And Rabinovitz? What about him?"

"He made his way back to Marseilles. That's his base. He's there now."

"What's your connection with him? May I know?"

Castelnuovo shrugged. "Why not? My father-in-law used to rent his films from that man Herbert Rose who went on the boat. When Rabinovitz ran short of money in Naples — what with delays, and repairs — Rose suggested that we might help him. Avram came up here by train. We gave him a lot of money."

"But one must be careful about such things," Sacerdote put in unhappily. "So incredibly careful! Our position here is delicate, *very* delicate."

The doctor said, "Well, that's it. Since then he and I have stayed in touch. He's a good man to know."

Castelnuovo talked of the growing danger to Italian Jews. Jews had no future anywhere in Europe, he said. He had decided that long ago, while going to medical school in Siena. That tough uphill fight had made him a Zionist. All of Europe was poisoned by nationalist hatred for the Jews; the Dreyfus case in ultraliberal France had been the warning sign, long ago. Under Mussolini's anti-Semitic laws, he himself could practice medicine only because the Siena health authorities had declared him essential. His father-in-law was retaining control of his property through tenuous legal fictions, which put him at the mercy of Christian associates. That very evening in the synagogue they had heard that the Fascist regime was preparing concentration camps for Italian Jews, such as already existed for Jewish aliens. The roundup squads would strike on Yom Kippur, four months hence, when the Jews could be caught in their synagogues. Once collected, they would be handed over to the Germans for shipping eastward, where terrible massacres were taking place.

Sacerdote broke in to insist the report was panicky nonsense. The man who had brought it was a rumormonger with no high connections. The stories of secret massacres were all foolishness. The archbishop himself had assured Sacerdote that the Vatican's intelligence net was the best in Europe; and that if the stories had any truth to them, the Pope would have long since denounced Nazi Germany and excommunicated Hitler.

"I've given fortunes to the archbishop's projects." Sacerdote turned moist and worried dark eyes to Jastrow. "I'm the chairman of the orphanage, his pride and joy. He would not lead me astray. You know him. Don't you agree?"

"His Excellency is an Italian gentleman, and a good soul." Jastrow again emptied his glass. He was very red in the face, but he spoke clearly. "I do agree. Even with a madman as their leader — for it has become my settled view that Hitler is unbalanced — the advanced culture of the Germans, their passion for order, and their legal scrupulosity preclude the truth of these rumors. The Nazis are indeed brutal open anti-Semites, and on such a base of fact, erecting gruesome fantasies becomes all too simple."

"Dr. Jastrow," said Castelnuovo, "what about Lidice? The work of an advanced culture?"

"This fellow Heydrich was a leader of the SS. Reprisal is commonplace in war," Jastrow answered, in a tone of cool academic riposte. "Don't ask me to defend the calculated military frightfulness of the Boche. He doesn't want it defended. He proclaims it. He has proclaimed with great fanfare the annihilation of that poor Czech village."

Castelnuovo came out with a burst of dry quick Italian. The archbishop didn't know all the Pope knew. The Pope had his reasons to keep silent, mainly the protection of the Church's property and influence in German-held lands; also, the old Christian dogma that the Jews must suffer down through history, to prove they had guessed wrong on Christ, and must one day acknowledge him. Miriam could not live much longer within reach of German claws; he and his wife had decided that. He was already communicating with Rabinovitz about ways and means of getting out.

Here again the old man struck in. The decision to leave would be a terrible one for himself and his wife. Siena was their home. Italian was their language. What was worse, Arnoldo was determined to remain; he was in love with a Sienese girl. The family would be torn apart, and the property gathered in a lifetime would be lost.

Louis and Miriam were laughing in a distant room. "Why, it's incredible that that child's still awake," Natalie said. "He's having the time of his life, but I must get him home and to bed."

"Mrs. Henry, why didn't you leave with the other Americans?" The doctor spoke with abrupt sharpness. "Rabinovitz is very puzzled and concerned. He has asked about you repeatedly."

She looked at her uncle, feeling color come into her cheeks. "We've been temporarily detained."

"But why?"

Jastrow answered, "Again, reprisal. Three German agents in Brazil, posing as Italian journalists, were arrested, and so —"

"German agents in Brazil?" Castelnuovo interrupted, wrinkling his forehead. "What has that got to do with you? You're Americans."

His wife said, "That makes no sense."

"None whatever," declared Jastrow. "Our State Department is pressing the Italian government through Bern to send us to Switzerland at once. And they're working on the release of those agents in Brazil, in case this pressure fails. I am not concerned."

"I am," said Natalie.

Jastrow said lightly, "My niece finds it hard to accept that our government has one or two other things on its mind besides our release. As, for instance, that it seems to be losing the war on all fronts, at the moment. But we have other protection. Protection of an unusual nature." He gave Natalie a teasing inebriated smile. "What do you say, my dear? Shall we confide in our pleasant new friends?"

"As you please, Aaron." Natalie pushed back her chair. His patronizing of these well-to-do but miserable people was annoying her. "The children are strangely quiet, suddenly. I'll have a look at Louis."

She found him asleep on Miriam's bed in his favorite slumber pose: face down, knees drawn up, rump in the air, arms sprawled. He looked very uncomfortable. Often she had straightened him out, only to watch him return to the pose, still fast asleep, as though he were a rubber baby rebounding to his manufactured shape. Miriam sat beside him, hands folded in her lap, ankles crossed, swinging both feet.

"How long has he been sleeping, dear?"

"Just a few minutes. Shall I cover him?"

"No, I'll take him home soon."

"If only he could stay!"

"Well, come to our house tomorrow and play with him."

"Oh, may I?" The little girl softly clapped her hands. "Will you please tell my mama that?"

"Of course. You should have a baby brother. I hope you will, one day."

"I did. He died," said the girl in a calm way that chilled Natalie.

She returned to the dinner table. Aaron was describing Werner Beck's intervention to quash the summons from the secret police, at the time when alien Jews had been interned. "We've been living in tranquillity ever since," Jastrow said. "Werner couldn't be more thoughtful and protective. He even brings us mail from home, illegally transmitted. Imagine! A high-placed German Foreign Service officer, keeping two Jews from being interned by the Fascists, because I once helped an earnest young history student with his doctoral thesis. Bread cast upon the waters!"

The old lady spoke up. "Then why doesn't he help you, Dr. Jastrow, with all this nonsense about Brazil?"

"He has, he has. He's been burning up the wires to Berlin. He assures us that this outrage will be corrected, that our release via Switzerland is only a matter of time."

"Do you believe that?" Castelnuovo addressed Natalie.

She gnawed her lower lip. "Well, we know that a diplomatic fuss is going on, and that he's taking an interest. I have a friend in the American legation at Bern who's written me as much."

"My guess would be," said the doctor, "that this Dr. Beck is preventing you from leaving Italy."

"How preposterous!" exclaimed Jastrow.

But Castelnuovo's words stirred a horrible dark sickness in Natalie. "Why? What would there be in it for him?"

"You ask the right question. It's to his advantage to have the famous Dr. Jastrow trapped in Italy and dependent on him. In what way, you will find out."

"You are quite a cynic," Jastrow said, beginning to bristle.

"About my Jewish identity, at this time, and in this place, I believe only the worst possibilities. It's not cynicism, it's common sense. Now I have a message for both of you from Avram Rabinovitz," the doctor said to Natalie. "He says, 'Get out, while you can.' "

"But how?" she almost shrilled at Castelnuovo. "Don't you think I want to get out?"

Jastrow looked at his watch, and said stiffly to the Sacerdotes, "You've taken us into the bosom of your family. I warmly thank you. We must go. Good-night."

23

Pug Henry stood in the reception line with his sons, Janice, and Carter Aster at a big lawn party on the grounds of the governor's mansion. Amid the palms, the flamboyant tropical shrubbery, the very noisy swanky crowd, the guest of honor visibly stood out. Alistair Tudsbury's ordeal in an open boat on the high seas had not slimmed him; or if it had, he had managed to eat himself back into shape with a net gain. He wore a yellow silk suit with a bright yellow tie; a yellow lei ringed his neck, and he leaned on a yellow malacca cane; and in the yellow sunshine of a late Hawaiian afternoon, he was altogether a rather blindingly buttery sight. A black patch covered his left eye.

When Pug came up, Tudsbury pulled him into a bear hug. "Awrr-hawrr! *Pug Henry,* by God! Late of Berlin, London, and Moscow! By God, Pug, how are you!"

Stepping forward to embrace Pug, he disclosed his daughter, standing there in a gray sheath dress. Until that moment Pug wasn't sure she was at the party, though the papers said she had arrived with Tudsbury. The correspondent, out of coyness or mischief, had not mentioned her over the telephone. Engulfed in the hug, losing sight of her in a perfumed crush of yellow flowers, Victor Henry thought how small she was, and how white those bare slender arms were; had she had no sun in all her months in the tropics? She wore her light brown hair as before, unfashionably piled up on her head.

"Well, Yank," boomed Tudsbury hotly and moistly in his ear, "you're in it with us now, aren't you? Up to your necks! In to the death!" He released Pug. "Awr-hawrr-hawr! And none too soon, none too soon, by God. Well! You do remember Pam, don't you? Or had you quite forgotten her?"

"Hello there." The voice was low, the clasp of her hand dry and brief. Her pale face was almost as calm, distant, and unrecognizing as it had been in their first meeting on the *Bremen.* But the illusion that she was tiny had been created by the eclipsing mass of her father. Pamela's green-gray eyes were almost level with his, and her bosom under the thin gray dress was fuller than he remembered.

Tudsbury said, "Governor, this is Captain Victor Henry of the *Northampton.* The confidant, as I've told you, of presidents and prime ministers."

The florid introduction was wasted on the governor, a wrinkled weary-look-ing man in seersucker, who gave Pug an empty smile suited to a mere cruiser captain. Tudsbury bellowed over the party noise, "What say, Pug, *three* stalwart sons, eh? I thought I remembered two. And hello, here's the senator's pretty daughter."

When Pug introduced Lieutenant Commander Aster the governor's bored eyes came alive. "Ah, the captain of the *Devilfish?* Really! Well, now, I've heard of *you.* Giving the Japs back some of their own, aren't you, skip-per? Well done!"

"Thank you, Governor." A modest bob of the head.

Tudsbury's good eye flashed alertly. "Submarine hero, eh? Let's have a chat later."

Aster answered with a frigid grin.

Under a palm tree far down the garden, Spruance was standing beside Admiral Nimitz, who had his hands folded before him. Spruance's were on the back of his hips, as though he did not know where else to put his hands. Both admirals wore pained squints. Spruance beckoned to Pug. He ap-proached Cincpac with some trepidation, for he had never met Nimitz.

"Sir, this is Captain Henry."

"Well! We'll be seeing you at the planning conference tonight, Cap-tain."

Dolphins were pinned over Nimitz's breast pocket and its bright layers of campaign ribbons. White close-clipped hair, ruddy skin, composed blue eyes, a square jaw, a flat waistline; here was a healthy hardy old submariner with a gentle look, yet a sufficient air of supreme command. Nimitz inclined his head toward the receiving line. "You're a friend of this newspaperman, I'm told."

"We became acquainted, Admiral, when I was serving in Europe."

"I was advised to show my face here because the Army was turning out in force." Nimitz's gesture took in the khaki uniforms clustering around Gen-eral Richardson, the military governor, and his hand swept out at the jocund mob of Hawaiian high society filling the lawn. "Is the man worth all this?"

"He has a world audience, sir."

"Public Information also wants me to talk to him tomorrow." The blue eyes probed. The statement was a question. The weight of the coming battle was already on Nimitz, Pug reflected. The request made him think of the little puff for Madeline in *Variety.*

"Admiral, if you have the time for any correspondent, he's a fine one."

Nimitz made a wry face. "Time is a problem. But they keep telling me we've got to keep up public morale back home."

"A good way to do that, Admiral, is with a victory."

Nimitz dismissed him with a flash of the eyes and a nod. A few minutes later, Pug saw the admirals thread through the crowd and slip out of the garden. Tudsbury now bulked yellow and huge at the tent bar beside General Richardson, in a ring of brightly dressed eagerly crowding women.

Pug stood alone, not drinking. To avoid being jostled by the throng of guests he backed up to the palm tree, and unconsciously put his knuckles to his hips as Spruance had, looking around with much the same pained squint. Pamela Tudsbury, drinking with Janice, his sons, and Aster, was telling a story; an anecdote of Singapore, Pug guessed, from the close attention of the others. He was glad to see Byron enjoying himself, for he had seemed sunk in gloom this afternoon, after a second unsatisfactory talk in two days with some evasive nobody in the State Department, who would not confirm or deny that Natalie was on her way home. As for Pamela, hungry though Pug was to talk to her, he would not intrude on that young group. Half a year had gone by since their parting in Moscow. A few more minutes didn't matter. How youthful she looked, after all! Her age was thirty-one, so she was older than his boys. But not by much; not by much.

Heavy on Pug's mind was awareness of the Japanese fleet plowing the high seas toward Midway. A ludicrous trifle by comparison, but weighing just as much on his spirit, was Pamela Tudsbury's distant greeting to him. He had not expected an affectionate outburst, but even in a receiving line a woman could signal feeling with a mouth twitch, a hand pressure, a glance. Nothing! At first glance Pam had looked less attractive than he had expected; a bit ordinary, even drab, and rather run-down. But now, a few yards away, animated in talk with young people, she was recovering the iridescent aura she had worn in memory and in fantasy; and he felt the same frustration that had ached in him at sea when daydreaming about her, though there she stood, solid and alive.

This whole twittery festive gathering, to his dour view, seemed a game of dressed-up children. There came vividly to his mind the Waterloo eve scene, recounted in poems, novels, and movies, of the grand ball in Brussels; beautiful women, handsome officers, music, wine, the Duke of Wellington himself dancing; and then the distant mutter of the French artillery, and the dissolution of the gaiety in panic, scurry, tears, farewells, and hasty arming. This noisy fancy crush in the garden of Washington Place might lack the rich glitter of Napoleonic times, but the oncoming battle muttered in Victor Henry's imagination like Waterloo. Its consequences, he thought, could be more cataclysmic for the side that lost.

"What, what, Pug Henry?" Alistair Tudsbury left the bar and came limping toward him. "Standing aside and alone, with the worries of the world on your manly phiz?"

"Hi there. Enjoying your party?"

"Oh, one sometimes can't say no." Tudsbury made a grotesque grimace.

"Bloody waste of an afternoon. Is that anniversary dinner still laid on for to-night?"

"It's laid on."

"Smashing."

"What about your eye, Talky?"

"Trifling irritation. Having it checked in your naval hospital tomorrow after I interview Nimitz."

"Sure you'll see him?"

"Why, Pug, the man came to this silly do, didn't he? These chaps are never too busy for me. They're always panting to get their ducks in a row for the public and for history. Why, Air Marshal Dowding talked to me at the height of Göring's September seventh raid! If I'd been at Waterloo, Napoleon would have talked to me on horseback while fleeing the field, I assure you. No matter how badly his piles were hurting him! Ah, hawr, hawr!"

Pug gestured at the jolly crowd all around them. "I've been thinking about Napoleon. About that ball in Brussels before the battle."

"Ah yes. '*There was a sound of revelry by night* —' But at the moment, at least, one doesn't hear the thunder of approaching cannon." The eye blinked and stared. "Or does one?"

"Not that I know of."

"Now come on, Pug!" A crafty tough look hardened the fat face. "Something's brewing on this island. Something damned tremendous. Tell me what you know."

"Can't help you."

"You do have the most damnably worried look."

A blonde girl came simpering up to Tudsbury in a cloud of white organdy, with an autograph book and a pen projecting in little pink hands from the cloud. "Would you, Mr. Tudsbury?" she tinkled. Snorting, he scrawled his signature. The cloud wafted away in giggles.

"I'll tell you what this reminds *me* of," growled Tudsbury. "*Pahits* and dances I attended in Singapore, while those little yellow devils were marching or bicycling down the peninsula. With all those smashed behemoths out there in your harbor, and a whole American army in the Philippines captured by the yellow men, who are also swarming over Southeast Asia and the Indies, sweeping up the wherewithal to wage war for a century; with Singapore gone, with the Empire shattered, with Australia naked as a bride for her deflowering, with the Japanese fleet four or five times as strong as anything you've got left in the Pacific — with all that, one would expect in Hawaii, shall we say a concerned air, a hint of urgency, a trace of resolve such as we showed in Old Blighty during the blitz? But the tropics unfit the white man for modern war." Tudsbury flipped the lei with a fat paw. "The natives seem so simple to handle, one gets a false sense of invincibility.

There's no such delusion in Australia. They are hellishly alarmed. They know that the Doolittle raid was a fine brave Yank stunt, but not a mosquito bite on Japan's war capacity. Every third person at this party has asked me about the Doolittle raid, popping buttons with pride. Why, man, the RAF's sending hundreds of bombers over Germany several times a month — in one night we sent a thousand bombers over Cologne — and we haven't dented the enemy's will yet. Perhaps my nerves are shot, but what I see about me here is more or less a Singapore with Yank accents and pineapples."

"Sounds like your next broadcast, Talky."

"It is, more or less. These people need waking up. I didn't like scuttling out of a falling British bastion under the artillery fire of Asians. Nor will they. I liked getting torpedoed by them even less. And I would gladly have skipped a week in a whaleboat on the open water, under an equatorial sun."

"If you get to talk to Nimitz you'll be reassured."

Pamela strolled by on Carter Aster's arm, both talking at a great rate. "How do you think my Pam looks?"

"Sort of tired."

"She's had a rotten time. We became separated when they sent off a drove of women in an old Greek tub bound for Java. Pam came down with dysentery on board, had to be hospitalized in Java, and then by God the Japs started landing there. So it was march aboard ship again when she could scarcely walk. Pam's resilient, and she's snapping back. I say, is that submarine hero coming to your dinner?"

"He hasn't been asked."

"Would you ask him, old cock? I do so want a word with him. Well, I must drivel a bit more with General Richardson. Awful stick, isn't he?"

As Tudsbury stumped off, Pug mulishly decided that he wouldn't invite Aster. He didn't like the *Devilfish* captain. Under his fawning politeness a hard ego jutted, with a hint of condescension to an older man commanding a treaty cruiser. The Navy tended to pound touchiness out of a man, and Pug Henry was used to letting the other fellow have his plaudits. But the snub from the governor of Hawaii in Pamela's presence, in favor of the younger officer, had nettled him.

Byron came weaving up, grasping a tall planter's punch. "Hi, old Dad! Get you a drink?" His eyes were sparkling and red, his grin foolish. "Great party, hey? What'll you drink, Dad?"

With a glance from the glass to his son's face, Pug said, "What's left?"

Byron laughed. "Dad, you can't put me down, not this afternoon. I'm feeling too damn good. I haven't felt so good in a year. Say, Dad, let's ask Lady Aster to the dinner, okay? He's peculiar, but in submarines you have to be somewhat goofy. He's a great skipper."

Through a gap in the crowd, Victor Henry could see Pamela and Aster at the bar, still in merry converse. All right, Pug thought. Suppose this able officer, back from a brilliant war patrol, likes Pam and she likes him? What's objectionable in that? What claim have I on her, and how would I propose to execute a claim if I had one?

"Sure, ask him, by all means. If you find yourself a nice girl, ask her."

"I've got one."

"Fine! And on second thought, bring me a rum collins with some hair on its chest."

"*Now* you're talking." Byron gave his father a one-armed hug, and startled Victor Henry to his bones by muttering indistinctly, "I love you," or "God love you." The father wasn't sure which.

Off Byron lurched toward the long bar under the striped tent, where Janice was talking to an Army general with thick white hair. Pug saw her wave excitedly to Byron. Beside her Pamela and Aster were laughing into each other's eyes. Victor Henry smiled at his own ridiculous pain; then he realized that the white-haired Army man was Senator Lacouture. He strode to the bar. "Hello there, General! Welcome, and congratulations."

"Why thanks, Pug." The brigadier general's uniform was bandbox new, the brass buttons too bright. The senator's plethoric face radiated good humor. "Yes, I'm still getting used to it! Why, General Richardson's driver met me at the airport, and zoom! — whisked me straight to this party. I think I'm going to like the Army, ha ha!"

Byron said to his father in a flat frigid sober voice, "She's not on that boat."

"What!"

"They detained her and Jastrow. She's still in Siena. All the other Americans are coming home but not her."

"Yes, but don't worry, young man," said Lacouture cheerily. "Somebody at State slipped up, not to notify you by cable. Sorry I had the wrong information. It's a temporary snag, so State assured me, a matter of weeks at most, some problem involving Italian journalists in Brazil."

"Senator, two very beautiful ladies here are absolutely dying to meet you," General Richardson called.

Lacouture hurried away.

"One rum collins with hair on its chest," said Byron calmly, his face ashen. "Coming up, Dad."

"Byron —"

Byron's back was to him, pushing through the brown Army crowd at the bar.

The main dining room of the Moana Hotel was a kaleidoscopic whirl of brass-buttoned uniforms and colored frocks, crowded to the walls and tumultuous with talk and brassy jazz. Young officers, mostly from the SubPac rest center in the nearby Royal Hawaiian Hotel, were spinning excited girls around and around in the Lindy Hop. The band's singer, in a strapless red dress that exposed billowy bosoms, was wriggling, jiggling, and howling "*and the boogie-woogie washerwoman washes away*" to an audience packed at tables around the dance floor; at which tables military uniforms predominated, and pretty laughing girls, bejewelled, bepainted, and dressed in splendid half-nude evening finery. Elderly civilians at a few tables, by their look wealthy and retired, were gazing wistfully at all this amorous wartime dazzlement, lit by a sinking sun through open windows. Though it was still day, the restaurant fizzed like a ballroom at midnight because the revelry, off to an early start, had to end at ten. The ten o'clock curfew had teeth.

Pug had reserved a large table by the dance floor. Carter Aster sat there alone. As Pug came into the room with the Tudsburys, the submariner jumped to his feet.

"Where's Byron?" Pug asked.

"Sir, I thought he must be with you. I couldn't find hide nor hair of him at the party." Aster pulled out a chair for Pamela with a gallant flourish. "I even went looking inside the governor's mansion. I figured he must have caught a ride with you."

"He didn't."

Dancing past them, Warren called, "Where's Briny, Dad?"

Pug turned up his hands.

"*And the boogie-woogie washerwoman washes away . . .*" Warren was blocked from sight by jostling dancers. Aster and Pamela fell at once into animated chatter. Pug thought that at this rate he might never get to talk to her. The Cincpac conference was scheduled for ten. The fleet was sailing for Midway in the morning. In the car Tudsbury had held forth without cease on Singapore, the Russian front, Rommel, the Japanese advance toward India, and such cheerful matters. Meantime Pamela had sat in the back seat mum as a fish. Now, putting his mouth almost to Pug's ear, Tudsbury began badgering him again for inside dope on what was brewing. "The Boogie-Woogie Washerwoman" gave way to total gibberish bawled by the gelatinously shaking singer. "*Hut-Sut rawlson on the riller-ah and a braw-la, braw-la soo-it*" were the approximate noises Pug heard. With this *Götterdämmerung* babble at one ear, with Tudsbury's pesky questions yelled into the other, with Aster and Pamela getting up to dance, with worry about Byron's disappearance plaguing him, with an ever-growing sense of the Japanese fleet's approach, Pug Henry was not having much fun.

Byron came in view, carrying a large brown envelope and leading a girl. "Hi, Dad. Hi, Mr. Tudsbury. This is Ursula Thigpen. Remember Ursula, Mr. Tudsbury? You gave her your autograph. Don't you think Ursula's a pretty name?"

Ursula plumped down in the chair beside the correspondent before he could reply. "Now, that's *Thigpen*, Mr. Alistair Tudsbury." She tapped his arm with a stiff little pink finger, spelling, "*T-h-i-g-p-e-n!* Thigpen! Not 'Pigpen,' see? Just in case you do broadcast about me. Hee hee!"

"Well, well, Briny, so you surfaced," said Aster, returning with Pamela. "Where the hell did you get off to?"

Warren and Janice came back to the table. "Like dancing in a subway rush," Warren said.

"*Hut-Sut rawlson on the riller-ah* . . ." Ursula inquired whether either Janice or Pamela cared to press their shoelaces. Byron had been driving her all over the island, she said. He had even brought her aboard the *Devilfish*, but there was no little girls' room on submarines. "My back teeth are floating," she elaborated.

Janice took her off, wondering why Byron had this imbecile in tow. While fixing her makeup in the powder room Ursula spilled a condom from her vanity case and unblinkingly put it back, tittering that in Hawaii you never knew when it was going to rain, did you? "Although frankly, your brother-in-law doesn't seem exactly the type," she said. "He's cute, but strange."

"What were you doing in the submarine?"

"Oh, he went to fetch a big wooden box. It's out in the jeep. Getting it up those ladders was a problem, but nothing like *my* problem, honey. Why, those awful submarine sailors! They could see everything. And they sure looked! I'll bet they've got eyestrain, the lot of them." Ursula chortled about this all the way back to the table, where a waiter was serving drinks.

Out on the floor Byron was now doing a Lindy Hop with Pamela, who, keeping him at arm's length, was observing his elegant antics with a half-dismayed, half-amused look.

Warren said to Janice, "Briny's flying to San Francisco tonight. He's brought his footlocker. At nine thirty we take him to the NATS terminal, he says, and pour him on board the plane."

Janice said to Aster, "But have you detached him?"

"There are his orders." Aster made a limp resigned gesture at the envelope on the table. "I've just signed them."

"What about air priorities?"

"He got himself an air priority. Byron does these things."

"Byron has two gaits," remarked his father, "a snail's crawl, and the speed of light in a vacuum." He was watching Byron dance, doing the best jitterbugging in sight, shaping the faddish angular prances and wild twirls of the Lindy Hop into fluid motions charming to watch. Pamela Tudsbury's sedate careful stepping-about, with her outstretched hand barely touching his, made a ludicrous contrast.

"Ursie Thigpen!" A fat perspiring lieutenant whose dolphins were green with sea tarnish wrapped a thick arm around her waist. "Good old Ursie! How about a dance, Urs? Will you excuse her, folks?" And away they gyrated.

Holding out a hand to Janice, Warren jumped up. "Well, let's go, anniversary girl. Tonight's your night."

"These damned Lindys!" bubbled Janice. "Don't they play anything for old married folks?"

"It's hopeless," Pamela said to Pug, dropping into a seat beside him, patting at her forehead with a wisp of gray handkerchief. She smiled up at Byron. "You were a darling to put up with me."

"I'm sorry you quit." Byron went back to his place, drank off a tall rum collins like a glass of water, and signalled at the waiter for another.

Aster and Tudsbury were in a low earnest colloquy quite drowned out by the music. Here was Pug's chance to talk to Pamela. How to start? She was looking away from him toward the dance floor. He had thought so much about her that here at his side, in the flesh, she had an unreal quality that disconcerted him; a minor actress, as it were, not quite filling the stupendous Pamela role of his yearnings and visions. Her face seen this close was strained and older; her cheeks were darkly hollow, her lipstick was carelessly applied, and on her upper lip there was a trace of moist down. He touched her bare white forearm.

"I'm sorry to hear you've been ill, Pam."

She faced him. Her tone was as low as his. "I do look it, don't I?"

"I didn't mean that. You look grand." Bad beginning! He lurched awkwardly on. "You didn't by chance get a letter I sent you from here, months ago?"

"A letter? No. I've never had a letter from you."

"I received one from you."

"Oh, did that missive actually reach you? Written in another epoch, wasn't it?"

"I was very glad to get it."

"How's your wife?"

"She asked me for a divorce."

Pamela stiffened, clenched her hands, and thrust her bare pale arms forward on the table, hectic eyes flaring at him. "How could she? You couldn't have given her any cause."

"Claimed she'd fallen in love with someone else."

"How ghastly for you."

"Well, she's since expressed regret about it, in a fashion. It's all up in the air."

Looking straight at Byron, whose eyes were on them, she murmured, "Do your sons know?"

"They haven't a notion."

"I'm terribly sorry to hear this. And you lost your battleship, too."

Victor Henry wanted to reply, *Now that you're here it's okay*, but her cool casual manner forbade it.

"How long will you and your father stay in Honolulu?"

"I'm not sure."

Janice and Warren glided by, a straight-backed pair in the crowd of flailing prancing couples. "Didn't you propose, on the *Bremen*, to match me up with a son of yours?"

"Oh, you recall that?"

"Warren, no doubt?"

"Yes. But meantime, Janice hogtied him."

Pamela's mouth wrinkled, and she shook her head. "Never. Byron, possibly. Though when you first told me about him and Natalie Jastrow, I confess I was surprised. I thought wow, Natalie, my contemporary, and a son of yours — a *son* —"

"I still think that."

She contemplated Byron, slumped low in his chair over a second rum collins, his dark red hair falling in his eyes. "Oh, I understand her now. Devastating charm. Quiet, effortless, lethal. As for Warren, he's fine, but formidable. Are Natalie and her baby in real danger?"

"I suppose they'll get out all right."

"Why's Byron going to the Atlantic? What can he do for them?"

"Don't ask me."

Waiters arrived with champagne bottles and shrimp cocktails. Ursula, holding down her skirt close by in an animated twirl, left her partner with a twiddle of her fingers. "Ooh, champagne, yum, yum! Bye-bye, Bootsie!" Byron ordered the champagne opened at once.

"Well, founder of the feast," he said to Pug, "how's for the first toast?"

"Okay. Raise your glasses. Janice, many happy returns. Of the day, and of your man. Warren, good hunting."

Next Byron held up his glass. It happened that the music just then stopped. "Mom," he said. The sharp clear word caught Victor Henry unaware.

Warren raised his glass. "And Madeline."

Janice said, "Natalie and her baby, and their safe return."

Byron gave her a dark glance, raised his glass to her, and drank.

Over the shrimp cocktails Pug lost Pamela to Aster. The submariner made some joke he didn't hear, Pamela threw her head back in hearty laughter, and soon they got up to dance again. So did the others. He was left at the table with Tudsbury, who leaned over and jogged his elbow. "I say, Pug, how well do you know this submarine man? Does he enjoy leading one up the garden path?"

"Pamela can take care of herself."

"Pamela? What the devil has she got to do with it? He's just told me the most astounding story about his last patrol."

"To what effect?"

Tudsbury shook his head. "Come up to our suite after dinner, won't you? Some things can't be bawled over music."

Thinking of the Cincpac conference, Pug said, "I will, if there's time."

More champagne arrived with the roast chicken. Pug wondered by what legerdemain Byron had lined up these scarce bottles of California wine. A frenetic spirit was animating and jamming the dance floor as nine o'clock approached. The waiter had trouble getting through to their table with the cake. In the white icing, a blurry blue aircraft trailed red skywriting: *Janice and Warren.*

"Lovely," said Janice.

"Wrong war," said Warren. "Biplane."

The waiter poured out the last of the wine as Warren cut the cake.

Tudsbury seized his glass. "Well, in concluding this splendid feast," he grandiloquently boomed, getting to his feet, "I propose our host, and his two sons. Gentlemen, your disguise of simple Yank sailors is convincing, but the Homeric marble shows through. You are three figures from the Iliad. I drink to your health, and to your victory."

"Jehosephat, that's some toast," said Pug.

"Three figures from what?" Ursula said to Byron.

"Three figures from *The Idiot*," he said. "It's a Russian novel."

Pamela burst into a shriek of laughter and spilled her champagne.

The room darkened for the floor show. A master of ceremonies trying to sound like Bob Hope told jokes about rationing, Hitler, Tojo, and the curfew. Two Hawaiian men played guitars and sang. Then half a dozen hula-hula girls came undulating barefoot into the pink spotlight, their grass skirts audibly swishing. They danced and sang, then broke their chorus line to move out along the cleared floor, inviting diners to dance with them. One by one men jumped up to face the girls and hula, some kicking off their shoes. Mostly they clowned. The most beautiful girl, who looked more Eurasian than Hawaiian, came weaving her hips toward the Henry table. Seeing the decorated cake at Warren's place, she turned a brilliant smile at him, and extended beckoning hands.

"Go ahead, darling," said Janice. "Show them how it's done."

With a serious expression Warren got to his feet and faced the grass-skirted girl. He did not take off his shoes. Moving with grace, maintaining the dignity of his gold-winged white uniform, he danced a cold correct hula-hula, bringing to Pug's mind the naval officer in *Madame Butterfly*, the imperturbable and lordly young white man toying with an Asian beauty.

"I didn't know men did this dance," said Pamela to Pug.

"It seems he does."

The fixed entertainer's grin on the hula-hula girl's face changed to a sweet smile of pleasure. She looked full into Warren's eyes, and impulsively hung her lei around his neck. Her dancing became sexier. Guests at other tables watched and whispered. Glancing around the table, Victor Henry saw that Janice, Pamela, and Ursula had admiring eyes fixed on Warren, while Aster and Tudsbury were gazing with appetite at the dancing girl. Byron was not looking at her. His face frozen in a drunken expression, he was staring at his brother, and tears were trickling down his cheeks.

24

PREDICTABLY, Tudsbury occupied the presidential suite, with the predictable huge living room full of overstuffed modernist sofas and armchairs, but with an unpredictable wallpaper of large red stallions charging around the room. The best feature of the suite, Tudsbury told Pug, was shrouded by the blackout curtains: a wide balcony facing the sea and Diamond Head. "Smashing view in the moonlight," he said, entering the suite with Pug as Pamela went off to her room down the hall. "What'll it be, Victor? Brandy? Or a warm whiskey and soda? There's a fridge, but it doesn't work. Shades of Singapore."

Since taking command of the *Northampton*, until this evening, Pug had drunk nothing. He asked for brandy. The first taste brought back a glimmer of his time of acute pain over Rhoda's divorce letter. Tudsbury flopped in an armchair, gulping dark whiskey and water. "Charming dinner, Victor, truly. Frightfully keen on your sons. One seldom runs into such a sense of family nowadays. Well, what cheer, old cock? What's the real news? Come on! There's a great sea battle making up, isn't there?"

"What was Aster's shocking story?"

"You really don't know? Why, my dear fellow, the second vessel the *Devilfish* sank was a hospital ship."

Sitting up straight, Pug jabbed a forefinger at Tudsbury's face. "He never told you that."

"But he did, dear boy."

"You misunderstood him."

"Softly, softly. It turned out to be a disguised ammunition ship. He's got photographs to prove it. Before it sank it popped off for half an hour like a pyrotechnics factory. And it was carrying tons of crude rubber. He retrieved samples."

"Was Aster very drunk?"

"No. Possibly Pam made him feel expansive. She rather took to him, I thought."

"Forget you ever heard that story."

"Why? Camouflaging an ammunition ship with the red cross is a filthy trick. Typical Jap insensitivity to civilized rules of war. They're barbarians, Pug." A fat fist waved in the air. "Lieutenant Commander Aster is one white fighting man who can be as ruthless as they are, an ingratiating young Yank with a killer's heart. Superb copy."

"Do you want him to go on killing?"

"Of course."

"Then blot the thing from your mind. Alcoholic babble. What are your plans, Talky? Where do you go from here?"

"San Francisco. Washington. And so home to Old Blighty, and thence to the desert army in North Africa." He leaned forward, his good eye popping, his paunch straining at the yellow silk, and dropped his voice to a hissing whisper. "See here, Pug Henry, *what's up?* I ask you man to man, *what's up?* Damn it all, I'm a friend of yours and a friend of your country."

A pleasant brandy fog wisped in Pug's brain. The battle was coming on, he thought, Tudsbury did happen to be here, and it would be a disservice to the Allies if he left. Ingrained total secrecy in this case could be modified. "Okay. You forget that hospital ship and I'll tell you something." He extended his hand. "Done?"

"But you're offering a pig in a poke."

"Yes."

"Well, for once, I'll trust a Yank." Tudsbury clasped hands. "Done! Now talk."

"Don't leave Honolulu."

"No? Good-o! Why not? Go on, *go on,* tell me all about it, dear fellow. I'm panting." Tudsbury was indeed breathing heavily, somewhat like a leaky bellows, with considerable wheeze.

"That's it."

"What's it?"

Henry reiterated, with the level droning emphasis of words issuing from a warship's bullhorn, *"Don't . . . leave . . . Honolulu."*

"That's *all?* But you're a damnable swindler!" Tudsbury's face contorted in a huge scowl. "I *know* I shouldn't leave. Your Cincpac building is boiling like an anthill, I saw that! What in hell have you given me?"

"Confirmation," Pug said.

Tudsbury's one-eyed indignant glare slowly faded into a crafty capitulating leer. "All right, dear boy. But it's *you* who's been diddled, you know, not me. I gave my word of honor to Aster not to use his story, before he'd tell me a word of it. No Allied correspondent could touch that tale. Heh heh. You're an easy mark." He leaned over and patted Henry's arm. "Tremendous battle cooking up, eh? Trafalgar of the Pacific, what? On their way already, the yellow beggars? Going to try to invade Hawaii?"

Pamela came in. Droplets of water clung to her hair at the forehead and temples. She looked very pale, almost ill. Pug stood up, and her father waved his glass.

"Ah, here's my charmer, my right hand. Nobody will ever know, Victor, how much I owe this girl. I've dragged her through fire and water in these past six months. She's never faltered or complained. Pour yourself a drink, Pam, and give me another stiff whiskey and soda."

"Talky, go to bed."

"I beg your pardon?"

"You've had a very long day. Go to bed."

"But Pam, I want to talk to Victor."

"So do I."

Tudsbury peered at his daughter's chill nervous face, and reluctantly pushed himself up out of his armchair. "You're being hard on me, Pamela, very hard," he whined.

"I must help him dress his eye," she said briskly to Pug. "I shan't be long. Take a look at our view."

Victor Henry slipped through the swaying blackout curtains. The night was starry, and the low moon cast a golden path on the calm sea. Eight or nine days from full; the Japs' battle plan called for full-moon nights, obviously. A deceitfully peaceful prospect here: the quiet plash and hiss of the phosphorescent surf, flower scents from the gardens below, the moonlit cone of Diamond Head beyond the blacked-out Royal Hawaiian Hotel. Under this same moon, lower in the sky thousands of miles to the west, the Japanese armada was even now plowing toward Midway, swells breaking and foaming on hundreds of iron bows — pagoda-masted battleships, crudely built carriers with flight decks propped by naked iron girders, tubby transports crowded with landing troops, and the vessels of the train swarming like waterbugs from horizon to horizon.

"I wondered where you'd got to." A touch on his shoulder. Pamela's voice, cool and low.

"Hi." He turned toward her dark shape. "That was quick. Is his eye bad?"

"Your Navy doctors call it an ulcer. They say it'll heal." A pause. "Your wife's demand for a divorce is shattering news."

"Well, it was blurred at the time by other things, Pamela, such as losing the *California*. And seeing Pearl Harbor from the air, a smoking junkyard."

"Something like my last glimpse of Singapore."

"I heard you broadcast from there. About the Mills bomb."

"Oh, did you?" Another awkward pause. Arms folded, she was staring out to sea.

"Last time we stood on a balcony like this the view was different," he ventured.

"I should say. The Thames docks on fire, searchlights on a black sky, sirens, AA popping, German planes falling —" She turned her face to him. "And then you went off to ride a bomber over Berlin."

"And that made you furious."

"Indeed it did. Look, I've lost my taste for tropic nights. The Southern Cross now signifies for me — and probably always will — nothing but god-awful sickness and fear. Let's go in." She led him through the french window and rustling blackout curtains. A streak of yellow light shone under the bedroom door.

A muffled call: "I say, Pam, is that you?"

"Yes, Talky. Why aren't you asleep?"

"Going over my notes. Where's Victor?"

"He's just leaving now."

"Oh, is he? Well, good-night there, Victor."

"Night, Talky," Pug called.

"Pamela, will you bring your pad and take just a little dictation?"

"No, I won't. Turn out the light. You're exhausted."

"Well, since you're so eager to go to bed, all right." The streak of yellow disappeared. "Pleasant dreams, Pam," Tudsbury called in a teasing tone.

"He's a small boy," Pamela muttered. "We'll go to my room."

The corridor smelled very hotel-like. The lights glared. As she took a key from a little gray purse, the elevator door slid open, and with a heart-thump Henry saw his son Warren step out. The discomfort lasted only a second or two. It wasn't Warren, but a tall young man in a white uniform with gold wings, who gave Pamela an admiring glance as he passed.

She unlocked her door and in they went. The room was small and dingy, as Pug expected it to be on the hotel's landward side: the gray paint faded and peeling, the red curtains in need of a dusting, the double brass bed hiding a threadbare carpet.

"I suspect it's a chambermaid's quarters," Pamela said. "I couldn't argue. The hotel was jammed and they did give him the royal suite. I wasn't expecting to entertain, anyway." She tossed aside key and purse, and held out her arms. "But I guess I am, at that."

Pug seized her.

"Oh, God Almighty, high time," Pamela gasped. She kissed him hard, sending sweet fire shooting all through him. Pug's awareness of other things — battle conference, oncoming enemy, sons, wife — was blotted out by a sensation forgotten since his honeymoon: the unique and fiercely exalting thrill of a woman in his arms signalling with mouth and body her love and her first surrender.

The worn lonely wounded man returned her kisses, crushing her close. Their rush of endearment, an incoherent blaze of kisses and broken words, at last slowed. They caught their breaths. There was the squalid little room again, and the big bed.

"This is one hell of a surprise," he muttered against her questing mouth.

"Surprise?" She leaned back in his arms, her eyes dancing with a joyous light. "How? Why? Didn't I declare myself very crudely in Moscow?"

"I thought tonight it was all off, from your manner."

"Dearest, your sons were *right there.*"

"I thought you liked young Aster."

"Oh? He was handy." She put caressing fingers to his face. "My problem was to keep my eyes off you. Now then. What's all this about a conference tonight?"

"I have to leave in half an hour."

"Half an hour! My God! Can we spend all day tomorrow together?"

"Pam, the fleet sails in the morning."

"NO! Damn! Oh, damn, damn!" She pulled free, and made an agitated gesture at a small seedy armchair. "What a disaster! Sit down. Damn! In the morning! There's *never* time, is there? Never! I should have hunted you up directly we got here." She sat on the bed, and struck the brass frame with a clenched white fist. "I *thought* of it, but I wasn't sure how you felt. It's been half a year, you know, and I'd never heard from you. What was in the letter you sent me?"

Pug said miserably, "I was giving you up."

"Had you heard from your wife when you wrote it?"

"No."

"She's reprieved me. Oh, how *could* the misguided woman do it? Do you know who the man is?"

"You met him at our house. That tall engineer, Fred Kirby. He's not a bad fellow."

"He made no impression on me. Half an hour! Oh, blast! Oh, hell!"

She swung up her legs and hugged them, leaning her back against the frame. The girlish pose troubled Pug. Madeline sat so, sometimes. Pam looked piercingly sweet and desirable, but young, young, hunched there with white slender arms clutching her folded legs and thighs outlined in gray silk.

"Now listen, darling," she said, talking fast. "Before I left London, I checked on ways and means of staying on in Honolulu. The chief of our military liaison here, a Commodore Alexander Pike, rather likes me. Also I've brought a high-powered letter from Lord Burne-Wilke. Milord's a dear boring man who'll do anything for me. In short, my love, I've got an offer of a job here. Just today I put down a month's rent to hold a sublease on a small flat. You see —" She was ticking off all this like an executive secretary, but at his headshake she stopped and grinned. "Have I been a trifle forward, *mon vieux?* My plan was to offer myself to you on a silver platter, all set, no problem. I couldn't foresee that we'd have so little time tonight. Or that your wife would go dotty on you. Exactly how does that stand, Pug?"

He repeated passages from Rhoda's divorce letter that were branded into his brain; and he spoke of the breezy tone of her writing since then, and of the anonymous notes.

"Oh, ignore that filth!" A disgusted headshake. "It's only what Rhoda writes that counts."

"She's stringing me along, Pam. That's my strong hunch. Maybe she feels it's her duty, because I'm out here fighting the war. Or maybe it's because the other fellow isn't nailed down yet. There's a phony note in her letters."

"You can't be sure. She's self-conscious, Pug. She's put herself in a false position. Can't you see that? Don't be too quick to judge her." Pamela glanced at her wristwatch. "Hell, time's burning down like a fuse. You're off to sea, and Talky will want to leave for the States. What a mess Rhoda's made! It's my golden opportunity, of course, but would it complicate your poor life if I stayed on?"

"Talky isn't going to leave. I've advised him to stay."

"You have?" She waited. He said nothing more. "Well. Interesting! Still, I'd better let old Alex Pike know about that job."

This lovely creature was no dream girl, Pug thought. She was almost as tough and pushy as her father. She sat there within reach, real as a rock, pale and anxious-looking, demanding a decision. Matters were blazing forward between them, after the long slow empty months.

"So the ball's in my court, then," he said.

Anger flashed across her face. "There's no ball and no court. This is no game." She sat up straight, her legs on the floor. "I'm here. If you want me, I'll stay. If you don't, I'll go. Is that explicit enough? I want to be where you are. *I love you.* To me you're life. You're distressed about Rhoda, and I can't blame you. Well, make your regulations and I'll obey them. But there's no place for me to go from here, Victor, unless you send me away. Do you understand, or don't you?"

How many men would give all they had to hear such words from such a woman? It was his God-granted chance to rebuild a ruined life. He got to his feet and pulled her up into an embrace. All but overwhelmed by the power of the moment and the joy of her body seeking his, he could only choke out, "I'm too damned old for you."

"I have to tell you something," she said, clinging to him hard, bowing her face on his white jacket. The words came muffled and fast. "In Singapore I went back to Phil Rule. He was there. I don't know why. It was the end of the world. He's the same old swine. Still, I went back to him. It happened once. I didn't plan it. I'm still sick about it." She raised her face. It looked as pale and ill as it had earlier.

Pug said, quelling agonized anger and hurt, "You didn't owe me anything. Now, you asked about regulations. Here's regulation number one. Never make me late for a Navy conference."

"Oh, Lord, that bloody conference! Is it time?" Her voice shook. "Be off with you, then. No, wait. Here." She darted at her purse, pulled out a white card and put it in his hand. "Here's where you'll find me when you get back. It's an apartment hotel."

" 'Dillingham Court,' " he read. "That still exists?"

"Yes. Seedy, but convenient and — why that peculiar smile?"

"Rhoda and I stayed there once. Before we had the kids."

She looked him straight in the eyes. "When will you return? Do you know?"

His face turned grave. "I'm telling this to you alone. We're heading out to fight a hell of a big battle, Pam. The odds are against us. I'm going now to Admiral Nimitz's headquarters."

Her face stiff with tension, her eyes huge and brilliant, she took his head in her hands and lingeringly kissed his lips. "I love you, Pug. I'll never change. When you come back, *and you will*, I'll be here."

She opened the door for him.

Thin brown smoke wisped from the *Northampton*'s stacks as it rode to a chain hove short. Through the smoke, the morning sun dappled a deck alive with sailors hurrying here and there under the long guns and the float planes on catapults, securing the heavy cruiser for sea. In his cabin, Victor Henry was downing a breakfast of fresh pineapple, oatmeal, ham and eggs, and hashed brown potatoes, as his amazed steward poured cup after cup of steaming coffee for him.

"Appetite fine this morning, Cap'n."

"Food's fine," said Pug.

The sunlight that fell through the porthole in a brilliant oval on the starchy white cloth seemed to be streaming into his spirit. He had slept only two or three hours, yet he felt wonderful; a half-year of funk was blasted away, like fog by a fresh sea wind. Before springing from his bunk for exercise and a cold shower, he had lain in the dark thinking it all over: an amicable settlement with poor fouled-up Rhoda, a second marriage, perhaps a second family — why not, *why not?* He knew men his age who lived in bliss with glowing young wives (none like Pamela Tudsbury!), even with fresh crops of babies around them. Fantasy was finished; fact was sweeter.

His concern about the battle was dissolving into nervy relish, now that his spirits were up, and he knew what would probably happen — that is, if Cincpac's cryptanalysts were right. Even with this intelligence break, the battle estimate went massively against the Pacific Fleet's chances of survival. Yet in the peculiar configuration of the Japanese attack plan there was some hope. Their power would be spread out from the Aleutians to the Marianas. In at least the first phase, carriers against carriers, the odds might be endurable, though the damaged *Yorktown* and the unblooded *Hornet* were weak sisters compared to the battle-hardened Japanese flattops. Anyway, he was heading for a fight, and he was a fighting man; and Pamela's love made him feel ready to take on any odds.

A ringing telephone broke into Pug's reverie.

"Sir, this is the OOD. Your son's come aboard."

"Send him along."

Warren appeared in the doorway in workaday khakis, with gold wings pinned on a faded shirt. "Hi, Dad. If you're too busy for me, say so."

"Come in. Have something to eat."

"No thanks." Warren held up a hand, dropping into an armchair. "Janice just gave me the royal send-off. Steak and eggs for breakfast." He looked around at the sunny cabin. "Hm! I've never yet seen you in your glory. Nice quarters."

"Well, you've been invited often enough."

"I know. My fault."

"Byron get away all right?"

"Oh, he's in San Francisco by now. With a historic hangover, no doubt."

Pug glanced at the steward, who bobbed his head and vanished. Warren lit a cigarette, saying quietly, "It's Midway, isn't it, Dad? And the whole damn Jap fleet?"

"Where'd you hear that?"

"Guy on Halsey's staff."

"Sorry to hear Halsey's staff is a sieve."

"What about this Admiral Spruance? You've been steaming around with him for months."

"What about him?"

"Well, to begin with, he's a battleship man, isn't he? The word is that he's an electrical engineer, a War College type. Not even qualified in aviation like Halsey. They say he's Halsey's buddy, and that's how he got the job. The staff's worried."

"Cincpac's choice of task force commander isn't your business or the staff's."

Warren's tone hardened like an echo. "Dad, the boss man of this show has to understand aviators. Halsey's flight qualification was just one of those things, but at least he went and did it. Actually he doesn't think like an aviator. When we struck the Marshalls he wanted to launch unescorted bombers beyond flight range, and at that his staff navigation was off. Half of us would have fallen in the drink getting back to Point Option. We staged a pilots' sit-down, damn near, and got the orders changed." His father shook his head in stern disapproval. Warren threw up both hands. "Well, that's what happened. You can't shoot off dive-bombers like sixteen-inch shells. They have to turn around and come back. It's a big difference, but admirals have no end of trouble remembering that."

"Spruance will remember it."

"Well, I'm glad you say that. If he'll just close the range and give us a chance, we'll do a job for him." Warren blew out a thick smoke ring. "Two carriers against the whole Jap navy. Should be interesting."

"Three carriers." Somewhat piqued, Pug added, "Also some nine cruisers, Warren."

"Three? The *Sara*? She's in California, isn't she?"

"The *Yorktown*."

"Dad, the *Yorktown* had her insides blown out. It's a six months' repair job."

"The Yard has promised to put her in combat shape in seventy-two hours."

Warren whistled. "I'll believe that when I see it. Incidentally, did you hear the morning news — that battle around Kharkov?"

"No."

"Biggest tank fight of all time. Both sides say that. Did you ever get to Kharkov?"

"The Germans held Kharkov when I was in Moscow. It's been taken and retaken since. I've lost track."

Warren nodded. "And Rommel's fighting still another tank battle in Africa. Where do the Germans get all these tanks? The RAF's supposed to be levelling their factories."

It struck Pug that this gossip had an empty, wandering note not like Warren. "See here, it's 0814. I'm getting underway at 0900. Shall I send you to Ford Island in my gig?"

"In a minute." Warren crushed his cigarette, audibly blowing out gray smoke. "Look, I was going to give Byron this, but he's gone." Warren pulled out a white envelope from a back pocket. "It's just some financial dope. Janice is a smart cookie, as you know, but arithmetic throws her into catalepsy." Victor Henry silently accepted the envelope and dropped it in a drawer. "Dad, coming back from a strike, I'll make a pass over the *Northampton* and waggle my wings. If I don't that won't mean anything. I may be in formation or low on gas, or something. But I'll try to do it."

"I understand perfectly. That'll be fine, Warren, but I won't count on it."

Warren's glance, avoiding his father's, rested on a desk photograph of Rhoda beside very young pictures of himself, Byron, and Madeline. "I missed Mom and Madeline last night."

"There'll be family reunions yet, Warren. And you'll do the hula again for us."

"The hula! *Ha!* It'll be some other dance by that time."

As they walked up to the passageway, Victor Henry could not resist asking, "What did you think of the Tudsburys?"

"He's sort of a blowhard. I liked the daughter."

"Oh, you did? Why?"

"Well, the way she devotes herself to her father. Also, though she's quiet, she strikes me as sexy as hell."

The comment gave Victor Henry a long-forgotten kind of male satisfaction, the pleasure of a midshipman hearing his girl praised.

In the sunlight on the main deck Warren squinted, put on dark glasses, and looked fore and aft along the busy six-hundred-foot deck. "It's a magnificent ship, Dad."

"It's not an aircraft carrier."

"Attention on deck!" The OOD rapped out the order. Hurrying sailors froze. As Victor Henry and his son shook hands at the gangway, Warren looked into the father's eyes and smiled. Never before had he smiled in quite this way at his parent: a remote reassuring smile, almost like a pat on the back, as though to say, *I'm not your little boy any more, though you don't quite believe it. I'm a dive-bomber pilot, and I'll do all right.*

Harry Hopkins's phrase leaped into Pug Henry's mind: *the changing of the guard.*

"Good hunting, Warren." The son tightened his grip, then turned and saluted the OOD. "Request permission to leave the ship."

"Permission granted, sir."

In his loose-limbed jaunty way Warren went down the ladder. "Carry on," Pug said, freeing the rigid sailors. He stood at the gangway, watching the gig pull away and head for Ford Island with his tall son standing arms akimbo in the stern sheets, steady despite the choppy waves.

The destroyers of the task force screen were steaming down channel for the sortie, signal flags flying. The long gray shape of a destroyer, passing close aboard, hid Warren from view. Pug felt self-conscious about lingering on the quarterdeck, just for another glimpse of his son. He went up to his bridge to take the *Northampton* out to sea.

25

WERNER BECK was having problems.

A letter had landed on his desk from subsection IV B-4 of the Reich Security Main Office, requesting a report on the possibilities of deporting Italian Jews to the east. For such ticklish matters, Beck handled liaison with Mussolini's comatose bureaucracy. It was he, for instance, who was getting drafts of Italian workers shipped to German factories. Beck knew how to handle Rome officials, those smiling eels whose life specialty was paralyzing positive action with charm, paperwork, and words. An electric shock of fear from the OVRA would cause the smiling eel to cease smiling and wriggling every time, straighten into a man, and get the desired job done.

However, Beck was no miracle worker; and this Jewish project he considered hopeless. No Italians, right up to Mussolini himself, were likely to cooperate in sending off the Jews to a shrouded fate. Even fanatical Fascists smirked at the anti-Semitic laws. Most Italians liked the Jews, or at least felt sorry for them. So Beck adopted the appropriate obfuscating tactics: he wrote official queries to the right bureaus, got official evasions in reply, made official appointments for useless secret talks, and wrote official minutes of these. He sent an official negative summary to the Reich Security Main Office, with a file of all the negative responses, and trusted that that would end the matter.

Back came another letter from the SS lieutenant colonel who headed Subsection IV B-4, saying that he would himself visit Rome. For a lieutenant colonel, the man wrote in peremptory style. SS rank was nothing like a genuine Wehrmacht commission. An offspring of Hitler's strong-arm squads, now a swollen private army of Nazi faithfuls, the SS was, in Beck's view, really just a phony "elite" of government police terrorists — even if reserve status in the SS had become a token of Nazi fealty, and Beck therefore was himself a reserve Sturmbannführer. But this Lieutenant Colonel Eichmann seemed to swing some weight, for the ambassador next received a terse tough top-secret letter from Heydrich — an SS general of frightening reputation second only to Himmler — saying in effect, "Do whatever Colonel Eichmann wants." Shaken, the ambassador demanded from Beck a detailed written rundown on Lieutenant Colonel Eichmann's Subsection IV B-

4. This compelled Beck to review the whole dreary and opaque tangle of security agencies, which puzzled the oldest heads in the Foreign Service.

It was all a mess of political empire-building. Division IV of Main Security was the old Gestapo, forged by Göring out of the Prussian political police into a secret service arm. Himmler and Heydrich of the SS had co-opted the Gestapo into Main Security, a bureaucratic octopus sprawling through Berlin's official buildings, combining the intelligence and police functions of both the government and the Nazi party. In no state structure had the Nazis made a worse hash of things. The RSHA was a sinister and ill-defined catch-all outfit, but it was obviously just what the party wanted: a secret total police power operating outside federal law, answerable only to Hitler.

Section B of the Gestapo was devoted to "sects." The fourth "sect" was the Jews. Subsection IV B-4 of the RSHA thus was the Gestapo desk for Jewish affairs. So this Lieutenant Colonel Eichmann governed the destiny of all the Jews in German-held Europe, for they were classed as a security matter. His peremptory style became more understandable; he held sway over eight to ten million souls, a larger domain than Sweden. Beck developed a somewhat anxious curiosity about him.

Eichmann arrived in Rome by car, shortly after the assassination of Heydrich. Despite the gasoline shortage, he had driven all the way from Berlin. One of his first remarks, in a meeting in the ambassador's grandly furnished reception suite, was that he never flew in airplanes; they were too unreliable. At this meeting there was only chitchat over coffee among the three men. Despite his ominous and splashy black-and-silver SS uniform, Lieutenant Colonel Eichmann looked and acted quite pleasant; scarcely military, rather with the brisk intelligent crispness of a high-level accountant. But he lacked class. He sipped coffee with a vulgar noise. The ambassador was an erect, ruddy, elderly gentleman of great affairs and polished deportment, descended from a field marshal; yet it was the old ambassador who deferred to this businesslike bureaucrat in his thirties, rather than the other way around. Assuring Eichmann that the embassy was at his disposal, begging him to convey his cordial regrets to Reichsführer SS Himmler over the sad death of General Heydrich, the ambassador fobbed the lieutenant colonel off on Werner Beck.

In Beck's office Eichmann turned peremptory again. About the negative responses of the Rome officials he was coarsely scornful. Italians were not to be taken seriously, he said; mere strutters and posers, with no conception of the Jewish problem. Security police and the Foreign Ministry would solve this Jew business in Italy despite the government. For in the Führer's view, said Eichmann, making frequent pedantic gestures with a stiff forefinger, the Jewish problem had no boundaries. Could a European epidemic of bubonic plague, for instance, be stamped out if the germs were allowed to multiply unchecked beyond invisible lines on the ground called "boundaries?" The Führer's unshakable will was to cleanse the continent of the Jews. Hence Herr Dr. Beck, as political secretary in Rome, would have to do better than file mere negative reports.

"But Italy is not an occupied country," Beck mildly rejoined. "It's a sovereign nation, I need hardly point out, a full military ally. And these Jews are still Italian nationals."

A trace of pleased approval widened Eichmann's broad thin mouth. Herr Dr. Beck was a realist, after all! Yes, in occupied capitals it was simpler. Main Security could put men in the German embassies to take over the Jewish question. But in Rome this would prick tender Italian feelings of national honor. So the delicacy of the task made the challenge all the more bracing.

He, Eichmann, had come to give Beck the guidelines. He had been dealing with this Jew business in all its aspects since well before the war. No government outside the Reich wholly understood the Führer's farseeing policy, said Eichmann, plying his forefinger like a schoolteacher. They were all more or less confused by Christian or liberalist notions. They were ready enough to revive the anti-Jewish laws that had once been in all European law codes; to kick their Jews out of the government, the professions, and the good neighborhoods, and to tax them into beggary. On more radical measures the politicians tended to drag their heels.

Beck should bear in mind, Eichmann went on, warming to his topic, smoking cigarette after cigarette, one crucial point: *it was imperative to get Italy to hand over some Jews, however few, and on whatever basis, to Germany at once.* Once the line was crossed, the principle established, the ice broken, resistance to the German policy would gradually crumble. That was his repeated experience. For despite the toughest taxes, Jews could cleverly hang on to their property with one dodge or another; but when they were physically removed, *kaputt!* The wealth remained behind for confiscation. Once a government could be induced to hand over some Jews and sample the surprising revenue that resulted, its attitude usually changed to warm enthusiasm. This had happened in country after country. The timid politicians simply had to learn for themselves how easy it was, how little their population really objected, how willingly the Jews complied, how blandly the rest of the world looked on, and above all, how much profit there was in the Führer's wise policy.

For example, Eichmann said, he was just now working up a deal with Bulgaria. That was a bad setup, a wobbly satellite ready to jump either way. Now that the Wehrmacht's summer offensive was rolling, the Bulgarian czar was softening up. The triumphs of Rommel and the big advances in the Crimea had really got him talking business at last. The key to hauling in all the

Bulgarian Jews was a handful of them now living in Germany. A swap was in the making. Bulgaria would get control of all German Jews who had fled there, and Germany would take charge of the Bulgarian Jews on Reich soil. The Bulgars were getting the better of it, profit-wise, *but they were officially acquiescing in the radical German policy; they were abandoning Bulgarian citizens who were Jews to the Germans.* That was the main point won. Italy was not too unlike Bulgaria, a bunch of treacherous politicians running a weak country. Hence Dr. Beck might try the same approach.

It was all a question, Eichmann went on, of the existing status of various Jews. Italian-born Jews now in Italy would be the toughest ones to nab. Alien Jews would be easier, but they still had sanctuary of a sort. The way to start was with *Italian Jews who were in Germany.* There were exactly one hundred eighteen of these delightful people, Eichmann said. He would send Dr. Beck dossiers showing each Italian Jew's place of origin, present place of German residence, age, health, important connections, and net worth statement. Dr. Beck should then propose the Bulgarian formula to the Fascist bigwigs. And Dr. Beck could use a fine humanitarian argument. If the German policy toward Jews was indeed so harsh — though of course he should deny that — this deal would only help the Jews, wouldn't it? A lot more would get out of German control than would pass under it, since there were many hundreds of German Jews in Italy. Eichmann added, with the sly grin of a close bargainer, that Beck needn't worry about the German Jews in Italy thus traded off; one way or another, they would be picked up in the end.

To sum up, Eichmann said, the opening wedge was what counted. Hadn't Herr Dr. Beck ever laid a virgin? That was the whole idea: gentle persuasion to start with, lots of soothing words and disarming talk, and then, at the proper moment — sock it home! After the first time, no problems! This Italian Jew situation called for a persuasive diplomat. The Labor Ministry had warmly recommended Herr Dr. Beck, and positive results were confidently expected by Reichsführer Himmler.

The clearer Eichmann's drift became, the less Werner Beck liked it. He had heard enough knowing hints about the Jewish camps in the east. Anti-Semites abounded in the Foreign Service, creatures of Ribbentrop. One of the worst was an undersecretary incongruously named Martin Luther, head of a high-security section called *Deutschland,* which was somehow involved in Jewish affairs. Beck had talked to this gross drunkard at a Berlin party. Very much in his cups, Luther had volunteered, with a gloating smile and a wink behind his hand, that the Jews were finally "getting it in the ass" in the eastern camps, just as the Führer had predicted. Among the better class of Germans, the subject was smothered in silence. Werner Beck had never asked anybody for details, and had tried to shut his mind to this whole unfortunate business. His army brother had lately dropped the entire subject.

Now this round-shouldered obscure functionary, with the long lean face, foxy nose, high balding forehead, and brisk manner, in a black uniform that heightened his paper-shuffler's pallor, was suggesting that he plunge himself up to his neck in that morass. One thing Beck never forgot, as a seasoned diplomat with a doctorate in history: all wars ended, and postwar accountings could be onerous. He was not quite at ease about his role in drafting Italian workers. The hardship pleas which he had vetoed wholesale had often upset him. War was war, and orders were orders, but this business with the Jews was entirely out of bounds.

He spoke up decisively, to nip the thing in the bud. "Let me point out one fact. In setting up the labor drafts I've had to give explicit written guarantees of destinations, wages, and working conditions of the laborers."

"Of course, but those were Italians. These are Jews."

The tone nonplussed Beck, for Eichmann might as well have said, "These are horses."

"Rome officials still regard them as Italian citizens. I'll be asked exactly where these one hundred eighteen Jews will be resettled, what they'll do there, and in what circumstances. I'll have to put an official written reply from the Foreign Ministry in the record."

"Fine!" Eichmann shrugged and smiled, quite unperturbed. "Just write whatever you please. What will all this shit ever amount to?"

Beck winced, but he tried to be patient. He was used to Nazi commonness, and perforce had to put up with it. "That's not how the Foreign Service works, you see. We've been very factual in the labor matter. We've made good on our representations. That's how we've gotten such favorable results."

The two men stared at each other. A change came over Lieutenant Colonel Eichmann's face. All the lines slightly stiffened, and into his narrow eyes there came a strange vacant look. "If you like," he said in deep sarcastic tones from his hollow chest, "I'll be glad to tell you exactly where the Jews will go, and what the disposition will be, by the Führer's direct orders. Then you can decide just what story to write for the Italians." There was no focus in the man's eyes. Behind the glitter of his glasses two dark caverns seemed to open, and in those caverns Dr. Werner Beck saw horror, a vision of mountains of dead bodies. Not a word passed between them, but the moment of silence told the political secretary what happened to deported Jews. It was disheartening to have to face this. With chills rippling on his backbone, he seized at a straw. "The ambassador would have to know."

"Oh, I can see what you mean." The long livid face relaxed. Eichmann said in a humorous familiar tone, "He's just the sort of backward old fart to make trouble for us, isn't he? Well, the Foreign Minister himself will put him in the picture. That'll squelch him, I assure you, and he'll be quiet as a mouse. He won't say 'boo' to Ribbentrop." Eichmann emitted a pleased sigh, and waved the forefinger. "I'll tell you this, you can look for a very positive effect on your career once you pull this off. Old fellow, do you happen to have a spot of brandy in the office? I drove two hundred kilometers this morning, and I've had no breakfast."

Producing a bottle and two glasses, Werner Beck did some fast thinking while he poured. He must not even seem to assent; otherwise, when he failed to deliver, disaster could befall him. The Italians would not budge on the Jews; of that he was all but sure. They might round them up in camps, treat them roughly, and so forth; but handing them over for deportation — no. As they clinked glasses and drank, he said, "Well, I'll try. But the Italians will have the last word. I can't help that. Nobody can, unless we occupy Italy."

"So? You can't help it." Brusquely, as to a barman, Eichmann held out his empty glass. Beck refilled it. The lieutenant colonel drank again, and folded his hands in his lap. "I now request from you," he said, "an explanation of the Jastrow case."

"The Jastrow case?" Beck stammered.

"You've sequestered in Siena, Herr Dr. Beck, a stateless Jew named Aaron Jastrow, aged sixty-five, a prominent author from the U.S.A., with a niece and her infant. You have visited them. You have written to them. You have telephoned them. Yes?"

In handling Jastrow Beck had of course repeatedly used his Gestapo contacts. He realized that this must be Eichmann's source. He had been open and aboveboard, and there was nothing to fear. The lieutenant colonel had simply startled him with his abrupt change of front and uncanny recall of detail. Eichmann was now sitting up straight, wrinkling his whole face in suspicion, the embodiment of a malevolent secret police officer.

As nonchalantly as he could, Beck explained what he had in mind for Aaron Jastrow.

Shaking a cigarette from a pack and slipping it in his mouth, Eichmann said, "But Dr. Beck, this is all very puzzling. You mention the poet Ezra Pound, and his shortwave broadcasts for Rome Radio. That's fine stuff, very fine. The Propaganda Ministry records and uses the broadcasts. But the poet Ezra Pound is a rarity, a very sophisticated American anti-Semite. He gives it in the ass to the Jewish bankers and to Roosevelt more than our own shortwave does. How can you compare this Jastrow person to him? Jastrow's a full-blooded Jew."

"Ezra Pound's talks are no good for American audiences. Please take my word for that. I know the United States. He must be regarded there as a traitor or a lunatic. What I plan for Jastrow —"

"We know you studied in the United States. We also know that Jastrow was your teacher."

Feeling that he was getting nowhere — that his conception was beyond the SS mentality — Beck yet had to plow on. What he hoped for, he said, was a farseeing, forgiving, Olympian broadcast, or series of broadcasts, picturing the Germans and Japanese as deprived and misunderstood proud peoples, the Allies as fat cats clutching riches gained by armed force, and the whole war as a useless bloodletting that should be settled at once by a "sharing of the hegemony." This brilliant phrase was Jastrow's own. Coming from a prominent Jewish author it would have great impact in America to weaken the war effort and encourage a peace movement. Perhaps other high-level alien intellectuals like Santayana and Berenson would follow Jastrow's example.

Eichmann looked unconvinced. Santayana's name clearly meant nothing to him. At "Berenson" his eyes sharpened. "Berenson? There's a smart millionaire Jew. Berenson has a lot of protection. Well, all right. When will this Jastrow make his first broadcast?"

"That's not definite yet." Under Eichmann's hard surprised gaze he added, "It's a question of persuading him, which takes time."

The lieutenant colonel gently smiled. "Really? Why should it? Persuading a Jew is simple."

"To be effective, this has to be done of his own free will."

"But Jews will do anything that you want them to do, of their own free will. Still, I believe I understand you now. He is your old teacher, a fine man. You have a soft spot in your heart for him. You don't want to upset or frighten him. It isn't that you're coddling or protecting a Jew —" Eichmann happily smiled, and waved the schoolteacher's forefinger — "it isn't that, but rather that you think you'll catch more flies with honey than with vinegar. Hm?"

Dr. Beck began to feel cornered. The man had a streak of the actor, and his changing moods and manners were hard to deal with. Yet he was *just an SS lieutenant colonel,* Beck told himself, whatever his role with Jews. He, Beck, must not let himself be bullied into an untenable commitment. His reply was as light and confident as he could make it. "I'm sure that my approach is correct and will get the right results."

Eichmann nodded and briefly giggled. "Yes, yes, providing you get the results before the war is over. By the way, is your family here with you in Rome?"

"No, they're at home."

"And where is home?"

"Stuttgart."

"And how many kids do you have?"

"Four."

"Boys? Girls?"

"Three boys. One girl."

"Girls are so sweet. I have three boys. No luck on girls." Eichmann sighed and produced the forefinger. "I try once a week, no matter what, to get home to the kids. Even if it's only for an hour, once a week religiously I must see the kids. Even General Heydrich respected that, and he was a god-damn hard boss." Eichmann sighed again. "I suppose you're as fond of your kids as I am." Every time Eichmann said "kids" he managed to edge the word with freezing menace.

"I love my children," said Beck, trying to control his voice, "but I don't get to see them once a week, or even once a month."

Eichmann's face took on a drawn, faraway look. "Enough, Dr. Beck. Let's talk straight. Can Reichsführer Himmler expect a progress report fairly soon on those one hundred eighteen Jews? You'll have all their docu-ments by courier tomorrow."

"I'll do my best."

With a wide friendly grin, Eichmann said, "I'm glad that I came here and we thrashed it out. This Jastrow business is not 'kosher.' " Eichmann repeated the Jewish word with rude amusement. "Not 'kosher,' Dr. Beck. When you walk in shit, it sticks to your shoes. So tell the old Yid to make his broadcast quick. Then let the OVRA put him and his niece away with the other Yids."

"But they have a guarantee of safe conduct back to America, as part of the journalist exchange."

"How can that be? All the American journalists have already left Italy. Anyway, he's no journalist, he writes books."

"I delayed their departure myself. It's a temporary thing, we tied it to a mess in Brazil which sooner or later is bound to clear up."

The lieutenant colonel's narrow face brightened into a jolly smile. "Well, but you did manage that delay! See? When you want to be, you're a live wire. So do a job now for the Führer."

Eichmann accepted another glass of brandy. As Werner Beck walked out with him to the entrance of the embassy, they exchanged banalities about the way the war was going. The colonel's walk was rather bowlegged in the varnished black boots; and as he creaked and clicked along on the marble floor, he was very much the preoccupied civil servant again. At the door he turned and saluted. "You have a big responsibility here, Dr. Beck, so good luck. Heil Hitler."

The greeting and the outstretched arm gesture were in almost total dis-use around the embassy. Both came rustily to Beck. "Heil Hitler," he said.

The black figure clumped down the steps, frightening away into the flow-ering shrubbery two peacocks that had the run of the embassy grounds. Beck hurried to his office and called Siena.

By mere chance, Natalie's hand was resting on the telephone when it rang. She stood by Jastrow's desk, holding the baby on her arm. Mrs. Castelnuovo, with Miriam clinging to her skirt, was admiring the Madonna and child over the mantel; and the little girl kept looking from the painted baby to the live one, as though wondering why the wrong one had the halo. Dr. Beck came on the line, gay and high-spirited. "Good morning, Mrs. Henry! I hope you're theeling well. Is Dr. Jastrow fere?" Beck had this odd speech defect of mixing up his f's and th's in moments of excitement or tension. Natalie had noticed it first when a highway patrol car had stopped the Mercedes on the drive from Naples to Rome.

"I'll call him, Dr. Beck." She went out to the terrace, where Jastrow was writing in the sunshine.

"Werner? Of course. Does he sound cheerful?"

"Oh, merry as could be."

"Well! Maybe it's news of our release." Laboriously he got out of the lounge chair, and began hobbling toward the house. "Why, bless me, both my legs are numb! I'm tottering like Methuselah."

Natalie took Miriam and Anna to her bedchamber, where the pink satin hangings and bedspread were getting threadbare with age, and the painted cherubs on the ceiling, what with the decay of the plaster, looked somewhat leprous and perspiring. She laid Louis in his crib, but he promptly pulled himself to his feet with tiny fists clenched on the rail. The women sat chatting while Miriam played with him.

Natalie was growing very fond of Anna Castelnuovo. Mere snobbish self-isolation, she realized, had deprived her of this warm bright companion in all her long Italian exile. What a waste! Neither she nor Aaron had imagined that the few shadowy Sienese Jews might be worth bothering with. No doubt because Dr. Castelnuovo had sensed this, he had not told her he was Jewish.

Aaron looked in. "Natalie, he's coming by overnight train for lunch tomorrow. He has letters for us from America. Also — so he hinted — great news he can't discuss by phone." Jastrow's wrinkled face was animated by hope. "So talk to Maria about the lunch, my dear, and tell her I'd like some tea and a little compote on the terrace now."

When Louis fell asleep in his rump-to-ceiling pose, Natalie strolled with Anna Castelnuovo and her daughter to the bus stop. They sat in the rickety wooden shed talking on and on, until the ancient bus wound smokily into sight, far up among the green vineyards along the ridge. Anna said, "Well, I hope your news will be truly good. It's so curious that a German official should be your benefactor."

"Yes, it's decidedly curious." They exchanged looks of wry skepticism.

The bus went off, and she walked back to the villa feeling very much alone.

When Dr. Beck arrived next day, he at once gave two letters to Natalie, and one to Dr. Jastrow. They were waiting for him on the terrace. "Don't be polite, please. Go ahead and read your mail." Smiling benignly, he sat on a bench in the sun while they ripped at the envelopes.

"*The Arch of Constantine!* It arrived safely!" Jastrow burst out. "Werner, you must tell Father Spanelli and Ambassador Titman. Natalie, just listen to this, from Ned Duncan. '*We can never thank the Vatican enough. . . . The Arch of Constantine is your best book yet . . . a permanent contribution to popular understanding of both Judaism and Christianity —*' I declare, what a satisfying description! '. . . *Of classic stature . . . certain book club selection . . . brilliant panorama of decadent Rome . . . honored to publish such a fresh and seminal work . . .*' Well, well, well! Isn't that capital news, Natalie?"

"That is good news," said Dr. Beck, "but not all the good news."

Natalie looked up alertly from Slote's discouraging letter. The German and Italian red tape over the Brazil affair seemed endless, he wrote; it would all work out, but he could no longer guess when. She passed this letter to Beck, who after a glance handed it back with a shrug and a smile. He looked very pale and his eyes were bloodshot, but his manner was jocose. "Yes, yes, but all that is quite out of date. May we have lunch? Otherwise we've so much to discuss, we may forget to eat."

Natalie was skimming a piece of microfilmed V-mail from Byron, poorly printed and scarcely readable, which had fallen out of the three-page scrawl from her mother. Nothing really new in either letter; Byron was writing from Australia in a lonesome mood, and her mother was complaining about the coldest Miami Beach spring in years, and fretting about Natalie's detention. She jumped up. "Lunch is only a soufflé and a salad, Dr. Beck."

"Ah, I didn't expect your veal coup to be repeated."

"But at any rate," Jastrow said, "we'll share the last of Berenson's coffee."

After lunch Beck asked Natalie's permission to light a heavy black cigar. With his first puff he leaned back, sighed, and gestured toward the open window. "Well, Dr. Jastrow, won't you be sorry to leave this view behind?"

"*Are* we leaving it?"

"That's why I've come."

He talked for a long while. His pace and tone were leisurely, with frequent long cigars puffs, yet he began mixing up his f's and th's. The official Italian radio, he disclosed, wanted to put Dr. Jastrow on the air! The shortwave section was planning talks by famous enemy aliens, to project abroad an image of intellectual tolerance in Fascist Italy. Speakers would have *carte blanche*. The plan called for big names: Bernard Berenson, George Santayana, and of course Aaron Jastrow. The OVRA had just come through with a written commitment to Beck that Jastrow, his niece, and the baby would leave for Switzerland directly after the broadcast. So this development was proving a quick solution of the departure snarl. If Jastrow would simply come to Rome with Mrs. Henry and her infant, and record a leisurely two-hour interview — or four half-hour broadcasts, whichever he preferred — the Brazil business would be set aside. Beck would arrange in advance three exit visas, and tickets on the Rome-Zurich plane. They would not even have to return to Siena! And the sooner this happened, the better. Rome Radio was very hot on the idea.

Having said all this, Beck sat back, relaxed and smiling. "Well, Prothessor? How does it strike you?"

"Dear me, I confess I'm bewildered. Would they want me to discuss something in my field of work, like Constantine?"

"Oh, no, no. Absolutely out of the question! They want a philosophical view of the war, simply showing that all the right is not on one side. Remember what you said in this very room, Dr. Jastrow, on the occasion of our famous veal dinner? That would precisely fill the bill."

"Oh, but Werner, I'd had far too much wine that night. I couldn't rail against my own country like that on enemy shortwave. You can see that."

Pursing his lips around the cigar, Beck cocked his head. "Professor, you're creating difficulties, aren't you? You're a genius in the use of words, and in the subtle elaboration of ideas. You have a great original vision of this world catastrophe, a remarkable God's-eye view of the whole tragic panorama. That theme of 'sharing the hegemony' is perfect. Once you put your mind to it, the words would come easily. I'm sure you'd not only please Rome Radio, but impress your own countrymen as well. And to state matters bluntly, you'd get out of Italy at once."

Jastrow turned to his niece. "Well?"

"Well, you and Ezra Pound," said Natalie.

An unpleasant expression flashed across Beck's jowly face. "Comparisons are odious, Mrs. Henry."

"What about Berenson and Santayana?" Jastrow asked. "Have they agreed to this?"

Beck took a long puff at the cigar. "The Italian radio people consider you the key personality. Santayana is very old, and as you know he lives up in the clouds, with his theory of essences and all that philosophical mumbo-jumbo. He'll just mystify people. Still, a great name. Berenson, well, Berenson's whimsical and very independent. Rome Radio feels they'll get Berenson once you agree. He thinks very highly of you."

"Then neither of them knows about this yet," Natalie said.

Reluctantly Beck shook his head.

"No, no, no!" Jastrow suddenly rapped out. "I can't possibly become bracketed with Ezra Pound. His critical writings are undeniably brilliant. He has an original mind, though his verse is willfully obscure. The few times we've met I've found him an untidy, overbearing egotist, but that's neither here nor there. The thing is, I've heard his broadcasts, Werner. His attacks on the Jews are worse than anything even on your Berlin broadcasts, and his wild ravings about Roosevelt and the gold standard are simple treason. After the war he'll be hanged or shut up in an insane asylum. I can't imagine what's gotten into him, but I'd rather rot here in Siena than become another Ezra Pound."

With a curl of his lips, and a total confusion of f's and th's, Beck retorted, "But there's also the question of Mrs. Henry and her baby 'rotting here.' And there's the more serious question of how long you can stay on in Siena." He pulled out a gold pocket watch. "I've made a long trip to put this before you. I didn't expect a rejection out of hand. I thought I had earned your confidence."

Natalie interjected, "What's the question about our staying in Siena?"

Deliberately crushing out the cigar, grinding it on the ashtray, Beck replied, "Why, the OVRA pressure never lets up on me, Mrs. Henry. You realize that you belong in a concentration camp with the rest of the alien Jews. I was reminded of this very pointedly, when the broadcasting idea came up, and —"

"But I can't fathom this!" Jastrow expostulated, his flecked little hands shaking on the table before him. "We're *guaranteed* eventual passage to Switzerland! Aren't we? Even Leslie Slote's new letter affirms that. How can Rome Radio blackmail me into wrecking my reputation? Just be firm, Werner. Tell them to put it out of their minds. I won't consider it."

Beck rolled his bloodshot eyes at Natalie. "That, I must tell you, is a grave statement, Professor."

"Nevertheless, that's my answer," cried Jastrow, his excitement mounting, "and it's final."

An auto horn sounded outside.

"Dr. Beck, are you expecting a taxi?" Natalie folded her napkin on the table. Her tone was low and calm. Her face seemed all bones and eyes.

"Yes."

"Let me walk out with you. No, Aaron, don't you come."

"Werner, if I seem obstinate, I'm sorry." Jastrow stood up and held out an unsteady hand to Dr. Beck. "Martin Luther once put it well. '*Ich kann nicht anders.*'"

Beck stiffly bowed, and went out after Natalie. On the terrace, she said, "He'll do it."

"He'll do what? The broadcasting?"

"Yes. He'll do it."

"Mrs. Henry, his resistance was very strong." Beck's eyes were hard, questing, anxious.

From behind the gate came the cracked wheeze of the horn again.

"I know him well. These explosive reactions pass. I set him off by mentioning Pound. I'm terribly sorry. When does Rome Radio want him?"

"That's not definite," Beck said eagerly, "but what I must imperatively have from him at once is a letter consenting to make the broadcasts. That will get the hounds off my back, and start the wheels turning — the wheels of your release, Mrs. Henry."

"You'll have the letter by the end of the week."

They were at the open gate, where a large old touring car was waiting. Beck said in harsh harried tones, "I'd rather bring the letter back to Rome now. That would take a vast load oth my mind. I'd even postpone my return."

"I can't press him when he's in this mood. I promise you the letter will come."

He stared at her, and with a decisive flourish held out his hand. "I must count on your good sense, then."

"You can count on my concern for my baby."

"The greatest pleasure for me," said Beck, pausing with his hand on the taxicab door, "will be to see you all off to Zurich. I'll be waiting anxiously for that letter."

She hurried back into the villa. Jastrow still sat at the dining table, wineglass in hand, staring out at the cathedral. With a hangdog look at her, he said in a voice that still trembled, "I just couldn't help it, Natalie. The proposal is outrageous. Werner can't think like an American."

"Indeed he can't. But you shouldn't have turned him down flat, Aaron. You'll have to equivocate and stall."

"Possibly. But I'll never make the broadcasts he's asking for. Never! He took my perverse half-serious tirade over the veal far too literally. There's a German for you! You had provoked me, I'd drunk a lot, and anyway I relish arguing on the wrong side. You know that. Of course I loathe the Axis dictatorships. I exiled myself to save money and live quietly. Clearly it was the mistake of my life. No matter how badly the State Department has mistreated me, I love the United States. I will not go on the air for the Axis, to disgrace my scholarship and mark myself a traitor." The old man lifted his bearded chin, and a stony look settled on his face. "They can kill me, but I won't do it."

Alarmed, and thrilled too, Natalie said, "Then we're in danger."

"That may be, and you had better consult Dr. Castelnuovo about his escape plans, after all."

"What!"

"Making a dash for it seems farfetched, but it may come to that, my dear." Pouring a glass of wine, Jastrow spoke with cheery vigor. "Rabinovitz is a very able man. This young doctor seems a resolute sort. It's best to be prepared. Chances are our release will come through meantime, but I can't say I like Werner Beck's new tune."

"Christ almighty, Aaron, this is a change."

Jastrow rested his head wearily on a hand. "I didn't bargain for adventuring in my old age, but the one important thing is to get you and Louis out safely, isn't it? I shall have this wine and take my nap. Please draft up a letter to Werner, dear, agreeing in principle, and apologizing for my outburst. Say I'm commencing now to lay out four broadcasts. Be terribly vague about a completion date, for I shall be weaving Penelope's cloth, you know. Then you had better go and talk to that young doctor. The OVRA may well be watching him, so it's best you make it look like an office visit. Take the baby."

Dumbly Natalie nodded. She went to the library to draft the letter, feeling — half with terror, half with relief — that the lead had in an eyeblink passed from her to her uncle, and that she and her baby were now in the dark rapids.

26

June flowers are springing up all over Auschwitz. Even in the muddy heavily trodden camp sectors, in nooks between the blockhouses missed by the wooden clogs of the prisoners, the flowers peep out.

The Auschwitz Interest Area of the SS spreads over some forty square kilometers of greenery and woodland, at the confluence of the Sola and the Vistula, where the Vistula begins its long meander north to Warsaw and the Baltic Sea. Everywhere inside the high barbed-wire fences of this huge enclave, spaced with signs in German and Polish warning of instant death to trespassers, wildflowers make bright splashes, except where construction crews are churning the marshy grassland into brown muck and putting up blockhouses. Berel Jastrow is working in one of these crews.

The peasants who dwelled in the villages within the enclave are gone. A few of their evacuated thatched houses still stand. Most have been razed and their rubble used in camp blockhouses. Near the mucky holes where the houses once stood, fruit orchards in bloom perfume the warm June winds. The sweet odors die in the rows of prison blocks with their terrible latrine huts. But out in the fields where Berel is working, the orchards still sweetly scent the air. In the past six months Berel has been gaining back some of his old gnarled strength. As an assistant foreman to Sammy Mutterperl, with the armband of a *Vorarbeiter,* a leading worker, he eats and sleeps better than most Auschwitz inmates, though wretchedly enough.

Mutterperl wears the armband of an *Unterkapo.* But he is something more. The *Arbeitskommando,* work gang, of SS Sergeant Major Ernst Klinger, is actually a construction crew managed by Mutterperl; six hundred inmates of two blockhouses in Camp B-I. The job here is the rush construction of Camp B-II-d Birkenau, one of six subcamps of thirty-two blockhouses each. Completed, the whole sector will have one hundred fifty blockhouses in all, planned by the Central Building Board for erection north of the main roadway. With a twin sector, B-III, not yet begun, and B-I, already standing, Birkenau is projected by the Central Building Board as the largest detention center on earth. More than a hundred thousand working prisoners will be housed in Birkenau as slave labor for SS factories.

Sammy Mutterperl is doing in the Oswiecim prison camp what he did when he was a free man in Oswiecim town. He was a contractor there; in a peculiar way he is a contractor here. His client now is the Commandant of Auschwitz, and Sergeant Major Klinger is the Commandant's deputy on the spot. In theory Reichsführer SS Himmler is the high ultimate Client, but Himmler is an unseen god in Auschwitz. Even the SS men speak his name seldom, and with awe. The Commandant's chauffeured black Mercedes, however, is a familiar intimidating sight in the area, fluttering the double lightning-flash insignia flags of the SS. Berel glimpses it often. The Commandant believes in personal supervision from the top — "the eye of the master" is his word.

The Klinger gang has been turning out good work for many months, laboring in all weather, in haste, silence, and submissiveness. The crew routinely endures curses and beatings from SS men and the kapos. Prisoners who weaken, faint, and fall get beaten bloody by the kapos for malingering. If they really look done for, the kapos finish them off with shovels or sticks, and other workers drag back their bodies for evening roll call. Fresh prisoners, of which the supply is endless, replace them on the next shift.

As Auschwitz goes, Mutterperl considers Klinger's a good kommando to serve in. He has been in Auschwitz for a year and a half. In 1941 the Commandant, desperate at the crazy expansion orders from Berlin, combed the countryside for builders and mechanics and put them to work at once —Jew, Pole, Czech, Croat, Rumanian, it made little difference, Mutterperl among them — in conditions of housing, nourishment, and discipline that were by outside standards unspeakable, but in Auschwitz something like luxury.

Sammy has come to know Auschwitz well. In on the ground floor, so to speak, he is surviving handily. Because of the rush to start construction he was spared quarantine camp, those fearsome isolation weeks of maltreatment and hunger which reduce many prisoners to bony automata, blank to any thought but self-preservation. Klinger as SS overseer and Mutterperl as Jew foreman have worked together since they did the SS barracks job a year ago. Both are wily burly fellows in their late fifties, anxious to produce results: Klinger to please his superiors, Mutterperl to stay alive. For his own benefit, Klinger has gradually pushed the Jew into an informal protected status as a construction foreman. As such, Sammy can recruit prisoners for the kommando. That is how he has rescued Berel. Pulling in a Russian prisoner is nonregulation procedure, but Auschwitz regulations have no consistency or coherence. SS noncoms and officers constantly trade off favors and loot, and bend the rules to suit themselves. Nobody is a better hand at such maneuvering than Hauptscharführer Ernst Klinger.

Klinger is an old file of the camps, a stout blond Bavarian going gray. Like the Commandant, he is a veteran of Dachau and Sachsenhausen; in fact, the Commandant requisitioned him for Oswiecim. Once a policeman in Munich, turned Nazi when he lost his job in the depression, Klinger found in the SS a haven. Since toughness was a requirement, this once easygoing family man became tough. In the line of duty Klinger has flogged the skin off prisoners' backs, wiping the blood-dripping whip with a casual grin as the victim sagged raw and unconscious. He has lined up with execution squads and shot condemned men. His normal tone of communication with prisoners is a menacing bellow. With a blow of a club he can collapse a man like a scarecrow of sticks. Nevertheless, Sammy Mutterperl considers him "all right." Klinger does not, like so many SS men and kapos, get his kicks from inflicting fear, pain, and death on terrified living skeletons. Moreover, he is very corrupt, which is a big help. You can do business with Klinger.

Klinger considers the Jew "all right," too, for a Jew. When getting drunk with his SS buddies, he can even boast about "my smart clipcock Sammy." For in the Central Building Board office back at the base camp, where several hundred German architects, engineers, and draftsmen work in comfort on Auschwitz's never-ending expansion plans, the word is "Give it to Klinger," when a job requires quick, visible results. Klinger's efficiency ratings have shot up since he left Sachsenhausen. Promotion to Untersturmführer, second lieutenant, is in the wind; a big leap at his age, from the noncom ranks to a commission, with big dividends in prestige and pay. How pleased his wife and kids will be, if it really comes off! He knows that he owes all this to his Sammy. So strictly in self-interest, he watches out for the Jew.

Klinger now has a big rush job going: to throw up all thirty-two blockhouse frames of Birkenau Camp B-II-d in a hurry. Never mind the walls and roofs, is the word from the board — just frames, frames, frames, as far as the eye can see. A big shot is coming to inspect. Klinger's gang is at the outer edge of new Birkenau construction. Farther west a horde of shaven-headed prisoners in striped ticking, knee-deep in marshy grass, are clearing rocks, pulling stumps, and levelling the ground with spades and hoes for still more camps, but those are only on the drawing-board. B-II-d is under construction, and the more actual structures in sight, the better for the Commandant.

Every day in Auschwitz can bring surprises; and on this day at the Klinger work site comes a frightening surprise. Seven covered gray trucks pull up on the road. Klinger orders Berel's subsection of seventy men — SS guards, kapos, and all — into the trucks, to load up studs and rafters at the timber yard. This is a very strange business. Human time and muscle are in infinite supply at Auschwitz, zero cost items. Prisoners carry lumber to building sites, if necessary several miles. The Germans do not waste gasoline and tires on such errands. So what is going on? Fear distorts their faces as the prisoners enter the trucks; some drag their feet, and the cursing kapos club them aboard.

But the trucks do go to the timber yard. Under the yells and the blows of the kapos, the prisoners rush about to load up, then jam aboard again pell-mell, and rumble back to B-II-d. Berel guesses that the deadline is drawing close, and for once, fast action matters. Ordinarily, Auschwitz is a slow machine-free world, paced by the human body. Over-slaves beat under-slaves, government taskmasters beat them both, and it is all — so he has thought often — a throwback to Pharaoh's Egypt, as the Torah pictures it. Only in this Egypt, twentieth-century trucks grind by sometimes, and the taskmasters have twentieth-century machine guns; and death is not for Jewish male babies only.

When the trucks arrive, another surprise. The Commandant himself stands there with a couple of green-uniformed aides, frowning in the sunlight at the strange sight of slaves riding. His Mercedes is parked by the roadside. Klinger is shuffling and scraping before him. The kapos and the guards pile on abuse and blows in the unloading. The prisoners run frantically with lumber several hundred yards to the northernmost framing sites, then scamper back for more. An old frog-faced kapo who has long had it in for Berel, a former Viennese bank robber who wears the high-status green trian-gle patch of a professional criminal, suddenly and blindingly clubs Berel's skull. *"Who do you think you are, you lazy old pile of shit, just because you've got a shitty armband? Grab a plank and shake your ass!"* Berel staggers, almost goes down, but seizes a brace and runs with it, dizzily think-ing that the kapo has picked his time well. With the Commandant looking on, there is no protection in Auschwitz. But the Commandant never stays long.

The Commandant for his part is in bad shape, though his square-hewn calm face shows no sign of it. Not since his own solitary confinement for a political murder in Brandenburg prison, under the Weimar regime, has he suffered such wrenching griping stomach pains. The agony is impervious to whiskey, sedatives, or any medicines he has tried. He simply must endure and go on.

He is busily muttering to an aide. After a while the aide takes Klinger aside. Fresh orders: work straight through the night, under floodlights! The Commandant is waiving the air defense rules. Halt work on framing. Switch to covering walls and putting on roofs. Put up wallboards only on the side facing the road, and only on every other blockhouse.

The Commandant gets in his Mercedes. Back to the Residence for lunch, he tells the chauffeur. Lunch! He will be lucky to hold anything on his stomach. All morning he has been driving over the route they will tra-verse tomorrow. He has been seeing every site for himself, anticipating questions, throwing questions at the SS overseers to get them on their toes.

The dam site is the worst problem. Berlin hasn't come up with the labor, materials, and supervision. I. G. Farben has been swallowing up everything for its Buna Werke at the Monowice subcamp. One can't flog starving unskilled Poles and Jews into building a dam. Flog them to death, yes, but the Vistula will still flow merrily on its way! If Reichsführer SS Himmler really wants to dam the Vistula, then let him see how far behind the project really is, and come up with the wherewithal. Dr. Kammler, chief architect of Auschwitz, is an SS major general, not a lowly major like the Commandant. Berlin can issue these impossible orders, but Kammler's deputies in Auschwitz have to implement them. Himmler will listen to Kammler. The Commandant feels fairly safe about the dam.

His one worry about the whole inspection visit is the damned Jewish transport. Himmler wants to see an action from the beginning to the end. The Commandant has tried to anticipate all the things that can go wrong, and that have gone wrong in the early months: the troublemakers who scream and cause panics, the sanitary squad idiots who fail to drop in enough stuff, so the people don't die, and the like. By now the process has been smoothed out and usually goes off all right. But if things get gummed up, nobody will be blamed but himself!

Then there is the disposal problem. This mass-grave burial technique is not going to work much longer; not in Auschwitz. This is no small cleanup of Jews like Chelmno or Sobibor. Those pen-pushers in Berlin don't picture what a disposal problem thousands and thousands of bodies can be. They don't care. All they want is impressive figures to show the boss. But these tons — many, many tons — of organic material, piling up week by week in Auschwitz soil, are a hell of a headache and a health hazard. And it's only the beginning! Let the Reichsführer see for himself.

And those Berlin pantywaists are plenty jittery about the big boss's visit. They've been giving him glowing reports, sidetracking the Commandant's desperate pleas for personnel and material and his complaints about impossible schedules. Now they have to pray that the Commandant will protect their asses. They wouldn't dream of soiling their own shiny boots with Auschwitz mud; not them, those desk-bound *Standartenführer* and *Obersturmbannführer*, leading the soft life back home! And he is just a major, running an establishment bigger than any army camp, bigger probably than any military installation in the world, and still growing! Berlin keeps telling him to go easy on the complaints, emphasize the positive things. The hell with them.

The Commandant is writhing in pain as the Mercedes drives up before the prettily flowering front garden of the Residence, where his wife is working in a sunbonnet. He knows very well what is causing these cramps. His career hangs on the next seventy-two hours. He can be relieved in disgrace and expelled from the SS; he can be promoted on the spot to Obersturm-bannführer — lieutenant colonel — a recognition scandalously overdue; those are the extremes, and in between are a lot of possibilities. A visit from Reichsführer SS Himmler doesn't happen every day.

His wife wants to show him how the roses are coming along, but he brusquely passes her by. His adjutant is standing in the bay window. She sees them talking inside. Her husband glances eagerly at a document the adjutant hands him. He looks happy, then suddenly he begins to glare. He lets out such a roar, throwing the document in the adjutant's face and waving both fists, that she hears him through the closed windows. He makes that old infuriated gesture: *Upstairs!* That means top-secret talk, in the den off the bedroom. She hurries inside to warn the cook not to dry out the roast.

The Commandant has in fact been pleased by his first glimpse of the fine paper and the good printing job. The schedule started off well:

REICHSFÜHRER VISIT
KONZENTRATIONSLAGER AUSCHWITZ

First Day

0800–0830.	*Aerodrome.* Arrival and reception. Motorcade to Base Camp.
0830–0845.	*Parade Ground.* Trooping of colors. Band serenade. Honor review of troops.
0845–0930.	*Officers' Mess.* Breakfast, with map demonstration of camp layout.
0930–1000.	*Architect's Office, Central Planning Board.* Reichsführer SS views models: Vistula dam, new drainage canal system, animal husbandry center, Birkenau Camp.
1000–1100.	*Motor Tour.* Monowice, Raisko, Budy. General view: I. G. Farben construction, dam site, agricultural areas, reclaimed lands, botanical laboratories, tree nurseries, stock breeding sector.
1100–1330.	SPECIAL.
1330–1500.	Lunch.

It was on seeing these last two items that the Commandant has thrown the schedule in his adjutant's face and ordered him upstairs.

Screaming so that the whole household hears him through closed doors, and his children quake in their rooms, and his wife and cook in the kitchen exchange scared looks, the Commandant demands an explanation. The trembling adjutant stammers that the railway directorate at Oppeln has scheduled the transport arrival before lunch, with instructions to expedite the return of the emptied train. If the Commandant will telephone Oppeln to see if the cars can be retained in the Auschwitz yards for a few more hours, then perhaps the Jews can just wait in the cars and get off after lunch.

The explosion that follows is the worst the Commandant's wife has ever heard. The Himmler visit, she thinks, is making nervous wrecks of everybody. How glad she will be when it is over! He has gotten dead drunk every night for a week, taken strong sedatives, and yet he has not slept. This job is too much. As for the children and herself, the sooner they get out, the better. The flood of new toys and picture books day by day for the young ones, the fine clothes for the big boy, the excellent servants, expert gardeners, the stacks of lovely expensive underwear and negligees for herself are all very well, but a decent home life would be better than any of that.

Upstairs the Commandant is roaring that the whole schedule will be printed again at once. The SPECIAL item will come *after* lunch as ordered. He, the Commandant, personally orders this. The train will remain in the freight yard as long as necessary! If the Oppeln railway directors have doubts, they can take a few months in the Auschwitz quarantine camp to think it over. This is REICHSFÜHRER SS BUSINESS! Understood? Nothing, *nothing* can interfere. What idiotic asshole could think of showing a special operation to the Reichsführer *before* lunch? What kind of appetite will he have to eat after that?

This is the gist of a ten-minute chewing-out that has the adjutant, himself a hardened SS captain with a Sachsenhausen background, whey-faced and shaking as a Jew before a quarantine camp flogging. Never has the Commandant thrown a fit like this. He himself is trembling all over when he dismisses the adjutant, who hurries out and barely makes it to the garden before throwing up everything in his stomach, with blood streaks in the vomited mess.

The Commandant gulps half a tumbler of brandy. It calms him. When he goes down to lunch the gnawing at his gut is gone. He eats well, and is pleasanter to his wife and children than he has been in a month. The rest of the schedule, after all, looks good. But God in heaven, if he had not insisted on seeing that printed schedule! His old rule never fails — *"the eye of the master!"*

The train has been waiting out of sight around the bend. Now its mournful whistle blows at five minutes to three.

The Reichsführer SS and his high-brass aides stand with the Commandant on the long wooden platform, waiting. Happily, it is another beautiful day. The leafy trees around the siding give pleasant shade from the hot afternoon sun. They have all lunched heartily at the senior officers' mess, and so far the whole inspection tour has been going smoothly. Himmler has been very gracious about the stalled dam. He has obviously been impressed by the camp's explosive growth. He has shown real delight in the agricultural installations, always his pet Auschwitz undertaking, farmer that he is. The impressive unfinished I. G. Farben structure at Monowice has won his approval, too. The Commandant is on pins and needles. If this business goes off without a hitch, positive results from the visit may well impend.

The smoke of the locomotive shows over the trees. The train pulls into sight. It is a small transport, deliberately planned that way by the Commandant; ten freight cars, about eight hundred people. The Kattowitz police have held them rounded up for several days. The bunker can take just about eight hundred, tightly packed. Himmler's personal letter to the Commandant was specific: *"a whole action, from the beginning to the end."* Two shifts would have dragged the thing out and depressed the Reichsführer SS. It will be bad enough as it is!

The Commandant has watched the process many times — *"the eye of the master"* — but he has never gotten quite used to it. He is tough. He knows that the Reichsführer is tough. He knows about Himmler's visit to a Special Action Unit in Russia during the dispatch of a lot of Jews. Crude stuff, that, from what he has heard: making them dig their own mass grave, then mowing them down and burying them, clothes and all. The Auschwitz process is far more humane, practical, *German*. Still, in its own way it is sad. The Commandant knows how hard it is on his own officers. He is intensely curious to see how Heinrich Himmler will take it. After all, it is a damn sticky proceeding. What if Germany loses the war? The Commandant never voices such doubts, naturally. He squelches the faintest hint from his subordinates. Still, these thoughts do trouble him every now and then.

The train stops. The Jews begin to descend. SS guards along the edge of the siding stand back, avoiding any bullying or menacing appearance. These are Jews from a big town, and they look prosperous. They blink in the sunlight as they clumsily tumble out of the cattle cars, helping down the old people, the cripples, and the youngsters. They peer around anxiously, the women holding their children close. But they show no great alarm, and listen intently to Untersturmführer Hössler's smooth announcement about where they will be housed, what skills are most in demand, and so on and so forth. It is convincing stuff at that. Hössler and his sidekick Aumaier keep polishing and improving the spiel.

Next, the Jews line up for the selection without difficulty. Soon the few men picked for the labor camp march off on foot through the thick trees toward Birkenau. The rest climb quietly into the waiting trucks. The abandoned platform is piled high with their baggage; handsome goods, a lot of real leather there. It will be quite a haul when the cleanup squad sorts it out. The Jews really seem to believe everything Hössler has said, down to the detail that the luggage will all be delivered to their living quarters. Living quarters! There is something very human in their credulity. Nobody wants to believe he is about to die, especially on such a pretty June day, with the sun shining and birds chirping in the trees. Some of the Jews cast apprehensive looks at the clump of SS officers watching the process; but it does not seem to the Commandant that any of them recognize the great Reichsführer SS Himmler. Maybe they are too preoccupied.

The loaded trucks wait while the SS party drives ahead to the bunker site for a quick look around. The Commandant is proud of its innocuous appearance. DISINFECTION, reads the large wooden sign by the roadside. One sees only a large thatched peasant cottage like thousands in Polish villages, set in an apple orchard. On the cottage door, a neat arrow sign says, *This Way to Disinfection*. The undressing huts, new structures of raw wood a few meters away, are not in the least scary. The inspection party enters the hut labelled *Women and Children*. Benches line the walls under numbered hooks where the Jews will hang and fold their clothes. A sign on the wall reads in several languages:

> *Remember your hook number, to recover your*
> *belongings after the disinfection!*
> *Fold clothes neatly!*
> *Be tidy!*
> *No unnecessary talking!*

The hot sun makes for a strong smell of fresh lumber in the hut, which mingles with the sweet scent of the apple blossoms drifting through the open door. Himmler offers no comments. His short, characteristically sharp and jerky nod shows he has seen enough: on to the next thing!

The SS officers cross the orchard and enter the cottage. Here the very heavy wooden doors on the four big empty whitewashed rooms, and the back door with a large sign reading *This Way to Bathroom*, look somewhat odd. An SS man in a white coat stands in the corridor beside a table piled with towels and bars of soap. The odor here is of some powerful disinfectant. The room doors are hooked open. The Commandant unhooks one, and shows Himmler the heavy bars that will screw the doors airtight. Wordlessly, he indicates the wall apertures where the gas crystals will tumble in. The Reichsführer SS nods. He makes an inquiring gesture at the sign about the bathroom. "Leads outside," says the Commandant. "Disposal."

Short jerky nod.

The trucks rumble up. The inspection party leaves the bunker and gathers under some apple trees, at a discreet distance, to watch the operation.

In the leading truck, as usual, are about a dozen of the Sonderkommandos, the squad of Jewish prisoners required to take part in the process. This small subsquad consists of Sonderkommandos who know several languages. They jump from their truck and run to assist their fellow Jews out of the other trucks. They are dressed respectably in civilian clothing: in this warm weather, good shirts, trousers, and leather shoes. No striped suits for these Sonderkommandos, and no wooden clogs, of course, only the obligatory striped camp cap. They help down the women and kids, talking in Yiddish or Polish about the disinfection procedure, the camp accommodations, the working conditions. By now the transport Jews have only a few minutes to live, so no chances are taken. The SS guards line up in a double cordon from the trucks to the undressing hut, with dogs, guns, and clubs. The Jews have no choice but to march straight on to the hut, accompanied by the Sonderkommandos, who are describing the food, the mail service, and the visiting privileges. These fellows will go all the way into the bunker with them, maintaining the humane hoax to the very last second, as the Commandant explains to the silent Himmler. They will dart outside only when the SS guards actually march in to bolt the gas-tight doors.

In his explanation the Commandant does not give credit to Aumaier and Hössler, the two SS officers who have worked up this really clever arrangement of the Sonderkommandos. After all, not they, but he himself will get the blame if something goes wrong! But these officers did create the whole concept. They train the Sonderkommandos in groups. Periodically they gas them and train more. Sonderkommandos are recruited from the new arrivals in the quarantine camp; the weak, the easily terrified, the ratty ones who tend to collapse under the shock of Auschwitz conditions, are the ones to look for. Hössler and Aumaier select them, isolate them in a special blockhouse, and confront them with this assignment in no uncertain terms. They can do as they are told and live, or they can be shot at once. That is their choice. There are always enough Sonderkommandos, though many prefer the *Kugel*, the bullet in the neck, terrorized though they are. They get their request. But even afterward there are those who break down on the job; try to warn the new arrivals, or even to undress and commit suicide with them. The SS keeps a sharp eye out for these, and usually catches them. They get a punishment designed to discourage the others; they are burned alive. Sound practice.

As the Commandant watches these wretches urging women and children along to their doom, he wonders at them, as always. How can they be so absolutely dead to all natural feelings, particularly toward their coreligionists? Jews are a riddle, that's all. He steals a look at Heinrich Himmler, and gets a nasty shock. Himmler is looking glassily and fixedly at him. The Commandant realizes with a cold shudder that this may be the decisive moment of the whole inspection, the only real point of it. The Reischsführer has come to see with his own eyes — *"the eye of the master"* — whether the Commandant of Auschwitz has what it takes. If he flinches now, shows the slightest nervousness or compunction, it is his career, possibly his neck. How long can he be allowed to live, knowing what he knows, if he can't cut the mustard? He has seen SS men — high-placed ones, too — get a *Kugel*.

The Jews are hurrying now in a drove toward the undressing hut. He sees a sight that unexpectedly tries his taut nerves. A dog lunges and barks at a child, no more than four or five years old, a little girl in a short blue dress who looks a lot like his own youngest daughter: fair hair, blue eyes, round German face, nothing "Jewish" about her. The pretty little thing shrinks against her mother and screams. The mother catches her up in her arms and to distract her, she breaks off a small branch of apple blossoms and holds it to the little girl's nose. So they disappear into the hut among the crowding Jews. The Commandant has seen dozens of pathetic incidents here; but something about the look of that little girl, the mother's impulsive seizing of the flowering branch — the mother, too, didn't look Jewish. The propaganda caricatures are stuff and nonsense; these mortal enemies of the Reich look like any other Europeans, most of them. He has found that out long ago. The Commandant feels a pain in his gut; the cramps are starting up again. He puts on his stoniest face.

Now at least it will go fast.

The SS double cordon lines up again in a tight path from the hut to the cottage. The naked men come out first, as always a sorry crowd — tubby ones, scrawny ones, cripples, gray or bald ones — their sorry circumcised cocks shrunken up with fright, no doubt. He seldom sees a Jew with a really big cock here. Maybe the ablebodied ones are more virile. The fully dressed Sonderkommandos among them are still talking, trying to cheer them up. But now these Jews are too close to death not to show it on their faces. The Sonderkommandos, too, have sick expressions. The Commandant is tough, but he never likes to look at the faces of the Jews walking to the bunker, especially the men.

Somehow the women have more courage. Or maybe the shock to their modesty distracts them; that, and concern for their kids. They do not look so ghastly as they come out next and troop naked through the two rows of young German uniformed men. These SS men are under strict orders to keep silent and serious, but nevertheless they can't help smirking at some of the lovely ones. There are always pretty ones among them, and after all, there is nothing in the world more charming than a naked woman; and when she is carrying or leading a nude child, in a strange way it adds to her beauty.

This, for the Commandant, has always been the supreme moment of the process, in its beauty, sadness, and terror — the walk of the naked women with their children to the bunker. He wants to look at Himmler, but he is afraid to. He keeps his face rigid, yet he almost loses his composure when, among the last of the women coming out of the cottage, he sees the mother who broke the branch. She has a sweet figure, poor creature. Like so many of the others, she has uncovered her tits so as to hold the child in one arm and protect her cunt with the other. Invariably they will let the tits go, if they carry a baby, to cover their bushes; it is a strange fact of feminine nature. But what shakes the Commandant is the sight of the naked little girl. She is still holding the branch of apple blossoms.

The last woman's pink backside disappears into the cottage. The SS men dash in, and out come the Sonderkommandos, with the white-coated man who stood by the soap and towels. The inspection party can hear the loud slamming of the doors, and the screeching of the bolts that fasten them tight. The Red Cross ambulance, which has driven up during the undressing time, now disgorges the SS men from the sanitary squad in their gas masks, carrying the cans of cyanide crystals. After the naked women, not a very handsome sight! But it's nasty stuff they handle. The precautionary rules are strict. They do their job in a few moments, opening the cans and dumping them into the wall slots. They pile back into the ambulance, and off it goes.

The Commandant, keeping his voice absolutely steady, asks the Reichsführer SS if he would like to listen at the bunker door and look in. Himmler goes with the Commandant, listens and looks. A transport of Jews sounds different inside; mournful, resigned, almost prayerful wails and groans, not the animal screeches and bellows of Russian prisoners or Polacks. As Himmler puts his eye to the peephole, his face contorts: a grimace of disgust or a smile of amusement, the Commandant cannot be sure.

Himmler does a surprising thing. He asks an aide for a cigarette. Like the Führer, Himmler does not smoke, or is reputed not to. But now he lights up and puffs calmly, as the Commandant takes him around to the back of the bunker, while they wait for the gas to do its work. He shows Himmler the enormous and ever-expanding area of the mass graves, and explains the mounting problems. For hundreds of meters in every direction, there are vast mounds of earth here and there in the grassy field. A rail track runs through them, ending near a large hole with earth piled high beside it, where the special kommandos are still digging. The expression on Himmler's face sharpens. His lips disappear as he puffs the skin around them in his curious fashion; a sure signal that he is intensely interested.

For the first time since their arrival at the bunker, he speaks; in a low calm voice, not to the Commandant, but to an aide, a tall good-looking colonel, who pulls off his black glove and makes rapid notes on a pad.

The gate in the back fence swings open. From the open back door of the bunker comes a cart heaped high with naked bodies rolling toward the inspection party on the rails, hauled and pushed by different Sonderkommandos, the burial detail. As the cart passes the SS officers, there is a whiff of the disinfectant, rather like carbolic acid. The naked people look not much different than they did less than half an hour ago, except that they are absolutely still now, streaked with excrement, and all jumbled together, some with jaws hanging open and wide eyes fixed and staring — old men, little children, pretty women, in an inert heap. One can still admire the looks of the women and the charm of the kids.

These Jew kommandos couldn't be more businesslike about the whole thing. Where the rails end, they crank the cart up so that the bodies slide to the ground in a tangle. A few of them push the cart back toward the bunker. The rest, together with the diggers who come climbing out of the pit, haul the bodies to the edge of the hole by an arm or a leg — some of them use big meat hooks, which the Commandant finds personally distasteful — and toss the dead down out of sight. Reichsführer Himmler is interested. He walks to the rim of the pit, and observes the kommandos laying out the warm naked bodies in rows, and sprinkling white powder on them. This, the Commandant explains, is quicklime. Something must be done, because the water table of the whole area is being contaminated. The bacteria count even of the drinking water at the SS barracks has gone up to the danger level. In the long run, as he has repeatedly complained to Berlin, burial is no answer; certainly it won't be once the actions that Lieutenant Colonel Eichmann has projected, on a scale of hundreds of thousands of Jews every few weeks, start to materialize.

The whole system will break down, he insists, if drastic steps are not taken at once. Nothing is adequate. The cottage bunker is a makeshift. Another one is being readied nearby, but it too is only a stopgap. The crematoriums remain pretty models in the Central Building Board office, and Berlin has simply been ignoring the disposal problem. The Commandant, in his honest preoccupation with this serious matter, pours out his heart to the Reichsführer SS, while the special kommandos continue to cart out bodies, throw them in the hole, and stack them in rows. So caught up is he in his pleas that when he sees the dead baby girl come tumbling out of the cart with the broken branch in her hand it does not bother him.

Sincerity pays off. He can see that he is making an impression. Himmler gives a sharp jerky nod; he puffs out his mouth so that his lips disappear, and he glances around at his aides.

"So?" says the Reichsführer. "And what is next?"

"The crematoriums will be built," he says next day to the Commandant, in a private meeting just before going to the aerodrome.

The meeting is almost over. The last serious request, for permission to use Jews in sterilization experiments, which the Commandant put with some trepidation, has been cheerfully granted. They are in an inner office at the Building Board. Only Schmauser, the SS general in charge of all of south Poland, and therefore of Auschwitz, is present.

"The construction of crematoriums will take priority even over I. G. Farben," Himmler states. "They will be completed before the end of the year. Schmauser will override all other projects in this province for labor and materials." Himmler waves his black swagger stick at the general, who hastily nods. "You will hear from me further about the disposal problem. You have told me all your difficulties, and given me an honest look at Auschwitz. I am satisfied that you are doing your best under very tough conditions. It is wartime, and we have to think in terms of war. Assign your best construction crews to the crematoriums. When they are completed, liquidate the crews. Understood?"

"Understood, Herr Reichsführer."

"I promote you to Obersturmbannführer. Congratulations. Now I am on my way."

Lieutenant Colonel! Spot promotion!

A week later, Ernst Klinger is promoted, too, to Untersturmführer. At the same time, he receives a different assignment for his construction crew. They have a new designation: *Arbeitskommando, Crematorium II.*

*   *   *

27

𝕸𝖎𝖉𝖜𝖆𝖞

(from *World Holocaust* by Armin von Roon)

One of the decisive battles in the history of the world was fought at sea at this time on the other side of the globe, almost unnoticed in Germany, even in our Supreme Headquarters. The failure of our Japanese allies to furnish us the truth about Midway amounted to bad faith. However, Hitler hated gloomy news, and most likely would have ignored an honest report of it. The serious German reader must grasp what happened at Midway in June 1942 to understand the course of the entire war.

Strangely, the democracies themselves gave Midway small play at the time. In the United States the news of the battle was scanty and inaccurate. To this day few Americans grasp that at Midway their navy won a sea victory to stand in military chronicles with Salamis and Lepanto. For the third time in planetary history, Asia sailed forth to attack the West in force, with ultimate stakes of world dominion. At Salamis the Greeks turned back the Persians; at Lepanto the Venetian coalition halted Islam; and at Midway the Americans stopped, at least for our century, the rising tide of Asiatic color. Pacific battles thereafter were in the main futile Japanese attempts to recover the initiative lost at Midway.

Before Midway, for all the missed chances and miscalculations of Adolf Hitler and the Japanese leaders, the war still hung in the balance. Had the United States lost this passage at arms, the Hawaiian Islands might well have become untenable. With his West Coast suddenly naked to Japanese might, Roosevelt might have had to reverse his notorious "Germany first" policy. The whole war could have taken a different turn.

Why then is this decisive event so underestimated? The anomaly stems from the nature of the battle. Victory at Midway turned partly on the analysis of Japanese coded radio traffic. The feat could not be revealed in wartime.* The United States Navy's version of Midway was foggy and guarded, and it

---

*In fact, a Chicago newspaper did dig out and print the story of the code-breaking. The Japanese missed it, evidently. President Roosevelt wisely ignored this treason, instead of prosecuting it in a blaze of publicity. — V.H.

came out several days late. A long time passed before the setback to Japanese war plans was fully assessed. So the realities of Midway were obscured. The war rumbled on, and the battle faded from sight, as Mount Everest can be obscured by a whirl of dust raised by a truck. But as time passes, this turning point looms ever larger and clearer in the military history of mankind.

"Flattop" Warfare

The German reader accustomed to land warfare needs a brief sketch of the tactical problem at sea. On the water of course there is no terrain. The battleground is all one smooth level unbounded field. This simplifies combat as the land soldier knows it, but adds weight to fundamental elements. The aircraft carrier developed as a radical advance in *range of firepower*.

In ancient sea fighting, warships rammed each other, smashed each other's banks of oars, cast arrows, stones, lumps of iron, or flaming stuff across a few feet of open water. Sometimes they came alongside each other with grappling hooks, and soldiers leaped across and fought on the decks. Long after guns were installed in men-o'-war, hand-to-hand waterborne fighting continued. John Paul Jones won the first big sea fight for America by grappling and boarding the British man-o'-war *Serapis,* exactly as a Roman sea captain would have done to a ship of Carthage.

But the great nineteenth-century revolutions in science and industry brought forth the *battleship,* a giant steam-driven iron vessel, with rotating centerline guns that could fire a one-ton shell almost ten miles to port or starboard. All modern nations hastened to build or buy battleships. The front-running race between our own shipyards and England's to build ever-bigger battleships was a prime cause of the First World War. Even before that, English capitalists had obligingly built a fleet of these monsters for the Japanese, who in 1905 used it to trounce czarist Russia at Tsushima Strait. Only one other large battleship engagement ever took place. At the Battle of the Skagerrak, in 1916, our High Seas Fleet outfought the British navy in a classic action. Twenty-five years later, at Pearl Harbor, the type went into final and futile eclipse.

The battleship was the dinosaur of sea warfare, misbegotten and short-lived. Each one was a drain on a nation's resources like the equipment for many army divisions. But it did bring long-range firepower into sea war. The trajectories of its big guns required a correction *for the curvature of the earth!* Thus the industrial age brought man face to face with the physical limits of his tiny planet.

After the First World War a few farseeing naval officers perceived that the airplane could far outrange the battleship's big guns. It could fly hundreds of miles, and the pilot could guide his bomb almost onto the target. Against the crusty advocacy of battleship admirals, they fought and won the argument for building "flattops," seagoing airdromes. Pearl Harbor settled the twenty-year dispute in an hour, and the Pacific conflict became an aircraft carrier war.

———————

TRANSLATOR'S NOTE: *I was a battleship man all my life. Roon ignores the role of the battleship in maintaining the balance of power for a turbulent half-century, though nobody can disagree that it failed at Pearl Harbor. His casual claim of German victory in the Jutland stand-off (Battle of the Skagerrak) is ridiculous. The Imperial German High Seas Fleet never sailed to fight after Jutland. Much of it was scuttled at Scapa Flow. Eventually Hitler scrapped the rest, after the* Bismarck *was sunk and the other battleships immobilized at their moorings by RAF bombs. — V.H.*

———————

Carrier Combat Tactics

All Pacific flattops, U.S. and Japanese, carried three kinds of airplanes.

The *fighter* plane was defensive. It escorted the attacking planes to the target, and protected them by knocking down fighters that tried to intercept them. It also protected its own fleet against enemy attackers, by hovering overhead in a combat air patrol.

There were two attacking types: the *dive-bomber* plane and the *torpedo* plane. The dive-bomber dropped its missile through the air. The torpedo plane aimed for the death blow below the waterline; its technique was riskier, its missile heavier. It had to fly for many minutes on a straight course low over the water, and slow down to drop its torpedo. During this approach, the torpedo plane pilot was suicidally vulnerable to AA fire or to a fighter plane attack. He therefore needed strong fighter protection.

Carrier battle doctrine was the same in both navies. The three types of aircraft were launched for a mission by squadrons. The fighters, dive-bombers, and torpedo planes would join up and wing together to the target. The fighters would engage the defending fighters, the dive-bombers would attack, and when the enemy was most distracted the vulnerable torpedo planes would slip in low for the kill. This was called *coordinated attack,* or *deferred departure.*

In this scheme there were variations: i.e., a fighter could carry a light bomb; and the Japanese from the start designed their torpedo plane, the Type-97 bomber, as a two-purpose machine. Instead of a torpedo, it could carry a very large fragmentation bomb, thus giving it a strong capability against land targets as well.

On this dual-purpose Japanese bomber, in the end, the whole battle turned.

Code Book C

Intelligence too was crucial. By analysis of encoded radio traffic and by fractional decipherment of the code, the Americans discerned the enemy battle plan. The Japanese should have foreseen and avoided this. In modern war all codes and ciphers must be frequently replaced. This was a standard rule in our Wehrmacht commands. One has to assume that the enemy is copying all the broadcast gibberish, and that what the mind of man can devise the mind of man can unravel. Japan's communication doctrine called for code replacement, but her navy's preparations for Midway were plagued by both overconfidence and hurry. The hurry resulted from the Doolittle raid.

Navy Code Book C had been in use by the Japanese since Pearl Harbor. Aided by pioneer use of IBM machines, American and British teams had worked on the texts for half a year. A Code Book D was supposed to go into use on April first. Had this been done the Japanese signals for the Midway attack would have been secure. But the replacement was postponed to May first and then to June first, in the post-Doolittle scramble. On June first the opaque curtain of Code Book D did at last fall, but by then only three days remained before the battle, and Japan's plan was largely known to the enemy.

The Damaged Carriers

The Japanese faults of overconfidence and hurry showed up after the Coral Sea battle, a carrier skirmish that took place when they tried to capture Port Moresby in New Guinea, to create an air threat to Australia. The expedition ran afoul of two American carriers. The Japanese had the better of the two-day melee, a comedy of blundering decisions and airborne blindman's buff in bad weather, during which the opposing vessels never sighted each other. The Japanese sank the big flattop *Lexington* and an oiler, and damaged the *Yorktown*. They lost a light carrier, and took bomb damage and aircraft attrition in the fleet carriers *Shokaku* and *Zuikaku*.

The flattops of both sides went limping home from the Coral Sea. Fourteen hundred Yankee workmen at Pearl Harbor, laboring around the clock, patched up the badly hit *Yorktown* in three days, and it fought at Midway. But the two damaged Japanese flattops were *dropped from the operation*. The high command refused a postponement to train and replace air crews, and ordered no urgent repair effort. To ensure a full moon for the landing, or for some such footling reason, the weight of two carriers was nonchalantly forgone.

Plan and Counterplan

Yamamoto's battle plan for Midway was the work of Captain Kuroshima, who had devised the great but aborted "westward" strategy. His judgment seems to have waned. The Midway scheme was grandiose in scope and dazzling in its intricacy, but it lacked two military virtues: *simplicity,* and *concentration of force.* It was a dual mission, always a hazardous business.

1. Capture Midway atoll.
2. Destroy the United States Pacific Fleet.

The plan started with a replay of Pearl Harbor, a surprise carrier strike at the atoll. Under Admiral Nagumo, four carriers — instead of the six originally called for — would approach from the northwest by stealth. They would wipe out the air defenses at a blow, and the landing force would then capture the atoll before Nimitz could interfere. It was assumed (quite soundly) that Nimitz would have to come out and fight, no matter how weak he was. Yamamoto himself planned to lie with his battleships several hundred miles astern of Nagumo, out of aircraft range, prepared to close and annihilate the Nimitz fleet elements that would survive Nagumo's air onslaught.

The plan included a feint at the Aleutian Islands off Alaska. There other carriers would blast American naval bases, and an invasion force would land. The feint might decoy Nimitz's meager forces far to the north, thus enabling Yamamoto to get between the Pacific Fleet and the Hawaiian Islands, a stupendous opportunity; if not, Japan would still seize and hold the Aleutians, thus tearing loose the northern anchor of the American line in the Pacific.

So, despite his overwhelming advantage in power, Yamamoto elected to base his operation on deception and surprise; but there was no surprise. Nimitz gambled that what his decoders told him was true, and that he might win against odds by surprising the surprisers. He thus cut the Gordian knot of military theory: should operations be based on what the enemy would *probably* do, or on the *worst* he could do? Chester von Nimitz even shrugged off the barbed nagging from Washington of Fleet Admiral King, who kept pointing out that the Japanese fleet might be heading for Hawaii. Had Nimitz proved wrong, his disgrace would have been greater than that of the Pearl Harbor commander-in-chief who was cashiered.

But Chester von Nimitz was made of good stuff. He was of pure German military descent, and he had bred true. His Texas family traced its line directly to one Ernst Freiherr von Nimitz, an eighteenth-century German major, with a crowned coat of arms. This ancestor in turn derived from von Nimitz military forebears going back to the Crusades. Recent generations of

Nimitzes, lacking the means to keep up the aristocratic style of life, had dropped the "von," and of course in Texas it would have been a handicap.

Nimitz made one simple grand decision: to ambush Yamamoto. He determined to position his carriers well northeast of Midway, as Nagumo's carriers were steaming down from the northwest. In this deadly game played around a wide water-girt bulge of the earth, much hung on who saw whom first. Placing his heavy pieces so, concealing them by distance, Nimitz seized a big advantage.

For Midway's land planes could search an arc of seven hundred miles, while Yamamoto's carrier craft could at best patrol three hundred miles. Also, Nimitz could receive patrol reports in Hawaii by underwater cable from Midway, so that no increase of broadcast traffic from the atoll would warn Yamamoto that the Americans were alerted. From Hawaii, Nimitz could then broadcast the patrol reports in code to his carriers, while Yamamoto's forces plodded within range, oblivious and unseeing.

Such was Nimitz's ambush. Yamamoto's fleet steamed right into it.

Yet not all ambuscades succeed. Surprise is a great but fleeting advantage. Yamamoto's powerful and battle-toughened forces quickly rallied from Nimitz's surprise, and in its opening phase the Battle of Midway took shape as a smashing Japanese victory.

TRANSLATOR'S NOTE: *Fleet Admiral Nimitz was a quiet man of broad vision, with a good sense of humor. Shortly before he died he read in manuscript my translation of this chapter. At Roon's usage of "von Nimitz" he enjoyed a hearty laugh, but he remarked that the details of his genealogy were accurate.*

A Navy adage runs, "If it works you're a hero, if it doesn't you're a bum." Actually there was much guesswork in the Midway intelligence break. Clues had to be teased out of the Japanese by deceptive signals. Admiral Nimitz's decision to act on this inconclusive "dope" was daring. He did not know the Japanese plan. Rather, he had a fair indication of what might be going on. He proceeded on hunches that proved brilliantly right.

The Wehrmacht coding precautions were not all that adequate. At this writing I can say no more, but the fact is that German communications were deeply penetrated. — V.H.

*   *   *

28

THE air squadrons flew out from Oahu to join the departing carriers in clear calm weather. On its approach, the leading *Enterprise* torpedo plane went into a spin, crashed, and tumbled overboard with pieces flying. To Warren, circling high above in a new dive-bomber, it looked like a toy breaking up. The plane guard destroyer rushed to the wreckage, boiling smoke like a locomotive and streaking the sea white. The plane crew was rescued, as he learned on landing. Such accidents were not uncommon, yet this one struck him as a bad omen.

TASK FORCE SIXTEEN IS PROCEEDING TO INTERCEPT A JAP LANDING ATTEMPT AT MIDWAY

Flashing across the teletype screens shortly after the pilots landed aboard, the words generated cheery excitement in the ready rooms. But in a long, long, dull week of northward zigzagging at standard speed, the excitement faded into an uncomfortable mix of boredom and mounting tension. The *Enterprise* and the *Hornet*, ringed by cruisers and destroyers, slowly moved from sunny tropical seas to gray swells, gray skies, and cool winds. Under the umbrella of the Hawaiian air patrol, there was nothing for the fliers to do. The newcomers, three-year Academy men or reserve ensigns, gloried in their prima-donna freedom from ship routine: sleeping late, playing acey-deucey and cards, fogging the ready rooms with tobacco smoke, drinking gallons of coffee and lemonade, eating big meals and great mounds of ice cream, killing time between drills and lectures with chatter of sex, shore leave, airplane mishaps, and the like, perpetrating ham-handed practical jokes; and generally mimicking, in their green self-consciousness, the Hollywood picture of combat fliers.

Usually Warren enjoyed the ready-room camaraderie play, but not this time out. Too many of the squadron mates with whom he had started the war were dead, missing, or transferred. The high-spirited recruits, mostly unmarried, made him feel old and irritable. The protracted idleness ate at him. He was flight operations officer, third in command, and he tried to keep busy reviewing tactics manuals, devising navigation problems and blackboard combat drills, exercising violently on the flight deck, and haunting the hangar deck to check and recheck the squadron's aircraft.

Idleness breeds gossip. Idleness plus tension is a bad brew. As the slow days passed, the talk in the ready rooms drifted to the topic of Rear Admiral Spruance. Word was trickling down from flag country that Halsey's staff was not cottoning to him. Halsey had built up the former screen commander, his old friend, to them as a brilliant intellectual. The staff was finding him a damned queer fish: cool, quiet, inaccessible, the Old Man's absolute opposite. He was content at meals to sit almost mum. He depressed Halsey's loyal and ebullient subordinates, who had absorbed their style from the rollicking Old Man. Why had Halsey pushed forward this taciturn nonflyer to fight a carrier battle, when red-hot aviators like John Towers had been available? Out of friendship? At lunch on the first day out, so rumor ran, Spruance had opened up after a long boring silence by saying, "Gentlemen, I want you to know that I'm not worried about any of you. If you weren't any good, Bill Halsey wouldn't have you." He seemed unaware that he himself was under worried scrutiny.

His ways were altogether odd. He tramped the flight deck alone by the hour, but otherwise he seemed rather lazy. He went to bed early and slept long and well. During an alarm over a night surface contact he had not turned out, merely ordered an evasive maneuver and gone back to sleep. Each day he ate an unvarying breakfast of toast and canned peaches, and drank only one cup of morning coffee; which he made himself, with the fussiness of an old maid, from special beans he had brought aboard. When it rained or blew hard topside, he sat in the flag mess reading old books from the ship's library. Almost, he seemed to be along for the ride. Halsey's chief of staff, Captain Browning, was running the task force, and Spruance was just initialling Browning's orders.

All in all, the staff was counting on Spruance for very little. Browning would fight the battle, and if the patched-up *Yorktown* got to the scene in time, Frank Jack Fletcher would take charge, since he was senior to Spruance. Fletcher had not done so well in the Coral Sea, but at least he had been blooded in carrier combat. Thus went the idle talk in the ready room; which irked Warren and troubled him too.

Arriving on station, a spot in the trackless sea designated "Point Luck," Task Force Sixteen steamed back and forth through two more tedious days, waiting for the *Yorktown*. This was the place of ambush, some three hundred twenty-five miles from the atoll; beyond the range of enemy carrier planes, yet close enough for a quick attack once Midway aircraft espied the foe. Dolphins frisking among the slow-moving ships found no scraps to eat; the crews were forbidden to throw so much as a paper cup overboard.

At last, making full speed, with no outward mark of its Coral Sea battering, the *Yorktown* hove into view. Like the ship, its decimated air squadrons were a patch job of Coral Sea survivors and *Saratoga* aviators hastily thrown together; but another flattop, patched or not, was mighty welcome. With

Fletcher now in tactical command, more fleet alarms began to break out. *Yorktown* warnings about enemy submarines or aircraft touched off the old frenzied routines time and again: sharp turns of all ships, flight decks crazily canting, crews scurrying to man and train guns, destroyers foaming and criss-crossing; then would come the bored wait, the standdown, the recovery of aircraft, and the resumed plan of the day. None of the alarms proved genu-ine. The two task forces milled around and around Point Luck: the *Yorktown* with its own screen of cruisers and destroyers called Task Force Seventeen, the *Hornet* and the *Enterprise* still designated Task Force Sixteen, under Spruance as subordinate to Fletcher.

Warren scheduled himself out on the first dawn search. When his new Dauntless bounded forward between lines of hooded yellow guide lights on the deck and roared off into the cold night toward the crowded stars and the Milky Way, his spirit lifted too. The new fliers had looked grave during the ready-room briefing when told of the absolute radio silence orders; the car-rier would send out no homing signals and if they had to make emergency water landings, distress calls were forbidden. Thus the chilly reality of the approaching enemy was thrust on them. Not having patrolled in an SBD-3 before, Warren too was uneasy at these tough rules. But the new machine purred out two hundred miles; then, in a soft lilac dawn and a beautiful sunrise, its new electronic homing device returned him dead on Point Op-tion. A pleasant sight, those two carrier islands nicking the horizon! He landed with a clean catch of the number three wire. A great airplane, sure enough: improved navigation gear, a sweet engine, self-sealing tanks, extra guns, thicker armor. Even his gunner, a gloomy Kentucky mountain boy named Cornett, who seldom spoke and seemed to be using a foreign lan-guage when he did, climbed smiling out of the rear seat.

"Not a bad crate at that," said Warren.

Cornett spat tobacco juice and said something like, "Rakn rat smat new dew."

"Warren! Warren! It's started. They're bombing Dutch Harbor."

"Jesus." Warren sat up on his bunk, rubbed his eyes, and seized his trousers. "What do you know! Alaska, hey? Screwed again."

His roommate's eyes shone. Peter Goff was an ensign new to the squad-ron, a youngster from upstate New York with a red beard like Byron's. He said eagerly, "Maybe we'll head north, cut off their line of retreat, and cream 'em."

"That's three days' steaming, fella." Warren jumped barefoot to the cold iron deck.

When they got to Scouting Six ready room the big reclining chairs were full. Silently the aviators stared at words crawling across the yellow teletype screen:

DIVERSION MOVE AT ALASKA EXPECTED MAIN THRUST WILL BE
AT MIDWAY DUTCH HARBOR PREPARED AND WELL DEFENDED

The commander of Scouting Six, a tough stocky old hand named Earl
Gallaher, hung the big Pacific chart over the blackboard to discuss time and
distance problems of a possible dash against the Japs to the north. The
younger fliers listened hungrily. This was getting down to business. But
Warren noted a new fleet course being chalked up: *120 degrees*, southeast,
away from the Aleutians, away from Midway, away from the wind. Just
another routine turn to hug Point Luck; no action.

Within the hour words were sliding across the screen again:

PBY PATROL PLANE REPORTS QUOTE MANY HEAVY ENEMY
SHIPS BEARING 237 DISTANCE 685 FROM MIDWAY UNQUOTE

The word "Midway" triggered shouts and rebel yells in the Scouting Six
ready room. Everybody started talking at once. The CO jumped to the chart
and drew a heavy red crayon ring at the point of the sighting. "Okay, here
we go. Range about one thousand miles. They'll be in striking range in sixteen, seventeen hours."

The fliers were still clustering at the chart, spanning distances with
fingers and arguing, when the teletype came to chattering life:

FROM CINCPAC URGENT THAT IS NOT THE ENEMY STRIKING
FORCE THAT IS THE LANDING FORCE THE STRIKING FORCE
WILL HIT FROM THE NORTHWEST AT DAYLIGHT TOMORROW

"Son of a bitch!" said Pete Goff at Warren's elbow. "How do they *know*
all that in Pearl Harbor?"

Night fell. Midnight drew on. Few Scouting Six pilots went to their
bunks. They were reading, or writing letters, or going on with the everlasting talk about women and flying; but the buzz of words had a different
sound, lower and more tense. Staff gossip kept drifting in. Spruance was
receiving the dispatches not in flag plot, but on a couch in the flag mess
where he sat reading a mildewy biography of George Washington, merely
initialling the message board. Meanwhile, in a flag plot like an overturned
beehive, Captain Browning was already making out the preliminary battle
orders.

The teletype now and then clicked out a burst of words about Dutch
Harbor, or about the oncoming Jap landing force; Army Air Corps bombers
from the atoll claimed to be pounding it and sinking battleships, cruisers,
and whatnot in high-level attacks. Nobody placed any stock in that. The
dive-bomber pilots had a word for high-level bombing at sea: it was like trying to drop a marble on a scared mouse. *What about the flattops? Where
are their carriers? Any dope about the goddamned carriers?"* All through the
ready rooms that was the restless litany.

Warren went topside to check the weather again. Moon almost full; stars, light clouds, cold crosswind, the Big Dipper on the starboard quarter. Loud splashing far below of a high-speed run. Closing the enemy fast now! On the flight deck aft, moonlight glinted on the wings of jammed-together planes, and here and there the pencil-thin red flashlight beams of repair work barely showed. The enlisted plane captains squatted in small knots, where sailor talk went on and on: about the better torpedo planes coming to the fleet in August, about religion, about sports, about family, about Honolulu whorehouses; not much talk about the subject most on every man's mind, the battle coming with the dawn.

Wide awake, Warren strode the breezy steady deck. The sea all around danced with moonlight. Passing through the hangar deck below, he had noted with peculiar clarity the quantities of explosive materials all about — bombs, gassed-up planes, full ammo racks, oil drums, torpedo warheads. The *Enterprise* was an iron eggshell eight hundred feet long, full of dynamite and human beings. Of this, he was edgily aware as never before. Jap eggshells just like it were probably only a few hundred miles away and closing.

Who would surprise whom? Suppose an enemy submarine had spotted this force? Far from unlikely! In that case Jap aircraft might strike at sunup. And even if this force did get the jump on the Japs, would the assault come off? In fleet exercises, even with no enemy opposition, a coordinated attack of fighters, dive-bombers, and torpedo planes had never yet worked. Some leader had failed to get the word, someone's navigation had gone wrong, or bad weather had scattered the formations. Too many *Enterprise* fliers were green recruits like Pete Goff. The battered *Yorktown*'s aviators were a sandlot team, scraped together off the beach after the Coral Sea losses. What would such a ragtag force do against seasoned Jap airmen who had wrecked Pearl Harbor and driven the British navy out of the Indian Ocean?

Yet there would be no more rehearsals, no more drills. This was it. Unless a surprise attack came off with total success, swift skilled Jap reprisal would explode the *Enterprise* into a grandiose fireball. He would either burn up in it, or if he was airborne he would fall in the sea when his fuel ran out. These were not fifty-fifty prospects.

And yet, Warren accepted them as all in the day's work. He no more expected to die in the coming battle than does a passenger who buys an air ticket from New York to Los Angeles. He was a professional flying man. He had flown through a lot of enemy fire. He thought he knew enough about it to get through the day alive, with any luck. At the after end of the flight deck, aft of the last dark row of planes, with the wind whipping his trousers, he stood and watched the broad moonlit wake rushing away. There was no place he would rather be, he thought, and nothing he would rather do than fly against the Japs tomorrow.

He wanted a cigarette. Returning to the island to go below, he glanced up again at the sky and he halted, his face turned upward, recalling a scene he had not thought of for years. He was a boy of seven, walking at night under just such a sky, on a wharf piled with fresh snow, hand in hand with Dad, who was telling him about the big distances and sizes of the stars.

"Dad, who put the stars there? God?"

"Well, Warren, yes, we believe the Lord God did that."

"You mean Jesus Christ himself stuck the stars up in the sky?" The boy was trying to picture the kindly long-haired white-robed man hanging gigantic balls of fire in black space.

He could recall his father's silence, then the hesitant reply. "Well, Warren, you sort of get into rocks and shoals there. Jesus is our Lord. That's true enough. He's also the son of God, and God created the universe and everything in it. You'll understand more about all this when you're older."

Warren could date the start of his doubts from that talk. In one of their rare arguments about religion, many years later, his father had cited the night sky as his old proof that there must be a God.

"Dad, I don't want to offend you, but to me those stars look pretty randomly scattered. And think about their size and distance! How can anything on this earth matter? We're microbes on a grain of dust. Life is a stupid and insignificant accident, and when it's over we're just dead meat."

His father had never again discussed religion with him.

The stars were majestically rocking over the prickly radar masts. They had never seemed so beautiful to Warren Henry. But despite the vivid patterns of the constellations, they still looked randomly scattered.

He lay in the dark in his cabin, chain-smoking. Pete Goff softly snored in another bunk. The third roommate, the squadron exec, was writing in the ready room. Warren yearned for just a couple of hours' sleep. He thought he had better try reading, and switched on the bunk light. Usually his glance passed over the black-bound Bible as though Dad's gift weren't in the book rack. Just the thing to make him drowsy! He propped himself up, and on a fortune-telling impulse opened the book at random. His eyes fell on this verse in the second Book of Kings:.

Thus saith the Lord, set thy house in order; for thou shalt die, and not live.

It gave him a turn. He had never quite stopped believing in God, though he thought He must be more like his father, for forbearance and a sense of humor, than the thundering blue-nosed God of the preachers. "Well, ask a silly question, hey?" he thought. "I better mind my own business and leave the rest to You."

He read the Creation chapters, then the stories of Noah and the Tower of Babel. He had not looked at these since Sunday school days. Surprisingly, they seemed not boring, but terse and perceptive. Adam's dodging of responsibility was something he saw every day in the squadron; Eve was a lovely troublemaker like too many he had tangled with; Cain was every envious hating son of a bitch in uniform; and the storm description in the deluge chapter was damned good, the real thing. He began to bog down in the patriarchs, and Jacob's troubles with Laban did the trick. He fell asleep clothed, his gold wings gleaming in the light he was too drowsy to turn off.

"Now General Quarters. General Quarters. Man your battle stations."

The dawn GQ call boomed over the windy flight deck. Stars still twinkled in the black sky, and in the graying east one cloud glowed pink. Pulling on helmets and life jackets, sailors poured out on the gloomy deck, some to the gun tubs, some to the aircraft, some rolling out fire-fighting equipment. Warren was in his plane, checking a balky canopy. Most of the aviators were still in the ready room; they had all long since breakfasted, and were just waiting. Warren, usually a sausage-and-eggs man, had taken toast and one cup of coffee to keep his insides quietly in order. In the dark morning hours the teletype had fallen silent. Of enemy carriers, still no word.

The canopy was moving freely, yet Warren lingered in the plane. The stars faded, the sky went from indigo to blue, the sea brightened. Starkly clear in Warren Henry's mind was a relative movement diagram of what was probably happening. The Jap carriers — if Pearl Harbor was right about a dawn strike — would now be about two hundred miles west of the *Enterprise.* In a God's-eye view, the two moving carrier forces and the motionless Midway atoll made an equilateral triangle on the sea, and the triangle shrank as both forces speeded toward the atoll. Some time this morning the distance between the forces would close to strike range, and that would be the flash point of the battle. Of course, the Japs might not be there at all. They might be down off Hawaii, in which case Admiral Nimitz had fallen for a historic sucker play.

The sun pushed a blazing yellow arc over the sharp horizon and mounted. Well, no Jap daybreak attack; one hazard passed! That was what Warren had really been waiting for. He went down to the ready room, and as he was walking in, the loudspeaker rasped, *"Pilots, man your planes."*

"Okay . . . This is it . . . Here we go . . ."

The fliers jumped from their chairs, boots thudding on the metal deck, faces taut and eager. This time by a common impulse they turned to each other and shook hands. Then, slapping shoulders and joking, about half of them had crowded through the door when in the passageway the loudspeaker bawled, *"Now belay that last word. Pilots return to their ready rooms."*

Angry and jumpy as racehorses pulled up short after a bad start, the aviators trudged back to their chairs, trading rude comments about "those idiots up there." A bad business, Warren thought, some nervous faltering on the command level.

What had happened "up there" was that Captain Miles Browning had given the order, and Rear Admiral Spruance had countermanded it.

Spruance had already discomfited Halsey's chief of staff well before dawn. Prior to the GQ alarm Browning and his operations officer had mounted to Halsey's flag shelter, a small steel eyrie high up above the flying bridge; and as Spruance had left no call, Browning had not disturbed him. A short shadowy form in the starlight outside the shelter had greeted them. "Good morning, gentlemen."

"Ah — Admiral?"

"Yes. Looks like we'll have good weather for it."

As day broke, Spruance leaned on the bulwark outside, watching the ship come to life. Captain Browning was nervily ready for battle, his head was full of contingency plans, but this early presence of the placid Spruance was unsettling. Halsey would be pacing now like a caged cat. The chief of staff, who was wearing a leather windbreaker like Halsey's, did all the pacing, smoking cigarette after cigarette with Halsey gestures, fuming at the lack of news, arguing with the operations officer about where the Jap carriers could be.

Abruptly he seized a microphone and issued the summons to the pilots that had greeted Warren in the ready room.

Spruance called in, "Why are we doing this, Captain?"

"If you'll look here, please, Admiral."

Spruance amiably came to the chart table.

"By now, sir, the Japs have certainly launched. It's broad day. They probably launched well before dawn. We know the range of their planes. They *must* be somewhere along this arc, give or take twenty miles." He swept a stiff forefinger in a slim circle near Midway. "They'll be sighted any minute. I want to be ready to hit them."

"How long does it take our pilots to man their planes?"

Browning glanced at the operations officer, who said with a touch of pride, "On this ship, Admiral, two minutes."

"Why not leave them in their ready rooms for now? They'll be in those cockpits a long time today."

Spruance walked out on the sunlit platform, and Browning testily broadcast the recall.

The flag shelter was a small area, cramped by the chart table and a couple of settees. A rack of confidential publications, a coffee maker, microphones, telephones, and radio speakers made up the equipment. One speaker, tuned to the frequency of the Midway patrol planes, was emitting a power hum and loud popping static. About half an hour after sunrise this speaker burst out in gargling tones, *"Enemy carriers. Flight 58 reports."*

"Kay, that's IT!" Browning again snatched the microphone. Spruance came inside. The three officers stared at the humming and popping receiver. Browning exploded, pounding the chart table with his fist, "Well? *Well*, you stupid son of a bitch? *What's the longitude and latitude?"* He glanced in angry embarrassment at Spruance. "Christ! I assumed the squirt would give us the location in his next breath. What kind of imbeciles are flying those Catalinas?"

"Their combat air patrol may have attacked him," said Spruance.

"Admiral, we've *got* the yellow bastards sighted now. Let's get the pilots to their planes."

"But if the enemy's out of range we'll have to close him, won't we? Maybe for an hour or more."

With a miserable grimace, as Spruance went out in the sunshine, Browning slammed the microphone into its bracket.

A dragging interval ensued; then the same voice, much clearer, broke through the random popping: *"Many enemy planes bearing 320 distance 150. Flight 58 reports."*

Again, humming silence.

More violently, the chief of staff cursed the PBY pilot for giving no position. He poured coffee, let it stand and cool; smoked, paced, studied the chart, paced some more, turned the pages of an old magazine and hurled it into a corner, while his operations officer, a burly quiet aviator, kept measuring with dividers and ruler on his chart. Spruance lounged outside, elbows on the bulwark.

"Flight 92 reports." It was a younger, more excited voice barking out of the speaker. *"Two carriers and battleships bearing 320 from Midway, distance 180, course 135, speed 25 Dog Love."*

"AH! God love *that* lad!" Browning plunged for the chart, where the operations officer was hastily marking the position.

Spruance came inside, took a rolled-up maneuvering board graph he had tucked in a wall rack, and spread it beside him on a settee. "What was that position again? And what is our present position?"

Rapidly measuring, scrawling calculations, barking questions into the intercom to flag plot several decks below, Browning soon rattled off the latitudes and longitudes to Spruance.

"Is the message authenticated?" Spruance asked.

"Authenticated, authenticated? Well, is it?" Browning snapped. The operations officer threw open a loose-leaf book while Spruance was spanning distances on his small graph with thumb and forefinger. " *The farmer in the dell,'* " the operations officer quoted, " *'any two alternate letters.'* The pilot gave us *Dog Love.* That works."

"It's authenticated, Admiral," Browning said over his shoulder.

"Launch the attack," said Spruance.

Startled, Browning jerked his head around from the chart to look at Spruance. "Sir, we've received no orders from Admiral Fletcher."

"We will. Let's go."

At the chart, the air operations officer lifted a worried face. "Admiral, I make the distance to the target one eighty. At that range our torpedo planes won't get back. I recommend we close at least to one fifty."

"You're quite right. I thought we were about there now." The admiral turned to Browning. "Let's put out a new fleet course, Captain Browning, closing them at full speed. Tell the *Hornet* we'll launch at a hundred and fifty miles."

A sailor in dungarees, life jacket, and helmet came thumping up the long ladder with a message board. Spruance initialled it and passed it to Browning. "Here are the orders from Fletcher."

URGENT. COM TF 17 TO COM TF 16. PROCEED SOUTHWEST AND ATTACK ENEMY CARRIERS WHEN DEFINITELY LOCATED. WILL FOLLOW AS SOON AS MY SEARCH PLANES RECOVERED.

Miles Browning was a fighting man, everybody acknowledged that, and he had been waiting most of his professional life to see such a dispatch. His ill humor vanished. A beguiling masculine grin lit his lean weathered face (he was a well-known ladykiller, too) and he squared his cap and saluted Raymond Spruance. "Well, Admiral, here we go."

Spruance returned the salute and went out in the sun.

In the ready rooms, when the carrier sighting printed out on the tele-types, the nervous irritation of the pilots cleared away. False alarm forgotten, they cheered, then fell to plotting and calculating. Guesses fired back and forth about probable time of launch. The range of the torpedo planes was of course the problem. Their chances of survival were reckoned poor at best, and the torpedo pilots deserved a decent chance to get back.

Visiting the ready room of Torpedo Squadron Six to kill the slow-grinding time, Warren found his friend Commander Lindsey in flying suit and life vest, his bandages gone, blood-caked scars on his hand and on his pale sunken face. This was the man whose plane had crashed on the first day out. "Ye gods, Gene, did Doc Holiwell shake you loose?"

Commander Lindsey said, unsmiling, "I've trained for this, Warren. I'm leading the squadron in."

The torpedo squadron room was unusually quiet. Some aviators were writing letters; some doodled on their flight charts; most of them smoked. Like the dive-bomber pilots they had stopped drinking coffee, to avoid bladder discomfort on the long flight. The effect here was one of taut waiting, as outside an operating room during surgery. At the blackboard a sailor wearing earphones was chalking new numbers beside RANGE TO TARGET: 153 *miles*.

Lindsey said to Warren, glancing at his own plotting board, "That checks. We're closing fast. I figure we'll close to a hundred thirty miles. So we'll be launching about an hour from now. This is for keeps, and we've got to get the jump on the little bastards, so even if we strain a bit —"

"Pilots, man your planes."

Glancing at each other and at the pallid squadron commander, the pilots of Torpron Six got out of their chairs. Their movements were heavy, not eager, but they moved. So alike were the expressions of grave hard resolve on their faces, they might have been nineteen brothers. Warren threw an arm around Lindsey's shoulder. His old instructor slightly winced.

"Happy landings, Gene. Give 'em hell."

"Good hunting, Warren."

The fliers of Scouting Six were trampling by in the passageway, shouting high-strung banter. Warren fell in with them. As the squadron ran out on the gusty sunny flight deck, a sight met his eye that always thrilled him: the whole task force turning into the wind, the *Enterprise*, the *Hornet*, the far-flung ring of cruisers and destroyers, all moving in parallel; and old Dad's *Northampton* right up there, swinging from the port beam to a station almost dead ahead in dazzling sun glare. With farewell shouts and waves the pilots climbed into their planes. Cornett nodded at Warren from the rear seat, placidly chewing tobacco in long bony jaws, his red hair flying in the wind.

"Well, Cornett, here we go to get ourselves a Jap carrier. You ready?"

"Stew lot yew dang sartin cummin," Cornett approximately replied, then broke into clear English to add, "The canopy is freed up."

Thirty-five dive-bombers were spotted on the flight deck, their motors coughing, roaring, and spitting dense blue fumes. Warren's plane, among those farthest aft, carried a thousand-pound bomb; as flight operations officer he had made sure of that. The take-off run for some of the others was too short, and their load was a five-hundred-pound bomb, with two more hundred-pounders. Warren's launch was heavy and lumbering. The SBD-3 ran off the end of the deck, settled much too close to the water, then began a wobbling climb. The rush of warm sea air into the open cockpit was soul-satisfying. A professional calm settled on Warren as he wound up the wheels and flaps, checked his dancing dial needles, and climbed skyward in a string of soaring blue bombers. The *Hornet* dive-bombers too were single-filing into the air in steep ascent about a mile away. Far above some shreds of high cloud, the gleaming specks of the combat air patrol circled.

At two thousand feet, as the squadron levelled and circled, Warren's exaltation dimmed. He could see, on the shrunken *Enterprise* far below, that the launch was lagging. In their square deck wells the elevators sank and rose, tiny men and machines dragged aircraft about, but the time crawled past seven thirty, seven forty-five. Soon almost an hour of gasoline was gone, and still no fighter escorts or torpedo planes were airborne! And still the two carriers plowed southeast into the wind, away from the atoll and the enemy, slaves to the wind in launch or recovery, no less than sailing ships of old.

A signal light flashed on the *Enterprise*, beaming straight up. Letter by letter, Warren read the message, addressed to the new group leader, Commander McClusky: *Proceed on assigned mission.*

A second shocker, after the very long-range launch — suddenly, no coordinated attack! What was going on? No fighter protection, no torpedo planes for the knockout punch: the *Enterprise* dive-bombers ordered to go in alone against the Jap interceptors! Rear Admiral Spruance was jettisoning — or allowing Halsey's staff to jettison — the whole battle plan at the outset, with the drills of a year, the fleet exercises of many years, and the entire manual of carrier warfare.

Why?

A barometer in Warren's spirit registered a quick sharp rise in the danger of this mission, and in the chances of his dying. He could not be sure what "those idiots down there" had in mind. But he suspected that between the inexperienced Spruance and the overeager Browning — who was something of a joke among the veteran pilots — the thirty-six *Enterprise* dive-bombers were being squandered in a jittery shot from the hip.

Warren Henry knew too much military history for a young flier. To him all this strongly smelled of the Battle of Balaclava:

> *Theirs not to reason why,*
> *Theirs but to do and die —*

Resignedly, he made hand signals to his wing mates. From planes roaring along a few yards below and behind him, they grinned and waved. They were both new ensigns; one was Pete Goff, clutching a cold corncob pipe in his mouth. McClusky waggled his wings and swooped around to the southwest. Warren did not know McClusky except to say hello. He had been the squadron CO of the fighters, but there was no telling how he would perform as group leader. The other thirty-five planes gracefully veered to follow McClusky. Making his turn over the screen, Warren saw from his tilted cockpit the tiny *Northampton* straight below, cutting a long white wake ahead of the *Enterprise*. "Well, old Dad," he thought, "there you are, sitting way down there, and here I go."

On the bridge of the *Northampton*, Pug Henry stood among crowding officers and sailors in gray helmets and life jackets. He had been watching the *Enterprise* since dawn. As the departing bombers dwindled to dots, he stared after them through binoculars. Everybody who served on the cruiser's bridge knew the reason.

The wind was smartly flapping the signal flags. Below, noisy swells were breaking on the hull like surf. Pug raised his voice to the exec at his elbow, "Secure from GQ, Commander Grigg. Maintain condition Zed. AA crews stand easy at their guns. Float plane pilots stand by the catapults ready to go. Double the regular lookouts for aircraft and submarines. All hands be alert for air attack. Where men remain on battle stations, serve out coffee and sandwiches."

"Aye aye, sir."

In a different tone Pug went on, "Say, incidentally, those SBDs won't be breaking radio silence till they're over the target. We've got the right crystals for the aircraft frequency, haven't we?"

"Chief Connors says that we do, Captain."

"Okay. If you hear anything, call me."

"Aye aye, sir."

In the sea cabin, Victor Henry slung helmet and life jacket on the bunk. His eyes smarted. His legs were leaden. He had not slept all night. Why were those dive-bombers flying off unescorted to face a cloud of Jap interceptors? His own prize lookout, Traynor, a sharp-eyed Negro youngster from Chicago, had spotted a Japanese float plane slipping in and out of low clouds. Was that the reason? Pug did not know what orders had gone out to the squadrons of the *Yorktown* and the *Hornet;* he could only hope the whole battle picture made more sense than he could yet discern. The game was on, that was sure.

From the old triple photograph frame on the chart table, between Madeline and Byron, Warren looked out at him sternly in the Academy graduation picture: a skinny solemn ensign in a big white officer's cap. Well, thought Pug, a damned good lieutenant was flying off against the Japs, with fitness reports that were a string of "outstandings," and a solid combat record. His next job would be as a Stateside flight instructor, no doubt. The air cadet programs were clamoring for combat veterans. Then he would rotate back to an air group in the Pacific, to gain command experience and reap medals. His future was radiant, and this day was the needle's eye of his destiny. Hardening himself to endure the wait for a break in radio silence, Pug took up a detective novel, reclined on his bunk, and numbly tried to read.

Why, in fact, did Spruance send off the dive-bombers?

The battle decisions of a commander are not easily analyzed; not even by himself, not even in reminiscent tranquillity. Not all men of war are at ease with words. Events evaporate and are *gone*, especially the evanescent moments of a battle. The memoirs composed long afterward are as often misleading as illuminating. Some truly proud men say or write little. Raymond Spruance left few words about his Midway conduct.

He was acting in the battle under a Nimitz directive that is on the record: *"You will be governed by the principle of calculated risk, which you shall interpret to mean the avoidance of exposure of your force to attack by superior enemy forces without good prospect of inflicting, as a result of such exposure, greater damage on the enemy."* The Navy had a sour slang translation for this: "Sock 'em and rock 'em, but don't lose your shirt"; a standard admonition to a weak force going out against odds. Boiled down, it meant little but "Try to win with conservative tactics." Few military orders are harder to obey. And he had unwritten orders from Nimitz not to lose his carriers, even if it meant giving up Midway. "We will get it back later," Nimitz had said. "Save the fleet."

Some hard truths had been squeezing Spruance, under these hobbling instructions. He was a stranger to the ship, to Halsey's staff, and to air operations. He could not force a speedup of the appallingly slow launches on the *Enterprise* or the *Hornet* merely by throwing an admiral's tantrum. In this matter he was in fact helpless. The *Yorktown* had drifted aft below the horizon while recovering its search planes, so he couldn't consult Fletcher. A Jap float plane had been sighted, and the special intelligence officer who knew Japanese said that it had sent a position report. So the edge of surprise was melting away like butter on a hot skillet. Midway atoll was reported under attack by enemy aircraft. His dive-bombers were circling and circling overhead, burning up gasoline.

Given the distances in the combat triangle, and the known aircraft ranges and speeds, Spruance could hope that his dive-bombers, if they left now, might reach the enemy in his moment of weakness, when his planes were getting back from Midway low on bullets and gas. But there was one grim catch to that. The PBY had seen only two carriers. Nimitz's intelligence staff had predicted four or five. *Where were those missing flattops?* Were they coming at Task Force Sixteen from the north, the south — even in an end run from the east? Would they pounce when all his dive-bombers were off, attacking the first two?

An oppressive urgent choice confronted him: either hold back the bombers for a full coordinated attack, and hope meanwhile for news of the missing carriers; or hit out now, gambling that they would show up near the two in sight.

Spruance hit out. It was hardly a "calculated risk." It was the steepest and gravest of gambles with the future of his Navy and his country. Such decisions — only such once-in-a-lifetime personal decisions — test a commander. Within the hour his far more experienced and stronger opponent, Vice Admiral Chuichi Nagumo, would face much the same hard choice.

29

A Jew's Journey
(*from Aaron Jastrow's manuscript*)

JUNE 4, 1942, MIDNIGHT.
SIENA.

I have just listened to the BBC and to Radio Berlin, hoping for I know not what — a last-minute turnabout in the war news, possibly, to justify putting off a desperate decision. There was none. Under the propaganda cosmetics — the German paint whorish, the British ladylike — one discerns the same grim face of events: *Germany and Japan triumphant.*

In my meeting with the archbishop today I encountered a subtle change. His Excellency is something of a peasant, with a red jowly face, a solid build, and an earthy vocabulary. But he is cultured and tolerant. I like him and tend to trust him. This time he received me not in his cozy wood-panelled study, but in his cold grand outer office. He sat behind a splendid old desk. When I came in he did not stand up, but motioned me to a chair. I understood. I am no longer the well-known American author at whose villa he can now and then enjoy a good dinner, fine wine, and jocose pedantic talk. I am a suppliant. The wheel has turned, and the archbishop with it.

Still, he has looked into the matter. As to the Italian authorities, no immediate harm threatens us. Of this he assures me. He knows of no new program to round up Jews. Our status as enemy aliens under house arrest is of course most singular. He has been told we are marked for privileged treatment, and for release to Switzerland when various problems are cleared up. The question of concealing ourselves may therefore not arise.

Still, if it does, hiding out in the countryside would be a possibility, he agrees. But taking refuge in Siena's environs would be unwise. The story of *il famoso scrittore americano* trapped by the war is common Sienese gossip, and no hiding place around here would be secure.

He has cautiously raised the topic with the bishop of Volterra, an old walled town some fifty miles to the northwest, on the winding mountain road down to Pisa. Many years ago, I visited the Etruscan antiquities in Volterra. An alabaster bowl I bought there sits on my desk now, filled with roses. It is a town forgotten by time. The inhabitants are a darkly handsome dour lot.

His Excellency jokes that they are probably Etruscan by blood and pagan at heart. Several people wanted by the Fascist regime are lying low in Volterra. Should the worst come to the worst, he can put us in touch with the Volterra bishop, who will be sympathetic. But he feels we should just keep calm and await our eventual release. He stood up smiling to see me out, thus cutting the meeting quite short.

I am shaken by his having talked to the Volterra prelate. How do I know that he can be trusted? Under all the bland reassurance, the archbishop offers us no hiding place himself; and as for future emergencies, he holds out only a promise of sympathy from the bishop of Volterra, a man I don't know, who owes me nothing. This dusty outcome brings me to the alternative.

[*The following passage in* A Jew's Journey, *eight and a half handwritten pages in all, is in the original manuscript a series of strange marks. Such sections occur all through the notebooks after June 4. The key to the cipher is given in the clear English text below. The first line of the passage looks like this:*

[//ᐧ ᒐ")ᒐᴕ ᑕᔑᴋ ᐟᔱ ᐊᒍᐟ ᔅᵖᵘᔆᑭᴔ ᔑᔑ ᐧᑊᴐᒍ ᔲᐟ ᑕᒍᴋ   ᔱ ᔑᔱᐧ ᴋᴋᒃ   ᴕ ᔑ ᐟᐟ   ᴕ ᒃ

I have avoided until now describing the alternative in these pages. Once it contains such things, my notebook becomes a ticking bomb. Bethinking me of Leonardo's mirror handwriting, I have decided to spell out perilous matters in English, but in the backward-running Yiddish alphabet, which will look to the uninitiated like hen scratchings: a temporary shield against prying eyes, or a sudden pounce by Italian police. A simple device, but the short-term security is good.

I scarcely dreamed, when I began *A Jew's Journey,* that I would be using spy tricks in writing it! My life's candle sputters and flares as it burns down, making melodramatic shadows leap about me. Yet I intend to record everything of consequence that happens from now on. By touching a match to tinder-dry faggots in my fireplace, I can in seconds reduce this book to ash.

To the alternative, then.

A Sienese doctor has revealed himself to us as a Jew and a secret Zionist. He plans to flee Italy with his family, hoping to reach Palestine; he is sure that all of Europe's Jews are doomed. Avram Rabinovitz, the tough Palestinian organizer of the *Izmir* voyage, has been in touch with this man, whose departure plans are now complete. Tomorrow he will send a confirming message to Rabinovitz. They are willing to include us in the flight arrangements. I must tell the doctor by morning whether we wish to come along.

The plan envisages an escape route via Piombino, Elba, Corsica, and Lisbon. The nub of it is a Turkish ship, once again; this time a freighter, which carries a cargo of Turkish tobacco from Istanbul to Lisbon every two months. This flavoring tobacco is important to the Allied war effort, so the vessel has British clearance. The ship's captain reaps a fortune by stopping at dead of night off Corsica and taking on Jewish stowaways for gold. In Lisbon we and our Zionist friends would part company. They would hope to go on to the Holy Land, one way or another, and we of course would simply walk into the American consulate.

The doctor does not blink at the hazards of this project. Italian and French underground groups are both involved. Rabinovitz deals with both. Sticky points abound from the start at the Siena bus station to the end at a Lisbon wharf. The whole thing could scarcely be less inviting.

Yet this is our last chance to struggle free; otherwise, in an ever-darkening war scene, we must helplessly wait. If I believed that release to Switzerland was genuinely in prospect, I would brave it out here. My rule, "When in doubt, *wait*," has served me well in life. But for a Jew in Europe, I begin to grasp, all rules are confounded. The compass needle spins in a violent magnetic storm. Even without those unthinkable broadcasts hanging over me, I would be tempted to flee. The archbishop pooh-poohs the stories of secret Nazi massacres of Jews; and anyway, he says, no Italian government will ever give Jews over into German hands, as the occupied countries are doing. So he thinks. He sits in an archdiocesan palace. My safety trembles on a thread.

If an Allied victory were in sight, if only as a glow from below the horizon, I would not budge. A month ago that was my resolve. Against the huge Allied array of raw materials, factories, and manpower, I couldn't see Germany and Japan ever winning. Rather, I was sure, Tocqueville's vision was coming to birth, of a world divided between America and Russia; these two great unions, aided by the doughty though sinking British imperium, would roar into central Europe, shatter the moonstruck Hitler tyranny, and set free not only the occupied countries, but the benighted bled-white Germans. Nor could Japan long survive the end of Hitler.

But what is now sinking in, after shock upon shock, is the example of Macedon. The forces of Alexander were small in number, compared to the hordes of Asia. But his phalanx smashed gigantic empires, and humbled the whole known world to his tiny state. Cortez, an adventurous butcher leading a handful of bravos, plundered and destroyed Montezuma's empire. Pizarro did the same to the great Inca civilization. Wars are won by will, by readiness to die, and by skill in killing, not by advantages, however lopsided, in numbers.

One hoped that the Russian winter, having halted the Germans outside Moscow, might have blunted the *furor Teutonicus* once for all. Alas, the monster was but leaning on his sword, catching his breath to spring again.

The Italian papers show mind-boggling photos of the siege of Sevastopol. Nightmarishly huge guns are throwing shells tall as houses at the city. A perfect rain of artillery fire and aircraft is blanketing Sevastopol with smoke like a volcano in eruption. Following on the Russian defeat near Kharkov, the grinning mannikin Dr. Goebbels is announcing astronomic bags of prisoners. On the high seas, Hitler's U-boats are so close to cutting the American supply route to Europe that the Allied press itself trumpets alarm, admitting that the sinkings are in the millions of tons. In North Africa, the British once again flee before Rommel.

Meanwhile, Japan grows in military stature like a genie towering up out of a bottle. The list of Japanese conquests is Kiplingesque: Singapore, Burma, Java, and now they threaten India! The photographs of defeated and captured white men look like the end of civilization. Dejected British prisoners in Singapore squat on the ground as far as the camera can focus; and on palm-lined Philippine roads, columns of unshaven, ragged, bowed Americans march to captivity from Bataan under the guns of scowling yellow dwarfs.

The lesson was writ plain by Thucydides centuries before Christ was born. Democracy satisfies best the human thirst for freedom; yet, being undisciplined, turbulent, and luxury-seeking, it falls time and again to austere single-minded despotism.

I may be giving way to gloom, blinded by scanty information and a dismal ambience. The pinched nagging shabbiness of life in wartime Italy, with the poor food and drink, weakens one's body and mind. I have not tasted decent meat or wine since the American journalists left. The rationed vegetables are stunted or rotten. The clayey bread sticks in one's throat. Still, I believe I am thinking straight. An Allied victory in the near future seems to me too silly to be discussed. The tides of war do not reverse so easily. The opposite is the more likely quick result: collapse of the Soviet Union, expulsion of the British from Asia and of the Americans from the Pacific, and an Axis triumph on terms. Otherwise the prospect is for stalemate. If the war drags on long enough, a tortuous Allied victory may ensue as Axis-plundered metals, fuel, and food run out. But the fall of Hitler in 1945 or 1946 will not help Natalie, her baby, or me. We would probably not survive such a long wait; but more than that, a showdown with Werner Beck cannot be put off many months, let alone several years.

I do not fear apocalypse. The armies of Germany and Japan are not going to land in New England and California. The oceans are broad, and America remains populous and strong, only impotent to wield its strength in time. Once the despots have swallowed their conquests there will be a pause for digestion and a peace of sorts, perhaps for a decade or two. Should the United States adopt a Vichy-like regime, there may be no third war at all, only a long gradual sucking dry of America's riches by the tyrannies. I need to plan for five or at most ten more years of life. *Après moi, le déluge.* And I must deliver Natalie and Louis if I can.

The decision does seem to be in my hands. Natalie is all but paralyzed. The hoyden who dashed to her lover in Warsaw while war was breaking out, who met another lover in Lisbon in wartime and married him on the spot, has become a mother. It has changed her. She says she will follow my lead. If she is willing to make this rash journey with an infant, it can only be because Avram Rabinovitz is involved, the man who awed and attracted her aboard the *Izmir.* Her submariner husband is half a world away, if indeed he is alive at all. For a bizarre and shadowy adventurer like Rabinovitz she can have only fugitive feelings, but I am glad this shred of moral assurance exists for her.

We will start for Lisbon, then. God help us! I wish I were on better terms with Him. But alas, as with the bishop of Volterra, I don't know Him and He owes me nothing.

If the worst comes to the worst, Natalie will learn that I am not altogether a blundering wool-head. Like Hamlet, when the wind is southerly, I know a hawk from a handsaw. There are the diamonds.

30

VICE ADMIRAL Nagumo's wartime photograph shows a stern bald old Japanese gentleman in a European-style admiral's uniform — thick gold epaulettes, diagonal sash, banks of medals — in which he looks choked and cramped. Nagumo far outclassed Raymond Spruance in rank and in achievement. He had not fought in the Coral Sea; that mess had been botched by lesser men. The victory record of his striking force from Pearl Harbor to the Indian Ocean was unstained. Of samurai descent, a destroyer and cruiser man of high repute, he was the veteran world master of carrier operations.

Steaming out of the melancholy rain and fog that had screened him for a week, Nagumo had launched his strike against Midway at dawn: half of each carrier's fighters, dive-bombers, and Type-97 torpedo planes; these last, dual-purpose machines having been loaded with fragmentation bombs for a land strike. Then he had ordered the remaining one hundred eight planes in the four flattops spotted on deck in readiness to attack any enemy warships that might show up; these Type-97s armed with their usual torpedoes, and the dive-bombers with armor-piercing bombs. But Nagumo and his staff did not expect to encounter the enemy; this was just a conservative precaution.

Just before the strike launch Nagumo in his own hand had drawn up an *Estimate of the Situation*:

1. *The enemy fleet will probably sortie to engage once the Midway landing operations are begun.*
4. *The enemy is not yet aware of our plan, and he has not yet detected our task force.*
5. *There is no evidence of an enemy task force in our vicinity.*
6. *It is therefore possible for us to attack Midway, destroy land-based planes there, and support the landing operation. We can then turn around, meet an approaching enemy task force, and destroy it.*
7. *Possible counterattacks by enemy land-based air can surely be repulsed by our interceptors and antiaircraft fire.*

Radioed victory reports, familiar but exhilarating, began to pour in from the Midway strike aviators. The atoll had sent up a large fighter force, but the Zeroes were mowing them down, and the bombers, without a single loss, were laying waste to the two little islands of Midway. Hangars, power plant, barracks were aflame, guns were silenced, ammunition and fuel dumps were exploding skyward, and the whole garrison was a smoking shambles.

There was one disappointing note. The Yank aircraft had not been caught on the ground as at Pearl Harbor; they had taken the alarm and scrambled out of sight. The hangars and runways had been found empty. Of course, those planes would soon have to land and refuel, and that would be the time to destroy them. So the strike commander had radioed, *"There is need for a second strike."*

Here was the first snag of the day. The Midway airpower had to be smashed, or the landing would be a delayed and bloody one. But the planes now spotted on deck were armed to hit ships. The Type-97s would certainly have to change weapons; torpedoes were no good for a strike on land. Nor were the armor-piercing shells in the dive-bombers as suitable as incendiary and fragmentation bombs.

Nagumo and his staff were debating this pesky problem when air raid bugles sounded, black smoke poured from destroyers to signal *Planes sighted,* and roaring enemy aircraft swooped in low over the wave crests, unmistakable blue U.S. attackers with white-starred wings. Unescorted by fighters, the enemy craft fell like shot fowl under AA and Zero attack. A few launched torpedoes before they went down in flames, but these weapons porpoised, broached, or broke in pieces on striking the water. Not one hit or ran true. It was a miserable display of American ineptness, a brilliant clean sweep by Nagumo's combat air patrol. One plane crashed on the flight deck of the *Akagi* right before Nagumo's eyes, cartwheeling harmlessly over the side. The vice admiral and his staff saw the twin engines, the white star on the flaming blue fuselage, and inside the canopy the blood-soaked pilot, probably already dead. This plane was too big for carrier launching. It was a B-26 medium bomber, and it could only have come from Midway.

That settled it for Nagumo. He would have to make that second strike. As for any enemy fleet nearby, search planes had been aloft since dawn and had reported nothing. Farfetched precautions had to go by the board. The planes now on deck would hit Midway, and to speed matters, only the Type-97 torpedo planes would be rearmed. The two big flattops of his division, the *Akagi* and the *Kaga,* had that chore to rush through. The Type-97s of the smaller *Hiryu* and *Soryu* in Division Two were all off over Midway. Their decks held only fighters and dive-bombers, ready to go. So the orders went out to Nagumo's division. The elevators whined up and down. The big Type-97s were struck below to the hangar deck. Crack crews swarmed to switch the weapons.

A decided surprise came at half past seven. The heavy cruiser *Tone* relayed word from its search plane that ten ships, "apparently enemy," had been sighted about two hundred miles to the east, heading southeast, away from Nagumo and the atoll. The message said nothing about carriers. Surface ships two hundred miles distant could not rescue Midway now. Once the atoll's air force had been obliterated, these vessels could be picked off; but first things first. The rearming of the Type-97s with bombs for land attack went on apace.

Then Nagumo or a staff officer had alarming second thoughts. Enemy course southeast — that course was *into the wind*. Could that float plane pilot have seen carriers and idiotically failed to specify them?

To the carriers: "*Suspend rearming! Leave torpedoes in Type-97 bombers!*"

To the float plane: "*Ascertain ship types and maintain contact.*"

So the chances of war froze the whole vast Japanese operation to the vagaries of one young pilot in one obsolescent cruiser scout plane. Half the Type-97s were already respotted on the flight decks with bombs. The rest were still below with their torpedoes. Now the air raid bugles blared once more, destroyers puffed black smoke balls, and dots in the sky grew to Douglas dive-bombers, approaching from the direction of Midway — again, with no fighter escort — at a peculiar shallow angle, contrary to the usual tactics of U.S. "hell-divers."

These planes were in fact being flown for the first time by raw Marine pilots, last-minute reinforcements for Midway, and their commander was trying to glide-bomb. A second massacre ensued; to the cheers of Japanese deckhands and gun crews, Zeroes picked off the blue planes one after another, and they burst into pretty rosettes of flame and arched smoking into the sea. Not a single bomb landed.

Perhaps this cold-blooded squandering of American pilots' lives in a second attack without fighter escort surprised Nagumo. It was not what one might expect of a soft decadent democracy. But then, the Zeroes had probably shot down all the fighters Midway had started with. The main point stood out: the skies this day were his. The Americans, though brave, were outmatched.

Now the far-off bumbler in the float plane answered up: *Enemy ships consist of five cruisers and five destroyers.* Well! No carriers; the rearming of Type-97s could proceed. But the air raid bugles sounded again, and this time a formation of gigantic land planes came drumming high, high overhead: B-17s by their silhouettes, the dreaded "Flying Fortresses." A harsh apparition; tiny Midway was peculiarly set for air combat! Yet what could the monsters actually do against moving ships with their high-level bombing? The test of this long peacetime debate was at hand as the huge bombers approached at twenty thousand feet.

They had no fighter escort. With their terrible gun-blisters they needed none. The Zeroes did not rise to challenge them. Ponderously, the four carriers scattered as heavy black bombs came showering down, plain to see, on the two smaller flattops, the *Soryu* and the *Hiryu*. Dark watery explosions engulfed them, again and again. The high-flying giants grumbled away in the sky, the splashes subsided; and out of the smoke into the sunlight, unscathed, the two carriers steamed!

With this historic defensive success, after slaughtering two low-level bomber waves, Nagumo was riding high. Obviously, however, Midway crawled with bombers. The second strike was imperative. He had been right to switch the Type-97s to bombs, and that process must now be speeded up.

Before he could act, four almost simultaneous jolts threw the old hero off balance again.

There was always much uproar around Nagumo during operations — clang of elevator warning bells, bark of flight deck loudspeakers, roar of engines warming up, chatter of radio receivers, shouts of flag bridge signalmen. Long habit enabled him to shut out this familiar racket, but the cataract of crises and tumult that burst on him now was something new. He had to make decision after decision — on some of which hung the future of his country, and indeed of the world order — in haste, in uncertainty, in a very hurricane of noise, alarm, confusion, upsets, and contradictory advice. A high commander lives for such moments, and he began to breast the storm with veteran calm.

First, still another wave of bombers came diving out of the clouds.

Second, as the bugles were shrilling and the remaining fighter planes on deck were scrambling to reinforce the combat air patrol, a stricken-faced officer brought Nagumo an addendum from the *Tone* pilot: *Enemy appears to be accompanied by a carrier bringing up the rear.*

Third, even as Nagumo was digesting this shocker, a different alarm signal flashed through the task force: *"Submarine!"*

Fourth, at precisely this juncture, his own first-strike airplanes began arriving back from Midway, winging in sight, low on fuel, some shot up and in distress, demanding to land on the cluttered carrier decks.

Nagumo found himself driven to the wall. A second strike on Midway? No, not *now;* not with an enemy aircraft carrier full of elite pilots within range! The order of his two missions was rudely reversed. No longer was he attacking the atoll; he himself was threatened with a crossfire of land-based bombers and carrier aircraft. Before anything else, he had to get that carrier.

The air raid proved to be only some old-type scout bombers buzzing a battleship of the screen and then running away from the Zeroes into the light clouds. Destroyers swarming over the supposed submarine found nothing. What to do now? The obvious course was to hit out at that carrier at once: turn into the wind, order the *Soryu* and the *Hiryu* to launch their planes all spotted and ready to go, and send off the Type-97s crowding his own decks. These now were armed with bombs, of course, not torpedoes — the ones with torpedoes were below — but bombs were better than nothing. That would clear the decks to recover the first strike, while getting right after the foe.

But it was such a weak gesture for the great Nagumo Force! A fraction of his power, without the punch of torpedoes, without fighter escort, for the fighters were mostly aloft and low on fuel. All morning Nagumo had been watching the slaughter of unescorted bombers. And what about that cardinal rule of war, the concentration of force?

Then again, he could keep calm, and call for cool heads and quick hands; clear *all* decks, including the *Soryu* and the *Hiryu*, by striking aircraft below; recover all planes from Midway, and all fighters of the combat air patrol; refuel and arm all aircraft, while closing the enemy at flank speed; and *then* hit him in the coordinated attack prescribed by doctrine, with his massed air might.

Of course, that would take time; perhaps as much as an hour. Delay in carrier warfare could be risky.

As Vice Admiral Nagumo weighed this momentous choice, surrounded on the flag bridge by the anxious faces of his staff — while all over the task force antiaircraft guns still rattled, and ships heeled and turned in a tangle of crisscrossing white wakes on the remarkably smooth blue sea, and the planes returning from Midway roared low, round and round the *Akagi*, and Zeroes drove off the last of the slow enemy bombers, and the thousand noises of a carrier in action rose all around him — at this fateful moment Nagumo got a message from his subordinate, the division commander of the *Soryu* and the *Hiryu*:

URGENT. CONSIDER IT ADVISABLE TO LAUNCH ATTACK FORCE IMMEDIATELY.

The officer who had to hand Nagumo this paper probably did not dare look him in the face. In any navy in the world, such a message from a subordinate in the heat of battle would have been an insult; in the Imperial Japanese Fleet it was suicidal effrontery. This man Yamaguchi was considered the most brilliant officer in the navy after Yamamoto, whom he was destined to succeed. Surely he knew the gravity of his act. He apparently thought that the battle might hang on this moment, and that sacrificing his career didn't matter.

Old men are not to be pushed that way. Nagumo immediately did the opposite: ordered all planes struck below — *including Yamaguchi's* — and directed the entire task force to recover aircraft. So the die was cast; it would be a full coordinated attack.

And now for the first time he broke radio silence to inform Admiral

Yamamoto, idling three hundred miles away with the seven battleships and one carrier of the Main Body, that he was heading to destroy an enemy force of one carrier, five cruisers, and five destroyers. Until that moment, ten long days after leaving Hiroshima Bay, the commander-in-chief had been utterly in the dark about what was happening to his attack plan.

So once again the Type-97s rolled to the elevators; once again they sank to the hangar decks; once again switching commenced. Bombs had at first replaced torpedoes, now torpedoes were replacing bombs, and still these airplanes had never left the ships. Possibly some Japanese muttering about "the idiots up there" went with the loaders' heavy labor, under the lash of loudspeakers howling exhortations from the flag bridge. But if so, it must have been good-natured. These sailors had seen American dive-bombers flying to pieces, dropping into the sea, streaking down afire like meteors, in defeated wave upon wave. They had watched the harmless fall of giant bombs from cowardly B-17s flying too high for the Zeroes, and the impotent American torpedoes floundering and breaking. Overhead they could hear the roar and the thud of the triumphant first strike returning from Midway. A more glorious victory than Pearl Harbor was in the making! So these hard-working youngsters, stripped to the waist and pouring sweat, undoubtedly felt as they scattered seventeen-hundred-pound bombs in disorder on the deck and feverishly strapped in place the heavy torpedoes.

In less than an hour the four carrier crews recovered all aircraft, rearmed them, refueled them, and spotted them on the flight decks ready to go. No doubt pleased with this superb performance, and with his own sturdy decision not to go off half-cocked, Nagumo was speeding northeast to pull away from Midway's annoying bombers and to strike at the American carrier.

The sun had now been up for almost four and a half hours.

The unescorted *Enterprise* dive-bombers, reaching the point where the staff navigators had predicted that they would intercept the enemy, saw nothing but cloud-flecked ocean, fifty miles in every direction. Onward and westward they flew. Warren's fuel-gauge needle was wobbling below the halfway mark. If within twenty minutes they turned back, he calculated, they might make it to the *Enterprise*, since it was steadily closing the range. But to go back with loaded bomb racks! For years he had imagined a combat dive at an enemy flattop, and now the reality was so goddamn close! Did anybody in charge, from Rear Admiral Spruance down to Lieutenant Commander McClusky, know what the hell he was doing? This harum-scarum Charge of the Light Brigade through the clouds was hardly a match for the Japs' brute professionalism. Would he even see the *Enterprise* again, without first dropping in the drink?

It seemed such a pitiful, stupid trap — a great flight of dive-bombers howling down the sky in disciplined echelons, loaded to strike, but heading nowhere except for the water. The enemy already lay behind and to the northeast, Warren was sure of that. Browning's staff navigators must have assumed that the Japs would continue to close the atoll at full speed, but obviously they had slowed to evade bomber attacks from Midway, and perhaps to launch aircraft. Gagged by radio silence, how could he point this out to McClusky, whose plane led the serried blue bombers hundreds of yards up ahead and above; was it his place to do it, and would the group commander listen to him, anyway?

Impulsively he slid back his oil-streaked canopy. The thin frigid air swept cigarette smoke and stale machine smells from the heated cockpit. He was breathing hard as on a mountain top, but he did not want to use oxygen; the soppy mask was irksome, and he preferred to smoke. His fuel predicament did not worry him too much. On the return from the Marcus raid his damaged engine had quit, and he had ditched, hitting into a foaming swell with an impact like a crash on land; but he and his rear gunner, Cornett's predecessor, had gotten the raft out of the sinking bomber and had floated for six hours, eating chocolate and swapping stories, before a destroyer had picked them up. Ditching was a nasty but manageable maneuver.

But this futile wandering of the two dive-bomber squadrons angered him to his heart. Stoically, he hoped that the *Hornet* and *Yorktown* planes, and maybe Gene Lindsey's torpedo squadron, would find the son-of-a-bitching Japs and do some harm; or that McClusky would turn northeast, or else go back and gas up for another try, instead of deep-sixing thirty-three Dauntlesses.

At this point, Wade McClusky did turn northeast.

Warren could not know — happily for him — what a sorry farce the whole American attack was degenerating into.

In the Japanese strike on Midway, one hundred eight aircraft from four carriers — fighters, dive-bombers, Type-97s — had joined up and flown out as a single attack group, performed their mission like clockwork, and returned in a disciplined formation. But in this American strike each carrier had sent off its own planes at odd times. The slow torpedo squadrons had soon lost contact with the fighters and the dive-bombers. No American pilot knew what other squadrons than his own were doing, let alone where the Japanese were. Disorganization could go little further.

The *Hornet* dive-bombers and fighters, in abysmal futility, had already fallen out of the fight. At the vacant intercept point their group leader had turned south toward the atoll, away from Nagumo's force. This group had then broken apart, some flying on to Midway to refuel, others turning back to the *Hornet*. Most of the latter would splash with dead engines.

While the *Enterprise* squadrons under McClusky were blundering westward, the *Yorktown* had finally launched, well after nine o'clock — but it had sent off only half its planes. Rear Admiral Fletcher was saving the rest for some emergency. Nagumo's carriers meanwhile were plowing northward, his intact air force fueled and rearmed, preparing to launch at half past ten a total coordinated attack with a hundred two planes.

Only one eccentric element — as it were, one wild card — remained in this all but played-out game: the three slow American torpedo squadrons. These were operating out of sight of each other, in a random and quite unplanned way. No torpron had any idea where another torpron was. The commanders of these weak and outmoded machines, three tough mavericks named Waldron, Lindsey, and Massey, were doing their own navigation. It was they who found the Japanese.

"Fifteen torpedo planes, bearing 130!"

Nagumo and his staff were not caught by surprise, though the absence — again! — of fighter escort must have astounded them. The bearing showed the planes were coming from the carrier Nagumo was closing to destroy. Fifteen planes, one squadron; naturally the Yank carrier would try to strike first. But the vice admiral, with an advantage, as he believed, of four to one in ships and planes, was not worried. He had no idea that he was closing three carriers. The float plane pilot from the cruiser *Tone* had never reported the other two.

There was an ironic fatality about this search pilot. He had been launched half an hour late, and so had made his crucial sighting late. He had failed at first to recognize the flattop he saw; and thereafter he had not mentioned the other carriers. Having turned in this sorry performance, he vanished from history; like the asp that bit Cleopatra, a small creature on whom the fortunes of an empire had briefly and sadly turned.

The fifteen aircraft sailing in against Nagumo were Torpedo Squadron Eight of the *Hornet*. Their leader, John Waldron, a fierce and iron-minded aviator, led his men in on their required straight slow runs — with what feelings one cannot record, because he was among the first to die — through a thick antiaircraft curtain of smoke and shrapnel, and a swarming onslaught of Zeroes. One after another, as they tried to spread out for an attack on both bows of the carriers, Waldron's planes caught fire, flew apart, splashed in the sea. Only a few lasted long enough to drop their torpedoes. Those who did accomplished nothing, for none hit. In a few minutes it was over, another complete Japanese victory.

But even as the fifteenth plane burst into flames off the *Akagi's* bow and tumbled smoking into the blue water, a strident report from a screening vessel staggered everybody on the flag bridge: *"Fourteen torpedo planes approaching!"*

Fourteen MORE? The dead, risen from the sea as in some frightful old legend, to fight on for their country in their wrecked planes? The Japanese mind is poetic, and such a thought could have flashed on Nagumo, but the reality was plain and frightening enough. American carriers each had but one torpedo squadron; this meant that *at least one more carrier was coming at him.* The report of the accursed *Tone* float plane was therefore worthless. There might be four more carriers, or seven. Who could tell what devilry the ingenious Americans were up to? Japanese intelligence had flatly failed. As Nagumo had once sneaked up on Pearl Harbor, could the enemy not have sneaked several new carriers into the Pacific Ocean?

"Speed all preparations for immediate takeoff!"

The panicky order, abandoning coordinated attack, went out to the four carriers. The air raid bugles brayed, the thick black-puffing AA thumped out from the screen, the carriers broke formation to dodge the attackers, and the Zeroes, halting the slow climb to combat patrol altitude, dove at this new band of unescorted craft. These were Gene Lindsey's squadron from the *Enterprise*. The scarred, unwell commander had led them straight to the enemy while McClusky groped westward. Ten planes went down, Lindsey's among them. Four evaded the slaughterers, dropped their torpedoes, and headed back for their ship. If any torpedo hit, it did not detonate.

Yet another big victory! But all steaming order was now gone from the Carrier Striking Force. Evasive maneuvering had pulled the *Hiryu* almost out of sight to the north, and strung the *Akagi*, the *Kaga*, and the *Soryu* in a line from west to east. The screening vessels were scattered from horizon to horizon, streaming smoke and cutting across each other's long curved wakes. The sailors and officers were working away on the carrier flight decks with unabated zest. They had already cheered the flaming fall of dozens of bombers from Midway, and now two waves of Yank torpedo craft had been minced up by the Zeroes! The four flight decks were crammed with aircraft; none quite set for launch, but all fueled and bomb-loaded, and all in a vast tangle of fuel lines, bombs, and torpedoes, which the deck crews were cheerfully sweating to clear away, so that the airmen could zoom off to the kill.

Warren Henry had thought of the *Enterprise* as an eggshell eight hundred feet long, full of dynamite and human beings. Here were four such eggshells; more nearly, four grandiose floating fuel and ammunition dumps, uncovered to the touch of a match.

"Enemy torpedo planes, bearing 095!"

This third report came after a short quiet interval. The Zeroes were heading up to the station whence they could repulse dive-bombers from on high, or knock down more low-skimming torpedo planes, whichever would appear. The four carriers were turning into the wind to launch; but now they resumed twisting and dodging, while all eyes turned to the low-flying attackers, and to the combat patrol diving in a rush for more clay-pigeon shooting. Twelve torpedo planes were droning in from the *Yorktown*. These did have a few escort fighters weaving desperately above them, but it made little difference. Ten were knocked down; two survived after dropping torpedoes in vain. All three torpedo squadrons were now wiped out, and the Nagumo Carrier Striking Force was untouched. The time was twenty minutes past ten.

"Launch the attack!"

The order went out all through the force. The first fighter escort plane soared off the deck of the *Akagi*.

At that very moment the almost unrecognizable voice of a staff officer uttered a scream which perhaps rang on in Nagumo's ears until he died two years later on the island of Saipan, under attack by another Raymond Spruance task force:

"HELL-DIVERS!"

In two slanting lines stretching upward into the high clouds, unopposed by a single fighter, dark blue planes were dropping on the flagship and on the *Kaga*. The Zeroes were all at water level, where they had knocked down so many torpedo planes and were looking for more. A more distant scream came from a lookout pointing eastward: *"HELL-DIVERS!"* A second dotted line of dark blue aircraft was arrowing down toward the *Soryu*.

It was a perfect coordinated attack. It was timed almost to the second. It was a freak accident.

Wade McClusky had sighted a lone Japanese destroyer heading northeast. It must be returning from some mission, he had guessed; if so, it was scoring a long white arrow on the sea pointing toward Nagumo. He had made the simple astute decision to turn and follow the arrow.

Meantime, the torpedo attacks of Waldron, Lindsey, and Massey had followed hard upon each other by luck. McClusky had sighted the Striking Force at almost the next moment by luck. The *Yorktown*'s dive-bombers, launched a whole hour later, had arrived at the same time by luck.

In a planned coordinated attack, the dive-bombers were supposed to distract the enemy fighters, so as to give the vulnerable torpedo planes their chance to come in. Instead, the torpedo planes had pulled down the Zeroes and cleared the air for the dive-bombers. What was not luck, but the soul of the United States of America in action, was this willingness of the torpedo plane squadrons to go in against hopeless odds. This was the extra ounce of martial weight that in a few decisive minutes tipped the balance of history.

So long as men choose to decide the turns of history with the slaughter of youths — and even in a better day, when this form of human sacrifice has been abolished like the ancient, superstitious, but no more horrible form — the memory of these three American torpedo plane squadrons should not die. The old sagas would halt the tale to list the names and birthplaces of men who fought so well. Let this romance follow the tradition. These were the young men of the three squadrons, their names recovered from an already fading record.

• • •

U.S.S. YORKTOWN

TORPEDO THREE

Pilots	*Radiomen-Gunners*
Lance E. Massey, Commanding Descanso, California	Leo E. Perry San Diego, California
Richard W. Suesens Waterloo, Iowa	Harold C. Lundy, Jr. Lincoln, Nebraska
Wesley F. Osmus Chicago, Illinois	Benjamin R. Dodson, Jr. Durham, North Carolina
David J. Roche Hibbing, Minnesota	Richard M. Hansen Lakefield, Minnesota
Patrick H. Hart Los Angeles, California	John R. Cole La Grange, Georgia
John W. Haas San Diego, California	Raymond J. Darce New Orleans, Louisiana
Oswald A. Powers Detroit, Michigan	Joseph E. Mandeville Manchester, New Hampshire
Leonard L. Smith Ontario, California	William A. Phillips Olympia, Washington
Curtis W. Howard Olympia, Washington	Charles L. Moore Amherst, Texas
Carl A. Osberg Manchester, New Hampshire	Troy C. Barkley Falkner, Mississippi
	Robert B. Brazier Salt Lake City, Utah

Survivors

Harry L. Corl Saginaw, Michigan	Lloyd F. Childers Oklahoma City, Oklahoma
Wilhelm G. Esders St. Joseph, Missouri	

U.S.S. ENTERPRISE

TORPEDO SIX

Pilots

Eugene E. Lindsey, Commanding
San Diego, California

Severin L. Rombach
Cleveland, Ohio

John T. Eversole
Pocatello, Idaho

Randolph M. Holder
Jackson, Mississippi

Arthur V. Ely
Pittsburgh, Pennsylvania

Flourenoy G. Hodges
Statesboro, Georgia

Paul J. Riley
Hot Springs, Arkansas

John W. Brock
Montgomery, Alabama

Lloyd Thomas
Chauncey, Ohio

Radiomen-Gunners

Charles T. Grenat
Honolulu, Hawaii

Wilburn F. Glenn
Austin, Texas

John U. Lane
Rockford, Illinois

Gregory J. Durawa
Milwaukee, Wisconsin

Arthur R. Lindgren
Montclair, New Jersey

John H. Bates
Valparaiso, Indiana

Edwin J. Mushinski
Tampa, Florida

John M. Blundell
Fort Wayne, Indiana

Harold F. Littlefield
Bennington, Vermont

Survivors

Albert W. Winchell
Webster City, Iowa

Robert E. Laub
Richland, Missouri

Edward Heck, Jr.
Carthage, Missouri

Irvin H. McPherson
Glen Ellyn, Illinois

Stephen B. Smith
Mason City, Iowa

Douglas M. Cossitt
Oakland, California

William C. Humphrey, Jr.
Milledgeville, Georgia

Doyle L. Ritchey
Ryan, Oklahoma

William D. Horton
Little Rock, Arkansas

Wilfred N. McCoy
San Diego, California

U.S.S. HORNET

TORPEDO EIGHT

Pilots	Radiomen-Gunners
John C. Waldron, Commanding Fort Pierre, South Dakota	Horace F. Dobbs San Diego, California
James C. Owens, Jr. Los Angeles, California	Amelio Maffei Santa Rosa, California
Raymond A. Moore Richmond, Virginia	Tom H. Pettry Ellison Ridge, West Virginia
Jefferson D. Woodson Beverly Hills, California	Otway D. Creasy, Jr. Vinton, Virginia
George M. Campbell San Diego, California	Ronald J. Fisher Denver, Colorado
William W. Abercrombie Merriam, Kansas	Bernard P. Phelps Lovington, Illinois
Ulvert M. Moore Bluefield, West Virginia	William F. Sawhill Mansfield, Ohio
William W. Creamer Riverside, California	Francis S. Polston Nashville, Missouri
John P. Gray Columbia, Missouri	Max A. Calkins Wymore, Nebraska
Harold J. Ellison Buffalo, New York	George A. Field Buffalo, New York
Henry R. Kenyon, Jr. Mount Vernon, New York	Darwin L. Clark Rodney, Iowa
William R. Evans, Jr. Indianapolis, Indiana	Ross E. Bibb, Jr. Warrior, Alabama
Grant W. Teats Sheridan, Oregon	Hollis Martin Bremerton, Washington
Robert B. Miles San Diego, California	Ashwell L. Picou Houma, Louisiana
	Robert K. Huntington South Pasadena, California

Survivor

George H. Gay, Jr.
Houston, Texas

● ● ●

Warren Henry had, of course, not a glimmer of this tactical miracle.

Shut in his cockpit, isolated by radio silence, locked into the array of blue bombers roaring through the sky over a thickening cloud cover, all he knew was that McClusky at last had — for one blessed reason or another — turned northeast; that radio silence had been broken by one weak garbled aircraft transmission and another, suggesting that somebody must have found the Japs, the next by a ship's high-powered radio, squawking in the unmistakable high-strung tones of Miles Browning, *"Attack! I say again, AT-TACK!"*

For the first time in over two hours, Warren then heard the baritone voice of McClusky, calm, clear, faintly sarcastic, the young professional cooling the excited old fud, *"Wilco, as soon as I find the bastards."* At once he felt a surge of warm confidence in McClusky. Within minutes the Japanese fleet burst into view, a stunning spread of ships from horizon to horizon, showing through breaks in the layer of clouds.

It looked just like the Pacific Fleet on a major battle exercise. That was Warren's first thought, and to dive-bomb them seemed like murder. McClusky droned orders to commence the descent to the attack point. The bomber group sank toward the dazzling white clouds, and broke through the upper layer for a panoramic view of the whole enemy force under wisps of low cloud.

The formation was in bad disorder. Long wakes curled and crisscrossed in the sea like a child's finger painting of white on blue, the screening ships raggedly headed this way and that; black AA puffballs floated all over the scene; and the pale yellow lights of gun muzzles winked everywhere. In his first glimpse Warren had seen only one carrier, but here were three almost in column, all heading into the wind, with black smoke and long, long white wakes streaming straight back; and far to the north was another big ship, possibly a fourth one, in a clump of escorts.

Tiny aircraft in a swarm were flitting and darting at wavetop height among the ships. Warren saw one trail smoke, another burst into flame; some kind of action was going on down there, but *where was the combat air patrol?* The sky was eerily vacant. McClusky was already issuing attack orders! One squadron to one carrier, Scouting Six for the rear flattop, Bombing Six for the second one; let that third one go for now. It was all happening fast, for there was McClusky starting to push over into his dive, and Warren's squadron leader was following him.

From here on this was familiar stuff, plain squadron attack drill, the ABC of dive-bombing. The one difference — so he told himself in these last seconds, with his hand on the diving brake lever, when he was beginning to feel better than he had ever felt in his whole life — the one difference now was that the oblong thing which he had to hit fifteen thousand feet down there on the sea wasn't a target sled but a carrier! That made the shot a hell of a lot easier. The flight deck was a hundred times the size of a sled. He had more than once splintered the edge of a sled with a dummy bomb.

Yet again, *where was the combat air patrol?* That had been his worry right along, unescorted as they were. This thing so far was an unbelievable cinch. He kept glancing over his shoulders for Zeroes pouncing out of the clouds. There wasn't a sign of them. McClusky and the first few bombers, already on their steep way down far below, one staggered behind the other, weren't even catching any AA. Warren had often pictured and dreamed of attacks on carriers, but never of a walkover like this.

He said into the intercom in high spirits, "Well here we go, I guess, Cornett. All set?"

"Yes, Mr. Henry." Matter-of-fact drawl. "Say, where the heck are the Zeroes, Mr. Henry?"

"Search me. Are you complaining?"

"No sir, Mr. Henry! Just you drop that egg in there, sir."

"Going to try. We'll have the sun on our starboard side. That's where they're likely to show up."

"Okay, Mr. Henry. I've got my eye peeled. Good luck."

Warren pulled the lever of his diving flaps. The perforated metal V opened all along his wings. The airplane mushily slowed. The flattop went out of sight beside the fuselage, under the wing. The nose came up, the plane gave its almost living warning shudder; Warren pushed over, dizzily dropped the nose straight toward the water far, far below, and straightened out in a roller-coaster plunge.

And there, by God, was the carrier in his telescopic sight, right over the little wobbling ball. Now if the telescope only wouldn't fog up as they plunged into the warmer air! Visibility through the oily film of the canopy wouldn't be very good.

It was an excellent dive. The danger was always overshooting and standing on your head, when the dive was almost impossible to control, but he was dropping toward the flattop at a beautiful angle, maybe sixty-five, seventy degrees, from almost dead astern, a little to port, perfect. He wasn't sitting on his seat now but hanging facedown in his straps, the pure dive sensation. He always thought it was like jumping off a high dive board. There was the same headfirst feeling, the same queaziness in gut and balls that you never got over. It was a long way down, almost a whole minute, and he had excellent controls to straighten out slips or wobbles, but this dive was going fine. With a pedal jammed in hard to neutralize the SBD's usual yaw, they were skimming down sweetly, the throttled-back engine purr-ing, the air whiffling noisily on the brakes — and that flight deck was sitting right there in his little lens, not fogging over at all, growing bigger and plainer, with the hardwood decking bright yellow in the sunlight, the big red ball conspicuous in the white oblong forward of the island, the planes crowded aft in a jumble, and minuscule Japs running around them like insects. As his altimeter reeled backward his ears popped and the plane warmed.

All at once he saw the great white splash of a near-miss jump up alongside the island; and then a huge fiery explosion ripped the white paint all around the meatball, with a blast of smoke. So there was one hit! He could see two bombers zooming away. His ears ached like hell. He swallowed, and they popped again. Right now that carrier was in trouble; one more good hit could really cream it. Warren was at five thousand feet. Doctrine called for the bomb drop at about three thousand feet, but he meant to bore down at least to twenty-five hundred. Joyously in control, watching his dials, watching the rapidly expanding deck almost straight below him, he was nerving himself for a split-second decision. He intended to slam the bomb in among those aircraft sitting there in his scope; but if this carrier took yet another hit first, then instead of plastering it again with a precious half-ton bomb, he might still veer over and try to hit the third carrier, far ahead.

But what a target, that mess of airplanes rushing up at him now in the telescopic sight, so clear that he could see white numbers on the fuselages, and the little Japs running and gesticulating as he plunged toward them! No other hits yet; *he'd go*. Now his heart was racing, his mouth was parched, and his ears seemed about to burst. He yanked the bomb release, felt the jolt of lightness as the missile flew clear, remembered to keep going to make sure he didn't throw the bomb, and he pulled up.

His body sagged to the seat, his head swam, his stomach seemed to plop against his backbone, the gray mist came and went; he kicked the plane's tail and glanced backward . . . Oh, *CHRIST!*

A sheet of white fire was climbing out of those airplanes, billowing black smoke; and even as he looked, the fire spread and exploded along the deck and arched into the air in beautiful colors, red, yellow, purple, pink, with varicolored smoke towering up into the sky. What a terrific change in a second or two! Debris was flying in every direction, pieces of airplanes, pieces of the deck, whole human bodies tumbling upward like tossed rag dolls; what a horrible unbelievable magnificent sight! The whole wild holocaust of fire and smoke went roaring skyward and streaming astern, for the stricken carrier was still rushing at full speed into the wind.

"Mr. Henry, there's a Zero at eight o'clock angels about one thousand." Cornett on the intercom. "He's making a run on us."

"Roger." Warren nosed over and dove for the water, violently jinking and yawing. The waves were breaking in long white crests, and he hurtled along through spume that spattered his canopy like hail, dodging erratically, grateful for the sturdy response of the SBD-3 to the crazy maneuvers. This was doctrine: hug the water, make the Jap miss, lure him to dive into the sea. The plane shook and his teeth jarred as Cornett's gun began a furious rattle. Warren saw bullets splashing a line in the water a few yards forward of his nose, and glancing up he caught sight of the Zero diving at him, squirting yellow flame and white smoke. The fighter that had knocked him down over Pearl Harbor had been a peacetime silver color; this was a dirty mottled greenish-brown, but those big red balls on the wings were just the same. The Zero pulled up smack at the waterline and disappeared into AA smoke; ye gods, those damned things were maneuverable.

Warren flew past a tragic sight, caught in a flash out of the corner of his eye — a blue wing with a white star, sticking out of the water; just the wing. It vanished, and a huge gray ship slid into view before his windshield with forty yellow lights blinking at him, surely a battleship or a heavy cruiser. Antiaircraft began bursting around him in sooty explosions that rocked and hammered the plane. In seconds the vessel stretched out dead ahead, blocking his way, a vast gray steel wall. Warren pulled up for dear life and the Dauntless soared over the forecastle, much lower than the crooked pagoda mast, barely clearing the forward turret of long gray guns.

So he was out of the screen now! If his luck would hold and he could outdistance the AA batteries that from behind were spattering shrapnel on the water all around him —

"Mr. Henry, that sumbitch is *back*. He been follerin' us all the way."

"Roger."

Warren tried to repeat his wild dodging, flying as close to the water as he dared, but the airplane was now acting sluggish. The red tracers from the Zero came raining down along his port side, kicking up white water spurts. He veered hard right and almost caught a wing in a wave top. The plane was not answering as before.

"*Yippee!* Mr. Henry, I think maybe I got the sumbitch." Cornett sounded like a kid at a high school ball game. "I swear he's headin' home to mama. Take a look, Mr. Henry, he's dead astern. He's smokin'."

The Dauntless turned and climbed. The attacker was shrinking away toward the enemy task force, trailing a smudge of smoke; and beyond it, beyond the ships of the screen, all three carriers were vomiting flame and black smoke upward into the blue sunny sky. Who had got the third carrier, he wondered? Had some other pilot done what he'd thought of doing? That third flattop was on fire, not a doubt in the world of it. Those three black

318 WAR AND REMEMBRANCE

smoke pillars were rising high over the task force like three black plumes on a hearse.

Now he looked at his watch, at the fuel gauge, and at the flight chart. It was 10:30, and he had winged over for the attack at 10:25; he had lived a lot of his life in five minutes! The fuel was too low to bear thinking about. He was sure the staff's Point Option position was wrong. Those stupid staff bastards had probably figured that Spruance would advance at full speed — same mistake as with the Japs — when chances were he had turned into the wind to recover the combat air patrol or returning aircraft. Warren headed for the 1000 position bearing, grimly noting that the craft's response was still sluggish.

"That was some hit, Mr. Henry. Gee, did that baby go up!"

"Say, Cornett, watch the tail assembly. I'm going to waggle the controls. Tell me if there's any damage to the surfaces."

"Yes, Mr. Henry. Oh, Judas Priest, you got no rudder, sir. Just a small ragged hunk."

"Well, okay." Warren quenched an upwelling of alarm. "We're heading home to mama ourselves."

"We gonna make it, Mr. Henry?"

"Dunno why not," Warren said with more cheer than he felt. "We may have to sling a couple of chocolate bars in the tank."

"Well, anyway, Mr. Henry," Cornett said with a most un-Cornett-like merry laugh, "whatever happens, it was worth it, just to get that hit, and watch them sumbitches burning back there."

"Concur."

Now the thought came to Warren as a gladsome surprise that radio silence was finished. He gambled the gasoline to climb to two thousand feet, and tuned in on the Enterprise's Y-E homing signal. Loud and clear, from the 1000 position dead ahead, came the Morse-code letter he expected. He throttled back near stalling speed, and settled down near the tossing white-capped swells. It would be a close thing, but there were always the rescue destroyers. In his exalted mood, a water landing held no terror for him. He could still see the flames billowing, the planes exploding, the bodies flying on that Jap carrier. He had done it; *done it*, and he was alive and heading back in glory.

Many miles astern, Vice Admiral Nagumo was being dragged off the flaming, listing *Akagi* by his staff officers. Picking his way among the broken corpses roasting with a kitchen stench on the red-hot deck plates, which still shuddered with explosions, he was fussily insisting that there was no real need yet to abandon ship. He had not authorized his subordinate Yamaguchi in the unhit *Hiryu* to take command, or even to launch at discretion. Climbing down a rope ladder to a cruiser's whale boat, the distraught old gentleman remained the commander-in-chief of the ruined Carrier Attack Force. But Yamaguchi was not waiting any longer for orders from Nagumo, who had probably just lost the war for Japan. On seeing the first bombs raise smoke and fire on the *Kaga*, he had commenced an immediate counterstrike.

*   *   *

31

Midway (Concluded)

(from *World Holocaust* by Armin von Roon)

Second Phase

The opening phase of the battle occupied most of the morning of June 4.

The middle phase lasted five minutes.

The end took four days.

The annals of military conflict, from their dim origins in Chinese and Egyptian accounts to the present era, show no equal to the world-historical second phase, the Five Minutes of Midway.

Between 10:25 A.M. and 10:30 A.M. of that fateful day, in that mere instant of combat time, three Japanese carriers, with their full complements of aircraft, were reduced to smoking flotsam. These giant victims embodied the national strength and treasure of Japan, the culmination of half a century of heroic effort to become a first-class military power. In those five explosive minutes, Japan's world status, laboriously built up from Tsushima Strait to Singapore, Manila, and Burma, was shattered; though she had yet to suffer three years of defeat and final atomic-blast horror before accepting this fact.

After Midway, as Admiral von Nimitz once put it, "We fought the Pacific war just as we had worked it out for twenty years in the War College" (a remark that sufficiently suggests the long-range aggressive intent of the Anglo-American plutocracies). The rest of that war is tangential to German readers' interests, but this brilliant classic of sea warfare must be studied.

Chance thrust an unknown junior flag officer into full command of the combined American task forces in mid-battle. Vice Admiral Halsey, a sort of seagoing General Patton full of dash and swagger, had fallen ill just before the fleet sortied, otherwise he would have led the fight. The replacement he suggested was his friend Raymond A. Spruance, a quiet man who commanded his screen. Rear Admiral Frank Jack Fletcher, commanding Task

Force Seventeen, was senior to Spruance. Nimitz intended that Fletcher run the battle. Luck dropped it into Spruance's hands, and Spruance proceeded to show himself one of the great admirals of world history. The United States of America has been a lucky nation, and this luck held remarkably on June 4, 1942. How long it will hold in the future, only the dark gods know who bestowed on this crass mercantile nation of mongrelized blood and cowboy culture a virgin continent with almost infinite natural resources.

Spruance made three historic decisions at Midway. This shy and reticent man, of no remarkable blood or background, unveiled an astounding capacity to think and act in the thick of battle. After Midway he won many victories in command of ever-vaster forces; yet in history, like Nelson of Trafalgar, he will remain Spruance of Midway.

The First Decision

Spruance's first great decision was to launch all the aircraft of the *Hornet* and the *Enterprise* at extreme range at seven o'clock in the morning, risking everything to get in the first surprise blow. The risk proved costly. Several of his squadrons could not even find the enemy. Almost half his planes ran out of gasoline and fell in the water, or returned with their bombs, or flew on to Midway atoll without fighting. Yet enough dive-bombers reached the Nagumo force to execute the blitz that left the *Akagi,* the *Kaga,* and the *Soryu* in flames. Nothing else mattered. Spruance won this world-historical gamble.

Here too he enjoyed American luck, for his wandering squadrons met up over the Japanese fleet for a combined attack by chance. The dive-bombers did all the damage. The torpedo planes were wiped out. By contrast, later that day, Japanese torpedo planes from the *Hiryu* drove home an attack and wrecked the *Yorktown.* Technically as well as numerically, the Americans were outclassed at Midway. This only highlights Spruance's leadership.

Rear Admiral Fletcher cautiously delayed his *Yorktown* launching for over an hour. He then sent out only half of his aircraft. When the torpedoed *Yorktown* had to be abandoned, Fletcher moved his flag to a screening cruiser, and passed command of all forces to Spruance. This was the only important act in the military career of Fletcher that this historian has been able to ascertain.

TRANSLATOR'S NOTE: *When Fletcher had to abandon the* Yorktown, *he signalled Spruance, "I will conform to your movements," thus generously yielding up leadership of a great battle. That was more than Nagumo ever did. Fletcher knew that Spruance had the staff, the communications, and the carriers to continue the battle. He did the sensible thing. — V.H.*

Nagumo's Dither

In even sharper contrast to Spruance stands the performance of Nagumo.

Here was a carrier flag officer as experienced as Spruance was green, commanding the best carrier force afloat. Under the same pressures that beset Spruance, with a seasoned staff that swiftly executed his every wish, with vessels and air squadrons that operated with ballet precision, Nagumo fell apart, and threw away a battle that almost could not be lost.

Here was more American luck. The catapult of the cruiser *Tone* was defective, so the search plane assigned to the sector where the Americans happened to be hiding did not get off on time. The pilot sent vague reports. But popular accounts make too much of the famous *"Tone* float plane." Nothing is commoner in warfare than unreliable scout or sentry reports. As soon as Nagumo learned of the presence of American ships, he should have assumed that they were carriers, and urgently prepared to attack. Instead, he dithered. Under air harassment from Midway that did him no harm, he kept changing his mind about his next move, and switching the armament of his Type-97 planes. Spruance's dive-bombers resolved his dilemma by destroying him.

Nagumo himself escaped with his life from the *Akagi* by climbing down a rope from his bridge. Unlike Fletcher, he clung to command, though in Rear Admiral Yamaguchi aboard the *Hiryu* he had a fine subordinate in position to fight on. One wonders what Vice Admiral Nagumo's feelings must have been as he boated in the open sea while three carriers burned in the morning sunshine before his eyes, the funeral pyres of Japan's first-line carrier pilots and aircraft, a loss beyond replacing. His conduct afterward suggests he was in shock, for he ordered pell-mell retreat and reported to Yamamoto at one point that five American carriers were chasing him. Yamamoto relieved him in the middle of the night. Yamaguchi, who might have won the battle, elected to go down with the *Hiryu*.

Aside from the dither, Nagumo committed another unpardonable mistake. Just prior to the fatal five minutes, he allowed the whole combat air patrol to abandon altitude and swarm down on the torpedo planes. Where torpedo planes appeared, dive-bombers could not be far behind. Had half the fighters stayed aloft, the whole story of the battle and possibly of the Second World War might have been different; but at the moment of maximum peril the upper sky was unguarded.

Spruance's Second Decision

The tragic dispatch of the disaster came to Fleet Admiral Yamamoto, three hundred miles away, after long tense hours of silence, during which he had every reason to suppose that Nagumo was enjoying his customary success. As though sensing trouble ahead, Yamamoto for days had been sick at his stomach. Now, learning the worst, the ailing old man rallied.

Very well, he seems to have decided, Japan had lost the first round. Aggressive American naval doctrine would undoubtedly draw Nagumo's conqueror westward in pursuit. Here then was a golden chance to counterambush and smash the thin Nimitz forces! He was on sound ground; many famous victories have followed on initial setbacks in the field. Yamamoto still had the enemy heavily outnumbered and outgunned in his Main Body. The four dispersed light carriers could be summoned. The *Hiryu* was intact. Urgent dispatches shot out to the scattered Imperial Fleet to close in around Yamamoto's battleships.

From then until nightfall of June 4, on the flag bridge of the great battleship *Yamato,* the mood seesawed with the flux of the news. The reply of the carriers in the Aleutians caused gloom. They could not join up for three days. The *Hiryu* reported that her pilots had dive-bombed an enemy carrier, and then that her torpedo planes had left a second carrier dead in the water. This caused great joy, but it was a mistake. The *Hiryu* had struck the *Yorktown* twice — once with dive-bombers, again and fatally with torpedo planes — but good American damage control had totally quenched the fires of the first attack. The glee died when at sunset the *Hiryu* reported that it too was hit and ablaze.

Still Yamamoto grimly bore eastward. His aim now was to force a night action. If only he could himself encounter the thin-skinned American carriers! His great guns could sink them like ferryboats, lay waste to the screening vessels, and turn defeat into victory; and he could then still take Midway. The whole hope now was that Americans in hot pursuit would spit themselves on the eighteen-inch guns of the *Yamato,* the tremendous firepower of the other battleships and cruisers, and the devastating "longlance" torpedoes of the Japanese destroyer squadrons.

Had Vice Admiral William F. Halsey been in command of the United States ships that probably would have happened. In such situations Halsey's nature was to fling himself with impetuous bellicosity after his wounded foe.

But Raymond Spruance was in command. Spruance steamed toward the oncoming Yamamoto force just long enough to catch the *Hiryu* and destroy it. He then recovered his aircraft *and reversed course to the eastward away from the enemy*. After midnight he again reversed course, and at dawn he was back in position to protect Midway with air cover from a possible landing.

This maneuver was the key to the victory at Midway; the finest command decision in the Pacific war, and one of the finest in the history of sea combat. It was wisdom itself, simplicity itself, with world consequences at stake.

It was not so regarded at the time. Spruance was chided even during the battle by his superiors in Pearl Harbor and Washington for failing to pursue the beaten foe that night. His own staff — or rather, Halsey's staff, which did not like or understand their new nonaviator admiral — was disconcerted by his decision. Afterward, staff officers asserted that radar would have detected oncoming surface forces, and so the task force should never have lost contact with the enemy. This view persists in American military literature, and Raymond Spruance is still sometimes called an overcautious officer.

The criticism is erroneous. Having already won a crucial battle with far inferior forces, this brilliant commander would not stake his victory on a new electronic gadget. Instead, he put his fleet where without question it remained both secure and dangerous. Neither Spruance nor Nimitz knew where Yamamoto's battleships were. Rear Admiral Spruance escaped Yamamoto's terrible trap by acting on perfect military instinct. Not till many months later did American intelligence ferret out the facts about Yamamoto's moves, which confirmed Spruance's blind second decision as a historic masterstroke.

Spruance's Third Decision

Shortly after midnight Yamamoto sensed that he had been foiled, that the night action would not take place, and that daylight might find him well within range of Midway's airplanes. Anguished flag conferences ensued. For Yamamoto and his staff, huddling in the luxurious undamaged flag country of the mightiest battleship afloat, leading a battle line of stupendous firepower through the night, there must have been a sickening sense of frustration. The combined fleet was like a gorilla confronting a cobra; if only once it could lay its paws on its puny foe and tear it to ribbons! But the cobra had struck and vanished.

Yamamoto's operations officer, the same Captain Kuroshima, now put forward a gallant proposal. Let the Imperial Fleet steam straight on to the atoll, and with dawn's first light let it pulverize the air installations with gunfire and proceed with the landing! The atoll's planes had failed against Nagumo, after all, and a swarm of them had splashed. The ones that remained must be poor stuff. As for the American carriers, they had suffered huge plane losses, and two (as he thought) were out of action or sunk. The concentrated AA of the Main Force, with cruiser float planes and the aircraft of two light carriers, could surely handle the surviving American carrier strength.

But the plan was hooted at as suicidal folly. There was little impulse for daring left in the staff. Yamamoto straightway rejected Kuroshima's idea, and with all respect to this great warrior's memory, the present writer wonders why. Spruance was in fact substantially weakened by plane losses. The Midway air strength was a shoddy mishmash of ineffective army and marine units. However, there is an inexorable rhythm to battles. The time for dash had passed on the Japanese side.

Nevertheless Yamamoto was more than ready to fight on in his own way. The atoll could not now be seized, but the small Pacific Fleet had been drawn far out beyond its Pearl Harbor air umbrella, and that was a great chance. If only it could be brought to battle and smashed, history would still call the Midway operation a success.

Yamamoto projected two more traps for the foe. He would retreat westward. No doubt the enemy would pursue with harassing tactics. He hoped now to lure the foe within the seven-hundred-mile airpower circle of Wake Island, and there pounce on him with his great force — battleships, heavy cruisers, and destroyer divisions. This giant force had not yet fired a gun or seen an enemy aircraft. That it was in retreat from two battle-worn American carriers and their escorts was grotesque.

Simultaneously, he ordered the carriers in the Aleutians to attack again. The capture of Attu and Kiska was to proceed. The American fleet might then be ordered north, where it would run into four heavy cruisers, a light carrier, and the formidable carrier *Zuikaku,* at last repaired, replenished with fresh pilots and aircraft, and making for the Aleutians at top speed.

The two arms of the gorilla, as it were, would grasp at the cobra from the west and the north.

Spruance did pursue. Naval men say that "a stern chase is a long chase." The last phase dragged on for two days as Yamamoto fell back and the American fleet hunted him. Spruance's surviving dive-bombers did very poorly against targets smaller than aircraft carriers. The only other sinking during the long chase, in fact, was an already damaged heavy cruiser, which had collided with a sister ship in a submarine scare. Kuroshima may have been profoundly right in guessing that Spruance was no threat to the heavy Main Force. But the staff on the *Enterprise* kept urging Spruance ever westward. The requirement to pursue and annihilate was for them holy writ.

Spruance's third major decision was to disregard this urging, and strong messages from Nimitz as well; to break off the pursuit, and end the battle. He would not enter the airpower circle of Wake Island. This seems a sort of clairvoyance. He is reported to have put it very simply to his staff:

"We have done just about all the damage we are going to do. Let's get out of here." His vessels were low on fuel; his aviators were exhausted; an enemy of unknown but heavy strength eluded him beyond the horizon; the known menace of land-based air cancelled out the doctrine of pursuit. So Rear Admiral Raymond Spruance decided, and so he sealed the Midway victory.

At the last moment his work was almost undone, for Chester von Nimitz took the Aleutian bait, and ordered Spruance north! Fortunately, Nimitz later thought better of this, and cancelled the order. On June 11th, Task Force Sixteen returned to Pearl Harbor to learn that Army Air Corps bombers had won the Battle of Midway by sinking four carriers, several battleships, etc., etc. The story was in every newspaper. It was in the weekly magazines. All Hawaii believed it. For a time, all America believed it. Raymond Spruance never issued a contradictory public account. In footnotes to postwar reports and memoirs, the Army Air Corps acknowledged that it did no damage at Midway..

Once, much later in life, when complimented on his victory, Raymond Spruance responded, "There were a hundred Spruances in the Navy. They just happened to pick me for the job." In fact, there was only one Spruance and luck gave him, at a fateful hour, to America.

Strategically, the great Nimitz-Spruance victory accomplished three things:

1. American submarines could continue to depart with full fuel bunkers from Midway instead of Pearl Harbor, a round-trip difference of 2300 miles. This multiplied their killing power in the war. William F. Halsey later wrote that the submarine campaign was the first cause of Japan's defeat.
2. Japan's first-line carrier squadrons were drowned or shot down off Midway. The loss of this cadre of leaders and trainers could never be made up.
3. Japan passed overnight, in morale, from élan to desperation. Morally, from 10:30 A.M. June 4, 1942, onward, Japan was on the run, though this brave race gave a good account of itself to the last.

Yamamoto: Vale

The trounced Imperial Fleet skulked back into Hiroshima Bay. Yamamoto still did not know that he had been beaten not by Nimitz, nor even by the famous Halsey, but by an anonymous replacement, plucked from the ranks of American rear admirals.

The Americans sent but four rear admirals into the fight: Fletcher,

Spruance, and the two screen commanders. By contrast, the Imperial Fleet sailed under the great Fleet Admiral Yamamoto himself, flanked by five vice admirals and thirteen rear admirals. In essence, Yamamoto took his headquarters to sea. Nimitz elected to keep his ashore, where it could use the radio, get information, and maintain broad perspective. Nimitz's course was the sounder.

Yamamoto, who had brought off the monumental air victory of Pearl Harbor, rode through Midway on a silenced giant, the world's biggest gunship. In retrospect, he seems not to have grasped the lesson of sea-air power which he himself taught the world. In his battle plan, the carriers were to clear away the land-based air menace; then he was to steam forward in massive grandeur with the Main Body, meet the Nimitz fleet head-on, and win the Pacific Battle of the Skagerrak. This delusory vision kept him out of action at Midway.

Radio Tokyo claimed a vast triumph, but the name of Midway was thereafter blotted from Japanese war reporting. The survivors were put into quarantine. So many records were suppressed or lost that the Japanese side of the battle will never be adequately documented. Yet Yamamoto did not fall. He was Japan's greatest military figure. He had been a naval attaché in the United States. He had represented Japan at the naval conferences of the 1920s, and had won equality for her with the white man's sea powers. He had been against the war with America, but given his sailing orders, he had done his best.

Yamamoto continued to lead his navy until April 1943, when Admiral von Nimitz, learning that Yamamoto was making an air tour of the South Pacific, ordered his plane ambushed and destroyed. So this great man perished. The final stain was on Nimitz. Between Achilles and Hector, there might have been more honor than this sneak murder.

At Midway, the colored man's dramatic military surge in the industrial age was thrown back; perhaps not for all time, since most of mankind is colored; but certainly for fifty or a hundred years. Midway was a solid recovery of the upper hand by the Caucasian after his collapse at Singapore.

Yet before the figure of Isoroku Yamamoto, the military analyst must pause. If Nagumo turned in the typical performance of the colored man under pressure — erratic, dilatory, dithering — Yamamoto rose to disaster with firmness, nobility, and ingenuity worthy of a Moltke or a Manstein. Europe and America should remember that Asia can produce such men.

Midway: The Final Lesson

The five-minute overturn that struck the Japanese nation at Midway compels a final reflection.

Industrial-scientific developments since that time have made possible

Midway-style lightning holocausts of entire countries. The new Midway which now threatens is, as is well known, atomic surprise and counter-surprise with colossal rockets, between U.S. capitalism and Russian Bolshevism. These twin brutish materialisms of our age are spiritual hells, incapable of controlling the forces they wield. Today both carry the logic of the aircraft carrier much further. Their entire land masses and their whole populations are now flattop and crew; and both nations are vulnerable and destructive to an unheard-of degree.

The tale must proceed to its dark end. Perhaps our own prostrate, sundered, and mutilated Fatherland will out of its great agony in World War II produce a new philosopher — a Kant, a Hegel, a Nietzsche — to point a way out of mankind's dread cul-de-sac. The German genius has always been for such Faustian reaching beyond the given.

Otherwise the prospect is grave. The Americans and the Russians are blood-brothers in uncultured hardness, though the Americans sometimes seem comfort-mad and the Russians woolly-headed. It means little or nothing to them that in their duel of dimwitted giants most life on earth is menaced, and all human advancement since Roman times seems condemned. As things stand now, one or another of their small allies will one unexpected day prove the Serbia or Poland of the Third World War. It will be no war in the old sense, however. It will be a lightning Midway of the continents.

TRANSLATOR'S NOTE: *Roon's racial viewpoint is beneath comment. The shooting down of Fleet Admiral Yamamoto was ordered by the Secretary of the Navy, Frank Knox, a former newspaper publisher. Chester Nimitz was apprised of the plan, and endorsed it on the grounds that Yamamoto was irreplaceable, and in military value to Japan, equal perhaps to four carriers. The Japanese joined Hitler's criminal attack on civilization and had to bear the consequences, Yamamoto among them. — V.H.*

＊　　＊　　＊

32

C APTAIN Henry sat slouched over the detective novel in the sea cabin, his head on his hand, a cigarette burning down in his fingers.

"The aviators are breaking radio silence, Cap'n." Hines, the quartermaster, saluting in the doorway.

"Very well." He leaped up and hurried to the wheelhouse, where his attempt to settle at ease in his high chair deceived nobody. The ship's clowns had long been mimicking his stooped posture and quick cigarette gestures when he was tense. Knowing glances went among the men on watch as he crouched and smoked, staring out to sea. Through the bridge loudspeakers came scratchy talk from the weak faraway aircraft transmitters: ". . . *Earl, you take that one on the left . . . Commencing our attack . . . Hey! Zeroes at eleven o'clock . . . Victor Sail Six, this is Tim Satterlee, I'm hit and ditching, wish me luck . . . Wow, look at that big bastard burn! . . .*"

"Sounds like they're doing pretty good, sir," ventured the exec, who was pacing and mopping sweat from his face.

Pug only nodded, straining his ears in vain for the timbre of his son's voice; the keyed-up youngsters out there all sounded alike. These garbled fragments peppered with hot obscenities brought laughter and noisy chatter on the bridge, which Pug for once overlooked in his own excitement.

When the transmissions petered out, Captain Henry glanced about him and the bridge talk died. Long silence, with crackling of static. Returning pilots began to give calm position reports, sometimes with a wry joke, as their fuel ran out and they prepared to ditch; from Warren, not a word. After a while radar reported "friendlies" approaching. The fleet swung ponderously into the wind. Pug's lookouts reported specks low in the western sky, which grew into airplanes roaring in over the screen to the carriers. The *Yorktown,* hull down far to the west, was landing its planes, too. As the aircraft came straggling into Pug's binoculars, he resolved *not* to worry if no SBD made a wing-waggling pass over him. Warren would have a fuel problem like the rest, and might be ditching. Still, as the *Enterprise* dive-bombers landed, he counted them. Thirty-two had departed. Ten . . . eleven . . . twelve . . . A long interval went by; long for him, anyway. Plane after plane kept landing on the *Hornet;* a few on the *Enterprise,* but no more dive-bombers . . .

"*Dauntless off the starboard bow, Captain!*" A shout of the quartermaster from the other wing. Pug darted through the bridge house. Rocking its white-starred wings, the plane thrummed over the forecastle and veered off toward the *Enterprise*, the goggled pilot waving a long arm. Victor Henry kept his face seaward, watching the aircraft come in to land. He would not put a hand up to his wet eyes. Nobody on the bridge came near him. So several minutes passed.

From the bridge house, the exec called, "*Yorktown* reports many bogies on radar, Captain. Bearing two seventy-five, distance forty. Closing speed two hundred knots."

Pug managed to articulate, "Very well. Go to General Quarters."

On the *Enterprise*, the landing officer sliced a paddle past his throat in a grinning cut. Warren's wheels thumped on the deck. Joy swept him as the drag of the arresting gear strained him against his belt. *Home!* He gunned forward over the flattened barriers, killed the engine, and jumped out with his chart board, slapping Cornett on the back as the radioman leaped to the deck. Quickly the handlers shoved the plane toward the elevator.

"Well, we made it," Warren tried to yell over the engine noise of another bomber slanting in to land. The sudden wailing of the general alarm drowned him out. Sailors streamed over the flight deck to battle stations, avoiding the Dauntless that slammed down (6-S-9, *Pete Goff, God bless him!*). Bells clanged, and the loudspeaker bellowed, "*Stand by to launch fighters.*"

Cornett trotted off. Warren dropped into the nearest AA tub. The helmeted gun crew turned surprised eyes at this aviator fallen among them, and the telephone talker gestured toward the flat gray hump on the horizon to the west. "Fire control reports a mess of bogies going for the *Yorktown*, Lieutenant."

"Sure, they've come on her first. Better look sharp, all the same."

"Bet your ass," said the sailor whose steel helmet was stencilled *Gun Captain*. "Sir," he added, showing white teeth, and they all laughed.

In his exaltation Warren thought that these were wonderful-looking American kids, that the weather was amazingly fine, that there was nothing to beat combat in the world, and that this victorious return in a damaged plane, with the fuel needle jammed at zero, was like starting life over with a million dollars. The launching of fighters commenced. Fingers to their ears, Warren and the gun crew peered toward the *Yorktown*, while planes howled off the deck one by one. They were still taking off when a smoke column grew out of the distant gray shape. "Shit, they got her," said the gun captain sadly.

"Maybe their screen's just making smoke," said another sailor.

"That ain't no smoke screen, you idiot," said the gun captain. "That's a goddamn bomb hit, and — *Jesus Christ!*" He frenziedly trained the weapon at a cluster of specks in the sunny sky. "Here comes a gang of the bastards. Straight *at* us."

"*All gun crews, attention.*" The loudspeaker took on an urgent tone. "*Planes approaching on the port quarter are not, repeat not, BOGIES, they are FRIENDLIES. Hold your fire. They are returning* Yorktown *aircraft, low on fuel and requesting emergency landing. The* Yorktown *has been hit. Repeat HOLD YOUR FIRE. Stand by to take planes on board.*"

Plane handlers scampered out on deck with red, yellow, and green jerseys showing under their life jackets. Warren jumped from the gun tub, sprinted across the windy deck, and went below. A glance into the torpedo squadron room sobered him. The teletype was clicking away, and on the unwatched screen words crawled,

YORKTOWN REPORTS THREE BOMB HITS HEAVY DAMAGE BELOW DECKS

Acey-deucey sets, packs of cards, girlie and sports magazines lay about the vacant leather reclining chairs. Ashtrays heaped with cigar and cigarette butts gave off a heavy stale smell. Good God, Lindsay's squadron must have had a bad time! Still, maybe they were elsewhere, in the wardroom or in sick bay, the ones who had got back. . . .

His own squadron room, though far from full, was lively and noisy. Of the ten fliers here, two were reserves who had not gone out. Eight of the eighteen returned so far, then. Only eight! They were talking, laughing, holding coffee or a sandwich in one hand and gesturing airplane maneuvers with the other. Overhead the *Yorktown*'s planes were thumping down with snarling engines, while the teletype clicked out a new damage report. She was on fire, dead in the water; damage control parties were beginning to master the blaze, but the *Enterprise* would have to land her search planes, too.

Warren gave the debriefing officer his combat account, chalking out his dive maneuver on the blackboard, while the jubilant pilot talk went on and on — who had gotten a hit, who had missed, who had been attacked by Zeroes, who had been seen on fire or going in the water, who might have ditched on the return leg. About Warren's hit there was no argument: solid, spectacular, confirmed. The rest of the attack was shrouded in dissent, even to the number of carriers observed — five, two, three, four, no consensus whatever; not about that, not about the hits, not even about the near-misses, and some disagreements verged on the acrimonious.

A telephone call from his squadron commander summoned Warren to Air Operations, and he hurried to the dark low crowded plotting room, clamorous with loudspeaker blare. Amid ozone-reeking, green-flashing radar scopes, and big Plexiglas compass roses still marked with orange grease-pencil tracks of the Jap attack, Gallaher was huddling with a refugee lieutenant from the *Yorktown*. McClusky had returned wounded, Gallaher said, so he would lead the group to attack the fourth carrier. Search planes were out to pinpoint its position now. His exec was missing, and Warren was next in line. Warren would have to scratch together a bomber squadron at once, with the surviving pilots of Bombing Six, Scouting Six, and the *Yorktown* aviators. Instant promotion to squadron command seemed quite normal to Warren on this radiant day. Gallaher went off at a call from Miles Browning. Warren sketched an attack plan with the *Yorktown* squadron leader, a hard-faced Southerner itching to strike back at the Jap flattop that had disabled his ship.

Back in Scouting Six room, Warren called together the *Enterprise*'s Dauntless fliers and the *Yorktown*'s refugees. Arms akimbo before the blackboard, he explained the new orders, and briskly warned against any further contention between Bombing Six and Scouting Six over hits in the morning strike. "Here's another shot for all hands," he said. "It's our asses if we don't operate together like old buddies, so save your pugnacity for the Japs."

The meeting went smooth as glass. From the first, the Bombing Six fliers and the *Yorktown* strangers accepted Warren's leadership. The aviators and their pro tem skipper quickly decided on new wing mates and section positions. He could sense them coalescing, as they talked, into a working make-do squadron. Warren forgot his fatigue. He almost forgot the missing pilots. The one thing he loved even above flying was leadership of any sort. He had not had a command since his Academy battalion.

Even the news that the *Yorktown*, after quelling the fires and resuming fleet speed, had been torpedoed in a second attack, was again ablaze and listing, and might be abandoned, could be taken in stride. The main thing was that the fourth carrier had been located, and the attack was on. Warren's last briefing to his hastily formed squadron went by like a dream, and he found himself in the cockpit of an SBD-2, with Cornett as usual in the rear seat. A dizzy, numbed but far from unpleasant sense filled Warren. He was riding a rocket of hours, staying alert on nervous energy, unafraid, and happy. Great events were swirling over his head, but he had to keep his part clear and simple: fly this plane, lead this squadron, find that carrier, and get a bomb hit.

On his launch the sense of heading out into the unknown was almost gone; Warren wryly thought that it was a little bit like the second time with a woman. There were no torpedo planes or fighters to wait for. The fighters had to stay behind to guard the *Enterprise* and the smoking *Yorktown*; and the torpedo aircraft were finished. A *Hornet* dive-bomber squadron was supposed to join the strike; but seeing no launch activity on the *Hornet*,

Gallaher decided to get going, and he led his group westward. It was a straight quiet flight into the sun over a cloudless blue sea. After an hour the Jap flattop showed on the horizon, straight ahead on the predicted bearing, in a heavy protective ring of ships. Southward in the distance, in a blaze of afternoon sunshine, the three ruined smoldering hulks of the other carriers still floated in a line, listing crazily this way and that: slaughtered bulls, dumped outside the bullring. Gallaher hooked all the way around the fourth flattop, so as to attack out of the sinking sun. With plenty of fuel, with only one carrier to attack, he could indulge in drilled doctrine, Warren thought, instead of making the pell-mell dives of the morning strike.

The sea winked with antiaircraft guns like a lawn full of fireflies. Black bursts filled the air. Zeroes swarmed up to meet them. Different business this time! The carrier, boiling out a thick white curving wake, heeled far over in a confusing flank speed turn. Now the newness of the squadron showed in ragged dives. Warren saw bomb after bomb splash. He went into his own dive, trying to shut out the distractions — the salvos of Cornett's gun, the green-brown Zeroes zooming and swooping like chicken hawks and spitting red tracers, the wild rattle of shrapnel on his wings, and the damned curving course of the carrier. He managed to hold the ship in his scope as he plunged thousands of feet, popping his ears and sweating; but the unfamiliar plane wobbled and the carrier kept sliding away. He made his decision to drop. Instantly he regretted it. As his hand obeyed his will and released the bomb he knew it would miss. When with a sinking stomach and aching loins he pulled up and looked back, a column of white water was kicking up ahead of the ship. But even as the water splashed on the tilting bow a giant fire sprang out of the afterdeck like a terrible red and yellow flower, and a second smoky explosion forward sent the whole elevator flying out of the deck and slamming back against the island, streaming flames and debris. So someone else had done it, thank Christ. Scratch another carrier.

Antiaircraft shrapnel was churning up the foamy blue waves as Warren dodged along the surface through the dark puffs, gunned straight between two big yellow-blinking ships — a battleship and a cruiser, he thought — and blasted out at full throttle to the open sea. Amazingly, despite the AA storm and the alerted Zeroes, when the straggling planes joined up and formed on Gallaher, Warren counted only three missing. Behind them, the thick smoke rolling up above the carrier was reddened within by leaping fire, and without by the low sun. The triumphant radio talk indicated four sure bomb hits, perhaps five. This was more like battle as he had pictured it: danger, losses, but victory with discipline unbroken. It was not too unlike an island raid. The morning attack by comparison had been a bloody botched mess. But of course this fourth carrier had been such a pigeon only because the first strike had already incinerated most of the Jap air force. Only the sight of the tardy

Hornet dive-bombers high overhead, heading the other way half an hour late in the red sunset light, recalled the morning foul-up.

Warren found the *Northampton* in the great spread of screening ships, and made his wing-wagging pass. When his wheels touched down in the last glow of sunset, exhaustion flooded him. Barely keeping his eyes open through a perfunctory debriefing, he stumbled off to his cabin. He thought he would drop off to sleep when he fell in his bunk. Instead he lay awake, though aching with fatigue, staring at the squadron exec's neat bunk. They had been roommates, but hardly close friends. There on the blanket was a half-empty pack of Camels. There on the bulkhead smiled the picture of his girl, Lois, a Navy junior. The short dark-haired sallow Ken Turner from Front Royal, Virginia, was gone. He would never manage that Hereford farm of his father's; or could he be alive somewhere out there on a raft? When Warren with an effort closed his eyes, yellow decks began coming up at him, and airplanes were exploding in rainbow spurts of flame.

"To hell with this," he said aloud and went to Gallaher's stateroom, where other wakeful pilots were discussing what was in store tomorrow; mainly, how to split up the search and the attack assignments. Obviously, there would be a high-speed pursuit all night; search at dawn, launch for attack at sunrise. The Japs must be given no respite. Without air cover, their battleships and cruisers were as vulnerable as the *Prince of Wales* and the *Repulse* had been. Here was the big chance of the war to smash the Nip fleet, and there would be plenty of hunting tomorrow for dive-bombers. So the talk went, mixed with exultation about the gutting of the four carriers. They had not been seen to sink, so finishing them off might also be in the next day's work. But Gallaher thought that destroyer torpedoes would do that job.

Fliers came and went in the room, *Yorktown* aviators and Bombing Six pilots joining the remnant of Warren's squadron. After a while someone suggested a raid on the wardroom for cold meats and coffee, and they marched off in great good humor. Warren dropped out, returned to his bunk, and fell fast asleep. When he awoke he foggily thought it must be the next morning, for he felt refreshed and slept out; but the glowing watch dial read 10:45. He had dozed off for less than half an hour.

This was no good, he thought. He showered, put on a uniform and a windbreaker, and went topside. A bright moon was paling the stars. Warren remembered wondering twenty-four hours ago whether he would live to see stars again. Well, there they were, and here he was. As he strode the cool breezy flight deck long mental vistas opened. This battle marked a divide in his life — truly "midway" it was! He'd been a hellion and tailhound, but an outstanding student, an outstanding engineer, an outstanding deck officer; and he had graduated to gold wings. With some cheerful departures from

Dad's prudish ideas and ways, he had really been aping his father. But he had gone past all that in the last twenty-four hours.

Flying was great, but a few more battles like this would give him a bellyful of glory and achievement. As a peacetime career the Navy was a sterile cramped long pull at bad odds. Dad had wasted his life and fine abilities, pretty much. In five combat minutes he, Warren, had done more for the country than Victor Henry had accomplished with his whole naval career. He didn't look down on his father — that could never be, he thought him a man superior to most — but Warren felt sorry for him. The model was out of date. His father-in-law was a better model. Ike Lacouture moved in the real world of money and politics. By comparison the Navy was a queer little planet whirling in an austere void. It served a purpose, but it was nothing but a tool for the real leaders.

The fresh wind, the rhythmic walking, relaxed Warren as these notions flickered in his tired mind. This battle wasn't over, and would still draw hard on his stamina and his luck. He knew that, but after the worst day the stars still shone on him. He stopped to stretch and yawn, and only then took notice that the Big Dipper and the North Star hung broad on the port beam, and that the yellow moon was sinking dead astern.

God Almighty, the task force was heading east. Admiral Spruance was withdrawing from a beaten enemy!

This discovery astounded Warren like nothing else in his life. It violated the first law of the Navy, gravely spelled out in *Rocks and Shoals:* never to withdraw from possible action; always to seek out a fight; a violation too of a basic maxim of war, to give no respite to a defeated foe. Was there some late word about gigantic Jap reinforcements — six fleet carriers or something — closing Midway?

He hurried down to the ready room, and found only Peter Goff, gloomily slouched on his back-tilted chair, puffing at his corncob and staring at the vacant teletype screen. "Where's everybody, Pete?"

"Oh, still in the wardroom chowing up, I guess."

"Is there any news?"

The ensign gave him a bleary sour look. "News? Just that we've got ourselves a chickenshit admiral. Do you know that we're retreating?"

"Yes. What's going on?"

"Who knows? All hell's breaking loose in flag country. You should hear the talk in the wardroom. They're saying Spruance can be court-martialled for this."

"What's his reason? He must have a reason."

"Look, this bird just has no stomach for fighting, Warren," said the ensign, his face pink with anger. "The staff could hardly get him to launch today. That's the word. He kept stalling and dillydallying. If not for Captain

Browning we'd never have gotten off the deck for the first strike. The Japs would have creamed us, instead of the other way around. Jesus, if only Halsey hadn't come down with the crud!"

"Where are we going? Any word on that?"

"I'm not sure. I think we reverse course again in the morning, so as to give air cover to Midway at dawn. By then, naturally, those yellow monkeys will be halfway back to Japan."

Warren yawned, picked up a sandwich from a piled tray, and lounged in the chair beside Goff. He was disappointed, but obscurely relieved, too. "Well, we did get the carriers. Maybe he wants to quit while he's ahead. That's not bad poker."

"Warren, he's blowing our chance to destroy the Jap fleet."

Warren was too weary to waste words with the youngster. "Look, maybe they'll still try to take Midway tomorrow. Then it'll be another big day. Better catch some shut-eye."

"Warren, what did it really feel like, getting that bomb in there?" Rubbing his bushy beard, Pete Goff callowly, awkwardly grinned. "I missed twice, by a country mile."

"Oh, it was a great feeling. Absolutely great. Nothing like it." Warren yawned and stretched. "However, Pete, I'll tell you something. On that long flight back, I got to thinking about all those Japs burning up, and their bodies flying around, and those planes going up like firecrackers, and that magnificent ship all wrecked up and frying and drowning everybody. Then I thought we get paid for doing some strange work in this fucking Navy."

The day broke cloudy. There was no dawn search, and so no daylight attack. At sunrise the task force was plowing through iron-gray swells at a sedate fifteen knots. No air operations whatever had been ordered. On the hangar deck the clang and shriek of all-night airplane repair still echoed. In the ready rooms a slump was taking hold. The edgy aviators, having breakfasted at 3 A.M., were waiting and waiting and waiting for something to happen. By ten the sun was breaking through. Still no orders came. There were no alarms. Except for the turns into the wind to launch and recover the overhead combat patrol, it was like peacetime steaming. The mutterings mounted that the admiral had let the Japs escape.

Meantime, the teletype burbled conflicting news.

Midway search planes had found the fourth carrier, smoking but still afloat, and under way.

No, that had actually been a *fifth* carrier, which Army B-17s had hit.

No, the fourth carrier had disappeared.

No, the Japanese fleet was splitting up, one force heading west toward Japan, the other withdrawing northwest with a smoking carrier.

The positions jumped about on the chart and made no sense. A feeling spread among the pilots that, after a glorious first day, something was going very, very wrong "up there."

In fact, Rear Admiral Spruance and Halsey's staff were at loggerheads.

To the staff officers, Raymond Spruance was still the screen OTC who by a fluke had been thrust into command of a battle that Halsey should have fought. The Old Man had assured them of Spruance's rare brilliance, but the night retreat had badly shaken them. Put to the test, he seemed to be muffing a historic victory.

Spruance for his part was losing confidence in them. He had assumed that they would execute combat operations with seasoned skill, but in reality this was their first battle. Until now, Vice Admiral Halsey had led only hit-and-run raids on atolls. The laggard first launch, the wrong estimate of the enemy's movements, the miscalculating of Point Option, had been disheartening bungles. The heavy damaging of four enemy carriers (for Spruance still had no confirmed news of sinkings) was a great result; but fuel exhaustion had put down more American aircraft than the enemy had done. Three torpedo squadrons had gone unescorted to the slaughter. The *Hornet* aviators, except for the suicidal Torpedo Eight, had entirely missed the battle. This was wretched work. Then in the second strike, the staff had — unbelievably — failed to notify the unlucky *Hornet* of the attack order, hence their tardy, useless flight.

Now the staff, still surly over the retreat at night, wanted to steam after the enemy at full speed, and launch search-and-attack sweeps at once, clouds or no clouds. But Spruance would not leave Midway unguarded until he knew the Japanese were out of air strike range; and he was keeping back his surviving machines and aviators for direct attacks, based on hard knowledge of where the foe was. This was the impasse in flag country. The restless aviators in the ready room, because their necks were at stake, quite accurately surmised that something was rotten "up there."

It was past one o'clock when orders at last came down. The fleet was speeding up to twenty-five knots. The squadrons would chase the Jap formation reported retreating with a "smoking carrier." The Dauntlesses were to sally forth on the cold trail, make a wide search, and hit anything they found; returning before dark, because they had not drilled in night landings. Glances soon began to pass among the pilots, as they plotted the orders on their flight charts. A peculiar silence fell.

Warren Henry was called to Earl Gallaher's stateroom. Pallid and weary, Wade McClusky sat in Gallaher's armchair, his khaki blouse bulging over bandages. Gallaher, chewing on a cold cigar, closed the door. "Had a chance to plot out the new attack plan, Warren?"

"Yes, sir."

"What do you make of it?"

"It's a plan for a swimming meet."

Wade McClusky, his face scored with worry lines, put in, "You know Spruance, don't you?"

"My father does, sir."

"That'll do." McClusky pushed himself up. "Let's go talk to the CO."

The captain of the *Enterprise* was waiting for them at his desk, in a large office bright with sunshine through open portholes. McClusky briskly stated the problem, asking him to intervene with Browning, and if necessary with Spruance. The captain stared at him, slowly nodding, his fingers idly expanding and contracting a thick rubber band. He was in an unenviable spot, squeezed between his aviators and his admiral's staff. "Well, okay, Wade," he said with a sigh that came out a groan. "I'm assuming you can use dividers and add. Maybe somebody on the staff can't. Let's go up to the flag shelter."

Perched on Halsey's favorite stool, Captain Miles Browning was looking over a large chart of the attack plan. For the first time since Halsey had left the ship, the chief of staff was happy. The admiral had been stalling and stalling, waiting for word of a definite enemy sighting from the Midway search planes. At last, in exasperation, Browning had pointed out that sunsets do not wait; that if they did not launch soon, a whole day of battle would pass without aggressive action; and that might take explaining soon in Pearl Harbor, not to mention *Washington*.

Quite casually, as though permitting an extra liberty for all hands, Spruance had thrown in the towel. "Very well, Captain. Prepare and execute an attack plan."

This chart was the result. Rapidly whipped up by the staff, beautifully drafted in blue and orange ink, it called for a majestic sweep of the widening triangle of ocean where the fleeing Nips might still be found. The area had fanned out like all hell with the passing hours, of course. If only Spruance had listened sooner! Yet the boys might still catch the Japs. Rear Admiral Spruance stood on the platform outside, elbows on the bulwark, watching the spotting of planes for the launch. At least the man did not resent being overborne. In his quiet way Spruance was even more stubborn than Halsey, but once he gave in he bore no grudge. Browning had to grant him that.

Trampling feet mounted the ladder, and the three aviators entered the shelter, led by the ship's captain. McClusky flatly told Miles Browning that the attack plan would splash every dive-bomber left on the *Enterprise*. Even with five-hundred-pound bombs, the distance, time, and fuel factors did not add up, yet the plan called for thousand-pound bombs. Nor was there any margin for gas consumption in combat. Mildly the ship's captain suggested that the staff might recheck the plan.

Browning retorted that there was nothing to recheck. The plan was an order. Let the fliers watch fuel economy and not botch their navigation, and there would be no splashes. Sharpening his tone in return, McClusky declared that if it meant a court-martial he would not take his air group out on those orders. Both men began shouting.

Rear Admiral Spruance strolled in and asked what the matter was. First Browning, then McClusky angrily put their cases. With a glance at the chronometer Spruance sat down in the armchair, scratching at his hairy face. Not to shave in combat was a Halsey staff custom, and he was conforming, though with his starched spotless khakis and gleaming black shoes the brown and gray bristles looked decidedly odd.

"Lieutenant Henry, you've been given your orders!" Spruance surprised them all by bursting out at Warren in a harsh grating voice, with a furious look. "What the devil does this temerity mean? What's your problem? Do you suppose the staff hasn't worked out this plan with the greatest care?"

Under Spruance's icy ugly stare, Warren spoke up shakily. "Admiral, the staff doesn't fly."

"That's an insubordinate response! Wouldn't your father in your place just carry out his orders? Just get in his plane and do as he'd been told?"

"Yes, Admiral, he would. But if asked — as you're asking me, sir — he'd mention that you wouldn't see any of your aircraft again. Because you won't."

Pursing his broad well-cut lips, his large sober eyes glancing around at the others, Spruance rubbed his chin, then clasped his hands behind his head. "Well," he said, turning to Wade McClusky, "I'll do what you pilots want."

"*What!*" The word broke from Browning like the cry of a stabbed man. He dashed his cap to the deck, stamped scarlet-faced out of the flag shelter, and his rapid steps thumped down the ladder. The cap rolled to the feet of Spruance, who picked it up and put it on the chair arm, saying placidly, "Call the operations officer, Wade."

In thickening weather, the dive-bomber squadrons finally left the *Enterprise* and the *Hornet* at three in the afternoon, on a modified plan. They saw only white clouds and gray patches of water in their wide sweep. Returning in a scarlet-flaring sunset, they came upon a lone Japanese destroyer and pounced on it. The vessel dodged and twisted under the hail of bombs, vomiting red AA tracers, even shooting down one plane, until darkness forced the air group commander to let it go unscathed. As the Dauntlesses roared off through the fast-falling night, homing on the Y-E signal, Warren wondered how the hell they would get back aboard. He stewed too about his own gross miss on this destroyer, and on the failure of an entire squadron to get even one hit.

On the *Enterprise*, Browning had thought better of his tantrum, and had returned to the shelter in a calm professional mood. Spruance's manner to him was as pleasant as always. As night fell and McClusky reported the search group on the way back, Spruance took to pacing like Halsey, for the first time in the battle. Both men strode here and there in the gloom until Browning burst out, "Admiral, we've got to turn on the lights."

The dim form of Spruance halted. "What about submarines?"

"Sir, we have a screen out there. If a son-of-a-bitching sub has gotten through the screen, that's too bad. The boys have to land."

"Thank you, Captain Browning. I agree. Illuminate at once."

In after years, in one of his rare specific statements on his war conduct, Raymond Spruance declared that he was concerned only once in the war, and that was when the planes were returning in the dark off Midway.

So to Warren's amazed relief, a white blaze suddenly starred the dark sea far ahead. The carriers stood out like perfect little ship models. The operations officer came on the radio with emergency instructions. Warily, nervously, the pilots came in for the first carrier night landings of their lives. The brilliant searchlight illumination made it seem a sort of circus stunt. Warren was surprised at how simple it actually was. He slammed down and caught the number two cable in the glare as though it were noon sunshine; then he hurried to the landing officer's platform to watch the other planes come in. The instant the last bomber touched down — with only one dropped in the sea, and its men handily rescued by the plane guard destroyer — the lights went out.

Ships, planes disappeared. The night sky leaped into view.

"What do you know?" Warren said to the landing officer. "Stars."

On the *Northampton*'s blacked-out bridge, Victor Henry happily told the exec to secure from General Quarters. The astonishing blaze-up, while forcing the cruiser on immediate submarine alert, had lifted a load from his heart. Pug didn't believe that the one unlucky plane had been Warren's. He sensed too that this spectacular night recovery was the real end of the battle. There might be mopping up of stragglers for a day or two, but the Japs were gone. Spruance would not follow them far. The screen destroyers were getting near their fuel limits, and in these waters he could not leave them behind. Pug had followed Spruance's maneuvers with intense if frustrated admiration. The withdrawal on the first night, and the cautious pursuit tactics, had secured a substantial victory against the Japanese powerhouse. He had socked them and rocked them, and not lost his shirt.

Now, standing out on the wing of his bridge under the stars, Pug Henry allowed himself to think about Warren again. This two-day vigil had aged him; he could feel it in his nerves, in his very breathing. On that fearful first morning a Bible verse had kept running through his mind, a verse over which he had once broken down, reading the Bible with his family long ago. Each morning a member of the family had taken a turn at a chapter, and the last battle of David and Absalom had fallen to him.

"O my son, Absalom, my son, my son, Absalom! Would God I had died for thee, O Absalom, my son, my son!"

Under the bright solemn eyes of the three children he had choked over the verse, slammed the book shut, and hurried from the room. Yesterday morning, as his agonized father-feeling had welled up, those words had repeated and repeated in his brain like a torturing old song; and like a smashed record, it had stopped at the sight of Warren's Dauntless flashing over the forecastle. Ever since, Pug had shut out thoughts of his endangered son, almost as he blocked away the hurtful remembrance of his faithless wife. He had even forced himself to stop watching the air operations on the *Enterprise*. Warren's second pass yesterday had been reassuring. Yet Pug knew he would not draw an easy breath until he saw his son again in Pearl Harbor. He was not absolutely sure that Warren was alive, and there was no seemly way of finding out. But the big risks were past, and now there was only the waiting.

Victor Henry thought he was not likely ever to endure a more harrowing time than these two days of futile steaming in command of a major warship with silent guns, while his son fought a battle at the highest hazard, as it were before his eyes.

In the flag shelter, the atmosphere had calmed. When Spruance set the pursuit speed for the night at a mere fifteen knots, there was no argument. He and the chief of staff now understood each other. Browning wanted hot pursuit at reckless fuel cost; oilers were bringing up the rear, in case fuel ran low. Spruance was conserving fuel for possible extended combat with no chance for refueling. The verdict between them now lay with their superiors and with history.

Early next morning an urgent Nimitz dispatch gave Miles Browning a sweet foretaste of that verdict, for Cincpac agreed with him. He hastened to deliver the message himself to Spruance, who was brewing coffee in his quarters before dawn. Nimitz said in the dispatch that the sole survivor of Torpedo Eight had been rescued, and had confirmed great damage to three Jap carriers. The time therefore was ripe to close the enemy and attack. Both men understood the veiled language of high command dispatches. This was a rough rebuke for excessive caution, and a warning of possible responsibility for letting a wounded enemy escape. The report of the rescued pilot was padding.

Calmly initialling the flimsy sheet, Spruance inquired, "What have you done about this?"

"Our dawn search is ready to launch, Admiral. The *Hornet's* bombers are standing by, armed with thousand-pound bombs, ready to attack at contact."

"Excellent." It was a word Spruance had rarely used. "Have the cruiser float planes follow up any sighting, Captain, and keep the enemy in view."

Warren put himself on the dawn search. Weary though he was, flying was pleasanter than fretting in the ready room. The starlit launch, the long flight in the dawn and the sunrise, gave him a sort of second wind. He saw nothing, but he heard Peter Goff radio a long excited report from the southern sector. Two large vessels, cruisers or battleships, had apparently collided in the night. They were moving slowly in a gigantic oil slick, screened by destroyers, and the bow of one appeared to be crushed. Poor Pete, flying without a bomb over a couple of huge unmaneuverable cripples! This would be the great chance for the *Hornet* bombers to improve their sad score. Approaching the screen on his return, he dropped once more to fly over the *Northampton,* and saw his father on the bridge nonchalantly wave. The *Hornet* bombers were already taking off.

In the *Enterprise* ready room, the fliers listened avidly to the jocular, occasionally obscene radio exchanges pouring from the loudspeaker as the *Hornet* planes found the two cripples and plastered them with half-ton bomb hits. When the attack ended, the patrolling cruiser plane reported the ships appallingly battered and on fire, but still under way at dead slow. The teletype, turning playful in the sunshine of victory, spelled out:

LOOKS LIKE MORE TARGET PRACTICE FOR ENTERPRISE

At this, Ensign Goff let out a rebel yell that raised a wave of guffaws, and some headshakes among the slumping red-eyed pilots.

"Well, Pete, here's your moment," Warren tiredly grinned. "Just lay it in there this time, nice and easy."

His face set and pale, Pete Goff said, "I'll put it down the smokestack."

As they were leaving the ready room, Warren tapped Goff's shoulder. "Look, Pete, belay that down-the-smokestack stuff. It's just another bombing run. You'll get a hundred more chances in this war."

Pulling on his helmet, the ensign set his red-bearded jaw with a youthful obstinacy that reminded Warren strongly and sadly of Byron. "I'm just tired of not earning my pay."

"You earn it when you fly."

The wind had now shifted to the west. Smoothly, swiftly, McClusky — back in action despite his injuries — led the group off to the attack. Bone-weary as the aviators were, Warren could see they were getting better and better at join-ups. Combat was the school, no doubt of that.

Over the horizon, after half an hour's flight, smoke pointed down at the victims. McClusky had three surviving torpedo planes in his group, but orders were to use torpedoes only if no AA was still firing. Seen through binoculars from ten thousand feet, the two vessels were unbelievably smashed up — guns askew, bridges dangling, torpedo tubes and catapults hanging crazily, amid drifting smoke and jumping flames. The *Hornet* fliers had reported them as battleships, but to Warren they looked much like a pair of ruined *Northamptons*. Both ships were putting up meager little squirts of AA tracers and a few black explosions.

"Well, that lets out the TBDs." McClusky's voice came in clearly. He assigned the dive-bomber sections to the two cruisers, and the attack began.

The first section, led by Gallaher, did a businesslike job: at least three hits sent up smoke and flame in billows, and the AA fire died away. As Warren prepared to lead his section down to the fiery shambles far below, he looked back at Peter Goff, and held up a palm outward, in a last friendly admonition to take it easy; then he pushed over in the familiar maneuver, straightened into a dive, and there was the blazing cruiser squarely in his telescope sight.

When he had dived about a thousand feet through sporadic and feeble AA, Warren's plane was hit. At the alarming jolt, and the grinding, gruesome noise of tearing metal, and the queer sight of a ragged piece of his blue wing flying away, with cherry-colored fire licking out of the stump, his first feeling was stupefied surprise. He had never thought he would be shot down, though he had known the risks. With his death sentence before his eyes he still could not believe it. His future stretched before him for so many years — so well-planned, so real, so important! But he had only a few more seconds to pull off something miraculous and even as these vertiginous thoughts whirled through his shocked brain and he jerked futilely at the controls, the fire flared all along the broken wing, and in the earphones he heard Cornett screaming something frightened but incomprehensible. The plane fell sideways and began to spin downward, shaking fearfully, with fire shooting from the engine. The blue sea turned round and round before Warren's eyes, framed in flames. He could see white breaking wave tops not far below. He tried frantically to open his canopy, but could not. He called to Cornett to jump, with no response. The cockpit grew hotter, and in the intense heat his rigid body hanging there in his straps struggled and struggled and struggled. At last it involuntarily relaxed. There was nothing more to do, after all. He had done his best, and now it was time to die. It was going to be tough on old Dad, but Dad would be proud of him. His last coherent thought was this one, of his father.

The water was thrusting up toward him in tossing revolving foamy waves. *All over already?*

Horrible pain seared Warren as fire leaped across his face, blinding his last living moments. The crash into the water was a terrific blow in the dark.

Warren's final sensation was a soothing cooling one: the sea, bathing his scorched face and hands. The plane exploded, but he never knew that, and his torn body began its long slow descent in peace to its resting place on the bottom of the trackless sea. For a few seconds, a thin black smoke plume marked the place where he fell. Then like his life the plume melted into the wind and was gone.

†   †   †

O my son, Absalom, my son, my son, Absalom! Would God I had died for thee, O Absalom, my son, my son!

PART THREE

Byron
and
Natalie

33

I N mid-July, still recovering from the terrible news, Rhoda left Washington by train for the West Coast. Madeline was in Hollywood and Byron was attending a submarine attack school in San Diego, so whenever he got leave, they could at least be together. Train journeys, even in wartime, were cheering, and just packing for this one relieved her agony. Her first dining-car meal woke a sluggish flow of life in her chilled veins. She knew that her black linen suit, dark hat, and dark stockings looked smart. After dinner men in the club car eyed her. A bemustached, beribboned Air Force colonel tried his luck at buying her a drink. What rotten taste! Couldn't the man see she was in mourning? She quenched him with one sad glance.

Bedding down between crisp heavy Pullman sheets, she was a long time dropping off. The clacking of the wheels, the rhythmic sway of the berth, the chugging and wailing of the locomotive, the old train smells in the upholstery and the green curtains, the vibrating roll through the night, bathed her in nostalgia. So she had lain as an engaged girl of nineteen, aquiver with love and with erotic visions, riding down to Charleston to visit Pug; so they had lain together in a lower berth, on their brief rapturous honeymoon; so she had lain as the mother of one infant, then two, then three, as the family dragged from one duty station to another. Now again she lay alone, on her way to the two grown-up children left to her.

Oh, Warren's wedding day, and the songs and the champagne in the car on the way to the Pensacola airport! Oh, that last glimpse of him, that last reunion of her little family to all eternity! He had looked so handsome driving the big Cadillac and singing along as the whole family, crowded in with his blonde bride and Byron's dark Jewish girl, were harmonizing

> *Till we meet, till we meet,*
> *Till we meet at Jesus' feet . . .*

Rhoda accepted the death of her son as a personal punishment. An excruciating, cleansing catharsis of remorse had been racking her for weeks. She was determined to cut her misconduct out of her life like a cancer. This resolve was turning the death of her firstborn son into a redeeming experience; she was spending much time and pouring out many tears in church.

Like most service wives and mothers, Rhoda had thought herself steeled against bad news, but the ringing doorbell at seven in the morning a few days after the Midway battle had frightened her, and the words on the yellow telegraph form had blasted her soul. Warren! The winner, the best, always carrying off prizes and top grades, going to the right schools, marrying the right girl, rising in the Navy faster than his father had — Warren, gone! *Dead!* Her firstborn son, lost to her, lying somewhere on the bottom of the Pacific, miles down, in the wreckage of an airplane! Would a funeral, and a last look at him in a coffin, have been easier or worse than this dry notification that her son, out of her sight for two years, was dead? She could not tell. The funerals of her mother, her father, and her older brother had not hit her like this. A funeral was a release of a sort, a vent for grief. Her only release had been one wild long flood of tears over Pug's letter.

She had meant to schedule an overnight stop in Chicago to break with Kirby, but he was away from his office, so she would have to do it on the way back. In the majestic shadow of her son's death, their middle-aged amour seemed not so much soiled and wicked as ridiculous. They had both needed it, or had thought they did, and so they had accommodated each other. That was the reality. The rest had been romantic illusion. Now it was finished. She was Pug's till death. He might be too good for her, his magnanimity might be crushing, but she hoped to become more worthy of him in the years that remained.

Buried under all this wholly sincere repentance was an intuition that the Kirby thing had peaked anyway. Forbidden fruit has its brown spots, but these are not seen in the dusky glow of appetite; one has to bite and taste the unpleasant mush. Her civilian lover had turned out not so very different from her military husband. He had less excuse for neglecting her, yet like Pug he had shut her out and absented himself for weeks at a time. Answering her fatal divorce letter, Pug had warned her that Fred Kirby was too much like himself for the thing to work. Wise old Pug! In fact, Palmer rather despised her. She knew this, though only with Warren's death had she squarely faced it. If she forced the issue he might marry her, but it would be a mere entrapment. When all was said and done, she had been a fortyish fool. It happened to lots of women, and it had happened to her. All she wanted now was to end the thing and save her marriage. Around and around this pivotal resolve her thoughts circled, chasing each other until she dozed off in the rocking berth, to the sad hoots of the whistle and the rhythmic clatter of the wheels.

Young men in white and khaki uniforms swarmed through the tumultuous mob in the sweltering Los Angeles terminal, three days later. Rhoda kept looking for a red beard as she wandered here and there, followed by a sweating porter with her bags.

"Here I am, Mom."

The shock when she turned and saw him so weakened her that she sagged into her smooth-shaven son's arms. He wore dress whites with a splash of campaign ribbons, his gold dolphins looked much like gold wings, his face had filled out, and a cigarette slanting from his mouth completed a frightening resemblance to Warren. They had never looked much alike to her, but this stern-faced tanned apparition was a shivery blend of the two. She buried her face against the starchy uniform and cried. When she could control herself she choked out, wiping her eyes, "I received the most beautiful letter from Dad. Have you heard from him?"

"No. Let's go. I've got Madeline's car."

At the wheel he slouched in a Byron-like way, and smiled with a mouth shape unchanged since infancy. "You've lost weight. You look very pretty, Mom."

"Oh, what does it matter how I look?" Her eyes overflowed again, and she put her hand on his. "It's so hot here, I'm perspiring like a NIGGER. I haven't had a proper bath in three days, Byron. I feel SLIMY."

His smile broadening, he leaned over and kissed her. "Old Mom." And he drove out into a brightly sunny avenue lined with palm trees and tall buildings; and into the thickest traffic jam she had ever seen.

"What news of Natalie?" Rhoda tried to sound naturally affectionate. Her Jewish daughter-in-law's name did not come easily to her tongue.

He took from an inside pocket and passed to her a long wrinkled airmail envelope half-covered with purple rubber stampings. "From that fellow Slote. I may have to go to Switzerland."

"Oh, Byron. SWITZERLAND? How can you? In wartime, and you under orders!"

"It's possible. Not easy, but possible. I can cross unoccupied France by train, or fly to Zurich from Lisbon. When this torpedo course finishes I've got thirty days' leave coming."

"But even so, dear. Once there, THEN what?"

Byron's face obstinately hardened. "Nobody cares about Natalie and that kid as I do. I can go there and see." When he looked like that, it was time to drop the subject, though his mother thought he was out of his mind. Slote's letter was a confused mess about exit visas and Brazil which she couldn't follow.

Rhoda had never before been to Hollywood. Walking through the lushly green hotel garden splashed with flowering hibiscus and bougainvillea she saw a real film star, Errol Flynn, sitting in swim trunks by the pool with a beautiful young girl, no doubt a starlet. She could not help being excited. "Before I do ANYTHING," she said as Byron carried her bags into the roomy villa Madeline had rented for them, "I must shower. I mean this SECOND."

"Where's Dad's letter?"

"You want to read it right now?"

"Yes."

The envelope was scuffed, the creases in the sheets of U. S. S. *Northampton* stationery were wearing through. Byron crouched in an armchair over the pages, written in his father's familiar firm clear Navy hand with heavily crossed *t*'s and plain capitals.

Dearest Rhoda:

By now you have the official word. I tried a couple of times to place a call to you, but it probably was for the best that I didn't get through. It might have been painful for both of us.

Our son made it through the worst of the battle. He would fly over my ship and rock his wings, coming back from sorties. Warren scored a direct bomb hit on a Jap carrier. He'll probably get a posthumous Navy Cross. Rear Admiral Spruance told me this. Spruance is a controlled person, but when he spoke of Warren there were tears in his eyes. He said that Warren turned in a "brilliant, heroic performance," and Raymond Spruance uses such words sparingly.

Warren was killed on the last day, on a routine mission of mopping up enemy cripples. An AA shell caught his plane. Three of his squadron mates saw him spin down in flames, so there's no hope that he ditched and is afloat on a raft, or cast up on some atoll. Warren is dead, we will never see him again. We have Byron, we have Madeline, but he's gone, and there will never be another Warren.

He came to see me just before the battle and gave me an envelope. When I found out he'd been killed (which wasn't until we got back to port) I opened it. It contained a rundown of his finances. Not that Janice had to worry, but he wasn't counting on his rich father-in-law. He'd arranged to transfer your mother's trust fund to her, and there's an insurance policy that guarantees Vic's education. How about that? He exuded confidence and cheer before the battle. I know he expected to make it through. Yet he did this. I can still see him standing in the door of my cabin, with one hand on the overhead, one foot on the coaming, saying with that easy grin of his, "If you're too busy for me, say so." Too busy! God forgive me if I ever gave him that impression. There was no greater joy in my life than talking to Warren, in fact just resting my eyes on him.

It's been awhile since I've heard from you, and almost six months since Madeline last wrote. So I feel sort of cut off, and don't know what to advise you. If you can stay with her in New York for a while, it might be a good idea. That girl needs somebody, and this is no time for you to be alone on Foxhall Road. Janice is behaving well, but she's kind of smashed up. Byron will probably mask his feelings as usual, but I'm worried about him. He worshipped Warren.

I've just written my ship's battle report. It's one page long. We never fired a gun. We never saw an enemy vessel. Warren must have flown a dozen search and attack sorties in three days. He and a few hundred young men like him carried the brunt of a great victorious battle. I did nothing.

Somewhere a character in Shakespeare says, "We owe God a death." Even if we could roll time back to that rainy evening in March 1939, Rhoda, when he was on leave from the *Monaghan,* and he told us he was putting in for flight training — in his typical fashion, just like that, no fuss, confronting us with the *fait accompli* — and even if we knew what the future held in store, what could we do differently? He was born to a service father. Boys tend to follow their dads. He chose the best branch of the Navy for effectiveness against the enemy; certainly he proved that! Few men in any armed force, on any front, will strike a harder blow for their country than he did. That was what he set out to do. His life was successful, fulfilled, and complete. I want to believe that, and in a way I truly do.

But ah, what Warren might have been! I'm a known quantity. There are a thousand four-stripers like me, and one more or less doesn't matter that much. I've had my family; you might say I've had my life. How can I compare to what Warren might have been?

Yes, Warren's gone. He won't have any fame. When the war's over, nobody will remember the ones who bore the heat of combat. They'll probably forget the names of the admirals, even of the battles that saved our country. I now feel that despite all the present discouraging news we'll eventually win the war. The Japs can't recover from the shellacking they took at Midway, and Hitler can't lick the world by himself. Our son helped to turn the tide. He was there when it mattered and where it mattered. He took his life in his hands, went in there, and did his duty as a fighting man. I'm proud of him. I'll never lose that pride. He'll be in my last thoughts.

Other things will have to wait for a different letter. God keep you well.

Love,
Pug

Emerging from her room in a silk robe, Rhoda said, "Isn't it a beautiful letter?" Byron did not reply. He sat smoking a cigar, staring emptily, his face wan, the letter on his lap. Disturbed by his silence and his look, she chattered cheerily, combing her hair at a large mirror. "I'm saving it. I'm saving everything — the telegram, the letter from the Secretary of the Navy, all the other letters, even the invitation from the Gold Star Mothers, and the story in the *Washington Herald.* It's a nice write-up. Now what is this party again, Byron? Isn't she working for Hugh Cleveland any more? I'm all confused, and — oh, to HELL with this hair! There's no light, and no time, and I don't *care,* anyhow."

"She is working for him. This party's something else, a volunteer thing." Byron got up, took a red and yellow circular from a pile on the coffee table, and handed it to her. "It's a buffet before this wingding starts."

AMERICAN COMMITTEE

FOR

A SECOND FRONT **NOW**

Hollywood Division

MONSTER RALLY

AT

THE HOLLYWOOD BOWL

There followed a large alphabetical list of participants: film stars, producers, directors, writers.

"My goodness! What a star cast. And Alistair Tudsbury, too, HE's here! Why, this is a very distinguished group, isn't it, Byron? '*Madeline Henry, program coordinator!*' My heavens! If that little snip hasn't come up in the world."

At this moment Madeline burst in. "Oh, Mother!" The intensity of the exclamation, and the clutching embrace that went with it, bridged their shared grief. She wore a dark wide-shouldered dress, her dark hair was elegantly styled, and her talk was cyclonic. "I'm so GLAD you came! Shoot, I hoped you'd be ready, but I'll just go, I guess, and then send Hugh's limousine back for you. Oh, God, there's so much to talk about, isn't there, Mom! This insane clambake will be all over tonight, thank Heaven, and then I can draw breath."

"Dear, we don't know these people, I'm tired, I have no clothes —"

"Mama, you're both *coming*. The Tudsburys will be sitting in your box. That's why they've stayed on, they want to see you. They won't be at the party, but you'll meet all the film stars. It's at Harry Tomlin's home on Lookout Mountain, a fabulous place, he's the biggest agent in the movie business. Wear anything! You must have a black suit."

"Well, I wore it to death on the train, but —" Rhoda went out.

Byron pointed to the pile of circulars. "Mad, isn't that a communist outfit?"

"Sweetie, not on your life. All Hollywood's in on it. It's a popular movement. With Soviet Russia doing all the real fighting and dying against Hitler, we *need* a second front now, and we've got to raise hell about it. Everybody knows Churchill hates the Bolsheviks, and wants to hold back and let the Soviet Union bleed itself white, fighting the Germans alone."

"Everybody knows that? I don't know it. How do you know it?"

"Oh, Lord, Byron, read your newspapers. Anyway, let's not argue, sweetie, it's not worth arguing about. I took this thing on because I thought it would be fun, and it *has* been fun in a bloodcurdling way. I've made some fantastic contacts. I don't want to be Hugh Cleveland's little sandwich-fetcher forever."

"I'm glad to hear that."

Madeline was making a long strident telephone call about the rally to a man she called "Lenny, darling," when Rhoda marched in, buttoning her jacket. "Let's go. Nobody will pay me the slightest attention. I'll pass as someone's poor aunt from Dubuque."

The home of Harry Tomlin was an opulent sprawl of redwood and glass angled around a flagstone terrace with a huge blue-tiled pool. Perched at the end of a scarily steep concrete road up into a canyon, it commanded a spectacular view of Los Angeles, which at the moment looked like a drowned city shimmering at the bottom of a brown lake. Madeline vanished in the babbling throng of guests, after introducing her mother and brother at the door to a man named Leonard Spreregen, the rally chairman, who — so she told them — had won two Academy Awards for screenplays. Rhoda saw that her concern over clothes was needless; Spreregen wore no tie, and his orange shirt collar flowed over his black and white houndstooth jacket. Madeline whirled into sight again and introduced her mother and brother to one star after another, all of whom were most cordial. To the astonished Rhoda they appeared peculiarly shrunken, seen as human beings rather than blown-up moving shadows.

"How on earth have you gotten to know them all, dear?" she exclaimed, catching her breath after a kind word and a smile from Ronald Colman.

"Oh, you do, Mom, when you mix into a thing like this. You just do. That's the fun of it. Ah, there we go."

White-coated butlers were sliding tall Chinese panels into wall slots, disclosing a long dining room and a heavily laden buffet table, where two chefs were sharpening knives over steaming hams and turkeys. As the guests drifted in toward the food, several men in sharply tailored Army uniforms fell into the line behind Madeline. She whispered to Byron that these were Hollywood types making training films. Hugh Cleveland was looking into this angle, she said. He had received a draft notice; if things got sticky he wanted an out. She blurted this artlessly, then caught the look on her brother's face. "Well, I realize how that must strike you, but —"

"How does it strike you, Madeline?"

"Briny, Hugh is totally unmechanical. He can't sharpen a pencil properly. He'd be an utter washout carrying a gun."

They brought their food to a little table on the terrace, where Leonard Spreregen joined them and talked with Madeline about the rally while she scratched notes on a pad. Spreregen's manner was bright and edgy, his speech pure New York. Madeline exclaimed, jumping up, "Omigawd, the trumpeters for the mass chant, of *course*. Sorry, Lenny. I *knew* there was something. Be right back."

"What a lovely party," Rhoda said to Spreregen, glancing around at French impressionist paintings crusting the walls, "and what a gorgeous home!"

He pleasantly smiled. He was a short lean man with thick curly blond hair and a hawklike face. His voice was deep, almost bass. "Well, Mrs. Henry, ten percent of my heart's blood is in it, but I don't mind, Harry's a terrific agent. Say, Lieutenant, how do you feel about the second front?"

"Well, I'm puzzled," Byron said, eating away at a heaped plate, "there are four or five fronts right now, aren't there?"

"Ah, the military precisionist speaks!" Spreregen nodded, with a keen glance at Byron that took in the ribbons and the dolphins. " 'The Committee for a Second Front against Germany in France Now' would be more exact, I guess. People know what we mean. You're for that, aren't you?"

"I don't know if it's feasible now."

"Why, any number of military authorities are clamoring for it."

"But the Allied chiefs of staff are the military authorities that matter."

"Exactly so," said Spreregen, as though to a clever pupil, "and the chiefs of staff can't buck their political bosses. Economic and political motives can cause stupid military decisions, Lieutenant. Then you fighting men have to pay the price. The reactionaries want to let Hitler destroy the Soviet Union, before they finish him off. The reactionaries have a strong voice, but the voice of the people is stronger. That's why rallies like this are vital."

Byron shook his head, saying mildly, "I doubt they can affect strategic policy. Why not put on a rally for the Jews in Europe? Such big propaganda shows might do them some real good."

Rhoda blinked at her son. At the word "Jews," Leonard Spreregen's eyes clouded, his mouth tightened, and he sat up straight, putting down the knife and fork on a slab of hot ham. "If you're serious —"

"I'm deadly serious."

Spreregen spoke fast, in a rattled way. "Well, I'm not sure what's happening over there, my friend, I don't think anybody here really knows, but the way to end all that misery is by smashing Hitler with a second front now."

"I see," Byron said.

"Excuse me. Nice meeting you," Spreregen said to Rhoda, and he departed, leaving his food behind.

Soon Madeline appeared, frowning at Byron. "Look, Briny, let's drop you off at the hotel on the way to the rally."

"What on earth!" Rhoda exclaimed. "Why suggest that?"

"He made an anti-Semitic remark to Lenny Spreregen."

Rhoda blinked in surprise. "What? Why, the man's a fool, all he said —"

"Forget it, Mom," Byron said. "I'll come along."

A gigantic yellow banner printed in red swayed above the main entrance to the Hollywood Bowl:

THE YANKS ARE NOT COMING TOO LATE.

Cars were streaming inside, and from nearby streets hordes of people on foot were converging toward the Bowl. But, although the entrance appeared mobbed, the audience in the big amphitheatre was sparsely clustering near the stage shell, below the tier of boxes. On the upper slope, slanting sunlight reddened rows upon rows of empty seats. Over the shell, which was draped with three large flags — the British ensign, the Stars and Stripes, and the red flag with its yellow hammer and sickle — huge cutout letters arched:

$$\mathrm{S}^{\mathrm{E}\,\mathrm{C}\,\mathrm{O}\,\mathrm{N}^{\mathrm{D}}\quad {}^{\mathrm{F}}\mathrm{R}_{\mathrm{O}_{\mathrm{N}_{\mathrm{T}}}}}$$
$$\mathrm{N\,O\,W}$$

Alistair Tudsbury, in a bulging seersucker suit and an eye patch, awkwardly got to his feet and kissed Rhoda when she came to the box. Pamela's smile was agreeable, but her eyes were puffy, her face was sagging and unpainted, and she was almost unkempt; she looked, Rhoda thought, as though she did not much care whether she lived or died. Madeline came dashing into the box. Grand panic backstage! Two stars had pulled out of the show, a third had laryngitis, and a frantic rearrangement of the program had placed Tudsbury in the closing spot, after the mass chant. Was that all right? Tudsbury agreed, remarking only that his talk would not be a high note.

"Oh, it will, it will. You have *authority*," Madeline said. "Sorry we didn't pull in more of an audience. Charging admission was a mistake." She scampered off.

It was a tedious patchy program, part singing and dancing to two pianos, part speech-making, with some labored comedy. The hit of the evening was a song, "The Reactionary Rag," in which actors dressed as paunchy nabobs in high hats and cutaways, with dollar signs on their white-waisted bellies, capered about expressing their sympathy with the Soviet Union, but finding funny reasons not to send military help. The mass chant was a business of many voices speaking up from all over the amphitheatre — a steel worker, a farm laborer, a schoolteacher, a nurse, a Negro, and so forth — each demanding a second front *now*; these solo declamations were punctuated with solemn unison readings from mimeographed sheets by the entire audience of quotes from Pericles, Shakespeare, Lincoln, Booker T. Washington, Tom Paine, Lenin, Stalin, and Carl Sandburg, while the orchestra softly played "The Battle Hymn of the Republic." The climax was a wildly syncopated audience shout, repeated in crescendo to the accompaniment of trumpets:

Open up that second FRONT
Open up that second FRONT

Open up that second FRONT
NOW! NOW! NOW!

It all ended in great applause and cheers.

Introduced by Leonard Spreregen, Tudsbury limped onstage to a standing ovation.

"On June 22nd, 1941, as you no doubt recall," his voice boomed on the loudspeaker over the great half-empty amphitheatre, now in twilight under a pale moon, "Nazi Germany invaded the Soviet Union.

"On June 23rd, 1941, my column in the *London Observer* bore the heading, 'Open Up a Second Front Now.'"

This brought the crowd to its feet again. But the Bowl grew very quiet as he talked. Military realities, he began, were not easy to grasp or to face. He had had to spend several months in Moscow during the worst of the German onslaught, a month in falling Singapore, and a week in Hawaii before and after the battle for Midway atoll, before he had gotten a grip on this global war.

A major assault on the French coast in 1942 was, he now knew, utterly out of the question. Only a trickle of green American forces had as yet arrived in England. The U-boats remained a formidable and merciless barrier to a rapid buildup of these forces. Mastering that menace was a long-range struggle. A cross-Channel attack now would have to be all-British. Britain was already spread far too thin. Singapore had proved that! Any British action in France would so weaken the China-Burma-India theatre that the United States would have to take over there — at once, and massively — with whatever forces it could get past the Japanese fleet. For if India or Australia fell to Japan, the defeat of Nazi Germany would not win the war, nor assure the survival of the Soviet Union.

"Eastern Asia is the center of gravity of the war, my friends," Tudsbury declared in weary firm tones. "World War Two started there at the Marco Polo Bridge, not in Poland. China has been fighting the war longer than anybody. If Japan wins there, Russia faces catastrophe. Japan will mobilize the incredible resources of India, China, and the East Indies against the Soviet Union. A new Golden Horde will storm across the Siberian border, armed with tanks, with Zeroes, and with manpower and natural resources outweighing the West ten to one. The China-Burma-India theatre is the true, the forgotten second front. We must hold it if civilization is to survive."

Several catcalls rose from the audience at this point.

"The long-range prospects are *good*," Tudsbury defiantly boomed. "Our soldiers who died in Singapore, and yours in the Philippines, did not die in vain. They upset the Japanese timetable for seizing India and Australia. The crux of the war now is a fight for time. Your country's productive power is awesome, but slow to gear up. I'm surprised to find so little interest here in your victory at Midway. Had your Navy lost that battle, you might be fleeing California this evening. Your fliers and sailors who died there gave their lives for all mankind."

Coughing was spreading in the amphitheatre, and people were yawning and looking at their watches.

"A second front in France? Yes, I'm warmly for it, too. The plight of the Soviet Union grows worse and worse. But the Russians are strong. They will hold on. It's delightful to visualize millions of stalwart Anglo-American troops storming across the English Channel *now*. But it's a pipe dream. We will overwhelm the Axis in good time with a cataract of men and firepower. Till then, we fight for time, and for the turn of the tide on many fronts, including the home front. My final word to this home front is, *Believe in the honor of your leaders, and trust them. They are great men, and they are fighting a great war.*"

As he limped off the stage, feeble brief handclapping ensued, with more catcalls. The crowd began dispersing, in a muttering mood. A loud bald man in a loud jacket was saying to a pretty girl as they left the box beside Byron's, "Still trying to hang on to their Empire, aren't they? Just pathetic."

Returning to the box with Madeline, Tudsbury said cheerfully, "Well, wasn't that a resounding flop!"

"Well done," Byron said.

Rhoda jumped up, kissed him, and said tremulously, "I'll never forget your words about Midway. Never."

"You made good sense," Madeline fumed. "This crowd doesn't change, and never will. Maybe it penetrated a thick skull here and there. I must go and pick up the pieces."

Pamela stood up as Madeline scurried off. "Was it fun, Talky?"

"It was, actually, watching them gradually realize that I wasn't one of them, but just another Limey snake in the grass. I quite enjoyed it."

"So courageous," said Rhoda. "Pug would have talked like that — without your lovely command of language, of course."

"Pug would have stayed away, and so should I have done," said Tudsbury. "However, we wanted to see you, Mrs. Henry, so let's have a drink now at our hotel, shall we? Pamela and I fly on to New York tomorrow."

As they walked out, the press of the crowd thrust Rhoda alongside Pamela, who spoke low fast words. "Mrs. Henry, may I have breakfast with you tomorrow — just the two of us?"

They faced each other next morning on the lawn beside the pool over melons, toast, and coffee on a wheeled linen-covered table. It was a perfect California day: hot sun, pellucid blue sky, scents of grass and palms, a cool breeze stirring the gaudy red flowers of the hibiscus hedges. Two youths and three girls dove and swam and laughed in the pool, their brown skins gleaming, their jokes as merry and simple as the mating calls of birds. Pamela looked better today, her face carefully made up, her hair falling behind her ears in long glossy waves. The sleeveless gray dress showed the cleft in her pale bosom. Rhoda recalled that this odd young woman, who fluttered in her father's wake like a gull behind an ocean liner, had a way of shifting between mousiness and allure. Perhaps, Rhoda thought, she was on her way this morning to meet a man. She gave the impression of very taut nerves.

As they idly chatted, Rhoda said she wished she had a copy of Tudsbury's speech to send to Pug.

"Nothing easier. I'll see that you get one." Pamela quickly replied in her educated British accent that so impressed and charmed Rhoda. "I wrote it."

"Why, it was his style to the life."

"Oh, yes, I fake for him when he's indisposed or lazy."

"Why the eye patch, Pamela?"

"That eye is ulcerating. He needs an operation. We'd be in London by now, but Madeline did mention that you were coming west, so we stayed. I desperately wanted to talk to you."

"Really? What about?"

"About your husband. I love him."

Rhoda yanked off her sunglasses and stared at the English girl, who sat up straight, her head high, her eyes wide and combatively shiny. Rhoda's first coherent thought, through the fog of amazement, was that Pamela was a formidable rival if Pug really liked her. Let her have her say, she thought, reveal what she would reveal. Rhoda played with the glasses and drank coffee, just eyeing her.

"I know that you wanted a divorce," Pamela said, "and that he's asked you to reconsider."

"I have reconsidered!" Rhoda leaped at the opening. "Long since. That's all over with. He's confided in you, it seems."

"Oh, yes, Mrs. Henry," Pamela replied gloomily. "He's confided in me."

"Have you had an affair with my husband?"

"No." Their glances met in mutual search. "*No*, Mrs. Henry. He's remained faithful to you, worse luck."

Rhoda saw truth in Pamela's eyes. "Indeed? You're terribly PRETTY."

"He's been an ass." Pamela turned off the compliment with a hitch of her shoulder. "It would have been heaven. What's more, honors would now be even between you two."

The tone and the words stung. Rhoda said acidly, "But isn't my husband much too OLD for you?"

"Mrs. Henry, your husband's the most attractive man I've ever met in every way, including his loyalty to you, which has defeated me."

The passion in her voice alarmed Rhoda. She could see the difference between Pamela's young skin and hers, admire the sweet slim form of Pamela's upper arms — Rhoda now had to conceal her own because of a growing, revolting limp bagginess — and could envy that bosom. A small voice within her said that Pug had indeed been an ass, though she blessed him for it. "Did you see him after — after Midway?"

"Yes, I saw a lot of him. Through all his agony he kept worrying about you, about how you were taking it, about what he could do to console you. He even considered asking for emergency leave. He packed me off, though I tried to stay. He's a family man to the bone. If you can get to Hawaii, do it. He needs you. If there ever was a chance for me, the death of your son has ended it."

Touching a handkerchief to her eyes, Rhoda barely articulated, "Poor Pug."

"You were foolish to risk losing him. I can't understand you, I think it was terribly stupid of you, but don't do it again." Pamela gathered up her purse. "You say all that's over with."

"Yes, yes. Absolutely and forever."

"Good. You have a well-wisher who's written your husband several anonymous letters about you and this man. If you have no better reason to straighten up, there's one."

"Oh, God," Rhoda groaned. "What did the letters say?"

"Guess!" It was a scornful snap. In a softer tone Pamela said, "I'm sorry to hurt you in your bereavement, but I don't want you hurting him any more. That's why I've talked to you. I'll send the speech text to you by messenger. Our plane leaves in a couple of hours."

"Will you promise never to see my husband any more?"

Ugly lines strained Pamela's face. She contemplated Rhoda's proffered hand — lean, long, wrinkled, strong-fingered — then glared at her. "That's impossible! The future can't be controlled. But I'm out of your way now, rest assured of that." She looked around at the youngsters, drying themselves and giggling on the pool's edge, and her manner turned gentle. "This has been a bizarre conversation, hasn't it? A wartime conversation."

"I'm STUNNED," Rhoda said.

They both got up.

"One more thing," Pamela said. "I met your son Warren only once, in Hawaii just before the battle. There was a strange light about him, Mrs. Henry. It wasn't my imagination, my father sensed it too. He was almost godlike. You've had an appalling loss. But you have two other wonderful children. I hope you and your husband will console each other, and in time be happy again." With a quick feline movement Pamela kissed Rhoda's cheek and hastened out of the garden.

Rhoda walked to a lounge chair in the sun and fell into it, half out of her senses with surprise. When had Pug mentioned Pamela Tudsbury in his letters? From London in the summer of 1940; from Moscow late in 1941; and then just lately, from Hawaii. Of course, the father and daughter had been in and out of Washington, too. In a letter about the party at the Moana before the battle, Pug had remarked on "the Tudsbury girl's" sickly appearance, due to dysentery.

Poor Pug! Camouflage? An effort to stamp out romantic stirrings in his own inhibited heart?

As in a crystal ball, Rhoda saw pictures in the sparkling blue bowl of the now-deserted swimming pool: Pug and Pamela together in those far-off places, not making love, perhaps not even kissing, but just being together, day after day, evening after evening, thousands of miles from home. The bitter knowing smile on the face of this woman was a picture of Eve with something on Adam. Pamela Tudsbury had told a good story, she thought, but old Pug couldn't have been quite the holy Joe she made him out. Rhoda knew better. The kind of passion that burned in Pamela Tudsbury did not kindle of itself. Pug had in some way, oblique or direct, wooed the girl. Perhaps indeed he had kept it platonic, so as to have his highminded cake and eat it; or perhaps they had slept together. It was hard to tell. As for the truthful look in Pamela's eyes, Rhoda knew all about truthful looks.

The anonymous letters were horrible to think about. What nasty biddy had done *that?* Nevertheless, the gap between her guilty self and her husband was narrower than she had dreamed, after all. She was jealous of Pamela, and scared of her; and Pug's desirability had shot up. She felt a warm unaccustomed stir of erotic longing for the taciturn old dog. The girl's renunciation meant little, of course. Pug had sent Pamela packing as she intended to do to Palmer Kirby. What had really gone on between them she might never know. It was a nice tactical problem, whether she should ever ask him.

With a start in her chair, Rhoda Henry realized she had forgotten for a little while that Warren was dead.

34

LOUIS stood fretting noisily in his crib, rattling the side bars. Siena in the summer was a bakeoven, and he took heat badly, his disposition becoming as rough and sore as the rashes that mottled him from head to toe. A diaper and a thin white shirt lay ready on the bureau top. He would probably howl when Natalie clothed him for the bus ride, so she was leaving that for last. As she tightened the suitcase straps, the sweat starting from this effort, Aaron looked in. "The car will be here in half an hour, my dear."

"I know. I'm ready."

In an old blue beret and a shabby gray suit he looked like any Italian bus passenger. Natalie had wondered whether to caution him about his usual flamboyant travelling clothes. He was showing good sense, happily, starting out. He glanced up at the mildewy ceiling with its peeling frescoed cherubs. "The whole place has certainly gone to seed. I hadn't really noticed until now." Gesturing at the open window and the distant cathedral, he added as he left, "But you won't soon have another view like this from your bedroom, will you?"

To Natalie the departure was not yet real. How often had she left this godforsaken Tuscan villa for good; how often had she seen once again, with sinking heart, the old gate with the wrought-iron peacock, the cracking yellow stucco garden wall, the red-tiled tower Byron had slept in! How lightly she had first set foot here in 1939, expecting to stay two or three months while she tried to recapture Leslie Slote; what a quicksand it had proved! Memories of her very first night in this room were haunting her — the musty smell of the satin-draped four-poster bed, the rat noisily gnawing in the wall, the crashing thunderstorm, lightning-lit Siena luridly framed in the open window like El Greco's Toledo.

Last-minute doubts were assailing her. Were they doing the right thing? They had just about settled down to a bearable house-arrest existence. Except for Werner Beck, nobody was bothering them. There was milk for the baby — goat's milk, but he thrived on it — and enough food. The Monte di Paschi bankers, aware of Aaron's wealth in New York, would not let them lack for money. All true. But she had acted out of instinct after that last meeting with Beck, and now the die was cast. Aaron had been handling Beck quite suavely since then, sending him outlines for broadcasts, flattering him by accepting his suggestions, and at last wheedling official permission to get away from Siena's heat, in a week or two by the sea, as guests of the Sacerdotes in their Follonica beach house.

The straps on the two suitcases were secure. One was full of Louis's stuff, the other contained her barest necessities. Rabinovitz's instructions were stark: *"no baggage you can't handle yourself walking twenty miles with the baby."* Since getting his message Natalie had been walking six miles a day. Her feet had blistered, then healed in calluses, and she felt very fit. What a shock when Castelnuovo had offered her the rolled-up cigarette paper with a magnifying glass! "Just like the cinema, eh?" he had said. Now was the time to get rid of that paper. She took it from her purse, and unrolled it on her palm.

> *dear natalie happy you are coming tell uncle travel very light you take no baggage you can't handle yourself walking twenty miles with the baby i care for your baby and i care for you it will be all right love*

The tiny words, barely discernible to the naked eye, stirred her yet. No letter had come from Byron in months. She had read to tatters the few she possessed. Her memories of Byron were as unchanging and repetitious as old home movies. Her life and his had been unfolding apart for the last two years and she was not even sure he was alive. His last letters that the Red Cross had forwarded — written from Albany, a tiny town in southwest Australia, months ago — suggested that combat was changing him; he sounded nothing like the lighthearted young dandy who had bewitched her. The news that Castelnuovo was in touch with Rabinovitz, and the cigarette-paper message, had thrown her in a turmoil that persisted, though common sense told her there was nothing in the Palestinian's words but Jewish kindness.

It was hard to give up the paper, but rolling it in a tiny ball, she flooded it down the bathtub drain. She dressed the baby; then she took a last look around at the big frilly candy box of a room, and stared long at the big bed in which for years she had not known a man's arms around her, only empty teasing dreams and fantasies.

"Come on, Louis," she said. "Let's go home."

There were no farewells to the servants. Aaron was leaving closets full of clothes, a whole untouched library, and stacked folders of the Luther book drafts on his desk. Natalie had given the maid and the gardeners orders for work to be finished when she returned in two weeks. But servants are wise, Italian servants especially. The cook, the maid, and the two gardeners were lined up at the iron gate. Their good-byes were cheery but their eyes were solemn and their manners fumbling. The cook gave the baby a stick of candy, and as they drove off she cried.

At the wheel of Sacerdote's car was the surly son who was remaining in

Siena, and — so his family suspected — taking Catholic instruction because of his Christian girl. The anti-Jewish laws forbade conversions, but in Siena Fascist edicts were often ignored. In a light open shirt, his hair thick and unruly, a cigarette hanging from a corner of his downturned mouth, the youth wordlessly drove them to the almost deserted Piazza del Campo, and left them there.

Siena had never been lively; now it scarcely seemed inhabited. The few vending stalls in the broad plaza stood empty and untended. Later, if a truckload of vegetables or fish came up from the coast there might be some buying and selling, but not much; rationing controlled everything down to garlic and onions. The long shadow of the Palazzo Pubblico tower oozed along the hot pavement, and mechanically the few gossipers moved with it, like toy figures on a huge sundial. Natalie and Aaron sat outside the one open café, drinking imitation orange soda with a metallic taste. She remembered the roaring mob of the Palio filling this amphitheatre of Renaissance palazzos, the rainbow parade of the *contrade*, the wild horse race: all stopped, all gone! Years of her life had melted away in this town bypassed by history. That Aaron had chosen to settle here was bizarre; that she had shared his exile was an aberration beyond fathoming.

The car came back, and the young man grumbled at them that the bus was about to leave. They had avoided waiting at the station because of the police. The permit to visit Follonica was an extraordinary document originating in Rome; the less they exposed it the better. At the station the bus driver impatiently waved them inside, and off they went under the eyes of a yawning policeman.

The bus chugged out through the high town wall and bumped down a narrow dirt road, heading west. The Sacerdotes, though dressed modestly, sat with the dignity of rich proprietors, their expressions abstracted and sad, and as in the faces of many old couples, very much alike. Louis fell asleep in Natalie's lap. Through the open windows of the bus sweet farmland odors swept in, mixed with the strangely pleasant gasogene fumes from the charcoal burner, like the scent of a wood fire. Miriam chattered happily to her mother, while her father stared out at the passing scenery. Grand panoramas of mountaintop villages, green hillside farms, and terraced vineyards opened up at every turn of the road. The bus ground down past Volterra in a steepening descent, and ended its run in Massa Marittima, a tiny old hilltop town quiet as Siena, its old gray stones shimmering in noon glare.

Here in the little square the futility of the Mussolini regime struck Natalie anew, in the contrast of the garish hollow victory posters and the old weathered façades of the church and town hall. Italy was too weary, too wise, too charming to play the armed bully. It had all been a showy fake and a waste. Unfortunately, the Germans had imitated the bloodthirsty charade with heavy Teutonic seriousness and run amuck with it; so Natalie tiredly thought, as she trudged to the railroad station holding the limp baby and one suitcase; Aaron was carrying the other, and one for himself.

A small narrow-gauge train tweeted into the station, and the conductor punched tickets with scarcely a glance at the passengers' faces. Nobody checked their papers either in the station or on the train. In all Massa Marittima they had seen only one policeman, dozing against his propped bicycle. Awake again, Louis looked out with mild interest at the farmers on the slopes, at the grazing sheep and cattle, and at the ugly gashes of mines in the hillsides, with their great brown rubbish heaps, tall conveyor belts, and rough wooden trestles and towers. The train wound around a rocky bend and there far below the Mediterranean glittered. Natalie caught her breath. Off on the hazy horizon she could see dots and humps of islands, their escape route to Lisbon.

The Sacerdotes' summer home in Follonica was a boxlike stucco house right on the beach, painted blue. Across the road a public park full of high old shade trees and wide-spreading palms gave exceptional privacy. Inside the boarded-up house all was stifling hot darkness and dank stale smells until Castelnuovo and his wife took down storm shutters and opened windows to a sea breeze. Natalie put Louis to bed in a crib that had once been Miriam's, and Sacerdote took her and Aaron to the small *carabinieri* station. The sleepy-eyed police chief, looking very impressed at the permit document from Rome, made the necessary stampings and notations, and stood up to shake hands with them. He had a brother in Newark, he said, a florist who made good money. Italy had no real quarrel with America. It was the Germans. What could you do with the damned Germans?

A week passed. No word came from Rabinovitz. Natalie sank into animal enjoyment of the beach as an anodyne for her mounting anxiety. As for Louis, playing in the sand with Miriam all day, and now and then getting dipped in the sea, he took on color and shed his rashes and his crankiness. On a Sabbath evening they were sitting down at the candle-lit table when the doorbell rang and a grimy man with a bluish three-day beard came in. His name was Frankenthal, he said, and he came from Avram Rabinovitz. His manner was matter-of-fact, tired, and abrupt until the Sacerdotes asked him to stay for dinner. Then he took off a ragged cap and looked pleasanter and slightly abashed. Pointing to the candles on the dining table he said, "*Sabato?* I have not seen that since my grandmother died."

He was a dock worker in Piombino, the iron-ore shipping port north of Follonica, he told them as he ate. His father too had worked on the docks. His grandfather had been a Hebrew scholar, but the family had dropped all that. He himself knew nothing but that he was a Jew. Once the children were put to bed he got down to business. The news was bad. The Turkish freighter that had been running refugees illegally from Corsica to Lisbon had lost its British navicert, and could not transit Gibraltar. That route was finished.

Still, they were to go on to Corsica via Elba as planned. Rabinovitz was arranging to bring them from Corsica to Marseilles, where most of the rescue agencies operated. Several routes existed for going on from Marseilles to Palestine or Lisbon. That was Rabinovitz's message. But Frankenthal told them of a more direct way to get to Marseilles. Vessels carrying iron ore from the mines of Elba and Massa Marittima for transshipment to the Ruhr made the run from Piombino every week or so. The British navy did not bother the ore boats. He knew a captain who would take them straight to Marseilles for five hundred dollars a passenger.

They were still at the table, drinking chicory by the light of the waning candles. Jastrow said drily, "I sailed from New York to Paris for five hundred dollars, first class."

"*Professore*, that was peacetime. The other way, God knows how long you'll be stuck in Elba or in Corsica. On the boat you'll sleep in beds, a direct trip, three days, the children safe."

He left to catch the last bus for Piombino, saying he would telephone in a day or two for their decision. "Take the ore boat," were his parting words.

Jastrow spoke first, with acid amusement, when he was gone. "If we do take the ore boat, this fellow will get a fat cut of our money."

"Do you trust him?" Natalie asked Castelnuovo.

"Well, I know he comes from Rabinovitz."

"How do you communicate with Avram?"

"Cables about innocuous matters. Otherwise, messengers like this fellow. Why?"

"I'm thinking of just going back to Siena."

Sacerdote said to his son-in-law, putting his arm around his frightened-looking wife, "She's right. You said we would go to Lisbon and never set foot in France."

"Yes, Papa, and now that has changed," Castelnuovo said with exaggerated forbearance, "and so, we're having a little chat."

Natalie turned to Jastrow. "When I went to meet Byron in Lisbon, the Vichy police pulled me off the train to check my papers. They were in order, luckily. My spine went icy when they asked whether I was a Jew." She turned to Castelnuovo. "What recourse would we have now in France, Jews travelling illegally? Suppose they jail us? I could become separated from Louis!"

"Avram will arrange transit visas for us," said Castelnuovo. "Papers can always be had."

"Fake papers, you mean," said Sacerdote.

"Papers that will pass."

Jastrow said, "Let's not be faint-hearted. We have set out. I confess I never liked the island-jumping plan. As long as we're going to Marseilles, I say let's take the ore boat. One big bribe, one comfortable trip, that's my notion."

Castelnuovo made an impatient gesture with both hands. "Now look, I already knew all about the ore boats. They dock in a maximum security area of Marseilles, behind a high fence with French military patrols, and German inspectors from the Armistice Commission. The captain cares nothing about you. It's just your money. If any danger arises to him — pauf! — his neck comes first. Going through the islands, we'll be in the hands of people Rabinovitz knows."

"I imagine my wife and I will go back," Sacerdote said very solemnly to Jastrow. "We must still talk it over, of course. But our son is there, you know." The old woman was sniffling into a handkerchief.

Jastrow quickly said, "It's natural. It's your home. For us it's safer to go on."

The old couple went upstairs. Jastrow and Castelnuovo debated some more about the ore boat. Castelnuovo hated to trust his family's lives, he said, to a bribed Italian. The price could jump in mid-passage; the man could take the money and fail to perform; he could in fact sell them out. Resistance people stood for something more than an itching palm.

At last Jastrow said, "Look here, is our organizing principle democracy or authority? If it's authority, you decide."

Castelnuovo sourly laughed, waving off the suggestion.

"Well, then, I vote for the ore boat."

Anna Castelnuovo said, "Two votes."

"You're a mule," her husband said, but the tone was wryly affectionate. He turned to Natalie. "Well?"

"The ore boat."

Castelnuovo pursed his mouth, lightly struck the table, and stood up. "Settled."

On a gray cool afternoon, coming back from an eight-mile walk, Natalie noticed from a distance a parked car near the house. There were few private cars in Follonica. Her steps quickened, and something like a prayer flitted through her mind: "Let it not be trouble." As she drew nearer she recognized the Mercedes. In the house Jastrow and Werner Beck sat at the dining table over tea and a platter of cakes. Yellow typescripts of Jastrow's broadcasts lay scattered on the bare table.

Werner Beck got up, smiling and bowing. "Delighted. It's been so long!" She could barely choke out a civil response. He glanced down at his SS uniform with an apologetic little laugh. "Ah, yes. Never mind my formidable masquerade. I'm on a tour of the western ports, Mrs. Henry, in connection with an unaccountable shortage of fuel oil, which my country has to supply to Italy one hundred percent. We're sure the black market is draining it off. Italians are more forthcoming with the truth when they see this uniform. My SS commission is purely honorary, but they don't know that. Well, now, the sea air has done wonders for you. And the baby? How is he? I'd love to see him."

Natalie said in as normal a tone as she could muster, "Shall I fetch him? How long can you stay?"

"Regrettably, not long. I have business in Piombino. Follonica's only a short way off the main road, so I thought I'd drop by and pay my respects."

"Let me get him, then."

On the second floor the Castelnuovos, their faces pallid and strained, sat in their bedroom with the door wide open. The doctor beckoned to her and whispered, "Is that the man?"

"Yes."

"I heard him mention Piombino."

"He's on an inspection tour."

In the other room Miriam was amusing Louis with a ragged toy bear. She looked up like a worried grown woman when Natalie lifted him from his crib. "Where are you taking him?"

"Downstairs, just for a moment."

"But downstairs there is a German."

Natalie put a finger to her lips and bore off the yawning Louis. She halted on the staircase, hearing Beck raise his voice. "But Dr. Jastrow, all four broadcasts are fine as they stand. Why, they're gemlike essays. You can't change a word. Why not record them now? At least the first two?"

Jastrow's voice, quietly serene: "Werner, a publisher once urged the poet A. E. Housman to print some essays he was discarding. Housman cut him off with these words: '*I did not say they were not good. I said they were not good enough for me.*' "

"That's all very fine, but for us time is a key factor. If you could not polish these talks to your taste before the war was over, it would all be pretty pointless, hm?"

Jastrow's chuckle was appreciative and jolly. "Very neat, Werner."

"But I'm absolutely serious! I'm shielding you from painful harassment. You told me that a week or two by the sea was all you'd need. If this matter is ever taken out of my hands, Dr. Jastrow, you'll be extremely sorry."

Silence.

Natalie hurried down the stairs and into the dining room. Beck stood up, beaming at the child. "My goodness, but he has grown!" He slipped his glasses into a breast pocket and extended his arms. "May I take him? If you knew how I miss my Klaus, my youngest!"

Putting her son into the hands of this uniformed man gave Natalie a sick qualm, but Dr. Beck's manner of handling the baby was knowing and gentle. Louis smiled beautifully at him. Dr. Beck's eyes moistened, and he spoke in an artificial little voice. "Well, hello there! Hello, little happy boy! We're friends, aren't we? No politics between us, hm? — Well! Want my glasses, do you?" He pried the frames out of Louis's tiny clutch. "Let's hope you never need glasses. Here, your mother looks anxious, go back to her. Tell her I've never dropped a baby yet."

Natalie clasped Louis with relief and sat down. Resuming his seat, Beck donned his glasses, and his face took on a severe cast. "Now then. I shall be returning from my tour in five days, and I propose to take you both with me to Rome. Dr. Jastrow, you must be ready to record the broadcasts. I've already made hotel arrangements, and I am going to be very firm about this."

With a resigned mock-humble gesture of bowed shoulders and out-stretched arms, Jastrow exclaimed, "Five days! Well, I can try to do something. But the second two scripts are out of the question, Werner. They're simply scattered notes. I can attempt to cobble up the first one or two, dear fellow, but if you insist on all four, I shall simply lie down in my traces like the overloaded horse."

Beck patted the old man's knee. "Just have the first two ready when I return. Then we'll see."

"Is it really necessary for me to come to Rome, too?" Natalie asked.

"Yes."

"Will we return to Siena afterward?"

"As you wish," Beck said absently, glancing at his wristwatch and standing up. Aaron walked outside with him.

Down the stairs came the Castelnuovos, with Miriam tiptoeing behind her mother's skirts. She poked out her head at Natalie and stage-whispered, "Did the German go away?"

"Yes, he's gone."

"Did he hurt Louis?"

"No, no, Louis is fine." Natalie was clutching the baby as though picking him up after a fall. "Suppose I put you two out on the porch."

"Can he have a cake?"

"All right."

The four adults held a quick conclave in the dining room. That this was a crisis, that Jastrow had to move on, they took for granted. Castelnuovo had to consult Frankenthal, they decided, but not over the telephone. The afternoon bus was leaving in half an hour. The doctor clapped on his hat and departed. A grim evening followed. He returned early the next morning, to the immense relief of his wife, who had not slept. Frankenthal's advice was that they had better go on to the islands after all, for an ore boat had sailed only last week. The next ferry to Elba was day after tomorrow.

"It's off to Corsica, then," said Natalie, covering the thumping of her heart with dogged gaiety.

"Off to Elba," said the doctor. "There we'll have to wait. Nothing is organized for Corsica as yet."

"Well," said Jastrow. "Napoleon made it off Elba, and so shall we."

It rained and blew hard the morning they left. Waves were breaking high over the sea wall of the Piombino waterfront when the passengers began straggling aboard the small ferryboat pitching in its slip. Far off under a shed three waterfront customs guards, dry and snug, sat smoking pipes and drinking wine. Frankenthal had excursion permits ready, as well as tickets; the permits were required because of the prison on Elba. But there was no checking of papers. The fugitives boarded the ferry among other travellers under umbrellas; chains rattled, the diesel coughed stinking smoke, the ferry pulled unsteadily away from the slip, Frankenthal waved at them and shouted a casual good-bye, and they were *out!*

Looking back at the mainland veiled by the downpour and by smoke from the Piombino blast furnaces, Natalie recalled how, the night before, the red flaming mouths of the furnaces outside the train window had scared Louis into a screaming fit, attracting an inspector examining passengers' papers. Miriam had distracted both Louis and the official by chattering Italian baby talk in her bell-clear Tuscan accent, and he had laughed and walked off without giving them trouble. For all her nightmarish fears, that had been the only narrow moment in leaving Italy.

A slow nauseating trip over stormy waters, and Elba loomed through the drizzle, a broad mist-shrouded hump of green. They disembarked on a windy U-shaped waterfront lined with old houses under a long frowning old fortress. On Frankenthal's instructions, Anna wore a white shawl and Natalie a blue one, and Aaron had a pipe in his mouth. A mule-drawn carriage driven by a gnarled old man drew up. He gestured at them to climb in, and he closed the carriage with very dirty canvas rain curtains. A long, long uphill ride ensued, with much bumping and sliding. Seen through isinglass panels, the hilly vineyards and farms were green blurs in fog. The air inside the canvas curtains was mildewy and close, the mule smell chokingly strong. The driver never spoke. Louis slept all the way. At last the carriage halted, the driver pulled back the curtains, and Natalie stiffly stepped down into a puddle, gulping the sweet damp country air. They were in the stone square of a sloping mountain village. There was nobody else in sight; not so much as a dog. Twilight was falling, the rain had stopped, the wet stone front of the old church looked violet, and the stillness was almost shocking.

"Where are we?" Natalie asked the driver in Italian. Her ordinary voice sounded like a shout.

He uttered his first word, "Marciana."

35

STABLEHANDS were grooming many neighing, stamping horses in the Bel Air Canyon Riding Academy, but no other riders were about except Madeline and Byron. Madeline's habit was bandbox-new: fawn jodhpurs, softly gleaming brown boots, mannish feathered hat. Byron wore Warren's Annapolis blazer with faded dungarees and sneakers. A withered groom in very dirty clothes, appraising him at a glance, brought out a large coal-black steed called Jack Frost. Byron adjusted the stirrups and mounted; whereupon Jack Frost, flattening his ears and redly rolling his eyes, took off up the canyon like a lunatic. He was a powerful animal with a smooth gallop, and Byron let him run free. Passing a white rag lying on the trail, Jack Frost reared, bucked, neighed, and snorted in a Hollywood enactment of acute panic. With some effort Byron stayed in the saddle. The horse, apparently concluding that he could ride, calmed down and glanced around at him inquiringly. Byron saw Madeline trotting along, far back on the trail, through Jack Frost's settling dust. "Okay, this was your idea, horse," he said with a kick. "Keep going."

Jack Frost lit out again, darted into a steep narrow switchback trail, and thundered up the side of the canyon in a hair-raising run to the summit, where he stopped short, head down, blowing like a whale. Shaken up and exhilarated, Byron got off, tied him to a tree, and perched on a rock. After a while he heard hooves scrambling below, and Madeline came in sight coated with dust. "What's with your horse?" she called.

"I think he wanted some exercise."

She giggled as he helped her off her mount. "I thought maybe he had a breakfast date in San Francisco."

They sat side by side on a wide flat rock, looking out over the canyon at sunlit wild hills. Lizards rustled on the rocks, and in the air below them vultures wheeled screaming. The horses stamped and puffed, jingling their harness. These sounds only heightened the prevailing hush.

Byron waited for her to speak. She had begged him to come on this ride, giving no reason. After a while he said, "Everything okay, Maddy?"

"Oh, Briny, I'm in a peck of trouble. But no! No!" She burst out laughing. "Your face! It's like a *teletype*, sweetie. Christ, did I ever get off on the wrong foot *that* time! I'm not pregnant, Briny. Put down that shotgun."

He scratched his head and managed a grin.

She shook a roguish finger at him. "Such evil thoughts about your own sister! No, it's a question of changing jobs, and"— she quickly lit a cigarette with a gold lighter —"it's something I can't discuss when Mom's around."

"Can you smoke here? I saw a sign about fire hazard in this canyon."

She shrugged, heavily inhaling. "You remember Lenny Spreregen?"

"I sure do."

"Universal's making him a producer. He wants me as an assistant."

"What about Cleveland?"

"Furious! Having kittens." She smiled at Byron. Her face was flushed, her eyes zestfully sparkled. "But I've got to consider it, don't I? Two hundred a week is a *beeg* jump from one fifty, you know."

"Why, that's munificent, Mad. And getting away from Cleveland sounds great."

Her face remained sweetly amiable, but the hard Henry note began to ring. "Oh, you've always underestimated Hugh, haven't you? The public *loves* him. Of course, making films beats selling soap and laxatives, but I have a sure thing where I am. Hugh's even given me a little stock ownership in his company. It's a really tough choice."

"Madeline, grab the job at Universal."

"Tell me one thing. Did Hugh ever do something to offend you? If so, it had to be unintentional. He thinks you're terrific."

"He doesn't know me."

"You know what? I bet it's that kiss he gave me in Janice's house. Isn't it?" She archly grinned. "I bet that still rankles. My God, when you told me you'd seen us, you had murder in your eye."

It was a memory Byron still preferred to blot out: the soft plump married man clutching Madeline to him, her skirt riding up behind, uncovering pink thighs and white garters. "Look, you asked for my advice. I gave it."

"Briny"— her voice softened —"Hugh Cleveland wants to marry me." Byron's face showed no reaction. She hurried on, blushing, *"That's* the complication. That's why I've got to talk to somebody. Mom's so straitlaced, she'd just fall over dead at the idea. Anyway, she has enough problems and — my, that's a grim silence, darling! But you don't know Hughie. He's *our kind*, honey, he's really a very intelligent, vulnerable, and lonesome man."

"Wife and three kids aren't that much company, eh?"

Madeline bitterly laughed. "That had to come, I guess."

"He's proposed to you?"

"Oh, darling, people don't *propose* nowadays." She waved a scornful hand. "Did you propose to Natalie?"

"I did, in so many words."

"Well, you're a weird old-fashioned type. All us Henrys are. Hugh's already working on his divorce."

"He is?" Byron got up and paced on the pebbly dirt with loud crunches. "You should be talking to Dad."

"Dad? Perish the thought. He'd visit Hugh with a horsewhip."

"Is he divorcing his wife because of you?"

"Oh, Claire, that's the wife, is just a horror, a total paranoid, a stupid woman he married when he was twenty-one. She's insanely afraid of losing him, yet she treats him like dirt. She's always running to psychoanalysts. She spends money like a duchess. Why, a year ago she was throwing fits about me, threatening I don't know what. He had to placate her with a sable coat. She is one unholy mess, Briny, take my word for it. And of course, she's turned his kids against him."

"Listen to me. Call Universal today." He halted and stood over her. "Tell the fellow you'll go to work for him Monday."

"I figured you'd say that." She looked up at him solemnly and her voice faltered. "I'm just not sure I can do it."

Feeling a wave of sickened, poignant sympathy for his sister, Byron said, "It's serious."

"Yes."

He spoke low. "How serious?"

"I *told* you." Her voice turned testy. "It's not a matter for horsewhips and shotguns. But it's serious."

He scanned her face, and heavily sighed. The gentle open look of the girl was as opaque as a leather mask. "How old is he?"

"Thirty-four." She glanced at her watch. "Honey, you have to pick up Mom and meet us in the Warner Brothers commissary at noon. Let's finish our ride."

"Maybe I'll talk to him at the studio."

The pretty leather mask faintly suggested wistful relief. "You? Whatever about?"

"About this."

Her mouth curled. "Shotgun in hand, sweetie?"

"No. If he wants to marry you, he should be glad to talk to me."

"I can't stop you. Do as you please." She put her foot in the stirrup. "Give me a leg up, Briny, we're late."

In the large, crowded, sunny cafeteria on the Warner Brothers lot, Rhoda gawked about, round-eyed, scarcely eating, saying things like, "Why, Maddy dear, isn't that Humphrey BOGART? — My stars, and there's Bette Davis! She looks so YOUNG off the screen."

Hugh Cleveland explained that though the stars had their own posh dining rooms, they liked to drop into the commissary now and then for a sandwich and a glass of milk. Like the stars, Cleveland was lunching in a dressing gown, his face painted up for filming. Byron disliked him again at sight, but his whimsical rumblings and chucklings clearly amused Rhoda, and his sleek happy air of success impressed her. Two radio shows — the old *Amateur Hour* and the military *Happy Hour* — were going strong, and the film shorts promised still more revenue. Madeline's hundred fifty a week was about twice Byron's submarine pay; and if she took the Universal offer she would be out-earning her own father, the captain of a heavy cruiser.

And for what? Watching the filming of a *Happy Hour* short after lunch, Byron was disgusted. The soldiers and sailors were the merest butts for Cleveland's supposedly spontaneous jokes, which were held up off camera on large printed placards. There was no audience. Later, Madeline explained, the director would splice in shots of attentive, laughing, or applauding onlookers. Byron couldn't believe that the films would be entertaining even if the fraud came off. Nothing was there but a radio announcer with a calculated folksy manner, poking condescending fun at untalented kids in uniform. The sights and sounds of show business, however low-grade, obviously enchanted his mother, and he was glad she had this distraction from grief; but as for him, he yawned and yawned until his jaws hurt, in an agony of irritated tedium.

A break came in the filming, and Cleveland approached them, grinning, with two paper cups of coffee. "You seem to need this more than I do, Admiral."

Madeline bustled up. "Mom, Byron! Humphrey Bogart is shooting on the next sound stage now. Want to watch?"

"Is it all right?" Rhoda asked eagerly.

"Of course."

"I'm DAZZLED by all this," Rhoda said, following her.

Cleveland said to Byron, who didn't stir, "Not interested?"

"Mr. Cleveland, can I talk to you?"

"What's up?"

"Madeline's told me about the Universal offer."

"Oh ho. Come along." Byron went with him into a plywood dressing room, and they both sat down on chairs by a lamp-bordered mirror. "Byron, don't let her take that job."

"Why not? It's more money."

"Lenny Spreregen's a passable screenwriter, but he's no executive. He's fast-talked himself into this thing. He's a communist, what's more, a notorious one. He'll never last at Universal, and the day he goes — bye-bye Madeline, broke and alone in Hollywood."

"She says you want to marry her."

"Oh, wow!" With a warm beguiling grin, Cleveland rubbed fingers in his back hair. "By the way, call me Hugh, won't you?" He looked at a cheap alarm clock on the dresser, swallowed coffee, and humorously rumbled as he stood up, "But let's not open that can of peas during a coffee break, huh, Admiral? How long are you going to be here?"

"My leave is up tonight." Byron rose, blocking the the narrow doorway. It was a casual act, but meanwhile Cleveland couldn't go out. "She says you're getting divorced."

Cleveland made a move toward the door, with a polite little gesture that Byron ignored. To leave he would have had to shove the submarine officer aside. His puffy face went sombre, then the charming grin with arched eyebrows reappeared. He rested a haunch on the dressing table, and rubbed his chin, looking quizzically at Byron's serious face. Rumpling his hair with both hands, he uttered a small groan. "Okay, Byron. Once over lightly, here goes. Claire, that's my wife, is a very unhappy and unfortunate woman. I'll say no more against her. We have three grand kids, but nothing else is left in common between us. Sexual interest is zero — not on my side. On hers. That's hell on earth, and I hope you never experience it. We've both been talking to lawyers, but these deals are messy and long. It's easy to get into marriage, but Christ on wheels, me lad, it's hard to get out."

"Do you love my sister?"

"You have a wonderful sister. She wasn't lying to you. I believe I can work this out, but it is one bitch of a bind. Now that's how it is, Byron." With his warmest radio chuckle, Cleveland stood up and lightly slapped his shoulder. "Back to the salt mine. Maybe the three of us can have a drink together later. Tell her not to take that Spreregen job, Byron. It's a stinker."

Madeline was rushing about outside, carrying a script board and talking to people over one shoulder and the other. She came darting to Byron, who leaned against a wall near the exit amid a snarl of cables and lights.

"Well?" It was a tone of mock conspiracy.

"Well, what? Where's Mom?"

"Oh, she won't budge. The director invited her to stay and meet Bogart. You talked to Hugh?"

"Oh, yes."

"Come on. What happened?" Her look was worried, excited, searching. "Did he get mad?"

"No."

She smiled. "No shotgun, then. He'd have blown his stack at that."

"Madeline, tell him you're quitting. Do it today. Hang it on me. Tell him I've got an insane temper. Tell him any goddamn thing you want."

Her face fell. "Did he deny that he wants to marry me?"

"He fudged. Quit, I tell you. If he's what you want, maybe that'll get him moving."

"Why, Byron Henry." Her eyes slyly narrowed. "That's how a girl thinks. Or should."

"And if he's stringing you along, you'll find that out, too."

She tossed her head, and the lithe hips in a pleated yellow skirt swished away.

In the villa, hours later, Byron was napping when a gentle knock at the door woke him. "Briny!" Madeline's voice, soft and excited. "Are you decent?"

Slant sunlight made big patches on the drawn red curtains: cocktail time. He sat up, stretching, naked except for shorts. "Oh, reasonably."

She swept in, and stood with her back to the closed door. "By Christ, I did it!"

"Great. Where's Mom?"

"I don't know. Not here. Briny, I never *dreamed* I could. It's incredible. I feel as though I've broken out of Alcatraz and swum ashore." The red glow through the curtains exaggerated the wild animation of her face. "And the way he took it! In a hundred years, I couldn't have predicted that. Byron, he was nice as pie! Utterly sweet! Not a harsh word! I'm in a daze. Can I have a drink?"

Byron put on a robe, and they went into the living room. He lolled on the couch, smoking, while she paced around and talked, highball in hand, yellow pleats flapping. She had done it in the dressing room, only an hour or so ago, upon finishing a review of the next day's script. Cleveland had been gentle, understanding, and not in the least surprised. "Oh, what a clever dog he is! You know what he said first thing? 'Well, kid, when you consulted your brother, that was it. That meant you already wanted to leave.' But, Byron — and this may really floor you — he says you're *right*. It's much better for me to get out while he pushes the divorce. Otherwise Claire could make real trouble about me. Thank Christ you came here."

"It's all set? It's definite? You've quit?"

"Absolutely. Isn't that terrific?"

"When do you go to work for this Asparagus person, or whatever?"

Madeline tried to hold her offended look, but her lips tightened and then she exploded in laughter. "*Asparagus!* Honestly, Byron, you're a sketch. What's so hard about Spreregen?"

"Sorry. When do you start with him?"

Still giggling, she said, "Next month. I called Lenny, he's agreed, and —"

"*Wait* a minute. Next month?" Byron sat up and swung his hairy naked legs to the floor.

"Sweetie, of course. I had to give a month's notice. I can't walk out overnight, that's childish." Byron crashed a fist on the coffee table so that books and ashtrays jumped. Frightened, Madeline raised her voice. "Oh, I can't *stand* you! How can you be so unreasonable? Could you or Dad walk off your ship without a replacement?"

Byron leaped to his feet. "Goddamn you, Madeline, are you comparing the garbage Cleveland does to what I do? To what Dad does? To what *Warren* did? I'll go see this fellow again."

"No! I don't want you to!" Madeline began to cry. "Oh, how ugly and cruel you can be! Did I mention Warren?"

"Hell, no, you haven't since I got here."

"*I can't bear to!*" Madeline screamed, shaking her fists at him. A storm of tears burst from her eyes. "And neither can you! Oh, God, why did you say that? Why?"

Rocked back by the outburst, Byron muttered, "Sorry," and tried to put an arm around her.

She pulled away, drying her eyes with a shaky hand. Her voice was tremulous but hard. "My work's important to me, Byron, and to millions of people. Millions! It's honest work. You're just bullying me, and you have no right to do it. You're not Dad. And even he doesn't have the right anymore. I'm not sixteen."

The door opened and Rhoda walked in, juggling large parcels. "Hi, kids, I've BOUGHT OUT Beverly Hills! Swept down Wilshire Boulevard like a typhoon! They'll be clearing the wreckage for WEEKS! Byron, I'm roasting, make me a nice tall gin and tonic, will you, dear?" She went on into her bedroom.

"Oh, Lord," Madeline muttered, wiping her eyes. She had turned her back as her mother entered.

"Go wash your face, Maddy."

"Yes. Fix me another drink, too. Strong."

In a new gay print robe, Rhoda soon looked into the kitchenette where Byron was mixing highballs. "Dear, are you really going back to sub school tonight? That's so awful. It seems I've barely laid eyes on you."

"I'll stay with you tonight, and drive down early. And I'll be back next Sunday."

"Oh, lovely! You and Maddy have brought me back from the DEAD, you truly have. In Washington I felt ENTOMBED. I've bought a RAFT of these California clothes, they're so smart, and light, and *different*. Amazing the stuff they've got out here, war or no war. It's a whole wardrobe for Hawaii. I intend to knock Dad's eyes out."

"You think you can get there?"

"Oh, I do. I do. There are ways and means, darling, and I'm absolutely determined — oh, thank you, pet. I may just dunk myself in the pool before I drink this."

Madeline said in a placating tone, when they were alone again sipping drinks, "Byron, will you really go to Switzerland after sub school? Will the Navy allow it?"

"I don't know. It depends on what I can find out from the State Department, and the legation in Rome. I won't start up with the Navy unless I have to."

She walked to his armchair, sat on the arm, and caressed his face. "Look, don't be so hard on me."

"Can't you quit in two weeks?"

"Trust me, Byron. You've been a big help. It'll work out, I swear." Madeline's voice shifted to loud cheerfulness as her mother came out in a bathing suit, carrying a towel. "Hey, Mom, big news! Guess what? I'm going to work at Universal Pictures!"

36

ARLY in August, in the American legation in Bern, the Jastrow-Henry case came to a sudden boil.

Dr. Hesse, Slote's friend in the Swiss Foreign Ministry, returned from Rome with the shocking news that Jastrow and his niece, having been granted the extraordinary privilege of a seaside holiday, had violated parole and vanished. A Jewish doctor from Siena, a secret Zionist, was involved. The Italian authorities were wrathful, and Dr. Hesse had been called in to the German embassy and asked what he knew. The roly-poly pink little diplomat was recounting all this to Slote in a sidewalk café, and half a chocolate éclair trembled on his fork as he described how he had told the German first secretary, a hard nasty customer named Dr. Werner Beck, to go to hell. The situation of Jastrow and his niece, in Hesse's opinion, was now hopeless. If they were hiding, they would be found; if they tried to leave Italy, they would be caught. On recapture, they would go straight to an Italian concentration camp. The government had confiscated Jastrow's villa, his bank account, and the contents of his safe deposit box.

Oh, God, thought Slote as he heard this upsetting tale, the same old Natalie, plunging headlong into incalculable risk, this time baby and all! He decided not to report this grave development to Natalie's mother or to Byron — who was writing him letter after letter — until he could find out more; and to do this, he decided, he would have to go to Geneva. There the big Jewish organizations, including the Zionists, had their Swiss offices. The American consulate dealt all the time with them; it had contacts too with the Jewish underground. He might learn nothing about the escape. On the other hand, one heard surprising things from the Jews in Geneva, and the information tended to be accurate.

It was through these contacts that the ghastly accounts of the German extermination camps were trickling in. Slote had been shutting his mind to these reports. After his failure to authenticate the Wannsee Protocol, and the strange death of Father Martin, he felt helpless, even threatened. Preserving himself and his sanity came first. Anyway, who was he to change history? Beyond the postcard beauty of the snowy Alps, there was not only a great war going on, but — he was all but sure — a vast secret slaughter. Meantime, the sun rose each day, one ate and drank, and one's desk was laden with work. There were diplomatic cocktail parties and dinner parties. War-time life wasn't bad in Bern, everything considered, and the town itself was so clean and quiet and charming! On the Zytglogge tower the little jester jingled the hours, the golden giant clanged the bell with his hammer, the puppets did their dance; in the bear pits the tame bears sadly stumbled through their waltzes for carrots. On days when the *Föhn* blew away the Alpine mists, the snowy Oberland ridge sprang into sight, white and pink and azure, looking like the approaches to Heaven. The only link to the terror beyond these pretty peaks was the permanent line of refugees with haunted eyes outside the door of the American legation.

Slote entrained for Geneva in a glum frame of mind. When he returned to Bern three days later, commercial work had piled up in his office. He ground through the heap with his secretary, grateful to be using his mind on rational matters. At the end of the day he declined a dinner with two other bachelors of the staff who had some visiting French ballet girls lined up. Telephoned at his flat by the married Swiss woman he now and then discreetly slept with, he stalled her off, too. After what he had learned in Geneva, petty sensualities seemed dirty to him. He ate some bread and cheese, then sank into an armchair with a bottle of Scotch.

What he had picked up about Jastrow and Natalie was only a vague third-hand report; still, it sounded plausible and cheering. Unfortunately, and unwillingly, he had also found out much more about the exterminations. The thought of resigning from the Foreign Service was circling in his mind, like a recurring slogan on an electric sign. Hard behind it there flashed the red reminder that he would at once be drafted into the Army.

Leslie Slote found himself reviewing his ambitions, his origins, his moral values, his hopes, in an agony of self-stripping, as before a decision to try a new career, or to give up a woman or marry her. He cared nothing for the Jews. He had grown up in a Connecticut suburban town where they could not easily buy homes. His father, a quiet philosophical Wall Street lawyer, had had no close Jewish friends. At Yale Slote had kept his distance from the Jewish students, and his secret society had tapped none. Natalie Jastrow's Jewishness had once seemed to Slote a flaw about half as bad as being a Negro.

Nor had he really changed. Now as always he was strictly out for himself, but by chance the Wannsee document had come his way. Because he knew German history and culture, what struck others as utter fantasy he believed to be true. Between the episode of the Minsk documents, and his stridency about the Wannsee Protocol, he was already suspect. If now he raised his voice about the new evidence, he would mark himself "Jew-lover" at the State Department for good. So Slote ruminated, sunk in his armchair, as the whiskey dwindled in the bottle.

Yet even the new Geneva evidence, though shocking and sickening, was not irrefutable. How could it be? *Where were the dead Jews?* Nothing surely proved murder except the *corpus delicti* — in this case great mounds of murdered people or mass graves full of them. How could one gain access to such proof? Photographs could be faked. There would never be irrefutable proof of this thing until the war ended; and then, only if the Allies won. The Geneva evidence, like the Wannsee Protocol, was only words: words spoken, words written, mixed with other words that were hysterical bosh, and still others, like the story of factories making corpses into soap, that were stale atrocity propaganda from the last war.

Slote could blame nobody for hesitating to believe in this weird gigantic massacre. Pogroms were an old story, but only a few people died in a pogrom. The Nazis did not bother to hide their persecution and looting of the Jews; still, they dismissed as Allied propaganda or Jewish ravings the ever-multiplying stories of secret murders in the hundreds of thousands. Yet these murders were happening, or at least Slote believed they were. The plan in the Wannsee Protocol was simply being carried out, in a grisly world of killers and victims as inaccessible as the unseen side of the moon.

Glass after glass of Scotch and water coursed down his throat, leaving a warm glowing trail, relaxing and comforting him, floating him above himself. Almost, he could look down like a released spirit at his skinny bespectacled self stretched on the chair and ottoman, and feel sorry for this clever chap whose future might be sacrificed for the goddamned Jews. How could he help it? He was a human being, and he was sane. If a sane man who knew about this insane thing didn't fight it, there was not much hope for the race of man, was there? And who could say what one man might not accomplish, if only he could find the right words to utter, to proclaim, to shout to the world? What about Karl Marx? What about Christ?

When a solitary boozing session got around to Marx and Christ, Slote knew it was running down. It was time to reel off to bed. He did.

Next morning he was in his shirt-sleeves, typing a letter to Byron Henry about what he had learned of Natalie, when his secretary came in, a fleshily sexy blonde girl named Heidi. Heidi kept flirting with Slote, but to him she was like a cream pastry in a skirt. "Mr. Wayne Beall from the Geneva consulate says you expect him."

"Oh, yes. Tell him to come in." He locked the letter in a drawer and donned his jacket. As Wayne Beall entered, Heidi made cow eyes at the handsome young American vice consul, a short man going very bald in front, but so straight-backed, flat-stomached, and bright-eyed that the bald brow didn't matter. He had dropped out of West Point on developing a heart murmur, but at thirty he still strode like a cadet, and kept trying to get back into the Army. Beall regarded Heidi's hind parts thoughtfully as she twitched out.

"You didn't bring your papers?" Slote closed the door.

"Hell, no, my hair stands on end to think of losing such stuff on a train. If the minister decides to act, I'll send him everything I've got."

"Your appointment is for ten o'clock."

"Does he know what it's about?"

"Certainly."

Beall's bald brow became corrugated with worry lines. "I'm in way over my head on this, Les. You'll join us, won't you?"

"Not a chance. I'm considered bonkers on this subject."

"Hell, Leslie, who considers you bonkers? You've read the files. You know who these informants are. You have a reputation for brilliance. I've never been suspected of that. Damn it, come along, Les."

Resignedly, and with a sense of foreboding, Slote said, "You'll do the talking, though."

The minister wore a Palm Beach suit and well-chalked white shoes. He was going to a garden luncheon, he said, so this interview would have to be a brisk one. He dropped into his swivel chair and keenly regarded with his living eye the two men sitting side by side on the couch.

"Sir, I appreciate your giving me this time out of your busy schedule," Beall began, somewhat overdoing the briskness in tone and gesture.

The minister made a tired deprecatory hand wave. "What new information have you?"

Wayne Beall launched into his report. Two hard separate confirmations of the massacre had come into his office from very high-level persons. From a third source, he had eyewitness affidavits of the mass murder process in action. He said this at length, with much talk about disaster, American humanitarianism, and the minister's wisdom.

Leaning his face on one hand like a bored judge, the minister asked, "What high-level persons gave you confirmation?"

The vice consul said that one was a well-known German industrialist, the other a top Swiss official of the International Red Cross. If the minister needed the names, he would try to get the gentlemen's consent to be identified.

"You've talked to them yourself?"

"Oh, no, sir! Neither one would level with an American official. Not unless they knew him very, very intimately."

"How did you get their reports, then? And how do you know they're authentic?"

With a trace of embarrassment Beall said that Jewish sources had given him the reports: the World Jewish Congress and the Jewish Agency for Palestine. Slote perceived the fall in the minister's interest: a wandering of the live eye, a slump of the shoulders. "Indirect reports again," Tuttle said.

"Sir," Slote spoke up, "what other kind can there be about a secret plan of Hitler's?" He could not keep irritation out of his voice. "As to this German industrialist, I spoke to the chap at the WJC myself, and he —"

"What's the WJC?"

"World Jewish Congress. He all but named the man. I know who he means. This man is very high up in German industry. I also read the file of eyewitness affidavits. They're substantial and shattering."

"And that's not the whole story yet, sir," said Beall.

"Well, what else?" The minister took an ivory paper cutter and slapped it on his palm.

Beall described how he and the British consul in Geneva had sent home identical coded cables about the new evidence, for confidential transmittal to Jewish leaders. The British Foreign Office had forwarded it at once to the designated British Jews, but the American State Department had suppressed the telegram. Now the Jewish leaders in both countries, besides being in a turmoil over the disclosures, were up in arms over the State Department's action, which had been found out.

"*That* I will look into," the minister declared, throwing the paper cutter down on his desk. "You'll be hearing further from me, Wayne, and now I'd like a word with Leslie."

"Certainly, sir."

"See you in my office, Wayne," Slote said.

When the door closed behind Beall, the minister said to Slote, looking at his watch and rubbing his good eye, "I've got to go. Now listen, Les, I don't like this business of suppressing cables. The Division of European Affairs puzzles me. It's already ignored two letters of mine, about the visa regulations, and about your photostats."

"You did write about the photostats?" Slote burst out. "When?"

"When the Polish government-in-exile's stuff came out. That gave me second thoughts. How on earth could they fabricate all that? The statistics, the locations, the carbon monoxide vans, the midnight raids on the ghettos? That business of searching the dead women's rectums and vaginas, for God's sake, for jewelry? How could anybody just imagine such things?" Slote stared dumbfounded at the minister. "But okay, let's assume the Poles are unreliable. Let's say they're blackening the Germans to cover their own misdeeds. What about that business in Paris? The Vichy police separating thousands of foreign Jews from their kids and shipping off the parents, God knows where! In front of news cameras, this was. Nothing secret about it. I got a YMCA report on the details. Just heartrending. That was when I wrote the department about your photostats, but it was like throwing a stone down a well. And the visa thing, Les, is just too much."

"Good God, I hope you mean the good conduct certificate!" Slote exclaimed. "I've been battling that nonsense for months."

"Exactly. I can't look these Swiss officials in the eye anymore, Leslie. We're not fooling them, we're simply disgracing our country. How can an escaped Jew produce a good conduct certificate from his hometown police in *Germany?* It's an obvious gimmick to keep the Jews piling up here. We're going to have to waive it."

Staring pallidly at Tuttle, Slote cleared his throat. "You're making me feel human again, sir."

The minister got up, combed his hair at a closet mirror, and fitted on his broad-brimmed straw hat. "Besides, the railroad intelligence is getting damned strange. These huge jammed trains really are hauling civilians from all over Europe to Poland, and then turning around and rattling back empty, while the German army's hurting for cars and locomotives. I know that for a fact. Something funny is going on, Leslie. I'll tell you something *entre nous.* I wrote a personal letter to the President about this business, but then I tore it up. We're losing the goddamned war, and he just can't be burdened with anything else. If these Germans do win, the whole world will become one big execution yard, and not just for Jews."

"I believe that, sir, but still —"

"Okay. You tell Wayne Beall to pull his material together. Go to Geneva and help him. Get that Red Cross big shot to put what he knows in writing, if you possibly can."

"I can try, sir, but these people are all petrified of the Germans."

"Well, do your best. I'll send the stuff straight to Sumner Welles this time. In fact, you may be the courier." The good eye sparked appraisingly at Slote. "Hey? How does that strike you? A nice little Stateside leave?"

Slote instantly recognized in such a mission the final ruin of his Foreign Service career. "Isn't Wayne Beall your man for that, sir? He's collected the stuff."

"The specific gravity isn't there. And he hasn't mastered this subject as you have."

"Mr. Tuttle, the car is waiting," the desk loudspeaker grated.

Tuttle left. Returning to his office, Slote heard merry laughter as he opened the door. Wayne Beall and Heidi stood there looking sheepish, and Heidi hurried out. Slote relayed the minister's instructions to Beall. "The sooner we get at it, the better, Wayne. The minister's hot on this at last, so let's keep up the momentum. Shall we go down to Geneva on the two o'clock train?"

"I just made a lunch date with your secretary."

"Oh, I see."

"In fact, Les, I thought I'd stay overnight, and —" He gave Slote a man-to-man grin. "Do you mind?"

"Oh, be my guest. We'll go tomorrow."

Soon Slote heard more laughter from the next room. One pretty girl on hand counted more than a million vague people suffering far away; nothing would ever change that fact of nature.

On his desk in the morning mail lay a formal report from Dr. Hesse, summarizing the Henry-Jastrow situation. Slote dropped it into a file marked *Natalie*, then tore up the unfinished letter to Byron. Perhaps good news would come in soon from some Mediterranean consulate, or even from Lisbon. For bad news there was always time.

37

PALMER FREDERICK KIRBY sat in shirt-sleeves at an old rented desk in a grimy office building near the University of Chicago campus, trying to finish a report before Rhoda's arrival by train. He was in a low mood; partly from dread of this encounter, partly because Vannevar Bush demanded facts and detested gloom in reports, and all the facts about the availability of pure graphite for a uranium reactor were gloomy. So was the weather. On this sultry gray August afternoon, opening the window admitted a gale off Lake Michigan warm as a desert sandstorm, and — what with Chicago's airborne dust and detritus — perhaps half as gritty; and shutting it gave him a gasping sense of taking a steam bath with his clothes on.

The graphite problem typified the grotesque enterprise in which Dr. Kirby was now passing his days. The languid trickling effort on uranium had become since Pearl Harbor a rising river of ideas, money, people, and problems tumbling along in murky secrecy. Kirby worked for the S-1 Section of Vannevar Bush's Office of Scientific Research and Development. To the initiated "S-1" meant uranium, but — and this was the root of his trouble — to everybody else it meant nothing. In his quest for materials and building sites, he could not beat out the tough procurement men from giant corporations and the armed forces. The Chicago scientists were blaming the repeated fizzling of their uranium reactor on the graphite, demanding purer stuff; but it was not to be had, and the large chemical firms capable of producing it were swamped with war orders from stronger bidders. This was the nub of Kirby's report to Bush, with some half-hearted optimistic suggestions to sugar the pill.

A telephone call from Arthur Compton at the Physics Department interrupted him. The Compton brothers were two crushingly brilliant men; this one had a Nobel Prize, the other headed the Massachusetts Institute of Technology. Kirby knew them both. He knew most of these dazzling physicists and chemists who were trying, at alarmingly wasteful cross-purposes, to make an atomic bomb before the Germans did. With some he had gone to school. They had not seemed much superior to himself at bull sessions and dances, or even in the laboratory; ambitious hardworking youngsters, as fond as he of girls, beer, and raw jokes. But in achievement they had pulled away from him like racehorses from a milkwagon nag. Being on first-name terms with them gave him no illusion of equality. On the contrary, it was a chronic sore in his ego.

"Fred, there's a Colonel Peters here." Compton, dry and direct as usual. "He'd like to come over and talk to you."

"Colonel Harrison Peters? Army Corps of Engineers?"

"That's the man."

"I just sent a stack of reports to him in Washington."

"He got them."

Kirby looked at his desk clock; Rhoda was arriving in two hours. This was how everything happened in the uranium project. "Tell him to come along, Arthur."

Soon Peters appeared, windblown and perspiring. Kirby seldom met men taller than himself, but Colonel Harrison Peters was one. The colonel was lean and long-skulled, with heavy graying hair, broad-shouldered, very erect; his grip was hard and his blue eyes were hard, too. Kirby gestured to his oversize armchair and ottoman. With a grateful sigh, Peters sank down, stretched out his legs, dusted his khaki uniform and pulled it straight, and clasped long muscular hands behind his head. "Thanks. This feels good! I've been on the go here since dawn. I've seen a lot, but I'm so ignorant that not much penetrates. You're a physicist, aren't you?"

"Well, I got my Ph.D. at Cal Tech. I'm an electrical engineer. A manufacturer, now."

"At least that's close, electrical engineering. I'm a civil engineer, West Point and Iowa State." Peters yawned, a picture of relaxed chattiness. "Bridge-building is what I do best, but I've done a lot of general construction. Also some hydraulics, with all the harbors and rivers stuff the Corps handles. But this high-powered physics is out of my line. I don't know what the hell I'm doing on this assignment. We'll be invading Europe or Africa or the Azores in the next six months. I've been counting on a field command. However" — the long arms waved wide — "*Befehl ist Befehl*, the Krauts say."

Kirby gave a short nod. "If you know German, that can be of use."

"Why, is there much literature on uranium in German? I can hardly make out the stuff in English. I was very grateful for your material. Reading it was like wiping a foggy windshield. I began to see where I was at."

"Glad it helped."

"Well, I still think somebody's crazy, Kirby, trying to play guessing games with triple-A priority materials, in the middle of a war, on a scientific riddle that may have no answer. I foresee nothing for myself but a knobby skull from butting stone walls. How's your skull?"

"All knobs." They both laughed, and Kirby added, spreading his hands, "I'm at your service."

Shoving the ottoman forward, Colonel Peters sat up, long legs crossed, elbows on the arms of the chair, fingers interlaced. Kirby, with his stocking feet up on the desk, felt a trifle sloppy under the big man's scrutiny. "Okay, Kirby. You and I have things in common." The tone now was curt. "We're both outsiders to chemical engineering and nuclear physics. We were both dragged into this thing. We both seem to have the same essential job, I on the Army side, you for this S-1 outfit of Vannevar Bush's. You've been in it a long time. I'd like to get some guidance from you before I plunge in."

"Ask me anything."

"Okay, now I've been travelling around the country getting a quick look-see at this whole undertaking. To start with, all these scientists grind axes like mad, don't they? Compton and his crowd here in Chicago are sure that this new Element 94, produced in a reactor, is the shortcut to the bomb. Only their reactor doesn't work; gets warm, then dies out. Dr. Lawrence's people out in Berkeley push electromagnetic separation of U-235. But they produce no U-235, with all that mess of big contraptions. The Columbia University crowd — and I take it, the British — think that diffusion is the way —"

"Gaseous diffusion, not thermal diffusion," Kirby put in with a chop of a flat palm. "Get that straight. Vastly different."

"Right. There's the Westinghouse thing, too, the ionic centrifuge. That makes the most sense to me, as an ignoramus. You've got two substances intermingled — natural uranium U-238 and the rare explosive isotope U-235. Okay? One's heavier than the other, so you spin 'em and get out the heavier one by centrifugal force. Cream separator principle."

"That one's pretty iffy, Colonel. Very complicated when you try to go to the large-scale mechanics. Ionized gas molecules don't act like butter fat." The colonel slightly grinned, and nodded in understanding. "I'm betting on gaseous diffusion myself," Kirby went on. "Simply because it's an established principle. Working with a corrosive gas like uranium hexafluoride you get into some nasty design problems, but there's no new concept to be tested. If you build enough stages and build them right — acres and acres of barriered chambers, I grant you, thousands of miles of conduits, and very difficult tolerances — you've *got* to end up with U-235. That magnetic separator of Lawrence's is a brilliant shortcut concept. I'm a Lawrence man, in fact a Lawrence worshipper, and my firm supplies him with high-performance equipment, but his whole idea just may not work. Nobody knows. It's a new principle. You're in green fields. Same thing with Compton's reactor. It has never been done anywhere on God's earth, unless the damned Germans have already brought it off."

"I spent two hours today," Peters said, "in that reactor setup under the football field bleachers. Ugly, sullen damned thing, this black heap towering to the ceiling, just standing there. Sooty technicians hovering around it, like devils fussing with a fire in hell that won't burn."

"Well put!" Kirby said with a sour smile. "There again, great concept. You nudge uranium with a neutron source and get it to splattering more neutrons around and splitting itself up. In theory if you design it right, you should get a chain reaction and blow up Chicago — except that the controls seem foolproof, so you just boil up a lot of heat and radiation and produce this new element, plutonium, that will also blow up with a hell of a bang, like U-235. That's what the pencil-and-paper gentlemen predict. Yet the thing keeps fizzling and dying out. Why? Nobody's sure. In a way I hope we're up against some fact of nature, some physical impossibility that nobody has discerned yet. That blank wall would stop the Germans, too. But is it really a solid wall? Or are we muffing the way through, while they're finding it? That's the damnable question."

"You rate gaseous diffusion first." Harrison Peters struck a stiff finger on the chair arm, as though to pin down Kirby's view.

"Yes, but I'm an ignoramus myself. We've got to assume the Germans are on all of these tracks, so we can't afford to bypass any of them. That's the position of the Office of Scientific Research and Development, so it's mine. I grind an axe too."

"Kirby, you keep looking at the clock. Am I keeping you?"

"I have to meet somebody at the Union Station at six. She hates to stand around waiting."

"Ah. A gal," said Colonel Peters. His smile turned to a goatish grin; he ran a hand along his handsome gray hair; his demeanor became charged with mischievous appetite. The Army brigadier general who had authorized Kirby to send Peters the secret reports had volunteered that "Big Pete" was a wild bachelor, with a plus score on pretty girls quite impressive in a man his age.

"Well, a lady," Kirby said.

"Good friend?"

"She's the wife of an old good friend. They just lost a son at the Battle of Midway, a naval aviator."

This wiped away, like a damp sponge swept over blackboard writing, the lecherous look of the colonel. His face went stiff and stern, his eyes clouded, and he shook his head. "That's rough."

"It's an all-Navy family. The father's commanding a cruiser, and another son's in submarines. She's been out on the West Coast, visiting the submariner and a daughter."

"Look, I won't hold you up then."

"I don't have to go yet."

"Can I pick your brain on one more point?"

"Shoot."

"If I understand it, the Army has come into this picture for the big production jobs. S-1 will carry on the experimental work, the pilot plants, and so forth."

"That's the general idea," Kirby said. "The Army should have been in long ago. I've learned *that* lesson, trying to get priorities for S-1. No corporation will pay attention to a pack of mad scientists with a secret Buck Rogers weapon, when the President's ordered sixty thousand planes a year, eight million tons of shipping, forty-five thousand tanks and God knows how many AA guns and shells. Yet this project begins to look like such a stupendous strain on this country's total resources, Colonel, that only the Army can handle it."

The colonel's eyes glinted. "Possibly, but won't S-1 and the Army be bucking each other? We'll want the same triple-A stuff, won't we? Won't you and I end up in a back-stabbing contest that I'll win, thus strangling your effort, which may be the key to the crucial advances?"

"Good question," Kirby replied, "but Vannevar Bush's uranium section can't last long now. The Army will soon take over in toto. I'm talking like a traitor, because Compton and Lawrence and company are having a great time running the whole thing themselves. Scientists have never played with such big chips. But at this point the problem is twenty percent theoretical science, and eighty percent industrial effort, a forced performance, Colonel, on a giant scale at top speed in dead secrecy." Kirby stood up, excited by his own words, and rapped the desk with a sweaty hand. "The muscle to ass-kick that performance out of American industry has got to come from the United States Army. In six months I'll be out of here, and glad of it. Maybe I'd better get down to Union Station now."

Peters got up too, stretching his great arms. "Are we going to make a bomb?"

Kirby put on a tie and a jacket as he replied, "Ask me some other time. Today I'm down. That black pile you saw, they just can't get it going. This has been happening for months. They try one thing and another, and now they're blaming the graphite. They say boron impurities absorb too many neutrons, so the thing fizzles out. You're going to be hearing a lot about neutrons, and —"

"My head's swimming with them now. Fast neutrons, slow neutrons — between two dunderheads, what the hell is a neutron?"

"If you're serious —"

"Sure I am. I'm ignorant as a horse about this stuff."

"It's a particle without a charge, in the nucleus of the atom. An Englishman named Chadwick discovered it in 1932. Neutrons are what radioactive substances give off. They can penetrate another nucleus and knock it apart into two other lighter substances. A couple of Germans did that first, back in

'39. That's splitting the atom, with a loss of mass and therefore a tremendous energy release."

"Einstein's law," Peters said, and he recited solemnly, as in a classroom, "*E equals mc squared.* I know that much."

"Okay. Neutrons aren't your job, of course. You'll just be looking at things like that dirty black pile and Lawrence's big electromagnet, all covered with dials and valves. Various Ph.D.'s and a Nobel laureate or two will yell at you for purer graphite or some bigger magnets or some other unobtainable thing. Someday something made out of uranium or Element 94 will probably go off with the biggest noise ever heard on earth. The smartest men alive think so. Whether it'll happen in our lifetimes, and whether we'll make that thing first — those are the crucial questions. If the Germans do it first, Hitler will shut down our effort rather rudely. And if they don't, and we don't make a bomb in time to use in this war — which is a real possibility, I assure you — well, Colonel, picture peace coming, and Congress learning that the Army blew in a few billion dollars on huge plants that produced a crock of horseshit. And start preparing your testimony."

Rhoda had spent two difficult hours in a swaying train compartment, grooming for this last encounter with the one guilty love of her life. Her charcoal shantung suit, a Beverly Hills purchase, set off her pretty figure with subtle charm; the purple hat added a sweet melancholy touch of color; gloves and shoes, still black. Her costume was appropriate for bereavement; also for an attractive widow getting ready to look around again. Two weeks of California sun and swimming had given her a rosy tan and cleared her eyes; and a nose veil so softened her features that a stranger might have taken her for a woman of thirty or so.

When a woman is about to discard a man — or to be discarded by him, for that matter — she often wants to look her best; arraying herself (so to say) for the last glimpse into the coffin of dead love. More prosaically, she simply prefers that he feel regret, not relief, if she can arrange it. The look on Palmer Kirby's face, when he first espied her at the train gate, rewarded her pains. Their talk in the taxicab was all about her family. Overshadowing Madeline's movie job was the news of Byron's orders to Gibraltar. He had telephoned it to her in great excitement from San Diego. His new duty, she supposed, was something hush-hush connected with submarines in the Mediterranean. He still meant to fly to Switzerland and work on freeing his wife and child; from Lisbon it was perhaps feasible, though Rhoda thought it a quixotic notion, and hoped they would get out of Italy before he tried it. Anyway, Byron had sounded happy, she said, for the first time since Warren's death. Those words slipped out. Then she and Kirby looked sadly at each other, and Rhoda turned away, her eyes watering.

The only hint of wartime in the famous Pump Room was the number of men in uniform, mostly bald or gray-headed colonels and captains. Expert waiters bustled about, chafing dishes flamed, rich roasts wheeled here and there, handsome bejeweled women devoured big lobsters, and the wine steward, clanking his brass tokens, hurried from table to table with bottles projecting from ice-filled buckets.

"We'll have wine, I suppose," he said to her when the waiter asked for their drink orders. "Would you like a drink first?"

"No wine tonight, I think," Rhoda returned with cool good cheer. "A very dry martini, please."

A long silence ensued between them, but the restaurant buzz made it tolerable. The drinks came. They lifted their glasses. Kirby shook his head, and spoke haltingly. "Rho, I keep thinking of the Berlin airport, the time you drove me there. I don't know why. There's no resemblance in the surroundings, God knows."

She peered at him through the veil, sipping at the martini. Delicately she put down the oversize glass. "That was a farewell."

"Well, we thought it was."

"Certainly I did," Rhoda sighed.

"Is this a farewell?"

Rhoda gave a slow bare nod. Her glance wandered away over the restaurant, and she began to prattle. "I once ate here with Pug, d'you know? We were on our way from San Francisco to Annapolis. BuOrd had stationed him in Mare Island to work on battleship turret design, and we were going back east for Warren's graduation from the Severn School. Ten years ago, I guess. Or is it eleven? All that's getting blurry." She stirred the martini, round and round. "You never know when you're happy, Palmer, do you? Imagine, I thought I had problems then! Byron kept failing in school. Madeline was fat, and her teeth were crooked. Big tragedies like that. Our house in San Francisco was too small, and on a noisy street. Dear me, I gave Pug a bad time about all those things. But how proud we were of Warren! He won the school sword, and a track medal, and the history prize — oh, hell." Her voice failed. She finished off her drink. "Please order me another, and then no more."

He signalled to the waiter for a second round, and said, slowly and gruffly, "Rhoda, let me speak my piece and get it over with. I won't embarrass you with a messy spill of my feelings. I have to accept your decision, and I do. That's all."

Rhoda's smile was sad and gentle. "Aren't you glad to be out of it, Palmer?"

"In your presence, I can't be."

Her eyes flashed at his intense look and tone. "A pretty speech, sir."

She held out her hand, and they shook hands as though sealing a bargain. "Well! Now I think we can enjoy our dinner," Rhoda tremulously laughed. "It would be a pity at that, wouldn't it, not to have a good time in the Pump Room?"

"Yes. Change your mind about the wine?"

"Oh, why don't you order us a half-bottle?"

"Hello, Kirby."

It was Colonel Peters, following the head waiter past their table with a tall girl in a green dress. Kirby knew her slightly by sight: a large colorless female who worked in Compton's office. Now her eyes were excited, her dark hair was piled up in a beauty-parlor do, and she was painted in a most nonacademic way. The green dress was a shade too tight on her lush figure. They sat down nearby, and Kirby and Rhoda could hear Peters jollying the girl. Their laughter rang across the noisy restaurant.

Over their dinner and the half-bottle of Chablis, Rhoda told Kirby of her plan to go to Hawaii, of the varying advice some admirals on the West Coast had given her, and of her intention to close up, and perhaps sell, the Foxhall Road house. Kirby made little comment, and the topic lapsed. They passed some of the time watching, with amusement and ironic remarks, the rapid progress of Colonel Peters with the green-clad girl. He clearly did these things by the book, using basic principles and tested materials: smoked salmon, champagne, shish kebab on flaming swords, crepes suzette, and brandy. The joking and the laughter of the couple seldom paused, and the girl was glowing with aroused delight. Peters had an eye for spotting the prey, thought Kirby, as well as skill at netting it. Kirby was not above a play for a secretary when he got lonesome, but he had never given this big Miss Chaney in Compton's outer office a second thought.

Rhoda's train did not leave until midnight. By ten they had finished the meal, and there seemed to be nothing else to do. In other days they might have gone to Kirby's apartment, but that was unthinkable. Their relationship had run out like a phonograph record; their chitchat was the last scratching of the needle. Rhoda was acting friendly, and she was even being lightly funny about Colonel Peters's amorous tactics; but woman to man, she had turned distant as a sister. There she sat, in an elusive way made more desirable than ever by time and by grief; an elegant quiet lady, so correct and serene that his irrepressible mental pictures of her naked in the throes of passion seemed indecent falsehoods, or contemptible peeks into a bedroom.

The Army man was leaning over Miss Chaney, whispering as he helped her out of her chair, and they were both laughing richly. They had no problem about what to do next, thought Kirby; but he was confronted with this problem of a remote woman for two more long hours.

"I'm going to suggest something strange, dear," Rhoda said, "and if you become cross, you'll distress me."

"Yes?"

"Did you see that little theatre in the Union Station that shows nothing but newsreels and cartoons? Let's go there. Or if you're terribly busy, I'll go, and you can get back to your work. Do you still sit up nights, writing reports about that horrible THING you're working on, whatever it is?"

"No, no, I have nothing to do." Rhoda's proposal would at least kill the time until midnight. "That sounds just right. I'm awfully full of duck and wild rice."

Colonel Peters stood alone in the restaurant lobby looking pleased with himself. He straightened when he saw Kirby and Rhoda, and his face turned self-conscious and solemn. Rhoda went off to the lounge.

"Kirby, is that the lady who lost a son?"

"Yes."

Peters made a grimace of incredulity. "You could have told me the naval aviator was her husband, I'd believe you."

"She's a handsome woman," Kirby said. "Your Miss Chaney's the surprise. I never imagined she could gussy herself up like that."

"Oh, Joan's not a bad sort. A lot of laughs. You know, Kirby, my nephew Bob went and joined the RAF in 1939. Army brat, twenty-one, couldn't wait to get into the scrap. Got himself killed in the Battle of Britain. My brother's only son. Wiped out the line, because I've never married. Bob was a fine boy, a splendid boy. It just about destroyed his mother, she's been in and out of sanatoriums ever since. Your friend seems to be handling it better."

"Well, she has other children. And in point of fact, she's a very strong woman."

Miss Chaney came out of the powder room, her hips swaying, her bust quaking under the shiny green silk. With a wolfish grin, Peters put out his hand to Kirby. "That was a good visit we had today."

"Any time, Colonel."

Miss Chaney wiggled her fingers at Kirby, and rolled her eyes. "Well, Dr. Kirby, so we meet in the Pump Room! Beats the Physics Department, doesn't it?"

"In every way I can think of," said Kirby. Miss Chaney accepted this as a salacious compliment, and went off on the colonel's arm in a flurry of giggles.

Soon Rhoda emerged. What a difference there was in women, Kirby thought; how it showed in the very way Rhoda stepped along and held her head. At a disadvantage of so many years, she was far more alluring than poor Miss Chaney. To Kirby the natural sway of her slim body was potent as ever, or more so. An intense notion struck him to fight this dismissal. He could look forward to only ten or fifteen more years. Without Rhoda they stretched ahead bleak as an Antarctic landscape.

But they went to the movie, and sat beside each other watching *Silly Symphonies*. Palmer Kirby, who had so often roughly taken this woman all naked in his arms to share raptures, now hesitated to take her hand. At last he did. Rhoda did not withdraw it, nor did she keep it unresponsively stiff or limp. But there was no sex in the clasp; Kirby was just holding a friendly hand. After a while, feeling foolish, he put it back in her lap. The three little pink pigs were gambolling on the screen singing, *"Who's afraid of the big bad wolf?"* and Palmer Kirby knew that he had lost Rhoda Henry for good.

She kissed him just once, standing on the steps of the Pullman car. It was a cool kiss, not quite empty of sex. She drew her head back, lifted her veil, and looked hard into his eyes. Her own were dry and rather glittery. He felt that she was savoring his regret, balancing off once for all the months when he had neglected her, the hesitation he had displayed over marrying her. The thing had oscillated back and forth but never had worked; it had always been wrong to cuckold another man, above all a fighting man in wartime. He was well served, thought Kirby, and he must face his Antarctic landscape.

"Good-bye, Palmer dear."

"Good-bye, Rhoda."

After Rhoda settled her things in her compartment, she walked up to the club car for a nightcap. There she came upon Colonel Harrison Peters.

38

I N Hollywood, Pamela had told Rhoda of her love for Victor Henry because
burning her bridges had seemed the best thing she could do, for both
these bereaved people. Now, sitting at her old portable, trying to start a letter to Victor Henry, it came very hard.

> Dearest Victor,
>   What is she doing in Cairo, do I hear you cry? I shall tell all, if heat pros-
> tration and a bout of Gyppy tummy don't finish me off first.

Slumped at the machine in a short shapeless Hawaiian flower-print, under
which she heavily perspired, Pamela paused over these jocose lines. The
heat and the damp seemed to be melting her bones. She had just ghosted an
article for her father, and she felt wrung out. After a long stare at the yellow
sheet, she ripped it from the typewriter, rolled in another, and began again,
shutting her senses as best she could to the street vendors' haunting wails,
and the spicy-fetid smells coming through the open french windows. Typing
hesitantly at first, she worked up to a rapid clatter.

> Dearest Victor,
>   We saw your son Byron almost a month ago in Gibraltar. I've been mean-
> ing to write you about it. In fact, he asked me to. Censorship is heavy on his
> ship, and he didn't want to entrust the news about his wife and son to some
> faceless snoop.
>   Perhaps by now he's gotten word to you, but if he depended on me, I'm
> sorry. We've been in an unrelieved rush since we got to Egypt. The climate is
> enervating, and as my poor plump father wilts — he's never at his best in the
> heat — I must take on more of the burden. In fact, he's shared a couple of
> recent by-lines with me.
>   I'll presume you haven't heard from Byron. He's on temporary duty with
> the Royal Navy, attached to *Maidstone*, a submarine depot ship (you call them
> "tenders"), servicing a flotilla which includes some old Lend-Lease S-boats of
> yours. He's there with other Americans to assist in maintaining the S-boats.
> Actually the *Maidstone* personnel are quite up to the job, he says, and he's
> fallen into sinfully soft and pleasant duty, including social forays to the Spanish
> side of the Rock. Of course food and bunks on a depot ship are of the best.
> Also, since the American mission on Gibraltar is chronically shorthanded, he's
> made some enjoyable air trips as a courier into unoccupied southern France.

He looks tanned and well, but he itches to get back to "the war," as he refers to Pacific operations, and he means to do so as soon as Natalie's situation clears up.

Now about that. Byron's information comes from Leslie Slote, who's now the political secretary at your legation in Switzerland. Some time ago, Natalie and her uncle disappeared from a seaside resort called Follonica, to the immense chagrin of the Italian authorities, who had extended very special privileges to them. Through contacts with Jewish organizations in Geneva, Leslie has ascertained that they may be making a run for Lisbon or Marseilles, aided by Resistance groups. All this has dissuaded Byron from attempting to go to Bern, where he could accomplish nothing, since the birds have certainly flown from Italy. Perhaps by now all has ended happily. At any rate, that was Byron's news a month ago.

It's always seemed passing strange to me, incidentally, that a son of yours married this girl, whom I knew long before I was aware you existed. Byron has much aged since I saw him in Hawaii. Removing the beard is part of it, for his mouth and chin are quite stern. The loss of his brother has hardened and thickened the texture of the young man. Less mercury than iron, now, one might say.

I should tell you, too, that we saw your family in Hollywood. Your wife said she would try to join you in Hawaii. I hope she has, and I must assume she's recounted a talk I had with her. Perhaps you're angry about that. It seemed to me that she'd better know there had been a risk of losing you. She asked me point-blank if we'd had an affair, so I told her. Whether she deserved your steadfastness is a closed question, but you should remember that for her the war when it broke out must have seemed the crash of everything.

That was how I felt in Singapore. Nothing mattered, *nothing*, with those snarling yellow men coming on. It was the worst moment of the war and of my life, until you returned from Midway; and I saw in your eyes what had happened, and felt that I was useless to you, and that it was over. That was worse.

Here in Cairo people are still rattled by the closeness of Rommel, but encouraged by your planes, tanks, and trucks pouring to our Eighth Army via the Cape of Good Hope, and on direct convoy past Malta. Talky has it straight from Churchill — Winnie flashed through here twice this month, raising a cloud of bloody nonsensical trouble — that all this is a drop in the bucket compared to the Niagara of equipment that you're flooding to the Russians. When or how your countrymen produce all this, I don't know. Your country baffles me: a luxurious unharmed lotus land in which great hordes of handsome dynamic people either wallow in deep gloom, or play like overexcited children, or fall to work like all the devils in hell, while the press steadily drones detestation of the government and despair of the system. I don't understand how America works, any more than Frances Trollope or Dickens did, but it's an ongoing miracle of sorts.

In London things are bad. The repair of the blitz devastation goes sluggishly. People drag themselves through the rubble in sticky weather on dwindling rations. Those in the know are frozen with fear of the U-boats. I'm not revealing secrets to you, I'm sure; Victor, they have sunk over *three million tons* just since you entered the war. In June alone they sank close to a million tons. At that rate you can't mount an attack against Europe, and we can't hold out much longer. The Atlantic's becoming impassable. It's a queer sort of menace, this invisible strangulation that shows up in thinner British bodies, fewer vehicles, sicklier faces, a general flavor of bad-smelling decay, and a creeping defeatism in Whitehall. There are mutters about coming to terms. When Tobruk fell, Churchill survived a no-confidence vote, but it was a red-light warning. Macaulayesque speeches won't keep him afloat much longer.

But bad as the surrender of Tobruk hit London, it was nothing to what went on here in Egypt. We missed the worst of it, but we hear it was like the fall of France. Rommel came roaring along the coast, all fueled up and rearmed with masses of stuff he captured at Tobruk. By the time he halted at El Alamein, two hours by car from Alexandria, government bureaus, military headquarters, and rich big shots were all fleeing eastward to Palestine and Syria in every available train and vehicle. Less-favored folk were clogging the roads on foot. In the cities there were strict curfews, empty hotels, abandoned streets and office buildings, looters, trigger-happy patrols, and all the rest. Little of this got past the tough censorship.

Things are less scary now. Some of the skedaddlers are sheepishly drifting back, but the more prudent ones are staying where they are. Obviously Rommel is retooling and gassing up for another try. There's little hope for a long respite, such as the Russians had once the Germans bogged down outside Moscow. It doesn't snow in Egypt.

Now, a little news about me, and I'll cease boring you. Duncan Burne-Wilke is in Cairo to take over the logistics of the air effort against Rommel. Unless I give him a discreet signal to desist, I suspect he's going to ask me to marry him. I saw quite a bit of him in London. Lady Caroline died of cancer a few months ago. I don't know whether you ever met her. She was a tremendous swell, most elegant, somewhat bossy and bristly, the daughter of an earl. Duncan married over his head, so to say, for he's "just" a viscount and his father, who made motor cars, bought the title.

The marriage hadn't worked well for a long time. In fact, Duncan once very sweetly proposed to me what we civilized Europeans call an arrangement. Well, I'm not very moral, but I've had my standards always. In all my misadventures (strike out Singapore) I've been passionately in love, or thought I've been. I was terribly in love with you at the time, you old iron man, and it would have been indecent to accept Duncan. The girls around the plotting table at Biggin Hill all sighed and languished after Duncan like a Gilbert and Sullivan female chorus, but the truth is I had no such feeling about him and I still don't.

Nevertheless, I suppose I must begin to think of what to do with my life. I can't go on and on with Talky; for I know he's failing. Duncan is a dear man, to be sure. I just don't see plunging into such a commitment now, though it would be ever so swanky a step up for me. Our family's respectable enough, in fact landed on my long-deceased mother's side, but I'm just a reasonably educated commoner, and my drawn face, alas, is my fortune. All that's fine, but Talky still needs me. We'll stay here for Rommel's onslaught, and I'm not looking past that. There's growing confidence here, based partly on Tommy At-kins's pluck, and partly on those heartwarming rows and rows and rows of olive-painted American trucks and tanks on the Alexandria wharfs.

Talky's slumbering noisily in the next room, having taken a sleeping ca-chet. Churchill's second whirl-through jangled and exhausted everybody. I must sleep, too. We leave before dawn tomorrow for Alexandria by train, and thence for a press-briefing by Montgomery out at his field headquarters. He's newly in command and opinions differ here about him. The buzz in the Shepheard's Hotel bar is about fifty-fifty pro and con; tactical genius, pompous eccentric showoff.

I really look forward to another trip out to the desert. Difficulties have been made about my gender, since the men strip naked out there to bathe in the sea, or wash, or just keep cool, and they perform natural functions casually. I was excluded from Talky's first trip, but he missed me and raised a great row, and now I go along. Presumably signals roll along the coast at my approach, "Female, take cover." I'm sure I'm a damned nuisance, but it's heartbreakingly beautiful out there — the glittering blue-green sea, the long white sand beach, blinding as snow, and then the slate-gray salt flats, the brackish lakes, the yellow and red sands of the desert dotted with brush — and oh, the sunsets and the clear starlit nights! The magnificent Australian troops stripped to trunks, bronzed as Indians! One of the rottenest aspects of this war, actually, is its beauty. Remember London on fire? And that tank battle in the snow we glimpsed in the distance outside Moscow, the flames from the burning tanks, reflected purple and orange on the mauve snow?

If not for the war what would I have been doing all these years? Some-thing dull in some dull London office building, or something domesticated in some suburban house or, with luck, town flat. And I would never have met you — an experience, which, with all its chiaroscuro, I treasure as the chief thing in my history.

I shall give this letter to a U.P. man who is going back to New York. He'll mail it to your Fleet Post Office address, so you should get it soon. Victor, if it isn't unreasonable I should like just a word from you that I have your blessing if I go on with Duncan. I myself thought silence the best way to close out our beautiful but guillotined relationship, but then I did have to write you about Byron, and I feel most enormously happy and relieved. You too may feel better writing to me, however briefly. I think we understand each other, though we had to part before we could explore the depths.

My love,
Pamela

The U.P. man did bring this letter to New York, and it entered the complex Navy system for delivering mail to the far-flung ships at sea. Gray sacks for the *Northampton* followed the cruiser all over the Central and South Pacific; but the letter never caught up before the ship went down off Guadalcanal.

*   *   *

39

Global Waterloo
1: Guadalcanal

(from *World Holocaust* by Armin von Roon)

November 1942! No German should ever hear that month mentioned without shuddering.

In that one ill-omened month, four concurrent disasters befell our brief imperium: two in North Africa, one in Russia, one in the South Pacific. On November 2 the British offensive at El Alamein, begun in late October, sent Rommel's Afrika Korps reeling out of Egypt, never to return. On November 8 the Anglo-Americans landed in Morocco and Algeria. From November 13 to 16, the tide turned at Guadalcanal. And on November 19 the Soviet hordes broke through at Stalingrad and began cutting off our Sixth Army.

Historians tend to miss the awful simultaneity of the fourfold smashup. Our German authors harp on Stalingrad, with casual treatment of the Mediterranean and silence on the Pacific. The communist pseudo-historians write as though only Stalingrad was happening then. Winston Churchill dwells on El Alamein, a minor textbook battle, decided by the lopsided British advantage in Lend-Lease supplies. The U.S. writers stress their walkover in French North Africa, and strangely neglect Guadalcanal, one of America's finest campaigns.

The Global Waterloo was in fact a swift, roaring, flaming reverse all around the earth of our war effort, history's greatest — on the seas, in desert sands, on beaches, in jungles, in city streets, on tropical islands, in snowdrifts. In November 1942, the world-adventurer Hitler, to whom we Germans had given our souls, lost the initiative once for all. Thereafter the hangmen were closing in on him, and he was fighting not for world empire but for his neck.

Militarily speaking, the situation even then was retrievable by sound military tactics, and we had great tacticians. Manstein's classic fighting withdrawal from the Caucasus after Stalingrad, to cite but one instance, will find a place one day in history with Xenophon's march to the Black Sea. But Hitler as warlord could only go on compounding his own pigheaded mistakes. Since nobody could loosen his terror-grip on our armed forces, he dragged the German nation down with him.

The Far Reach of the Third Reich

To understand Hitler's swollen pride before his fall, one must picture Germany's situation before November 1942.

For the modern-day German reader, this is difficult. We are a cowed people, ashamed of our mighty though Faustian past. Our defeated and shrunken Fatherland is sundered. Bolshevism bestrides one half; the other half cringes to the dollar. Our economic vigor has revived, but our place in world affairs remains dubious. Twelve brief years of Nazi mistakes and crimes have eclipsed the proud record of centuries.

But in the summer of 1942, we were still riding high. On the eastern front, the Wehrmacht was rebounding to the attack. After storming Sevastopol and clearing the Kerch peninsula, we were thrusting two gigantic armed marches into the Soviet southern gut; one across the Don toward the Volga, the other southward to the Caucasus oil fields. Stalin's armies were everywhere fading back before us with big losses. Rommel's stunning capture of the Tobruk fortress had opened the way to the Suez Canal and had all but toppled Churchill.

Our comrade Japan had won Southeast Asia, and in Burma was advancing to the borders of India. Her grip on prostrate China's coastal provinces was solid. Her defeat at Midway was shrouded by the fog of war. Her armies were still triumphing wherever they marched. All Asia trembled at the shift of world forces. India was rent with riots. Its Congress voted for the immediate withdrawal of the British, and an Indian government-in-exile was forming to fight on the Japanese side.

In Arctic waters, with the famous rout of the PQ-17 convoy at the end of June, we severed the Lend-Lease supply route to Murmansk, a body-blow to the already staggering Red Army. This defeat epitomized the British decline at sea. The convoy screening force, warned that our heavy surface ships were approaching, ordered the merchant vessels to disperse and hightailed it home to England! The shades of Drake and Nelson must have wept in Valhalla. The slaughter that ensued was mere rabbit-shooting by our aircraft and submarines. The cold seas closed over twenty-three merchant vessels out of thirty-seven, and one hundred thousand tons of war matériel, with much loss of life. Churchill's shamed message to Stalin cancelling the Murmansk run brought an angry Slav howl. The grotesque alliance of capitalism and Bolshevism was sorely strained.

On the visible evidence, then, we were triumphing in the summer and autumn of 1942 against all the odds, even with the United States thrown into the balance against us, even with all of Hitler's miscalculations.

———————

TRANSLATOR'S NOTE: *The Murmansk run was suspended during the summer months of long Arctic daylight, then resumed. In December, British destroyers escorting another convoy outfought a German task force, including a pocket battleship and a heavy cruiser. Hitler waxed so wroth at this fiasco that he ordered the fleet scrapped, and the guns put to use on land. Admiral Raeder resigned. Dönitz took over, but the German surface fleet never recovered from Hitler's tantrum.*

Roon's appreciation of Guadalcanal which follows is detached and reliable. No Germans were fighting there. — V.H.

The Pacific Theatre

All of Europe from the Bay of Biscay to the Urals could be sunk without a trace between Honolulu and Manila, yet the Pacific campaigns were fought over far greater distances than that. Unheard-of military space, unprecedented forms of combined land, sea, and air combat: such is the fascination of the Pacific conflict. The period in history when such operations were feasible came and went quickly. A high point was the six-month melee which raged in the skies, on the water, under the water, and in the jungle, for the possession of a small airfield that accommodated sixty planes: Henderson Field on Guadalcanal.

Guadalcanal is a neglected campaign, a small Pacific Stalingrad swirling around that landing field. Had it been a British victory, Churchill would have written a volume about it. But Americans are apathetic toward their military history. They lack the European sense of the past, and writers of broad culture.

In my restricted research* I have yet to come upon an adequate relating of the Stalingrad and Guadalcanal campaigns, but one might say that the Second World War turned on those poles. We reached the Volga just north of Stalingrad in August. The Americans landed on Guadalcanal in August. General Paulus surrendered at Stalingrad on February 2, 1943; the Americans secured Guadalcanal on February 9. Both battles were desperate and successful defenses of a waterfront perimeter: the Russians with their backs to the Volga, the Americans on a beachhead with their backs to the sea. Both battles were head-on clashes of national wills. With both outcomes the tide in a war theatre turned, for all the world to witness.

German readers must never forget that the war had a global dimension. We are obsessed with Europe, and that is how the Bolshevik historians also write. But under Adolf Hitler's flawed but kinetic leadership, our nation broke the ice of the entire world imperial system. For six years a world storm raged, and all was fluid. The land masses of the planet, fifty-eight

*General von Roon wrote in prison. — V.H.

million square miles of real estate, were at hazard. The Asian samurai surged forward to form an alliance with the Nordic soldier, seeking a just redistribution of the earth's habitable surface. That two martial showdowns should simultaneously explode on two sides of the globe therefore lay in the nature of this wrenching world convulsion. The stunning halt of the Japanese onrush at Midway resembled our halt before Moscow in December 1941. These were chilly warnings. But the fatal crunches came later and in parallel, at Stalingrad and Guadalcanal.

The differences of course are substantial. If we had defeated the Red Army at Stalingrad, history in its present form would not exist; whereas had the Americans been thrown off Guadalcanal, they would probably have returned later with new fleets, air groups, and tank divisions, and beaten the Japanese elsewhere. Stalingrad was a far vaster battle, and more truly a decisive one. Still, the parallels should be borne in mind.

Admiral King

It was a wheeze in the American navy that Admiral Ernest King "shaved with a blowtorch." A naval aviator with a long record of achievement, including the raising of a sunken submarine in the open sea, King had been put out to pasture on the General Board, an advisory panel for old admirals with no place to go. His cold driving personality had not made him loved. He had bruised egos and damaged careers. Shortly after Pearl Harbor, Roosevelt appointed him Commander-in-Chief of the United States Fleet. King is said to have observed, "When things get tough they send for the sons of bitches." In the Wehrmacht, alas, when "things got tough" the Führer sent for the sycophants.

Besides the problem of the rampaging Japanese, King had to contend with the fixed Roosevelt-Churchill policy, *Germany First*. The Combined Chiefs of Staff were neglecting "his" war in favor of the bigger conflict. King's cold-blooded solution was the attack on Tulagi, which evolved into the Guadalcanal campaign.

Japanese War Aim

Despite some blustering rhetoric, the Japanese were not seeking to crush the United States of America in war. Their aim was limited. In their view, Southeast Asia was none of America's business. Thanks to our conquest of Europe the time had come to throw out the imperialist exploiters, and to found a peaceful Greater East Asia for the Asians, including a pacified China; a so-called Co-prosperity Sphere under Japanese leadership, friendly to the coming world master, Germany.

Their military aim was a quick conquest of the desired areas, then a tough perimeter defense on interior lines. The hope was that the far-off prosperous Americans would tire of a costly war in which they were not very interested, and would make a face-saving peace. This might well have worked, except for the attack on Pearl Harbor, which roused in the proud Yanks, and especially in their fine navy, an irrational cowboy thirst for frontier vengeance.

———————

TRANSLATOR'S NOTE *to the third edition, October 1973: The Viet Nam experience is making me wonder whether Roon is not absolutely right about this. — V.H.*

———————

American War Aim

On the other hand, for twenty years the United States Navy had been plotting to destroy Japan if American hegemony was ever challenged by "the yellow peril." Assuming the Japanese would be maneuvered into striking first, their war games had produced a cut-and-dried plan of counterattack. After the war, as has been said, Chester von Nimitz claimed the U.S.A. had won the war along the exact lines planned at the Naval War College. The plan was:

1. *Hold a line of communication to the main forward bases in Australia and New Zealand, with installations along a curve of islands outside Japanese aircraft range.*
2. *Batter northward through the archipelagoes of the southwest Pacific in flank attack.*
3. *Thrust the main assault westward across the Central Pacific atolls, in an island-hopping strike toward Luzon and Japan.*

But King had trouble getting enough force in his theatre to execute the plan. General George Marshall, the Chief of Staff of the United States Army, an able planner and organizer, was adamant on "Germany First," and a full-scale invasion of France in 1943. He wanted to concentrate on an immediate buildup in England of American manpower and matériel.

Happily for King, all the British leaders from Churchill down kept waffling on the invasion. They remembered the Somme and Dunkirk all too well. In July 1942, Marshall in great disgust therefore recommended to President Roosevelt that the Americans throw their weight into the Japanese conflict. King seized this favoring moment to push the execution of a quick modest aggressive move in the Pacific: the capture of a Japanese seaplane base in the Solomons, the small island of Tulagi. Though already authorized, the Tulagi operation had stalled in an army-navy argument over supreme command. Now it went forward, with a complicated deal on command, which temporarily dodged the impasse. Soon afterward the American and British war planners settled on the North African landings called

"Torch," but King's operation meantime went ahead. It was called Operation Watchtower. His forces were so meager that in the field they dubbed it Shoestring.

TRANSLATOR'S NOTE: *I omit here a long Roon analysis of the conflict between the Army and the Navy over the Pacific command issue and the Tulagi idea. MacArthur wanted to try a more ambitious shot, the capture of the big Japanese air base of Rabaul. Roon comments, "Vanity of leaders can divert or wreck campaigns. The divided command problem between MacArthur and Nimitz haunted the Pacific war and resulted in the stupendous botch at Leyte Gulf." In a later chapter I include a controversial essay by Roon on the Battle of Leyte Gulf. — V.H.*

First Blood

Combat preparations for taking Tulagi were well along, when a coast-watcher intelligence report greatly raised the stakes of the operation. Only a few miles from Tulagi, the Japanese were building an airfield on the large island of Guadalcanal.

This was explosive news. Pacific combat turned on local air superiority, and air power meant either carriers or airfields in the battle zone. Flattops could move about, bringing power where needed; also, they could flee from strong threats. On the other hand, airfields were unsinkable, and land-based planes could fly farther than carrier aircraft, with heavier bombs. An operational airfield was the strongest piece in Pacific chess.

Seven hundred miles northwest of Guadalcanal, the Rabaul air base threatened the line to Australia and barred an advance toward Japan. Hence MacArthur's dashing plan, which King had vetoed, to strike there. But an airfield as far south as Guadalcanal was a menace King could not accept. Denying it to the foe, he would gain local air superiority in the Solomons, and American airpower could trade punches at long range with Rabaul. Shoestring forces already embarked received added orders: *Capture and hold the Guadalcanal airfield.*

And so America sidled, as it were, into its most arduous Pacific campaign.

Guadalcanal itself, a potato-shaped island a hundred miles long and half as wide, was never the prize. For months the land fighting raged along a narrow plantation strip of the northern coast flanking the airfield. The rest of the mountainous island was left to the mosquitoes, the jungle wildlife, and the natives, who were probably both frightened and entertained by the noisy flaming fireworks along the north shore.

The small, ill-equipped Shoestring expedition had little trouble capturing Tulagi and the Guadalcanal airfield, but the severe counterstroke from nearby Japanese bases came fast. In a night action called the Battle of Savo Island, Japanese warships sank the entire U.S. fire support force, four heavy cruisers, and departed unscathed. They could have finished the job and extinguished Shoestring by sinking the helpless half-emptied transports, but they had to assume that American aircraft carriers were steaming close by in the darkness and would attack at dawn. So they left, giving the Americans the brief breathing spell that saved their campaign. In war, when a strong enemy is down, one is well-advised to cut his throat. In point of fact, Vice Admiral Fletcher was out of combat range with his carriers, preparing to fuel. Fearing air attack from Rabaul, he had left while the transports were still unloading.

Reprimanded by King earlier in the war for lack of aggressiveness, missing his chances in the Coral Sea, failing to launch all aircraft at once at Midway, Fletcher's career seems to have had one good moment: when he signalled Spruance at Midway, *I will conform to your movements.* By abandoning the transports at Guadalcanal he nearly lost the campaign at the outset. Whenever danger impended, this admiral seems to have been seized by an uncontrollable urge to steam away a couple of hundred miles and fuel. He fades from sight after Guadalcanal.

———————

TRANSLATOR'S NOTE: *Roon continues to make a goat of Frank Jack Fletcher here. My cruiser* Northampton *missed the Battle of Savo Island, but I know that the Japanese leadership, gunnery, and torpedo fire were good at Savo, and ours were miserable. That was why we lost four cruisers. It is true that Fletcher might have struck a counterblow, and that his retreat was conservative. — V.H.*

———————

Land Operations August 1942–February 1943

Like their navy, the Japanese army seems to have been plagued by overconfidence; probably they wrote off Midway as mere navy ineptness. After all, white men had yet to defeat the Japanese on land. Busy with plans to assault New Guinea and threaten Australia, the army committed troops only piecemeal to Guadalcanal, not enough and not adequately supported; and the United States forces formed a perimeter around the airfield, often dented but never broken by wild and bloody *banzai* charges.

Still, for a long time it was touch and go for the Americans. In effect they were stranded. Air bombardment, naval shelling, enemy night attack overland — and above all, malaria and other tropical illnesses — decimated them. Their weakened navy could sneak in only scanty supplies and reinforcements. Hungry, thirsty, feeling forgotten and abandoned, they lived off captured Japanese rice, and burned Japanese gasoline. The few fresh aircraft and pilots that slipped in were quickly worn down or shot down. On one black day, Admiral Halsey's account avers, there was *one operating aircraft* on Henderson Field. President Roosevelt began publicly talking of Guadalcanal as a "minor" operation, a most ominous and pusillanimous signal. But the beleaguered marines and exhausted airmen clung to the perimeter until the tide turned.

In view of the poor record of American soldiers elsewhere, this epic defense of Henderson Field is striking. These defenders were marines, the navy's elite amphibious combat corps. The words of the American naval historian, Samuel Eliot Morison, perhaps explain all: *Lucky indeed for America that in this theater and at that juncture she depended not on boys drafted or cajoled into fighting but on "tough guys" who had volunteered to fight and who asked for nothing better than to come to grips with the sneaking enemy who had aroused all their primitive instincts.*

TRANSLATOR'S NOTE: *Roon's slurs on our army are intolerable. The Germans never won a victory against us in two wars, if one ignores the brush at Kasserine Pass. We even won the Battle of the Bulge. We marched to the Elbe. We could have taken Berlin, had the Allies not already agreed that it would belong in the Russian occupation zone.*

Considering our social and political background, and the traditional distaste of Americans for war, our soldiers became damned good. They were irreverent and ingenious, they had initiative, and they fought hard without hate. Roon's mentality cannot absorb American combat policy, which is quite simple and non-European: to lose as few lives as possible, yet win battles and wars.

Morison does get carried away by Guadalcanal, where the United States Marines in truth put up one hell of a show. —V.H.

Battle at Sea

At sea, the war took on a bizarre form. The sea mission of both sides was support of the troops fighting for Henderson Field. Holding the field, the Americans controlled the daylight hours, when their supply ships could move under the thin air umbrella. But the Japanese, with a much stronger surface force, traversed the Solomons in the darkness so regularly that the Americans called it the "Tokyo Express." Though missing each other in this alternation of night and day maneuvers, the two navies had numberless brushes, and the Japanese generally had the better of this fighting. But the

Americans won the one all-out clash that counted, the Battle of Guadal-canal.

This was a diffuse four-day explosion of carnage at sea by day and by night. Both sides threw in almost everything they had; the Japanese, to land at last a massive troop reinforcement, the Americans, to prevent it. Eyewitness accounts tell of eerily picturesque nocturnal sea fights: red tracer showers in the darkness, blue-white searchlight beams stabbing for miles, detonating ship's magazines turning night into day, flaming ships drifting over wide areas of black waters. The losses on both sides were high. In the end only one thing mattered: American airplanes, carrier and land-based, sank seven out of the eleven Japanese troop transports, while the rest were driven up on the beaches and bombed to burned-out hulks. So ended the last Japanese try to retake the island.

Thereafter, as the American forces built up, the Mikado's troops became the stranded ones. In the end the Tokyo Express brought off this harried remnant in a tropical Dunkirk. But Japan had no rich and idle major power to come to her rescue, as England had had. She never recovered from Guadalcanal.

Admiral King had accomplished his purpose. The marines cursing and sweating under Japanese fire in the tropical night, the airmen spinning to their deaths, the naval officers and men whose bones litter the sea bottom off Guadalcanal, doubtless died damning the higher-ups who had sent them against such odds to such an out-of-the-way place. In the vulgar talk of American fighting men, Guadalcanal was and remains "*that fucking island.*" But war theatres tend to be self-generating, and once King had committed Franklin Roosevelt to the Pacific with Guadalcanal, he was assured of enough men and ships to fight the Japanese while our beleaguered Third Reich was going down; not afterward, when the Japanese would have been entrenched and the Allies war-weary. King may have, in this way, deprived Japan of the negotiated settlement that was her war aim.

TRANSLATOR'S NOTE: *Roon puts the above vulgarism in quotes in English. Considering the language prevalent in current literature I think the readers of this volume will not be too outraged. Incidentally, that remains my own exact opinion of Guadalcanal.*

In view of his biting criticism of Admiral Halsey later on in the Leyte Gulf chapter, I wish Roon had given him his due here. The turnabout in the Guadalcanal campaign occurred when Halsey relieved Vice Admiral Ghormley as ComSoPac. Fatigue had made Ghormley a defeatist, and MacArthur's spirit was down, too. Halsey's belligerent and inspiring leadership got everybody going again. — V.H.

*   *   *

40

NATALIE had pictured a flight via an "underground railroad" as something swift, organized, secretive, hairbreadth, and romantic. All they did in Marciana was wait for a very long time, not communicating with anybody, not even with the villagers. The little walled hamlet of old stone cottages, straggling along a spur halfway up Elba's highest peak, was picturesque and pleasant enough. The fugitives might have come for a rusticating vacation, except that they weren't paying.

This delay wore on and on. Castelnuovo seemed unconcerned. He had told Natalie and her uncle little about the plan of escape or the people helping them, and she could understand that. The less she knew, if they happened to be caught, the better. Once when they were alone — almost a month had then passed — he remarked, "Look here, Natalie, everything is all right. Just don't worry." She tried not to.

They were housed in a tumbledown cottage of stone and cracked plaster at the end of a steeply climbing alley, which beyond the house became a donkey path through terraced truck gardens and vineyards; where, from sunup to sundown, silent villagers harvested, loading little donkeys with produce and sometimes riding them about. The views were magnificent, though the villagers ignored them as they ignored the newcomers: off to the west the crags of Corsica poking above the water, eastward a hazy line of mainland ridges, north and south green islands of the archipelago, like Capraia and Montecristo, with their little wreaths of cloud; and down the mountainside the blue sea breaking on the wooded coast dotted with fishing villages. Natalie passed much time climbing around up here among the gardens and orchards, enjoying the panoramas, the birdsong, and the sight and fragrance of September fruits and flowers.

During the first week a fat very ugly girl, who had more warts than words, brought them net bags of vegetables and fruit, coarse bread, goat's milk and cheese, and sometimes fish wrapped in wet seaweed. After that Anna Castelnuovo foraged and shopped in the small marketplace. If rationing existed on Elba, there was no way of knowing it in Marciana; if there were *carabinieri*, they were incurious about the mountain towns. Natalie's edginess faded. The cottage had only two dark moldy-smelling rooms — one for the Castelnuovos, one for herself and her uncle — with an outdoor privy, and a wood-burning stove layered with black grease. She had to fetch water in pails from a communal pump, sometimes standing in line with barefoot children, and she slept on straw. But she and her baby were free from the menace of Werner Beck in a quiet remote hideout. For the time being, that was enough.

Aaron Jastrow took to the halt with philosophic placidity. Old Sacerdote had given him as a parting gift a mildewed Bible in Hebrew and Italian from the Follonica beach house. All day he sat on a bench under an apple tree with this Bible and his dog-eared Montaigne. Toward evening, he would walk out on the donkey paths. He seemed to have shed, with his tight work routine, his irritating traits. He was calm, undemanding, cheerful. He was letting his beard grow out, and looking more and more like an aging peasant. When Natalie one sunny morning late in September fretted to him about the inaction he shrugged and said, "Would you mind waiting out the whole war on Elba? I wouldn't. Unlike Napoleon, I've no delusion that the world greatly misses or needs me."

The Bible was open on his lap. She peered at the pages of heavy Hebrew lettering and old-fashioned Italian print, all stained and mottled with time and sea damp. "Why are you reading that, exactly?"

"Aristotle said" — Aaron faintly grinned — "that in his old age he became more interested in myth. Care to join me?"

"I haven't studied Hebrew since I walked out of the temple's Sunday school when I was eleven."

He made room on the bench. She sat down, saying, "Oh, what the hell, why not?"

He turned the book to the first page. "Do you remember anything? Read."

"Let's see. That's a *B. Beh-ray-shis.* Right?"

"Summa cum laude! 'In the beginning.' Next?"

"Oh, Aaron, I'm a dolt at this, and I'm really not interested."

"Come now, Natalie. If you don't like to learn, I like to teach."

Heavy double knocks at the wooden door.

A young man smiled at Natalie in the doorway, stroking a droopy black mustache. The pudgy olive face was insolent and uncultured; the brown eyes took her in with a gleam of appetite; the baggy corduroy trousers and short red jacket were like stage clothes. *"Bonjour, de la part de Monsieur Rabinovitz. Prêts à partir?"* Strange harsh accent.

An open hay wagon blocked the alley, hitched to a bony mule twitching long ears.

"Eh? Partir? Tout de suite? Je crois que oui, mais — entrez?"

He shook his head, grinning. *"Vite, vite, je vous prie."*

Castelnuovo sat at the table with the others in the back room, eating the monotonous daily lunch of bread and vegetable soup. "Good!" He wiped his mouth and stood up. "I've been expecting him for a week. Let's pack up."

Aaron said, "Who is he?"

The doctor made a vague gesture. "He's a Corsican. Please hurry."

The fugitives bumped downhill for hours in the slow wagon, heading west. Miriam and Louis larked about in the hay. They stopped and got off at a fishing settlement, a few houses on a stony beach. Nobody was around, but rough clothes drying on lines and damp nets draped on beached rowboats showed it was inhabited. The Corsican led them aboard a sailing boat piled with fishing tackle, tied to a rickety wooden pier. Two unshaven men in ragged sweaters came out of the blue-painted deckhouse and hoisted a filthy gray sail. The boat heeled and went slipping out to sea, as the two men shouted hoarse gibberish at each other. The mule, left tied to a tree, stared after the boat like an abandoned child.

Natalie braced herself against the deckhouse, watching Miriam and the baby play on a pile of dry nets. The young Corsican, whose throaty patois sometimes lost her, said the worst was over. They had met no police, and the coast guard seldom patrolled here, so they were free of the Fascists now. Once in Corsica she and her friends would be safe, and they could remain as long as they chose. Corsica had rigid traditions about fugitives, *les gens qui prennent le maquis.* Corte, where he lived, was an old rebel citadel in the mountains. German and Italian armistice commissioners avoided Corte for their health. His own name was Pascal Gaffori. His older brother, Orlanduccio, who lived in Marseilles, had shipped often with Monsieur Rabinovitz on French freighters in peacetime. Now Orlanduccio had a job in the harbor master's office. The Marseilles waterfront was full of Corsicans, and the Resistance in the port was very strong.

The wind was plastering Natalie's old brown wool dress against her, and as he talked the Corsican was taking in with relish the curves of her breasts and thighs. Natalie was used to the eyes of men, but this blunt stare was unsettling. Still, there was no menace in his gaze, only strong Latin appreciation — so far.

Did he know, she asked, trying to distract him, what the further plans were? He did not. They would stay with his family until some message came from Monsieur Rabinovitz. Had he talked to Rabinovitz? No, he had never met Monsieur Rabinovitz, all this had been arranged by his brother. Were the two men in the deckhouse also his brothers? He snorted. They were Bastia fisherman, doing this for money. Times were bad, the armistice commission had beached the fishing boats. Hulls were drying up, seams were opening; these fellows had spent two days secretly caulking their bottom. They were tough guys, but she need have no fear of them.

Natalie was starting to wonder how much she had to fear Pascal. She was at sea with three ruffians in international waters, with no legal record of their departure. What of Aaron's well-stuffed money belt? What of the zipped-up compartment of dollars in her own suitcase? The boat was hissing along on the swells toward the sun sinking behind the Corsican mountaintops, the sail hummed and slapped, and all this was really happening, but how dreamlike it was, the sudden ride on the sea after the long stagnation in Marciana! This brigandlike stranger could easily rape her if he chose. Who could stop him? Poor Aaron? The genteel doctor? The two coarsely laughing horrors in the deckhouse, who were now passing a jug back and forth? They would only cheer him on and probably await their turns. Natalie's vivid anxious imagination ran through the scenario: this fellow knocking her down on the nets, shoving up her skirt, forcing apart her bared thighs with those big hands —

Spray from the roughening swells flying over the deck stung Louis's eyes and he wailed. She pounced on him and comforted him, and then Pascal let her alone.

The sun disappeared in a glow behind Corsica. The wind freshened. The boat canted steeply and ran fast. Swells broke over the gunwale. Anna became seasick, retching over the side while Castelnuovo patted her back and Miriam looked on in alarm. Aaron staggered to Natalie in the lee of the deckhouse, sat down beside her, and commenting on the pretty view of Elba astern, began to philosophize about Napoleon. Napoleon had left Corsica to rampage through Europe, he said, destroying the old regimes, spreading waste and death, turning the French Revolution into a reactionary comic opera of tinsel empire, only to come full circle and end up on Elba within sight of his native island. The same sort of thing would happen to Hitler; these upstart monsters inevitably generated the counterforces to crush them.

It was hard for Natalie to pay attention amid the noise of wind and water, but she had heard most of it before, in interludes of their Hebrew readings, and all she had to do was nod now and then. If only this scary passage would end! The coastline of Corsica was still below the horizon, and it was getting dark. Louis was whimpering in her arms. She was hugging him to keep off the cold, and feeling remorse at risking him in a tiny wallowing boat on the open sea; but these fishermen surely had been out here in worse weather a hundred times. Pascal came groping to them with a flask. She took a swig of raw brandy, and in the kindling warmth of it forgave him the presumably accidental grope at her breasts.

Made sleepy by the brandy, the rocking, and boredom, Natalie numbly endured the slow passage of time, the wetting of her feet and legs, the pitching of the boat, for she could not tell how long. At last the boat moved into calmer water. On the dark coast ahead, she could discern moonlit trees and boulders. Another half hour or so, and the boat closed the shore. One fisherman dropped the sail; the other jumped with a manila line to a big flat rock. Pascal helped the passengers off with their meager luggage. At once the boat hoisted sail and slipped off into the night.

"Well, now you are in Corsica, and so you are in France," he said to Natalie, taking her suitcases, "and we must walk about three kilometers."

With Louis in her arms, she easily kept pace with him along a footpath through swampy-smelling fields, but they had to slow down for the others. The ground rocked under her feet after the long sail. So they walked for almost an hour. At a dark farmhouse Pascal led them to a hut in back. "Here you will sleep. There is some supper at the house."

The food was soup and bread which Pascal served out. Nobody else appeared. In the candlelight at the plank table Natalie could see octopus tentacles in the tureen; loathsome, but she ate every scrap in her bowl. Pascal gave Louis bread dipped in goat's milk, which he devoured like a dog; and they all bedded down in the hut fully clothed, on straw.

Next morning they had only a glimpse of Bastia's narrow streets and old houses, very like a Tuscan town, as Pascal drove them through in an old truck. A train of three small cars carried them up a hair-raising mountain pass. The passengers, some dressed like Pascal and others in shabby city garb, were amused by Louis, who in his merry morning mood prattled nonsense on his mother's lap and clapped his hands, looking wisely about him. Pascal joked with the conductor, handing him the tickets, and the man ignored the fugitives. Natalie felt in nervous high spirits. She had slept like a rock, and breakfasted on bread, cheese, and wine. Grand mountain views were unfolding outside the open window and an exquisite, pungently flowery odor was drifting in. Pascal told her that she was smelling the *maquis,* the famous aroma which Napoleon in St. Helena had sadly yearned to breathe again.

"I understand him," she said. "It smells like Paradise."

Pascal gave her a heated look through half-closed eyes. She could hardly contain her laughter, he so much resembled Rudolph Valentino emoting in a silent movie. For all that, he rather scared her.

Pascal's father was the son, thirty years older; stouter, also dressed in corduroy, with white mustache and hair, with the same oval face and the same uncivilized brown eyes, set in aged leathery pouches. His manner was courtly, and his house on three levels of a steep street below the hilltop fortress of Corte had the look and the furnishings of prosperity. In a ceremonious lunch around a long polished oak table in a gloomy room, he welcomed the fugitives. His wife, a shapeless figure in black, and two silent-walking daughters, also in black, brought the food and drink: identified by Pascal with some provincial pride as blackbird paté, goat stew, a cake of chestnut flour, and Corsican wine.

Over the first glass of wine Monsieur Gaffori made a little speech, sitting erect in his heavy carved armchair. *Le docteur Jastrow*, he understood, was a famous American author, in flight from the infamous Fascisti. America would one day rescue Corsica from its oppressors. The Corsican people would rise up and do their part by cutting many German and Italian throats; as in the past his ancestors in Corte had cut Genoese throats, Spanish throats, Turkish throats, Saracen throats, and Roman and Greek throats. The old gentleman's soft fierce repetition of *gorges* — "*des GORGES espagnoles, des GORGES romaines, des GORGES grecques*" — gave Natalie the chills. Meanwhile, to help the famous author and his friends, said old Gaffori, was a privilege. The Gaffori house was theirs.

Pascal conducted them up a postern stair to a separate apartment. "Mine is the room exactly below," he said to Natalie, repeating the Rudolph Valentino look, as he showed her into a room with a crib. But under his father's roof, his menace had vanished; he was just a plump youngster suffering from endemic Mediterranean oversexiness, and he was, after all, her rescuer. She was on French soil, that was what mattered. She felt a pulse of gratitude toward Pascal.

"*Vous êtes très aimable, monsieur.*" She shook his hand, holding Louis in one arm, and gave him a brief kiss on the cheek. "*Merci mille fois.*"

His eyes glowed like blown-on coals. "*Serviteur, madame.*"

Avram Rabinovitz rode the little three-car train up to Corte the other way, from the port of Ajaccio. The single-track road was reputed a scenic wonder, but he slumped with closed eyes at a window seat, chain-smoking vile Vichy French cigarettes as the splendid valleys and crags slid by. Shutting out the sunlight and the moving scenery somewhat relieved a migraine headache, which was clacking in his skull to the rhythm of the wheels. Some of the most beautiful views in the world had been wasted on Avram Rabinovitz: the Pyrenees, the Tyrol, the Dolomites, the Alps, the Danube valley, the Turkish coast, the Portuguese backcountry, and the Syrian mountains. In all these sublime settings his preoccupation had been finding enough food and water to keep fugitive Jews alive and on the move.

Not only was his taste for pretty scenery extinct; Rabinovitz's outlook on geography and nationality was altogether peculiar. Countries, borders, passports, visas, languages, laws, currencies, were to him unreal elements in a tawdry risky game played on the European land mass. His attitude was in that sense criminal. He recognized the law of rescue and no other. He had not always been such a freebooter; quite the contrary. His parents had come to Marseilles from Poland after the First World War. His father, a tailor, had taken to making naval and merchant marine uniforms. So Avram had grown up with French schooling and French friends, and had gone into the French merchant marine as a cabin boy, working his way up to a chief engineer's certificate. Well into his twenties he had remained a conforming Frenchman, only dimly aware of his Jewish origins.

With the coming of Hitler, and with anti-Semitism rising in Marseilles like the seep of sewer gas, Rabinovitz had wakened to reluctant Jewish consciousness. A wealthy Swiss Zionist had recruited him to run Jews illegally to Palestine. He had taken three hundred people down the Danube and across the Black Sea to Turkey in a hulk like the *Izmir*, and thence through the Turkish and Syrian backcountry to the Holy Land. The exploit had changed his life. Thereafter he had done nothing else.

Settling in Palestine, he learned some Hebrew and married a Haifa girl. He changed his Frenchified name, André, back to Avram. He tried joining the Zionist movement, but the party quarrelling bored him and put him off. He was at heart a French Jew still, baffled by the fast-spreading hatred for Jews in Europe, and determined to do something about it. He looked no further than the saving of lives. In those days he was hearing the complacent Jewish byword about Hitler's threats in many languages, *It's always hotter cooked than eaten*, but to him the Nazis meant business. He stopped arguing with the Zionists about doctrine and politics, and used their money and connections for rescuing Jews, as he had done with Herbert Rose and the Sacerdotes.

After the fall of France he had returned there and joined the Resistance in Marseilles, as the best base for continuing rescue work. In effect he had been a Resistance man for years. He was already a competent forger, smuggler, spy, liar, confidence man, and thief. Once, to save more than forty people, he had killed an informer in Rumania who was blackmailing him for hush money; striking him harder with a piece of iron than he intended and leaving the man in an alley gasping, his eyes glazing. The episode recurred to him in low moments — the feel of bone cracking under metal, the gush of blood from the bushy hair of the fallen extortionist — but he felt no conscious regrets.

Rabinovitz's migraines tended to come on him when he was overtired, or frustrated, or doing something he knew was stupid. He had no business reason to be riding this Corsican train. He merely wanted to see Mrs. Henry. Though he had talked with her on the *Izmir* only a couple of times, she remained a radiant memory. For Rabinovitz, as for many European men, American women were glamorous. Natalie Henry fascinated him: a

Jewess, an unmistakable darkly glowing Jewess, yet as American as Franklin D. Roosevelt, niece of a famous writer, married to a United States submarine officer! In Marseilles in peacetime, visiting American warships had brought with them an aura of distant power. The young officers in white and gold walking in twos and threes on the boulevard had seemed to Rabinovitz almost the kind of supermen the Germans fancied themselves to be. Byron Henry, an image on a snapshot, added much to Natalie's magic in Rabinovitz's eyes.

He had no designs on her; she seemed a very proper wife and mother. He was just greedy for the sight of her. He had done his best on the *Izmir* to suppress his pointless feelings, even though he thought she liked him. That Naples situation had been complicated enough, without the addling of his wits in a futile romance. Nevertheless her disembarking had been a blow.

The news from Siena in June — first, that Mrs. Henry and her uncle were still there, and then, that they were coming with the Castelnuovos — had deeply stirred him. For a week after learning that Mrs. Henry had reached Corsica, he had resisted the urge to go there. Then he had given in. The migraine had hit him on the overnight boat; and as the little train groaned up the hairpin turns and steep grades toward Corte, what with the turmoil in his heart and the throbbing agony in his head, he had to wonder at his folly. Yet he was happier than he had been since the death of his wife.

When he arrived at the Gaffori house, the object of his infatuation was in the small upstairs apartment in an old gray wool wrapper, bathing her baby in the kitchen sink. She had just washed her hair and put it up in pins. Splashed all over with soapy water by the frolicsome baby, she was not just then an erotic dream figure.

A knock. Aaron's voice through the door. "Natalie, we have a visitor."

"Who?"

"Avram Rabinovitz."

"Christ!"

She heard Jastrow laugh. "He makes no such claim, dear, though he is a savior of sorts."

"Well, I mean, how long will he be here? Louis is all soap from head to foot. So am I. I'm an absolute fright. What's the news? Are we leaving?"

"I gather not. He's staying for lunch."

"Well — oh, blast, I'll be down in a quarter of an hour."

She dressed hurriedly in the white wool dress with the scarlet brass-buckled belt that she had bought in Lisbon for her meeting with Byron. For a long time after Louis's birth she had been too plump to get into it. Packing up in Siena, she had on a last-minute impulse slammed it into a suitcase; *some* time in her wanderings she might want to look well! She put on Louis a little corduroy suit Madame Gaffori had given her, and she strode into the garden, carrying him in her arms. Rabinovitz rose from a bench in the grape arbor where he sat with the others. He looked rather different from her recollection of him: younger, not so stout, not so desperately drawn.

"Hello, Mrs. Henry."

Her dark hair, still damp despite furious towelling, was swept up over her head. He remembered this heavy beautiful hair, and the slant of the huge eyes, now twinkling at him in the friendliest way, and the shape of the generous mouth when she smiled, and the way her cheeks curved. The feel of her brief cool handshake was enchanting.

"I've got a surprise for you," she said, setting Louis down on the brown grass. "Stretch out your arms to him."

Rabinovitz obeyed. She let go, and Louis, with a keen excited look on his chubby face, took a few uncertain steps and fell into the Palestinian's arms, laughing and crowing. Rabinovitz swept him up.

"He's starting to talk, too," Natalie exclaimed. "Imagine, it's all happened in one week! Maybe it's the Corsican air. I feared I was raising an idiot."

"You never did." Jastrow sounded indignant.

"Say something," Rabinovitz told Louis, who was inspecting him with sharp eyes.

Louis pointed a finger at Rabinovitz's broad nose. "Daddy."

Natalie turned scarlet. Even the Castelnuovos, sitting in glum silence, burst out laughing. Natalie gasped, "Oh, God! I've been showing him a snapshot of his father."

Delighted with the sensation he had produced, Louis shouted, "Da-dee! Da-dee!" pointing at Castelnuovo and at Jastrow.

"Horrors, that'll do, you little beast!"

The old man and Pascal ate in farming clothes. Pascal, grimy and tousle-haired in his old goatskin jacket, was giving Natalie his Valentino looks again. In his father's presence he had until now been more careful. The dress, she thought uneasily, was setting him off, and she kept glancing at Rabinovitz, who took no visible notice. The conversation around the table was about the war news. The latest rumor in Corsica, said old Gaffori, was that all the North Africa hints were a deception. The Allies would hit Norway, drive across Scandinavia and Finland, and link up with the Russians. This would relieve Leningrad, open up a good Lend-Lease supply route to the Red Army, and put Allied bombers close to Berlin. What did Monsieur Rabinovitz think?

"I don't believe the Norway story. Too late in the year. Your son and I once served in a freighter that made port in Trondheim in November. We got icebound for weeks."

"Orlanduccio told us about that," said Gaffori, reaching for a stone jug and filling Rabinovitz's glass and his own. "He told us about some other things, monsieur, such as the little affair in Istanbul." He raised his glass to Rabinovitz. "You are always welcome in this house, as long as you live. Thank you for sending us the great American author and his friends."

Jastrow said, "We feel we're a burden."

"No. You may stay, monsieur, until we are all freed together. And now Pascal and I must go back to work."

Natalie said quietly to Rabinovitz as they stood up from the table, "I must talk to you. Have you time?"

"Yes."

He walked with her up the steep cobbled steps of the street outside, which led to the open gateway of the ruined fortress. "Shall we climb up?" she said. "The view is marvelous from the top."

"Okay."

"What was the business in Istanbul?" she asked as they began to mount a narrow stone staircase along an inner wall.

"Nothing much."

"I'd like to know."

"Oh, well, this guy Orlanduccio used to drink a lot and raise hell when we made port. This was before he married and settled down. I was on deck working on a broken winch, and I saw him come staggering along the wharf about midnight. Some hoodlums jumped him. Those waterfront rats are all cowards, they pick on drunks, so I just ran down there with a crowbar and broke it up."

"Why, then, you saved his life."

"His money, maybe."

"And the Gafforis are being kind to us on your account."

"No, no. They're in the Resistance, the whole family."

On a level terrace choked with brown grass and weeds, goats were wandering in and out of the broken walls of a roofless stucco structure with bars in the windows.

"Guardhouse," said Rabinovitz. "Not much good now."

"Tell me about the *Izmir*," she said, leading him across the terrace to another staircase that went higher.

"The *Izmir*? That's long ago." He shook his head, looking sad and troubled. "It wasn't so bad when we started out, but the weather got pretty wild by the time we reached Haifa. We had to unload the people into boats at night in a storm. That damned Turkish captain was making trouble, threatening to leave. There were some drownings, a few, I don't know just how many. Once the people reached the shore they scattered. We never got an accurate count."

Natalie asked soberly, "Then I was right to get off, after all?"

"Who can say? Here you are in Corsica now."

"Yes, and what happens next?"

The higher staircase, its steps ground deep by climbers, was very steep. He spoke slowly, breathing hard, "The American consul general in Marseilles knows you're here. He's a good fellow, James Gaither. I've had dealings with him. He's all right. Some of the other people in that consulate are no damn good. He's handling your problem himself, on a strict confidential basis. When all your papers are in order you'll come to Marseilles and proceed by train the same day to Lisbon. That's Gaither's idea."

"When will that be?"

"Well, the tough thing is the exit visa. Up to a month or so ago you could have gone by train to Lisbon like any tourist. But now the French have stopped issuing exit visas. German pressure. Your embassy can get things done in Vichy, so you'll receive visas, but it'll take a while."

"You've already managed all that!"

"Don't give me credit." It was a sharp sour reply. "Gaither had a cable from the U.S. legation in Bern to be on the lookout for you. When I told Gaither you were in Corsica, he said, 'Hooray!' Just like that." They were at the top now. Over windswept battlements, they looked down on a valley floor of farms and vineyards, surrounded by wild forested mountains. "Well, I see what you mean. Fine view."

"What about the Castelnuovos?"

He cupped a cigarette in his palms to light it. "Much tougher proposition. The German armistice commission made a raid on Bastia in September, because refugees were escaping to Algeria through there. That broke up my arrangements, so you got stuck in Marciana. Still, it's good they left Siena. The OVRA started pulling in Italian Zionists in July. They'd be in a concentration camp by now. I'm working something out for them, so please try to keep the doctor from getting impatient. If the worst comes to the worst, the Gafforis will always look after them." He puffed the cigarette and glanced at his watch. "We'd better start back. You wanted to talk to me? The train leaves for Ajaccio in about an hour."

"Well, yes. That young fellow, Pascal —" she hesitated, gnawing a knuckle.

"Yes, what about him?"

"Oh, hell, I must confide in you. And I couldn't talk in the house. Night before last, I woke up and he was in my room, sitting on my bed. With a hand on the covers. On my leg." She began rushing out the words as they went down the windy steps. "Just sitting there! My baby's crib wasn't two feet from us. I didn't know whether I was dreaming or what! I whispered, 'What is it? What are you doing here?' And he whispered, *Je t'aime. Tu veux?*" Rabinovitz stopped short on the steps. To her astonishment he was blushing. "Oh, don't worry, he didn't rape me or anything, in fact I got rid of him." She tugged at his elbow. Frowning, he resumed the descent. "It may have been my fault. Even in Elba he was making eyes at me, and on the boat he got sort of fresh. I did one damn fool thing when we got to the house. The trip was over, I'd made it safely, and I was grateful to him. I kissed him. Well, he looked at me as though I'd taken off my skirt. And since then, it's as though I've never put it back on. And now this thing the other night —"

"How did you get rid of him?"

"Well, it wasn't so easy. First thing I whispered was, 'It's impossible, you'll wake my baby.' " Natalie took a quick side glance at Rabinovitz. "Now, maybe I should have gotten on my high horse and just thrown him out, yelled for his father, whatnot. But I was sleepy and surprised, and I didn't want to wake Louis, and I felt more or less at these people's mercy. So then he whispered, 'Oh, no, we'll be as quiet as two little pigeons.' " Natalie nervously giggled. "I was scared as hell, but it was just too ludicrous, '*deux petites colombes*' —"

Rabinovitz was smiling, but not pleasantly. "So what broke it up?"

"Oh, we whispered like that, yes, no, back and forth. He wouldn't leave. I thought of appealing to his Corsican honor not to harm a fugitive under his roof. Or threatening to tell his father. All that seemed long and complicated. So I just said, 'Look, it mustn't be, I'm unwell.' He snatched his hand off my leg and jumped from the bed as though I'd pleaded leprosy."

For a seafaring man, she thought, Rabinovitz was oddly prudish. He looked very ill at ease at this.

"Then he stood over me and whispered, 'You're telling the truth?' 'Of course.' 'Madame, if you are simply refusing me, you are making a grave mistake. I can promise you ecstasy.' " She assumed a baritone voice. " '*Je peux te promettre l'extase.*' His very words. With that, thank God, he tiptoed out. I fear he's going to try again. What shall I do? Shall I talk to his father? The old man's so formidable."

Rabinovitz was rubbing a palm on a very worried face. "I'm thinking where I can put you in Marseilles. Unless you want to try that ecstasy." She said nothing, and again the puffy face reddened. "Sorry, I shouldn't make fun of you, I'm sure it's distressing."

She replied a touch mischievously, "Oh, well, it's made me feel young and so forth. But no, I'll forgo Corsican ecstasy."

He gave her a curious smile, with much sadness in it. "Good. Not for nice Jewish girls."

"Oh, you don't know me," Natalie retorted, though not — to her surprise — annoyed by the description. On Rabinovitz's lips the words had a caressing sound. "I've always done exactly as I pleased, or God knows I wouldn't have married Byron Henry. Or put myself through other wringers that nice Jewish girls usually avoid. Anyway, you think you'll move us to Marseilles?"

"Yes. I don't want trouble with the Gafforis. They're very important to me, especially Orlanduccio. And at the moment they're my one sure place for the Castelnuovos. Orlanduccio's told me about this Pascal, he's no good. You might be better off in Marseilles anyway. When your papers come through, you can leave, one two three. That's an advantage."

"And the Castelnuovos?"

"They stay here."

"But I don't want to abandon them."

"*Abandon* them?" Rabinovitz's voice turned harsh as they walked across the terrace past the tumbledown guardhouse. "Don't use such a silly expression, please. The U.S. consul general will step in for you if anything goes wrong, but they'd have no protection, none whatever. Marseilles is full of police and informers. I can't possibly move them there. Please don't encourage the doctor with such ideas. I'm having enough trouble with him as it is."

"All right. Don't be angry with me. Louis and Miriam are like brother and sister now."

"I know. Listen, that Bastia raid was rotten luck. If the doctor will be sensible, he and his family will be all right."

"While we're in Marseilles, will we see you now and then?"

"Sure."

"Well, that will be good."

He hesitated, and spoke very gruffly. "I was disappointed when you left the *Izmir*."

Natalie suddenly kissed his cheek. It felt bristly and cold.

"Mrs. Henry, doing that is what got you into trouble."

"I don't think I'll wake to find you in my bedroom."

"To a Frenchman that's no compliment."

They smiled uncertainly at each other, and descended into the town.

That evening it was Natalie's turn to cook. As she served out a scrappy ratatouille in the little upstairs kitchen, a recipe from her Paris days, there was little talk. Even Miriam was grave. She went off to bed while the adults lingered in the kitchen over a coffee substitute made of roasted grains, mere sour brown water. Castelnuovo said, "Well, it'll be hard on the children, won't it?" This was the first open reference to their coming separation.

She had stopped noticing his appearance from day to day, but now she was struck by the alteration in him since Siena. Then he had been a self-assured, charming, handsome Italian doctor. His good looks were fading, his eyes were hollow, the lids were heavy.

"It'll be hard on me, I know that," she said.

Aaron Jastrow said, "Isn't it possible we'll still rejoin, and go out together?"

Castelnuovo's headshake was slow, emphatic, and weary.

"What are his plans for you?" Jastrow insisted. "Can't we be frank with each other?"

"In Marciana we still hoped to go by ship to Algiers," said the doctor, "and make our way east to Palestine. But that's closed off. It seems we can go out illegally either to Spain or Switzerland. People go in groups, with guides who sneak them through the woods. I guess Spain's better. At least it's on the way to Lisbon."

"The trouble is," Anna said, with a pointless smile, "that to get to Spain we have to cross the Pyrenees on foot. In November. There's no other way. Miles of walking in the wilds, with snow and ice, and the border patrols to watch out for."

"What about Switzerland?" Natalie asked.

"If they catch you, back to France you go," said Anna. "Into the hands of the French police."

"Not necessarily!" Her husband spoke angrily to her. "Don't exaggerate. Every group has a different experience. There are rescue agencies in Switzerland, too, who can help you. Rabinovitz prefers Spain, but Anna is worried about Miriam walking over the mountains."

"But the vessels that were going to South America," said Jastrow, "the fishing boats to Morocco — all those other possibilities we've talked about?"

Castelnuovo's hopeless shrug and dark empty look made Natalie herself feel trapped as never before. "You'll be all right," she said, very cheerfully. "I trust him."

"So do I," said the doctor. "He tells the truth. He knows what he's doing. It was I who decided to leave Italy, and I was right. We're not in a concentration camp. If Miriam has to walk over the Pyrenees in the snow, why, she'll walk over the Pyrenees. She's a strong healthy girl." He got up and hurried out.

Natalie said to Anna Castelnuovo, whose eyes were wet, "Anna, can I take Miriam into my bed tonight?"

Anna nodded. The drowsy little girl came to Natalie's bed herself later, without a word, and fell asleep in a moment. Natalie loved the feeling of the small warm body snuggled beside her. When the sun woke Natalie next morning Miriam was gone. The girl had crawled into the crib and was sleeping with Louis in her arms.

41

A GRAND armada was now on the high seas, converging upon North Africa. Not since the Japanese Imperial Fleet had set out for Midway, and before that never in all history, had the oceans of earth borne such a force. Aircraft carriers, battleships, cruisers, troop transports, and newfangled landing ships crammed full of small craft, tanks, trucks, and mobile guns; also destroyers, minesweepers, submarines, and assorted supply vessels; from several directions, in far-flung formations, these warships of frowning shapes and many sizes, painted gray or in gaudy camouflage colors, were crawling the watery curve of the planet. They came thronging south from the British Isles, and, in an ocean-borne assault new in size and reach, they came steaming east from North America. Axis intelligence knew nothing of all this. The speculations at a Corsican dining table were being echoed aboard Hitler's command train heading for a Party rally in Munich. Though mounted in chatterbox democracies, the great attack was being kept as secret as the Japanese assault on Pearl Harbor.

Winston Churchill had closed his defiant oration after Dunkirk with a pledge to carry on the struggle *until, in God's good time, the New World, with all its power and might, steps forth to the rescue and the liberation of the Old."* Now it was happening, two and a half years later, the Churchillian dithyramb coming to majestic life: a swarm of fresh seapower with the ever-rising roar of American technology behind it, bearing veteran British divisions and the first wave of America's newly recruited soldiery. If romance could exist in industrialized war, this was a romantic hour, the approaching hour of Torch.

But the American invaders, despite a Patton here and there, would have been embarrassed by Churchillian dithyrambs about what they were doing. The career challenges and the technical risks interested the professional soldiers; otherwise, generals and privates alike regarded Torch and the whole war as a dirty job to get over with. George Marshall disapproved altogether of Torch as a diversion from the big landing in France, and the commander-in-chief of the expedition himself, a newcomer on the world scene named Dwight Eisenhower, feared that the decision for Torch "might go down as the blackest day in history." Still, given their orders, he and his staff had methodically set about the business.

Loading the odds in their favor was much to be desired, however unromantic; and if a fight could be avoided altogether, so much the better. So the notion had arisen to bring into the combined Anglo-American high command a famous French general in a window-dressing role, to induce the Vichy forces in North Africa not to fight, no matter what their German-ruled government might order. Thus began a comedy worthy — except for the magnitude of the stakes — of a Parisian boulevard farceur's pen.

In this scherzo interlude in the heavy march of the war, Byron Henry became caught up. The reader therefore needs a brief sketch of what the foolery was about.

For this role of high-brass catspaw Charles de Gaulle was available in London, where he was sounding forth as the voice of "Free France," exhorting his countrymen to resist their conquerors. The trouble with de Gaulle was that Vichy's generals and admirals loathed him to a man. Nor did the Resistance much love him. Sonorous defiance from a London hotel suite did not greatly charm French hearts just then. The personage the Allies hit on instead was one General Henri Giraud. Giraud had fought well against the Germans in 1940, had been captured, and had escaped from a German prison. He was now lying low in France, and the plan was to hunt him up, spirit him from his hideout to the Mediterranean coast, take him aboard an Allied submarine, and speed him to Gibraltar to join Eisenhower.

This was a complicated project, and when secretly approached, Giraud made it more complicated. On points of honor General Giraud turned out to be a fussy man. Earlier in the war British warships had bombarded a French fleet to prevent its falling into German hands. Henri Giraud therefore would not consent to be rescued by a British submarine. But the only suitable subs on hand at the moment flew British flags. A British submarine had to be put under nominal command of an American captain, with a couple of other American officers along for verisimilitude, to fetch the Frenchman. The British skipper and crew naturally operated the boat as before; the Americans rode along and tried to act busy. This "American" submarine duly picked up General Giraud off the coast near Toulon, and brought him to Gibraltar.

There — to round out the Giraud epic, before narrating Byron Henry's small part in it — on being ushered into the presence of Eisenhower in his command-post cave, Giraud calmly thanked the American generalissimo for his services to date, and informed him that he, Henri Giraud, would now relieve him as commander-in-chief, and would himself conduct the invasion of North Africa. This happened less than forty-eight hours before the start of the assault, with some four hundred fifty ships approaching the landing beaches. Details of this remarkable chat are lacking, but we know that Giraud was deaf to argument. Taking supreme command was, he insisted, a point of honor with him. But Eisenhower insensitively declined to be relieved. The Frenchman thereupon went into a profound sulk and played no part in the invasion.

As things turned out he was not missed. In the early hours of the landing a certain Admiral Darlan, the most influential Vichyite in Northwest Africa, noted chiefly for his extraordinary hatred of England, America, and Jews, fell into the invaders' hands. Knife to his throat, they pressed him into the Giraud role. He did a fine job of pacifying the French forces, terminating the sporadic resistance, and establishing order under the Allies. Willy-nilly, Darlan prevented the deaths of many American and British soldiers, far better than Giraud could have.

A loud long cry at once went up in the Allied press against this cynical use of such a bad man. Political trouble ensued. General Eisenhower contemplated resigning, and President Roosevelt underwent prolonged newspaper savaging, more strident than usual. Then by another lucky chance of war the matter was cleared up. An idealistic French student shot Darlan. Some time afterward, at the Casablanca Conference, General Giraud, yielding to a lot of coaxing, consented to pose sullenly for pictures with Churchill, Roosevelt, and de Gaulle. So it is that one knows today what the man of honor looked like. He was tall and thin, but not as tall and thin as de Gaulle. He had the larger mustache.

It was during the frantic spate of communications back and forth about Giraud's honor that Byron Henry got sucked into the affair. Oddly, his submarine experience had nothing whatever to do with it. He was swept like a cork in an eddying stream, from Gibraltar to Marseilles, around and around, with no inkling of what the propelling force was, simply because he had a high American security clearance. Gibraltar was chronically short of American couriers; with invasion imminent, even more so. Since his encounter with the Tudsburys, Byron had been sent on several of these errands, but never before to Marseilles, though he had been in touch with the consulate by mail and telephone, inquiring about Natalie.

Like everybody at the Rock he knew that a big operation was afoot. The power hum vibrating throughout the base, the gathering of warships and warplanes, the descent of high brass with their scurrying self-important staffs, all brought to his mind Pearl Harbor before Midway. But whether the objective was Africa, Sardinia, the south of France, or even Italy, Byron did not know. He had never heard of General Henri Giraud. Nor was the name mentioned to him now. At eight in the morning, black with grease, he was aboard a decrepit S-boat alongside the *Maidstone*, trying to get a defunct air compressor to work; and by noon, hastily cleaned up and in civilian clothes, with the courier's leather pouch once more chained to his wrist and the diplomatic passport in his pocket, he was on his way to Marseilles.

He had heard nothing from Leslie Slote in over two months. His repeated inquiries to the Marseilles consulate had proven fruitless. Still, since he was going there, he meant to check around. His instructions were to hand the locked pouch of documents to a certain vice consul, wait for a coded reply, and bring it back posthaste. He would have time, he figured, to press a few inquiries. And so it was that he did find Natalie, though the final linkup was fortuitous. Had she not left Italy, and had he not gotten himself to Gibraltar, it naturally could not have happened, but the gap was closed by luck.

Arriving in a pouring cold rain at the consulate, he unchained the pouch and delivered it to the vice consul, a man named Sam Jones, with a nondescript face and nondescript clothes to match; a good inconspicuous sort to be handling covert military intelligence. As Byron doffed his dripping raincoat he asked Jones, "Is Lucius Babbage still stationed here?"

"Luke Babbage? Sure. Why?"

"I want to talk to him. How much time have I got?"

An incongruous foxy look creased Jones's average face; the intelligence man, peeping through the drab vice consul. "You've got time. Luke's office is down the hall. Frosted glass panel door."

A pinch-faced woman with a tight net on her grizzled hair was typing away inside the frosted glass door, at a desk stacked with official forms. Refugees crowded the anteroom, most of them looking as though they had been sitting there for days. The secretary's cold glance dissolved in a charming smile as she took in his face, and the American sport jacket and slacks in which he ran his courier errands. He had no trouble getting past her to see Babbage.

Pale watery light from the wide windows of the inner office fell on life-sized framed photographs of President Roosevelt and Cordell Hull; also on a large bad reproduction of *George Washington Crossing the Delaware*. Behind the desk a plump bald pink man rose to shake hands with Byron, his blue eyes twinkling through gold-rimmed glasses. "Lieutenant Henry, eh? I recall your letter, Lieutenant. Your phone calls, too. Lousy connection to Gibraltar. Good old American name, Henry. No relation to Patrick? Ha ha! Submariner, isn't it? My son wanted to join the Navy but couldn't make it. Eyes. He's in the Air Corps, quartermasters. How's the war looking from Gibraltar? I guess these courier trips are interesting, but I'd think you'd be out in the Pacific. Well, sit down, sit down."

Lucius Babbage wanted to know when Byron had last been in the States and whether he had seen any major league baseball games. Rocking back and forth in a squeaky swivel chair, he said that agitation to draft stars like DiMaggio and Feller was fomented by people of dubious motives. If a few great ball players could keep millions of laborers diverted while turning out planes and tanks, where was the sense in marching them off to carry rifles in the mud, leaving the big leagues to Army rejects and misfits? During this aimless persiflage the prominent eyes stared through the gold rims, and Babbage kept rubbing the back of his hand on jowls as smooth-shaven as a priest's.

"Well!" Babbage said, changing his tone as though with a flip of a switch, "the problem is your wife, as I recall it. Suppose you tell me the story again, and save me pulling out your letter again? There's an uncle, too, isn't there?"

"Yes. His name's Aaron Jastrow. He's the author," Byron said. "Hers is Natalie. Mrs. Byron Henry. My son is Louis, an infant in arms. I've lost track of them, but I have reason to think they might be in or around Marseilles."

Babbage kept nodding through all this, his face blankly beaming. "They're Americans?"

"Of course."

"Passports in order?"

"Yes."

"What would they be doing in the free zone, then? We sent everybody home ages ago."

"Then I take it they've not turned up?"

Babbage pulled a yellow pad from a drawer, and picked up a pen in his left hand. He nodded at Byron with a warm smile, his eyes squeezed almost shut. "Why not give me all the facts, as long as you're here? When and where you last had news of their whereabouts, and so on and so forth? The more I know, the more thoroughly I can look into it."

Some instinct made Byron tread cautiously. "Dr. Jastrow was living in Siena, retired from teaching history at Yale, writing his books. Natalie worked as his secretary. They were caught there when we got into the war. So —"

"Let me interrupt you right there, Lieutenant. All the Americans who were interned in Italy were exchanged in May." Babbage was smiling and scrawling as he spoke, his left hand curled around the pen. "So they should be home by now, no problem."

"Well, I was out in the Pacific then. I don't know what happened, but they weren't exchanged."

"How odd."

"And last anybody heard, they were going to try to get to France."

"You mean illegally?"

"I really don't know any more details."

"What's her uncle's name again?"

"Jastrow."

"Spell it, please."

"J-A-S-T-R-O-W."

"Well-known author?"

"The Book-of-the-Month Club took one of his books."

"Good enough. Which book was that?"

"*A Jew's Jesus.*"

This did bring a reaction from Babbage. His smile flared out, his eyebrows went up, and his eyes shone. "Oh? He's a Jew?"

"Not a practicing one."

"Few of them are, it's a question of nationality, isn't it?" Slight pause, and a happy grin. "Your wife is one, too?"

"Yes, she is."

"You're not, obviously."

"No."

The left hand scrawled and stopped. With a genial nod and a wink, Babbage got up and walked into the anteroom, saying, "Half a sec." He was gone about five minutes, while Byron stared at George Washington, at Roosevelt, at Hull, and at the grimy rain-beaten buildings across the street. Babbage returned, sat behind his desk, and clasped his hands before him. "No, they're not in Marseilles. And there's no record of them anywhere in the unoccupied zone. Have you checked with the International Red Cross? What with their being Jewish, and the kind of books he writes, they may well have landed in an Italian concentration camp."

"Suppose they'd made it to Toulon, or Algiers? Would you know?"

"If they'd reported in to American authorities, I'd know. The roster of all Americans in the area is my responsibility. Now, if they attempted an *illegal* transit of France — well, let's just hope they didn't, Lieutenant. The French police are getting damned tough with Jews on the run." He cheerily smiled. "But I don't know why they should have done such a silly thing, if their papers were in order. Right?"

"Right." Byron abruptly stood up.

"Well, it's an unusual case." Babbage rubbed his jowl with the back of his hand. "You a submariner, your wife working for this relative who writes these leftist books, and —"

"What? There's nothing in the least leftist about *A Jew's Jesus.*" Byron allowed hard annoyance into his voice. "It's a historical work, and very brilliant."

"Oh? Well, I'll have to read it. I thought it might be one of those tripey things that make out Our Lord to be a revolutionary. That's the old leftist line, isn't it?"

"Much obliged." Byron stalked out, galled by this frustrating finale to the long trek from Australia: a bureaucratic stone wall, mildewy with snide anti-Semitism, in a Marseilles consulate. He had the addresses of a Quaker agency and a Jewish committee, and he decided to walk off his irritation, though it was still raining. He had last visited Marseilles in 1939, in his vagabonding after dropping out of graduate school in Florence, and he retained pleasant memories of the Canebière boulevard with its opulent window displays and seafood restaurants, and the noisy cheerful people, so unlike the glum French elsewhere. Rain or shine, Marseilles had been a delight.

It had much changed. The people appeared peaked, weary, and impoverished. The long, wide, quiet Canebière, all but empty of auto traffic, had a plague-stricken look. The rain-blurred shop windows offered scanty dusty things like badly made garments, cheap Vichy propaganda books, and cardboard luggage. The famous food markets were pitifully shrunken. The meat stalls that were not barred shut vended horrid scraps caked with black blood: tails, ears, guts, lungs. The few vegetables for sale were sparse, wilted, and wormy-looking. There was no fruit. Amazingly, there was no fish. All the famous stalls, which once had been piled with gleaming bright-eyed fish wet from the sea, and all manner of shellfish in beds of seaweed, were shuttered. The cancer of German conquest was visibly eating at Marseilles.

Outside the Quaker office Byron found a great jam of children on the streaming sidewalk, blocking the entrance; children by the dozens, from toddlers to adolescents, huddled under dripping umbrellas. Inside, typewriters were clattering amid much high-pitched French gabble. A fat American woman herding the children into a line said that she had no time for him; Congress had passed a special resolution, allowing five thousand Jewish children into the United States: no parents, only children, and the Quakers were rounding them up as fast as possible, before Vichy changed its mind about releasing them, or the Germans grabbed them to ship them east, or the State Department threw in a new monkey wrench. Byron despaired of accomplishing anything here, and he left.

The Jewish office, called the "Joint," was in a different neighborhood. He had to ask directions. The first two Frenchmen he approached skulked off without a reply. He persisted, and found his way to the place. In so doing he walked right past the building where Rabinovitz had ensconced his wife and child; just one more wet gray four-story Marseilles apartment house in blocks and blocks of them. He strode by, hunched against the rain, in a close blind chance miss, as two submarines running silent can pass each other in the undersea dark by inches and not know it.

In the small crowded anteroom of the agency office, a hollow-eyed young woman at one desk frantically banged at a typewriter, but Byron could not approach her; a long line waited at the desk, coiling all around the room and snaking through people sitting in chairs or lounging on their feet, some holding battered valises, all talking every known language (or so it seemed to Byron) but English. Sad fear pervaded this crowd, visible in faces and sounding in voices. Byron leaned against the wall, wondering how to proceed. A plump dark young man in a trench coat came out of a door behind the desk, looked busily about, and shouldered toward the street entrance. Passing Byron, he stopped and said, "Hi."

The American monosyllable was clear as a bell. Byron replied, "Hi."

"Got a problem?"

"Sort of."

"I'm Joe Schwartz."

"I'm Lieutenant Byron Henry."

The man arched a heavy black brow. "Had lunch?"

"No."

"Ever eat couscous?"

"No."

"It's pretty good, couscous."

"Okay."

Schwartz led him a block away to what looked like a tailor shop; at least there was a headless unclothed dummy in the narrow gloomy window, and a yawning cat. They passed through the shop to a back room where at small oilcloth-covered tables people were eating. The couscous, served by an unshaven man in a skullcap, was a sort of farina with vegetables and a hot spicy meat gravy. Acting again on instinct, Byron told this stranger his story, including everything he had withheld from the American consul. Schwartz kept nodding as he ate with appetite. "Leslie Slote. Bern. Thin blond fellow," he said. "I know him. Very smart. Nervous type, very nervous, but he's all right. That fellow Babbage is bad news. These fellows here in Marseilles vary. It's an individual thing, some are fine guys, and the man you want to talk to here is Jim Gaither. If anybody knows anything about your wife, it'll be Gaither."

"Who's Gaither?"

"The consul general. He's not here now, though. He had to go to Vichy."

"I must return to Gibraltar today."

"Well, maybe you can phone or write to him."

"What do you do?"

"Right now I'm organizing thirty typewriters. One thing the Germans have is typewriters, so they trade them with the French."

"What do you need thirty typewriters for?"

"The Joint office in Lisbon. That's where I work. The American consulate in Lisbon has a total of three typewriters. It's unbelievable. So we're going to have plenty of typewriters from now on, and volunteer typists to fill out papers. Jews aren't going to be stuck in Lisbon any more, when a ship becomes available, because of a lack of typewriters."

"If my wife passed through Lisbon, would you know?"

"I'd know about her uncle." Schwartz looked thoughtful. "*A Jew's Jesus.* Who hasn't read it? Now listen, Lieutenant. Some decent Italian or French people could well be hiding them. Be optimistic."

"How bad is the situation?"

"You mean, of the Jews?"

"Yes."

Joe Schwartz's voice went deep, the face stony. "Very bad. In the east Jews are being murdered, no question about it, and the French are letting the Germans take them away. However" — he returned to his goodnatured manner, even smiling — "there are many decent Christians, willing to risk their lives to help. Things can be done. It's a complicated picture, and we do what we can. Did you enjoy the couscous? How about some tea?"

"Sure. Thanks. The couscous was good."

"What's he like, Aaron Jastrow?"

Byron hesitated. "Very regular in work habits. Quite a scholar."

"That shows in his work. Informative. But *A Jew's Jesus* is a best-seller for Christians. You know? It's bland. Vanilla-flavored. Nice. Christianity has been hard on the Jews. The Crusades, the Inquisition, and now this. The Germans are supposed to be Christians."

"I'm a Christian. Or rather, I try to be," Byron said.

"I didn't mean to offend you."

"You didn't, but nothing Jesus taught leads to Hitler."

"That's very true, yet if Jesus hadn't walked the earth, would such things have happened? Europe is a Christian continent, isn't it? Well, what's going on? Where's the Pope? Mind you, there's one Catholic priest right here in Marseilles who's a saint, a one-man underground. I only hope the Gestapo doesn't murder him." Looking at his watch, Joe Schwartz shook his head. "How did we get into this? Yes, *A Jew's Jesus.* Well, anyhow, it's a good book. It brings Jesus down from the stained glass, the big famous paintings, the huge crosses, where's he's always dying or dead. It shows him walking around among Jews, a poor Talmud scholar, a boy prodigy, a real living Jew. That's important. Maybe it's enough. More tea?"

"I've got to get back to the consulate."

The rain was blowing in slant sheets outside. They paused in the doorway to turn up their collars. Schwartz said, "I know where you can hire a cab."

"I'll walk. Thanks for lunch. Tell me something," Byron said, looking hard at Schwartz. "What can somebody like me do?"

"You mean about us, about the Jews?"

"Yes."

The heavy lines reappeared in Schwartz's face. "Win the war."

Byron held out his hand, and Joe Schwartz shook it. They went their separate ways in the rain.

Back in Gibraltar, Byron boarded the *Maidstone* dog-tired, after turning in his pouch at Allied headquarters. He meant to collapse on his bunk in his clothes, but a dispatch lying on his desk jolted him alert.

FROM: BUPERS

TO: CO HMS MAIDSTONE

VIA: COMLANT

LIEUTENANT (JG) BYRON (NONE) HENRY USN DETACHED TEMPORARY LIAISON DUTY ROYAL NAVY X PROCEED SANFRAN REPORT CO USS MORAY PAREN SS 345 PAREN X CLASS TWO AIR PRIORITY AUTHORIZED

Aster!

In a recent U.S. Fleet letter, Byron had seen a roster of new-construction submarines and their skippers, including *USS MORAY (SS 345)* — *Carter W. Aster, Lt. Cdr. USN.* This was Aster's style, to ask BuPers for officers he wanted, instead of taking what he got. Byron dropped on his bunk, not to sleep but to ponder. A gladsome, an electrifying prospect, suddenly; putting one of these new fleet subs in commission, to sail again with Lady Aster against the Japs!

He could leave the *Maidstone,* he knew, when he pleased. The tender captain had not requested the American technicians, didn't really need them to maintain the S-boats, and faintly resented the whole arrangement. Had this dispatch come a few days earlier, Byron would have packed and left at sunrise. But another courier trip to Marseilles was scheduled, and he decided he would make that last trip, in the hopes of seeing Consul General Gaither. That fellow Joe Schwartz seemed to know what he was talking about.

42

A MASTER plumber named Itzhak Mendelson owned the flat and the building where Natalie was holed up with her baby and her uncle. A Polish Jew, Mendelson had come to Marseilles in the 1920s and had done very well. His firm serviced the municipal buildings; he spoke excellent French; he knew magistrates, police chiefs, bankers, and all the most important criminals. So Rabinovitz had told Natalie. Mendelson was no Resistance man, and the Jews who slept on his parlor furniture or randomly on the floor were not underground types wanted by the Gestapo or the French police. They were objects of compassion, innocuous drifters like Jastrow and Natalie, lacking the proper papers to reside in Marseilles or to get out of France legally.

The apartment was enormous, for Mendelson had knocked down walls and merged several flats to fashion this labyrinthine warren, where Louis kept disappearing down dim corridors with racketing children who yelled in Yiddish. Two other younger families, refugee relatives of Mendelson, lived in the place. Natalie had trouble sorting out the transients from the residents, but it didn't really matter. The common tongue in the flat was Polish-Yiddish; in fact, the master plumber prided himself on a Yiddish historical romance he had written in his Warsaw youth, about the false Messiah Shabbatai Zvi. He had evidently paid to have it translated into French, for yellow-bound copies of *Le Faux Messie* lined the walls of the small room where Jastrow, Natalie, and Louis now dwelled. Glancing at this version, Natalie found it very silly stuff, though not bad for a plumber. Aaron, of course, with his flawless Yiddish, was right at home in the Mendelson ménage; and as *der groiser shriftshteller* he received immediate deference. Louis had a boil of children to play with, Natalie could get along with her rusty Yiddish, and all in all it was a warm, noisy, homey milieu. She was grateful to Pascal Gaffori, when she thought about it, for having driven her to this little Jewish oasis in Marseilles to await her freedom.

At first she didn't feel that way. The third night they were there, the police made a sweep of the neighborhood to round up alien Jews. Warned by his high-placed friends, Mendelson had notified as many Jews as he knew; and he assured Natalie and Aaron that his building would not be entered. When at midnight she heard excited talk in the front rooms, she jumped from her bed and went to watch. Peeking through the curtains with the others, she saw two police vans surrounded by a docile crowd, much like onlookers at an accident, except for the valises they carried, and the small children among them. Under the eyes of a few gendarmes, they all peaceably got into the vans. The only odd detail was the frills of nightgowns, the legs of pajamas, and even bare feet, showing below the overcoats of some. Mendelson was right, the police never entered his building. The vans drove off, leaving the blue-lit street empty, and Natalie frightened.

She cheered up next day when Rabinovitz came with the news that the American consul general was expected back from Vichy in a day or two. Jim Gaither was a man of his word, the Palestinian said, a decent guy, a bonded officer with money and authority to deal with the Resistance. Since he had taken over the consulate, hundreds of people had received visas whose departure would otherwise have been blocked. A great admirer of *A Jew's Jesus*, Gaither was handling the Jastrow-Henry file himself, taking no chances on a leak. Nobody else in the consulate knew anything about it. Once Gaither got back they could count on a prompt departure.

About the Castelnuovos Rabinovitz was less sanguine. The headstrong doctor was negotiating directly for passage to Algiers with the Bastia roughnecks who had brought them from Elba. Rabinovitz said these fellows were unreliable, even dangerous, except when dealing with old Gaffori. He wanted the Castelnuovos to stay where they were until some safer way to leave opened up. Corsica was a good refuge, with enough to eat and drink. But Castelnuovo was becoming obsessed with an itch to move on. "So far, luckily, those scoundrels are asking for more money than he's got," Rabinovitz said. "So maybe he'll stay put. I hope so."

When Byron returned to Marseilles with another pouch for Sam Jones, the vice consul told him that Gaither had returned; and that, on hearing the name and rank of the expected courier from Gibraltar, he had exclaimed, "Hooray!"

"He wants you to report to his office at once. Second floor. You'll see the sign," Jones said. "*Without fail* were his words. Is he an old friend of your family, or something?"

"Not that I know of," Byron replied, with the greatest false show of nonchalance in his life. "Tell him I'm coming." He leaped up the stairs to the second floor.

"Well!" exclaimed the consul general, standing up and extending a hand over his desk. "D'Artagnan!" In his yellow pullover and gray slacks he looked like an old tennis pro: tall, stringy, brown, with close-cut straight white hair.

Byron blurted, "Where are they?"

"What? Sit down." The consul general laughed at the impetuous question. "They're in Corsica. Or they were, last I heard. They're fine, the three of them. How the devil have you pulled this off?"

"Corsica!" Byron gasped. "Corsica! God Almighty, so close? How do I get there? Is there a boat? An airplane?"

Gaither laughed again, very agreeably. "Take it easy, young fellow."

"You say they're fine? You've seen them?"

"I've been in touch. They're quite okay. There's no airplane to Corsica. The boat runs three times a week, and it takes eleven hours. They'll be leaving for Lisbon in a few days, Lieutenant, and —"

"They will? Why, that's marvelous, sir. Are you sure? I have orders to return to the States. I'll get to work on priorities, and maybe take them with me."

"Could be." Gaither shook his head, smiling. "You're an energetic fellow. Aren't you in submarines? How do you come to be in Gibraltar?"

"Can I talk to them on the telephone? Is there phone service to Corsica?"

"I wouldn't recommend that." Gaither leaned back in his chair, pulling at his lower lip. "Now look, Sam Jones has got an urgent job for you. You'll have to return to Gibraltar tonight. Sam will bring you to my house for dinner about six. How's that? We'll have a long talk. I repeat, they're fine, just fine, and they'll be out of here in a few days. Incidentally, Sam Jones knows nothing about all this. Nobody does. Keep it that way."

Impulsively Byron grasped his hand. "Thanks."

"All right. Steady does it. Don't get impatient."

Jones gave Byron two sealed envelopes to deliver by hand to an unnamed place. A silent ghost-pale young man in a ragged sweater drove him out along the coast in an old taxicab, ceaselessly glancing at the rearview mirror. The ride took over an hour, ending in a bumpy ride down a dirt road to a small villa within sight of the blue calm sea, almost hidden by overgrown shrubs and vines. A wary woman half-opened the door to Byron's knock. He could see behind her a tall mustached man looking keenly toward the door, hands jammed in the pockets of a red dressing gown. So he caught a good look at General Henri Giraud; though only long afterward, coming on a picture story of the Casablanca Conference in an old *Life* magazine, did he realize what his courier errands had been about, and who the man had been. It was after five o'clock when he returned to the consulate. Sam Jones said, rubbing his eyes and yawning, "Ready to go to the boss's house? He's waiting to give you dinner."

Natalie put on the white dress for the Friday night meal, and arrayed Louis in his cleanest shirt and jumper. Rabinovitz was coming, and they were going afterward to his apartment in the Old Town. She had herself proposed this in all innocence, during their last chat in the clamorous living room. She wanted to be alone with him, to talk in unhurried peace. Yet the last time she had invited herself to a man's flat, her love affair with Slote had ensued; and, a bit laggardly, this thought was troubling her. On impulse she pinned to her dress the brooch of purple stones that Byron had given her in Warsaw.

On this night she did something she had not done before in her life; she lit Sabbath candles. It seemed more mannerly to do it than to decline, when Mrs. Mendelson, a stout, incessantly busy, incessantly cheerful red-faced woman, came to tell her the candles were ready. Scrubbed and dressed-up children crowded around their mothers by the long dining table, where eight candlesticks stood on a fresh white cloth. Covering her head with a kerchief, putting the match to two cheap sputtering candles, stammering the Hebrew blessing as Louis watched her with enormous eyes, Natalie felt decidedly peculiar. Mrs. Mendelson elbowed her and made a genial joke to the others: "*Zeh, zi vert by unz a ganzer rebbitzin.*" ("Look, we're making her into a rabbi's wife.") Natalie sheepishly joined in the laughter.

While the children were being fed, Rabinovitz arrived. Above the piping tumult of the children, he said, "Jim Gaither's back. I missed him at the consulate, but I'll go and see him tomorrow morning. That's a pretty piece of jewelry."

When the children swarmed out of the dining room, the adults gathered at the reset table. Rabinovitz was just sitting down beside Natalie when the doorbell rang. Mendelson answered it. He came back to tap Rabinovitz on the shoulder, and without a word Rabinovitz got up and left. He tended to come and go like a wraith, and nobody commented. The seat was left vacant beside Natalie. Twelve people, including several famished new transients, fell to the meal. It was all black market fare, obviously: baked fish, fish soup, and boiled chickens, the bones of which the transients loudly gnawed to splinters. Brown bottles of fiery potato spirits went round, and Aaron Jastrow quaffed more than his share.

Ever since his arrival, Aaron had been holding forth at table, overawing even Mendelson. Tonight he was in good form. The sacrifice of Isaac came up, for it was in the Sabbath Torah reading. Mendelson had a brash atheist of a son-in-law named Velvel, his partner in the plumbing business, characterized by a lot of bushy red hair and strong opinions. Velvel said the story exposed the Jewish God as a fictive Asian despot, and the author as a Bronze Age savage. Coolly Aaron put Velvel down. "The story's about Abraham, not God, don't you understand, Velvel? Even a *goy* like Kierkegaard could see that. Read *Fear and Trembling* some time. The people of Father Abraham's time burned children to their gods. Archaeology confirms it. Yes, Abraham took up the knife. Why? To show for all time that he cared no less for God than the pagans did for their bloody idols. He trusted God to make him drop the knife before he hurt the boy. That's the whole point of the story."

"Beautiful," said Mendelson, adjusting a large black yarmulka on his white hair. "That's a beautiful interpretation. I must read Kierkegaard."

"And suppose," Velvel grumbled, "God hadn't told the old fanatic to drop the knife?"

"Why, the Bible would end at Genesis twenty-two," Aaron retorted, smiling. "There'd have been no Jewish people, no Christianity, no modern world. Holocausts of children might still be going on. But you see, He did tell him to drop it. Western civilization turns on that stark fact. God wants our love, not the ashes of our children."

"What a depressing conversation," said Mrs. Mendelson, jumping up to collect dishes. "Burning children, slaughtering a boy! *Feh!* Velvel, play something happy."

Velvel got his guitar and struck up a Sabbath hymn, *Yah Ribon*, which everyone sang. Even Natalie knew that this instrument playing violated orthodox rules. In the Mendelson ménage everything went eccentrically. The women cleared the table and brought on tea and coarse cakes, and the singers grew very jolly in a ditty about an Old King Cole sort of rabbi sending for fiddlers, drummers, fifers, and so on. Natalie joined the women in the kitchen to get the dishes and pots washed before the electricity went off. In the dining room Velvel began to play an old lullaby, *Rozhinkes mit Mandlen* (Raisins and Almonds). This song was now Aaron's solo; he was vain about knowing all the Yiddish verses. Softly accompanied by the guitar, Aaron began the haunting nonsense refrain that stirred Natalie's heart with powerful childhood echoes:

> *Under my darling's cradle*
> *Lies a little white goat.*
> *The little goat went into business,*
> *That will be your career.*
> *Raisins and almonds,*
> *Sleep, little boy, sleep, dear.*

She heard the outside door open and close. Avram Rabinovitz appeared in the kitchen doorway, his face pale and smiling. "Natalie?" She came to the doorway, drying her hands on her apron. In the hallway, redolent of Sabbath food aromas, dim light from a wall bracket fell slantwise on Byron in his gray raincoat, standing with a large valise in one hand, and a leather pouch in the other. Natalie's legs almost gave way at the shock. He looked much changed, but there was no mistaking him.

"Hi, darling," Byron said.

*   *   *

43

Global Waterloo
2: Torch

(from *World Holocaust* by Armin von Roon)

The Torch assault on North Africa was an Anglo-American gesture to placate Stalin. Since the day we invaded the Soviet Union, he had been nagging the British to open a "second front NOW in Europe." This demand was empty noise and Stalin knew it. The British were too weak for that.

But once Japan was goaded into the Pearl Harbor attack, enabling Roosevelt to make the gleeful plunge into world war, Stalin's demand became clamorous. The unscathed American Union, sitting prosperous and happy beyond bomber range, could field ten million men. Its capacity for making the tools of war was immense, and the Soviet Union was hard-pressed.

Yet the warmongering President had only a half-trained expanding army of green recruits, led by an unblooded officer cadre. Civilian morale was unstable. Mild rationing ordinances brought wails of protest; austerities that we Germans had been taking for granted for years seemed to the spoiled Americans the end of the world. What was worse — and this was fundamental, and Roosevelt knew it — like the Italians, *the American people were incapable of accepting substantial battle losses. This fact shaped all of Franklin Roosevelt's war decisions, including the North African landing.*

Roosevelt's solution of his problems can be starkly stated. The formula that won world empire for the U.S.A. was twofold:

1. Germany First.
2. Shed German blood by shedding the blood of others.

How Roosevelt did it will be an enduring study for political and military historians.

Roosevelt In Trouble

Roosevelt's people did not share his aim of "Germany First." They wanted to avenge Pearl Harbor. As Wake Island and the Philippines fell to yellow-skinned attackers, the racial outrage of the Americans grew intense.

Thousands of Japanese Americans were thrown into concentration camps, precisely like Jews behind the German lines, and for precisely the same reason: they were wartime security risks. The weepy indignation with which Roosevelt protested our security measures concerning the Jews was not in evidence on this matter.

TRANSLATOR'S NOTE: *The Nisei were abominably treated because of war hysteria. They were not murdered en masse, they all survived the war, and they got their property back. It was an indefensible business, but the distinction seems to escape General von Roon. — V.H.*

Moreover, the President soon discovered that war was not all beer and skittles.* Along his Atlantic coast and in the Caribbean, our U-boats played havoc at night, when the glow from the brightly lit coastal cities set up the targets. Strident calls for arms and action poured in on Roosevelt from the retreating Philippine defenders, from the forces in Hawaii, from the hard-pressed Chinese, from England's home front, from the British in Africa, Burma, Australia, India, and — loudest and ugliest — from the Soviet Union. Yet American war production was not in gear, and Roosevelt had his own army and navy to equip. He was in trouble.

Still, the Anglo-American planners had to go to work on a second front. The American General Staff officers, who had yet to smell gunpowder, were thinking in textbook terms: force the Channel coast as soon as possible, and smash across the northern plains to Berlin. But the British hated that notion. They proposed operations in Norway, in North Africa, in the Middle East; anywhere, in fact, but where we stood in force. Let the Red Army grind up the Wehrmacht; and if that meant a weak postwar Russia, all the better!

The "transatlantic essay contest" between the two staffs, as it came to be known, swayed back and forth. Roosevelt allowed the letters, memoranda, visits, and conferences to run on and on. He never strongly backed General Marshall in the American proposal:

1. A vast buildup of men and supplies in Britain;
2. A contingent scheme for an emergency landing in France in 1942, if Russia seemed about to collapse;
3. Otherwise, an all-out cross-Channel attack in 1943.

Roosevelt did not push for this because something very different was in his mind.

---

*German: *Krieg ist kein Honiglecken.*

Roosevelt's Basic War Plan

The Battle of Midway set him free to destroy Germany in his own fashion.

Before that, with an all-triumphant Japan menacing his rear, he could make no big move against us. Had Yamamoto won at Midway — as by all the odds he should have — public opinion would have forced Roosevelt to go all-out in the Pacific. But with the great Nimitz-Spruance victory in hand, he could devote his "forested mind" to winning world rule with other people's blood. In effect, this meant at all costs keeping the Soviet Union in the war.

Franklin Roosevelt's basic plan for winning the Second World War was to take Germany from the rear with a brute mass of Russian troops. Everything else was secondary. He saw his main chance cold and straight. Militarily, it was a clear and brilliant plan; and brilliantly, alas, did it work.

This explains his hardheaded distribution of American supplies. He starved his Pacific forces so that they barely made it through the fierce Guadalcanal campaign, while he lavished matériel on the ungrateful and ever-demanding Russians through the Persian Gulf and the northern route. And he amply supplied the British in Egypt via the Cape of Good Hope and the Red Sea, while Rommel's stalled army withered under Hitler's neglect. Thus Roosevelt made sure that when his raw troops went ashore in French North Africa against feeble Vichy opposition, our tough and dashing Afrika Korps would be embroiled at a disadvantage, two thousand miles away at El Alamein.

Rooseveltian Chicanery

Moreover, he skillfully put the blame on the British for reneging on the second front in France.

He allowed the "transatlantic essay contest" to drag on until Marshall reported to him from London that the two staffs were stalemated. Admiral Ernest King had long been pushing for a turn to the Pacific; and the frustrated and infuriated Marshall, a stiff autocrat in the George Washington image, advised the President that an all-out shift to the Pacific was the only answer to British obduracy.

This was the moment Roosevelt had been playing for. In his lordly fashion, he notified his Joint Chiefs through his gray eminence, Harry Hopkins, that it would be wrong to "pick up our dishes and leave." Roosevelt loved to use homely phrases to mask his subtle machinations. The western Allies had to fight the Germans somewhere in 1942, to keep faith with Russia. If the British were really all that cautious and battle-worn, why, he would graciously give in and accept one of their proposals: French North Africa was all right with him.

Marshall warned that opening the Mediterranean theatre meant cancelling the cross-Channel attack in 1943; but in soldierly fashion he did Roosevelt's bidding. So Torch took form as a concession by Roosevelt to the British, when in fact it was just what he wanted.

TRANSLATOR'S NOTE: *General von Roon here ventures into mind reading. Mr. Roosevelt as I observed him — sometimes from close at hand — was an astute improviser, solving problems day by day with common sense, and a good grasp of historical facts and logistical limits. For the long view he was smart enough to trust long heads like Marshall and King, which sufficed. — V.H.*

Churchill shouldered the responsibility to bring Stalin the bad news, for Roosevelt was ostensibly "giving in" to him, by sending the American army into an operation which could not fail. French North Africa was the softest of touches. Not one German soldier faced the invaders. It was out of Luftwaffe range. All Roosevelt had to worry about was French "honneur" (which his deal with the arch-collaborator Darlan neutralized), and some freak of weather or tides that might drown some of his G.I. Joes, or wet their feet and give them pneumonia as they plodded ashore. True, the logistical mounting of the armada was impressive. Mass production and organization were and still are the American forte.

In Moscow Stalin vented much rage on Churchill; but of course he was not really angry. It was all political show. Stalin always tended to defer genially to Roosevelt; possibly because, being the world's greatest mass murderer himself, he bowed to this master politician who could get others to do his slaughter for him.

In an engaging passage of his history, Churchill describes how Stalin, after treating him with barbarous rudeness at a long Kremlin conference, invited him to his private apartment, called for wine and vodka, invited in Molotov as a butt for jokes, and had a jolly midnight snack of a whole roast suckling pig; of which Churchill, who had a splitting headache, declined to partake. The picture lingers — the relish of the arch-Bolshevik consuming a pig, and the weary nausea of the aged arch-imperialist.

The British were wise to balk at the landing in France at that time. The Dieppe raid in August, when we killed or captured most of the Canadian raiders, suggests the warm welcome that would have awaited the Anglo-Americans, especially the neophyte G.I. Joes, in a landing attempt in France in 1942 or even 1943. But in the North Africa landing they had exactly the tea party that Roosevelt planned; they did, that is, until Rommel crossed the vast deserts after El Alamein and gave them their first rude taste of real war.

TRANSLATOR'S NOTE: *Roon deliberately belittles the largest, most difficult, most successful long-distance sea-borne invasion in history. If it looked easy, that was because it was well planned and well executed. It could have been a gigantic Gallipoli. — V.H.*

*   *   *

44

S HE threw herself into his arms. The dangling pouch struck her hip. The blow, the hard embrace, the warm eager kiss on her mouth, all scarcely registered, she was so shattered and dazed.

"Where's the boy?" Byron asked.

Clutching his hand, unable to talk, trying to infuse all her astounded love in her grip, she pulled him past the dining room down the gloomy halls. A romp was going on in the back of the flat: laughing and shouting boys were chasing squealing girls around a big bedroom. On the bed one little girl sat holding a baby in a clean blue jumper.

"There. That's your son."

In the dining room, many voices were joining in the chorus:

> The little goat went into business,
> That will be your career.
> Raisins and almonds,
> Sleep, little boy, sleep, dear.

Byron stood staring at the infant. At the sight of him the children stopped running, and their hubbub subsided. Exerting all her willpower not to cry, Natalie said, "Well, what do you think?"

"I guess he looks like me."

"God, does he ever! He's a stamped-out miniature."

"Will he be afraid if I pick him up?"

"Try it!"

Byron walked to the baby through the silent children, and lifted him. "Hello, boy. I'm your dad."

The girl who released the baby wrinkled her face at the English words. Louis looked from his mother to his father, then put his tiny hands to Byron's cheeks.

"He's a heavy kid," Byron said. "What have you been feeding him?"

"You wouldn't believe me if I told you. Octopus. Blackbirds. Anything!" She was unaware of the tears springing from her eyes till he brushed her cheek with his knuckles, and she felt the sliding wetness. "He's a travelling man, you see. A hell of a lot of goat's milk and cheese. Byron, do you like him?"

"He's all right," Byron said.

The other children were watching and listening with scarcely a whisper or a smile, their faces set in solemn curiosity. And Natalie could see Byron as it were through their grave wide eyes: a tall tanned Gentile with a tough countenance, in alien clothes, with a leather bag chained to his wrist; in looks and language not of the tribe, yet handling one of themselves in a fatherly way.

"Come, you've got to see Aaron! Then we'll go to my room and talk, my God, we've got to talk! You've got to tell me how you did this, I'm still gasping." As she took the baby from him, the leather pouch swung between them. "Byron, what is this thing?"

"I'll tell you about that, too."

Byron's visit to the dining room was a protracted and tumultuous sensation. Aaron's drunken amazement, his excited explanation in Yiddish — *"Natalie's mann fun Amerika, fun Amerikaner flot!"* — the general babble, the handshaking all around, the setting of a new place beside Rabinovitz, the parade of food and drink for them, the rousing welcome song in Yiddish while Byron forced down a few bites he didn't want; all this took time, but one couldn't fight off Jewish hospitality.

Bemused, Natalie stood in the doorway, holding Louis. There he sat amid the Mendelson ménage, Byron Henry, at a table where eight Sabbath candles burned, two of which she had herself lit — the most amazing sight in her life. Out of place though he obviously was, he was making cordial responses to the Yiddish compliments from all sides as Jastrow translated, and these people were warmly accepting him. He was her husband. That was enough. He was also an American naval officer. If the American consulate had rebuffed the applications of some visas, it didn't matter. Like the French, like most of Europe, they were waiting for the American counterattack against Hitler as their believing ancestors had waited for the Messiah. Nor did they seem surprised at Byron's thunderbolt appearance. Americans were supermen. Anyway, startling events were an everyday thing for these people; life was in chaos, and no one occurrence was very much stranger than another.

The contrast between Rabinovitz and Byron bit deep into her as the two men sat there side by side in candlelight, for the electricity had now shut off. The white-faced stumpy Palestinian, his shoulders bowed, his expression in repose a mixture of weariness, sadness, and resolve, was of another breed than Byron. Her husband had the clear-eyed self-assured naïve air of an American. His face bore new marks of experience she had yet to hear about, but Byron Henry, if he lived to be ninety, and if all his years were hard, would never look like Avram Rabinovitz.

"Sorry, now I go." Byron stood up. They let him leave, with a clamor of good-nights. Carrying Louis, she led him to the little room lined with yellow books. There Mrs. Mendelson, by the light of a tall candle burning on a dresser, was gathering Aaron's pajamas and dressing gown from a closet. The double bed Aaron usually slept in had been freshly made up. Natalie's cot was folded away. "Your uncle will sleep somewhere else, good Shabbas, good-night," she rattled in Yiddish, and she walked out, giving Natalie no time to smile, or blush, or thank her.

"I didn't understand a word," Byron said, "but there's a fine woman. How does that door lock?"

"With two bolts," Natalie said uncertainly, putting the yawning Louis down in his crib.

"Okay, lock them." He undid the chain from his wrist with a key and dropped the pouch on a chair. "I'm a temporary diplomatic courier, Natalie. That's what this thing is, and that's how I got here. I'm stationed on a submarine tender in Gibraltar. I've been there since August."

"But how did you manage that? And how did you find me? And — oh, sweetie —"

"All in good time." He was sweeping her into his arms.

She yielded to his powerful embrace, to his kisses, trying to please him, stupefied as she was. She thought of the revolting underwear he might uncover if they made hasty love right now; gray heavy cotton things, fit for a sow, all one could find in Siena. She still had her treasured pretty lingerie from Lisbon, but how could she stop him to change? Natalie would have lain naked on the worn carpet for him then and there, she was flooded with marvelling admiration and gratitude, but what she could not do was feel aroused. He had smashed back into her life like a cannon shell.

Unexpectedly his kisses stopped, his embrace loosened. "Natalie, that kid's watching us."

Louis indeed was standing up, holding the crib rail, regarding them with a lively expression.

"Oh, it's all right, he's only a year old," she murmured. "He's just curious as a raccoon."

"Raccoon, hell. He looks as though he's taking notes."

Natalie couldn't contain a giggle. "Maybe he is, dear, at that. It'll be his turn one day, you know."

"I swear I'm embarrassed," Byron said, and he let her go. "It's ridiculous, but it's the truth. That kid has grown-up eyes."

"Actually, honey," Natalie said, trying to keep her deep relief out of her voice, "why don't I clean him up for bed? Would you mind that? We can talk, and I can get a little used to you."

"Sure, go ahead. That's better than my idea, which was to cover his crib like a parrot's cage."

"Look, love, you should feel reassured," she giggled. Byron's drolleries had always amused her, and her nerves were stretched fiddlestring-tight. "The procedure is obviously quite new to him."

"I guess so. Is it true that he walks and talks?"

She took him from the crib and set him down on his feet. Louis toddled a few steps, looking to Byron for applause; for which, it was clear, he had developed a great taste.

"Well done, sprout. Now say something."

"Oh, you wouldn't understand him." She caught Louis up, and at a sink in the corner stripped and began washing him. "He babbles a mishmash of Yiddish, Italian, and French."

"I'd like to hear it."

With a shy sidewise glance she said, "You look so trim."

"You've grown far more beautiful."

Sweet warmth washed through her. "And your father, and Warren? Have you heard from them? Are they all right?"

"Warren? What do you mean? Didn't the Red Cross forward my letters? I wrote to Slote too about Warren."

His harsh tone made her turn scared eyes at him. "I got your last letter in May."

"Warren's dead. He died in the Battle of Midway."

"Oh! Oh, *darling* —"

"He got a posthumous Navy Cross." Glancing at his watch, Byron began to pace the narrow room. "Look, the train for Barcelona leaves at midnight. That's four and a half hours from now. You'd better start thinking about packing, Natalie. You won't have to take a lot. The shopping in Lisbon is still good."

She said dizzily, "Packing?"

"Aaron will have to wait till the consul general clears him, but I'm taking you and the baby with me."

"What! My God, Byron, did the consul general *say* you could?"

"We're going to his apartment now."

Like the dwellers in the Mendelson flat, James Gaither was hard to surprise. Wartime Marseilles was such a bubbling stew of political double-dealing, financial corruption, racial and nationalist crisscrossings, refugee agonies and tragedies, and Mediterranean finagling dating back to Phoenician times, that compared to Gaither's daily grind, melodramas and spy yarns paled. And this was only his legitimate work. In his covert dealings with the Resistance groups his experiences were right out of cheap cinema; of a drab sort, since sexy eyefuls never got into the action. All in all, in his two Marseilles years he had seen — so he liked to say — just about everything.

Still, Byron Henry's story was something new, and he was writing an account of it in his diary, in pajamas and dressing gown, when a knock came at the door. There stood Lieutenant Henry, pouch under his arm.

"Sorry to disturb you, sir."

"You again?"

"Sir, my wife and baby are downstairs."

"What! Out at night, without papers?"

"Rabinovitz is with them." Glancing down at the consul general's pajama legs, Byron said, "I regret the intrusion, sir."

"Never mind that. Get them all up here, fast."

Mrs. Henry came in with the baby in her arms, giving him a sweet apprehensive smile. Though her clothes were shabby, her hair carelessly combed, her whole aspect flustered and disarrayed, one look at her made the submariner's romantic feat easier to grasp. Well might a man work his way around the world for this one! The fair infant she carried was a babyish replica of the lieutenant. Avram Rabinovitz slouched in behind Mrs. Henry, looking unusually depressed and anxious.

Byron was still explaining his plan when Gaither began to wonder how best to quash it. It was a terrible idea, rash and highly dangerous. Yet with Natalie Henry sitting there holding that baby, he quite understood the young husband's impetuosity. Gently does it, he thought. "Lieutenant, the chargé d'affaires in Vichy has the exit visas. The telex came in confirming that today. We'll be getting them any day now. Perhaps as soon as tomorrow."

"Yes, sir, so you told me at dinner. But I've been thinking, and I don't see why I shouldn't just take Natalie and Louis along now. The thing is, I believe I can get them on the plane to the United States with me."

The wife cleared her throat and said in a charming husky voice, "He's good at that sort of thing."

"No doubt, Mrs. Henry, but there's the problem of crossing the border."

Byron sat beside his wife on the sofa, tense, erect, but collected. "Sir, flashing my diplomatic passport will suffice. It cuts through immigration red tape like a hot knife through butter. You know that yourself."

"Not always. Suppose you run into a nasty French border inspector or a German agent? I have myself. There's a lot of both kinds on that railroad route. You've got your transit visa. Your wife and child have nothing."

"I'll have a story."

"What's the story?"

"The baby got sick as hell in Gibraltar. We rushed him to Marseilles at night. We didn't bother with visas. I'll talk in broken French. I'll yell. I'll be the dumb angry American official. I'll make it stick, that I can promise you."

"But their passports have no Gibraltar stamps, no French stamps, only Italian stamps months old."

"Sir, all that flummery won't matter, I promise you. I can handle it."

"And unfortunately for your story, I've never seen a healthier-looking baby, Lieutenant. He's in the absolute pink."

On Natalie's lap, Louis was yawning like a crocodile. He did have excellent color, and his blinking eyes were clear and bright.

"It could have been appendicitis, something like that, just a false alarm."

Gaither turned on Natalie. "Are you prepared to sustain this story?"

Byron quickly struck in as she hesitated, "By the time we get to Perpignan we'll have it all rehearsed and down cold. Please don't worry, sir."

Gaither went to a telephone and summoned the consulate car and driver. "How about something to drink, all around?" he asked. "Chilly night."

Byron said, "Thanks, but we'd better keep clear heads."

"I'll take something," Natalie said. "Thank you."

"So will I," said Rabinovitz.

Gaither mixed drinks, still thinking, *Gently does it.* Walking up and down the room, whiskey in hand, white hair in disorder, dressing gown flapping, he said, "Lieutenant, I want to talk plainly to your wife."

"By all means, sir."

"Mrs. Henry, as I said, there are Gestapo agents on the trains and at the border. When they're on the trains, they do exactly as they please. They ignore all regulations. Rabinovitz knows that. Your husband may indeed get you by. He's a resourceful man, that's clear. On the other hand, the Gestapo has a keen nose for Jews travelling illegally. Those agents are hard and cruel men. You may be pulled off the train."

"She won't be," Byron interrupted, "and if she is, I'll go along."

"In that case," Gaither went on to Natalie, as though Byron hadn't spoken, "when you're questioned, your baby may be taken away from you. That's how the Germans do things." At the look of horror that passed over her face Gaither added, "I'm not predicting this will happen. But it may. You can't rule it out. Can you sustain a fake story once they do that?" Her eyes were reddening as she sat silent. He went on, "And once you and your baby are taken into custody, I can't protect you. We have a file of such cases pending now — people halted with questionable American documents. Some are still in police custody. A few, unhappily, are already in Rivesaltes."

"Rivesaltes?" Natalie choked the word at Rabinovitz.

"French concentration camp," he said.

Byron stood up and faced Gaither. "You're trying to frighten her."

"I'm trying to be honest with her. Are you, young fellow? You're carrying classified documents. Once you're detected in this bluff, the Gestapo can take the position that you're an imposter, confiscate that pouch, and slash it open."

Byron's face was getting pale and drawn. "It's a negligible risk," he said after a pause. "I'm ready to take it."

"It's not up to you."

Byron adopted a quieter, almost pleading manner. "Mr. Gaither, you're raising bugaboos. It'll all go smooth as oil, I assure you. Once we're across and out, all this will be forgotten. You'll laugh at your fears. We're going to chance it."

"You are not. I'm the senior American officer in this area, and I have to order you not to do this. I'm very sorry."

"Byron," Natalie said, in a faltering tone, her eyes wide with alarm, "it'll be a few more days at most. Go. Wait for us in Lisbon."

He whirled on her. "Damn it, Natalie, all hell's about to break loose in the Med. There's hundreds of planes lined up wing to wing in Gibraltar. At the first sign of trouble they'll close the borders." She was looking desperately at him, as though hoping for a convincing word and not yet hearing it. "Good God, darling, we went from Cracow to Warsaw with the war blowing up all around us, and you never turned a hair."

"We've got Louis now."

Byron faced Avram Rabinovitz. "Don't you think we can make it?"

The Palestinian, crouched over a cigarette, turned his head sideways to look up at Byron. "You're asking me?"

"Sure."

"I'm afraid."

"*You're* afraid?"

"I've been taken off that train to Barcelona by the Germans."

Byron stared long at him. "I guess this is why you told me to come here first."

"Yes, it is."

Dropping into a chair, Byron said to Gaither, "I'll take that drink, sir."

"I have to go," Rabinovitz said, and with a last sombre glance in Natalie's eyes and a caress of Louis's cheek, he departed.

Pouring more whiskey and soda, Gaither thought of a leading article in *Le Cahier Jaune*, the French anti-Semitic journal that he had glanced through on the train coming back from Vichy. The photographs had been taken at a French government exhibit in Paris called "Jewish Traits and Physiognomies": huge plaster models of hook noses, blubber lips, and protruding ears. Louis Henry didn't fit the specifications; but if French immigration inspectors, or the Gestapo, laid hands on him, he would be just a Jew like his mother. Otherwise, of course, Mrs. Henry could bluff her way through any border point, even without the lieutenant; a beautiful woman, a mother, an American; ordinarily no problem! But the Germans had turned routine travel in Europe, for Jews, into a risk like jumping from a burning building. Trivial bits of paper could mean life or death; Gaither knew Jews with valid passports and exit visas who were staying on in France merely for fear of facing the Gestapo at the borders.

The silence in the room was leaden as Gaither passed the drinks. To ease the strain, he talked about how he had gotten British pilots out of France on this train to Barcelona, posing as firemen and engineers. But they were tough men, he explained, trained in the escape art, prepared to confront the Gestapo; and still there had been some bad incidents. When the consulate car arrived, Gaither became all business again. It still lacked an hour of train time, he said. Byron could get to the terminal in twenty minutes. Would he like some time alone with his family? The driver would bring up Mrs. Henry's luggage; now that she was here, she had better remain until the exit visas came. In the morning he would send for Jastrow, too, and keep the three of them under his eye until they left for Lisbon. He would himself go with them to the border, or send someone trustworthy in his place.

He showed Byron and Natalie into a small bedroom, and closed the door. Not looking at Byron, Natalie laid the sleeping baby on the bed, and covered him with her coat.

Byron said, "You surprised me."

She faced him. He leaned against the doorway, hands in his pockets, one leg crossed over the other, in the exact pose in which she had first laid eyes on him, when she had called for him on a Siena street in Jastrow's car.

"You're terribly angry."

"Well, not really. He frightened you. But I think we could have made it. Cigarette?"

"I don't smoke any more."

"I recognize that pin."

"Warsaw seems a million years ago."

"I'll wait for you in Lisbon, Natalie. I've got thirty days' leave, and I'll just wait. I'll inquire every day at the consulate." His smile was gracious and distant. "I doubt I can book that honeymoon suite in Estoril."

"Try."

"All right, I will."

That started them on reminiscences. Carter Aster's name came up. Byron chatted about his orders to the *Moray*, and about how fine the new fleet submarines were. Natalie did her best to act interested, to respond, but it was lifeless talk. He made no move to take her in his arms. She was afraid to move first herself. She was afraid of him, ashamed of her cowardice. The wretched suspicion was growing on her that his spectacular feat in finding her was the worst thing that could have happened to them, given the time and the circumstances. Yet what could she have done about this miserable turn of events? To the Germans and the Vichy French agents, the baby was a Jew. That was a terror impossible for Byron Henry to grasp. On that rock their marriage might split, but there it was.

"I suppose I ought to think about moving along," he said at last, in a dry cold manner, getting up.

That triggered a reaction from Natalie. She ran to him, clutched him in her arms, and kissed him wildly on the mouth, again and again. "Byron, I'm sorry, I'm sorry, I can't help it. I can't defy Gaither. I think he's right. I'll be there in a week or less. Wait for me! Forgive me! Love me, for God's sake! I'll love you till I die. Do you doubt me?"

He returned her kisses gently; and he said with his strange melancholy smile, the smile that had intoxicated her from the first, "Why, Natalie, you and I will never die. Don't you know that?" Walking over to the bed, he looked down at the flushed slumbering infant. "Good-bye, sprout. I'm glad I got a look at you."

They went into the living room together, and after a handshake with Gaither, he was gone.

PART FOUR

Pug and Rhoda

45

I N helmet and life jacket, Victor Henry stood on the port wing, watching red tracer shells of his main battery salvo streak off into the sultry night. The shadowy line of enemy ships off Guadalcanal showed up under a drifting cluster of green-white star shells, partly obscured by smoke and splashes of straddles from the *Northampton*'s guns.

"*Torpedoes! . . . Torpedoes one point on the port bow! . . . Torpedoes to port, Captain, target angle ten!*"

The clamor broke from the lookouts, from the telephone talkers, from officers and sailors all over the bridge. Though Pug's ears were half-deafened by salvos and his eyes half-blinded by muzzle flame, he heard the cries and saw the approaching wakes. On the instant he barked, "*HARD LEFT RUD-DER!*" (Turn toward the wakes, and hope to comb them; the only chance now.)

"Hard left rudder, Captain." The helmsman's voice was loud and firm. "Rudder is hard left, sir."

"Very well."

The two phosphorescent lines cut through the glassy black water almost dead ahead, at a slight angle to the ships' course. It would be a close thing! Three other heavy cruisers, already torpedoed, were burning astern in blotches of yellow under dense high smoke columns: the *Minneapolis*, the *Pensacola*, and the *New Orleans*. Torpedoes were shoaling like herrings around the task force. Where in God's name were they all coming from? A pack of submarines? In its first fifteen minutes this action was already a catas-trophe, and now if his own ship went — ! As the vessel rolled, the two green wakes disappeared, then came in sight sliding past far below, directly under the captain's gaze. Confused shouts rose all around him. Christ, this was going to be close! He gripped the bulwark. His breath stopped —

LIGHT!

The night exploded into sun glare.

• • •

The night action on November 30, 1942, in which the *Northampton* went down has faded from memory. The Japanese navy is extinct, and the

United States Navy has no reason to celebrate the Battle of Tassafaronga, a foolish and futile disaster.

At the time, the United States already dominated Guadalcanal by sea, in the air, and on land. To supply their starved sick garrison, Japanese destroyers were skulking past the cove called Tassafaronga, tossing overboard drums of fuel and food for small craft to come out and retrieve. They were not looking for a fight. But on Halsey's orders an American cruiser flotilla came six hundred miles from the New Hebrides to Guadalcanal, to halt and sink a large new enemy landing force. In fact, there was no such force. It was a phantom of false intelligence.

The rear admiral commanding the flotilla had taken over only two days before. His force was formed of broken units, remnants of many Guadalcanal sea fights. He was new to the area, and his ships had not trained together. Still, with the advantages of radar, surprise, and superior firepower, his Task Force Sixty-seven should have wiped out the enemy. With four heavy cruisers, a light cruiser, and six destroyers, he faced only eight Japanese destroyers.

But his operation plan assumed that the Japanese destroyer torpedo, like the American weapon, had a range of twelve thousand yards. Actually, the Japanese torpedo could go about twenty thousand yards, and twice as far on slow setting; and its warhead was much more destructive. At the admiral's conference before the run north, Victor Henry had mentioned this; he had written an intelligence memorandum in 1939 on the Japanese torpedo, which had altered his whole career. But the new admiral had coolly repeated, "We will close to twelve thousand yards, and open fire." Pug could argue the point no further.

So the Japanese destroyer admiral, trapped against the coast without sea room on the night of November 30, heavily outgunned, with eight-inch cruiser shells raining around him, star shells glaring overhead, splashes and smoke enveloping his force, desperately launched all torpedoes toward the distant muzzle flashes. This shotgun blast of warheads caught all four American heavy cruisers. The Japanese fled victorious and all but unscathed.

•   •   •

The thundering concussion tore at Pug Henry's ears. He was thrown to his knees. He sprang up, staggering. The whole ship was shuddering like a train off its track, and worse than that, worse than the fire shooting up on the port side, was the sudden list. Ten degrees or more, he groggily estimated — in seconds. What holes those torpedoes must have blown!

Seared into his memory was the story of the *Juneau*, torpedoed and vanishing in a giant explosion. He darted into the bridge house and seized a microphone. *"This is the captain speaking."* He heard the grating bellow of his own voice over the deck loudspeakers. "*Flood magazines of number three turret and jettison five-inch ready ammo. Repeat, flood magazines of number three turret and jettison five-inch ready ammo! Acknowledge!*"

A telephone talker shouted that the orders had been heard and were being carried out. The deck was still quivering. Almost, the *Northampton* might be bumping over a reef, but Pug knew that he was out in six hundred fathoms of water. When he strode out on the port wing, microphone in hand, the heat hitting his face surprised him. It was like opening a furnace door. The fire was roaring all over the stern, casting an orange glow far out on the dark water.

"*Now, all hands, this is the captain speaking. We've taken a torpedo hit, possibly two, on the port quarter. Expedite damage reports. Forward fire-fighting and damage control parties, lay aft to help control fires and set flooding boundaries. Exec, lay up to the bridge —*"

The orders formed readily in Pug's mind after months of hard drilling. Drills were a hell of a nuisance to the crew, but they would pay off now. In the bridge house the telephone talkers were relaying damage reports in controlled tones. The OOD and the quartermaster were hunched at the chart table over the ship's diagram, hatching the lower deck compartments with red and black crayons; black for salt water penetration, red for fire. Bad first reports: three propeller shafts stopped, communication and power failing, water and oil flooding on C and D decks. As Pug kept issuing orders he was already thinking of a salvage strategy. Holding back fire and flood long enough to make port was the thing to try for. Tulagi was eighteen miles away. The three other cripples were already heading there.

"*After fire room, secure ruptured fuel and steam lines. All stations that have power pump fuel port to starboard. Pump overboard all port side water ballast,* and —"

Another *BLAST!* jerked the deck under his feet. Far aft behind the boat deck a thick geyser of black oil climbed like a Texas gusher and toppled in the firelight, drenching the mast, the gun director housings, the boat deck, and number three turret in a thick gummy rain. Flames began climbing the oil-soaked mast, making a tower of bright rising fire against the smoky sky. More sheets of oil sprang from below-deck explosions, feeding the flames.

The ship could not live long at this rate. Despite her formidable length and big guns, she was a vulnerable monster. Her stability and her damage control characteristics were poor. She had been built not to military requirements, but to the stupid limits of a politicians' treaty. Pug had known that all along, hence his zealotry for disaster drills. Alas, the torpedoes had lucked into the heavy cruiser's weakest spot, just aft of the skimpy armor belt, tearing open main fuel-oil bunkers and — almost certainly — the cavernous engine and fire rooms. It would be all uphill to Tulagi. The sea must be cascading in below.

But the pumping had yet to take hold. This long hull contained some two million cubic feet of air space. That was a lot of buoyancy. If his vessel wasn't about to blow up, if the enemy didn't put more torpedoes in her, if the fires didn't break out of control, he might make port. Even if he had to beach her, the *Northampton* was of immense salvage value. The fire-fighting parties, clumps of moving shadows in the glare, were dragging their handybillies and hoses here and there on the slippery deck, and sparkling streams were raising great clouds of orange-red vapor. Damage reports were pouring up to the bridge house, and the tones of officers and sailors were becoming businesslike. The forward engine room still had power; one propeller was enough to shove this cripple into Tulagi.

For all the heartsickness at the torpedoing of his ship, and the defeat in the making, for all the macabre light and sound of a warship stricken at night — the glare, the crackling tumult, the shouts, the alarms, the smell of burning, the eye-stinging smoke, the worsening list, the nightmare glow on the black sea, the cacophony on the bridge of TBS and sailors' voices — for all the acute peril, for all the drastic decisions he had to make fast, Victor Henry was not bewildered or beset; on the contrary, he felt himself coming fully alive for the first time since Midway. Back in the bridge house he spoke over the TBS, *"Griffin, Griffin, this is Hawkeye, over."*

In reply, a formal drawl: *"Hawkeye from Griffin, come in, over —"* An older voice broke through. "Hold on, son, that's Pug Henry over on the *Northampton*. I'll talk to him. . . . Say, Pug, is that you?" Admirals ignored communication procedure. "How are you doing, fella? You look pretty bad from over here."

"Over here" was the *Honolulu*, the one unscathed cruiser left in the task force, a lean long shadow to the northwest, racing with the destroyer screen out of the torpedo water.

"I've got one engine room and one propeller, Admiral. I'll head for Tulagi too. We're effecting repairs, or trying to, as we go."

"That's one hell of a fire there on your stern."

"We're fighting it."

"Do you require assistance?"

"Not now."

"Pug, radar shows these bandits retiring westward. I'll sweep around Savo Island to engage them beyond torpedo range. If you need help, holler, and I'll send you a couple of my small boys."

"Aye aye, sir. Good hunting. Out."

"Good luck, Pug."

During this talk the executive officer arrived on the bridge, his moon face under the helmet streaked with soot and sweat, and he took charge of damage control while the captain conned the ship. Through battles, bombardments, long voyages, and a Navy Yard overhaul, Pug had developed confidence in this quiet chubby man from Idaho, though their personal relationship remained by mutual choice a distant one. In Grigg's last fitness report, Pug had reported him qualified for command. The latest Alnav had promoted Grigg to four stripes, and they expected him to get the *Northampton* any day. Pug already had orders to fly back to Washington for reassignment "when relieved." With Grigg handling damage control, Pug had time to reflect. His evil luck was certainly holding! Grigg's orders were probably on the way, but the delay had pushed him into this ill-omened night battle as captain. If he lost his ship, he would have to answer to a court of inquiry, and he could not plead that an inept admiral with an ill-conceived op-plan had led him into torpedo water.

The fires were no longer spreading so rapidly, and the main bulkheads were holding out the sea; so the reports went. But Pug was watching two indicators: the clinometer, which kept creeping left, and a plumb line that he had rigged which showed the ship settling by the stern. He was trying to head around northeast to Tulagi. All the telephone systems had failed, even the sound-powered lines; grounded by salt water, burned out, jarred loose. Messengers were carrying each order down the foremast, along the main deck, through black smoky passageways awash in water or oil, down several more decks to the forward engine room. Conning his ship by this slow process was exasperating, yet she was coming around. Meantime, Grigg was sending rescue teams to release trapped men from flooding compartments. The wounded were being brought topside. The fire-control crews, caught in the oil-drenched gun directors on the buring mainmast, were being saved from roasting alive by asbestos-clad rescuers, slowly mounting the mast behind fog nozzles and helping them down.

Dead ahead on the horizon, Florida Island bulged, with Tulagi lost in its shadow. The list was now up to twenty degrees, about as far as the heavy cruiser rolled in a gale. The *Northampton* hung lifelessly to port in a sea smoothed by leaking oil. It would be a race between the flooding and the remains of the power plant. If Grigg could keep the ship afloat till dawn it might make Tulagi behind the three other cripples, far ahead and brightly smoking. So Pug was thinking when Grigg came to him, mopping his brow with a sleeve. "Sir, we'd better lie to."

"Lie to? I've just now got her on course."

"Shoring is giving way on C and D decks, sir."

"But what do we do, Grigg, sit here and drift, filling up? I'll take some turns off the engine."

"Also, Captain, Chief Stark says the lube oil supply to number four engine is failing. The pump can't overcome the list."

"I see. Well, in that case maybe I will ask the admiral for a couple of destroyers."

"I guess you should, sir."

Grigg's news about the lubricating oil was close to a death sentence. Both men knew it. They both knew, too, that the lube oil system was poorly designed. Long ago, to no avail, Pug had requested an alteration.

"Yes, but meantime let's close Tulagi, even if we burn out our bearings."

"Captain, with any way on, we won't hold out the sea."

"Then what's to be done?"

"I'll counterflood all I can. We're low on pumping capacity, is the trouble. If I can right her five degrees and double up the shoring we can try getting under way again."

"Very well, I'll lay below for a looksee. You ask Griffin for the destroyers. Tell him we're afire, dead in the water, listing twenty-two degrees, and down hard by the stern."

Pug descended to the steeply slanting main deck, and slipped and slid ankle-deep in malodorous black oil past the fire-fighters to the huge rip in the afterdeck through which the oil had spouted up. Leaning outboard, he could see ragged hull plates sticking straight out into the water, blown out by the torpedoes. That was a sight he would never forget: a black hole in his ship, rimmed in broken metal like a crudely opened can. The other hole below the water line was reported to be yet larger. Leaning over the lifelines, Pug dizzily felt that the ship might capsize then and there. The list was rapidly getting worse, no doubt of that. He passed horribly wounded and burned men lying in rows on the fantail deck, tended by the pharmacist's mates. Time was needed to get those men off. Sadly, he returned to the bridge, called the executive officer aside, and told him to prepare to abandon ship.

About an hour later, Victor Henry took his last look around the deserted bridge. The little steel structure was quiet and clean. The quartermaster and the officers of the deck had taken away all the logs and records. The secret publications had been thrown overboard in weighted bags. Below, the crew was mustering at abandon-ship stations. The sea was a black still lake, with four scattered vessels burning on it like fallen yellow stars. The rescue destroyers were on their way. Sharks would be a hazard, and some sixty officers and men, at last muster, would never leave the ship; missing, or killed by fire, water, or explosion. Still, the loss of life would be low if nothing else went wrong.

By now Pug was in a fever to get his crew off. Crippled heavy ships were a prime prey of submarines. The last thing he did was to take from his sea cabin a pair of gloves and the folding photograph frame, containing Warren's Academy graduation picture and an old photograph of the whole family, in which Warren and Byron were gangling boys, and Madeline a little girl in a paper crown. Tucked into the frame were two small snapshots: Pamela

Tudsbury, huddled in gray fur in the snow outside the Kremlin, and Natalie holding her baby in the Siena garden. About to descend the ladder, he noticed the *Northampton*'s battle flag folded on a flagbag. He took that.

Grigg was waiting for him, firelight flickering on his face, on a main deck slanted like a ski slide. He gave an unhurried muster report.

"Okay, let's abandon ship, Grigg."

"You're coming, then, Captain?"

"No." He gave Grigg the battle flag. "I'll get off in due course. Take this. Fly it in your next command. And here, try to keep my family dry for me, will you?"

Grigg tried to argue that counterflooding was still possible, that a number of pumps were working, and that damage control was his specialty. If the captain wouldn't leave, then the first lieutenant could man the motor whaleboat and look after the men down in the sea. He wanted to remain.

"Grigg, abandon ship," Pug interrupted in sharp cold tones.

Grigg stood as straight as he could and saluted. Pug returned the salute, saying, in an informal tone, "Well, good luck, Jim. I guess that turn west was a mistake."

"No, *sir!* You couldn't do anything else. We had the range. We had the bastards straddled. How could you let them retire scot-free? Pete Kurtz claims we hit a cruiser with that last salvo. He saw the explosions, just after we took those fish."

"Yes, so he told me. Maybe we can get that verified. Still, we should have hauled ass like the *Honolulu*. But it's done."

The exec looked forlornly up and down the steep-slanting deck. "I'll miss the *Nora-Maru*."

Surprised, Pug smiled. This was the sailors' nickname for the ship, and neither he nor Grigg had used it before. "Go ahead, over the side with you."

Swung out on the davits, the motor whaleboat loaded with wounded was so close to the water that the sailors had only to cut the falls. Balsa rafts flew over the side. Hundreds of nearly naked sailors went swarming down nets, sliding down ropes, many crossing themselves before they went. Below, there was a great sound of splashing, and those in the water cried thinly to each other and to the men on deck.

Soon they all were down in the sea. Rafts, boats, and bobbing heads drifted away on the current. In the distance the two destroyers shadowily approached. The crew's voices carried up on the slight warm breeze — men shouting for help, blowing whistles, calling out to each other in the dark. Well, none would die by fire now, Pug thought, and few if any by water, though sharks might be a hazard. Fortunately the floating oil had not ignited.

Pug was remaining aboard with a small volunteer salvage party of sailors and one chief. Strange things happened to damaged ships. Fires could burn out. Vagaries of flooding could even right a listing hulk. At Midway the captain of the *Yorktown* had in some embarrassment climbed back aboard his ship long after abandoning it, and if not for a submarine attack next day he might have salvaged it. Pug and his volunteers might be caught in a capsizing or a torpedoing, but if the *Northampton* stayed afloat till dawn they could rig the line for a tow.

The silence, the unprecedented filth on the vast empty deck, were strange and dreamlike. Clutching at cleats, stanchions, lifelines — for to keep his footing was becoming harder all the time — he groped his way to the forecastle to see how the towing rig preparations were coming along. Looking back at his sinking ship, he observed that his guns, arrested in the elevation of the last portside salvo, paralleled the sea, so steep was the list. Here the *Northampton* looked like her old self, except for the crazy tilt and the yellow glow that silhouetted the masts and the guns. Good-bye, then, to the *Nora-Maru!*

Around abandoned hand pumps and over coiling hoses he staggered aft, amid heaps of detritus — clothes, food, cigarette wrappings, books, papers, shell cases, coffee mugs, half-eaten sandwiches, oil-soaked life jackets, shoes, boots, helmets, all in a rotten stink of garbage and excrement, for the men had been relieving themselves topside; but the prevailing smells were of burning and of oil — above all *oil, oil, oil!* The sour stench of disaster would forever, for Victor Henry, be the smell of crude petroleum.

For another hour he watched the salvage party stumble about their work, mainly pumping and fire-fighting. The sailors had to move monkey-fashion, using hands and feet on deck projections to keep from sliding on the oily plates. Firelit faces stern, mouths taut, they kept looking out to sea at the two destroyers picking up survivors. Pug at last decided, at a quarter to three, that the *Northampton* was a dead loss. Staying on any longer, he would only risk sailors' lives to make himself look good. She might or might not float for another hour; she might also capsize with little warning.

"Chief, let's abandon ship."

"Aye aye, *SIR.*"

At the word the sailors pitched the last large balsa raft overboard. It sailed down and struck with a loud splash. The chief, a gray-headed big-bellied man, the best machinist on the ship, urged the captain to go first. When Pug brusquely refused, the chief kicked off his shoes, stripped to oil-smeared jockey shorts, and tied his life jacket around his thick sweaty white rolls of fat. "Okay, you heard the boss man, let's go." He scrambled like a boy down the straight-hanging cargo net, the sailors after him.

In this last minute alone on deck, Pug tasted a bitter private savor of farewell. Going down with the ship was out of the question; in the United States Navy you saved yourself to fight another day. The other tradition was stupid, though romantic and honorable. He could not help the war effort by drowning. Pug murmured a prayer for the dead men he was leaving in the hulk. He stripped to shorts, and drew on the gloves he had fetched from the bridge. In abandon-ship drills, he had always gone hand over hand down a dangling hawser. Aside from gratifying his petty vanity — he was agile at it — this had set many of the crew to imitating him, a useful thing. In emergencies ladders and nets might not be available when ropes were.

Rough manila slithering through his bare legs, Pug lowered himself into the black tropical sea. As he let go and splashed, the water felt good; warm as a bath and very salty. He swam through sticky gobs of petroleum to the raft, which still rode to a long painter tied to a cleat on deck. Naked sailors jammed the raft and swimmers surrounded it clinging to loops of cord.

"Chief, are all the men here?"

"Yes, Captain."

Several sailors offered to make room for him on the raft.

"Stay where you are, the lot of you. Cast off!"

A knife flashed in the firelight. The painter fell away. The men paddled the raft from the foundering ship. Trying to wipe foul oil from his hair and face and to rinse the taste from his mouth, Victor Henry watched her sinking. Seen from below she was a grandiose spectacle, a vast black shape stretching across half the horizon in sluggish toppling agony, with one end burning like a torch. The men on the raft were chanting long wailing halloos and blowing on shrill whistles at the nearby destroyers and motorboats. A swell washed over Pug, and oil got in his eyes. He was bathing them when he heard yells of *"There she goes!"*

Rearing up on his wrist cord, he saw the *Northampton* roll over and lift her dripping bow high. The fire went out, and she slid downward. The men ceased hallooing and whistling. It was so quiet on the raft that, over the lapping of the water, as the bow sank from sight, Pug heard the mournful sighing rush and roar of the vortex that swallowed his ship.

46

A YELLOW blaze lights the night sky in a different part of the world.

Berel Jastrow, ankle-deep in snow outside the hideously stinking latrine blockhouse, stops in his tracks and stares at the high flare. It is the test: scheduled, postponed, rescheduled, postponed again. All week long SS bigwigs have been stomping through the puddles in the ice-cold raw cement structure, down in the enormous underground chambers and up above at the untried furnaces, their impatient brusque comments echoing to the splash and thump of boots.

The Commandant himself has been there with his frozen-faced entourage, watching civilian technicians work their heads off on twenty-four-hour shifts side by side with the shaven-headed bone-skinny inmates in their striped pajamas. Very strange they have looked in Auschwitz, these well-fed healthy outsiders with full heads of hair, wearing the almost forgotten polite costume of overcoats, trousers, jackets, ties, or else workmen's overalls; cheerful businesslike Poles or Czechs, talking technical jargon with the German supervisors about retorts, generator gases, fire bricks, draft cross-sections, and so forth; normal fellows, doing a normal job, acting normally.

Normally, except for the way they look at the prisoners. It is as though the striped ticking gives a man the invisibility of a fairy-tale cloak. The technicians do not seem to see you. Of course they are not allowed to talk to inmates, and they fear the SS overseers. Still, not even to show, with a flicker of the eyes, that they see fellow human beings? To look through them as though they are air? To walk around them as though they are posts, or piles of bricks? A strange thing.

The high red-yellow flare at the chimney top flutters and almost dies as clouds of black smoke swirl in the fire; then it burns clear again. No mistaking what this sight is. The tall square chimney shows up plain in the smoky glow from the disposal pits out beyond. Successful test; and why not? The best German workmanship has been going into this installation, the finest machinery and equipment — generators, ovens, blowers, electric hoists, giant ventilators, novel cradles that roll on rails right into the oven mouths — all first-class. Berel has himself been working at cementing this factory-new apparatus into place. He knows quality when he sees it. German wartime shortages have not affected this job. Highest priority! Down in the lower level, those long cavernous chambers are rough work by comparison, except for the airtight doors; excellent workmanship in those heavy doors, in the stout frames, in the double rubber gaskets.

Swinging his club, a trusty slogs by Jastrow toward the latrine, giving him an ugly look. Jastrow has his armband pinned on; rank has its privileges, he can relieve himself after dark. But armband or no, a trusty can crack you on the ass if he pleases, or for that matter smash in your skull and leave you bleeding to death in the snow, and there will be no fuss. Hurrying back to his barrack, Jastrow looks into the block chief's room: clean comfortable digs, with German travel posters of the Rhine, the Berlin Opera, and the Oktoberfest on the plank walls.

The block chief, a tall thin horribly pimpled *Volksdeutscher* burglar from Prague, is smoking a pipe in an old wicker chair, muddy boots up on a stool. Plenty of tobacco around in the camp now; also soap, food, Swiss francs, dollars, medicine, jewelry, gold, clothes; all manner of precious things, available at great risk, at high price. The SS men and the trusties are skimming the cream, naturally, but the inmates trade also; some to eat better, some to grab profit, a daring few to implement resistance or escape. This tide of goods has been sweeping in with the Jewish transports from the west, which have been mounting in number and size month by month. During the summer typhus epidemic, all camp discipline sagged. The trickle of contraband from "Canada," the luggage disposal barracks, became a corrupting flood. The Auschwitz black market, though a mortally dangerous racket, is now unstoppable.

The block leader blows out a sweetly fragrant gray cloud, and with a wave of his pipe dismisses Jastrow, who makes his way down the long frigid crowded blockhouse, his wooden clogs sliding in the ropy mud of the floor. Not an unendurable trusty, he thinks, this old green-triangle type from Dachau and Sachsenhausen, ready as a whore to do anything for money or luxuries except risk his neck or his job. At roll call he puts on a tough show for the SS, clubbing inmates about, but in the block he is just a lazy good-for-nothing. Now and then he messes behind his closed door with one or another of the *peipls*, the perverted boy inmates who drift through the blocks. The prisoners do not even slyly grin at that any more. Old stuff.

Many inmates are already snoring in their bunks, lying three and four to a tier like sardines. Jastrow pushes past the men roosting on the long central brick pipe which doesn't warm the place, but slightly mitigates, together with all the body heat of the prisoners, the subzero night. All the Birkenau huts — he has worked on constructing more than a hundred of them — are built on one German army plan: the field shelter, *Pferdestall*, for horses. These drafty barns, knocked up on the bare marshy ground with wood and tarpaper, are designed to shelter fifty-two animals. But a man needs less room than a horse. Three shelves per stall gives a hundred fifty-six spaces. Put three prisoners on a tier, deduct space for the trusty's room, the block office, the food service area, the slop vat area; result, about four hundred men per *Pferdestall*.

That's the regulation number, more or less; but regulations in Auschwitz are elastic, and heavy overcrowding is the usual thing. Sammy Mutterperl rescued Jastrow from a block where over a thousand men, mostly newcomers sick in the bowels, turned and squirmed all night in every inch of space, in the tiers and on the mud floor, faces jammed to assholes in the dark; where every morning ten or twenty glassy-eyed open-mouthed corpses had to be dragged outside to the roll call, and piled up for the meat wagons. Skilled artisans and foremen like Mutterperl are in the less crowded block-houses like this one. The mushrooming camp needs these surveyors, locksmiths, carpenters, tanners, cooks, bakers, doctors, draftsmen, linguist-clerks, and the like; so life in their huts may include fuel for the stoves, endurable food, and good water and latrine privileges. Some of those fellows may even survive the war, if the Germans will let anyone survive Auschwitz.

The block of the Klinger kommando is bad enough. The lukewarm morning ersatz coffee, watery evening soup, and single slice of sawdusty bread are the usual Auschwitz ration: in itself, a sentence to slow death. But the kitchen has special orders about hard workers and skilled men: distribution twice a week of extra slices of bread, salami, or cheese to the privileged list. This enriched dole is still less than the "regulation" ration, for the SS consumes, or steals and sells, half the food consigned by Berlin for prisoners. Everybody knows that. They steal all food parcels for Jews from the outside, too; other prisoners, especially British inmates, can end up with part of their parcels. Still, the Klinger gang does well on the added calories, though some of them do gradually dwindle to *Musselmen*. These are a familiar Auschwitz type, the Musselmen; men starved down to dreamy emaciated moving mummies, doomed to be clubbed or kicked to death for slow work, when they don't simply drop and die at random.

Men like Mutterperl and Jastrow are not going to fade to Musselmen. A different fate awaits them. The sardonic word has long since leaked down from the Labor Section: when the work is done, the kommando will have the great honor of going up the chimney first. Auschwitz humor! Also probably the truth; a variation of the Sonderkommandos' fate.

With a practiced movement Jastrow slides feet first into the middle bunk that he shares with Mutterperl, who lies asleep in the blankets which he "organized" from Canada; and which, despite the prevailing thievery, nobody steals from him. The tier shakes. Mutterperl opens his eyes.

Jastrow murmurs, "They just tested."

Mutterperl nods. They avoid words if they can. Above them are three old inmates, but below with two old-timers lies a recent arrival speaking a fine Galician Yiddish, who claims to be a lawyer from Lublin. His skin color is fresh, not the Auschwitz gray, and his shaved scalp is white and unweathered. He bears no scars of quarantine camp. There is an odd expression in his eyes. Chances are, an informer for the Political Section.

The SS keeps searching out the feeble undergrounds that are stirring in Auschwitz; tiny secret groups germinating like weeds in some common ground — political, national, or religious. They endure and grow until the Political Section detects and squashes them. Some last awhile, make contact with the outside, and even smuggle out documents and photographs. Betrayal is their usual end. In this narrow world of disease-ridden famished slaves jammed in horse stalls in the snow, bounded by electrified barbed wire and guarded by machine gun towers and killer dogs, where life hangs by a hair and torture is as common as parking fines elsewhere on earth, informers of course exist. What is surprising is the number of straight fellows.

Mutterperl murmurs, "Well, never mind. It's set."

"When?"

"Tell you later." The words are barely breathed in Jastrow's ear. Closing his eyes, the foreman turns over.

Jastrow knows nothing about the escape scheme except what Mutterperl has so far told him. That is very little. The bakery is the goal, a structure outside the barbed wire, near the woods by the riverbank. Berel's skill in baking will be important. He knows no more than that. Mutterperl will have the films, so if caught and hauled off to the barracks of the Gestapo's Political Section, Berel will have almost nothing to betray; not when the cross-examiners threaten to cut off his penis and testicles; not as the hedge-clipper blades are pushed into his crotch and coldly closed on his scrotum, and they give him his last chance to talk.

That's the rumor: the instrument is a plain crude garden hedge-clipper, sharpened like razors. They threaten you with it, and then they really use it. Who can say if it's true? Nobody would survive such a wound to tell the tale. Mutilated corpses are rushed straight to the old crematorium; nobody sees them but the Gestapo men and the Sonderkommandos. What is beyond German interrogators? If this isn't true, something just as bad is true.

One thing is sure: the flame in the night means death very soon for the Klinger kommando. Berel is prepared to try the escape; nothing to lose! So far Mutterperl has been his good angel. A Jew has to hope. Hungry, freezing, exhausted, he prays and falls asleep.

The test has in fact not gone well.

Chief Engineer Pruefer — from J. A. Topf and Sons of Erfurt, a fine company with international furnace patents — is embarrassed. The blowback has belched black smoke and scraps of burning flesh all over the damn place! Only by luck were the Commandant and Colonel Blobel standing clear. The disgusting stuff has spattered SS officers, civilian technicians, even Pruefer himself. Everybody has inhaled the nauseous greasy smoke. A real mess!

Yet Pruefer's conscience is clear. He knows he was right to fire off a mix of lumber, waste oil, and cadavers for the first test. In the new superheated retorts, the corpses will become fuel to accelerate the process; that's the whole point of these big-volume installations. For a serious test he needed actual conditions. As to the blowback, whatever the defect that caused it, he'll put it to rights. Tests show up problems, why else make tests? That Colonel Blobel was on hand is too bad. Topf and Sons did not invite him.

The Commandant and Colonel Blobel leave, coughing rancid smoke from their lungs. The Commandant is beside himself with rage. Civilian swine! Two months behind in delivery; then three postponements of the test; and by the worst luck Colonel Blobel himself has to show up, just today, for this fiasco. Oh, that buggering Erfurt engineer! In his nice comfortable tweed overcoat, English shoes, and fedora, assuring the Commandant that the test would go off all right! What he needs is a few months in Auschwitz, to teach him what lackadaisical performance in wartime means. Straight to Block 11, the swine!

Colonel Blobel says nothing. His disapproving smirk is enough.

They drive in the Commandant's car to the vicinity of the pits, flaring red and smoky over a broad area. Together they walk out on the fields, upwind, and — oh, hell, another foul-up. The Sonderkommandos are using flame-throwers. The Commandant gave strict orders: no flame-throwers while Colonel Blobel is in the camp! These old rotten bodies, some of them from pits dug in 1940 and 1941, just won't burn away. That's the plain fact. When the fire dies you're left with big piles of charred slop and bones. Yet the order from Berlin is, *Eradicate.* What else is there to do but clean up the mess with flame-throwers? But it's a waste of fuel, a confession of poor work. Does Blobel have to know that Auschwitz Establishment can't solve a combustion problem? The Commandant has asked Berlin in vain, over and over, for some decent officer material. They just ignore him, they send him the dregs. He can't do everything himself.

In the crimson firelight, Blobel stares at the flame-throwers, a supercilious look on his face. Well, he is the expert. Now he knows, let him do his worst. Let him tell Müller. Let him tell Himmler! Better yet, let him make suggestions on how to improve things. The Commandant is only human. He has fifteen square miles of installations to worry about. Big munitions and rubber factories going full blast, and more under construction. Dairy farms, plant nurseries. New subcamps and factories springing up. More political prisoners dumped on him by the thousands all the time. Major shortages of lumber, cement, pipes, wiring, even nails. Serious health and discipline problems, all over the area. And to top it all, Jews keep arriving by the trainload, in bigger and bigger batches. The special treatment facilities get overloaded, naturally. More mess! That tough guy Eichmann is no real planner. He runs a jerky hit-or-miss operation, always either no action or too much. Dirtiest part of the whole assignment. Has to be done, but not productive, except for the stuff in Canada.

What a pyramid of responsibilities! How can a man do a decent job under these conditions?

Fortunately, Blobel is an architect, an intellectual. He's no Eichmann. As they drive back to the villa for dinner, he has the taste to avoid criticism. He senses the Commandant's feelings. Once they've bathed and dressed and are having drinks in the library, he turns cordial. Colonel Blobel likes his drop, as the Commandant knows, and before the Polish maid curtseys to announce dinner, he has downed almost half a bottle of Haig and Haig. Fine, let him get mellow. One thing Blobel can have here is liquor, all he can guzzle. Surprising what the Jews manage to bring along in their suitcases. Even wine. At dinner the Colonel tells the Commandant's wife that not since peacetime has he drunk such a succession of wines at table. She blushes with pleasure. Blobel praises the roast veal, the soup, the cream chocolate cake. Cook has done herself proud, in fact. Blobel makes little jokes with the boys about their studies, and about their appetite for cake. His forbidding manner is melting away. He's a good fellow, after all, once he's had a few! The Commandant is feeling more optimistic about the unpleasant business talk still to come, but then —

AOW! AOW! AOW! The damned escape siren!

Even here, way down by the river front, the wailing, screaming escape alarm of Auschwitz shakes the windows and the walls, and all but drowns out the distant spatters of machine gun fire. *Of all times!* Stiffening in his armchair, Colonel Blobel turns a hard face to the Commandant, who excuses himself and tramples upstairs to his private telephone, seething. The dinner ruined, too.

A plane flying low over Auschwitz now — though no such thing is possible, the air space over these fifteen square miles of Polish backcountry is strictly off limits, even to the Luftwaffe — would come on a striking sight: thousands upon thousands of men and women ranked on the long parade grounds of the Birkenau camps under glaring floodlights in gently falling snow; a quasi-military sight, except for the unmilitary costumes of vertical-striped thin cotton rags.

The scream of the sirens has really startled the inmates, who have come tumbling out under the clubbing and curses of the SS and the trusties. Escape roll calls have been discontinued for months. Why now, all of a sudden?

Roll call is daily torture. One day the books will play up more gruesome aspects of Auschwitz: the medical experiments on women and children, the collecting of tons of female hair and the skeletons of twins, the mutilating tortures of the Gestapo, the casual sadistic murders of slave workers, and of course the covert asphyxiation of millions of Jews. All these things happen, but most working prisoners do not encounter them. Roll call is as bad as anything they endure. They stand motionless in ranks morning and evening for a couple of hours in all weathers. The hardest work is preferable. At least you warm yourself when you're in the swing, and distract your mind. At roll call hunger gnaws, bowels and bladder agonize, cold eats into bones, and time stops. Roll call is when Musselmen tend to keel over. By the time roll call ends on a bitter winter morning, bodies litter the ground. The meat wagons collect the dead; the inmates carry the living into the blockhouses, or drag them off to work if clubbing revives them.

But there are big rush jobs under way in Auschwitz, and killing off workers with roll calls is no help. The authorities therefore decided way back during the typhus epidemic to cut down on these extra roll calls at an escape alarm.

So what now?

What has happened is that the Commandant has telephoned his deputy and warned that if the swine who escaped isn't promptly caught, there will be summary death sentences for negligence in the SS. Someone will pay! Heads will roll! As for the prisoners, call them out! Let them stand at attention until morning, the shitasses! Then let them march off to work.

It's ten below zero outside. The Commandant knows he's cutting off his nose to spite his face, for these orders will kill a lot of marginal working hands. Never mind! Paul Blobel of Kommando 1005 is his guest. Stern measures are in order. Auschwitz Establishment cannot be disgraced. The roll call shows he means business. When the SS gets scared, it produces. They'll catch the shitass.

•   •   •

Are escapes then possible from Auschwitz?

Yes. As concentration camps go, Auschwitz is a sieve.

One day Auschwitz will acquire an awesome name in the world as an impenetrable fortress of macabre horrors. In actuality it is a sloppy industrial sprawl, always expanding, always anarchic. Something like seven hundred escapes will be recorded in its history. A third of those will succeed. The unrecorded ones may add up to twice as many. Nobody will ever know.

There is no other German concentration camp like Auschwitz.

The German camps early in the Nazi era simply imitated the gulags of Lenin's Bolsheviks; they were isolation and terror dumps for political opponents. But in wartime these camps have swollen, proliferated into hundreds dotting all Europe, filled up with foreigners, and become slave pens for German-run factories; where, to be sure, prisoners die in droves from bad conditions. But in only six camps, all in Polish backcountry, does the SS murder Jews en masse upon arrival, with an elaborate hygienic hoax of disinfection.

The German names for these six places are Chelmno, Belzec, Sobibor, Treblinka, Maidanek — and Auschwitz.

Auschwitz is in a class by itself, and not only because of its reliance on a cyanide pest-killer gas, while the other five massacre centers use exhaust fumes from truck engines. That is a minor distinction. The main thing is that the other camps serve no purpose but slaughter, though there may be some slave use of overflow Jews for a while. So from the others escape is very tough.

Auschwitz stands alone: at once the biggest asphyxiation center, the biggest corpse-robbing center, and the biggest slave-factory center of German-ruled Europe. It is the colossus. Hence its laxness. It is too huge, too complex, too improvised, for proper control. The effect of the Jewish plunder is also very unsettling. There is too much of it. Most of the Jews are poor, and they bring only two suitcases apiece; but in such multitudes, the loot adds up. The gold from the teeth alone is mounting into the millions of reichsmarks. SS training and morale break down, more even than from the temptation of scared submissive Jewesses in the women's work camp. Despite the fiercest penalties, the little gold ingots keep disappearing from the smelting laboratory and floating through Auschwitz, a strange secret currency for perilous deals.

The fact is, the Commandant lacks the manpower to run his show. His complaints are just. The battle of Stalingrad is on, and the army is demanding more and more men. Himmler is forming SS battle divisions, too. Which Germans are left from the comb-out? The stupid, the feeble, the elderly, the disabled, the criminal — frankly, the scum. And even of those there's not enough. The trusty system has to expand and take in foreign prisoners.

There is the trouble. Certainly a lot of these bootlick the SS and brutalize other prisoners to save their own skins. Auschwitz is a machine for debasing human nature. Still, too many of these non-German trusties remain soft. Hence the Resistance. Hence the escapes. Poles, Czechs, Jews, Serbs, Ukrainians, they're all alike. Not really trustworthy. They even soften up some confused Germans.

Yes, there are plenty of escapes from Auschwitz.

The Commandant hears from Himmler about them, time after time. The

problem threatens his career. So he wants to impress Colonel Blobel with a
recapture, at least. The man who heads Kommando 1005 has Himmler's ear.

• • •

An hour passes.

An hour and a half.

Two hours.

In the library, the Commandant keeps glancing at his recently acquired antique clock, as Colonel Blobel talks on; or rather maunders on, for he is consuming an amazing quantity of brandy. At another time, the Commandant would be relaxed and happy, hearing such alcoholic confidences from such a high-placed insider. But he is on pins and needles. He really cannot enjoy the talk, nor the twenty-year-old Courvoisier. He has airily assured the colonel that his garrison will "catch the bugger straight off." Risky thing to say! Now his head is on the chopping block.

Out on the parade ground there are only crude ways to gauge the passage of time. Snow piling on shoulders, for instance; or the spread of frozen numbness in your limbs, your nose, your ears; or the count of prisoners falling to the ground. Otherwise how can you tell time? Motion measures time. There is no motion here but the tread of a passing trusty on guard, no sound but his boots squeaking in the snow. No stars move overhead. Light white snow falls randomly in white glare on striped-clad immobile shuddering ranks. By the feeling that he has no legs below the knees, Berel Jastrow guesses that about two hours must have passed. Klinger will be unhappy at morning roll call. Berel can see thirteen men down.

The new fellow from Lublin, between Jastrow and Mutterperl, suddenly takes his life and theirs in his hands, exclaiming, *"How long does this go on?"*

In the silence the strangled gasp is like a shout, like a pistol shot. And at this moment the block chief walks by! Berel can't see him, but he hears the boots behind him, he knows the footfall, he smells the pipe. He waits for the club to crash on the fool's thin cotton cap. But the trusty walks on, does nothing. German blockhead! He should have slammed him with the club. He didn't have to hurt him. One good result of the roll call: the SS plant identified.

But SS plant or not, the man isn't shamming agony. Not much later he plops down with a groan on his knees and tumbles over on his side, eyes rolling and glassy. Well fed, new to the camp, he should have done better than that. Camp weakens or toughens you. If the Resistance doesn't murder that one, he'll end as a Musselman.

Colonel Blobel is well into his cups now: slumped in the armchair, slurring his words, drooping his glass at an angle that slops brandy. His assertions and boasts are getting wild. The Commandant suspects that, drunk as he is, Blobel is cutely playing cat-and-mouse with him. He still has not mentioned the problem that has brought him to Auschwitz. The escape will give him some nasty leverage, if it isn't foiled — and soon.

Blobel is now claiming that the whole Jewish program is his idea. In the Ukraine, where he headed an *Einsatzgruppe* in 1941, he grasped how shoddy the original SS plan was. Back in Berlin on sick leave, he presented a top-secret memorandum to Himmler, Heydrich, and Eichmann, three copies only — so hot that he didn't dare keep a copy himself. Therefore he can't prove that he conceived the present system. But Himmler knows. That's why Blobel now heads Kommando 1005, the hardest of all SS tasks. Yes, the honor of Germany rests in Paul Blobel's hands. He realizes his responsibility. He wishes more people would.

What Blobel saw in the Ukraine, so he says, was terrible. He was then an underling following orders. They assigned him to Kiev. Just ordered him to go in there and do a job. His part went off smoothly. He found a ravine outside the town, collected the Jews in batches and got them out to the ravine, called Babi Yar or something, a few thousand at a time. It took days to get it done. There were more than sixty thousand Kiev Jews, the biggest job anybody had yet tried. But everything he didn't organize himself was bungled. Not only did the army fail to keep Ukrainian civilians away from Babi Yar; half of the crowds of onlookers were German soldiers. Disgraceful! People watching the executions as though they were at a soccer game! Laughing, eating ice cream, even taking pictures! Pictures of women and children kneeling to be shot in the back, tumbling into the ravine! This was damn hard on the morale of the rifle squads; they didn't appreciate getting into such snapshots. He had to call a halt, raise hell with the army, and get the place cordoned off.

Moreover, the Jews were shot with their clothes on, and with God knows what money and jewelry concealed on them, and sand was bulldozed over them. Idiotic! As to their empty homes in Kiev, why, the Ukrainians just walked in and helped themselves. The Reich got nothing of their property. Everybody knew what was happening to the Jews.

Blobel perceived then and there that Germany was going to lose billions in Jewish property, if the whole thing wasn't done with more system. His memorandum laid the plan out properly, and Himmler jumped at it. Auschwitz and the whole revised Jewish solution resulted.

The Commandant isn't about to argue with Blobel, but all this is eyewash. Maybe not about the Ukraine; but long before the Wehrmacht ever got near Kiev, he met with Himmler about the Jewish question, and afterward with Eichmann. It was Eichmann's setup in the Vienna Jewish Emigration Office, way back in 1938, that was the economic model for Auschwitz. The Commandant has heard all about that Vienna setup. The Jews went in one door of the building rich proud bourgeois, passed down a row of offices signing papers, and came out the other end with bare asses and passports. As for the *Aktion Reinhardt*, the official general collection of the property of the Jews after special treatment, Globocnik has always handled that. So when Blobel tries to claim —

R-R-R-RING!

The sweetest sound the Commandant has heard in his life! He jumps to his feet. The telephone doesn't ring in the villa at midnight to report failure.

The sound of the drum is muffled by the snow, so Berel doesn't hear it until it starts up in the next camp. So they've nabbed him, and are marching him through Birkenau already! Well, if he had to be caught — God pity him — better now than later. For the first time in months, Berel has been fearing his knees would give way. Hearing the drum gives him strength. Two SS men are carrying the flogging frame out on the parade ground now. It will soon be over.

And here the guy comes. Three officers lead him, three follow him, leaving him plenty of room for his solo performance. One prods him with a sharp stick, to keep him dancing as he beats the drum. The poor devil can scarcely stay on his feet, but on he comes, jigging and drumming.

The clown suit is getting bedraggled with use. The bright yellow cloth is stained in the seat and the legs with blood. Still, it is a terribly ludicrous sight. Around his neck the usual sign dangles — HURRAH, I'M BACK —in big black German lettering. Who is he? Hard to tell, through the crude paint on his face, the red mouth, the exaggerated eyebrows. As he dances by, feebly whacking the drum, Berel hears Mutterperl hiss.

The flogging is short. The fellow's behind, when they bare it, is raw bleeding meat. He gets only ten more blows. They don't want to weaken him too much. The Gestapo interrogation comes first. They want him to stay lively enough so that the torture will make him talk. They may even feed him for a while to build him up. In the end, of course, he'll be hanged at a roll call, but there won't be much of him left to hang. Ticklish business, escaping. But if the alternative is going up the chimney, a man has little to lose, seeking another way to leave Auschwitz.

The chilled ranks break. The SS men and the trusties curse, club, and whip the slow-moving inmates back to the barracks. Some stumble and fall. Their rigid legs held them up while they didn't move. Bend those frozen joints, and down you can go! Berel knows about this. He found it out on the march from Lamsdorf. He walks on his own numb ice-cold legs as though they are iron braces, swinging them clumsily along with his hip muscles.

The block, where the temperature must be about zero, but at least the snow isn't falling, seems a warm refuge: in fact, home. When the light is turned off, Mutterperl pokes Berel, who rolls close and puts his ear to the foreman's mouth.

Warm breath; faint words. "It's off."

Berel changes position, his mouth to Mutterperl's ear. "Who was the guy?"

"Never mind. All off."

The Commandant laughs uproariously with relief and with genuine amusement, as he hangs up. The dogs tracked the fellow down, he tells Blobel. The poor bugger tried to escape in one of the big cistern carts that carry off the crap from the mass latrines. He didn't get far, and he's so covered with shit that it's taken three men to hose him off. Well, that's that!

Blobel slaps his shoulder. An escape that fails, he says wisely, is not a bad thing for discipline. Make an example of the bastard. This is the psychological moment, the Commandant thinks, and he invites Blobel upstairs to his private office. He locks the door, unlocks the closet, and brings out the treasure. Lovingly he spreads it out on the desk. Colonel Blobel's bleary eyes widen in an envious admiring gleam.

The stuff is women's underwear: exquisite fairylike things, soft works of art, lacy pretty nothings that give a man a hard-on just to look at them. Panties, brassieres, shifts, slips, garters, in filmy pastel silks, perfectly laundered, ready for movie stars to put on! The best in the world! The Commandant explains that in the undressing room he has a man just to collect the sweetest stuff he sees. Some of these Jewesses are ravishing. And oh, Christ, what lovely stuff comes off their asses. Just look.

Colonel Paul Blobel scoops up a double handful of panties and girdles, crushing them against his crotch like a woman's rump, with a wide grin at the Commandant and a masculine growl — RRRRRR! The Commandant says that the stuff is a present for Colonel Blobel. There's plenty more, tons of it. But this is the best of the best. The SS will deliver a package to the colonel's airplane with a good selection, also some decent Scotch and brandy, a few boxes of cigars, and so forth.

Blobel shakes his hand, gives him a little hug, becomes a different man. They sit down and talk turkey.

First he lectures the Commandant on the merits of crematorium versus burning pit. He has definite and informed ideas. He gives some technical tips on how to improve the pit performance. Damn useful! Then he comes to the point. Auschwitz has been sending him garbage, not workers. Kommando 1005 duty is very hard work. These fellows he's been getting don't last three weeks, whereas it takes three weeks just to show them the techniques. He is tired of complaining to Berlin. He knows that the way to get things done right — as the Commandant has been saying — is to do them himself. So he has come to Auschwitz to settle this thing. It has to be straightened out.

The tone is friendly. The Commandant responds that he will do what he can. He is caught in a bind himself. Himmler can't make up his mind what the function of Auschwitz is. Is he trying to eliminate Jews? Or put them to work? One week the Commandant gets a bawling out from Eichmann for sending too many Jewish arrivals to the work camp, instead of to special treatment. The next week, or the next day, for that matter, Pohl from the Economic Section will be down on him for not putting enough Jews into the factories. A directive has just come in, four pages long, with orders to nurse sick Jews back to health on arrival, and put them to work, if there's six months of potential labor in them. To a person who knows Auschwitz, it's utter nonsense. Just bureaucratic bumpf! But there you are. He has a dozen factories to man, and a perpetual labor shortage.

Blobel waves all this aside. Kommando 1005 has the highest priority. Does the Commandant want to ask Himmler? Blobel is not leaving Auschwitz — and now the tone is not so friendly — without an assurance that he will get four or five hundred ablebodied Jews in the next shipment. *Ablebodied!* Fellows who can deliver three or four months of hard labor before you have to get rid of them.

The Commandant is resourceful under pressure. In this business he has to be. He has a brainstorm. Colonel Blobel has seen the kommando at work in Crematorium II, he says. There's a fine working gang, well-fed fellows with strong backs, no better stuff in the camp. They are due to be liquidated when their work is done. The crematorium fires off next week. How about it? Kommando 1005 can have the Crematorium II kommando. Will that do?

This is highly satisfactory to Blobel. The two officers shake hands on it, and open another bottle of brandy.

Before they stagger off to bed, at three o'clock in the morning, they have agreed at length that their work is dirty but honorable, that the SS is the soul of the nation, that front-line soldiers don't have it as tough, that obedience to the Führer is the only salvation for Germany, that the Jews are the Fatherland's eternal enemy, that this war is the historic chance of a thousand years to root them out for good; that it only seems cruel to kill women and children, that it's one hell of a rotten job, but the future of European civilization and culture is at stake. They are seldom this frank about the things that trouble them, but to a surprising extent they find themselves kindred spirits. Arms around each other's shoulders, they lurch to the bedrooms with almost loving good-nights.

A week later, trucks take the crematorium construction kommando to Cracow. Before the work gang leaves Auschwitz, word comes down from the Labor Section about Kommando 1005. It is just a postponed sentence of death. Still, escapes from 1005 are reputedly easier. In Cracow they board trains for the north. Mutterperl and Jastrow carry identical rolls of undeveloped film, slipped to them after they were searched, stripped, and issued different clothes for departure. Both men have memorized Resistance names and addresses in Poland and Czechoslovakia, and a destination for the films in Prague.

* * *

47

Global Waterloo 3: Rommel

(from *World Holocaust* by Armin von Roon)

The Hinge of Fate

In his history, Winston Churchill calls the Battle of El Alamein "The Hinge of Fate." Actually, it was an interesting textbook encounter, a revival of World War I tactics in a desert setting. The double political impact of El Alamein and Torch was certainly serious. Just as America was dipping a gingerly toe into the European war at one end of North Africa, the legendary Desert Fox was driven from Egypt at the other end. The world was amazed. Spirits rose among the Allies and fell in Germany; Italian morale collapsed.

Nevertheless, despite the great distances and colorful battles, North Africa was a secondary theatre. Once Hitler backed off from the Mediterranean strategy, his last chance to win the war, the front dwindled to a costly and tragic sideshow; and when he too late plunged into Tunis in force, it became a military hemorrhage. Typically, Churchill devotes some twenty pages to El Alamein, and about seven pages to Stalingrad and Guadalcanal combined. Historical myopia can go little further.

Churchill's Greatest Blunder

What Churchill fails to mention at all, of course, is that his own stupid interference with his army commanders created the North African situation in the first place.

Mussolini took Italy into the war in 1940 as France was falling, after the British had left their ally in the lurch at Dunkirk. The Italian dictator thought he could snatch spoils on the cheap from two defunct empires, so from his huge arid territory in Libya he launched an invasion of Egypt. It was a case of the hyena mistaking an ailing lion for a dead one, and biting prematurely. The British air force and navy were still almost intact. So was their Middle Eastern army. They not only counterattacked by land and air and sent the Italians fleeing westward; they also marched light forces south and took Somaliland and Abyssinia. This cleared the Red Sea and the whole East African coastline for British shipping.

Meantime, along the Mediterranean coast the Italians were routed. Wherever the British armored columns appeared the Italians gave up in droves, though greatly outnumbering the enemy. It appeared that England had North Africa won, to the very border of neutral French Tunisia. This meant sea and air control of the Mediterranean, with the gravest consequences for us.

Absorbed though Hitler was at that time with his plan to invade Russia, these events roused him to dispatch an air wing to Sicily, and a small armored force to Tripoli to stiffen the collapsing Italians. And so it was that there came on the scene the immortal ROMMEL. In February 1941, when the then little-known junior panzer general landed in Tripoli, the Italians were on their last legs. His Afrika Korps of ten thousand men was quite inadequate to hold off the fast-approaching British forces. But Churchill, with his worst blunder of the entire war, gave Rommel his historic chance.

At that time, the feckless Mussolini was in trouble in Greece, and Hitler wanted to pacify the Balkans before our assault on Russia. That we might invade Greece to clean things up was apparent. Anticipating this, *Winston Churchill halted the march of his victorious African forces, yanked out four of their strongest divisions, and shipped them to Greece!* His old Balkan mania, which had led to his Gallipoli disgrace in World War I, was cropping out again.

In both wars Churchill was haunted by the absurd fantasy that the polyglot squabblers of the Balkan peninsula, that patchwork of small countries formed of the debris of the Ottoman Empire, could be induced to unite and "rise up against Germany." This time his folly cost England a disastrous defeat in Greece and Crete, the "little Dunkirk," and her chance to secure North Africa as well. By the time the defeated divisions returned to Libya, their equipment battered, their élan gone, Rommel was entrenched, and the Desert War was on. It would take two years of hard fighting and the whole gigantic Anglo-American invasion to retrieve Churchill's idiocy, and win for England what she had in hand before he threw it away.

TRANSLATOR'S NOTE: *No great man fails to make mistakes. Churchill's shift of forces from Africa to Greece was mistimed. Churchill doesn't admit this, in his unabashedly self-serving though fine six-volume history called* The Second World War. *One has to read a few other books, including works like Roon's, to get a clearer idea of what really went on. — V.H.*

Desert Warfare

The North African desert war oscillated for a year and a half between two port bases fourteen hundred miles apart: Tripoli in Libya, Alexandria in

Egypt. A game of hare and hounds went on turn and turn about. First the Afrika Korps, then the British, stretched their supply lines to attack, ran low, and withdrew to base. *Supply* so far governed this war that Rommel wrote, *"Any desert campaign was won or lost by the Quartermaster Corps before a shot was fired."*

In Erwin Rommel's masterly desert tactics, the ruling concept was the *open southern flank*. On the north lay the Mediterranean. To the south lay the sandy void. Conventional rules of land war melted before the oceanlike open flank. It was Rommel's flank moves that won victory after victory, as he kept varying his tricks to bedazzle his stolid foe.

But a desert army's range, like a fleet's, is dictated by the amount of fuel, food, and water it can carry along, with the reserve needed to double back to base. The dashing Rommel was somewhat neglectful of this limitation; fortunately his good staff kept it in mind. It was something Adolf Hitler could never understand. His mentality was that of a World War I foot soldier. In Europe adequate supply lines were taken for granted, and our troops could live off fruitful invaded lands like France and the Ukraine. The picture of armored columns proceeding through vast sterile flat voids was beyond Hitler. He saw the newsreels regularly at Headquarters, but they made no dent in his obtuseness.

I was present on two occasions when Rommel flew to the Führer's HQ in East Prussia to plead for more supplies. Göring was there once. The bored uncomprehending glaze in the eyes of the two politicians must have sickened Rommel. Hitler's response each time was the same: airy-fairy chaffing of this great field general as a "pessimist," voluble promises to improve supplies, warm assurances that Rommel would "pull it off no matter what," and a new medal.

Göring reacted only once, when Rommel was describing the power of the new American Tomahawk fighter-bomber that the British were using. At this pinch of his Luftwaffe toes he smirked, "Nonsense, the Americans are good at making only refrigerators and razor blades."

Rommel retorted, "Reichsmarschall, the Afrika Korps will appreciate a large issue of such razor blades."

But Rommel's fearless talk to the bigwigs came to nothing. To save Mussolini's face, the African theatre was maintained as an Italian command; and the Italians broke promises of more supplies as fast as Mussolini made them.

Tobruk: Poisoned Fruit

Rommel's great storming of Tobruk in June 1942 marked the high tide for us. Coming when Sevastopol was falling to Manstein and our U-boat sinkings were spiking upward, the fall of Tobruk shook the world. The British retreated all the way to the El Alamein line in Egypt, only eighty miles from Alexandria. The Tobruk booty was lavish — gasoline, food, tanks, guns, ammunition, in quantities known only to the enemy, never to us. The worn and spent Afrika Korps, like a starving lion that has caught and devoured a gazelle, came back to roaring life. Rommel demanded freedom to drive for decisive victory. Hitler gave him the green light. On to Suez; maybe to the Persian Gulf!

Those were heady days in the map room. In my mind's eye the pallid puffy-faced Führer still leans on the table map of North Africa with stiff arms, his favorite posture, wearing the very thick reading glasses the public never saw, lifting a pudgy white hand to sweep it with a slight tremor from Tobruk across Suez, Palestine, and Iraq to the mouth of the Euphrates. Unfortunately, the Führer tended to fight his wars with just such visionary arm sweeps. Logistics bored him. He either dismissed these gritty supply realities, or terrorized with screaming fits generals who pressed him too hard about such mundane details. Since his fearsome willpower did sometimes work wonders, he had become accustomed to demanding the impossible.

This time he really demanded the impossible of Rommel, for he used the fall of Tobruk as an excuse to cancel "Operation *Herkules*," the capture of Malta. The small but strong fortress island base lay athwart Rommel's supply line, a hundred miles off Sicily. Mussolini yearned to capture it. But Hitler, his mind on the eastern front, had hemmed and hawed for a year, and now he dropped the plan. This was a radical error. Malta's interdiction was ceaseless, and each tanker, each ammunition ship, that was sunk weakened Rommel. Hitler believed that Luftwaffe bombardment would neutralize Malta, but the British patched their airstrips, flew in more aircraft, slipped in more submarines, fought through in convoys, and kept the garrison supplied.

Tobruk convinced Hitler and Mussolini that the superman, Rommel, could manufacture victories out of thin air, and that his complaints about supply were prima donna tantrums. Pressure for supplying him relaxed. The Tobruk cache melted away as he drove up to El Alamein, and made an assault late in August which barely failed. And still supplies did not come. His own reputation was strangling him.

The British Buildup

On the British side, the fall of Tobruk had the opposite effect.

Churchill was in Washington at the time, and Roosevelt asked how he could help. Never bashful, Churchill at once demanded three hundred Sherman tanks, the U.S. Army's brand-new weapon. Over the army's grumbling, Roosevelt granted this request; added another hundred Grant tanks, and a lot of new antitank guns and other matériel. At highest priority a big convoy sailed off for Egypt via the Cape of Good Hope. When this convoy unloaded in September, the munitions and supplies it delivered *alone outweighed everything the Afrika Korps had on hand to fight the Battle of El Alamein.* Meanwhile, the British had been heavily rearming Montgomery too, via the Mediterranean. Moreover, Persia's refineries and the military reserves in Palestine were there to draw on.

In fact it was now no contest. Rommel has been much criticized for not declining battle and withdrawing from El Alamein, for the British buildup was becoming monstrous.

TRANSLATOR'S NOTE: *Roon here gives a table showing British advantages of five to one or better at El Alamein in tanks, planes, and troops. Dubious, but the figures in British accounts are lopsided enough. — V.H.*

But Rommel *could not* leave. So poor were his logistics, so badly had the Supreme Command failed him, so costly was the interdiction from Malta, that the Afrika Korps virtually lacked the gasoline to pull across Libya. Rommel had to stand and fight, using up in battle what fuel he had. Beyond El Alamein lay Alexandria, a richer supply dump than Tobruk; beyond that, Suez still beckoned. He had beaten the British often. He had their measure. One more fight, one more victory, and all might yet be well!

El Alamein was a long-prepared British fall-back position, well fortified and mined. The front stretched some forty miles from the coast to the Qattara Depression, where steep cliffs dropped to a vast bog of salt marsh and quicksand, two hundred feet below sea level. It was perfect for the World War I mentalities in charge of England's forces, and unsuited to Rommel's desert tactics.

He too sowed stupendous mine fields nine miles deep all along the front, mainly with captured British mines. He fortified the high ground, husbanded the fuel and ammunition, begged and pleaded and raged for more supplies, and waited for the enemy to attack. But his opponent, Bernard Montgomery, was in no hurry. Montgomery combined a flair for flamboyant and belligerent rhetoric with extreme caution in planning and fighting. Eisenhower once called him a good "set-piece commander." Montgomery wanted his set piece against Rommel to be a sure thing.

Erwin Rommel was not a well man, and his health gave way. He flew back to Germany on sick leave. When the battle began he was still in the hospital, and the Anglo-American armada was already on the high seas, bound for French North Africa.

El Alamein Erupts

Montgomery attacked on the October full moon. One thousand massed artillery pieces laid down a Verdun-like barrage; waves of infantry then crossed the mine fields to seize advanced positions; sappers cleared mines yard by yard in narrow corridors; and behind them came crawling the tanks. It was heavy, unimaginative, slogging warfare, orthodox as a Sandhurst field exercise. Montgomery had the weight of men, shells, and metal, and was not trying tricks. Our troops and some superior Italian divisions, well dug in all along the line, stoutly resisted. By daylight the attack was bogged down in the mine fields, facing rings of heavy antitank guns.

Hitler ordered the Desert Fox from his sickbed to fly to El Alamein and resume command. The unequal battle raged for a week. Throwing in men and machines with World War I abandon, Montgomery failed to break through. Rommel fought back brilliantly, switching his dwindling handful of tanks here and there, virtually counting his shells and gasoline jerrycans before each counterattack.

In London, Churchill was impatiently waiting for the breakthrough. He wanted to order the victory bells rung throughout England, for the first time in the war; just as Mussolini had flown over to Libya in July — entourage, white horse, and all — for his grand entry into Alexandria. But as the days dragged on, the bell-ringing had to be put off. In plain fact, the Afrika Korps had Montgomery stopped. Concern in Alexandria and in London grew that the engagement might have to be broken off, a desert stalemate very much like the Western Front in 1916.

But the attrition became too much for Rommel. His tank force was shrinking away. His shells were almost gone. He had no air support; and the RAF pounded him at will. Having no tanks left to consume gasoline, he could now use what fuel remained to truck his forces back to Libya. This he decided to do, but he made the terrible mistake of telegraphing Hitler for permission to withdraw. The answer of course shot back, *Hold fast at all costs, no retreat, the troops must write a glorious new page in German history,* and so forth and so on.

This delayed the loyal Rommel's escape by a full forty-eight hours, and forced him to abandon his Italian infantry division in order to save the Afrika Korps. Two days earlier he might have extricated the lot, but now he had to put first things first and preserve his striking arm. Montgomery was slow in pursuit, and the Desert Fox made good his retreat to Libya and to Tunis.

Such in truth was the vaunted "Hinge of Fate" Battle of El Alamein.

By October 1942, the Afrika Korps was already all but done for, due to the criminal failures of supply. After the most formidable preparations, Montgomery placed the pistol of the Eighth Army at the prostrate Rommel's temple, pulled the trigger — and missed. The Desert Fox sprang up and escaped. That is essentially what happened.

That the needed supplies could always have been sent in a flood — troops, tanks, fuel, aircraft, antitank guns — was amply proved, too late, once the Anglo-Americans landed. Stung in their sensitive political nerves, Hitler and Mussolini rushed whole armies to Tunis by air and sea, gradually building up to almost three hundred thousand men. Such reinforcements to Rommel in July would have carried German arms to the Persian oil fields and to India. Slipping away from his dawdling pursuers, Rommel crossed the continent in a great fighting retreat, took command of the Tunis pocket, and made a shambles of the Allies' Mediterranean timetable. But the dream of Suez and beyond was over.

Torch: Summary

The Anglo-American North African campaign was a poor show even before Rommel entered the picture. The key was the Bizerte-Tunis port area at the Sicilian Narrows, scarcely one hundred miles from Europe. The British wanted to land near there and dash for the objective. But the American army, facing its first battle test, feared venturing so far inside Gibraltar Strait. What about German air power, the inexperienced Yank generals asked; what about possible intervention by Spain, which could cut off the expedition's supply lines? They wanted a cautious landing in the rough Atlantic surf at Casablanca, on the outer bulge of Africa, connected to the key terrain only by a single rickety railroad line. The final compromise plan retained the Casablanca landing, with beachheads inside Gibraltar much too far from the main objective. Axis reinforcements crossed the Mediterranean by sea and air and seized Tunisia first.

Yet winning the race for Tunis was but a snare into which the two dictators blundered. With all of Fortress Europe to defend, we could not in the long run triumph in North Africa against the rich and untouched American industrial system. Our armies in Tunis were foredoomed to become as big a prisoner bag as the Sixth Army at Stalingrad. Even Rommel's generalship could not avert this, though he did wreck the Allies' plan for a quick win. North Africa was our most useless defeat, under our best general; another disaster of the *Führerprinzip* in war.

Triumph of Roosevelt

Roosevelt got out of the Torch landing just what he wanted: a "victory" to pep up his home front, a battleground where his raw recruits and bright-buttoned generals could make their first mistakes (they made many) at a light price, and a plausible second front to placate the Russians. Marshall was right in predicting that the sideshow would lengthen the war by at least a year, but meantime the politician Roosevelt reaped his profits. The easy Torch success froze Spain in her neutrality, kept Turkey quiet, and ensured the early fall of Mussolini.

All this Roosevelt accomplished in French North Africa at a cost of about twenty thousand Americans killed or captured, and less than half as many British casualties. When one adds that in four years of war that brought the U.S.A. de facto world hegemony, America lost in all theatres less than three hundred thousand men in battle deaths — *about equal to the force we lost at Stalingrad* — while the Russians sacrificed something like eleven million soldiers, and we lost perhaps four million, one must call Franklin Roosevelt's overall war strategy a work of malevolent genius.

Churchill never did ring his bells. Rommel had pummelled the Eighth Army too badly before retreating. Moreover, with Torch about to go with green American troops, Churchill may have feared a debacle there. In any case, he thought better of it, and even in defeat, Rommel silenced the church bells of England.

TRANSLATOR'S NOTE: *In view of Roon's exalted estimate of General Rommel, one sentence from Rommel's* Memoirs *may be in order here: "The battle which began at El Alamein on the 23rd October, 1942, turned the tide of war in Africa against us and, in fact, probably represented the turning point of the whole vast struggle." In this matter Rommel evidently shared Churchill's "myopia."*

Rommel is an important and controversial figure in any discussion of military ethics. He was implicated in the generals' plot on Hitler's life in 1944. Most of the generals remained slavishly loyal to Hitler, and the Führer sent two of these to finish off Rommel. They offered him the choice of a public trial for treason, or a quiet death by poison (with a cover story of a heart attack) and a "hero's funeral," with safety guaranteed to his family. He took the poison, and they delivered him dead to a hospital. Hitler duly proclaimed a day of national mourning for the great Desert Fox.

Rommel had fought for Hitler to the last. When he was murdered, he was already a broken man, done in by illness and a bad automobile accident. He knew about the extermination camps. He considered the Führer incompetent to command. He bemoaned the waste of life and property in continuing a lost war. He hated the whole Nazi gang that was sacrificing what was left of Germany to prolong their clutch on power. Yet he went on fighting until he was incapacitated; and then he took the poison that the Führer sent him by the hands of his fellow generals.

Rommel's career is some sort of object lesson for military men in the difficult borderline between steadfast loyalty and criminal stupidity.

As for Roon's assertion that "Americans cannot take battle losses," I have heard that a little too often from Europeans. A Russian general once told Eisenhower that his way of clearing a mine field was to march a couple of brigades through it. We Americans fight differently, when we can. Yet in the Civil War we fought some of the most sanguinary battles in history, and the South was living on grass and acorns when it quit. Nobody knows yet what the American people can do in the last extremity.

Our moral climate does seem to be going to hell in a handbasket — I am writing in 1970, the "counterculture" era — but my superiors were making that complaint in the 1920s, the "flaming youth" era, which then more or less included me. — V.H.

*   *   *

48

JANICE answered a ring at the front door and blinked. Victor Henry stood there hunched, his eyes troubled and weary, his face as gray as his ill-fitting work uniform. He carried a wooden footlocker and a bulging leather portfolio.

"Hi." The voice too was troubled and weary.

Clutching at her open housecoat collar, she exclaimed, "Dad! Come in, come in! What a surprise! The place is a mess, and so am I, but —"

"I tried to telephone. I know the rule against surprising the female persuasion. The line was busy, and I'm crowded for time. I had a problem finding where you'd moved."

"I wrote to you."

"I never got it." He glanced around the small living room, his eyes jerkily avoiding Warren's photograph on the wall. "Furniture's sort of jammed in here."

"Does it seem a comedown? It's all Vic and I need now."

"Have you stored my stuff?"

"No, it's all there in Vic's room."

"Good. I'll need my dress blues and bridge coat."

"How long will you be in Honolulu?"

"A few hours."

"Wow! No more?"

He raised heavy eyebrows in which Janice saw new flecks of gray. "I've got orders back to Washington. Class One air priority." The quick tart grin, with a flick of a knuckle across his nose, was a Warren mannerism that gave her a turn. "In the Nouméa NATS terminal I bumped an Australian newspaper editor. He was madder'n hell."

"Why the rush?"

"Beats me."

"Well, there's a whole closet full of your Stateside things."

"Good. I can use whatever's here. That footlocker is empty. Even this outfit is borrowed."

It was her opening to say softly, "I'm sorry about the *Northampton*."

"Was it in the papers?"

"Grapevine." Embarrassed, she hurried on, "How about some breakfast?"

"Well, let me think now." He dropped in a chair, rubbing his eyes. "I could use a hot bath. I've spent three days and nights in NATS planes." His head down on a hand, he spoke in a remote exhausted tone. "The thing is, I'm wanted at Cincpac at two, and my plane takes off at five."

"My Lord, they're pushing you!"

"Where's the baby?"

"Out there." She pointed to french doors opening on a sunlit garden. "He's no baby, though. He's grown like King Kong."

"Jan, suppose I see him, then clean up and rest a bit before I pack? If you'll wake me and just give me some scrambled eggs about noon, we can talk and — what's the matter?"

"Why, nothing. That's just fine."

"Got something else on?"

"No, no, that's just what we'll do."

She picked up the telephone as he went out to the grassy yard. His grandson, in swimming trunks in the blazing sun, was making a coal-black Scottie jump for a red rubber ball. A young Hawaiian girl sat watching the tanned plump child.

"Hi, Vic. Remember me?"

The child turned his head to inspect him, said, "Yes, you're Grandpa," and threw the ball for the dog to chase. He had Warren's eyes and jaw, but his cool response struck Pug as pure Byron.

"You know who has a dog like that, Vic? The President of the United States. What's your doggie's name?"

"Toto."

The dog chased the ball under a clothesline, where Janice's pink two-piece swimsuit dangled beside a man's flower-print trunks. Janice came out in the sunshine, pushing up her thick blonde hair with both hands. "Well, what do you think of him?"

"Perfect physical specimen. Mental giant."

"How unprejudiced. This is Lana." The Hawaiian girl smiled and bobbed her head. "She follows him around, or tries to. Problem about lunch. You remember Lieutenant Commander Aster?"

"Sure."

"We were going on a picnic today. I was making the sandwiches when you arrived. So —"

"Well, just go ahead with it, Jan."

"No, no. I'll call it off. The thing is, his room at the Royal Hawaiian doesn't answer. He may get here while we're eating. That won't matter, will it?"

"Why scrub the picnic?"

"Oh, it couldn't be more casual. We're a five-minute walk from the hotel. You know, SubPac's taken it over. Carter was teaching Vic to swim there yesterday, so sort of to thank him I suggested a picnic, but we can do that any time."

"I see. Well," Victor Henry said, "me for that hot bath."

In the Tulagi hospital cot, and dozing in iron bucket seats on the planes, he had kept dreaming of the *Northampton*. His nap now was broken by such a nightmare. He and Chief Stark were aboard as the ship dizzily heeled up on its beam ends, and black warm water came rushing along the deck, engulfing them to their thighs. The feeling in his dream of being drenched was real and not unpleasant, like settling into a bath. The chief seized a sledgehammer and banged at the brackets that held a life raft, his eyes bulging with terror, and Pug Henry woke with a shudder. The hammering became a knocking at the door. Relieved to find himself dry and in bed, he could not at first recollect how he came to be in this yellow nursery room decorated with animal pictures.

"Dad? Dad? It's a quarter past twelve."

"Thanks, Jan." Memory flooded in. "What about Aster?"

"Come and gone."

He appeared in the yard in a white dress uniform. He was spruce and straight, and his color was better. The clothesline was empty. The Hawaiian girl sat by Vic on the grass as he fed himself yellow mush from a tray, smearing half the stuff on his nose and chin. "Got his appetite back, eh?"

"Oh, yes, long since. Do you mind eating in the kitchen?"

"I'd like it."

They talked haltingly over eggs and sausages. There were so many sore topics — the unknown whereabouts of Natalie, the sinking of the *Northampton*, the uncertainty of Pug's future, above all the death of Warren — that Janice had to force voluble chatter about her job. She was working for the Army. A colonel with the sonorous title of Director of Materials and Supplies Control had met her at a party and pirated her away from Cincpac. Martial law now ruled the territory, and under the jolly surface of Honolulu — the leis, the brass bands, the luaus, and the beautiful scenery — there was a cold tough dictatorship. Her colonel had the newspapers cowed. He and he alone decided how much paper to import, and who would get allotments, so the editors grovelled to him and to the Military Governor. There was no criticism in the editorials. Military tribunals, called "provost courts," had superseded the law, handing out strange verdicts like sentencing offenders to buy war bonds or donate blood.

"It's all more or less benign," she said. "The Army does keep order, and takes good care of us. There's nothing rationed but booze and gas. We eat like lords, and most everybody's happy as a clam, but it's disturbing, when you see its inner workings as I do. It's not America, you know? If we ever get a Stateside dictatorship, God forbid, it'll start as a military emergency measure."

"Mmph," said her father-in-law. His end of this conversation was nothing but such grunts. Perhaps, she thought, he disliked criticism of the military. She was just trying to keep the talk going. The change in him hurt her to see. There was about the quiet man an air of loss, a smell of ash. His accustomed silence now seemed a threadbare cloak against misfortune. Despite his impeccable air and the dogged toughness in the worn face, she pitied him. Once Warren's father had seemed so formidable — this brilliant senior naval officer, this intimate of President Roosevelt who had talked with Churchill, with Hitler, with Stalin . . . how he had dwindled! He looked all right. He was eating. His core of strong energy showed in this bounce back after a short nap. He was a hard nut to crack, but he was being squeezed hard. So his daughter-in-law thought, without knowing anything of the betrayal by his wife.

Over coffee, she showed him Rhoda's latest letter, hoping the warm sprightly run of chitchat would cheer him up. Rhoda had taken to church work; details of this, and some Navy gossip, filled three sheets. A postscript mentioned that Madeline's movie job had fizzled out, and that she had returned to New York to work for Hugh Cleveland.

Pug's face darkened over the letter. "Damned idiot of a girl."

"I thought you'd be pleased about Madeline. Hollywood's such a sinkhole."

He threw the letter on the table. "Incidentally, what's that canal out in front of your house?"

"The Ala Wai Canal. It runs down to the yacht harbor."

"Got trouble with mosquitoes?"

"You would think of that. I didn't. Monsters, by the millions."

"Rhoda and I have rented a lot of tropical houses. You learn."

"Well, I got it for a steal. A fighter pilot from the *Yorktown* had it. His wife went home after —" Janice's voice wavered. "Actually, Toto was their dog."

"You don't want to go home?"

"No, I feel I'm in the war here. When you and Byron come back, here I'll be. You'll both have a place near the beach. Vic will get to know you."

"Well, that'll be nice for Byron." Pug cleared his throat. "About me, I dunno. I'd guess I've had my shot at the blue water."

"But why? That's not fair."

Again the quick acid grin. "Why not? The parade moves fast in wartime. You lose step once, you drop to the sidelines. I can make myself useful in

BuOrd or BuShips." He drank coffee, and spoke on thoughtfully. "My judgments under fire may be questioned at Cincpac today. I just don't know. Our loss of life was small. Still, my portfolio contains fifty-eight letters I've written to next of kin. That's how I passed the time, flying here. I regret every man we lost, but we took two torpedoes in a running gun battle, and that was it. I'll be moseying along. Thanks for lunch."

"Let me drive you to Cincpac."

"I cadged a Navy car." He went into the bedroom and brought out the footlocker and portfolio, carrying over his arm a heavy brass-buttoned blue coat that smelled of camphor. "You know, I started out for Moscow over a year ago in this coat, going the other way. It's circling the world." Halting before Warren's picture, he briefly looked at it, then at her. "Say, tell me about Lieutenant Commander Aster."

"Carter? Oh, he's becoming one of the famous submarine skippers. The *Devilfish* sank twenty thousand tons under his command. Now he's putting a new fleet sub in commission, the *Moray*. In fact, he's gotten orders for Byron to the *Moray*."

"Then what's Aster doing here? New construction's in the States."

"There's a flap with BuOrd about some radar he wants. He flew here to twist arms at SubPac. Carter doesn't fool around."

"What's the fellow like? I've never quite figured him out."

"Neither have I. But he's nice to Vic and to me."

"Do you like him? Not that it's my business."

"Yes, it is." Her jaw was set, her eyes faraway and clouded. Pug Henry had seen this sort of look on her face often after Midway. "You're asking me if it's serious, aren't you? No. I'm not interested in becoming widowed twice in one war."

"He'll be rotated to the beach after a year or so."

"Oh, no!" She spoke with swift flat assurance. "ComSubPac sends the high-scoring skippers back out as often as they'll go. I'm sort of sorry Byron's been ordered to the *Moray*. No doubt he'll love it, but Carter's too adventurous for me. Vic and I swim with him, and every now and then he takes me dancing. I'm the widow lady, the backup date when there's no hotter action." Her crooked-tooth smile was wryly pretty. "Okay?"

"Okay. Does Aster have any word on when Byron's due back?"

"Not that I know of."

"Well, I'll take my leave of the senior officer present."

Vic slept on a spread-out blanket in the shade, still holding the red ball, with the dog curled at his feet. It was very hot. Lana drooped dozing over her magazine, and the child was perspiring. Victor Henry contemplated him for perhaps a minute. Glancing at Janice, he saw her eyes glittering with unshed tears. A look like a long conversation passed between them.

"I'll miss you," she said, walking out with him to a gray Navy sedan. "Give my love to my folks. Tell them that I'm all right, will you?"

"I'll do that." He got in and closed the car door, whereupon she tapped on the glass. He rolled down the window. "Yes?"

"And if you see Byron, tell him to write. I treasure his letters."

"I will."

He drove off, never having mentioned Warren. It didn't surprise her. Since the Battle of Midway, the name of his dead son had not once, in her presence, passed his lips.

Pug had no notion of what to expect at Cincpac. At three that morning, in mid-flight, the co-pilot had brought him a scrawled dispatch: PASSENGER VICTOR (NONE) HENRY CAPTAIN USN REPORT CINCPAC DUTY OFFICER 1400. In the red beam of the flashlight the words had looked ominous. A favorite saw of Pug's had once been, "I've had a lot of troubles in my life, and most of them never happened," but this incantation had lately lost its force.

The new gleaming white Cincpac building, high on Makalapa Hill above the submarine base, showed the way the war was going. It had been built fast, it was a work of power and wealth, and the lanais encircling the upper stories were sophisticated adaptations to the tropics. Inside, the building still smelled of fresh plaster, paint, and linoleum. The thronging staff — officers sporting aiguillettes, enlisted men in whites, and many pretty Waves — had a sprightly look and walk. Midway and Guadalcanal, and the bristling array of new warships in the Yard, all showed in that bouncy new pace. It was not a change to triumph or even to optimism yet. Rather, the open confident look of Americans at work had come back. Gone were the stricken expressions of the days following Pearl Harbor, and the driven tension of the months before Midway.

Ensconced in the glass-partitioned cubicle of the duty officer, inside a bastion of junior officers and Waves, sat the youngest three-striper Victor Henry had ever laid eyes on, with lanky blond hair and a creamy face that appeared never to have been shaved. "A full commander," thought Pug, "and the Cincpac duty officer? I'm really out of step."

"My name is Victor Henry."

"Oh, Captain *Victor Henry!* Yes, sir." In the inquisitive eyes, at the utterance of that name, Pug could see the burning *Northampton* going down. "Please have a seat." The fellow gestured at a wooden chair and pressed an intercom button. "Stanton? Find out if the chief of staff is available. It's Captain Victor Henry."

So Spruance would be the interrogator. A tough man to face; old acquaintance would count for exactly zero. Soon the intercom gabbled, and the duty officer said, "Sir, Vice Admiral Spruance is in conference. Please wait."

While sailors and Waves scurried to and fro, and the duty officer answered the telephone, made calls, and scrawled in a log book, Victor Henry sat reviewing possible lines of questioning. If Spruance was taking time to see him, the battle had to be the topic. The duty officer's commiserating peeps at him were like wasp stings. So a very long half hour went by before Spruance summoned him. Pug remembered into old age the narrow girl-smooth face of the duty officer, the furtive pitying glances, and the tension of that wait.

Spruance was signing letters at a stand-up desk by a window. "Hello, Pug. Just a minute," he said. He had never used Henry's first name before; he addressed almost nobody that way. Spruance looked trim in starched khakis: face gaunt, color high, waist board-flat. Again Pug thought, as he had so many times, how ordinary this victor of Midway looked and acted, compared to Halsey with his battering-ram jaw, glaring eye, bushy brows, and imperious or rollicking humors.

"Well, now." Carefully inserting the pen in a holder, Spruance faced him, hands on hips. "What the Sam Hill happened out there off Tassafaronga?"

"I know what happened to me, Admiral. The rest is sort of a blur." The truthful words were scarcely out of his mouth when he regretted them. Wrong tone of levity.

"You're to be commended on the *Northampton*'s small loss of life."

"It's nothing I ever hoped to be commended for."

"We're going to be able to repair those other three CAs."

"Good. I wish I could have made port, too, Admiral. I tried."

"What went wrong in the battle, exactly?"

"Sir, we found ourselves in torpedo water after we'd opened fire at twelve thousand yards. That was supposed to be beyond torpedo range. Now, either we were ambushed by submarines — which seems unlikely in view of our sizable destroyer screen — or else the Japs have a destroyer torpedo that far outranges ours. We've had intelligence about such a weapon."

"I recall your memo to BuShips about that, and your recommendation on the battleship blisters."

Victor Henry allowed himself a short thankful smile. "Well, Admiral, now I've been on the business end of a couple of those things. They exist."

"Then combat doctrine should be modified accordingly." The large eyes scrutinized Pug. The stand-up desk served the purpose of keeping conversations short, Pug thought. He was making an effort not to shift from foot to foot, and he decided, if ever his time became valuable again, to have a stand-up desk, too. "A word with Admiral Nimitz might be in order," Spruance said. "Let's go."

Hurrying to keep up, Victor Henry followed Spruance down the corridor to tall royal-blue double doors with four affixed gold stars. Admiral Kimmel had received him in such an office in the old building, he remembered, all brave smiles and good humor, as his blasted fleet smoked in the sunshine beyond the windows. Pug had walked in to see Kimmel with calm confidence. He felt very shaky now. Why? He was now more or less in Kimmel's shoes, that was why. Another loser.

They went straight in. Nimitz stood alone, arms folded, at a window. To all appearances he was sunning himself. His handshake was cordial, his square tanned face pleasant; but the direct blue eyes under the thatch of sunlit white hair had a slaty look. That kindly, almost gentle face with those hard eyes, half in sunshine and half in shadow, made Victor Henry yet more nervous.

"Captain Henry says the Japs have a destroyer torpedo of very long range," Spruance said. "That's how he explains Tassafaronga."

"How long is very long?" Nimitz asked Pug.

"Possibly as much as twenty thousand yards, Admiral."

"What do we do about it?"

Forcing words through a tight throat, Pug replied, "In future engagements, Admiral, once our destroyers have made their torpedo attack, the battle line should open fire at much longer range, and make radical evasive turns during the action."

"Did you make radical evasive turns after you saw the other CAs get hit?" Nimitz spoke in an easy Texas-tinged drawl, but there was nothing easy in his look or manner.

"No, sir."

"Why didn't you?"

Victor Henry now had to answer, face to face with Cincpac, the question on which his career hung. He had already tried to handle this question in a fifteen-page action report.

"Admiral, it was a mistake made in the heat of battle. All my guns were bearing. I was straddling the enemy. I wanted vengeance for the three cruisers he had set afire."

"Did you get your vengeance?"

"I don't know. My gunnery officer claimed two hits on two cruisers."

"Confirmed?"

"No, sir. We'll have to await the task force report. Even then I'll have my doubts. Gunnery officers are troubled with creative eyesight."

Nimitz's eyes glinted at Spruance. "Any other observations?"

"I've listed a few in my report, sir."

"For example?"

"Admiral, flashless powder was a BuOrd project way back in '37 when I was there. We still don't have it. The enemy does. We discourage use of searchlights in night action, so as not to show where we are. Then we fire a few salvos and disclose our bearing, target angle, and speed of advance. Our battle line that night looked like four erupting volcanoes. It was a glorious sight, sir, very soul-satisfying. It also gave the Japs their torpedo solution."

Nimitz turned to Spruance. "Get off a dispatch to BuOrd today, and a personal follow-up letter to Spike Blandy on the flashless powder."

"Yes, sir."

Rubbing a stringy hand, which was missing a finger, across his square chin, Nimitz said, "Why the devil was our own destroyer attack a total failure? They achieved surprise with radar, didn't they? They had the drop on the other fellow."

Pug felt himself — so to say — back in torpedo water. This question might well become the crux of a court of inquiry on Tassafaronga. "Admiral, it was a reverse action, forces moving on opposed courses. Relative closing speed fifty knots or better. The torpedo problem developed very fast. When the destroyer commander requested permission to attack with torpedoes, Admiral Wright preferred to close first. The enemy was abaft the beam before he let him go. So it became an up-the-kilt shot at extreme range. That's how it looked in the *Northampton* plot."

"Yet the enemy had the identical problem, and he got an excellent solution."

"They won the torpedo duel hands down, Admiral."

After an excruciating pause Nimitz said, "Very well." He moved away from the window and offered Pug his hand. "I understand you lost an aviator son at Midway, who distinguished himself in combat. And that you've got another son serving in submarines." He bent his head toward the dolphins on his own khaki blouse.

"Yes, Admiral."

Holding Pug's hand in a lingering clasp, looking deep in his eyes, Chester Nimitz said, "Good luck, Henry," in a sad personal tone.

"Thank you, sir."

Spruance took him to the crowded smoky operations room. "There's your battle," he said, pointing to a heavily marked chart of Guadalcanal on the wall, "as we've reconstructed it." They passed into a small anteroom, where they sat down together on a sofa. "The *Northampton* was a beautiful ship," Spruance said. "But there were stability problems."

"I can't fault my damage control people, Admiral. We were unlucky. We took two torpedoes aft of the armor belt. I should have turned away. Gotten the hell out of there, the way the *Honolulu* did. Maybe I'd still have my ship."

"Well, the rage of battle is a factor. Your blood was up. You tried to reverse a rout."

Victor Henry made no comment, but it was as though Spruance had cut ropes holding a heavy burden on his back. He took a deep breath and audibly sighed.

Spruance went on, "Where to next?"

"I have orders back to BuPers for reassignment, Admiral."

"Last time around you were fighting shy of staff duty. I need a deputy chief of staff for planning and operations."

Unable to help it, Victor Henry blurted like a boy, "Me?"

"If you're interested."

"Good God." Pug involuntarily put a hand to his eyes. In the light of the huge growth of the Pacific Fleet, Spruance was offering him a golden prize; a long leap toward flag rank, toward responsibility on the scale of great men; precisely the second chance he had told Janice he could not expect. Victor Henry was not three weeks away from splashing naked through black oil toward a crowded raft, with his ship afire and sinking behind him. After a moment he said hoarsely, "You've achieved surprise, Admiral. I'm interested."

"Well, let's hope BuPers will go along. We've got some fine battle problems ahead, Pug. You should start thinking about them. Come."

Dazed, Victor Henry followed Spruance back into the operations room, to a large yellow and blue table chart of the Pacific. Spruance began to talk with a curious enthusiasm, half-pedantic and half-martial. "At the College, did you get in on the old problem, the recapture of the Philippines after Orange invades and occupies? That's more or less the war we've got."

"No, sir, in my tour we did the Wake Island problem."

"Oh, yes. Well, the thing boils down to two lines of attack. The geography dictates that. A drive across the Central Pacific, reducing the Jap island strong points, and consolidating in the Marianas for the jump to Luzon." Spruance's right hand moved over the chart as he talked, traversing thousands of ocean miles to pantomime a sweep through the Marshalls, the Marianas, and the Carolines to the Philippines.

"And a campaign northward from Australia — New Guinea, Morotai, Mindanao, Luzon." His left hand passed from Australia across New Guinea, with the fingers doing a slow crawl as though to suggest — as they vividly did to Pug — armies slogging over tropical mountains. "General MacArthur naturally is hot for that second strategy. Land fighter. But in the water route you've got a mobile flank attack on the enemy supply lines that keeps him guessing. He can't be sure where you'll hop next. Makes him scatter his strength. The other is a frontal assault overland through mountainous jungle. Jap fleet on *your* flank, alert Jap armies opposing you." Spruance shot Pug a puckish look. "To be sure, the general would strongly desire to lick some Jap armies."

Spruance's right index finger now stabbed at an island off New Guinea. "Still, even he concedes that the way is barred by Rabaul. That's what he saw in the Guadalcanal operation, a stepping-stone toward Rabaul. In any case, we're tooling up here for the Central Pacific. It'll be a big effort. Meantime MacArthur will pursue his drive, of course."

For Victor Henry, still shaken by this turn in his life, the unfolding horizons were magnificent. From command of a cruiser, a cramping task, he foresaw passing to the planning of gigantic sea campaigns. Ideas boiled up in his mind from War College problems and studies of Pacific war. Thin abstractions they had then seemed, algebraic toying with forces and situations that would never exist. Now they were materializing in thick and flaming realities. There surged in him a reviving sense of global combat as his own job to do, in an anonymous slot; all he could ask for.

Spruance tapped the chart at Guadalcanal. "You know, Tassafaronga was a pretty sour note for Admiral Halsey, after the magnificent way he turned that campaign around. Did you see him at all?"

"Yes, sir, when I passed through Nouméa he sent for me."

"How is he?"

"On top of the world. He's got everybody in SoPac on their toes, I'll say that. When I got to his office he was roaring mad about something or other. Everybody in sight was quailing. Next minute with me he was gentle as a parson. Very sympathetic about the *Northampton.*" Pug hesitated and added, "Said at least I went after the bastards."

"How is Warren's wife?"

"I've just seen her." Pug's voice roughened. "She's all right. She's working for the Military Government."

"What about your submariner's wife? Did she ever get out of Europe?"

"I'm hoping there'll be news of her at home, sir."

"Warren was an outstanding fighting man." Spruance shook hands. "I'll never forget him."

Victor Henry said abruptly, "Thank you, Admiral," and he left. It was less than an hour to his plane time. He turned in the car at the pool office, and caught a cab to the NATS terminal. There, at a small newsstand inside the shed, he picked up a *Honolulu Advertiser,* not having read a newspaper in months. Banner headlines bawled of Allied breakthroughs in Morocco, the flight of Rommel, the encirclement of the Germans at Stalingrad. These things he had seen, put in less bubbling terms, on the Cincpac teletype board. Lower on the page a smaller headline hit him like a blow in the face.

ALISTAIR TUDSBURY
KILLED AT EL ALAMEIN

49

Alistair Tudsbury's sixty-year-old secretary put her white head in through the doorway. "A Mr. Leslie Slote is here, Pamela."

In the tiny old office on Pall Mall, Pamela sat in her father's big swivel chair, crying. A cold wind was rattling the loose windows, purple with December gloom at midday. Even bundled in her gray lambskin coat, with a wool shawl tied over her head and ears, she was chilled. The ancient oil heater was having little effect in the room; the place smelled hot, so to say, but no more.

Dabbing her eyes with both hands, Pamela jumped up as Slote came in. He carried a Russian fur-lined greatcoat and a big brown fur hat. He had always been lean, but now his pinstripe suit hung in folds on him, and his eyes burned redly in black sockets.

"Hello, Leslie."

"I'm very sorry about your father, Pam."

"I wasn't weeping over his death. I'm used to that. What brings you to London? Are you finished in Bern so soon? Will some whiskey warm you up?"

"God, it'll save me."

She pointed at a typescript on the desk. "That's the last thing he wrote. He didn't quite finish it. The *Observer* wants it. I'm winding it up, and I'm afraid it brought on the tears."

"What is it? A news dispatch?"

"Oh, no, that would be dead as mutton. It's a battlefield sketch. He called it 'Sunset on Kidney Ridge.' " She handed him half a tumbler of neat whiskey, and gestured with another. "Cheers. He was dictating it, actually, when Monty's press chap rang to say that the interview was on."

Pamela's careworn countenance, the swollen eyes, the slipshod hair, the flat voice, could be ascribed to grief, Slote was thinking, but she seemed altogether quenched. At her lowest in other days — and Pamela had been very low — she had not lost a certain defiant sparkle, an enticing bravura beneath the quiet surface. Slote was looking now at a dull sad woman past thirty.

"Do you believe in presentiments?" Her voice was hoarse from the whiskey.

"I'm not sure. Why?"

"Talky had one. I know. I was supposed to go in that jeep. I'd even been cleared by Montgomery's press chap, quite a break for a female. Talky suddenly, mulishly, bumped me. He was downright nasty about it, and I got nasty too. We parted in anger, and that's why I'm alive, sitting here now, drinking with you." She raised her glass sadly, and drained it. "I'm an utter skeptic, Leslie, I believe only in things you can see and hear and measure, and all that. Still, he knew. Don't ask me how. Hitting a land mine is a random accident, I realize, yet he knew. That piece on Kidney Ridge is a deathbed sort of thing."

"You remember Byron Henry?" Slote asked.

"Why, of course."

"I met him in Lisbon last week. I fear there's more bad news. The *Northampton's* gone down." Slote had been looking forward with sour relish, of which he was slightly ashamed, to making this disclosure. Not that he wished her ill, or Victor Henry either, but in their romance he had briefly figured as a feeble also-ran, and the bad taste lingered. She showed no emotion. "You're very well connected here, Pam, aren't you? Can you find out whether Captain Henry survived, and cable Byron? The only word he could get in Lisbon, from some Navy people there, was that the ship was sunk in battle."

"What about your naval attaché here?"

"He's off in Scotland."

"All right," she said briskly, almost gaily, "let's find out about Captain Henry." It was a peculiar reaction to grave news, Slote thought; mighty peculiar. Merely talking about the man animated her. She told the secretary to call Air Vice Marshal Burne-Wilke. "Well! And what news about Byron? And Natalie?"

"He found her. Found her, and the baby."

"I'll be damned. *Found* her! Where?"

"In Marseilles. Told me about it for two hours over dinner. It's a saga."

"Honestly, that family! How did he do it? Where's Natalie now?"

Slote had just started on Byron's tale when the telephone rang. It was Burne-Wilke. Pamela told him about Pug Henry and Byron in a quick affectionate way, calling him "darling." She hung up and said to Slote, "They have a direct line through to Washington. He'll get on it as soon as he can. Have you ever met my fiancé?"

"Once. On a receiving line at your embassy in Washington. You were there, but he wasn't your fiancé then."

"Oh, of course. And Captain Henry was there, and Natalie, too. Now go on with what happened in Marseilles. More whiskey?"

"Absolutely, if you can spare it."

"People have been kind. I've bottles and bottles."

Slote told the story of the encounter at some length, and said Byron was still trying to learn his family's fate. On the day the Allies had invaded North Africa, the telephone lines to Marseilles had shut down. Intermittent contact had since been restored, with long delays, but none of his calls had gone through. He had thirty days' leave, and he was spending them hanging around the rescue agencies' offices in Lisbon.

"What on earth came over Natalie to balk like that? I don't blame Byron for being furious," Pamela said.

Slote stared at her. Blankly he repeated, "What came over her?"

"Leslie, that's the girl who climbed up to your second-story window on the rue Scribe, when you lost your latch key. Remember? Remember how she faced down the gendarmes in Les Halles, when I cracked Phil's head open with a soup bowl? The lioness, we called her."

"What's all that got to do with it? She'd have been insane to try to run the border with Byron."

"Why? He had his diplomatic pass. How could she be worse off than she is now?"

The eyes in the dark sockets luridly flared. Slote looked to Pamela as though he were running a high temperature. He replied with soft exaggerated calm, "Why, sweetheart, I'll try to tell you exactly how much worse off she could be. Can I have just a tot more of your firewater?"

He pulled a pen from his breast pocket, and while she poured, he sat down at her desk and began to sketch on a yellow sheet. "Look, this is prewar Poland. All right? Warsaw to the north, Cracow to the south, Vistula connecting them." It was a skilled rough map, drawn as quickly as the hand could move. "Hitler invades. He and Stalin partition the country. Zip! To the west of this line is German-held Poland. The Government General." The irregular stroke cut Poland in two. Slote drew three heavy ink circles on the western side. "Now, you've heard about concentration camps."

"Yes, I have, Leslie."

"You haven't heard of these. I've just spent four days talking to Polish government-in-exile people here. That's actually why I came to London. Pam, this is quite a news story. You're carrying on your father's work, aren't you?"

"Trying to."

"Well, this may prove the biggest story of the war. The reporter who breaks it will have a place in history. In these three places — there are more, but the Polish government-in-exile has eyewitness accounts on these right here in London — the Germans are exterminating human beings like rats, in multitudes. They ship them here from all over Europe in trains. It's a massacre by railroad. When the Jews arrive, the Germans kill them with carbon monoxide or rifle squads, and they burn up the bodies." The pen darted from circle to circle. "This place is called Treblinka. This one is Lublin. This is Oswiecim. As I say, there are more, but on these there is *proof.*"

"Leslie, concentration camps aren't news. We've had these stories for years."

Slote gave her a ghastly smile. "You don't grasp what I'm saying." He achieved emphasis by dropping his voice to a grinding whisper. "I'm talking about the *systematic execution of eleven million people. It's well under way as you and I are talking.* A fantastic plan, a gargantuan secret operation with vast facilities built to carry it out! You don't call that a story? What is a news story then? This is the most enormous crime in the history of the human race. It dwarfs all wars that have ever been fought. It's a new aspect of life on this planet. And it's *happening.* It's about half-accomplished right now. Isn't that a news story, Pamela?"

Pamela had read stories of gassing chambers and of mass rifle slayings. There was nothing new about any of it. Of course, the Gestapo was a gang of monstrous thugs. The war was worth fighting, just to rid the world of them. The plan to wipe out all the Jews of Europe was naturally a morbid exaggeration, but she had read of this, too. Somebody obviously had sold the whole package to Slote; and, perhaps because his career was going badly, or because he had never gotten over Natalie, and was now having guilt feelings about having jilted a Jewess he adored, he had fastened on this thing. She murmured, "It's quite beyond me to handle, dear."

"Well, I don't think so, but we were discussing Natalie. Refusing Byron took amazing guts, a hell of a lot more than climbing to a second-story window. She didn't have her exit visas. The Gestapo swarms on those trains. If there'd been a snag, they'd have taken her and her baby off the train. Then they might have put her in a camp. Then they might have put her on another train going east. Then they might have murdered her and her baby, and burned them to ashes. Now that was a bad risk, Pam, and if she didn't know the details she sensed that in her bones. She knew that exit visas were coming. She knew the Germans have a lunatic respect for official paper, it's the one talisman that restrains them. She did the right thing. When I tried to tell Byron that, he turned white with rage, and —"

The telephone was ringing. She made an apologetic silencing gesture.

"Hello? What, so *quickly?*" Her eyes opened enormously, and went brilliant as jewels. She nodded hard at Slote. "Well! Marvelous. Thank you, thank you, dearest. See you at eight." She hung up, and smiled radiantly at Slote. "Captain Henry's all right! You know, getting that information out of our Admiralty would have taken a week. Your War Department put Duncan through to Navy Personnel, and he had the answer almost at once. Captain Henry is on his way back to Washington. Shall I cable Byron, or will you?"

"Here's his address in Lisbon, Pam. You do it." Slote hastily scrawled in a notebook and tore out the sheet. "And look, the Poles here are amassing a book of their documents. I can get you the galley proofs. What's more, they've got a man who escaped from Treblinka, this camp up here" — a skinny finger jabbed at the sketch on the desk — "near Warsaw. He made his way clear across Nazi Europe on sheer nerve, just to bring photographs and tell the story. I've spoken to him through interpreters. It's impossible not to believe him. His story is an Odyssey. A terrific scoop, Pamela."

Pam was finding it hard to pay attention. *Pug Henry alive and safe! Returning to Washington!* This put a new light on her plans, on her life. As for Slote's "scoop," he seemed to her more than a bit obsessed. She could almost hear her father saying, *"No chance. None whatever. Old stuff."* The new stuff was victory — victory in North Africa, in Russia, in the Pacific; victory too against the U-boats, after four years of catastrophe, the true great turn of the war. That the Germans were terrorizing Europe and maltreating the Jews was as familiar as the tide tables.

"Leslie, I'll talk to my editor-in-chief tomorrow."

Slote thrust an emaciated hand straight at her. The palm was wet, the grip loose. "Splendid! I'll be here two more days. Call me either at the Dorchester or the American embassy, extension 739." As he put on his fur coat and cap, the old Paris smile lit the gaunt face and haunted eyes. "Thank you for the booze, old girl, and for listening to the Ancient Mariner."

He stumbled out.

The editor-in-chief listened to her next day in a bored slump, gnawing at his cold pipe, nodding and grunting. The Polish government-in-exile, he said, had long since offered him all this material. He had run some pieces. She could see these in the files, standard propaganda stuff. By any journalistic standards the stories could not be verified. The business about the plan to kill all the Jews was coming from Zionist sources, to pressure Whitehall into opening up Palestine for Jewish immigration. Still, he would be willing to see Mr. Slote next week. Oh, the man was leaving tomorrow? Too bad.

But when she offered to go to Washington and write some stories on the war effort there, he brightened. "Well, why not? Do try your hand, Pam. We know you were drafting Talky's copy toward the last. When will you let us have 'Sunset on Kidney Ridge'? We're frightfully anxious for it."

Slote knew of two Foreign Service officers who had disappeared on ferry command bomber flights between Scotland and Montreal. The North Atlantic sky was not the route of choice, certainly not in midwinter. Big comfortable airliners flew the southern route — down to Dakar, a hop across sunny seas to the bulge of Brazil, then north to Bermuda and so on to Baltimore. But that was for big shots. The choices offered him were a ten-day voyage in a convoy, or an RAF ferry command trip.

On the train to the Scottish airport, he fell in with an American ferry pilot going the same way: a wiry middle-sized Army Air Corps captain with a toothbrush mustache, a wild eye, three banks of ribbons on his khaki tunic, a richly obscene vocabulary, and a great store of flying stories. The two men had a compartment to themselves. The ferry pilot kept nipping brandy, explaining that he was getting plastered and intended to stay plastered until they were well off the Prestwick runway. Crashing on takeoff was a hazard at Prestwick. He had attended two mass funerals of pilots who had died on the runway. Dangerous overloads of gasoline had to be accepted, when you were flying westward into North Atlantic gales. The ferry command had to keep hauling pilots back, because shipping disassembled aircraft by sea was slow and cumbersome, and the U-boats got too many of them. It was the ferry pilots who were really building up the Allied air forces in the war zones. Nobody gave a shit about them, but they were the key to the whole war.

As the old dusty train clanked its slow way through snowy fields, the pilot regaled Slote with his autobiography. His name was Bill Fenton. A barnstormer before the war, he had since 1937 been doing various flying jobs, civilian and military, for various governments. He had flown cargo carriers on the India-China run ("over the hump," he called it); taking off from a runway that had to be cleared of cows and water buffalo by a honking jeep, then climbing five miles and more to get over icy storms that whirled higher than Everest. He had joined the Royal Canadian Air Force to ferry planes to England. Now he was flying bombers for the Army Air Corps via South America to Africa, and on across to Persia and the Soviet Union. He had crash-landed in the desert. He had floated for two days in the Irish Sea on a rubber raft. He had parachuted into Japanese-held territory in Burma, and walked out to India on foot.

By the time they reached Prestwick in a snowstorm, Slote was not only tired, sleepy, and drunk from his share of Bill Fenton's brandy; he had a whole new vision of the war. In his fumed brain pictures reeled of aircraft crisscrossing the globe — bombers, fighters, transports, by the thousands — battling the weather and the enemy, bombing cities, railroads, and troop columns; crossing oceans, deserts, high mountain ranges; a war such as Thucydides had never imagined, filling the skies of the planet with hurtling machines manned by hordes of Bill Fentons. He had not until now given the war in the air a thought. For once, the everlasting Wannsee Protocol, the map of Poland with the three black circles, and the European trains carrying hundreds of thousands of Jews each month to their deaths faded from his mind. He was moreover so scared at the prospect of the flight that he could hardly walk off the train.

When they arrived at the airfield the plane was warming up. Waddling out of the check-in office in cumbersome flying suits, heavy gloves, and life vests, with parachutes dangling behind their knees, they could not at first see the aircraft through the falling snow. Fenton led him toward the motor sound. It was inconceivable to Leslie Slote that a machine could take off in this weather. Inside the four-engine bomber there were no seats. On the board floor about a dozen returning ferry pilots sprawled on pallets. Slote's armpits coldly dripped and his heart raced as the plane heavily took off. Fenton screamed into his ears, over the engine roar and the groan of retracting wheels, that the weather briefing predicted headwinds of a hundred miles an hour. They might well have to put down in Greenland, the asshole of the Arctic.

Leslie Slote was a coward. He knew it. He had given up fighting it. Even riding in a car with a fast driver gave him bad nerves. Every airplane ride, just a one-hour hop in a DC-3, was an ordeal. This man now found himself in a stripped-down four-engine bomber, setting out to cross the Atlantic westward in December; a howling rattletrap that sucked in the cold through whining and whistling air leaks, climbed through hail that made a machine gun racket on the fuselage, and bucked, dipped, and swerved like a kite. Slote could see, in dim light from iced-up windows, the greenish faces of the sprawled pilots, the sweat-beaded foreheads, the shaking hands bringing cigarettes or bottles to tight mouths. The fliers looked fully as terrified as he felt.

Fenton had explained on the train that the North Atlantic head winds were strongest at low altitudes. Planes flew high to climb over the weather and conserve fuel in the thinner air; but up there they could accumulate ice too fast for the de-icers to work. Also, the carburetors could get chilled from pulling in subzero air, and they could ice up. Then the engines would quit. That no doubt was the way so many planes vanished. When ice began to build up you could keep trying to climb above the wet cold into the dry cold, where one needed an oxygen mask to survive. Otherwise you had to drop back down fast, maybe down to the wave tops, where warmer air would melt your ice. Against his better judgment, Slote had asked him, "Can't the icing conditions prevail right down to the water?"

"Hell, yes," Fenton had answered. "Let me tell you what happened to me." And he had launched into a long hideous anecdote about a near-spin into the water off Newfoundland under a heavy ice load.

The plane kept climbing and climbing; loose things persisted in sliding toward the rear. Some pilots huddled under ragged blankets and snored. Fenton too stretched out and closed his eyes. A sudden metallic crashing and banging along the fuselage stopped Slote's heart, or so he felt. Fenton blinked, grinned at Slote, and pantomimed ice forming along the wings, and rubber de-icers cracking it off.

Slote wondered how anybody could sleep in this howling torture chamber in the sky, hammered at by breaking ice. He could as soon sleep, he thought, nailed to a cross. His nose was freezing. There was no sensation in his hands or feet. Yet he did doze, for a nasty sensation woke him: a smell of rubber, a cold thing pressed to his face as in anesthesia. He opened his eyes in the dark. Fenton's voice yelled in his ear, "Oxygen." Somebody lit a dim battery lamp. A shadowy figure was stumbling here and there with masks that trailed long rubber tubes. Slote thought he had never been so cold, so numb, so sick all over, so ready to die and get it over with.

All at once the plane dived, roaring. The pilots sat up and looked about with white-rimmed eyes. It was an obscure comfort in Slote's agony that these skilled men were so scared, too. After a horrendously steep long dive, ice crashed along the fuselage once more. The floor levelled off.

"Never make Newfoundland," Fenton yelled in Slote's ear. "Greenland it is."

· · ·

> *Ven Der Fuehrer says,*
> *"Ve iss der Master Race,"*
> *Ve Heil (phfft!)*
> *Heil (phfft!)*
> *Right in Der Fuehrer's face.*

In the wooden barracks beside the Greenland runway, this song was grinding out of the phonograph, hour after hour. It was the only record on hand. The airfield, a treeless spread of steel netting sunk into mud and drifted over with snow, was a drearier place than Slote had imagined could exist on earth. The runway was short and chancy, so the refueled aircraft had to wait for endurable takeoff conditions.

> *Not to luff Der Fuehrer*
> *Iss a great disgrace*
> *So ve Heil (phfft!)*
> *Heil (phfft!)*
> *Right in Der Fuehrer's face.*

Here in this witless ditty, Slote thought, was the fatally soft American idea of Hitler and the Nazis — the ranting boob, the dumbbell followers, the *heils* and the razzes. The musical arrangement mixed various funny noises — cowbells, toy trumpets, tin cans — with the oom-pahs of a German band. The pilots were playing cards or lolling about, and when the record ended somebody simply moved the needle back to the start.

Fenton lay on the bunk underneath Slote's, leafing a girlie magazine. Slote leaned over and asked him what he thought of "Der Fuehrer's Face."

Fenton yawned that it was getting to be a pain in the ass. Climbing down, Slote sat beside the captain and unburdened himself about the massacre of the Jews, bitterly observing that when a song like that could amuse people, it was small wonder that nobody believed what was happening.

Turning the pages of naked females, Bill Fenton calmly remarked, "Shit, man, who doesn't believe it? *I* believe it. Those Germans have to be weird people, to follow a nut like Hitler. Some of them are fine aviators, but taken as a nation they're a menace."

> *Ven Herr Goebbels says,*
> *"Ve own de Vorld und Space,"*
> *Ve Heil (phfft!)*
> *Heil (phfft!)*
> *Right in Herr Goebbels' face.*

> *Ven Herr Goering says,*
> *"Dey'll neffer bomb dis place,"*
> *Ve Heil (phfft!)*
> *Heil (phfft!)*
> *Right in Herr Goering's face . . .*

"But what can anybody do about the Jews?" Fenton tossed the magazine aside, stretching and yawning. "Fifty million people will die before this war's over. The Japs have been fighting the Chinese since 1937. Do you know how many Chinese have starved to death? Nobody does. Maybe ten million. Maybe more. You ever been to India? There's a powder keg. The British can't keep the lid on much longer. When India blows, you're going to see Hindus and Sikhs and Moslems and Buddhists and Parsees cutting each other's throats till hell won't have it. The Germans have killed a lot more Russians than Jews. This world is a slaughterhouse, man, it always has been, and that's what all these fucking pacifists keep forgetting."

> *Iss ve not der Supermen?*
> *Aryan pure, Supermen?*
> *Yah! ve iss der Supermen*
> *Sooper DOOPER Supermen!*

Fenton enjoyed the sound of his own voice, and he was getting worked up. He sat erect and poked Slote on the shoulder. "Tell me this. Is Stalin any better than Hitler? I say he's the same kind of murderer. Yet we're fly-ing half of the bombers we're producing over to him — free, gratis, and for nothing, and some damn good pilots are getting killed at it, and I'm risking my own ass. And why? Because he's *our* murderer, that's why. We're not doing it for humanity, or for Russia, or for anything except to save our own asses. Christ, *I* feel sorry for the Jews, don't think I don't, but there just isn't a thing we can do about them but beat the shit out of the Germans."

> *So ve Heil (phfft!)*
> *Heil (phfft!)*
> *Right . . . in . . . Der . . . Fuehrer's . . . face.*

· · ·

At the enormous Canadian Air Force Base outside Montreal, Slote telephoned the Division of European Affairs, and the division chief told him to hurry along to the Montreal airport and catch the first plane to New York or Washington. While this was going on, Fenton passed the telephone booth. A tall pretty girl in a red fox coat was clinging to his arm, hips rolling with each step, devouring the pilot with lustrous green eyes. A casual wave with his smoking cigar at the booth, a man-to-man grin, and the ferry pilot passed from view. A short life and a merry one, thought Slote, with a flicker of rueful envy.

To his pleased surprise, Slote found that he did not mind the takeoff of the DC-3, or the bumpy climb through heavy clouds. The airliner seemed so huge, the interior so luxurious, the seat so broad and soft, the stewardess so entrancing, that it was more like being on the *Queen Mary* than on something flying through the air. He cold not tell whether the bomber ride had cauterized, as it were, his fear of flying, or whether he just had no nerves left, and was on the verge of a total crack-up. Anyway, not to be frightened was delightful.

He had snatched a *Montreal Gazette* from the newsstand. Now he unfolded it, and a picture of Alistair Tudsbury and Pamela on the first page made him sit up. They stood beside a jeep, Tudsbury grinning in balloonlike army fatigues, Pamela looking pinched and bored in slacks and a shirt.

SUNSET ON KIDNEY RIDGE

By Alistair Tudsbury

By wireless from London. This dispatch, dated November 4, 1942, the famous British correspondent's last, was dictated shortly before he was killed by a landmine at El Alamein. Edited by his daughter and collaborator, Pamela Tudsbury, from an unfinished draft, it is reprinted by special permission of the London Observer.

The sun hangs huge and red above the far dust-streaked horizon. The desert cold is already falling on Kidney Ridge. This gray sandy elevation is deserted, except by the dead, and by two intelligence officers and myself. Even the flies have left. Earlier they were here in clouds, blackening the corpses.

They pester the living too, clustering at a man's eyes and the moisture in the corners of his mouth, drinking his sweat. But of course they prefer the dead. When the sun climbs over the opposite horizon tomorrow, the flies will return to their feast.

Here not only did these German and British soldiers die, who litter the ground as far as the eye can see in the fading red light. Here at El Alamein the Afrika Korps died. The Korps was a legend, a dashing clean-cut enemy, a menace and at the same time a sort of glory; in Churchillian rhetoric, a gallant foe worthy of our steel. It is not yet known whether Rommel has made good his escape, or whether his straggle of routed supermen will be bagged by the Eighth Army. But the Afrika Korps is dead, crushed by British arms. We have won here, in the great Western Desert of Africa, a victory to stand with Crécy, Agincourt, Blenheim, and Waterloo.

Lines from Southey's "Battle of Blenheim" are haunting me here on Kidney Ridge:

> They say it was a shocking sight
> After the field was won,
> For many thousand bodies here
> Lay rotting in the sun;
> But things like that, you know, must be
> After a famous victory.

The bodies, numerous as they are, strike the eye less than the blasted and burned-out tanks that dot this weirdly beautiful wasteland, these squat hulks with their long guns, casting elongated blue shadows on the pastel grays, browns, and pinks of the far-stretching sands. Here is the central incongruity of Kidney Ridge — the masses of smashed twentieth-century machinery tumbled about in these harsh flat sandy wilds, where one envisions warriors on camels, or horses, or perhaps the elephants of Hannibal.

How far they came to perish here, these soldiers and these machines! What bizarre train of events brought youngsters from the Rhineland and Prussia, from the Scottish Highlands and London, from Australia and New Zealand, to butt at each other to the death with flame-spitting machinery in faraway Africa, in a setting as dry and lonesome as the moon?

But that is the hallmark of this war. No other war has ever been like it. This war rings the world. Kidney Ridge is everywhere on our small globe. Men fight as far from home as they can be transported, with courage and endurance that makes one proud of the human race, in horrible contrivances that make one ashamed of the human race.

My jeep will take me back to Cairo shortly, and I will dictate a dispatch about what I see here. What I am looking at, right now as the sun touches the horizon, is this. Two intelligence officers, not fifty yards from me, are lifting the German driver out of a blasted tank, using meat hooks. He is black and charred. He has no head. He is a trunk with arms and legs. The smell is like gamy pork. The legs wear good boots, only a bit scorched.

I am very tired. A voice I don't want to listen to tells me that this is England's last land triumph; that our military history ends here with a victory to stand with the greatest, won largely with machines shipped ten thousand miles from American factories. Tommy Atkins will serve with pluck and valor wherever he fights hereafter, as always; but the conduct of the war is passing out of our hands.

We are outnumbered and outclassed. Modern war is a clangorous and dreary measuring of industrial plants. Germany's industrial capacity passed ours in 1905. We hung on through the First World War by sheer grit. Today the two industrial giants of the earth are the United States and the Soviet Union. They more than outmatch Germany and Japan, now that they have shaken off their surprise setbacks and sprung to arms. Tocqueville's vision is coming to pass in our time. They will divide the empire of the world.

The sun going down on Kidney Ridge is setting on the British Empire, on which — so we learned to say as schoolboys — the sun never set. Our Empire was born in the skill of our explorers, the martial prowess of our yeomanry, the innovative genius of our scientists and engineers. We stole a march on the world that lasted two hundred years. Lulled by the long peaceful protection of the great fleet we built, we thought it would last forever. We dozed.

Here on Kidney Ridge we have erased the disgrace of our somnolence. If history is but the clash of arms, we now begin to leave the stage in honor. But if it is the march of the human spirit toward world freedom, we will never leave the stage. British ideas, British institutions, British scientific method, will lead the way in other lands, in other guises. English will become the planetary tongue, that is now certain. We have been the Greece of the new age.

But, you object, the theme of the new age is socialism. I am not so sure of that. Even so, Karl Marx, the scruffy Mohammed of this spreading economic Islam, built his strident dogmas on the theories of British economists. He created his apocalyptic visions in the hospitality of the British Museum. He read British books, lived on British bounty, wrote in British freedom, collaborated with Englishmen, and lies in a London grave. People forget all that.

The sun has set. It will get dark and cold quickly now. The intelligence officers are beckoning me to their lorry. The first stars spring forth in the indigo sky. I take a last look around at the dead of El Alamein and mutter a prayer for all these poor devils, German and British, who turn and turn about sang "Lili Marlene" in the cafés of Tobruk, hugging the same sleazy girls. Now they lie here together, their young appetites cold, their homesick songs stilled.

> *"Why, 'twas a very wicked thing!"*
> *Said little Wilhelmine.*
> *"Nay, nay my little girl!" quoth he —*

Pamela Tudsbury writes: "The telephone rang just at that moment, as my father was declaiming the verse with his usual relish. It was the summons to the interview with General Montgomery. He left at once. A lorry

brought back his body next morning. As a World War I reserve officer,
he was buried with honors in the British Military Cemetery outside Alex-
andria.

The London Observer *asked me to complete the article. I have tried.*
I have his handwritten notes for three more paragraphs. But I cannot do
it. I can, however, complete Southey's verse for him. So ends my father's
career of war reporting —

"It was a famous victory."

•   •   •

The airplane was humming above the weather now, the sky was bright
blue, the sunlight blinding on the white cloud cover. Slote slumped sadly in
his chair. He had come a long way from Bern, he was thinking, not only in
miles but in perception. In the hothouse of the Swiss capital, under the comfortable glass of neutrality, his obsession about the Jews had sprouted like
some forced plant. Now he was coming back to realities.

How could one arouse American public opinion? How get past the
horselaugh of "Der Fuehrer's Face," the acid cynicism of Fenton? Above all,
how overcome the competition of Kidney Ridge? Tudsbury's piece was touching and evocative, describing a great slaughter; but there was no Kidney
Ridge for the Jews of Europe. They were unarmed. It was no fight. Most of
them did not even comprehend that a massacre was going on. Sheep going
to the slaughter were uncomfortable to contemplate. One turned one's eyes
elsewhere. One had an exciting world drama to watch, a contest for the
highest stakes, in which the home team was at last pulling ahead. Treblinka had small chance against Kidney Ridge.

50

I N September 1941, Victor Henry had left a country at peace, but with isolationists and interventionists in a screechy squabble, the production of munitions a trickle, despite all the "arsenal of democracy" rhetoric; the military services shuddering over Congress's renewal of the draft by one vote; a land without rationing, with business booming from defense spending, with lights blazing at night from coast to coast, with the usual cataracts of automobiles on the highways and the city streets.

Now as he returned, San Francisco from the air spelled War: shadowy lampless bridges under a full moon, pale ribbons of deserted highways, dimmed-out residential hills, black tall downtown buildings. In the dark quiet streets and in the glare of the hotel lobby the swarms of uniforms astounded him. Hitler's Berlin had looked no more martial.

Newspapers and magazines that he read next day on the eastbound flight mirrored the change. In the advertisements, all was bellicose patriotism. Where heroic-looking riveters, miners, or soldiers and their sweethearts were not featured in the ads, a toothy Jap hyena, or a snake with a Hitler mustache, or a bloated scowling Mussolini-like pig took comic beatings. The news columns and year-end summaries surged with buoyant confidence that at Stalingrad and in North Africa the tide of the war had turned. The Pacific was getting short treatment. Sketchy references to Midway and Guadalcanal, perhaps through the fault of the closemouthed Navy, miserably missed the scope of these battles. As for the sinking of the *Northampton*, Pug saw that if released the story would have been ignored. This calamity in his life, this loss of a great ship of war, would have been a dark flyspeck on a golden picture of optimism.

And it was all mighty sudden! Island-hopping across the Pacific in recent days, he had been reading in airplanes and waiting rooms scuffed periodicals of the past months. With one voice they had bemoaned the dilatory Allied war effort, the deep German advances into the Caucasus, the pro-Axis unrest in India, South America, and the Arab lands, and Japan's march across Burma and the Southwest Pacific. Now with one voice the same journals were hailing the inevitable downfall of Adolf Hitler and his partners in crime. This civilian change of mood struck Pug as frivolous. If the strategic turn was at hand, the main carnage in the field was yet to come. Americans had only begun to die. To military families, if not to military columnists, this was no small thing. He had called Rhoda from San Francisco, and she had told him that there was no news of Byron. In wartime, no news, especially about a son in submarines, was not necessarily good news.

His orders to BuPers and the talk with Spruance were much on his mind as the plane bounced and tossed through the wintry gray skies. The key man at the Bureau for four-striper assignments was Digger Brown, his old Academy chum. Pug had drilled the ambitious Brown, who couldn't learn languages, through three years of German, boosting him to top grades which had raised Brown's class standing and helped his whole career. Pug expected to be ordered back to Cincpac without trouble, for nobody in the Navy swung much more weight right now than Nimitz and Spruance; still, if there were any bureaucratic shuffling about it, he meant to look Digger Brown in the eye and tell him what he wanted. The man could not refuse him.

What about Rhoda? What could he say in the first moments? How should he act? He had been puzzling over this while he flew halfway around the globe, and the quandary was still with him.

In the dark marble-tiled foyer of the big Foxhall Road house, she wept in his arms. His bulky bridge coat was flecked with snow, his embrace was awkward, but she clung to him against the cold wet blue cloth and the bumpy brass buttons, exclaiming through sobs, "I'm sorry, oh, I'm sorry, Pug. I didn't mean to cry, truly I didn't. I'm so glad to see you I could DIE. Sorry, darling! Sorry I'm such a crybaby."

"It's all right, Rho. Everything's all right."

And in this first tender moment he really thought everything might turn out all right. Her body felt soft and sweet in his embrace. In all their long marriage he had seen his wife in tears only a few times; for all her frothy ways she had a streak of stoical self-control. She clutched him like a child seeking comfort, and her wet eyes were large and bright. "Oh, damn, *damn*, I was going to carry this off with a smile and a martini. The martini is probably still a SCRUMPTIOUS idea, isn't it?"

"At high noon? Well, maybe, at that." He tossed his coat and cap on a bench. She led him hand in hand into the living room, where flames leaped in the fireplace, and ornaments glittered on a large Christmas tree that filled the room with a smell of childhood, of family joy.

He took both her hands. "Let's have a good look at you."

"Madeline's coming here for Christmas, you know," she chattered, "and not having a maid and all, I thought I'd just buy a tree early and trim the darn thing up, and — well, well, SAY something!" She shakily laughed, freeing her hands. "This captain's inspection is giving me the WIM-WAMS. What do you think of the old hulk?"

It was almost like sizing up another man's wife. Rhoda's skin was soft, clear, scarcely lined. In the clinging jersey dress her figure was as seductive as ever; if anything, a shade thin. Her hip bones jutted. Her movements and gestures were lithe, fetching, feminine. Her comic waggle of ten spread fingers at him when she said "WIM-WAMS" brought back her roguish charm in their first dates.

"You look marvelous."

The admiring tone brought instant radiance to her face. She spoke huskily, her voice catching, "You would say that. And you look so smart! A bit grayer, old thing, but it's attractive."

He walked to the fire, holding out his hands. "This feels good."

"Oh, I'm being ever so patriotic. Also practical. Oil's a problem. I keep the thermostat down, close off most of the rooms, and burn a lot of wood. Now, you WRETCH! Why didn't you call me from the airport? I've been pacing the house like a LEOPARD."

"The booths were jammed."

"Well, I've been FALLING on the phone for an hour. It kept ringing. That fellow Slote called from the State Department. He's back from Switzerland."

"Slote! Any news of Natalie? Or of Byron?"

"He was in a terrific hurry. He's going to call again. Natalie seems to be in Lourdes, and —"

"What? Lourdes? France? How'd she get to Lourdes?"

"She's with our interned diplomats and journalists. That's all he said about her. Byron was in Lisbon, trying to get transportation back, last Slote heard. He's got orders to new construction."

"Well! And the baby?"

"Slote didn't say. I asked him to dinner. And do you remember Sime Anderson? He called, too. The phone never stopped ringing."

"The midshipman? The one who ran me all over the tennis court while Madeline giggled and clapped?"

"He's a lieutenant commander! How about that, Pug? I declare, these days if you've been WEANED you're a lieutenant commander. He wanted Madeline's phone number in New York."

Staring into the fire, Pug said, "She's back with that monkey Cleveland, isn't she?"

"Dear, I got to know Mr. Cleveland in Hollywood. He's not a bad fellow." At her husband's ugly look she faltered, "Besides, she's having such fun! And the MONEY the child makes!" The firelight was casting harsh shadows on Victor Henry's face. She came to him. "Darling, how about that drink? I'm frankly all of a QUIVER."

His arm went round her waist, and he kissed her cheek. "Sure. Just let me ring Digger Brown first, and find out why in hell I'm here on Class One priority."

"Oh, Pug, he'll only tell you to call the White House. Let's just pretend your plane's late and — why, what on EARTH is wrong, sweetie?"

"The White House?"

"Well, sure." She clapped a hand to her lips. "Oh, LORDY. Lucy Brown will have my HEAD. She swore me to secrecy, but I just assumed you knew."

"Knew *what?*" His tone changed. He might have been talking to a quartermaster. "Rhoda, tell me exactly what Lucy Brown told you, and when."

"Dear me! Well — it seems the White House ordered BuPers to get you back here, p.d.q. This was early in November, before, well, before you lost the *Northampton*, Pug. That's all I know. That's all even Digger knows."

Pug was at a telephone, dialling. "Go ahead and make that drink."

"Dear, just don't let on to Digger that Lucy told me. He'll ROAST her over a slow fire."

The Navy Department switchboard was long in answering. Victor Henry stood alone in the big living room, recovering from his surprise. *The White House* was still for him, as for any American, a magic expression, but he had come to know the sour aftertaste of serving a President. Franklin Roosevelt had used him like a borrowed pencil, and in the same way had dropped him; paying off, politician fashion, with the command of the unlucky *California*. Victor Henry bore the President no grudge. Near or far, he still regarded the masterful old cripple with awe. But he was resolved to fight off, at any cost, further presidential assignments. Those sterile shorebound exercises as flunky to the great had all but wrecked his professional life. He had to get back to the Pacific.

Digger was out. Pug went over to the fireplace and stood with his back to the blaze. He did not feel at home, yet in Janice's cramped cottage he had. Why was that? Before going to Moscow he had spent less than three months in this house. How huge it was! What had they been thinking of, to buy such a mansion? Once again he had allowed her to chip in some of her own trust money, because she wanted to live in a style beyond his means. Wrong, wrong. There had been talk of putting up lots of grandchildren. What a bitter memory! And what were the summer slipcovers doing on the furniture in chill December, in a room smelling of Christmas? He had never liked this garish flower pattern on green chintz. Though he could feel the fire heat on his jacket, the chill in the house seemed to pierce to his marrow. Maybe it was true that serving in the tropics thinned the blood. But he could not remember feeling so cold before, on returning from Pacific duty.

"Martinis," Rhoda announced, marching in with a clinking tray. "What about Digger?"

"Not there."

The first sip made a fiery streak down Pug's throat. He had not tasted alcohol in months; not since a spell of heavy self-numbing after Warren's death. "Good," he said, but he regretted agreeing to the martini. He might need all his wits at BuPers. Rhoda offered him a plate of open-face sandwiches, and he commented with assumed heartiness, "Hey, caviar! Really cosseting me, aren't you?"

"You don't remember?" Her smile was archly flirtatious. "You sent it from Moscow. An Army colonel brought me six tins, with this note from you."

"For when we meet again," the scrawl on shoddy Russian paper read. *"Martinis, caviar, a fire, AND . . . especially AND . . . ! Love, Pug."*

It all came back to him now: the boisterous afternoon when the Harriman party had shopped in the one tourist store still functioning, in the National Hotel, months before Pearl Harbor. Pamela had vetoed all the shawls and blouses; an elegant woman like Rhoda, she had said, wouldn't be caught dead in these tacky things. The fur hats had seemed made for giantesses. So he had bought the caviar and scrawled this silly note.

"Well, it's damn good caviar, at that."

Rhoda's warm glance was inviting a pass. That much, Victor Henry had often pictured: the sea captain home from the wars, Odysseus and Penelope heading for the couch. Her voice was dulcet. "You look as though you haven't slept for days."

"Not all that much." He put both palms to his eyes and rubbed. "I've come a long way."

"Haven't you ever! How does the good old U.S.A. look to you, Pug?"

"Peculiar, especially from the air at night. Solid blackout on the West Coast. Inland you begin to see lights. Peaceful blaze in Chicago. Past Cleveland they start dimming down again, and Washington's dark."

"Oh, that's so typical! No consistency. This ungodly mess with shortages! All the talk about rationing! Off again, on again! You never know where you're at. And the HOARDING that's going on, Pug. Why, people BOAST about how clever they've been, piling up tires, and meat, and sugar, and heating oil, and I don't know what all. I tell you, we're a nation of spoiled HOGS."

"Rhoda, it's a good idea not to expect too much of human nature."

The remark cut his wife short. A doubtful look, a silent moment. She put her hand on his. "Darling, do you feel like talking about the *Northampton?*"

"We got torpedoed and sank."

"Lucy says most of the officers and crew were saved."

"Jim Grigg did a good job. Still, we lost too many men."

"Did you have a close call yourself?"

Her face was eager, expectant. In lieu of some affectionate move, for which he felt no impulse, he began to talk about the loss of his ship. He rose and paced, the words running free after a while, the emotions of the terrible night reviving. Rhoda listened shiny-eyed. When the telephone rang he halted in his tracks, staring like a wakened sleepwalker. "I guess that's Digger."

Captain Brown boomed heartily, "Well, well, Pug. Made it, did you? Great."

"Digger, did you get a dispatch from Cincpac about me?"

"Look, let's not do any business over the phone, Pug. Why don't you and Rhoda just take it easy and enjoy yourselves today? It's been a long time, and so on and so forth. Heh heh! We'll talk tomorrow. Give me a ring about nine in the morning."

"Are you tied up today? Suppose I come down right now?"

"Well, if that's what you want." Pug heard his old friend sigh. "But you do sound tired."

"I'm coming, Digger." Pug hung up, strode to his wife, and kissed her cheek. "I'd better find out what's doing."

"Okay." She cupped his face in her hands, and gave his mouth a lingering kiss. "Take the Oldsmobile."

"It still runs? Fine."

"Maybe you'll get to be the President's naval aide. That's Lucy's guess. Then at least we'd see something of each other for a while, Pug."

She walked to a little desk and took out car keys. The unselfconscious pathos of Rhoda's words got to him more than all the flirting. Alone in a cold house, bereaved of her firstborn son — whom they still hadn't mentioned, whose picture smiled from the piano top; her husband home after more than a year away, rushing out about his business; she was being very good about all this. This sway of her slender hips was beguiling. Pug wondered at his own lack of desire for her. He had an impulse to throw off the bridge coat he was donning, and to seize her. But Digger Brown was expecting him, and she was dropping the keys into his hand with an arch little flip. "Anyway, we'll dine at home, won't we? Just the two of us?"

"Sure we'll dine at home, just the two of us. With wine, I trust, and —" he hesitated, then forced a ribald lift of the eyebrows, "especially *and.*"

The flash in her eyes leaped across the gulf between them. "On your way, sailor boy."

Outside it was the same old Navy Building, the long dismal "temporary" structure from the last war still disfiguring Constitution Avenue, but inside it had a new air: a hurrying pace, a general buzz, crowds of Waves and callow-looking staff officers in the corridors. Lurid combat paintings that hardly seemed dry hung on the dusty walls: dogfights over carriers, night gun battles, bombardments of tropic islands. During most of Pug's career, the decor had been mementos of the Spanish-American War, and of Atlantic action in 1918.

Digger Brown looked every bit the king of the hill that he was: tall, massive, healthy, with a thatch of grizzled hair, with a year of battleship command under his belt (Atlantic service, but good enough), and now this top post in BuPers. Digger had flag rank in the bag. Pug wondered how he must seem to Brown. He had never been overawed by his fast-moving old friend, nor was he now. Much passed unspoken as they shook hands and scanned each other's faces. The fact was, Pug Henry made Captain Brown think of an oak tree in his own back yard, blasted by lightning yet still vigorous, and putting forth green shoots each spring from charred branches.

"That's hell about Warren," Brown said.

Henry made an elaborate business of lighting a cigarette. Brown had to get the rest spoken. "And the *California*, and then the *Northampton*. Christ!" He gripped Pug's shoulder in awkward sympathy. "Sit you down."

Pug said, "Well, sometimes I tell myself I didn't volunteer to be born, Digger, I got drafted. I'm all right."

"And Rhoda? How'd you find her?"

"Splendid."

"What about Byron?"

"Coming back from Gib to new construction, or so I hear." Pug cocked his head at his old friend, squinting through smoke. "You're riding high."

"I've yet to hear a gun go off in anger."

"There's plenty of war left out there."

"Pug, it may be a reprehensible sentiment, but I hope you're right." Captain Brown put on horn-rimmed glasses, thumbed through dispatches on a clipboard, and handed one to Pug. "You asked me about this, I believe?"

FROM: CINCPAC
TO: BUPERS
DESIRE ASSIGNMENT STAFF DUTY THIS COMMAND VICTOR (NONE) HENRY
CAPTAIN USN SERIAL 4329 EX CO NORTHAMPTON X NIMITZ

Pug nodded.

Brown unwrapped a stick of chewing gum. "I'm supposed to quit smoking. Blood pressure. It's got me climbing the walls."

"Come on, Digger, are my orders to Cincpac set?"

"Pug, did you wangle this on the trip home?"

"I didn't wangle it. Spruance sprang it on me. I was amazed. I thought I'd catch hell for losing my ship."

"Why? You went down fighting." Under Pug's hard inquiring look, Digger Brown chewed and chewed. The big body shifted in the swivel chair. "Pug, you ducked Cincpac staff duty last year, according to Jocko Larkin."

"That was then."

"Why do you suppose you were recalled with Class One air priority?"

"You tell me."

Slowly, with a portentous air, Brown said, "*The . . . Great . . . White . . . Father.*" Then more lightly, "Yessir! The boss man himself. You're supposed to report in to him soonest, in full feathers and war paint." Brown laughed at his own humor.

"What's it about?"

"Oh, blast, give me a butt. Thanks." Brown dragged at the cigarette, his eyes popping. "You know Admiral Standley, I believe. The ambassador to Russia, that is."

"Sure. I went there with him last year on the Harriman mission."

"Exactly. He's back for consultations with the President. Even before the *Northampton* was lost, Rear Admiral Carton was telephoning us from the White House in a big sweat about you. Standley was inquiring about your availability. Hence the Class One priority."

Pug said, trying to keep the irritation out of his voice, "Nimitz should draw more water around here than Standley does."

"Pug, I have my instructions. You're to call Russ Carton for an appointment to see the President."

"Does Carton know about the Cincpac dispatch?"

"I haven't told him."

"Why not?"

"I wasn't asked."

"Okay, Digger. I'm asking you to notify Russ Carton about that Cincpac dispatch. Today."

A brief contest of cold stares. With a deep drag on the cigarette, Digger Brown said, "You're asking me to get out of line."

"Why? You're derelict in not telling the White House Cincpac wants me."

"Christ on a bicycle, Pug, don't give me that. When that man up on Pennsylvania Avenue snaps his fingers, we jump around here. Nothing else signifies."

"But this is just a whim of old Bill Standley's, you say."

"I'm not sure. Tell Russ Carton about Cincpac yourself when you see him."

"N.G. He must get the word from BuPers."

Captain Brown sullenly avoided his eyes. "Who says he must?"

Victor Henry intoned as in a language drill, "*Ich muss, du musst, er muss.*"

An unhappy grin curled Brown's mouth and he picked up the chant, *"Wir müssen, ihr müsst, sie müsst."*

"Müssen, Digger."

"Müssen. I never could hack German, could I?" Brown pulled deeply on the cigarette and abruptly ground it out. "God, that tasted good. Pug, I *still* think you should find out first what the Great White Father wants." He hit a buzzer in an annoyed gesture. "But have it your way. I'll shoot a copy to Russ."

The house was warmer. Pug heard a man talking in the living room.

"Hello there," he called, very loud.

"Oh, hi!" Rhoda's cheery voice. "Back so soon?"

A deeply tanned young officer was on his feet when Pug walked in. The mustache puzzled him, then he put together the blond hair and the bright new gold half-stripe of a lieutenant commander. "Hello there, Anderson."

Pouring tea at a table by the fire, Rhoda said, "Sime just stopped by to drop off Maddy's Christmas present."

"Something I picked up in Trinidad." Anderson gestured at the gaily wrapped box on the table.

"What were you doing in Trinidad?"

Rhoda gave the men tea and left, while Anderson was telling Pug about his destroyer duty in the Caribbean. U-boats had been having fat pickings off Venezuela and the Guianas, and in the Gulf of Mexico: oil tankers, bauxite carriers, freighters, and passenger liners. Emboldened by the easy pickings, the German skippers had even taken to surfacing and sinking ships with gunfire, so as to save torpedoes. The American and British navies had now worked up a combined convoy system to control the menace, and Anderson had been out on that convoy duty.

Pug was only vaguely aware of the Caribbean U-boat problem. Anderson's tale made him think of two large photographs in the Navy Building, showing Eskimos bundled in furs watching the loading of a Catalina flying boat in a snowstorm, and Polynesians naked but for G-strings staring at an identical Catalina moored in a palm-fringed lagoon. This war was a leprosy spreading all over the globe.

"Say, Anderson, weren't you working with Deak Parsons at BuOrd on the AA proximity fuse, advanced hush-hush stuff?"

"Yes, sir."

"Then why the Sam Hill were you shipped off to the Caribbean on an old four-piper?"

"Shortage of deck officers, sir."

"That fuse is fantastic, Sime."

The bright blue eyes glowed in the brown face. "Oh, has it gotten out to the fleet?"

"I saw a demonstration off Nouméa against drone planes. Sheer slaughter. Three out of three drones splashed in minutes. Downright spooky, those AA bursts opening up right by the planes every time."

"We worked pretty hard on it."

"How the devil did Deak Parsons get a whole radio signal set inside an AA shell? And how does it survive a jolt of muzzle velocity, and a spin in trajectory of five hundred times a second?"

"Well, sir, we figured out the specs. The industry fellows said, 'Can do,' and they did it. As a matter of fact, I'm going down to Anacostia now to see Captain Parsons."

Victor Henry had never liked any of Madeline's gosling suitors, but this one looked pretty good to him, especially by contrast with Hugh Cleveland. "Any chance you can come and have Christmas dinner with us? Madeline will be here."

"Yes, sir. Thank you. Mrs. Henry's been kind enough to invite me."

"She has? Well! Give Deak my regards. Tell him SoPac's buzzing about that fuse."

In the stuffy office of the Naval Research Laboratory, looking out over the mud flats to the river, Captain William Parsons complimented Anderson on his suntan, and nodded without comment at Pug Henry's message. He was a man in his forties with a wrinkled pale brow and receding hair, run-of-the-mill in appearance but the most hardworking and brilliant man Anderson had ever served under.

"Sime, what do you know about uranium?"

Anderson felt as though he had stepped on a third rail. "I've done no work in radioactivity, sir. Nor in neutron bombardment."

"You do know that there's something funny going on in uranium."

"Well, when I did my postgrad work at Cal Tech in 1939, there was a lot of talk about the fission results of the Germans."

"What sort of talk?"

"Wild talk, Captain, about superbombs, also about atomic-powered propulsion, all very theoretical."

"D'you suppose we've left it at that? Just a theoretical possibility? Just a promising freak of nature? With all the German scientists working around the clock for Hitler?"

"I hope not, sir."

"Come with me."

They went outside and hurried with heads down toward the main laboratory building, through a bitter wind blowing from the river. Even at a distance, an eerie hissing and whistling sounded from the lab. Inside, the noise was close to deafening. Steam was escaping from a forest of freestanding slender pipes reaching almost to the very high roof, giving the place the dank warmth of the Caribbean. Men in shirt-sleeves or coveralls were pottering at the pipes or at instrument panels.

"Thermal diffusion," Parsons shouted, "for separating U-235. Did you know Phil Abelson at Cal Tech?" Parsons pointed to a slender man in shirt-sleeves and tie, about Anderson's age, standing arms akimbo at a wall covered with dials.

"No, but I heard about him."

"Come and meet him. He's working with us in a civilian capacity."

Abelson gave the lieutenant commander a keen look when Parsons explained over the noise that Anderson had worked on the proximity fuse. "We've got a chemical engineering problem here," Abelson said, gesturing around at the pipes. "That your field?"

"Not exactly. Out of uniform I'm a physicist."

Abelson briefly smiled and turned back to his instrument panel.

"I just wanted you to see this setup," Parsons said. "Let's get out of here."

The air outside seemed arctic. Parsons buttoned his bridge coat to his chin, jammed his hands in his pockets, and strode toward the river, where nests of gray Navy ships rode to anchor.

"Sime, you know the principle of the Clusius tube, don't you?"

Anderson searched his memory. "That's the lab tube with the doughnut-shaped cross-section?"

"Yes. That's what Abelson's got in there. Two pipes one inside the other, actually. You heat the inside pipe and chill the outside one, and if there's a liquid in the space between, the molecules of any lighter isotope will move toward the heat. Convection takes them to the top, and you skim them off. Abelson's put together a lot of giant Clusius tubes, a whole jungle of them in series. The U-235 gradually cooks out. It's damned slow, but he's already got measurable enrichment."

"What's his liquid?"

"That's his original achievement. Uranium hexafluoride. He developed the stuff and it's pretty touchy, but stable enough to work with. Now, this thing is getting pretty hot, and BuOrd wants to station a line officer here. I've recommended you. It's a shore billet again. You young fellows can always get sea duty if you prefer."

But Sime Anderson had no seafaring ambitions. He had gone to the Academy to get a superior free education. Annapolis had stamped him out in the standard mold, and on the bridge of a destroyer he was just another OOD; but inside this standard replacement part a first-class young physicist was imprisoned, and here was his chance to leap out. The proximity fuse had been an advance in ordnance, but not a thrust into a prime secret of nature. Abelson with his messy array of steam pipes was hunting big game.

At Cal Tech there had been speculation about a U-235 bomb that could wipe out a whole city, and of engines that could drive an ocean liner three times around the world on a few kilograms of uranium. Among Navy men the talk was of the ultimate submarine; power without the combustion that needed air. This was a grand frontier of applied human intelligence. A more mundane inducement occurred to young Anderson. Stationed in Anacostia, he could see a lot more of Madeline Henry than he had been doing. "Sir, if the Bureau considers me qualified, I've no objection."

"Okay. Now what I'm going to tell you next, Anderson, blows away on the wind." Parsons rested his elbows on an iron railing that fenced off a rocky drop to the river. "As I said, our interest is propulsion, but the Army's working on a bomb. We're excluded. Compartmentalized secrecy. Still, we know." Parsons glanced at the younger man, hurrying his words. "Our first objective and the Army's are the same, to produce pure U-235. For them the next step is making a weapon. A battery of theoreticians is already working on that. Maybe some fact of nature will prevent it. Nobody can say for sure yet."

"Does the Army know what we're doing?"

"Hell, yes. We gave them their uranium hexafluoride to start with. But the Army thinks thermal diffusion is for the birds. Too slow, and the enrichment is too low-grade. Their assignment is to beat Hitler to a bomb. A prudent notion, that. They're starting from the ground up, with untried designs and new concepts that are supposed to be shortcuts, and they're doing it on a colossal industrial scale. Nobel Prize heavyweights like Lawrence, Compton, and Fermi have been supplying the ideas. The size of the Army effort really staggers the mind, Anderson. They're commandeering power, water, land, and strategic materials till hell won't have it. Meantime we've got enriched U-235 in hand. Low enrichment, not bomb material as yet, but a first stage. The Army's got a lot of big ideas and big holes in the ground. Now if the Army falls on its face it'll be the biggest scientific and military bust of all time. And then — just conceivably, mind you — then it could be up to the Navy to beat the Germans to atomic bombs, right here in Anacostia."

"Wow."

Parsons wryly grinned. "Don't hold your breath. The Army's got the President's ear, and the world's greatest minds working on it, and they're outspending us a million dollars to one. They'll probably make a bomb, if nature was careless enough to leave that possibility open. Meantime we'll keep our little tinpot operation cooking. Just keep the other remote contingency in your mind, and pick up your orders at BuPers tomorrow."

"Aye aye, sir."

By candlelight Rhoda's face was like a young woman's. As they ate cherry tarts she had baked for dessert, Pug was telling her, through a fog of fatigue, about his stop in Nouméa on his way home. They were on their third bottle of wine, so his description of the somnolent French colony south of the equator, overrun by the carnival of American war-making, was not very coherent. He was trying to describe the comic scene in the officers' club in an old fusty French hotel, of men in uniform clustering four and five deep around a few Navy nurses and Frenchwomen, captains and commanders up close, junior officers hovering on the outer edges just to stare at the females. Pug was so weary that Rhoda's face seemed to be blurrily wavering between the candle flames.

"Darling," she interrupted quietly and hesitantly, "I'm afraid you're not making very good sense."

"What? Why not?"

"You just said you and Warren were watching all this, and Warren cracked a joke —"

Pug shuddered. He had indeed been drifting into a doze while he talked, fusing dreams with memory, picturing Warren alive in that jammed smoky Nouméa club long after Midway, holding a can of beer in his old way, and saying, *"Those gals are forgetting, Dad, that once the uniform comes off, the more stripes, the less action."* It was pure fantasy; in his lifetime Warren had never come to Nouméa.

"I'm sorry." He vigorously shook his head.

"Let's skip the coffee" — she looked concerned — "and put you to bed."

"Hell, no. I want my coffee. And brandy, too. I'm enjoying myself, Rhoda."

"Probably the fire's making you sleepy."

Most of the rooms in this old house had fireplaces. The carved wooden mantelpiece of this large dining room, in the flicker of light and shadow from the log fire, was oppressively elegant. Pug had grown unused to Rhoda's style of life, which had always been too rich for him. He stood up, feeling the wine in his head and in his knees. "Probably. I'll take the Chambertin inside. You deploy the coffee."

"Dear, I'll bring you the wine, too."

He dropped in a chair in the living room, by the fireplace heaped with gray ashes. The bright chandelier gave the trimmed Christmas tree a tawdry store-window look. It was warm all through the house now, and there was a smell of hot dusty radiators. She had put up the thermostat with the comment, "I've gotten used to a cool house. No wonder the British think we steam ourselves alive like SEAFOOD. But of course you've just come from the tropics."

Pug wondered at his macabre waking vision of Warren. How could his dreaming mind have invented that wisecrack? The voice had been so recognizable, so alive! *"Once the uniform comes off, Dad, the more stripes, the less action!"* Pure Warren; neither he himself nor Byron would ever have said that.

Rhoda set the bottle and glass at his elbow. "Coffee will be right along, honey."

Sipping at the wine, he felt he could fall into bed and sleep fourteen hours without moving. But Rhoda had gone to so much trouble, and the dinner had been so good: onion soup, rare roast beef, baked potatoes with sour cream, au gratin cauliflower; her new form-fitting red silk dress was a stunner, her hair was done up as for a dance, her whole manner was loving and willing. Penelope was more than ready for the returned wayfarer, and Pug didn't want to disappoint or humiliate his wife. Yet whether because he was aging, or weary, or because the Kirby business lay raw and unresolved, he sensed no stir of amorousness for her. None.

A shy touch on his face, and he opened his eyes to see her smiling down at him. "I don't think coffee'll help much, Pug."

"No. Most discouraging."

Getting ready for bed half-woke him. Coming from the bathroom, he found her, fully dressed, turning down his twin bed. He felt like a fool. He tried to embrace her. She fended him off with the laughing deftness of a coed. "Sweetie pie, I love you to little pieces, but I truly don't believe you'd make it. One good night's sleep, and the tiger will be back on the prowl."

Pug sank into bed with a sleepy groan. Softly she kissed him on the mouth. "It's good to have you back."

"Sorry about this," he murmured, as she turned out the light.

Not in the least put out, rather relieved than otherwise, Rhoda took off the red dress and donned an old housecoat. She went downstairs and cleaned up every trace of the dinner, and of the day gone by; emptied the living room ashtrays, shovelled the fireplace ashes into a scuttle, laid a new fire for the morning, and put out the ashes and the garbage. She enjoyed the moment's breath of icy air in the alley, the glimpse of glittering stars, and the crunch of snow under her slippers.

In her dressing room, with a glass of brandy at hand, she ran a hot bath and set about the dismantling job under glaring lights between large mirrors. Off came the rouge, the lipstick, the mascara, and the skin makeup which she wore down to her collar bone. The naked woman stepping into the vaporous tub was lean, almost stringy, after months of resolute starving. Her ribs unattractively showed; but her belly was straight, her hips slim, her breasts small and passably shaped. About the face, alas, there was nothing girlish. Still, Colonel Harrison Peters, she thought, would find her desirable.

To Rhoda's view desirability was nine-tenths in the man's mind, anyway; the woman's job was to foster the feeling, if she detected it and if it suited her purpose. Pug liked her thin, so she had damned well gotten thin for this reunion. Rhoda knew she was in trouble, but about her sexual allure for her husband she was not worried. Given Pug's dour fidelity, this was the rock on which their marriage stood.

The warm water enveloped and deliciously relaxed her. Despite her outer calm she had been taut as a scared cat all evening. In his gentleness, his absence of reproach, his courteous manner, and his lack of ardor, Pug had said it all. His silences disclosed more than other men's words. No doubt he had forgiven her (whatever that might mean) but he had not even begun to forget; though it seemed he was not going to bring up the anonymous letters. Adding it all up, she was not unhappy with this first day. It was over, and they were off the knife-edge, on a bearable footing. She had dreaded the first encounter in bed. It could so easily have gone wrong, and a few silly minutes might have exacerbated the estrangement. Sex as pleasure, at this point, mattered to her not at all. She had more serious concerns.

Rhoda was a woman of method, much given to lists, written and mental. The bath was her time for review. Item one tonight was nothing less than her marriage itself. Despite Pug's kind letters, and the wave of reconciling emotion after Warren's death — now that they had faced each other, was it salvageable? On the whole, she thought so. This had immediate practical consequences.

Colonel Harrison Peters was amazingly taken with her. He was coming to Saint John's Church on Sundays just to see more of her. At first she had wondered what he wanted of her, when (so she had heard) plenty of round-heeled Washington girls were his at a push. Now she knew, because he had told her. She was the military man's lady of his dreams: good-looking, true, decorous, churchgoing, elegant, and brave. He admired the way she was bearing the loss of her son. In their moments together — she was keeping them infrequent and public, having learned her lesson with Kirby — he had gotten her to talk about Warren, and sometimes had wiped away his own tears. The man was tough and important, doing some highly secret Army job; but when it came down to cases, he was just a lonesome bachelor in his mid-fifties, tired of fooling around, too old to start a family, but wistful to settle down. There the man was for the having.

But if she could hold on to Pug, that was what she wanted. He was her life. She had worked out with Palmer Kirby her romantic yearnings. Divorce and remarriage were messy at best. Her identity, her prestige, her self-respect, were bound up with remaining Mrs. Victor Henry. Moving to Hawaii had proven too difficult and complicated; but maybe it was just as well that time had passed before a reunion, and the newest wounds had somewhat healed. Pug was a real man. You could never count Pug Henry out. Why, here was the White House calling him again! He had had a rotten run of luck, including her own misconduct; but if ever a man had the stuff to weather it, he did. In her way Rhoda admired and even loved Pug. The death of Warren had enlarged her limited capacity for love. A broken heart sometimes stretches when it mends.

The way Rhoda now sized matters up, soaking in her tub, it appeared that after a touch-and-go reconciliation they would make it. After all, there was the Pamela Tudsbury business; she had something to forgive too, though she did not know just what. When they had talked of Tudsbury's death at dinner she had carefully watched Pug's face. "I wonder what Pamela will do now," she had ventured. "I saw them when they passed through Hollywood, you know. Did you get my letter? The poor man gave a BRILLIANT speech at the Hollywood Bowl."

"I know. You sent me the speech."

"Actually, Pug, she wrote it. So she told me."

"Yes, Pam was ghosting a lot for him toward the end. But he gave her the ideas." No surprising the old fox, tired or not; his tone was perfectly casual.

Not that it mattered. Rhoda had digested Pamela Tudsbury's astounding revelation in Hollywood more or less in this wise: if a passionate young beauty like that one — who by the look of her knew plenty about men — could not snag Pug right after poor Warren's death, when he was far from home, vulnerable, estranged by the Kirby affair, and no doubt drunk every night, then the marriage was probably safe. Colonel Harrison Peters, all handsome six feet three of him, could go hang if she could keep Pug. Harrison's admiration was like an accident insurance policy. She was glad she had it, and hoped she would never have to fall back on it.

In the dim glow of the bedroom nightlight, the grim lines of Pug's face were smoothed by sleep. An unwonted impulse came to Rhoda's mind: should she slip into his bed? She had seldom done this down the years; mostly a long time ago, after too much to drink or an evening of flirting with someone else's husband. Pug took her rare advances as great compliments. He looked handsome and sweet. Many a breach between them had quickly closed with lovemaking.

Yet she hesitated. It was one thing for the modest spouse to yield to a yen for her man back from the war. For her — on probation, seeking forgiveness — wasn't it something else; a bribing use of her body, a hint of coarsened appetite? None of this was articulated by Rhoda, naturally. It raced through her mind in a sort of female symbolic logic, and she got into her own bed.

Pug snapped awake, the alcohol wearing off and his nerves jangling an alarm. Rhoda, dead to the world, wore a wrinkly cap on her hair. No use turning over. He would have to drink more or take a pill. He found the warmest bathrobe in his closet, and went to the library where the movable bar was. On the antique desk lay a big leather-bound scrapbook, with Warren's photograph worked into the cover over gold-stamped lettering:

Lieutenant Warren Henry, USN

He mixed a stiff bourbon and water, staring at the album as at a spectre. He walked out of the room, snapping off the light; then he went back, groped to the desk, and lit the reading lamp. Standing drink in hand, he went through the scrapbook leaf by leaf. On the inside front cover, bordered in black, was Warren's baby picture; on the inside back cover, his obituary in the *Washington Post*, with a blurry photograph; and facing this, the citation for his posthumous Navy Cross, boldly signed in black ink by the Secretary of the Navy.

In this album Rhoda had marshalled their firstborn son's whole short life: the first attempt at lettering — MERRY CHRISTMAS — in red and green crayon on coarse kindergarten paper; the first report card in Grade One of a school in Norfolk — Effort A, Work A+, Conduct C; pictures of children's birthday parties, pictures at summer camps, honor certificates, athletic citations, programs of school plays, track meets, and graduations; sample letters, with penmanship and language improving from year to year; Academy documents and photographs, his commission, promotion letters, and transfer dispatches, interspersed with snapshots of him on ships and in the cockpits of airplanes; half a dozen pages devoted to pictures and mementos of his engagement and marriage to Janice Lacouture (an unexpected photograph of Natalie Jastrow in a black dress, standing beside the white-clad married pair in the sun, gave Pug a turn); and the last pages were full of war souvenirs — his squadron posing on the deck of the *Enterprise*, Warren in his cockpit on deck and in the air, a jocular cartoon of him in the ship's newspaper reporting his lecture on the invasion of Russia; and finally, centered on two pages, also bordered in black, his last letter to his mother, typed on *Enterprise* stationery. It was dated in March, three months before his death.

Shaken at finding these fresh words from his dead son, Pug avidly read them. Warren had always hated to write letters. He had filled the first page by recounting Vic's bright doings and sayings, and housekeeping problems in Hawaii. On the second page he had warmed up:

I fly dawn patrol, so I had better sign off, Mom. Sorry I haven't written more often. I usually manage to see Dad when we're in port. I assume he keeps you up to date. Also I can't write much about what I do.

But I'll say this. Every time I take off over the water, and every time I come in for a deck landing, I thank my stars that I made it through Pensacola. There are just a handful of naval aviators in this war. When Vic grows up and reads all about it, and he looks at the gray-headed old crock he calls Dad, I don't think he'll be ashamed of the part I played.

I certainly hope that by the time Vic's a man the world will be getting rid of war. This exercise used to be fun, and maybe even profitable for the victor, I don't know. But mine's the last generation that can get a kick out of combat, Mom, it's all getting too impersonal, and complicated, and costly, and deadly. People have to figure out a saner way to run this planet. Armed robbers like the Germans and the Japs create problems, but hereafter they'll have to be snuffed out before they get rolling.

So I almost hate to confess how much fun it's been. I hope my son never knows the fear and the glory of diving a plane into AA fire. It's a hell of a stupid way to make a living. But now that I'm doing it, I have to tell you I wouldn't have missed it for all the tea in China. I'd like to see Vic become a politician and work at straightening the world out. I may even have a shot at it myself when all this is over, and cut a trail for him. Meantime, dawn patrol.

Love,
Warren

Pug closed the album, tossed off his second drink, and passed his hand over the rough leather as over the cheek of a child. Turning off the lights, he trudged upstairs to the bedroom. Warren's mother was asleep as before, on her back, the pretty profile cut off by the grotesque hair bag. He stared at her as though she were a stranger. How could she have endured putting that album together? It was a wonderful job, like everything she did. He could not yet trust himself to speak his son's name aloud, and she had done all that: dug up the mementos, faced them, handled them, made a nice ornamental arrangement of them.

Pug got into bed, face buried in the pillow, to let the whiskey whirl him down into a few more hours of oblivion.

51

THE broad gold admiral's stripe on Russell Carton's sleeve was very shiny. His overheated little office in the west wing of the White House was crusted with many paint jobs, the latest oyster gray. This newly minted rear admiral was only two Academy classes senior to Pug. The face was jowlier, the body thicker than in the days when Carton had marched by on the Annapolis parade ground shouting orders to his battalion. He had been stiff then and he was stiff now. Seated at a metal desk under a large autographed picture of the President, he shook hands without rising, and made pointless chitchat, not mentioning the Nimitz request. So Pug decided to risk a probe. "Admiral, did BuPers notify you of a dispatch from Cincpac about me?"

"Well, yes." Guarded and grudging answer.

"Then the President knows that Admiral Nimitz wants me for his staff?"

"Henry, my advice to you is simply to go in there and listen when summoned," Carton said testily. "Admiral Standley is with the President now. Also Mr. Hopkins and Admiral Leahy." He pulled a basket of correspondence forward. "Now until we're buzzed, I do have these letters to get out."

Pug had his answer; the President did not know. The wait went by without another word from Carton while Pug reviewed his situation and planned his tactics. In over a year he had received no comment on his battlefront report to Harry Hopkins from Moscow, nor a reply to his letter to the President about the evidence of a Jewish massacre in Minsk. He had long since concluded that that letter had finished him with the White House, showing him up as a sentimental meddler in matters not his concern. That had not bothered him much. He had never sought the role of a minor presidential emissary, and had not relished it. Evidently old Admiral Standley was behind this White House summons. The countering tactic must be simple: disclose the Nimitz dispatch to nullify Standley, pull out and stay out of the President's field of force, and return to the Pacific.

The buzzer sounded twice. "That's us," said Carton. The White House hallways and stairways appeared quiet and unchanged, the calm at the eye of the hurricane. Secretaries and uniformed orderlies moved softly at a peacetime pace. In the Oval Office the gadgets and ship models cluttering the big desk did not seem to have been moved in nearly two years. But Franklin Roosevelt was much altered: the gray hair thinner, the eyes filmy in purple pouches, the whole aspect strikingly aged. Harry Hopkins, slouching waxen-faced in an armchair, wearily waved at Pug. The two admirals emblazoned with gold and ribbons, sitting rigidly on a couch, barely glanced at him.

Roosevelt's tired big-jawed face took on lively pleasure as Victor Henry came in with Carton. "Well, Pug, old top!" The voice was rich, lordly, Harvardish, like all the boring radio comedians' imitations. "So the Japs made you swim for it, eh?"

"I'm afraid so, Mr. President."

"That's my favorite exercise, you know, swimming," Roosevelt said with a waggish grin. "It's good for my health. However, I like to pick my own time and place."

Nonplussed for a moment, Pug realized that the heavy pleasantry was intended as a kindness. Roosevelt's eyebrows were expectantly raised for his answer. He forced the lightest riposte he could think of. "Mr. President, I agree it was an ill-timed swim, but it was pretty good for my own health."

"Ha, ha!" Roosevelt threw back his head and laughed with gusto, whereupon the others also laughed a little. "Well put! Otherwise you wouldn't be here, would you?" He delivered this as though it were another joke, and the others laughed again. Russell Carton withdrew. The President's expressive face went grave. "Pug, I regret the loss of that grand ship, and of all those brave men. The *Northampton* gave a bully account of herself, I know that. I'm terribly glad you came away safe. You must know Admiral Leahy" — Roosevelt's lean, dry-looking chief of staff gave Pug a wooden nod suited to his four stripes and sunken ship — "and of course Bill Standley. Bill's been singing your praises ever since you went with him to Moscow."

"Hello, Henry," said Admiral Standley. Leathery, wizened, a bulky hearing aid in his ear, his thin lipless lower jaw thrust out over a corded, wattled neck, he looked a bit like an angry tortoise.

"You know, Admiral Standley grew so fond of the Russians on that Harriman mission, Pug" — Roosevelt signalled another joke with arched eyebrows — "that I had to send him back to Moscow as ambassador, just to keep him happy! And though he's been home on leave, he misses them so much he's hurrying back there tomorrow. Right, Bill?"

"Right as rain, Chief." The tone was coarsely sarcastic.

"How did you like the Russians, Pug?"

"I was impressed by them, Mr. President."

"Oh? Well, other people occasionally have been, too. What impressed you most about them?"

"Their numbers, sir, and their willingness to die."

Glances darted among the four men. Harry Hopkins spoke up in a weak hoarse voice, "Well, Pug, I guess at this point the Germans at Stalingrad might agree with you."

Standley gave Pug a peevish look. "The Russians are numerous and brave. Nobody disputes that. They're also impossible. That's the basic problem, and there's a basic answer. Firmness and clarity." Standley waved a bony finger at the tolerantly smiling President. "Words are wasted on them. It's like dealing with beings from another planet. They understand only the language of deeds. Even that they can get wrong. I don't think they understand Lend-Lease to this minute. It's available, so they simply demand and demand, and grab and grab, like kids at a party where the ice cream and cake are free."

Cocking his head, the President almost gaily replied, "Bill, did I ever tell you about my talk with Litvinov, way back in 1933? I was negotiating recognition of the Soviet Union with him. Well, I'd never dealt with such people before. Gracious, I got mad! It was over the issue of religious freedom for our nationals in Russia, as I recall. He was being slippery as an eel. I simply blew up at him. I've never forgotten his comeback, as cool as you please.

"He said, 'Mr. President, right after our revolution, your people and mine could hardly communicate. You were still one hundred percent capitalistic, and we had dropped to zero.' " Roosevelt spread his meaty hands vertically in the air, far apart. " 'Since then we've come up to here, to about twenty, and you've come down to about eighty. In the years to come I believe we'll narrow it to sixty and forty.' " The President's hands converged. " 'We may not get any closer,' he said, 'but across that gap we'll communicate quite well.' Now Bill, I see Litvinov's words coming true in this war."

"So do I," said Hopkins.

Standley fairly snapped at Hopkins, "You fellows don't stay long. Their company manners are fine with you vodka visitors. Working with them day to day is something else. Now, Mr. President, I know my time's up. Let me summarize, and I'll take my leave." He ticked off brisk pleas for stricter administration of Lend-Lease, for promotion of his attachés, and for direct control by the embassy of visiting VIPs. He mentioned Wendell Willkie with special abhorrence, and shot Hopkins a sour look. Nodding, smiling, Roosevelt promised Standley that it would all be done. As the two admirals went out, Standley gave Pug a pat on the shoulder and a crabbed grin.

Sighing, the President pressed a button. "Let's have some lunch. You too, Pug?"

"Sir, my wife just gave me a late breakfast of fresh trout."

"You don't say! Trout! Well, I call *that* a nice welcome! How is Rhoda? Such an elegant and pretty woman."

"She's well, Mr. President. She hoped you'd remember her."

"Oh, she's hard to forget." Taking off his pince-nez and rubbing his purple-rimmed eyes, Franklin Roosevelt said, "Pug, when I heard from Sec-Nav about your boy, Warren, I felt terrible. That's the one I never met. Is Rhoda bearing up?"

The old politician's trick of remembering first names, and the sudden reference to his dead son, threw Pug off balance. "She's fine, sir."

"That was a remarkable victory at Midway, Pug. It was all due to brave youngsters like Warren. They saved our situation in the Pacific." The President abruptly changed his tone and manner from the warmest sympathy to straight business. "But see here, we've lost far too many warships around Guadalcanal in night actions. Haven't we? How is that? Are the Japs better night fighters than we are?"

"No, sir!" Pug felt the question as a personal jab. Glad to get off the subject of Warren, he answered crisply, "They started the war at a much higher level of training. They were geared up and ready to go. We weren't. Even so, we've stood them off. They've given up trying to reinforce Guadalcanal. We're going to win there. I admit we have to do better in night gun battles, and we will."

"I agree with all you say." The President's look was cold and penetrating. "But I was terribly worried for a while there, Pug. I thought we might have to pull out of Guadalcanal. Our people would have taken that very hard. The Australians would simply have panicked. Nimitz did just the right thing, putting Halsey in there. That Halsey's a tough bird." The President was fitting a cigarette into his holder. "He's done splendidly on a shoestring. Rescued the whole picture there. *One* operational carrier! Imagine! We'll not be in that fix much longer, our production is starting to roll. It's taken a year longer than it should have, Pug. But just as you say, they were plotting war, and I wasn't! No matter what some newspapers keep hinting. Ah, here we are."

The white-coated Negro steward wheeled in a servidor. Putting aside the cigarette holder, Roosevelt startled Pug by complaining, "Just *look* at this portion, will you? Three eggs, maybe four. Darn it all, Pug, you're going to have to divide this with me. Serve it for two!" he ordered the steward. "Go ahead and have your soup, Harry. Don't wait."

The steward, looking scared, slid out a shelf from a corner of the desk, pulled up a chair, and served Victor Henry eggs, toast, and coffee, while Hopkins listlessly spooned soup from a bowl on a tray in his lap.

"This is more like it," said Franklin Roosevelt, eagerly starting to eat. "Now you can tell your grandchildren, Pug, that you shared a Presidential lunch. And maybe the staff will get the idea, once for all, that I don't like wasteful portions. It's a constant battle." The loose lukewarm eggs lacked salt and pepper. Pug ate them down, feeling historically privileged if not at all hungry.

"Say, Pug," said Hopkins in a faded voice, "we ran into a heck of a shortage of landing craft for North Africa. There was talk of a crash program to turn them out, and your name came up. But now the invasion's a success, and the U-boat problem has gotten more acute. So destroyer escorts are the number one shipyard priority. Nevertheless, the landing craft problem won't go away, so —"

"Absolutely not," the President cut in, dropping his fork with a clunk. "It haunts every discussion of the invasion of France. I remember our talks way back in August '41, Pug, aboard the *Augusta* before I went to meet Churchill. You knew your stuff. One forceful man riding herd on the landing craft program for the Navy, with my full backing, is what I need. But here old Bill Standley has come along, quite by coincidence, and asked for you as a special military aide." Roosevelt glanced up over the rim of his coffee cup. "Do you have a preference?"

After weeks of wondering, here was a tumble of revelations for Victor Henry. So they had whisked him back from the Pacific to put him into landing craft production; an important but dreary BuShips job, a career dead end. The Standley request was just an unlucky complication. How to bring up the Nimitz dispatch at this point? Torpedo water!

"Well, Mr. President, this goes to my head a bit, being offered such a choice, and by you."

"Why, that's most of what I do, old fellow," the President chuckled. "I just sit here, a sort of traffic cop, trying to direct the right men to the right jobs."

Roosevelt said this with pleasantly flattering intimacy, as though he and Victor Henry were boyhood friends. Cornered though Pug was, he yet could admire the President. The whole war was on this aging cripple's mind; and he had to run the country, too, and wrestle with a fractious Congress at every point to get things done. Harry Hopkins was growing restless, Pug could see. Probably some major meeting was scheduled next in this office. Yet Roosevelt could chat on with an anonymous midget of a naval captain, and make him feel important to the war. It was Pug's way with a ship's crew; he tried to give every sailor a sense that he mattered to the ship. But this was leadership magnified to a superhuman dimension, under unimaginable pressure.

It was very hard to cope with. It took all the willpower Victor Henry had, to remain silent under the scrutiny of those wise, weary eyes, two astrally remote sparks in a mask of intimate good fellowship. Mentioning the Nimitz dispatch was beyond him. It meant undercutting Carton and in a sense turning Roosevelt down flat. Let the President sense his hesitation, at least.

Roosevelt broke the slight tension. "Well! You've got to take ten days' leave first, in any case. Show Rhoda a good time. Now that's an order! Then, get in touch with Russ Carton, and one way or another we'll put you to work. By the bye, how's your submariner?"

"He's doing well, sir."

"And his wife? That Jewish girl who was having difficulties in Italy?"

A drop in the President's tone, a shift of his eyes to Hopkins, told Pug he was now overstaying his time. He jumped up. "Thank you, Mr. President. She's all right. I'll report in ten days to Admiral Carton. Thank you for lunch, sir."

Franklin Roosevelt's mobile face settled into lines that looked carved on stone. "Your letter from Moscow about the Minsk Jews was appreciated. Also your eyewitness report from the front to Harry. I read it. You proved right in predicting that the Russians would hold. You and Harry. A lot of experts here were wrong about that. You have insight, Pug, and a knack for putting things clearly. Now, the Jewish situation is simply terrible. I'm at my wits' end about that. That Hitler is a sort of satanic person, really, and the Germans have gone berserk. The only answer is to smash Nazi Germany as fast as we can, and give the Germans a beating they'll remember for generations. We're trying." His handshake was brief. Chilled, Pug left.

"If you think I'm a bold hussy, that's too bad," said Rhoda. "I'm just not easily discouraged."

Logs were burning in the living room fireplace, and on the coffee table were gin, vermouth, the mixing jug, and a jar of olives; also a freshly opened tin of caviar, thin-cut squares of bread, and plates of minced onions and eggs. She wore a peach negligee. Her hair was done up, her face lightly touched with rouge.

"A beautiful sight, all this," said Pug, embarrassed and yet stimulated, too. "Incidentally, the President sent you his best."

"Oh yes, I'll bet."

"He did, Rho. He said you're an elegant and pretty woman, and not easy to forget."

Blushing to her eartips — she very rarely blushed, and it gave her a fleeting girlish glow — Rhoda said, "Well, how nice. But what happened? What's the news?"

Over the drinks he gave her a deliberately laconic report. All Rhoda could gather was that the President had a couple of jobs in mind for him, and meantime had ordered him to take ten days' leave.

"Ten whole days! Lovely! Will either job keep you in Washington?"

"One would."

"Then that's the job I hope you land. We've been separated enough. Too much."

When they had eaten a lot of caviar, and finished the martinis, Pug was in the mood, or thought he was. His first gestures were rusty, but this soon passed. Rhoda's body felt delicious and exciting in his arms. They went upstairs to the bedroom and drew the blinds — which nevertheless let through much subdued afternoon light — and laughing at each other and making little jokes as they undressed, they got into her bed together.

Rhoda swept ahead with her old pleasing passionate ways. But from the moment he saw his wife's naked body, for the first time in a year and a half — and it still seemed dazzlingly pretty to him — an awareness seized Victor Henry that this body had been penetrated by another man. It was not that he bore Rhoda a grudge; on the contrary, he thought he had forgiven her. At least now, of all times, he wanted to blot the fact out. Instead, with her every caress, her every murmured endearment, her every lovemaking move, he kept picturing her doing exactly this with the big engineer. It did not interfere with what was happening. In a way — in a pornographic way — that enjoyment even seemed to be enhanced, for the moment. But the end was faint disgust.

Not for Rhoda, though. She gave every evidence of ecstatic gratification, covering his face with kisses and babbling nonsense. After a while, yawning like an animal and laughing, she snuggled down and fell asleep. The sun coming through the crack in the curtains blazed a bar of gold on one wall. Victor Henry left her bed, shut out the sunlight, returned to his own bed, and lay staring at the ceiling. So he was staring when she awoke an hour later with a smile.

52

LESLIE SLOTE woke in his old Georgetown flat, put on old trousers and a tweed jacket hanging in a closet he had locked away from subtenant use, and made toast and coffee in the airless little kitchen as he had done a thousand times. Carrying the old portfolio swollen with papers as usual, he walked down to the State Department in commonplace midwinter Washington weather; low gray clouds, cold wind, a threat of snow in the air.

It was like returning to normal life after a long illness. The sights and sounds and smells of upper Pennsylvania Avenue, in other times ordinary and dreary, were beautiful to him. The people who walked past him, Americans all, stared at his Russian fur hat, and this delighted him; in Moscow and in Bern nobody would have noticed. He was home. He was safe. Not since the start of the German march on Moscow, he now realized, had he drawn an easy breath. Even in Bern the pavement underfoot had seemed to quake to the near thump of German boots. But the Germans were no longer just beyond the Alps, they were an ocean away; and the Atlantic headwinds were roaring their icy throats out at other scared men.

The rash of small pillars all over the façade of the State Department building did not, this once, seem ugly to Slote, but quaint and naïve and homey; an American architectural abomination, and therefore charming. Armed guards inside halted him and he had to draw a celluloid pass. This was his first brush with the war in Washington. He stopped in the office of the Vichy desk for a look at the confidential list of some two hundred fifty Americans, mostly diplomatic and consular personnel, confined in Lourdes.

Hammer, Frederick, Friends Refugee Committee
Henry, Mrs. Natalie, journalist
Holliston, Charles, vice consul
Jastrow, Dr. Aaron, journalist

Still there! He hoped the omission of the baby, as in the list at the London embassy, was an oversight.

"Well, here you are," said the Division Director for European Affairs, standing up and scrutinizing Slote with an oddly excited air. Ordinarily he was a phlegmatic professional who had stayed cool and quiet even when they had played squash together years ago. In his shirt-sleeves, shaking hands over the desk, he disclosed the beginnings of a pot belly. His handshake was sweaty and rather convulsive. "And here *it* is." He handed Slote a two-page typed document scarred with red-ink cuts.

December 15, 1942 (tentative)
JOINT UNITED NATIONS STATEMENT ON
GERMAN ATROCITIES AGAINST JEWS

"What on earth is this?"

"A keg of dynamite, that's what. Official, approved, ready to go. We've been at it day and night for a week. It's all set at this end, and we're waiting for confirming cables from Whitehall and the Russians. Then, simultaneous release follows in Moscow, London, and Washington. Maybe as soon as tomorrow."

"Jesus, Foxy, what a development!"

People at State had always called the director Foxy. It was his nickname from Yale days. Slote had first encountered him as an alumnus of his secret society. Then Foxy Davis had seemed a debonair, remotely superior, and glamorous personage, a career Foreign Service officer just returned from Paris. Now Foxy was one among many men grayish of hair, face, and character who strolled State's corridors in grayish suits.

"Yes, it's a hell of a breakthrough."

"Seems I've crossed the ocean for nothing."

"Not in the least. The fact that you were coming"— Foxy jabbed a thumb toward the portfolio Slote had laid on the desk — "with that stuff gave us a lot of leverage. We knew from Tuttle's memoranda what you were bringing. You served. And you're needed here. Read the thing, Leslie."

Slote sat down on a hard chair, lit a cigarette, and conned the sheets while Foxy worked on his mail, chewing his lower lip in his old way. Foxy for his part noticed Slote's unchanged habit of drumming fingers on the back of a document as he read it; also that Slote looked yellow, and that his forehead was wrinkling like an old man's.

The attention of His Majesty's Government in the United Kingdom, of the Soviet Government, and of the United States Government has been drawn to reports from Europe ~~which leave no room for doubt~~ that the German authorities, not content with denying to persons of Jewish race, in all the territories over which their barbarous rule has been extended, the most elementary human rights, are now carrying into effect Hitler's oft-repeated intention to exterminate the Jewish people in Europe. From all the countries Jews are being transported, ~~irrespective of age and sex and~~ in conditions of appalling horror and brutality, to Eastern Europe. In Poland, which has been made the principal Nazi slaughterhouse, the ghettos are being systematically emptied of all Jews except a few highly skilled workers required for war industries. None of those taken away are ever heard of again. The ablebodied are slowly worked to death in labor camps. The infirm are left to die of exposure and starvation or are deliberately massacred in mass executions.

His Majesty's Government in the United Kingdom, the Soviet Government, and the United States Government condemn in the strongest possible terms this bestial policy of cold-blooded extermination. They declare that such events can only strengthen the resolve of all freedom-loving peoples to overthrow the barbarous Hitlerite tyranny. They reaffirm their solemn resolution to ensure, in common with the governments of the United Nations, that those responsible for these crimes shall not escape retribution, and to press on with the necessary practical measures to this end.

Dropping the document on the desk, Slote asked, "Who made those cuts?"

"Why?"

"They castrate the thing. Can't you get them put back?"

"Les, that's a very strong document as it stands."

"But those strikeouts are malevolent surgery. Reports *'which leave no room for doubt'* says that our government believes this. Why cut that? *'Irrespective of age and sex'* is crucial. Those Germans are exterminating women and children wholesale. Anybody can respond to that! Otherwise the thing's just about 'Jews.' Far-off bearded kikes. Who cares?"

Foxy grimaced. "Now *that's* an overwrought reaction. Look, you're tired, and I think slightly biased, and —"

"Come on, Foxy, who made those cuts? The British? The Russians? Can we still fight?"

"They came from the second floor here." A serious look passed between them. "I went to the mat on this, my friend. I headed off a lot of other cuts. This thing will make an explosion in the world press, Leslie. It's been torture getting three governments to agree on the wording, and what we've ended with is remarkable."

Slote gnawed on a bony knuckle. "All right. How do we back it up?" He tapped his portfolio. "Can I prepare a selection of this stuff to release with the statement? It's hard confirmation. I can pull together a devastating selection in a few hours."

"No, no, no." Foxy shook his head. "We'd have to put all that on the wires to London and Moscow. Weeks could go by in more arguments."

"Foxy, without documentation that release is just a propaganda broadside. Mere boiler plate. That's how the press will take it. Milktoast stuff anyway, compared to what Goebbels puts out."

The division director spread his hands. "But your material all comes from Geneva Zionists or London Poles, doesn't it? The British Foreign Office raises its hackles at any Zionist material, and the Soviets foam at the very mention of the Polish government-in-exile. You know all that. Be practical."

"No backup, then." Slote struck a fist on the desk in frustration. "Words. Just words. The best the civilized nations can do against this horrible massacre, with all the damning evidence in hand."

Foxy got up, slammed his door shut, and turned on Slote, thrusting out a stiff arm and forefinger.

"Now look here. My wife is Jewish, as you know"— Slote didn't know it —"just as Mr. Hull's is. I've given this thing agonized thought, sleepless nights. Don't wave off what we've accomplished here. It will make a hell of a difference. The Germans will think twice before proceeding with their barbarities. It's a signal to them that'll sink in."

"Will it? I think they'll ignore it or laugh it off."

"I see. You want a world howl, and a big rescue push by the Allied governments."

"Yes. Especially of Jews piled up in neutral countries."

"Okay. You'd better start thinking in Washington terms again." Foxy slumped in his chair, looking irritated and sad, but he took a cool even tone. "The Arabs and the Persians are already over on Hitler's side, as you well know. In Morocco and Algeria right now there's hell to pay about our so-called pro-Jewish policy, simply because our military authorities removed the Vichy anti-Semitic laws. The Moslems are up in arms. Eisenhower's got Moslems all around his armies and up ahead in Tunis. If a world howl leads to a popular push to open Palestine for the Jews, that will *really* kick over the crock in the whole Mediterranean and Middle East. It will, Leslie! What's more, it'll alienate Turkey. It's an unacceptable political hazard. Do you disagree?"

At Slote's scowling silence, Foxy sighed and talked on, ticking off points on his fingers. "Now. Did you follow the elections while you were over there? President Roosevelt almost lost control of Congress. He squeaked through in both houses, and that nominal Democratic majority is riddled with rebelliousness. There's a big reaction gathering force in this country, Les. The isolationists are feeling their oats again. There's a record defense budget coming up. Big Lend-Lease appropriations, especially for the Soviet Union, which aren't popular at all. Renewal of price controls, rationing, and the draft, vital things the President must have to fight the war. Start a cry in this country to let in more Jews, Les, and just watch the counterblast in Congress against the whole war effort!"

"Well delivered, Foxy," Slote all but sneered. "I know the line well. Do you believe a word of it?"

"I believe all of it. Those are the facts. Unfortunate but true. The President saw Woodrow Wilson frustrated and his peace plans blown to hell by a Congress that got out of control. I'm sure the spectre of Wilson haunts him. The Jewish question is right on the red line, Leslie, in this government's basic political and military policies. The working room is narrow, fearfully narrow. Within those cramped limits, the document' s an achievement. The British drafted it. Most of what I did was fight to keep the substance. I think I succeeded."

Suppressing the old sense of hopelessness, Slote asked, "Okay, what do I do next?"

"You have an appointment at three with Assistant Secretary Breckinridge Long."

"Any idea what he has in mind for me?"

"Not a clue."

"Fill me in on him."

"Long? Well, what do you know about him?"

"Just what Bill Tuttle told me. Long recruited Tuttle to organize the Republicans for Roosevelt in California. They both raced thoroughbred horses, or something, and that's how they got acquainted. Also, I know Long was ambassador to Italy. So I guess he's rich."

"His wife's rich." Foxy hesitated, then gave a heavy sigh. "He's a man on a hot seat."

"In what way?"

Foxy Davis began to pace his small office. "All right, short *curriculum vitae* on Breckinridge Long. You'd better know these things. Gentleman-politician of the old school. Fine Southern family. Princeton. Lifelong Missouri Democrat. Third Assistant Secretary of State under Wilson. Flopped trying to run for the Senate. In electoral politics, a washout." Foxy halted, standing over Slote, and poked his shoulder. "BUT — Long's an old, old, *old* Roosevelt man. That's the key to Breckinridge Long. If you were for Roosevelt before 1932 you're in, *and* Long goes back to 1920, when FDR ran for Vice President. Long's been a floor manager for him at the conventions. Ever since Wilson's time he's been a big contributor to Democratic campaigns."

"I get the idea."

"Okay. Reward, the post in Italy. Record, so-so. Admired Mussolini. Got disillusioned. Got recalled. Ulcers was the story. Actually, I believe he behaved ineptly during the Ethiopian war. Came back and raced his thoroughbreds. But of course he wanted back in, and FDR takes care of his own. When the war came, he created a job for Long — Special Assistant Secretary of State for emergency war matters. Hence the hot seat. The refugee problem is smack in his lap, because the visa division is his baby. Delegations in an unending parade — labor leaders, rabbis, businessmen, even Christian clergy — keep urging him to do more for the Jews. He has to keep saying no, no, no, in polite doubletalk, and he's too thin-skinned for the abuse that's ensued. Especially in the liberal press." Foxy sat down at his desk. "That's the drill on Breck Long. Now, until you get set, if you want an office —"

"Foxy, is Breckinridge Long an anti-Semite?"

A heavy sigh; a prolonged stare, not at Slote but into vacancy. "I don't think he's an inhumane man. He detests the Nazis and the Fascists. He really does. Certainly he's not an isolationist, he's very strong for a new League of Nations. He's a complicated fellow. No genius, not a bad guy, but the attacks are hurting and stiffening him. He's touchy as a bear with a sore nose."

"You're ducking my question."

"Then I'll answer it. *No.* He's not an anti-Semite. I don't think so, though God knows he's being called that. He's in a rotten spot, and he's overburdened with other work. I'm sure he doesn't know half of what's going on. He's one of the busiest men in Washington, and personally one of the nicest. A gentleman. I hope you go to work for him. I think you can get him to eliminate some of the worst abuses in the visa division, at the very least."

"Good Lord, that's inducement enough."

Foxy was looking through papers on his desk. "Now. Do you know a Mrs. Selma Ascher Wurtweiler? Formerly of Bern?"

It took Slote a moment to remember. "Yes. Of course. What about her?"

"She'd like you to telephone her. Says it's urgent. Here's her number in Baltimore."

Heavily pregnant, Selma came waddling behind the headwaiter to Slote's table, followed by a short red-faced almost bald young man. Slote jumped out of his chair. She wore plain black, with one brooch of big diamonds. Her hand was as cold and damp as if she had been making snowballs. Despite the huge bulge of her abdomen, the resemblance to Natalie was still marked.

"This is my husband."

Julius Wurtweiler put warm force into the banal greeting, "It's a pleasure to meet *you!*" As soon as he sat down, Wurtweiler called the waiter and began ordering the drinks and the lunch. He had to see several congressmen and two senators, he said, so he would eat and run, if that was all right, leaving Slote and Selma to chat about old times. The drinks came, with tomato juice for Selma. Wurtweiler lifted his glass toward Slote. "Well, here's to that United Nations statement. When's it coming out? Tomorrow?"

"Ah, what statement would that be?"

"Why, the statement about the Nazi massacres. What else?" Wurtweiler's pride in his inside knowledge glowed on the healthy face.

Better let the man disclose his hand, such as it was, Slote quickly decided. "You have a private line to Cordell Hull, I gather."

Wurtweiler laughed. "How do you suppose that statement originated?"

"I'm actually not sure."

"The British Jewish leaders finally got to Churchill and to Eden with some incontrovertible evidence. Terrible stuff! Churchill's heart is in the right place, but he has to buck that damned Foreign Office, and this time he did it. Of course, we've been kept informed."

"We?"

"The Zionist Councils here."

Before the food came — it took a while, because the restaurant was packed — Wurtweiler did a lot of talking over the loud chatter all around them. His manner was forceful and pleasant, his accent faintly Southern. He served on several committees of protest and rescue. He had given scores of personal affidavits for refugees. He had twice been in Cordell Hull's office with delegations. Mr. Hull was a thorough gentleman, he said, but aging and rather out of things.

Wurtweiler was not in total despair about the massacres. The Nazi persecution would prove a turning point in Jewish history, he believed. It would create the Jewish homeland. The political line of the Jews and their friends, he said, now had to be strong and single: *Repeal the White Paper! Open Palestine to European Jewry!* His committee was thinking of following up the Allied statement with a massive popular descent on Washington, and he wanted Slote's opinion of this. It would be called the "March of the Million." Americans of all faiths would take part. It would present a petition to the White House, signed with a million names, demanding — as the price of continuing Lend-Lease to the British — that London repeal the White Paper. Many senators and congressmen were ready to support such a resolution.

"Tell me candidly what you think," Wurtweiler said, attacking a cheese omelette while Selma picked at a fruit salad and gave Slote what seemed a warning glance.

Slote put a few mild questions. Assuming the British yielded, how could the Jews in German-held Europe actually be moved to Palestine? No problem, retorted Wurtweiler; plenty of neutral shipping was available: Turkish, Spanish, Swedish. For that matter, empty Allied Lend-Lease ships could carry them under a flag of truce.

But would the Germans honor a flag of truce or release the Jews?

Well, Hitler did want to clear Europe of Jews, said Wurtweiler, and this plan would do it, so why shouldn't he cooperate? The Nazis would demand a big ransom, no doubt. All right, the Jews in the free countries would beggar themselves to save Hitler's captives. He would himself. So would his four brothers.

Slote found himself, to his surprise, thinking in Foxy's "Washington terms" about the matter, in a reaction to this man's naïve self-assurance. He pointed out that such a large transfer of foreign currency would enable the Nazis to buy a lot of scarce war materials. In effect, Hitler would be bartering Jewish lives for the means to kill Allied soldiers.

"I don't see that at all!" Wurtweiler's answer shaded into impatience. "That's weighing remote military conjectures against the certain deaths of innocent people. It's a plain question of rescue before it's too late."

Slote mentioned that Arab sabotage could close the Suez Canal overnight. Wurtweiler had a brisk answer to "that old chestnut." The threat to the canal was finished. Rommel was running away from Egypt. Eisenhower and Montgomery were closing a nutcracker on him. The Arabs veered with the winds of victory, and they wouldn't dare to touch the canal.

They were now talking over coffee. As pleasantly as he could, Slote cautioned Wurtweiler against the charm of this one big simple answer, the "March of the Million" to open Palestine. He did not think the British would do it, or that there was any way for Jews in Nazi Europe to go there if they did.

"You're a total pessimist, then. You think they must all die."

Not at all, Slote replied. There were two things to work for: in the long range to destroy Nazi Germany, and in the short range to frighten the Nazis into stopping the murders. In the Allied world there were many thousands of sparsely settled square miles. Five thousand Jews, to start with, admitted to twenty countries — perhaps even including Palestine — would add up to a hundred thousand rescued souls. There were more than that many piled up in neutral lands. A concerted Allied decision to give them haven at once would jolt the Germans. At the moment, the Nazis kept jeering at the outside world, "If you're so worried about the Jews, why don't you take them in?" The only answer was shamed silence. That had to end. If America would lead, twenty countries would follow. Once the Allies showed they really cared about the fate of the Jews, that might scare Hitler's executioners, and slow down or even stop the killing. Agitation to open Palestine was futile and therefore beside the point.

Wurtweiler listened, his brow furrowed, his eyes intent on Slote, who thought he was making some headway. "Well, I get your point," he said at last, "and I completely disagree with you. A hundred thousand Jews! With millions facing doom! Once we support such a program, with the little strength we've got, it'll mean the end for Palestine. Your twenty havens would back out at the last minute anyhow. And most Jews wouldn't want to go to them."

With the friendliest farewell, Wurtweiler left after paying the bill, kissing his wife, and urging Slote to come to dinner soon in Baltimore.

"I like your husband," Slote ventured, as the waiter poured them more coffee.

Selma had eaten almost nothing, and she had turned very pale. She burst out, "He has a wonderful heart, he's given a fortune to rescue work, but his Zionist solution is a dream. I don't argue any more. He and his friends are so full of plans, meetings, projects, demonstrations, marches, rallies, this, that! They mean so well! There are so many other committees with different plans, meetings, rallies! He thinks *they're* so misguided! These American Jews! They run in circles like poisoned mice, and it's all too late. I don't blame them. I don't blame the Congress, or even your own State Department people. They aren't bad or stupid, they just can't imagine this thing."

"Some of them are pretty bad and pretty stupid."

She held up a protesting hand. "The Germans, the Germans are the killers. And you can't even blame them, exactly. They've turned into wild animals driven by a maniac. It's all too hopeless and horrible. I'm sorry we spent our whole lunch discussing it. I'll have nightmares tonight." She put both hands to her temples, and forced a smile. "What's happened to the girl who looked like me? And her baby?"

Her expression hardened at his reply. "Lourdes! My God! Isn't she in terrible danger?"

"She's as safe as our own consular people are."

"Even though she's Jewish?"

Slote shrugged. "I believe so."

"I'll dream about her. I dream all the time that I'm back in Germany, that we never got out. I can't tell you what awful, awful dreams I have. My father is dead, my mother's sick, and here I am in a strange country. I dread the nights." She looked around the restaurant in a stunned way, and gathered up bag and gloves in some agitation. "But it's a sin to be ungrateful. I'm alive. I'd better get my shopping done. Will you accept Julius's invitation to come to dinner in Baltimore?"

"Of course," Slote said too politely.

Her look was skeptical and resigned. On the sidewalk outside she said, "Your idea about refugees is not bad. You should push it. The Germans are losing the war. Soon they'll start worrying about saving their individual necks. Germans are very good at that. If America and twenty other countries would really take in a hundred thousand Jews now, that could worry those SS monsters. They might start looking for excuses to save Jews, so they could show good records. It's very sensible, Leslie."

"If you think so, I'm encouraged."

"Is there any chance of it happening?"

"I'm going to find out."

"God bless you." She held out her hand. "Is it cold?"

"Ice."

"You see? America hasn't changed me so much. Good-bye. I hope that your friend and her baby will be saved."

Walking back to the State Department under a clearing blue sky, leaning into a frigid wind, Slote paused and stared through the White House fence across the snowy lawn, trying to imagine Franklin Roosevelt at work somewhere inside that big edifice. For all the fireside chats, speeches, newsreels, and millions of newspaper words about him, Franklin Roosevelt remained for Slote an elusive man. Wasn't there a trace of fraud about a politician who could seem to Europeans a great humanitarian deliverer, yet whose policies, if Foxy was right, were fully as cold and inhumane as Napoleon's?

Tolstoy's grand theme in *War and Peace* — so Slote thought, as he hurried on — was the sinking of Napoleon in Pierre Bezukhov's mind from liberal deliverer of Europe to bloodthirsty invader of Russia. In Tolstoy's dubious theory of war, Napoleon was a mere monkey riding an elephant; an impotent egomaniac swept along by time and history, mouthing orders he couldn't help giving, winning battles that were bound to be won, because of small battlefield events that he didn't know about and couldn't control; then later losing wars with the same "strokes of genius" that had brought him "victories," because the stream of history had changed course away from him, stranding him in failure.

If Foxy was accurately reflecting Roosevelt's policy on the Jews, if he wouldn't even risk a clash with Congress to halt this vast crime, then wasn't the President Tolstoy's monkey after all — an inconsequential man, inflated by history's strong breath into a grandiose figure, seeming to be winning the war only because the tides of industrial prowess were moving that way; time's puppet, less free in confronting the Hitler horror than a single frightened Jew escaping over the Pyrenees, because that Jew at least was lowering the toll of murder by one?

Slote did not want to believe any of that.

The sunlight streaming through the tall windows of Breckinridge Long's office was no more pleasant to the eye, or more warm and cheery, than the Assistant Secretary himself, as he strode across the room like a young man to shake hands. Long's patrician face, thinly chiselled mouth, neat curling iron-gray hair, and short athletic figure went with a well-tailored dark gray suit, manicured nails, gray silk tie, and white kerchief in breast pocket. He was the very model of an Assistant Secretary of State; and far from appearing harried, or bitter, or in any way on a hot seat, Breckinridge Long might have been welcoming an old friend to his country home.

"Well, Leslie Slote! We should have met long ago. How's your father?"

Slote blinked. "Why, he's very well, sir." This was a disconcerting start.

Slote did not remember his father's ever mentioning Breckinridge Long. "Haven't seen him since God knows when. Dear me! He and I just about ran Ivy Club, played tennis almost every day, sailed, got in hot water with the girls —" With a melancholy charming smile, he waved at a sofa. "Ah, well! You know, you look more like Timmy Slote than he himself does now, I daresay. Ha-ha."

With an embarrassed smile, Slote sat down, searching his memory. At Harvard Law School the father had developed a scornful regret for his "wasted" years at Princeton: a country club, he would say, for rich feather-heads trying to avoid an education. He had strongly advised his son to go elsewhere, and had spoken little of his college experiences. But how strange not to mention to a son in the Foreign Service that he knew an ambassador, an Assistant Secretary of State!

Long offered him a cigarette from a silver case, and leaning back on the sofa, fingering the handkerchief in his breast pocket, he said jocularly, "How did you ever happen to go to a tinpot school like Yale? Why didn't Timmy put his foot down?" He chuckled, regarding Slote with a fatherly eye. "Still, despite that handicap, you've made an admirable Foreign Service officer. I know your record."

Was this heavy sarcasm?

"Well, sir, I've tried. I feel pretty helpless sometimes."

"How well I know the feeling! How's Bill Tuttle?"

"Thriving, sir."

"Bill's a sound man. I've had some distressing communications from him. He's in a sensitive spot there in Bern." Breckinridge Long's eyes drooped half-shut. "You've both handled matters prudently there. If we'd had a couple of these radical boys out in that mission, the stuff you've been turning up might have been smeared all over the world press."

"Mr. Assistant Secretary —"

"Great day, young fellow, you're Tim Slote's son. Call me Breck."

In a memory flash Slote now recalled his father's talking of a "Breck," in conversations with his mother long, long ago; a shadowy figure from his racketing youth. "Well, then, Breck — I consider that material I've brought authentic and appalling."

"Yes, so does Bill. He made that clear. All the more credit to both of you for sensing where your duty lies." Long fingered his breast-pocket hand-kerchief and smoothed his tie. "I wish some of these wild-eyed types we're getting in Washington were more like you, Leslie. At least you know that a man who eats the government's bread shouldn't embarrass his country. You learned that lesson from that little episode in Moscow. Quite understandable and forgivable. The Nazi oppression of the Jews horrifies me, too. It's repul-sive and barbaric. I was condemning that policy back in 1935. My memoranda from those days are right here in the files. Now then, young fellow. Let me tell you what I have in mind for you."

It was a while before Slote found out. Long first spoke of the nineteen divisions he headed. Cordell Hull actually had him drawing up a plan for the new postwar League of Nations. *There* was a challenge! He was working nights and Sundays, his health was suffering, but that didn't matter. He had seen Woodrow Wilson destroyed by Congress's rejection of the League in 1919. That must not happen to his great old friend, Franklin Roosevelt, and his grand visions for world peace.

Also, Congress had to be kept in line, and the Secretary had delegated to him most dealings with the Hill. *There* was a backbreaker! If Congress balked at Lend-Lease aid to Russia, Stalin might make a treacherous separate peace overnight. This war would be touch and go till the last shot was fired. The British could not be trusted, either. They were already intriguing to put de Gaulle into North Africa, so that they could control the Mediterranean after the war. They were in this war strictly for themselves; the British never changed much.

After this global rambling, Breckinridge Long came to the point at last. Somebody in the Division of European Affairs should be disposing of Jewish matters, he said, not passing them up to him — all these delegations, petitions, correspondence, important individuals who had to be treated with kid gloves, and the like. The situation required just the right man to keep it on an even keel, and he thought Leslie was that man. Leslie's reputation as a sympathizer with the Jews was a wonderful asset. His discretion in Bern had demonstrated his soundness. He came from good stock, and he had bred true. He had a shining future in the Department. Here was a chance to take on a really prickly job, show his stuff, and earn brilliant advancement.

Slote was appalled by all this. Taking over as a buffer for Breckinridge Long, *"saying no, no, no, in polite doubletalk"* to Jewish petitioners, was a disgusting prospect. The end of his career seemed now no farther off than the door of Long's office, and he hardly cared.

"Sir —"

"Breck."

"Breck, I don't want to be placed in such a spot unless I can help the people who come to me."

"But that's exactly what I want you to do."

"But what do I do besides turn them down? Say 'No,' every devious way I can think of?"

Breckinridge Long sat up straight, giving Slote a stern righteous stare. "Why, when you can possibly help somebody, you're to say yes, not no."

"But the existing regulations make that almost impossible."

"How? Tell me." Breckinridge Long inquired, his manner very kindly. A muscle in his jaw worked, and he fingered first his handkerchief, then his tie.

Slote started to explain the preposterousness of requiring Jews to produce exit permits and good conduct certificates from the police of their native lands. Long interrupted, his brow wrinkled in puzzlement, "But, Leslie, those are standard rules devised to keep out criminals, illegal fugitives, and other riffraff. How can we bypass them? Nobody has a God-given right to enter the United States. People have to show evidence that if we let them in they'll become good Americans."

"Breck, Jews have to get such papers from the Gestapo. That's obviously an absurd and cruel requirement."

"Oh, the New York bleeding hearts have made that a scare word. *Gestapo* simply means federal Secret Service, *Geheime Staatspolizei*. I've had dealings with the Gestapo. They're Germans like any others. I'm sure their methods are mighty tough, but we have a mighty tough Secret Service ourselves. Every country does. Besides, not all Jews come from Germany."

Battling a ragged-nerve impulse to walk out and seek another livelihood — because he did sense in Long a peculiar streak of honest if perverse reasonableness — Slote said, "Wherever the Jews come from, they've fled for their lives. How could they have stopped to apply for official documents?"

"But if we drop these regulations," said Long patiently, "what's to prevent saboteurs, spies, dynamiters, and all sorts of undesirables in the thousands from getting into the country, posing as poor refugees? Just answer me that. If I were in German intelligence, I wouldn't miss that bet."

"Require other evidence of good character. Investigation by the Quakers. Affidavits of personal histories. Endorsements by the local U.S. consul. Or by some reliable relief agency, like the Joint. There are ways, if we'll look for them."

Breckinridge Long sat with his hands clasped under his chin, thoughtfully regarding Slote. His reply was slow and cautious. "Yes. Yes, I can see merit in that. The regulations can be onerous for deserving individuals. I've had other things on my mind, like the structure of the postwar world. I'm not pigheaded and" — his smile now was rather harried — "I'm not an anti-Semite, despite all the smears in the press. I'm a servant of the government and of its laws. I try to be a good one. Would you prepare a memorandum on your ideas for me to give the visa division?"

Slote could scarcely believe he was moving Breckinridge Long, but the man spoke with warm sincerity. Emboldened, he asked, "May I offer another idea?"

"Go ahead, Leslie. I find this talk refreshing."

Slote described his plan for the admission of a hundred thousand Jews to twenty countries. Breckinridge Long listened carefully, fingers moving from his tie to his handkerchief, and back to his tie.

"Leslie, you're talking about a second Evian, a major international conference on refugees."

"I hope not. Evian was an exercise in futility. Another conference like that will consume a lot of time while people are being slaughtered."

"But the political refugees are a more acute problem now, Leslie, and there's no other way to get such a thing going. A major policy can't be developed on the departmental level." Long's eyes were narrowed almost shut. "No, *that* is an imaginative and substantial suggestion. Will you let me have a confidential paper on it? For my eyes only, now. Put in all the practical detail that occurs to you."

"Breck, are you really interested?"

"Whatever you've heard of me," the Assistant Secretary replied with a shade of weary tolerance, "I'm not given to wasting my time. Nor that of anyone who works with me. We're all carrying too heavy a load."

But the man might be brushing him off; *write me a memorandum* was a very old departmental dodge. "Sir, you know about the joint Allied statement on the Jews, I suppose?"

Long silently nodded.

"Do you believe — as I do — that it's the plain truth? That the Germans are murdering millions of European Jews, and intend to murder them all?"

A smile came and went on the Assistant Secretary's face; an empty smile, a mere agitation of the mouth muscles.

"I happen to know quite a bit about that statement. Anthony Eden drew it up under pressure, and it's nothing but a sop to some prominent British citizens of that race. I think it will do more harm than good, just provoke the Nazis to harsher measures. But we can't pass judgment on that unfortunate race, we must help them if we can, within the law, in their time of agony. That's my whole policy, and that's why I want a memo on that conference idea right away. It sounds practical and constructive." Breckinridge Long stood up and held out his hand. "Now will you help me, Leslie? I need your help."

Getting to his feet and accepting the handshake, Slote took the plunge. "I'll try, Breck."

The four-page letter that Slote wrote that night to William Tuttle ended this way:

So perhaps you were right, after all! It's almost too good to be true, this possibility that I can have some influence on the situation, root out the worst abuses, and enable thousands of innocent people to go on living, largely due to the accident that my father was Princeton '05, and Ivy Club. Sometimes things do work out that way in this Alice-in-Wonderland town. If I'm pitifully deceived, I'll know soon enough. Meantime, I'll give Breckinridge Long my full allegiance. Thanks for everything. I'll keep you informed.

53

SLOTE and Foxy Davis were reviewing the early press clippings about the United Nations statement for a first report to the Secretary on the national reaction, when Slote remembered that he was dining at the Henry home. "I'll take these with me," he said, stuffing the batch into his portfolio, "and draft the thing tonight."

"I don't envy you," said Foxy. "Bricks without straw."

"Well, all the returns aren't in."

Walking to the corner to catch a cab, Slote noticed a stack of the new *Time* magazines, still tied with string, on the sidewalk by a newsstand. He and Foxy had been hungering for a look at it, since a *Time* reporter had interviewed Foxy on the telephone for almost an hour about the evidence for the massacre. He bought a copy, and in the light of a streetlamp, despite a drizzle that made the pages limp and sticky, he thumbed the issue eagerly. Nothing in the news section; nothing under features; front to back, *nothing*. How could that be? The *New York Times* had at least run it on the front page; a disappointing single-column story, overshadowed by a right-hand streamer on the flight of Rommel, and a two-column story about a cut in gas rationing. Most of the other big papers had dropped it inside, the *Washington Post* on page ten, but they had all done something with it. How could *Time* utterly ignore such an event? He paged through the copy again.

Not one word.

In the *People* section the picture of Pamela and her father that he had seen in the *Montreal Gazette* caught his eye.

Pamela Tudsbury, fiancée of Air Vice Marshal Lord Duncan Burne-Wilke (*Time*, Feb. 16), will leave London for Washington next month, to carry on the work of her late father as a correspondent for the *London Observer*. Until a land mine at El Alamein ended Alistair Tudsbury's career (*Time*, Nov. 16), the future Lady Burne-Wilke, on leave from the WRAF corps, globetrotted with eloquent, corpulent Tudsbury, collaborated on many of his front-line dispatches, barely escaped Jap capture in Singapore and Java.

Well, he thought, this may just interest Captain Henry. The flicker of malice slightly assuaged his disappointment. Slote did not like Henry much. To him, military men by and large were grown-up boy scouts; hard-drinking time-servers at worst, efficient conformists at best, banal narrow-minded conservatives to a man. Captain Henry bothered Slote because he did not quite fit the pigeonhole. He had too incisive and agile a mind. On that memorable night in the Kremlin, Henry had talked up to the awesome Stalin quite well, and he had pulled off a feat in getting to the front outside Moscow. But the man had no conversation, and anyway he reminded Slote of his galling defeats with Natalie and Pamela. Slote had accepted the dinner invitation only because in all conscience he thought he ought to tell Byron's family what he knew.

Welcoming Slote at the door of the Foxhall Road house, Henry scarcely smiled. He looked much older and peculiarly diminished in a brown suit and red bow tie.

"Seen this?" Slote pulled the magazine from his overcoat, open to the photograph.

Henry glanced at the page as Slote hung up his damp coat. "No. Too bad about old Talky, isn't it? Come on in. I believe you know Rhoda, and this is our daughter, Madeline."

The living room was astonishingly large. Altogether, this establishment looked beyond a naval officer's means. The two women sat on a sofa near a trimmed Christmas tree, drinking cocktails. Captain Henry handed his wife the magazine. "You were wondering what Pamela would do next."

"Bless me! Coming here! Engaged to Lord Burne-Wilke!" Mrs. Henry gave her husband a sidewise glance and passed the magazine to Madeline. "Well, she's done all right for herself."

"Christ, she looks so old, so tacky," Madeline said. "I remember when I met her, she was wearing this mauve halter dress"— she waggled one little white hand at her own bosom —"all terribly terrific. Wasn't Lord Burne-Wilke there, too? A blond dreamboat with a beautiful accent?"

"He was indeed," said Rhoda. "It was my dinner party for the Bundles for Britain concert."

"Burne-Wilke's an outstanding man," Pug said.

Slote could detect no trace of emotion in the words, yet he was sure that in Moscow Pamela Tudsbury and this upright gentleman had been having a hot little time of it. Indeed, it had been his pique at Henry's success with Pamela that had impelled him to drop his professional caution, and slip the Minsk documents to a *New York Times* man, thus starting his slide to his present nadir. Pamela's reaction in London to the news about Henry had indicated that the romance was far from dead. If Victor Henry did not have the soul of a wooden Indian, he was very good at simulating it.

"Oh, his lordship's unforgettable," exclaimed Madeline. "In RAF blue, all campaign stars and ribbons, and so slender and straight and blond! Sort of a stern Leslie Howard. But isn't that a screwy match? He's as old as you, Dad, at least. She's about my age."

"Oh, she's older than that," said Rhoda.

"I saw her in London, briefly," Slote said. "She was rather broken up over her father."

"What news of Natalie?" Pug asked Slote abruptly.

"They're still in Lourdes, still safe. That's the nub of it. But there's a lot to tell."

"Madeline, dear, let's get the dinner on." Rhoda rose, carrying her drink. "We'll talk at the table."

The candle-lit dining room had fine sea paintings on the walls and a log fire flaming in the fireplace. The mother and daughter served the dinner. The roast beef seemed a luxurious splurge of money and red points, and the plate and china were far more elegant than Slote had expected. While they ate, he narrated Natalie's odyssey as he had gathered it from her early letters, some Swiss reports, the Zionist rumors in Geneva, and Byron's story. It was a sketchy version patched together with a lot of guesswork. Slote knew nothing of Werner Beck's pressure on Jastrow to broadcast. A German diplomat had befriended Natalie and her uncle, as he told it, and settled them safely in Siena. But they had illegally disappeared in July, escaping with some Zionist fugitives, and had popped up months later in Marseilles, where Byron had caught sight of them for a few hours. They had planned to join him in Lisbon, but the invasion of North Africa had brought the Germans into Marseilles and prevented their departure. Now they were in Lourdes with all the American diplomats and journalists caught in southern France. He passed over Natalie's refusal to go with her husband; let Byron tell that to the family, Slote thought.

"Why Lourdes?" Captain Henry asked. "Why are they interned there?"

"I don't really know. I'm sure Vichy put them exactly where the Germans wanted them."

Madeline said, "Well, then, can't the Germans take her from Lourdes whenever they feel like it, with her uncle and her baby, and ship them off to some camp? Maybe cook them into soap?"

"Madeline, for heaven's SAKE!" exclaimed Rhoda.

"Mom, those are the gruesome stories going around. You've heard them, too." Madeline turned on Slote. "Well, what about all that? My boss says it's a lot of baloney, just stale British propaganda from the last war. I just don't know what to believe. Does anybody?"

Slote contemplated with heavy eyes, across his half-eaten dinner and a centerpiece of scarlet poinsettias, this bright comely girl. For Madeline Henry, clearly, these were all happenings in the Land of Oz. "Does your boss read the *New York Times?* There was a front-page story about this day before yesterday. Eleven Allied governments have announced it as a fact that Germany is exterminating the Jews of Europe."

"In the *Times?* You're sure?" Madeline asked. "I always read it straight through. I saw no such story."

"You overlooked it, then."

"I didn't notice that story, and I read the *Times*, too," Victor Henry observed. "It wasn't in the *Washington Post*, either."

"It was in both papers."

Even a man like Victor Henry, Slote thought in despair, had unconsciously blocked out the story, slid his eyes unseeing past the disagreeable headlines.

"Well, then they are in a pickle. From what you say, their papers are phony," Madeline persisted. "Really, won't the Germans get wise and haul them off?"

"They're still in official French custody, Madeline, and their position's not like that of other Jews. They're interned, you see, not detained."

"I can't follow you," Madeline said, wrinkling her pretty face.

"Neither can I," said Rhoda.

"Sorry. In Bern the distinction became second nature to us. You're *interned*, Mrs. Henry, when war catches you in an enemy country. You've done nothing wrong, you see. You're just a victim of timing. Internees get traded off: newspapermen, Foreign Service officers, and the like. That's what we expect to happen with our Americans in Lourdes. Natalie and her uncle, too. But if you're *detained* when a war starts — that is, if you're arrested — for anything from passing a red light to suspicion of being a spy, it's just too bad. You have no rights. The Red Cross can't help you. That's the problem about the European Jews. The Red Cross can't get to them because the Germans assert that the Jews are in protective custody. *Detained*, not *interned*."

"Christ Almighty, people's lives hanging on a couple of goddamned words!" Madeline expostulated. "How sickening!"

This one lethal technicality, Slote thought, had penetrated the girl's hard shell. "Well, the words do mean something, but on the whole I agree with you."

"When will she ever get home, then?" Rhoda asked plaintively.

"Hard to say. The negotiations for the exchange are well along, but —"

The doorbell rang. Madeline jumped up, giving Slote a charming smile. "This is all wildly interesting, but I'm going to the National Theatre, and my friend's here. Please forgive me."

"Of course."

The outer door opened and closed, letting cold air swirl through the room. Rhoda began to clear away the dinner, and Pug took Slote to the library. They sat down with brandy in facing armchairs. "My daughter is a knucklehead," Pug said.

"On the contrary," Slote held up a protesting hand, "she's very bright.

Don't blame her for not being more upset about the Jews than the President is."

Victor Henry frowned. "He's upset."

"Is he losing sleep nights?"

"He can't afford to lose sleep."

Slote ran a hand through his hair. "But the evidence the State Department has in hand is monstrous. What gets up to the President, of course, I don't know, and I can't find out. It's like trying to catch a greased eel with oily hands in the dark."

"I report back to the White House next week. Can I do anything about Natalie?"

Slote sat up. "You *do?* Do you still have your contact with Harry Hopkins?"

"Well, he still calls me Pug."

"All right, then. There was no point in alarming you before." Slote leaned forward, clutching the big brandy glass so hard in both hands that Pug thought he might smash it. "Captain Henry, they won't remain in Lourdes."

"Why not?"

"The French are helpless. We're actually dealing with the Germans. They've caught some fresh American civilians, and they're squeezing that advantage. They want in exchange a swarm of agents from South America and North Africa. We've already had strong hints from the Swiss that the Lourdes people will soon be taken to Germany, to build up the bargaining pressure. That will enormously heighten Natalie's danger."

"Obviously, but what can the White House do?"

"Get Natalie and Aaron out of Lourdes before they're moved. It might be done through our people in Spain. The Spanish border isn't forty miles away. Informal, quiet deals can be made, sometimes indirectly even with the Gestapo. People like Franz Werfel and Stefan Zweig have been spirited across borders. I'm not saying it'll work. I'm saying you'd better try it."

"But how?"

"I could attempt it. I know whom to talk to at State. I know where the cables should go. A phone call from Mr. Hopkins would enable me to move. Do you know him that well?"

Victor Henry drank in silence.

Slote's voice tightened. "I don't want to sound frantic, but I urge you to try this. If the war goes on two more years, every Jew in Europe will be dead. Natalie's no journalist. Her documents are fraudulent. If they break down she'll be a goner. Her baby, too."

"Did this *New York Times* story say the German government plans to kill all the Jews they can lay their hands on?"

"Oh, the text was fudged, but the implication was to that effect, yes."

"Why hasn't such an announcement created more noise?"

With an almost insane jolly grin, Leslie Slote said, "You tell me, Captain Henry."

Leaning his chin on a hand and rubbing it hard, Henry gave Slote a long quizzical look. "What about the Pope? If such a thing is happening, he's bound to know."

"The Pope! This Pope has been a lifelong reactionary politician. A decent German priest I talked to in Bern said he prayed nightly for the Pope to drop dead. I'm a humanist, so I expect nothing of any Pope. But this one is destroying whatever was left of Christianity after Galileo — I see that offends you. Sorry. All I want to impress on you is, this is a time to cash whatever credit at the White House you have. *Try to get Natalie out of Lourdes.*"

"I'll think about it, and call you."

Slote nervously leaped to his feet. "Good. Sorry if I got worked up. Will Mrs. Henry think me rude if I leave? I've got a lot to do tonight."

"I'll give her your apologies." Pug stood up. "Incidentally, Slote, when is Pamela getting married? Did she tell you?"

Slote suppressed the grin of a huntsman who sees the fox break from cover. In his overwrought state, he took this almost as comic relief. "Well, you know, Captain, *la donna è mobile!* Pam once complained to me that his lordship's a slave driver, a snob, and a bore. Maybe it won't come off."

Pug saw him out the front door. He could hear Rhoda pottering in the kitchen. On the coffee table in the living room, the copy of *Time* lay. Pug opened it and sat hunched over the magazine.

He had lost the snapshot of Pamela in the *Northampton* sinking, but the image was fixed in his memory, a little icon of dead romance. This story of her marriage had hit him hard. Acting indifferent had been tough. She didn't look good at all in this chance shot; with her head down, her nose appeared long, her mouth prissily thin. The desert sun overhead put dark shadows around her eyes. Yet this small poor picture of a woman four thousand miles away could wake a storm in him; while toward his very attractive flesh-and-blood wife in the next room he was numb. A hell of a note! He trudged back to the library, and was sitting there reading *Time* and drinking brandy when Madeline and Sime Anderson returned from the theatre in a rollicking mood. "Is that spook from the State Department gone? Thank heavens," she said.

"How was the play? Shall I take your mother to see it?"

"Christ, yes, give the old girl some giggles, Pop. You'll enjoy it yourself, these four girls in a Washington apartment, popping in and out of closets in their scanties —"

Anderson said, grinning uncomfortably, "There's not much to it, sir."

"Oh, come on, you laughed yourself silly, Sime, and your eyes about fell out of your head." Madeline noticed the Warren album, and her manner sobered. "What's this?"

"Haven't you seen it yet? Your mother put it together."

"No," Madeline said. "Come here, Sime."

Their heads together, they went through the scrapbook, at first silently; then she began exclaiming over the pages. A gold medal reminded her of how Warren had been borne off the field on his schoolmates' shoulders after winning a track meet with a spectacular high jump. "Oh, my God, and his birthday party in San Francisco! Look at me, cross-eyed in a paper hat! There was this horrible boy, who crawled under the table and looked up girls' dresses. Warren dragged him out and almost murdered him. Honestly, the memories this brings back!"

"Your mother's done an outstanding job," said Anderson.

"Oh, Mom! System is her middle name. Lord, Lord, how *handsome* he was! How about this graduation picture, Sime? Other kids look so sappy at that age!"

Her father was watching and listening with a cold calm expression. As Madeline turned the pages, her comments died off. Her hand faltered, her mouth trembled; she crashed the album shut, dropped her head on her arms, and cried. Anderson awkwardly put an arm around her, with an embarrassed glance at Pug. After a few moments, Madeline dried her eyes, saying, "Sorry, Sime. You'd better go home." She went out with him and soon returned. She sat down, crossing shapely legs, quite self-possessed again. It still jarred Victor Henry to see her light up a cigarette with the automatic gestures of a boatswain's mate. "Say, Pop, a Caribbean sunburn does things for Sime Anderson, eh? You should talk to him. He tells wild tales about hunting the U-boats."

"I've always liked Sime."

"Well, he used to remind me of custard. You know? Sort of bland and blond and blah. He's matured, and — all right, all right, never mind the grin. I'm glad he's coming to Christmas dinner." She dragged deeply on the cigarette and gave her father a hangdog glance. "I'll tell you something. *The Happy Hour* is beginning to embarrass me. We tool from camp to camp, making money off the naïve antics of kids in uniform. These wise-guy scriptwriters I work with laugh up their sleeves at sailors and soldiers a lot better than they are. I get so goddamned mad."

"Why don't you chuck it, Madeline?"

"And do what?"

"You'd find work in Washington. You're an able girl. Here's this nice house, almost empty. Your mother's alone."

Her expression disturbed him — sad, timorous, with a touch of defiant mischief. She had looked like this at fourteen, bringing him a bad report card. "Well, frankly, that very thought crossed my mind tonight. The thing is, I'm pretty involved."

"They'll get someone else to handle that fol-de-rol."

"Oh, I like my work. I like the money. I like those numbers jumping up in my little brown bank book."

"Are you happy?"

"Why, I'm just fine, Pop. There's nothing I can't handle."

Victor Henry was seeing her on this visit for the first time in a year and a half. The letter he had received at Pearl Harbor, warning him that she might be named in a divorce action, was going unmentioned. Yet Madeline was flying distress signals, if he knew her at all.

"Maybe I should go and have a talk with this fellow Cleveland."

"What on earth about?"

"You."

Her laugh was artificial. "Funnily enough, he wants to talk to you. I was almost ashamed to mention it." She flicked ash from her skirt. "Tell me, how does the draft work? Do you know anything about it? It seems so cockeyed. There are young fellows I know, unmarried, healthy as horses, who haven't gotten their draft notices yet. And Hugh Cleveland's got his."

"Oh? Fine," Pug said. "Now we'll win the war."

"Don't be mean. The chairman of his draft board is one of these creeps who enjoy hounding a celebrity. Hugh thinks he'd better get into uniform. Volunteer, you understand, and just keep on with *The Happy Hour* and everything. Do you know anyone in Navy public relations?"

Victor Henry slowly, silently shook his head.

"Okay." Madeline sounded relieved. "I've done my duty, I've asked you. I said I would. It's his problem. But Hugh really shouldn't carry a gun, he's all thumbs. He'd be more of a menace to our side than to the enemy."

"Doesn't he have all kinds of military contacts?"

"You wouldn't believe how they fade away, once they know he's got his draft notice."

"Glad to hear that. You should get away from him yourself. He's nothing but trouble."

"I'm having no trouble with Mr. Cleveland." Madeline stood up, tossed her head exactly as she had done when she was five, and she kissed her father. "If anything, the shoe's on the other foot. Night, Pop."

A really grown-up woman, Pug thought as she left, could lie better than that. Undoubtedly she was in a wretched mess. But she was young, she had margins for error, and there was nothing he could do about it. Shut it from mind!

He picked up *Time* to look yet again at the little picture of Pamela and her dead father. "The future Lady Burne-Wilke," coming to Washington.

Something else to shut from mind; and one excellent reason to duck the landing craft job and return to the Pacific. Rhoda had adroitly laid the true basis for salvaging their marriage in the scrapbook there on the table, in the pool of yellow lamplight, where Madeline had slammed it shut. They were linked by the past and by death. The least he could do was cause her no more pain. He might not make it through the war. If he did, they would be old. There would be five or ten years to live side by side in cool decay. She was pitifully contrite, she would surely not slip again, and there was nothing she could do about what had happened. Let time repair what it could. He tossed the magazine in a leather wastebasket, suppressing as kid stuff a notion to tear out the picture, and went off to his dressing room.

In her boudoir, Rhoda was thinking, too. Weary from kitchen work, she was more than ready for sleep. But should she tell Pug of her talk with Pamela? It was the old marital question: have something out, or let it lie? As a rule, Rhoda thought the less said the better, but this time might be the exception. She was getting tired of remorse. Were those nasty anonymous letters on his mind? Well, he had been no saint himself. It might clear the air if she put that truth before him. The news of Pam's engagement was an opening. The scene might be a rough one. Fred Kirby would come up, and possibly the letters. Still, she was wondering if even that might not be better than the dead thick heaviness of Pug's long silences. Their marriage was going out, like the candle under the glass jar in the high school experiment, for want of air. Even the lovemaking at night was making little difference. She had a horrid sense that her husband with some effort was being polite to her in bed. Rhoda put on a lace-trimmed black silk nightgown, brushed out her hair for looks instead of pinning it up for the pillow, and out she went, ready for peace or a sword. He was sitting up in bed with his old bedside Shakespeare in the cracked maroon binding.

"Hi, honey," she said.

He laid the book on the night table. "Say, Rhoda, this fellow Slote has an idea about helping Natalie."

"Oh?" She got in bed and listened, her back to the headboard, her brow furrowed.

Pug was honestly consulting her, by way of trying to grope back to their old footing. She heard him out, nodding and not interrupting. "Why not do it, Pug? What's there to lose?"

"Well, I don't want to make more trouble for the White House than they've got."

"I don't see that. Harry Hopkins may turn you down, for his own reasons. MOUNTAINS of such requests must come his way. But they're your family, and they're in danger. To me the real question is, suppose he's willing to try? Do you trust Slote that much?"

"Why not? It's his field."

"But he's so, I don't know, so OBSESSED. Pug, I'd worry about rocking that boat. You're far away. You can't know what's going on. By singling them out — I mean the WHITE House, honestly! — won't you throw a spotlight on them? And isn't their game to stay inconspicuous, just two more names in that batch of Americans, until they get exchanged? Besides, Natalie's a pretty woman with a baby. The worst fiends in the world would lean over backward for her. Maybe it's tempting fate to interfere."

He took her hand and squeezed it. "That's good thinking."

"Oh, I'm not sure I'm right. Just be very careful."

"Rhoda, Madeline is getting to like Sime Anderson. Has she talked to you? Isn't she in a mess in New York?"

Rhoda could not readily share with Pug her own suspicions, and misconduct was a high-voltage topic. "Madeline's a cool one, Pug. That radio crowd really isn't her kind. If she takes up with Sime, she'll be fine."

"She says the show's very dirty. I'll get us tickets down front."

"Well, how lovely." Rhoda laughed uncertainly. "You're an old RIP, and I always knew it." She was deciding, as she said it, to let the Pamela matter lie.

When she emptied the wastebaskets next day, she couldn't resist turning the pages of *Time* to the picture of Pamela Tudsbury. It was still there, of course. She felt like a fool. Not all that attractive a woman, at that; aging fast, and badly. Engaged to Lord Burne-Wilke, besides. Let it lie, she thought. Let it lie.

54

A Jew's Journey
(*from Aaron Jastrow's manuscript*)

CHRISTMAS DAY, 1942.
LOURDES.

I awoke this morning thinking of Oswiecim.

The Americans in all four hotels were permitted, just this once, to go to church together, to the midnight Mass at the basilica. As usual we were accompanied by our reasonably pleasant Sûreté shadows, and by the surly German soldiers who since last week have been following us on our walks, shopping trips, and visits to the doctor, dentist, or barber. The soldiers were clearly irked at drawing such disagreeable duty on Christmas Eve (it is very cold up here in the Pyrenees, and of course neither the basilica nor the hotel lobbies are heated) when they might have been greeting the birth of their Savior with drunken wassail, or perhaps with animal raptures on the bodies of the few poor French whores who service the conquerors here. Well, Natalie would not go to the Mass, but I did.

It is a very long time since I attended a Mass. In this pilgrimage town you get the real thing, with a crowd of real worshippers; and because of the shrine, those who come include the paralyzed, the crippled, the blind, the deformed, the dying, a terrible parade; a parade of God's cruel jokes or inept mistakes, if you seriously maintain that He heeds the sparrow's fall. Cold as it was in the basilica, the air was warm as May compared to the chill in my heart as the Mass proceeded; chants, bells, elevations, genuflections, and all. It would have been only courteous to kneel at the proper time, as all did, since I had voluntarily come; but for all the disapproving glances, I, the stiff-necked Jew, would not kneel. Nor would I go afterward to a Christmas party for our group at the Hôtel des Ambassadeurs, where, I was told, the black-market wine would flow free, and there would be black-market turkey and sausage. I returned to the Gallia, accompanied to the door of my room by a grumpy German with a hideous breath. I went to sleep, and I awoke thinking of Oswiecim.

It was in the yeshiva at Oswiecim that I first broke with my own religion. I remember it all as though it were yesterday. I can still feel my cheek stinging from the slap of the *mashgiakh*, the study hall supervisor, as I trudge in the snow on the town square in the purple evening, having been ordered out of the *bet midrash* for impudent heresy. I have not thought about all this for years, yet even now it rises in my mind as an intolerable outrage. Perhaps in a yeshiva in a larger city — say Cracow or Warsaw — the *mashgiakh* would have had the sense to smile at my effrontery, and pass it off. Then the whole course of my life might have been different. That slap was the twig that turned the torrent.

It was so utterly unfair! After all, I was a good boy; a "silken boy," as they would say in Yiddish. I excelled in expounding the abstruse legal distinctions that are the meat and the glory of the Talmud, the subtle ethical nuances that the foolish call "hair-splitting." These arguments have an austere, almost geometrical elegance for which one acquires not only a taste, but a thirst. I did have that thirst. I was a star Talmud student. I was brighter and quicker than the *mashgiakh*. Possibly he was glad of the chance, narrow thick-skulled black-capped bearded fool that he was, to take me down a peg; so he slapped my face, ordered me out of the study hall, and set my foot on the path to the Cross.

I remember the passage: page one hundred eleven, Tractate *Passover Offerings.* I remember the subject: demons, and how to avoid them, foil them, and conjure them away. I remember why I was slapped. I asked, "But Reb Laizar, are there really such things as demons?" I remember the bearded fool bawling at me, as I lay on the floor stunned, with a flaming cheek, "Get up! Get out! *Shaygetz!*" (nonbeliever, abomination!) And so I stumbled out into dreary snowy Oswiecim.

I was fifteen. To me, Oswiecim was still a big town. I had visited the grand metropolis of Cracow only once. Our village of Medzice, some ten kilometers up the Vistula, was all wooden houses and crooked muddy pathways. Even the Medzice church — which we children steered clear of as though it were a leprosarium — was built of wood. Oswiecim had straight paved streets, a large railroad station, brick and stone houses, shops with lighted glass windows, and several churches of stone.

I did not know the town well. We lived a strictly regimented life in the yeshiva, seldom venturing beyond the mews on which it faced, bounded by our little dormitory and the teachers' houses. But my rebellious anger that day carried me out of the mews into the town. I walked all over Oswiecim, seething at my ill-treatment, giving way at last to the suppressed doubts that had been plaguing me for years.

For I was no fool. I knew German and Polish, I read newspapers and novels, and precisely because I was a bright Talmudist I could look beyond the *bet midrash* to the world outside; a world glittering with strange dangers and evil temptations, but nevertheless a broader world than one saw in the everlasting straight and narrow march down black columns of Talmud, hemmed in by wise but wearying commentators, who absorbed all one's young wit and energy in exhaustive microanalysis of a main text fourteen centuries old. Between my eleventh year and the moment of the slap, I had been ever more painfully wrenched between the natural yeshiva boy's ambition to become a world-famous *ilui* (prodigy), and a wicked whisper in my soul that I was WASTING MY TIME.

Thinking of all this as I trudged ankle-deep in snow, freed by the *mashgiakh's* anger to wander like a homeless dog, I halted in front of Oswiecim's largest church. Strange that I should have forgotten its name! The one nearest the yeshiva was called *Calvaria;* that I recall. This was another, and much more imposing, edifice on a main square.

My anger had not cooled. Rather, as the rebelliousness of four years came bursting through the bounds of lifelong drilling and a very tender religious conscience, I did something that a few hours earlier would have been as unthinkable as cutting my wrists. I slipped into the church. Wrapped against the cold, I did not look very different from a Christian child, I suppose. In any case some sort of service was going on, and everybody was looking to the front. Nobody paid attention to me.

So long as I live, I shall not forget the shock of seeing a great bloody naked Christ hanging from a cross on the front wall, where in a synagogue the Holy Ark would stand; nor the strange sweetish Gentile smell of incense; nor the big painted saints on the side walls. I was stunned to think that for the "outside" world (as I then regarded it), this was religion, this was the way to God! Half-horrified, half-fascinated, I stayed a long time. Never since have I felt so alien and alone, so dizzily on the brink of a shattering irreversible change in my soul.

Never, that is, until last night.

Whether it was the cumulative effect of living for weeks in the appalling commercialism of Lourdes, which still garishly pervades the town, even off-season, even in wartime; or whether it was the pathetic gathering of the maimed in the basilica; or whether, as once my rebelliousness surfaced, so everything that has been happening to me and Natalie broke through a suppressing instinct in my spirit — however all that may be, the fact is that at midnight Mass last night, familiar as Christ on his cross now is to me, and much as I have written about Christianity, and much indeed as I have loved the religious art of Europe, I felt last night as alienated and alone as I did at fifteen in the Oswiecim church.

I woke this morning thinking of it. I am writing this note as I drink my morning coffee. It is not bad coffee. In France, in the depths of war, under the conqueror's heel, money can still buy everything. The illegal prices are not even very high in Lourdes. It is off-season.

I have neglected this diary ever since our arrival in Lourdes; hoping — to be honest — that I would resume it on a steamship bound for home. That hope is dimming. Our situation is probably worse than my niece and I admit to each other. I hope her good cheer is more real than mine. She knows less. The consul general wisely avoids upsetting her with the ins and outs of our problem, but he is fairly straight with me.

What has gone wrong is a matter far beyond anybody's control. It was of course the most ghastly misfortune that we failed by a few days to leave Vichy France legally. All was in order, the precious papers were in hand, but with the first news of the American landings all train schedules were suspended and the borders were closed. Jim Gaither acted with coolness and dispatch to protect us, by providing us with official journalists' documents predated to 1939, accrediting us to *Life* magazine, which has in fact published a couple of my essays on wartime Europe.

But he went further than that. In the consulate files which they were burning, they turned up some letters from *Life*, requesting courtesies for various writers and photographers. In Marseilles there is a most accomplished ring of document fakers for refugees, run by a remarkable Catholic priest. The consul general, despite everything else he had to do in the sudden crisis, obtained through his underground contacts forged letters on the *Life* letterhead, establishing both Natalie and myself as regularly employed correspondents; papers authentic-looking to the extent of being rubbed, folded, and faded as though they were several years old.

James Gaither did not anticipate that these concocted papers would have to shield us for any very long time, but he thought they would stand up until we got out. However, as time passes, the risk increases. At first he expected that our release would be a matter of days or weeks. After all, we are not at war with Vichy France. There is but a rupture of relations, and so Americans are not "enemies" and should not be "interned" at all. But the group here in Lourdes, about a hundred and sixty of us, most definitely is interned. We have been under strict French police surveillance from the start, unable to move about except under the eyes of a uniformed inspector. And a few days ago, Gestapo men took station around all four hotels where we Americans are sequestered. Ever since, we have been under German guard, as well as in official French police custody. The French act vaguely humiliated and embarrassed by all this, and in small ways try to make us more comfortable. But the Germans are there always, stolidly marching with us wherever we move, staring at us in the lobbies, and ordering us about severely if one of us happens to trespass on a Boche regulation.

Only gradually have I learned what the long delay is all about. For a while Gaither himself did not know. The American chargé d'affaires, who was brought here from Vichy with our entire embassy staff, lives in another hotel, and telephone communication is forbidden. The chargé, an able man named Tuck — a great admirer of my writings, though that is neither here nor there — is apparently allowed one telephone talk a day, of short duration, with the Swiss representative in Vichy. So we are virtually cut off, especially here at the Gallia, and are very much in the dark.

The snag turns out to be simple enough. The Vichy personnel in the United States who should have been swapped for us refused almost to a man to go back to France; understandably, since the Hun now occupies all of it. This has created great confusion, into which the Germans have stepped to seize an advantage. Thus far they still talk through their Vichy puppets, but it is plainly they who are bargaining over us.

We might have gotten away in the first week or two, if the French had simply sent us off the thirty miles to the Spanish border. That would have been a decent return for the food and medical supplies America has lavished on this government for years. But the Vichy men are a loathsome form of life — crawling, sycophantic, pretentious, lying, self-righteous, anti-Semitic, reactionary, feebly militaristic, and altogether base and unworthy of French culture — the very slimy dregs of the anti-Dreyfusards of old. In short, we didn't get out. Here we are, counters in German haggling for assorted Nazi agents being held abroad; and that they will drive a close and savage bargain goes without saying.

I woke thinking of Oswiecim for yet another reason.

During our long stay in the Mendelson apartment in Marseilles, a stream of refugees kept passing through, usually staying not more than one or two nights. In consequence, we heard a lot of the grisly talk that circulates in the European Jewish grapevine about the atrocities in the east, the mass shootings, the gassing in sealed vans, the camps where everybody who arrives is either murdered outright or starved and worked to death. I have never known how much credit to give to these reports and still don't, but one thing is sure: a place name that keeps recurring, and that is never uttered except in hushed terms of the most profound horror and dread, is Oswiecim; usually in its ugly Germanization that I remember well, *Auschwitz.*

If these rumors amount to more than mass paranoid fears brought on by suffering, then Oswiecim is the focal point of the whole horror; my Oswiecim, the place where I studied as a boy, where my father bought me a bicycle, where the whole family sometimes came to spend a Sabbath and hear a great traveling cantor or *maggid*, a revivalist Yiddish preacher; and where I first saw the inside of a church and a life-size Christ on the cross.

The ultimate menace that faces us, in that case, is transportation to the mysterious and frightful camp at Oswiecim. There would be a neat closing of the circle for me! But our random existence on this petty planet does not move in such artistic patterns — that thought really consoles me — and we are a continent away from Oswiecim, and only thirty miles from Spain and safety. I still have faith that we will end by going home. It is vital to keep up one's hopes in a time of danger; to remain alert, and ready to face down bureaucrats and brutes when one must. That takes spirit.

Natalie and the baby, who had a chance to escape, are trapped because at a crucial moment she lacked spirit. I wrote a decidedly intemperate journal entry on Byron's thunderbolt visit and its miserable outcome. My anger at Natalie was fueled by my guilt at having mired her and her baby in this ever-worsening predicament. She will never let me express it; invariably she cuts me off by saying that she is grown up, acted of her own free will, and bears me no grudge.

Now we have been shadowed and ordered about by Germans for a week; and while I still think she should have taken the chance and gone with Byron, I can sympathize more with her reluctance. It would be a fearful thing to fall into the hands of these hard uncouth men without legal papers. All policemen, in relation to those they guard, must seem more or less wooden, hostile, and cruel; for to carry out their orders they must suppress fellow feelings. There has been nothing attractive about the Italian and French police I've dealt with during the past two years, nor — for that matter — about certain American consuls.

But these Germans are different. Orders do not seem merely to guide their actions; orders, as it were, fill their souls, leaving no room for a human flicker in their faces or eyes. They are herdsmen, and we are cattle; or they are soldier ants, and we are aphids. The orders cut all ties between them and us. All. It is eerie. Truly, their cold empty expressions make my skin crawl. I understand that one or two of the higher-ups are "decent sorts" (Gaither's words), but I have not met them. I too once knew "decent sorts" who were German. Here one sees only the other face of the Teuton.

Natalie might well have chanced it with Byron; I know no more resolute or resourceful young man, and he had special diplomatic papers. It was a question of a fast dash through the flames. If she had been the old Natalie, she would have done it, but she balked because of the baby. James Gaither still maintains (if with less assurance as the days pass) that he advised her correctly, and that all will yet be well. I think he's beginning to wonder. We talked the whole matter out again last night, Gaither and I, as we slogged through the snow to the midnight Mass. He insists that the Germans, wanting to recover as many of their agents as possible in this swap, are not at any point going to examine anybody's papers too closely. Natalie, Louis, and I are three warm bodies, exchangeable for perhaps fifteen Huns. They will be satisfied with that, and will look no further.

He does think it is important that I remain inconspicuous. So far we are dealing with very low-grade Frenchmen and Germans, none of whom is likely to have read any books in years, let alone one of my books. He says that my credentials as a journalist are holding, and that none of the police officers has yet singled me out as a "celebrity" or person of consequence, nor as a Jew. For this reason he quashed a suggestion that I give a lecture to our hotel group. The United Press man is arranging a lecture series here at the Gallia, to pass the time. The topic he suggested to me was Jesus, naturally. This was a few days ago, and but for Jim Gaither's veto, I might have consented.

But since my experience at the midnight Mass, I would under no circumstances — even back in the States, and offered a large fee — lecture about Jesus. Something has been happening to me that I have yet to fathom. In recent weeks I have found it harder and harder to work even on Martin Luther. Last night that something began to surface. I have still to focus on it and determine what it is. One of these days I shall trace in this journal the path from my first glimpse of Christ crucified in Oswiecim, to my brief conversion to Christianity in Boston, eight years later. Just now Natalie has come in from her bedroom with Louis, all bundled up for her morning walk. In the open doorway our surly German shadow glowers.

55

ON New Year's Eve Pug surprised Rhoda by suggesting that they go to the Army-Navy Club. She knew he detested the rigmarole of paper hats, noisemakers, and alcoholic kissing; but tonight, he said, he wanted distraction. Rhoda loved the New Year's Eve nonsense, so she happily got herself up; and in the merry crowd of senior military men with their wives moving through the lobby, she felt that few women looked as pretty or glittery as she did in the silver lamé dress from the old Bundles for Britain days. She had an uneasy moment when, as she and Pug entered the dining room, Colonel Harrison Peters stood up and waved to them to join him. Her conduct with Peters had been snowily blameless, but might he not mention Palmer Kirby, or show too much warmth?

Arm in arm, feeling her hesitate, Pug gave her a questioning look. She decided she didn't give a damn. Let it come out at last! "Well, bless me! There's Colonel Peters. Let's join him, by all means," she said cheerily. "He's a fine man, I've met him at church. But where on earth did he get that CHORUS GIRL? Can I trust you at the same table with her?"

Peters towered a head and a half over Pug Henry, shaking hands with him. His blonde bosomy young companion, in a white Grecian-drapery sort of dress that showed much rosy skin, was a secretary at the British Purchasing Council. Rhoda mentioned that they knew Pamela Tudsbury. "Oh, really? The next Lady Burne-Wilke?" the girl trilled, and her accent stirred an ache in Victor Henry. "Dear Pam! You could have knocked us all over with a feather at the Council. Pamela used to be our office mutineer. Always muttering against the old slave driver! Now his lordship will pay for all that overtime, won't he just?"

The hour before midnight melted away in dull war talk over dull club food and very flat champagne. An Army Air Corps colonel with purple bulldog jowls, sitting at this table by chance with his highly rouged wispy wife, railed at the neglect of the "CBI" theatre from which he had just returned, by which he meant China, Burma, and India. Half the human race lived there, said the colonel; even Lenin had once called it the richest war prize in the world. If it fell to the Japs, the white man had better find himself another planet to live on, because Earth would soon be too hot for him. Nobody in Washington seemed to grasp that.

An Army brigadier general, with conspicuously more ribbons than either Peters or the CBI colonel, held forth on the assassination of Admiral

Darlan; whom, he said, he had come to know very well in Algiers. "It's a great pity about Popeye. That's what we on Ike's staff all called Darlan, Popeye. The fellow looked like an insulted frog. Of course he was a plain pro-Nazi, but he was a realist, and once we nabbed him, he delivered the goods, saved a whole lot of American lives. This de Gaulle fellow, now, thinks he's Joan of Arc. We'll get nothing from him but rhetoric and grief. Try telling that to all these pinko typewriter strategists."

Rhoda might have spared herself any concern about Colonel Peters. He was scarcely looking her way, sizing up instead the squat husband with the forbidding tired face. Pug was saying nothing at all. Peters at last asked how he thought the war was going.

"Where?" asked Pug.

"All over. How does the Navy see it?"

"Depends, Colonel, on where you sit in the Navy."

"From where you sit, then."

Puzzled by the idle probing of this big good-looking Army man, Pug answered, "I see plenty of hell behind and plenty ahead."

"Concur," said Peters, as the lights in the noisy dining room blinked and darkened, "and that's a better year-end summary than I've read in all the newspapers. Well, five minutes to midnight, ladies and gentlemen. Allow me, Mrs. Henry." She was sitting beside him, and in an oddly gentle and pleasing way, to which she felt Pug couldn't possibly take exception, he placed on her head a paper shepherdess's bonnet, then tilted a gilt cardboard helmet on his own handsome gray hair. Not everybody at the table put on paper hats, but to Rhoda's astonishment her husband did. Not since the children's early birthday parties had she seen that happen. On Victor Henry's head a pink hat with gold frills, far from looking playful or funny, brought out a terrible sadness in his face.

"Oh, Pug! No."

"Happy New Year, Rhoda."

Champagne glasses in hand, the guests stood up to kiss all around and sing *"Auld Lang Syne"* in candlelight. Pug gave his wife an absent kiss, and yielded her to a polite buss from Colonel Peters. His mind was drifting back over 1942. He was thinking of Warren leaning in the doorway of the cabin on the *Northampton*, with one hand on the overhead, saying, *"Hi, Dad. If you're too busy for me, say so"*; and of the officers and men lying entombed in the sunken hull of the *Northampton*, in the black waters off Guadalcanal. And he was thinking, in the depths of bitter sorrow, that he would ask Hopkins to try to get Natalie and her baby out of Lourdes, after all. She at least was alive.

Harry Hopkins's bedroom in the White House was at one end of a long dark gloomy hall, a few doors down from the Oval Office. In a gray suit that hung on him like a scarecrow's rags, he stood looking out toward the sunlit Washington Monument. "Hello there, Pug. Happy New Year."

He kept skinny hands clasped behind his back as he turned. This stooped, shabby, emaciated, yellow-faced civilian made a sharp contrast to the beefy Rear Admiral Carton, red of cheek and straight as a pole, standing near him in tailored blue and gold with a golden froth of shoulder cords. In newspaper accounts Hopkins sometimes seemed a Dumas figure, a sort of shadowy gliding Mazarin in the presidential back rooms; but face to face he looked to Pug more like a debauched playboy, by the glint in his eye and his fatigued grin still hoping for fun. At a glance Pug took in the dark Lincoln painting and the plaque saying the Emancipation Proclamation had been signed here; also the homey touches of a rumpled red dressing gown flung over the unmade four-poster bed, a frilly negligee beside it, pink mules on the floor, and bottles of medicines lined up on the bedside table.

"Thank you for seeing me, sir."

"Always a pleasure. Sit you down." Carton left, and Hopkins faced Pug on a wine-colored couch seedily worn at the arms. "So! Cincpac wants you, too. Popular fella, aren't you?" Caught by surprise, Pug made no comment. "I suppose that would be your choice?"

"I naturally prefer combat operations."

"What about the Soviet Union?"

"I'm not interested, sir."

Hopkins crossed bone-thin legs and rubbed a hand over his long curving jaw. "Do you remember a General Yevlenko?"

"Yes. Big burly gent. I met him on my trip to the Moscow front."

"Just so. He's now Russia's top dog on Lend-Lease. Admiral Standley thinks you could help a lot in that area. Yevlenko has mentioned you to Standley. Also Alistair Tudsbury's daughter, who I gather went along on that trip."

"Yes, she did."

"Well, you both made quite an impression on him. You know, Pug, your report about the Moscow front last December was a big help. I was a lonely voice around here, maintaining that the Russians would hold. The Army's intelligence estimate was all wrong. Your paper impressed the President. He thinks you have horse sense, which is always in short supply around these parts."

"I thought I'd queered myself by my gratuitous letter about the Minsk Jews."

"Not at all." Hopkins casually waved away Pug's words. "Between you and me, Pug, the whole Jewish situation is a fearsome headache. The President has to keep dodging delegations of rabbis. The State Department tries to deflect them, but some do get through. It's all terribly pitiful, but what can he tell them? They just go over and over the same depressing ground. Invading France and breaking up that insane Nazi system is the only way to keep faith with the Russians, save the Jews, and end this damned war. And the key to *that* is landing craft, my friend." Hopkins leaned back on the couch with a shrewd look at Pug.

Trying to stave off that tricky topic, Pug asked, "Sir, why don't we take in a lot more refugees?"

"Modify the immigration laws, you mean," Hopkins replied briskly. "That's a tough one." He picked a blue book off a side table, and handed it to Pug. The title was *America's Ju-Deal*. "Ever see this?"

"No, sir." Pug made a disgusted face and dropped it. "Nazi propaganda?"

"Possibly. The FBI says it's been widely circulated for years. It came in the mail, and should have gone into the wastebasket, but it reached my desk, and Louise saw it. It sickened her. My wife and I get a flood of hate mail, Pug. Half of it in various filthy ways calls us Jews, which would be funny if it weren't tragic. It's hit a peak since the Baruch dinner."

Victor Henry looked puzzled.

"Were you still abroad? Barney Baruch threw a sort of belated — and frankly, ill-advised — wedding dinner for us. Some reporter got hold of the menu. You can imagine, Pug, a Baruch blowout! Pâté de foie gras, champagne, caviar, the works. With all the discontent about rationing and shortages, I took my lumps again. That, plus the damned lie that Beaverbrook gave Louise an emerald necklace worth half a million as a wedding present, really made things rough around here. I've got a rhinoceros hide, but I've exposed Louise to all this by marrying her. It's terrible." He made a gesture of loathing at the book. "Well, try to pass a new immigration law, and that poison will boil up all over the land. We'd probably get beaten on the Hill. Certainly the war effort would suffer. And in the end what good would it do? We can't pry the Jews out of the German clutches." He gave Victor Henry an inquisitive glance. "Where's your daughter-in-law now?"

"Sir, that's why I asked to see you."

Pug described Natalie's predicament, and Slote's idea for getting her out of Lourdes. Asking a favor came hard to him, and he somewhat fumbled his words. Hopkins listened with his thin mouth pursed. His reaction was quick and hard. "That's negotiating with the enemy. It would have to go to the President, and he'd bump it over to Welles. Lourdes, eh? Who's this fellow at State, again?" He pencilled Leslie Slote's name and telephone number on a bit of paper fished from his pocket. "Let me look into this."

"I'm very grateful, sir." Pug made a move to rise.

"Sit where you are. The President will call me soon. He has a cold and he's sleeping late." With a grin Hopkins unfolded a yellow sheet from his breast pocket. "Just an average basket of crabs for him today. Like to hear it? *One. Chinese calling home their military mission.* Now, there's a bad business, Pug. Their demands for aid are just moonshine, in view of what we need in Europe. On the other hand, the Chinese front is a running sore for Japan. They've been fighting this war longer than any of us, and we have to keep them placated.

"*Two. Heating oil crisis in New England.* God, what a flap! The weather's fooled us, it's been a much colder winter than predicted. Everybody's freezing from New Jersey to Maine. The Big Inch pipeline has fallen behind half a year. More controls, more trouble."

Thus he read off and commented dourly on a list of topics:

3. *Snag over the Siberian route for Lend-Lease.*
4. *Sudden acute shortage of molybdenum.*
5. *Pessimistic revised report on rubber.*
6. *Another rash of U-boat sinkings in the Atlantic.*
7. *German reinforcements in Tunisia throwing back Eisenhower's advance, and famine in Morocco threatening his supply lines.*
8. *General MacArthur again, more troops and air power in New Guinea desperately needed.*
9. *Revision of the State of the Union speech.*
10. *Plans for a meeting with Churchill in North Africa.*

"Now that one's top secret, Pug." Hopkins rattled the paper at him. "We'll be going in about a week to Casablanca, Joint Chiefs of Staff and all. Stalin begged off because of the Stalingrad battle, but we'll keep him informed. We're going to settle strategy for the rest of the war. The President hasn't been in an airplane in nine years, not since he took office. What's more, no President has *ever* flown abroad. He's as excited as a boy."

Victor Henry was wondering at Hopkins's chatty expansiveness, but now came the explanation. Hopkins hunched forward and touched Pug's knee. "You know, Stalin's howling for a Channel crossing this year. That'll get thirty or forty German divisions off his back, and then he probably could throw the Germans out of Russia. He claims we welshed on a second front in '42. But we didn't have the landing craft, and we weren't ready in any respect. The British hate the whole idea of invading France. At Casablanca they're bound to plead the landing craft shortage again."

Drawn in despite himself, Pug asked, "What are the numbers now, sir?"

"Come here." Hopkins led Henry into another room, small, airless, full of dowdy old furniture, with one incongruous card table piled with files and papers. "Have a seat. The Monroe Room, they call this, Pug. He signed the

Doctrine here — now, what the devil! I was just looking at those figures." He shuffled papers on the table, and some fell off. Hopkins ignored these, pulling out and brandishing an ordinary file card, while Pug marvelled at this slapdash casualness at the hub of the war. "Here you are. Figures as of December fifteenth. They're cloudy, Pug, because the losses in North Africa aren't firmed up yet."

Victor Henry knew by heart the landing craft projections he had brought to the Argentia conference, and he was shocked by the statistics on the card that Hopkins read off. "Mr. Hopkins, what in God's name has happened to production?"

Hopkins threw down the card. "A nightmare! We've lost a year! Not only in landing craft, but across the board. The trouble was priorities. Tugs of war between the Army, industry, the home economy, squabbles between this board and that board, jealous infighting among some fine men. All at each other's throats. Everybody was brandishing triple-A priorities, and nobody was getting anything delivered. We had a crazy sort of priority inflation, Pug. Priorities were getting meaningless as old German marks. The mess was beyond description. Then along came Victor Henry."

Hopkins laughed at Pug's astonished blink. "Not really you, of course. Your sort. Ferdie Eberstadt is his name. One of these fellows nobody hears about, who can get things done. You'll have to meet him. A stockbroker, would you believe it? A Princeton type straight out of Wall Street. Never in government. They got him down here on the War Production Board, and Ferdie worked out a brand-new priorities scheme. The *Controlled Materials Plan,* he calls it. It gears all production plans to the flow of three materials — steel, copper, and aluminum. That stuff's being allotted now in a vertical pattern, according to the thing that's being produced. Destroyer escort, long-range bomber, heavy truck for the Soviets, whatever it is, those materials get allotted to make every single component of the thing. Not horizontally, some here, some there, some to the armed forces, some to the factories"— Hopkins waved his long arms wildly about —"depending on who has the coziest inside track in Washington. Well, it's a miracle. Production figures are shooting up all over the country."

He was pacing as he talked, his lean clever face electrically alive. He dropped in a chair beside Henry's. "Pug, you can't imagine what was going on before Eberstadt did this. Piecemeal insanity! Waste to frighten the gods! Ten thousand tank tracks, and no tanks to put them on! A football field full of airplane frames, without engines or controls even being manufactured! A hundred LCIs docked and rusting away, for want of winches to drop and raise the ramps! That awful time is over, and we can get the landing craft we need, but the Navy has to run a coherent show. That means one good man, a Ferdie Eberstadt, in charge. I've talked to Secretary Forrestal and to Vice

Admiral Patterson. They know your record. They're for you." Hopkins leaned back in his chair, spectacle frames to his mouth, his eyes twinkling. "Well, old top? Will you sign on the dotted line?"

The telephone on the card table rang. "Yes, Mr. President. Right away. As it happens, Pug Henry's here . . . Yes, sir. Of course." He hung up. "Pug, the boss will say hello to you."

They walked out into the dark book-lined hall and down a rubber-padded ramp toward the Oval Office. Hopkins took Pug's elbow. "What say? Shall I tell the President you're taking it on? There are a lot of Navy captains who can do Cincpac's staff work, you know that. There's only one Pug Henry who has a grasp of landing craft from A to Z."

Victor Henry had never before had a clash of wills with Hopkins. The great seal of the Presidency was in this man's pocket. Yet he was not the Commander-in-Chief, or he would be issuing orders, not cajoling. The affable insiders' talk, the flattery about Eberstadt, and now this arm-twisting were tactics of a powerful subordinate. Hopkins had taken it into his head to put him in landing craft, and the visit about Natalie had given him his opening. He probably did this sort of persuasion all the time. He was damned good at it, but Victor Henry meant to go to Cincpac. Hopkins's airy dismissal of that job was civilian talk. There were plenty of good men in the landing craft program, too.

They were walking past the Oval Office toward the open door of the President's bedroom. The President's rich resonant voice sounded hoarse today. Pug felt a touch of awe and affection at hearing Franklin Roosevelt's accents.

"Mr. Hopkins, this probably means the rest of my war service. Let me talk it over down at BuShips."

Harry Hopkins smiled. "Oke. I know they're all for it."

They entered the bedroom just as the President violently sneezed into a large white handkerchief. Rear Admiral McIntire, the President's physician, stood beside the bed in full uniform. He and several elderly civilians in the room chorused, "God bless you."

Pug recognized none of the civilians. They all stared at him, looking self-important, while McIntire, whom he had known in San Diego, gave him a slight nod. Wiping his reddened nose, the President glanced up blearily at Pug. He was sitting propped on cushions, wearing over wrinkled striped pajamas a royal blue cape, with *FDR* monogrammed on it in red. Picking pince-nez glasses off a breakfast tray, he said, "Well, Pug, how are you? Did you and Rhoda have a nice New Year?"

"Yes, thank you, Mr. President."

"Good. What were you and Harry cooking up just now? Where are you going next?"

It was an offhand polite question. The other men in the room were look-ing at Henry as at an interloper, like a Roosevelt grandchild who had wan-dered in. Despite the President's cold, which showed in his irritated nose and rheumy eyes, he had a gay air, a look of relish for the new day's busi-ness.

Victor Henry plunged, fearing Hopkins might overcommit him by speaking up first. "I'm not sure, Mr. President. Admiral Nimitz has requested my services as Deputy Chief of Staff for Operations."

"Oh, I see! Really!" The President arched his heavy brows at Hopkins. Clearly this was news to him. A shade of vexation flickered over Hopkins's face. "Well, then, that's where you'll go, I suppose. I certainly couldn't blame you for that. All the best."

Roosevelt rubbed his eyes with two fingers, and put on his glasses. This changed his aspect. He looked younger, more formidable, more the familiar President of the newspaper pictures, less an old man with mussed gray hair in bed with a cold. Obviously he was finished with Victor Henry, and ready to get on with his morning's work. He was turning toward the other men.

It was Pug who took the matter further, with a few words that haunted his memory always. There was a touch of disappointment in the President's reaction, a resigned acceptance of a naval officer's narrow human desire to promote his own career during a war, that stung him into saying, "Well, Mr. President, I'm always yours to command."

Roosevelt turned back to him with a surprised and charming smile. "Why, Pug, it's just that Admiral Standley really did feel he could use you in Moscow. I had another cable from him about you only yesterday. He has his hands full over there." The President's jaw lifted and stuck out. A formidable aspect came over him, as he straightened up under the cape. "We're fighting a very big war, you know, Pug. There's never been anything like it. The Russians are difficult allies, Heaven knows, perfectly awful to deal with sometimes, but they are tying down three and a half million German sol-diers. If they go on doing that, we'll win this war. If for some reason they don't, we may lose it. So if you can help out in Russia, and my man on the spot seems to think so, why, maybe that's where you should be."

The faces of the other men were turned to Victor Henry with mild curi-osity, but he was scarcely aware of them. There was only the sombre face of Roosevelt before him; the face of a man he had once known as a handsome Assistant Secretary of the Navy, scrambling up a destroyer's ladders like a boy; now the visible face of American history, the face of a worn old cripple.

"Aye aye, sir. In that case, I'll go from here to the Bureau of Personnel, and request those orders."

A pleased light came into the President's eyes. He held out his hand with a sweep of a long arm from under the cape, gesturing manly gratitude and admiration. It was all the reward Victor Henry ever got. When he thought about this scene in after years, it seemed enough. A love for President Roosevelt welled up in his heart as they shook hands. He tasted the acrid pleasure of sacrifice, and the pride of measuring up to the Commander-in-Chief's opinion of him.

"Good luck, Pug."

"Thank you, Mr. President."

A friendly nod and smile from Franklin Roosevelt, and Victor Henry was walking out of the bedroom, the course of his days turned and fixed. Hopkins, near the door, drily said, "So long, Pug." His eyes were narrow, his smile cool.

Rhoda jumped up as her husband walked into the living room. "Well? What's the verdict?"

He told her. At the way her face fell, Pug felt a passing throb of his old love for her, which only told him how nearly it was gone.

"Oh, dear, and I was so hoping for Washington. Was that what you wanted — Moscow again?"

"It's what the President wanted."

"That means a year. Maybe two years."

"It means a long time."

She took his hand, and twined her fingers in his. "Oh, well. We've had a lovely couple of weeks. When do you take off?"

"As a matter of fact, Rho"— Pug looked uncomfortable —"BuPers used some muscle and put me on the Clipper that leaves tomorrow."

"Tomorrow!"

"Dakar, Cairo, Tehran, Moscow. Admiral Standley really seems to want me there."

They drank their best wine at dinner, and fell into reminiscing about old times, about their many separations and reunions, retracing the years until they were back to the night when Pug proposed. Rhoda said, laughing, "Nobody can say you didn't warn me! Honestly, Pug, you talked on and on about how AWFUL it was to be a Navy wife. The separations, the poor pay, the periodic uprooting, the kowtowing to the wives of big brass, you reeled it all off. At one point, I SWEAR, I thought you were trying to talk me out of it. And I said to myself, 'Fat chance, mister! This was your idea, now you're HOOKED.' "

"I thought you should know what you were getting into."

"I've never regretted it." Rhoda sighed, and drank her wine. "It's such a pity. You'll miss Byron. That convoy should be getting here any day."

"I know. I don't like that much."

They were relaxed enough, and Rhoda was female enough, and it was near enough to the end, so that she couldn't resist adding, very casually, "And you'll miss Pamela Tudsbury."

He looked her straight in the eye. What they had never yet talked about suddenly lay, as it were, out on the table — his romance with Pamela, and her affair with Palmer Kirby, a name that had not crossed his lips, any more than Warren's had. "That's right. I'll miss Pamela."

Long seconds passed. Rhoda's eyes dropped.

"Well, if you can stand it, I've made an apple pie."

"Great. I won't get that in Moscow."

They went to bed early. The lovemaking was self-conscious and soon past, and Pug fell heavily asleep. After smoking a cigarette, Rhoda got up, put on a warm robe, and went downstairs to the living room. The album of records she pulled out from a low shelf was dusty. The record was scratched and slightly cracked, and the faded orange label was scrawled over with crayon, for at one point the kids had gotten at this album, and had played the records to death. The old recording was tinny and high-pitched, a ghostly voice from the distant past, coming weak and muffled through the worn surface:

> *It's three o'clock in the morning*
> *We've danced the whole night through*
> *And daylight soon will be dawning* •
> *Just one more waltz with you . . .*

She was back in the officers' club in Annapolis. Ensign Pug Henry, the Navy football star, was taking her to some big dance. He was much too short for her, but very sweet and somehow different, and crazily in love with her. It showed in his every word and look. Not handsome, but virile, and promising, and sweet. Irresistible, really.

> *That melody so entrancing*
> *Seems to be made for us two*
> *I could just keep right on dancing*
> *Forever dear with you.*

The antique jazz band sounded so thin and old-fashioned; the record ran out so fast! The needle scratched round and round and round, and Rhoda sat there staring dry-eyed at the phonograph.

PART FIVE

Pug and Pamela

56

PUG didn't miss Byron by much.

Two days after the Clipper left for the Azores on the first leg of his circuitous flight to Moscow, the destroyer *Brown* came steaming up-channel into New York harbor. Happy sailors crowded the flying bridge, hands jammed in the pockets of their pea jackets, feet stamping, breath smoking in eager ribald talk about shore leave. Byron stood apart from them in a heavy blue bridge coat, white silk muffler, and white peaked cap, staring up at the Statue of Liberty as the green colossus slid past, starkly lit by a clear cold midwinter sunrise. The crew were wary of this passenger officer. Because the wardroom was short-handed he had stood deck watches under way; a cool shiphandler who spoke little and smiled less while on the bridge. Joining the watch list had made Byron feel that he was getting back in the war, and the officers of the *Brown*, relieved of a grinding one-in-three, had gratefully treated him as one of themselves.

As the convoy scattered, the merchant vessels heading for the New Jersey shore or the sunlit skyscrapers of Manhattan, the screening ships toward Brooklyn, Byron impatiently jingled in a coat pocket a fistful of sweaty quarters. When the *Brown* tied up at a fueling dock, he was the first man down the gangway and into the lone telephone booth on the wharf. A queue of sailors was lined up at the booth by the time his call got through the State Department switchboard.

"Byron! Where are you? When did you get back?" Leslie Slote sounded hoarse and harried.

"Brooklyn Navy Yard. Just docked. What about Natalie and the kid?"

"Well —" at Slote's hesitation, Byron immediately felt sick, "— they're all right, and that's the main thing, isn't it? The fact is, they've been moved to Baden-Baden with those other Americans who were in Lourdes. Just temporarily, you understand, before they're all exchanged, and —"

"*Baden-Baden?*" Byron broke in. "You mean Germany? Natalie's in *Germany?*"

"Well, yes, but —"

"GOD ALMIGHTY!"

"Look, there are reassuring aspects to this. They're in a superb hotel, getting A-one treatment. The Brenner's Park. They're still classed as journalists, still in with diplomats, newspapermen, Red Cross workers, and such. Our chargé d'affaires who was in Vichy, Pinkney Tuck, heads the group. He's a top man. A Swiss diplomat is at the hotel, looking out for their rights. Also a German Foreign Ministry man and a French official. We're holding plenty of Germans that their government wants back very badly. It'll just be a haggling process."

"Are there any other Jews in that group?"

"I don't know. Now, I happen to be busy as hell, Byron. Phone me at home tonight, if you like." Slote gave him the number and hung up.

As Byron's white forbidding face passed through the wardroom full of officers dressed for going ashore, the raillery died. Alone in his cabin, folding uniforms into his footlocker, he tried to plan his next move, but he could scarcely think straight. If one brush with Germans on a French train had been too grim a risk for Natalie to take, what about now? She was in Nazi Germany, over the line, over on the other side! It was beyond imagining; she must be scared out of her mind. In Lisbon Slote had told a bloodcurdling tale of what was happening to the Jews, even claiming that he was returning to Washington to deliver evidence to President Roosevelt. Byron found the story beyond belief, a hysterical exaggeration of what was probably going on in Germany in the fog of war. He did not fear that his wife and son really risked being caught in a continent-wide process of railroading Jews to secret camps in Poland, where they would be gassed to death and their bodies burned up. That was a fairy tale; even Germans could not do such things.

But he did fear that their diplomatic protection might fail. They were illegal fugitives from Fascist Italy, and their journalist credentials were phony. If the Germans turned ugly, they might be singled out first for harsh treatment, among those Americans trapped in Baden-Baden. Louis might sicken or die from mistreatment; he was such a little thing! Byron left the *Brown* sunk in wretchedness.

Trudging through the Navy Yard with his footlocker, amid laborers thronging off their jobs for lunch, he decided that if he could locate Madeline, he would stay in New York overnight; then go to Washington, and from there fly to San Francisco, or to Pearl Harbor if the *Moray* had departed. But how to get hold of Madeline? His mother had written that she was back working for Hugh Cleveland, and had sent him an address on Claremont Avenue, just off the Columbia campus. He could drop his stuff at his old fraternity house, he figured, and spend the night there if he couldn't track her down. Since their parting in California, he had not heard from her.

The cab wound through Brooklyn, came out on the Williamsburg Bridge for another brilliant view of the skyscrapers, then plowed into the lower east side of Manhattan, where Jews in numbers were hustling along the sidewalks. His mind circled back to Natalie. She had struck him from the start as a sophisticated American, all the more alluring for a dusky spicy trace of Jewishness — to which she had never alluded in the old days except in self-mockery, or in contempt for Slote because he had allowed it to matter. Yet in Marseilles she had appeared overpowered, paralyzed, by her Jewishness. Byron could not understand. He took little account of race differences; he thought it was all bigoted nonsense, and his attitude toward the Nazi doctrines was one of incredulous contempt. He felt out of his depth in this thing, but the residue was anger and frustration at his stiff-necked wife, and scarcely endurable concern for his son.

The fraternity house had the same old dusty banners and trophies on the walls. The brick fireplace was piled as ever with cold wood ashes, fruit peelings, cigarette packages and butts, and over the mantel, the portrait of an early benefactor was much darkened by more years of wood smoke and tobacco fumes. As always, two collegians clicked away at the ping-pong table, watched as always by idlers on broken-down sofas; and as always blaring jazz shook the walls. Surprisingly callow and pimply high school boys seemed to have taken over the place. The spottiest of these introduced himself to Byron as the chapter president. He had obviously never heard of Byron, but the uniform impressed him.

"Hey," he bellowed up the stairs, "anybody using Jeff's room? Old grad here for overnight."

No answer. The spotty president ascended with Byron to a back bedroom where the same sepia picture of Marlene Dietrich hung, wrinkling and askew. The president explained that the occupant Jeff, about to flunk all his midterms, had abruptly joined the Marines. The wise-guy Columbia grin that went with this disclosure made Byron feel more at home.

One o'clock. No use trying to track down Madeline now, all those radio types would be out to lunch. Byron had stood the midwatch, and had stayed awake ever since. He set his alarm for three and stretched out on the dingy bed. The discordant crash and bleat of jazz did not keep him from falling fast asleep.

Cleveland, Hugh, Enterprises, Inc. 630 Fifth Avenue. The directory at the telephone under the staircase was a couple of years old, but he tried the number. A blithe girlish voice came on. "Program coordinator's office, Miss Blaine."

"Hello, I'm Madeline Henry's brother. Is she there?"

"You ARE? You're Byron, the submarine officer? Really?"

"That's right. I'm in New York."

"Oh, how terrif! She's at a meeting. Where can she reach you? She'll be back in an hour or so."

Byron gave her the number of the pay telephone, hunted up the spotty president through the smoke, and got his promise to take any message that came in. He escaped from the jazz din into the windy freezing street, where he heard very different music: the "Washington Post March." On South Field, blue-coated ranks of midshipmen were marching and counter-marching with rifles. In Byron's time the only marching on South Field had been for anarchic antiwar rallies. These fellows might be a year getting out to sea, Byron thought, and then months would pass before they could stand watch under way. This marching mass of unblooded reservists made him feel pretty good about his combat record; then he wondered, in his low frame of mind, what was so praiseworthy about repeated exposure to getting killed.

Why not walk to the *Prairie State,* scene of his own reserve training? Nothing else to do. He strode up Broadway, and over to the river on 125th Street. There was the old decommissioned battleship, tied up and swarming with midshipmen. The smells from the Hudson, the piping and loudspeaker announcements, deepened his nostalgia. On the *Prairie State,* in the long bull sessions at night, there had been so much talk of the kind of wife one wanted! Hitler and the Nazis then had been ludicrous figures in the newsreels; and the Columbia demonstrators had been signing pledges right and left not to fight in any wars. Natalie's predicament seemed, in the familiar scene at the foot of 125th Street, a dim incredible nightmare.

It occurred to Byron that he could go back to the fraternity house through Claremont Avenue, and slip a note under Madeline's door telling her where he was staying. He found the house, and pressed the outside call bell beside her name. The door buzzed in reply; so she was in! He opened the door, leaped up two flights of stairs, and rang her bell.

It is almost never a good idea to walk in on a woman without warning her: not a sweetheart, not a wife, not a mother, and certainly not a sister. Madeline, in a fluffy blue negligee, with her black hair down to her shoulders, looked out at him. Her eyes rounded and popped, and she exclaimed "EEK!" exactly as though he had come upon her naked, or as though he were a rat or a snake.

Before Byron could say anything, a deep rich male voice rumbled from inside, "What is it, honey?" Hugh Cleveland came in sight, nude to the waist, and below that clad in a flopping flowery lava-lava, scratching his hairy chest.

"It's *Byron,*" Madeline gasped. "How are you, Byron? My God, when did you get back?"

Fully as disconcerted as she was, Byron asked, "Didn't you get my message?"

"What message? No, nothing. Well, Jesus Christ, now that you're here, come in."

"Hi, Byron," said Hugh Cleveland, with the charming smile that showed all his big white teeth.

"Say, are you two married already?" Byron said, walking into a well-furnished living room where an ice bucket, a bottle of Scotch, and soda bottles stood on a table.

Cleveland and Madeline exchanged a look, and Madeline said, "Sweetie, how long will you be here, anyway? Where are you staying? Jesus Christ, why didn't you write or telephone or something?"

A door was open to a bedroom, and Byron could see a big rumpled double bed. Though abstractly he accepted the possibility that his sister was misbehaving, he literally did not believe his eyes. He said to Madeline, with clumsy blundering bluntness, "Madeline, come on, are you married, or what?"

Hugh Cleveland might have been well-advised to keep quiet at this point. But he smiled a big white smile, spread his hands, and rumbled warmly, "Look, Byron, we're all adults, and this is the twentieth century. So if you'll —"

Byron swiftly drew back his arm despite the bulk of his bridge coat, and crashed a fist into Cleveland's smiling face.

Madeline gave another "EEK!" louder and shriller than before. Cleveland went down like a poled ox, but he was not really knocked out, because he landed on his hands and knees, crawled about, and got up. As he did so his lava-lava fell off, and he was standing stark naked, with a sizable white paunch protruding over his spindly legs and private parts. This unprepossessing sight was quite eclipsed by the astounding transformation of his face. He looked like Dracula. All his upper front teeth were filed to sharp little points, with slightly longer fangs at either end.

"Jesus CHRIST, Hugh," Madeline cried out, "your teeth! Look at your *teeth!*"

Hugh Cleveland stumbled to a wall mirror, grinned at himself, and uttered an eerie wail. "Jethuth Chritht, my bridge! My porthelain bridge. It cotht me fifteen hundred fucking dollarth! Where the hell ith it?" He glanced wildly around the floor, turned on Byron and lisped in great indignation, "Why the hell did you thock me? How ridiculouth can you get? Let'th find that bridge, and damned fatht!"

"Oh, Hugh," Madeline said nervously, "put something on, for Heaven's sake, will you? You're prancing around naked as a jaybird."

Cleveland blinked down at his bare body, snatched the lava-lava, and fastened it on as he strode around searching the floor for his bridgework. Byron saw a white thing lying on the carpet under a chair. "Is this it?" he said, picking up the object and offering it to Cleveland. "Sorry I did that." Byron wasn't really very sorry, but the man was a pitifully idiotic sight with his sharpened-down tooth stumps, and the lava-lava carelessly dragging on his bulging belly.

"That'th it!" Cleveland went back to the mirror, and with two thumbs pressed the thing into his mouth. He turned around. "How's that, now?" He looked normal again, flashing the celebrated smile that Byron had seen in so many magazine advertisements of Cleveland's radio sponsor, a toothpaste company.

"Oh, heavens, that's better," said Madeline, "and Byron, you *apologize* to Hugh."

"I did," Byron said.

After grimacing at himself in the mirror and gnashing his teeth to test the fixity of the bridge, Cleveland turned to them. "Well, it's just a damned good thing it didn't break. I've got that U.S. Chamber of Commerce banquet tonight to toastmaster, and that reminds me, Mad, Arnold never did give me my thcript. What am I thuppothed to do if — oh, Chritht, there it goeth. It'th thlipping! I'm loothing it!" As he talked, Byron could indeed see the bridge come loose and drop out of his mouth. Cleveland lunged to catch it, stepped on the hem of the lava-lava, and fell on his face naked again, the flowery cloth pulling off and crumpling under him.

Madeline clapped her hand to her mouth and glanced at Byron, her wide eyes sparkling with their sense of fun shared since childhood. Hurrying to Cleveland, she spoke in tones of tender concern, "Are you hurt, honey?"

"Hurt? Thit, no." Cleveland got to his feet, the bridge clutched in his fingers, and strode to the bedroom, his plump white bottom waggling. "Thith ith damned theriouth, Mad. I'm calling my dentitht, and he better be in! I'm getting paid a thouthand buckth to be toathtmathter tonight. Thon of a bith!"

He slammed the door.

Picking up the lava-lava, Madeline snapped at Byron, "Oh, YOU! How could you be such an ANIMAL!"

Byron glanced around the room. "Honestly, what is this setup, Madeline? Does he live here with you?"

"What? How can he? He's got a family, stupid."

"Well, what are you doing then?" Pouting, she did not answer. "Mad, are you just having a toss now and then with this fat old guy? How is that possible?"

"Oh, you don't understand anything. Hugh is a friend, a dear good friend. You'll never know how good he's been to me, and what's more —"

"You're committing adultery, Mad."

A fleeting miserable look came and went on her face. Madeline flipped a hand, shook her head, and smiled a super-wise female smile. "Oh, you're so naïve. His marriage is better now than it was, MUCH better. And I'm a much better person. There's more than one way to live, Briny. You and I come from a family of fossils. I know Hugh would marry me if I pushed him, he's daffy about me, but —"

Half-dressed, Cleveland looked out of the bedroom and lisped loudly at Madeline that his dentist was driving in from Thcarthdale. "Call Tham right away. Tell him to get hith ath over here in ten minuteth. Chritht, what a meth!"

"Tham?" Byron said as Cleveland closed the door.

"Sam's his chauffeur," Madeline said, hurrying to a telephone and dialling. "Oh, Byron, are you disowning me? Can I cook you a dinner? Shall we get blind drunk tonight? Want to stay here? There's a spare room. When are you leaving? What's the news of Natalie? — Hello, hello, let me talk to Sam . . . Well, *find* him, Carol. Yes, yes, I KNOW my brother Byron's in town. Jesus Christ, do I know it . . . Never mind, just find Sam, and tell him to get the Cadillac over here in ten minutes flat."

She said as she hung up, "Byron, I've worked for Hugh for four years, and I didn't know he had bridgework."

"Live and learn, Mad."

"If the whole thing weren't so awful," she said, "and if you weren't such a disgusting neanderthal, it would be the funniest goddamned thing I've been through in my life." Her mouth was wrinkling, suppressing laughter. "I've nagged him for years to get rid of that horrible stomach. Look at you, now! Flat as a boy, just like Dad. Will you give your adulterous sister a kiss?"

"Lechery, lechery; still, wars and lechery; nothing else holds fashion," rails the sour Thersites. *"A burning devil take them!"*

Janice had some warning, so she was able to receive Byron in poised innocence; as Madeline could have done too, given half a chance.

When her father-in-law had passed through Honolulu, dissembling to him about her affair with Carter Aster had given her not a qualm. It was none of his business. No man could think like a woman about these things, least of all Captain Victor Henry, who wouldn't even play cards on Sunday. Frankness would have led only to embarrassment, and no possible useful purpose would have been served. But Byron's cable posed a problem to Janice.

Aster had told her that her brother-in-law would be reporting to the *Moray.* Byron was altogether a peculiar sort, fully as dashing as Warren, but with a sweetly idealistic attitude toward women which could prove a nuisance. His moral views seemed as narrow as his father's. His tale about the girl in Australia had been all but incredible, but Janice had believed it. What would have been the point of a lie that made him out a prudish simpleton?

Yet, when a war was on, when men were far from home and lonely, when everywhere there was great activity in what Aster robustly called "unauthorized ass" — a phrase that much amused Janice, though she pretended to bridle at it — why should Byron have denied himself a natural and beautiful relationship? The Aster affair had sprung up more or less accidentally. After Midway an attack of dengue fever had laid her low, and Carter Aster had visited her every day and had seen to her needs of food and medicine, and one thing had led to another.

She knew that Byron would be scandalized if he found out. Janice didn't understand that side of Byron; he was damned different from his brother. She regarded his prudishness as a quaint minor foible, and she certainly did not want to disillusion or estrange him. She considered herself a Henry, she liked that family better than her own, and she had always found Byron a very attractive man. It was wonderful to have him around.

So as Aster was getting dressed to return to the submarine late one night, Janice decided to take things in hand. She was smoking a cigarette in bed, nude under a sheet.

"Byron's due in the morning, honey."

"He is?" Aster paused in pulling on khaki trousers. "So soon? How do you know that?"

"He cabled me from San Francisco. He's getting a ride on NATS."

"Well, great! It's high time. We need him aboard."

It was past midnight. Aster never stayed till morning. He liked to be up and about on the submarine at reveille; also, he was tender of Janice's reputation, living as she did in a row of houses with early-rising neighbors. Janice loved Aster, or at least loved her hours with him, but she wanted nothing permanent with him. He had nothing like Warren's breadth, he read trash, and his talk was pure Navy. He reminded her of the many Pensacola pilots who had bored her before Warren had come along. Aster was an able naval engineer, with an urge to excel and to kill, born for submarining. And he was a considerate and satisfying lover; the perfect partner for unauthorized ass, so to say, but not much more. If Aster sensed her qualified regard for him, he wasn't complaining.

"The point is, dear," Janice said, "that hanky-panky has to be out for a while." He gave her a cool inquiring look, tucking in his shirt. "I mean, you know Byron. I love him dearly. I don't want him getting all upset and disapproving. I can't have it."

"Now let me understand you. Are you calling it off?"

"Oh, would you mind, all that much?"

"Hell, yes, I'd mind, Janice."

"Well, don't look so tragic. Smile."

"Why does Byron have to know?"

"When you're in port, he'll be spending nights here."

"He'll have the duty every other night."

"Yes, I suppose he will. All the same —"

Aster came to the bed, sat down, and gathered her in his arms.

After a breathless few kisses she murmured, "Well, we'll see, we'll see. One thing, Carter. Byron must never, *never* find out. Understand?"

"Sure," Aster said. "No need for it."

The morning he arrived Byron stayed only long enough to have breakfast, then went on to the submarine; but in that short time he unburdened with frank and deep bitterness of heart the gist of what had happened in Marseilles. The news that Natalie and her baby were caught in Germany horrified Janice. Automatically she defended what her sister-in-law had done, and tried to reassure Byron that it would all turn out well. But she feared Natalie was doomed. Watching him play with Vic in the garden before he left, she had to exert willpower not to cry. The instant mutual magnetism between the uncle and the child was poignant to behold. When Byron said he had to go, Victor clung to him with arms and legs as he had never done with Warren.

The *Moray* stayed around Pearl Harbor for several more weeks, most of the time out at sea in the training areas. When the submarine came into port Byron spent every other night at Janice's cottage. The first time he remained aboard, Aster telephoned. Janice did not know what to do. She told him to come over, but not until after little Vic was asleep in bed. His visit was a failure. She was uneasy, Aster quickly discerned it, and after a couple of drinks he left without touching her. She saw him only once after that before the *Moray* left on patrol. When Byron told her that they were sailing in the morning, she said, "Oh! Well, why don't you ask Carter to come to dinner, then? He's been awfully kind to me and Vic."

"That's nice of you, Jan. Can he bring a girl?"

"If he wants to, sure."

Aster brought no girl. The three of them dined by candlelight, drinking a lot of wine and working up to a jolly mood. Byron's spirits were improving with his return to submarine duty. Aster's correct mixture of informality and aloofness won Janice's gratitude. At one point they turned on the radio for the war news, and heard that the Germans had at last surrendered at Stalingrad. They opened another bottle of wine on that.

"There go the Krauts," Byron said, lifting his glass, "and none too soon." To his wine-flushed mind, this news signalled the early deliverance of his family.

"Damn right. Now we get the Japs," said Aster.

When the evening was over and Janice was left alone, her head reeled with wine, and she was feeling in delighted girlish confusion that the death of her husband was behind her, and that she truly loved two men.

*   *   *

57

𝕲lobal 𝖂aterloo 𝖄: 𝕾talingrad

(from World Holocaust by Armin von Roon)

TRANSLATOR'S NOTE: *General von Roon's discussion of Stalingrad concludes the strategic analysis section of* World Holocaust. *The original book sketches all campaigns and battles to the end of the war. But as it happens, this subsequent ground is covered briefly, and with much more anecdotal interest, in the epilogue to Roon's magnum opus: a personal memoir of his dealings with Adolf Hitler called "Hitler as Military Leader." This gives interesting glimpses of the Führer in decay during the mounting collapse of Germany on all fronts. My translation continues with excerpts from the memoirs, adding only Roon's essay on the Battle of Leyte Gulf.*

I have taken some liberties with Roon's writing on Stalingrad. Seen in isolation, the battle was a senseless five-month grinding of whole German armies to hamburger in a remote industrial town on the Volga. One needs the context of the 1942 summer campaign to grasp what happened there. But Roon's Case Blue analysis is so fogged with names of Russian cities and rivers, and with German army movements, that American readers cannot get through it. So I have inserted some passages of "Hitler as Military Leader" to illuminate the picture, employing only the words of Armin von Roon, and I have tried to cut out as many confusing technical and geographical references as possible. — V.H.

Stalingrad fulfilled on the battlefield Spengler's prophetic vision of the decline of the West. It was the Singapore of Christian culture.

The true tragedy of Stalingrad is that it need not have happened. The West had the strength to prevent it. It was not like the fall of Rome, or of Constantinople, or even of Singapore: not a world-historical crushing of a weak culture by a stronger one. On the contrary! We of the Christian West, had we but been united, could readily have repulsed the barbaric Scythians out of the steppes in their new guise of Marxist predators. We could have pacified Russia for a century and changed its essential menacing nature.

But this was not to be. Franklin Delano Roosevelt's one war aim was to destroy Germany so as to win unimpeded rule of the world for American monopoly capital. Rightly he perceived that England was finished. As for the menace of Bolshevism he was either blind to it, or saw no way to eradicate it, and decided that Germany was the competitor he could destroy.

The great Hegel has taught us that it is irrelevant to challenge the morality of world-historical individuals. Morally, if one values the Christian civilization now being swamped by Marxist barbarism, Franklin Roosevelt was unquestionably one of mankind's archcriminals. But in military history, one regards only how well the political aim of a war leader was achieved. However shortsighted Roosevelt's aim, he certainly achieved the destruction of Germany.

Sunset Glow

Our second great assault on the Soviet Union, called "Case Blue,"* led to Stalingrad. It was an insightful concept, it was mainly Hitler's, and it came close to success. Hitler himself ruined it.

The contrast of Franklin Delano Roosevelt and Adolf Hitler in their warmaking is altogether Plutarchian. Spidery calculation versus all-out gambling; steadfast planning versus impulsive improvising; careful use of limited armed strength versus prodigal dissipation of overwhelming strength; prudent reliance on generals versus reckless overruling of them; anxious concern for troops versus impetuous outpouring of their lives; a timid dip of a toe in combat versus total war with the last reserves thrown in; such was the contrast between the two world opponents as they at last came to grips in 1942, nine years after they both took power.

In retrospect the world sees Hitler as the disgusting 1945 figure in the bunker: Roosevelt's trapped victim, a distintegrating, trembling, unrepentant horror lost in dreams, maintaining his grip on a prostrate Reich by sheer terror. But this was not the Hitler of July 1942. Then he was still our all-masterful FÜHRER: a remote, demanding, difficult warlord, but the ruler of an empire unmatched by those of Alexander, Caesar, Charlemagne, and Napoleon. The glow of German victory lit the planet. Only in retrospect do we see that it was a sunset glow.

Case Blue

Case Blue was a summer drive to end the war in the east.

Our great 1941 drive, Barbarossa, had aimed to destroy the Red Army

*The code name was altered to *Braunschweig* (Brunswick) during the campaign. This translation retains "Blue" throughout. — V.H.

and shatter the Bolshevik state in one grand three-pronged summer campaign. We had tried to do too much at once. We had hurt the enemy, but the Russian is a stolid fatalist, with an animal ability to resist and endure. The Japanese unwillingness to attack Siberia — duly reported to Stalin by his spy Sorge from our embassy in Tokyo — had enabled the Red dictator to denude his Asian front and hurl fresh divisions of hardy brutish Mongol troops at us. These winter counterattacks, though halting us in the snows outside Moscow, had petered out. When the spring thaw came we still held an area of the Soviet Union roughly analogous to the entire U.S.A. east of the Mississippi. Who can doubt that under such an occupation the flighty Americans would have collapsed? But the Russians are a different breed, and they needed one more convincing blow.

Case Blue carried forward Barbarossa in its southern phase. The aim was to seize southern Russia for its agricultural, industrial, and mineral wealth. The theme was limited and clear: *Hold in the north and center, win in the south.* Granted that Hitler's continental mentality could not grasp the Mediterranean strategy, it was the next best thing to do. We were in it, and we had to attack. Moreover, it did not appear that we could fight the war to a finish without the Caucasus oil.

Under all the muddled political verbiage of Hitler's famous Directive Number 41, rewritten by his own hand from Jodl's professional draft, the governing concepts of Case Blue were:

1. Straighten out the winter penetrations;
2. Hold fast, north and center, on the Leningrad–Moscow–Orel line;
3. Conquer the south to the Turkish and Iranian borders;
4. Take Leningrad, and possibly Moscow;
5. The main objectives in Russia thus achieved, if the enemy still fights on, fortify the eastern line from the Gulf of Finland to the Caspian Sea, and go on the defensive against an emasculated foe.

Essentially then, the original Barbarossa goal now shifted to a slanting Great Wall of fortified positions from the Gulf of Finland to the great Baku oil fields on the Caspian, sealing off our "Slavic India." Other vital benefits, if the campaign succeeded, would be cutting off Lend-Lease via the Persian Gulf, tilting Turkey to our side, and denying our enemies Persian oil. An advance to India might even be in the offing, if all went well, or a northward sweep east of the Volga to take Moscow from the rear. Admittedly, this was adventurous policy. We had failed once, and were trying again with weaker forces. But Russia was weakened, too. The whole grandiose drive of the German people under Hitler for world empire was only a pyramiding of gambles.

If only we could change the war balance by seizing Russia's wheat and oil, and then stabilize the eastern front, two political solutions of the war could open up: an Anglo-Saxon change of heart at the prospect of facing our full fury, or a realistic peace by Stalin. Roosevelt's fear of such a separate eastern peace governed all his war-making. And Stalin remained suspicious to the end that the plutocracies were planning to leave him in the lurch. It was uncertain right up to our surrender whether the bizarre alliance of our foes would not fall apart.

Why in fact did the Americans and British never grasp that only by letting us win against Russia could the world flood of Bolshevism be stemmed? Churchill at least wanted to land in the Balkans to forestall Stalin in middle Europe. If this was bad strategy, because we were too strong and the terrain too difficult, it was at least alert politics. Roosevelt would have none of it. Since he could not annihilate us, he wanted to help the Bolsheviks to do it. So he sacrificed Christian Europe to American monopoly capital for a brief gluttonous feast, at the price of a new dark age now fast falling on the world.

Answers to Critics of Blue

After every war, the armchair strategists and the history professors have their pallid fun, telling those who bled in battle how they should have done it. Certain shallow criticisms of Case Blue have been repeated until they have taken on a false aura of fact. Stalingrad was a great and fatal turn in world history, and the record leading up to it should be clear.

Strategically, Blue was a good plan.

Tactically, Blue went awry, because of Hitler's day-to-day interference.

Critics carp that the one acceptable objective of a major campaign is the destruction of the enemy's armed forces. In the summer of 1942 Stalin had concentrated his armies around Moscow, assuming we would try to end the war by smashing the bulk of his forces and occupying the capital. Our critics assert we should have done so. This would indeed have been orthodox strategy. By striking south we achieved massive surprise. That too is orthodox strategy.

TRANSLATOR'S NOTE: *Russian sources bear out Roon. Stalin was so positive that the attack in the south was a feint to draw off Moscow's defenses, and he hung on to this idea so long, that only Hitler's botch of the tactics saved Stalingrad, and possibly the Soviet Union. — V.H.*

We are also told that the strategic aim of Case Blue was *economic,* and therefore wrong. One must destroy the enemy's armed force, then one can do as one pleases with his wealth; so the banal admonition goes. These critics miss the whole point of Blue. It was a plan to enforce a *gigantic land blockade of the poor but governing north rump of the Soviet Union,* by depriving it of food, fuel, and heavy industry. Blockade, if one can enforce it, is a tedious but tested way to humble an enemy. When Blue was planned, the Japanese were running wild in the Pacific and in Southeast Asia. We assumed that they would neutralize the United States for a year or more. Alas, the stunning early turnabouts at Midway and Guadalcanal freed Roosevelt to flood Lend-Lease aid to the Russians in 1942, past our blockade. That made a powerful difference.

Finally, critics contend that Blue's double objective, Stalingrad and the Caucasus, required a stretching out of the southern front far beyond the capacity of the Wehrmacht to hold it, so that the outcome of the campaign was foredoomed.

But Stalingrad was not an objective of Case Blue. It became Hitler's objective when he lost control of himself in September.

Strategy of Case Blue

Near Stalingrad, the rivers Don and Volga converge in a very striking way. The two great bends point their *V*'s at each other over a forty-mile space of dry land. The first phase of Blue called for capture of this strategic land bridge, so as to block attacks from the north on our southern invasion forces; also, to cut the Volga as a supply route of fuel and food to the north.

At the *V* of the Volga, a medium-sized industrial town straggled along the bluffs of the west bank: *Stalingrad.* We did not need to occupy it, we needed merely to neutralize it with bombardment in order to dominate the bottleneck. Our general plan was to thrust two heavy fast-moving pincers along the two arms of the enormous *V* of the Don, thus trapping and destroying most of the Soviet forces defending south Russia. The first pincer, the Volga Force — jumping off first, since it had the longer distance to go — would march down the upper arm of the Don. The second, the Caucasus Force, would advance along the lower arm. They would meet between the rivers, near Stalingrad. After defeating and mopping up the trapped forces, these two great army groups would divide responsibilities for the second or conquest phase. The Caucasus Force would wheel south, cross the Don, and drive down to the Black Sea, to the Caspian, and through the high passes to the borders of Turkey and Iran. The Volga Force would defend the dangerous flank opened up all along the Don, which would be manned during our advance by three satellite armies: Hungarian, Italian, and Rumanian.

Here was the weak link in Blue, and we knew it. But we had already lost nearly a million men in the war, and we were near the limit of German manpower. We had to use these auxiliaries on the flanks while the Wehrmacht struck ahead. But we did not plan that they should man the Don against a full assault by the Red Army. That happened only because the Führer lost his head, and disrupted the timetable of the campaign.

TRANSLATOR'S NOTE: *In editing Roon, I have omitted Manstein's conquest of the Crimea and Sevastopol, and the failure of Timoshenko's May attack against Kharkov. These big German victories weakened Russia in the south, making Blue a much more promising operation. I have called "Army Group A" Caucasus Force, and "Army Group B" Volga Force. The technical Wehrmacht designations are hard to follow, especially as regroupings occurred in mid-campaign. — V.H.*

•   •   •

(From "Hitler as Military Leader")

What Went Wrong

. . . Supreme Headquarters is an edgy place during a campaign. One waits in a map room for developments, day after day. The war seems to drag and drag. Out in the field is reality: hundreds of thousands of men marching over fields and through cities, moving masses of equipment, coming under fire. In Headquarters one sees the same faces, the same walls, the same maps, one eats in the same place with the same elderly tired men in uniform. The atmosphere is strained and quiet, the air stale. There is a remoteness and abstraction about this nerve center of the war. The perpetual tension of deferred hope gnaws at the heart.

At our advance headquarters at Vinnitsa in the Ukraine all this was doubly true. "Werewolf," as Hitler named the installation, was a crude compound of log cabins and wooden huts in the open pine country near the southern River Bug. Socially, there was no relief. Physically, we could go splash in the slow muddy river, if we cared to expose our naked skins to clouds of stinging insects. The weather was blazing hot and sticky, too much so for Hitler even to walk his dog, his only exercise.

We moved there in mid-July, at the height of the campaign. Hitler did not take the heat well, strong sunlight bothered him, and altogether it was an uncomfortable situation. His digestion was worse than ever, his flatulence a trial for everybody in a room with him. Even the dog, Blondi, was out of sorts and whiny.

But even before that, while we were still in our cooler and more comfortable compound in the East Prussian woods, he had already shown signs of strain and instability, by his drastic change of plan for the Caucasus Force and for the Fourth Panzer Army. . . .

・   ・   ・

(From *World Holocaust*)

The faltering of Blue can be dated precisely to the thirteenth of July.

Hitler's anxiety had been mounting day by day. He could not understand why we were not hauling in the hordes of prisoners that our great enveloping movements had yielded in 1941. Whether Stalin had learned at last not to order his troops to stand fast and be captured; or whether the southern armies were fading away before us in undisciplined rout; or whether the front was just weakly manned; or whether, finally, the Russians were resorting to their classic tactic of trading space for time, the fact was we were capturing Russians in the tens of thousands, instead of the hundreds of thousands.

On July 13, Hitler suddenly decided to divert the *entire eastward campaign away from the Stalingrad land bridge, southwest toward Rostov!* Thus he hoped, by a tighter enveloping move, to bag a supposed enormous Red Army force in the Don bend. The whole Caucasus Force wheeled off on this mission. He even peeled off the Volga Force's panzer army, the doughty Fourth, and sent it clanking toward Rostov, too, although Halder bitterly opposed piling so much armor against one minor objective. The Volga Force slowed to a standstill, very low on gasoline, for the main supplies had to go to this adventure of catching Russians.

The huge power thrust captured Rostov and netted some forty thousand prisoners. But precious time had been lost, and the whole Blue plan was in disarray. The Caucasus Force and the Fourth Army were milling around Rostov, choking the transit arteries, and creating unimaginable difficulties in improvised organization and supply.

At this critical point Adolf Hitler sprang on our stupefied Headquarters his notorious and catastrophic Directive Number 45, perhaps the worst military orders ever issued. It abrogated the Blue plan altogether. A responsible General Staff would have analyzed, war-gamed, and organized such an operation for months, or even for a year. Hitler airily scrawled it all out in a day or two, and so far as I know, all by himself. If Jodl helped him with it, he never boasted of it!

In essence, Directive Number 45 consisted of three points:

1. A mere *assertion* (contrary to known fact) that the first aim of the campaign had been achieved: i.e., that the Red Army in the south had been "largely destroyed."

2. The Volga Force was to resume the drive toward Stalingrad, with the Fourth Panzer Army rejoining it.
3. The Caucasus Force under List was to proceed southward at once, with additions to its original difficult task, such as securing the entire Black Sea coast.

This was Hitler's last attack directive. It was at this point that we at Supreme Headquarters began to lose heart, though in the field things still looked rosy. Halder, the Army Chief of Staff, was scandalized. He noted in his diary — and he said baldly to me — that these orders no longer bore any resemblance to military realities.

The *conditions* for carrying out our summer campaign in any reasonable form had now melted away. Neither the upper bend of the Don, nor the crucial land bridge, had been secured. The Caucasus Force, the lower pincer of the Don phase, had been scheduled to move south *only* when the Don flank stretching to Stalingrad was secure. Now the two great forces were to separate and operate in different directions with unsecured flanks — leaving a constantly widening gap between them as they pursued diverse missions!

Moreover, the Blue plan had called for Manstein's Eleventh Army, which had conquered the Crimea and captured Sevastopol, to cross to the Caucasus and support List in his drive. But Hitler, in his glee at the capture of Rostov, had decided that things were going too well in the south to waste Manstein there; and *he had ordered Manstein to take most of his army eleven hundred miles north to attack Leningrad!*

Hitler's numbered directives end with Number 51, dated late in 1943; but in fact, after this fatal Number 45, they trail off in defensive measures. This was his final wielding of the initiative. Lack of experience, and the strain of arrogating to himself all the political and military authority of Germany, had told at last on a high-strung temperament, a very adept mind, and a fearsome will. The order was madness. Yet only in our innermost HQ councils was the picture clear in all its folly. The Wehrmacht obeyed, and marched off into the remotest depths of southern Russia on two separate roads to its sombre fate.

Arrival at Stalingrad

With awesome inevitability, the tragedy now began to unfold.

The Caucasus Force performed wonders, marching across vast steppes blazing with midsummer heat, climbing to the peaks of snowcapped mountain ranges, investing the Black Sea coast, and actually sending patrols as far as the Caspian Sea. But it fell short of its objectives. What Hitler had ordered was beyond its manpower, its firepower, and its logistical support. The force stood still for as much as ten days at a time, for want of gasoline, and of supply trucks to bring up the fuel. At one point, with true Greek irony, gasoline was even being brought to the Caucasus Force on the backs of camels! List's great armies stalled in the mountains, harried by elusive tough Red units, and unable to advance.

Meanwhile, on August 23 the Volga Force, driving on toward Stalingrad, reached the riverbank north of the city, and the neutralization phase began with heavy air and artillery bombardment. Resistance was at first meager. For a day or two it looked as though Stalingrad might fall to a *coup de main*. But it did not happen. We were at a far stretch ourselves, and Stalingrad held against the first shock.

TRANSLATOR'S NOTE: *These dry words of Roon scarcely convey the reality as the Russians saw it.*

The advance of the Sixth Army on Stalingrad was apparently the most terrifying event of what the Russians call the Great Patriotic War. The army commanders, the populace, and Stalin himself were astounded at this renewed powerful thrust of the Germans into the vitals of their country. The August twenty-third bombardment was one of the most horrible ordeals by fire the Russians ever endured. Some forty thousand civilians were killed. The flaming streets of the town literally "ran with blood." All communication with Moscow was cut off. For several hours Josef Stalin believed that Stalingrad had fallen. But though the city was to undergo one of the worst punishments in the history of warfare thereafter, that was the low point.

Most military writers conclude that if Hitler had not interfered with the Blue plan, the Volga Force would have reached the river weeks earlier, while Stalin was still under the delusion that the southern attack was a feint. Stalingrad would have fallen, a fruit of the massive initial surprise, and the whole war might have gone differently. Hitler disembowelled the Blue campaign by the diversion to Rostov. — V.H.

Catastrophe at Stalingrad

As previously stated, the capture of Stalingrad was *not* a military necessity.

Our aim was to take the land bridge between the rivers, and to deny the Soviets the use of the Volga as a supply route. Now we were at the Volga. All we had to do was invest the city and bombard it to rubble. After all, we invested Leningrad for more than two years. About a million Russians fell in Leningrad streets from starvation, and for all intents and purposes of the war, the city was a withered corpse. There was no *military* reason not to treat Stalingrad the same way.

But there was increasing *political* reason. For as the Caucasus Force came to a halt in the wild mountain passes despite all Hitler's savage urging; as Rommel stalled at El Alamein, failed in two assaults, and at last underwent the grinding assault of the British; as the RAF increased its barbaric fire raids on our cities, slaughtering thousands of innocent women and children and pulverizing important factories; as our U-boat losses suddenly and alarmingly shot up; as the Americans landed in North Africa with world-shaking political effect; as all these chickens came home to roost, and Adolf Hitler's great summer flush of triumph waned, and the first cracks in his gigantic imperium appeared, the embattled Führer felt a more and more desperate need for a prestige victory to turn all this around.

STALINGRAD!

STALINGRAD, bearing the name of his strongest foe! STALINGRAD, symbol of the Bolshevism he had fought all his life! STALINGRAD, a city appearing more and more in world headlines as a pivot of the war!

The capture of Stalingrad became for Adolf Hitler an unbelievably violent obsession. His orders in the ensuing weeks were madness compounded and recompounded. The Sixth Army, which with its mobile striking power had won an unbroken string of victories in Poland, France, and Russia, was fed division by division into the meat grinder of Stalingrad's ruined streets, where mobile tactics were impossible. Slav snipers mowed down the veterans of the great Sixth in a house-to-house "rat war." The Russian General Staff poured in defenders across the Volga to keep up this annihilation, while methodically preparing a stupendous counterstroke against the weak satellite armies on the Don flank. For Josef Stalin had finally grasped that Hitler, with his obsessive cramming of his finest divisions into the Moloch-maw of Stalingrad, was giving him a glorious opportunity.

Late in November the blow fell. The Red Army hurtled across the Don into the Rumanian army, guarding the flank of the Volga Force, northwest of Stalingrad. These unwarlike auxiliaries gave way like cheese to a knife. A similar attack routed the Rumanian flank corps in our Fourth Panzer Army, on the southern flank. As the attack developed into December, the Russians smashed into our lines all along the Don where Italians and Hungarians were protecting the Sixth Army's rear; and a steel trap closed on three hundred thousand German soldiers, the flower of the Wehrmacht.

· · ·

(From "Hitler as Military Leader".)

Transformation of Hitler

. . . As it happened, I was away from Supreme Headquarters during much of this trying period, on a long inspection tour. When I left late in August, all was going well enough in Russia. Both forces were advancing rapidly on their diverging fronts; the Red Army still seemed to be fading away, taking no advantage of the great gap opening up in our line; and Hitler, though understandably tense and nervous, and suffering dreadfully from the heat, seemed in good spirits.

I returned to find a shocking change at Werewolf. Halder was gone, fired. Nobody had relieved him. General List of the Caucasus Force had been fired. Nobody had relieved him, either. Hitler had assumed both posts!

Adolf Hitler was now not only head of the German State, head of the Nazi Party, and Supreme Commander of the armed forces; he was now his own Army Chief of Staff, and he was in direct command of the Caucasus Force, stymied six hundred miles away in the mountains. And this was not a nightmare; it was all really happening.

Hitler was not speaking to Jodl, his erstwhile pet and confidant. He was not speaking to anybody. He was taking his meals alone, spending most of his time in a darkened room, brooding. At his formal meetings with the staff, secretaries came and went in relays, writing down every word; and it was with these secretaries and nobody else that Hitler was conversing. The break with the army was complete.

Gradually I pieced together what had happened. Halder's objections to Hitler's senseless pressing of the Stalingrad attack had at last resulted in his summary dismissal in September; and so the last level head among us, the one senior staff officer who for years would talk up to Hitler, was gone.

As for the pliable Jodl, the Führer had sent him by plane to the Caucasus Force, to urge General List to resume the advance at all cost. But Jodl had come back and, for once in his life, had told Hitler the truth — that List could not advance until logistics improved. Hitler had turned nasty; Jodl, in an amazing burst of spirit, had rounded on his master, reeling off all Hitler's orders which had led to this impasse. The two men had ended screeching at each other like washerwomen, and thereafter Jodl had been barred from the great man's presence.

It was several days before I was summoned to appear at a briefing. I was quite prepared, even at the cost of my head, to give my report on the bad state of Rommel's supply. As it happened, Hitler did not call on me to speak. But I will never forget the glance he fixed on me when I first entered the room. Gray-faced, red-eyed, slumped in his chair with his head sunk between his shoulders, holding one trembling hand with the other, he was searching my face for the nature of my news, for a ray of optimism or hope. What he saw displeased him. He gave me a menacing glare, uncovering his teeth, and turned away. I was looking at a cornered animal. I realized that he knew in his heart that he had botched the Blue campaign, thrown away Germany's last chance, and lost the war; and that from all quarters of the globe, the hangmen were approaching with the rope.

But it was not in his nature to admit mistakes. All we heard, in the dreadful weeks that dragged on until the Sixth Army surrendered — and indeed until he shot himself in the bunker in 1945 — was how we generals had failed him; how Bock's delay at Voronezh had lost Stalingrad; how incompetent List was; how battle nerves had incapacitated Rommel; and so on without end. Even when the Stalingrad pocket, cut to pieces, began surrendering piecemeal, all he could think of was to promote Paulus to Field Marshal; and when Paulus failed to kill himself rather than surrender, he threw one of his worst fits of rage. That ninety thousand of his best soldiers were going into captivity; that more than two hundred thousand more had been hideously lost for his sake; all that meant nothing to the man. Paulus had failed to show proper gratitude for promotion, by blowing his brains out. That upset Hitler.

• • •

(From *World Holocaust*)

Post Mortem

Hitler would never allow the Sixth Army its one chance, which was to fight its way out to the west; either early in the entrapment, when it might have broken out by itself, or in December, when Manstein at the head of the newly formed Don Force battled his way through the snow to within thirty-five miles of a join-up. Not once would he give Paulus permission to break out. The screeching refrain that echoed through Headquarters until Paulus surrendered was, "*I won't leave the Volga!*"

He kept prating of "Fortress Stalingrad," but there was no "fortress," only a surrounded and shrinking army. He boasted in a national broadcast, late in October, that he had actually captured Stalingrad, and was reducing pockets of resistance at leisure because "he did not want another Verdun," and time was of no consequence. Thus he burned his public bridges, condemning the Sixth Army to stand and die.

Some military analysts now lay the disaster to Göring, who promised to supply the trapped Sixth Army at a rate of seven hundred tons of supplies a day. The Luftwaffe effort never reached two hundred tons, and Göring blamed the bad weather. Of course Göring's promise was just a jig to his master's tune. They were old comrades-in-arms. He knew what Hitler wanted him to say, so he said it, and condemned large numbers of Luftwaffe pilots to useless deaths. Hitler never reproached Göring for this. He wanted to stay at the Volga until tragedy befell, and Göring's transparent lie helped him to do it.

Jodl testified at Nuremberg that as early as November Hitler privately admitted to him that the Sixth Army was done for; still it had to be sacrificed to protect the retreat of the armies in the Caucasus. What balderdash! A fighting retreat from Stalingrad would have made far more sense. But the propagandist in Hitler sensed that a heartrending drama of a lost army might rally the people to him, whereas an ignominious swallowing of his boasts with a retreat would sully his prestige. On some such reasoning, he sacrificed a superb striking arm of battle-hardened veterans which could never be replaced.

Roosevelt Triumphant

Franklin Roosevelt's proclamation at this time of the slogan "Unconditional Surrender," at the Casablanca conference in January, was in every way a masterstroke. Critics of the slogan — including the august General Eisenhower — fail to understand what Roosevelt accomplished with this thunderous stroke; which, with his usual guile, he passed off as a casual remark at a press conference.

In the first place, he drove home to the entire world, and above all to the German people, the fundamental fact that we were now losing the war. The entire Global Waterloo turnabout was crystallized in those two simple words. This was in itself a stunning propaganda success.

Secondly, he publicly signalled to Stalin an Anglo-American pledge against a negotiated peace in the west. No doubt Stalin remained skeptical, but it was as loud and powerful a commitment as Roosevelt could give him.

Third, Roosevelt reassured the wavering nations like Turkey and Spain, and the subject peoples all over Europe, and the ever-veering Arabs, that the Western powers would not relax at the turn of the tide in Russia, and allow Bolshevism to sweep the continent and the Middle East.

Fourth, he gave his own spoiled and soft nation, in its first moment of success against us, a clear and simple war aim, which appealed to its naïve psychology, and discouraged notions of a short war or a compromise peace.

It is objected that the German people were stiffened to resist to the last under Hitler's leadership; that Roosevelt should have appealed over his head to them and to the army to topple the Nazi regime and make an honorable peace. This objection shows fatuous ignorance of what the Third Reich really was.

Hitler had made Germany over in the only form he ever wanted; a system of headless structures, including the army, with all power concentrated in himself. *There was nobody to topple the Nazis. There was nobody to appeal to.* Our national destiny was bound up with this man. This had been the one aim of all his actions since attaining power, and this he achieved.

He was Germany. The armed forces were pledged to him with their sacred honor. The assassination attempt that failed in July 1944 was witless and traitorous. I took no part in it, and I have never regretted that decision. It should have been plain to every general, as it was to me, that to order men to die in the field for a Leader, and then to murder this same Leader (however unsatisfactory he might be) was a betrayal of principle.

More than once, at bad moments in Headquarters, I thought of how relatively easy it would be for one of us to shoot Hitler. But he knew he could rely on two pillars in the German character: Honor and Duty.

The German people were in a tragic trap of history, condemned to fight for two and a half more fearful years, simply to keep alive the Head of State who had led them to destruction. Too late did we learn the fatal mistake of the *Führerprinzip*. A monarch can sue for peace and preserve his nation's honor and stability in defeat, as the Japanese emperor did. A dictator who fails in war is only a beleaguered usurper, who must fight on to the last like Shakespeare's Macbeth, wading ever deeper in blood.

Hitler could not step down; and none of the Nazis could step down. Their secret massacres of the Jews had rendered that impossible. "Unconditional Surrender" made not the slightest difference either to them or to the German people. Nothing could now sunder Hitler and the Germans, and put an end to the war, but *Götterdämmerung*.

TRANSLATOR'S NOTE: *General von Roon's operational sketch of the fate of the Caucasus Force, which follows the Stalingrad account, he calls "Epic Anabasis of Army Group A." It is the longest essay in* World Holocaust. *I do not believe the American reader would be as interested in it as Roon's German readers are. Essentially, once Paulus's army surrendered at Stalingrad, the Caucasus Force faced a complete cutoff of their line of retreat. After considerable dithering, Hitler put the very able General von Manstein in charge of the northern and most threatened of these luckless armies, to pull him out of the mess. This Manstein did, with some brilliant maneuvering under the worst winter conditions. Another general, Kleist, led the retreat of the southern forces to a bridgehead on the Black Sea. In the end the Caucasus Force got out in good order, inflicting strong blows on the Red Army as it retreated; and the Germans found themselves more or less back on the jumping-off line of Case Blue. It was a stupendously futile military exercise, thanks to Germany's supreme "intuitive" genius who ordered it and then messed it up. A bitter name for the campaign gained currency in the Wehrmacht: "the Caucasus round trip."*

I had occasion to meet Hitler, so I know how plausible and even amiable he could be, like a gangster boss; he had all the forcefulness and cunning of a master criminal. But that is not greatness in my book. Hitler's early "successes" were only the startling depredations of a resolute felon be-

come a head of state and turned loose with the power of a great nation to back him up.

Why the Germans committed themselves to him remains a historical puzzle. They knew what they were getting. He had spelled it all out in advance, in Mein Kampf. He and his National Socialist cohorts were from the start a gang of recognizable and very dangerous thugs, but the Germans by and large adored and believed in these monsters right up to the rude Stalingrad awakening, and even long afterward. — V.H.

*   *   *

58

A Jew's Journey
(from Aaron Jastrow's manuscript)

FEBRUARY 20, 1943.
BADEN-BADEN.

. . . I shall never forget the moment when the train passed through opened barrier gates over which a large red swastika flag fluttered, and signs in German began appearing along the track. We were in the dining car, eating an abominable lunch of salt fish and rotten potatoes. The American faces all around us were a study. I could hardly bear to look at my niece. She has since told me that she was already in such shock that she scarcely noticed the crossing of the border. So she says now. I saw then on her face the terror of a person being swept over Niagara Falls.

For me it was not quite such a plunge. My memories of pre-Hitler Germany were pleasant enough; and during my brief reluctant trip to the 1936 Olympics to write a magazine piece, when swastikas were flying wherever the eye turned, I had encountered no problems beyond my own uneasiness. I knew some Jews who travelled in Hitler's Germany on business, and a thick-skinned few for perverse pleasure. Nor were they at much risk. The German moves on tracks; that is at once his virtue and his menace. The travelling Jews were on the track of tourism, as I was on the track of journalism, and therefore safe. I am counting much on this Teutonic trait. Even if the worst stories of German brutality prove true, we are on the diplomatic track. I cannot see anti-Semitism jumping its track and harming us on this one, especially since we are being bargained off for Nazi agents, probably at a rate of four or five to one.

All the same, in our first days here I did not draw a quiet breath. Natalie did not sleep or eat for a week. The defiant haunted gleam in her eyes when she held her son on her lap seemed not quite sane. But after a while we both calmed down. It is the old story, nothing is as terrifying as the unknown. The thing you have most feared, once it is upon you, is seldom as bad as imagined. Life here in Brenner's Park Hotel is dismal enough, but we are used to it now and mainly bored to death with it. If ever asked whether fear or boredom oppressed me more in Baden-Baden, I shall have to reply,. "Boredom, by a wide margin."

We are quarantined off from the local inhabitants. Our shortwave radios have been confiscated, and we hear no news except the Berlin broadcasts. Our only newspapers and magazines are Nazi publications, and a couple of French papers full of the crudest German lies, set forth in the language of Molière, Voltaire, Lamartine, and Hugo. It is a prostitution worse than any poor French whore's submission to the pumping and thumping of a hairy Hun. If I were a French journalist, they would have to shoot me before I would so stain my own honor, and the honor of my elegant language. At least I hope that is true.

With so little to read, and no news, and nothing to do, all the Americans immured in Baden-Baden are deteriorating, myself perhaps more than others. In five weeks I have not written in this journal. I, who once prided myself on my work habits; I, who produced words as unfailingly as Anthony Trollope; I, who have nothing else to do, and worlds to tell; I have let this record slide like a schoolgirl who starts a diary, then slacks off and lets the almost empty notebook molder in a desk, to be found and giggled over by her own schoolgirl daughter twenty years later.

But sound the trumpets! The first Red Cross food packages came in yesterday, and everybody has snapped out of the doldrums. *Canned ham! Corned beef! Cheese! Canned salmon! Canned sardines! Canned pineapple! Canned peaches! Powdered eggs! Instant coffee! Sugar! Margarine!* I love just writing down the words. These American staples are beautiful to our eyes, exquisite to our palates, reviving to our fading physiques.

How on earth do the Germans fight a war on their everlasting black bread and potatoes and spoiled vegetables? No doubt the soldiers get whatever good food there is; but the civilians! Our ration, we are told, is fifty percent more than the average German's. One can fill up on starch and cellulose, but eating such food a dog could not thrive. I say nothing of the disgusting cookery in this famous hotel. The Swiss representative assures us that we are not being mistreated, that hotel food all over Germany nowadays is worse than ours. Another time I shall describe what we have been eating, the strange dining room arrangements, the wretched wine, the black-market potato schnapps, the whole way we live under our German "hosts." It is all worth recording. But first I want to make up lost ground.

It is eleven in the morning, and very cold. I am out on the balcony in pale sunshine, well wrapped up as I write. Those Red Cross proteins and vitamins are coursing through my system, and I am myself again, craving the sun, the fresh air, and the moving pen. Thank God!

My digestion has been poor since we left Marseilles. In Lourdes I thought it was only nervous tension. But I was taken terribly ill on the train after that awful lunch, and my bowels have been in grave disorder ever since. Yet today I feel fit as a boy. I have had (ridiculous to set down, but true) a gloriously normal stool, over which I felt inclined to crow like a hen over her egg. It is not just the nourishment, I am sure, that has worked such healing magic. There is something psychic to it; my stomach recognizes American food. I could congratulate it on its sensitive politics.

About Louis.

He is the pet of the hotel. He grows in dexterity, vocabulary, and charm from week to week. He began to cast his spell over the group on the train. In Lourdes nobody had seen much of him; but at the station someone gave him a fine toy monkey that squeaked, and he went toddling up and down the train, keeping his balance admirably as our car swayed, offering his monkey to people to squeeze. He was having such fun that Natalie let him roam. He quite broke up the glumness in the car. He even brought the monkey to our uniformed Gestapo man, who hesitated, then took the monkey and unsmilingly made it go *Squeak!*

It would require another treatise like Meredith's on the comic spirit to explain why it was that everyone in the car burst out laughing. The Gestapo man looked around in embarrassment, then he laughed, too; and the horrible absurdity of the war seemed to strike us all, even him, for just that moment. The incident was talked about all over the train, and the little boy with the monkey became our first celebrity at the Brenner's Park Hotel.

I have given more space to a trivial incident than it perhaps warrants, to suggest the beguiling nature of the child. In my bouts of illness in recent weeks (some have been severe) one cardinal thought has kept me from sinking into apathy. I cannot and will not go under until Natalie and Louis are safe. I will guard them to the death, if I must, and I will fight depression and illness to be able to protect them. Our flimsy journalists' credentials rest on my few magazine pieces. The special treatment we are getting — this two-room suite on a high floor with a balcony, overlooking the hotel garden and a public park — can only be due to my literary standing, such as it is. Our lives in the end may hang on my jump, with a book-club selection, from academic obscurity to a name of sorts.

There are many children in the group, but Louis stands out. He is a privileged imp, getting more and better food than the others from a master scrounger, the naval attaché. When this man found out Natalie was a Navy wife, he was enslaved. They are quite close in an intimacy of (I am certain) antiseptic purity. He brings milk, eggs, and even meat for Louis. He brought a forbidden electric hot plate too, and Natalie cooks on the balcony to dissipate the odors. Now he is coaxing her to take the role of Eliza in *Pygmalion*, which he wants to put on with the dramatic group. She is actually considering it. Often the three of us play card games or anagrams. All in all, considering that we are on the soil of Hitler's Germany, Natalie and I are living a strangely banal existence, like people on an endless cruise aboard a third-rate ship, forever seeking ways to kill time. Boredom is the repeating bass note of our days, fear an intermittent piccolo shriek.

Our Jewish identity is known. The German Foreign Ministry man stationed here in the Brenner's Park has made a point of complimenting me on *A Jew's Jesus*. In fact, he talked rather intelligently about it. At first I was appalled, but granted the thoroughness of the Germans, it now seems naïve to have hoped that I would pass unnoticed. I am listed in *The International Who's Who*, the *Writers Directory*, and various academic reference tomes. So far my Jewishness has made no difference, and my semi-celebrity has helped. Germans respect writers and professors.

This must account for the assiduous medical attention I have been receiving. Our American doctor, a Red Cross man, was inclined to shrug off my gastric troubles as "detentionitis," his own facetious term for the malaise that afflicts our group. But in the third week I became so violently ill that he requested my hospitalization. So it was that at the Baden-Baden Municipal Hospital I met Dr. R————. I will not write down his real name even in this bothersome Yiddish-letter cipher. I must draw a portrait of Dr. R———— when I have more time. Natalie is calling me to lunch. We have given some of our precious Red Cross food to the hotel kitchen, which has promised to cook it up in style. We are to have corned beef hash; at last, at last, a way to doctor up those infernal potatoes.

FEBRUARY 21.
BADEN-BADEN.

I was very ill last night, and I am far from recovered today. However, I am determined to keep writing this record, now that I have started again. Moving a pen across a page makes me feel alive.

The hotel kitchen's execrable bungling of the corned beef hash upset me. Anger no doubt triggered the indigestion. How could a dish be simpler to prepare? But it was burned, lumpy, cold, greasy, altogether odious. We have learned our lesson. Natalie, the attaché, and I will pool our Red Cross food, and cook and eat it in our rooms, and to hell with the Boches. Others are doing it; the aroma drifts in the corridors.

The latest rumor is that the exchange and release will take place at Easter time, to show Germany's civilized respect for religion. Pinkney Tuck himself has told me this is sheer wishful fantasy, but the rumor mill grinds on. The psychology of this group is fascinating. A novel as good as *The Magic Mountain* could be made of it; pity I have no atom of creativity in me. If Louis were older he could well be our Thomas Mann, and possibly his acute little mind is recording more than we can discern.

The mention of Easter reminds me that in my Lourdes entry I started the topic of my abortive conversion to Catholicism. It is an old sad dreary story, a stirring up of cold ashes. Still, since these pages, if they survive me, may be the last testament of my brief and insignificant passage through the world, let me scrawl out the main facts. They should take but a paragraph or two. I have already described my alienation from the Oswiecim yeshiva, the key to it all.

I could not tell my father about that. Respect for parents was too deep in the grain for us Polish Jews. He was a lovable man, a dealer in farm implements, with a lively trade in bicycles. We were well-to-do, and he was pious and learned in an unquestioning way. It would have shattered him to know that I had become an *epikoros,* an unbeliever. So I went on being a star Talmud pupil, while laughing up my sleeve at Reb Laizar and the conforming young noddies around me.

Our family doctor was a Yiddishist agnostic. In those days Jewish doctors often returned from the university smelling of pork. One day on impulse I went and asked him to lend me Darwin's book. *Dar-veen,* the yeshiva whisper went, was the very Satan of modern godlessness. Well, "Dar-veen" was hard going in German; but I devoured *The Origin of Species* on the sly by candlelight, or away from the house by day. The first actual Sabbath violation of my life was carrying the Darwin book in my pocket down to the meadow by the river. Sabbath law forbids the bearing of burdens in "the public domain," and a book counts as a burden. Strange to say, though in spirit I was already far from the faith, the physical deed of carrying that book out of my father's house on Saturday was a terribly hard thing to do.

Next, the doctor loaned me Haeckel, Spinoza, Schopenhauer, and Nietzsche. I raced through those books as adolescents do through pornography, with mixed feelings of appetite and shame, thumbing eagerly for the irreligious parts: sneers at miracles and at God, attacks on the Bible, and the like. Two books I shall never forget, cheap German anthologies in green paper covers: *Introduction to Science,* and *Great Modern Thinkers.* Galileo, Copernicus, Newton, Voltaire, Hobbes, Hume, Rousseau, Kant, the whole radiant company burst on me, a fifteen-year-old Jewish boy lying alone on the grass by the Vistula. In a couple of weeks of feverish reading, my world and the world of my father fell in ruins: demolished, devastated, crumbled to dust, no more to be restored than the works of Ozymandias.

So my mind opened up.

When my family came to the United States, I was the precocious wonder of a Brooklyn high school. I learned English as though it were the multiplication table, sped through the school in two years, and won a full scholarship to Harvard. By then my parents had seen me turn Yankee Doodle in speech, dress, and manners. They were proud of the Harvard scholarship, but fearful, too. Yet how could they stop me? Away I went.

At Harvard I was a prodigy. The professors and their wives made much of me, and I was invited to wealthy people's homes, where my yeshiva-accented English was a piquant novelty. I took all the petting as my due. I was a good-looking young man then, with something of Louis Henry's unforced charm, and a great gift for conversation. I could make the Brahmins feel my own excitement in discovering western culture. I loved America; I read prodigiously in American literature and history; I knew most of Mark Twain by heart. My yeshiva-trained memory retained everything I read. I talked with a fluency of ideas and richness of allusion that the Bostonians found dazzling. I could spice my talk with Talmudic lore, too. In that way I stumbled on the perception that later made my name; to wit, that Christians are fascinated when one presents Judaism to them, with dignity and a touch of irony, as a neglected part of their own background. Thirty years later I wrote my *Talmudic Themes in Early Christianity*, which metamorphosed into a best-seller with a catchier title, *A Jew's Jesus*.

I am not proud of what happened next, and I shall be brief. Anyway, how repetitious life is! What story is more threadbare than an infatuation between a wealthy girl and a poor tutor? Comic operas, novels, tragedies, films abound on that simple plot. I lived it. She was a Catholic girl of a prominent Boston family. In one's early twenties one is not wise, and in love one is not honest, not with others or with oneself. My own fluency of ideas and argumentation, turned in upon myself, persuaded me that Christ had come into my heart. The rest was simple. Catholicism was the true tradition, the treasure house of Christian art and philosophy; and it was a strongly elaborated ritual system, the only sort of faith I really understood. I went through a conversion.

It was a shallow dream. The awakening was ghastly, and I pass over it in silence. At heart, through all the instruction I remained — as I still remain — the Oswiecim yeshiva boy, who came into a church out of the snow, and was shocked to his soul at seeing on the far wall the image of the crucified Christ, where in a synagogue the Holy Ark would be. If her family had not thrown me out, and if she had stood by me instead of liquefying in tears like a candy figure in the rain, I should still have lapsed. My essential condition for admiring, pitying, loving, and endlessly studying and writing about Jesus of Nazareth, as I have done, has been that I cannot believe in him.

According to the Nuremberg Laws, since all this happened before 1933 and I never did anything about "de-converting," I may be technically safe from persecution as a Jew. The exemption, as I understand it, applies to German half-Jews, and as an American I might well get the benefit, too, if it came to that. When my passport problems grew sticky in 1941, a good friend in the Vatican procured for me photocopies of the Boston documents that recorded my conversion. I still have those dark blurry papers. I have never yet officially produced them, because I might in some way become separated from Natalie. That must not happen. If I can help her with them, I will.

As for saving my own life — well, I have lived most of it. I shall not return to the Martin Luther book. I meant to round out, with this Reformation figure, my picture of Christ moving through history. But the coarse strident Teutonism of my hero was giving me greater and greater pause, quite aside from his diatribes against the Jews, indistinguishable from the bawlings of Dr. Goebbels. That he was a religious genius I do not doubt. But he was a German genius, therefore a destroying angel. Luther's best brilliance goes to smashing the Papacy and the Church. His eye for weaknesses is terrifying, his eloquence explosive. His bold irreverent hatred of old institutions and structures sounds the true German note, the harsh bellow out of the Teutoburg Forest, the ring of the hammer of Thor. We shall hear it again in Marx, the Jew turned German and combining the fanatic elements of each; we shall hear it in Wagner's music and writings; and it will shake the earth in Hitler.

Let other pens tell of what was great in Luther. I should like to write next some dialogues in the Platonic manner, ranging in the casual fashion of my Harvard conversations over the philosophical and political problems of this catastrophic century. I could contribute nothing new; but writing as I do with a light hand, I might charm a few readers into pausing, in their heedless hurry after pleasure and money, for a look at the things that matter.

Another rambling entry! But I have done my six pages. I have been writing in great abdominal pain, clenching my teeth to get the words down. I shall find it hard to rise from this chair, I feel so weak and poorly. There is something gravely wrong with me. These are not psychosomatic spasms. Alarm thrills through my system. I shall certainly see the doctor again.

FEBRUARY 26, 1943.
BADEN-BADEN.

I am feeling a little better than I did in the hospital. Actually, it was a relief to get away for three days from the boredom of Brenner's Park Hotel and the smell of the bad food. The hospital jellies and custards went down well, though I am sure they were distilled by German inventive genius out of petroleum waste or old tires. I was put through every possible gastrointestinal test. I still await the diagnosis. The hospital time passed quickly because I talked a lot with Dr. R———.

He wants me to bear witness, when I return to the United States, that the "other Germany" lives on, shamed, silenced, and horrified by the Hitler regime; the Germany of the great poets and philosophers, of Goethe and Beethoven, of the scientific pioneers, of the advanced social legislators of Weimar, of the progressive labor movement that Hitler destroyed, of the good-hearted common people who in the last free election voted by an increased majority against the Nazis; only to be betrayed by the old-line politicians like Papen and the senile Hindenburg who took Hitler into the government when he had passed his peak, and brought on the great disaster.

As for what ensued, he asks me to picture the Ku Klux Klan seizing power in the United States. That is what has happened to Germany, he says. The Nazi Party is an enormous German Ku Klux Klan. He points to the dramatic use of fire rituals at night, the anti-Semitism, the bizarre uniforms, the bellicose know-nothing hatred of liberal ideas and of foreigners and so forth. I rejoined that the Klan is a mere lunatic splinter group, not a major party capable of governing the nation. Then he cited the Klan of Reconstruction days, a respectable widespread movement which many of the leading Southerners joined; also the role of the modern Klan in the Democratic politics of the twenties.

Extremism, he says, is the universal tuberculosis of modern society: a world infection of resentment and hatred generated by rapid change and the breakdown of old values. In the stabler nations the tubercles are sealed off in scar tissue, and these are the harmless lunatic movements. In times of social disorder, depression, war, or revolution, the germs can break forth and infect the nation. This has happened in Germany. It could happen anywhere, even in the United States.

Germany is sick unto death of the infection, the doctor says. Millions of Germans know it and are grieved by it. He himself is a Social Democrat. One day Germany will return to that path, the only road to the future and to freedom. German culture, and the German people as a whole, must never be condemned for producing Hitler, and for what he is doing to the Jews. The greatest misfortune of the Hitler era has befallen the Germans themselves. There is Dr. R———'s thesis.

What of Hitler's popularity with the Germans? Well, he argues that terror, and total control of the press and radio, produce a mere simulacrum of popularity. But I wrote magazine pieces on Hitler. I know facts and figures. I know how the universities in a body went over to Hitler, how eagerly Germany's best minds began touting this great man of destiny, how readily and enthusiastically the civil service, the business world, the judiciary, and the army swore allegiance to him. I said to the doctor that in future study of this insane era, the chief phenomenon to explain will be the almost general spiritual surrender to Hitler of the German nation. If you call his movement a Ku Klux Klan, then all Germany overnight either turned Klansmen or cheered the Klan, as though liberalism, humanism, and democracy had never existed on this soil.

His retort: the American mind cannot comprehend the Germans' predicament. They are imprisoned on a narrow patch of central Europe's poorest earth, living for centuries under the pressure of the Russian threat, with France harrying them at their back. Their two great cultural foci, Prussia and Austria, were trodden under the boots of Napoleon's armies. England intrigued with czarist Russia for a century to keep the German people weak. This led to the ascendancy of Bismarck; and because of his stubborn preservation of absolutism when all of Europe was swept by liberalism, the German people remained politically immature. When the amorphous Weimar "system-time" began to fall apart in the Depression, and Hitler's clear strong voice of command rang out, there was a reflex of energy and enthusiasm. Hitler played upon the best qualities of the nation to bring about an economic recovery much like Roosevelt's New Deal. Unfortunately his military successes, to a nation hungry for self-respect, swamped resistance to his evil tendencies. Were not the Americans themselves worshippers of success?

On my bed lay a copy of the Propaganda Ministry's foreign-language magazine, *Signal*, with a long obfuscated account in French of the Stalingrad surrender. The story made it sound almost like a victory. Of course here in Baden-Baden one cannot learn much about Stalingrad, but obviously it was a towering defeat, possibly the pivot of the war. Yet *Signal* declares it all went according to plan; the sacrifice of the Sixth Army strengthened the eastern battle line and foiled the Bolsheviks' campaign. Did Dr. R——— think the German people would swallow that, I asked, or would resistance to Hitler grow now?

He commented that my very impressive historical insight did not extend to current military expertise. In point of fact the Stalingrad operation *had* stabilized the eastern front. His own son, an army officer, had written him to this effect. It was in any case irrelevant to the discussion of the nature and culture of the German people. It was very important to him, he said, that a man of my standing should grasp these ideas, for a time was coming when the world should be told them by a powerful literary voice.

It has occurred to me that the doctor may be a Gestapo agent, but he does not strike me as such. His manner is immensely earnest and sincere. He is a big blond chap with thick glasses, and small eyes that peer with eager seriousness as he makes his points. He speaks in low tones, unconsciously looking over his shoulder now and then at the blank wall of my room. I think he has approached me in all ingenuousness to convince me that the "other Germany" survives. No doubt it does, and I believe he is part of it. Pity it counts for so little.

FEBRUARY 27.

The tentative diagnosis is diverticulitis. The treatment: a special diet, bed rest, and continuous medication. Ulcers and similar digestive ailments have afflicted several other members of our group. One of the U.P. correspondents, a heavy drinker, was taken to Frankfurt last week under Gestapo guard for an operation. If my condition greatly worsens, I also could be sent to Frankfurt for surgery. Would this mean separation from Natalie? I shall take that up with Pinkney Tuck. It must not happen, if I have to die here.

59

SINCE the day Miriam Castelnuovo arrived at the children's home outside Toulouse, she has been a favorite of the director. In happier times long ago Madame Rosen — not married, not pretty, not hopeful — spent her vacations in Italy, loved Italian art and music, and once almost married a nice Italian Jewish man, who was too ill with heart trouble to go through with it. Miriam's clear Tuscan speech brings back those golden days, and Miriam's disposition is so sweet that Madame Rosen, who tries not to play favorites — the home was built for three hundred children, and more than eight hundred are jammed in now — despite herself rather dotes on this newcomer.

It is the free play period before bedtime. Madame Rosen knows where Miriam probably is. The girl has a favorite herself, a little French orphan named Jean Halphan, barely a year and a half old. Jean resembles Louis Henry, above all in the way his large blue eyes light up when he smiles. While Miriam was still with her parents she never stopped talking about Louis. She soon ceased asking questions, because she saw that they saddened her mother and irritated her father. But she endlessly reminisced, reliving her time with him, displaying a memory like a film library. Now that her parents are gone, and she has nobody, she has fastened on Jean. The little boy adores her, and when she is with him she is happy.

Madame Rosen finds them on the floor of Jean's big dormitory room, carefully building blocks amid milling children. She chides Miriam for sitting on the cold floor, though both children are bundled up as though they were outside in the snow. The home has not yet received its meager fuel ration this month. What little coal is left must be used to keep the water pipes from freezing, and to cook the meals. Miriam wears the fringed red shawl Madame Rosen gave her. It is so big it quite hides her face, but it is very warm. Miriam and Jean perch on a cot, and Madame Rosen talks to the girl in Italian. Miriam always likes that; she holds Jean on her lap, playing with his hands, and making him repeat Italian words. This visit of Madame Rosen's does not last long. She returns to the office, warmed and cheered to face her problems.

They are the old administrative ones, many times magnified: overcrowding, shortages, staffing difficulties, lack of funds. Now that the small

Toulouse Jewish community is almost gone, she is all but overwhelmed. Happily, the mayor of Toulouse is a kindly man. When matters get desperate, as they are now regarding fuel, medicine, bed linen, and the milk supply, she appeals to him. She sits at her desk to resume writing her letter, this time with dimmed expectations. The French friends of the Jewish children have become very wary of showing their sympathy. This wizened yellow-faced little woman in her late fifties, wrapped in a faded coat and a torn shawl, weeps as she writes. The situation seems hopeless when she puts it down on paper. But she must do something, or what will become of the children?

Worse yet, warnings have been chilling the remaining Jews in the area for a week: *another action impending.* Madame Rosen feels safe herself. She has an official position, and clear papers of native French citizenship. So far, only foreign Jews have been taken, though in the last action some of the deportees were naturalized citizens. Her concern is for the children. Nearly all the newcomers are foreigners. Hundreds of them! For about a third she has no papers at all. They were dumped on her by the police; the French government separates children from parents being deported to the east, and puts them anywhere. The Jewish orphanages are becoming swamped. The regulation seems humanely intended, despite the anguish for the torn-apart families, for horrible stories circulate about the east; but why is so little provision made for the children?

And now supposing that in this new action, the police come and ask for the foreign tots? Dare she claim she has no records of any child's origin? Or since that is so farfetched in bureaucratic France, can she plead that she burned her records in panic when the Allies landed in North Africa? Shall she actually burn the records now? Will that save the foreign waifs, or merely condemn the French-born children to be taken off with them?

Madame Rosen has no reason to believe that the Germans are collecting foreign children. She has not yet heard of such a thing, and the fact that they have been dumped on her argues that they are meant to be spared deportation. But the anxiety haunts her. It is about midnight, bitter cold, and she is folding the letter up with numbed fingers in the candlelight (the electricity has long since gone off) when she hears crashing knocks at the street door.

Her office is close to the street. The knocks startle her out of the chair. Crash! Crash! Crash! My God, all the children will wake up! They will be frightened to death!

"*Ouvrez! Ouvrez!*" Loud coarse male shouts. "*Ouvrez!*"

SS Obersturmführer Nagel has a problem too.

A tremendous flap is going on: a quota unfilled, and a partly empty train scheduled to pass through Toulouse in the morning. The top SS man in Jewish affairs in Paris is in a gigantic rage, but there just aren't that many Jews left in this prefecture. They have melted into the countryside, or fled to the Italian-occupied zone. There is just no way to fill three entire freight cars. The Toulouse action so far has collected five hundred. The demanded count from Paris is fifteen hundred.

Fortunately, the Toulouse police records show that the children and the staff here add up to nine hundred and seven Jews. Nagel has obtained permission from Paris to pick them up, while a squad combs Toulouse for the balance needed; any Jews, no protection applicable. So the SS lieutenant sits in a car across the street from the children's home, watching the French policemen knocking at the door. Given half a chance, those fellows would report back with some lame excuse and no results. He will sit here until the police chief comes out and reports to him.

The story Nagel has given the chief to tell is a good one. The occupation authority needs the building as a convalescent home for wounded German soldiers. Therefore the children and staff will be moved to a ski resort in the Tyrol, where all the hotels have been converted into an enormous special care center for children, with a school, a hospital, and many playgrounds; and where thousands of children from the bigger camps near Paris are already settled. In transporting Jews, standard procedure requires giving them some kind of reassuring story. Secret circulated instructions from Berlin emphasize that the Jews are very trusting, and eagerly believe any kind of flimsy official information. This greatly facilitates the processing of the Jews.

The door opens, the police disappear inside. Lieutenant Nagel waits. He is on his third cigarette, very chilled despite his warm new greatcoat and wool-lined service boots, and he is nervously thinking of going over there himself, though the uniform may scare the Jew staffers, when the door opens again, and out comes the police chief.

That fellow manages to stay nice and fat on French rations; plenty of black-market fat on that belly. He comes to the car, and reports with very garlicky breath that it is all arranged. The staff people will pack their belongings, and the central records of the institution. Nagel emphasized that touch about taking the records; it makes the story more plausible. The children will be wakened at three, dressed, and given a hot meal. The police vans and the trucks will come for them at five. They will all be on the railroad station platform at six. The Frenchman's fat face in the pallid moonlight is expressionless, and when Lieutenant Nagel says, *"Bon,"* the drooping mustache lifts in a nasty sad smile.

So all is well. The train is due at a quarter to seven, and at that hour most people of the town won't be up and about. That is a bit of luck, Nagel thinks, as he drives back to his apartment to catch a few winks before the morning's business. Orders are to avoid arousing sympathy in the population when transports leave. Repeated bulletins from Berlin caution that there can be unpleasant episodes, especially if children are moved about by day in populous places.

In fact, it turns out to be a gloomy morning, and when the train pulls in it is still almost dark. The Jews are shadowy figures, climbing into the cars. The station lights have to be turned on to speed up the loading of the children. They march quietly up the wooden ramps into the freight cars, two abreast, hand in hand as they have been told to do, the staff women carrying the youngest ones. Miriam Castelnuovo is walking with little Jean. She has been moved several times in this fashion, so she is used to it. This is not as bad as when they took her from her parents. Jean's hand in hers makes her happy. Madame Rosen walks behind her carrying a baby, and that too is reassuring.

Lieutenant Nagel wonders at the last minute whether there is any point in shoving those twelve big cartons of records into the freight car. They will just be a nuisance, and they may puzzle the fellows at the other end. But he sees the white terrorized face of Madame Rosen, who is staring out of the freight car at the cartons, as if her life hung on what happened to them. Why panic her? She's the one to keep the children quiet all the way to the end. He gestures with his stick at the cartons. The SS men load them into the car, and shut the big sliding doors on the children. Black gloved hands seize the frigid iron levers, rotate them, lock the doors in place.

The train starts with no whistle sound, only the chuffing of the locomotive.

60

PUG HENRY had made a fast departure for the Soviet Union. However, he was awhile getting there.

As the Clipper slapped and pounded clear of Baltimore harbor and roared up into low gray January murk, he pulled from his dispatch case two letters which he had had no time to read. He opened the bulky White House envelope first to skim the typewritten pages, a lengthy harangue by Hopkins on Lend-Lease.

"I'm taking breakfast orders, sir." A white-coated steward touched his elbow. Pug ordered ham and eggs and pancakes, though his uniform was tight after two weeks of Rhoda's food and wine. One should fatten up for Soviet Union duty, he thought, like a bear for the winter sleep. His career was damned well going into hibernation, he was damned well hungry, and he would damned well eat. And Harry Hopkins's disquisition could damned well wait while he found out what was on Pamela Tudsbury's mind. The spiky handwriting on the airmail envelope from London was obviously hers, and Pug tore it open with more eagerness than he wanted to feel.

December 20th, 1942

Dear Victor,

This is a mere quick scrawl, I'm just off to Scotland to do a story on American ferry pilots. You surely know that my father's gone, killed by a land mine at El Alamein. The *Observer* has generously given me a chance at carrying on as a correspondent. No use writing about Talky. I've pulled myself together, though for a while I felt that I had died too, or might as well have.

Did my long letter from Egypt ever reach you, before you lost your ship? That news horrified me, but luckily hard upon it I learned that you were safe and en route to Washington, where I myself will shortly be heading. I said in that letter, among other things, that Duncan Burne-Wilke wanted to marry me. In effect, I guess, I asked for your blessing. I received no answer. We have since become engaged, and he's off to India as Auchinleck's new deputy chief of staff for air.

I may not stay in Washington long. The great crunch at Stalingrad has given my editor the notion of sending me back to the Soviet Union. But I've run into mysterious visa problems which the *Observer* is working on, and meantime here I come. If I can't ever return to Moscow, for inscrutable Marxist reasons, my usefulness will dim; and I may then just pack it up and join Duncan for a tour of duty as memsahib. We'll see.

No doubt you know that Rhoda and I met in Hollywood, and that I told her about us. I just wanted to take myself out of the picture, and I trust you're not angry at me. Now I'm engaged to a darling man, with my future all settled, so that's that. I'll be at the Wardman Park Hotel on or about January 15th. Will you give me a ring? I can't tell how Rhoda would feel about my telephoning you, though obviously I'm no threat to her. About meeting you of course I want to be open and aboveboard. I just don't propose to pretend you don't exist.

Love,
Pamela

So, Pug thought — astonished, amused, impressed — Rhoda knew all along and said nothing. Good tactics; good girl. Perhaps she had noticed the London postmark, too, when she handed him the letters. About the disclosure, he felt sheepish; innocent, but sheepish. Rhoda was quite a woman, take her for all in all. Pamela's letter was proper, calm, friendly; in the situation, well put. He ate the large breakfast very cheerily, despite grim clouds tumbling past the window of the bumping Clipper, because of the slight chance that he might see the future Lady Burne-Wilke in the Soviet Union.

Then he read the Hopkins letter.

THE WHITE HOUSE

Jan. 12

Dear Pug,

You pleased the Boss greatly the other morning, and he'll remember it. The landing craft problem won't go away. You might still tackle it, depending on how long Ambassador Standley wants you. The special request about your daughter-in-law went through, but the Germans queered the effort by moving those people to Baden-Baden. Welles says they're in no hazard, and that negotiations for exchanging the whole crowd are well along.

Now to business:

Admiral Standley came back to Washington at his own request because he thinks we're mishandling Lend-Lease. But there are only two ways to handle Lend-Lease: unconditional aid, or aid on a quid pro quo basis. It burns up the old admiral that we give, give, give, asking for no accounting, no justification of requests, no trade-offs. That's our policy, all right. Standley's a wise and salty old bird, but the President as usual is miles ahead of him.

The President's overall policy toward the Russians is three-pronged, and very simple. Remember it, Pug:

(1) <u>Keep the Red Army fighting Germany</u>
(2) <u>Bring the Red Army in against Japan</u>

(3) Create a stronger postwar League of Nations with the Soviet Union in it.

Lenin walked out of World War I in 1917, you know, by making a deal with the Kaiser. Stalin opted out of this war in 1939 by making a deal with Hitler. He'd still be out of it if Hitler hadn't attacked him. The President doesn't forget those things.

Stalin's rhetoric notwithstanding, I doubt that Hitlerism is such a great evil to him. He too is a dictator running a police state, and he got cozily into bed with Hitler for two whole years. Now Russia's been invaded, so he has to fight. He's a total pragmatist, and our intelligence is that they've been exchanging peace feelers over there. A separate peace on that front is always possible, if Germany makes a substantial offer.

That may not be in the cards just yet. Hitler would have to show his people some territorial gains for all the German blood he's spilled. The more we strengthen the Russians, the less likely it is that Stalin will make such a deal. We want him to throw the Germans clear out of Russia, and not stop there, but drive on to Berlin. This will save millions of American lives, because our war aim is to eradicate Nazism, and we won't quit till we do.

So, it's a confusion of objectives to look for quid pro quos from Lend-Lease. The quid pro quo is that the Russians are killing large numbers of German soldiers who won't oppose us one day in France.

We have not exactly lived up to our commitments on Lend-Lease. We're at about 70 percent. We've tried, and our aid is massive, but the U-boats have taken a big toll, the Japanese war is a drain, and we had to cannibalize Lend-Lease to mount the North African landings. Nor have we lived up to our promise of a second front in Europe, not yet. So we are in no position to get tough with the Russians.

Even if we were, it would be bad war-making. We need them more than they need us. Stalin can't be fooled about such a fundamental reality. He is a very complicated figure, very difficult to deal with, a sort of Red Ivan the Terrible, but I'm damn glad we've got him and his people in the war on our side. I'm candid about that in public, and take a lot of lumps for it.

Admiral Standley will want you to try to obtain quid pro quos. He has a high opinion of your ability to handle Russians. It's true that they could loosen up a lot on air transport routes, military intelligence, shuttle bases for our bombers, release of our airmen downed in Siberia, and so on. Perhaps you'll make Standley happy by succeeding where others have failed. But on the basic issue, General Marshall has told the President that nothing the Russians can give us as a Lend-Lease trade-off would change our strategy or tactics in this war. He approves of unconditional aid.

The President wants you to know all this, and to resume sending him informal reports, as you did from Germany. He mentioned again your prediction of the Hitler-Stalin pact in 1939, and he requested (not wholly humorously) that if your crystal ball warns you of any moves toward a separate peace over there, to let him know fast.

Harry H.

Scarcely an encouraging letter; Pug was on his way to serve under a former CNO, and here was an order right at the start to bypass the old admiral with "informal reports" to the Commander-in-Chief. This new post promised to be nothing but a quagmire. Pug took from his dispatch case a sheaf of intelligence documents on the Soviet Union, and dug into them. Work was the best refuge from such thoughts.

The Clipper was diverted to Bermuda; no explanation. As the passengers were lunching in a beach hotel they could see, through the dining room windows, their flying boat heavily lifting away into the rain. They remained in Bermuda for weeks. In time they learned that the aircraft had been recalled to take Franklin Roosevelt to the Casablanca Conference. The conference by then was the great news on the radio and in the press, sharing the headlines with the growing German collapse at Stalingrad.

Pug did not mind the delay. He was in no great hurry to get to Russia. This little green isle far out in the Atlantic, in peacetime a quiet flowery Eden without automobiles, was now an American naval outpost. Jeeps, trucks, and bulldozers boiled around in clouds of exhaust and coral dust; patrol bombers buzzed overhead, gray warships crowded the sound, and sailors jammed the shops and the narrow town streets. The idle rich in the big pink houses seemed to have gone underground, waiting for the Americans to sink all the bothersome U-boats, win the war, and go away; the black populace looked prosperous and happy, for all the fumes and noise.

The commandant put up Pug in his handsome newly built quarters, complete with tennis court. Besides playing occasional tennis or cards with the admiral, Pug passed the time reading up on the Soviet Union. The intelligence papers he had brought were thin stuff. Poking around in Bermuda's library and bookstores, he came on erudite British books highly favorable to the Soviets, written by George Bernard Shaw, and a man named Laski, and a couple named Beatrice and Sidney Webb. He ground sedulously through these long stylish paeans to Russian socialism, but came on little substance that a military man could use.

He found harshly negative books, too, by various defectors and debunkers; lurid accounts of fake trials, mass murders, gigantic famines engineered by the government, and secret concentration camps all over the communist paradise, where millions of people were being worked to death. The crimes ascribed to Stalin in these books seemed worse even than Hitler's reputed malefactions. Where did the truth lie? This blank wall of contradiction brought back vividly to Victor Henry his last trip to the Soviet Union, with the Harriman mission; the sense of baffled isolation there, the frustration of dealing with people who looked and acted like ordinary human beings, who even projected a hearty if shy charm, and yet who could suddenly start behaving like Martians, for sheer inability to communicate, and for icy remote hostility.

When his flight was rescheduled, he bought a three-volume paperbound history of the Russian Revolution by Leon Trotsky to read on the way. Pug knew of Trotsky as a Jew who had organized the Red Army, the number two man under Lenin during the revolution; he knew too that on Lenin's death Stalin had outmaneuvered Trotsky for power, had driven him into exile in Mexico, and — at least according to the unfriendly books — had sent assassins who had brained him there. He was surprised at the literary brilliance of the work, and appalled by its contents. The six days of his trip across the Atlantic, over North Africa, and up through the Middle East to Tehran passed easily; for when clouds shut off the magnificent geography unreeling far below, or he was waiting for a connection, or spending a night in a dismal Quonset hut on an air base, he had Trotsky to turn to.

This intermingling of a flight across much of the globe with a flaring epic of czardom's fall was quite an experience. Trotsky wrote of sordid plots and counterplots by squalid formidable men to seize power, which gripped like a novel; but there were long passages of stupefying Marxist verbiage which defeated Victor Henry's earnest efforts to get through them. He did dimly grasp that a volcanic social force had broken loose in Russia in 1917, reaching for a grand utopian dream; but it seemed to him that on Trotsky's own testimony — and the book was intended to celebrate the revolution — the thing had foundered in a sea of sanguinary horror.

Except for hopping from one hot dusty base to another, Pug saw little of the war in North Africa, where, from radio reports, Rommel was giving the invaders a bad time. Green jungles slipped by, empty deserts, rugged mountains, day after day. The Pyramids and the Sphinx at last drifted past far below, and the Nile, glittering in its band of greenery. A half-day delay in Palestine enabled him to drive to old Jerusalem, and walk the crooked streets where Jesus Christ had borne his cross; then he was back in an aircraft high above the earth, reading about plots, imprisonments, tortures, poisonings, shootings, all in the name of the socialist brotherhood of man, inevitable under Marxism. When he got to Tehran he was just beginning the third volume, and he left the unfinished book on the plane. At his next stop, Trotsky was not a welcome import.

"The whole point, Henry," said Admiral Standley, "is to get through to this General Yevlenko. If anyone can do it, you can."

"What's Yevlenko's official position, Admiral?"

Standley made a frustrated gesture with gnarled hands. "If I knew and I told you, you'd be no better off. He's Mister Big on Lend-Lease, that's all.

He's a hero, I gather. Lost a hand in the battle for Moscow. Wears a fake hand in a leather glove."

They were at the long dinner table in Spaso House, just the two of them. Arrived from Kuibyshev scarcely an hour earlier, Pug would have been glad to forgo dinner, take a bath, and turn in for the night. But it was not to be. The little old admiral, who looked lost in this grand and spacious embassy, formerly the mansion of a czarist sugar merchant, had developed a great head of steam about Lend-Lease, and with Pug's arrival the safety valve popped.

In Washington, said Standley, he had gotten the President's promise that the Lend-Lease mission would be subordinated to him. The orders had gone out, but the head of the mission, one General Faymonville, was blandly ignoring the President. Growing red in the face, hardly touching his boiled chicken, Standley struck the table with a fist over and over, declaring that Harry Hopkins must be at the bottom of this, must have told Faymonville that the order didn't mean anything, that the prodigal handouts should continue. But he, Standley, had come out of retirement to take this post at the President's request. He was going to fight for America's best interests come hell or Harry Hopkins.

"Say, incidentally, Pug," said Standley with a sudden glare, "when I've talked to this General Yevlenko socially, he's referred to you more than once as Harry Hopkins's military aide. Hey? How's that?"

Pug answered cautiously, "Admiral, when we came over with Harriman in 1941, the President wanted an eyewitness report from the front. Mr. Hopkins designated me to go, because I'd taken a crash course in Russian. I met Yevlenko out in the forward area, and maybe the Nark man who accompanied me put that idea into his head."

"Hm. Is that so?" The ambassador's glare slowly metamorphosed into a cunning wrinkled grin. "I see! Well, in that case, land's sakes, don't ever disabuse the fellow. If he really thinks you're *Garry Gopkins*'s boy, you may get some action out of him. *Garry Gopkins* is Father Christmas around here."

Pug could remember first meeting William Standley ten years ago, when as Chief of Naval Operations he had visited the *West Virginia;* a straight austere little four-star admiral in white and gold, number one man in the Navy, saying a kind word to the lowly Lieutenant Commander Henry about the battleship's gunnery record. Standley was still full of fire, but what a change! During that dinner it seemed to Victor Henry that he had relinquished the post at Cincpac in order to help a tetchy old man cannonade at gnats. On and on the grievances poured out. The gifts of the Russian Relief Society, which Standley's own wife had worked hard for, weren't being acknowledged. The American Red Cross aid wasn't getting enough thankful publicity in the Soviet Union. The Russians weren't giving any quid pro quos for Lend-Lease. Bone-weary after the elaboration of these gripes for perhaps an hour and a half, Pug ventured to ask Standley over coffee what the purpose would be in seeking out General Yevlenko.

"That's business," said the ambassador. "We'll get to it in the morning. You look a bit bushed. Get some sleep."

Possibly because the sun shone brightly into the ambassador's library, or because he was at his best in morning hours, their next meeting went better. There was in fact a touch of the CNO about Standley.

Congress was debating the extension of the Lend-Lease act, he explained, and the State Department wanted a report from the Soviets on how Lend-Lease supplies had helped them on the battlefield. Molotov had agreed "in principle"— a fatal Russian phrase, which meant an indefinite stall. Molotov had referred the request to Yevlenko's Lend-Lease section. Standley had been hounding Faymonville to keep after Yevlenko, and Faymonville claimed he was doing his best, but nothing was happening.

Worse than nothing, actually. In Stalin's latest Order of the Day, the dictator had stated that the Red Army was bearing the whole weight of the war alone, with no help from its allies! Now, how would *that* go down with Congress? These damned Russians, said Standley coolly, just didn't comprehend the depth of anti-Bolshevik feeling in America. He admired their fighting spirit. He just had to save them from themselves. One way or another he had to get that statement about the battlefield benefits of Lend-Lease. Otherwise, come June there might be no more Lend-Lease. The whole alliance might collapse, and the whole damned war might be lost. Pug did not argue, though he thought Standley was exaggerating. No doubt the Russians were being boorish, and his first thankless task was to hunt down General Yevlenko, force him to face that fact, and try to get something done about it.

It took him two days of trudging through the Moscow streets ridged with black unremoved ice, amid crowds of shabby pedestrians, from one official structure to another in the government's uncharted maze, just to find out where General Yevlenko's office was. He could not obtain a telephone number, not even an accurate address. The British air attaché, whom he had known in Berlin, finally took him in hand and pointed out the building where Yevlenko had not long ago given him a red-hot dressing-down, over the diversion of forty Lend-Lease Aircobra fighters to the British forces in the North African landings. But when Pug tried to enter the building, a silent burly red-cheeked young sentry put a bayonetted rifle athwart his chest, and was deaf to his protests in sputtering Russian. Pug went back to his office, dictated a long letter, and brought it to the building. Another sentry accepted it, but days passed without an answer.

Meantime, Pug met General Faymonville, an affable Army man not much like the monster Standley had described. Faymonville said that he understood Yevlenko was in Leningrad; and that, in any case, Americans never saw Yevlenko on business. One dealt with him through his liaison officer, a general with a jawbreaker of a name. But Standley's attachés had already warned Pug that General Jawbreaker was a waste of time, a dead end; his sole job was to absorb questions and demands like a feather pillow with no comeback, and he was matchless at it.

After about a week of this frustration, Pug awoke in his bedroom in Spaso House and found a note under his door.

Henry —
Some American correspondents are returning from a tour of the southern
front; and I'm seeing them this morning at 0900 in the library. Be there at
0845.

He found Standley alone at his desk, dark red in the face and glaring dangerously. The admiral slung a pack of Chesterfield cigarettes across the desk at him. Pug picked it up. Stamped in bright purple ink on the package were these words: FROM THE FELLOW WORKERS PARTY, NEW YORK.

"Those are Red Cross *or* Lend-Lease cigarettes!" The admiral could barely choke out the words. "Can't be anything else. We're giving them by the millions to the Red Army. Yet I got that from a Czech last night. The fellow said a Red Army officer gave it to him, and told him that the generous communist comrades in New York are keeping the whole army supplied."

Victor Henry could only shake his head in disgust.

"Those reporters will be here in ten minutes," grated Standley, "and they'll get an earful."

"Admiral, the new Lend-Lease act comes to a vote this week. Is this a time to blow the whistle?"

"It's the only time. Give these scoundrels a jolt. Show 'em what ingratitude can lead to, when you deal with the American people."

Pug pointed at the cigarette package. "Sir, this is a bit of knavery on a very low level. I wouldn't magnify it."

"That? I quite agree. Not worth discussing."

The reporters came in, a bored lot obviously disappointed in their trip. As usual, they said, they had gotten nowhere near the front. In the chat over coffee Standley asked whether they had seen any American equipment out in the countryside. They had not. One reporter inquired whether the ambassador thought the new Lend-Lease act would pass in Congress.

"I wouldn't venture to say." Standley glanced at Victor Henry, and laid all ten bony fingers straight before him on the desk, like a main battery trained for a broadside. "You know, boys, ever since I've been here, I've been looking for evidence that the Russians are getting help from the British and us. Not only Lend-Lease, but also Red Cross and Russian Relief. I've yet to find any such evidence."

The reporters looked at each other and at the ambassador.

"That's right," he went on, drumming the fingers before him. "I've also tried to obtain evidence that our military supplies are actually in use by the Russians on the battlefield. I haven't succeeded. The Russian authorities seem to want to cover up the fact that they're receiving outside help. Apparently they want their people to believe that the Red Army is fighting this war alone."

"This is off the record, of course, Mr. Ambassador," said a reporter, though they were all pulling out pads and pencils.

"No, *use* it." Standley spoke on very slowly, virtually dictating. The drumming of his fingers quickened. In his pauses, the scribbling was an angry hiss. *"The Soviet authorities apparently are trying to create the impression at home and abroad that they are fighting the war alone, and with their own resources. I see no reason why you should not use my remarks if you care to."*

The reporters asked a few more excited questions, then bolted from the room.

Next morning, as Pug walked through the snow-heaped streets from the National Hotel to Spaso House, he was wondering whether he would find that the ambassador had already been recalled. Breakfasting with the reporters at the hotel, he had been told that Standley's statement had hit the front pages all over the United States and England, that the State Department had refused comment, that the President had cancelled a scheduled press conference, and that Congress was in an uproar. The whole world was asking whether Standley had spoken for himself or for Roosevelt. One rumor had it that the Russian censors who had allowed the statement out had been arrested.

In these wide quiet Moscow streets drifted high with fresh snow, amid the hundreds of Russians slogging past and the usual truckloads of soldiers coming and going, the whole fuss seemed petty and far-off. Still, Standley had done an incredible thing; on an explosively delicate issue between the United States and the Soviet Union, he had publicly vented his personal irritation. How could he survive?

In the small room assigned to him as a temporary office, he found a note on the desk from the telephone operator: *Call 0743*. He placed the call, heard the usual cracklings, poppings, and random noises of the Moscow telephone system, and then a harsh bass voice, *"Slushayu!"*

"Govorit Kapitan Victor Genry."

"Yasno. Yevlenko."

This time the sentry stiffly saluted and let the American naval officer pass without the exchange of a word. In the large marbled lobby an unsmiling army man at a desk looked up, pressing a button. *"Kapitan Genry?"*

"*Da.*"

An unsmiling girl in uniform came down a broad curved staircase, and spoke prim stiff English. "How do you do? Well, General Yèvlenko's office is on the second floor. If you please to come with me."

Ornate iron balustrades, marble stairs, marble pillars, high arched ceilings: another czarist mansion, brought up-to-date by red marble busts of Lenin and Stalin. Large thick patches of peeling old paint gave the edifice the general wartime look of neglect. Typewriters clattered behind closed doors all down the bare long corridor to Yevlenko's office. Pug remembered him as a giant of a man, but as he stood up unsmiling, holding out his left hand across the desk, he did not look so big; possibly because the desk and the room were enormous, and the photograph of Lenin behind him was many times lifesize. Pictures on other walls were black and white reproductions of old czarist generals' portraits. Tall dusty red curtains shut out the gray midwinter Moscow daylight. In a high curlicued brass chandelier naked electric bulbs glared.

The awkward clasp of Yevlenko's left hand was strong. The big jowly face looked even wearier and sadder than it had on the Moscow front with the Germans breaking through. He wore many decorations, including the red and yellow wound stripe, and his trim greenish-brown uniform was festooned with new gold braid. They exchanged greetings in Russian, and Yevlenko gestured at the girl. "Well, shall we have the translator?"

She woodenly returned Pug's glance: pretty face, heavy blonde hair, a charming red mouth, a fine bosom, blank cool eyes. Since leaving Washington, Pug had been drilling two hours a day on vocabulary and grammar, and his Russian was again about as good as it had been after the crash course in 1941. On instinct he replied, "*Nyet.*" Like a clockwork figure the girl turned and walked out. Pug assumed that microphones would still record everything he said, but he had no reason to be cautious, and Yevlenko no doubt could look after himself. "One less pair of eyes and ears," he said.

General Yevlenko smiled. Pug at once thought of the evening of drinking and dancing in the cottage near the front, and Yevlenko clodhopping around with Pamela, smiling in that big-toothed way. Yevlenko waved toward a sofa and a low table with the artificial right hand, shocking to see, projecting from his sleeve in a stiff brown leather glove. On the table were platters of cakes, fish slices, and paper-wrapped candy, bottles of soft drinks and mineral water, a bottle of vodka, and large and small glasses. Though Pug didn't want anything, he took a cake and a soft drink. Yevlenko took exactly what he did, and said, puffing at a cigarette clipped in a metal ring on his fake hand, "I received your letter. I have been very busy, so forgive my delay in answering. I thought it would be better to talk than to write."

"I agree."

"You asked for information about the use of Lend-Lease matériel on battlefields. Of course we have made very good use of Lend-Lease matériel on battlefields." He was slowing his speech and using simple words, so that Pug had no trouble understanding him. The deep rough voice brought timbres of the combat zone into the office. "Still, the Hitlerites would be very grateful to know the exact quantity, quality, and battlefield performance of Lend-Lease matériel used against them. As is known, they have access to the *New York Times*, the Columbia Broadcasting System, and so forth. The enemy's long nose must be reckoned with."

"Then don't disclose anything the Germans can use. A general statement will suffice. Lend-Lease is very costly, you see, and our President needs popular support if it is to continue.

"But haven't victories like Stalingrad gained enough American public support for Lend-Lease?" Yevlenko passed his good hand over his nearly bald close-barbered head. "We have smashed several German army groups. We have turned the tide of the war. When you open your long-delayed second front in Europe, your soldiers will face greatly weakened opposition, and will take far smaller losses than we have. The American people are clever. They understand these plain facts. Therefore they will support Lend-Lease. Not because of some 'general statement.'"

Since this was exactly what Pug thought, he found it hard to respond. A rotten job, shooting at Standley's gnats! He poured his soft drink and sipped the sickly-sweet red concoction. General Yevlenko went to his desk, brought back a thick file folder, and opened it on the table. With his good hand, he riffled gray clippings glued to sheets of paper. "Besides, are your Moscow correspondents asleep? Here are just a few recent articles from *Pravda*, *Trud*, and *Red Star*. Here are general statements. Read them yourself." He took a final puff at the clipped stub, and ground it out in practiced motions of the lifeless hand.

"General, in Mr. Stalin's recent Order of the Day, he said the Red Army is bearing the brunt of the war, with no help from its allies."

"He was speaking after Stalingrad." The retort came sharp and unabashed. "Wasn't he telling the truth? The Hitlerites stripped the Atlantic coast to throw everything they had against us. Still, Churchill would not move. Even your great President could not budge him. We had to win all by ourselves."

This was getting nowhere, and a riposte about North Africa would not help. Since Pug would have to report back to Standley, he decided he might as well fire at all gnats. "It's not just a question of Lend-Lease. The Red Cross and the Russian Relief Society have made generous contributions to the Soviet people, which have not been acknowledged."

Grimacing incredulously, Yevlenko said, "Are you talking about a few million dollars in gifts? We are a grateful people, and we show it by fighting. What else would you have us do?"

"My ambassador feels that there has been insufficient publicity for the gifts here."

"Your ambassador? Surely he is speaking for your government, not for himself?"

Less and less comfortable, Pug replied, "The request for a statement on battlefield use of Lend-Lease comes from the State Department. Renewal of Lend-Lease is before Congress, you know."

Yevlenko inserted another cigarette into the clip. His lighter failed, and he muttered till he struck a flame. "But our Washington embassy has told us that Lend-Lease renewal will pass Congress easily. Therefore Admiral Standley's outburst is most disturbing. Does it signal a shift in Mr. Roosevelt's policy?"

"I can't speak for President Roosevelt."

"And what about Mr. Hopkins?" Yevlenko gave him a hard wise look through wreathing smoke.

"Harry Hopkins is a great friend of the Soviet Union."

"We know that. In fact," said Yevlenko, reaching for the vodka and turning very jolly all at once, "I would like to drink to Harry Hopkins's health with you. Will you join me?"

Here we go, Pug thought. He nodded. The vodka streaked down inside him, leaving a warm tingling trail. Yevlenko smacked thick lips, and startled Pug by winking. "What is your rank, may I ask?"

Pointing to the shoulder bars on his bridge coat — the room was cold and he still wore it — Pug said, "Four stripes. Captain, U.S. Navy."

Yevlenko knowingly smiled. "Yes. That I see. I'll tell you a true story. When your country first recognized the USSR in 1933, we sent as military attachés an admiral and a vice admiral. Your government complained that their high rank created protocol difficulties. Next day they were reduced in rank to captain and commander, and everything was fine."

"I'm nothing but a captain."

"Yet Harry Hopkins, next to your President, is the most powerful man in your country."

"Not at all. In any case, that has nothing to do with me."

"Your embassy is already fully staffed with military attachés, isn't it? Then what is your position, may I ask? Aren't you representing Harry Hopkins?"

"No." Pug figured there was no harm, and there might be some good, in adding, "As a matter of fact, I'm here by direct personal order of President Roosevelt. Nevertheless I'm just a Navy captain, I assure you."

General Yevlenko gravely stared at him. Pug endured the stare with a solemn face. Let the Russians try to figure us out for a change, he thought. "I see. Well, since you are an emissary of the President, please clarify his misgivings on Lend-Lease," said Yevlenko, "which led to your ambassador's disturbing outburst."

"I have no authority to do that."

"Captain Henry, as a courtesy granted to Harry Hopkins, you toured the Moscow front at a bad moment in 1941. Also at your request, a British journalist and his daughter, who acted as his secretary, accompanied you."

"Yes, and I remember well your hospitality within sound of the guns."

"Well, by a pleasant coincidence, I can offer you another such trip. I am about to leave Moscow to inspect the Lend-Lease situation in the field. I will visit active fronts. I won't enter any zones of fire" — briefly the big-toothed grin — "not intentionally, but there may be hazards. If you wish to accompany me and render an eyewitness report to Mr. Hopkins and to your President on battlefield usage of Lend-Lease, that can be arranged. And perhaps we can then agree on a 'general statement' as well."

"I accept. When will we start?" Though surprised, Pug seized the chance. Let Standley veto it, if he had some objection.

"So? American style." Yevlenko stood up and offered his left hand. "I'll let you know. We'll probably go first to Leningrad, where — I may say — no correspondent, and I believe no foreigner, has been for over a year. It is still under siege, as you know, but the blockade has been broken. There are ways through that are not too dangerous. It is my birthplace, so I welcome a chance to go there. I have not been there since my mother died in the siege."

"I'm sorry," Pug said awkwardly. "Was she killed in the bombardment?"

"No. She starved."

61

STARVED.

It may have been the worst siege in the history of the world. It was a siege of Biblical horror; a siege like the siege of Jerusalem, when, as the Book of Lamentations tells, women boiled and ate their children. When the war began, Leningrad was a city of close to three million. By the time Victor Henry visited it, there were about six hundred thousand people left. Half of those who were gone had been evacuated; the other half had died. Gruesome tales persist that not a few were eaten. But at the time there was little outside awareness of the siege and the famine, and to this day much of the story remains untold, the records sealed in the Soviet archives or destroyed. Probably nobody knows, within a hundred thousand people, how many died of hunger, or the diseases of hunger, in Leningrad. The figure falls between a million and a million and a half.

Soviet historians are caught in an embarrassment over Leningrad. On the one hand, in the city's successful three-year resistance lie the makings of a world epic. On the other hand, the Germans rolled over the Red Army and arrived at the city in a matter of weeks, thus setting the stage for the drama. How does the infallible Communist Party explain that? And how explain that this great water-locked city was not mobilized for siege by rapid evacuation of the useless mouths, and by stockpiling of necessities for the garrison facing huge powerful armies drawing near?

Western historians are free and quick to blame their leaders and their governments for defeats and disasters. The Soviet Union, however, is governed by a party which has the invariably correct approach to all situations. This creates a certain awkwardness for its historians. The Party alone decides the allotment of paper for the printing of histories. The siege of Leningrad is something of a bone in the throat of Soviet historians who want to see their work in print. Thus a magnificent Russian feat of heroism goes half-told in its grim and great truth.

Lately, these historians have in gingerly fashion touched things that went wrong in the Great Patriotic War, including the total surprise of the Red Army in 1941, its near-collapse, and its failure for nearly three years to free half of Russia from the Germans, a much smaller people at war on other fronts as well. The explanation is that blunders were made by Stalin. Yet this too is a hazy business. As the years pass, and obscure shifts in high Soviet policy come and go, Stalin's stock as a wartime leader falls and rises again. He has yet to be blamed directly for what happened at Leningrad. The Party is by dogma blameless.

What is undeniable is that the Germans of Army Group North, some four hundred thousand strong, drove to the outskirts of the city in a quick summer campaign, and cut it off by land from the "Great Earth," the unconquered Soviet mainland. Hitler decided against an immediate grand assault. His orders were to blockade the city into submission, starve the defenders or wipe them out, and level it stone by stone to an extinct waste.

The people of Leningrad knew they could expect little more than that. Declaring it an open city like Paris, as showers of enemy leaflets kept urging, was out of the question. As winter drew on, the people started bringing in supplies under the German guns, across the frozen surface of Lake Ladoga. The invaders tried to smash the ice with artillery shells, but ice seven feet thick is tough stuff. Convoys kept running on the ice road through the winter, through darkness, blizzards, and artillery barrages; and Leningrad did not fall. As food came in, useless mouths departed on the empty trucks. By the time the ice melted in the spring there was something like a balance between mouths and food.

In January 1943, shortly before Victor Henry's visit, Red Army units defending Leningrad pushed back the German lines a short distance, at terrible cost, and freed a key railroad junction. This broke the blockade. Under the invaders' artillery pounding, rail supply resumed along a strip of roadbed called the "corridor of death," cut by the German shelling over and over, and always reopened. Most cargoes and travellers got through safely, and that was how Victor Henry entered the city. General Yevlenko's ski plane landed near the freed rail depot, where Pug saw immense stacks of food cartons, with U.S.A. stencillings; also arrays of American jeeps and Army trucks marked with red stars. They took the train into Leningrad at night in an absolute blackout. Outside the train windows on the left, German guns flared and muttered.

The breakfast in the chilly barracks was black bread, powdered eggs, and reconstituted milk. Yevlenko and Pug ate with a crowd of young soldiers at long metal tables. Gesturing at the eggs, Yevlenko said, "Lend-Lease."

"I recognize the stuff." Pug had eaten a lot of it aboard the *Northampton* when the cold-storage eggs ran out.

The artificial hand waved around at the soldiers. "Also the uniforms and boots of this battalion."

"Do they know what they're wearing?"

Yevlenko asked the soldier beside him, "Is that a new uniform?"

"Yes, General." Quick reply, the young ruddy face alert and serious. "American-made. Good material, good uniform, General."

Yevlenko glanced at Pug, who nodded his satisfaction.

"Russian body," observed Yevlenko, eliciting a rueful laugh from Pug.

Outside it was growing light. A Studebaker command car drove up, its massive tires showering snow, and the driver saluted. "Well, we will see what has happened to my hometown," said Yevlenko, turning up the collar of his long brown greatcoat and securing his fur cap.

Victor Henry did not know what to expect: another dreary Moscow, perhaps, only burned, battered, and scarred like London. The reality struck him dumb.

Except for silvery barrage balloons serenely floating in the still air, Leningrad scarcely seemed to be inhabited. Clean untracked snow covered the avenues lined with imposing old buildings. No people and no vehicles were moving. It was like Sunday morning back home, but in his life Pug had never seen a Sabbath peace like this. An eerie blue silence reigned; blue rather than white, the blue of the brightening sky caught and reflected by the pristine snow. Pug had not known of the charming canals and bridges; he had not imagined magnificent cathedrals, or splendid wide thoroughfares rivalling the Champs-Elysées, white-mantled in crystalline air; or noble houses ranged along granite embankments of a frozen river grander than the Seine. All the breadth, strength, history, and glory of Russia seemed to burst on him at a glance when the command car drove out on the stupendous square before the façade of the Winter Palace, a sight more extravagantly majestic than Versailles. Pug remembered this square from films of the revolution, roaring with mobs and czarist horse guards. It was deserted. There was not one track in the acres of snow.

The car halted.

"Quiet," said Yevlenko, speaking for the first time in a quarter of an hour.

"This is the most beautiful city I have ever seen," said Pug.

"Paris is more beautiful, they say. And Washington."

"No place is more beautiful." Impulsively Pug added, "Moscow is a village."

Yevlenko gave him a very peculiar look.

"Is that an offensive remark? I just said what I think."

"Very undiplomatic," Yevlenko growled. The growl came out rather like a purr.

As the day went on Pug saw much shell damage: broken buildings, barricaded streets, hundreds of windows patched with scrap wood. The sun rose, making a blinding dazzle of the thoroughfares. The city came to life, especially in the southern sector nearer the German lines, where the factories were. Here the artillery scars were worse; whole blocks were burned out. Pedestrians trudged in the cleared streets, an occasional trolley car bumped by, and there was heavy traffic of army trucks and personnel vehicles. Pug heard the intermittent thump of German guns, and saw stencilled on buildings, CITIZENS! DURING ARTILLERY SHELLING, THIS SIDE OF THE STREET IS MORE DANGEROUS. Yet the sense of an almost empty, almost peaceful great city persisted even here; and these later and more mundane impressions did not erase — nothing ever erased — Pug Henry's vivid morning vision of wartime Leningrad as a sleeping beauty, an enchanted blue frosty metropolis of the dead.

Even the Kirov Works, which Yevlenko said would be very busy, had a desolate air. In one big bombed-out building, half-assembled tanks stood in rows under the burned rubble from the cave-in, and dozens of shawled women were patiently clearing away the debris. One place was very busy: an immense open-air depot of trucks under an elaborate camouflage netting that stretched for blocks. Here maintenance work was proceeding at a hot pace in a tumult of clanking tools and shouting workmen, and here was Lend-Lease come to life: an outpouring from Detroit, seven thousand miles away beyond the U-boat gauntlet; uncountable American trucks showing heavy wear. Yevlenko said most of these had been running on the ice road through the winter. Now the ice was getting soft, the rail line was open, and that route was probably finished. After reconditioning, the trucks would go to the central and southern fronts, where great counterattacks were beating back the Germans. Yevlenko then took him to an airdrome ringed with antiaircraft batteries that looked like U.S. Navy stuff. Russian Yak fighters and Russian-marked Airacobras were dispersed under camouflage all over the bomb-plowed field.

"My son flies this airplane," said Yevlenko, slapping the cowl of an Aira-cobra. "It is a good airplane. You will meet him when we go to Kharkov."

Near sundown they picked up Yevlenko's daughter-in-law, a volunteer nurse coming off duty at a hospital. The car wound through silent streets that looked as though a tornado had swept them clean of houses, leaving block after block of shallow foundations and no rubble. All the wooden houses here, Yevlenko explained, had been pulled down and burned as fuel. At a flat waste where rows of tombstones stuck out of the snow, the car stopped. Much of the graveyard was randomly marked with bits of debris — a piece of broken pipe, a stick, a slat from a chair — or crude crosses of wood or tin. Yevlenko and his daughter-in-law left the car, and searched among the crosses. Far off, the general knelt in the snow.

"Well, she was almost eighty," he said to Pug, as the car drove away from the cemetery. His face was calm, his mouth a bitter line. "She had a hard life. Before the revolution she was a parlor maid. She was not very educated. Still, she wrote poetry, nice poetry. Vera has some poems she wrote just before she died. We can go back to the barracks now, but Vera invites us to her apartment. What do you say? The food will be better at the barracks. The soldiers get the best we have."

"The food doesn't matter," said Pug. An invitation to a Russian home was an extraordinary thing.

"Well, then, you'll see how a Leningrader lives nowadays."

Vera smiled at Pug, and despite poor teeth she all at once seemed less ugly. Her eyes were a pretty green-blue, and charming warmth brightened her face, which might once have been plump. The skin hung in folds, the nose was very sharp, and the eye sockets were dark holes.

In an almost undamaged neighborhood they entered a gloomy hallway smelling of clogged toilets and frying oil, and went up four narrow flights of a black-dark staircase. A key grated in a lock. Vera lit an oil lamp, and by the greenish glow, Pug saw one tiny room jammed with a bed, a table, two chairs, and a pile of broken wood around a tiled stove, with a tin flue wandering to a boarded-up window. It was colder here than outside, where the sun had just gone down. Vera lit the stove, broke a skin of ice in a pail, and poured water into a kettle. The general set out a bottle of vodka from a canvas bag he had carried up the stairs. Frozen through, despite heavy underwear and bulky boots, gloves, and a sweater, Pug was glad to toss off several glassfuls with the general.

Yevlenko pointed to the bed where he sat. "Here she died, and lay for two weeks. Vera couldn't get her a coffin. There were no coffins. No wood. Vera would not put her in the ground like a dog. It was very cold, much below zero, so it was not a health problem. Still, you would think it was horrible. But Vera says she just looked asleep and peaceful all that long time. Naturally the old people went first, they didn't have the stamina."

The room was rapidly warming. Frying pancakes at the stove, Vera took off her shawl and fur coat, disclosing a ragged sweater, and a skirt over thick leggings and boots. "People ate strange things," she said calmly. "Leather straps. Glue off the wallpaper. Even dogs and cats, and rats and mice and sparrows. Not me, none of that. But I heard of such things. In the hospital we heard awful stories." She pointed at the pancakes starting to sizzle on the stove. "I've made these with sawdust and petroleum jelly. Terrible, you got very sick, but it filled your stomach. There was a small ration of bread. I gave it all to Mama, but after a while she stopped eating. Apathetic."

"Tell him about the coffin," said Yevlenko.

"A poet lives downstairs," Vera said, turning the sputtering cakes. "Lyzukov, very well-known in Leningrad. He broke up his desk and made Mama a coffin. He still has no desk."

"And about the cleanup," said the general.

The daughter-in-law snapped with sudden peevishness, "Captain Henry doesn't want to hear of these sad things."

Pug said haltingly, "If it makes you sad, that's different, but I am interested."

"Well, later, maybe. Now let us eat."

She began setting the table. Yevlenko took from the wall a photograph of a young man in uniform. "This is my son."

The lamplight showed a good Slavic face: curly hair, broad brow, high cheekbones, a naïve clever expression. Pug said, "Handsome."

"I believe you told me you have an aviator son."

"I had. He was killed in the Battle of Midway."

Yevlenko stared, then gripped Pug's shoulder with his good hand. Vera was setting a bottle of red wine on the table from the canvas bag. Yevlenko uncorked the bottle. "His name?"

"Warren."

The general got to his feet, filling three glasses. Pug stood up, too. "*Varren Viktorovich Genry,*" said Yevlenko. As Pug drank down the thin sour wine, in this wretched lamplit room growing stuffy from the stove heat, he felt — for the first time — something about Warren's death that was not pure agony. However briefly, the death bridged a gulf between alien worlds. Yevlenko set down his drained glass. "We know about the Battle of Midway. It was an important United States Navy victory which reversed the tide in the Pacific."

Pug could not speak. He nodded.

With the pancakes there were sausages and American canned fruit salad from the general's bag. They rapidly emptied the bottle of wine and opened another. Vera began to talk about the siege. The worst thing, she said, had been when the snow had started to melt last spring, late in March. Bodies had begun to appear everywhere, bodies frozen and unburied for months, people who had just fallen down in the streets and died. The garbage, the rubble, and the wreckage, emerging with the thousands of bodies, had created a ghastly situation, a sickening smell everywhere, a big threat of an epidemic. But the authorities had severely organized the people, and a gigantic cleanup had saved the city. Bodies had been dumped in enormous mass graves, some identified, many not.

"You see, whole families had starved," Vera said. "Or only one would be left, sick or apathetic. People wouldn't be missed. Oh, you could tell when a person was getting ready to die. It was the apathy. If you could get them to a hospital, or put them to bed and try to feed them, it might help. But they would say they were all right, and insist on going out to work. Then they would sit or lie down on the sidewalk, and die in the snow." She glanced at Yevlenko and her voice dropped. "And often their ration cards would be stolen. Some people became like wolves."

Yevlenko drank wine and thudded his glass on the table. "Well, enough about it. Big blunders were made. Crude stupid unforgivable blunders."

They had been drinking enough so that Pug was emboldened to say, "By whom?"

Immediately he thought he had committed a fatal offense. General Yevlenko gave him a nasty glare, showing his big yellow teeth. "A million old people, children, and others who weren't ablebodied should have been evacuated. With the Germans a hundred miles away, and bombers coming around the clock, food stores shouldn't have been left in old wooden warehouses. Six month's rations for the whole city burned up in one night. Tons of sugar melted and ran into the ground. The people ate that dirt."

"I ate it," said Vera. "I paid a good price for it."

"People ate worse than that." Yevlenko stood up. "But the Germans did not take Leningrad, and they will not. Moscow gave the orders, but Leningrad saved itself." His speech was growing muffled and he was putting on his greatcoat with his back to Pug, who thought he heard him add, "Despite the orders." He turned around and said, "Well, starting tomorrow, *Kapitan*, you will see some places that the Germans took."

Yevlenko travelled at a gruelling pace. Place names melted into each other — Tikhvin, Rzhev, Mozhaisk, Vyazma, Tula, Livny — like American midwestern cities, they were all settlements on a broad flat plain under a big sky, one much resembling another; not in peaceful and banal sameness, as in the American repetition of filling stations, diners, and motels, but in horror. As they flew on and on for hundreds of miles, descending to visit an army in the field, or a headquarters in a village, or a depot of tanks and motor transport, or an operating airfield, Pug got a picture of the Russian front colossal in scale and numbing in wreckage and death.

The retreating Germans had executed a scorched-earth policy in reverse. Whatever was worth stealing, they had carried off; what would burn, they had burned; what would not, they had dynamited. For thousands and thousands of square miles they had ravaged the land like locusts. Where they had been gone for a while, buildings were rising again. Where they had recently been pushed out, shabby haggard Russians with shocked eyes were poking in the ruins or burying their dead; or they were being fed by army field kitchens in queues, under the open sky on the flat snowy plain.

Here was the problem of a separate peace, written plain across the devastated land. That the Russians loathed and despised the Germans as a form of invading vermin was obvious. Each village or city had its horror stories, its dossier of atrocity photographs of beatings, of shootings, of rapes, of heaps of bodies. The pictures numbed and bored by their grisly repetition. That the Russians wanted vengeance was equally obvious. But if after a few more bloody defeats like Stalingrad, the hated invaders would agree to leave the Soviet earth, stop torturing these people, and pay for the damage they had wrought, could the Russians be blamed for making peace?

Pug saw vast quantities of Lend-Lease matériel in use. Above all, there were the trucks, the trucks everywhere. Once Yevlenko said to him, at a depot in the south where olive-painted trucks, not yet marked with Russian lettering and red stars, stretched literally out of sight in parallel rows, "You have put us on wheels. It is making a difference. Now Fritz's wheels are wearing out. He is going back to horses. One day he will eat the horses, and run out of Russia on foot."

In an army HQ in a large badly shattered river town called Voronezh, they were eating an all-Russian supper: cabbage soup, canned fish, and some kind of fried grits. The aides were at another table. Yevlenko and Pug sat alone. "*Kapitan Genry*, we will not be going to Kharkov after all," the general said in a formal tone. "The Germans are counterattacking."

"Don't alter your itinerary on my account."

Yevlenko gave him the unsettling glare he had flashed in Leningrad. "Well, it's quite a counterattack. So instead we will go to Stalingrad."

"I'm sorry to miss your son."

"His air wing is in action, so we would not see him. He is not a bad young fellow. Maybe some other time you will meet him."

From the air, the approaches to Stalingrad were a moonscape. Giant bomb craters, pustular rings by the thousands, scarred a snowy earth littered with machines. Stalingrad itself, straggling along a black broad river flecked with floating ice, had the roofless broken look of a dug-up ancient city. As Yevlenko and his aides stared down at the ruins, Pug recalled his own dismaying airplane arrival over Pearl Harbor. But Honolulu had been untouched; only the fleet had been hit. No city on American soil had known such destruction. In the Soviet Union it was everywhere, and worst in this scene below.

Yet as they drove into the city past burned-out huts and buildings, tumbled masonry, and piles of wrecked machines, all in a vile stink of destruction, the crowds of workers clearing away the debris looked healthful and high-spirited. Merry children were playing around the ruins. There were many traces of the vanished Germans: street signs in their heavy black lettering, smashed tanks, guns, and trucks piled about or jammed in the rubble, a soldiers' cemetery in a crater-pocked park, with painted wooden grave markers topped by simulated iron crosses. High on one broken wall, Pug noticed a half-scraped-off propaganda poster: a school-age German girl in blonde braids, cowering before a slavering ape in a Red Army uniform, reaching hairy talons for her breasts.

The jeep pulled up before a bullet-riddled building, on a broad central square where all the other structures were entirely bombed out. Inside, Soviet bureaucracy was regenerating itself, complete with file cabinets, noisy typewriters, pasty men at rough desks, and women carrying tea. Yevlenko said, "I will be very busy today. I will turn you over to Gondin. During the battle Gondin was secretary to the Central Committee. He did not sleep for six months. Now he is quite sick."

A big very tough-looking gray-headed man in uniform, his face graven with deep lines of fatigue, sat behind a plank desk under a photograph of Stalin. Resting a large hairy fist on the desk, he looked pugnaciously at the stranger in the blue bridge coat. Yevlenko introduced Victor Henry. Gondin sized the newcomer up with a lengthy stare, thrust out a heavy jaw, and sardonically inquired, *"Sprechen Sie Deutsch?"*

"Govaryu po-russki nemnogo" ("I speak a little Russian"), Pug mildly returned.

The official raised thick eyebrows at Yevlenko, who put his good hand on Victor Henry's shoulder. *"Nash,"* he said. ("Ours.")

Pug never forgot that, and never understood what had prompted Yevlenko to say it. At any rate, *"Nash"* worked on Gondin like magic. For two hours he walked and rode with Pug around the wrecked city, out into the hills, down into the ravines that sloped to the river, and along the waterfront. Pug could scarcely follow his rapid Russian talk about the battle, spate of commanders' names, unit numbers, dates, and maneuvers, all poured out with mounting excitement. Gondin was reliving the battle, glorying in it, and Victor Henry did get the general idea: the defenders backed up against the Volga, surviving on supplies and reinforcements ferried across the broad river or brought across the ice; the fighting slogan, *There is no land east of the Volga;* the long horror of Germans on the hills in plain view, on rooftops of captured sections, or rumbling in tanks down the streets; the bloody deafening house-by-house, cellar-by-cellar fighting, sometimes in rain and in blizzards, the unceasing artillery and air bombardment, week upon week, month upon month. In the outskirts of the city, the German defeat was written in the snow, in long trails winding westward of smashed tanks, self-propelled guns, howitzers, trucks, half-tracks, and most of all in gray-clad bodies by the thousands, still strewn like garbage over the quiet cratered fields, miles upon miles. "It's a tremendous job," said Gondin. "I suppose in the end we'll have to pile up and burn these dead rats. We're still taking care of our own. They won't be back to bury theirs."

That night, in a cellar, Pug found himself at the sort of feast the Russians seemingly could produce in any place, under any circumstances: many varieties of fish, some meat, black and white bread, red and white wine, and endless vodka, served up on plank tables. The feasters were army officers, city officials, Party officials, about fifteen men; the introductions went fast, and obviously didn't matter. It was Yevlenko's party, and three themes ran through the boisterous talk, singing, and toasts: the Stalingrad victory, gratitude for American Lend-Lease, and the imperative need of a second front. Pug gathered that his presence was the excuse for some relaxation by these big shots. He too bore a heavy burden of emotion and tension. He let go, and ate and drank as though there were no tomorrow.

Next morning when an aide woke him in the frigid darkness, a blurry recollection made him shake his aching head. if it was not a dream, he and Yevlenko had staggered down a corridor together, and Yevlenko had said as they parted, "The Germans have retaken Kharkov."

After Pug's swift passage through war-torn Russia, Moscow appeared to him about as untouched, peaceful, well-kept, and cheery as San Francisco, despite the unfinished buildings abandoned and deteriorating, the sparseness of traffic, the difficulty of getting around, the dirty humps and ridges of ice, and the whole look of wartime neglect.

He found the ambassador ebullient. *Pravda* had printed every word of the Stettinius Report on Lend-Lease, leading off with it on the front page! A rash of stories on Lend-Lease was breaking out in the Soviet press! Moscow Radio was broadcasting Lend-Lease items almost every day!

Back home the Senate had passed the renewal of Lend-Lease unanimously, the House with only a few dissenting votes. Standley was snowed under with congratulations for speaking out. American and British newspapers had officially but gently disowned him. The President had passed it all off with an ambiguous joke to reporters about the tendency of admirals to talk too little or too much. "By God, Pug, maybe my head will roll yet for what I did, but by God, it worked! They'll think twice before kicking us around anymore."

Thus Standley, in the warm pleasant library at Spaso House, over excellent American coffee and white rolls and butter; his wrinkled eyes bright, his corded neck and face red with pleasure. He got all this out before Victor Henry said anything about his trip. Pug's account was brief He would at once write up his observations, he said, and submit them to Standley.

"Fine, Pug. Well! Leningrad, Rzhev, Voronezh, Stalingrad, hey? By God, you covered ground. Won't this ever put Faymonville's nose out of joint! Here he sits on his ditty box, the grand high mucky-muck of Lend-Lease, never gets a look-see at what's really happening and here you come along, and go right out and get the dope. Outstanding, Pug."

"Admiral, I'm the beneficiary of a delusion around here that I'm somebody."

"By God, you are somebody. Let me see that report soonest. Say, how about the Germans retaking Kharkov? That confounded maniac Hitler has nine lives. Lot of down-in-the-mouth Russkis at the Swedish embassy last night."

Among the letters piled on Pug's desk, a State Department envelope caught his eye with *Leslie Slote* handwritten in red ink on a corner. He first read a letter from Rhoda. The change in tone from her former false-breezy notes was marked.

"I did my best to make you happy while you were here, Pug darling. I was very happy, God knows. But I honestly don't know how I rate with you anymore." That was the key sentence in a couple of subdued pages. Byron had passed through, and had told her about Natalie's removal to Baden-Baden. *"I'm sorry you missed Byron. He's a man, every inch of him. You'd be proud. Like you, though, he's capable of scary silent anger. Even if Natalie gets home safe with that child, as Mr. Slote assures me she will, I'm not sure she can ever make it up to him. He's in an agony of worry over the baby, and he feels she let him down."*

Slote's letter was written on long yellow sheets. The red ink, unexplained, made the contents seem more sensational than they perhaps were.

March 1, 1943

Dear Captain Henry:

The pouch is a handy thing. I have some news for you and a request.

The request first. Pam Tudsbury is here, as you know, working for the *London Observer*. She wants to go to Moscow, where indeed all the major war stories are to be found these days. She applied for a visa some time ago. No soap. Pam sees her journalist's career going glimmering, whereas she's developed an interest in her work and wants to keep at it.

Quite simply, can you, and will you, do something about this? When I suggested to Pam that she write you, she turned colors and said not a chance, she wouldn't dream of pestering you. But having observed you in action in Moscow, I had a notion that you might pull it off. I told Pamela that I would write you about her, and she turned more flamboyant colors and said, "Leslie, don't you dare! I won't hear of it." I took that as British female doubletalk for "Oh, please, please do."

One can never be sure why the Narkomindel turns deaf or sulky. if you want to have a go at this, the problem may be a matter of some forty Lend-Lease Airacobras. These planes were earmarked for the Soviet Union, but the British managed to divert them for the invasion of North Africa. Lord Burne-Wilke had a hand in this. Of course that may not turn out to be the hitch at all. I mention it because Pam did.

I come to my news. The attempt to get Natalie and her uncle out of Lourdes fell through, because the Germans moved the whole group to Baden-Baden, quite against international law. A month or so ago Dr. Jastrow fell dangerously ill with an intestinal ailment requiring surgery. Operating facilities in Baden-Baden evidently were limited. A Frankfurt surgeon came and looked him over, and recommended that he be moved to Paris. The best man in Europe for such surgery is in the American Hospital there, we're told.

The Swiss Foreign Office has handled this very smoothly. Natalie, Dr. Jastrow and the baby are in Paris now. The Germans were quite decent about allowing them to remain together. Apparently his life was in some danger, because there were complications. He was operated on twice, and he is slowly recuperating.

Paris must be far pleasanter for Natalie than Baden-Baden. She is under Swiss protection, and we are not at war with France. There are other Americans living in Paris under such special circumstances, awaiting the grand Baden-Baden swap, in which they will be lumped. They have to report to the police and so forth, but they are warmly treated by the French. The Germans keep hands off so long as the legalities are observed. If Aaron and Natalie can stay in Paris until the swap comes off, they'll probably be the envy of the Baden-Baden crowd. There is the problem of their Jewish identity, and I can't pretend it isn't worrisome. But that existed in Baden-Baden too, perhaps more acutely. In short, I remain concerned, but with a little luck all should go well. The Lourdes thing was worth a try, and I regret it didn't come off. I'm very impressed at the water you draw with Harry Hopkins.

I saw Byron as he whistled through Washington. For the first time I noticed a physical resemblance to you. He used to look like an adolescent movie actor. And I had a long phone talk with your wife about Natalie, which calmed her somewhat. Natalie's mother calls me every week, poor lady.

About myself there is little to tell, none of it good, so I will pass that by. I hope you can do something for Pamela. She does yearn to go to Moscow.

Yours,
Leslie Slote

General Yevlenko did not rise or shake hands, but nodded a welcome, waving off his aide and motioning Pug to a chair with the dead hand. There were no refreshments in sight.

"Thank you for agreeing to see me."

A nod.

"I'm looking forward to the Lend-Lease statistical summary you said you'd let me have."

"It is not ready. I told you that on the telephone."

"That is not why I am here. You mentioned last week the correspondent who came to the Moscow front with me, Alistair Tudsbury."

"Yes?"

"He was killed in North Africa by a land mine. His daughter is carrying on his work as a correspondent. She is having difficulties obtaining a journalist's visa to the Soviet Union."

With a cold incredulous little smile, Yevlenko said, "*Kapitan Genry*, that is something to take up at the visa section of the Narkomindel."

Pug rode over this predictable brush-off. "I would like to help her."

"She is a *particular* friend of yours?" A man-to-man insinuating note on the Russian word *osobaya*.

"Yes."

"Perhaps I am mistaken, then. I have heard from British correspondents here that she is engaged to be married to the Air Vice Marshal, Lord Duncan Burne-Wilke."

"She is. Still, we are good friends."

The general laid his living hand over the artificial one on his desk. He was wearing what Pug thought of as his "official" face: no smile, eyes half-closed, heavy mouth pulled down. It was his usual aspect, and a truculent one. "Well. As I say, visas are not my concern. I am sorry. Is there something else?"

"Have you heard from your son on the Kharkov front?"

"Not as yet. Thank you for inquiring," Yevlenko replied in a final tone, standing up. "Tell me, does your ambassador still feel we are suppressing the facts of Lend-Lease?"

"He is gratified by recent Soviet press and radio coverage."

"Good. Of course some facts are best suppressed, as, for example, when the United States breaks a pledge to send Lend-Lease Aircobras urgently needed by our squadrons, and allows the British to divert the planes instead to themselves. To publicize such facts would only delight our enemies. Nevertheless, wouldn't you say such bad faith between allies is a very serious matter?"

"I have no information on such an occurrence."

"Really? Yet Lend-Lease seems to be your sphere of duty. Our British friends are afraid, of course, to let the Soviet Union become too strong. They are thinking, what about after the war? That is very farsighted." Yevlenko was standing with both hands on the desk, grating out sarcastic words. "Winston Churchill tried to stamp out our socialist revolution in 1919. No doubt he has not changed his low opinion of our form of government. That is most regrettable. But meantime, what about the war against Hitler? Even Churchill wants to win that war. Unfortunately, the only way to do that is to kill German soldiers. As you have now seen with your own eyes, we are killing our share of German soldiers. But the British are very reluctant to fight German soldiers. Those Aircobras were diverted by Lord Duncan Burne-Wilke, as it happens, for the landings in French North Africa, where there are no German soldiers."

In this tirade, Yevlenko's intonation on each repetition of *nemetskie soldati*, "German soldiers," was intolerably coarse and sneering.

"I said I know nothing about this." Pug reacted in a quick hard fashion. He had his answer on Pamela's visa, but the thing was going much beyond that. "If my government broke a pledge, that is a grave matter. As for Prime

Minister Churchill, the British under his leadership fought against Germany for a whole year alone, while the Soviet Union was supplying Hitler. At El Alamein and elsewhere they have killed their share of German soldiers. Their thousand-bomber raids on Germany are causing great damage and tying down a great force of antiair defenders. Any misunderstanding like this Aircobra affair certainly should not be publicized, but corrected among ourselves. Lend-Lease must go on despite such things, and despite our heavy losses. One of our Lend-Lease convoys has just suffered the worst U-boat onslaught yet in this war. Twenty-one ships sunk by a wolf pack, thousands of American and British sailors drowned in icy waters so that Lend-Lease can reach you."

Yevlenko's tone slightly moderated. "Have you reported yet to Harry Hopkins on your tour with us?"

"I have not completed my report. I shall include this complaint on Aircobras. Your statistical summary will go with it."

"You will have that on Monday."

"Thank you."

"In return, may I have a copy of your report to Mr. Hopkins?"

"I will deliver a copy to you myself."

Yevlenko offered his left hand.

Pug wrote a twenty-page report. Admiral Standley, delighted with this cornucopia of Lend-Lease intelligence, ordered it mimeographed for a large political distribution list back home, including the President.

Pug also wrote a letter by hand to Harry Hopkins. He sat up late one night scrawling it, fueled by sips of vodka, and he intended to put it in the pouch an hour before the courier departed. Such surreptitious bypassing of Standley was distasteful, but it was his job, if in this formless assignment anything was his job.

27 March 1943

Dear Mr. Hopkins:

Ambassador Standley is forwarding to you and to others my intelligence report on a recent eight-day observer trip through the Soviet Union with General Yuri Yevlenko. All my facts are in that document. I add, at your request, some "crystal ball" footnotes.

As to Lend-Lease: the trip convinced me that the President's policy of freehanded giving, without demanding any quid pro quo, is the only sane one. Congress did itself proud by showing how well it understood that. Even if the Russians weren't slaughtering great numbers of our foes, it would be churlish to tie strings to our help. This war will end, and we will have to live with the Soviet Union. If we now start bargaining about the price of a lifeline, before we throw it to a man struggling in deep waters, he may pay anything, but he'll remember.

As I see it, the Russians are starting to break the backbone of Hitlerism, but at terrible cost. I keep picturing the Japs rampaging ashore on our Pacific Coast and sweeping halfway across the country, killing or capturing maybe twenty million Americans, ravaging all the foodstuffs, taking over the factories, sending a few million people back to Nippon as slave labor, and spreading destruction and atrocities everywhere. That's roughly what the Russians have been going through. That they've hung on and come back is amazing. No doubt Lend-Lease has helped, but it wouldn't have helped a gutless country. General Yevlenko showed me some soldiers in new Lend-Lease uniforms, and he dryly remarked, "Russian bodies." So far as I'm concerned, that's the first and last word on Lend-Lease.

Just as amazing, however, is the German war effort. We see these things on maps and read about them, but it is another thing to fly along a battlefront for more than a thousand miles and view the reality. Considering that Hitler is also maintaining large forces in western Europe from Norway to the Pyrenees, and conducting massive operations in North Africa and a ferocious large-scale U-boat campaign — and that I didn't visit the Caucasus at all, which has been another huge front in itself — this sustained onslaught on a country ten times as big as Germany, twice as populous, and highly industrialized and militarized, boggles the mind. It may be history's most remarkable (and odious) military feat. Could we and the British stamp out this monstrous predatory force without Russia? I wonder. Again, the President's policy of keeping the Soviet Union fighting at all costs is the only sane one.

This raises the question of a separate peace, on which you have specifically asked for a judgment. Unfortunately the Soviet Union baffles me; the people, the government, the social philosophy, everything about it. Of course I'm not alone in that.

I don't feel that the Russians love or even like their Communist government. I think they're stuck with it by the accidents of a revolution that went wrong. Despite the blanket of propaganda, I think they sense too that Stalin and his brutal gang bungled the start of the war and almost lost it. Maybe one day this great patient people will have a reckoning with the regime, as they did with the Romanoffs. Meantime Stalin remains in the saddle, providing harsh driving leadership. He'll make the separate peace decision, one way or the other. The people will obey. Nobody's going to rebel against Stalin, not after the way the Germans have behaved here.

At this point such a peace would be perfidious, and when I'm among Russians I don't sense or fear perfidy. War-weariness is something else. The German resilience as shown in the recapture of Kharkov is ominous. I ask myself, why did the Russian authorities permit me to go on this unusual trip? And why did General Yevlenko invite me to the squalid flat of his daughter-in-law in Leningrad, and prod her to tell me horror stories of the siege? Possibly to make our complaints of Russian ingratitude seem shameful. Possibly to drive home to me — for as described in my main report, I've been treated as your unofficial aide — that there may be limits even to Russian endurance. The hints here, sometimes subtle but usually very crude, about a second front in Europe are interminable.

I've been through some cruel warfare in the Pacific, but that's mainly a war of professionals. This one is all-out — two entire nations at each other's jugulars. The Russians don't mean to do us a favor by fighting for their lives, but it's working that way. Lend-Lease is an inspired and historic policy. But bloodshed on the battlefield remains the decisive thing in wars, and people can stand only so much of it without hope of relief.

My "crystal ball" says therefore something very obvious: if we can convince the Russians that we're serious about a second front in Europe soon, we can forget about a separate peace. Otherwise it's a risk.

Sincerely,
Victor Henry

"The matter of the Aircobras," Pug said, "is discussed on pages seventeen and eighteen."

A weekend had passed. He and Yevlenko were exchanging papers: a copy of his report to Yevlenko, a thick-bound document to him. Riffling through Yevlenko's summary, Pug saw pages on pages of figures, graphs, and tables, with long pages of solid text in Russian.

"Well, of course I cannot read your report myself." Yevlenko's tone was chatty but hurried. He slipped the report into his travelling portfolio, which lay on the desk; his fur-lined greatcoat and a valise were on the sofa. "I am off to the southern front, and my aide will translate at sight on the plane."

"General, I have also written a personal letter to Harry Hopkins." Pug pulled more papers from his portfolio. "I have translated it myself into Russian for you, though I had to use a dictionary and a grammar."

"But why? We have excellent translators."

"So have we. I don't want to leave a copy with you. If you care to read it and hand it back to me, that is what I prepared it for."

Yevlenko looked puzzled and suspicious, then gave him a slow patronizing smile. "Well! That is the sort of cautious secrecy we Russians are often accused of."

Pug said, "Possibly it's infectious."

"Unfortunately, I have very little time just now, *Kapitan Genry*."

"In that case, when you return, I'll be at your service."

Yevlenko took the telephone and growled quick words; hung up, and held out his hand. Pug gave him the translated letter. Inserting a cigarette in the clip, still wryly smiling, Yevlenko began to read. The smile faded. A couple of times he shot at Pug the nasty glare he had first flashed in the Leningrad apartment. Turning over the last page, he sat staring at the letter, then handed it back to Pug. His face was expressionless. "You have to work on your Russian verbs."

"If you have any comment, I will transmit it to Harry Hopkins."

"You might not like what I would say."

"That doesn't matter."

"Your political understanding of the Soviet Union is very superficial, very prejudiced, and very uninformed. Now I must go." Yevlenko stood up. "You asked about my son on the Kharkov front. We have heard from him. He is all right."

"I'm absolutely delighted to hear it."

Yevlenko barked an order into the telephone and began putting on his coat, dead hand first. An aide entered and gathered up his luggage. "As for Miss Pamela Tudsbury, her visa has been issued. Your driver will return you to your flat. Good-bye."

"Good-bye," Pug said, too startled to react about Pamela. He thought Yevlenko was offering him the live hand, but it went up to his shoulder for a brief almost painful squeeze. Then Yevlenko left.

62

No locomotive will ride the steel tracks that Berel Jastrow, Sammy Mutterperl, and the other Jews of Kommando 1005 are handling, nor will the heavy wooden ties piled nearby support the weight of rolling trains. The rails and ties are for railroad bed repair, but Standartenführer Blobel has found another use for them.

Since first light the kommando has been out at the job, setting up the steel frame. The frame is the secret of the 1005 operation. For a professional architect like Paul Blobel it was a simple thing to design, build, and put into use, but the thick heads at Auschwitz and the other camps still cannot grasp the advantage of it. Blobel has offered copies of the drawings to the camp commandants. So far, they have shown little interest, though that fellow Hoess at Auschwitz has indicated he will give it a try. The frame is the answer to the disposal problem about which he whines and makes so many excuses, and which in fact is a serious health problem. But the fellow obviously did not grasp the idea when Blobel described it, and was afraid to admit his stupidity, so he nodded and smiled and passed the thing off. Just an old concentration camp hand, no culture or imagination.

This morning Standartenführer Blobel is at the site when work begins. That is unusual. The procedure is cut-and-dried, and this latest squad from Auschwitz — a sturdy gang of Jews at last, hardworking physical specimens with smart work leaders — has caught on fast. Usually at this hour Blobel is in his van or at quarters in town if the section is not too far out in the sticks, quaffing schnapps to chase off the morning chill. This duty is lonely, repetitious, boring, and very hard on the nervous system. The SS men get their schnappps ration at night; during work hours they have to keep an eye on the Jews. The escape rate is very bad, worse than Blobel reports to Berlin. Rank has its privileges, and SS Colonel Blobel likes to start the day with a few shots, but this morning is special. He is cold sober.

The pit was opened yesterday. Fortunately, the snowfall at night wasn't much. There are the bodies in rows, lightly snowed over. A medium-sized job, maybe two thousand. The smell as usual is awful, but the cold and the snow keep it down some, and the frame stands to windward, which helps. Blobel is pleased to observe how quickly the frame takes form. The Jew work leader "Sammy" had a good idea, cutting numbers into the rails for sorting and matching. It is up, bolted, braced, and ready to go in less than half an hour — a long narrow sturdy structure of rails held together with steel cross-beams, like a section of track on stilts. Next will come the pileup: a layer of wooden ties, a layer of bodies and fuel-soaked rags, wood, bodies, wood, bodies, with a row or two of heavy steel rails to hold the mass down, until you have all the bodies out of the hole, or until the pyre is toppling-high.

What Blobel has come to watch is the new search procedure. The looting has been getting out of hand. These are all early graves around the Minsk district, from the 1941 executions. Nobody had any know-how then. Jews were taken out by the hundreds of thousands, and shot and buried with their clothes on, without even being searched. Rings, watches, gold coins, old paper money (plenty of American dollars, too) stiff with black blood but still good, are all over White Russia in these mass graves. Up the assholes and in the cunts of these cheesy bodies you are apt to find valuable gems, no fun to make the search, but worth it! Here and there the local population has already been robbing the graves; to discourage the practice Blobel has had to shoot a few kids, who tend to be adept at such ghoulishness. Germany needs all the wealth it can acquire to carry on its world-historical struggle. They are collecting pots and pans back home for the Führer, and here is real buried treasure, amid all this rotting garbage that now has to be burned up.

Until today the treasure has been picked over randomly, a lot of it carelessly given to the flames, some going into the pockets of the SS underlings; and some Jews have even become so bold in their Yiddish greed that they have been caught with loot. Blobel suspects that escapees may have bribed their way past the guards with looted jewels and money; on this duty SS morale and training tend to break down. He has had to make an example and shoot seven perfectly healthy Jews, who will be missed in the work force.

He observes the new system go into action. Excellent! Jewish body-searchers, Jewish loot-collectors, Jewish inventory-writers, Jews with pliers for the gold teeth, all under close SS supervision, go to work on the corpses as they are handed up and laid out on the snow in rows. Untersturmführer Greiser is in charge. From now on that young fellow will do nothing else but attend to the "economic processing," as Blobel has termed it, so long as Kommando 1005 is obliterating the 1941 graves. Greiser is a good-looking idealistic rookie from Breslau, a fine SS type with whom Blobel enjoys philosophical discussions. Formerly an accountant with a university degree, he can be relied upon to handle this business. Kommando 1005 will be remitting plenty of stuff to the central bank depository in Berlin, and Blobel's promotion file will duly record this.

The search adds some time to the whole process, but less than he expected. It goes fast. Most of the people were poor and had nothing on them.

The thing is, you never know when you'll come on a loaded one. The Standartenführer's orders are, *"Search them all, even the kids!"* It's an old Yid trick to hide valuables on the children.

Well, something accomplished!

It is finished. The rifled bodies are all piled up with the railroad ties and rails. As the Jews climb their ladders to pour waste oil and gasoline over the pyre, Blobel waves to his chauffeur. Gasoline for the pyre is getting to be a real problem. The Wehrmacht is becoming stingier all the time about this, just as it won't ever provide enough soldiers to cordon off a work area. Without gasoline the blaze just doesn't get going. You can have a terrible smoldering mess for days. But today there is plenty. In a moment, as it seems, the pile of more than a thousand long-dead Jews bursts into towering flame. Blobel has to recoil a bit from the blast of heat.

He is driven back to his van. Downing many glasses of schnapps, he drafts a report to Berlin on his procedure. It pays to get these things on the record. Nobody else can claim credit for the frame; he wrote a long report on it, pointing out that the great problem in the combustion of corpses, especially old ones, was getting enough oxygen to the conflagration. Those open pits in Auschwitz — well, he has used open pits, too: slow, visible far and wide at night, soaking up four times as much oil and gasoline as the frame does because oxygen can't get down in there. The pits at Chelmno burned cherry-red for three days, and there was still a big problem with bones. All he can say for a pit is it beats a crematorium.

He has argued in vain against the Auschwitz crematoriums, and given up. He knows more about this business than anyone, but to hell with it. The gas-chamber concept is fine, it does a quiet smooth job with large numbers; but the damned fools who designed the installation gave it a gassing capacity four times the burning capacity. The overload in peak periods must end in a tremendous mess. Well, let those wiseacres in Berlin spend money and waste scarce material and machinery. Let them find out for themselves that no chimney linings will hold up against the heat of combustion of hundreds of thousands of human bodies, dead meat burning by the hundreds of metric tons on a twenty-four-hour basis. Those big complicated structures will give nothing but trouble. The height of foolishness; amateur architecture, amateur disposal techniques! Bureaucrats a thousand miles from the job dreaming up fancy installations when all they ever needed was plenty of God's open air and Paul Blobel's frame.

Depending on the wind, the burning time on the frame can be two to ten hours. Some Jews tend the crackling pyre with iron forks. Others, including Jastrow and Mutterperl, are down in the long narrow pit, passing up more bodies. It is starting to snow again. Black smoke and red flames climb into the white snowfall, a beautiful sight if any eye here can see beauty. But the forty-odd SS men surrounding the job, guns in hand, are bored and numb, waiting for their reliefs; and the Jews — those who are sane enough to notice things — are all driven and busy.

Many of these Jews are now quite harmless madmen. They work because they will be fed if they do, and starved and beaten if they don't. Uncovering and descending into hideously foul mass graves; handling desiccated rotted corpses that can come apart in one's leather-gloved hands, that drip fat worms; piling up one's murdered fellow Jews and setting them afire, day in and day out; these things have been too great a strain. Minds and spirits have given way, fallen apart like old corpses. These docile lunatic automatons are no more trouble to their guards than cattle; which is how the SS men handle the squad, with shouts and with dogs.

But not all minds and spirits are gone. There are tough-willed fellows among them who mean to survive. They too obey the SS, but with eyes and ears alert for self-protection. For Jastrow and Mutterperl, working down in the graves has advantages, once one is steeled to handling gap-mouthed limp skeletal bodies all day. The SS allows you to wear a cloth over nose and mouth, and the guards, having no great zest for the sight and smell of the bodies, stand well clear of the holes. Slave workers can be shot to death without warning for talking on the job, but Jastrow and Mutterperl carry on long free conversations behind their masks.

Today they are rehashing an old argument. Berel Jastrow is against trying a getaway here. True, he knows the forests, he knows partisan pathways and hiding places, and he even recalls old passwords. That is Sammy Mutterperl's argument; this is Jastrow's territory, and it's a good place to make the try.

But Berel is thinking ahead. It is not a question of taking to the woods to save their skins. Their mission is to bring the photographs and documents of Auschwitz to Prague, where the organized Resistance can get the material to the outside world, above all to the Americans. But Kommando 1005 has been moving farther and farther from Prague. Escaping here, they will have to traverse all of Poland through the woods, behind German lines. Some of the Poles are all right, but many of their partisan bands in the forests are unfriendly enough to Jews to kill them, and the Polish villagers cannot be trusted not to turn Jews in. Berel has heard talk among the SS officers about an impending transfer of Kommando 1005 to the Ukraine. That is many hundreds of miles closer to Prague.

Mutterperl doesn't want to rely on SS gossip. The transfer may not happen. He wants to act. He does most of the talking as they work their way down the row, lifting each maggoty body with what reverence they can, and passing it up to waiting hands above; signalling, when the corpse is a loose disintegrating one, for a canvas sling to hold it together.

While he does this work, Berel Jastrow recites psalms for the dead. He knows the psaltery by heart. Several times each day he goes through all hundred and fifty *t'hilim*. The dead hold no terrors for Berel. In the old days, as an officer of the burial society, the *hevra kadisha*, he washed and prepared for interment many bodies. Here the terrible odor, the disgusting condition of these long-buried corpses, cannot mar his deep affection for them. They cannot help the way they died, these pitiful Jews, many still streaked with black blood from visible bullet holes.

For Berel Jastrow these rotten remains possess all the sad sacred sweetness of the dead: poor cold silent mechanisms, once warm happy creatures sparkling with life, now dumb and motionless without the spark of God in them, but destined one day in His good time to rise again. So the Jewish faith teaches. He goes about this gruesome task with love, murmuring psalms. He cannot give these dead the orthodox purification by water, but fire purifies too, and the psalms will comfort their souls. The Hebrew verses are so graven in his memory that he can listen to Mutterperl, or even break off to argue, without missing a word of a psalm.

Mutterperl is beginning to alarm Berel Jastrow. Sammy's health is good; the man is burly, and Kommando 1005 feeds its exhumers well, before (as they all realize) their turn comes to be shot and burned on the frame. Until recently Sammy has seemed to be retaining his hard sanity, but he is talking really wildly now. The idea of crossing Poland through the forests is not enough for him today. He wants to organize the strongest Jews in the kommando and make a break in a body; *seize some guards' guns, and kill as many SS men as they can before plunging into the forest.*

Sammy is talking so vehemently that his breath makes risky telltale smoke through the cloth mask. This situation is nothing like Auschwitz, he argues. There are no electrified wire fences. The SS men are a stupid, lazy, drunken, altogether careless gang. The cordon of soldiers is far off, and alerted only to keep the peasants away from the grave. They could kill a dozen Germans before getting away — maybe twice as many — if they could seize two or three machine guns.

Berel replies that if organizing an uprising and killing a dozen Germans will help a getaway, fine, but how can it? The chances of being informed on and caught will increase with every Jew they approach. A silent escape always has the best chance of succeeding. Killing Germans will raise a hue and cry and start the whole military police force in Byelorussia after the fugitives. Why do it?

Sammy Mutterperl is handing up out of the grave a little girl in a lilac dress. Her face is a peering grinning skull patched with shreds of greenish skin, but her dark streaming hair is feminine and pretty. "For her," he says, as a Jew above takes the girl. The wide-eyed glittery look he gives Berel Jastrow above his mask is more horrible than the dead girl's face.

Berel does not answer. He heaves up body after body — they are light, these long-dead Jews, one seizes a body by the waist and twitches it readily into the air, into the waiting hands above — and goes on murmuring psalms. This is how Berel Jastrow holds on to his sanity. He is doing *hevra kadisha* work; his religious structure can contain and support even this heavy horror. Why such strange death has befallen so many Jews he cannot fathom. God will have much to answer for! Yet God did not do this, the Germans did it. Why did God not pass a miracle and stop the Germans? It may be that the generation did not deserve a miracle. So things went naturally, and the Germans broke loose all over Europe, murdering Jews. In this narrow squirrel-cage of question and answer Jastrow's mind runs when he allows himself such vain thoughts. He does his best to suppress them.

Mutterperl says after a long silence, "I intend to talk to Goodkind and Finkelstein tonight, to start with."

He is serious, then!

What can one say to him? Mutterperl knows as well as Jastrow that beyond this grave where living Jews in a long file are handing up dead Jews, beyond the pyre which is now burning down to glowing ash, the ring of SS men stands always with tommy guns at the ready, with leashed dogs that if released will kill any moving prisoner. There are different ways that this work changes men. There are the crazy ones: Berel understands them. There are the ones who have been robbing the bodies, and — usually the same ones — sucking up to the SS, informing on other Jews, doing anything to get more food, more comfort, more assurance of surviving. He even understands them. God did not make human nature strong enough to stand what the Germans are doing.

The bullying Jewish kapos in Auschwitz, the *Judenrat* officials in Warsaw and the other cities who picked people to go on the trains, and protected their relatives and friends, are all a product of the German cruelty. He can understand them. The mysterious crazy ferocity of the Germans is too much to endure; it turns normal people into treacherous animals. The hundreds of thousands of Jews that now lie in these graves meekly marched out to the pits and stood on the brink to let themselves be shot, with their wives, children, old parents, and all. Why? Because the Germans were acting beyond human nature. The surprise was too numbing. It could not be happening. People didn't do such things for no reason. On the brink of the hole, with the Germans or their Latvian or Ukrainian shooters pointing the guns at them, these Jews, clothed or naked, probably thought that it was all a mistake, or a hoax, or a dream.

Now Mutterperl wants to fight. Good, maybe that is the way, but with sense, not crazily! When Berel was with the partisans they killed some Germans. But what Mutterperl is talking about is a suicide rush; the work has gotten to him, and he really wants to die, whether he knows it or not; and this is wrong. They do not have the right to the surcease of death. They have to get to Prague.

"There he is," Mutterperl says with hoarse hate. *"Ut iz er."*

An SS man with gun tucked under an arm has come to the edge of the hole. He looks down, yawning, then takes out a pale penis and urinates over the bodies. This same fellow does this every day, usually several times. It is either his idea of humor, or a special way he has to show contempt for Jews. He is not a bad-looking young German, with a long narrow face, thick blond hair, and bright blue eyes. They know nothing else about him; they call him the Pisser. Marching to and from the work sites he is like the other SS men, tough and harsh, but not one of the sadists who look for excuses to beat a Jew. It is just his fancy to piss on the dead.

Mutterperl says, "Him, I want to kill."

Later, when both men are on the bone-disposal detail, raking warm fragments or whole collarbones, thighs, and skulls out of the smoking ash heap and feeding them into the bone-crushing mill, Mutterperl pokes Jastrow with an elbow.

"Ut iz er."

At the pit, the SS man is urinating again, picking a spot where the bodies still lie.

Mutterperl repeats, *"Him,* I want to kill."

The sun has gone down. It is almost dark, and bitter cold. The last fire of the day is flickering low all along the frame, lighting up the faces and arms of the Jews who are raking the fallen ashes for bones. The trucks have arrived. This grave is too far out from town to march the kommando there and back; not that one has to coddle Jews, but time is important. Blobel has even taken criticism for "taxiing" Jews with precious gasoline, as one critical SS inspector put it; but he has a tough hide and he runs his show as he pleases. Only he knows the true magnitude and urgency of the job. He knows more about it than the great Himmler, who assigned it to him, because he is the man on the spot, and he has all the maps and reports of the execution squads.

So the Jews will ride back to the cow barns at an abandoned dairy in Minsk. There are of course no cattle or horses in occupied Russia. The Germans have long since taken them off. Blobel's far-roaming Kommando 1005 has no trouble quartering its Jews in one animal stall or another, and its SS contingent merely turns out of their homes as many Russians as may be necessary. Food for the field kitchens is a chronic problem, because the Wehrmacht is so stingy about it, but Blobel's officers are now old hands at smelling out and requisitioning victuals from the local people. Even in this scrubby and devastated part of the Soviet Union there is food. People must eat. One has to know how to lay hands on their stores, that is all.

By the last light of the fire, Untersturmführer Greiser is himself locking up the valuables collected from the corpses, in heavy canvas bags used for transporting secret SS correspondence.

More of this disagreeable work tomorrow; a pretty deep grave, after all, two layers of bodies left. Half a day's work to clean them up, shovel in the ashes, level off the pit with dirt and scatter grass seed. By next spring it will be hard to find the place. In two years brush will cover it; in five years the woods will obliterate it with new growth, and that will be that.

Standartenführer Blobel's car drives up. In the dim firelight, the chauffeur gets out and salutes. Untersturmführer Greiser is to report to the Standartenführer at once, and the car has come for him. Greiser is surprised and concerned. The Standartenführer seems to like him, but any summons from a superior can be bad news. Probably the boss wants a report on the economic processing. Greiser puts his master sergeant in charge of the sacks, keeping the keys himself. The car drives off with him toward Minsk.

How Greiser would love a bath before he makes his report! It's no use keeping clear of the pit, the bodies, the smoke; the smell infects the air all around a work area. It haunts the nerves of your nose. You're still smelling it even after a bath, when you sit down to try to enjoy your dinner. Rough duty!

Untersturmführer Greiser reported to Kommando 1005 with a high rating for loyalty and intelligence. His father is an old National Socialist, a top official in the post office. Greiser was brought up in the Hitler movement. The special treatment of Jews was a hard concept to swallow when he first heard of it in a secret SS training program. But now he understands it. Still, he has had trouble with the Kommando 1005 mission. Why conceal and obliterate the graves? On the contrary, once the New Order triumphs these places should all have monumental markers to show where the enemies of mankind perished, at the hands of the German people, Western civilization's rescuers. He once ventured to say this to the Standartenführer. Blobel explained that once the new day dawns for mankind, all these evildoers and the world wars they caused must simply be forgotten, so that innocent children can grow up in a happy Jew-free world, without even a memory of the bad past.

But, Greiser objected, what will the world think happened to Europe's eleven million Jews, that they just vanished into thin air? Blobel, with an indulgent smile, advised the young man to read *Mein Kampf* again, on the stupidity and short memory of the masses.

Standartenführer Blobel, well along in his evening boozing, is poring over his SS maps of the Ukraine while he waits for Greiser to arrive. He finds the loyal naïveté of the young officer very engaging. Blobel could not tell him the truth about the 1005 operation, which he himself has surmised but has never breathed to a soul; and which is, that Heinrich Himmler now thinks Germany may lose the war, and is taking steps to preserve Germany's reputation. Blobel thinks the Reichsführer is very wise. One can hope the Führer will still pull it off, in spite of all the odds, and in spite of the hard Stalingrad blow. But now is the time to prepare for an unfavorable result of the war.

Whatever happens, doing away with the Jews will remain Germany's historic achievement. For two thousand years the European nations tried converting them, or isolating them, or driving them out. Yet when the Führer took power there they were still. Only the leader of Kommando 1005 can appreciate the true grandeur of Adolf Hitler to the fullest. As Himmler said, "We will never talk about this to the world." Even the mute evidence of the corpses must not exist. For otherwise the decadent democracies will pretend holy horror at Germany's special measures against the Jews, should they find out, though they have no use for the Jews themselves; and the Bolsheviks of course will make crude distorted propaganda of anything that can be turned to the Reich's discredit.

In short, Kommando 1005 has become the custodian of the great and sacred Reich secret; indeed, of Germany's national honor. He, Paul Blobel, is in the last analysis as great a guardian of that honor as the most famous general in the war; but the difficult work he must do will never get the praise it merits. He is a German hero who must go unsung. Drunk or sober, this is what Paul Blobel truly thinks. He is, in his own mind, no common concentration camp plug-ugly; nothing like it. He is a cultivated professional man, in peacetime an independent architect, a loyal German who understands German world-philosophy and is serving heart and soul in a very demanding war job. One honestly needs nerves of iron.

Greiser learns, on arriving at the house in Minsk which the Standartenführer is occupying, that Blobel is not interested in a report on the economic process. There is big news. Kommando 1005 is going to the Ukraine! The Standartenführer has been nagging Berlin for a month to issue these orders. He is in a jovial mood, and presses a large glass of schnapps on the young officer, who is glad enough to get it. Down in the Ukraine things will hum, because that is his own territory, Blobel says. He was a leading officer of *Einsatzgruppe* C, and he insisted from the start on keeping decent maps and accurate body-count reports. As a result the Ukraine sweep can be done with system. All this groping around for grave sites wastes precious time, and the ground in the north is still frozen, and the whole thing is stupid. While they are cleaning out the Ukraine, he will send an officer detail back to Berlin to make a thorough review of all the confused records, maps, and reports of *Einsatzgruppen* A and B. That detail will then return and search out and mark every northern grave site *in advance*.

Hope stirs in Greiser that he is being detailed back to Berlin, but that is not it. Blobel has another mission for him. The graves in the Ukraine are enormous, much bigger than any Greiser has seen. One frame will not do down there, they will have to work with three for best results. Greiser is to proceed at once to Kiev with a detachment of a hundred Jews from the section, a suitable number of SS guards, and report to the office of the Reich commissar for the Ukraine. Blobel will issue to him the necessary top-priority authorizations for steel rails and the use of a foundry. The Jew work leader "Sammy" is a construction man, and Greiser will have no trouble manufacturing the frames in a week or so. Blobel wants them finished and ready for use when Section 1005 arrives in Kiev. Meanwhile, it will clean out one more small grave to the west of Minsk, which was found today.

Greiser diffidently asks about the economic processing of the new grave. Very little to do, says Blobel; the bodies in that grave are naked.

But Standartenführer Blobel's plan for the move to the Ukraine is delayed at the outset by a grave accident at the Minsk railroad station.

At about nine o'clock in the morning, when the train has already failed to show up for two hours, and the Jews in striped suits are drooping sleepily on their feet in two long lines that stretch the length of the platform, and the SS guards are grouped in desultory talk to kill time, a burly figure bursts from the Jews, grabs a machine gun from one of the guards, and begins shooting! It is never known whose gun he snatched, because several guards fall and their guns go clattering over the platform. But no other Jews have time to snatch up the fallen guns and make real trouble. From both ends of the platform SS men come running, pumping bullets into Sammy Mutterperl. He topples, still holding the machine gun, blood flowing over his striped suit. The surviving guards surround him in rage and riddle his body with bullets; possibly a hundred slugs enter his already lifeless body. They boot and stamp and kick the corpse all around the platform, kicking and kicking at his face until it is a mere pulp of blood and broken bone, as a hundred Jews look on in dumb paralyzed fear. Yet they do not quite kick off the wrecked face the contours of a grin.

Four SS men are sprawled dead on the platform; one crawls around wounded, trailing blood, crying like a woman. It is the Pisser; and after a few moments he lies still across the track, dead as any corpse he ever pissed on, his blood spurting on the steel rails and the wooden ties.

In his report Greiser fixes the blame on the SS noncom in charge of the armed guards, who drifted together instead of holding spaced positions along the double line of Jews as regulations require. The Jew work leader "Sammy" was a privileged character who got special food rations. The incident demonstrates again that the subhuman Jews are totally unpredictable.

Therefore the harshest and most vigilant severity, as with wild animals, is the only safe method of handling them.

The detachment marches back from the station carrying the bodies. The dead SS men are left in Minsk, to receive honored burial in a German military cemetery. Mutterperl's blood-soaked and bullet-riddled remains go on the truck with the Jews to the grave site, to be burned on the frame with the day's corpses. Berel Jastrow sees the body, hears the whispered story down in the pit, and makes the blessing on evil news, *Blessed be the true judge.* He places himself at the frame when the pyre has burned down, and himself rakes out what he believes are Mutterperl's bone fragments. As he shoves them into the crusher, he murmurs the old burial service:

"Lord, full of mercy, dweller on high, grant true rest, under the wings of the Presence among the holy and pure ones, to the soul of Samuel, son of Nahum Mendel, who has gone to his eternity. . . . Blessed is the Lord who created you justly, fed and sustained you justly, gave you death justly, and in the future will resurrect you justly . . ."

So the faith teaches. But what resurrection can there be for these burned atomized remains? Well, the Talmud takes up the question of bodies destroyed by fire. It teaches that in each Jew there is one small bone that no fire can consume, that nothing can shatter; and that out of this minute indestructible bone, the resurrected body will grow and rise.

"Go in peace, Sammy," Berel says when it is finished.

Now it is up to him to get to Prague.

63

AMERICAN torpedoes were still failing when the *Moray* set forth on its first war patrol. The two problems that haunted SubPac were dud torpedoes and dud captains. The service was secretive about both alarming deficiencies, but the submariners themselves all knew about the unreliable magnetic exploders of the Mark Fourteen torpedo, and about the captains who either had to be beached for overcaution or, on the Branch Hoban pattern, fell apart under attack. Aces like Captain Aster who combined cold courage with skill and luck in battle were few. Such men of picturesque sobriquets — Mush Morton, Fearless Freddie Warder, Lady Aster, Red Coe — were setting the pace in SubPac, inspiring the rest of the skippers despite the damnable torpedo failures. Within broad limits, they could get away with murder.

A large sign over Admiral Halsey's advance headquarters in the Solomons read:

KILL JAPS
KILL JAPS
KILL MORE JAPS

A photograph of this sign hung on the bulkhead of Captain Aster's cabin in the *Moray*.

• • •

April 19, 1943; one more day of war; a day burned into Byron Henry's memory. For others elsewhere it was also a fateful day.

On April 19 the International Bermuda Conference was opening, after much delay, to decide on ways and means of helping "war refugees," and Leslie Slote was there in the American delegation. And on that selfsame April 19, Passover Eve, the Jews in the Warsaw Ghetto were rising in revolt, having been warned that the Germans were about to wipe the ghetto out — a few underground fighters taking on the Wehrmacht, seeking only the death of a Sammy Mutterperl in fighting and killing Germans.

On April 19 sorrowing Japanese were cremating Admiral Yamamoto. The Japanese still could not grasp that their codes were being broken, and so the plan for Yamamoto's risky air tour of forward bases had been broadcast in code. American fighter planes ambushed him in the sky, shot their way past escorting Zeroes, and gunned down the bomber he rode in. The search party groping in the Bougainville jungle came on Yamamoto's scorched corpse in full-dress inspection uniform, still gripping his sword. So perished the best man Japan had.

On April 19 the American and British forces in North Africa were closing the ring around Rommel's armies in Tunis, a German defeat as big as Stalingrad.

And on April 19 the Soviet government was reaching the point of breaking relations with the Polish government-in-exile. Nazi propagandists had been trumpeting the discovery of some ten thousand corpses in the uniforms of Polish army officers, buried in the Katyn woods in territory that the Russians had occupied from 1941 onward. Expressing righteous horror at this Soviet atrocity, the Germans were inviting neutral delegations to come and view the terrible mass graves. Since Stalin had openly shot multitudes of his own Red Army officers, the charge was at least plausible, and the Polish politicians in London had joined in suggesting an investigation. The fury of the Russian government at this idea was volcanic, and on April 19 the sensation was cresting.

So things were happening; yet in general, on the worldwide fronts the war simply went on, sluggishly here, actively there. No great turning point occurred on April 19. But nobody aboard the *Moray* was likely to forget that day.

• • •

It started with the down-the-throat shot.

"Open the doors forward," Aster said.

Goose pimples rose all over Byron's body. Submariners talked a lot about down-the-throat shots; usually in the calm safety of bars on dry land, or in wardrooms late at night. Aster had often said that in extremis he might try it; and in the training of his new vessel off Honolulu, he had taken many practice shots at a destroyer charging straight for him. Even those dummy runs had been hair-raising. Only a few skippers had ever tried it against the enemy and returned to tell the story.

Aster took the microphone. His voice was quiet, yet vibrant with controlled rage. "All hands hear this. He's heading for us along our torpedo wakes. I'm going to shoot him down the throat. We've been tracking this convoy for three days, and I'm not about to lose it because of those torpedo failures. Our fish ran straight, but they were duds again. We've still got twelve torpedoes on board, and there are major targets up there, a troop transport and two big freighters. He's the only escort, and if he drives us down and works us over they'll escape. So I'm going to shoot him with contact exploders on a shallow setting. Look alive."

The periscope stayed up. The executive officer reeled off ranges, bearings, target angles, his voice tightening and steadying; Pete Betmann, a man of thirty, bald as an egg, taciturn and quick-witted. Hastily Byron cranked the data into the computer, giving the destroyer an estimated flank speed of forty knots. It was a weird problem, evolving with unbelievable rapidity. No down-the-throat exercise in the attack trainer, or at sea off Honolulu, had gone this fast.

"Range twelve hundred yards. Bearing zero one zero, drifting to port."

"*Fire one!*"

Thump of the escaping torpedo; jolt of the deck underfoot. Byron had no confidence in his small gyro angle. Luck would decide this one.

"The wake is missing to starboard, Captain," said Betmann.

"Hell!"

"Range nine hundred yards . . . Range eight hundred fifty yards . . ."

Aster's choices were melting like a handful of snow in a fire. He could still order, "*Go deep — use negative,*" and plunge, or he could make a radical turn, probably take a terrific blast from a pinpointed depth-charging, and then hope to go deep and survive. Or he could fire again. Either way the *Moray* was already on the brink.

"Range eight hundred yards."

Could a torpedo still work? It shot out of the tube locked on safety. At eight hundred yards and closing so fast, it might not arm before it struck . . .

"*Fire two! Fire three! Fire four!*"

Byron's heart was beating so hard, and seemed to have swelled so huge in his chest, that he had to gasp for air. The closing speed of the destroyer and torpedo must be seventy knots! Propellers approaching, *ker-da-TRUMM, ker-da-TRUMM, ker-da-TRUMM —*

BLAMMM!

The exec in a scream: "HIT! My God, Captain, *you blew his bow off!* He's in two pieces!"

Thunderous rumbling shakes the hull.

"HIT! Oh, Captain, he's a shambles! His magazines must be going up! There's a gun mount flying through the air! And wreckage, and bodies, and his motor whaleboat, end over end —"

"Let me have a look," Aster snapped. The exec stepped away from the periscope, his face red and distorted, his naked scalp glistening. Aster swung the periscope about, droning, "Kay, the two freighters are hightailing it away, but the transport is turning *toward* us. That captain must be demented or in panic. Very good. Down scope!"

Folding up the handles, stepping away from the smoothly plunging shaft of the periscope, Aster bit out clear level words over the microphone. "Now all hands. The U.S.S. *Moray* has scored its first victory. That Jap destroyer is sinking in two sections. Well done. And our prime target, the transport, is heading this way. He's a ten-thousand-tonner, full of soldiers. So here's a big chance. We'll shoot him, then pursue the freighters on the surface. Let's get them all this time, and make up for the convoy we lost and for all those dud fish. Clean sweep!"

Eager yells echoed through the ship. Aster, curt and loud: "Knock it off! Celebrate when we've got 'em. Make ready the bow tubes."

The attack developed like a blackboard drill. Betmann exposed the periscope time after time, crisply rattling off data. The Jap came plodding into position. Perhaps because he was heading away from the sinking pieces of the destroyer he thought he was on an escape course.

"Open the outer doors."

The attack diagram was clear and perfect in Byron's mind, the eternal moving triangle of submarining: the transport steaming along in the sunshine at twenty knots, the *Moray* half a mile on its beam and some sixty feet under water, slinking toward it at four knots, and the torpedoes in the open flooded stern tubes, ready to race from the one to the other at forty-five knots. Only malfunction, massive malfunction of American machinery, could save the Jap now.

"Final bearing and shoot."

"Up periscope! Mark. Bearing zero zero three. Down scope!"

Aster fired a spread of three torpedoes. Within seconds explosions rocked the conning tower, and heavy shocking detonations rang along the hull. Whoops, cheers, rebel yells, laughter, whistles, shouts broke out all over the submarine. In the crowded tower sailors punched each other and capered.

The exec shouted, "Captain, two sure *hits*. On the quarter, and amidships. I see *flames*. She's afire, smoking, listing to starboard, down by the bow."

"Surface and man all guns."

The rush of fresh air at the cracking of the hatch, the shaft of sunlight, the drip of sparkling seawater, the healthy growl of the diesels starting up, touched off in Byron a surge of exhilaration. He seemed to float up the ladder to the bridge.

"God in heaven, what a sight!" said Betmann, coming beside him.

It was a beautiful day: clear blue sky with a few high puffy clouds, gently swelling blue sea, blinding white sun. The equatorial air was humid and very hot. Close by, the transport steeply listed under a cloud of smoke, its red bottom showing. A strident alarm siren was wailing, and yelling men in life jackets were climbing over the side and down cargo nets. A couple of miles away the forecastle of the destroyer still floated, with forlorn figures clinging to it and crowded boats tossing close by.

"Let's circle this fellow," said Captain Aster, chewing on his cigar, "and see where the freighters have got off to."

His tone was debonair, but as he took the cigar from his mouth Byron could see his hand shake. The patrol was a success right now, but by the look of Carter Aster he was ravening for more; tightened grinning mouth, coldly shining eyes. For thirty-seven days, sharpened by the torpedo failure, this greed for action had been building up in him. Until a quarter of an hour ago, a goose-egg first patrol threatened him. No more.

As they rounded the stern, passing the huge brass propeller lifted clear out of the water, a wild sight burst on them. The transport was disgorging its troops on this side. In covered launches, in open landing craft and motor-boats, on wide gray rafts, Jap soldiers crowded in the thousands. Hundreds more were swarming on the deck and fleeing down the dangling cargo nets and rope ladders. "Like ants off a hot plate," Aster gaily observed. The blue sea was half-gray with troops bobbing in kapok life vests.

"Good Lord," Betmann said, "how many of them does it hold?"

Aster said absently, peering through binoculars at the two distant freighters, "Oh, these Japs are cattle. They just pack 'em in. What's the range to those freighters, Pete?"

Betmann looked through a dripping alidade. A burst of machine gun fire drowned out his reply, as smoke and flame spurted from a covered launch jammed with soldiers.

"I'll be damned," said Aster, smiling, "he's trying to put a hole in us! He just might, too." Cupping his hands, he shouted, "Number two gun, sink him."

The forty-millimeters opened up, and the Japanese began leaping off the launch. Pieces flew from its hull, but it went on firing for a few seconds, and then the silent smoking little wreck sank. Many inert bodies in green uniforms and gray life vests floated off it.

Aster turned to Betmann. "What's that range, now?"

"Seven thousand, Captain."

"Okay. We'll circle, charge our batteries, and get our pictures of this transport." Aster glanced at his watch and at the sun. "We can overtake those other two monkeys before dusk, easy. Meantime let's sink these boats and rafts, and send all the floaters to join their honorable ancestors."

Byron was more sickened than surprised, but what the exec did surprised him. Betmann firmly put his hand on Aster's forearm as the captain was lifting the bridge microphone to his mouth. "Captain, don't do it." It was said *sotto voce*. Byron, at Aster's elbow, barely heard it.

"Why not?" Aster was just as quiet.

"It's butchery."

"What are we out here for? Those are combat troops. If they're picked up, they'll be in action against our guys on New Guinea in a week."

"It's like shooting prisoners."

"Come on, Pete. What about the guys on Bataan? What about the guys still inside the hull of the *Arizona*?" Aster shook off Betmann's hand. His voice rang out over the deck. "Now gun crews, hear this. All these boats, barges, and rafts are legitimate targets of war, and so are the men in the water. If we don't kill them, they'll live to kill Americans. *Fire at will.*"

On the instant every gun barrel on the *Moray* was spitting yellow fire and white smoke.

"All ahead slow," Aster called down the tube. "Maximum charge on the batteries." He turned to Byron. "Call away the quartermaster. Let's get pictures of that tin can while he's still afloat, and of this fat boy."

"Aye aye, sir." Byron passed the order on his telephone.

The Japanese were leaping frantically off the boats and rafts. The four-inch gun was methodically picking off boats, and at this point-blank range they were flying apart one by one. Soon the rafts and launches were empty, the troops were all in the water, and some were shucking their life jackets to dive deep. Machine gun bullets were drilling rows of white spurts in the water. Byron saw heads bursting redly open like dropped melons.

"Captain," Betmann said, "I am going below."

"Very well, Pete." Aster was lighting a fresh cigar. "Go ahead."

By the time the transport reared its stern up and sank, uncountable lifeless Japanese floated all around the *Moray* on the bloodstained water. A few still swam here and there like porpoises harried by a shark.

"Well, I guess that's that," Carter Aster said. "Time's a-wasting, Byron. We'd better catch those freighters. Secure the gun crews. Set cruising watch. All ahead full."

The sun was low when the *Moray*, overhauling the freighters in an end run at long range, submerged. The unprotected ships were making only eleven knots. Lieutenant Betmann came back on the periscope, good-humored and accurate as though the events of the morning had made no difference to him. But among the crew, they had made a difference. During the daylong chase, whenever Byron had come on a group of sailors, he had been met with silence and odd looks, as though he were interrupting talk not meant for an officer's ears. They were a new crew, just working in together, and they should have been buoyant and noisy over the victories, but they were not.

Lieutenant Betmann was a hard one for Byron to figure out. He had come to the *Moray* from BuOrd; he was a Christian Scientist, and he had initiated voluntary (and ill-attended) Sunday services on the submarine. Whatever his scruples about the morning slaughter, he was now all crisp aggressiveness once more.

Aster gambled three of his remaining five torpedoes on an overlapping shot at the two ships steaming close together. Betmann reported one hit flaring up in the night; the explosion rumbled through the *Moray*'s hull.

"Surface!"

The light in the conning tower was dim and red to protect night vision, but Byron could see the disappointed grimace on Carter Aster's face. The *Moray* came up in moonlight on a choppy sea. The undamaged ship was turning away from its stricken companion, dark smoke pouring out of its funnel and obscuring the stars.

"All ahead full!"

Both freighters began firing wildly at the black shape cutting the swells in phosphorescent spray. Judging by the muzzle flames, they were armed not only with machine guns but also with three-inch cannon; a solid hit from one of these could sink a submarine. But Aster bore on through the red tracers and whirring shells as though they were the ticker tape of a hero's parade, and pulled abreast of the fleeing freighter, which swelled big as an ocean liner and blazed with gunfire.

"Left full rudder. Open the stern tubes." The submarine swung around under a fusillade of crimson tracers and high-whining bullets. The lookouts were cowering behind their bullet shields. So was Byron. Aster, erect and staring astern, fired one torpedo. The night burst into thundering red day. The freighter flamed up amidships.

"Dive, dive, dive!"

Byron, shaking in his shoes, had to admire this. With both targets hit and halted, Aster was taking no more gunfire.

"Okay, after torpedo room," Aster said into the microphone, as the submarine slanted down into the sea, "we got him. Now comes our last torpedo. Our last shot of the patrol. It's the freighter we hit before, and he's a sitting duck. He needs one more punch. So, no foul-ups. Let's sink him and head for the barn."

Aster crept up on the cripple, reversed the submarine, and made his shot at six hundred yards. The *Moray* rocked in the very close underwater explosion, and the crew cheered.

"Surface! Surface! Surface! And I'm so proud of the whole lot of you, I could damn near cry." Indeed, Aster's voice was choking with unabashed emotion. "You're the greatest submarine crew in the Navy. And let me tell you something, the *Moray* has only BEGUN to kill Japs."

Whatever the roiled emotions of the day, the crew was with him again. The cheering and whooping and hugging and handshaking went on and on until the quartermaster cracked the hatch, the diesels coughed and roared, and moonlit seawater dripped down the ladder.

Coming out into the hot night, Byron saw both vessels dead in the water and burning. There was no gunfire. One freighter sank fast, its flame going out like a spent candle. But the other burned on, its broken hulk staying obstinately afloat, until Aster with a yawn told Betmann to finish it off with the four-inch gun. Peppered with blazing hits, it still took a long time to sink. At last the sea went dark, except for the yellow path of a low half-moon.

"Now hear this, gentlemen of the U.S.S. *Moray*," Aster announced, "we will come to zero six seven, the course for Pearl Harbor. When we pass channel buoy number one, ten days from now, we'll tie a broom to the periscope. All engines ahead standard, and God bless you all, you marvelous gang of fighting fools."

Such was the April 19th of Byron Henry.

The broom was up there when they entered Pearl Harbor. On a long streamer behind the broom, four small Japanese flags fluttered. Sirens, foghorns, steam whistles, serenaded the *Moray* all the way up-channel. On the dock at the sub base, a stunning surprise: Admiral Nimitz, in dress whites, stood amid the entire khaki-clad staff of SubPac. When the gangplank went over, Aster called the men to quarters. Nimitz marched aboard alone. "Captain, I want to shake the hand of every officer and man on this ship." He did, passing along the forecastle with his wrinkled eyes agleam; then the SubPac staff came crowding on deck. Somebody brought a *Honolulu Advertiser*. The lead headline was

CLEAN SWEEP ON FIRST PATROL

Sub Wipes Out Convoy and Escort
"One-boat Wolf Pack" — Lockwood

The picture of Aster, grinning in strong sunlight, was recent, but the newspaper had dug up Betmann's Academy graduation photograph, and he looked decidedly odd with all that hair.

Dry land felt good underfoot. Byron made slow progress to the ComSubPac building. The word was spreading fast about the killing of the Jap troops in the water, and the long walk became a sort of straw poll on Aster's deed. Officers kept stopping him to talk about it, and reactions ranged from nauseated disapproval to bloodthirsty enthusiasm. The vote seemed to go against Aster, though not by much.

Later in the day, Janice flung herself at Byron when he arrived with a wild kiss that dizzied, thrilled, and shot fire through him.

"Holy smoke," he gasped. *"Janice!"*

"Oh, hell, I love you, Briny. Don't you know that? But don't be afraid of me, I won't eat you." She broke loose, eyes glowing, yellow hair tumbled this way and that. Her thin satiny pink dress swished as she darted to a table and brandished the *Advertiser*. "Seen this?"

"Oh, sure."

"And did you get my message? Is Carter coming for dinner?"

"He's coming."

Aster showed up far from sober, wearing several leis that had been piled on him at the officers' club. He draped one flowery wreath on Byron and another on Janice, who gave him a decorous kiss. They washed down a feast of shrimps, steak, baked potatoes, and apple pie à la mode, with four bottles of California champagne, joking randomly and laughing themselves helpless. Afterward Janice donned an apron and ordered them to let her clear up herself. "Conquering heroes," she said a bit thickly, "stay the hell out of my kitchen. Go out on the lanai. No mosquitoes tonight, offshore wind."

On the dark porch facing the canal, as they sank into wicker chairs with the wine bottle between them, Aster said in a flat sober tone, "Pete Betmann has asked to be transferred."

After a silence Byron said, "And? What do we do for an exec?"

"I told the admiral I wanted you."

"Me?" Byron's head was spinning from the wine. He tried to collect himself. "That's impossible."

"Why?"

"I'm too junior. I'm a reserve. Battle stations, sure, I'd love the periscope, but I'm a zilch administrator."

"The roster shows you qualified, and you are. The admiral's considering it. You'd only be the third reserve exec in SubPac, but he's inclined to give me what I want. The other two guys are senior to you, they've been on active duty since '39. But you've done a lot of combat patrolling."

"I had all that dead time in the Med."

"Maintenance at an advance base isn't dead time."

Byron poured for both of them. They drank in darkness. Over the clinking and splashing in the kitchen they could hear Janice singing "Lovely Hula Hands."

After a while Aster said, "Or do you agree with Pete Betmann? Don't you want to sail with me again? That can be arranged, too."

In the long voyage back to base there had been very little talk in the wardroom about the slaughter episode. Byron hesitated, then said, "I haven't asked off."

"We go out there to kill Japs, don't we?"

"They didn't have a fighting chance in the water."

"Horseshit." The word had harsh force because Aster tended to avoid obscenities. "We're in a war. The way to end it, to win it, and to save lives in the long run, is to kill large numbers of the enemy. Right? Or wrong?" No answer from Byron. "Well?"

"Lady, you loved it."

"I didn't mind doing a job on the bastards, no. I admit that. The war was their idea."

Silence in the dark.

"They killed your brother."

"I said I haven't asked off. Drop it, Captain."

Janice sat up talking with Byron long after Aster left, about the patrol, and then about Warren, reminiscing affectionately as they had never done before. He said nothing about Natalie, except that he meant to call the State Department in the morning. When he went off to bed he held out his arms and gave her a passionate kiss. Surprised, moved, she looked into his eyes. "That's for Natalie, isn't it?"

"No. 'Night."

Before she left she looked into his room and listened to his quiet breathing. The Military Government pass on her car eliminated the curfew problem, and she drove through the blackout to the small hotel Aster now stayed at for their meetings. She slipped back into her house a few hours later, weary, spent, aglow with the transient rapture of unauthorized ass. Again she listened to Byron's breathing; heavy, regular, no change. Janice went to bed blissful in body and soul, yet with an irrational wisp of guilty feeling, almost as though she had committed adultery.

The controversy over Aster's killing of the Jap troops went on for a long time within SubPac. It never spilled over to the newspapers, or even to the rest of the Navy. The submariners kept it a family secret. Long after the war, when all patrol reports were declassified, it came out at last. Carter Aster's report described the killing in candid detail, and ComSubPac's endorsement was one of unqualified high praise. The draft endorsement by the chief of staff was also declassified. He had written a long paragraph disapproving of the slaughter of helpless swimmers. The admiral had struck it out with an angry scratch of the pen; the ink splatters still stain the page moldering in the Navy's war files.

"If I had ten more aggressive killers like Aster in this command," the admiral said to the chief of staff at the time, "the war would end a year sooner. I will not criticize Lieutenant Commander Aster for killing Japs. This was a great patrol, and I will recommend him for his second Navy Cross."

64

ARLY in July, the minister of the American legation in Bern heard from Leslie Slote after a very long silence. Ordinary mail from the United States had been cut off since the German seizure of southern France, and there were no official pouches anymore. But the pouches of neutral diplomats were an irregular recourse for getting letters and reports back and forth. One of Slote's old friends in the Swiss Foreign Ministry brought Tuttle the thick envelope — handing it to him, after a meeting on another matter, without a word as he left.

June 3, 1943

Dear Bill,

I'll start by apologizing for the illegibility of my enclosed memorandum on the Bermuda Conference. I'm writing in bed, nursing a sprained ankle. I've resigned from the Foreign Service, so I have no office or secretary.

My sprained ankle is due to a parachute jump. An altered Leslie Slote scrawls these lines! I have always been — to put it charitably — a timid sort. But on quitting the Department I landed in the Office of Strategic Services. I've been on the run ever since, with no notion of where I'll fetch up, but with a novel if somewhat alarmed sense of euphoria, such as a man might have upon falling out of an airplane and finding himself enjoying — however briefly —the panoramic view and cold breeze of the plunge. Images of falling come to me readily, after my parachute jump yesterday: an utter nightmare, yet in a blood-curdling way quite exhilarating.

Of course you know about the OSS. As I recall, General "Wild Bill" Donovan rather ruffled your feathers when he whirled through Bern last year. It is an improvised intelligence outfit, bizarre in the extreme. Obviously I can tell you very little about what I'm doing. *But I am doing something;* and that, after the State Department, is a good feeling. I've been through a professional catastrophe, but things have been moving too fast for me to give much time to self-pity.

Bill, the State Department is a seraglio from which the beauties have all been kidnapped, leaving behind a drove of squeaking eunuchs with nothing to do. Mr. Roosevelt and Mr. Hopkins between them preempt most of foreign policy; General Donovan's outfit is moving in on the rest; and the castratos at State impotently continue to pass papers around which might as well be toilet tissue.

If all this sounds bitter, remember that I've destroyed my career, relinquished ten years of precious seniority, because I think it's the truth. What the State Department did at the Bermuda Conference finished me off, though it was probably only a question of time before I'd have quit anyway. The Jewish problem had grown for me into a cancerous obsession, and Breckinridge Long was aggravating my condition to dementia. Now I am *out,* and recovering.

Long drafted me into the Division of European Affairs, as you know, to handle Jewish problems. He was then under very heavy pressure to break the visa logjam facing refugees from Hitler, and also to do something about the Jews being railroaded to extermination. He's a beset man who has taken to clutching at straws. I guess he wanted one plausible figure in the division with a "pro-Jewish" reputation, who could speak sympathetically to Jews without having any power to help them. And I guess he counted on me, as a good loyal State Department hack, to follow his policies no matter how they went against my grain. The real question is why I accepted the job. The answer is, I don't know. I suppose I hoped that Long meant what he said, and that I could be a loosening, liberalizing, moderating voice on Jewish matters.

If so, I was self-deceived. From the first, and until I left the Bermuda Conference in mid-session, I ran into a blank wall. On the whole, I now feel sorry for Breckinridge Long. I don't even regard him as the villain of the piece. He can't help being what he is. He sent me to Bermuda to be a sort of Gentile Sol Bloom, a support diplomat with demonstrable pro-Jewish sympathies, to be cited at future congressional investigations, if any. My resignation is not going to look very good on the record, but of course I have no interest now in keeping up the State Department façade.

And what a façade it was! How carefully it was stage-managed by our Department and the British Foreign Office to screen out pressure, challenge, and controversy! Newspapermen couldn't get there. Labor leaders, Jewish leaders, protest marchers — the broad ocean protected the conference from all that. Bermuda was lovely with spring flowers, and we met in charming hotels far from the new military bases, with plenty of time off to swim in the pools and drink the island's rum concoctions. In the social evenings amid Bermuda's smart set one could almost forget there was a war on.

Poor Dr. Harold Dodds — the president of Princeton, dragooned for the chairmanship of our delegation — beseeched me to stay on, but by the third day I had had enough. I told him that I was either going to raise the question of the Jews threatened with extermination (*these Jews were a forbidden topic at the conference!*) or I was going to fly back to Washington and resign from the Foreign Service. Dodds was helpless. He couldn't authorize me to go against the policies that bound him. So I left, and at least I brought away a small shred of my self-respect.

The proceedings of the conference haven't yet been published. The Department is now frenziedly pleading a need for secrecy "to protect the measures to aid political refugees." What Messrs. Hull and Long really hope is that interest in the conference will die out, and they'll never have to come clean. But it will not. The pressure for disclosure will build, and there is going to be a hell of an explosion when the truth is uncovered.

My memorandum will give you an inkling of what really happened at Bermuda. You remember that horrible document I received in the Bern movie theatre, describing the Wannsee Conference? I could not authenticate it, but events have since done so with a vengeance. Unless President Roosevelt acts quickly, history will say that the Jews of Europe were destroyed between the hammer of the Wannsee Conference and the anvil of the Bermuda Conference. The American people under Roosevelt will be blamed, equally with the Germans under Hitler, for the massacre! That is a cruel distortion, but it is exactly what Breck Long is bringing about.

You know President Roosevelt well. I send you this memorandum, to do with what you will. It is a clear and true warning of what impends after Bermuda, not only for the European Jews, but for the historical reputation of Franklin Delano Roosevelt, and certainly for the postwar moral position of America in the world. Please read it carefully, and consider whether — in any form you choose to revise or amplify it — it should go to the President.

Hurricanes never find people prepared, Bill, and by the time improvised safety measures are taken, the storm has wreaked its worst. The German massacre of the Jews is a hurricane. There has never been anything like it. It is going on behind the smokescreen of a world war, in a rogue nation cut off from civilized society. It could not be happening otherwise. Recognition of it has been slow, measures to deal with it laggard. But all these mitigating facts will be lost in later years. Seen in retrospect, the Bermuda Conference will be perceived as a ruthless, heartless farce, perpetrated by America and England to avoid taking any action while millions of innocent people were being slaughtered.

So long as the responsibility is not taken from Breck Long this distortion will deepen and harden, yet the final disgrace will not rest with him, for he will be a forgotten small man. If the Bermuda Conference remains the Allies' last word on the Nazi barbarity, Franklin Roosevelt will go down as the great American President who led his country out of depression and into world triumph; but who, with full knowledge of this horrendous massacre, failed the Jews. Don't let it happen, Bill. Warn the President.

For the sake of my own sanity, with this memorandum I sever my accidental involvement in the most terrible crime in the history of the world. The burden was never mine, except in the sense that it is every man's. The world so far refuses to shoulder it. I have tried and failed, because I am nobody and powerless. This memorandum written in blood — the Jews', and mine — is my legacy of the experience.

Sincerely,
Leslie Slote

William Tuttle could readily see in the enclosed memorandum, scrawled on legal-length yellow sheets, the exasperated outpouring of a subordinate quitting his job in anger. The style was hurried, the tone intemperate. That this careful and timorous man had taken a job involving parachutist training sufficiently showed how shaken up he was.

Nevertheless, the memorandum disturbed Tuttle. He had been wondering about the Bermuda Conference. He did not sleep well for a couple of nights, wondering what to do about all this. Breck Long had always seemed to him a sound enough person; a polished self-assured gentleman, very much an insider, a good judge of horseflesh, and all in all anything but a villain.

But Tuttle still resented the recent orders that had come from the State Department to stop transmitting through Department codes the Jewish reports out of Geneva about the exterminations; and he was well aware that all the information he had sent to the Division of European Affairs had vanished into silence. He himself did not like to dwell on the Jewish horror, and he had let the lack of response pass as bureaucratic delay and inattention. But if Long was at the bottom of it, and doing it purposefully, the President perhaps ought to know. How to tell him?

In the end he heavily cut Slote's memorandum, toning down the bitter diatribes against Breckinridge Long. He sent the typed revision to Washington via the Swiss pouch, with a handwritten covering letter marked *Personal and Urgent,* for the President.

August 5, 1943

Dear Mr. President:

The author of the enclosed document served at the Bermuda Conference and resigned from the Foreign Service in protest. He is a Rhodes Scholar who worked with me here in Bern. I found him a man of rare intelligence, always thoroughly reliable.

I hesitate to add to your grave burdens, but a twofold concern compels me to do so: firstly, for the terrible fate of the European Jews; secondly, for your own place in history. This report may help fill in for you a true picture of what happened at the Bermuda Conference, behind the official reports. I am afraid I tend to believe Leslie Slote.

With deepest respect and admiration,

Sincerely,
Bill

CONFIDENTIAL MEMORANDUM
The Bermuda Conference: American and British Complicity in the Extermination of the European Jews

1. *Historical Background*

Since early 1941 the German government has been engaged in a secret systematic operation to murder Europe's Jews. This stark fact goes so far beyond all previous human experience that no social machinery exists to cope with it.

Because of the war the German government is an international outlaw, answerable only to the German people. By police state terror the Nazi regime has reduced them to docile compliance in its savage acts. Yet the sad truth is, popular resistance to the Nazi policy against Jewry has been minimal since Hitler took power.

The roots of the massacre lie in a broad and deep German cultural strain, a sort of desperate romantic nationalism, an extreme reaction to the humane liberalism of the West. This body of thought extols a brutish self-glorification of warlike German "Kultur," and implies, where it does not openly express, virulent anti-Semitism. This is a complex and dark subject. The philosopher Croce traces this uncivilized strain to an event in Roman times, the victory of Arminius in the Teutoburg Forest, which cut off the German tribes from the meliorating influence of Roman law and manners. Whatever the origin, Adolf Hitler's rise and popularity indicate how that strain persists.

2. Embarrassments of the Allies

The Bermuda Conference took place because the secret of the massacre leaked out. On December 17, 1942, the governments of the United Nations publicly and jointly warned that its perpetrators would be punished. This official disclosure sparked a strong public demand in the United States and Great Britain for action

Unfortunately, in his Jewish policy Adolf Hitler struck at the Achilles' heel of Western liberalism.

Quite aside from the Jews, the call for action has come from press, church, progressive politicians, intellectuals, and the like. But other forces, glacially silent and immovable, have prevented action.

What the Jews want from England is the opening of Palestine to unrestricted Jewish immigration, an obvious step to relieve the Nazi pressure. But the British Foreign Office believes it cannot risk Arab opposition, at this stage of the war, to such a step. An equally obvious move for the United States would be emergency legislation to admit the threatened victims of Hitler. But our drastic restrictive laws are the will of Congress, which is against changing the "racial composition" of our country.

If Allied liberalism were government policy, rather than something between an ideal and a myth, these steps would be taken. As realities stand, Adolf Hitler has put the Allies on the spot.

Hence, the Bermuda Conference. It was launched with fanfare as the Allied response to the Nazi horrors. The Conference produced an appearance of action, to placate the demand; and the fact of inaction, to conform to policy. It was a mockery. The diplomatic menials went through the motions with very bad consciences, to which they adjusted with bravado, mendacity, or ulcers.

In all this there was not so much villainy as a pathetic inability to come to grips with history's most monstrous villainy.

That is the heart of the matter. The Nazi massacre of the Jews is still far-fetched newspaper talk to most people, obscured by big battle stories. The German action is so savage, so incomprehensible, so far from the mild dislike of Jews which is an old story everywhere, that public opinion shuts it out of mind. The glare of war makes that easy.

3. *The Conference*

The agreed purpose of the Conference was "*to deal with the problem of political refugees.*" Great emphasis was placed on the avoidance of the word "Jews" in the agenda. Moreover, the only "political refugees" that could be discussed were those in neutral countries; that is, people whose lives were already safe! These rules were secret. No word of them ever got out to the press.

Someday the minutes will have to come to light. They will show nothing but a dreary sham, a repulsive exercise in diplomatic dodging, shadowboxing, and double-talking. Every attempt to expand the agenda is beaten down; every suggestion for real action — even to relieve the pileup of refugees in neutral countries — is frustrated. There are no funds; or there is no shipping; or there is no place to send people; or they pose too great a security problem, because of possible spies and saboteurs among them; or the action in question might "interfere with the war effort."

A game of buck-passing goes on and on. The Americans push for North Africa and the Near East as a place to dump refugees. The British insist on an opening up of the western hemisphere. In the end they cordially agree on negative conclusions; and to produce the illusion of action, they agree to revive the moribund Committee on Refugees established by the Evian Conference, a similar fiasco perpetrated in 1938.

It is easy to condemn the delegates who had to go through this contemptible charade. But they were puppets, acting out the policies of their governments, and ultimately the public will of their nations.

4. *The Need for Further Steps*

After the disaster of the Conference, what can still be done?

At best, very little can be done. The Germans are bent on their savage deed. They have most of Europe's Jews in their grip. Only Allied victory can prevent their carrying out their purpose. But *if we will but do with vigor what little we can do, we will be absolved of complicity in the Nazi crime.* As things stand now, the Bermuda Conference has made the United States government a passive bystander at murder.

Some sixteen months from now, there will be a presidential election. The massacre of the European Jews may by then be almost an accomplished fact. The American people will have had another year and a half to overcome their lag in awareness of this incredible horror. Evidence will have mounted to a flood. Conceivably Europe will have been invaded, and some murder camps captured. The American public is a humane one. Though today it does not want to "admit all those Jews," by the end of 1944 it will be looking for somebody to blame for letting the thing happen. The blame will fall squarely on those in power now.

The author of this memorandum knows the President to be a true humanitarian, who would like to help the Jews. But in this vast global war, the problem is a low-priority one. Since so little can be done, and since the subject is so ghastly, Mr. Roosevelt can hardly be blamed for attending to other things.

The agitation to open Palestine or to change the immigration laws seems hopeless. Extravagant mass ransom schemes, and proposals to bomb nonmilitary targets like concentration camps, run afoul of major war-making policies. Still, some things can be done, and must be done.

5. *Short-term Steps*

The single most urgent and useful thing that President Roosevelt can do at once is *to take the entire refugee problem out of the State Department*, and above all away from Mr. Breckinridge Long.

He is now in charge of this problem, and be is a disaster. This unfortunate man, forced out on a limb of negativism, is resolved to do as little as possible; to prevent anybody else from doing any more; and to move heaven and earth to prove that he is right and has always been right, and that nobody could be a better friend of the Jews. At heart he still seems to think that talk of the Nazi massacre is mostly a clever trick to get around the immigration laws.

State personnel have had this viewpoint drummed into them. Too many share his rigid restrictionist convictions. The Department's morale, and its capacity to perform in humanitarian matters, are low. An executive agency must be created, empowered to explore any possibility to save Jewish lives, and to act with speed. Commonsense adjustment of visa rules in itself can at once rescue a larger number of Jews *eligible to enter the United States under existing quotas.* They will be no financial burden. Relief funds in almost any magnitude will be procurable from the Jewish community.

Latin America's restrictionism is based on our own. Once the new agency projects to Latin American countries the changed attitude of the United States, some of those countries will follow suit.

The new agency should at once move as many refugees as possible from the four neutral European havens — Switzerland, Sweden, Spain, and Portugal — to relieve the strain on them, and change their present attitude of "the lifeboat is full" to one of welcome to those hunted Jews who can still reach their borders.

The new agency should work on congressional leaders for the temporary admission of perhaps twenty thousand refugees. If ten other countries around the world will follow such a lead, this will be a loud and clear signal to the slaughterers themselves, and to the satellite governments which have not yet handed over their Jewish citizens to the Germans, that the Allies mean business.

For as the tide of war shifts, the murders are bound to slow, and at last stop. Sooner or later, the murderers and their accomplices will take fright. That turning point can come when ninety-nine percent of the Jews are gone, or when sixty or seventy percent are gone. No better figure can probably be hoped for; but even that much would be a historic achievement.

Leslie Slote

•   •   •

William Tuttle received no acknowledgment of his letter to the President, and never found out whether it had reached him. As a matter of history, the public reaction gradually swelled to a roar during 1943, as the facts of the Bermuda Conference came out. On January 22, 1944, an Executive Order from the White House took the refugee problem out of the State Department's hands. It created the War Refugee Board, an executive agency empowered to deal with "Nazi plans to exterminate all the Jews." A new policy of forceful American rescue action began. By then the hurricane had long been blowing its worst.

65

THE Swiss diplomat who walked into the hospital alongside Jastrow's wheelchair brought a letter from the German ambassador to the director, Comte Aldebert de Chambrun. "You know, of course," said the Swiss casually, "Monsieur's masterpiece, *Le Jésu d'un Juif.*"

Comte de Chambrun was a retired general, a financier, an old-line aristocrat, and an in-law of Premier Laval, all of which made him fairly imperturbable, even in these disordered times. He nodded as he glanced over the letter, which called for the finest possible treatment for the "distinguished author." Since the abrupt departure of most of the staff after Pearl Harbor, the comte had taken on the directorship of the American Hospital. The few Americans left in Paris came there for treatment, but Jastrow was the first from the Baden-Baden group. The comte did not keep up with current American literature and wasn't sure he had ever heard of Jastrow. *A Jew's Jesus!* Strange letter, in the circumstances.

"You will note," went on the Swiss, as though reading his mind, "that the occupying authority considers racial origin irrelevant."

"Just so," replied the comte. "Prejudice cannot pass the doorway of a hospital."

The Swiss received this sentiment with a face twitch, and left. Within the hour the German embassy telephoned to inquire about Jastrow's condition and accommodations. That settled it. When Jastrow began to mend, after difficult two-stage surgery and a few bad days, the director placed him in a sunny room and had him nursed around the clock.

Comte de Chambrun discussed this odd German solicitude for Jastrow with his wife, a very positive American woman with a quick answer for everything. The comtesse was a *grande dame:* a Longworth, related by marriage to the Roosevelts, sister of the former Speaker of the House. She was whiling away the war by managing the American Library, and pursuing her Shakespearean studies. Their son was married to the daughter of Pierre Laval. The comtesse had long since taken on French citizenship, but in talk and manner she remained pungently American, with a patina of rabid French old-nobility snobbishness; a walking anomaly of seventy, begging for the pen of a Proust.

There was nothing in the least odd about the thing, the comtesse briskly told her husband. She had read *A Jew's Jesus,* and didn't think much of it, but the man did have a name. He would soon be going home. What he had to say about his treatment would be widely quoted in American newspapers and magazines. Here was a chance for the Boches to counter the unfavorable propaganda about their Jewish policy; she was surprised only at the good sense they were showing, for she regarded the Germans as a coarse and thickheaded lot.

General de Chambrun also told her about Jastrow's niece. Chatting with her in visiting hours, he had been struck by her haggard sad beauty, perfect French, and quick intelligence. The young lady might work at the library, he suggested, since Jastrow's convalescence would take time. The comtesse perked up at that. The library was far behind in sorting and cataloguing piles of books left behind in 1940 by hastily departing Americans. The Boches might veto the idea; then again, the American niece of a famous author, wife of a submarine officer, might be quite all right, even if she was Jewish. The comtesse consulted the German official who supervised libraries and museums, and he readily gave her permission to employ Mrs. Henry.

Thereupon she lost no time. Natalie was visiting Aaron at the hospital when the comtesse barged into the room and introduced herself. She liked the look of Natalie at once; quite chic for a refugee, pleasantly American, with a dark beauty that might easily be of Italian or even French origin. The old Jew in the bed looked more dead than alive; gray-bearded, big-nosed, with large melancholy brown eyes feverishly bright in a waxy sunken face.

"Your uncle seems to be very sick indeed," said the comtesse in the director's office, where she invited Natalie for a cup of "verbena tea" which tasted like, and perhaps was, boiled grass.

"He almost died of internal hemorrhaging," said Natalie.

"My husband says he can't return to Baden-Baden for a while. When he's well enough he'll be moved to our convalescent home. Now then, Mrs. Henry, the general tells me that you're Radcliffe, with a Sorbonne graduate degree. *Pas mal.* How would you like to do something useful?"

She walked with Natalie to her boardinghouse; declared the place unfit for an American to be caught dead in; cooed, or rather croaked, over Louis; and undertook to move them to decent lodgings. Marching Natalie to an old mansion near the hospital, converted to flats occupied by hospital staff, she then and there arranged room and board for her and the baby. By nightfall she had moved them to the new place, executed the necessary papers at the prefecture, and checked them in with the German administrator of the Neuilly suburb. When she left, she promised to return in the morning and take Natalie to the library by Métro. She would arrange, she said, for someone to look after Louis.

Natalie was quite overborne by this crabbed old fairy godmother materializing out of nowhere. Her transportation into Germany had put her into a state of mild persisting shock. In the Baden-Baden hotel with its unfriendly German staff, incessant German talk, German menus and signs, Gestapo men in the lobby and the corridors, and glum American internees, her nervous system had half-shut down, narrowing her awareness to herself and Louis, to their day-to-day needs, and to possible dangers. The opportunity to go to Paris had seemed like a pardon from jail, once the Swiss representative had assured her that several special-case Americans dwelled freely in German-occupied Paris, and that she would be under Swiss protective surveillance there, just as in Baden-Baden. But before the comtesse burst upon her, she had seen little of Paris. She had cowered in her room, playing with Louis or reading old novels. Mornings and evenings she had scurried to the hospital to visit her uncle and scurried back again, fearing police challenge and having no confidence in her papers.

A new time began with her employment at the library. She had work, the best of anodynes. She was moving about. The first scary check of her papers in the Métro went off without trouble. After all, Paris was almost as familiar to her as New York, and not much changed. The crushing crowds in the Métro, including many young German soldiers, were a disagreeable novelty, but there was no other way to get around Paris now except for bicycles, decrepit old horse carriages, and queer bicycle-taxis like rickshaws. The library task was simple, and the comtesse was enchanted with her speed and ready grasp.

Natalie had mixed feelings about the strange old woman. Her literary talk was bright, her run of anecdotes about famous people tartly amusing; and she was an impressive Shakespeare scholar. Her political and social opinions, however, were hard to take. France had lost the war, she averred, for three reasons; Herbert Hoover's moratorium on German war reparations, the weakening of France by the socialist Front Populaire, and the treachery of the British in running away at Dunkirk. France had been misled by the English and her own stupid politicians into attacking Germany (Natalie wondered whether to believe her ears at that remark). Still, if the French army had only listened to her husband and massed its tank forces in armored divisions, instead of scattering them piecemeal among the infantry, an armored counterstroke in Belgium could have cut off the panzer columns in their dash to the sea, and won the war then and there.

She never troubled to coordinate or justify her opinions and judgments; she just let them off like firecrackers. Pierre Laval was the misunderstood savior of France. Charles de Gaulle was a posturing charlatan, and his statement, "France has lost a battle, not a war," was irresponsible rubbish. The Resistance was a riffraff of communists and bohemians, preying on their fellow Frenchmen and bringing reprisals on them without hurting the Germans. As to the occupation, despite its austerities, there was something to be said for it. The theatre was much more wholesome now, offering classics and clean comedies, not the sexy farces and depraved boulevardier dramas of other days; and the concerts were more enjoyable without all the horrid modern dissonance which nobody really understood.

Anything Natalie said touched off a monologue. Once as they worked together on cartons of books left by an American movie producer, Natalie remarked that life in Paris seemed curiously close to normal.

"My dear child, normal? It's ghastly. Of course the Boche wants to make Paris *seem* normal, even charming. Paris is the showpiece, don't you see, of the 'New Order.' " She uttered the phrase with acid sarcasm. "That's why the theatres, the opera, and the concerts are encouraged and even subsidized. That's why our poor little library is staying open. Dear me, the poor Boches do try so hard to act civilized, but they're such animals, really. Of course, they're a lot better than the Bolsheviks. Actually, if Hitler had just had the common sense not to invade France, just to finish off the Soviet Union, which he obviously could have done in 1940, he'd be a world hero today and there'd be peace. Now we must wait for America to rescue us."

Natalie saw her first yellow star while walking to lunch with the comtesse along a busy boulevard. Two women in smart tailored suits passed them, one talking vivaciously, the other laughing. On both women's suits, over the left breast, the star glared. The comtesse took no notice whatever. As time passed Natalie saw a few more; not many, just an occasional yellow star worn in the same matter-of-fact way. Rabinovitz had told her of a tremendous public roundup of Jews in Paris a year ago; either most of them had been swept away by that, or they were staying out of sight. The placards barring Jews from restaurants and public telephone booths were curling and dusty. Every day, the casually ferocious anti-Semitism in familiar papers like *Paris-Soir* and *Le Matin* startled her, for the front pages looked no different than in peacetime, and some of the columnists were the same.

Occupied Paris did have its peculiarly charming aspect: quiet clean streets free of honking taxicabs and jammed-up automobiles, clear fumeless air, brightly dressed children playing in uncrowded flowery parks, horse carriages bearing women in striking Parisian finery, all as in old paintings of the city. But the leprous trace of occupation was everywhere: large black-lettered signs like CONCORDE-PLATZ and SOLDATEN KINO; yellow wall posters with long lists of executed saboteurs; crimson swastika flags fluttering on official buildings and monuments, on the Arc de Triomphe, on the Eiffel Tower; chalked menus in German outside restaurants, German army machines driving down the wide empty boulevards, and off-duty Wehrmacht soldiers in their green-gray uniforms sloppily strolling the sidewalks with cameras. Once Natalie came on a fife and drum corps leading a goose-stepping guard up the Champs-Elysées toward the Arc de Triomphe with rat-tat-tat and shrill martial music, swastika banners streaming; the occupation was summed up in that one strange glimpse.

The adaptability of the human spirit is its saving. So long as Natalie was buried in work at the library, or spending the evening with Louis, or strolling after lunch along the Seine looking at the bookstalls, she was all right. Once a week she checked in at the Swiss legation. On a day when Louis was ill and she stayed home, a tall well-dressed young Swiss diplomat came calling, to make certain all was well. That was reassuring. Paris seemed less frightening than Marseilles; the people looked less hunted and better fed, and the police acted more civilized.

After three weeks Aaron was moved to the convalescent home and given a room overlooking the garden. Weak and lethargic still, hardly able to talk, he appeared to take the luxurious treatment quite for granted. But it puzzled Natalie. She had accepted the move to Paris as innocuous, since the doctor in Baden-Baden had explained that the American Hospital had an excellent staff, and that her uncle would be better off there than in Frankfurt. Paris itself was incomparably pleasanter than Baden-Baden. Nevertheless, a shadowy dread never quite left her, a dread like that of a child's about the mystery of a locked room, a dread of the unknown; an uneasy sense that the gracious treatment of her uncle and her own freedom in a German-occupied city were not bits of good luck, but a riddle. When the answer came at last at the American Library it was less a surprise than the fright of opening the dark locked room.

The comtesse called from the outer office, "Natalie! We have a visitor. An old friend of yours."

She was squatting amid piles of books in a back room, writing up lists. Pushing the hair away from her face, she hurried out to the office. There Werner Beck stood, bowing, clicking his heels, wrinkling his eyes shut in an amiable smile.

"The minister of the German embassy," said the comtesse. "Why didn't you tell me you knew Werner?"

She had not dressed in formal clothes since leaving Siena; where, despite the casual Italian house arrest, she had sometimes put on a faded long dress for an evening out. By now living out of suitcases, alternating the same few travelling clothes, had become her way of life. In Natalie's shocked and frightened frame of mind that evening, putting on the Cinderella finery which the comtesse had obtained for her seemed a grotesque mockery, a morbid last farewell to her femininity before getting hanged. The stuff fitted; the comtesse's cousin was just her size. Drawing smooth pearly silk stockings on her legs and up her thighs to the garters gave Natalie a very queer feeling. Where did even a rich Parisienne get such stockings nowadays? What would it be like to dress like this for an evening out with Byron in peacetime, instead of for this chilling nightmare?

She did her best to paint herself to match the high-fashion gray crepe silk dress, but she had only rudimentary cosmetics, dry and cracking with disuse: a rouge pot, a lipstick, the stub of an eyebrow pencil, and a little mascara. Louis watched her making up with wide wondering eyes, as though she were setting fire to herself. She was still at this task when the grayheaded baby-sitter looked in. "Madame, your gentleman is here in his car downstairs — oh, madame, but you are ravishing!"

There had been no alternative to accepting Beck's staggering invitation; and had there been, she would have been too frightened to try. To the comtesse's wry comment when he left the library — "Well! The German minister, and *The Marriage of Figaro! Pas mal*" — Natalie had blurted, "But how can he possibly do this? Aside from my being an enemy alien, he knows I'm Jewish."

With a curving grin of her thin wrinkled old mouth — they had never referred to this topic before — the comtesse replied, "My dear, the Germans please themselves, *ils sont les vainqueurs*. The thing is, what will you wear?"

Not a question about Natalie's relation with Beck, not a catty remark; just a brisk getting down to the business of equipping a fellow female for a fashionable night out in Paris. The comtesse's cousin, a dark bucktoothed young woman, was quite buffaloed by the comtesse's sudden appearance at her flat with the American girl. Without many words, if also without visible joy, she meekly produced the finery demanded of her. The comtesse passed judgment on every item, even insisting on a bottle of good scent. Whether the comtesse was doing this out of kindness, or to curry favor with the German minister, Natalie had no way of discerning. She just did it, quickmarch.

Louis stared in a hurt way when his mother left without kissing him. Her lips felt thick and greasy, and she was afraid to smear him up, and herself, too. Down the stairs she went in a wine-colored velvet cowled cloak, feeling after all the womanly excitement of dressing up. She did look beautiful, he was a man, and she was under Swiss protection. This was the scariest thing that had happened to her yet in these endless months of trouble, but she had survived much, and she felt ready for a desperate defense.

The Mercedes stood there in the blue streetlight and the light of a full moon. Murmuring compliments, he stepped out and opened the door for her. The night was warm, and smelled of flowering trees in the railed front garden of the old house.

Natalie said as he started the car, "This may be a tactless question, but how can you be seen with a Jewess?"

His serious face, dimly lit by the glow of the dashboard dials, relaxed in a smile. "The ambassador knows that you and your uncle are in Paris. The Gestapo of course knows, too. They also know I am taking you to the opera tonight. Who you are is nobody else's business. Are you uneasy?"

"Horribly."

"What can I do to reassure you? Or would you rather not go? The last thing I want to do is force a disagreeable evening on you. I thought you might enjoy this. I intended it as a friendly, or at least reconciling, gesture."

Natalie had to find out what this man was up to, if she possibly could. "Well, I'm dressed up now. It's very kind of you."

"You do like Mozart?"

"Of course. I haven't heard *The Marriage of Figaro* in years."

"I'm happy I've hit on a pleasant amusement."

"How long have you known that we were in Paris?"

"Mrs. Henry, I knew that you were in Lourdes." He was driving slowly down the empty black streets. "Winston Churchill, you know, paid General Rommel a handsome compliment during the Africa campaign. 'Across the gulf of war,' he said, 'I salute a great general.' Your uncle is a brilliant scholar, Mrs. Henry, but he isn't a strong or practical man. Getting from Siena to Marseilles surely was your doing. Your escape caused me terrific embarrassment. However, 'across the gulf of war' I salute you. You have courage."

Left hand on the wheel, Beck offered Natalie his pudgy right hand. Natalie could do nothing but shake it. It felt damp and cold.

"How did you find out we were in Lourdes?" Involuntarily she wiped her hand on the cloak, then hoped he didn't notice.

"Through the effort to get you released. The French brought it to our attention at once, naturally, and —"

"What? What effort? We didn't know about any such effort."

"You're sure?" His head turned in surprise.

"It's complete news to me."

"That is interesting." He nodded several times. "Well, there was an approach from Washington to let you cross quietly into Spain. My reaction when you turned up was one of relief. I feared you had come to harm."

Natalie was stunned. Who had tried to get them released? What bearing did it have on their predicament now? "So that betrayed our presence to you?"

"Oh, I was bound to find out. At the embassy we've kept close watch on your group right along. Quite a mixture, eh? Diplomats, journalists, Quakers, wives, babies, whatnot! By the way, the doctor at the Victoria Home informed me today that your uncle is much on the mend."

Natalie said nothing, and after a while Beck spoke again. "Don't you find the Comtesse de Chambrun an interesting woman? Very cultured?"

"A character, certainly."

"Yes, that's an apt word for her."

That ended the chitchat. Walking out of the blackout into the blaze of the opera foyer dazzled Natalie. A time machine, as it were, hurtled her back to the Paris of 1937. Nothing was different from her opera-going evenings with Leslie Slote, except the scattering of German uniforms. Here was the essence of the Paris she remembered, this grandiose lobby with its marble columns, magnificent staircase, and rich statuary; the hairy students in raincoats with their short-skirted girl friends, crowding amid working people toward the entrances to the cheap seats; the middle-class comfortable-looking couples heading for the orchestra; and the thin glittery stream of the beau monde threading through the crowd. The noise was animated and very French, the faces — perhaps a shade more pinched and pallid than in the old days — were mostly French, and the smart few were pure French top to toe; especially the women, the eternal elegant Parisiennes, beautifully coiffed and made up, displaying in every flash of eye, turn of bare arm, quick laughter, the arts of shining and pleasing. Some were with Frenchmen in dinner jackets, some with German officers. In the commoner crowd German soldiers also escorted French girls, prettily gotten up and glowing with kittenish vivacity.

Perhaps because Natalie was in an aroused state, with the adrenalin pumping at the alarming proximity of Dr. Beck, this plunge into the opera lobby dazzled her not only with light, but with a searing mental flash. Who then, she thought, were the "collaborationists," derided and excoriated by the Allied press and the de Gaulle broadcasts? Here they were. Wasn't it so? They were the French. They were the people. They had lost. They had spilled rivers of blood to win the first war, paid their taxes for twenty years, done what their politicians had demanded, built the Maginot Line, gone to war under prestigious generals; and the Germans had taken Paris. *Eh bien, je m'en fiche!* If the Americans would come to the rescue, well and good. Meantime, they would pursue their French ways under the Boches. And since the hardships were many and the pleasures few, these few were all the more to be savored. In this moment Natalie felt she half-understood the Comtesse de Chambrun. There was one difference from 1937, she realized, as she and Beck moved through the crowd to their seats. Then there had been many Jewish faces in every opera audience. Here there was not one.

The first notes of the overture swept across her nerves like a wind through harp strings, setting up shuddery vibrations; the more so because of her terrific tension. She tried to give herself to the music, but within a few measures her mind was racing back over Beck's disclosures. Who could have made that futile and damaging approach when they were in Lourdes? As she puzzled and wondered and worried, the curtain rose on a setting as opulent as any in peacetime. Figaro and Susanna, both excellent singers, launched into their immortal high-spirited antics. Natalie did not get much out of this *Marriage of Figaro*, though it was a polished performance. Her mind kept darting here and there over her predicament.

For the entr'acte Beck had reserved a little table in one of the smaller lounges. The waiter greeted them with an amiable smile and bow. "*Bonsoir, Madame, bonsoir, Monsieur le Ministre.*" He whisked away the *reservé* sign, and brought champagne and sugar cakes.

"By the bye," Beck said, after some judicious comments on the singers as he ate cakes and sipped wine, "I've been rereading your uncle's broadcast scripts. He was truly prescient, do you realize that? The things he wrote a year ago are being said now all over the Allied world. Vice President Henry Wallace recently gave a speech that might have been lifted from your uncle's pages. Bernard Shaw, Bertrand Russell, many such first-class minds, have been saying these things. Astonishing."

"I haven't had much contact with the Allied world."

"Yes. Well, I have the press cuttings. When Dr. Jastrow is stronger, he ought to see them. I've been sorely tempted to publish his scripts. Really, all that talk about further polishing was silly. They are gems. Memorable essays, with a beautiful intellectual progression to them." Beck paused as the waiter refilled his glass. Natalie wetted her lips with wine. "Don't you think he might want to broadcast them now? Perhaps over Radio Paris? Really, he owes me that much."

"He's too weak to discuss anything like that."

"But his doctor told me today that he should have his strength back in a couple of weeks. Is he comfortable at the Victoria Home?"

"He has had the best of everything."

"Good. I insisted on that. The Frankfurt hospital is very good, but I knew that he'd be happier here — ah, the first bell already, and you've hardly touched your wine. Isn't it all right?"

Natalie drank off her glass. "It's very good."

The torrent of brilliant music thereafter passed by Natalie like distant train noises. Fearful possibilities crowded on her, as the singers on the stage capered through their farcical disguises and misunderstandings. Once again, the worst possibility was proving the reality. The move to a hospital in Paris had not been innocuous. Dr. Beck had wanted to get them here, had bided his time, and had used the mischance of Aaron's illness to do it, since more brutal tactics might have embarrassed him with the Swiss. And what now? Aaron would still balk at broadcasting; and even if he agreed, wouldn't that only seal his fate and probably hers? Obviously he could repudiate the broadcasts as soon as he returned to the United States, and Dr. Beck was smart enough to know that. Therefore once the Germans had those recordings, they would hold on to Aaron in one way or another, and very likely to herself as well. Could the Swiss "protection" hold in such a case, considering their dubious status?

Yet what would happen if Aaron confronted Werner Beck with an outright refusal? In Follonica he had played out the procrastination game.

The trap, in fact, had sprung, or so it seemed to her. It was the most horrible imaginable sensation to be sitting there in the Paris Opera in a borrowed Worth original, with a thickly painted face, with a nervous stomach rebelling at the glass of wine she had gulped, beside a polite and intelligent man, a former Yale graduate student, in every nuance of word and manner a cultivated and civilized European, who nevertheless when it came right down to it was threatening her and her baby with a veiled hideous future. And this was not a preposterous dream from which she would wake up; it was reality.

"Perfectly charming," said Dr. Beck, as the curtain descended to great applause, and the singers came out to bow. "And now for a bite of supper, eh?"

"I must get home to my baby, Dr. Beck."

"You'll be home very early, I promise you."

He took her to a crowded dim restaurant nearby. Natalie had heard about it in the old days: far too expensive for student purses, requiring reservations a day in advance. Here the uniformed German customers were bald or grizzle-haired generals, and the Frenchmen tended to potbellies and naked pates. She recognized two politicians and a famous actor. Some of the women were gray and plump, but for the most part they were, once again, exquisite young Parisiennes, dressed to kill and bubbling with charm.

The very smell of food nauseated Natalie. Beck advised her to try the Loire salmon; this was the only place in Paris where one could get Loire salmon just now. She begged off, asking for an omelette, and when it came she ate only a fragment, while Beck devoured his salmon with serene appetite. Around them the Germans, the prosperous French insiders, and their women were eating duck, whole fresh fish, and roast meats, quaffing good wines, arguing, laughing, on top of the world. It was an incredible sight. Rationing was very severe in Paris. The papers were full of feature articles and sourly humorous pieces on the food shortage. At the convalescent home Aaron's daily ration of custard, requiring an egg, was regarded as royal fare. But for enough influence or money, at least in this obscure oasis, Paris was still Paris.

Natalie drank a little white wine to quiet Beck's urging. There was something so gross, she thought, about what he was doing; the swanky entertainment to soften her up, and the simultaneous harsh pressure of his demands, which he kept up over supper in wheedling tones. Even before the food came, he was at it again. When they had first turned up in Lourdes, he said, Gestapo headquarters in Paris had wanted to take them into custody at once, as Jewish fugitives from Italy with faked papers. Luckily, Ambassador Otto Abetz was a cultured and spiritual man. Thanks only to Dr. Abetz they had gone on to Baden-Baden. Dr. Abetz had read Dr. Jastrow's broadcast scripts with tremendous enthusiasm. In Dr. Abetz's view, the only way to achieve a positive outcome of the war now was for the Anglo-American allies to realize that Germany was fighting their fight, the fight of Western civilization, against brutish Slav imperialism. Anything that could promote understanding with the West was of huge importance to Ambassador Abetz.

That was the sugar. The pill came as they were eating. Beck let her have it casually, while smacking his lips over the salmon. The Gestapo pressure to arrest them had never ceased, he informed her. The Gestapo was exceedingly anxious to question them about their trip from Siena to Marseilles. Policemen, after all, had their job to do. Dr. Abetz had been shielding Dr. Jastrow thus far, said Beck, and if he withdrew his protection, the Gestapo would at once sweep them in. Beck could not be responsible for what happened after that, though he would be most enormously distressed. Swiss diplomatic protection, in such a case, would be like a straw fence against a fire. The Swiss had the whole record of their illegal escape from Italy. In view of Natalie's and Dr. Jastrow's clear criminal record the Swiss would be powerless. Dr. Otto Abetz was their shield and their hope.

"Well," Dr. Beck said, turning off the motor as he parked outside her house, "I trust the evening proved not so bad, after all."

"Thank you very much for the opera and the supper."

"My pleasure. Despite all your vicissitudes, Mrs. Henry, I must say you look more lovely than ever."

Good God, was he going to make a pass at her, too? She said hastily and coldly, "Every stitch I'm wearing is borrowed."

"The comtesse?"

"Yes, the comtesse."

"So I assumed. Dr. Abetz will be awaiting a report from me on our evening. What can I tell him?"

"Tell him I enjoyed *The Marriage of Figaro*."

"That will charm him," Beck said with his eye-shutting smile, "but he will be strongly interested in your position on the matter of the broadcasts."

"It will be up to my uncle."

"You yourself are not rejecting the idea out of hand?"

Natalie bitterly thought how much simpler it would be — however skin-crawling — if all he really wanted was to sleep with her.

"I don't have much choice, do I?"

He nodded, a pleased look on his shadowy face. "Mrs. Henry, our evening has been well spent if you understand that. I would love to have a glimpse of your delightful boy, but I suppose he is asleep now."

"Oh, for hours."

After a long moment, during which Beck silently smiled at her, he got out and opened the door.

The flat was dark.

"*Maman?*" A wide-awake voice.

Natalie turned on a light. In a chair in the sitting room beside Louis's cot, the old lady dozed under a blanket. Louis was sitting up, blinking and joyously smiling, though his face was tear-streaked. The light woke the old woman. She apologized for going to sleep and waddled out, yawning. Quickly Natalie rubbed off all the paint with a ragged towel, and scrubbed her face with soap. She came to Louis and hugged and kissed him. He clung to her.

"Louis, you must go to sleep now."

"*Oui, maman.*" Since Corsica, she had been *maman*.

As he snuggled down under his blanket, she began to sing in Yiddish the lullaby that had become his bedtime ritual in Marseilles, and ever since:

> *Under Louis's cradle*
> *Lies a little white goat.*
> *The little goat went into business,*
> *That will be your career.*
> *Raisins and almonds,*
> *Sleep, little boy, sleep, dear.*

Louis drowsily sang along, mangling the Yiddish in his babyish way.

> *Rozhinkes mit mandlen,*
> *Shlof, mein ingele, shlof.*

One glance at Natalie's face next day told the comtesse that the opera evening had not been an unalloyed delight. She asked, as Natalie set down the two bags of clothing by the desk, how it had gone.

"All right. It was terribly generous of your cousin."

With that, Natalie went silently to work on catalogue cards in her own tiny office. After a while the Comtesse de Chambrun came in and shut the door. "What's up?" she twanged, sounding very little like a French noblewoman.

Turning haunted eyes on her, Natalie did not reply. In her fog of fear she hesitated to take any step, not knowing what pits surrounded her. Could she trust this collaborationist woman? That question, with others as hard, had kept her awake all night. The comtesse sat down on a small library stool. "Come on, we're both Americans. Let's hear."

Natalie told the Comtesse de Chambrun the whole story. It took a long time. She was under such strain that twice she lost her voice, and had to drink water from a carafe. The comtesse listened wordlessly, eyes bright as a bird's, and said when she finished, "You had better go back to Baden-Baden at once."

"Back to Germany? How will that help?"

"Your best protection is the chargé d'affaires. Tuck's a flaming New Dealer but he's competent and tough. You have no advocate here. The Swiss can only go through the motions. Tuck will fight. He's got the threat of the German internees in the U.S.A. You're in a situation where once things happen, it's too late to protest. Can your uncle travel?"

"If he must, he will."

"Tell the Swiss you want to rejoin your group. Your uncle misses his fellow journalists. The Germans have no right to hold you here. Move quickly. Ask them to get in touch with Tuck right away, and to arrange your return to Baden-Baden. Or I will."

"It's risky to involve yourself, Comtesse."

With a grim writhing smile of ribbon lips, the comtesse stood up. "Let us go and talk to the comte."

Natalie went along. It was a plan; otherwise she was at the end of the road. The comtesse stopped at the hospital, and Natalie went on to the convalescent home. Aaron's vitality was too low for a violent reaction to the news about Beck. He shook his head wearily and murmured, "Nemesis." To the proposal that they return to Baden-Baden, he said he left it in Natalie's hands; they must do whatever was best for herself and Louis. He felt strong enough for the journey, if that was the decision.

When Natalie rejoined the comtesse at the hospital, her husband had already talked to the Swiss minister, who had promised to get in touch with Tuck and arrange for the return to Baden-Baden, anticipating no difficulty.

Nor did there seem to be any. The Swiss legation telephoned Natalie next day at the library to say that everything was in order. The Germans had approved the return, the railroad tickets were in hand. Telephone communication with Tuck in Baden-Baden was limited, and had to be routed through the Berlin switchboard, but they expected to be able to notify him before Jastrow left Paris. That same afternoon the Swiss telephoned again: a snag. Ambassador Abetz was personally interested in the famous author, and was sending his own physician to examine Jastrow and certify his fitness for travel.

When she heard that, Natalie knew the game was lost. So it was. The Swiss legation reported the following day that the German doctor had declared Jastrow was in very poor condition and should not be moved for a month. Ambassador Abetz therefore felt he could not take the responsibility of permitting him to leave Paris.

*   *   *

66

𝔉𝔬𝔯𝔱𝔯𝔢𝔰𝔰 𝔈𝔲𝔯𝔬𝔭𝔢 ℭ𝔯𝔲𝔪𝔟𝔩𝔢𝔰

(from "Hitler as Military Leader," the epilogue to *Land, Sea, and Air Operations of World War II*, by General Armin von Roon)

TRANSLATOR'S NOTE: *Armin von Roon's epilogue gives a vivid picture of the Führer in action, especially as he was falling apart. In this reminiscence Roon is much harder on Hitler than in the operational analysis. His German editor notes that Roon drafted this memoir on his last sickbed, and did not revise it.*

The memoir opens with these words:

For more than four years I observed Adolf Hitler at close hand in Supreme Headquarters. Keitel and Jodl, who had the same opportunity, were hanged by the Allies. Most of the generals who knew the Führer well were executed by him, or sickened and died from the strain, or fell on the battlefield. I have seen no military memoir which truly portrays him as a man. The books of Guderian and Manstein pass over his personal aspects in understandable silence.

In my military history I have acknowledged his adroitness and his inspiring force as a politician, and have cited his flare for strategic and tactical decision-making in war, especially involving surprise. I have indicated that at his peak he seemed to us the soul of Germany reborn. I have also suggested his serious failings as a supreme commander that led to catastrophe.

Personally, he more and more revealed himself in adversity as a low and ugly individual. In his behavior after the July 20, 1944, assassination attempt he showed his true colors. Nobody who sat beside him as I did, and saw him gloat and giggle and applaud at motion pictures of great German generals, my revered superiors and friends, strangling naked in nooses of piano wire, their eyes popping from their discolored faces, their purple tongues thrust out, blood, urine, and feces streaking down their jerking bodies, could thereafter feel anything for Adolf Hitler but distaste.

If Germany is ever to rise again, we must uproot the political and cultural weaknesses that led us to follow a man like this to defeat, disgrace, and partitioning. Hence I have written this unsparing personal description of the Führer as I saw him in his headquarters.

This is a far cry from Roon's encomiums in the first volume of Land, Sea, and Air Operations; *such as, "A romantic idealist, an inspiring leader dreaming grand dreams of new heights and depths of human possibilities, and at the same time an icy calculator with iron willpower, he was the soul of Germany."*

Roon seems to have decided to level about the Führer before he died. Or possibly he felt more kindly toward him in writing about the victorious years; then, as he worked through the second volume, the bitterness of collapse came back to mind. At any rate, the epilogue is a warty picture of Hitler and a brisk recapitulation of the war. My translation of World Holocaust *concludes with excerpts which sketch the war to the end.* — V.H.

Tunis and Kursk

Hitler's phantom "Fortress Europe," a pure propaganda bluff, began to crumble visibly in July 1943, when the Red Army smashed our big summer offensive at Kursk, the Anglo-Americans landed in Sicily, and Mussolini fell.

These disasters stemmed straight from Hitler's two most colossal and pigheaded blunders: Stalingrad and Tunis. When I returned from my inspection trip to Tunis I told Hitler that Rommel was right, that our successes against the green American soldiers at Kasserine Pass were ephemeral, that in the long run we couldn't supply three hundred thousand Italian and German troops across a sea dominated by enemy navies. But Göring airily assured Hitler that Tunis was "just a hop" from Italy, and that the Luftwaffe would keep the armies supplied. Despite Göring's abject failure to make good the identical boast at Stalingrad, Hitler accepted this and kept pouring troops into North Africa, when he should have been evacuating the ones who were there. Had he taken out all those troops to Italy as an operating reserve, they might well have pushed the Allies off Sicily, and kept Italy in the war. We never recovered in the south from the Tunis bloodletting.

The Kursk offensive was just as ill-advised. My son Helmut fell there on July 7 at the head of a tank battalion under Manstein. He was a studious gentle lad who perhaps would not have been a professional soldier if not for his father's example. He died for Germany in the gigantic and futile operation called *Citadel,* the last gasp of German strategic initiative.

Like Guderian and Kleist, I was against Citadel. The Anglo-Americans were bound to attack the continent somewhere soon, and we had to stay uncommitted and mobile till we knew where the blow would fall. The sensible course was to straighten our lines in the east, gather strong reserves, let the Russians commit themselves, and then smash them with a counterattack as we did at Kharkov. Manstein was the master of this backhand stroke;* another such bloody setback and the Soviets might have proved more flexible in the secret peace talks. The Russians were showing interest, but their demands were still too cocky and unrealistic. No doubt what Hitler wanted at Kursk was a big victory that would improve his bargaining position with Stalin.

But Manstein and Kluge fell in love with the Citadel plan. As an actor offered a star part in a bad play will take it and hope to pull off a success, so generals become intoxicated by plans for large-scale operations which they will command. In the hinge of our front between Manstein's Army Group South and Kluge's Army Group Center, the Russians in their winter counterattacks had punched a deep westward bulge around the city of Kursk. Manstein and Kluge were to drive armored pincers in from north and south, cut off this bulge of territory, bag a reverse Stalingrad of Russian prisoners, and then drive on to God knows what great victories through this gaping hole torn in the Soviet lines.

A charming vision, but we lacked the means.

Hitler loved to reel off figures of divisions available for combat. We had hordes of such "divisions," but the figures were poppycock. Nearly all these divisions were understrength, and the men they had lost were the best troops, the fighting head, leaving the flabby administrative tail. Other divisions had been wiped out and were mere names on charts. But Hitler had ordered these "reconstituted"; and behold, by the breath of his mouth, they were again — in his mind — the full-strength trained fighting forces he had squandered forever on the Volga, in the Caucasus, and in Tunis. He was retreating into a dream world where he was still the triumphant master of the continent, commanding the strongest army on earth. This retreat went on until it ended in outright paranoia. But out of that private dreamland, until April 1945, there issued a stream of insensate orders which the German fighting man had to carry out on the harsh and bloody field of battle.

Moreover, while the Wehrmacht had been going downhill, the Red Army had been reviving and growing. The Soviet generals had been studying our tactics for two years. American Lend-Lease trucks, canned food, tanks, and planes, together with new Russian tanks from factories behind the Urals, had stiffened the real, not phantom, fresh divisions from Russia's limitless manpower. Of all these adverse factors our intelligence warned us, but Hitler paid no attention.

Still, the Kursk attack might have had a chance in May, as first planned,

---

* German — *aus der Rückhand schlagen,* a military term borrowed from tennis. — .V.H.

when the Russians were worn out by their counterattacks and had not yet dug into the salient. But he put it off for six weeks so as to use our newest tanks. I warned Jodl that this would put Citadel squarely into the time-frame of the probable Anglo-American landing in Europe, but as usual I was ignored. The Russians used the time well to harden up the haunches of the Kursk bulge with mine fields, trenches, and antitank emplacements, while bringing in more and more forces.

Our intelligence spoke of *half a million railroad cars* entering the salient with troops and matériel! Hitler's response was to commit more and more divisions and air wings to Citadel. As in an American poker game, the stakes of this gamble kept building up on both sides, until Hitler had thrown in as many tanks as we had used in the entire 1940 campaign in the west. At last, on July 5, despite serious second thoughts of even Manstein and Kluge because of the two-month delay, Hitler unleashed the attack. What ensued was the world's biggest tank and air battle, and a total fiasco. Our pincers made very heavy weather against the Russian static defenses and swarms of tanks, achieving penetration of only a few miles. The attack was five days old and going very badly, north and south, when the Allies landed in Sicily.

What was Hitler's reaction? At a hurriedly summoned conference, he announced with great assumed glee that since the Anglo-Americans had now presented him with an opportunity to smash them in the Mediterranean, "the true theatre of decision," Citadel would be called off! That was his way of wriggling out of his failure. Not a word of apology, regret, or acknowledgment of error. Eighteen of our best remaining armored and motorized divisions, a striking force which we could never replace, and which should have been hoarded as a precious operational reserve, had been thrown away in the Kursk battle on a dreamy echo of the grand summer campaigns of the past. With Citadel all German offensives were over. Any attacks we made for the rest of the war were tactical counterthrusts to stave off defeat.

Hitler soon learned that we could not just "call off" a major offensive. There was the little matter of the enemy. On both sides of the Kursk salient the Russians struck back, and within a month freed the two central anchors of our eastern line, the cities of Orel and Belgorod. After Citadel our whole front slowly and inexorably crumbled before a Russian advance that stopped only at the Brandenburg Gate. If Stalingrad was the psychological turning point in the east, Kursk was the military pivot.

My feelings about my son have no place here. He died advancing at Kursk. Thereafter millions of Germany's sons were to die retreating, so as to keep the heads of men like Hitler and Göring on their shoulders.

The Fall of Mussolini

Meantime, my inspection trip to Sicily and Rome convinced me that Italy was about to drop out of the war or change sides. I saw that we must cut our losses and form a strong defense line in the Apennines at the northern end of the Italian boot. There was nothing to be gained by trying to hold on to Italy. From the start of the war this nation had been one gigantic *bouche inutile,* gulping enormous quantities of Germany's war resources to no result. The southern front was a chronic abscess. The Anglo-Saxons were welcome to occupy and feed Italy, I wrote in my summary report, and our forces thus released would help stabilize the eastern front and defend the west.

When I told this to Keitel at Berchtesgaden, he drew a face like an undertaker's and warned me to change my tune. But I was past caring. My only son was dead. I was suffering seriously from high blood pressure. To be transferred from Supreme Headquarters to the field seemed to me a welcome prospect.

So at the briefing conference I presented the picture as I had seen it. The Allies had total air superiority over Sicily, and Palermo had been flattened. The Sicilian divisions assigned to defend their island were fading into the countryside. In the German-held sector of Sicily the civilians were cursing and spitting at our soldiers. Rome looked like a city already out of the war, for soldiers were scarcely to be seen on the streets. Our German troops were staying out of sight, and the Italian soldiers were shedding their uniforms wholesale. I had encountered only evasiveness from Badoglio on the whole question of bringing more German divisions into Italy, and the Italians were *strengthening their Alpine fortifications,* an action which could only be directed against Germany. Such was the situation report I presented to Hitler.

He listened with his head down between his shoulders, glaring at me from under his graying eyebrows, now and then curling one side of his mouth in the half-smile, half-snarl that distorted his mustache, showed his teeth, and signalled extreme displeasure. His only comment was that "there still must be some worthwhile people in Italy. They can't have all turned rotten." As for Sicily, his inspiration was to assume command himself. Of course this made not the slightest difference.

Still, my report must have sunk in, because he arranged a meeting with Mussolini. It took place in a country house in northern Italy a few days before Il Duce fell, and it was a dismal affair. Hitler had nothing new to offer the sick-looking disheartened Mussolini and his staff. He spewed out optimistic statistics by the hour on manpower, raw materials, arms production, details of improved or new weaponry while the Italians looked at each other with their expressive miserable dark eyes. The end was written on their faces. During the meeting Mussolini received a dispatch saying that the Allies were making their first air raid on Rome. He handed the message to Hitler, who barely glanced at it, then resumed his boasting about our rising arms production and marvelous new weapons.

The scenes in Supreme Headquarters when Mussolini fell were horrendous. Hitler was beside himself with rage, howling and storming at the treachery of the Italian court, and the Vatican, and the Fascist leaders who had deposed Mussolini. His crude language and his threats were frightful. He would take Rome by force, he said, and get hold of "that rabble, that scum" — by which he meant King Victor Emmanuel, the royal family, and the whole court — and make them creep and crawl. He would seize the Vatican, "clean out all that pus of priests," shoot the diplomatic corps hiding in there, lay hands on all the secret documents, then say it was a mistake of war.

He kept trying to get Göring on the phone. "There's an ice-cold fellow," he said. "Ice-cold. At times like these you need a man who's ice-cold. Get me Göring, I say! Hard as steel. I've been through any number of tough ones with him. Ice-cold, that fellow. Ice-cold." Göring hurriedly came, but all he did was agree with everything Hitler said, using vulgar language and bad jokes. That constituted being ice-cold.

The hundred urgent decisions and moves for keeping Italy in the war, at least while we peaceably introduced enough German troops to take over the country, were hammered out in our OKW headquarters. Hitler spent that time feverishly plotting a coup d'etat in Rome to restore Mussolini, which was impossible to execute and which he dropped; also the parachute rescue of the imprisoned Duce, which did come off and may have made them both feel better, but accomplished nothing. In fact, the photograph flashed around the world of a jolly uniformed Hitler, greeting the shrunken cringing ex-Duce in an ill-fitting black overcoat and black slouch hat, with a sickly smile on his white face, proclaimed louder than any headlines that the famous Axis was dead, and that Fortress Europe was doomed.

My Rise

All this had the surprising and unwelcome effect of restoring me to Hitler's favor. He asserted that I had seen through the Italian treachery before anybody else, that "the good Armin has a head on his shoulders," and so on. Also, he had heard of Helmut's death, and he put on a tragic face to commiserate with me. He praised me at briefings, and — a rare thing for a General Staff officer in those days — invited me to dinner. Speer, Himmler, and an industrialist were his other guests that night.

It was a miserable experience. Hitler must have talked for five consecutive hours. Nobody else said anything except a perfunctory word of agreement. It was all a high-flown jumble of history and philosophy, with a great deal about the Jews. The real trouble with the Italians, he said, was that the marrow of the nation had been eaten out by the cancer of the Church. Christianity was just a wily Jewish scheme to get control of the world by exalting weakness over strength. Jesus was not a Jew, but the bastard son of a Roman soldier. Paul was the greatest Jewish swindler of all time. And so on, ad nauseam. Late in the evening he made some interesting observations about Charlemagne, but I was too numbed to pay close attention. Everybody was stifling yawns. All in all the verbal flatulence was as unbearable as the physical flatulence. No doubt that was a weakness he could not control, due to his bad diet and irregular habits, but sitting near the Führer at table was no privilege. How a man like Bormann endured it for years I cannot imagine.

I was not asked again, but my hope of escaping from Headquarters and serving in the field went by the board. Jodl and Keitel now were all smiles to me. I did get a month's medical leave, and so was able to see my wife and console her. By the time I returned to Wolfsschanze, Italy had surrendered and our long-planned Operation Alaric to seize the peninsula was in full swing.

And so the drain to the south was to go on to the last. Adolf Hitler could not face the political setback of giving up Italy. While our armies humiliated the far stronger Anglo-Saxons there, forcing them to inch up the boot with heavy losses, it was all a terrible military mistake. This obtuse political egotism of Hitler, wasting our strength southward when we could have held the Alps barrier with a fraction of Kesselring's forces, set the stage for total national collapse under the squeeze from east and west.

*　　*　　*

67

THOUGH plunged in passion often, Pamela Tudsbury had experienced romantic love just once; and she flew from Washington to Moscow in August for a last glimpse of Captain Henry, the man for whom she felt that love, before she married somebody else.

Long after she had given up on the Soviet Union, in fact after she had given on journalism and had decided to join Burne-Wilke in New Delhi, the visa suddenly came through. At once she changed her travel route so as to include Moscow, and to justify that, she put off quitting her job with the *Observer*. If Pamela's nature was excessively passionate, her head was on fairly straight, and she now knew beyond a doubt that her writing was but a thin echo of a dead man's. Cobbling up her father's dispatches when he was ill or weary had been one thing; but producing fresh copy with his insights and his verve was beyond her. She was not a journalist, but a ghost. Nor did she deceive herself about her reasons for marrying Burne-Wilke. Like the attempt at journalism, that decision had whirled into the vacuum left by Tudsbury's death. He had proposed at a vulnerable moment, when her life had loomed sad and empty. He was a gracious man, an extraordinary catch, and she had consented. She did not regret it. They could be happy enough together, she thought, and she was lucky to have attracted him.

Why then was she detouring to Moscow? Mainly because of what she had seen of Rhoda Henry in casual encounters at dances and parties, usually in the company of a tall gray-haired Army colonel. Rhoda had acted sprightly and cordial toward her, and — so it had struck Pamela — rather proprietary toward the imposing Army man. Before leaving Washington Pam had telephoned her, figuring she had little to lose. Rhoda had told her gaily that Byron was exec of his submarine now; Pamela must be sure to give Pug this news, and "tell him to watch his weight!" Not a trace of jealous concern or artificial sweetness; very puzzling. What had happened to the marriage? Had the reconciliation been so complete that Rhoda could act as she pleased? Or was she betraying Pug again, or working up to it? Pamela had absolutely no idea.

Since Midway she had had no word from him, not so much as a note of condolence on the much-publicized death of her father. Wartime mails were uncertain. In her letter from Egypt about Burne-Wilke, she had invited him to object to the engagement; no answer. But had it reached him before the sinking of the *Northampton?* Again, she had absolutely no idea. Pamela wanted to know how things stood with Victor Henry, and the only way to find out was to face the man. The thousands of extra miles of wartime travel in midsummer were nothing.

Nothing, yet prostrating. She all but collapsed into the embassy car that met her at the Moscow airport. Flying stop-and-go across North Africa, and then waiting three days in the dusty fly-ridden inferno of Tehran, had done her in. The driver, a little Cockney dressed in proper black, not visibly suffering from the Moscow heat, kept glancing at her in his rearview mirror. Weary though she was, Lord Burne-Wilke's slim fiancée, so un-Russian and so elegant in a white linen suit and white straw hat, looked to the homesick man every inch a future viscountess, and he was thrilled to be driving her. He was sure she must be doing newspaper work as a lark.

Moscow itself appeared much the same to the exhausted Pamela: flat stretches of drab old buildings, many unfinished structures abandoned to wind and weather because of the war, and fat barrage balloons still floating in the sky. But the people were changed. When she and her father had hastily left in 1941, with the Germans nearing the city and all the big shots skedaddling to Kuibyshev, the bundled-up Muscovites had looked a pinched harassed lot, trudging through the snowdrifts or digging tank traps. Now they strolled the sidewalks in the sunshine, the women in light print dresses, the men in sport shirts and slacks if they were not in uniform; and the pretty children were running and playing with carefree noise in the streets and the parks. The war was far away.

The British embassy, on a fine river-front site facing the Kremlin, had once been a czarist merchant's mansion like Spaso House. When Pamela stepped through the french windows in the rear, she came on the ambassador lounging stripped to the waist in the sunshine amid a loudly clucking flock of white chickens. The formal gardens had been turned into an enormous vegetable patch. Philip Rule, slouched on a campstool beside the ambassador, got up with a mock bow. "Ahhh! Lady Burne-Wilke, I presume?"

She returned drily, "Not quite yet, Philip."

The ambassador gestured around at the garden as he rose to shake hands. "Welcome, Pam. You see some alterations here. One's most likely to eat regularly in Moscow when food grows in the back yard."

"I can imagine."

"We tried to book you into the National, but they're jammed. Next Friday you'll get in, and we'll put you up here meantime."

"Very kind of you."

"Why do that?" Rule said. "I didn't know there was a problem. The

U.P. just gave up a suite at the Metropole, Pam. The living room's an acre in size, and there's not a fancier bathroom in Moscow.

"Can I get it?"

"Come along, and let's see. It's five minutes from here. The manager's a distant cousin of my wife."

"The bathroom decides me," Pamela said, passing a hand over her wet brow. "I'd like to soak for a week."

The ambassador said, "I sympathize, but be sure to come to our party tonight, Pam. Best spot for watching the victory fireworks."

In the car Pam asked Rule, "What victory?"

"Why, the Kursk salient. You know about it, surely."

"Kursk didn't get much play in the States. Sicily's been the big story."

"No doubt, typical Yank editing. Sicily! It toppled Mussolini, but militarily it was a sideshow. Kursk was the biggest tank battle of all time, Pamela, the true turn of the war."

"Wasn't it weeks ago, Phil?"

"The breakthrough, yes. The counterattack swept into Orel and Belgorod yesterday. Those were the key German strong points of the salient, and the backbone of Jerry's line is broken at last. Stalin's ordered the first victory salute of the war, a hundred and twenty artillery salvos. It'll really be something."

"Well, I'd better come to the party."

"Why, you've got to."

"I'm perishing for sleep, and I feel rotten."

"Too bad. The Narkomindel's taking out the foreign press on a tour of the battlefields tomorrow. We'll be on the hop for a week. You can't miss that, either."

Pamela groaned.

"Incidentally, the whole Yank mission's coming to the embassy to watch the fireworks, but Captain Henry won't be there."

"Oh, won't he? You know him, then?"

"Of course. Short, athletic-looking, fifty or so. A bit dour, what? Doesn't say much."

"That's the man. Is he the naval attaché?"

"No, that's Captain Joyce. Henry does special military liaison. The inside word is that he's Hopkins's man in Moscow. Right now he's off in Siberia."

"Just as well."

"Why?"

"Because I look like death."

"Now, Pam, you look smashing." He touched her arm.

She pulled it away. "How's your wife?"

"Valentina? Fine, I guess. She's out touring the front with her ballet group. She dances on flatcars, on the backs of trucks, on air strips, wherever she can do a leap without breaking an ankle."

The suite at the Metropole was as Philip Rule had described it. The drawing room contained a grand piano, a vast Persian rug, and a cluttered array of very poor statues. Pamela said, peering into the bathroom, "Look at that tub! I shall be doing laps."

"Do you want the suite?"

"Yes, whatever it costs."

"I'll arrange it. And if you'll give me your papers, I'll check you in at the Nark for the battlefield tour. Suppose I call for you at half past ten? The guns and fireworks go off at midnight."

She was taking off her hat at a spotty mirror, and behind her he was frankly admiring her. Rule was going to fat, his blond hair was much thinner, his nose seemed bigger and broader. Except as a disagreeable memory, he meant nothing to her. Since the episode in the rainstorm on Christmas Eve in Singapore, she felt squeamish at being touched by him, that was all. She knew she still attracted him, but that was his problem, not hers. Kept at a distance, Philip Rule was quite tame, even helpful. She thought of his flowery eulogy for her father at the Alexandria cemetery: *An Englishman's Englishman, a reporter's reporter, a bard with a press card, singing the dirge of Empire to the thrilling beat of a triumphal march.*

She turned and with an effort gave him her hand. "You are kind, Phil. See you at ten-thirty."

Pamela was used to being undressed by men's glances, but a stripping by female eyes was a novelty. The Russian girls at the British embassy party stared her up and down, hair to shoes. She might have been a model, paid to go on display under hard scrutiny. There was no bitchiness in the looks, no deliberate rudeness, only intense wistful curiosity; and no wonder, considering their evening dresses; some long, some short, some flouncy, some tight, all atrociously cut and hideously colored.

Men soon surrounded Pam: Western correspondents, officers and diplomats relishing the sight of a chic woman from their world, and Russian officers in uniforms as smart as their women's dresses were dowdy, silently gazing at Pamela as at an objet d'art worth millions. The long wood-panelled room was not at all crowded by the forty or fifty guests, many clustered at a silver punch bowl, others dancing to an American jazz record on a bared patch of parquet floor, the rest talking and laughing, glasses in hand.

A big handsome young Russian officer, strung with medals and very fresh-faced, broke through the circle around Pamela and asked her in stumbling English to dance. Liking his nerve and his smile, she nodded. He was a very bad dancer, like herself, but the delight on his healthy red face at holding the beautiful Englishwoman by the waist, at an extremely respectful distance, charmed her.

"What are you doing in the war?" she asked, straining her rusty Russian to compose the sentence.

"*Ubivayu nemtsev!*" he returned, then hesitantly translated, "I — killing Chormans."

"I see. Lovely."

He nodded with a savage grin, eyes and teeth gleaming.

Philip Rule waited at the edge of the dance floor with two glasses of punch. When the record ended the Russian gave up Pamela with a bow. "That's one of their great tank commanders," said Rule. "He fought at Kursk."

"Really? He's hardly more than a boy."

"Boys fight the wars. We'd have the brotherhood of man tomorrow if the politicians had to get out and fight."

Rule was slipping, thought Pamela. Five years ago he would not have uttered the bromide with an air of saying something clever. Another record began: "Lili Marlene." They looked in each other's eyes. For Pamela, this song meant North Africa, and the death of her father. Rule said, "Strange, isn't it? The only decent war song of this whole bloody holocaust. A cheap weepy Hun ballad." He took the glass from her hand. "What the hell, Pamela, let's dance."

"Oh, all right."

To Pug Henry, who was just coming in with Ambassador Standley and an Air Corps general, "Lili Marlene" meant Pamela Tudsbury. The plaintive all-too-German melody had by some freak captured the bittersweet essence of fugitive wartime romance, the poignant sense of a fighting man's lovemaking in the dark before going off to battle, the sort of lovemaking he and Pamela would never know. He heard the tinny phonograph bleating as he walked in.

> *Bugler, tonight don't play the call to arms,*
> *I want another evening with her charms.*
> *Then we must say good-bye and part.*
> *I'll always keep you in my heart*
> *With me, Lili Marlene, with me, Lili Marlene.*

He was dumbfounded to come upon Pamela, of course. So the visa had gone through! Seeing her in Rule's arms intensified the surprise. Pug quietly loathed the man because of the Singapore episode; his reaction was not exactly a jealous one, for he had given up his dreams of Pamela, but the sight disgusted as well as amazed him.

Noticing the squat figure in blue and gold go by, Pamela guessed he had seen her, and was passing on because she was dancing with Rule. God in heaven, she thought, why did he have to turn up like this? Why does it never go right with us? And since when has he become so gray? She broke away and hurried after Pug, but he and the tall Air Corps general went into the crowd at the punch bowl, which closed around them. She hesitated to elbow through, but was about to try when the lights blinked several times. "Five minutes to midnight," the ambassador announced as the talk subsided. "We shall darken the room now, and open the curtains."

Pamela was swept by the excited guests to a railed open window. The night was starry, and a blessedly cool breeze was blowing. She stood there boxed in by noisy chatterers, unable to move, looking across the river toward the black mass of the Kremlin.

"Hello, Pamela." His voice, Victor Henry's voice, spoke in the dark beside her.

Rockets shot up into the sky at that moment and burst in a great crimson glare. Guns thundered. The floor shook beneath them. The party crowd cheered. A volcanic barrage rose from all over the city, not of fireworks but of ammunition: star shells, signal rockets, crimson tracers, shells that burst dazzling yellow, a canopy of colored battlefield fire, making a din that all but drowned out the gargantuan booming of a hundred and twenty big guns.

"Hello, there. Remind you of anything?" she gasped to the shadowy figure at her side. So they had stood watching the firebombing of London in 1940, when for the first time he had put his arm around her.

"Yes. That wasn't a victory display, though."

BOOM . . . BOOM . . . BOOM . . .

The barrage was exploding and blazing all over the sky, eerily lighting up the river, the cathedral, and the Kremlin. He spoke again between the roars of the big guns. "I'm sorry about your father, Pam, terribly sorry. Did you get my letter?"

"No. Did you ever get any of mine?"

BOOM . . .

"Just one that you wrote to me in Washington, saying you'd become engaged. Are you married?"

"No. I wrote another letter, a long one, to the *Northampton* —"

BOOM . . .

"That one I never got."

The salvos thundered on and on, and at last ceased. The eruption of fire died down, leaving puffs of black smoke spread across the stars. In the sudden quiet, a rattling and clattering started up on the embankment outside. "Great God, it's shrapnel falling!" the ambassador's voice rang out. "Away from the windows, everybody!"

When the lights came on, the Air Corps general, a tall lean man with wavy blond hair like Burne-Wilke's, and an unpleasantly cold expression, stood at Pug's elbow. "Lavish display of flak," he said. "Pity they're not that free with useful information."

Pug introduced him to Pamela. The general all at once looked pleasanter. "Well! I was with Duncan Burne-Wilke three weeks ago in New Delhi. He'd just gotten word you were coming, and he was a very happy man. I now see why."

She smiled. "Is he well?"

"Getting along. But that's a thankless war theatre, the CBI. Pug, we'd better get back at those charts. I'll make my farewells."

"Yes, sir."

The general went off. Pug said to her, "Sorry, I've got him on my hands, Pam. I'm pretty tied up. Business of getting new air routes for flying in Lend-Lease aircraft. Can we meet day after tomorrow, sometime?"

She told him about the Kursk tour. His face fell, and that slightly encouraged her. "A whole week, eh?" he said. "Too bad."

"I saw your wife in Washington. You've heard from her?"

"Oh, yes, now and then. She seems to be fine. How'd she look?"

"Very well. She told me to tell you that Byron's become the executive officer of his ship."

"Exec!" He raised heavy brows. Like his hair they were grayer now, and his face was heavier. "That's odd. He's very junior, and he's a reserve."

"Your general looks ready to go."

"So I see."

His handshake was friendly. She wanted to grip hard, to say in an act what would not come in words. But in this botched meeting, even that much might seem offensive disloyalty to Burne-Wilke. Oh, fiasco, she thought; fiasco, fiasco, fiasco!

"Well, see you in a week," he said. "If I'm not out of town again. So far I've nothing scheduled."

"Yes, yes. We have worlds to talk about."

"We do. Call me when you get back, Pam."

She rang the American embassy a week later, minutes after she returned to the Metropole suite, which she had wastefully retained and paid for. She was sure he would be away again, that they would go on missing each other, that this Moscow side trip would end as a doomed waste of time and spirit. But he was there, and he sounded glad to hear from her.

"Hello, Pam. How did it go?"

"Horribly. It's no good without Talky, Pug. What's more, I'm sick to my soul of devastated cities, smashed-up tanks, and stinking German corpses lying about. I'm sick of photographs of Russian women and children strung up on gallows. I'm sick of this whole insane and vile war. When do we see each other?"

"How about tomorrow?"

"Hasn't Philip Rule called you about tonight?"

"Rule?" His voice flattened. "No, he hasn't."

Hastily she said, "He will. His wife's back. It's her birthday, and he's having a party for her here in my suite. It's gigantic, and he got it for me, so I could hardly refuse. There'll be correspondents, a few embassy people, her ballet friends, that sort of thing. I'll gladly duck it if you'd rather not, and meet you somewhere else."

"N.G., Pamela. The Red Army's throwing a farewell banquet for my general. At the Metropole, in fact. We've got the agreement he came here to work out."

"How marvelous."

"That remains to be seen. Russian draftsmanship of an agreement can be surrealistic. Meantime there's this eating and drinking brawl to celebrate, and I can't possibly get out of it. I'll call you tomorrow."

"Damn," said Pamela. "Oh, bloody hell."

He chuckled. "Pam, you do sound like a correspondent."

"You don't know how I can sound. All right, tomorrow, then."

Rule's wife was almost too beautiful to be real: a perfect oval face, enormous clear blue eyes, heavy yellow hair, exquisitely molded hands and arms. She sat in a corner, hardly speaking or moving, never smiling. The suite was crowded, the music was blasting away, the guests were drinking and eating and dancing, but there was no real merriment in any of it, perhaps because the birthday girl was so conspicuously glum.

Far from showing any ballet grace in their Western dancing, the Russians were elephantine. Pamela danced with a man she had once seen as the prince in *Swan Lake*. He had a faun's face, a handsome shock of black hair and, even in his ill-fitting clothes, a superb physique; but he didn't know the steps, and he kept apologizing in incomprehensible Russian. The whole party was going like that. Phil was throwing down vodka, dancing awkwardly with one girl after another, and forcing foolish laughter. Valentina was beginning to look as though she wished she were dead. Pamela could not fathom what was wrong. Some of the trouble might be Russian awkwardness at socializing with foreigners, but there must be a strain between Rule and his fairy-tale beauty that she didn't know about.

Captain Joyce, the American naval attaché, a jolly Irishman with a knowing eye, asked Pamela to dance. Placing herself in his arms, she said, "Too bad Captain Henry is stuck downstairs."

"Oh, you know Pug?" Joyce said.

"Quite well." The knowing eye sparked at her. She added, "He and my father were good friends."

"I see. Well, the man is terrific. He's just pulled off a great feat."

"Can you tell me about it?"

"If you won't put it in your paper."

"I won't."

Speaking in Pamela's ear over the music as they shuffled here and there, Joyce said that Ambassador Standley had been trying in vain for months to get action on the Siberian route for the Lend-Lease aircraft. In a previous visit to the Soviet Union to push the thing, General Fitzgerald too had accomplished nothing. This time Standley had turned the problem over to Pug, and an agreement was now in hand. It meant that instead of flying a tough route via South America and Africa with a lot of crack-ups, or coming crated on convoy vessels which the U-boats could sink, the aircraft would now funnel in directly over a safe straight route. Fewer delays, more deliveries, and a cooling of much ill feeling on both sides would result.

"Will the Russians keep their word?" asked Pamela, as the music paused and they walked to the refreshment table.

"Remains to be seen. Meantime, that's a real love feast down below. Pug Henry is damn good at handling these tough ones." Pamela refused vodka. Tossing down a sizable glassful, Joyce coughed and glanced at his watch. "Say, they should be starting to carry them out of that fracas downstairs round about now. Why don't I try to fetch Pug?"

"Oh, please. *Please.*"

About ten minutes passed. Then into the room burst four Red Army officers in full regalia, followed by Joyce, Pug Henry, and General Fitzgerald. One of the Russians was an enormous bald general with a blaze of decorations, and an artificial hand in a leather glove. The others were much younger, and they did not seem nearly as jolly as the general, who entered with a roar in Russian of "*Happy Birthday!*" He marched up to Rule's wife, bowed over her hand, kissed her, and asked her to dance. Valentina smiled — for the first time, it seemed to Pamela, and it was like dawn over icy peaks — jumped up, and put herself in his arms.

"Recognize him?" Pug said to Pamela, as the pair went pounding out on the floor to "The Boogie-Woogie Washerwoman."

"Isn't he the one who gave us dinner in his field HQ, and then danced like mad?"

"Right. Yuri Yevlenko."

"By God, he's a live wire," said Captain Joyce. "That squinty little officer with the scar must be his political aide. Or an NKVD man. He tried to stop him from coming up. Muttered about fraternizing with foreigners.

You know what the general said? He said, 'So? What can they do to me? Cut off my other hand?' "

  . . . And the boogie-woogie washerwoman washes away . . .

"Seems to me," Pug said to Pamela, "that we've heard that imbecile noise before. Dance?"

"Must we?"

"You'd rather not? Thank God." He twined fingers in hers and led her to a small sofa. "They caught me at my white wine trick during the toasts. I had to switch back to vodka, and I'm reeling."

As Yevlenko clomped eccentrically about with the beaming Valentina, some Russians were abandoning their wooden fox-trots for the Lindy Hop. It better suited their springy dancing muscles. Though nobody could mistake them for Americans, several were flailing expertly away.

Pamela said, "You look sober enough." He sat erect in dress whites with bright gold buttons and shoulder-board stripes, and a rainbow bank of starred ribbons. The vodka had livened his eyes and heightened his color. Nothing had changed in fourteen months except for the grayed hair and added poundage. "By the way, your wife told me to admonish you about your weight."

"Ah, yes. She knows me. Go ahead, give me hell. When I've got duty like this, I eat and drink. On the *Northampton* I was a rail."

Nearly everybody was dancing now, except the three young Red Army officers ranged frozen-faced against the wall, and General Fitzgerald, who was flirting with a beautiful ballet girl in a ghastly red satin dress. Such was the noise that Rule had to turn up the music. Pamela all but shouted, "Tell me about the *Northampton,* Victor."

"Okay." As he talked about what had happened at sea after Midway, even about the Tassafaronga disaster, he glowed, or so it seemed to her. He told her of the post under Spruance that he might have had, and how he had taken this job instead at Roosevelt's request. He talked without bitterness or regret, laying out for her his life as it was. The party bubbled about them, and she sat listening, supremely content to be by his side, warmed by his physical presence, and sweetly disturbed by it, too. This was all she wanted, she kept thinking, just this closeness to this man until she died. She felt wholly alive again because she was sitting with him on a sofa. He was not happy. That was clear. She felt that she could make him happy, and that doing it would justify her own life.

Meantime, in a lull in the phonograph music, Yevlenko and the ballet people were talking excitedly around the piano. A girl sat down and rippled out-of-tune sour chords that brought general laughter. Yevlenko shouted,

"Nichevo! Igraitye!" ("It doesn't matter! Play!") She drummed out a Russian melody, Yevlenko bawled an order, and all the Russians, even the three junior officers, formed up and performed a whirling group dance: everyone shouting, stamping, crisscrossing, spinning, while the Westerners in a circle clapped time and cheered them on. After that there was no ice left to be broken. Yevlenko stripped off his bemedalled coat, and in his sweat-stained blouse did the dance he had performed in the house at the Moscow front, squatting and bounding to applause; only, he held his lopped limb awkwardly and lifelessly. Next Valentina caused howls by putting on his coat, and improvising a wicked little dance burlesquing a pompous general.

More excited consultation at the piano, and Valentina gestured for silence, and friskily announced that she and her friends would do the ballet created for their tour of the fronts. She would dance Hitler, another girl Goebbels, a third Göring, and a fourth Mussolini, though they didn't have their masks. Four men would be dancing the Red Army.

Pug and Pamela broke off their talk to watch this satiric pantomime. The four villains strutted in to martial music, miming an invasion; gloated over their victory; argued about a division of the spoils; came to slapstick blows. Enter the Red Army, prancing to the "Internationale." Extravagant pantomime of cowardice and fear by the villains. Comic circular chase, round and round. Death of the four villains; and as they fell one by one, their four crooked bodies formed a swastika on the floor. Sensation!

Amid the applause the *Swan Lake* prince stripped off his coat and tie, kicked off his shoes, and signalled to the pianist. In open white shirt, trousers, and stocking feet, he launched into a stunningly brilliant dance with leaps and twirls that brought cheer after cheer. It was a climax impossible to top, or so it seemed. As he stood panting, surrounded by congratulations while refills of vodka were poured all around, the piano struck a harsh chord. Out on the floor stalked the ramrod-straight much-ribboned General Fitzgerald. He did not take off his coat. At his brusque signal the pianist began a fast *kozotzki;* whereupon the lean Air Corps general squatted and danced, arms folded, blond hair flying, long legs athletically kicking out and in, with appropriate sideward leaps. The surprise was magnificent. The *Swan Lake* prince dropped beside Fitzgerald and they finished the dance as a duo to a tumult of encouraging shouts, stamping, and clapping.

"I like your general," said Pamela.

"I like these people," said Pug. "They're impossible, but I like them."

General Yevlenko presented a glass of vodka to Fitzgerald and clinked with him. They drained their glasses to great applause. Fitzgerald walked to a refreshment table beside Pug's sofa and picked off two open vodka bottles — not very large, but full — saying, "Here goes for Old Glory, Pug." He strode back and handed Yevlenko a bottle with a challenging flourish.

"Eh? *Horoshi tshelovyek!*" ("Good fellow!") bellowed Yevlenko, whose big face and naked pate were now bright salmon color.

With all the guests urging them on — except, Pug noted, the Red Army officer with the scar, who looked as vexed as a disobeyed governess — the two generals tilted the bottles to their mouths, eyeing each other. Finishing first, Fitzgerald crashed his bottle into the brick fireplace. Yevlenko's bottle came flying after it. They embraced amid cheers, while the girl at the piano thumped out a barely recognizable "Stars and Stripes Forever."

"Christ, I'd better get him back to the embassy," Pug said. "He's been dodging booze ever since he got here."

But somebody had put "Tiger Rag" on the phonograph, and Fitzgerald was already dancing with the girl in red satin, who had cruelly mimicked the club-footed Goebbels in the ballet. Yevlenko took Pamela on the floor. It was past two in the morning, so this last burst of dancing did not last long. The guests began to leave, the party to dwindle down. Dancing again with the *Swan Lake* prince, Pamela noticed Pug, Yevlenko, and Fitzgerald huddled in talk, with Rule listening. Her dimming journalist instinct woke, and she went over to sit down beside Pug.

"Okay. Are we talking straight?" Fitzgerald said to Pug. The two generals were on facing settees, glaring at each other.

"Straight!" barked Yevlenko, with an unmistakable gesture.

"Then tell him I'm fed to the teeth, Pug, with this second front stuff. I've been getting it here for weeks. What about North Africa and Sicily, the two greatest amphibious attacks in history? What about the thousand-plane air raids on Germany? What about the whole Pacific war, where we're keeping the Japs from jumping on their backs?"

"Here goes for Old Glory," Pug muttered, bringing a chill grin to Fitzgerald's face. He translated, and kept translating as fast as he could during the ensuing exchange.

Yevlenko nodded and nodded at Pug's words, his face hardening. He thrust a finger at Fitzgerald's face. "*Concentrate forces and strike at the decisive point! Schwerpunktbildung!* Do they teach that principle at West Point? The decisive place is Hitlerite Germany. Yes or no? The way for you to strike at Hitlerite Germany is through France. Yes or no?"

"Ask him why Russia didn't open a second front for a whole year when England stood alone against Hitlerite Germany."

Yevlenko grated at Fitzgerald, "That war was an imperialist quarrel over world markets. It was of no concern to our peasants and workers."

Philip Rule, who kept refilling his own glass with vodka as he listened, now said to Fitzgerald rather thickly, "Should you go on with this?"

"He can call it quits. He started it," Fitzgerald snapped. "Pug, ask him why we should break our necks to help a nation that's committed to the destruction of our way of life."

"Oh, gawd," murmured Rule.

Yevlenko's glare grew more bellicose. "We believe your way of life will destroy itself through its inner contradictions. We won't destroy it, but Hitler can. So why don't you cooperate to beat Hitler? In 1919 Churchill tried to destroy our way of life. Now he is entertained in the Kremlin. History goes in steps, Lenin said. Sometimes forward, sometimes backward. Now is a time to go forward."

"You don't trust us for sour apples, so how can we cooperate?"

Pug had trouble with "sour apples," but Yevlenko got the idea. He sneered, "Yes, yes. An old complaint. Well, sir, your country has never been invaded, but we have been invaded over and over, invaded and occupied. Most of our allies have historically proved treacherous, and sooner or later have turned and attacked Russia. We have learned a little caution."

"America won't attack Russia. You have nothing we want."

"Well, we want nothing from you, once we beat Hitler, but to be left alone."

"On that note, can we all have a last drink?" said Rule.

"Our host is getting tired," said Yevlenko, dropping the harsh debating tone for a sudden amiable aside at Fitzgerald.

Rule began pontificating in Russian, with drunken gestures, and Pug muttered a running translation to Fitzgerald. "Oh, this is all talk in a vacuum. The white race is having another big civil war. Race, General Yevlenko, not economics, rules human affairs. The white race is mechanically brilliant but morally primitive. The German is the purest white man, the superman, Hitler's dead right about that. The white man like the red man is destined to fade from history, after laying waste half the planet in his civil wars. The white man's drivel about democracy is finished, too, after democracy elected creatures like Chamberlain, Daladier, and Hitler. Next will come China's turn. China is the Middle Kingdom, the center of gravity of the human race. The only genuine Marxist of world consequence is now living in a cave in Yenan. His name is Mao Tse-tung."

Rule delivered himself of this pronouncement with insufferable alcoholic positiveness, glancing often at Pamela as Pug translated.

Fitzgerald yawned and sat up, straightening his blouse and tie. "General, will I be able to fly my planes through Vladivostok, or won't I?"

"Keep your end of the bargain. We'll keep ours."

"Another thing. Are you going to make another deal with the Nazis, as you did in 1939?"

Pug was nervous about translating that, but Yevlenko retorted in a level tone, "If we get wind that you're negotiating another Munich, we'll turn the tables again and it'll serve you right. But if you fight, we'll fight. If you don't, we'll crush the Hitlerites ourselves."

"Okay, Pug. Now tell him I argued myself black in the face, as a war planner, against the North African campaign. Tell him I fought six long months for a second front in France this year. Go ahead. Tell him that."

Pug obeyed. Yevlenko listened, narrowed his eyes at Fitzgerald, and tightened his mouth.

"Tell him he'd better believe America is different from all other countries in history."

An enigmatic smile was Yevlenko's only reaction.

"And I hope his tyrannical regime will let his people realize that. Because it's the one chance for peace in the long run."

The smile faded, leaving a face of stone.

"And you, General," said Fitzgerald, standing and offering his hand, "are one hell of a guy. I am dead drunk. Any words of offense I spoke don't count. Pug, lead me back to Spaso House. I've got to pack up fast."

Yevlenko got to his feet, stretched out his left hand, and said, "*I will take you back to Spaso House.*"

"Really? Most handsome of you. In the name of Allied amity, I accept. Now I'll say good-bye to the birthday beauty."

By now only the Red Army officers and Valentina had not yet left the suite. Yevlenko growled some words at the junior officers, whereupon they stiffened. One of them spoke to Fitzgerald — in fair English, Pug noted, using the language for the first time that evening — and the Air Corps general went out with him. Valentina pulled Rule from a slump in an armchair, and led him stumbling out. Pug, Pamela, and General Yevlenko remained alone amid the desolation of the ended party.

Yevlenko took Pamela's hand in his left, saying, "So you will marry Air Vice Marshal Duncan Burne-Wilke, who stole forty Airacobras from us."

Getting the grammar wrong, Pam replied, "General, we are fighting the same enemy with those Airacobras."

"*I yevo?*" ("And him?") Yevlenko directed his lifeless hand at Pug Henry.

She opened wide eyes and mimicked his gesture. "*Sprasitye yevo!*" ("Ask him!")

Pug spoke rapidly to Yevlenko. Pamela interrupted, "Now, now, what's all that?"

"I'm saying he misunderstands. That we're dear old friends."

Yevlenko spoke in slow clear Russian to Pamela, thrusting an index finger into Pug's shoulder. "You are in Moscow, dear lady, because *he* got you your visa. *Genry*," he went on, buttoning the top of his tunic, "*ne bood durakom!*"

Abruptly he walked out, closing the door.

"*Ne bood durakom* — don't be — what?" asked Pamela. "What's *durakom?*"

"Goddamned fool. Instrumental case."

"I see." Pamela burst out with a throaty peal of female joy. She put her arms around his neck and kissed his mouth. "So you brought me to Moscow because we're dear old friends." He crushed her to him, kissed her hard, and let her go. Walking to the windows, he pulled back the curtains. It was day, the early Russian day of midsummer. The cool light made the after-party scene sadder and drearier. Pamela came beside him, looking out at clouds faintly flushed with sunrise. "You love me."

"I don't change much."

"I don't love Duncan. That's what I wrote you in the letter to the *Northampton.* He knows I don't. He knows about you. In that letter I asked you to speak, or forever hold your peace. But you never got it."

"Why are you marrying a man you don't love?"

"I wrote you that, too. I was sick of floating, I wanted to land. That's doubly true now. I had Talky then, now I have nobody."

It was a while before he spoke. "Pamela, when I got home, Rhoda acted like a Turkish harem girl. She was my slave. She's guilty, and sorry, and sad, and bereft. I'm sure she has nothing to do with that other fellow any more. I'm not God. I'm her husband. I can't chuck her out."

Guilty and sorry! Sad and bereft! How little that resembled the woman Pamela had seen in Washington! Pug was the sad and bereft one, it was written in every line of his face. *And if she's unfaithful to you again?* The question was on the tip of Pamela's tongue. Looking into Pug Henry's seamed decent face and somber eyes, she couldn't utter it. "Well, here I am. You got me here. What do you want of me?"

"Look, Slote wrote that you were having trouble with your visa." She was facing him, staring into his eyes. "All right, do I have to say it? I wanted you here because to see you is happiness."

"Even when I'm dancing with Phil Rule?"

"Well, that just happened."

"Phil means nothing to me."

"I know."

"Pug, we have the rottenest luck, don't we?" Her eyes filled with tears that did not fall. "I can't hang around Moscow just to be near you. You don't want lovemaking, do you?"

With an ardent and bitter look he said, "I'm not free for lovemaking. Neither are you."

"Then I'll go on to New Delhi. I'll marry Duncan."

"You're so young. Why do that? There'll be a man you'll love."

"God almighty, there's no *room.* Don't you understand me? How explicit do I have to be? Duncan's sexual taste runs to pretty young popsies, and they swarm and swoon around him, so that more or less solves a difficulty for me. He wants a lady in his life, and he's very affectionate and romantic about me. He thinks I'm a dashing creature, decorative as hell." She put both hands on Pug's shoulders. "You are my love. I'd help it if I could. I can't."

He took her in his arms. The sun came through low clouds and made a yellow patch on the wall.

"Ye gods, sunup," he said.

"Victor, just keep your arms around me."

After a long, long silence he said, "This may not come out right in words. You said we've had rotten luck. Well, I'm grateful as things are, Pam. It's a miraculous gift from God, what I feel for you. Stay here awhile."

"A week," Pamela said, choking. "I'll try to stay a week."

"You will? A week? That's a lifetime. Now I've got to go and pour General Fitzgerald on an airplane."

She caressed his hair and eyebrows and kissed him. He strode out without looking back. At her window she watched until the erect small figure in white came in view, and vigorously walked out of sight on the quiet sunlit boulevard. The melody of "Lili Marlene" was running over and over in her head, and she was wondering when he would find out what was happening to his wife.

68

I N a wild ravine high in the Carpathian Mountains, wan light diffused through yellowing leaves shows a meandering forest path which might be a hunters' trail or an animal track, or no path at all but a trick of the light falling among the trees. As the sun sets and clouds redden overhead a bulkily clad figure comes striding down this trail carrying a heavy pack, with a rifle slung on a shoulder. It is a woman of slight build, her face close-wrapped by a thick gray shawl, her breath smoking. Passing a lightning-blasted oak trunk, she vanishes like a forest spirit sinking into the earth.

She is no forest spirit, but a so-called forest wife, a partisan commander's woman; and she has jumped down into a dugout, through a hole so masked by brush that if not for the ruined oak she herself might have missed it in the gloom. Partisan discipline forbids such creature comforts to lesser men, but a woman sharing his bed is a prestige symbol of the leader, like a new Nagant pistol, a separate dugout, and a leather windbreaker. Major Sidor Nikonov has grown quite fond of Bronka Ginsberg, whom at first he more or less raped; besides using her body he talks a lot to her, and listens to her opinions. He has been waiting for her, in fact, to help him decide whether or not to shoot the suspected infiltrator lying tied up in the cook dugout.

This fellow swears he is no infiltrator, but a Red Army soldier who escaped from a prison camp outside Ternopol, and joined a partisan band which the Germans wiped out. He got away, so he says, and has been wandering westward in the mountains, living on roots and berries or handouts from peasants. His story is plausible, and he is certainly emaciated and ragged enough; but his Russian accent is odd, he looks over sixty, and he has no identification at all.

Bronka Ginsberg goes to size up the man. Hunched in the dirt in a corner of the cook dugout, more tortured by the food smells than by the ropes cutting his ankles and wrists, Berel Jastrow takes one look at her face and decides to gamble.

"*Yir zeit a yiddishe tochter, nane?*" ("You're a Jewish daughter, no?")

"*Richtig. Und ver zeit ir?*" ("Right. And who are you?")

The Galician Yiddish, toughly rapped out, falls on his ears like song. He gives straight answers to Bronka's probing questions.

The two bearded cooks stirring the soup vats exchange winks at the Yiddish gabble. Bronka Ginsberg is an old story to them. Long ago the major dragged this thin-lipped, hard-faced creature out of the family camp of Jews up in the mountains, to nurse men wounded in a raid. Now the damned Jew-bitch bosses the whole show. But she is a skilled nurse, and nobody makes trouble about her. For one thing Sidor Nikonov would shoot any man who looked cross-eyed at the woman.

As she jaws away in Yiddish with the infiltrator, the cooks lose interest. Since the fellow is a Yid, he can't really be an infiltrator; so they won't get to take him out in the woods and shoot him. She'll see to that. Too bad. It can be fun when they beg for mercy. These two are Ukrainian peasants drafted into the band; in the cook dugout they stay warm, fill their bellies, and avoid the food raids and railroad dynamitings. They loathe Bronka Ginsberg but aren't about to cross her.

Why, she is asking Jastrow, didn't he tell his captors the truth? The partisans know about the mass graves; why did he make up that yarn about Ternopol? Glancing at the cooks, he says she ought to know how treacherous the Ukrainian backwoods are, worse even than in Lithuania. The Benderovce gangs are just as apt to kill a Jew as to feed him or to let him go on his way. In Auschwitz some of the worst guards were Ukrainians. So he invented that story. Other partisan bands have believed him and given him food. Why is he tied up here like a dog?

Bronka Ginsberg explains that a unit of turncoat Russian soldiers led by Germans infiltrated the ravine a week ago to destroy Nikonov's band. One fellow doublecrossed the Fritzes, and alerted the partisans. They ambushed the outfit, killed most of them, and have been hunting the stragglers ever since. Jastrow is lucky, she says, that he wasn't shot at sight.

Berel is untied and fed. Later in the command dugout he repeats his story in Russian to Major Nikonov and the political officer, Comrade Polchenko, a wizened man with black teeth. Bronka Ginsberg sits by, sewing. The officers make Berel cut the slender aluminum cylinders containing the film rolls out of his coat lining. They are peering at the cylinders by the oil lamp when the evening Central Partisan Staff broadcast from Moscow starts up. They put aside the film containers to listen. Through a square wooden box that whistles and squeals, dispatch orders come gargling out in plain language to various code-named detachments; also cheery bulletins about a victory west of recaptured Kharkov, big bombing raids on Germany, and the surrender of Italy.

Their discussion about Berel resumes. The political officer is for sending the films to Moscow in the next ammunition delivery plane, and turning the Jew loose. Major Nikonov is against that; the films will get lost or nobody will know what they mean. If the films go to Moscow, the Jew should be sent along.

The major is curt with Polchenko. Political officers in partisan detachments are an irritation. Most of these bands consist of Red Army soldiers trapped behind German lines who have taken to the woods to survive. They attack enemy units or the local gendarmerie to seize food, arms, and ammunition, or to take revenge for peasants who are punished for helping them. But the heroic partisan stories are propaganda romance, by and large; these men have mostly turned forest animals, thinking first of their safety. This does not suit Moscow, naturally; hence men like Polchenko have been airlifted to the partisan forests, to stir up activity and see that Central Staff orders are obeyed.

As it happens, Nikonov's band is a brave and venturesome one, with a good record of sabotaging German communications. Nikonov himself is a regular Red Army officer, thinking of his own future once the tide of war has turned. But the Carpathians are far from Moscow, and the Red Army is far from the Carpathians. The Soviet bureaucracy, represented by the black-toothed man, doesn't swing much weight; Nikonov is boss here. So Berel Jastrow observes, listening anxiously to the talk. Polchenko is civil, almost ingratiating, as he argues with the leader.

Bronka Ginsberg looks up from her sewing. "You're both talking nonsense. Why bother with this fellow? What's he to us? Did Moscow ask for him or his films? Send him up to Levine's camp. They'll feed him, and then he can go on to Prague, or to the devil. If his Prague contact can really reach the Americans, then maybe the *New York Times* will have a story about the heroic Sidor Nikonov band. Eh?" She turns on Berel. "Wouldn't you give Major Nikonov credit? And his partisan detachment, that's blowing up Fritz's trains and bridges all over the western Ukraine?"

"I will get to Prague," says Berel, "and the Americans will hear about the Nikonov partisan brigade."

Major Nikonov's band is far from a brigade — a mere four hundred men, loosely held together by Nikonov. The word pleases him.

"All right, take him to Levine tomorrow," he says to Bronka. "You can use mules. The fellow's half-dead."

"Oh, he'll drag his own carcass up the mountain, don't worry."

The political officer makes a disgusted face, shakes his head, and spits in the dirt.

Dr. Levine's Jews, refugees from the last massacre in Zhitomir, are squatting in a tumbledown hunters' camp by a small lake, not far from the Slovakian border. The carpenters have long since repaired the leaky roofs of the abandoned cabins and main lodge, sealed the walls, put in shutters, knocked together rough furniture, and made a habitable retreat for the survivors of some eighty families, much reduced by frost, malnutrition, and disease in their long westward trek. Sidor Nikonov raided these Jews when they first came here, took most of their food and weapons, and dragged off Bronka. Bronka pointed out to him, after her rape, that Levine's men are craftsmen spared by the Germans in Zhitomir; electricians, carpenters, blacksmiths, mechanics, a gunsmith, a baker, a watchmaker, and the like. Ever since, the partisans have supplied food, clothing, bullets, and weapons to the Jews — very little, but sufficient to keep them alive and able to fight off intruders — and in return the Jews have serviced their machines, fashioned new weapons, made crude bombs, and repaired their generators and signal equipment. They are like a maintenance battalion, very useful.

The partnership has paid off both ways. Once when an SS patrol, tipped off by an anti-Semite down in the flats, climbed the mountain to scoop in the Jews, Nikonov warned them. They melted into the woods with their children, their aged, and their sick. The Germans found an empty camp. While they were still engaged in stealing everything they could lift, Nikonov's men fell on them and murdered them all. Germans have not come again looking for Jews. On the other hand, while Nikonov was off attacking a troop train, a gang of renegade Ukrainians happened upon his dugouts, and in a brief fierce fight with the guards set fire to the weapons cache. It burned for hours, leaving a smoking pile of twisted red-hot gun barrels. The Jews straightened the barrels, repaired the firing mechanisms, made new stocks, and restored the weapons to Nikonov's arsenal, usable again in a fashion until he could steal more guns.

Such are the stories that Bronka Ginsberg tells Jastrow while toiling up the mountain trail. "Sidor Nikonov is really not a bad man, for a *goy*," she sums up, sighing. "Not a wild beast like some. But my grandfather was a rabbi in Bryansk. My father was the president of the Zhitomir Zionists. And look at me, will you? A forest wife. Ivan Ivanovitch's whore."

Jastrow says, "You are an *aishess khayil*."

Bronka, ahead of him on the trail, looks back at him, her weatherbeaten face coloring, her eyes moist. *Aishess khayil,* from the Book of Proverbs, means "woman of valor," the ultimate religious praise for a Jewess.

Late that night, the only woman in the council circle at the lodge is Bronka Ginsberg. The other firelit faces, except for the clean-shaven doctor's, are bearded, rough, and grim. "Tell them about the chains," she says. Her face is as hard as any man's there. "And about the dogs. Give them the picture."

Jastrow is talking to the executive committee of Dr. Levine's band, seated around a big stone fireplace where massive logs blaze. The prompting is helpful. What with the long climb and the bellyful of bread and soup, he is dropping off with fatigue.

Blobel's Jews had to work in chains, he relates, after his pal broke free, seized a gun, and shot some SS guards. Every fourth man in the gang, counted off at random, was hanged; the rest were chained in sections by the neck, with ankle chains on each man. The number of guard dogs was doubled.

Still, the escape of his section was planned for months. They waited for two minimum simultaneous conditions: a river nearby, and a heavy rainstorm. They worked during those months on their chains with screwdrivers, keys, picks, and other tools filched from the clothes of the dead. Though they were a sick, beaten, frightened lot, they knew that they were overdue to be shot and burned up, so the feeblest of them was game to try the break.

A thunderstorm just before sunset, in the woods outside Ternopol, at a mass grave on a bluff near the Seret River, gave them their chance. A thousand bodies, piled up on two frames with timber and waste oil, had just been put to the torch. The cloudburst caused dense dark clouds of stinking smoke to roll over the SS men, who backed off with their dogs. Jastrow's gang shed its chains amid the smoke and downpour, scattered into the woods, and made for the river. As Jastrow scrambled and slid down the bluff he heard the dogs, and shouts, and shots, and screams; but he reached the water and plunged in. He allowed the current to sweep him far downstream, and crawled ashore on the other side in darkness. Next morning, groping through dense dripping woods, he came on two other escapees, Polish Jews who were heading for their home towns, hoping for food and concealment there. As to the others, he feels that perhaps half got away, but he never saw them again.

"You still have the films?" asks Dr. Levine, a round-faced, black-haired man in his thirties, dressed in a patched Wehrmacht uniform. With his rimless glasses and kindly smile he looks like a city intellectual rather than the leader of the roughnecks around the fire. According to Bronka, he is a gynecologist, and also a dental surgeon. In the mountain hamlets, and in the villages down in the flats, the inhabitants like Levine: he will come great distances to treat their sick.

"Yes, I have them."

"You'll let Ephraim develop them?" Levine jerks a thumb at a long-nosed man with red whiskers bristling all over his face. "Ephraim is our photography specialist. Also a professor of physics. Then we can have a look at them."

"Yes."

"Good. When you're stronger, we'll send you on to people who'll get you over the border."

The red-whiskered man says, "Do the pictures show the crematoriums?"

"I don't know."

"Who took them? And with what?"

"Auschwitz has thousands of cameras. Mountains of film." Berel's reply is weak and weary. "Auschwitz is the biggest treasure house in the world, all the stuff robbed from our dead people. Jewish girls sit in thirty big warehouses, sorting out the loot. It's all supposed to go back to Germany, but the SS steals a lot. We steal, too. There is a very good Czech underground. They are good Jews, those Czechs. They are tough, and they stick together. They stole the cameras and the films. They took the pictures." Berel Jastrow is so tired that as he talks his eyes droop, and he half-dreams, and seems to see Auschwitz's long rows of horse stalls in floodlit snow, the trudging bent Jews in their striped suits, and the big "Canada" warehouses with the loot piled up outside them under snow-covered tarpaulins, and in the distance dark chimneys vomiting flames and black smoke.

"Let him rest," he hears Dr. Levine say. "Put him in with Ephraim."

Berel has not lain in a bed for weeks. The straw mattress and the ragged blanket in a rude three-tier bunk are blissful luxury. He sleeps and sleeps. When he wakes an old woman brings him hot soup with bread. He eats and dozes again. Two days of this and he is up and about, bathing in the lake at high noon when the sun warms the icy water, then walking around the camp dressed in the German winter uniform Ephraim gives him. It is a curiously peaceful scene, this lakeside cluster of mountain cabins surrounded by peaks russet with autumn. Ragged clothes dry in the sun, women scrub, sew, cook, and gossip, men in small workshops saw and hammer and clank, a blacksmith makes his forge blaze as little children watch. Older children drone in open-air classes: Bible, mathematics, Zionist history, even Talmud. There are few books, no pencils, no paper; the instruction is rote oral repetition in Yiddish. The pinch-faced shabby children look as bored and harassed here as in any schoolroom, and here as everywhere some are at surreptitious mischief. The Talmud boys sit in a circle around one large tome, some reading aloud from the upside-down text.

Young men and women armed with rifles patrol the camp. Ephraim tells Berel that radio-equipped sentinels are posted far down the trails and passes. The camp is not likely to be surprised. The armed guards can take care of infiltrators or small bands, but for protection from serious threats they must signal Nikonov. Their best young people are gone. They wanted vengeance for the killings at Zhitomir; some have joined Kovpak's famous partisan regiment, others the one led by the legendary Jew, Uncle Moisha. Dr. Levine approved their going.

In the week that Berel stays he hears a flood of stories, most of them horrible, a few heroic, some funny, drawn from the Jewish forest grapevine. He too has his adventures to relate. In this way, as he is reminiscing at supper one evening about his days with the early Jewish partisans outside Minsk, he learns that his own son is alive! There is no mistake about it. A skinny, pimply young fellow with an eyepatch, who served with Kovpak until a German grenade half-blinded him, marched with a Mendel Jastrow, through the Ukraine for months. So it comes out that not only is Mendel alive, but a partisan — quiet Mendel, the super-religious yeshiva boy — and that the daughter-in-law and her child, from what this young fellow last heard, are in hiding on a peasant's farm outside Volozhin.

This is the first word Berel has had of his family in two years of wanderings and imprisonment. Through all the abuse, pain, and hunger that have ground him down, he has never totally lost hope that things would yet turn around. He takes the news quietly, but it seems a signal that the darkest part of the dark night may be starting to pass. He feels stronger, and he is ready to forge on to Prague.

In the big room of the main lodge, the night before he leaves, Ephraim puts on a lantern-slide show for selected adults: Berel's developed films, copied to larger slides, and flashed on a sheet gray with age and washings, through a crude projector using the arc light of two battery carbons. The sputtering and flickering of this improvised light lends a bloodcurdling animation to the slides. The naked women appear to shiver, marching into the gas chamber with their children; the prisoners wrenching gold from the corpses' teeth under SS guard seem to heave and strain; over the long open pit, where huge rows of human bodies burn, and Sonderkommandos with meat hooks are dragging up more bodies, the smoke wavers and billows. Some pictures are too blurred to show much, but the rest tell the story of the Oswiecim camp in crushing truth.

The bad light makes the photographed documents hard to read. A long ledger page shows several hundred deaths of "heart attacks" in the same day; there are inventories of jewels, gold, furs, currency, watches, candlesticks, cameras, fountain pens, itemized and priced in neat German; six pages of a report of a medical experiment on twenty identical twins, with measurements of their response to extremes of heat, cold, and electric shock, length of time for expiring after phenol injection, and elaborate comparative anatomy statistics after autopsy. Berel Jastrow has never seen the documents nor witnessed the scenes pictured. Horrified and sorrowful, he is yet reassured to know that the material is so utterly and unanswerably damning.

Silently, those who have watched the slides trudge out of the main house, leaving only the council. Dr. Levine stares at the fire for a long time. "Berel, they know me in the villages. I'll take you over the border myself. The Jewish partisans in Slovakia are well organized, and they'll get you to Prague."

The train from Pardubice to Prague is crowded, the aisles of the second-class carriages jammed with standees. Czech policemen patiently work their way down the compartments, examining papers. In this docile Protectorate, betrayed at Munich, gobbled up before the war by the Germans, crushed by the reprisals for the Heydrich assassination, nothing ever turns up in the train inspections. Still, the Gestapo headquarters in Prague continues to require them.

An old man reading a German paper has to be nudged for his papers by a policeman entering the compartment. Absentmindedly he pulls out a worn wallet containing his cards and permits, and hands it over while continuing to read. Reinhold Henkle, German construction worker from Pardubice, mother's maiden name Hungarian, which goes with the broad smooth-shaven Slavic face; the policeman glances at the threadbare suit and toilworn hands of the passenger, returns the papers, and takes the next batch. So Berel Jastrow surfaces.

The train bowls along the valley of the Elbe by the glittery river, through fruit-laden vineyards and orchards full of harvesters, and grain fields spiky with stubble. The other people in the compartment are a fat old lady with an irritated look, three young women giggling together, and a uniformed young man with crutches. This confrontation with the policeman, for which Berel rehearsed for a week, has come and gone like a quick bad joke. He has been through grotesque times, but this passage from the wild world of mass graves and mountain partisans to what he once took for everyday reality — a seat on a moving train, girls in pretty dresses diffusing cheap scent and laughing, his own tie, creased hat, white shirt that cuts his neck — what a jolt! Coming back from the dead would have to be something like this; normal life seems a mockery, a busy little make-believe game that shuts out a terrible truth beyond.

Prague astounds him. He knows it well from business trips. The lovely old city looks as though the war has never happened, as though the past four years recorded in his mind have been a long bad dream. The swastika flags flapping noisily in a high wind were all too visible in Prague in peacetime, when the Nazis were agitating for the return of the Sudetenland. Just as always the people crowd the streets in the afternoon sunshine, for it is just about quitting time. Well-dressed, looking stolidly content with things as they are, they fill the sidewalk cafés. If anything, Prague is more serene now than in the turbulent days when Hitler was breathing fire against Beneš. In the sidewalk crowds Berel sees not one Jewish face. That is new. That is the one clear sign in Prague that the war is no dream.

His memorized instructions give him an alternate address if the book-shop should be gone; but there it is, in a crooked alley of the Mala Strana, the Little Town.

N. MASTNY

BOOKS

NEW AND SECOND-HAND

The opening door jangles a bell. The place is packed with old books on shelves, in piles on the floor, and the smell is very musty. A white-haired woman in a gray smock sits at a desk heaped with books, marking catalogue cards. She looks up benignly, with a smile that is more like a twitch, and says something in Czech.

"Sprechen Sie Deutsch?"

"Ja."

"Do you have, in your second-hand section, any books on philosophy?"

"Yes, quite a number."

"Do you have Immanuel Kant's Critique of Pure Reason?"

"I'm not sure." She blinks at him. "Forgive me, but you do not look like a man whom such a book would interest."

"It is for my son Eric. He is writing his doctoral thesis."

After a long appraising stare, she gets up. "Let me ask my husband."

She goes out through a curtain in the back. Soon a short, stooped, bald man in a torn sweater, wearing a green eyeshade, emerges sipping from a cup. "Excuse me, I just made my tea and it is still hot."

Unlike the other dialogue, this is not a signal. Berel makes no reply. The man potters about among the shelves, noisily drinking. He takes down a worn volume, blowing off dust, and hands it to Berel, open to the flyleaf, on which a name and address are inked. "People should never write in books." The volume is about travels in Persia, and the author's name is meaningless. "It is such a desecration."

"Thank you, but that is not what I had in mind."

The man shrugs, murmurs a blank-faced apology, and vanishes behind the curtain with the book.

The address is on the other side of town. Berel takes a trolleybus there, and walks several blocks through a shabby section of four-story houses. On the ground-floor entrance of the house he seeks, there is a dentist's sign. A buzzer admits him. Two doleful elderly men sit waiting on a bench in the foyer. A housewifely woman in a dirty uniform comes out of the dentist's office, from which groans and the noise of a drill can be heard.

"I'm sorry, the doctor can see no more patients today."

"It's an emergency, madam, a very bad abscess."

"You'll have to wait your turn, then."

He waits almost an hour. The doctor, his white coat spattered with blood, is washing his hands at a sink when Berel comes into the office. "Sit down, I'll be right with you," he says over his shoulder.

"I come from Mastny, the bookseller."

The doctor straightens and turns: bushy sandy hair, a heavy square face, a hard big jaw. He scans Berel with narrowed eyes, and says words in Czech. Berel gives the memorized reply.

"Who are you?" asks the dentist.

"I come from Oswiecim."

"Oswiecim? *With films?*"

"Yes."

"My God. We've long since given you fellows up for dead." The doctor is tremendously excited. He laughs. He seizes Berel by the shoulders. "We expected two of you."

"The other man is dead. Here are the films."

With a sense of solemn exaltation, Berel hands the aluminum cylinders to the dentist.

That night, in the kitchen on the second floor of the house, he sits with the dentist and his wife at a supper of boiled potatoes, prunes, bread, and tea. His voice is giving out, for he has been talking so much, recounting his long journey and his adventures along the way. He is dwelling on his week in Levine's camp, and the great moment when he learned that his son was alive.

The wife, bringing glasses and a bottle of slivovitz to the table, casually says to her husband, "It's an odd name, at that. Didn't someone at the last committee meeting tell about a Jastrow they've got in Theresienstadt now? One of the *Prominente?*"

"That's an American." The dentist makes a gesture of dismissal. "Some rich Jewish writer who got himself caught in France, the damn fool." He says to Berel, "What route did you take to get over the border? Did you go through Turka?"

Berel does not reply.

The two men look at each other.

"What's the matter?" asks the dentist.

"Aaron Jastrow? In Theresienstadt?"

"I think his name is Aaron," says the dentist. "Why?"

PART SIX

The Paradise Ghetto

69

U NLIKE Auschwitz there is really nothing secret about Theresienstadt. The German government has even been at some pains to publicize, with news stories and photographs, the "Paradise Ghetto" in the Czech fortress town of Terezin near Prague, where Berel now hears his cousin is immured.

This anomalous Nazi-sponsored haven for Jews, also called *Theresienbad* ("Terezin Spa"), is almost a byword in Europe. Jews of influence or means desperately try to get sent there. The Gestapo collects enormous fees for selling them commodious Terezin apartments with guaranteed lifetime medical care, hotel service, and food allotments. Jewish leaders of some large cities are shipped there, once disease, hunger, and transportation "to the east" have erased their communities. Half-Jews, deserving old people, distinguished artists and scholars, decorated Jewish war veterans, dwell in this town with their families. Privileged Jews of the Netherlands and Denmark also end up there.

News pictures in European journals show these fortunate Jews, some recognizable by name or face, all wearing yellow stars, sitting at their ease in small cafés, attending lectures and concerts, happily at work in factories or shops, strolling in a flowery park, rehearsing an opera or a play, watching a local soccer game, wrapped in their prayer shawls and worshipping in a well-appointed synagogue, and even dancing in crowded little nightclubs. Outside Nazi Europe information about the place is distorted and sparse, but its existence is known through favorable Red Cross reports. European Jews who have not yet gone "east" would joyously trade places with Aaron Jastrow, and throw into the bargain all they possessed.

Such a comfortable resort for Jews in the midst of a Europe swamped in anti-Semitic propaganda and wartime hardships has naturally caused resentment. Dr. Goebbels has given voice to this in a speech:

. . . *While the Jews in Terezin are sitting in the café, drinking coffee, eating cake, and dancing, our soldiers have to bear all the miseries and deprivations, to defend their homeland* . . .

Hints are not lacking in neutral and Allied countries, to be sure, that Theresienstadt is just a Potemkin village, a cynical show staged by the Nazis;

so German Red Cross representatives have been invited to come and see for themselves, and have publicly confirmed the existence of this curious sanctuary. The Germans claim that Jewish camps in "the east" are all like Theresienstadt, just not quite so luxurious. For this the Red Cross and the world has to take their word.

There are few American Jews in Theresienstadt, or indeed anywhere in Nazi Europe. Most of them fled before the war. As for the scattering that remain, some are surviving by dint of influence, reputation, wealth, or luck, like Berenson and Gertrude Stein; some have gone into hiding and are making it through the war that way; some have already been gassed in Auschwitz, their American citizenship a useless mockery. Natalie, her uncle, and her baby have landed in the Paradise Ghetto.

·   ·   ·

National Socialist Germany seems to have been something new in human affairs. Its roots were old, and the soil was old, but it was a mutant. In the ancient world, Sparta and Plato's imaginary Republic were but the dimmest foreshadowings. Despite Hitler's copious borrowings from Lenin and Mussolini, no modern political comparisons hold. No philosopher from Aristotle to Marx and Nietzsche ever foresaw such a thing, and none gave an account of human nature that could accommodate it. The Third Reich erupted into history as a surprise. It lasted a mere dozen years. It is gone. Historians, social scientists, political analysts, still stammer and grope in the mountainous ruins of unprecedented facts about human nature and society that it left behind.

Ordinary people prefer to forget it: a nasty twelve-year episode in Europe's decline, best swept under the rug. Scholars force it into one or another academic pigeonhole: populism plus terror, capitalist counterrevolution, recrudescence of Bonapartism, dictatorship of the right, triumph of a demagogue; bookish labels without end, developed into long heavy tomes. None really accounts for the Third Reich. The still-spreading, still-baffling, sinister red stain on all mankind of National Socialist Germany — more than the population explosion, nuclear bombs, and the exhaustion of the environment — is the radical though shunned question in present human affairs.

Theresienstadt sheds light on it, because unlike Auschwitz, the Paradise Ghetto is not unfathomable. It was a National Socialist deed; but by an effort of the imagination, because it had a trace of recognizable sense, we can grasp it. It was just a hoax. The resources of a great government went into it, and so it worked. Natalie Henry's best hope for survival with her child lay, strangely enough, in this enormous fake painstakingly staged by the Germans.

The intention to kill every Jew in Europe — and every Jew in the world, as German domination expanded — was, for Hitler and his trusted few, probably never in doubt. It crystallized in deeds and documents early in the war. The paper trail remains exiguous, and Hitler apparently never signed anything; but that the order came down from him to execute his threats in *Mein Kampf* appears self-evident.

However, old-fashioned notions in the world outside Germany presented difficulties: mercy, justice, the right of all human beings to life and safety, horror of killing women and children, and so forth. But for the National Socialists, killing was the nature of war; German women and children were dying under bombs; the definition of *enemy* was a matter of government decision. That the Jews were Germany's greatest enemy was an article at the core of National Socialist policy. This was why, even as Germany in 1944 began to crumple, crucial war resources continued to go to murdering Jews. To the critical military mind this made no sense. To the leaders whom the German nation passionately followed to the last it made total sense. In the last will and testament that Adolf Hitler wrote, before blowing his brains out in his Berlin bunker, he boasted of his "humane" massacre of the Jews — he used that word — and exhorted the defeated German people to go on killing them.

In dealing with the softhearted prejudices of the benighted outside world during the great slaughter, the essential National Socialist policy was *hoax*. Wartime secrecy made possible the job of covering up the actual killings. No reporters travelled with the *Einsatzgruppen,* or got into Auschwitz. It was a question first of counteracting the ever-growing flood of leaks and rumors about the slayings, and second of getting rid of the evidence. The corpse-burning squads of Paul Blobel, and the Paradise Ghetto of Terezin, were complementary aspects of the great hoax. Theresienstadt would show that the slaughter was not happening. The corpse-burning squads would erase any evidence that it had ever happened.

Today the notion of forever concealing the murder of many millions of people may seem utterly crazy. But the energy and ingenuity of the entire German nation were at Hitler's disposal. The Germans were performing many other prodigious mad feats for him.

The most triumphant part of the hoax was directed at the Jews themselves. All through the four years of the giant slaughter, most of them never knew, few suspected, and fewer truly believed that the trains were taking them to their deaths. The Germans soothed them with the most diverse and elaborate lies about where they were going, and what they would do when they arrived. This faking lasted to the final seconds of their lives, when they were led naked into the "disinfection shower baths" which were asphyxiation dungeons.

Today, again, the millions of doomed Jews may seem crazily simpleminded to have swallowed the hoax and walked like oxen to the knife. But as the patient refuses to believe he has leukemia but grasps at any straws of reassurance, so the European Jews willed not to believe the ever-mounting rumors and reports that the Germans meant simply to kill them all.

To believe that, after all, they had to believe that the legal government of Germany was systematically and officially perpetrating a homicidal fraud gigantic beyond imagining. They had to believe that the function of the state itself, created by human society for its self-protection, had mutated in an advanced Western nation to the function of secretly executing multitudes of men, women, and children who had done nothing wrong, with no warning, no accusation, and no trial. This happened to be the truth, but to the last most of the Jews who died could not grasp it. Nor can we, even in hindsight, altogether blame them, since we ourselves still find this one stark fact absolutely incomprehensible.

The Theresienstadt part of the hoax was complex, and in the tangle of its cross-purposes lay Natalie's chance of living.

The Paradise Ghetto was nothing but a transit camp, a way station to "the east." The Jews there called it a *"schleuse,"* a sluice or floodgate. But it was a transit camp with a difference. The privileged Jews on arrival were cordially received, served a meal, and encouraged to fill out forms detailing what sort of hotel accommodations or apartments they preferred; also what possessions, jewelry, and currency they had brought with them. Then they were robbed down to their bare skins, and their bodily orifices searched for valuables. The cordial prelude of course facilitated the plundering. Thereafter they were treated exactly like the ordinary Jews who overflowed the houses and streets of the ghetto.

When large transports of Jews arrived the welcoming farce was sometimes omitted. The newcomers were simply herded into a hall, robbed en masse of whatever they had brought, issued cast-off clothing, and marched out into the crowded, verminous, disease-ridden town, to find shelter in four-tier bunks, in drafty attics already swarming with sick starving people, or in a room for four now housing a writhing mass of forty, or in a hallway or on a staircase just as jammed with wretched living bodies. Still, the arrivals were not asphyxiated straight off. To that extent it was a Paradise Ghetto.

Things unplanned by the Germans added to the paradisal façade. At the outset, the well-organized Jews of Prague had persuaded the SS to let them set up a Jewish municipality in the fortress town, a government half-joke and half-real; a joke, because it simply had to do whatever the Germans ordered, including drawing up lists for shipment "to the east"; yet real, since the departments did manage health, labor, food distribution, housing, and culture. The Germans cared only about tight security, their own comfort and pleasure, the production quotas of the factories, and the delivery of live bodies to fill up the trains. In other matters the Jews could look after themselves.

There was even a bank that printed special decorative Theresienstadt currency, with an astonishing engraving on all the bills, made by some anonymous artist, of a suffering Moses holding the tablets. The money was a ghetto jest, of course. One could buy nothing with it. But the Germans required the bankers and the Jewish workers to keep elaborate records of salaries, savings accounts, and disbursements, which also looked good to the casual eye of a casual Red Cross observer. The German effort in Terezin was a total hoax first to last; it never extended to raising the food ration above the starvation level, or providing medicines, or keeping down the incoming torrents of Jews.

Terezin was a pretty town; not, like Auschwitz, an expanse of horse stalls in a sandy marsh. The stone houses and long nineteenth-century barracks set along rectilinear streets pleased the eye, if one did not look inside at the crowds of sick and hungry inhabitants driven out of sight whenever visitors came. Including the soldiers quartered in the barracks, Terezin in normal times could house four or five thousand people. The ghetto averaged fifty or sixty thousand souls. It was like a town on the edge of a flood or earthquake area, overrun with disaster survivors; except that the disaster kept mounting and the survivors piling in, their numbers relieved only by the enormous mortality rate and by the sluice gate "to the east."

The lectures, the concerts, the plays, the operas, did actually go on. The talented inmates were permitted by the Germans to forget the hunger, the sickness, the crowding, the fear, in these paradisal activities. The cafés and the nightclub existed. There was nothing to eat or drink, but musicians abounded, and the Jews could go through the ghostly motions of peacetime pleasure till their turn came to be shipped off. The library in which Aaron Jastrow worked was a fine one, for the books were all looted from the arriving Jews. There were even shop façades, with windows full of goods stolen from the half-dead throngs drifting by. Naturally, nothing was for sale.

For a while only German Red Cross commissioners were allowed into Theresienstadt. No great effort was needed by the SS to elicit favorable reports from them. However, the very success of the hoax put the Germans in an unanticipated fix. A very pressing demand developed for a visit to the Paradise Ghetto *by neutral Red Cross observers.* This led to the most bizarre episode in Theresienstadt's bizarre history, the *Verschönerungsaktion,* or Great Beautification. On this Natalie's fate turned.

70

NATALIE is unrecognizable at work because a handkerchief masks her face below the eyes. The mica dust drifts from trimming and grinding machines over rows of long tables where women sit all day splitting the laminated mineral into sheets. Natalie is one more bent back in this large shabby array. The work takes dexterity and it is very boring, but not hard.

What the Germans use the stuff for she is not sure. Something to do with electrical equipment. It is evidently a rare material, for scraps and table sweepings go to the grinder, and the powder is crated and shipped to Germany like the trimmed sheets. Her job is to take a block or "book" and split the laminations into thinner, more transparent sheets until the tool will not wedge off another layer; and in the process to avoid tearing a sheet and getting clubbed by the armbanded French-Jewish harridan who patrols her section. Simple enough.

In this long low crowded shed of rough wood she spends eleven hours a day. Dimly lit by low-wattage bulbs hanging on long black wires, unheated and almost as cold as the snowy outdoors, damper because of the muck underfoot and the breath of the close-packed women, stinking from one loathsomely overflowing latrine, which is cleaned out only once a week by the pitiful squad of yellow-starred college professors, writers, composers, and scientists whom the Germans delight to put at hauling ordure; malodorous too from the body smells of the crowded ragged unwashed females who can scarcely get water to drink, let alone to bathe in or to launder their clothes — to a visitor from the outside this shed would seem a very hell. Natalie is used to it.

Most of the women are of refined background like hers. They are Czech, Austrian, German, Dutch, Polish, French, Danish. Terezin is a true melting pot. Many were once wealthy, many are as highly educated as Natalie. The mica factory is for favored women in the ghetto. The grisly ill-defined menace of "transport to the east" hangs over Terezin, much as death haunts normal life. The transport toll is spasmodic, cutting deep wide sudden swaths like a plague; but mica workers and their families do not go. As yet, anyway, they have not.

Most of the women doing this easy handwork are elderly, and Natalie's assignment to the mica factory suggests some veiled *"protectsia."* So does

Aaron's library job. Their chute into Theresienstadt, though baffling and terrible, is not a random mischance. Something is behind it. They do not know what. Meantime, from day to day they endure.

The six o'clock bell.

The machines stop. The bent women get up, store their tools, and shuffle outside in a mob, clutching shawls, sweaters, rags around them. They move stiffly but fast, to get to the food queues while the slops are still warm. Outside, Natalie pulls the handkerchief off an almost unchanged face: sharper, paler, still beautiful, the mouth thinner, the jaw set harder. A brisk wind has swept from these straight snowy streets the prevailing Theresienstadt stench of clogged sewers, random excretions, rotting garbage, and sick filthy people; a slum smell with added gruesome whiffs of the dead from hand-pulled hearses that roll night and day, and of the crematorium beyond the wall that disposes of them; Jews dead of "natural" causes, not murder, at a mortality rate that extermination camps do not greatly surpass.

Between the straight lines of the barrack roofs, as she strikes out across the town to the toddlers' home, stars glitter overhead. A crescent moon hangs low over the fortress wall, beside a brilliant evening star. Rare clean sweet air rushes into her grateful lungs, and she thinks of Aaron's wry remark that morning, "Do you know, my dear, that today is Thanksgiving? Take it all in all, we have things to be thankful for."

She detours around the high wooden walls that shut Jews out of the main square, where she can hear the musicians playing at the SS café. At mealtime the streets are quiet and less crowded, though some of the feeble old people who poke in the rubbish heaps are still creeping around. The long food lines curl from some courtyards into the street. People stand scooping messes from tin dishes into their mouths, eyes popping with eagerness. It is one of the sadder sights of the ghetto, these cultured Europeans gulping slops like dogs.

A lean figure in a long ragged coat and cloth cap comes up beside her. "*Nu, wie gehts?*" ("So, how goes it?") says the man called Udam.

In Yiddish intonations no longer self-conscious she replies, "How should it go?"

She is beginning to talk the language as readily as her grandmother did. Now and then a Dutch or French inmate will even take her for a Polish Jewess. When she uses English she switches back easily to her old American tones, but they sound odd here. She and Aaron often fall into Yiddish, for he too uses it a lot in the library and in his Talmud course, though he lectures in German and French.

"Jesselson's string quartet is playing again tonight," Udam says. "They want us afterward. I have some new material."

"When can we rehearse?"

"Why not after we see the kids?"

"I teach an English class at seven."

"It's simple stuff. Won't take long."

"All right."

Louis is waiting in the doorway of his dormitory room. With a yell of joy, he leaps into her embrace. Feeling his sturdy body in her arms, Natalie forgets mica, boredom, misery, fear. His high spirits flood her and cheer her. Whatever hell winds blow, this is not a flame destined to be snuffed out.

Since his birth, Louis has been the light of her life, but never so much as here. Separated from her in the toddlers' home amid several hundred children, seeing her for only a few minutes most evenings, regimented by strange women in this damp dark old stone house, sleeping in a wooden box like a coffin, fed coarse scrappy food — though the children's rations are the best in the ghetto — Louis is thriving like a weed. Other little children pine, sicken, fall into listlessness and stupor, weaken in uncontrollable fits of crying, starve, die. The mortality in this home is terrible. But whether his travels — with the ever-changing water, air, food, bedding, and company — have hardened him, or whether, as she often thinks, the crossbreeding of the tough Jastrows and the tough Henrys has produced a Darwinian super-survivor, Louis is blazing with vitality. He leads in his classes. Finger painting, dancing, singing, are all one to him. He excels without seeming to try. He leads in mischief, too. The house women love him, but he is their despair. More and more he looks like Byron, with his mother's enormous eyes. His smile, at once enchanting and melancholy, is just his father's.

This is where she eats, since she takes turns on the night-duty staff. Udam eats here, too. He usually manages to fix things his way, and this is how he spends extra time with his three-year-old daughter. His wife is gone, transported. Tonight the soup is thick with potatoes, spoiled by frost and rotten-tasting, but substantial. As they eat he runs through his new dialogue, while his daughter plays with Louis. The portable puppet theatre is folded away in the basement playroom, and afterward the two children come down to watch them rehearse. Natalie's puppet show, a Punch and Judy which she got up to amuse the children, has become, with Udam's corrosive dialogue, a sub-rosa ghetto hit. It has given her more distinction than her American identity, which was briefly a wonder and soon taken for granted. Unlucky or stupid, here she is, and that is that to the ghetto people.

Natalie can become happily and totally absorbed in this revival of a teenage pastime neglected for years: making the dolls, dressing them, manipulating them, working up comic gestures to match Udam's words. Once she even put on a show in the SS café where he sings. She had to sit trembling through Udam's salacious German songs at which the boisterous

SS men roared, and some sentimental ballads like "Lili Marlene" that had them all misty-eyed; and then her hands shook so that she could scarcely work the puppets. Happily the show wasn't a success. Udam left out all his good material, and they weren't asked again. There are other, far more masterly puppet shows in the ghetto that the SS can commandeer. Natalie's little display is feeble without Udam's bite.

Udam is a Polish cantor's son, a cadaverous crane of a man with burning eyes and a red mop of curly hair. A composer and singer of racy, even obscene songs, he nevertheless conducted the Yom Kippur service in the synagogue. He came to Theresienstadt with the early shipments from Prague, in the Zionist crowd that organized and ran the shadowy Jewish municipality. Berlin and Vienna types are now edging them out, for the SS favors the German Jews. Udam works in the farcical Theresienstadt bank, though it is a fief of these latecoming Jews, who still cling to their sense of superiority and tend to exclude others. Udam knows more about ghetto politics and angles than Natalie can absorb. His name is Josef Smulovitz, but everyone calls him "Udam." She has even heard the SS address him so.

Tonight he is adding new jokes to their most popular sketch, *The King of Frost-Cuckoo Land.*

Natalie puts a crown on Punch, and a very long red nose edged with icicles, and that is the king. Frost-Cuckoo Land is losing a war. The king keeps blaming the reported disasters on the Eskimos in the country. "Kill the Eskimos! Kill them all," he rages and rages. The comedy lies in the rushing in and out of a minister puppet in a vague uniform, also with an icicle-draped red nose, alternately announcing shortages, rebellions, and defeats, which make the king weep and bellow, and reports of more Eskimos killed at which he jumps with glee. At the end the minister bounces in to declare that all Eskimos have at last been liquidated. The king starts to rejoice, then abruptly roars, "Wait, wait! Now who can I blame? How will I run my war? This is terrible! Rush a plane to Alaska for more Eskimos! Eskimos! I need lots and lots of Eskimos!" Curtain.

Strange to say, the Jews find this crude macabre parallel extremely funny. The disasters resemble the latest news about Germany. The minister reports them in the orotund double-talk of Nazi propaganda. This sort of risky underground humor is a great relief to ghetto life; there is a lot of it, and nobody seems to inform, because it goes on and on.

Natalie works the puppets with bitter zest. She is no more an American Jewess terrified of falling into German talons, and hugging the talisman of her passport for safety. The talisman has failed. The worst has happened. In a strange way she feels freer at heart, and clearer in her mind. Her whole being has a single focus now: to make it through with Louis, and live.

Udam's new dialogue refers to recent ghetto rumors: Hitler has cancer, the Germans are running out of oil to fight the war, the Americans will make a surprise landing in France on Christmas Day; the sort of wishful thinking that abounds in Theresienstadt. Natalie works up puppet business to match Udam's jokes, while his daughter and Louis, to whom the words mean nothing, chortle at the red-nosed dolls. Rehearsal done, she hugs Louis, feeling an invigorating electricity in the embrace, and goes on to her English class.

At the teenage boys' house lessons proceed day and night. Education of Jewish children is officially forbidden, but there is nothing else for them to do. The Germans do not really check, knowing what the ultimate destiny of the children is, and not caring what noises they make in the slaughter pen. These big-eyed scrawny boys put out a small newspaper, learn languages and instruments, work up theatricals, debate Zionism, sing Hebrew songs. On the other hand, they are for the most part cynical, accomplished scroungers and liars, believe in nothing, know their way around the ghetto like rats, and are sexually very precocious. Their greeting glances sometimes make Natalie uneasy, though in her baggy brown yellow-starred wool suit she considers herself a sexless, not to say a revolting, female object.

But once the boys get down to the lesson they are all sharp attention. They are bright volunteers, beginners, a mere nine of them, who want to know English "to go to America after the war." Two are missing tonight, off at a rehearsal of *Abduction from the Seraglio*. This ambitious Mozart opera is being undertaken to follow up on the big hit of the ghetto, *The Bartered Bride*, which even the SS enjoyed. Natalie saw a weak performance of this favorite because the cast had just been decimated by a transport. She has even heard that Verdi's *Requiem* is being rehearsed somewhere in a barracks cellar, though that seems fantastic. The class over, she hurries through the windy starry night to the loft where she will perform.

The quartet is already playing at the far end of the long low slope-roofed room, which was once usable for big gatherings, but is now filling up with bunks as more and more Jews sluice into the ghetto; far faster, as yet, than they are sluicing out "to the east." The whole hope of the ghetto Jews is that the Americans and the Russians will smash Frost-Cuckoo Land in time to save those piling up in the Theresienstadt floodgate. The object of life meantime is to avoid being transported, and to make the days and nights bearable with culture.

Jesselson's quartet makes excellent music: three gray-headed men and a very ugly middle-aged woman, playing on instruments smuggled into the ghetto, their shabbily dressed bodies swaying to the brilliant Haydn melodies, their faces intent and bright with inner light. The loft is packed. People hunch or lie on the bunks, squat on the floor, line the walls on their feet, beside the hundreds sitting jammed together on long wooden benches. Natalie waits for the piece to end, so as not to cause a commotion, then pushes through the crush. People recognize her and make way.

The puppet stage stands ready behind the musicians' chairs. She sits by Udam on the floor in front, and lets the balm of the music — Dvorak now — flow over her soul: the sweet violins and viola, the sobbing and thundering cello, weaving a pretty arabesque of folksong. After that the musicians play a late Beethoven quartet. The Theresienstadt programs are long, the audiences rapt and grateful, though here and there the sick or the elderly nod off.

Before the puppet show begins Udam sings a new Yiddish composition, *Mi Kumt* ("They're Coming"). This is another of his ingenious double-meaning political numbers. A lonely old man is singing on his birthday that everybody has forgotten him, and he is sitting sadly alone in his room in Prague. Suddenly his relatives begin to arrive. He turns joyful in the refrain, capering about the stage and snapping his fingers:

> *Oy they're coming, they're coming after all!*
> *Coming from the east, coming from the west,*
> *English cousins, Russian cousins,*
> *American cousins,*
> *All kinds of cousins!*
> *Coming in planes, coming in ships —*
> *Oy what joy, oy what a day,*
> *Oy thank God, from the east, from the west,*
> *Oy thank God, they're coming!*

Instant hit! In the encore, the audience takes up the refrain, clapping in rhythm: *Coming from the east, coming from the west!* On this high note the puppet show commences.

Before *The King of Frost-Cuckoo Land,* they do another favorite sketch. Punch is a ghetto official, in the mood to have sex with his wife. Judy puts him off. There is no privacy, she's hungry, he hasn't bathed, the bunk is too narrow, and so forth, familiar ghetto excuses which bring roars of laughter. He takes her to his office. Here they are alone; she coyly submits, but as their lovemaking commences, his underlings keep interrupting with ghetto problems. Udam's amorous coos and grunts of man and wife, alternated with Punch's irascible official tones and Judy's frustrated squawking, with some ribald lines and action, add up to a very funny business. Even Natalie, crouched beside Udam manipulating the dolls, keeps bursting into giggles.

The revised *Frost-Cuckoo Land* draws great laughter, too; and Udam and Natalie emerge flushed from behind the curtains to take bow after bow.

Calls arise here and there in the loft: "Udam!"

He shakes his head and waves protesting hands.

More calls: "Udam, Udam, Udam!"

Gesturing for quiet, he asks to be excused, he is tired, he is not in the mood, he has a cold; another time.

"No, no. Now! *Udam! Udam!*"

This happens at every puppet performance. Sometimes the audience prevails, sometimes Udam does beg off. Natalie sits. He strikes a somber singer's attitude, hands clasped before him, and in a deep cantorial baritone begins a mournful chant.

Udam . . . udam . . . udam . . .

Chills creep along Natalie's spine each time he starts it. This is a passage of the Yom Kippur liturgy. *"Udam yesoidoi may-ufar vay soifoi lay-ufar . . ."*

> *Man is created of the dust, and his end is in the dust. He is like a broken potsherd, a fading flower, like a floating mote, a passing shadow, and like a dream that flies away.*

After every pair of images comes the refrain of the opening melody, which the audience softly chants:

Udam . . . udam . . . udam.

It means

Man . . . man . . . man. The word in Hebrew for *man* is *adam*. *Udam* is a Polish-Yiddish variant of *adam*.

This brokenhearted low chant from the throats of the Theresienstadt Jews — *Adam, adam, adam* — all in the shadow of death, all recently howling with mirth, now murmuring what may be their own dirge, stirs deeps in Natalie Henry that she never knew were there before her imprisonment. As he works into the florid cantorial passage, Udam's voice sobs and swells like a cello. His eyes close. His body weaves before the little puppet stage. His hands stretch out and up. The agony, the reverence, the love of God and of humanity in his voice, are beyond belief in this man, who minutes before was performing the rawest ribaldry.

"Like a floating mote, a passing shadow . . ."

Udam . . . udam . . . udam . . .

He rises on tiptoe, his arms stiffen straight upward, his eyes open and glare at the audience like open furnace doors:

"And like a DREAM . . ."

The fiery eyes close. The hands fall, the body droops and all but crumples. The last words die to a crushed whisper

". . . that flies away."

He never does an encore. He acknowledges the applause with stiff bows and a strained white face.

This wrenching liturgical aria, words and melody alike, once seemed to Natalie a strange, almost gruesome way to close an evening of entertainment. Now she understands. It is pure Theresienstadt. She herself feels the catharsis she sees on the faces around her. The audience is spent, satisfied, ready to sleep, ready to face another day in the valley of the shadow. So is she.

"What the devil is *that?*"

A gray yellow-starred woolen suit lies across her cot. Beside it are lisle stockings and new shoes. A man's suit and shoes are on Aaron's cot opposite. He sits at the little table between the cots, poring over a large brown Talmud volume. He holds up a hand. "Just let me finish this."

The *protectsia* hovering over them is most apparent here; a separate room for the two of them, though it is only a tiny space with one window, partitioned off with wallboard from a larger chamber, formerly the dining room of a prosperous Czech family's private house. Beyond the partition hundreds of Jews are crowded in four-tier bunks. Here are two cots, a dim little lamp, a table, and a cardboard wardrobe like a telephone booth, the acme of ghetto luxury. Council officials do not live better. There has never been an explanation for this kind treatment, other than that they are *Prominente*. Aaron gets his food here, but not by standing in line. The house elder has assigned a girl to bring it to him. However, he scarcely eats. He seems to be living on air. Usually when Natalie returns there are scraps and slops left, if she cares to choke them down. Otherwise the people beyond the partition will devour the stuff.

Now what is this gray suit? She holds it up against her; excellent material, well cut; a fair fit, a bit loose. The suit exudes a faint charming rose scent. A woman of quality owned this garment. Alive? Dead? Transported?

Closing the volume with a sigh, Aaron Jastrow turns to her. His hair and beard are white. His skin is like soft mica; bones and veins show through. Ever since his recovery he has been placidly frail, yet capable of surprising endurance. From day to day he teaches, lectures, attends concerts and plays, and puts in a full day's work on the Hebrew cataloguing.

He says, "Those things arrived at dinnertime. Quite a surprise. Eppstein came by later to explain."

Eppstein is Theresienstadt's present head of the municipality, a mayor of sorts with the title of *Ältester*. Formerly a lecturer in sociology, and the head of the "Association of Jews in Germany," he is a meek, beaten-down man, a survivor of Gestapo imprisonment. Trapped in subservience to the SS, he tries in his unnerved way to do some good, but the other Jews see him as hardly more than a puppet of the Germans. He has little choice, and little strength left to exercise what choice he has.

"What did Eppstein say?"

"We're to go to SS Headquarters tomorrow. But we're *not* in danger. It will be pleasant. We're due for more special privileges. So he swears, Natalie."

Feeling cold in her stomach, in her very bones, she asks, "Why are we going?"

"For an audience with Lieutenant Colonel Eichmann."

"*Eichmann!*"

The familiar SS names around Theresienstadt are those of the local officers: Roehn, Haindl, Moese, and so forth. Lieutenant Colonel Eichmann is a remote evil name only whispered; despite the modest rank, a figure standing not far below Himmler and Hitler in the ghetto mind.

Aaron's expression is kindly and sympathetic. He shows little fear. "Yes. Quite an honor," he says with calm irony. "But these clothes do bode well, don't they? Somebody at least wants us to look good. So let's do that, my dear."

71

"Mark! Haleakala, zero eight seven. Mark! Mauna Loa, one three two." Crouched at the alidade, Byron was calling out bearings to a quartermaster writing by a red flashlight, as the *Moray* scored a phosphorescent wake on the calm sea. The warm offshore breeze smelled to Byron — a pleasant hallucination, no doubt — like the light perfume Janice often wore. The quartermaster went below to plot the bearings, and called up the position through the voice tube. Byron telephoned Aster's cabin.

"Captain, the moon's bright enough so I got a fix of sorts. We're well inside the submarine restricted area."

"Well, good. Maybe the airedales won't bomb us at dawn. Set course and speed to enter the channel at 0700."

"Aye aye, sir."

"Say, Mister Executive Officer, I've just been going over your patrol report. It's outstanding."

"Well, I tried."

"You're no dud at paperwork, Briny. Not anymore. Unfortunately, the clearer you put the story the lousier it comes out."

"Captain, there'll be other patrols." Aster's irritable depression had been troubling Byron all during the return voyage. The captain had holed up in his cabin, smoking cheap cigars by the boxful, reading tattered mysteries from the ship's library, leaving the running of the sub to the exec.

"Zero is zero, Byron."

"They can't fault you for aggressiveness. You volunteered for the Sea of Japan."

"I did, and I'm going back there, but next time with electric torpedoes. Otherwise the admiral can beach me. I'm all through with the Mark Fourteen." Byron could hear the slam of the telephone into the bracket.

Driving in a pool jeep to Janice's cottage next day, Byron was afire to crush his sister-in-law in his arms and forget the patrol. Loneliness, the passage of time, the disappearance of Natalie, the warmth of Janice's home, the quiet shows of affection by his brother's pretty widow — all these elements were fusing into something like an undeclared romance, mounting in sweetness each time he came back from the sea. The flame was feeding on an explosive mixture of intimacy and unfulfillment. Guilt tormented Byron over his flashes of thought about a life with Janice and Victor, if it should happen that Natalie never came back. He suspected Janice of harboring similar notions. Normal relationships can be wrenched out of shape or destroyed by the tensions and separations of war, and what Byron was experiencing was very commonplace just now, all over the world. Only his conscience pangs were slightly unusual.

Something was wrong this time. He knew when she opened the door and he saw her serious unpainted face. She was expecting him, for he had telephoned, but she had not changed out of a drab blue housedress, nor in any way smartened herself up; nor did she hand him the usual planter's punch in welcome. He might have interrupted her at her cooking or cleaning. She said straight off, "There's a letter from Natalie, forwarded by the Red Cross."

"What! My God, finally?" Through the International Red Cross he had written several letters to Baden-Baden, with this return address. Everything about the envelope she handed him was disturbing: the flimsy gray paper; the purple block lettering of the address and of "N. HENRY" in a corner; the overlapping rubber stamps in different colors and languages, almost obliterating the Red Cross symbol; above all, the postmark. "Terezin? Where's that?"

"Czechoslovakia, near Prague. I've telephoned my father about this, Byron. He's talked to the State Department. Read your letter first."

He sank on a chair and slit the envelope with a penknife. The single gray sheet was block-lettered in purple.

> KURZESTRASSE, P–I
> THERESIENSTADT
> SEPT. 7, 1943

DEAREST BYRON SPECIAL PRIVILEGE FOR "PROMINENTS" MONTHLY HUNDRED-WORD LETTER. LOUIS WONDERFUL. AARON ALL RIGHT. MY SPIRITS GOOD. YOUR LETTERS DELAYED BUT LOVELY TO HAVE. WRITE HERE. RED CROSS FOOD PACKAGES EXTREMELY DESIRABLE. DON'T WORRY. THERESIENSTADT SPECIAL HAVEN FOR PRIVILEGED WAR HEROES ARTISTS SCHOLARS ETC. WE HAVE GROUND-FLOOR SUNNY APARTMENT BEST HERE. AARON LIBRARIAN HEBRAIC COLLECTION. LOUIS KINDERGARTEN STAR ALSO CHIEF TROUBLEMAKER. MY WAR FACTORY WORK TAKES SKILL NOT BRAWN. LOVE YOU HEART SOUL. LIVE FOR DAY HOLD YOU IN ARMS. TELEPHONE MY MOTHER. LOVE LOVE NATALIE.

Byron glanced at his watch. "Would your father still be at the War Department?"

"He gave me a message for you. You're to call a Mr. Sylvester Aherne at the State Department. The number's by the telephone."

Byron rang the operator and put in the call. Lunch on his return from a patrol had developed into a merry ritual: strong rum concoctions, a Chinese meal, a bowl of scarlet hibiscus on the table, a laughing exchange of anecdotes. But this time neither the drinks nor Janice's tasty egg foo yong and pepper steak could lift the pall of the letter. Nor could Byron talk about the failed patrol. They ate glumly, and he leaped at the telephone when it rang.

Sylvester Aherne's way of talking made Byron picture a little man in a pince-nez, pursing his mouth and dancing his fingers together. As Byron read the letter to him, Aherne said, "Hm! . . . Hmmmm! Hmm! . . . *Hmmm!* Well! Quite a ray of light, that — isn't it? Reassuring, all in all. Very reassuring. Gives us something solid to work on. You must airmail a copy to us at once."

"What do you know about my family, Mr. Aherne, and about Theresienstadt?"

Speaking with slow prim care, Aherne disclosed that some months ago Natalie and Jastrow had failed to check in with the Swiss in Paris, simply dropped from sight. Insistent inquiries by the Swiss, and by the American chargé in Baden-Baden, had brought no response as yet from the Germans. Now that State knew where they actually were, efforts on their behalf could be redoubled. Since hearing from Senator Lacouture, Aherne had been looking into the Theresienstadt situation. The Red Cross had no record of any releases from the model ghetto; but the Jastrow case was unique, he said, and — so he concluded with a high little giggle — he always preferred to be an optimist.

"Mr. Aherne, are my wife and baby safe in that place?"

"Considering that your wife is Jewish, Lieutenant, and that she was caught travelling illegally in German-occupied territory — for as you know, her journalist credentials were trumped up in Marseilles — she's lucky to have landed there. And as she herself writes, at the moment all is well."

"Can you switch me to another officer in your division, Mr. Leslie Slote?"

"Ah — Leslie Slote? Leslie resigned from the State Department, quite awhile ago."

"Where can I reach him?"

"Sorry, I can't say."

Byron asked Janice to try to call his mother, who might know where Slote was; and he went back to the *Moray* in as low a frame of mind as he had ever been.

As soon as he left Janice began the beautifying routine that she had skipped for Byron's visit. Whether the feeling between them would ever warm up again she could not tell, but she knew that right now she had to keep her distance. Janice was very sorry for Natalie. She had never intended to steal Byron from her. But what indeed if she did not come back? The

Theresienstadt letter struck Janice as ominous. She honestly wished Natalie would extricate herself and come home safely with the baby, but the chances seemed to be fading. Meantime, she enjoyed the cornucopia sense of pouring herself out to two men, each time the *Moray* made port. She preferred Byron on the whole; but Aster had his points, and he certainly deserved a good time when he returned from combat. Janice was, in fact, doing a very fair job of eating her cake and having it. She had given Byron his ritual lunch, and the next thing was the ritual rendezvous with Aster.

Byron found Aster waiting in the *Moray's* wardroom, dressed for the beach and hollowly cheerful. "Well, Briny, the admiral was okay. All is forgiven. We get our Mark Eighteens, and a target ship for training runs. Two weeks for turnaround, and back to the Sea of Japan." He made a bravura flourish with his cigar. "Tomorrow, captain's inspection. Friday Admiral Nimitz comes aboard to give us a unit citation for the first patrol. Saturday, under way at 0600 for electric torpedo exercises. Questions?"

"Hell, yes, what about rest and recreation for the crew?"

"Coming to that. One week in drydock for the new sonar head, and repairs to the stern outer doors. Liberty for all hands. Three more days of training, and we're off to Midway and La Pérouse Strait."

"One week for the men isn't enough."

"Yes, it is," Aster snapped. "This crew has been hurt in its pride. It needs victories a lot more than R and R. Why are you so down in the mouth, anyway? How's Janice?"

"She's all right. Look, Captain, I thought we'd be getting a telephone line over from the dock today, but Hansen just told me no soap. Would you give her a ring while you're ashore? Tell her to call me at the officers' club about ten o'clock."

"Will do," Aster said with a strange grimace, and he left.

Byron assumed that Aster had a woman in Honolulu, but it had never once crossed his mind that the woman might be Janice. So far Aster had been playing along with Janice's pretense, but not liking it much. He thought she was making a fool of her brother-in-law. Byron's naïve obtuseness troubled him; couldn't he sense what was going on? Aster saw nothing wrong in what he and Janice were doing. They were both free, and neither wanted marriage. He didn't think that Byron would mind, but Janice claimed that he would be shocked and alienated, and she insisted on discretion. That was that. It was a subject they no longer talked about.

But he was in an evil mood and a lot of drinking did little to improve it. It grated on him when she telephoned the officers' club at ten o'clock, sitting up on the bed naked, her skin still glistening with amorous perspiration.

"Hi, Briny. Leslie Slote will be waiting for your call in his office tomorrow afternoon at one," she said with sweet calm, as though she sat at home with knitting in her lap. "That's seven in the morning our time, you know. Here's the number." She read it off a slip of paper.

"Did you talk to Slote?"

"No. Actually it was a Lieutenant Commander Anderson who tracked him down, and called me back. Do you know him? Simon Anderson. He seems to be living temporarily at your mother's place. Something about a fire in his apartment house, and she's putting him up for a couple of weeks."

"Simon Anderson's an old beau of Madeline's."

"Oh, well, maybe that explains it. Your mother wasn't there. Madeline came on the line first, sounding all bubbly. She was about to go out for a job interview, so she put Anderson on."

"Madeline's back in Washington to stay, then?"

"She seems to be."

"Why, that's marvelous."

"Will you come to lunch tomorrow, Briny?"

"No can do. Captain's inspection."

"Call me and tell me what Slote says."

"I will."

Aster had been around women; he had been in such a situation with the sweethearts of other men, and with a wife, too. He usually felt sympathy, tinged with contempt, for the poor fish on the other end of the line; but this was Byron Henry being taken in by Janice's coy charade.

"Jesus Christ, Janice," Aster said when she hung up, "are you still playing games with Byron, when Natalie's in a goddamn concentration camp?"

"Oh, just shut up!" Aster had been peevish and difficult all evening. He had said nothing whatever about the patrol, and he had gotten quite drunk; the sex in consequence had been a sputtering business, and Janice was feeling testy herself. "I didn't say she was in a concentration camp."

"Sure you did. In Czechoslovakia, you said."

"Look, you're too smashed to know what I said. I'm sorry you had a disappointing patrol. The next one will be better. Suppose I just go home now?"

"Do as you please, baby." Aster rolled on his side and went to sleep. After thinking it over, Janice did the same.

By the next morning a telephone had been rigged aboard the *Moray*. Byron got his call through to Leslie Slote, though it took several hours. The connection was a scratchy one, and when he finished reading Natalie's letter there was such a long noisy pause that he asked, "Leslie, are you still there?"

"I'm here." Slote uttered a sigh close to a groan. "What can I do for you, Byron? Or for her? What can anybody do? If you want my advice, just put all this from your mind."

"How can I?"

"That's up to you. Nobody knows much about that model ghetto. It does exist, and it may in fact prove a haven for her. I just can't tell you. Send her the letters and Red Cross packages, and keep sinking Japs, that's all. It doesn't help to go out of your head."

"I'm not going out of my head."

"Good. Neither am I. I'm a new man. I've made five training parachute jumps. Five! Remember the incident on the Praha road?"

"What incident?" Byron asked, though he never talked to Slote without thinking of his cowardly collapse under fire outside Warsaw.

"You don't recall? I'll bet you do. Anyway, do you see me making parachute jumps?"

"I'm in submarines, Leslie, and I always hated the Navy."

"Bah, you're from a warrior family. I'm a diplomat, a linguist, altogether a bespectacled cream puff. I die forty deaths in every jump. Yet I enjoy myself in an eerie fashion."

"Parachute jumps for what?"

"OSS. Intelligence. Fighting a war is the best way to forget what it's all about, Byron. That's a novel perception for me, and enormously illuminating."

"Leslie, what are Natalie's chances?"

Another very long scratchy pause.

"Leslie?"

"Byron, she's in a damnable situation. She has been, ever since Aaron wouldn't leave Italy in 1939. As you recall, I begged him to. You were sitting right there. They've done stupid and rash things, and now the fat's in the fire. But she's tough and strong and clever. Fight the war, Byron. Fight the war, and put your wife from your mind. Her, and all the other Jews. That's what I've done. Fight the war, and forget what you can't help. If you're a praying man, pray. I wouldn't talk like this if I were still employed at State, naturally. Good-bye."

When the *Moray* sailed, there were more defections from the crew than there had been in all previous patrols put together: requests for transfers, sudden illnesses, even some AWOLs.

The sky over Midway was low and gray, the wind dankly cold. Fueling was almost complete. Hands jammed in his windbreaker pockets, Byron paced the deck in a strong stench of diesel oil, making a last topside inspection before the long pull to Japan. Each departure from Midway made him think long dark thoughts. Somewhere around here, on the ocean floor in a shattered airplane, his brother's bones lay. Leaving Midway meant sallying forth from the last outpost, on the long lonely hunt. It meant calculation of distances, chances, fuel capacity, food stores; also of the state of nerves of the captain and the crew. Aster emerged on the bridge in fresh khakis and overseas cap, with eyes cleared and color restored by a few sober days under way; very much the killer-captain, Byron thought, even laying it on a bit to cheer up his depressed and edgy sailors.

"Say, Briny, Mullen's going with us, after all," he called down to the forecastle.

"He is? What changed his mind?"

"I talked to him."

Mullen was the *Moray*'s first-class yeoman. His orders to chiefs' school had arrived, and he was due to fly back to the States from Midway. But like all submarine sailors, the *Moray* crew were a superstitious lot, and many of them believed that this yeoman was the ship's good-luck charm, simply because his nickname was Horseshoes. The name had nothing to do with his luck; Mullen tended to lose at cards and dice, also to fall off ladders, get himself arrested by the shore patrol, and so on. Nevertheless, Horseshoes he was, so dubbed at boot camp years ago because he had won a horseshoe-pitching contest. Byron had overheard many foreboding comments by crewmen on the transfer of Mullen, but it jarred him that Aster had gone and worked the man over. He found Mullen thumping a typewriter in the tiny ship's office, a cigar thrust in his round red face; if Byron was not mistaken, one of the captain's Havanas. The tubby little sailor had been dressed in whites to go ashore, but he was wearing his washed-out dungarees again.

"What's all this, Mullen?"

"Just thought I'd grab one more patrol on this hell ship, sir. The food is so lousy I'll lose weight. The Stateside gals will like that."

"If you want to get off, say so, and you'll go."

The yeoman took a long puff at the expensive cigar, and his genial face toughened. "Mr. Henry, I'd follow Captain Aster to hell. He's the greatest skipper in SubPac, and now that we've got those Mark Eighteens, this is going to be the *Moray Maru*'s greatest patrol. I'm not about to miss it. Sir, where is Tarawa?"

"Tarawa? Down in the Gilberts. Why?"

"Marines are catching hell there. Look at this." He was making carbon copies of the latest news broadcast from Pearl Harbor. The tone of the bulletin was grave: *fierce opposition . . . very heavy casualties . . . outcome in doubt. . . .*

"Well, the first day of a landing is the worst."

"People think we've got rough duty." Horseshoes shook his head. "Those Marines sure bought the shit end of this war."

The *Moray* left Midway in a melancholy drizzle. For days the weather kept worsening. The submarine never rode well on the surface, and in these frigid stormy latitudes, shipboard life was a bruising routine of treacherous footing, seasickness, cold meals half-spilled, and chancy sleep through interminable dull days and nights. In the northwest Pacific, an inactive waste of tempestuous black water, the Japanese were unlikely to be doing much patrolling, and visibility was poor. Still, Aster maintained a combat alert all day. Frostbitten lookouts and OODs were coming off watch cracking ice from their clothes.

Making a transit of the rocky Kuriles within air range of Japan, Aster sailed on at fifteen knots, merely doubling the lookouts. The *Moray* was not a submarine, but a "submersible," he liked to say — that is, a surface ship that could dive — and skulking under the sea was no way to get places. Byron agreed, but he thought Aster sometimes crowded the line between courage and rashness. By now several submarines had patrolled the Sea of Japan; the *Wahoo* had disappeared there; the enemy might well have an air patrol out. Fortunately the *Moray* was travelling most of the time in fog and sleet. Byron's dead reckoning was getting a hard workout.

Seven days out of Midway, a shift in the wind thinned the fog, and the hills of Hokkaido ridged the gray horizon ahead. To starboard a higher black lump showed: the headlands of Sakhalin.

"*Soya Kaikyo!*" Aster jocularly hailed La Pérouse Strait by the Japanese name, and clapped Byron's shoulder. "Well done, Mister Navigator." The *Moray* was wallowing on heavy quartering swells, and a bitter stern wind whipped the captain's thick blond hair as he squinted landward. "Now then, how close do we go before we pull the plug? Do the Japs have radar yet on those hills, or not?"

"Let's not find out," said Byron. "Not now."

With a slow reluctant nod, Aster said, "Concur. Clear the bridge."

Riding at periscope depth was a restful change after a week of plunging and rolling. Seasick sailors climbed out of their bunks and ate sandwiches and hot soup at level tables. At the periscope, Byron was struck by the romance of the view in the glass. As the *Moray* neared the eastern entrance, the setting sun shot red rays under the low clouds, haloing in rosy mist the Hokkaido hill called Maru Yama. Across Byron's mind there flashed an old lovely vision. Japanese art had charmed him in his undergraduate days; the paintings, novels, and poetry had conjured up fairyland landscapes, delicately exotic architecture, and quaintly costumed little people with perfect manners and subtle esthetic tastes. This picture did not mesh at all with "the Japs," the barbarians who had smashed Pearl Harbor, raped Nanking, taken the Philippines and Singapore, killed his brother, and stolen an empire. He took grim pleasure in torpedoing "Japs." But this glimpse of misty Maru Yama in the sunset brought back that early vision. Did "the Japs" — it occurred to him to wonder — consider Americans barbarians? He did not feel like a barbarian, nor did the dungareed sailors on watch look barbarous. Yet the *Moray* was approaching the quaint fairyland to murder by stealth as many "Japs" as it could.

In short, war.

Byron summoned the captain to show him through the scope two vessels steaming eastward with running lights on: sparks of red, green, and white vivid in the twilight.

"Russkis, no doubt," said Aster. "Are they in the designated Russian route?"

"Dead on," said Byron.

"Good. That's where the mines aren't."

Last time, Aster had commented wryly on this freak aspect of the war: Soviet ships plying the Lend-Lease run through Jap waters with impunity, though Germany's defeat was bound to drag down Japan. Now, peering through the periscope, he remarked in businesslike tones, "Say, why don't we go through showing lights? If the Nips have installed radar up here, that's better deception than running darkened."

"Suppose we're challenged?"

"Then we're stupid Russians who didn't get the word."

"I'm for it, Captain."

In full view of the Japanese coast, about an hour after dark, the dripping *Moray* turned on its lights. For Byron, standing on the bridge in the strong freezing wind, it was the strangest moment of the war. He had never yet sailed on an illuminated submarine. The white masthead lights fore and aft dazzled like suns; the red and green glows seemed to shoot out to port and starboard half a mile. The ship was so visibly, so horribly a *submarine!* But only from the bridge; surely nothing could be seen from the Japanese headland ten miles away but the lights, if that much.

The lights were seen. As the *Moray* plunged along through the coal-dark strait, a signal searchlight on Hokkaido blinked. Aster and Byron were flailing their arms and stamping on the bridge. The signaller blinked again. And yet again. "No spikka da Joponese," said Aster.

The signalling ceased. The *Moray* bore on into the Sea of Japan, doused its lights before dawn, and submerged.

Toward noon as they were crawling southward they spotted a small freighter, perhaps eight hundred tons. Aster and Byron debated whether to shoot. It was worth torpedoing, but the attack might trigger SOS signals and a full air-and-sea submarine search in the Sea of Japan. If the Japs were not alerted now, the pickings further south tomorrow would be easier and fatter. Aster was calculating on three days of depredations, and one day to escape. "The Mark Eighteen can use a firing test," he said at last, lighting up a Havana. "Let's have an approach course, Mister Navigator. We'll shoot one fish." He returned a frigid defiant grin to Byron's quizzical look. "The Mark Eighteen leaves no wake. If it misses, our Nip friend up there will know from nothing, right? If it hits, he may get too busy to send messages."

Aster ran off the attack in a curt businesslike way, and Byron was heartened by the crew's spirited responses. The electric torpedo was longer-legged than the Mark Fourteen, but slower. Byron was not used to the additional lag before impact; watching in the glass, he was about to report a miss, when a column of smoke and white water burst over the freighter; and a second or so later a destructive rumble sounded through the *Moray*'s hull. He had never seen a vessel go down so fast. Less than five minutes after the hit, while he was still taking periscope photographs, it sank out of sight in a cloud of smoke, flame, and steam.

Aster seized the loudspeaker microphone. "Now hear this. Scratch one Jap freighter. And score one victory for the Mark Eighteen electric torpedo, the first of many for the *Moray Maru!*"

The yells sent prickling thrills through Byron. It had been a long time since he had heard this triumphant male baying, the war cry of a submarine.

That night Aster ran south to get athwart the ship lane to Korea, where the targets had been so numerous and the results so dismal on the last patrol. Toward dawn the OOD reported running lights ahead; so as yet, despite the attack on the freighter, there was no submarine alert in the Sea of Japan. Aster ordered a dive. In the periscope, brightening day showed what he called a mouth-watering sight, ships moving peaceably and unescorted wherever the glass turned. Byron found himself with a problem in relative movement worthy of an Annapolis navigation course: how to attack one target after another, with maximum scoring and minimum warning to the victims.

From the captain downward the *Moray* came alive. The killing machine was back in swing. Aster chose first to attack a large tanker; he bore in to nine hundred yards, fired a single torpedo, and struck. Leaving the cripple ablaze, settling, and pouring volcanic black smoke from the flammable cargo, he swung around in a long approach to what looked like a big troop carrier, by far the fattest target in sight. Maneuvering to close this prize took hours. Aster paced the conning tower, went below to his cabin, came up and paced again, gobbled a large steak from the galley at the chart desk, and ripped the pages of a girlie magazine with his impatient flipping. In attack position at last, with Byron at the periscope, he fired a spread of three torpedoes as soon as he could, at extreme range. After a prolonged wait Byron cried, "*Hit!* By God, he's *disappeared!*" When the obscuring curtain of smoke and spray cleared, the vessel was still there, sharply down by the bow and listing, clearly a dead loss. Aster's announcement brought more lusty cheers.

He had selected this target with a view to two others, a pair of large freighters steaming on the same course not far off. These vessels now turned away from the stricken troopship and put on speed.

"I can't catch them submerged. We'll pursue on the surface after nightfall," Aster said. "They're running back east for home and air cover. Things will be tougher tomorrow. *However*" — he slapped Byron on the back — "not a bad day's haul!"

This buoyant spirit was everywhere in the submarine: in the conning tower, the control room, the wardroom, even down in the engine rooms, when Byron laid below for a routine check. The perspiring half-naked grease-streaked sailors greeted him with the happy grins of football players after a big win. While he was below the submarine surfaced, and the diesels churned into deafening action. He hurried topside. On the bridge, in a parka and mittens, Carter Aster was eating a thick sandwich. The night was starry, with one dim red streak of sunset, and dead ahead on the horizon were the two tiny black blobs of the freighters.

"We'll nail both those monkeys at dawn," said the captain. "How are we on fuel?"

"Fifty-five thousand gallons."

"Not bad. This roast beef is great. Get Haynes to make you a sandwich."

"I think I'll grab some sleep."

"Staying in character, eh?"

Aster had not laughed much in recent weeks, nor poked fun at Byron. Actually, Byron had been getting by on very little rest, but the sleepyhead joke was permanent, and he was glad that Aster was in a joshing mood again.

"Well, Lady, it's a stern chase. Not much doing till about 0300." Looking up at the sky, Byron leaned on the bulwark. He felt relaxed and in no hurry to go below. "Nice night."

"Beautiful. One more day's hunting like today, Briny, and they can rotate me to the States any time."

"Feeling better, eh?"

"Christ, yes. How about you?"

"Well, on a day like today, I'm just fine. Otherwise, not so hot."

Long silence, except for the splash of the sea and the sighing of the wind.

"Natalie's on your mind."

"Oh, she always is. And the kid. And for that matter, Janice."

"Janice?" Aster hesitated, then asked, "Why Janice?"

They could barely see each other's faces in the starlight. The OOD stood close by, his binoculars trained on the horizon.

Byron's reply was scarcely audible. "I've treated her abominably."

Aster called down for another sandwich and coffee, then said, "In what way, for Pete's sake? I think you've been a downright Sir Galahad around Janice." Byron did not answer. "Well, you don't have to talk about it."

But in the release of long tension, Byron did want to talk about it, though the words came hard. "We're in love, Lady. Haven't you seen that? It's all my doing, and it's a stupid dream. That letter from Natalie woke me up. I've got to cut it off, and it'll be rotten for both of us. I don't know what the hell's possessed me, all these months."

"Look, Byron, you're lonesome," Aster commented after a pause, in a low gentle tone not like him. "She's a beautiful woman, and you're quite a guy. You've been sleeping under the same roof, for crying out loud! You ask me, you rate a Bronze Star for staying faithful to Natalie."

Byron gave his captain a light punch on the shoulder. "Well, that's how you'd figure it, Lady. Superlative fitness report. But from my viewpoint, she's fallen for me because I've encouraged her. I've been damned obvious about that. Yet while Natalie's alive, it's hopeless, isn't it? And do I want Natalie dead? I've been a shit."

"Jesus Christ and General Jackson," exclaimed Aster, "that tears it. Briny, in some ways I admire you, but on the whole you're to be pitied. You live off on some other planet, or you've never grown up, I don't know which, but —"

"What's all this, now?"

Byron and Aster were side by side, leaning elbows on the bulwark and looking out to sea. Aster glanced over his shoulder at the shadowy OOD.

"Listen, you fool, I've been laying Janice for a year. How could you be so goddamned blind, not to realize that?"

Byron straightened up. "*Wha-a-at!*" The word was an animal growl.

"It's true. Maybe I shouldn't tell you, but when you —"

At this moment the wardroom steward came up the ladder with a sandwich on a plate and a steaming mug. Aster picked off the sandwich, and took a gulp of coffee. "Thanks, Haynes."

Byron stood staring at Aster, rigid as an electrocuted man.

Aster resumed as the steward left, "Christ, man, with all your troubles, the idea of you eating out your heart because you've misled Janice! It would be hilarious, if it weren't so pathetic."

"For a year?" Byron repeated, dazedly shaking his head. "A year? You?"

Biting into the sandwich, Aster spoke with a half-full mouth. "Jesus, I'm hungry. Yes, I guess about a year. Since she got over the dengue fever. Between that, and your brother's death, and you off in the Med, she was a mighty sad cookie at that time. Now, don't get me wrong, she *likes* you, Byron. She missed you a lot when you were in the Med. Maybe she does love you, but Christ, she's *human*. I mean what harm have we done? She's a great kid. We've had a lot of laughs. She's been afraid of you and your father. Thought you'd disapprove." He drank coffee, and took another bite, peering at the silent and unmoving Byron. "Well, maybe you do, at that. Do you? I still don't know how your mind works. Just don't waste any more energy feeling guilty about Janice. Okay?"

Byron abruptly left the bridge.

At three o'clock in the morning he came into the control room and found Aster at the plotting board with the plot party, smoking a stogie and looking white and tense. "Hi, Briny. The SJ radar has picked one hell of a time to fail. We're socked in again. Visibility down to a thousand yards. We're trying to track them by sonar, but listening conditions stink. Our last position on them is two hours old, and if they change course we can lose them." Aster peered through smoke at Byron. "I don't know why they would change course. Do you?"

"Not if they're returning to port."

"Okay. We agree. I'm holding course and speed."

He followed Byron into the wardroom. Over coffee, after a lengthy silence, he asked, "Sleep?"

"Sure."

"Sore at me?"

Byron gave him a straight hard look that reminded Aster of Captain Victor Henry. "Why? You took a load off my mind."

"That was the idea."

At dawn they were topside, straining their eyes through binoculars. The radar still was not functioning. The visibility had improved, though heavy clouds still hung low over the sea. The freighters were not in sight. It was Horseshoes Mullen, their best lookout, who sang out from the cigarette deck, *"Target! Broad on the starboard bow, range ten thousand!"*

"Ten thousand?" said Aster, swinging his binoculars to starboard. "Son of a bitch. They did change course. And one of them's gone."

Byron discerned in his glass the faint small gray shadow. "Yes, that's one of those freighters. Same samson posts."

Aster yelled down the hatch, *"All ahead flank! Right full rudder!"*

"Five miles," Byron said. "Unless he zigzags, he's made it."

"Why? We can overtake him."

Byron turned to peer at him. "You mean on the *surface?*"

Aster jerked his thumb up at the low thick cloud cover. "What kind of air searches can they be running in this?"

"Lady, those freighters took evasive action. There's probably a full submarine alert on. You've got to assume that that freighter's been reporting his course, speed, and position all night, and that planes are in the area."

"*Steady on one seven five!*" Aster called.

Byron persisted, "They can swarm down like bees through any break in the clouds. What's more, we don't even know that they haven't got airborne radar."

The submarine was heeling and speeding up. Green water came crashing over the low forecastle, dousing everyone on the bridge with spray. Aster grinned at Byron, patted his arm, and snuffed the air. "Great morning, hey? Sound the happy hunting horn."

"Listen, we're still in the shipping lane, Lady. Plenty of other targets will be coming along. Let's submerge."

"That freighter's our pigeon, Briny. We've been tracking him all night, and we're going to get him."

The surface chase lasted almost an hour. The lighter the day grew, the more nervous Byron felt, though the clouds stayed low and solid overhead. They came close to overtaking the freighter, close enough to confirm that it was certainly the same ship. Byron never saw the planes. He heard Mullen yell, "*Aircraft dead astern, coming in low,*" and another, "*Aircraft on the port —*" The rest was drowned out in the stutter, whine, and *zing!* of many bullets. He threw himself on the deck, and as he did so a monstrous explosion almost broke his eardrums. Water showered over him; the heavy splash from a close miss, a bomb or a depth charge.

"*Take her down! Dive, dive, dive!*" Aster bawled.

Bullets went pinging all over the wallowing ship. The sailors and officers, staggering and leaping for the hatch, one by one dropped through in a rapid automatic routine. Within seconds the conning tower was crowded with the dripping deck watch.

BAMMMM!

Another close miss. Very close.

RAT-TAT-TAT! PING! PING! A hail of bullets topside. Solid water flooded down through the open hatch, sloshing all over the deck, wetting Byron to his knees.

"The captain! Where's the captain?" he bellowed.

As though in answer, an anguished voice shouted out on the deck, "BYRON, I'M HIT! I CAN'T MAKE IT! *TAKE HER DOWN!*"

Stunned for an instant, then wildly glancing around, Byron shouted at the crew, "Anybody else missing?"

"Horseshoes is dead, Mr. Henry," the quartermaster yelled at him. "He's out on the cigarette deck. He got it in the face. I tried to bring him down, but he's dead."

Byron roared. "Captain, I'm coming up for you!" He darted into the water showering down the ladder and began to climb.

"Byron, I'm *paralyzed*. I can't move!" Aster's voice was a cracking scream. "You can't help me. There's five planes diving at this ship. TAKE HER DOWN!"

BAMM!

The *Moray* rolled far over to starboard.

A torrent of salt water cascaded through the hatch, flooding up against control instruments. Sparks flew in smoke and sudden stink. The crewmen were slipping and stumbling about in swirling water, white-rimmed eyes on Byron as he desperately calculated the time he would need to fight his way topside and drag the paralyzed captain to safety. In this attack, probably in seconds, the *Moray* would almost surely be lost with all hands.

"Take her down, Byron! I'm done for. I'm dying." Aster's voice was fading.

Byron thrust himself up the ladder against the foaming waterfall in a last effort to climb out. He could not do it. With terrific exertion he barely succeeded in slamming the hatch shut. Drenched, coughing salt water, his voice breaking with grief, he gave his first order in command of a submarine.

"Take her to three hundred feet!"

The only knell for Captain Aster was the sound he perhaps loved best, though nobody could know whether he heard it.

A-OOOGHA . . . A-OOOGHA . . . A-OOOGHA . . .

72

October 1, 1943

Dear Pug:

Bill Standley has come home singing your praises. I am ever so grateful for all you've gotten done over there.

Now I have asked Harry to write the attached letter to you. At least it will get you out of Moscow! You have a feeling for facts, so please take on this job and do what you can. A cable about Tehran very soon would be much appreciated.

By the way, we are launching several splendid new battleships nowadays. One will be for you, as soon as we can shake you loose.

FDR

THIS was scrawled on one sheet of the familiar pale green notepaper. Hopkins's typewritten letter was much longer.

Dear Pug:

You've certainly been doing some grand work with the Russians. Thanks to your survey of shuttle-bombing sites the Joint Chiefs' planners are already working on the Poltava idea. General Fitzgerald wrote me a fine letter about you, and I sent the Bureau of Personnel a copy. Also, getting our servicemen's hospital and rest center finished up at Murmansk was a triumph over the ways of their bureaucracy. I'm told it has improved convoy morale.

Now about the forthcoming heads of state conference: Stalin won't travel farther than Tehran, just south of his Caucasus frontier. He claims he has to stay in close touch with his military situation. Whether that's true, or he's being coy, or worrying about his prestige we can't tell, but he absolutely will not budge on this.

The President will travel almost anywhere to get this damnable war won, but Tehran poses a constitutional snag. If Congress passes a bill he wants to veto, he has to do this with his own hand in ten days, or it automatically becomes law. A cabled or telephoned veto won't work. Tehran is reachable from Washington in less than ten days, with all equipment pushing in fair weather. But we're told Tehran weather is unpredictable and horrendous. We're also told it's not all that bad. Nobody around here seems to know much about Persia. To Washington types it's like the moon.

I suggested that you fly down there, look around, ask some questions, and shoot us a word on the weather prospects at the end of November, and on the security angle too, since we hear the place crawls with Axis spies. Also, the President is fortifying himself with facts and figures for talking with Stalin, and Lend-Lease is bound to come up. We have sheaves of reports, but we could use a good eyewitness account of how things are really going in the Persian supply corridor. Unlike most report-writers you have no axe to grind!

General Connolly is the man in charge at our Amirabad base outside Tehran. He's a good man, an old Army engineer. I knew him well years ago when I headed the WPA and he handled some big construction projects. I have cabled him about you. Connolly will give you a rapid tour of our Lend-Lease port facilities, rail and truck routes, factories, and depots. You can ask any questions, go anywhere, talk to anybody. The President will want to see you before he meets Stalin; and if you can sum up your observations on one sheet of paper that will be a real help.

Incidentally, the landing craft problem has now reached a critical stage, as I foresaw. It's the strangling bottleneck of all our strategic plans. Production is increasing, but it could be a lot better. However, you'll soon be returning to your first love, the sea. The President is aware that you feel like a stranded whale.

> Yours,
> Harry Hopkins

The letters came as a cheering reprieve. Admiral Standley had not lasted long after his outburst; Harriman had succeeded him, bringing a large military mission headed by a three-star general, which spelled the end of Victor Henry's job. But as yet he had received no orders, and he was beginning to think BuPers had lost track of him. Moscow was again snowbound. He had not heard from Rhoda or his children in months. At last he could escape from the boredom of Spaso House talk, the bitching of the frustrated vodka-soaked American newspapermen, and the unfriendly deviousness and obduracy of the Russian bureaucrats. The same afternoon that he got the letters he was on a Russian military plane to Kuibyshev, thanks to a last assist from General Yevlenko. Next day General Connolly met Pug at the airport, put him up in his own quarters on the huge newly built base in the desert, served him venison for dinner, and over coffee and brandy handed him an itinerary that made him blink.

"It'll take you a week or so," said Connolly, a bluff West Pointer in his sixties who bit out rapid words, "but then you'll have something to tell old Harry Hopkins. What we're doing here is sheer lunacy. One country, the U.S.A., is trying to deliver stuff to another country, the USSR, under the control, or rather interference, of a third country, England, through the territory of a fourth country, Persia, where none of us have any goddamned business being. And —"

"You lose me. Why should England interfere?"

"You're new to the Middle East." Connolly blew out an exasperated breath. "Let me try to explain. The British are here by right of invasion and occupation, see? So are the Russians. They partitioned this country by armed force back in 1941, so as to suppress German activity here. That was the reason given, anyhow. Now, follow me carefully. *We* have no right to be here, because we *haven't* invaded Persia. See? Clear as mud, what? Theoretically we're merely helping the British help Russia. The striped-pants boys are still dingdonging about all that. Meantime we're just shoving the goods through any old way, insofar as the Limeys will let us, and the Persians don't steal it, and the Russkis will come and get it. It keeps piling sky-high in the Soviet depots."

"It does? But in Moscow they keep screaming for more."

"Naturally. That has nothing to do with their own transport foul-up. It's monumental. I had to call an eight-day rail embargo back in August, till they came and took away a mountain of stuff at the northern railhead. Once their pilots, drivers, and railroad men get out of the workers' paradise they tend to linger outside. Being fresh from Moscow, you probably can't understand that."

"Beats me." They grinned tart American grins at each other. Pug said, "I also have to look into the weather here."

"What about the weather?"

As Pug described the President's legal difficulty, General Connolly's face wrinkled in a pained frown. "Are you kidding? Why didn't somebody ask me? The weather's changeable, and the dust storms are a nuisance, sure. But we've had maybe two scheduled military flights held up all year. He and Stalin must be playing games. Stalin wants to make him come all the way to his back fence, and the Great White Father is standing on his dignity. I hope he sticks to that. Old Joe should move his tail himself. Russians don't admire people they can shove around."

"General, there's a lot of ignorance about Persia in Washington."

"Christ, you said a mouthful. Well, look, even assuming big winter storms at both ends" — Connolly scratched his head with a hand holding a thick smoking cigar — "that bill he might want to veto could be delivered to Tunis in five days, and we could fly him there in a B-24. He'd go there and back and miss maybe one day here. It's not a real problem."

"Well, I'll cable all that to Hopkins. I have to check into security here, too."

"No sweat, I'll give you the whole drill. How's your backgammon game?" Connolly asked, pouring more brandy for both of them.

Pug had played a lot of acey-deucey over the years. He beat the general two games running, and was winning the third when Connolly said, looking up at him from the board and half-closing one eye, "Say, Henry, we have a mutual acquaintance, don't we?"

"Who?"

"Hack Peters." At Pug's blank look he elaborated, "Colonel Harrison Peters, Engineers. Class of 1913. Big tall guy, bachelor."

"Oh, right. I met him at the Army-Navy Club."

Connolly heavily nodded. "He wrote me about this Navy captain who was Harry Hopkins's boy in Moscow. Now here we meet in this godforsaken neck of the woods. Small world."

Pug played on without further comment, and lost. The general happily folded away the elegantly inlaid board and the ivory counters. "Hack's working on something that can end this war overnight. He's cagey about it, but it's the biggest job the Army engineers have ever tackled."

"I don't know anything about that."

Bedding down in the chilly desert night on an austere Army-issue bed under three coarse blankets, Pug wondered what Colonel Peters could have written about him, after meeting him for a casual raucous hour of drinking champagne and wearing paper hats at a club table. Rhoda had mentioned Peters now and then as a church acquaintance. A possible connection with Palmer Kirby through the uranium bomb crossed Pug's mind, giving him a sick ugly qualm. After all, why had Rhoda's letters ceased? Communication with Moscow was difficult, but possible. Three silent months . . . His fatigue and the brandy helped him blot out these thoughts in sleep.

General Connolly's itinerary called for Pug to traverse Iran, south to north, by railroad and truck convoy; a man from the British legation, Granville Seaton, would go along partway on the train trip. The truck convoys were an all-American show to back up the railroad, which suffered — so Connolly said — from sabotage, washouts, pilfering, breakdowns, collisions, hijacking raids, and the general inefficiency built in by the Germans, and compounded by Persian and British mismanagement.

"Granville Seaton really knows the whole Persian setup," said Connolly. "He's a history scholar, a strange duck, but worth listening to. He loves bourbon. I'll give you some Old Crow to pack along."

On the flight down to Abadan the small plane was too noisy for talk. In the long sweaty tour of an astonishingly large American airplane assembly plant on the desolate seaside flats, where the temperature must have been well over a hundred degrees, Granville Seaton trudged alongside Pug and the factory manager, smoking and saying nothing. Then they drove up to Bandar Shahpur, the rail terminal on the Persian Gulf. Seaton chatted over their dinner at a British officers' mess, but the flutey sing-song words came out so blurry and strangled that he might as well have been talking Persian. Pug had never seen a man smoke so much. Seaton himself looked rather smoked; dried-out, brownish, weedy, with a wide gap between large yellow upper front teeth. Pug had the fancy that if injured the man would bleed brown as a tobacco stain.

Next day at breakfast Pug produced the bottle of Old Crow. At this Seaton smiled like a boy. "Most decadent," he said, and held out his water glass.

The single-track railway crossed dead salt flats and twisted up toward dead mountains. Seen from an airplane the barrenness of this country was bad enough, but from a train window it was worse. No brush grew, miles without end; sand, sand, sand. The train halted to take on another diesel locomotive, and they got off to stretch their legs. Not so much as a jackrabbit or a lizard moved on the sand. Only flies swarmed.

"This may have been the actual garden of Eden," Seaton suddenly spoke up. "It could be again, given water, energy, and a people to work the ground. But Iran lies on this landscape inert as a jellyfish on a rock. You Americans could help. And you had better."

They got back aboard. Clanking and groaning, the train ascended a rocky gorge on a hairpin-turning roadbed. Seaton unwrapped Spam sandwiches, and Pug brought out the Old Crow.

"What should we do about Iran?" Pug asked, pouring bourbon into paper cups.

"Save her from the Russians," replied Seaton. "Either because you're as altruistic and anti-imperialist as you say, or because you'd rather not see the Soviet Union come out of this war dominating the earth."

"Dominating the earth?" Pug asked skeptically. "Why? How?"

"The geography." Seaton drank bourbon, giving Pug a severe stare. "That's the key. The Iranian plateau bars Russia from warm-water ports. So she's landlocked half the year. Also bars her from India. Lenin hungrily called India the depot of the world. Said it was the main prize of his policy in Asia. But Persia, jammed by a thoughtful Providence against the Caucasus like a huge plug, holds back the Bear. It's as big as all western Europe, and mostly it's harsh mountains and salt deserts, such as you're looking at. The people are wild mountain tribes, nomads, feudal villagers, wily lowlanders, all very independent and unmanageable." His paper cup was empty. Pug quickly poured more bourbon. "Ah, thank you. The prime truth of modern Persian history, Captain, is simply this and remember it: *Russia's enemy is Iran's friend.* That's been the British role since 1800. Though on the whole we've bungled it, and come off as perfidious Albion."

The train howled into a long inky tunnel. When it clattered back into the sunglare, Seaton was toying with his empty paper cup. Pug refilled it. "Ah, lovely."

"Perfidious Albion, you were saying."

"Just so. You see, from time to time we've needed Russia's help in Europe — against Napoleon, against the Kaiser, and now against Hitler — and each time we've had to turn a blind eye to Persia, and the Bear each time has seized the chance to claw off a chunk. While we were allied against Napoleon, the Czar snatched the whole Caucasus. The Persians fought to regain their land, but we couldn't support them just then, so they had to quit. That's how Russia happens to possess the Baku and Maikop oil fields."

"All this," said Pug, "is complete news to me."

"Well, the tale gets sorrier. In 1907, when Kaiser Bill was getting nasty, we needed Russia in Europe again. The Kaiser was probing the Middle East with his Berlin-Baghdad railway, so we and the Russians partitioned Persia: sphere of influence in the north for them, in the south for us, with a neutral desert belt in between. Quite without consulting the Persians. And now again we've divided the country by armed invasion. Not pretty, but the Shah was decidedly pro-German, and we had to do it to secure our Middle East position. Still, one can't blame the Shah, can one? From his viewpoint, Hitler was striking at the two powers who've gnawed at Persia north and south for a century and a half."

"You're being very frank."

"Ah, well, among friends. Now look at it from Stalin's viewpoint for a moment, if you can. He partitioned Poland with Hitler. That we consider sinful. He partitioned Persia with us. That we consider quite all right. Appeals to his better nature may therefore confuse him a bit. You Americans have just got to take this thing firmly in hand."

"Why should we get into this mess at all?" asked Pug.

"Captain, the Red Army now occupies northern Iran. We're in the south. The Atlantic Charter commits us to get out after the war. You'll want us to comply. But what about the Russians? Who gets them out? Czarist or communist, Russia acts exactly the same, I assure you."

He gave Pug a long solemn stare. Pug stared back, not replying.

"Do you see the picture? We vacate. The Red Army stays. How long will it be before they control Iranian politics, and advance by invitation to the Persian Gulf and the Khyber Pass? Changing the world balance beyond recall, without firing a shot?"

After a gravelled silence, Pug asked, "What do we do about it?"

"Here endeth the first lesson," said Seaton. He tilted his yellow straw hat over his eyes and fell asleep. Pug dozed, too.

When the train jolted them awake, they were in a huge railway yard crowded with locomotives, freight cars, flatcars, tank cars, cranes, and trucks, where a great noisy activity went on: loading, unloading, shunting about of train sections on sidings, with much shouting by unshaven American soldiers in fatigues, and a wild gabble from crowds of native workers. The sheds and carbarns were newly erected, and most of the rails looked freshly laid. Seaton took Pug on a jeep tour of the yard. Breezy and cool despite a strong afternoon sun, the yard filled hundreds of acres of sandy desert, between a little town of mud-brick houses and a range of steep brown dead crags.

"Yankee energy endlessly amazes me. You've conjured up all this in months. Does archeology bore you?" Seaton pointed at a flinty slope. "There are Sassanid rock tombs up there. The bas-reliefs are worth a look."

They got out of the jeep and climbed in gusty wind. Seaton smoked as he went, picking his way upward like a goat. His stamina violated all physical rules; he was less out of breath than Pug when they reached the dark holes in the hillside, where the wind-eroded carvings, to Pug's unpracticed eye, looked Assyrian: bulls, lions, stiff curly-bearded warriors. Here all was quiet. Far below, the railroad yard clanged and squealed, a small busy blotch on the ancient silent desert.

"We can't stay in Iran once the war's won," Pug remarked, pitching his voice above the wind. "Our people don't think that way. All that stuff down there will just rust and rot."

"No, but there are things to do before you leave."

A loud hollow groan sounded behind them in the tomb. Seaton said owlishly, "The wind across the mouth of the sepulchre. Odd effect, what? Rather like blowing over an open bottle."

"I damned near jumped off this hill," said Pug.

"The natives say it's the souls of the ancients, sighing over Persia's fate. Not inappropriate. Now look here. In 1941, after the invasion and partition, the three governments — Iran, the USSR, and my country — signed a treaty. Iran promised to expel the German agents and make no more trouble, and we and Russia agreed to get out after the war. Well, Stalin will just ignore that scrap of paper. But if *you* join in the treaty — that is, if Stalin promises *Roosevelt* he'll get out — that's something else. He may actually go. With grunts, shoves, and growls, but it's the only chance."

"Is it in the works?"

"Not at all."

"Why not?"

Seaton threw up skinny brown hands.

Toward evening the train passed a string of smashed freight cars lying twisted and overturned by the roadbed. "This was a bad one," said Seaton. "German agents planted the dynamite. Tribesmen looted the cars. They had good intelligence. The cargo was food. Worth its weight in gold, in this country. The big shots are hoarding all the grain, and most other edibles. The corruption here boggles the Western mind, but it's how things are done in the Middle East. Byzantium and the Ottomans have left their mark."

He talked far into the night about the ingenious pilfering and raiding devices of the Persians, which were a real drain on Lend-Lease. To them, he said, this river of goods suddenly rushing through their land, south to north, was just another aspect of imperialist madness. They were fishing in it for dear life, knowing it couldn't last. Copper telephone wire, for instance, was stolen as fast as it was strung up. Hundreds of miles of it had vanished. The Persians loved copper trinkets, plates, and bowls, and the bazaars were now flooded with them. These people had been robbed for centuries, said Seaton, by conquerors and by their own grandees. *Loot or be looted* was the truth they knew.

"Should you succeed in getting Stalin out," he said, yawning, "for God's sake don't try to install your free enterprise system here, with party elections and the rest. By free enterprise, Persians mean what they're doing with your copper wire. A democracy in a backward or unstable country simply gets smashed by the best-organized power gang. Here it'll be a communist gang that will open the gates of Asia to Stalin. So forget your antiroyalist principles, and strengthen the monarchy."

"I'll do my best," said Pug, smiling at the cynical candor of the man.

Seaton smiled sleepily back. "One is told you have the ear of the great."

The Tehran Conference was an off-again, on-again thing until the last minute. Suddenly it was on. A presidential party of seventy fell out of the sky on General Connolly: Secret Service men, generals, admirals, diplomats, ambassadors, White House stewards, and assorted staff people, swirling through the Amirabad base in unholy confusion. Connolly told his secretary that he was too busy to see anybody, but on hearing that Captain Henry had reappeared he jumped up and went out to the anteroom.

"Good God. Look at you." Pug was unshaven, haggard, and covered with grime.

"The truck convoy got caught in a dust storm. Then in a mountain blizzard. I haven't been out of my clothes since Friday. When did the President get here?"

"Yesterday. General Marshall's in your room, Henry. We've moved you over to the officers' quarters."

"Okay. I got your message in Tabriz, but the Russians sort of garbled it."

"Well, Hopkins asked where you were, that's all. I thought you'd better get the hell back here. So the Russians did let you through to Tabriz?"

"It took some talking. Where's Hopkins now?"

"Downtown in the Soviet embassy. He and the President are staying there."

"In the *Soviet* embassy? Not here? Not in our legation?"

"Nope. There are reasons. We've got nearly everybody else."

"Where's the Soviet embassy?"

"My driver will take you there. And I think you should hurry." Pug rubbed a hand over his grimy stubby face. Connolly gestured at a bathroom door. "Use my razor."

Despite a few new boulevards which the deposed Shah had bulldozed through Tehran, most of the city was a maze of narrow crooked streets lined by blank mud-wattle walls. Seaton had told Pug that this Persian way of building a town was meant to slow and baffle an invading horde. It slowed the Army driver until he struck a boulevard and roared downtown. The walls around the Soviet embassy gave it a look of a high-security prison. At the entrance, and spaced all along the street and around the corners, frowning soldiers stood with fixed bayonets. One of these halted the car at the iron gates. Victor Henry rolled down the window and snapped in clear sharp Russian, "I am a naval aide to President Roosevelt." The soldier fell back in a stiff salute, then leaped on the running board to guide the driver through the compound, a spacious walled park with villas set here and there amid autumnal old trees, splashing fountains, and wide lawns dotted with ponds.

Russian sentries and American Secret Service men blocked the veranda of the largest villa. Pug talked his way into the foyer, where civilians and uniformed men, British, Russian, American, bustled about in a polyglot tumult. Pug spied Harry Hopkins slouching along in a gray suit by himself, hands in his pockets, looking sicker and skinnier than ever. Hopkins saw him, brightened, and shook hands. "Stalin just walked over to meet the Chief." He gestured at a closed wooden door. "They're in there. Quite a historic moment, hey? Come along, I haven't unpacked yet. How's the Persian Gulf Command doing?"

Behind the door, Franklin Roosevelt and Joseph Stalin sat face to face. There was nobody else in the room but two interpreters.

Across the narrow street that separated the Russian and the British compounds, Winston Churchill sulked in a bedchamber of his legation residence, nursing a sore throat and a sorer spirit. Since arriving in separate planes from Cairo, he and Roosevelt had not spoken. He had sent an invitation to Roosevelt to stay at his legation. The President had declined. He had asked urgently for a meeting before any talks with Stalin. The President had refused. Now those two were meeting without him. Alas for the old intimacy of Argentia and Casablanca!

To Ambassador Harriman, who went across the street to calm him, Churchill grumbled that he was glad to "obey orders," that all he wanted was to give a dinner party two nights later on his sixty-ninth birthday, get thoroughly drunk, and leave the next morning.

Why was Franklin Roosevelt staying in the Russian compound?

Historians casually note that on arrival he had declined invitations from both Stalin and Churchill, so as to offend neither. At midnight Molotov had urgently summoned the British and American ambassadors to warn them of an assassination plot afoot in Tehran. Stalin and Churchill were scheduled to come to the American legation in the morning for the first conference session. It was over a mile from the British and Russian compounds, which adjoined each other. Molotov urged that Roosevelt move to one of these, hinting that otherwise business could not safely proceed.

So when Roosevelt woke in the morning, a choice was thrust on him: either move in with Churchill, his old trusted ally, offering comfortable English-speaking hospitality and reliable privacy; or with Stalin, the ferocious Bolshevik, Hitler's former partner in crime, offering a goldfish bowl of alien attendants and perhaps of concealed microphones. An American Secret Service man had already checked the Russian villa Roosevelt was being offered; but could such a cursory inspection detect the sophisticated Soviet bugging?

Roosevelt chose the Russians. Churchill writes in his history that the choice pleased him because the Russians had more room. Chagrin is not something a great man often acknowledges.

Was there an assassination plot?

Nobody really knows. A book by an aged Nazi ex-agent asserts that he was part of one. Of making such books there is no end. At the least, Tehran's streets were risky; German agents were there; public men do get killed riding through streets; the First World War had started that way. The weary disabled Roosevelt no doubt was better off staying downtown.

Yet — *why with the Russians,* when the British were across the street?

Franklin Roosevelt had come all the way to Stalin's back fence. So he had bowed to the brute fact that Russia was doing the main suffering and bleeding against Hitler. To take this last step, to accept Stalin's hospitality, to show openness and trust to a tyrant who knew only secrecy and distrust, was perhaps the subtle gamble of an old lion, the ultimate signal of goodwill across the political gulf between east and west.

Did it signal to Stalin that Franklin Roosevelt was a naïve and gullible optimist, a soft touch, a man to push around?

Stalin seldom disclosed his inner thoughts. But once, during the war, he told the communist author Djilas, "Churchill merely tries to pick your pocket. Roosevelt steals the big things."

The grim ultra-realist was not unaware, it would seem from this, that

Russians were dying by the millions and Americans by the thousands, in a war that would give world preeminence to the United States.

We have a record of the first words they exchanged.

ROOSEVELT: *I have been trying for a long time to arrange this.*
STALIN: *I'm sorry, it is all my fault. I have been preoccupied with military matters.*

Or, translated into plain terms, Roosevelt was saying, as for the first time he shook hands with the second most powerful man on earth, *"Well, why have you been so difficult and mistrustful for so long? Here I am, you see, under your very roof."*

And Stalin, whom even Lenin called rude, was drawing instant first blood in his retort: *"We've been doing most of the fighting and dying, that's why."*

So these two men in their sixties met at Stalin's back fence in Persia and chatted: the huge crippled American in a blue-gray sack suit, the very short potbellied Georgian wearing an army uniform with a broad red stripe down the full trousers; the one a peaceful social reformer three times elected, guiltless of any trace of political violence, the other a revolutionary despot with the blood of unthinkable millions of his own countrymen on his hands. A strange encounter.

Tocqueville had predicted that America and Russia would between them rule the earth, the one as a free land, the other as a tyranny. Here was his vision made flesh. What drew these opposites together was only the mutual need to crush a mortal menace to the entire human race, Adolf Hitler's Frost-Cuckoo Land, coming from the east, and coming from the west.

A Secret Service man looked into Hopkins's room. "Mr. Stalin just left, sir. The President's asking for you."

Hopkins was changing his shirt. Hurriedly he tucked the shirttail inside baggy trousers, and pulled over his head a red sweater with a hole in one elbow. "Come along, Pug. The President was inquiring about you this morning."

Everything about this villa was oversize. Hopkins's bedroom was huge. So was the crowded foyer. The room in which Roosevelt sat might have accommodated a masquerade ball. Tall windows admitted a flood of golden sunshine through the sere leaves of high trees. The furniture was heavy, banal, randomly scattered, and none too clean. In an armchair in the sun Roosevelt smoked a cigarette with the holder in his teeth, exactly as in the caricatures.

"Why, hello there, Pug. Grand to see you." His arm swept out for a hearty handclasp. The President looked drawn, lean, much older, but a massive man still, radiating strength and — at the moment — triumphant good humor. The color of the big-jawed face was high. "Harry, it went beautifully. He's an impressive fellow. But bless me, the translation does eat up the time! Terribly tedious. We're meeting at four for the plenary session. Does Winnie know that?"

"Averell went over to tell him." Hopkins glanced at his wristwatch. "That's in twenty minutes, Mr. President."

"I know. Well, Pug!" He gestured at a sofa on which seven men might have sat. "We get gorgeous statistics about all the Lend-Lease aid going to Russia through this Persian corridor. Did you see any sign of it out there? Or is it all just talk, as I strongly suspect?"

The facetiousness went with a broad smile. Roosevelt clearly was still winding down from the excitement of meeting Stalin.

"It's all out there, Mr. President. It's an unbelievable, a magnificent effort. I'll have a report for you later today on one sheet of paper. I'm just back from the road."

"One sheet, eh?" The President laughed, glancing at Hopkins. "Grand. The top sheet is all I ever read, anyway."

"He toured Iran from the gulf to the north," said Hopkins. "By rail and by truck."

"What can I tell Uncle Joe, Pug, if Lend-Lease comes up?" Roosevelt said a shade more seriously. In an aside he remarked to Hopkins, "I don't think it will today, Harry. That wasn't his mood."

"He's changeable," Hopkins said.

Pug Henry swiftly described the pile-ups he had seen at the northern depots, especially at the truck terminal. The Russians had refused to permit the truck convoys to drive any distance into their zone of Iran, he said, allotting only one unloading terminal far from the Russian frontier. That was the big bottleneck. If the trucks could go straight on to Caspian ports and Caucasus border points, the Russians would get more matériel, much faster. Roosevelt listened with sharp attention.

"That's interesting. Put it on your one sheet of paper."

"Don't worry," said Pug without thinking, making Roosevelt laugh again.

"Pug's been boning up on Iran, Mr. President," Hopkins said. "He's on to Pat Hurley's idea, that we should become a party to the treaty guaranteeing withdrawal of foreign armies after the war."

"Yes, Pat keeps harping on that." On Roosevelt's expressive face impatience fleetingly came and went. "Didn't the Russians reject the notion at the Moscow Conference?"

"They stalled." Hopkins, sitting beside Pug, held out a bony hand in an argumentative gesture. "I agree, sir, that we can hardly initiate it. That would be pushing ourselves into the old imperialist game. Still —"

"Exactly. And I won't have that."

"But what about the Iranians, Mr. President? Suppose *they* ask for a guarantee that we'll get out? Then a new declaration would be in order, which would include us."

"We can't ask the Iranians to ask us," Roosevelt replied with casual candor, as though he were in the Oval Office, and not in a Soviet building where all his words were almost certainly being overheard. "That won't fool anybody. We've got three days here. Let's stick to essentials."

He dismissed Victor Henry with a smile and a handshake. Pug was making his way out through the noisy crowded foyer when he heard a very British voice: "I say, there's Captain Henry." It sounded like Seaton. He glanced about, and first noticed Admiral King, standing straight as a telephone pole, looking around with visible lack of love at the swarming uniformed Russians. Beside him a tanned man in a beribboned RAF blue uniform was smiling and beckoning. Pug had not seen Burne-Wilke in several years, and remembered him as taller and more formidable-looking. Beside King the air vice marshal appeared quite short, and he had a mild harassed look. "Hello, there," he said as Pug approached. "You're not on your delegation's roster, are you? Pamela said she'd looked, and you weren't."

"Henry, I thought you were in Moscow," Admiral King said in cold harsh tones. In their rare encounters King always made Pug uneasy. It was a long time since he had thought of the *Northampton*, but now in a mental flash he saw his burning cruiser going down, and sensed a hallucinatory stench of petroleum in his nostrils.

"I came to Iran on special assignment, Admiral."

"You're in the delegation, then?"

"No, sir."

King stared, not liking the vague responses.

Burne-Wilke said, "Pug, if we can manage it, let's get together while we're here."

As coolly as he could, Pug replied, "Pamela's with you, you say?"

"Yes indeed. I was summoned from New Delhi on very short notice. Problems with the Burma campaign plans. She's still sorting out the maps and reports that we hustled together. She's my aide-de-camp now, and jolly good at it. One realizes what she must have done for poor old Talky."

Despite King's look of distaste for this chitchat, Pug persisted, "Where is she?"

"I left her at our legation, hard at work." Burne-Wilke gestured toward the open doorway. "Why don't you pop over and say hello?"

73

A Jew's Journey
(from Aaron Jastrow's manuscript)

It will not be easy to record my meeting with Obersturmbannführer Adolf Eichmann. In a sense I am starting this narrative over; and not only this narrative! Whatever I have written, all my life long, now seems to have been composed in a child's dream.

What I must put down is so dangerous that the former hiding place of my papers will not do. As for the encipherment in Yiddish transliteration, the SS here would penetrate the poor mask instantly. Any one of a thousand wretches in Theresienstadt would read it all off for a bowl of soup or to avoid a beating. I have discovered a more secure place. Not even Natalie will know about it. If I go in one of the transports (at the moment this still seems unlikely) the papers will molder until wreckers or renovators, probably long after this war is over, let sunlight into the walls and crevices of Theresienstadt's mournful old buildings. If I survive the war, I will find these papers where I hid them.

Eppstein himself came by this morning, to accompany us to the SS headquarters. He tried to be agreeable, complimenting Natalie on her looks and on the healthy appearance of Louis, whom she was clutching in her arms. Eppstein is in a pitiful position: a Jewish tool, the figurehead "mayor" (Ältester) who carries out the SS orders; a shabby Jew like the rest of us with his yellow star, making a point of wearing a clean if frayed shirt and a threadbare tie to show his high position. His wan, puffy, worried face is a truer badge of office.

We had never been in or near SS headquarters before; a high wooden fence separates it and the entire town plaza from the Jews. The sentry passed us through the fence and we went along a street bordering the park, past a church and into a government building with offices and bulletin boards and stale-smelling corridors echoing with typewriter noise. It was very strange to come out of the grotesque and squalid ghetto into a place that, except for the large picture of Hitler in the lobby, belonged to the old familiar order of things. In its ordinariness, it was almost reassuring; the last thing I expected of SS headquarters. Of course I was very, very nervous.

Despite a balding broad forehead, Lieutenant Colonel Eichmann looks surprisingly young. The remaining hair is dark, and he has the alert, live-wire air of a middle-level official who is ambitious and on the climb. When we came into the office he sat behind a wide desk, and beside him in a wooden chair sat Burger, the SS boss of Theresienstadt, a cruel rough man one avoids if at all possible. Without getting up, yet not disagreeably, Eichmann motioned Natalie and me to chairs in front of the desk, and with a tilt of his head directed Eppstein to a grimy settee. So far, except for the cold nasty look of Burger, and the black uniforms on both men, we might have been calling on a bank manager for a loan, or on a police supervisor to report a theft.

I remember every word of the German conversation that followed, but I mean to put down only essentials. First Eichmann made businesslike inquiries about our health and accommodations. Natalie did not utter a word; she let me reply that we felt well-treated. When he glanced to her she jerkily nodded. The child, completely at his ease, sat in her lap looking wide-eyed at Eichmann, who then said that conditions in Theresienstadt did not satisfy him at all. He had made a thorough inspection. In the next weeks we would see remarkable improvements (*"gewaltige Verschönerungen"*). Burger had instructions to treat us as very special *Prominente*. As things improved in Theresienstadt we would be among the first to benefit.

Next he cleared up — as much as it ever will be, I fear — the mystery of how we come to be here. We were brought to his attention, he says, when I was in the hospital in Paris. The OVRA demanded that the Gestapo hand us over as fugitives from Italian justice. As he tells it, Werner Beck wanted first to extract recordings of my broadcasts from me, and then let the Italian secret police take us away. He paints a very black picture of Werner, which may well be distorted.

At any rate, our case fell in his lap for disposition. To hand us over to the Italians might well have meant our deaths, and could have complicated the negotiations for exchanging the Baden-Baden group. Yet to allow us to return to Baden-Baden, once we were discovered, would have offended Germany's one European ally; for Italy was then still in the war. Sending us to Theresienstadt, while taking the Italian request "under advisement," seemed the most considerate solution. He had brushed aside Werner Beck's pleas to extort the broadcasts from me. That was no way to treat a prominent personage, even a Jew. He always tried, Eichmann said, to be as fair and humane as possible in carrying out the strict Jewish policies of the Führer; with which, he was frank to say, he totally agreed. Moreover, he did not believe the broadcasts would have served any purpose. So in short, here we were.

Now, he said, he would let Herr Eppstein talk.

The *Ältester*, sitting hunched on the sofa, proceeded to reel off words in a monotone, occasionally looking at me and Eichmann, but throwing many worried glances at Burger, who was glaring at him. The Council of Elders had recently voted, he said, to split off the Culture Section from the Education Department. Cultural activities had greatly increased; they were the pride of Theresienstadt; but they were not properly supervised or coordinated. The council wanted to designate me as an Elder to head the new Department of Culture. My lectures on Byzantium, Martin Luther, and Saint Paul were the talk of the town. My status as an American author and scholar commanded respect. No doubt in my university career I had learned administration. Abruptly Eppstein stopped talking, looking straight at me with a mechanical smile, a mere lifting of the upper lip from stained teeth.

My only possible motive for accepting the offer would have been pity for the man. Clearly he was doing as he had been ordered. It was Eichmann who for some reason wanted me to head this new "Department of Culture."

I do not know how I summoned the courage to reply as I did. Here is almost exactly what I said. "*Herr Obersturmbannführer*, I am your prisoner here, bound to obey orders. Still, I permit myself to point out that my German is only fair. My health is frail. I have little appreciation for music, which is the backbone of Theresienstadt's cultural activities. My library work, which I enjoy, absorbs all my time. I am not refusing this honor, but I am ill-suited for it. Do I have a choice in this matter?"

"If you did not have a choice, Dr. Jastrow," Eichmann answered briskly, without annoyance, "this conversation would be pointless. I am a rather busy man. Sturmbannführer Burger could have given you an order. However, I think this job would be a fine one for you."

But I was appalled at the prospect of becoming one of the wretched Elders, who for a few miserable privileges — most of which I already enjoy — bear the awful burden of the ghetto on their consciences, transmit to the Jews all the harsh SS decrees, and see that these are carried out. It meant giving up my obscure but at least endurable existence for the limelight of the council, for daily dealing with the SS, for unending wrangling over terrible problems which have no decent solution. I screwed up my nerve for one more try.

"Then, if I may, sir, and only if I may, I should like to decline."

"Of course you may. We'll say no more about it. We do have one other matter to discuss." He turned to Natalie, who was sitting through all this with a face of white stone, gripping the boy. Louis was behaving like an angel. That he sensed his mother's terror and was doing his best to help seems to me beyond doubt. "But we are keeping you from your work. The mica factory, I believe?" Natalie nodded. "How do you like it?"

She had to speak. The voice came out hoarse and hollow. "I am very glad to be working there."

"And your son looks well, so it seems the children of Theresienstadt are properly treated."

"He is very well."

Lieutenant Colonel Eichmann stood up, gesturing to Natalie, and walked with her to the door. There he spoke a few offhand words to an SS man in the corridor, with whom she passed from sight. Eichmann closed the door and walked to his seat behind the desk. He has a thin mouth, a long thin nose, narrow eyes, and a sharp chin. Not a good-looking man; but now, all at once, he looked very ugly. His mouth was crazily twitched to one side. He burst out in a terrible roar, "WHO DO YOU THINK YOU ARE? WHERE THE DEVIL DO YOU THINK YOU ARE?"

Burger jumped up at this, charged at me, and slapped me. It made my ear ring, and as he raised his hand I winced, so that the blow knocked me off the chair. I fell hard on my knees. My glasses dropped off, so what happened next I saw very blurrily. Burger kicked me, or rather shoved me, with a boot so that I rolled over on my side. Then he kicked me in the stomach; not with all his might, though it hurt and nauseated me, but in utter contempt, as though kicking a dog.

"*I'll* tell you what you are," Burger shouted down at me. "You're nothing but AN OLD BAG OF FILTHY JEWISH SHIT! You hear? Why, you stinking old pile of shit, did you think you were still in America?" As he walked around me I could barely see the moving black boots. Next he kicked me hard in the backside. "You're in THERESIENSTADT! Understand? Your life isn't worth a pig's fart if you don't get that through that old shithead of yours!" With this, he delivered a really ferocious kick with the point of his boot. It struck my spine. Red-hot pain shot all through me. I lay there, stunned, blinded, agonized, shocked. I heard him walking away, saying, "Get up on your knees."

I obeyed, shaking all over.

"Now tell me what you are."

My throat was clamped shut by fear.

"Do you want more? Say what you are!"

God forgive me for not letting him kill me. The thought pierced my fog of shock that if I were to die now, Natalie and Louis would be in still greater danger.

I choked out, "I'm an old bag of filthy Jewish shit."

"Louder. I didn't hear you."

I repeated it.

"Scream it, shit pile! Scream it at the top of your lungs! Or I'll kick you, you stinking Jew pig, until you do scream it!"

"I'M AN OLD BAG OF FILTHY JEWISH SHIT."

"Give him his glasses," Eichmann said in a matter-of-fact tone. "All right, get up."

As I staggered to my feet, a hand caught my elbow to steady me. I felt the glasses placed on my eyes. Into my vision there sprang the face of Eppstein. On that pale face, in those haunted brown eyes, were scarred two thousand years of Jewish history.

"Sit down, Dr. Jastrow," said Eichmann. He was sitting at the desk, smoking a cigarette, looking quite composed and bank-managerial. "Now let's talk sensibly."

Burger sat down beside him, grinning with enjoyment.

What happened after that is less clear in my recollection, for I was dazed and in great pain. Eichmann's tone was all business still, but with a new sarcastic edge. What he said was almost as upsetting as the physical abuse. The SS knows that I have been teaching the Talmud; and since education in Jewish subjects is forbidden, I could be sent to the dread prison in the Little Fortress, from which few return alive. Even more staggering, he disclosed that Natalie takes part in scurrilous underground shows mocking the Führer, for which she could be arrested and forthwith executed. Natalie has never talked to me about this. I only knew that she did puppet shows for children.

Obviously Eichmann told me these things to drive home the lesson of Burger's brutal assault: that no vestige remains of our rights as Americans, or as human beings in Western civilization. We have crossed the line. Any claim to our former Baden-Baden status has been erased by our offenses, and the sword hangs over our heads. With peculiar acid frankness he commented, "Not that we really give a damn how you Jews amuse yourselves!" He told me to teach away, and added that if Natalie ceases her satires it will only go harder with both of us, for I am not to tell her what happened after she left SS·headquarters. I must never breathe a word of it to anybody. If I do, he will be sure to find out, and that will be too bad. He said that Eppstein would show me the ropes of my new Elder status; and so, with an offhand wave, he dismissed me. I could hardly rise from the chair. Eppstein had to help me hobble out. Behind us we could hear the two Germans joking and laughing.

As we left SS headquarters together, Eppstein said not a word. Passing the sentry at the fence, I forced myself to walk more normally. The pain was less, I found, if I stood straight and took firm strides. Eppstein brought me to the barber shop to have my hair and beard trimmed. We went on to the council chamber, where a photographer was setting up for news pictures of the gathered Elders. A reporter, a rather pretty young German woman in a fur coat, was asking questions and scrawling notes. I posed with the Elders. I had my own picture taken. The reporter chatted with me and with the others. I'm sure that these two newspaper people were genuine, and that they left with a highly plausible story — which they may even have believed — about the Jewish council which governs the Paradise Ghetto, a serene well-dressed group of distinguished gentlemen, including the eminent Dr. Aaron Jastrow, author of *A Jew's Jesus.*

That Natalie and I are beyond diplomatic rescue is self-evident in this public use of my name and face. Even if the story is meant for European consumption, word is bound to seep back to the United States. The slight gloss I lend to Theresienstadt seems to outweigh any trouble the State Department can now give the Germans about us. Exchanges of official correspondence can go on for years. Our fate will be decided before anything comes of that footling process.

Some notes on all this, before I proceed to write about the counterweight to all this shock, pain, and degradation: my cousin Berel's return from the dead.

In all my sixty-five years I have encountered strangely little physical violence. The last instance that I can recall, in fact, was the slap Reb Laizar gave me in the Oswiecim yeshiva. Reb Laizar slapped me out of my Jewish identity, as it were, and an SS officer kicked me back into it. What I did when I returned to my room will perhaps make no sense to anybody but me. Since leaving Siena I have carried a well-concealed pouch of last resort, containing the diamonds and the photocopied documents of my juvenile conversion to Catholicism. As *Prominente* we have never yet, thank God, been bodysearched. I got out those worn folded conversion papers dated 1900, and tore them to bits. This morning for the first time in about fifty years I put on phylacteries. I borrowed them from a pious old man next door. I mean to do this in all the days remaining to me on this sick and stricken earth.

Is this a return to the old Jewish God? Never mind. My Talmud teaching has certainly not been that. I drifted into it. Young people in the library began to ask me questions. A circle of questioners gradually formed, I found I enjoyed the elegant old logical game, and so it became a regular thing. The phylacteries, the old black-stained leather boxes containing Mosaic passages, gave me no intellectual or spiritual uplift as I tied them on head and arm. In fact, though I was alone, I felt self-consciously showy and silly. But I will persist. Thus I answer Eichmann. As for the old Jewish God, He and I both have accounts to settle, for if I have to explain my apostasy, He has to explain Theresienstadt. Jeremiah, Job, and Lamentations all teach that we Jews tend to rise to catastrophe. Hence phylacteries. Let it go at that.

It says much about human nature — or at least about my own personal foolishness — that for many years I have refused to believe the stories of Nazi atrocities against the Jews, and even the evidence of my eyes; yet now I am certain that the most alarming reports are the true ones. Why this turnabout? What was so very convincing about the encounter with Eichmann and Burger?

After all, I have already seen much atrocious German conduct here. I have seen an SS man clubbing an old woman to her knees in the snow because he caught her peddling cigarette butts. I have heard of children being hanged in the Little Fortress for stealing food. Then there was the census. Three weeks ago, the SS marched the entire ghetto population out into the fields, in blowing freezing weather, counted us over and over for about twelve hours, and left upwards of forty thousand persons standing around in the rainy night. Rumors swept the huge famished crowd that we were all about to be machine-gunned in the dark. A stampede to the town gates ensued. Natalie and I ducked the mob and got back without incident, but we heard that the field in the morning was littered with sleet-covered bodies of trampled old people and children.

Yet none of this signalled to me the truth. My meeting with Eichmann did. Why? It is the oldest psychological fact, I suppose, that one cannot really feel another's misery. And worse; let me face for once in my life this raw reality; the misery of others can make one glad and relieved that one has been spared.

Eichmann is not a low police brute. Nor is he a banal bureaucrat, though that is the role he brilliantly puts on when it suits him. Much more than the flamboyant fanatic Hitler, this businesslike Berlin official is the dread figure that has haunted the twentieth century and precipitated two wars. He is a reasonable, intelligent, brisk, even affable fellow. He is one of us, a civilized man of the West. Yet in a twinkling he can order horrible savagery perpetrated on an old feeble man, and look on calmly; and in another twinkling can return to polite European manners, without the slightest sense of any inconsistency, even with a sardonic smirk at the discomfiture of the victim who cannot conceive of this version of human nature. Like Hitler, he is an Austrian. Like him, in this dread century, he is *the German.*

I have grasped this difficult truth. Nevertheless, I will go to my death refusing to condemn an entire people. We Jews have had enough of that. I will remember Karl Frisch, the historian, who came to Yale from Heidelberg, a German to the bone, a sweet, liberal, profound man with a superb sense of humor. I will remember the wonderful yeasting of art and thought in Berlin in the twenties. I will remember the Hergesheimers, with whom I stayed for six months in Munich, people of the first quality with — I will swear — no taint of anti-Semitism, at a time when it was becoming a volcanic political rumble. Such Germans exist. They exist in large numbers. They must, to have created the beauty of Germany, and the art, and the philosophy, and the science; what was known as *Kultur* long before it became a name of execration and horror.

I do not understand the Germans. Attila, Alaric, Genghis Khan, Tamerlane, in the fury of conquest exterminated all who resisted them. The Moslem Turks slaughtered the Christian Armenians during the World War, but the Armenians were taking the part of the enemy, czarist Russia, and it happened in Asia Minor.

The Germans are part of Christian Europe. The Jews have passionately embraced and enriched the German culture, the arts, the sciences. In the World War the German Jews had a record of insensate loyalty to the Kaiser. No, there has been nothing like this before. We are caught in a mysterious and stupendous historical process, the grinding birth pangs of a new age; and as at the dawn of monotheism and of Christianity, we are fated to be at the heart of the convulsion, and to bear the brunt of its agony.

My lifelong posture of learned agnostic humanism was all very fine. My books about Christianity were not without merit. But taking it all in all, I have spent my life on the run. Now I turn and stand. I am a Jew. A fine earthy vulgarism goes, "What that man needs is a swift kick in the arse." It would seem to be my biography.

Berel Jastrow is in Prague.

That is almost all I know: that he is there, working in the underground, having escaped from a concentration camp. He sent me word through a communist grapevine that links Prague and Theresienstadt. To identify and authenticate himself, he used a Hebrew phrase that on Gentile tongues (for the Czech gendarmerie is the main transmitter) became almost undecipherable. Still, I puzzled it out: *hazak ve'emats*, "Be strong and of good courage."

It is amazing that this iron-willed resourceful cousin of mine is alive, close by, and aware of my incarceration here; but nothing is too amazing in the chaotic maelstrom that the Germans have made of Europe. I have not seen Berel in fifty years, yet Natalie's description has made him a commanding presence in my mind. That he can do anything for us is unlikely. My health would not endure an escape effort, even if such a thing were possible. Nor could Natalie risk it, with the child on her hands. What, then? My hope is only that of every other Jew in this trap: that the Americans and British will land in France very soon, and that National Socialist Germany will be smashed between assaults coming from the east and the west, in time to set us free.

Still, it is wonderful that Berel is in Prague. What an odyssey he must have lived, since Natalie last saw him in falling Warsaw, four eternal years ago! His survival must be called a miracle; the fact that he is so near, another miracle. Such things give me hope; make me, in fact, *"strong and of good courage."*

74

Pug Henry had been feverish for days, victim of some endemic Persian bug. Riding trains and trucks day and night through towns, farmlands, dust storms, blistering deserts, and snowy mountain passes, he had fallen into a lethargy in which — especially at night — fever dreams and reality had run together. He had arrived at Connolly's headquarters light-headed, and had been hard put to it to stay alert even talking to Hopkins and Roosevelt. Through those long whirling hours on the convoy route, Pamela and Burne-Wilke had come and gone in his hectic visions much as his dead son and his living family had. Pug could consciously seal off Pamela, like Warren, in a forbidden section of memory, but he could not help his dreams.

So the sight of Burne-Wilke in the Russian embassy villa was startling: a fever-dream figure, standing there beside the cold real Ernest King. *Pamela in Tehran!* He could not, under King's hard eye, ask straight out, "Are you married?" He left Roosevelt's villa not knowing whether he should inquire at the British legation for Lady Burne-Wilke or Pamela Tudsbury.

Stalin and Molotov were approaching on a gravel path as Pug came out, Molotov talking earnestly, Stalin smoking a cigarette and glancing about. Seeing Pug he nodded and half-smiled, his wrinkled eyes flashing clear recognition. Pug was used to politicians' memories, but this surprised him. It was over two years since he had delivered Hopkins's letter to Stalin. The man had borne the weight of a gigantic war all that time; yet he really seemed to remember. Tubby, gray, shorter than Victor Henry, he strode bouncily up the steps into the villa. Pug had had almost a year of the Moscow iconography — statues, paintings, gigantic photographs — presenting Stalin as a remote legendary all-wise Savior, one of a cloud-riding trinity with the dead Marx and Lenin; and there went the flesh and blood reality, a small paunchy old fellow in a beige uniform with a broad red stripe down the pants. Yet the icons in a way were more true than that reality; so Pug thought, recalling scenes on the vast Russian front that Stalin's will controlled, and remembering too his history of murdering millions. A stone-hearted colossus had gone by in that little old man.

Winston Churchill, whom he had met more often, did not recognize

Pug. Accompanied by two stiff-striding generals and a pudgy admiral, chewing on a long cigar, he left the British compound as Pug was identifying himself at the gate. The filmy shrewd eyes looked straight at Pug and through him, and the stooped rotund figure in a white suit ambled on. The Prime Minister appeared dull and unwell.

Inside the British legation a few armed soldiers walked about the gardens, and civilians in little knots chatted in the sunshine. This was a much smaller and quieter establishment. Pug paused to take thought under a tree shedding golden leaves. Where to find her? How to ask for her? He was able to grin wryly at his own pettiness. An earth-shaking event was happening here, yet on this peak of high history, what excited him was not the sight of three world giants, but the prospect of laying eyes on a woman he saw once or twice a year by the chances of war.

Their week in Moscow, cut to four days by a whim of Standley's, remained in his memory as a burst of beauty like his honeymoon: serene, sweet, nothing but companionship at meals, in long walks, in Spaso House, at the Bolshoi, at a circus, in her hotel suite. They had talked endlessly, like lifelong friends, like husband and wife, meeting after a separation. In the last evening at her hotel he had even talked about Warren. The thoughts and feelings had broken from him. In Pamela's face, and in her brief gentle comments, he had found comfort. They had managed to part next day with smiles and casual words. Neither had said that it was an ending, but to Pug, at least, it had been nothing else. Now here she was again. He could no more resist looking for her than he could will to stop breathing.

"Hullo! There's Captain Henry." This time it really was Granville Seaton, standing with some men and women in uniform. Seaton came and took his arm, with far more warmth than he had displayed in their journeying together. "What cheer, Captain? Wearing business, that truck route, what? You look fairly done up."

"I'm all right." Pug gestured in the direction of the Soviet embassy. "I just told Harry Hopkins your ideas about a new treaty."

"You did? You actually did? Smashing!" Seaton hugged his arm close, exhaling a strong tobacco breath. "What was his reaction?"

"I can tell you the President's reaction." In his light-headedness Pug blurted this. His temples throbbed and his knees felt weak.

Seaton spoke intensely, his eyes searching Pug's face. "Tell me, then."

"The thing was discussed at the Moscow Conference of foreign ministers last month. The Russians stalled. That's that. The President won't thrust the United States into your old rivalries. He's got a war to win and he needs Stalin."

Seaton's face fell into lines of sadness. "Then the Red Army will never leave Persia. If what you say is accurate, Roosevelt's pronouncing a long-range doom on all free men."

Victor Henry shrugged. "I guess he figures on fighting one war at a time."

"Victory is meaningless," Seaton exclaimed, "except in its effect on the politics of the future. You people have yet to grasp that."

"Well, if an initiative came from the Iranians that might be different. So Hopkins said."

"The Iranians?" Seaton grimaced. "Forgive me, but Americans are tragically naïve about Asia and Asian affairs. The Iranians won't take the initiative, for any number of reasons."

"Seaton, do you know Lord Burne-Wilke?"

"The air vice marshal? Yes, they've brought him here on the Burma business. He's over at the plenary session now."

"I'm looking for his aide, a WAAF."

"I say, Kate!" Seaton called and beckoned. A pretty woman in a WAAF uniform left the group he had been chatting with. "Captain Henry here is looking for the future Lady Burne-Wilke."

Green eyes snapped in a snub-nosed face, giving Pug a quick pert inspection. "Ah, yes. Well, everything's in such a muddle. She brought masses of maps and charts and whatnot. I think they installed her in the anteroom outside the office that Lord Gore is using."

"I'll take you there," Seaton said.

Two desks jammed the little room on the second floor of the main building. At one of them a pink-faced officer with a bushy mustache was hammering at a typewriter. Yes, he said peevishly, the other desk had been shoved into the room for Burne-Wilke's aide. She had worked at it for hours, but had left not long ago to shop at the Tehran bazaar. Seizing a scrap of paper on Pamela's desk, Victor Henry scrawled, *Hi! I'm here, at the U.S. Army base officers' quarters. Pug,* and jammed it on a spike. He asked Seaton as they walked outside, "Where's this bazaar?"

"I don't recommend that you go looking for her there."

"Where is it?"

Seaton told him.

General Connolly's driver took Pug into the old part of Tehran, and left him at the bazaar entrance. The exotic mob, the heavy smells, the foreign babble, the garish multitudinous signs in a strange alphabet, dizzied him. Peering past the stone arcades at the entrance, he saw crowded gloomy passageways of shops receding out of sight. Seaton was right. How could one find anybody here? Yet the conference was due to last only three days. This day was already melting away. Communication in this Asian city, especially amid the helter-skelter doings of an improvised conference, was chancy. They might even miss each other entirely if he did not make an effort to find her. "The *future* Lady Burne-Wilke," Seaton had called her. That was what mattered. Pug went plunging in to look for her.

He saw her almost at once, or thought he did. He was passing by shop after shop of tapestries and linens, when a narrow passageway opened off to the right, and glancing down it past the crowd of black-veiled women and burly men, through hanging leather coats and sheepskin rugs, he spotted a trim little figure in blue, wearing what looked like a WAAF cap. Shouting at her was hopeless, above the din of merchant cries and bargaining. Pug shouldered through the mob and came to a broader cross-gallery, the section of carpet dealers. She was not in sight. He set off in the direction she had been moving. In an hour of sweaty striding through the pungent, crowded, tumultuous labyrinth, he did not see her again.

Had he not been in a fever it would still have seemed dreamlike, this frustrated quest for her through a thronged maze. All too often he had had just such nightmares about Warren. Whether he was looking for him at a football game, or in a graduation crowd, or aboard an aircraft carrier, the dream was always the same: he would glimpse his son just once, or he would be told that Warren was close by, and he would pursue and pursue and never find him. As he tramped sweatily round and round the galleries, feeling ever lighter in the head and queerer about the knees, he came to realize that he was not behaving normally. He groped back to the entrance, bargained in sign language with a cab driver in a rusty red Packard touring car, and paid a crazy price for a ride to the Amirabad base.

The next clear thing that happened to Pug Henry was that somebody shook him and said, "Admiral King wants to see you." He was lying clothed on a cot in the officers' quarters, bathed in sweat.

"I'll be with him in ten minutes," Pug said through chattering teeth. He took a double dose of pills that were supposed to control the ailment, and a heavy slug of Old Crow; showered and rapidly dressed, and hurried through the starlit darkness in his heavy bridge coat to General Connolly's residence. When he came into King's suite, the admiral's glowering glance changed to a look of concern. "Henry, get yourself to sick bay. You're damned green around the gills."

"I'm okay, Admiral."

"Sure? Want a steak sandwich and a beer?" King gestured at a tray on the desk between piles of mimeographed documents.

"No, thank you, sir."

"Well, I saw history made today." King talked as he ate, in an unusually benign vein. "That's more than Marshall and Arnold did. They missed the opening session, Henry. Fact! Our Army Chief of Staff and the boss of the Air Corps flew halfway around the world for this meeting with Stalin, then, by God, they didn't get the word, and tooled off sightseeing. Couldn't be located. Ha ha ha! Isn't *that* a snafu for the books?"

King emptied his glass of beer and complacently touched a napkin to his mouth. "Well, *I* was there. That Joe Stalin is one tough gent. Completely on top of things. Doesn't miss a trick. He put a hell of a spoke in Churchill's wheel today. *I* think all the talk about pooping around in the Mediterranean is finished, over, done with. It's a new ball game." King looked hard at him. "Now you're supposed to know something about landing craft."

"Yes, sir."

"Good." Searching through piles of documents, King pulled several out as he talked. "Churchill turns purple, just talking to me about landing craft. I spoil his fun. We've got thirty percent of new construction allotted to the Pacific, and I have to be a son of a bitch about them, or they'd melt away in his wild invasion schemes." He brandished a sheaf of documents. "Here's a British op-plan for a landing on Rhodes, for instance, which I consider absolutely asinine. Churchill asserts that it'll pull Turkey into the war, set the Balkans aflame, and blah blah blah. Now what I want you to do —"

General Connolly knocked, and entered in a heavy checkered bathrobe. "Admiral, Henry here has been invited to dinner by the Minister of the Imperial Court. This just arrived by hand. A car's waiting."

Connolly gave Pug a large cream-colored unsealed envelope.

"Who's the Minister of the Imperial Court?" King asked Pug. "And how do *you* know him?"

"I don't, Admiral." A scrawled note clipped to the crested card explained the invitation; but he did not mention it to King.

Hi — I'm a houseguest here. Talky and the minister were old good friends. It was this or the YWCA for me. Do come. P.

"Hussein Ala is the second or third man in the government, Admiral," said General Connolly. "Sort of a grand vizier. Better send Pug along. The Persians have peculiar ways of doing things."

"Like the heathen Chinee," said King. He threw the documents on the desk. "Okay, Henry, see me when you return. No matter what time."

"Aye aye, sir."

The black Daimler driven by a silent man in black went twisting through the walls of old Tehran, and halted in a narrow moonlit street. The driver opened a small door in a wall; Victor Henry had to stoop to go through. He walked down into a lantern-lit garden spacious as the Soviet embassy, with fountains spouting sparkling waters, rivulets murmuring in canals among the towering trees and sculptured shrubbery, and at the other side of this opulent private park, many lighted windows showing. A man in a long crimson garment, with enormous drooping black mustaches, bowed to Pug as he came in, and led him around the fountains and through the trees. In the foyer of the mansion Pug got a peripheral impression of inlaid wood walls, a high tiled ceiling, and rich tapestries and furniture. There stood Pamela in uniform. "Hi. Come and meet the minister. Duncan's late for dinner. He's staying at the officers' club."

The mustachioed man was helping Pug take off the bridge coat. Unable to find words for the joy he felt, Pug said, "This is somewhat unexpected."

"Well, I got your note, and I wasn't sure I'd see you otherwise. We're flying back to New Delhi day after tomorrow. The minister was very sweet about inviting you. I told him a thing or two about you, of course." She put her hand to his face, looking worried, and he saw the glitter of a large diamond. "Pug, are you all right?"

"I'm fine."

Despite a well-tailored dark British suit and pleasant clear English, it was a grand vizier who welcomed Pug in a magnificent sitting room: a commanding nose, wise brilliant brown eyes, thick silvering hair, a lordly bearing, an antique smooth manner. They settled in a cushioned alcove and the minister fell to talking business almost at once, while Pug and Pamela drank highballs. Lend-Lease, he said, had its very bad aspect for Iran. The American wages were causing a wild inflation: prices spiking, shortages mounting, goods vanishing into the warehouses of hoarders. The Russians were making matters worse. They occupied much of the best farming lands, and they were taking the produce. Tehran was not far from food riots. The Shah's one hope lay in the generosity of the United States.

"Ah, but the United States is already feeding nearly the whole world," Pamela remarked. "China, India, Russia. Even poor old England." The sound of her voice speaking these simple words enthralled Pug. Her presence transformed time; every moment was a celebration, a drunkenness; this was his reaction to seeing her again, perhaps fevered but true.

"Even poor old England." The minister nodded. His faint smile, the tilting of his head, conveyed ironic awareness of the dwindling of the British empire. "Yes, the United States is now the hope of mankind. There has never in history been a nation like America. But with your generous nature, Captain Henry, you must learn not to be too trusting. There truly are wolves in the woods."

"And bears," said Pug.

"Ah, just so." Ala smiled the formal bright smile of a grand vizier. "Bears."

Lord Burne-Wilke arrived, and they went in to dinner. Pug feared that he faced a heavy meal, but the fare was plain, though everything else was grand — the vaulted dining room, the long dark table polished to a mirror shine, the hand-painted china, and what looked like platinum or white-gold plate. They had a clear soup, a chicken dish, and sherbet, and with the help of wine Pug managed to eat.

Burne-Wilke did most of the talking at first, in an autumnal vein. The conference had started very badly. Nobody was to blame. The world had come to a "discontinuity of history." Those who knew what should be done lacked the power to do it. Those who had the power lacked the knowledge. Pug discerned in Burne-Wilke's gloom the spoke that Stalin had put in Churchill's wheel, to the glee of Ernest King.

The minister took up the theme and discoursed mellifluously on the ebb and flow of empires; the inevitable process by which conquerors became softened by their conquests, and dependent on their subjects to keep them in luxury, and so sooner or later fell to a new nation of hard rude fighters. The cycle had rolled on from Persepolis to the Tehran Conference. It would never end.

During all this Pug and Pamela sat silent opposite each other. Each time their eyes met it was a thrill for him. He thought she was tightly controlling her eyes and her face, as he was; and this necessity to mask his feelings only intensified them. He wondered what there could ever be again in life to match what he felt for Pamela Tudsbury. She wore Burne-Wilke's large diamond on her finger, as she had once worn the smaller diamond of Ted Gallard. She had not married the aviator, and she had not yet married Burne-Wilke, four months after the wrenching farewell in Moscow. Was she still caught as he was? This love kept triumphing over time, over geography, over shattering deaths, over year-long separations. A random meeting on an ocean liner had led step by step to this unlikely meeting in Persia, to these profoundly stirring glances. Now what? Would this be the end?

Pug scarcely knew Duncan Burne-Wilke, and the excited warmth with which the man began to expatiate on Hinduism astonished him. The air vice marshal grew flushed, his eyes softened and moistened, and he spoke for a long time, while his sherbet melted, about the *Bhagavad-Gita*. Serving in India, he said, had opened his eyes. India was old and full of wisdom. The Hindu view of the world was a total break from Christian and Western ideas, and wiser. The *Bhagavad-Gita* offered the only acceptable philosophy he had ever come upon.

The warrior hero of the *Gita*, he said, disgusted with the senseless killing of war, wanted to throw down his arms before a great battle. The god Krishna persuaded him that as a warrior his task was to fight, however stupid the cause and however revolting the murders, leaving the sorting out of the whole to Heaven and to destiny. Their long dialogue, said Burne-Wilke, was greater poetry than the Bible; it taught that the material world was not real, that the human mind could not grasp the workings of God, that death and life were twin delusions. A man could only face up to his lot, and act according to his nature and his place in life.

With a slight face twitch, Pamela conveyed to Pug that all this meant little to her, that Burne-Wilke was off riding a hobbyhorse.

"I know the *Bhagavad-Gita*," said the minister placidly. "Some of our Persian poets write much in that vein. It is too fatalistic. One cannot control all the consequences of one's actions, true. But one must still think about them, and make choices. As to the world's not being real, I always humbly ask, '*Compared to what?*' "

"Compared to God, possibly," said Duncan Burne-Wilke.

"Ah, but by definition, He is beyond compare. So that is no answer. But we are caught in a very old revolving door. Tell me, what will come out of the conference to benefit Iran? We are your hosts, after all."

"Nothing. Stalin is dominating the proceedings. The President is just drifting with him, I suppose to show his good intentions. Churchill alone, great as he is, can't pull against two such weights. An ominous state of things, but there you have it."

"Perhaps President Roosevelt is cleverer than we know," said the minister, turning shrewd old brown eyes at Victor Henry.

Now Pug felt as he had in his Berlin post, just before sending in his report on the combat readiness of Germany. It had been a presumptuous thing to do. It had led to his meeting with Roosevelt. It had probably destroyed his naval career. Yet there sat Pamela opposite him, and that was how he had met her. Perhaps there was something to the *Bhagavad-Gita*, to the working of destiny, to the need for a man to act according to his nature. He was a plunger at crucial moments. He always had been. He plunged.

"Wouldn't it be a good thing to come out of the conference," he said, "if the United States joined in your treaty with England and Russia? If all three countries agreed to pull out their troops after the war?"

The minister's somewhat hooded eyes glinted. "A wonderful thing. But this idea has been rejected at the Moscow meeting of foreign ministers. We were not present, but we know."

"Why doesn't your government ask the President to take it up with Stalin?"

Glancing at Burne-Wilke, who was regarding Pug quizzically, the minister said, "Let me ask you an indiscreet question. On your tour of the Lend-Lease installations here, were you not a personal emissary of President Roosevelt?"

"Yes."

The minister nodded, contemplating him through eyes lidded almost shut. "Do you actually know your President's views on this matter of a new treaty?"

"Yes. The President won't initiate such a move, because it might look to the Russians like an imperialist intrusion. But he might respond to Iran's request for reassurance."

The minister's next words came rapid-fire. "But that idea has already been explored. A hint to your legation not long ago met no encouragement. It was not pressed. It is an extremely serious thing to push a powerful nation in such a delicate matter."

"No doubt, but the conference will break up in a couple of days. When will such a chance come again for Iran? If the President's doing everything Stalin's way, as Lord Burne-Wilke says, then Stalin might be in a mood to oblige him."

"Shall we have coffee?" The minister stood, smiling, and led them into a glassed-in veranda facing the garden. Here he left them, and was gone for about a quarter of an hour. They lolled on cushioned divans, and servants brought them coffee, brandy, and confections.

"Your point is well-taken," Burne-Wilke commented to Pug as they settled down. "The conference is such an utterly disorganized muddle that by sheer luck the Iranians might just pull it off. It's worth a try. There's no other way the Soviet Union will ever get out of Persia."

He talked about the China-Burma-India theatre. It was always feast or famine there, he complained; the forces were either starved, or suddenly glutted with supplies and asked to perform miracles. President Roosevelt was obsessed with keeping China in the war. It was bloody nonsense. Chiang Kai-shek wasn't fighting the Japanese. Half the Lend-Lease aid was lining his pockets, the other half was going to suppress the Chinese communists. General Stilwell had told Roosevelt the brute facts at Cairo. Yet the President had promised Chiang a campaign to reopen the Burma Road, though the only troops on hand to fight such a campaign were British and Indian, and Churchill opposed the whole idea. Mountbatten had wisely avoided coming to Tehran, unloading the whole wretched Burma tangle on Burne-Wilke. The discussions with the American staff were going round and round in circles. He was heartily sick of it, and looked forward to escaping in a day or two.

"Pug, you don't look well," Pamela said quite suddenly, sitting up.

There was no use denying it. The relief of bourbon, Scotch, and wine, and the pulse of adrenalin from seeing Pamela, were all ebbing away. The room was swimming, and he felt like death. "It comes and goes, Pam. The Persian crud. Maybe I'd better get back to base."

The minister just then returned, and he at once ordered the car and driver brought around to the garden door.

"I'll walk with you to the car," Pamela said.

Wearily, with a gracious intelligent smile, Burne-Wilke rose to shake hands. The minister accompanied them through the ornate foyer.

"Thanks for dinner," Pug said.

"I am pleased you could come," said Hussein Ala, with a penetrating look into Pug's face. "Very pleased."

In the garden Pamela paused in a darkened space between lanterns, seized Pug's sweaty hand, and turned him toward her.

"Better not, Pam," he muttered, "I'm probably infectious as hell."

"Really?" She took his head in her hands and pulled his mouth down on hers. She kissed him three times, light sweet kisses. "There. Now we've both got the crud."

"Why haven't you married Burne-Wilke?"

"I'm going to. You've seen my ring. You couldn't take your eyes off it."

"But you're not married."

Her tone turned exasperated. They were both talking breathlessly and low. "Oh, look, when I got to New Delhi, Duncan had this blinding imbecile of an aide who was driving him bonkers. He asked me to step in. I've done a fair job. He seems pleased. It would be sort of sticky, Lady Burne-Wilke manning the outer office, but this way it's okay. We're together constantly. Everything's fine. When it seems suitable we'll get married, but possibly not till we go back to England. There's no hurry."

"He's a grand fellow," Pug said.

"He's terribly depressed tonight. That brought on the *Bhagavad-Gita*. He's a brilliant administrator, a fearless flier, and altogether a lamb. I love him."

"You saw Rhoda several times in Washington, didn't you?"

"Yes, three or four times."

"Was she ever with an Army colonel named Peters? Harrison Peters?"

"Why, no. Not that I know." She turned and started to walk.

"You're sure?" He put his hand on her arm.

She shook it off and strolled on, speaking nervously. "Don't do this. What a pointless question! It's wretched of you to fish like that."

"I'm not fishing. I want to know."

"About *what?*" She halted and turned to him. "Look, didn't we explore this haunting — *thing* — of ours to weariness, darling, in Moscow? There's a bond between you and Rhoda that nothing can break. Nothing. Not since Warren died. I understand. It's taken me a while, but I've got the idea. It's a terrible mistake to open it all up. Don't do it."

They stood by a large fountain in the middle of the garden. The tall man in the crimson robe was waiting, a dim figure, at the steps to the garden door.

"Why did you get the minister to ask me to dinner?"

"You damned well know why. I won't change till I'm dead. Maybe not then. But I'm not raving with fever, and you are, so *go*. Get yourself doctored. I'll look for you tomorrow."

"Pamela, I've lived four days this year, those four days in Moscow. Now what about this Colonel Peters? You're not very good at pretending."

"But what brings this on? Have you had more poison-pen letters?" He did not answer. She took both his hands, looking him straight in the eyes. "All right, listen. Once at a big dance — I don't remember what it was — I ran into Rhoda, and a tall gray-haired man in Army uniform was escorting her. Very casual, very correct. All right? She introduced him, and I think the name was Peters. That's it. That's *all* of it. A woman can't go to a dance without an escort, Pug. You startled me with your abrupt question, or I'd have told you that straight off."

He hesitated, and said, "I don't think that's all of it."

Pamela burst out at him, "Pug Henry, these fleeting encounters of ours are all very romantic, and I freely confess I'm as dotty as you are. I can't help it. I can't hide it. I don't. Duncan knows all about it. Since it's utterly hopeless, and since we've had the best of it, why not just *forget it?* Call it a chimera feeding on loneliness, separation, and these tantalizing glimpses. Now for God's sake, *go!*" Her cold hand touched his cheek. "You're terribly sick. I'll look for you tomorrow."

"Well, I'd better go, at that. They'll think you've fallen in a fountain." They walked through the garden. She was clutching his hand like a child.

"What about Byron?"

"So far as I know, he's all right."

"Natalie?"

"No news."

The crimson-robed man went up the steps and opened the garden door. Moonlight glinted on the Daimler. They halted at the steps.

"Don't marry him," Pug said.

Her eyes opened wide, gleaming in the moonlight. "Why, I most certainly will."

"Not until I get back to Washington, and find out where Rhoda stands."

"You're delirious. Just go back to her and make her as happy as you can. When this ghastly war ends, maybe we'll meet again. I'll try to see you tomorrow before I go."

She kissed him on the mouth and strode off into the garden.

The car roared through the quiet chilly town and out into the desert silvered by the moon. At the gate to the Amirabad base, a soldier on guard came to the window and saluted. "Cap'n Henry?"

"Yes."

"General Connolly lak to see you, suh." The Virginia accent gave Pug a homesick twinge.

In the checkered bathrobe, wearing horn-rimmed glasses, Connolly was writing at a desk in his sitting room on the ground floor of the residence, his feet in heavy stockings stretched toward a small oil stove. "Hello, Pug. How are you feeling?"

"I could use a slug of booze."

"Christ, you're shivering! Sit by this stove. It gets damned cold toward midnight, doesn't it? Don't disturb Admiral King, he's turned in. What was on Hussein Ala's mind?"

"A British friend of mine is staying with him. We all dined together."

"That's all?"

"That's all." Pug downed the whiskey. "Incidentally, General, what did Hack Peters write you about my wife?"

Connolly was settling back in his desk chair. He took off his glasses and stared at Pug. "Beg your pardon?"

"You mentioned last week that Peters wrote you about us."

"I said nothing about your wife."

"No, but he's her friend, actually, not mine. They met at church, or something. What did he say? Is she all right? It's been a long time since I've heard from her." The general was flushing, and looking very uncomfortable. "Why, what's the matter? Is she ill?"

"Not in the least." Connolly shook his head and rubbed a hand on his brow. "But this is blasted awkward. Hack Peters is my oldest friend, Pug. We write each other with our hair down. Your wife seems to be some kind of paragon. He's taken her dancing and whatnot, Hack's a great dancer, but — oh, hell, why pussyfoot around? Here's what he wrote about her. I'll read you every word, though I probably shouldn't have mentioned the letter."

Rummaging in his desk, Connolly pulled out a small dark V-mail sheet, and read from it with a magnifying glass. Pug listened, sitting hunched in his bridge coat by the smelly stove, the whiskey flaming in his stomach and chills racking his frame. It was a sentimental, flowery picture of a perfect woman — beautiful, poised, sweet, clever, modest, rigidly faithful to her husband, unapproachable as a vestal virgin, and yet a marvelous companion at dances, the theatre, and concerts. Peters praised her gallantry about Warren's death at Midway, the long silences of her submariner son, and the prolonged absence of her husband in Russia. The gist of all this was a moan that, after a long frivolous bachelor existence, he had found the one impossible right woman; and she was totally out of reach. He had to be grateful that she would even let him take her out now and then.

Connolly tossed down the letter and the magnifying glass. "I call that a superb tribute. I wouldn't mind a man writing it about my wife, Pug! Your gal must be quite something."

"She is. Well, I'm glad he's giving her some diversion. She's entitled to it, she's got a rotten deal. I thought the admiral was expecting me."

"No, he seems to be coming down with what you've got. The President got taken queer at dinner tonight, too. Had to leave Churchill and Stalin chewing the fat without him. The Secret Service had a poison scare, but I hear he's sleeping it off all right. Just the crud. Persia's kind of hard on newcomers."

"It is that."

"If you're not better in the morning, go to the hospital, Pug, and get some blood tests."

"I have a report to finish before I turn in. The President expects it in the morning."

Connolly looked impressed, but his reply was offhand. "No sweat. Call the base duty officer and it'll be picked up, any hour of the night."

Coming into the officers' quarters, Pug said to a sergeant sleepily reading a comic book at the entrance desk, "Is there a typewriter in this place?"

"This desk has a fold-away typewriter, sir."

"I'd like to use it."

The sergeant squinted at him. "Now, sir? It makes a racket."

"I won't be long."

He went to his room, took a dram of strong bourbon, and returned to the silent lobby with his notes on the Lend-Lease tour. His ailment tended to retreat before alcohol, leaving him briefly euphoric; and the one-page report that he thunderously clattered off seemed brilliant to him. That it might look like drunken drivel in the morning was a risk he had to accept. He sealed it up and called the duty officer. In his unheated small room he tumbled into the cot, piling on every blanket and also his bridge coat.

He woke in sweat-soaked sheets. By the blurry look of his wristwatch, the spinning of the sunlit room, and his weakness when he tried to stand, he knew he had no choice but the hospital.

75

THE "spoke in Churchill's wheel" was nothing less than the expulsion of the British Empire from its leading position in world affairs, all in a few hours of polite talk around a table in the Soviet embassy.

Churchill had met Stalin before. Roosevelt had not. With the first face-to-face encounter of Stalin and Roosevelt, the center of gravity of the war and of the world's future shifted. The one person who felt this shift in its full crushing force was Winston Churchill. Hints had not been lacking from the start at Tehran that his intimacy with Roosevelt in war leadership was fading: the President's private first meeting with Stalin, for one thing, and his acceptance of Russian hospitality for another. But only in the plenary sessions did the change bite into Churchill's role in history.

A great man, an astute historian, Churchill at Tehran could play only the cards he held. They were relatively weak. Roosevelt might feel affection for him, and total distrust toward Stalin. But in this new deal, shuffled up by world war, of the ancient great game, the Soviet Union now held the cards of manpower and willpower. At Tehran the British were dealt out; some three hundred years of Western European leadership in history ended; and the present day gloomily dawned.

The very hardest thing to imagine, in looking back on this old war, is that it could have gone other than it did. Yet the overwhelming reality during the war — which one must try to grasp, to get a sense of the time — is that nobody knew how it would go. Franklin Roosevelt had done well to journey to the Bolshevik's back fence. Fighting men were dying in masses all over the world, tanks were burning, ships sinking, planes falling, cities toppling, resources wasting; yet the outcome was still very much in doubt, and no plan for winning existed among Hitler's foes. After two years of talk, the American and British staffs remained at loggerheads: the Americans adamant for an all-out smash into France in 1944, the British holding out for less risky operations in the Balkans and the eastern Mediterranean. Roosevelt had no assurance that the Soviet Union would not make a separate peace, or like the Chinese quit fighting beyond a point; and that Stalin would ever declare war on Japan, or join a union of nations after the war, were mere hopes.

Tehran changed all that. In the space of three days, in three round-table strategy meetings lasting but a few hours, the President with bland art —

and what looks in the record like simulated clumsiness — led Josef Stalin to veto once for all Winston Churchill's proposed nibblings at Europe's periphery, and to swing the decision at last for *Overlord,* the grandiose cross-Channel landing in France. Stalin promised a synchronized all-out smash from the east; also, once Germany was beaten, an attack on Japan. He pledged, too, that Russia would join a postwar United Nations. The long suspicious fencing among the Big Three ended at Tehran in a tough solid alliance, with a firm plan for wiping out National Socialism. The alliance would not last in the riptides of postwar change, but it would win the war. Franklin Roosevelt went to Tehran to win the war.

The plan rode roughshod over Churchill's cherished ideas. In the opening session, Roosevelt almost chattily asked Stalin whether he preferred the great assault on France, or one or another Mediterranean plan; and when the formidable Russian approved the Overlord attack, Churchill found himself outvoted two to one, with his vote the least powerful of the three. It was the "spoke in the wheel," the quietus on his long dogged struggle to conduct the war so as to preserve his old Empire.

Next day in the second formal meeting he fought back, arguing long and frantically for his Mediterranean proposals, until Stalin stopped him cold by asking, "Do the British really believe in Overlord, or are they only saying so to reassure the Russians?" It was such a raw moment that Roosevelt said they had all better get ready for dinner. Stalin rode Churchill hard, all during the meal that evening, about his tenderness for the Germans. The Prime Minister at last stalked in fury from the room; whereupon the Russian followed and good-humoredly brought him back.

Early on the third morning Hopkins visited Churchill. Perhaps he brought the crusty old battler word from Roosevelt that it was time to quit; we do not know. Anyway, at the combined Chiefs of Staff meeting shortly after that, the British all at once conceded that the staff had better set the date for Overlord or go home. Thus the two-year wrangle ended. The Americans showed no elation or triumph. A one-page agreement on Overlord was rushed to Churchill and Roosevelt. At lunch, Churchill gamely suggested that Roosevelt read it to Stalin, and he did. With grim delight, Stalin responded that the Red Army would show the gratitude of Russia by a full-scale matching attack from the east.

That night Churchill's birthday dinner took place in the British legation. Churchill presided, with Roosevelt at his right, Josef Stalin at his left, and military leaders and foreign ministers ranged up and down the glittering table. All was conviviality and wassail, optimism and friendship. The sense of a great turn in history was strong. The toasts went round and round. It was Churchill's prerogative to give the last one, but Stalin surprised the gathering by requesting the privilege. These were his words:

"I want to tell you, from the Russian point of view, what the President and the United States have done to win the war. The most important things in this war are machines. The United States has proven that it can turn out from eight thousand to ten thousand airplanes per month. Russia can only turn out, at most, three thousand airplanes per month. England turns out three thousand to thirty-five hundred, which are principally heavy bombers.

"The United States, therefore, is a country of machines. Without these machines, through Lend-Lease, we would lose the war."

It was more than Stalin ever said publicly to his own people about the American contribution to the war until he died. He might have been expected, given the occasion, to compliment Churchill and the British; instead the old monster chose to praise America and Lend-Lease. He had never allowed Churchill to forget his enmity to Bolshevism; perhaps this was his oblique last thrust at the aging Tory.

There would be another day of political chaffering, leaving the sore issue of Poland uppermost and unresolved, but the Tehran Conference was over. All three leaders could go home in triumph. Stalin had his full-scale invasion of France, which was what he had been demanding since the day Germany had invaded his country. Put down though Churchill was, he could bring to the British people assurance of victory in the war they had all but lost; and if his Mediterranean plans had been subordinated to Overlord, he would fight on for them, and push some through.

The chief gain was Roosevelt's. He had a firm alliance against Germany at last, the exact Allied strategy he wanted, elimination of a separate peace, Stalin's pledge to attack Japan, and his commitment to join the United Nations: a clean sweep of objectives. Franklin Roosevelt bore himself at Tehran, the memoirs suggest, as though it were his finest hour. Perhaps it was.

Yet no human mind can peer very far into the coming time; less so, in the smoke of war. In the end, the United States would not need Russia's help in the Pacific, indeed would be embarrassed by it. But now the atomic bomb project was a limping question mark, and capturing one small atoll, Tarawa, had been a very bloody business. The war against Japan was expected to go on after Germany's fall for a year or more, ending in an invasion of the Tokyo plain that might cost a million casualties. Stalin's pledge seemed a godsend. As for the eventual dismal decline of the United Nations, who could foresee that? What was there to do but try?

For the Jews still alive in Europe's dreadful night, Tehran was also a dawn; but for them, too, a gloomy dawn. The Overlord assault could not traverse the stormy English Channel before the mild weather of May or June. Roosevelt jocosely observed to Stalin, in breaking this bad news, that the Channel was "a disagreeable body of water." Churchill interjected that the British people had reason to be glad it was so disagreeable. On this waggish byplay turned countless Jewish lives. By the time of Tehran the "territorial solution" was going full blast. Most of Europe's Jews were dead or en route to their deaths. Yet multitudes might yet be saved by the quick smashing of Nazi Germany.

Nobody talked at Tehran about the Jews, but among the high stakes of the conference was this race for the rescue of a remnant. Franklin Roosevelt had made sure that Hitlerism would not much longer darken the earth; but meantime the German murder machinery was working very fast.

What remains of the Tehran Conference, besides old words and old photographs, is the shape of the modern world. If you would see the monument of Tehran, look around. The quaint Persian city in which it took place has been engulfed by a roaring metropolis. The war leaders, having strutted and fretted their hour, are gone. Their work still turns history's wheels. The rest is for the tellers of tales.

• • •

A fat pale Army doctor, moving along the double row of beds, came upon Pug Henry sitting up in a khaki hospital gown. "How are you?" the doctor wearily said. He was himself a newcomer, and had a touch of some Persian ailment.

"Hungry. Can I order breakfast?"

"What have you in mind?"

"Ham and eggs and hashed brown potatoes. Maybe I should go over to the officers' mess."

The doctor sadly grinned, felt his pulse, and handed him a letter. "Will you settle for powdered eggs, dehydrated potatoes, and Spam?"

"Sounds great." Pug was eagerly tearing open the envelope, addressed in Pamela's mannish vertical hand. It was dated the previous day.

My love,

I am beside myself. They won't let me see you!

They tell me you're still too sick to come out to the visitors' room, and a female can't enter the ward. Blast, hell, damn! They say you don't have amoebas, malaria, or any of the other local horrors, so that's a relief, but I'll worry about you all the way back to New Delhi. *Please* go to the British legation before you leave, look for Lieutenant Shinglewood (a nice green-eyed girl) and tell her you're all right. She'll get word to me.

Duncan is abysmally disgusted with the way the conference has gone. He says it's the end of the Empire. I am hearing a lot of the *Bhagavad-Gita*.

Now *listen*, very quickly and no doubt very clumsily, here it is. I put on an idiotic show that other night in the garden. Possibly there was no "right" way to behave when you threw those questions about Rhoda at me. I reacted on pure instinct, squirting an ink cloud like an alarmed octopus. Why? Not sure. Solidarity of the sex, reluctance to stick a knife into a rival, whatever. Now I've thought it over. Matters are too serious for any of that. The happiness of several people may be at stake. Anyway, you obviously know something, possibly more than I do.

I *don't* know that Rhoda's done anything wrong. I *did* meet her with a Colonel Harrison Peters, and not once but several times. Their relationship may be innocent. In fact I would venture from her demeanor that it is. However, I don't think it's trivial. You had better get back to Washington by hook or by crook, and have it out with her.

Meantime, my love, I *cannot* sit on the sidelines holding my breath for news. I am in very deep with Duncan. We'll probably be married before you and I see each other or even communicate again. I confess this tenuous but iron tie between us is beyond me. It's like a fairy-tale thread that giants cannot break. But there's nothing we can do about it, except to be glad that we've known such painful and exquisite magic.

Write me when you settle something, anyway. With all my heart I urge you to give Rhoda the benefit of every doubt. She's a remarkable woman, she gave you stunning sons, and she's had a terrible time. I'll always love you, always want to hear from you, always wish you well. We've lived five days now this year, haven't we? So many people never live a day from the cradle to the grave.

> I love you.
> Pamela

Pug was downing the breakfast, thinking that Spam was a grossly maligned delicacy — especially with powdered eggs, another underrated treat — when the doctor looked into the ward and said that he had a visitor. Pug walked out as fast as he could on shaky legs, the hospital bathrobe flapping. On a cheap settee in the deserted outer room, Harry Hopkins sat. He raised a tired hand. "Hi. We're flying off to Cairo in half an hour. The President asked me to see how you are."

"That's incredibly thoughtful of him. I'm better."

"Pug, your Lend-Lease memo was a dandy. He wants you to know that. He didn't use it, but I did. Molotov started to gripe to me about Lend-Lease at a foreign ministers' meeting. I socked him with your facts, and not only did I shut him up, but he apologized and said the bottlenecks would be eliminated fast. When I told the President he laughed like anything. Said it made his day. Now, you haven't talked to Pat Hurley, have you?"

"No, sir. I've been pretty much out of things."

"Well, that idea for a new agreement on troop withdrawals has worked out. The Iranians asked for a statement of intent from the three occupying powers, and that was all the President needed. He got an okay from Stalin, and Hurley rushed hither and yon getting the thing drafted and signed. It's called 'The Declaration of Iran.' The Shah signed at midnight."

"Mr. Hopkins, what about the landing craft situation?"

"That's shot up in importance and urgency at this conference." Hopkins gave him an acute questioning glance. "It'll be top priority next year. Why?"

"That's what I'd like to do next."

"That, rather than command a battleship?" The long lean sickly face expressed lively skepticism. "You, Pug? You're up for a command, I know that."

"Well, for narrow personal reasons, Mr. Hopkins, yes. I'd like to spend some time with my wife."

Hopkins stuck out a bony hand. "Come back by fastest transportation."

The first situation ever brought before the United Nations, in April 1946, was a complaint by Iran that the Soviet Union, unlike America and Great Britain, had failed to withdraw its troops in accordance with the Tehran agreement, and was trying to set up a puppet communist republic in the north. President Harry Truman forcibly backed up Iran. The Russians, with considerable snarling, finally got out. The puppet republic collapsed. Iran recovered its territory. During that crisis, Victor Henry wondered whether a few words at a Persian dinner table might have been his chief contribution to the war. He could never know.

76

SOME twenty seedy men wearing yellow stars sit around a long table in the Magdeburg barracks, Aaron Jastrow among them, awaiting their first meeting with the new commander of Theresienstadt. After several days of driving around in gray February gloom and slush, making a thorough inspection of the ghetto, the new man has summoned the Council of Elders. The Board of Three heading the table — Eppstein and his two deputies — are not saying much, but their faces are long.

The newcomer, SS Sturmbannführer Karl Rahm, is not unknown here. For years he ran the Registry for Jewish Property, in the Central Office for Jewish Affairs of nearby Prague. The registry is the official German government office for despoiling Jews. Most European capitals have such agencies, patterned after Eichmann's pioneer bureau in Vienna, and men like Rahm manage them. By reputation he is a run-of-the-mill Nazi, an Austrian, with a dangerous way of exploding on small provocation; but his manners are reputed a bit less coarse and cold than Burger's.

These Elders, the sham government of Theresienstadt, are worried about the change of commanders. Burger was a devil they were used to. The ghetto was functioning under him on a wretched but stabilized basis. There have been no transports for many weeks. What will the unknown devil bring? That is the question written on the faces around the table.

Major Rahm enters the room with the camp inspector, Haindl. The Elders rise.

Only the black dress uniform with silver flashes and buttons, Jastrow thinks, gives this very common-looking fellow Rahm any presence. One saw such types by the thousands in the old days, jowly thirtyish blonds with bulging stomachs and haunches, strolling on the boulevards of Munich or Vienna. But Scharführer Haindl looks as evil as he is: a real plug-ugly. This Austrian inspector with the cigarette obsession is a feared and loathed man. He will jump through barracks windows to catch Jews smoking; spy on field gangs with binoculars; pop into hospitals, cabarets, even latrines. For possessing a single cigarette he will beat a victim half to death, or send him or her off to the Little Fortress to be tortured. Nevertheless people smoke voraciously in Theresienstadt; cigarettes rate just below gold and jewelry as currency; but a very sharp watch is kept for Haindl. Today he has a mild look, and his gray-green uniform is less sloppy than usual.

Major Rahm tells the Elders to sit down. From the head of the table he addresses them, feet apart, black swagger stick clutched behind him. His opening words are an amazement. He means to make Theresienstadt the Paradise Ghetto in fact as well as in name. The Elders know the town. They know their departments. It is up to them to give him ideas. Present conditions are disgraceful. Theresienstadt is run-down. He is not going to tolerate it. He is initiating a great beautification (*eine grosse Verschönerungsaktion*).

Jastrow is struck by this Eichmann phrase. Rahm's entire speech echoes what Eichmann said two months ago. Under Burger too there was talk about "beautification," but the idea was so preposterous, and Burger himself seemed so uninterested, that the Elders took it as just one more mendacious German façade of words; and the Board of Three gave only desultory orders for cleaning up the streets and painting some huts and barracks.

Rahm is talking a different language. "The Great Beautification" is going to be his prime concern. He has issued important orders. The old Sokol hall will be rebuilt at once as a community center, with studios, lecture halls, and an opera house and theatre with fully equipped stages. All Theresienstadt's other auditoriums and meeting halls will be smartened up. The cabarets will be enlarged and newly decorated. More orchestras will be created. Operas, ballets, concerts, and plays will be scheduled, also various amusements and art exhibits. Materials for costumes, settings, paintings, and so forth will be provided. The hospitals are going to be spic-and-span. A children's playground will be built. A beautiful park will be laid out for the old folks' leisure.

As Jastrow listens to this astonishing harangue, wondering whether it can be serious, the catch in the whole business becomes clear. Rahm is not mentioning any of the things that really make Theresienstadt a hell instead of a paradise: the starvation diet, the hideous overcrowding, the lack of warm clothes, of heat, of latrines, of care centers for mental cases and for the old and crippled, all generating the terrible death rate. Of these things, not a word. He is proposing to paint a corpse.

Jastrow has long suspected that Eichmann made him a figurehead Elder, and possibly even sent him to Theresienstadt, in anticipation of a visit from the Vatican or the neutral Red Cross. Something like that must be in the wind now. Even so, Rahm's approach seems simpleminded. No matter how laboriously he renovates the buildings and grounds, how can he conceal the overwhelming squalor, the crowding, the sickly faces, the malnutrition, the death rate? A little more food, some attention to health, would quickly and easily create a sunburst of happiness in the ghetto that would fool anybody. But the concept of treating the Jews themselves any better, even to create a brief useful illusion, seems beyond the Germans.

Rahm finishes up and asks for suggestions. Around the table eyes shift in gray faces. Nobody speaks. The so-called Elders — in actuality department heads of varying ages — are a mixed lot: some decent, some corrupt, some narrowly self-seeking, some humane. But all hug their posts. Private living quarters, exemption from transport, the chance to give and receive favors, outweigh the tension and guilt of being SS tools. None will risk opening his mouth first, and the silence grows nasty. Outside, a gray sky; inside a gray silence, and the ever-prevailing Theresienstadt smell of dirty bodies. Faintly from afar one can hear "The Beautiful Blue Danube"; the town orchestra is starting the morning concert, off behind the fence in the main square.

Jastrow's department does not deal in the vital things Rahm has ignored. He will do nothing that might hurt Natalie and her child, but for himself, since the encounter with Eichmann, he is strangely unafraid. The American in him still finds this European nightmare in which he is caught disgusting and ludicrous; and the miasma of fear all around him, pathetic. For the barking fat-faced mediocrity in the stagy black uniform he feels chiefly contempt, modified by caution.

He raises his hand. Rahm nods. He stands up and salutes. "*Herr Kommandant,* I am the stinking Jew, Jastrow — "

Rahm interrupts, pointing a thick finger at him. "Now then! That kind of shit will cease at once." He turns to Haindl, who is smoking a cigar in an armchair. "New regulations! No more idiotic saluting and removing of caps. No more 'stinking Jew' talk. Theresienstadt is not a concentration camp. It is a comfortable and happy residential town."

Haindl's malevolent face twists in surprise. "*Jawohl, Herr Kommandant.*"

Surprise, too, on all the Elders' countenances. Hitherto, failure to pull off one's head-covering and to salute in a German's presence has been a major ghetto offense, punishable by instant clubbing. Sounding off as a "stinking Jew" has been mandatory. The reflexes will take much unlearning.

"I beg leave to mention," Jastrow goes on, "that in my department the music section badly needs paper."

"Paper?" Rahm's face wrinkles up. "What kind of paper?"

"Any kind, *mein Kommandant.*" Jastrow is speaking the truth. Scraps of wallpaper, even of linen, are being used to note down music. It is a small harmless item, worth a try. "The musicians will rule it themselves. Though of course, ruled musical score paper would be best."

"Ruled musical score paper." Rahm repeats this as though it were a foreign language. "How much?"

Jastrow's deputy, a cadaverous orchestra leader from Vienna, whispers from the seat beside him.

"*Mein Kommandant,*" says Jastrow, "for the kind of great cultural expansion you are planning, five hundred sheets to start with."

"See to it!" Rahm says to Haindl. "And I thank you, sir. Gentlemen, that is the kind of idea I want. What else?"

One by one the other Elders now timidly rise with innocuous requests, which Rahm receives warmly. The atmosphere improves. On cue, the day brightens outside and the sun shines into the room. Jastrow rises again. May the music section also request more musical instruments, of better quality? Rahm laughs. By all means! The Central Registry in Prague has two big warehouses stuffed with musical instruments: violins, cellos, flutes, clarinets, guitars, pianos, the lot! No problem at all; just put in a list.

Not one Elder mentions food, medicine, or living space. Jastrow feels capable of bringing up these things, but what good could come of it? He would quench the sunny moment, bring trouble on himself, and accomplish nothing. Not his department.

When Rahm and Haindl leave, Eppstein rises. On his face the fixed obsequious smile fades. There is one more thing, he announces. The new commander has found the overcrowding of the town most unhealthy and unsightly, so five thousand Jews must at once be transported.

In an ordinary town of fifty thousand, struck by a tornado that wiped out five thousand inhabitants, the people might feel somewhat as the Jews do at a transport.

There is no getting used to this intermittent scourge. Each time the fabric of the ghetto is torn apart. Optimism and faith dim. The sense of doom rises again. Though nobody is sure what "the east" really means, it is a name of terror. The unlucky ones move around in shock, making their farewells, giving away what meager belongings they cannot pack into one suitcase. The Central Secretariat is besieged by frantic petitioners pulling every string and trying every loophole to get exemptions. But an iron proscenium of number frames the tragedy: *five thousand*. Five thousand Jews must get on the train. If one is exempted, another must take his place. If fifty are excused, fifty who thought themselves safe must be struck as by lightning with gray summons cards.

The Jews who run the Transport Section are a sad harried lot. They are their brothers' keepers, saviors, and executioners. It is a ghetto joke that in the end Theresienstadt will shrink to the commander and the Transport Section. Everybody smiles on them; but they know they are cursed and despised. They have life-and-death power they never wanted. They are Sonderkommando clerks, disposing of Jews' living bodies with pens and rubber stamps.

Are they to blame? Many desperate Jews stand ready to seize their places. Some of these transport bureaucrats belong to the communist or Zionist undergrounds, spending their nights in vain plots for uprisings. Some never think of anything but their own skins. A few brave ones try to correct the worst hardships. Some wretched ones show favoritism, take bribes, satisfy grudges.

In this spectrum of human nature blasted by German cruelty, what man can say where he would have fit? What man who was not there can judge the *Judenräte*, the Central Secretariats, and the Transport Sections? *"God pardons the coerced,"* says an ancient Jewish proverb, distilled from bitter millennia.

A parody of German thoroughness, the Central Secretariat reaches everywhere with its gray summons cards. In half a dozen different catalogue systems, Jews are indexed and cross-indexed by other Jews. Wherever a body can lie down for the night, that space is catalogued, with the name of the body occupying it. Each day a roll call of the town is taken. The dead and the transported are neatly crossed off the cards. Newcomers upon arrival are indexed as they are robbed. One can get out of the card catalogues only by dying or "going east."

The real power in Theresienstadt under the SS is not Eppstein, or the Board of Three, or the Council of Elders; it is the Central Secretariat. Yet the Secretariat is nobody you can talk to. It is friends, neighbors, relatives, or just other Jews. It is a Bureau, bureaucratically carrying out the orders of the Germans. The Complaint Section of the Secretariat, a row of sour Jewish faces behind desks, is an impotent mockery; but it provides a lot of jobs. The Secretariat is monstrously overstaffed because it has been a refuge. Yet this time the gray cards strike even inside the Secretariat. The monster is starting to eat its own bowels.

The strangest thing is that a few people actually apply to go in each transport. In a previous shipment their spouses, parents, or children have gone. They are lonesome. Theresienstadt is not such a bed of roses that they should want to stay on at all costs. So they will brave the unknown, hoping to find their loved ones in the east. Some have received letters and postcards, so they know that those they seek are at least still alive. Even from the mica factory, the most reliable refuge in Theresienstadt, several women have volunteered and gone east. That is one request about which the Germans are invariably gracious.

When Natalie meets Udam outside the children's home after work he stuns her by showing her his gray card. He has already been to the Secretariat. He knows Eppstein's two deputies. The head of the transport section is an old Zionist pal from Prague. The bank manager has intervened. Nothing helps. Perhaps the SS got irked by his performances. Anyway, it is all finished. Tonight they give their last show. At six in the morning he must collect his daughter and go to the depot.

Her first reaction is cold fright. She too has been performing; has a gray card come to her apartment during the day? Seeing the look on her face, Udam tells her he has inquired, and there is no summons for her. She and Jastrow have the highest exempt classification. If nobody else is here when "the cousins arrive from the east and the west," they will be. He has some new topical jokes for Frost-Cuckoo Land, and they may as well rehearse, and make this last show a good one.

She lays a hand on his arm as he starts inside, and suggests that they call it off. Jastrow's audience will be small and in no mood to laugh. Maybe nobody will come. Aaron's lecture subject, "Heroes of the *Iliad*," is heavily academic, and hardly inspiring or cheering. Aaron requested the puppet show because he has never seen it, but Natalie suspects that professorial vanity dies hard, and that he really wants to draw an audience. It is his first lecture since he became an Elder, and he must know that he is unpopular.

Udam won't hear of cancelling. Why waste good jokes? They go in to the children. Louis greets her with the usual wild joy, in the great moment of his day. During their meal, Udam talks optimistically about "the east." How much worse can it be, after all, than Theresienstadt? His wife's postcards, coming about once a month, have been short but reassuring. He shows Natalie the last card, dated only two weeks ago.

Birkenau, Camp II-B

My dearest

    Everything is all right. I hope Martha is well. I miss you both. Much snow here.

Love,
Hilda

"Birkenau?" Natalie asks. "Where is that?"

"Poland, outside Oswiecim. It's just a village. The Jews work in big German factories around there, and get plenty of food."

Udam's tone does not match his words. Natalie passed through Oswiecim with Byron years ago, on the way to the wedding of Berel's son in Medzice. She barely remembers it as a flat dull railroad town. There is remarkably little talk in the ghetto about "the east," the camps there, and what happens there; like death, like cancer, like the executions in the Little Fortress, these are shunned topics. Nevertheless, the word *"Oswiecim"* vibrates with horror. Natalie does not press Udam. She does not want to hear any more.

They rehearse in the basement, while Louis romps with the playmate he will not see after tonight. Udam's new jokes are pallid, except for the touch about the Persian slave girl. The Frost-Cuckoo minister has brought her for the king's pleasure. She comes in, a veiled waggling female puppet. Natalie puts on a husky sexy voice for the billing and cooing she does with the amorous king. He asks her name. She is coy and reluctant. He teases it out of her. "Well, I'm named after my home town." "And that is?" She giggles. "Tee-hee. Tehran." The king shrieks, the icicles fall off his nose — a standard trick Natalie has worked up — and he chases her off the stage with a club. That will go well. Reports of the Tehran Conference have much cheered the ghetto.

Afterward Natalie hurries back to the new apartment, still fearing a gray card may be there. Who was safer than Udam? Who had more inside contacts? Who could have felt more protected? But she sees at once on Aaron's face that there is no gray card; though he says nothing, merely looking up and nodding, at the quite decent desk where he is marking his lecture notes.

The luxury of these two rooms and a bath still makes Natalie uneasy. Ever since Jastrow reversed himself and accepted the post and privileges of an Elder, there has been a coldness between them. She saw Eichmann accept his refusal. He has never explained why he changed his mind. Did his old selfish love of comfort overcome him? Being an SS tool does not seem to trouble him at all. The religiosity is the only change. He puts on phylacteries, spends a lot of time over the Talmud, and has withdrawn into a quiet frail placidity; perhaps, she thinks, to shut out her disapproval, or his own self-contempt.

Jastrow knows what she thinks. He can do nothing about it. The explanation would be too terrifying. Natalie already lives on the brink of panic; she is young, and she has the baby. Since his illness he is reconciled to dying when he must. Let her go about her business, he had decided, not knowing the worst. If the SS chooses to pounce, her scurrilous performances have already condemned her. It is now a race against time. His aim is to last, until rescue comes from the east and the west.

She tells him about Udam, and without much hope asks him to intercede. He replies drily that he has very little influence; that it is a bad business to venture prestige and position on a request likely to be refused. They hardly talk again until they set out together for the barracks where Aaron is to lecture in the loft.

A large silent audience has gathered, after all. Usually there is lively chatter before the evening's diversion. Not tonight. They have turned out in surprising numbers, but the mood is funereal. Behind the crude lectern, off to a side, stands the curtained puppet theatre. As Natalie takes the vacant seat beside Udam, he gives her a little smile that cuts her heart.

Aaron places his notes on the lectern and looks about, stroking his beard. Softly, in a dry classroom manner, speaking slow formal German, he begins.

"It is interesting that Shakespeare seems to find the whole story of the *Iliad* contemptible. He retells it in his play, *Troilus and Cressida,* and he puts his opinion in the mouth of Thersites, the cynical coward — *'The matter is only a cuckold and a whore.'* "

This quotation Aaron Jastrow cites in English, then with a prudish little smile translates it into German.

"Now Falstaff, that other and more celebrated Shakespearean coward, thinks like Emerson that war in general is nothing but a periodic madness. *'Who hath honor? He that died o' Wednesday.'* We suspect that Shakespeare agreed with his immortal fat man. *Troilus*, his play of the Trojan war, is not in his best tragic vein, for madness is not tragic. Madness is either funny or ghastly, and so is much war literature: either *The Good Soldier Schweik*, or *All Quiet on the Western Front*.

"But the *Iliad* is epic tragedy. It is the same war story as *Troilus*, but with one crucial difference. Shakespeare has taken out the gods, whereas it is the gods who make the *Iliad* grand and terrible.

"For Homer's Hector and Achilles are caught in a squabble of the Greek deities. The gods take sides. They come down into the dust of the battlefield to intervene. They turn aside weapons hurled straight to kill. They appear in disguises to make trouble or to pull their favorites out of jams. An honorable contest of arms becomes a mockery, a game of wits among supernatural, invisible magicians. The fighting men are mere helpless pieces of the game."

Natalie glances over her shoulder at the listeners. No audiences like these! Famished for diversion, for light, for a shred of consolation, they hang on a literary talk in Theresienstadt, as elsewhere people do on a great concert artist's recital, or on a gripping film.

In the same level pedantic way, Jastrow reviews the background of the *Iliad:* Paris's awarding of the golden apple for beauty to Aphrodite; the hostilities on Olympus that ensue; the kidnapping by Paris of Helen, the world's prettiest woman, Aphrodite's promised reward; and the inevitable war, since she is a married Greek queen and he a Trojan prince. Splendid men on both sides, who care nothing for the cuckold, the whore, or the kidnapper, become embroiled. For them, once it is war, honor is at stake.

"But in this squalid quarrel, what gives the heroes of the *Iliad* their grandeur? Is it not their indomitable will to fight, despite the shifting and capricious meddling of the gods? To venture their lives for honor, in an unfair and unfathomable situation where bad and stupid men triumph, good and skilled men fall, and strange accidents divert and decide battles? In a purposeless, unfair, absurd battle, to fight on, fight to the death, fight like men? It is the oldest of human problems, the problem of senseless evil, dramatized on the field of battle. That is the tragedy Homer perceived and Shakespeare passed over."

Jastrow pauses, turns a page, and looks straight at the audience, his emaciated face dead pale, his eyes large in the sunken sockets. If the audience has been silent before, it is now as quiet as so many corpses.

"The universe of the *Iliad*, in short, is a childish and despicable trap. The glory of Hector is that in such a trap he behaves so nobly that an Almighty God, if He did exist, would weep with pride and pity. Pride, that He has created out of a handful of dirt a being so grand. Pity, that in His botched universe a Hector must unjustly die, and his poor corpse be dragged in the dust. But Homer knows no Almighty God. There is Zeus, the father of the gods, but who can say what he is up to? Perhaps he is off mounting some bemused mortal girl in the disguise of her husband, or a bull, or a swan. Small wonder that Greek mythology is extinct."

The disgusted gesture with which Jastrow turns his page surprises an uncertain laugh from the rapt audience. Thrusting his notes into his pocket, Jastrow leaves the lectern, comes forward, and stares at his listeners. His usually placid face is working. He bursts out in another voice, startling Natalie by shifting to Yiddish, in which he has never lectured before.

"All right. Now let us talk about this in our mother-language. And let us talk about an epic of our own. Satan says to God, you remember, 'Naturally, Job is upright. Seven sons, three daughters, the wealthiest man in the land of Uz. Why not be upright? Look how it pays. A sensible universe! A fine arrangement! Job is not upright, he is just a smart Jew. The sinners are damned fools. But just take away his rewards, and see how upright he will remain!'

" 'All right, take them away,' God says. And in one day marauders carry off Job's wealth, and a hurricane kills all his ten children. What does Job do? He goes into mourning. 'Naked I came from the womb, naked I will return,' he says, 'God has given, God has taken away. Blessed be God's name.'

"So God challenges Satan. 'See? He remained upright. A good man.'

" 'Skin for skin,' Satan answers. 'All a man really cares about is his life. Reduce him to a skeleton — a sick, plundered, bereaved skeleton, nothing left to this proud Jew but his own rotting skin and bones —' "

Jastrow loses his voice. He shakes his head, clears his throat, passes a hand over his eyes. He goes on hoarsely. "God says, 'All right, do anything to him except kill him.' A horrible sickness strikes Job. Too loathsome an object to stay under his own roof, he crawls out and sits on an ash heap, scraping his sores with a shard. He says nothing. Stripped of his wealth, his children senselessly killed, his body a horrible stinking skeleton covered with boils, he is silent. Three of his pious friends come to comfort him. A debate follows.

"Oh, my friends, what a debate! What rugged poetry, what insight into the human condition! I say to you that Homer pales before Job; that Aeschylus meets his match in power, and his master in understanding; that Dante and Milton sit at this author's feet without ever grasping him. Who was he? Nobody knows. Some old Jew. He knew what life is, that's all. He knew it as we in Theresienstadt know it."

He pauses, looking straight at his niece with sad eyes. Shaken, perplexed, on the verge of tears, Natalie is hungry for his next words. When he speaks, though he looks away, she feels he is talking to her.

"In Job, as in most great works of art, the main design is very simple. His comforters maintain that since one Almighty God rules the universe, it must make sense. Therefore Job must have sinned. Let him search his deeds, confess and repent. The missing piece is only what his offense was.

"And in round after round of soaring argument, Job fights back. The missing piece must be with God, not with him. He is as religious as they are. He knows that the Almighty exists, that the universe must make sense. But he, poor bereft boil-covered skeleton, knows now that it does not in fact always make sense; that there is no guarantee of good fortune for good behavior; that crazy injustice is part of the visible world, and of this life. His religion demands that he assert his innocence, *otherwise he will be profaning God's name!* He will be conceding that the Almighty can botch one man's life; and if God can do that, the whole universe is a botch, and He is not an Almighty God. That Job will never concede. He wants an answer.

"He gets an answer! Oh, what an answer! An answer that answers nothing. God Himself speaks at last out of a roaring storm. *"Who are you to call me to account? Can you hope to understand why or how I do anything? Were you there at the Creation? Can you comprehend the marvels of the stars, the animals, the infinite wonders of existence? You, a worm that lives a few moments, and dies?'*

"My friends, Job has won! Do you understand? God with all His roaring has *conceded Job's main point, that the missing piece is with Him!* God claims only that His reason is beyond Job. That, Job is perfectly willing to admit. With the main point settled, Job humbles himself, is more than satisfied, falls on his face.

"So the drama ends. God rebukes the comforters for speaking falsely of Him, and praises Job for holding to the truth. He restores Job's wealth. Job has seven more sons and three more daughters. He lives a hundred and forty more years, sees grandchildren and great-grandchildren, and dies old, prosperous, revered."

The rich flow of literary Yiddish halts. Jastrow goes back to the lectern, pulls the notes from his pocket, and turns over several sheets. He peers out at the audience.

"Satisfied? A happy ending, yes? Much more Jewish than the absurd and tragic *Iliad?*

"Are you so sure? My dear Jewish friends, what about the ten children who died? Where was God's justice to them? And what about the father, the mother? Can those scars on Job's heart heal, even in a hundred and forty years?

"That is not the worst of it. Think! What was the missing piece that was too much for Job to understand? *We* understand it, and are we so very clever? Satan simply sneered God into ordering the senseless ordeal. No wonder God roars out of a storm to silence Job! Isn't He ashamed of Himself before His own creature? Hasn't Job behaved better than God?"

Jastrow shrugs, spreads his hands, and his face relaxes in a wistful little smile that makes Natalie think of Charlie Chaplin.

"But I am expounding the *Iliad.* In the *Iliad,* unseen powers are at odds with each other, and that brings about a visible world of senseless evil. Not so in Job. Satan has no power at all. He is not the Christian Satan, not Dante's colossal monster, not Milton's proud rebel, not in the least. He needs God's permission to make every move.

"Then who is Satan, and why does God leave him out of the answer from the storm? The word *satan* in Hebrew means *adversary.* What is the book telling us? Was God arguing with Himself? Was He asking Himself whether there was any purpose in the vast creation? And in reply pointing, not to the dead glittering galaxies that sprawl over thousands of light-years, but to man, the handful of dirt that can sense His presence, do His will, and measure those galaxies? Above all to the upright man, the speck of dirt who can measure himself against the Creator Himself, for dignity and goodness? What else did the ordeal establish?

"The heroes in the *Iliad* rise superior to the squabbling injustice of weak and contemptible gods.

"The hero in Job holds to the truth of One Almighty God through the most senseless and horrible injustice; forcing God at last to measure up to Himself, to acknowledge that injustice is on His side, to repair the damage as best He can.

"In the *Iliad* there is no injustice to repair. In the end there is only blind fate.

"In Job God must answer for everything, good and bad, that happens. Job is the Bible's only hero. There are fighting men, patriarchs, lawgivers, prophets, in the other books. This is the one man who rises to the measure of the universe, to the stature of the God of Israel, while sitting on an ash heap; Job, a poor skeletal broken beggar.

"Who is Job?

"Nobody. '*Job was never born and never existed,*' says the Talmud. '*He was a parable.*'

"Parable of what truth?

"All right, we have come to it now. Who is it in history who will never admit that there is no God, never admit that the universe makes no sense? Who is it who suffers ordeal after ordeal, plundering after plundering, massacre after massacre, century after century, yet looks up at the sky, sometimes with dying eyes, and cries, 'The Lord our God, the Lord is One'?

"Who is it who in the end of days will force from God the answer from the storm? Who will see the false comforters rebuked, the old glory restored, and generations of happy children and grandchildren to the fourth generation? Who until then will leave the missing piece to God, and praise His Name, crying, 'The Lord has given, the Lord has taken away, blessed be the Name of the Lord'? Not the noble Greek of the *Iliad*, he is extinct. No! Nobody but the sick, plundered skeleton on the ash heap. Nobody but the beloved of God, the worm that lives a few moments and dies, the handful of dirt that has justified Creation. Nobody but Job. He is the only answer, if there is one, to the adversary challenge to an Almighty God, if there is One. Job, the stinking Jew."

Jastrow stares in a stunned way at the still audience, then stumbles toward the first row. Udam jumps up and gently helps him to his seat. The audience does not applaud, does not talk, does not move.

Udam begins to sing.

Udam . . . udam . . . udam . . .

So there will be no puppet show. Natalie joins in the chorusing of the tragic refrain. Udam sings his song for the last time in Theresienstadt, driving it to a heartrending crescendo.

When it ends, there is no reaction. No applause, no talk, nothing. This silent audience is waiting for something.

Udam does something he has never before done; an encore; an encore to no applause. He starts another song, one Natalie has heard in Zionist meetings. It is an old simple syncopated refrain, in a minor key, built on a line from the liturgy: *"Let the temple be rebuilt, soon in our time, and grant us a portion in Your law."* As he sings it, Udam slowly begins to dance.

> *Sheh-yi-boneh bet-hamikdash*
> *Bim-hera b'yomenu —*

He dances as an old rabbi might on a holy day, deliberately, awkwardly, his arms raised, his face turned upward, his eyes closed, his fingers snapping the rhythm. The people softly accompany him, singing and clapping their hands. One by one they rise to their feet. Udam's voice grows more powerful, his steps more vigorous. He is losing himself in the dance and the song, drifting into an ecstasy terrible and beautiful to see. Barely opening his eyes, twisting and swaying, he moves toward Aaron Jastrow, and holds out a hand. Jastrow gets to his feet, links his hand with Udam's, and the two men dance and sing.

It is a death dance. Natalie knows it. Everybody knows it. The sight both freezes and exalts her. It is the most stirring moment of her life, here in this dark malodorous loft in a prison ghetto. She is overwhelmed with the agony of her predicament, and the exaltation of being Jewish.

> *Oy let the temple be rebuilt*
> *Oy speedily in our time*
> *Oy and grant us a portion in Your law!*

When the dance ends, the audience starts to leave. Everybody slowly goes from the loft, as if from a burial. There is almost no talking. Udam folds up the puppet theatre, and gives Natalie one kiss in farewell.

"I did not think they wanted my jokes," he says. "I'll put this back in the children's home. Keep up your shows for the children. Good-bye."

"Tehran was a good joke," she says, through a choked throat.

Aaron leans heavily on her as they go down the stairs and into the shadowy street. Amid the dispersing crowd, a burly man sidles up to them, and says in Yiddish, *"Gut gezugt, Arele, und gut getantzed."* ("Well said, little Aaron, and well danced.") "Natalie, *sholem aleichem.*"

In the gloom she sees a square tough elderly smooth-shaven face, a total stranger.

"Who are you?" she asks.

Aaron Jastrow, who has not seen him in fifty years, says, "Berel?"

77

Pamela, my love —

Here I am in a place you never heard of, doing what I've been doing ever since I returned to the States — namely, persuading various obtuse or confused sons of bitches to do things they ought to be doing anyway, if this country's to get the landing craft it urgently needs.

This is my first chance to write you, because Rhoda and I didn't get down to cases until recently. I've been on the run since I got back. Besides, Rhoda has a sort of genius for keeping her mouth shut when in doubt or in trouble; and as you know, I'm not a ready talker about such things.

Brigadier General Old came to Washington from New Delhi last week, to blast loose more transport planes for Burma. He has great regard for Burne-Wilke, and rather likes you, too. To my immense relief he called you Pamela Tudsbury, not Lady Burne-Wilke. Hence, all that follows. Rhoda's supposed to telephone me tonight or tomorrow about her situation with Peters. Then I can spell it all out for you. Meantime, my other news — quite a lot since Tehran:

To begin with, I'm now the Deputy Chief, Production Branch, Office of Procurement and Materials; and collaterally, Material and Products Control Officer; that is, another anonymous man in uniform running around Washington's corridors. My task boils down to industrial liaison and troubleshooting.

I came into this business late, with the landing craft program well along. So I'm the outsider, the roving player, with no bureaucratic position to build up or protect; SecNav's professional alter ego, you might say, watching for problems, cutting across agency lines, forestalling major delays. When I do my job right, there's no sign of it; disasters just fail to occur.

Our industrial mobilization has become an absolute marvel, Pam. We've sprung to life, turning out weapons of war, ships, planes, internal combustion engines in quantities that add up to the eighth wonder of the world. But it's all been improvised; new people in new factories doing new jobs. Tempers are short, pressure is terrific, and everybody's competitive and tight-nerved as hell. When priorities clash, whole agencies harden into battle posture. Big shots get their dander up and memos start flying.

Well, I know a good deal about landing craft, as an engineer and as a war planner, and about available factories and materials. Serving on the main war boards I can usually spot developing trouble. The tough part is persuading hard-charging bosses to do as I say. As the secretary's man I have a lot of leverage. I seldom have to go to Hopkins, though I've done it on occasion. The Navy is going to come up with an amazing number of landing craft for Eisenhower, Pamela. Our civilian sector is unruly and spoiled, but ye gods, it turns out the stuff.

No doubt I'll stay in production until the war ends. I've fallen behind in the career race. My classmates will fight the remaining battles at sea. There's a lot of life left in the Japs, but I've passed up my last chance at the blue water. It doesn't matter. For every star performer in this war you need a dozen good backup men in industrial logistics, or you don't get your victories.

One A.M. and old Rhoda hasn't called. My plane to Houston leaves at the crack of dawn, so I'll break off. More tomorrow.

> 3 March
> Houston

Hi.

Wild rainstorm here. Wind whipping the palm trees outside my room, rain lashing the windows. Texas weather, like the inhabitants, tends to extremes. However, Texans are okay once they understand (a) that you're right, (b) that you mean business, and (c) that you have some negotiating strength. Haven't heard from Rhoda yet, but expect to tonight, for sure.

More news: Byron's passed through Washington, en route to his new duty post, exec of a submarine undergoing overhaul in Connecticut. He's come through some bad personal ordeals.

[*The letter narrates the death of Carter Aster, and the news about Natalie in Theresienstadt.*]

I've obtained the record of the court of inquiry about Aster's death. It was touch-and-go for Byron. He made a very poor witness for himself. He would not say that he *couldn't* have saved the captain by a delay in submerging. But the old chief of the boat wrapped the thing up in his testimony when he said: "Maybe Captain Aster was wrong and he could have survived, but he was right that the *Moray* couldn't have. He was the greatest submarine skipper of this war. He gave the right orders. Mr. Henry only obeyed them." That's what the court concluded. Forrestal is proposing a posthumous Congressional Medal of Honor for Aster. Byron may get a Bronze Star, but it won't help his spirits much.

Warren's widow came back around Christmastime, and Rhoda took her in. She's planning to go back to law school in the fall. She's a beautiful woman with a fine son and her whole life ahead of her. Usually she's very cheerful, but when Byron was with us she went into a deep depression. Byron looks more and more like Warren as he fills out. No doubt that got Janice down. A couple of times Rhoda came on her crying. Since he left she's been okay.

And what a kid that Vic is! Handsome, affectionate, and deep. He's very active and naughty, but in a stealthy way. His mischief is not impulsive but *planned*, like tactics, for maximum destruction and minimum detection. He'll go far.

Madeline finally dropped that grinning, pot-bellied, oleaginous radio mountebank I told you about, relieving me of the need to horsewhip him, which I was working up to. She's living at home, working in a Washington radio station, and she's taken up again with an old admirer, Simon Anderson, a first-rate naval officer who's on duty here in new weaponry. Last week she had a long tearful talk with Rhoda on whether, and what, she should tell Simon about the radio man. I asked Rhoda what her advice was. She gave me a funny look and said, "I told her, wait till he asks you." I would have advised Madeline to have it out with Sime, and start on an honest basis. No doubt that's why she consulted Rhoda.

There goes the telephone. It has to be my wife.

It was.

Okay. Now I can backtrack and tell you what happened last week. We were sitting around after dinner, the same day General Old let me know you were still unmarried. I said, "Rho, why don't we talk about Hack Peters?" She didn't turn a hair. "Yes, why not, dear? Better mix us a couple of stiff drinks." Rhoda-like, she waited until I asked her. But she was quite ready for this showdown.

She acknowledged the relationship, declared it's the real thing, not guilty but deep. I believe her. Colonel Peters has been an "irreproachable gentleman," thinks she's twenty times as good as she is, and in short looks on her as the perfection of womankind. Rhoda says that it's embarrassing to be so idolized, but also very sweet and rejuvenating. I asked her point-blank whether she'd be happier divorcing me and marrying Peters.

Rhoda took a very long time to answer that one. Finally she looked me in the eye and said, yes, she would. The main reason, she said, is that she's lost my good opinion and can't get it back, though I've been kind and forgiving. After being loved by me for years, it's wretched just to be tolerated. I asked her what she wanted me to do. She brought up that talk you had with her in California. I said that I had great affection for you, but since you were engaged, that was that. I told her to decide on her own best prospects for happiness, and that I would do whatever she wanted.

She apparently had been waiting for this sort of green light from me. Rhoda's always been a bit afraid of me. I don't know why, since it seems to me I've been rather henpecked. Anyway, she said that she'd need some time. Well, she didn't need much. That was what the phone call was about. Harrison Peters is dying to marry her. No question. She's landed him. She expects to talk to our lawyer, and then to Peters's lawyer, in the next couple of days. Peters also wants to talk to me "man to man" when I get back to Washington. I may forgo that delight.

Well, Pamela darling, so I'll be free, if by some miracle you'll still have me. Will you marry me?

I'm not a rich man — serving one's country one doesn't get rich — but we wouldn't be badly off. I've saved fifteen percent of my salary for thirty-one years. Working in BuShips and BuOrd I could observe industrial trends, so I've invested and done well. Rhoda's in fine shape, she's got a substantial family trust. Anyway, I'm sure Peters will take excellent care of her. Am I being too mundane? I'm not expert at proposing. This is only my second try.

If we do marry, I'll take an early retirement so that we can be together all the time. There are many jobs for me in industry; I could even work in England.

If we did have a kid or two, I'd want to give them a church upbringing. Is that all right? I know you're a freethinker. I can't make much sense out of life, myself, but none whatever without religion. Maybe in my fifties I'd make a hard-shelled mossy crab of a father; still, I get along pretty well with little Vic. I might in fact spoil kids now. I'd like the chance to try!

So there it is! If you're Lady Burne-Wilke by now, take my letter as a wistful farewell compliment to an unlikely and wonderful love. If I hadn't casually booked passage on the *Bremen* in 1939, mainly to brush up on my German, I'd never have known you. I was happy with Rhoda, in love with her, and not inclined to look further. Yet despite the differences in age, nationality, and background, despite the fact that over four years we've spent perhaps three weeks together in all, the simple truth is that you seem to be my other half, found when it was all but too late. The bare possibility of marrying you is a glimpse of beauty that stops my breath. Very likely Rhoda's been groping for that beauty outside our marriage, because it wasn't quite there; she's been a good wife (till she fell away) but a discontented one.

In the Persian garden you suggested that this whole thing might be a romantic illusion. I've given that a lot of thought. If we'd been snatching at our rare meetings to go to bed together, I might agree. But what have we ever done but talk, and yet feel this closeness? Marriage will not be, I grant you, like these tantalizing encounters in far-off places; there'll be shopping, laundry, housekeeping, the mortgage, mowing the lawn, arguments, packing and unpacking, headaches, sore throats, and all the rest. Well, with you, all that strikes me as a lovely prospect. I don't want anything else. If God gives me that much, I'll say — with everything that's gone wrong with my life, and all my scars — that I'm a happy man, and I'll try to make you happy.

I hope this letter doesn't come too late.

All my love,
Pug

The battle for Imphal was already on when Pug wrote. Since Burne-Wilke's headquarters was no longer in New Delhi but at the forward base at Comilla, the letter did not reach her until mid-April, after Burne-Wilke had disappeared in a flight over the jungle, and while a search was still on for him.

* * *

Luck figures not only in war, but in the writing of war journalism and history. Imphal was a British victory which lifted the cloud of Singapore; a classic showdown like El Alamein, fought out on worse terrain over a larger front. It was unique among modern battles, in that the RAF did at Imphal what the Luftwaffe failed to do at Stalingrad: it supplied a surrounded army by air for months until breakout and victory. But the Normandy invasion and the fall of Rome, with hordes of reporters and cameramen in attendance at both events, spanned the same block of time. So at Imphal, in a remote valley near the Himalayas, two hundred thousand men fought a long series of sanguinary engagements unnoticed by the newspapers. History continues to overlook Imphal. The dead of course do not care. The survivors with their faded recollections are passing from the scene unnoticed.

Imphal itself is a real-life Shangri-La, a cluster of native villages around golden-domed temples, on a fertile and beautiful plain in the northeast corner of vast India bordering Burma, ringed by formidable mountains. The freakish tides of world war brought the British and the Japanese to death-grips there. Ignominiously kicked out of Malaya and Burma by the Japanese in 1942, the British had one war aim in Southeast Asia, to retrieve their Empire. The conquering Japanese armies had halted at the great mountain ranges that separate Burma from India. The Americans, from Franklin Roosevelt down, had no interest in the British war aim, regarding it as backward-looking, unjust, and futile. Roosevelt had even told Stalin at Tehran that he wanted to see India free. But the Americans did want to clear a corridor through northern Burma to keep China supplied and fighting, and to set up bases on the China coast for bombing Japan.

The beautiful plain of Imphal was the key to such a supply corridor, a gateway among the mountain passes. The British had been building up here for counterattack, and perforce they accepted the American strategy. Their commanding general, a brilliant warrior named Slim, piled in a large army of mingled English and Asian divisions, with the mission of fighting through northern Burma to join hands with Chinese divisions driving south under the American General Stilwell, thus opening the supply corridor. At this, the Japanese too moved up north in force to confront Slim. His appetizing buildup offered a chance to destroy India's defenders with a counterstroke; and then perhaps to march in and set up a new puppet government of India under Subhas Chandra Bose, a red-hot Indian nationalist who had defected to Japan.

The Japanese attacked first, employing their old jungle-fighting tactics against the British: rapid thrusts far beyond supply lines with quick flanking encirclements, feeding and fueling their army from captured supply dumps as they advanced. But this time Slim and his field commander, Scoones, accepting battle on the Imphal plain, bloodily fought the Japanese to a standstill there, denying them their usual replenishment until they starved, wilted, and ran. This took over three months. The battle evolved into two epic sieges — of a small British force surrounded at a village called Kohima, and of Slim's main body at Imphal itself, invested by a seasoned and fierce Japanese jungle army.

Airlift tipped the balance of the sieges. The British consumed supplies more rapidly than the Japanese, whose soldiers could survive for a while on a bag of rice a day; but American transport planes daily flew in hundreds of tons of supplies, landing some at overburdened airfields, the crews kicking the rest out of open plane doors to parachute down. Burne-Wilke's tactical command protected the airlift, and harried the Japanese army with bombing and strafing.

· · ·

Upon investing Imphal, however, the Japanese overran several radar warning outposts, and for a while the air picture was not good. Burne-Wilke decided in a conference at Comilla to fly into Imphal to see things for himself. His Spitfire squadrons stationed on the plain were reporting that without adequate radar warning, maintaining control of the air was becoming a problem. He took a reconnaissance aircraft and flew off solo, ignoring Pamela's mutterings.

Burne-Wilke was a seasoned pilot, a World War I flyer and a career RAF man. The premature death of his older brother had made him a viscount, but he had stayed in the service. Too senior now to fly in combat, he seized chances to fly alone when he could. Mountbatten had already reprimanded him once for this. But he loved flying over the jungle without the distracting chatter of a co-pilot. It afforded him something like the calming peace of flight over water, this solid green earth cover passing underneath for hours, unbroken except by the rare brown crooked crawl of a river speckled with green islands. The bouncing curving ride through mountain passes amid thick-timbered peaks towering high above his wings, ending in a sudden view of the gardened valley and the gleaming gold domes of Imphal, with here and there on the broad plain a smoky plume of battle, gave him a dour delight that helped shake off his persisting fatalistic depression.

For to Duncan Burne-Wilke, Imphal was a battle straight out of the *Bhagavad-Gita*. He was not an old Asia hand, but as an educated British military man he knew the Far East. He thought American strategic ideas about China were pitifully ignorant; and the gigantic effort to open the north Burma corridor, into which they had pushed the British, a futile waste of lives and resources. In the long run, it would not matter much who won at Imphal. The Japanese, slowly weakening under the American Pacific assault, now lacked the punch to drive far into India. The Chinese under Chiang Kai-shek would not fight worth a damn; Chiang's concern was holding off the Chinese communists in the north. In any case, Gandhi's unruly nationalist movement would shove the British out of India, once the war was over. The handwriting was on the wall; so Burne-Wilke thought. Still, events had swirled into this vortex, and a man had to fight.

As usual, talking to the combatants on the spot proved worth it. Burne-Wilke gathered his pilots in the large bamboo canteen at Imphal, and asked for complaints, observations, and ideas. Out of the crowd of hundreds of young men came plenty of response, especially complaints.

"Air Marshal, we'll take the red ants and the black spiders, the heat rashes and the dysentery," spoke up one Cockney voice from the rear, "the short rations, the itches and the sweat, the cobras, and the rest of this jolly show. All we ask in return, sir, is enough petrol to fly a combat air patrol from dawn to dusk. Sir, is that askin' so bleedin' much?" This brought growls and applause, but Burne-Wilke had to say that Air Transport could not bring in that much fuel.

An idea surfaced, as the meeting went on, which the fliers had been discussing among themselves. The Japanese raiders came and went over the Imphal plain through two passes in the mountains. The notion was to scramble not after the raiders, but directly into patrol positions in the passes. Returning Jap pilots would either face the superior Spitfires in these narrow traps, or they would crash from engine failure or lack of fuel, trying to evade over the mountains. Burne-Wilke seized on the idea, and ordered it put into effect. He promised alleviation of other shortages, if not of fuel, and he flew off to cheers. On this return flight, he disappeared in a thunderstorm.

Pamela endured a bad week before word came from Imphal that some villagers had brought him in alive. It was during this week that Pug's letter arrived from New Delhi, in a batch of delayed personal mail. She was busier than usual, working for the deputy tactical commander. The disappearance of Burne-Wilke was preying on her mind. As his fiancée, she was the focus of all the concern and sympathy on the base. These pages typed on stationery of the Jeffersonville Plaza Motor Hotel seemed to come from another world. For Pamela, everyday reality was now Comilla, this hot mildewy Bengali town two hundred miles east of Calcutta, its walls stained and rotting from monsoons, its foliage almost as green and rank as the jungle, its main distinction a thick sprinkling of monuments to British officials murdered by Bengali terrorists, its army headquarters aswarm with Asian faces.

Jeffersonville, Indiana! What did it look like? What sort of people were there? The name was so like Victor Henry himself — square, American, obscure, unprepossessing, yet with the noble hint of "Jefferson" in it. Pug's marriage proposal, with its sober financial statement and brief clumsy words of love, both amused and dizzied Pamela. It was endearing, but she could not cope with it at this bad time, so she did not write an answer. When she thought about the letter, in the ensuing turbulence of Burne-Wilke's return, it seemed less and less real to her. At bottom, she could not believe that

Rhoda Henry would bring off this latest maneuver. And it was all happening so far, far away!

After a few days in the Imphal hospital, Burne-Wilke was flown to Comilla. His collarbone was broken, both ankles were fractured, and he was running a high fever. Worst of all, at least to look at, were his suppurating sores from leeches. He ruefully told Pamela that he had done this to himself, tearing the leeches off his body and leaving the heads under his skin. He knew better, but he had regained consciousness in a swamp with his uniform almost torn off, and black fat leeches clustering on him. In dazed horror he had begun plucking at them, before remembering the rule to let them drink their fill and drop off. The plane had spun in, he said, but he had managed to level off at the tree tops for a stalling crash. Coming to, he had hacked through the jungle to a riverbed, and stumbled along it for two days until the villagers came on him.

"I was rather lucky, actually," he said to Pamela. He lay in a hospital bed, swathed in bandages, his wanly smiling face puffed and hideously discolored by the leech sores. "One's told the Nagas are headhunters. They could have helped themselves to my head, and nobody would have been the wiser. They were dashed kind. Frankly, my dear, I don't care if I never see another tree."

She was at his bedside for hours every day. He was very low, and movingly dependent on her for affection and encouragement. They had been close before in a quiet way but they now seemed really married. Pamela finally and rather despairingly wrote to Pug on her plane trip from New Delhi to London. After two weeks in hospital, Burne-Wilke was being sent back, very much against his will, for further treatment. She recounted what had happened to explain her delay in replying, and went on,

> Now, Pug, about your proposal. I put my arms around your neck and bless you. I find it very hard to go on, but the fact is that it mustn't be. Duncan's sick as a dog. I can't jilt him. I don't want to. I'm terribly fond of him, I admire him, and I love him. He's a superb man. I've never pretended to him — or to you — that I feel for him the strange love that has bound us. But I'm about ready to give up passion as a bad job. I've not had much luck with it!
>
> He's never pretended, either. At the outset, when he proposed, I asked, "But why do you want me, Duncan?" With that shy subtle smile he answered, "Because you'll do."
>
> My dear, I really don't quite believe your letter. Don't be angry with me. I just know that Rhoda hasn't landed her new fellow yet. Until he's marched her into a church, she won't have done. There's many a slip! The unattainable other man's wife, and the prospective spouse, may look very different to a confirmed bachelor threatened with the altar.
>
> You will always take Rhoda back, and actually I feel you should. It's impossible to blame you. I can't give you a Warren (I *wouldn't* mind the church

upbringing, you dear thing, but — oh well) and whatever ties us, it's nothing like that thick rope of memories between you and Rhoda.

I look back at these hastily scrawled paragraphs and find it hard to believe my blurring eyes.

I love you, you know that, and I always will. I've never known anyone like you. Don't stop loving me. The whole thing was just fated not to be; bad timing, bad luck, interfering commitments. But it was beautiful. Let's be great friends when this damned war ends. If Rhoda does get her man, find some American beauty who will make you happy. They abound in your country, oh my sweet, like daisies in a June meadow. You have just never looked around. Now you can. But don't ever forget

> Your poor loving
> Pamela

78

A Jew's Journey

(*from Aaron Jastrow's manuscript*)

APRIL 22, 1944.

I am waiting for Natalie to return from a clandestine Zionist meeting; waiting and worrying on a cool spring night, with pleasant scents drifting into the apartment from window boxes of geraniums, placed on our sills only yesterday by Beautification workers. I think she is stumbling into acute danger. Though it may cause a scene for which I haven't the strength, I intend to have it out with her when she returns.

How long is it since I wrote a diary entry? I'm not sure. The last sheets are hidden away, long since. The Beautification has more or less overwhelmed me, both at the library and in the council. Also, Berel's stunning appearance after my *Iliad* lecture was a very difficult thing to write about, so I put it off, put it off, and let the whole diary slide. Now I will try to fill it in. I've prepared tomorrow's Talmud section, and this is the best way left to kill time. I won't sleep till she shows up.

Berel gave me the start of my life that night, coming out of the gloom. What an eerie encounter! I had not seen him for close to fifty years. Alas, the transformations of time; the red-cheeked plump boy has become a hard-looking elderly man with bushy gray hair, a big outthrust jaw, heavy frowning eyebrows, and deep lines scored on a clean-shaven face. There's a ghostly familiarity in the smile, and that is all. Shabbily dressed, with a yellow star for camouflage on his torn sheepskin jacket, be looked more Polish then Jewish, if there is anything to these notions of racial physiognomies; a formidable suspicious old Silesian peasant. He was nervous and wary in the extreme. While he walked with us he kept looking around and behind. He had a mission to perform in the ghetto, he said, and would leave before dawn; no explanation of when and how he had come, or how he would go.

He walked to our apartment with us, and there without ado he offered to get Louis out of Theresienstadt! Natalie paled at the very thought. But a new transport had just been ordered, she was in a shaken mood, and she was willing to listen. Berel's idea was to place the child with a Czech farm family, as some Prague Jews managed to do with their tots before being hauled off to

Theresienstadt. It has worked well; the parents hear news of the children from time to time, and even receive smuggled letters from the older ones. To get Louis out, he would be hospitalized on some fraudulent diagnosis, for which Berel says he has the necessary connections in the Health Department. A death certificate would be provided to satisfy the Central Secretariat index, and there might be a faked burial or cremation. The child would be removed from the hospital in secret and spirited to Prague. There Berel would receive him and take him to the farm, visit him regularly, and send news about him to Natalie. The war might go on another year or more; but whatever happened, Berel would watch over him.

Natalie's face grew longer and grimmer as Berel talked. Why, she asked, was this necessary? Louis was adaptable and thriving. Seeing his mother every day was the best thing for him. Berel did not argue about any of that, but he urged that, all in all, the best thing was to let Louis go. Sickness, malnutrition, transport, and German cruelty were ever-present dangers here, worse than the temporary risk of getting him out. Natalie gave no ground. I am abstracting here a low-toned Yiddish conversation that took more than an hour, before Berel dropped it and said he had business with me. She went off to bed. We talked Polish, which she doesn't understand.

Now my pencil halts. How to write down what he told me?

I will not try to recapitulate his journeyings and ordeals. Imagination numbs, belief fails. Berel has passed through all seven circles of the inferno that Germany has made of eastern Europe. The very worst rumors about the Jewish fate are not only true, but very pale and gentle intimations of the truth. With his own hands my cousin has disinterred from mass graves and burned thousands of murdered men, women, and children. Such graves dot all of eastern Europe near cities where Jews once lived. A million and a half buried corpses, is his conservative guess.

In certain camps, including the one outside our old yeshiva town of Oswiecim, huge poison gas cellars exist for killing thousands of people at a time. A crowd to fill a great opera house, crammed into an enormous basement and asphyxiated all at once! Arriving fresh off sealed trains from all over Europe, they are murdered then and there. Great crematoriums burn up the bodies. Tall chimneys dominate the camp landscape, vomiting flames, greasy smoke, and human scraps and ash twenty-four hours a day, when an "action" is on. Berel was not recounting rumors. He worked in a construction gang that built such a crematorium.

The Jews who are not killed at once are worked to death as slave labor in gigantic armaments factories, on rations calculated to murder them by rapid attrition.

We Theresienstadt Jews, he says, are oxen in the pen, waiting our turn. The Beautification is a lucky reprieve, but the day after the neutral Red Cross visit the transports will again roll. Our hope is an Allied victory. The war is certainly going against the Germans, but the end is a way off, and the destruction of the Jews is accelerating. His organization, which he did not identify (I would guess the communists), is planning an uprising in case of a mass transport order, or a killing action launched by the SS here in Theresienstadt. But that will be a desperate business in which Natalie and Louis are unlikely to survive. The Jewish people must look to the future, he said. Louis is the future. He is the one to save.

He did not want to tell Natalie about the murder camps because he could see that her spirits are good, and that is the secret of survival under the Germans. I must try to persuade her to let Louis go, without frightening her too much.

I asked him how widespread in Theresienstadt was knowledge of the murder camps. He said that high-placed people had been told of it; he had spoken to two himself. The usual reaction was incredulity, or anger at the tellers of such "scare stories," and a quick change of subject.

I asked if the outside world yet had any inkling. Newspaper stories were just starting to appear abroad, he replied, and radio broadcasts. The microfilmed documents and pictures he brought from Oswiecim did reach Switzerland and these may be figuring in the accounts. But the people in England and America seem no more inclined as yet to believe the thing than are the Jews right here in Theresienstadt, who know the SS so well. In the Oswiecim camp itself, Berel said, where one saw the chimneys flame out at night, and smelled the burning hair, meat, and fat, many inmates shunned the topic of the gassings, or even denied that they were happening.

(My hand has been shaking as I write these things, that is why the words straggle on the page.)

To wind up quickly the visit of Berel, we had a sad interlude of family gossip. Except for himself and one son's family, our Jastrow clan in Europe has been extirpated, root and branch. His eldest son fights with Jewish partisans behind the German lines in White Russia. The daughter-in-law and grandson are safe on a Latvian farm. Berel has lost everyone else, and so have I; a network of clever and lovable relatives I never saw after I went to America but pleasantly remembered. Through all his wanderings he has preserved a tattered picture of the grandchild, so scuffed and water-stained that one sees only a vague blurred infant face. "The future," Berel said as he showed it to me. *"Der osed."*

He explained how I could notify him if Natalie changed her mind about Louis. We embraced. I had last hugged Berel half a century ago in Medzice, when we left for America; nothing is stranger than what actually happens. As he released me, he shot me the kind of keen look, with head aslant, that in the old days preceded an acute question about the Talmud; and one shoulder humped up, a mannerism unchanged by years and sufferings. "Arele, I heard you wrote books about that man." (*Oso ho-ish,* Jesus.)

"Yes."

"Why did you *dafka* have to write about that man?"

Dafka is an untranslatable Talmud word. It means many things: *necessarily, for that very reason, perversely, defiantly, in spite of everything.* The Jews have a tendency to do things *dafka.* That is the essence of the stiff-necked people. They had to worship the golden calf *dafka,* for instance, at the foot of Mount Sinai.

It was a moment of truth. I answered, "I wrote to make money, Berel, and a name for myself among the Gentiles."

"See how it helped you," he said.

I took from a drawer the phylacteries for which I recently gave a diamond, and showed them to him.

"So?" He sadly smiled. "In Theresienstadt?"

"In Theresienstadt, *dafka,* Berel."

We embraced again, and he slipped out. In two months I have heard nothing more from him or about him. I assume he got safely away. In the First World War Berel escaped twice from prisoner-of-war camps. He is made of wiry stuff, and he is very ingenious.

Past midnight. No sign of her. It is unwise to be walking the streets at this hour, though I suppose her nurse's aide card covers her.

Now let me hurriedly sketch the Beautification. This is a story which in years to come must be told. Future generations may find it harder to believe even than the Oswiecim gassing cellars. After all, however gruesome, those are but the natural end product of National Socialism. One has simply to grasp that Hitler meant it, and that the obedient Germans went and did it.

The Beautification is stranger. It is a painstaking pretense that the Germans are Europeans just like the others, conforming to the tenets of Western civilization; that the rumors and reports about the Jews are too silly for words, or else cruel Allied atrocity propaganda. The Germans are playacting here an elaborate denial of their central effort in this war, the eradication of a people and of two world religions. Yes, two. I believe with whole faith that Jews and Judaism will in the end live on; but Christianity cannot survive this deed by a Christian nation. Nietzsche's Antichrist has come, in boots and swastika armband. In the flames and smoke of the Oswiecim chimneys, all the crucifixes of Europe are going up.

Our new commander, Rahm, is a coarse but thorough brute. His planning of this Beautification carries hypocrisy into new realms. Because I am the Elder in charge of culture, I am much involved. I have spent hours in his office over a table map of the town, where the route of the visitors is marked in red, with every stopping place numbered. A wall chart shows the progress of renovation and new construction at each numbered halt. My department is staging the musical and dramatic events along the route, but my deputies are doing the real work. My role on "the day" will be to show the visitors around a marvelously renovated library; I already have twenty people working on the catalogue, and beautiful books keep pouring in. We are amassing the finest Judaica collection left on European soil, all for one day's fakery.

The visit is being planned like a Passion play; it will be a spectacle involving an entire town. The action, however, will be limited to the route traced in red on the map. A hundred yards on either side of that route, the old filth, illness, overcrowding, and starvation will prevail. A narrow simulacrum of an idyllic spa is being created with immense labor, and no expense spared, wherever the visitors' eyes may look. Do the Germans really expect to get away with this grotesque fake? It seems so. Previous inspections by German Red Cross officials proved no problem, of course. The visitors came and went and spread glowing reports about the Paradise Ghetto. But this time the visitors will be neutral outsiders. How can the Germans be sure of controlling them? A determined Swede or Swiss Red Cross man has only to say, "Let us go down that street," or "Let us have a look in yonder barracks," and the bubble will pop. Beyond the iridescent film of fakery will lie horror to make a neutral's hair stand on end; though we of course are used to it, and thought it is nothing compared to an Oswiecim.

Does Rahm have some wily plan to deflect such embarrassing requests? Does he count on suave bullying to keep the visitors in line? Or, as I strongly suspect, is this whole Beautification just a master instance, a paradigm, of the idiot thoroughness which has characterized what the Germans have done since Hitler took power?

In their ability to get things done, their energy, their attention to detail, their sheer scientific and industrial prowess, they equal and perhaps surpass the Americans. Moreover, they are capable of the greatest charm, intelligence, and taste. It is their peculiarity as a people that with no reservations, with whole hearts, with singular élan, they can throw themselves into the executing of plans and orders crazy or monstrous beyond previous human conceptions. Why this should be, the world may be a thousand years puzzling out; meantime it is happening. It has loosed a holocaust of war which must almost certainly end in the destruction of Germany. At the heart of that vast hecatomb is what they are doing to my people. And at the heart of the heart is this Beautification, the German face turned innocently to the outside world, with the plaintive statement, "See how unjust you are, to accuse us of doing bad things?"

The idiot thoroughness of this Beautification is awesome. There is nothing Rahm and his advisers haven't thought of, assuming that he can hold his visitors to the red line. Very little is finished yet, but the scenario is all laid down. The bustling disorder in Theresienstadt these days is that of a stage halfway ready for a dress rehearsal. Two or three thousand ablebodied Jews are toiling from dawn to dusk for the Technical Department — and, here and there, all night under floodlights — to build this fantastic narrow path of illusion.

The itinerary of the visitors has been fixed for months. Rahm carries around a thick document bound in black and red striped cloth, which we of the council call (among ourselves) the "Beautification Bible." All our department heads have contributed to it, but the final minuteness of detail could only be German. It includes the selections the municipal orchestra will play in the town square, though the Technical Department is only now laying the foundation for the pavilion. Our musicians are busy copying out the parts — two Rossini overtures, some military marches, several Strauss waltzes, and potpourris from Donizetti and Bizet. Copying paper is now available in profusion. Excellent new instruments have flooded in. Theresienstadt, like Prospero's magic island, is becoming a place where melody fills the air.

Looking into the opera house in the Sports Hall, the visitors will observe a full orchestra and large chorus rehearsing Verdi's *Requiem:* more than a hundred fifty talented Jews in neat clean clothing, yellow stars and all, producing music worthy of performance in Paris or Vienna. Downstairs in a smaller theatre they will happen upon a costumed run-through of the delightful original children's opera, *Brundibar,* the hit of the ghetto. Walking in the flower-lined streets, they will hear a string quartet in one private house doing Beethoven, a superb contralto singing Schubert lieder in another, a great clarinetist practicing Weber in a third. In the cafés they will come on costumed musicians and singers performing, as patrons sip coffee and eat cream pastries. The visitors will refresh themselves at one café, where customers will pay, depart, and arrive in a thoroughly drilled natural fashion.

The visitors will see shops well-stocked with all manner of fine goods, including luxury foods, and shoppers casually coming and going, buying what they please, paying in the Theresienstadt paper currency engraved with a picture of Moses. This worthless currency is the sourest joke of the ghetto, of course, and Rahm's Bible contains a stern warning that as soon as the visitors depart these "customers" must return all the "purchases." Any shortage will be punished. For a missing food item, the offender will go to the Little Fortress.

The plan ramifies through every phase of ghetto life. A mock superclean hospital, a mock children's playground, a mock printing plant for men, a mock clothing factory for women, a mock sports field, are all in the works.

The bank is being redecorated. A mock boys' school is already finished, a new building complete to the last detail of blackboards, chalk, and textbooks, which has never been and will never be used, except for musicians' rehearsals. A "main mess hall," a commodious hut, is being erected for the serving of exactly one meal, the visitors' lunch, where Jews all around them will also heartily dine. The SS have yet to figure out a way to avoid feeding some Jews just this once. It is the only lapse in Rahm's Bible. The café customers, of course, are to indulge in coffee and cakes only while the visitors are in sight, otherwise they will go through motions over brown slop, and plates of cakes they may not touch.

It is after one o'clock. Why do I go on with this bitter drivelling? Well, even the gallows jest of the Beautification is some relief from thoughts of Berel's disclosures, and my worry over Natalie's tardiness. She must get up at six. Before she goes to work at the mica factory, she has to rehearse for the visit, at the children's playground and the kindergarten. She has just received that assignment, with several other attractive women. They will have their work cut out for them, training the kids to speak their little pieces and simulate happiness. At lunch, she tells me, the kids are supposed to cry out, "What, sardines again?" A whole twenty-minute charade like that has been written out. Here the Beautification is doing some real good, for the SS have increased the rations of the children. They want the visitors to see roly-poly tots at play; so they are stuffing them as the witch did Hansel and Gretel.

I cannot believe that so blatant a comedy can hoodwink anybody. Yet say it does succeed: what are the Germans hoping to gain by it? The Jews are disappearing, millions are gone, and can this vast horror be long concealed? I cannot understand it. There is no sense to it. No, it is the backward child, on a monumental and terrible scale; the backward child caught at the empty jam jar, his face, hands, clothes smeared red, smiling and denying that he ate the jam.

For that matter, what sense is there to the Oswiecim gas cellars? I have thought and thought about that for weeks, with dizzied brain. Calling the Germans sadists, butchers, beasts, savages explains nothing, for they are men and women like us. I have an idea, and I will scribble it down, with much more certainty than I feel. The root of the matter cannot be Hitler. I start with that premise. Such a thing must have been brewing for centuries, to have encountered so little resistance among the Germans when it happened.

Napoleon forced liberty and equality on the Germans. From the outset they gagged on it. With cannon and tramping boots, he invaded a patchwork of absolutist states hardly out of feudalism. He ground the faces of the Germans in the brotherhood of man. Freeing the Jews was part of this new liberal humanism. It was not natural to the Germans, but they conformed.

Alas, we Jews believed in the change, but the Germans in their hearts never did. It was the conqueror's creed. It swept Europe, but not Germany. Their Romantic philosophers inveighed against the un-German Enlightenment, their anti-Semitic political parties sprouted, while Germany grew and grew to an industrial giant, never convinced of the "Western" ideas.

Their defeat under the Kaiser, and the great inflation and crash, generated in them a terrible frustrated anger. The communists threatened chaos and overthrow. Weimar was falling apart. When Hitler rose from this witches' brew, like an oracular spook in Macbeth, and pointed at the Jews in the department stores and the opera promenades; when he thundered that not only were they the visible beneficiaries of Germany's wrongs, but the actual cause of them; when that frenzied historical formula rolled forth, as mendaciously simple as the Marxist slogans, but more candidly bloodthirsty; then the German rage was released in an explosion of national energy and joy, and the plausible maniac who had released it had his murder weapon in hand. Bottomless lack of compunction in the Germans peculiarly fitted the weapon to the man. Awareness of this baffling trait had to be kicked into me. I am still puzzling over it.

Does my work on Luther shed light on it? Only Luther, before Hitler, ever so wholly spoke with the national voice to release plugged-up national rage; in his case, against a corrupt Latin-droning popery. The resemblances in the forceful, coarse, sarcastic rhetoric of the two men gave me anxious pause even when I was Luther's admiring biographer. Luther's Protestantism is a grand theology, a sonorous earnest hardheaded Christianity, well worthy of the Christ whom Luther claimed to be rescuing from the Whore of Babylon. But even this homegrown product sat hard on the German stomach, did it not?

The German has never been quite at home in Christian Europe, has never quite made up his mind whether he is Vandal or Roman, the destroyer from the north or the *comme il faut* Western man. He oscillates, vacillates, plays the one or the other role, as historic circumstances change. To the Vandal in him, Christian compunction and British and French liberalism are nonsense; the reason and logic of the Enlightenment are a veneer over real human nature; destruction and dominance are the thing; slaughter is an ancient joy. After centuries of Lutheran restraint, the rude rough German voice bellowed forth once again, in Nietzsche, radical revulsion from Christianity's meek tenets. Quite accurately Nietzsche blamed all this kindness and compunction on Judaism. Quite accurately he foretold the coming death of the Christian God. What he failed to foresee was that the freed Vandal, in lunatic industrialized vengeance, would set out to nail eleven million Christs to the cross.

Oh, scribble, scribble, scribble! I look back over these hastily pencilled pages and my heart sinks. No wonder I have neglected the diary; my small mind cannot cope with what I now know. How can one move on this theme without a general theory of nationalism? Without tracing socialism to its sources, and demonstrating how the two movements converge in Hitler? Without giving the menace of the Russian Revolution its due weight?

Have I made any contact whatever with the German in all this glib scrawling? Am I, the stinking Jew Jastrow, putting on phylacteries in Theresienstadt, and he, striking out all over Europe with clanking armies and roaring air fleets, really following the same human impulse, to preserve a threatened identity? Is that why he wants to kill me, because the Jew and Judaism are the everlasting challenge, reproach, and hobble to primitive Germanism? Or is all this an empty conceit, the vaporings of the tired and overwrought brain of a lifelong liberal, trying to find one shred of sense in Oswiecim and in the Beautification, trying to bridge the gulf between myself and Karl Rahm, because the truth is that though he slay me we are brothers, in Darwinian taxonomy if not under God?

Here is Natalie!

NEXT MORNING.

It is even graver than I thought. She is in very deep. She came back weary, but in a glow. These Zionist meetings have been debating ways and means to defeat the Beautification, to signal the truth about Theresienstadt to the Red Cross visitors, without alerting the SS. She thinks they have hit on something. At each of the stops, a Jew in charge will be primed to say one and the same sentence, in response to any Red Cross comment: *"Oh yes, it is all very, very new. And there is much more to see."*

They worked this out, I gather, with great wrangling and revisions. They voted on words. These exact repetitions, they believe, will strike the visitors as a signal. The Jews will speak the sentence casually, with meaningful looks, if possible beyond SS earshot. The hope, or rather the fantasy, is that the visitors will catch on that they are seeing brand-new faked installations, and will push beyond the planned route, because of the "much more to see."

I listened patiently. Then I told her that she was slipping into the endemic ghetto dreaminess, and endangering her life and Louis's. The Germans are trained wary prison guards. The visitors will be soft polite welfare executives. The Beautification is a major German effort, and the most obvious thing to guard against is just such Jewish schemes to tip off the visitors. So I argued, but she retorted that one way or another the Jews must fight back. Since we have no weapons but our brains, we must use them.

Then I took the drastic step of disclosing Berel's revelations about Oswiecim. My intent was to shock her into greater awareness of her danger of being transported. She was, of course, badly shocked; not quite flabbergasted, since such stories do float around. But she took it the wrong way. All the more reason, she said, to waken the suspicions of the Red Cross; anyway, Berel's story must be exaggerated, because Udam had received postcards from his wife in Oswiecim, and her friends were getting cards now from relatives in the February transport.

I repeated what Berel told me: that the Oswiecim SS keeps up a "Theresienstadt family camp," in case the Red Cross ever manages to negotiate a visit to that terrible place; that on arrival in Oswiecim everyone must write postcards dated months ahead; and that the Theresienstadt camp is periodically cleared of the sick, the weak, the elderly, and the children, all gassed in a body, to make room for further Theresienstadt transports. Udam was undoubtedly getting mail from a cremated woman.

Next she asserted that her group has heard, via their grapevine to Prague, that according to German military intelligence, the Americans will definitely land in France on May 15. This may well touch off uprisings all over Europe, and lead to the rapid collapse of the Nazi empire. In any case, the SS officers will begin worrying about their own necks, and so further transports are unlikely.

Against such wishful thinking hardened into delusion there is no arguing. I urged her, if she meant to go on with this business, at least to send word to Berel to get Louis out. She wouldn't hear of it; denied that she was putting Louis in any greater danger than he already faced; turned decidedly snappish, and went off to bed.

That was only a few hours ago. She was in a better mood when she awoke, and apologized before she left for her display of short temper. She said nothing more about Louis. Nor did I.

Far from objecting to her newfound Zionism, I am glad of it. It seems to be for her the assertion of threatened identity that I have found in my old religion. One needs some such spiritual stiffening to survive in the ghetto, if one is not a conniver or a black marketeer. But suppose her circle is penetrated by an informer? With scurrilous puppetry already on record in her SS dossier, that will be the end of her.

I myself was never a Zionist. I remain enormously skeptical of the notion of returning the Jews to that desolate patch of the Middle East inhabited by unfriendly Arabs. True, the Zionists did foresee this European catastrophe, when it was a cloud no bigger than a man's hand. But does it follow that their visionary solution was a possible or correct one? Hardly. Only a handful of dreamers ever went to Palestine before Hitler. Even they were driven there by pogroms, rather than drawn by the desiccated Holy Land.

I am no longer sure about this, I confess, or about any of my former notions. Certainly Jewish nationalism is a powerful means of identity, but I regard nationalism as the curse of modern times. I simply cannot believe that we poor Jews are ever meant to have an army and a navy, a parliament and ministers, boundaries, harbors, airports, universities, on Mediterranean sands. What a sweet and hollow dream! Let Natalie dream it, if it helps her get through Theresienstadt. She says that if a Jewish state the size of Liechtenstein had existed, all these horrors wouldn't be happening; and that such a state must arise to prevent their happening again. Messianic rhetoric; my fear is only that this new febrile enthusiasm, overcoming her usual tough good sense, may lead her into rashness that will destroy her and Louis.

79

THROUGH the closed bedroom door it sounded like crying, but Rhoda cried so seldom that Victor Henry shrugged and passed on to the guest room where he now slept. It was very late. He had sat up for hours in the library after dinner, working on landing craft documents for his meeting with Colonel Peters; something he was not looking forward to, but a priorities conflict was forcing it. He undressed, showered, drank off his nightcap of bourbon and water, and before turning in stopped to listen at Rhoda's door. The sounds had become unmistakable: keening moans, broken by sobs.

"Rhoda?"

No answer. The sounds ceased as though switched off.

"Rho! Come on, what is it?"

Muffled sad voice: "Oh, I'm all right. Go to sleep."

"Let me in."

"The door's not locked, Pug."

The room was dark. When he turned on the light Rhoda sat up in an oyster-white satiny nightdress, blinking and dabbing a tissue at swollen red eyes. "Was I making a racket? I tried to keep it low."

"What's up?"

"Oh, Pug, I'm done for. Everything's in ruins. You're well rid of me."

"I think you can use a drink."

"I must look GRUESOME. Don't I?" She put her hands to her tumbled hair.

"Want to come down to the library and talk?"

"You're an angel. Scotch and soda. Be right there." She thrust shapely white legs and thighs out of bed. Pug went to the library and mixed drinks at the movable bar. She soon appeared in a peignoir over her nightgown, brushing her hair in familiar charming gestures he had not seen since moving to the guest room. She was lightly made-up and she had done something to her eyes, for they were bright and clear.

"I washed my face and FLUNG myself into bed hours and hours ago, then I couldn't sleep."

"But why? Because I have to see Colonel Peters? It's just a business meeting, Rhoda. I told you that." He handed her the drink. "Maybe I shouldn't have mentioned it, but I won't make any trouble for you."

"Pug, I'm in such distress!" She took a deep gulp of her drink. "Somebody's been writing Hack anonymous letters. He's received, oh, five or six. He tore up the first ones, but he showed me two. With abject apologies, but he showed them. They've gotten under his skin."

Rhoda gave her husband one of her most melting, appealing looks. He thought of mentioning the anonymous letters he too had received, but saw no purpose in that. Pamela might have told Rhoda about them; in any case, no use stirring up that mud. He did not comment.

She burst out, "It's so unfair! I didn't even KNOW Hack, then, did I? Talk about your double standard! Why, he's slept with all KINDS of women, to hear him talk. Single, married, divorced, he makes no bones about it, even reminisces, and the point always is how different I am. And I am too, I *am!* There was only Palmer Kirby. I still don't know how or why THAT happened. I'm not one of those cheap flirts he's run around with all his life. But these letters are wrecking everything. He seems so unhappy, SO CRUSHED. Of course I denied everything. I had to, for HIS sake. For such an experienced man, he's strangely NAIVE."

What surprised Pug most was that this casual outright admission of her adultery — "There was only Palmer Kirby" — could give him pain; not the agony of the first shock, her letter asking for a divorce, but still, real pain. Rhoda had skirted a specific admission until this very moment. Her habit of silence had served her well, but the words had slipped out because Peters was now the man who mattered. This was the real end, thought Pug. He, like Kirby, was part of her past. She could be careless with him.

"The man loves you, Rhoda. He'll believe you, and forget about the letters."

"Oh, will he? And suppose he asks *you* about them tomorrow?"

"That's unthinkable."

"Not so unthinkable. You're meeting for the first time since all this happened."

"Rhoda, we've got a very urgent priorities problem to thrash out. He won't bring up personal matters. Certainly not those anonymous letters. Not to me. His skin would crawl at the idea."

She looked both amused and miserable. "Male pride, you mean."

"Call it that. Forget it. Go to sleep, and pleasant dreams."

"May I have another drink?"

"Sure."

"Will you tell me afterward what happened? I mean, what you talked about?"

"Not the business part."

"I'm not interested in the business part."

"If anything personal comes up, I'll tell you, yes." He handed her the drink. "Any idea who's writing the letters?"

"No. It's a woman. Some vicious bitch or other. Oh, they abound, Pug, they abound. She uses green ink, writes in a funny up-and-down hand on little tan sheets. Her facts are all cockeyed, but she does mention Palmer Kirby. Very nastily. Dates, places, all that. Disgusting."

"Where's Kirby now?"

"I don't know. I last saw him in Chicago when I was coming back from California, right after — after Midway. I stopped there for a few hours to break it off once for all. Funnily enough, that's how I met Hack."

As she drank, Rhoda described the encounter in the Pump Room, and finding Colonel Peters afterward on the train to New York.

"I'll never know why he took a fancy to me, Pug. I was *very* distant in the club car that night. Actually, I FROZE him. I was feeling wretched about Palmer, and you, and the whole mess, and I was by no means over Warren. I wouldn't accept a drink. Wouldn't get into conversation. I mean, he was so OBVIOUSLY fresh from a roll in the hay with that creature in green! He still had that glint in his eye, and I wasn't about to give him IDEAS. Then next morning in the dining car the steward seated him at my table. It was crowded for breakfast, so I couldn't object, although I don't know, maybe he SLIPPED that steward something. Anyway, that was it. He said Palmer had told him about me, and he admired my brave spirit so much, and all that. I still kept my distance. I always have. He really PURSUED me, in a gentlemanly way, showing up at church, and Navy affairs, and Bundles for Britain, and so on. It was a very gradual business. It was MONTHS before I even agreed to go to the theatre with him. Maybe that's what intrigued Hack, the sheer novelty of it all. It couldn't have been my girlish charm. But when he thinks back to when we met, there I WAS, after all, visiting Palmer Kirby. It makes those horrid letters so PLAUSIBLE."

This was more than Rhoda had said about her romance in all the months that Pug had been back. She was being positively chatty. Pug said, "Feeling better now, aren't you?"

"Heaps. You're sweet to be so reassuring. I'm not a crybaby, Pug, you know that, but I am in a STATE about those letters. When you told me you were meeting him tomorrow, I panicked. I mean, Hack can't possibly ever ask Palmer. That's not done. Palmer wouldn't tell, anyway. You're the only other one who knows. You're the aggrieved husband, and, well, I just got to thinking of all kinds of awful possibilities." She had finished her drink and was slipping pink mules back on her bare feet.

"I really didn't know anything, anyway, Rhoda. Not until tonight."

She went rigid, staring at him, one mule in her hand, her mind obviously racing back over the conversation. "Oh, nuts." She slammed the slipper down on the floor. "Of course you knew. Don't be like that, Pug. How could you NOT know? What was it ever all about?"

Pug was sitting at the desk where the big leather-bound Warren album still lay, beside a pile of his file folders. "I'm sort of waked up now," he said, picking up a folder. "I'll do a little more work."

MANHATTAN ENGINEER DISTRICT
Brig. Gen. Leslie R. Groves, U.S.A., Chief
Colonel Harrison Peters, Deputy Chief

The signs on the two adjoining doors, on an upper floor in the State Department building, were so inconspicuous that Pug walked by them and had to backtrack. Colonel Peters strode from behind his desk to shake hands. "Well! High time we met again."

Pug had forgotten how tall the man was, perhaps six feet three, and how handsome: brilliant blue eyes, healthily colored long bony face, straight body in a sharply tailored uniform, no trace of a bulge at the middle. Despite the gray hair the general effect was youthful, manly, and altogether impressive, except for an uncertain quality in his broad smile. No doubt he was embarrassed. Yet Pug felt very little resentment toward the Army man. It helped a lot that the fellow had not cuckolded him. Pug did believe he hadn't, mainly because that had been the only way for Rhoda to play this particular fish.

The small desk was bare. The only other furniture was an armchair. There were no pictures on the wall, no files, no window, no bookcase, no secretary; a low-level operation, one would think, assigned to a run-of-the-mill colonel. Pug declined coffee, and sat in the armchair.

"Before we get down to business," said Peters, flushing a little, "let me say one thing. I have the greatest respect for you. Rhoda is what she is, a woman in a million, because of her years with you. I regret we haven't yet talked about all that. We're both busy as hell, I know, but one of these days we'll have to."

"By all means."

"Do you smoke cigars?" Peters took a box of long Havanas from a desk drawer.

"Thanks." Pug did not want a cigar, but accepting it might improve the atmosphere.

Peters took his time about lighting up. "Sorry I was slow getting back to you."

"I guess the phone call from Harry Hopkins helped."

"That would have made no difference, if your security clearance hadn't checked out."

"Just to shortcut this a bit," Pug said, "when I was naval attaché in Berlin I supplied the S-1 committee, at their request, with dope on German industrial activity in graphite, heavy water, uranium, and thorium. I know the Army's working on a uranium bomb, with a blank-check triple-A priority power. That's why I'm here. The landing craft program needs those couplings I mentioned over the telephone."

"How do you know we've got them?" Peters leaned back, clasping his long arms behind his head. A harder professional tone came into his voice.

"You haven't got them. They're still warehoused in Pennsylvania. The Dresser firm wouldn't say anything except that they're on Army order. The prime contractor, Kellogg, wouldn't talk at all. I ran into a blank wall at the War Production Board, too. The fellows there just clammed up. The landing craft program hasn't conflicted with the uranium bomb before. I figured it couldn't be anything else. So I called you."

"What makes you think I'm in the uranium bomb business?"

"General Connolly told me in Tehran that you were working on something very big. I took a shot in the dark."

"You mean," Peters asked, tough and incredulous, "that you telephoned me on a guess?"

"Right. Do we get the couplings, Colonel?"

After a long pause, and a mutual staring contest, Peters replied, "Sorry, no."

"Why not? What are you using them for?"

"Jesus Christ, Henry! For a manufacturing process of the highest national urgency."

"I know that. But is this component irreplaceable? All it does is connect pipes. There are many ways to connect pipes."

"Then use another way on your landing craft."

"I'll tell you my problem, if you'll listen."

"Sure you won't have coffee?"

"Thanks. Black, no sugar. This is a fine cigar."

"Best in the world." Peters ordered coffee over the intercom. Pug was liking the man better as he toughened up. This rapid exchange over the desk was a little like a long point in tennis. Peters's returns so far were hard but not sneaky or tricky.

"I'm listening." Peters leaned back in his swivel chair, nursing a knee.

"Okay. Our shipyards have gotten so jammed that we've subcontracted some construction to Britain. We're sending sections which can be put together by semiskilled help and launched in a few days. That is, *if* the right components are on hand. Now, these Dresser couplings go in faster than welded or bolted joints. They require little experience or strength to install. Also, uncoupling them to check faulty lines is simple. The *Queen Mary* sails Friday, Colonel, with fifteen thousand troops aboard, and I've reserved cargo space for shipping that stuff. I've got trucks standing by in Pennsylvania, ready to take the lot to New York. I'm talking about components for forty vessels. If they're launched on schedule, Eisenhower will hit the French beaches with more force than he'll have otherwise."

"We hear this kind of thing all the time," Peters said. "The British will connect up those lines, one way or another."

"Look, the decision to put these vessels together in England turned on hard specifications for speed of assembly. When we shipped the sections those couplings were available. Now you've overridden our priority. Why?"

Peters puffed at his cigar, squinted through the smoke at Pug, and replied, "Okay. For a very large network of underground water lines. Our requirements for speed and simplicity are the same as yours, and our urgency is greater."

"I have an idea for solving this," Pug said, "less messy than going to the President, which I'm also prepared to do."

"Let's hear your idea."

"I checked all the stuff Dresser has on hand. They could modify a larger coupling to meet your specs. Delivery would be delayed ten days. Now, I have samples of that substitute coupling. Suppose I take them to your plant, and talk to the engineers in charge?"

"Christ, not a chance."

"Why not? Peters, the fellows on the spot can clear this thing up, yes or no, in a few hours. President Roosevelt has other things on his mind, and anyway, General Groves wouldn't appreciate being overruled by him. Why not try to avoid that?"

"How do you know what the President will do?"

"I was at Tehran. The landing craft program is a commitment not only to Churchill but to Stalin."

"Clearing you for such a visit — if it could be done at all — would take a week."

"N.G., Colonel. Those trucks have to load up and leave Bradford, Pennsylvania, Thursday morning."

"Then you'll have to go to the President. I can't help you."

"Okay, I will," Pug said, grinding out his cigar.

Colonel Peters stood up, shook hands, and walked out with Pug into the long hallway. "Let me look into one possibility, and ring you before noon."

"I'll wait for your call."

Peters telephoned Pug about an hour later. "Can you come with me for a little trip? You'd be away from Washington two nights."

"Sure."

"Meet me at Union Station at five to seven, track eighteen. I'll have the Pullman berths."

"Where are we going?"

"Knoxville, Tennessee. Fetch along that substitute coupling."
Match point, thought Pug.

Oak Ridge was a huge backwoods area on a little-known Tennessee river, cordoned off from the world, where a secret industrial complex had sprung up to effect mass murder in a new way, on an unprecedented scale. Some would therefore argue today that it was comparable to Auschwitz.

Nobody was being murdered at Oak Ridge, to be sure. Nor was there any slave labor. Cheerful Americans were working at very high pay, constructing enormous buildings and installing gigantic masses of machinery, with no idea of what it was all for. The secret of Oak Ridge was better kept than that of Auschwitz. Inside, only very high-level personnel knew. Outside, few rumors leaked.

As in Germany it was bad form to talk about the state of the Jews, so in Oak Ridge it was antisocial to discuss the purpose of the place. In Germany, people did know that something ghastly must be happening to the Jews, and the Germans in Auschwitz knew exactly what was happening; whereas the Oak Ridge workers were in the dark until the day the bomb fell on Hiroshima. In beautiful wooded country they drudged by day in ankle-deep mud, and amused themselves as they could by night in rude huts and trailers, asking no questions; or they passed jocular rumors, such as that they were creating a plant for mass-producing front ends of horses, to be shipped to Washington for assembly.

Still, the postwar argument goes that when one contemplates the results of Auschwitz and Oak Ridge, there is little to choose between the Americans and the Nazis; both were equally guilty of the new barbarism. It is a challenging point. After every war there is a great and sensible revulsion at the whole horrible bloodletting. Distinctions tend to blur. All was atrocity. All were equally criminal. That is how the cry runs. It was in truth a nasty war; so nasty that mankind does not want another; which is a start, anyway, toward abolishing this old human craziness. But it really should not be seen in remembrance as a mere blur of universal guilt. There were differences.

The Oak Ridge effort, to begin with, broke new ground in physics, chemistry, and industrial invention by producing uranium-235. As a feat of applied engineering and of human scientific genius, it was remarkable, possibly unique in scale and brilliance. The German gas chambers and crematoriums were not brilliant innovative works of genius.

Again, once one is attacked in war one can either give up and submit to looting, or one can fight. To fight means to try to frighten the other side, by a lot of murder, into stopping the war. Political conflicts between states must occur; and certainly, in an age of reason and science, they should be resolved by some more sane means than wholesale murder. But that was the means the German and Japanese politicians chose, thinking it would work, and they could only be dissuaded by the same means. When the Americans began their race to make uranium bombs, they had no way of knowing that their attackers would not make and use them first. It was a scary and highly motivating thought.

So on the whole, the analogy between Auschwitz and Oak Ridge seems forced. Resemblances exist. Both were stupendous secret wartime improvisations for slaughter; both opened terrible new problems in human experience that remain unsolved; and if not for National Socialist Germany, neither would have existed. But the purpose of Auschwitz was insane useless killing. The purpose of Oak Ridge was to stop the global war unleashed by Germany, and it worked.

However, when Pug Henry came to Oak Ridge in the late spring of 1944, the Manhattan Project loomed as a vast wartime bust, the boondoggle of the ages. The whole thing was uneconomical to the point of lunacy. Only the rush for a decisive new weapon could justify it. Fear was fading in 1944 that the Germans or Japanese might beat America to the bomb; the new goal was to shorten the war. So on three different theories, the Army had built three different giant industrial complexes for making bomb stuff. The Hanford plant on the Columbia River was striving to produce plutonium. A dubious enough venture, it was a bright hope compared with the two colossal installations at Oak Ridge intended to separate uranium-235 by two different methods, both still sputtering and failing.

Few people even at the highest levels knew the extent of the threatening failure. Colonel Peters knew. The scientific mastermind of the bomb project, Dr. Robert Oppenheimer, knew. And the resolute, thick-hided Army man bossing the show, Brigadier General Leslie Groves, knew. But nobody knew what to do about it. Dr. Oppenheimer had an idea, and Colonel Peters was going to Oak Ridge to meet with Oppenheimer and a small senior committee.

As against this crisis, Captain Henry's request for the Dresser couplings was small potatoes. Rather than risk trouble with the White House, Peters was taking him along, since Pug's security clearance was flawless. Oppenheimer's idea involved bringing in the Navy, and Army–Navy relations were touchy. A cooperative gesture made some sense at this point.

Peters knew nothing about the Navy's thermal diffusion system. "Compartmentalization" was General Groves's first rule: noncommunication walls between sections of the bomb effort, so that people in one track would not know what was happening elsewhere. Groves had investigated thermal diffusion in 1942 and concluded that the Navy was wasting its time. Now Oppenheimer had written to Groves suggesting a second very urgent look at the Navy's results.

Pug Henry had been passing through military checkpoints all his life, but the Oak Ridge roadblock was something new. The gate guards were processing a crowd of new workmen in a considerable uproar, letting them through one by one like counted gold coins, to buses waiting beyond the gate. The substitute coupling Pug had brought along was scrutinized by hardfaced MPs and passed before a fluoroscope. He himself went through a body search and some stiff questioning, then got back into Peters's Army car, wearing various badges and a radiation gauge.

"Let's go," Peters said to the sergeant driver. "Stop at the overlook."

They went bowling along a narrow tarred road through dense green woods, flowering here and there with redbud and dogwood.

"Bob McDermott will be at the castle. I phoned," said Peters. "I'll turn you over to him."

"Who's he? What's the castle?"

"He'll have to pass on your request. He's the boss engineer. The castle is the administration building."

The ride through wild woods went on for miles. The colonel worked on papers as he had on the train, and during the drive from Knoxville. The two men had scarcely spoken since leaving Washington. Pug had his own paper sheaf, and silence always suited him. It was a warm morning, and the forest scent through the open windows was delightful. The car climbed a twisting stretch of road through solid dogwood. Rounding a bend, the driver pulled off the road and stopped.

"God Almighty," Pug gasped.

"K-25," said Peters.

A long wide valley stretched below, a chaotic muddy panorama of construction centered around an unfinished building that looked like all the airplane hangars in America put together in a U-shape; the most gigantic edifice Pug had ever seen. Around it sprawled miles of flat-roofed huts, acres of trailers, rows of military barracks, and scores of buildings, clear out of sight. The general look, from this distance, was a strange mélange of Army base, science-fiction vision, and gold-rush town, all in a sea of red mud. A sense of an awesome future rose from this view like the shock wave of a bomb.

"The water lines are for that big plant," said Peters. "Something, hey? The technicians get around in there on bicycles. It's operating, but we keep adding units. Over the ridge there's another valley, and another installation. Not quite as big, different principle."

They drove down through the booming valley past rough huts interlined with wooden boardwalks built over the mud, past long queues of workingmen and women at bus stops and stores, past a hundred noisy construction jobs, past the gigantic K-25 structure, to the "castle." Pug was not expecting to encounter a familiar face, but there in the corridor was Sime Anderson in uniform, talking to shirt-sleeved civilians. Sime returned a salute to Pug's startled informal wave.

"Know that young fellow?" asked Peters.

"Beau of my daughter's. Lieutenant Commander Anderson."

"Oh, yes. Rhoda's mentioned him."

It was the first reference to Rhoda on the trip.

The walls of the chief engineer's small office were covered with maps, his desk with blueprints. McDermott was a heavyset mustached man with a grimly amused look in bulging brown eyes, as though he were hanging on to his sanity by regarding Oak Ridge as a great mad joke. His neatly pressed suit trousers were tucked into rubber knee boots crusted with fresh red muck. "Hope you don't mind walking in mud," he said to Pug as he shook hands.

"If it'll get me those couplings, not at all."

McDermott looked over the substitute coupling Pug showed him. "Why don't you use this on your landing craft?"

"We can't accept the delay needed for modification."

"Can we?" McDermott asked Colonel Peters.

"That's the second question," Peters replied. "The first question is whether you can use that thing."

McDermott turned to Pug, and pointed a thumb at a pile of muddy boots. "Help yourself and let's go."

"How long will you be?" Peters asked.

"I'll bring him back by four."

"Good enough. Did the new barriers come in from Detroit?"

McDermott nodded. Grim amusement came on his face like a mask. "Unsatisfactory."

"Jesus God," said Peters. "The general will go up in smoke."

"Well, they're still testing them."

"Ready," Pug said. The boots were too large. He hoped they would not come off in the mud.

"On our way," said McDermott.

In the corridor, a short bespectacled colonel, almost bald, with a genial very sharp expression, had joined Anderson and the civilians. Peters introduced Pug to the Army boss of Oak Ridge, Colonel Nichols.

"Is the Navy going to get those landing craft made in time?" Nichols asked Pug, his bluntness modified by a pleasant manner.

"Not if you keep preempting our components."

Nichols asked McDermott, "What's the problem?"

"The Dresser couplings for the underground water lines."

"Oh, yes. Well, do what you can."

"Gonna try."

"Hi, there," Pug said to Anderson. The junior officer diffidently grinned. Pug went off with McDermott.

A frail-looking, young-looking man smoking a pipe entered the building as Pug left. The prospect of addressing a meeting that included Dr. Oppenheimer had Sime Anderson shaking at the knees. Oppenheimer was, in Anderson's view, probably the brightest human being alive; his mind probed nature as though God were his private tutor, and he was cruel to fools. Sime's boss, Abelson, had casually sent Sime off to Oak Ridge to describe the thermal diffusion plant for a few key Oak Ridge personnel and corporation executives. Only on arriving had Sime learned that Oppenheimer would be there.

There was no help for it now. Feeling appallingly ill-prepared, he followed Dr. Oppenheimer into the small conference room, where a blackboard gave the place a classroom look. Some twenty men, mostly in shirtsleeves, made it crowded, smoky, and hot. Anderson was sweating in his heavy blue uniform when Nichols introduced him and he got to his feet. But chalk in hand, talking about his work, he soon felt all right. He avoided looking at Oppenheimer, who slouched smoking in the second row. By the time Anderson paused for questions, forty minutes had sped by, and the blackboard was covered with diagrams and equations. His small audience appeared alert, interested, and puzzled.

Nichols broke the short silence. "That separation factor of two — that's the theoretical performance you're hoping for?"

"That's what our system is putting out, sir."

"You're getting that concentration of U-235? *Now?*"

"Yes, sir. One point four. One part in seventy."

Nichols looked straight at Oppenheimer.

Oppenheimer stood, walked forward, and shook hands with Sime, smiling in remote recognition. "Well done, Anderson." Sime sat down, his heart swelling with relief.

Oppenheimer looked around with large sombre eyes. "The figure of one point four is the reason for this meeting. We have made a very fundamental, very serious, very embarrassing mistake," he said in a slow weary voice, "all of us have, who share responsibility for this effort. It seems we were bemused by the greater elegance and originality of gaseous diffusion and electromagnetic separation. We were obsessed, too, with going to ninety percent enrichment along a single path. It didn't occur to us that combined processes might be a speedier way. Now here we are. From the last word on barriers, K-25 will not work in time for this war. Hanford too is a question. Out in

New Mexico we're testing bomb configurations for an explosive that doesn't yet exist. Not in usable quantities."

Picking up chalk, Oppenheimer went on, "Now thermal diffusion itself won't provide the enrichment we need, but a combination of thermal diffusion and the Y-12 process will give us a bomb by July 1945. That is clear." He rapidly scrawled on the board figures that showed a fourfold increase in the electromagnetic separation of the Y-12 plant, given feed enriched to one part in seventy. "The question is, can a thermal plant on a very large scale be erected within a few months to feed Y-12? I've recommended this urgently to General Groves. We're here to discuss ways and means."

Stooped, skinny, melancholy, Oppenheimer returned to his seat. Now that the meeting had a direction, ideas and questions sparked around in quick insiders' shorthand. Sime Anderson was called on to answer many questions. The meeting pressed him hard on the core of the Navy system, the forty-eight-foot vertical steam pipes of concentric iron, copper, and nickel cylinders.

"But the Navy's using only a hundred of them, hand-fashioned at that," exclaimed a big red-faced civilian in the front row. "That's lab equipment. We're talking here about several thousand of the damn things, aren't we? A whole forest of them, factory-made! It's a plumber's nightmare, Colonel Nichols. You won't get a corporation in this country to take on such a contract. Three *thousand* pipes of that length, with those tolerances, in a few *months?* Forget it."

The meeting split into two groups for lunch: one to talk about design with Oppenheimer and Anderson, one to confer with Nichols and Peters on construction and manufacturing. "The general wants this thing done," Colonel Nichols summed up in adjourning. "So it will be. We'll all meet back here at two o'clock, and start making some decisions."

With a wave of his pipe, Oppenheimer stopped Sime from leaving the room. When they were alone he said, walking to the blackboard, "A-minus, Anderson." He picked up chalk, corrected an equation with a nervous rub of a fist and a scrawl of symbols; then asked a series of quick questions, dazzling the naval officer with his total grasp of thermal diffusion in every aspect. "Well, let's get on to the cafeteria," he said, dropping the chalk, "and join the others."

"Yes, sir."

Leaning against the desk, arms folded, Oppenheimer made no move to go. "What next for you?"

"I'm returning to Washington tonight, sir."

"I know that. Now that the Army will get into thermal diffusion, what about a new challenge? Come and join us out in New Mexico."

"You're sure the Army will do it?"

"They have to. There's no alternative. The weapon itself still poses some nice problems in ideas. Not lion hunting, so to say, but a lively rabbit shoot. Are you married, Anderson?"

"Ah — no, I'm not."

"Better so. The mesa is a strange place, quite isolated. Some of the wives take to it, but others — well, that won't concern you. You'll soon be hearing from Captain Parsons."

"Captain Parsons? Is he in New Mexico now?"

"He's a division head. You'll come, won't you? There's a lot of excellence out there."

"I go where I'm ordered, Dr. Oppenheimer."

"Orders won't be a problem."

All the trudging in ropy mud wore Victor Henry down. McDermott drove a jeep, but the narrow rutted roads ended abruptly in brush or muck, sometimes far from where they wanted to go. Pug didn't mind the slogging here and there, because they were getting the answers he wanted. One after another, the technicians concurred that with a modified sleeve and a thicker gasket, the substitute coupling would answer. It was the old story — administrative rigidity in Washington, good-humored horse sense among the men with hard hats, dirty hands, and muddy shoes. Pug had broken many a supply impasse this way.

"I'm convinced," McDermott shouted over the grinding and bumping of the jeep, as they headed back under lowering storm clouds. They had been at this for hours, pausing only for sandwiches and coffee at a field canteen. "Now convince the Army, Captain."

80

SHARING a drawing room on the train back to Washington, Pug and Peters hung up wet clothes as the train started, and Pug declined the whiskey the Army man offered him. He did not feel much like drinking with his wife's current love. Sime Anderson came in, summoned by the colonel. "Stay here," Peters said to Pug, when their discussion began and he offered to leave. "I want you in on this."

Pug quickly gathered that the Army was taking a sudden urgent interest in a Navy system for processing uranium. He kept his mouth shut while the colonel, whose frame bulked large in the tiny room, puffed at a cigar, sipped whiskey, and asked Anderson questions. The train picked up speed, the wheels clattered, rain beat on the black windows, and Pug began to feel hungry.

"Sir, I'm on special detached duty, assigned directly to the lab," Anderson replied to a query about the Navy chain of command on the project. "You'll have to talk to Dr. Abelson."

"I will. I see only one way through this mess," Peters said, putting his notebook into a breast pocket. "We'll have to build twenty Chinese copies of your plant. Just duplicate it and string 'em in series. Designing a new two-thousand-column plant can take many months."

"You could design for greater efficiency, sir."

"Yes, for the next war. The idea is to make a weapon for this one. All right, Commander. Many thanks."

When Anderson left, Peters asked Pug, "Do you know Admiral Purnell? I'm wondering how I go about getting the Navy's blueprints for thermal diffusion real fast."

"Your man is Ernest King."

"But King may not even be clued in on uranium. Purnell's the Navy man on the Military Policy Committee."

"I know, but that doesn't matter. Go to King."

"Will you do that?"

"What? Approach Admiral King for the Army? *Me?*"

At the incredulous tone, Colonel Peters's fleshy mouth widened in the grin which no doubt charmed the women; the naïve, cheery grin of a mature man who had not known much grief, a gray-haired boyish man. "Look,

Henry, I can't proceed through channels in the uranium business, and I can't write letters. Ordinarily I'd go with this thing to the next meeting of the Military Policy Committee, but I want to get moving. The trouble is — and it hasn't been my doing — we've cold-shouldered the Navy for years. We've shut Abelson out. We even got snotty about giving him a supply of uranium hexafluoride, when it was Abelson, for Christ's sake, who first produced the stuff for us. I just found that out today. Stupid policy, and now we need the Navy. You know King, don't you?"

"Quite well."

"I have a feeling you could broker this thing."

"Look, Colonel, just getting in to see Ernest King can take days. Tell you what, though. You release those couplings — I mean telephone that firm in Pennsylvania from Union Station tomorrow — and I'll get right in a cab and try to break in on the CNO."

"Pug, only the general can waive this priority." Peters's wide grin was wary and uncertain. "I could get my head cut off."

"So you said. Well, I can get my head cut off for barging in on Ernest King without an appointment. Especially with an Army request."

Staring at Pug, Colonel Peters rubbed his mouth hard, then burst out laughing. "Hell, those Oak Ridge fellows approved your coupling, didn't they? You're on. Let's have a drink on it."

"I'd rather have dinner. I'm hungry as a bear. Coming?"

"Go ahead." Peters clearly did not like this second refusal. "I'll be along."

Sime Anderson stood in the queue outside the dining car, pondering a common quandary of wartime — whether to propose marriage before going off to serve in a distant place. He could take Madeline out to that mesa in New Mexico, but would she agree to go, and even if she did, would she be happy in such a place? Oppenheimer had hinted at difficulties with wives. When Madeline's father showed up on the queue, Sime seized the chance to sit with him in the jammed dining car at a table for two. While they ate tepid tomato soup and very greasy fried pork chops, and the car swayed and rattled, and rippling rain slanted in streaks on the window, he told Pug his problem. Pug did not speak until he finished, and not for a while after that.

"You love each other?" he asked at last.

"Yes, sir."

"Well, then? Navy juniors are used to living in strange places."

"She went to New York to break the mold of a Navy junior." Sime said nothing as yet about Hugh Cleveland. His sad tone, his miserable glance at the father, revealed to Pug that Madeline had told all, and that it had gone down hard.

"Sime, she came home."

"Yes. To another big city, and another radio job."

"Are you asking for my advice?"

"Yes, sir."

"Ever hear about faint hearts and fair ladies? Take your chances. I think she'll go with you, and stay with you." The father offered his hand. "Good luck."

"Thank you, sir." They gripped each other's hands.

In the club car, Pug drank a large brandy in a contented glow. Madeline for years had seemed an irretrievable disaster; and now this! He mulled over images of Madeline through the years: the enchanting girl baby, the fairy princess in the school play, the disconcerting flirt with budding breasts, shining eyes, and inexpert makeup going to her first dance, the brassy horror in New York. Now it seemed that poor Madeline would make it; at least there was a damned good chance for her, after a rotten start.

Pug did not want to spoil his good mood by spending the night bedded down in a room with Colonel Harrison Peters. He was used to sleeping sitting up in trains and planes, and he decided to snooze in the club car. Peters had not appeared for dinner; probably he had quaffed several whiskeys and turned in. Pug dozed off with the lights on and drinkers' noise all around him, having slipped the barman ten dollars to buy his peace.

The car was dimmed, and quiet except for the rapid clacking of the wheels, when he was poked awake. A tall figure in a bathrobe swayed over him. Peters said, "There's a nice berth all made up for you."

Yawning, stiff, Pug could think of no gracious way out. He stumbled after Peters to the drawing room, which for odors of whiskey and stale cigars was no better than the club car; but the crisply sheeted upper berth looked good. He quickly undressed.

"Nightcap?" Peters was pouring from an almost empty bottle.

"No, thanks."

"Pug, don't you want to drink with me?"

Without comment Pug accepted the glass. They drank, got into their berths, and turned out the lights. Pug was glad to be under covers after all. He relaxed with a sigh, and was sinking into sleep.

"Say, Pug." Peters's voice from below, warm and whiskeyish. "That Anderson's a comer. Rhoda thinks he and Madeline are serious. You'd approve, wouldn't you?"

"Yep."

Silence. Train sounds.

"Pug, can I ask you a very personal question?"

No reply.

"Sorry as hell to disturb you. This is damned important to me."

"Go ahead."

"Why did you and Rhoda ever break up?"

Victor Henry had tried to avoid a night with the Army man, to duck the risk of just such a probe. He did not answer.

"It wasn't my doing, was it? It's unbelievably shitty to move in on a guy's wife when he's overseas. I understood you were already estranged."

"That's true."

"Otherwise, believe me, attractive as she is, I'd have steered clear."

"I believe you."

"You and Rhoda are two of the finest people I know. What happened?"

"I fell in love with an Englishwoman."

Pause.

"That's what Rhoda says."

"That's it."

"It doesn't seem like you."

Pug was silent.

"Are you going to marry her?"

"I thought I was, but she refused me." So Peters wrung from Victor Henry his first reference to Pamela's astounding letter, which he had tried to bury from mind.

"Jesus! You never know with a woman, Pug, do you? Sorry to hear that."

"Good-night, Colonel." It was a sharp cut-off tone.

"Pug, just one more question. Did Dr. Fred Kirby have anything to do with all this?"

There it was. The thing Rhoda had feared was coming to pass because of this forced intimacy. What Victor Henry said next could make or break the rest of Rhoda's life; and he had to answer fast, for every second of hesitation was a slur on her, on him, and on their marriage.

"What the hell does that mean?" Pug hoped he put the right puzzlement, tinged with anger, in his tone.

"I've been getting letters, Pug, damnable anonymous letters, about Rhoda and Dr. Kirby. I'm ashamed of myself for paying them any attention, but —"

"You should be. Fred Kirby's an old friend of mine. We met when I was stationed in Berlin. Rhoda had to come home when the war broke out. Fred was in Washington then, and he played tennis with her, and took her to shows and such, sort of the way you've been doing, but with no complications. I knew about it, and I appreciated it. I don't like this conversation much, and I'd like to turn in."

"Sorry, Pug."

"Okay."

Silence. Then Peters's voice, low, troubled, and drunk. "It's because I idolize Rhoda that I'm so upset. I'm more than upset, I'm tortured. Pug, I've known a hell of a lot of women, prettier than Rhoda, and sexier. But she's virtuous. That's where her preciousness lies. That sounds strange coming from me, but that's how I feel. Rhoda's the first lady in every sense of the word that I've ever known, except for my own mother. She's perfect. She's elegant, modest, decent, and truthful. She never lies. Christ, most women lie the way they breathe. You know that. You can't blame them. We keep trying to screw them, they play a desperate game, and all's fair. Don't you agree?"

Peters had drunk up the bottle, Pug thought, to nerve himself for this. The maundering could go on all night. He made no reply.

"I mean I'm not talking about these stodgy wives, Pug. I'm talking about stylish women. My mother was a knockout till she was eighty-two. Christ, she looked like a chorus girl in her coffin. Yet I want to tell you, she was a saint. Like Rhoda, she went to church every Sunday, rain or shine. Rhoda's as stylish as a movie queen, yet there's something saintly about her, too. That's why this thing's hit me like an earthquake, Pug, and if I've offended you I'm sorry, because I think the world of you."

"We've got a busy day tomorrow, Colonel."

"Right, Pug."

In a few minutes Peters was snoring.

There were two admirals in King's outer office, when Pug came there straight from Union Station. He prevailed on the flag lieutenant to send in a short note, and King at once summoned him inside. The CNO sat behind his large desk in the bleak room, smoking a cigarette in a holder. "You look better than you did in Tehran," he said, not offering Pug a chair. "What's this about uranium now? I've shredded your note into the burn basket."

Pug sketched the situation at Oak Ridge in spare sentences. King's bald long head and seamed face turned very pink. His severe mouth puckered strangely, and Pug surmised that he was trying not to smile. "Are you saying," King broke in harshly, "that the Army, after commandeering all the nation's scientists and factories, and spending billions, hasn't got a bomb, while we've cooked one up in that tinpot Anacostia lab of ours?"

"Not quite, Admiral. There's a technical gap in the Army's method. The Navy process closes that gap. They want to take our system and blow it up on a huge industrial scale."

"And that way they'll get this weapon made? Not otherwise?"

"So I understand. Not in time for use in this war."

"Hell, I'll give 'em anything they need, then. Why not? This should make us look pretty good in the history books, hey? Except the Army will write the history, so we'll probably get left out. How did you become involved in it?"

King listened to the tale of the couplings, nodding and smoking, his face rigid again. "Colonel Peters has telephoned the Dresser company," Pug concluded. "It's all set. I'm flying to Pennsylvania to make sure that the stuff gets on the trucks and rolls out."

"Good idea. Flying how?"

"Navy plane out of Andrews."

"Got transportation?"

"Not yet."

King picked up the telephone and ordered a car and driver for Captain Henry. "Now then. What do you want me to do, Henry?"

"Assure Colonel Peters of Navy cooperation, Admiral. Before pushing this idea of duplicating our plant, he wants to be sure of his ground."

"Give his phone number to my flag lieutenant. I'll call the man."

"Yes, sir."

"I've heard about your expediting of the landing craft program. The Secretary is pleased." King got up and held out a long lean arm crusted with gold to the elbow. "On your way."

As Pug was paying off the taxicab on his return from Pennsylvania, Madeline opened the front door. She looked almost as she had, going to her first dance: flushed, shiny-eyed, too painted-up. She said nothing, but gave him a hug and led him into the living room. There sat Rhoda, looking very dressy for a weekday at home, behind a coffee table on which champagne was cooling in a silver bucket. Sime Anderson stood beside her with a bewildered, foolishly pleased look on his face.

"Good evening, sir."

"Well! Return of the warrior!" said Rhoda. "You remembered you had a FAMILY! How nice! Are you busy next Saturday?"

"Not that I can think of, no."

"Oh, no! Well, fine. How about coming to Saint John's Church, then, and giving Madeline away to this sailor boy?"

Mother, daughter, and suitor burst into joyous laughter. Pug seized Madeline in his arms. She clung to him, hugging him hard, her wet cheek to his. He shook hands with Sime Anderson and embraced him. The young man wore the shaving lotion Warren had used; the smell gave Pug a small shock. Rhoda jumped up, kissed Pug, and exclaimed, "OKAY! Surprise is over, now for the champagne." Practical talk followed: wedding arrangements, trousseau, caterer, guest list, accommodations for Sime's family, and so forth; Rhoda kept making neat notes in a stenographic pad. Then Pug took Anderson off into the library.

"Sime, how are your finances?"

The young man confessed to two expensive hobbies: hunting, which he had learned from his father, and classical music. He had put more than a thousand dollars into records and a Capehart, and almost as much into a collection of rifles and shotguns. No doubt it hadn't been sensible to clutter up his life that way; he could hardly turn around in his apartment; but then, he hadn't bothered much with girls. Now he would store the stuff, and one day sell it off. Meantime he had saved only twelve hundred dollars.

"Well, that's something. You can live on your salary. Madeline has savings, too. Also some stock in that damned radio show."

Anderson looked very uncomfortable. "Yes. She's better off than I am."

"Don't live higher on the hog than your own salary warrants. Let her do what she likes with her money, but not that."

"That's my intention."

"Now, look, Sime, I've got fifteen thousand dollars put aside for her. It's yours."

"Ye gods, that's marvelous!" An innocently greedy pleasure lit the young man's face. "I didn't expect that."

"I'd suggest you buy a house around Washington with it, if you plan to stay in the Navy."

"Sure, I'm staying in the Navy. We've talked that all out. R and D will be very big after the war."

Pug put his hands on Anderson's shoulders. "She's said a thousand times, down the years, that she'd never marry a naval officer. Well done."

The young couple went off in a happy flurry to celebrate. Pug and Rhoda sat in the living room, finishing the wine.

"So," said Rhoda, "the last fledgling takes wing. At least she's made it before the mother flew off." Rhoda blinked archly over the rim of her wineglass at Pug.

"Shall I take you out to dinner?"

"Oh, no. I've got shad roe for the two of us. And there's another bottle of champagne. How was your trip? Was Hack helpful?"

"Decidedly."

"I'm so glad. He has got a big job, hasn't he, Pug?"

"Couldn't be bigger."

Fresh-cut flowers from the garden on the candle-lit table; a tossed salad with Roquefort dressing; perfectly done large shad roe with dry crisp bacon; potatoes in their jackets, with sour cream and chives; a fresh-baked blueberry pie; obviously Rhoda had planned all this for his return. She cooked and served it herself, then sat and ate in a gray silk dress, with beautifully coiffed hair, looking like a chic guest at her own table. She was in a wonderful mood, telling Pug her ideas for the wedding, or else she was giving a superb performance. The champagne sparkled in her eyes.

This was the Rhoda who, for all her familiar failings — crabbiness, flightiness, moodiness, shallowness — had made him a happy man, Pug was thinking, for twenty-five years; who had captivated Kirby and Peters, and could ensnare any man her age; beautiful, competent, energetic, attentive to a man's comforts, intensely feminine, capable of exciting passion. What had happened? Why had he frozen her out? What had been so irreparable? Long, long ago he had faced the fact that the war had caused her affair with Kirby, that it was a personal mischance in a world upheaval; even Sime Anderson had shrugged off Madeline's past, and made a happy start on a new life.

The answer never changed. He did not love Rhoda any more. He had no use for her. He could not help it. It had nothing to do with forgiveness. He had forgiven her. But a live nerve now bound Sime Anderson and Madeline, and Rhoda had severed the nerve of their marriage. It was withered and dead. Some marriages survived an infidelity, but this one had not. He had been ready to go on with it because of the memory of their lost son, but it was better for Rhoda to live with someone who loved her. That she was in trouble with Peters only made him pity her.

"Great pie," said Pug.

"Thank you, kind sir, and you know what I propose next? I propose coffee and Armagnac in the garden, that's what. All the iris have popped open, and the smell is sheer HEAVEN."

"You're on."

It had taken Rhoda a couple of years to weed out and replant the neglected quarter-acre. Now it was a charming brick-walled nook of varied colors and delicious fragrances, around a musically splashing little fountain she had installed at some cost. She carried the coffee service out to a wrought-iron table between cushioned lounge chairs, and Pug brought the Armagnac and glasses.

"By the bye," she said as they settled down, "there's a letter from Byron. In all the excitement, I clean forgot. He's fine. It's just a page."

"Any real news?" Pug tried to keep relief out of his voice.

"Well, the first patrol was a success, and he's been qualified for command. You know Byron. He never says much."

"Did his Bronze Star come through?"

"Nothing on that. He worries and worries about Natalie. Begs us to cable any word we get."

Pug sat staring at the flower beds. The colors were dimming in the fading light, and a breeze stirred a rich scent from the nodding purple iris. "We should call the State Department again."

"I did, today. The Danish Red Cross is supposed to visit Theresienstadt, so maybe some word will come through."

Pug was experiencing the sensation of a slipped cog in time, of reliving an old scene. Rhoda's *"By the bye, there's a letter from Byron"* had triggered it, he realized. So they had sat drinking Armagnac in twilight before the war, the day Admiral Preble had offered him the attaché post in Berlin. *"By the bye, there's a letter from Byron,"* Rhoda had said, and he had felt the same sort of relief, because they had not heard from him in months. It had been the first letter about Natalie. That day, Warren had announced he was putting in for flight training. That day, Madeline had tried to go to New York during the school week, and he had stopped her with difficulty. In hindsight, quite a turning point, that day.

"Rhoda, I said I'd report any personal talk I had with Peters."

"Yes?" Rhoda sat up.

"There was some."

She gulped brandy. "Go ahead."

Pug narrated the conversation in the dark train compartment. Rhoda kept taking nervous sips of her brandy. She sighed when he described Peters's subsiding into snores. "Well! You were very, very gallant," she said. "It's no more than I expected of you, Pug. Thank you, and God bless you."

"That wasn't the end of it, Rho."

She stared at her husband, her face white and strained in the gloom. "He went to sleep, you said."

"He did. I woke early, and slid out of there for some breakfast. The waiter was bringing me orange juice when your colonel showed up, all shaved and spruce, and sat down with me. We were the only two people in the diner. He asked for coffee, and right off he said — in a very sober and calm way — 'I take it you preferred not to give me a straight answer last night about Dr. Kirby.' "

"Oh, God. What did you say?"

"Well, he caught me off guard, you realize. I said, 'How could I have been any straighter?' Something like that. Then here's what he answered — and I'm trying for his exact words — 'I'm not about to cross-examine you, Pug. And I'm not about to throw over Rhoda. But I think I should know the truth. A marriage shouldn't start with a lie. If you get a chance to tell Rhoda that, please do. It may help clear the air.' "

"And what did you say to that?" Her voice shook, and her hand shook as she poured her glass full.

"I said, 'There's no air to clear, except in your mind. If poison-pen letters can get to you, you don't deserve any woman's love, let alone Rhoda's.' "

"Beautiful, darling. Beautiful."

"I'm not sure. He looked me in the eye and just said, 'Okay, Pug.' He changed the subject and talked business. He never referred to you again."

Rhoda drank deeply. "I'm lost. You're not a good liar, Pug, though God knows you tried."

"Rhoda, I can lie, and on occasion I do it damned well."

"In the line of duty!" She flipped her hand in scorn. "That's not what I'm talking about." She drank, and poured more, saying, "I'm sunk, that's all. That accursed woman! Whoever she is, I really could kill her — oops!" The glass was overflowing.

"You'll be blotto."

"Why not?"

"Rhoda, he said he's not throwing you over."

"Oh, no. He'll go through with it. Soul of honor, and all that. I'll probably have to let him. What's my alternative? Still, it's all ruined."

"Why don't you just tell him, Rhoda?"

Rhoda sat and peered at him without replying.

"I mean that. Look at Madeline and Sime. She told him. They couldn't be happier."

With some of her old feminine sarcasm she said, "Pug, my dear dumb love, what kind of comparison is THAT? For God's sake, I'm a HAG. Sime's not thirty years old, and Madeline's a luscious girl. Hack's fastened on to me, and it's all been terribly charming, but at our age it's mostly mental. Now I'm CORNERED. I'm damned if I do and damned if I don't. I'm a good wife, *you* know I am, and I know I could make him happy. But he had to have this perfect picture of me. It's GONE."

"It was an illusion, Rho."

"What's WRONG with illusions?" Rhoda's voice strained and broke. "Sorry. I'm going to bed. Thank you, darling. Thank you for trying. You're a grand man, and I love you for it."

They stood up. Rhoda took a lithe step or two, put her arms around him and gave him a sensuous brandy-soaked kiss, pressing her body to his. They had not kissed like this in a year. So far as it went, it still worked. Pug could not help pulling her close and responding.

With a husky laugh, she broke half-free. "Save it for Pamela, honey."

"Pamela turned me down."

Rhoda went rigid in his arms, opening eyes like saucers. "Is THAT what was in that letter last week? She DIDN'T!"

"Yes."

"My God, you're close-mouthed. Why? How *could* she? Is she marrying Burne-Wilke?"

"She hadn't yet. Burne-Wilke was wounded in India. They're back in England. She's been nursing him and — well, Rhoda, she said no. That's it."

Rhoda uttered a coarse chuckle. "You accepted that?"

"How do I not accept it?"

"Honeybunch, I'm potted enough to TELL you how. Woo her! That's all she wants."

"I don't think she's like that. The letter was pretty final."

"We're ALL like that. I declare, I am STONE drunk. You may have to help me up the stairs."

"Okay, let's go."

"Just fooling." She patted his arm. "Finish your brandy, dear, and enjoy that gorgeous moon. I can navigate."

"You're sure?"

"Sure. Night, love."

A cool gentle kiss on the mouth, and Rhoda walked unsteadily inside.

When Pug came upstairs almost an hour later, Rhoda's door was wide open. The bedroom was dark. The door had not been open since his return from Tehran.

"Pug, is that you?"

"Yes."

"Well, good-night again, darling."

It was all in the tone. Rhoda was a signaller, not a talker, and Pug read the signal, loud and clear. Clearly she had weighed her chances again, in the light of Peters's suspicions, Pam's refusal, and the family glow of Madeline's happiness. Here was his old marriage, asking him back in. It was Rhoda's last try. *They play a desperate game,* Peters had said. True enough. It was a powerful game, too. He had only to step through the doorway, into the remembered sweet odors of that dark room.

He walked by the door, his eyes moistening. "Good-night, Rhoda."

81

PAST midnight. Overhead the full moon rides, silvering the deserted streets; silvering too the long, long freight train that comes clanking and squealing into the Bahnhofstrasse and jars to a halt outside the Hamburg barracks. Reverberating through the straight streets, the noises awaken the restless sleepers. *"Did you hear that?"* In many languages these words are whispered through the crowded rows of three-tier bunks.

There has not been a transport in a long time. The train could be bringing more materials for the crazy Beautification. Or perhaps it has come to take away the products of the factories. So the worried whispers go, though trucks and horse-drawn wagons, not trains, usually haul in and out everything but human beings. Of course it could be an arriving transport, but those usually come by day.

Aaron Jastrow, poring over the Talmud in his preposterously well-furnished ground floor apartment on the Seestrasse (it is to be a stop for the Red Cross visitors) hears the train. Natalie does not wake. Just as well! The Council of Elders has been wrestling for days with the transport order. The controlling figures are burned in Jastrow's brain:

All Jews now in Theresienstadt	35,000
Protected by Germans (*Prominente, half-Jews, Danes, medal bearers, wounded war veterans and their families*)	9,500
Protected by the Central Secretariat (*officials bureaucrats, staff artists, war factory workers*)	6,500
Total protected	16,000
Available for transport	19,000

Seven thousand, five hundred persons must go — almost half of the "available," one-fifth of the whole ghetto. The grating irony of the dates! The expectation of an Allied landing on May 15 has swept Theresienstadt. People have been waiting and praying for that day. Now the Transport Section is frantically shuffling and reshuffling index cards for the first shipment on May 15 of twenty-five hundred; the transport will go in three trains on three successive days.

This transport will badly disrupt the Beautification. The Technical Department will lose much of the work force that is repainting the town, laying out flower beds, putting down turf, building and renovating. The orchestras, the choruses, the drama and opera casts, will be cut to pieces. But the SS is unconcerned. Rahm has warned that the work will be done and the performances will shape up, or those in charge will be sorry. The Beautification is the cause of the transport. As the Red Cross visit draws nearer, the commander is getting nervous about his ability to steer it along a restricted route. The whole ghetto is being cleaned up, and to relieve the overcrowding, the sluice to the east has once more been opened.

Jastrow is heartsick over the general tragedy, and over a private bereavement. Headquarters has ordered all orphans in the town shipped off. Red Cross visitors asking a child about its parents must not hear that they are dead or — forbidden word — "transported." Half of his Talmud class are orphans. His star student, Shmuel Horovitz, is one: a shy gaunt lad of sixteen with long hair, a silky beard, huge infinitely sad eyes, and a lightning mind. How can he bear to lose Shmuel? If only the Allies will indeed land! If only the shock will delay or cancel this transport! Saving seven thousand, five hundred Jews out of the massacre would be a miracle. Saving Shmuel alone would be a miracle. In Jastrow's fond view, the blaze of this boy's brain could light up the future of the whole Jewish people. He could be a Maimonides, a Rashi. To lose such a mind in a brief horrible flare over Oswiecim!

Natalie departs for the mica factory in the morning, unaware of the waiting train. Jastrow goes to the newly located, superbly equipped library, which would not disgrace a small college: whole rooms full of new steel book stacks, bright lighting, polished reading tables, good chairs, even carpeting; and a richly varied collection of books in the major European languages, as well as the stunning Judaica collection, all smartly indexed and catalogued. Of course nobody is using this luxurious facility. Readers and borrowers will be suitably rehearsed in due time, to make it all look natural for the Danish visitors.

Nobody on Jastrow's staff mentions the train. The day fades into late afternoon. Nothing has happened, and he begins to hope that all will be well. But they come, after all: two shabby Jews from the Transport Commission, a big fellow with wavy red hair carrying the bundle of summons cards, and a yellow-faced gnome with the roster to be signed. Their expressions are bitter. They know they move in an aura of hatred. They plod about the rooms, hunting down each transport recruit, serving him with his card, and getting his signature. The library is badly hit; out of seven staff workers Jastrow loses five, including Shmuel Horovitz. With the gray card on the desk before him,

Shmuel strokes his youthful beard and looks to Jastrow. Slowly he turns his palms up and outward, his dark eyes wide, black-rimmed, and grieving as the eyes of Jesus in a Byzantine mosaic.

When Jastrow returns to the apartment, Natalie is there. Regarding him with eyes like Shmuel Horovitz's, she holds out two gray cards to him. She and Louis are assigned to the third train, departing on the seventeenth "*for resettlement in the direction of Dresden.*" Their transport numbers are on the cards. She must report with Louis to the Hamburg barracks on the six-teenth, bringing light luggage, one change of linen, and food for twenty-four hours.

"This is a mistake," says Jastrow. "I'll go to Eppstein."

Natalie's face is as gray as the card. "You think so?"

"No doubt of it. You're a *Prominent,* a mica worker, and the head-mistress of the children's pavilion. The Transport Commission is a mad-house. Somebody pulled the wrong card. I shall be back within the hour. Be cheerful."

Outside the Magdeburg barracks, there is a riotous crush. Cursing ghetto guards are trying to shove the people into a queue, using fists, shoul-ders, and here and there rubber clubs. Jastrow passes through a privileged entrance. From the far end of the main hallway comes the angry anxious tumult of petitioners jamming the transport office. Outside Eppstein's suite there is also a line. Jastrow recognizes high officials of the Economic and Technical Departments. This transport is biting deep! Jastrow does not get in line. The rank of Elder is a wretched burden, but at least it gives one access to the big shots, and even — if one has real business with them — to the SS. Eppstein's pretty Berlin secretary, looking cross and worn, manages a smile at Jastrow, and passes him in.

Eppstein sits with hands clasped on his handsome new mahogany desk. The office would suit a Prague banker now, for furnishings and decoration; a long briefing for the Red Cross is scheduled here. He looks surprised to see Jastrow, and is cordial and sympathetic about Natalie. Yes, a mistake is not at all unlikely. Those poor devils in transport have been running around with-out heads. He will look into it. Has Jastrow's niece been up to any mischief, by chance? Jastrow says, "Nothing of the kind, certainly not," and he tries to give Eppstein the gray cards.

The High Elder shrinks from them. "No, no, no, let her keep them, don't confuse things. When the error is corrected she'll be notified to turn the cards in."

For three days no further word comes from Eppstein. Jastrow tries over and over to see him, but the Berlin secretary turns cold, formal, and mean. Pestering her is useless, she says. The High Elder will send word when he has news. Meantime Natalie learns, and reports to Jastrow, that every member of her Zionist circle has received a transport card. Sullenly she acknowledges that Jastrow was prescient; an informer must have betrayed them, and they are being gotten rid of. They include the hospital's head of surgery, the deputy manager of the food administration, and the former president of the Jewish War Veterans of Germany. No protection avails this group, obviously.

The first two trains leave. Natalie's little cabal, except for herself, are all shipped off. A third long string of cattle cars squeals into the Bahnhofstrasse. All over Theresienstadt, transportees trudge toward the Hamburg barracks in bright afternoon sunshine, carrying luggage, food, and small children.

Jastrow returns to the apartment from a last try to see Eppstein. He has failed, but there is a ray of hope. One of his students, who works in the Central Secretariat, has whispered news to him. Gross errors were made by the Transport Commission. Over eight thousand summonses went out, but the SS has contracted with the Reichsbahn, the German railroad company, for exactly seven thousand five hundred transportees. The Reichsbahn calls the transports *Sonderzüge*, "special trains," charging the SS reduced third-class group fares. There are cars for only seventy-five hundred in all. So at least five hundred summonses may be cancelled; five hundred transportees reprieved!

Natalie sits on the couch sewing, with Louis beside her, as Jastrow pours out this news. She does not react with joy. She hardly reacts at all. Natalie has withdrawn into the old shell of narrow-focused numbness that protects her in bad times.

Right now she is wondering, she tells Jastrow, what to wear. She has dressed Louis up like Little Lord Fauntleroy, buying or borrowing clothes from families who are not going. With calm, dreamy, almost schizoid logic, she explains that her appearance will be important, since she will no longer be shielded by a famous uncle. She will be on her own. She must look her best. If only she can find instant favor in the eyes of the SS men where she is going, identify herself as an American and a *Prominent*, then her sex appeal and Louis's charm, and sympathy for a young mother, can all work for her. Shall she wear her rather seductive purple dress for the journey? She is sewing a yellow star on the dress as they talk. In this warm weather, she says, it might just do for the trip. What does Aaron think?

He gently falls in with her frame of mind. No, the purple dress might provoke liberties from the Germans, or even from low Jews. The tailored gray suit is elegant, Germanic, and it sets off her figure. She and Louis will stand out when they arrive. Solemnly nodding as he talks, she agrees, and folds away the starred dress in her suitcase, saying it may come in handy yet. She continues fussing at her packing, talking half to herself about the choices she must make. Aaron unlocks a desk drawer, takes out a knife, and severs a couple of stitches in the stout walking shoe on his right foot. Numb as she is, this strikes her as strange. "What are you doing?" The shoe is too tight, he says, going off into his own room. When he comes out, he is wearing his best suit and his old fedora. He looks rather like a transportee. His face is very grave, or upset, or scared, she cannot tell which.

"Natalie, I'll follow up on this matter of the cancelled summonses."

"But I must go to the Hamburg barracks soon."

"I shan't be long, and anyway, I can visit you there tonight."

She peers at him. "Honestly, do you think there is any hope?" Her tone is skeptical and detached.

"We'll see." Aaron drops on a knee beside Louis, who is playing with Natalie's Punch puppet on the floor. "Well, Louis," he says in Yiddish, "good-bye, and God watch over you." He kisses the boy. The tickling beard makes Louis laugh.

Natalie finishes her packing, closes the suitcases, and ties the bundles. Now she has nothing to do. This is what she finds hard to bear. Keeping busy is her best surcease from dread. She knows well that she and Louis are on a brink. She has not forgotten Berel's account, reported by Aaron, of what happens "in the east." She has not forgotten it, but she has suppressed it. She and Aaron have not referred to Oswiecim again. The transport summons says nothing about Oswiecim. She has shut her mind and heart to the thought that she is probably going there. She does not even yet repent of her involvement with the underground Zionists. It has kept her spirits high, given her a handle on her fate, made some sense of it.

The great German oppression is due to the homelessness and defenselessness of the Jews. Bad luck has caught her up in the catastrophe. But Western liberalism was always a mirage. Assimilation is impossible. She herself has lived an empty Jewish life until now, but she has found herself. If she survives, her life will go to restoring the Jewish nation to its ancient soil in Palestine.

She believes this. It is her new creed. At least, she believes she believes it. A small resistant mocking American voice has never quite died in her, whispering that what she really wants is to survive, go back to Byron, and live in San Francisco or Colorado; and that her sudden conversion to Zionism is mental morphine for the agony of entrapment. But morphine or creed, she has risked her life for it, is about to pay the price, and still does not regret it. She regrets only that she did not jump at Berel's offer to deliver Louis. If only she might still do it!

She can wait no longer for Aaron. With Louis toddling beside her, she sets out for the Hamburg barracks, a bundle of food and toilet things on her back, a suitcase in either hand. She falls into a stooped shabby procession of Jews with their packs, all headed that way. It is a beautiful balmy afternoon. Flowers bloom everywhere, bordering fresh green lawns that have been laid down in the last couple of weeks. Theresienstadt's streets are clean. The town smells like springtime. The buildings gleam with new yellow paint. Though the Beautification has a long way to go, the Red Cross visitors could almost be fooled right now, Natalie dully thinks, as she squints into the sinking sun dead ahead in the street; fooled, that is, if they would not enter the barracks, or if they would not inquire about the railroad spur into the town, or about the mortality rates.

She gets into the long line outside the Hamburg barracks, holding tight to Louis, pushing her suitcases forward with a foot. Across the street under the terminal shed stands the black locomotive. At the courtyard entrance, under the eyes of SS men, Transport Commission Jews at raw lumber tables are officiously checking in the transportees — asking questions, calling out names and numbers, slamming papers with rubber stamps, all with the worn-down irritability of emigration inspectors at any border.

Natalie's turn comes. The official who takes her papers is a small man wearing a red cloth cap. He shouts at her in German, stamps the papers, and scrawls notes. He collects her cards, and bawls the numbers over his shoulder. A man with a three-day stubble brings him two cardboard signs looped with string. The numbers of Natalie's gray cards are painted on the signs in huge black digits. Natalie hangs a number around her neck, and the other on Louis.

At the SS headquarters, Aaron Jastrow stands hat in hand outside the commander's office, the adjutant having ordered him to wait in the hall. Uniformed Germans pass him without a glance. A Jew Elder summoned to Sturmbannführer Rahm's office is no uncommon sight, especially during the Beautification push. Fear weakens the old man's knees, yet he does not dare lean against the wall. A Jew in a lounging attitude in the presence of Germans invites a fist or a club, Beautification or no. The wariness is soaked into his bones. With great effort, he holds himself stiffly straight.

The fear was worst when he made the decision back at the apartment. His hand trembled so, when he cut into the shoe, that at first try the knife slipped and gashed his left thumb, which still oozes blood through the rag he has tied over it. That, happily, Natalie did not notice in her stunned state, though she did see him sever the stitches. But the decision once taken, he has mastered the fear enough to go ahead. The rest is in God's hands. The time for the ultimate gamble is upon him. *The Allies will land;* if not in May, then in June or July. On all fronts the Germans are losing. The war may end quite suddenly. Natalie and Louis must not go in this transport.

"Doron, t'fila, milkhama!"

Over and over Aaron Jastrow keeps muttering these three Hebrew words. They give him courage. *"Doron, t'fila, milkhama!"* He remembers them from a childhood Bible lesson about Jacob and Esau. After a twenty-year separation, the brothers are about to meet, and Jacob hears that Esau is coming with four hundred armed men. Jacob sends ahead huge gifts, whole herds of cattle, donkeys, and camels; he arrays his caravan for combat; and he implores God for help. Rashi comments, "The three ways to prepare for the foe: tribute, prayer, and battle — *doron, t'fila, milkhama.*"

Jastrow has prayed. He has brought costly tribute with him. And if he must, he is ready to fight.

The adjutant, a big pink-faced Austrian who cannot be twenty-five, yet whose Sam Browne belt strains his green-clad paunch into two rolls, opens the office door. "All right, you. Get in here."

Jastrow walks through the anteroom, and through the open door to Rahm's office, where the scowling commander sits writing at his desk. Behind Jastrow, the adjutant shuts the door. Rahm does not look up. His pen scratches and scratches. Jastrow has a bad urge to urinate. He has never been in this office before. The big pictures of Hitler and Himmler, the swastika flag, the double lightning-flash insignia of the SS, blown up on the wall in a large silver and black wall medallion, all unnerve him. In almost any other circumstances he would beg the use of a bathroom, but he dare not open his mouth.

"What the devil do you want?" Rahm all at once shouts, glaring up at him and going red in the face.

"*Herr Kommandant,* may I respectfully — "

"Respectfully what? You think I don't know why you're here? Say one word on behalf of that Jew-whore niece of yours, and you'll be thrown out of here covered with blood! You understand? You think because you're a shitty Elder you can barge into these headquarters, to beg for a Jewish sow who plotted treason against the German government?"

This is Rahm's way. He has a fulminating temper and at such moments he can be very dangerous. Jastrow is near collapse. Pounding the desk, rising to his feet, Rahm screams at him, "WELL, JEW? You asked to see the commander, *ja?* I give you two minutes, and if you mention that cunt of a niece even once, I'll knock your teeth down your swinish throat! TALK."

In low tones, Jastrow gasps out, "I have committed a serious crime, which I want to confess to you."

"What? What? A crime?" The choleric face distorts in a look of puzzlement.

Jastrow pulls from his pocket a small velvety yellow pouch. With a violently shaking hand, he lays it on the desk before the commander. Glaring from him to the pouch, Rahm picks it up, and empties out on the desk six sparkling stones.

"I bought them in Rome, *Herr Kommandant,* in 1940, for twenty-five thousand dollars. I lived in Italy then. In Siena." Jastrow's voice slightly firms as he talks. "When Mussolini entered the war, I took the precaution of putting money into diamonds. As a *Prominent,* I was not searched on arrival in Theresienstadt. Regulations required the turning in of my jewelry. I know that. I regret this very serious offense, and I have come to make a clean breast of it."

Rahm sits down in his chair, contemplating the diamonds with a sour grin.

"I thought I had better turn them in directly to the *Herr Kommandant,*" Jastrow adds, "because of their value."

After a long, cynical stare at Jastrow, Rahm abruptly laughs. "Value! Probably you bought them from a Jew swindler, and they're glass."

"I bought them at Bulgari, Herr Kommandant. No doubt you have heard of the finest jeweler in Italy. The trademark is on the pouch."

Rahm does not look at the pouch. He brushes the stones aside with the back of his hand, and they scatter on his blotter.

"Where did you keep them hidden?"

"In my shoe."

"Ha! An old Jew trick. How much more have you got hidden away?" Rahm's tone is conversationally sarcastic. This is his way, too. Once his rage blows over, one can talk to him. Eppstein says, *"Rahm barks more than he bites."* However, he does bite. There lies the bribe on the desk. Rahm is not taking it. Jastrow's fate is in the balance now.

"I have nothing more."

"If your balls got twisted in the Little Fortress, you might remember something you overlooked."

"There is nothing else, *Herr Kommandant.*" Jastrow is convulsed with shivers; but his reply is persuasive in its steady tone.

One by one Rahm picks up the diamonds and holds them to the light. "Twenty-five thousand dollars? You were swindled blind, wherever you got them. I know cut stones. These are shit."

"I had them appraised in Milan, a year later, for forty thousand, *Herr Kommandant.*" Jastrow is here putting in a beautification touch of his own. Rahm's eyebrows lift.

"And your whore of a niece knows all about the stones, naturally."

"I never told her. It was wiser so. Nobody in the world knows of them, *Herr Kommandant,* but you and me."

Sturmbannführer Rahm's bloodshot eyes bore at Jastrow for long seconds. He drops the stones into the pouch, the pouch into a pocket. "Well, the whore and her bastard go in the transport."

"Herr Kommandant, there was an excess of summonses, I understand, and many will be cancelled."

Obstinately Rahm shakes his head. "She goes. She's lucky not to get sent to the Little Fortress and shot. Now clear out of here." He takes a pen and resumes writing.

Yet the *doron* has had some slight effect. The dismissal is curt but not fierce. Aaron Jastrow now has to make a quick judgment at highest hazard. Of course Rahm cannot acknowledge that the bribe has worked. But will he in fact see to it that Natalie does not go?

"I said, get your shitty ass out of here," snaps Rahm.

Jastrow decides to wield his pitiful weapon.

"*Herr Kommandant,* if my niece is transported, I must tell you I will resign as Elder. I will resign from the library. I will take no part in the Beautification. I will not talk to the Red Cross visitors in my apartment. Nothing will force me to change my mind." In nervous rapid-fire, he blurts out these rehearsed sentences.

The audacity catches Rahm by surprise. The pen drops. A horrible ferocity rumbles in his voice. "You are interested in committing suicide, Jew? Right away?"

More rehearsed sentences tumble out. "*Herr Kommandant,* Obersturmbannführer Eichmann went to great trouble to bring me from Paris to Theresienstadt. I make good window dressing! My picture has been taken by German journalists. My books are published in Denmark. The Red Cross visitors will be very interested to meet me, and —"

"Shut your dribbling asshole," Rahm says in an oddly unemotional way, "and get out of here this instant, if you want to live."

"*Herr Kommandant,* I don't value my life much. I'm old and not well. Kill me, and you'll have to explain to Herr Eichmann what became of his window dressing. Torture me, and if I survive, what impression can I make on the Red Cross? If you cancel my niece's summons, I guarantee our cooperation when the Red Cross comes. I guarantee she will do no more foolish things."

Rahm presses a buzzer and picks up his pen. The adjutant opens the door. At Rahm's murderous glare and dismissive gesture with his pen, Jastrow rushes out.

The square in front of the HQ is a mass of blossoming trees. As Jastrow emerges on the street, the sweet smell fills his nostrils. The band is playing the evening concert; at the moment, a waltz from *Die Fledermaus.* The moon hangs red and low over the trees. Jastrow staggers to the outdoor café, where Jews may sit and drink black water. As an Elder he can walk past the queue of waiting customers. He falls in a chair, and buries his face in his hands in exhausted relief. He is alive and unhurt. What he has accomplished he does not know, but he has done his all.

Searchlights blaze down on the lawn from the roof of the Hamburg barracks. Blinded, frightened, Natalie snatches up her sleeping son. He whimpers.

"*On your feet! Form a queue by threes!*" Ghetto guards are stalking the lawn and yelling. *"Everybody out of the barracks! Into the courtyard! Queue up! Hurry up! On your feet! Line up by threes!"*

Transportees swarm into the courtyard, hastily pulling on clothes. These are the foresighted ones who have reported in early to grab bunks, knowing the SS has cleared the barracks for use as an assembly center. The two thousand or more Jews who lived there are gone, staying wherever they can.

Word sweeps among the transportees, *"Exemptions!"* What else can be happening but that? Everybody knows by now about the excessive summonses. The Elders, led by Eppstein himself, are trooping into the courtyard, as guards set up two tables on the cleared grass. Transport officials sit down with their stacks of cards and papers, their wire baskets, their rubber stamps. Commander Rahm arrives, swinging a swagger stick.

The line of three thousand Jews commences a shuffling march around the yard before Rahm. He points his stick to exempt this one and that. The freed ones go to a corner of the yard. Sometimes Rahm consults the Elders, otherwise he simply picks handsome men and pretty women. The entire line passes in review, and starts around again. It takes a long time. Louis's legs give out, and Natalie has to sling him on her back, for she is dragging the suitcases, too. As she comes around again, she sees Aaron Jastrow address Rahm. The commander menaces him with the stick and turns his back on him. The march goes on and on under the floodlights.

Suddenly, tumult and confusion!

The guards shout, "Halt!" Sturmbannführer Rahm is bellowing obscenities and swinging his stick at squirming, dodging transport officials. There has been some kind of miscount. A long delay ensues. Whether Rahm is drunk, or the Jews at the tables are incompetent or terrorized, this botch with people's lives has now gone on past midnight. At last the line starts moving again. Natalie trudges in a hopeless daze, following the back of a limping old lady in a ragged coat with a black feathery collar, the same back that she has been trailing for hours. A rough tug at her elbow all at once spins her stumbling out of line. "What's the matter with you, you stupid bitch?" mutters a whiskered guard. Commander Rahm is pointing his stick at her, with a sneering expression.

The floodlights go out. The commander, the Elders, the transport officials leave. The exempted Jews are trooped off into a separate bunk room. A transport official, the same redheaded man who distributed summonses, tells them that they are now "the reserve." The commander is very angry about the bungled count. There will be another tally tomorrow when the train loads up. Till then they are confined to this room. Natalie spends a hideous sleepless night with Louis slumbering in her arms.

Next day the official returns with a typewritten list, and calls out fifty names to proceed to the train. The list is not alphabetical, so until the last name is read off, the tension on the listening faces deepens. Natalie is not called. The fifty unfortunates pick up their suitcases and go out. Another long wait; then Natalie hears the wail of the train whistle, the chuffing of the locomotive, and the clank of moving cars.

The redheaded man looks into the room and shouts, "Pile your numbers on the table and get out of here. Go back to your barracks."

Sick at heart as she is about the people on the train, especially those with whom she spent the night, taking Louis's number off his neck gives Natalie the greatest joy of her life.

Aaron Jastrow waits outside the barracks entrance amid a crowd of relatives and friends. The reunions all about them are subdued. He only nods to her. "I'll take the suitcases."

"No, just pick up Louis, he's exhausted." She lowers her voice. "And for God's sake, let us get in touch with Berel."

At the mica factory about noon, a few days later, a ghetto guard comes to Natalie and tells her to report to SS headquarters at eight in the morning with her child. When the workday ends, she runs all the way to the Seestrasse apartment. Aaron is there, murmuring over the Talmud. The news does not seem to upset him. Probably she is due for a warning, he says. The SS knows, after all, about the scheme to alert the Red Cross, and she is the only one of the group left in the ghetto. She must be humble and contrite, and she must promise to cooperate from now on. That is undoubtedly all the Germans want of her.

"But why Louis? Why must I bring him?"

"You brought him there last time. The adjutant probably remembers that. Try not to worry. Keep your spirits up. That's crucial."

"Have you heard from Berel yet?"

Jastrow shakes his head. "They say it may take a week or more."

Natalie does not close her eyes that night, either. When the windows turn gray she gets up, feeling very ill, puts on the gray suit, and does her best with her hair, and with touches of color from her dry old rouge pot, to look presentable.

"All will be well," Jastrow says, as she is about to go. He looks ill himself, for all his reassuring smiles. They do something unusual for them; they kiss.

She hurries to the children's house, and dresses and feeds Louis. As the clock on the church strikes eight, she enters SS headquarters. The boredlooking SS man at the desk by the door nods when she gives her name. "Follow me." They go down the hall, descend a long staircase, and walk through another gloomier hall. Louis, in his mother's arms, is looking around with bright-eyed curiosity, holding a tin soldier. The SS man halts at a wooden door. "In here. Wait." He shuts the door on Natalie. It is a windowless whitewashed room, with a cellar smell, lit by a bulb in a wire mesh. The walls are stone, the floor cement. There are three wooden chairs against a wall, and in a corner a mop and a pail full of water.

Natalie sits on a chair, holding Louis on her lap. A long time goes by. She cannot tell how long. Louis prattles to the tin soldier.

The door opens. Natalie gets to her feet. Commander Rahm comes in, followed by Inspector Haindl, who closes the door. Rahm is in black dress uniform; Haindl wears the usual gray-green. Rahm walks up to her and roars in her face, "SO, YOU'RE THE JEWISH WHORE WHO PLOTTED AGAINST THE GERMAN GOVERNMENT! YES?"

Natalie's throat clamps shut. She opens her mouth, tries to talk, but no sounds come.

"ARE YOU OR AREN'T YOU?" Rahm bellows.

"I — I —" Low hoarse gasps.

Rahm says to Haindl, "Take the shitty little bastard from her."

The inspector pulls Louis from Natalie's arms. She is losing any belief that this is really happening, but Louis's wail forces hoarse words out of her throat. "I was insane, I was misled, I will cooperate, don't hurt my baby —"

"Don't hurt him? He's GONE, you dirty cunt, don't you realize that?" Rahm gestures at the mop and the pail of water. "That's for cleaning up the bloody garbage he'll be in ONE MINUTE. You'll do that yourself. You thought you got away with it, did you?"

Haindl, a squat burly man, turns Louis upside down, holding one leg in each hairy hand. The boy's jacket hangs around his face. The tin soldier clinks to the floor. He utters muffled cries.

"He is DEAD," shouts Rahm at her. "Go ahead, Haindl, get it over with. Rip him in half."

Natalie shrieks, and rushes toward Haindl, but she trips and falls to the cement. She raises up on her hands and knees. "Don't kill him! I'll do anything. *Just don't kill him!*"

Rahm, with a laugh, points his stick at Haindl, who is holding the wailing child upside down still. "You'll do anything? Fine, let's see you suck the inspector's cock."

It does not shock her. Natalie is nothing but a crazed animal now, trying to protect a baby animal. "Yes, yes, all right, I will."

Haindl takes both of Louis's ankles in one hand, holding the whimpering boy head down like a fowl. Unbuttoning, he pulls out a small penis in a bush of hair. On her hands and knees, Natalie crawls to him. The exposed penis is limp and shrunken. Odious and unspeakable as all this would be if she were sane and conscious, Natalie only knows that if she takes that object in her mouth her child may not be hurt. Haindl backs away from her as she crawls. Both men are laughing. "Look, she really wants it, *Herr Kommandant,*" he says.

Rahm guffaws. "Oh, all these Jewesses are cocksuckers at heart. Go ahead, let her have her fun. German cocks is what they want most."

Haindl halts. Natalie crawls to his feet and raises her mouth to do the horrible thing.

Haindl lifts a boot, puts it in her face, and pushes her tumbling backward on the floor. Her head hits the cement hard. She sees zigzag lights. "GET away from me. Think I'd let your Jewish shit-mouth dirty my cock?" He stands over Natalie, spits down at her face, and drops Louis on her stomach. "Go suck off your uncle, the Talmud rabbi."

She sits up, clutching at the child, pulling the jacket away from his purpled face. He is gasping, his eyes are red and staring, and he has vomited.

"Get to your feet," says Rahm.

Natalie obeys.

"Now LISTEN, Jew-sow. When the Red Cross comes, YOU will be the guide for the children's department. You will make the finest impression on them. They will write you up in their report, you will be such a happy American Jewess. The children's pavilion will be your pride and joy. *Ja?*"

"Of course. Of course. Yes."

"After the Red Cross goes, if you've misbehaved in any way, you'll come straight here with your brat. Haindl will tear him in half like a wet rag before your eyes. You'll clean up the bloody crap with your own hands and take it to the crematorium. Then you'll go to the hut of the POW road gang. Two hundred stinking Ukrainians will fuck you by turn for a week. If your whore's carcass survives, you'll go to the Little Fortress to be shot. Understand, cunt?"

"I will do everything you say. I'll make a wonderful impression."

"All right. And one word about any of this, to your uncle or anybody else, and you're *kaputt!*" He shoves his face directly into her spittle-wet face, and howls with a corpse-smelling breath, so loud that her ears ring, "DO YOU BELIEVE ME?"

"I do! I do!"

"Get her out of here."

The inspector pulls her by the arm out of the room, up the stairs, along the hall, and shoves her, with the inert child in her arms, out into the square glorious with spring blossoms. The band is playing the morning concert, selections from *Faust.*

Jastrow is waiting when she returns. The child, his face still smeared with vomit, looks stunned. Natalie's face sickens Jastrow; the eyes are round and white-rimmed, the skin dirty green, the expression one of deathbed fright.

"Well?" he says.

"It was a warning. I'm all right. I must change my clothes and go to work."

He is still there a half hour later, when she comes out in her threadbare brown dress with the child, who is washed and seems better. Her face is dead gray but the hellish look has faded. "Why aren't you at the library?"

"I wanted to tell you that word has come from Berel."

"Yes?" She grasps at his shoulder, her eyes wild.

"They'll try."

*   *   *

82

Finis Germaniae

(from *World Holocaust* by Armin von Roon)

TRANSLATOR'S NOTE: *Roon treats the Normandy landings and the Soviet attack in June as a combined operation. This is valid only in a very general sense. At Tehran the Grand Alliance did agree to strike at Germany simultaneously from east and west. But the Russians did not know our operational plans, nor we theirs. Once we landed it was touch and go for two weeks whether Stalin would actually keep his word and attack.*

This chapter combines passages from Roon's strategic essay and his concluding memoir about Hitler. — V.H.

In June 1944, the iron jaws of the vise forged at Tehran began to close. The German nation, the last bastion of Christian culture and decency in middle Europe, was assailed from west and east by the long-plotted double onslaught of plutocratic imperialism and Slav communism.

In Western writings, the Normandy landings and the Russian assault still pass as a triumph for "humanity." But serious historians are beginning to penetrate the smokescreen of wartime propaganda. At Tehran, Franklin D. Roosevelt delivered eastern Europe into Red claws. His motive? To destroy Germany, the strongest rival on earth to American monopoly capital. England was already skinned like a rabbit, in Hitler's colorful phrase, by her overstrained war-making, and by Roosevelt's wily anticolonialism. Brave Japan was sinking to her knees in the unequal contest with von Nimitz's ever-swelling fleets. Only Germany still blocked the way to the world hegemony of the dollar.

It is a shallow commonplace that Roosevelt was "outsmarted" at the later conference in Yalta and gave away too much to Stalin. In fact, he had already given everything away at Tehran. Once he pledged the assault on France, he made the Red Asian sweep into the heart of Europe inevitable.

To assure this, he flooded Lend-Lease to the Soviet Union. The figures still beggar the imagination: some four hundred thousand motor vehicles, two thousand locomotives, eleven thousand railway cars, seven thousand tanks, and more than six thousand self-propelled guns and half-tracks, with the two million seven hundred thousand tons of petroleum and other products required to put the primitive Slav horde on wheels; to say nothing of fifteen thousand aircraft, and millions of tons of food, together with raw materials, factories, munitions, and technical equipment beyond calculation.

The picture of Roosevelt as a naïve outwitted humanitarian in his dealings with Stalin was his greatest propaganda swindle. These two icy butchers thoroughly understood each other; they just struck dissimilar poses for domestic consumption and for history. Of the two, Roosevelt always had the upper hand, because Soviet Russia was half-devastated and in desperate straits, while America was rich, strong, and untouched. Stalin had no choice but to sacrifice millions of Russian lives to clear the way for world rule by American monopolists. He did explore the possibility of making peace with us on reasonable terms, in very secret parleys that we at Headquarters knew nothing about at the time; but here Roosevelt's Lend-Lease "generosity" frustrated us. Naturally Hitler was not prepared to yield all our gains. Given all that matériel, Stalin decided he would do better by fighting on, at the cost of rivers of German and Russian blood.

The quarrelsome and impoverished lands of eastern Europe were Roosevelt's sop to Stalin for his country's terrible sacrifices. Roosevelt's policy was simply to let them fall to the Russians. Of course, the treacherous Balkans were a dubious prey. The Soviets already belch with indigestion from those swallowed but intransigent nationalities. The strategic importance of that turbulent peninsula is not what it was in past centuries, or even to us in 1944 as a conduit for Turkish chrome. But even so, to invite Slav communism to march to the Elbe and the Danube was monstrous. Churchill's itch to funnel the main Allied thrust into the Balkans at least showed some political sensitivity, and some sense of responsibility for middle Europe and for Christian civilization. His blood was not as cold as Roosevelt's. Roosevelt cared nothing for the Balkans or for Poland; though in a strange moment of candor he told Stalin at Tehran that he had to make some sort of fuss about Poland's future, because of the large Polish vote in the election he faced.

Clash of the Warlords

Franklin Roosevelt took a great risk with the Normandy landings. This is not well-known. When one weighs the opposing forces, the elements of space and time, and the sea–land transfer problem, one sees that Churchill's foot-dragging made sense. The landings were very chancy and might have ended disastrously. A pyramiding of mistakes and bad luck on our side gave Roosevelt success in his one audacious military move.

Eisenhower himself knew the riskiness of Overlord. Even as his five thousand vessels were steaming toward the Normandy coast in the stormy night, he drafted an announcement of the operation's failure, which by chance has been preserved: *"Our landings in the Cherbourg–Havre area have failed to gain a satisfactory foothold and I have withdrawn the troops. My decision to attack at this time and place was based upon the best information available. The troops, the air, and the Navy did all that bravery and devotion to duty could do. If any blame or fault attaches to the attempt it is mine alone."*

That this document did not become the official Allied communiqué was due to several factors, chiefly:

a. Our abominable intelligence;
b. Our confused and sluggish response to the attack in the first decisive hours;
c. Unbelievable botching by Adolf Hitler;
d. Failure of the Luftwaffe to cope with Allied air superiority.

The mounting of the invasion armada was certainly a fine technological achievement; as was the production of the huge air fleets, with crews to man them. General Marshall's raising, equipping, and training of the land armies that poured into Normandy showed him to be an American Scharnhorst. The U.S. infantryman, while requiring far too luxurious logistical support, put up a nice fight in France; he was fresh, well fed, and unscarred by battle. The British Tommy under Montgomery, though slow-moving as usual, showed bulldog courage. But essentially what happened in Normandy was that Franklin Roosevelt beat Adolf Hitler, as surely as Wellington beat Napoleon at Waterloo. In Normandy the two men at last clashed in head-on armed shock. Hitler's mistakes gave Roosevelt the victory; just as at Waterloo it was less Wellington who won than Napoleon who lost.

The core of Franklin Roosevelt's malignant military genius lay in these simple rules: to pick generals and admirals with care; to leave strategy and tactics to them, and attend only to the politics of the war; never to interfere in operations; never to relieve leaders who encountered honorable reverses; and to allow all the glory to those who won victories. When Roosevelt died, his supreme command in the field was virtually the original team. This steadiness paid dividends. Shake-ups in military command can cost much momentum, élan, and fighting effectiveness. The shuffling of generals by Hitler was our plague.

For the Führer had arrogated supreme operational command to himself, and we were suffering bad reverses. He could never admit that he was responsible for any setback. Hence, heads had to keep rolling. Ambitious rising commanders abounded, eager to plunge in where their elders had been sacked for Hitler's failures. I watched these temporary Führer favorites come and go, taking over with zest, only to be worn down by Hitler's meddling and at last fired for his bad moves; likely as not to kill themselves or die of heart failure. It was a sad business, and absurd war-making.

The Normandy Landings

Three questions governed the invasion problem, on which the fate of our nation hung:

1. Where will they land?
2. When will they land?
3. Where do we fight them?

By all military logic, the place for the Anglo-Americans to land was the Pas de Calais, opposite Dover. It offered the shortest route to the Ruhr, our nation's industrial heart. The Channel is there at its narrowest. Waterborne troops are all but helpless, and common sense demands getting them ashore the quickest way. The turnaround time for ships and for air support would have been shortest on the Dover-Calais axis. The Normandy coast, where the enemy struck, was a much longer pull by sea and air.

By preparing so well for invasion at the Pas de Calais, we set our minds in one groove, and gave the foe the chance to spring a surprise. Hitler somehow guessed that Normandy might be the place. At one staff meeting he literally put his finger on the map and said, "They will be landing here," with what we used to call his undeniable *coup d'oeil*. But he made many such guesses during the war, as often as not extremely wild. Of course he remembered only the ones that turned out right, and made a great noise about them. Rommel, charged with repelling the invasion, also became concerned about Normandy. So, very late, we hardened up those beaches, and augmented the armed forces poised there; and we could have crushed the landings despite the surprise, except for the unspeakable manner in which the first day was bungled.

The chief British planner of the landings, General Morgan, has written: "One hopes and plans for battle as far inland from the beach as may be, *for if the invasion battle takes place on the beach, one is already defeated.*" I confess that we of the OKW staff erred on this. We agreed with Rundstedt that the mobile reserve should lie in wait far enough inland to avoid the naval and close air bombardment; and that once Eisenhower was ashore and moving inland in force, we should attack and wipe out the whole enterprise, as we had repeatedly bagged Russian armies. It was an "eastern front" mentality. Rommel knew better. In North Africa he had tried to fight a war of maneuver against an enemy controlling the air. We were between the devil and the deep, and the only time to stop the Normandy invasion was when the enemy was floundering ashore under our guns. Rommel fortified the so-called Atlantic Wall and made all his plans on that principle. Had we fought D-day as he planned it, we might have won and turned the war around.

TRANSLATOR'S NOTE: *Roon gives no credit to the superb deception tactics, mainly British, that encouraged the Germans in their wishful "logic" about where we would land. An enormous effort was laid on: air attacks and naval bombardment of the Pas de Calais exceeding those in Normandy, aerial bombing of the railroads and highways leading to it, vast arrays of dummy landing craft and fake army hutments near Dover, and a variety of still-secret intelligence tricks. The Germans were not very imaginative. They swallowed all hints confirming their clever judgment that we were coming to the Pas de Calais. — V.H.*

What Went Wrong — Preparations

We German generals are sometimes accused of blaming Hitler, the dead politician, for losing the war it was our job to win. Still, the defeat in France was Hitler's work. He fumbled the one slender chance we had. This fact cannot be blinked in a professional analysis.

His *fundamental* estimate was not bad. As far back as November he issued his famous Directive Number 51 for shifting strength to the west. Quite properly he pointed out that we could trade space for time in the east, whereas an enemy lodgment in France would have immediate "staggering" implications; the Ruhr, our war-making arsenal, would come within enemy reach. The directive was sober, its program realistic. If only he had followed through on it! But from January to June he dithered and waffled, actually draining western forces into three other theatres: the occupation of Hungary, the eastern front, and the Allied front south of Rome. Also, he froze large forces in Norway, the Balkans, Denmark, and the south of France to ward off possible landings, instead of massing all these near the Channel coast.

Certainly he was under pressure. Europe's three thousand miles of coastline lay exposed to assault. In the east the Russians were fighting on, in Hitler's phrase, like "swamp animals"; freeing Leningrad, recapturing the Crimea, and threatening our whole southern flank. Partisan activity was making all Europe restive. The satellite politicians were wavering. In Italy the enemy kept crawling up the boot. The barbarous Allied air bombings were intensifying in size and accuracy, and for all Göring's loud mouth, his battered Luftwaffe was tied down in the east and over our factory cities. Like England in 1940, we were stretched too thin with diminishing troops, arms, and resources. The tables had turned, and there was no untouched ally beyond the seas to pull our chestnuts out of the fire.

At such times a great leader should supply the steadying hand. If Directive Number 51 was correct, Hitler's course was clear:

1. Firm up political faltering with victory, not with wasteful armed occupation as in Hungary and Italy;
2. Withdraw in Italy to the easily defended line of the Alps and Apennines, and send the released divisions into France;
3. Slow the enemy in the east with elastic harrying tactics, instead of rigid costly stands for prestige;
4. Leave skeleton forces in unlikely invasion areas, and gamble all strength at the Channel.

That is how von Nimitz and Spruance won the Battle of Midway against odds; by accepting great risks to concentrate at the decisive point. This principle of warfare is eternal. But Hitler's nervousness precluded adhering to principle. Obstinate he was, but not firm.

His much-vaunted "Atlantic Wall" along the Channel was ill-conceived. In his solitary wisdom he decided that the invasion forces would head for a major port. A million and a half tons of concrete and countless man-hours went into pillboxes and heavy gun emplacements, designed by the supreme genius himself, that bristled around the main French harbors. Rommel presciently ordered the open beaches fortified too: belts of mines on land in the sea, underwater obstacles to tear up and blast approaching vessels, sharpened stakes in areas behind the beaches to destroy gliders, myriads of more pillboxes and gun emplacements along the shore.

But lack of manpower hampered this new effort, because of the excavating of grandiose bomb-proof caverns for aircraft factories, and the repair of bomb damage in our cities. Compared to INVASION, how important were such things? Yet Hitler did not back up Rommel's supplementary Atlantic Wall orders, and the "Wall" remained largely a propaganda phantom. One instance suffices. Rommel ordered fifty million mines planted in the glider areas behind the beaches. Had he been obeyed the airborne landings would have failed, but not even ten percent of the mining was done, and they succeeded.

On paper we had a force of about sixty divisions to defend France; but the static divisions strung along the coast consisted mainly of substandard troops scraped from the bottom of the barrel. Some attack infantry divisions were scattered here and there, but with the ten motorized and armored divisions lay our hope. Five of these, stationed not far from the Channel coast, could strike at either the Pas de Calais or Normandy. Rommel intended to annihilate on the beaches the first wave arriving in landing craft; actually, as it turned out, only five divisions in all. He therefore pleaded for operational control of the panzers.

In vain. Rundstedt, the overall *Ob West,* advocated hitting the invaders after they were well-lodged. Dithering between the two tactical concepts, Hitler came down on neither side. He issued orders dividing the panzers among three different commands; and *he reserved to himself, six hundred miles away in Berchtesgaden, operational control of the four panzer divisions nearest the Normandy beaches.* This decision was a grievous one. It tied Rommel's hands, when all depended on a quick free-swinging punch. But the invasion found the German command in such a state of chaos that it is hard to say which omission, which mistake, which folly, brought *finis Germaniae.* Invasion day was a cataract of omissions, mistakes, and follies.

What Went Wrong — D-day

The overwhelming failure was the Pas de Calais mistake. That we lacked agents in England to ferret out a "secret" involving two million men; that deception measures took us in, and that our reconnaissance could not pinpoint the direction of an attack organized a few score miles away in plain sight; there is a bitter mystery!

We failed to discern that they would land at low tide. Our guns bore on the high-tide line; the thought was, why should they elect to slog across eight hundred additional yards of mushy sand under fire? They did. Eisenhower's shock troops came in when our formidable underwater obstacles were exposed for swift clearing by sappers, and his troops made it across the sand.

We abjectly failed on the question, *When?* As the enemy armada was crossing the Channel, Erwin Rommel was visiting his wife in Germany! A near-gale was blowing on the fifth of June, predicted to last three days. This bad weather lulled Rommel and everyone else. Eisenhower had meteorological intelligence showing a marginal break in the weather. He risked a go-ahead. The scattered airborne descents in the wee hours of the morning somehow did not alarm us. Not till our soldiers in the Normandy pillboxes saw with their naked eyes the monstrous apparition of Overlord — thousands and thousands of vessels, approaching in the misty gray dawn — did we go on battle alert.

Actually we had one intelligence break which was pooh-poohed. Our informers in the French Resistance had obtained the BBC signals that would call for D-day sabotage. Our monitoring posts heard these signals. All operational commands received the warning. In our Supreme Headquarters the report went to Jodl, who thought nothing of it. Later I heard that Rundstedt, laughing off the alarm, remarked, "As though Eisenhower would announce the invasion on the BBC!" This was the general attitude.

* * *

My Trip to the Front

(from "Hitler as Military Leader")

. . . It seemed that Hitler would never wake up that morning. Repeatedly I telephoned Jodl to rouse him, for Rundstedt was demanding the release of the panzers. Obviously the Normandy attack was serious! Jodl put off Rundstedt, a decision for which historians now excoriate him. Yet when Hitler did see Jodl at about ten o'clock, after a leisurely private breakfast, he quite approved denying Rundstedt's frantic requests.

The Berchtesgaden command situation was absurd. Hitler was up at his mountain eyrie, Jodl in the "Little Chancellery," and operational headquarters were in a barracks at the other end of town. We were never off the telephone. Rommel was out of touch, returning to the front; Rundstedt in Paris, and Rommel's chief of staff, Speidel, at the coast, and the panzer general, Geyr, were all scorching the telephone lines and teleprinters to Berchtesgaden. The midday briefing conference was scheduled for Klessheim Castle, a charming spot about an hour out of town, in honor of some Hungarian visitors of state. It never occurred to Hitler to call this off. No, the staff had to motor out there to meet him in a small map room, where he rehearsed the "show" briefing for the visitors; then we had to hang around for the briefing, while our troops were dying under Allied bombs and naval shelling, and enemy lodgments were expanding by the hour.

I can still see the Führer bouncing into that map room about noon, his bloated pasty face wreathed in smiles, his mustache aquiver, greeting the staff with some such remark as, "Well, here we go, eh? Now we've got them where we can hit them! Over in England they were safe." He showed no concern whatever over the grave reports. This landing was all a fake that we had anticipated long ago. We weren't fooled! We were all ready for them at the Pas de Calais. This feint would turn into another bloody Dieppe fiasco for them. Splendid!

So he also declaimed in the large briefing chamber, with its soft armchairs and impressive war maps. He bombarded the Hungarians with disgusting boasts about the strength of our forces in France, the superiority of our armaments, our miraculous "new weapons" soon to be launched, the greenness of the U.S. army, etc. etc. etc. He pooh-poohed the fall of Rome two days earlier, even making a coarse joke about his relief at turning over a million and a half Italians, syphilitic whores and all, for the Americans to feed. What the obsequious Hungarians thought of all this, nobody could tell. To me, Hitler was convincing only himself, talking his daydreams aloud. As soon as this charade was over, I requested permission to go to Normandy. Not only did the unpredictable Führer agree, he waived the rule against airplane travel by senior officers. I could fly as far as Paris, and find out what was going on.

When my plane circled down several hours later over the swastika fluttering on the Eiffel Tower, I couldn't help thinking, *How long will it fly there?* In Rundstedt's situation room everything was at sixes and sevens. Hitler had meantime released *one* panzer division, and a staff argument was raging about where to use it. Junior officers rushed about in a din of teleprinters and shouting. The battle map bristled with little emblems of ships and parachute-drops. Red infantry markers delineated a fifty-mile front in surprising depth, except in one spot where we had the Americans pinned down at the waterline.

Rundstedt appeared calm enough, and as usual bandbox-neat, but weary, thin, and pessimistic. He did not act at all like the *Ob West;* rather, like an old man with worries but no power. He tried to argue that I should not risk capture by paratroopers, but he was half-hearted about that, too. He still believed this was a diversion in force. But throwing the invaders back into the sea would buck up the Fatherland and give the enemy pause, so it had to be done.

Next morning the beautiful French landscape, with its fat cows and drudging peasants, was strangely quiet. The young aide of Rundstedt's who was riding with me had to order the chauffeur to detour time and again around knocked-out bridges. The damage from the weeks of methodical Allied air bombings was manifest: devastated railroad yards, smashed trestles, burned-out trains and terminals, overturned locomotives, Churchill's "railway desert" with a vengeance. Tactically the ground was a blotch of islands, rather than a terrain suited to overland supply. No wonder; *fifteen thousand enemy air sorties on D-day alone,* with virtually no opposition! So the postwar records show.

Passing through Saint-Lô, I fell in with trucks carrying our paratroopers toward Carentan. I took the major into my car. French saboteurs had cut his telephone lines, he said, and he had been out of touch on invasion day, but late at night had gotten through to his general. His mission now was to counterattack the thin American beachhead east of Varreville.

The strange bucolic quiet persisted as we neared the coast. The major and I climbed the steeple of a village church to have a look around. A stunning panorama greeted us: the Channel dotted with enemy ships from horizon to horizon, and boats like a million water-insects swarming between the shore and the vessels. Through field glasses a colossal and quite peaceful operation was visible on the beach. Landing craft were lined up hull to hull as far as one could see, disgorging men, supplies, and equipment. The shore was black for miles with crates, boxes, bags, machines, and soldiers doing stevedore labor, and a crawling parade of trucks heading inland.

The "Battle of France" indeed! These troops were preparing to destroy Germany, and they looked like picnickers. I heard no gunfire but a scattering of rifle shots. What a contrast to the Führer's gory boasts at Klessheim Castle about "squashing the invaders into the sand," and "meeting them with a curtain of steel and fire"!

As we drove eastward small gun duels sputtered and villages burned in the persisting quiet. Interrogating officers wherever I could, I learned the reason for the strange calm. A vast combined naval and air bombardment at dawn had poured a deluge of shot and shell on our defenses. The wounded I spoke to had horror-stricken faces. One older noncom with a smashed arm told me that he had lived through Verdun and experienced nothing like it. Everywhere I encountered fatalism, apathy, lost communications, broken-up regiments, and confusion over orders. The gigantic sea armada, the air fleets roaring overhead, and the fearful bombardments had already spread a sense of a lost war.

That a possibly fatal crisis was at hand I could no longer doubt. Speeding back to Paris I told Jodl over the telephone that this was the main assault, and that we must concentrate against it, moving at night to evade the air interdiction, and effecting transport repair on a crash basis. Jodl's response was, "Well, get back here, but I advise you to be very careful about what you say." It was unnecessary advice. I never got a hearing. At the next few briefing conferences I was not called on. Hitler pointedly avoided my eye. The Normandy situation deteriorated rapidly, and my information was soon out of date.

Two impressions remain with me of this lovely June, when our German world was crumbling while Hitler socialized over tea and cakes in Berchtesgaden. On June 19 a great storm blew up on the Normandy coast and raged for four days. It set back the invaders far more than our forces had. It broke up the artificial harbors, and threw almost a thousand vessels up on the beach. Reconnaissance photographs showed such a gigantic disaster that I felt my last flicker of hope. Hitler was in seventh heaven, reeling off giddy disquisitions on the fate of the Spanish Armada. When the weather cleared, the enemy resumed his attacks by land, sea, and air, as though a summer shower had passed by. His resources, pouring out of the unreachable U.S. cornucopia, were frightening. We heard no more about the Spanish Armada.

Stamped on my memory too is a briefing conference about the time Cherbourg was falling. Hitler was standing at the map, wearing his thick glasses, and with a compass and ruler he was gleefully showing us what a small part of France the invaders held, compared to the area we still occupied. This he was telling to senior generals who knew, and who had been warning him for weeks, that with the defensive crust at the coast smashed, and a major port gone, the rest of France was open country for enemy operations, with no tenable German position short of the West Wall at the border and the Rhine. What a sorry moment; scales fell from my eyes, and I knew once for all that the triumphant Führer had degenerated to a pathological monster, trembling for his life behind a mask of bravado.

•   •   •

Normandy: Summary

(from World Holocaust)

. . . Had Hitler accepted the suggestions of Rommel and Rundstedt late in June to end the war, we would have had to kneel down to a draconic peace. We might have ended up partitioned as we are now, we might not have; but certainly our people would have been spared a year of savage air bombings, including the gruesome horror of Dresden, and Eisenhower's ruinous march to the Elbe; and from the east, the horror of universal Bolshevik pillage and rape, which the world smiled at and overlooked, while millions of our civilians had to flee westward from their homes, never to return.

In 1918, while we stood on foreign soil, Ludendorff and Hindenburg had similarly counseled surrender, before others could inflict on German territory the ruin of war. But in 1918 there had been a political state and a military arm; and by the abdication of the Kaiser, the politicians could effect this timely surrender. Now there was no political state, no military arm; all was merged in Hitler. Politically, how could he surrender, and stretch out his neck to the hangman? He could only fight on.

Very well, what of his strategy in fighting on: was it good, or bad? It was rigid, complacent, and dull-witted. He lost Normandy. Only five divisions in the landing force! Had the panzers been freed and concentrated, then in spite of all — intelligence failure, enemy air superiority, naval bombardment — Rommel's able chief of staff, Speidel, could have unleashed them against the floundering G.I.'s and Tommies. The result would have been a historic bloodbath. At Omaha Beach, the Americans were almost thrown back into the sea by one attack infantry division, the 352nd, which happened to be operating there. What would a planned concentrated counterattack in those first hours not have achieved?

Had we smashed those five divisions, that might well have been the turning point. The Anglo-Americans were not Russians; politically and militarily they could not take such bloodletting. If all those fantastic preparations, all that outpouring of technology and treasure, could not prevent the slaughter of their landing force on that crucial first day, I believe Eisenhower, Roosevelt, and Churchill would have quailed and announced a face-saving "withdrawal." The political results would have been spectacular: the fall of Churchill, Roosevelt's defeat in the election, charges of bad faith by Stalin; even some kind of endurable separate peace in the east, who can say? But Adolf Hitler wanted to control the panzers from Berchtesgaden.

As doom closed in, Hitler clung to, and interminably mouthed, three self-comforting fantasies:

1. The breakup of the Alliance against us;
2. The turning of the tide by miraculous new weapons;
3. A sudden outpouring from the factory caverns of new jet fighters that would sweep the enemy from the skies.

For seven fatal weeks he insisted on immobilizing the Fifteenth Army at the Pas de Calais awaiting the "main invasion," because the launching platforms for his precious V-1 and V-2 rockets were there. But the rockets, when they finally flew, were minor terror weapons, causing random death and damage in London without military effect. The fighter planes came trickling out of the caverns only in 1945, much too late. As for the only new weapon that mattered, the atom bomb, Hitler had frittered away our scientific lead in atom-splitting by failing to support the project, and he had driven out the Jewish scientists who produced it for our enemies.

The breakup of the enemy coalition had indeed been our one escape hatch; but Franklin Roosevelt's supreme political stroke at Tehran had slammed it shut and sealed it. And so there burst on us from the east on June 22, three years to the day after we invaded the Soviet Union, the worst catastrophe yet, the Battle of White Russia, Stalin's assigned role in the Tehran plan.

To this grim tale I now turn.

TRANSLATOR'S NOTE: *In this much-abridged compilation of Roon's views, I have tried to highlight how the Germans saw the Normandy landing, omitting much operational detail familiar from popular history and movies. Stalin's telegram to Churchill remains as good a summary as any of the grandeur of Overlord: "The history of war knows no other like undertaking, from* the point of view of its scale, its vast conception, and its masterly execution."

The blaming of Hitler can be overdone. Even if the panzers had been released to Rommel, our forces would probably have known it. Our intelligence – from air reconnaissance, the French Resistance, and code penetration — was superb. We might have battered up the panzers from the air before they ever went into action. This is not to say that the landing was not a close thing. It was an extreme risk calculated to a cat's whisker, and it succeeded.

As for Hitler "degenerating" into a pathological monster, he never was anything else, though he had a good run in his first flush of brigandage. Why his demagogic bunkum ever spurred the Germans to their wars and their crimes remains a vastly puzzling question.

The scales did not fall from Roon's eyes. They had to be shot off. — V.H.

* * *

83

JEDBURGH TEAM "MAURICE"

U.S.A.: *Leslie Slote, OSS*
French: *Dr. Jean R. Latour, FFI*
British: *Leading Aircraftsman Ira N. Thompson, RAF*

When Pamela saw Slote's name in the top-secret schedule of the Jedburgh air drops, she at once decided to go and see him. She was getting desperate for some word of Victor Henry. Since sending her letter of refusal, the thought of which was making her more and more miserable as time passed, she had heard nothing. Utter silence. She found an official reason to go to Milton Hall, the stately home some sixty miles north of London where the Jedburghs trained, and she went whizzing out there next day in a jeep. At Milton Hall she quickly attended to her official business. Leslie Slote, she was told, was off on a field exercise. She left a note for him with her telephone number, and was walking disconsolately back to her jeep, when she heard from behind her, "Pamela?"

Not a hail; an uncertain call. She turned. Heavy drooping blond mustache, close-cropped hair, no insignia on the untidy brown uniform; a very different Leslie Slote, if the same man. "Hello! It is Leslie, isn't it?"

The mustache spread in Slote's old frigid grin. He came and shook her hand. "I guess I'm a bit changed. What the devil are you doing at Milton Hall, Pam? Got time for a drink?"

"I'd rather not, thanks. I have to drive forty miles. My jeep's just down in the lot."

"Is it Lady Burne-Wilke yet?"

"Well, no, he's still recuperating from an air crash in India. I'm going to Stoneford now, that's his house in Coombe Hill." She glanced curiously up at him. "So you're a Jedburgh?"

His face stiffened. "What do you know about that?"

"Sweetie, I'm in the Air Ministry section that's arranging to drop you in."

He laughed, a coarse hearty guffaw. "How much time have you got? Let's sit down and talk somewhere. Christ, it's wonderful to see an old face. Yes, I'm a Jed."

Here was an opening of sorts for Pamela.

"Victor Henry mentioned that you were in some branch of the OSS."

"Ah, yes. Seeing much of the admiral these days?"

"I've had an occasional letter. Nothing lately."

"But Pamela, he's here."

"Here? In England?"

"Of course. Didn't you know that? He's been here quite a while."

"Really! Would we be out of the wind down at that lily pond? I see a stone bench. We can chat for a few minutes."

Slote well remembered Pamela's great urge to go to Moscow when Henry was there. Her nonchalance seemed overdone; he guessed that the news was a hell of a jolt. They strolled to the bench and sat down by the pond, where frogs croaked as the sun sank behind the trees.

Pamela was indeed silenced by pure shock, and Slote did all the talking. He foamed words. For months he had had nobody to talk to. He told Pam, who sat listening with grave brilliant eyes, that he had joined the OSS because his knowledge of the German massacre of the Jews — which more and more each month was coming to public light, proving he hadn't been a monomaniac after all — and the callous inertness of the State Department had been driving him crazy. The drastic move had transformed his life. He had discovered to his surprise that most men were as full of fear as himself. He had done no worse in parachuting than anybody else, and better than some. As a boy he had loathed violence; bullies had discerned this, he said, picked on him, and fixed him in a timorousness which had fed on itself and became an obsession. Other men concealed their fears even from themselves, for a hearty swagger was the American male way; but he had always been too self-analytical to pretend that he was anything but a coward.

"I've come a long way, Pam!"

On the first airplane jump, back in the States, the man ahead of him in line, a beefy Army captain who had done very well in training, had refused; had looked out at the landscape far below and had frozen, resisting the dispatcher's shove with hysterical obscene snarling. Once he was pushed aside, Slote had jumped out into the roaring slipstream with, in his words, "imbecile joy"; the static line had opened his chute, and the shock had jerked him upright; he had yanked on his webs, floated down in proud ecstasy, and landed like a circus acrobat. Afterward he had shivered and sweated and gloried for days. He had never made another jump half as good. To him, jumping was a hideous business. He hated it. Quite a few OSS men and Jeds felt as he did, and were ready to admit it, though others liked to jump.

"Passing the psychological tests really stunned me, Pamela. I was having very shaky second thoughts about volunteering. I told the Jedburgh board straight out that I was a high-strung coward. They looked skeptical and asked why I had put in for the duty. I gave them my song and dance about the Jews. They rated me 'questionable.' After weeks of being observed by psychiatrists, I passed. They must have been damned hard up for Jeds. Physically I'm very fit, of course, and my French is dazzling, at least to Americans."

It was obvious to Pamela that he would go on and on in this vein and say no more about Victor Henry. "I've got to go, Leslie. Walk me to my jeep." Over the whirring of the motor, as she turned the key, Pamela asked, "Where is Captain Henry, exactly? Do you know?"

"It's Admiral Henry, Pam," said Slote, suppressing a smile. "I told you that."

"I thought you were being facetious."

"No, no. Rear Admiral Henry, ablaze with gold braid, battle ribbons, and stars. I ran into him at our embassy. Try the U.S. Amphibious Base in Exeter. He said he was going there."

She reached out and clasped his hand. He gave her a quick kiss on the cheek. "Till we meet again, Pam. Lord, isn't it a million years since Paris? I did some drinking with Phil Rule last month in London. He's gotten utterly gross."

"It's the liquor. I saw him in Moscow last year. He was all stout and tallowy then, and he got falling-down drunk. Victor wrote me that Natalie's waiting out the war in a Czech ghetto."

"Yes, so he told me." Slote nodded, his face falling. "Well, Pamela, we were young and gay in Paris, anyway."

"Were we? I think we labored awfully sweatily at being Ernest Hemingway characters. Too too raffish and mad. I remember how Phil would hold that black comb under his nose and do Hitler reciting Mother Goose, and we would roar." She ground the jeep into gear, and raised her voice. "Very funny. Those were the days. Good luck on your mission, Leslie. I admire you."

"I had a time tracking you down." Pamela's voice over the telephone was affectionate and cheerful. Hearing those husky tones was very painful to Victor Henry. "Will you by some chance be in London on Thursday?"

"Yes, Pamela, I will be."

"Wonderful. Then come to dinner with us — with Duncan and me — at Stoneford. It's only half an hour from town."

Pug was sitting in the admiral's office in the Devonport dockyard. Seen from the window, landing craft stretched out of sight in the gray drizzle, tied up in the estuary by the hundreds; an array of floating machinery so thick that no water was visible from shore to shore. Back home

Pug had dealt in abstractions: production schedules, progress reports, inventories, projections. Here was the reality: multitudes on multitudes of ungainly metal vessels — LCIs, LCMs, LSTs, LCVPs — strange shapes, varying sizes, seemingly numberless as the wheat grains of an American harvest. But Pug knew the exact number of each type here, and at every other assembly point along the coast. He had been hard at work, travelling from base to base, exerting willpower not to telephone Pamela Tudsbury; but she had found him.

"How do I get there?"

"Take one of the SHAEF buses to Bushey Park. I'll pick you up at four or so, and we can talk a bit. Duncan sleeps from four to six. Doctor's orders."

"How is he?"

"Oh — not too well. There will be a few others for dinner, including General Eisenhower."

"Well! Exalted company for me, Pamela."

"I don't think so, Admiral Henry."

"That's two stars, and only temporary."

"Leigh-Mallory will be coming, too, Eisenhower's commander for air." A silence. Then Pam said jocularly, "Well, let's both get on with the war, shall we? See you Thursday at four, out at SHAEF."

Pug could not guess what this invitation was really about. Nor was Pamela free to tell him. She was dying to see him, of course, but bringing him into the high-brass dinner had a special purpose.

During these anxious last days before D-day, the planned airborne attack at "Utah Beach," the westernmost American landing area, was in hot controversy. A swampy lagoon behind the beach was passable only over narrow causeways. These had to be seized by airborne troops before the Germans could block them or blow them up. Otherwise, the landing force could be stranded on the sands, unable to advance and vulnerable to quick destruction. Utah Beach was the closest landing area to Cherbourg. In Eisenhower's view it had to be captured for Overlord to succeed.

Sir Trafford Leigh-Mallory, who had the responsibility for flying in the gliders and parachute troops, opposed the air operation. It would run into devastating flak over the Cotentin peninsula, he argued; the losses would exceed fifty percent; the remnant who got through would be overwhelmed on the ground; it would be a criminal waste of two crack divisions. Even if it meant cancelling the Utah Beach landing, he wanted the air assault dropped. The American generals would not hear of abandoning the Utah landing or its air operation. But Leigh-Mallory had been fighting the Germans in the air for five years. His knowledge and his fortitude were beyond dispute. It was a deadlock.

In the history of coalition warfare such impasses have been common, and sometimes disastrous. Adolf Hitler could well hope to the last that his foes would fall out in some such way. The Anglo-American invasion was riven by disagreements from start to finish, but Dwight Eisenhower held the grand assault together until his troops met the Russians at the Elbe. So he won his place in military history. To wind this matter up — for the Utah Beach attack is no part of our narrative — Eisenhower in the end took the responsibility and ordered Leigh-Mallory to do it. With the air reinforcement, Utah was a swift smooth landing. The causeways were secured. The airborne casualties were lighter than the estimates. Leigh-Mallory apologized to Eisenhower next day by phone "for adding to his burdens." Years later, Eisenhower said that his happiest moment in the whole war was the news that the two airborne divisions had gone into action at Utah Beach.

When Pamela called Pug, Leigh-Mallory was still resisting the Utah operation. Burne-Wilke had contrived the dinner with Eisenhower so that his old friend might urge his case. Telegraph Cottage, Eisenhower's country place, was near Stoneford. The ailing Burne-Wilke kept a good stable, and Eisenhower liked to ride; Burne-Wilke was a passable bridge player, and that was Eisenhower's game. They had hit it off as neighbors, having already worked together in North Africa.

Burne-Wilke too thought that the Utah Beach air drop was a calamitous idea. In general, Burne-Wilke was seeing the world and the war through a veil of invalid gloom. To him the torrent of American manpower and weaponry flooding England had an end-of-the-world feeling; he saw the pride of Empire crumbling before candy bars, chewing gum, Virginia cigarettes, and canned beer. Still, when Pamela suggested inviting Pug Henry he warmly approved. The bone of jealousy was either missing in Lord Burne-Wilke's makeup, or concealed beyond detection. He thought Rear Admiral Henry's presence might dilute the tension of the dinner.

Pug had briefly met Eisenhower once; on arriving in England, he had brought him an oral message from President Roosevelt about bombing the French railway yards, terminals, locomotives, and bridges. The political consequences of slaughtering Frenchmen, their former comrades-in-arms, was troubling the British, and they were pressing Eisenhower to let up on the French. Roosevelt sent word by Victor Henry that he wanted the bombing to go on. (Later, since Churchill kept making trouble, the President had to put this hard-boiled view in writing.) At their meeting Eisenhower received the grim message with a cold satisfied nod, and made no other comment. He said some genial words about Pug's football prowess against Army in the old days; then he queried him sharply on the close-support bombardments in the Pacific, and asked incisive questions about the Overlord naval fire-support plans. Pug left after half an hour feeling that this man had a trace of

Roosevelt's leadership aura; that under a mild warm manner and a charming smile he was at least as tough a customer as Ernest King; and that the invasion was going to succeed.

The prospect of dining with him gave Pug no thrill. He had had enough of the war's heavyweights. He was not sure how he would react to seeing Pamela again. Of one thing he was sure: that she would not inflict on him twice the pain of rejection; that by no word or gesture would he try to change her mind.

As she drove Burne-Wilke's Bentley to Bushey Park Pamela was dreading, and at the same time yearning, to look on Pug Henry once more. A woman can handle almost anything but indifference, and the revelation that he was in England had all but shattered her.

Since returning to England, Pamela had been finding out the gritty aspects of her commitment to Duncan Burne-Wilke. His family, she now knew, included an abrasively vigorous mother of eighty-seven who talked to Pam, when she visited, as to a hired nurse; and a numerous train of brothers and sisters, nephews and nieces, all of whom seemed unanimous in snobbish disapproval of her. By and large she and Burne-Wilke still enjoyed the old easy RAF intimacy, though illness and inactivity were making him querulous. In the stress of war she had become extremely fond of him; and bereft of any other future, she had accepted him. Pug's abrupt proposal had come much too late. Still, Stoneford struck her as a big burden, however imposing; Duncan's family was another burden; both bearable had she been deeply in love, but as things stood, gloomily disconcerting. The real trouble was that her letter of rejection to Pug had really settled nothing in her own mind. Not a word in reply for weeks! And then to learn from somebody else that he was here! Could he have turned stone-cold after that one letter, her only offending move, as he had with his wife? What a scary man! In this state of turmoil she drove into Bushey Park and saw Victor Henry standing at the bus stop.

"You look smashing." The schoolgirl words and tones gushed from her.

His smile was wry and reserved. "The big gold stripe helps."

"Oh, it isn't that, Admiral." Her eyes searched his face. "Actually, you're a bit war-worn, Victor. But so *American*. So totally American. They should carve you on Mount Rushmore."

"Kind words, Pam. Isn't that the suit you wore on the *Bremen?*"

"So! You remember." Her face burned with a blush. "I'm out of uniform. I *felt* like being out of uniform. There it was in the closet. I wondered whether I could still get into it. How long will you be here?"

"I'm flying back tomorrow night."

"Tomorrow! So soon?"

"Overnight in Washington, and on to the Pacific. Tell me about Duncan."

Thoroughly rattled (*tomorrow!*) she described Burne-Wilke's puzzling symptoms as calmly as she could while they drove: the abdominal pains, the recurring low fevers, the spells of extreme fatigue alternating with days of seemingly restored health. At the moment he was low again, scarcely able to walk around the gardens. The doctors guessed that injury and shock had allowed some tropical infection to get going in his bloodstream. Months or a year could go by before he shook it off; then again, it might suddenly clear up. Meantime, an invalid regime was mandatory: curtailed activity, much sleep, long bed rest every day, and many pills.

"He must be going mad."

"He was. Now he reads and reads, sitting in the sun. He's taken to writing, too, rather mystical stuff à la Saint-Exupéry. Flying plus the *Bhagavad-Gita*. Aviation and Vishnu really don't mix, not to my taste. I want him to write about the China-Burma-India theatre, it's the great untold story of this war. But he says there are too many maggots under the rocks. Well, here's Stoneford."

"Pam, it's magnificent."

"Yes, isn't the front lovely?" She was driving the car between brick pillars and open wrought-iron gates. Ahead, bisecting a broad green lawn, stretched a long straight gravel road lined with immense oaks, leading to a wide brick mansion glowing rose-red in the sun. "The first viscount bought the place and added the wings. Actually it's a wreck inside, Pug. Lady Caroline took in masses of slum children during the blitz, and they quite laid waste to the place. Duncan's had no chance to fix it up. We live in the guest wing. The little savages never got in there. I have a nice little suite. We'll have tea there, then walk in the garden until Duncan wakes up."

When they mounted to the second floor, Pamela casually pointed out that she and Burne-Wilke lived at opposite sides of the house; he looked out on the oaks, she on the gardens. "No need to tiptoe," she said as they walked past his door. "He sleeps like a dormouse."

An elderly woman in a maid's costume served the tea very clumsily. Pug and Pamela sat by tall windows overlooking weed-choked flower beds. "It's all going to jungle," she said. "One can't hire the men. They're fighting all over the world. Mrs. Robinson and her husband look after the place. She's the one who bungled the tea, she used to be the laundress. He's a senile drunk. Duncan's old cook has stayed on, so that's good. I have a job in the ministry, and I manage to come out most nights. That's my story, Pug. What's yours?"

"Madeline married that young naval officer."

"Wonderful!"

"They're in New Mexico. Pleasantest turnabout in my life. Byron's got his Bronze Star, and by all accounts he's a good submariner. Janice is in law school. My grandson at three is a formidable genius. There's some hope about Natalie. A neutral Red Cross delegation will visit her camp, or ghetto, or whatever it is, very soon, so maybe we'll get some word. If the Germans are letting the Red Cross in, the place can't be too bad. That's my story."

Pamela could not help it, though Pug's tone was so final. "And Rhoda?"

"In Reno, getting her divorce. You said something about a walk in the gardens."

Getting her divorce! But his manner was so estranged, cold, and discouraging, she could say no more about that.

They were outside before he spoke again. "This isn't jungle." The terraced rose garden was massed with well-tended bushes coming into bud.

"Roses are Duncan's hobby. When he's well he spends hours here. Tell me about your promotion."

Pug Henry brightened. "Actually, that's quite a yarn, Pam."

The President, he said, had invited him to Hyde Park. He had not seen Roosevelt since Tehran, and had found him shockingly withered. They had dined at a long table with only one other person, his daughter. Afterward in a small study Roosevelt had talked about the landing craft program. A curious anxiety was haunting the haggard President. He feared enemy action in the first few days might damage or sink a large number of the craft. Weeks might pass before Cherbourg was captured and big supply ships could take over the logistics; meantime speedy salvage and relaunching of sunk or damaged landing craft would be imperative. He had asked for reports on such arrangements and had gotten nothing satisfactory. He would "sleep better" if Pug would go to England and inspect the facilities. In the morning as Pug took his leave, the President had said something jocose and puzzling about "fair sailing weather ahead." Immediately on Pug's return to Washington from Hyde Park, Admiral King had summoned him to tell him face to face that he was getting his two stars and a Pacific battleship division.

"A battleship *division*, Pug!" They were walking through a densely blossoming apple orchard. Pamela seized his arm. "But that's absolutely marvelous! A *division!*"

"King said it was my reward for work well done, and he knew I could fight a BatDiv if I had to. It's two ships, Pam. Two of our best, the *Iowa* and the *New Jersey*, and — what the devil is the matter?"

"Nothing, nothing at all." Pamela was putting a handkerchief to her eyes. "Oh, Pug!"

"Well, it's the best I could hope for in my career. A monumental surprise." Pug wearily shrugged. "Of course it's a carrier war out there, Pam.

The battlewagons mainly bombard beaches. I may just ride around in fancy flag quarters till the war ends, initialing papers and acting pompous. An admiral afloat can be a futile fellow."

"It's terrific," Pamela said. "It's absolutely, utterly, bloody flaming terrific."

Pug gave her the bleak smile she had loved on the *Bremen* and loved now. "I agree. Won't Duncan be waking up?"

"Good Lord, six o'clock. Where did the time go? Let's run like deer."

They had drinks before dinner on the terrace. Eisenhower arrived late, looking pale and acting edgy. He declined a highball, and when his driver, Mrs. Summersby, cheerfully accepted one, he gave her a grumpy glance. This was Pug's first glimpse of the woman that all the gossip was about. Even in uniform Kay Summersby looked like the fashion model she had been before the war: tall, lissome, with a seductive high-cheekboned face and big eyes that glinted self-assurance; a professional beauty to her fingertips, with a faintly mischievous military veneer. Since the general wasn't drinking, the others gulped their highballs and conversation lagged.

The small dining room opened out on the gardens, and through the french doors pleasant flower scents drifted in. For a while this was the only pleasant thing going on. Sunburned, scarred, spectral, Burne-Wilke talked with Mrs. Summersby while the laundress waddled about clumsily serving lamb, boiled potatoes, and brussels sprouts. Pamela, with Eisenhower on her right and Leigh-Mallory on her left, could not get a rise out of either. They just sat there eating glumly. The dinner seemed to Pug Henry a disaster. Leigh-Mallory, a stiff correct RAF sort, stocky and mustached, kept furtively shifting his eyes at Kay Summersby beside him, as though the woman were sitting there stark naked.

But Burne-Wilke's good claret and Pug's presence in time helped matters. Leigh-Mallory mentioned that the drive to relieve Imphal was picking up steam, and Burne-Wilke observed that perhaps only Leningrad had been besieged longer in this war. Pamela piped up, "Pug was in Leningrad during the siege."

At that Eisenhower shook his head and rubbed his eyes like a man wakened from a doze. "You were, Henry? In Leningrad? Let's hear about it."

Pug talked. The imminent invasion was apparently weighing down the two high commanders, so a yarn was in order. His account of silent snowy Leningrad, the apartment of Yevlenko's daughter-in-law, the horror tales of the siege, rolled out easily. Leigh-Mallory's rigid face relaxed to lively attention. Eisenhower stared straight at Pug, chain-lighting cigarettes. He commented when Pug finished, "Most interesting. I was unaware that any of our fellows had gotten in there. I saw no intelligence on this."

"Technically I was a Lend-Lease observer, General. I did send a supplement on combat aspects to ONI."

"Kay, tell Lee tomorrow to get that stuff from the Office of Naval Intelligence."

"Yes, General."

"This chap, Yevlenko — he took you to Stalingrad too, you say?" asked Leigh-Mallory.

"Yes, but the fighting had already ended there."

"Tell us about that," said Eisenhower.

Burne-Wilke signalled the laundress to bring more claret. The atmosphere was clearing by the minute. When Eisenhower laughed at Pug's description of the rough drinking party in the Stalingrad cellar, Leigh-Mallory too uttered a reluctant chortle.

Eisenhower said, his face hardening, "Henry, you know these people. Once we go, will they attack in the east? Harriman's assured me that the attack is on, but there's a lot of skepticism around here."

Pug took a moment to think. "They'll go, sir. That's my guess. Politically, they're unpredictable, and may strike us as treacherous. They truly don't see the world, or use language, as we do. That may not change, ever. Still, I think they'll keep this military commitment."

The Supreme Commander emphatically nodded.

"Why?" asked Leigh-Mallory.

"Self-interest, of course," Eisenhower almost snapped. "I agree, Henry. The time to hit the other fellow is when he has his hands full. They're bound to go."

"Also," said Pug, "out of a sense of honor. That they've got."

"If they've got that much in common with us," Eisenhower said soberly, "we'll eventually get along with them. We can build on that."

"I wonder," said Leigh-Mallory in a heavily jesting tone. "Look at the trouble we have getting along, General, and we have the English language in common."

Kay Summersby remarked sweetly, in Mayfair accents, "It only seems we do."

Turning on her, Sir Trafford Leigh-Mallory genuinely laughed, and raised his glass to her.

Eisenhower gave Mrs. Summersby a wide warm grin. "Well, Kay, now I have to talk for a while with these two RAF fellows — in sign language, of course." A joke from the Supreme Commander naturally brought loud laughter. Everybody stood up. Eisenhower said to Burne-Wilke, "Maybe we can get in a rubber afterward."

Pamela invited Pug and Mrs. Summersby to the terrace for brandy and coffee, but once outside Kay Summersby did not sit down. "See here, Pam," she said with an ironic little glance from Henry to Pamela, "they'll be talking for quite a while. I have simply masses of things to do at the cottage. You and the admiral will forgive me, won't you, if I just pop over there and come back for the bridge?"

And she was gone. The general's car rattled down the gravel road.

Pamela was perfectly aware that Mrs. Summersby, with sharp intuition, was giving her what might be her last chance at Victor Henry in this life. She went right on the attack. She had to provoke a scene to accomplish anything. "No doubt you deeply disapprove of Kay. Or do you bend your rules for great men?"

"I know no more about her than meets the eye."

"I see. As a matter of fact, and I know them rather well, I'm sure that's all there is to it." Pug made no comment. "Pity you couldn't be more broadminded about your wife."

"I was ready to stick it out. You know that. Rhoda chose differently."

"You froze her."

Pug said nothing.

"Will she be happy with the fellow?"

"I don't know. I'm worried, Pam." He told her about the anonymous letters, and his talk with Peters on the train. "I've met him once since then, the day Rhoda left for Reno. He came to take her to the station, and while she primped we talked. He didn't act happy. I think at this point he's doing the honorable thing."

"Poor Rhoda!" This was all Pamela could say, in the rush of emotion at what Pug Henry was now telling her. Here was the last bit of the jigsaw puzzle. Colonel Peters had looked to Pamela like a hard and clever man; and her instinct had been that he would see through Rhoda Henry before she got him to the altar, and would drop her. He *had* seen through her; yet the marriage was on. Victor Henry was really free.

The night was dark now. They sat in starlight. A bird nearby was pouring out rich song. "Isn't that a nightingale?" Pug asked.

"Yes."

"Last time I heard one was on the airfield, before I took off on the flight over Berlin."

"Oh, yes. And didn't you put me through the hell of an ordeal *that* time, too. Only it lasted twenty hours, not six weeks."

He peered at her. "Six weeks? What are you talking about?"

"Six weeks and three days, exactly, since I wrote you. Why didn't you ever answer my letter? Just a word, any word? And why did I have to find out by chance that you've been in England? Do you hate me that much?"

"I don't hate you, Pam. Don't be ridiculous."

"Yet all I deserved was to be cast into the outer darkness."

"What could I have written you?"

"Oh, I don't know. Let's say, a gallant good-bye. Conceivably, even, a dashing refusal to take 'no' for an answer. Any little sign that you didn't loathe and despise me for an agonized decision. I told you I was blinded with tears when I wrote. Didn't you believe me?"

"I wrote the gallant good-bye," he said dully. "Can't you imagine that much? I wrote the refusal to take 'no' for an answer. I tore up many letters. There was no graceful way to answer. I don't see begging a woman to change her mind, and I don't imagine begging helps. Anyway, I'm no good at it."

"Yes, you do find it awkward to write your feelings, don't you?" Gladness surged through Pamela to hear of the torn-up letters, and she drove on in forcible tones. "That marriage proposal of yours! The way you went on and on about money —"

"Money's important. A man should let a woman know what she may be getting into. Anyhow, what is all this about, Pamela?"

"Goddamn it, Victor, I'll have my say! Your letter couldn't have been more horribly mistimed. I've been wretched ever since I answered you. I've never been more shocked in my life than when Slote said you were here. I thought I'd expire of the pain. Seeing you is incredibly sweet, and it's sheer torture." Pamela stood up. Stepping to Pug, who remained in his chair, she held out her arms to him, dim white in the light of the rising moon. "I told you in Moscow, I told you in Tehran, I tell you for the last time that I love you and not Duncan. Now there it is, and now *you* talk. Speak up, Victor Henry, at long last! Will you have me, or won't you?"

After a pause, he said blandly, "Well, I'll tell you, Pamela. I'll think about it."

It was such an unexpected deflating response that it took Pam a second or two to suspect teasing. She pounced on him, seized his shoulders, and shook him.

"You're shaking Mount Rushmore," he said.

"I'll shake it down! The damned stuffy banal Yankee monument!"

He gripped her hands, rose, and embraced her for a long hard kiss. Then he held her a little away from him, keenly scanning her face. "Okay, Pamela. Six weeks ago you refused me. What's changed?"

"Rhoda's gone. I couldn't believe that. Now I know she is. And you and I are here together, not separated by the whole damned planet. I've been sad since I wrote you, and now I'm happy. I've got to do Duncan dirt, that's all. It's my life."

"This is astounding. Old Rhoda said all you needed was some wooing."

"She said that? Wise woman, but I've never gotten it, and I never would have done. It's a good thing I'm such a forward slut, isn't it?"

He sat on the parapet and pulled her beside him. "Now listen, Pamela.

That Pacific war can last a long time. The Japs are still raising plenty of hell out there. If it comes to a fleet action, I'll probably be in it, and I could come out on the short end, too."

"So? What are you saying? That I'd be prudent to keep Duncan on the string? Something like that?"

"I'm saying you needn't make up your mind. I love you, and God knows I want you, but just remember what you said in Tehran."

"What did I say in Tehran?"

"That these very rare meetings of ours generate an illusion of romance, a wartime thing of no substance, and so on —"

"I'll gamble the rest of my life that it's a lie. I'll have to tell Duncan straight off, darling. There's no other possibility now. He won't be surprised. Hurt, yes, damn it, and I dread that, but — oh, Christ, I hear them." The voices of the other men sounded faintly in the house. "They weren't at it long, were they? And we've arranged nothing, nothing! Pug, I'm dizzy with happiness. Call me at the Air Ministry at eight o'clock, my dear sweet love, and now for God's sake kiss me once more."

They kissed. "Is it possible?" Pug murmured the words, looking searchingly into her face. "Is it possible that I'm going to be happy?"

He rode back to London with Leigh-Mallory. All the while the car raced down the moonlit highway to the city, and twisted through blacked-out streets to Pug's quarters, the air marshal said not a word. The meeting with Eisenhower clearly had not gone well. But the lack of talk was a blessing for Pug, who could dwell on the amazed supreme joy suffusing him.

When the car stopped, Leigh-Mallory spoke hoarsely and abruptly. "What you said about the Russian sense of honor interested me, Admiral. D'you think we British have a sense of honor, too?"

The emotion in his voice, his strained expression, forced Pug to collect himself fast.

"Marshal, whatever we Americans have, we learned from you."

Leigh-Mallory shook his hand, looked him in the eye, and said, "Glad we met."

The night before D-day. Ten o'clock.

In a lone Halifax bomber flying low over the Channel, the Jedburgh team "Maurice" was on its way. The Jeds were a small cog in the giant invasion machine. Liaison with the French Resistance was their mission; to arm and supply the maquisards and link them to the Allied attack plan. These three-man teams parachuted into France from D-day onward, had colorful adventures, did some good, had some losses. Without them the war would doubtless have been won, but the thorough Overlord plan had provided for this small detail, too.

And so it was that Leslie Slote — a Rhodes Scholar, a resigned Foreign Service officer, a man who had despised his own timidity all his life — found himself crouching in the noisy Halifax with a baby-faced aircraftsman from Yorkshire, his radio operator, and a French dentist, his contact with the Resistance; calculating, as the plane roared over moonlit water toward Brittany, his chances for living very long. A Rhodes Scholar had had to excel in sports, and he had always kept up his physical fitness. His mind was nimble. He had mastered the guerrilla crafts in a fashion: jumping, knife and rope work, silent movement, silent killing, and the rest. But to the last, to this moment when he found himself going in, it had all seemed strenuous make-believe, a simulation of Hollywood combat. Now here was the real thing. His uppermost feeling was relief, whatever the dread that was muttering underneath; the waiting at least was over. The hundred twenty-five thousand embarking troops probably felt much the same way. There were few hurrahs on D-day. Honor consisted in keeping one's head in the convulsive maelstrom of machinery, explosives, and fire, and doing one's assigned job unless shot or blown up.

Leslie Slote did his assigned job. The moment came, and he jumped. The opening shock of the chute was violent; and seconds later, so it seemed, the ground hit him another hard shock. Dropped too damned low by the damned RAF again; made it, anyway!

Powerful arms embraced him, even as he was unhooking the parachute. Whiskers scratched him. There was a gabble of idiomatic French, a smell of wine and garlic on heavy breaths. The dentist appeared out of the night, and the young Yorkshireman, in a mill of happy armed Frenchmen with wild faces.

I've done it, thought Leslie Slote. *I want to live, and by God I'm going to.* The surge of self-confidence was like nothing he had known before. The dentist was in command. Slote carried out his first joyous order, which was to drink down a stone mug of wine. Then they set about gathering up the dropped supply containers in the peaceful fragrant meadow under a glittery moon.

84

A Jew's Journey
(from Aaron Jastrow's manuscript)

JUNE 22, 1944.

I am utterly spent from the day's "dress rehearsal." Tomorrow the Red Cross comes. Cleanup and painting squads are still at work under floodlights, though already the town looks far better than Baden-Baden did. The spanking new paint everywhere, the clipped lawns, the lush flower beds, the fine sports fields and children's playgrounds, together with the artistic performances and the well-dressed Jews playacting vacationers at a happy peacetime spa, all add up to a musical comedy in the open air, utterly unreal. Not knowing what humaneness is, the Germans have worked up an elephantine parody of humaneness. It shouldn't deceive anybody who is not determined to be deceived.

Rabbi Baeck, the wise and gentle old Berlin scholar, a sort of spiritual father of the ghetto, hopes for much from this visit. The Red Cross people will not be taken in, he is sure; they will ask searching questions and probe behind the façade; and their report will force genuine changes in Theresienstadt, and perhaps in all the German camps. He reflects the prevailing optimism. We are an unstable lot in Theresienstadt. The prison mentality, the overcrowding, the haunting fear of the Germans, the subhuman nutrition and medical care, and the nerve-wracking jumbling together of Jews from many countries with little more than the yellow star in common, all make for unrealistic gusts of mood. What with the Allied landings in France and this imminent visit from the "outside," the mood is for the moment manic.

But I try to keep a grip on reality. The Allied invasion of Normandy has in fact bogged down. The Russians have in fact failed to attack in the east. What treachery is beyond Stalin? Has the monster decided to let a death struggle waste both sides in France, after which he can roll over all Europe at his leisure? I greatly fear so.

Today, June 22, three years ago, the Germans sprang at the Soviet Union. Today, if ever, the Russians, with their love of dramatic anniversary gestures, should have launched their Tolstoyan counterblow. No sign of it. The BBC evening bulletin was glum and vague. (BBC is always covertly monitored here and the word quickly spreads, although the penalty for listening is death.) Radio Berlin was cock-a-hoop again, crowing that Eisenhower's armies are trapped in the bocage and marsh country of Normandy; that Rommel will soon drive them into the sea; and that Hitler's new "wonder weapons" will then deliver a frightful knockout to the Anglo-Americans. As for the Russians, the Germans say that they paid "with oceans of blood" for their drive in the Crimea and the Ukraine, and have now come to the end of their strength, hence their long halt. Is there any truth to that? Even the German home front cannot tolerate total nonsense in war bulletins. Unless the Russians do attack very soon, and in great force, we will yet again know the foul taste of hope soured to despair.

Oh, what a revolting farce this long day was! Some small-fry German officials from Prague stood in for the visitors. Only Rahm was in uniform. It was absolutely dreamlike to watch Haindl and the other SS thugs in ill-fitting suits, ties, and felt hats bowing and scraping to us Elders, helping us in and out of our chauffeured cars, stepping aside smilingly for Jewish women in the cafés, in the streets, or in corridors. The whole thing went off like clockwork. Concealed messenger boys, as the party progressed, ran ahead and triggered off a singing chorus, a café performance, a string quartet in a private house, a ballet workout, a children's dance, a soccer game. Wherever we passed we saw happy, well-dressed, good looking holiday strollers smoking cigars and cigarettes. "Clockwork" is just the word. The Jews played their little happy parts with the stiffness of living dolls; and the "visitors" once past, their motions stopped, and they froze into poor seared Theresienstadt prisoners waiting for the next signal.

Three battered Red Cross parcels from Byron are piled on the floor beside me. Trucks trundled through the ghetto tonight heaped high with the packages, withheld by the Germans for months. Thus the visitors will see a ghetto swamped with Red Cross provisions. The Germans have thought of everything. From the Prague storehouses of Jewish loot they have brought a great load of finery for those inmates who will be on show. Right now I am wearing a superb suit of English serge and two gold rings. A beauty parlor has been set up for the women. Cosmetics have been distributed. Pretty Jewesses with neat yellow stars on their elegant clothes strolled today like queens on the arms of well-dressed escorts in the flower-bordered squares. Almost, I could believe I was back in peacetime Vienna or Berlin. Poor females! Despite themselves, they glowed in the brief delight of being bathed, perfumed, coiffed, decked out, and gemmed. They were as pathetic in their way as the wagonloads of dead bodies that used to pass by day and night, before all the sick were transported.

At the children's pavilion Natalie wears a beautiful blue silk dress, and Louis, in a dark velvet suit with a lace collar, is a joy to watch at his games. The SS have fattened up the tots like Strasbourg geese. They are rotund, red-cheeked, and full of vim, none more so than Louis. If anything can fool the visitors it will be this lovely pavilion, completed only a few days ago, charming and quaint as a dollhouse, and its enchanting little children playing on the swings and roundabout or splashing in the pool.

Natalie has just come in with the news that the Russians have attacked, after all! Two separate radio reports were picked up at midnight; an exultant BBC bulletin, and a long Czech-language broadcast from Moscow. The Soviets called the attack "our drive to crush the Hitlerite bandits in cooperation with our Allies in France." When she told me this, I murmured the Hebrew blessing on good news. Then I asked her if she would go ahead with the plans for Louis. Who knows, I said — suddenly manic myself — but what Germany may now quickly collapse? Is the risk still worth it?

"He goes," she said. "Nothing will change that."

I drop my pen with poor Udam's song running in my brain: *"Oy they're coming, they're coming after all! Coming from the east, coming from the west . . ."*

God speed them!

• • •

From World Holocaust
by Armin von Roon

Bagration

On the night of June 22, 1944, the third anniversary of Barbarossa, the Russians struck at us with full fury in the east. Partisan uprisings all over White Russia derailed our troop trains and blew up bridges. Reconnaissance probes stabbed at Army Groups Center and North from the Baltic Sea to the Pripet Marshes. Next day rolling artillery barrages from perhaps a hundred thousand big guns, massed in some places wheel to wheel, turned the four-hundred-fifty-mile front into an inferno. Then rifle divisions, tank divisions, and motorized divisions advanced in hordes, under a sky dark with Soviet aircraft. No Luftwaffe fighters rose to oppose them. The Russians were attacking us with a million two hundred thousand men, five thousand tanks, and six thousand airplanes. Here with a vengeance was the other jaw of Roosevelt's vise, grinding westward to meet the eastward thrust of Overlord.

BAGRATION! Revenge of Barbarossa!

Like us, the Soviets invoked the name of a great war leader, their hero of the Battle of Borodino, for their June 22 assault. Like us, they aimed at the speedy capture of all of White Russia, and the envelopment of the armies stationed on that vast wooded plain. Indeed, Bagration as it unfolded on our OKW maps was a spine-chilling mirror image of Barbarossa, reflecting back in our amazed faces the military lessons we had taught the Soviets only too well.

In their gory winter campaign to relieve Leningrad, and in their slogging rout of Manstein's forces from the Ukraine and the Crimea in the spring, we had seen their frightening resilience, and Stalin's brute resolve to go on squandering lives. But here in White Russia was something new: our own best tactical concepts, skillfully turned against us. To make the mirror image complete, Adolf Hitler would repeat the wooden-headed orders of Stalin in 1941 — "Stand where you are, no retreat, no maneuvers, hold or die" — with the identical catastrophic results, in the opposite direction.

The Soviets even achieved the same kind of surprise.

In 1941, expecting Hitler to strike for the Ukrainian breadbasket and the Caucasus oil fields, they had weighted their forces to the south. Thus our main thrust through White Russia had quickly shattered their central front. This time, despite the big Red buildup in the center, the infallible Hitler "knew" that the Russians would exploit their salient in the south to drive at the Rumanian oil fields and the Balkans. The central buildup he dismissed, in his usual airy-fairy way, as a feint, and he concentrated our forces to face the Soviet front in the Ukraine.

The anxious intelligence warnings by Busch, the commanding general of Army Group Center, and his pleas for reinforcements, went unheeded. When the Russian blow fell and the front caved in, Hitler of course fired Busch for his own pigheaded miscalculation; but the new commander, General Model, was just as hamstrung by Hitler's meddling, especially by his insistence that our divisions hole up in "strong points," towns left behind by the swift Russian onslaught — Vitebsk, Bobruisk, Orsha, Mogilev — instead of fighting their way out. This folly wrecked the front. The "strong points" fell in days, and all the divisions were lost. Gaping holes opened in our line, through which the Soviets came roaring like Tatars, on their limitless Lend-Lease wheels.

My operational analysis of Bagration, called "The Battle of White Russia," is very detailed, for I consider this little-studied event the pivot of Germany's final collapse in World War II, even more than the much-touted Normandy landings. If there was a true "second Stalingrad" in the war, it was Bagration. In less than two weeks the Russians advanced some two hundred miles. Sweeping pincer thrusts closing on Minsk trapped a hundred thousand German soldiers, and in the fighting we lost perhaps a hundred fifty thousand more. The remnants of Army Group Center reeled westward beyond Minsk, its formations sliced and skewered by Soviet armored spear points. By the middle of July Army Group Center had virtually ceased to exist. Melancholy ragged columns of German prisoners were again parading in Red Square. The Red Army had recaptured White Russia and marched into Poland and Lithuania. It was threatening the east Prussia frontier, and Army Group North faced being cut off by a Red thrust to the sea. All this time, the Anglo-Americans were still struggling to break out of Normandy.

And all this time Adolf Hitler kept his eyes obsessively on the west! The swelling eastern crisis he brushed off, at our briefing conferences, with short-tempered snap judgments. Our controlled press and radio drew a veil over the catastrophe. As for the Americans and the British, they were preoccupied then, and their historians still are, with operations in France. The Soviets put out little more than the bald facts of their advances; and after the war, during Stalin's decline into bloodthirsty lunacy, their military historians were gagged by fear. Not much useful writing about the war emerged from that wretched land for a long time.

So it happens that Bagration has slipped into obscurity. But it was this battle that irretrievably broke our front in the east, toppled Finland out of the war, and set the Balkan politicians plotting the treachery that led to our even larger disaster the following month in Rumania. And Bagration was the real fuse that, on July 20, set off the bomb in Supreme Headquarters.

———————

TRANSLATOR'S NOTE: *In recent years the Soviets have been putting out more and better books on the war. Marshal Zhukov's memoirs treat Bagration at length. These books, while informative, are not necessarily truthful by our standards. The communist government owns all the printing presses in Russia, and nothing sees the light that does not extol the Party; which, like Hitler, never makes mistakes. — V.H.*

•   •   •

At the first gray light on June 23, Natalie gets up and dresses for the Red Cross visit, in a bedchamber befitting a good European hotel: blond wood furniture, a small Oriental carpet, gay flowered wallpaper, armchair, lampshades; even vases of fresh flowers, delivered last night by the gardening crew. The Jastrow flat will be a stop in the tour. The noted author will show the visitors through the rooms, offer them cognac, and take them to the synagogue and the Judaica library. So Natalie tidies the place as for military inspection before hurrying off. There is much yet to do at the children's pavilion. Rahm has ordered a last-minute rearrangement of the furniture and many more animal cutouts for the walls.

It is just sunrise. Squads of women are out on the streets already, scrubbing the pavements on their hands and knees in the slant yellow light. The stench of these tattered scarecrows from the overcrowded lofts fouls the morning breeze. Their work done, they will vanish, and the perfumed pretty ones in fancy clothes will come out. Natalie's senses are too blunted to register such Beautification ironies. A recurring nightmare has been destroying her sleep for a month — Haindl, swinging Louis by the legs and smashing his skull on the cement floor. By now the picture of the child's head splitting apart, the blood spurting, the white brains spattering, is as real to her as her memory of the SS cellar; in a way even more familiar, because that short horror came and went in a blur of shock, whereas she has seen this ghastly vision a score of times. Natalie is a reduced creature, scarcely normal in the head. One thing keeps her going, and that is the hope of getting Louis out of the ghetto.

The Czech gendarme who conveys Berel's messages says the attempt is set for the week after the visit. Louis will sicken and disappear into the hospital. She will not see him again. She will be told only that he has died of typhus. Then she has to hope that she will one day hear he is safe. It is like sending him off to emergency surgery; no help for it, whatever the risk.

From a handcart parked outside the Danish barracks, gardeners are unloading rose bushes full of blooms, carrying them into the courtyard, and tamping them down into holes in the lawn. Heavy rose perfume deliciously sweetens the air as Natalie walks by. Clearly something special is going on with the Danish Jews. But that is not her concern. Her concern is to get through this day without a mistake, without angering Rahm and endangering Louis. The children's pavilion is the last stop on the scheduled tour, the star attraction.

As it happens, the Danish Jews are the important ones today: a handful, four hundred fifty Jews amid thirty-five thousand, but a special handful.

The whole story of Danish Jewry is astonishing. All but these few are free and safe in neutral Sweden. The Danish government, getting wind of an impending roundup of Jews by the German occupying force, secretly alerted the population; and in an improvised fleet of small craft, in one night, Danish volunteers ferried some six thousand Jews across a narrow sound to neutral and hospitable Sweden. So only this tiny group was caught by the Germans and sent to Theresienstadt.

Ever since, the Danish Red Cross has been demanding to visit its Jewish citizens in the Paradise Ghetto. The Danish Foreign Ministry has been forcefully pressing this demand. The Germans, curiously enough, instead of shooting a few Danes and squelching the nuisance, have acted irresolute in the face of such unprecedented moral courage on behalf of Jews, displayed by this one small nation and by no other. Though postponing the visit time and again, they have, in fact, at last knuckled under.

Four men, dim in history, but their names still on record, make up the visiting party.

Frants Hvass, the Danish diplomat who has been pressing Berlin about Theresienstadt.

Dr. Juel Henningsen, of the Danish Red Cross.

Dr. M. Rossel, of the German office of the International Red Cross in Berlin.

Eberhard von Thadden, a German career diplomat. Thadden handles Jewish affairs in the Foreign Ministry. Eichmann transports Jews to their deaths; Thadden pries them out of the countries where they hold citizenship, and delivers them to Eichmann.

The tour begins at noon. It lasts eight hours. It is to impress these two Danes and these two Germans, in these eight hours, that the whole stupendous six-month Beautification has been carried out. It proves well worth it. The written reports of Hvass and the Red Cross man have survived. They glow with approbation of the splendid conditions in Theresienstadt. "More like an ideal suburban community," one sums up, "than a concentration camp."

And why not?

The four visitors, with a train of high Nazi officials from Berlin and Prague, traverse Rahm's route by the timetable without a hitch. Their approach sets off one charming sight after another — pretty farm girls singing as they march with shouldered rakes to the truck gardens, masses of fragrant fresh vegetables unloading at the grocery store and Jews happily queueing up to buy, a robed chorus of eighty voices bursting forth with a breathtaking "Sanctus," a soccer goal shot to the cheers of a joyous crowd, just as the visitors reach the sports field.

The hospital looks and smells Paradise-clean, the linen is snow-white, the patients are cheerful and comfortable, replying to all questions by praising the superb treatment and meals. Wherever the visitors go — the slaughterhouse, the laundry, the bank, the Jewish administration offices, the post office, the ground-floor apartments of the *Prominente*, the Danish barracks — they see order, brightness, cleanliness, charm, and contentment. The Danish Jews outdo each other in assuring Hvass and Henningsen that they are well off and handsomely treated.

And the outdoor scenes are so pleasant! The quaintly decorated street signs are a treat to the eye. Well-dressed Jews stroll at leisure in the sunshine, as few Europeans can do in the harsh wartime conditions. The café entertainment is first-class. The cream pastries are delicious. Of the coffee Herr von Thadden remarks, "Better than you can get in Berlin!"

And what a fine last impression the children's pavilion makes! The lovely svelte Jewess in charge, the niece of the famous author, appears so happy in her work, and is so quick with positive responses to questions! Clearly she is on the friendliest terms with Commander Rahm and Inspector Haindl. It is a beguiling close to the visit: healthy pretty children swinging, sliding, dancing in a circle, splashing in the pond, riding a roundabout, casting comic long shadows in the sunset light on the fresh grass of the playground, their laughter chiming like light music. Pretty young matrons watch them, but none half as handsome or cheerful as the one in the blue silk dress. With the commander's permission, the Berlin Red Cross man takes photographs, including one of her holding her son in her arms, a lively imp with a heart-melting smile. In a burst of good feeling, Herr Rossel tells her that a print will be forwarded to her family in America.

* * *

After the war, challenged in the Danish Parliament to explain how he was duped by the Germans, Frants Hvass replies that he was not in the least fooled. He could see the visit was staged. He turned in a favorable report to assure continued good treatment for the Danish Jews and the flow of food parcels to them. That was his mission, not the exposure of German duplicity. Hvass confesses to Parliament, nevertheless, that he was relieved by the visit. In view of the terrible reports of the German camps already in the hands of the Red Cross, he had half-feared seeing corpses lying all over the streets, Musselmen stumbling about in a miasma of filth and death. Despite all the fakery, there was none of that.

The world keeps wondering why the International Red Cross — and for that matter, the Vatican — kept silent all through the war when they certainly knew about the great secret massacre. The nearest thing to an explanation is always Frants Hvass's: that accusing the Germans of crimes that could not be proven in wartime would only have made matters worse for the Jews still alive in their hands. The Red Cross and the Vatican knew the Germans well. Possibly they had a point, though the next question is, "How could matters have been made worse?"

* * *

The success of the Great Beautification gives the higher-ups in Berlin an idea. Why not shoot a film in Theresienstadt showing how well off the Jews are under the Nazis, giving the lie to all the mounting Allied atrocity propaganda about murder camps and gas cellars? Orders go out to prepare and shoot such a film at once. Title: *Der Führer schenkt den Juden eine Stadt,* "The Führer Grants the Jews a Town." Assigned to the script committee is Dr. Aaron Jastrow; and the children's pavilion will be prominently featured.

From "Hitler as Military Leader"

July 20 — The Attempt to Kill Hitler

. . . The briefing conference was taking place in a wooden hut, because the heavy concrete command bunker was being reinforced against air attack as the Russian front drew nearer Rastenburg. This saved Hitler's life. In the bunker we would all have been wiped out by the confined explosion.

It was a familiar boring scene until the bomb went off. Heusinger was droning on glumly about the eastern front. Hitler leaned over the table map, peering through his thick spectacles, and I stood beside him among the usual staff officers. There came a shattering noise, and the room was swathed in yellow smoke. I found myself lying on the wooden floor in terrible pain, involuntary groans issuing from my throat. I thought we had been bombed from the air. My first idea was to save myself from being burned alive, for there was a crackling of flame and a smell of burning. Despite my broken leg I dragged myself outside, stumbling over fallen bodies in the smoke and gloom. The groans and screams all around me were frightful. On the ground outside I collapsed in a sitting position. I saw Hitler come out of the smoke leaning on somebody's arm. There was blood on his face, his hair stood on end caked with plaster dust, and I could see his naked legs through his ripped black trousers. Those white spindle legs, those pudgy knees, for the moment made him seem an ordinary and pathetic man, not the ferocious warlord.

A favorable literature has sprung up about the conspirators. I myself cannot sentimentalize over them. That I was almost killed is beside the point. Count von Stauffenberg certainly was brave and ingenious to get by the formidable gate systems and security checks of Wolfsschanze and to place the briefcase full of explosives under the table; but to what avail? He was already a mutilated wreck, as is well known, minus an eye, a right hand, and two fingers on the left, lost in North Africa. Why did he not give his all? True, he was the head of the conspiracy, but the whole purpose was to kill Hitler; and the only sure way to do that was to walk up to him, camouflaged bomb in hand, and detonate it. The count's vague Christian idealism, it seems, did not extend to martyrdom. Ironically, he only lived a few more hours, anyway. He was caught and executed that same night in Berlin.

I knew nearly all the Wehrmacht conspirators. That some of them turned out to be involved astounded me. The identity of others I would have guessed, for I too was sounded out, early on. I silenced the inquirer and was not approached again. The concept of ending the war by murdering the Head of State — whatever his defects, so evident to us insiders — I considered treasonous, contrary to our oath as officers, and unsound. I still do.

On July 20, 1944, the Wehrmacht stood everywhere deep in foreign territory, nine million strong, fighting magnificently despite erratic leadership. The Fatherland, though battered from the air, was intact. The political spine of Germany was, for better or worse, the bond between the German people and Hitler. Murdering him would have let loose chaos. Himmler, Göring, and Goebbels, who still controlled all the state machinery, would have launched a vengeful blood bath beyond imagining. Every German's hand would have been against his brother. Our leaderless armies would have collapsed. The military situation, bad as it was, did not call for such a solution, really no solution at all: to plunge ourselves into anarchy, and invite the Bolshevik barbarians to spread rapine and pillage to the Rhine!

In fact, the July twentieth bombing boomeranged into a second Reichstag Fire. It gave Hitler the one excuse he needed to slaughter all surviving opposition. At least five thousand people died, most of them innocent. The General Staff and the independent intellectual elite — politicians, labor leaders, priests, professors, and the remnants of the old German aristocracy — were all but exterminated. My judgment is that July twentieth may have prolonged the war. We were at the very brink of the August disasters, which might have forced the Nazis themselves to ease out Hitler for an orderly capitulation. Instead, July twentieth shocked all Germany into rallying around the Führer. This lasted until he shot himself nine fearful months later. Among the German people, there was no support for the bungled attempt. The conspirators were execrated, and Hitler was riding high again.

In the infirmary at Wolfsschanze, as I can well recall, Hitler sat not ten feet from me talking to Göring, while doctors worked on his burst eardrums. "*Now I have got those fellows where I want them,*" he said, or words to that effect. "*Now I can act.*" He knew that the fiasco had reprieved his regime.

Hitler's apologists claim he did not see the films he ordered taken of the generals' executions, but I myself sat beside him during the screening. His giggles and remarks were more appropriate to a Charlie Chaplin comedy than to the ghastly distortions of my old comrades-in-arms, going through death agonies naked, in nooses of piano wire. I could never respect him after that. I cannot respect his memory when I recall it.

For me, the July twentieth affair was in every way a calamity. I have walked with a bad limp ever since. I lost the hearing in my right ear, and I am subject to dizzy spells and falling episodes. Also, it ended my chances of getting out of Supreme Headquarters. Coming from a conservative landowning family like most of the July twentieth men, I might well have fallen victim to Hitler's irrational suspicions and been executed myself. But possibly my injuries made my innocence seem self-evident. Or perhaps the Gestapo knew that I was in the clear. At any rate, I became again "the good Armin," different from those "others," treated more decently by Hitler than almost any general except Model and Guderian; and I was forced to witness his progressive degeneration down to the bitter end in the Berlin bunker, swallowing every day the foulest abuse of my profession and my class.

———————

TRANSLATOR'S NOTE: *The tiny band of conspirators had a sort of Keystone Cops quality. They kept setting bombs that failed to go off, planning actions in which someone goofed, and generally falling all over themselves. But they were very brave men, and their story is complex and fascinating. Roon's disapproval of them is not widely shared in Germany. I get the impression that Roon feels guilty about staying out of it, and protests too much. — V.H.*

• • •

From **A Jew's Journey**

JULY 23.

Rahm toured the ghetto today with the Dutch Jew who will direct the film. The script calls for a big scene at the children's pavilion. Natalie knew they were coming, and by the time the two cars arrived, she tells me, she was close to nervous prostration. But Rahm took very airily the news that Louis was dead. "Well, too bad. Use one of the other brats, then," was all he said. "Pick a lively one, and teach him that French song your kid sang." It seemed quite a matter of course to him that the child had died of typhus; no condolences, and apparently no suspicions. Of course we must wait and see. He may still investigate. Meantime, the relief is enormous.

Possibly none of Natalie's macabre precautions have been necessary: the urn of Louis's ashes in her bedroom, the memorial candles, the consultations with the rabbi on mourning procedures, the synagogue attendance to say *kaddish*, and the rest. But they have eased her mind. Nor has she had to playact! The continuing uncertainty has been crushing her. In three weeks there has been no further word; just the official death notice, and the grisly offer from the crematorium of his ashes, at a price. For all we know as yet, those really are Louis's ashes in Natalie's room. Of course we don't believe that; still, it has been all too convincing a business, first to last.

(Alas! Whose are they?)

The war news is becoming glorious. One wakes each day hungry for the latest word. German newspapers, smuggled in or pilfered from SS quarters, are now passed eagerly from hand to hand, for they have become fountains of good cheer. Whatever the Goebbels press admits *must* be true; and recent stories cause one to blink with amazed happiness. It is an absolute fact that a cadre of German generals have tried to kill Hitler! I read a full account in the scrawny *Völkischer Beobachter*, boiling with moral indignation at the "tiny clique of crazy traitors." German army morale is clearly cracking. In the far-off Pacific — the BBC, again — our Navy has won another victory while capturing the Mariana islands, which brings Japan within the range of American B-29s; and the Japanese government has fallen.

Meantime, the whole mad Beautification extravaganza is on again; rehearsals, refurbishing, and construction of even more fake Theresienstadt delights: a public "beach" on the river, an open-air theatre, and Heaven knows what else. The film is a God-given reprieve. Preparing for it will take a month; shooting, another month. The Germans are as fully bent on it as they were on the Beautification. If somebody in the collapsing Berlin regime doesn't think of countermanding the film, the cameras may be inanely grinding away when Russian or American tanks come crashing through the Bohusovice Gate.

For the Anglo-Americans have at last begun to break out of their Normandy bridgehead. The German papers tell of heavy fighting around Saint-Lô, a new place-name. On the eastern front, old place-names of my youth fill the German communiqués, as the Soviets have driven deep into eastern Poland. Pinsk, Baranovitch, Ternopol, Lvov — great Jewish cities, homes of famous yeshivas and eminent Hassidic dynasties — have been recaptured by the Red Army.

From Lvov, as the crow flies, Theresienstadt is some four hundred miles.

In the past three weeks, the Russians have advanced two hundred miles. *In three weeks.*

It is a race. Because of the film, we have a chance. Thank God — this once — for the Nazi passion for crude fraud!

AUGUST 6.

I have been drafted to work on the film script, hence the gap in this record. I suggested a simple visual running theme — the flow of water, in and out of the ghetto — thinking that some clever viewers might catch the symbolism of the "sluice." The director grasped it without words; I saw it in his eyes. The blockhead Rahm approves. He is taking childish pleasure in the film project; especially in selecting the bathing girls for the beach scene.

And still no word about Louis. Nothing. He disappeared into the hospital a month ago yesterday. Natalie puts in her day's work at the mica factory, then plods to the children's pavilion for film rehearsals. She does not eat, she never mentions Louis, and she looks gaunt and haunted. A few days ago in desperation she went to the hospital and demanded to talk to the doctor who wrote Louis's death certificate. She was very roughly turned away.

AUGUST 18.

Filming began. I have been rewriting the half-witted script night and day with four collaborators, under the interminable meddling of the dullard Rahm. No time to breathe, but thank God still for the film. Eisenhower's armies have swarmed out over France and surrounded the German armies at a place called Falaise. The BBC talks of a "western Stalingrad." The Allies have now landed in southern France, too, and the Germans there are retreating in panic. "The south of France is going up in flames," says the Free French radio, and the Russians have reached the Vistula. They are in Praga, across the river from Warsaw, in great force. The Poles are rising against the Germans. In Warsaw there is bloody street fighting. One's hopes brighten and brighten.

AUGUST 30.

Louis is all right! Paris is liberated!

This is the brightest day in all my years.

During a filming session in the library today, a Czech cameraman — I honestly don't know which one, it happened so fast, in the glare of the klieg lights — shoved into my pocket an off-focus photograph of Berel and the boy. They stand by a haystack in strong sunlight. Louis looks plump and well. As I write these words, Natalie sits opposite me, still weeping with joy over the picture.

The good news from the battlefields is becoming a cataract. The American armies moved so fast across France that they captured Paris undamaged. The Germans simply pulled out and fled. Rumania has suddenly changed sides, and declared war on Germany. This caught the Nazi regime by surprise, it seems. Between the invading Red Army and the Rumanian turncoat forces, so says the Moscow radio, the Germans are snared in a colossal Balkan entrapment. They are being shattered on all fronts, no doubt of that. The Allied air bombing, complains the *Völkischer Beobachter*, is the most horrible and remorseless in history. How pleasant! The Goebbels editorials take on a strident tone of *Götterdämmerung*. This war can end at any moment.

SEPTEMBER 10.

How far off can the end be now? Bulgaria has declared war on Germany. Eisenhower's armies are driving for the Rhine, scarcely opposed by the fleeing Wehrmacht. The uprising in Warsaw goes on. Somehow the Russians have not managed to cross the Vistula to help the Poles. Of course those lightning advances strained their supply lines. No doubt that is the reason for the lull.

Now Rahm, after much meddling and dawdling, has abruptly ordered the film finished. No explanation. I can think of only one. When the Soviets captured Lublin, they overran a vast concentration camp for Jews there called Maidanek. They found gas chambers, crematoriums, mass graves, thousands and thousands of living skeletons, and countless corpses lying about, all exactly as Berel described Oswiecim. The Russians brought in thirty Western correspondents to see the horror for themselves. The details are being told and retold on Radio Moscow. The worst reports and rumors turn out to have been plain fact.

So the gruesome German game is up. "The Führer Grants the Jews a Town," an idyllic documentary of the Paradise Ghetto almost two hours long, will probably never be shown. After the Lublin exposure the film is a self-evident, clumsy, hopeless fabrication. Our reprieve expires in five days. Then what? Nobody knows yet.

It is very strange. All these crashing war developments are for us distant thunder. We read words on paper, or we hear whispers of what was said on some foreign radio. Theresienstadt itself remains a stagnant little prison town where every sticky summer day is the same; a noisome ghetto jammed with undernourished, sick, scared people; faintly animated by the filming nonsense, but otherwise quiet as a morgue.

• • •

From 𝔚𝔬𝔯𝔩𝔡 𝔥𝔬𝔩𝔬𝔠𝔞𝔲𝔰𝔱

The September Miracle

During August our doom appeared to some giddy Western journalists "a question of days." The jaws of the east-west vise had closed to the Vistula and the Meuse. On the southern fronts the Anglo-Americans were driving up the Rhone valley almost unchecked, and ascending the Italian boot far north of Rome; and the Russians, wheeling in a great mass through our wide-open southern flank in the treacherous Balkans, had arrived at the Danube. On nearly every active front large numbers of our forces were either retreating or encircled.

Later Hitler himself called August 15 "the worst day of my life." That was the day the Allies landed in the south of France, and in the north General von Kluge disappeared into the Falaise pocket. Pathologically suspicious after July 20, the Führer feared that Kluge might have vanished to negotiate; the situation actually looked that bad at Headquarters. But the gallant Kluge soon managed to restore communications with us. Shortly afterward he killed himself; whether in despair over Hitler's stupid commands which were destroying his army, or because he was really involved in the bomb plot, I do not know. In August, I confess, the thought of suicide more than once crossed my own mind.

But September passed and no enemy soldier had yet set foot on German soil!

After Rundstedt's forces brilliantly repulsed Montgomery's foolhardy narrow thrust with airborne troops at Arnhem, trying to flank the Westwall through Holland, Eisenhower's rush toward the Rhine faded away. Gas tanks were empty, generals at loggerheads, strength dispersed from the Low Countries to the Alps. The Russians were halted along the Vistula, coping with our counterattacks, while across the river the Waffen SS levelled Warsaw with fire and explosives to wipe out the uprising. The southern drives against us were all halted. Under the worst pounding and against the worst odds of modern history, Germany stood bloodied and defiant, holding its ring of foes at bay.

If the lone British stand in 1940 merits praise, why not this heroic rebound of the Wehrmacht in September 1944?

The analytical elements of the "September miracle" are clear. West and east, our enemies outran their supplies in their spectacular and speedy advances; while German discipline hardened and total mobilization took place, under the threat to our sacred soil. Nor can one overlook the letdown in the invaders' fighting morale, especially in the west: the euphoric feeling of "well, we've won the war, we'll be home by Christmas," induced by long advances, the fall of Paris, and the attempt on Hitler's life. Also, Hitler's onesided insistence on hardening up the French ports was at last paying some dividends. Eisenhower had two million men ashore, but through the distant bottlenecks of Cherbourg and an artificial harbor he could not supply an all-out assault on the Westwall. He needed Antwerp, and we still dominated the Scheldt estuary.

In postwar military writings there is much armchair scoffing at Eisenhower. These authors dwell on map distances and troop counts, overlooking the sweaty, gritty, complex logistics that decide modern war. Eisenhower was the typical American military man, a plodder in the field but something of a genius in organization and supply. His caution and broad-front strategy were not unsound, if scarcely Napoleonic. We were still a very dangerous foe, and he deserves credit for resisting specious gambles in September.

Advocates of both Montgomery and Patton argue that given enough gasoline, each of their heroes could have thrust on to Berlin and quickly ended the war. General Blumentritt told British interrogators that Montgomery could certainly have done it. I shall demonstrate in my operational analysis the decisive adverse factors. Briefly, the flanks of such a narrow thrust on extended supply lines would have invited a disastrous repulse, a much greater Arnhem. I knew Blumentritt well, and I doubt that those were his professional views. He was telling his conquerors what they wanted to hear. Given the port facilities and communications available to Eisenhower, the thing could not be done. The consumption rate of his troops was quite shocking: seven hundred tons per division per day! A German division did its fighting on less than two hundred tons a day.

Eisenhower could not afford a massive risk and setback; not with hundreds of American correspondents breathing down his neck, and a presidential election two months away. The enemy coalition was unstable enough. All through the summer campaign the Anglo-Americans pulled and tugged at bad cross-purposes. And the Russian failure to aid the Warsaw uprising — and what was worse, their refusal to allow the Anglo-Americans even to send airborne assistance — already planted the poison of the Polish question, which would in time destroy the strange alliance of capitalists and Bolsheviks.

Unfortunately we lacked the punch to exploit these strains among our foes. Hitler's mulish "stand or die" policy on the battlefield had bled us too much. In the three colossal summer defeats — Bagration, the Balkans, and western France — and a score of smaller entrapments, one million five hundred thousand German front-line troops had been killed, captured, cut off, or routed in disorder without arms. Had these battle-hardened forces fought an elastic defense instead, harrying our foes' advance while withdrawing in good order to the Fatherland, we might well have salvaged something from the war.

As it was, the "September miracle" could not avert *Finis Germaniae,* it could only postpone the doom. Yet even as he went down, Hitler retained the hypnotic power to draw suicidal reserves of nervous energy and fighting heart from Germany. Already at the end of August he had issued his startling directive for the Ardennes counterattack. With heavy hearts we were making plans and issuing preliminary orders at Headquarters. However badly the man was failing, his feral willpower was not to be opposed.

———————

TRANSLATOR'S NOTE: *This Ardennes operation became the "Battle of the Bulge." It is interesting that Roon commends Eisenhower's cautious broad-front strategy, which many authorities condemn. The true judgment would lie in unravelling very complicated logistical statistics of Overlord. Fortune favors the bold, but not when they are out of gas and bullets. The strange Red Army inaction while Warsaw was destroyed by the Germans in plain sight across the river remains controversial. Some say that from Stalin's viewpoint the wrong Poles were leading the uprising. The Russians maintain that they had reached the limit of their supplies, and that the Poles did not bother to coordinate their uprising with Red Army plans. — V.H.*

• • •

From **A Jew's Journey**

OCTOBER 4.

The fourth transport since the filming ended is now loading. I have just come from the Hamburg barracks, where I said my last good-bye to Yuri, Joshua, and Jan. That is the end of my Theresienstadt Talmud class.

We stayed up all night in the library, studying by candlelight until dawn broke. The boys had packed their few belongings, and they wanted to learn to the last. A strange and abstruse topic we had reached, too: the *met-mitzva*, the unidentified body found in the fields, whose burial is a strict duty to all. The Talmud drives to a dramatic extreme to make the point. A high priest, enjoined by special laws of ritual purity against contact with a corpse, is forbidden to bury even his own father or mother. So is a man under Nazirite vows. Yet a high priest who has taken a Nazirite vow — thus being doubly restricted — is commanded to bury a *met-mitzva* with his own hands! Such is the Jewish regard for human dignity, even in death. The voice of the Talmud speaks across two thousand years to teach my boys, as its last word to them, the gulf between ourselves and the Germans.

Joshua, the brightest of the three remaining lads, asked abruptly as I closed the old volume, "Rebbe, are we all going to be gassed?"

That yanked me back to the present! The rumors are rife in the ghetto now, though few people are tough-minded enough to face up to them. Thank God I was able to answer, "No. You're going to join your father, Joshua — and you, Yuri and Jan, your older brothers — at a construction project near Dresden. That's what we in the council have been informed, and that's what I believe."

Their faces shone as though I had set them free from prison. They were high-spirited still at the barracks, with the transport numbers around their necks, and I could see that they were cheering up other people.

Was I deceiving them, as well as myself? The Zossen construction project outside Berlin — temporary government huts — is a fact. The workers from Theresienstadt and their families are being very well treated there. This labor project in the Dresden area, Rahm has firmly assured the council, is the same sort of thing. Zucker heads the draft; an able man, an old Prague Zionist and council member, very supple at handling the Germans.

The pessimists in the council, who tend to be Zionists and long-term ghetto inmates, don't believe Rahm at all. The draft of five thousand able-bodied men, they say, denudes us of the hands needed for an uprising, should the SS decide to liquidate the ghetto. There have been uprisings in other ghettos; we hear the reports. When Eppstein was arrested after the filming stopped, and the order came down for this huge labor draft, the false security of the Beautification and the movie foolishness dissolved, and the council was plunged in dismay. We had had no transport order in almost five months. I heard mutinous mutterings around the table that astonished me, and there were Zionist meetings about an uprising to which I was not invited. But the draft went off on schedule in three transports, with no disturbance.

This fourth transport is extremely worrisome. True, they are the relatives of the construction workers who have gone. But last week the SS permitted relatives to volunteer to go along, and about a thousand did. These are being railroaded out willy-nilly. The one shred of reassurance is that the four shipments do make up one group, the big labor draft and its families. Rahm explains that it is the policy to keep families together. This may be a soothing lie; conceivably it could still be true.

The endless talk in the council about our probable fate comes down to two opposed views: (1) Despite the lull in the war, the Germans have lost, and they know it; and we can expect a gradual softening of our SS bosses as they start thinking of self-preservation. (2) The lust of the Germans to murder all the Jews of Europe will only be aggravated by looming defeat; they will rush to complete this "triumph" if they can gain no other.

I hesitate between the two probabilities. One is sensible, the other insane. The Germans have both faces.

Natalie is a total pessimist. She is recovering much of her old toughness, now that Louis is gone and safe; eating the worst slops voraciously, and gaining weight and strength every day. She means to survive, she says, and find Louis; and if transported, she intends to be strong enough to survive as a laborer.

OCTOBER 5.

A fifth transport was ordered *two hours* after the fourth left; a random selection of eleven hundred people. No explanation this time, nothing to do with the Dresden construction project. Many families will have to be broken up. Large numbers of the sick, and women with small children, will go. Natalie probably would have gone, if Louis were still here. The Germans simply lied again.

I will not yield to despair. Despite the strange lull on the battlefronts, Hitler's Reich is falling. The civilized world can yet smash into this lunatic enclave of Nazi Europe in time to save our remnant. Like Natalie, I want to live. I want to tell this story.

If I do not, these scrawls will speak for me in a distant time.

85

THE wind was high, the swells huge, as Battleship Division Seven stood in to Ulithi atoll with the *Iowa* in the van, and the *New Jersey* in column astern flying Halsey's flag. When the battleships pitched, gray water broke clear over their massive forecastles, and the dipping long guns vanished in spray. The screening destroyers were bobbing in and out of sight on the wind-streaked black swells of the typhoon's aftermath. Blue patches were just starting to show in the overcast after the storm.

Ye gods, Victor Henry was thinking — as the warm sticky wind, sweeping salt spray all the way up to the *Iowa*'s flag bridge, wetted his face — how I love this sight! Since the newsreels of his boyhood days showing dreadnoughts plowing the seas, battleships under way had always stirred him like martial music. Now these were *his* ships, more grand and strong than any he had ever served in. The accuracy of the radar-controlled main batteries, in the first gunnery exercises he had ordered, astounded him. The barrage thrown up by the bristling AA made a show like the victory blaze over Moscow. Halsey's staff in its happy-go-lucky fashion had not yet put out the Leyte operation order, but Pug Henry was convinced that this landing in the Philippines meant a fleet battle. Avenging the *Northampton* with the guns of the *Iowa* and the *New Jersey* was a grimly pleasing prospect.

Signal flags ran snapping and fluttering up the halyards, ordered by Pug's chief of staff: *Take formation to enter channel*. Responding flags showed on the *New Jersey* and the carriers and destroyers. The task group smoothly reshuffled its stations. Pug had one reservation about his new life; as he had told Pamela, there wasn't enough to do. Paperwork could keep him as busy as he pleased, but in fact his staff — nearly all reserves, but good men — and his chief of staff had things under control. His function was close to ceremonial, and would continue so until BatDivSeven got into a fight.

He could not even explore the *Iowa* much. At sea he had an ingrained busybody instinct, and he yearned to nose around the engine spaces, the turrets, the magazines, the machine shops, even the crew's quarters of this gargantuan vessel; but it would look like snooping on the work of the *Iowa*'s captain and exec. He had missed out on commanding one of these engineering marvels, and his two stars had lifted him forever beyond the satisfying dirty work of seagoing, into airy spotless flag quarters.

As the *Iowa* steamed up Mugai channel, Pug had his eye out for submarines; he had not seen Byron or heard from him in months. Fleet carriers, new fast battleships, cruisers, destroyers, minesweepers, support vessels, were awesomely arrayed in this lagoon ten thousand miles from home; one could scarcely see the palms and coral beaches of the atoll for the warships. But no subs. Not unusual; Saipan was their forward base now. The dispatch that his flag lieutenant brought him as the anchor rattled down was therefore a disquieting surprise.

> FROM: CO BARRACUDA
> TO: COMBATDIV SEVEN
> RESPECTFULLY REQUEST PERMISSION CALL ON YOU.

It had come in on the harbor circuit. The submarine was berthed in the southern anchorage, the flag lieutenant said, blocked from view by nests of LSTs.

But why the commanding officer, Pug wondered? Byron was the exec. Was he ill? In trouble? Off the *Barracuda?* Pug uneasily scrawled a reply.

> FROM: COMBATDIV SEVEN
> TO: CO BARRACUDA
> MY BARGE WILL FETCH YOU 1700 DINNER MY QUARTERS

For Halsey's command conference, deferred by the typhoon sortie, long black barges fluttering white-starred blue flags came bouncing through the choppy waters to the *New Jersey.* Soon admirals in starched open-collared khakis ranged the long green table of Halsey's quarters. Pug had never seen so many starred collar pins and flag officers' faces in one room. There was still no operation order. Halsey's chief of staff, standing with a pointer at a big Pacific chart, described the forthcoming strikes at Luzon, Okinawa, and Formosa, intended to squelch land-based air interference with MacArthur's landing. Then Halsey, though looking very worn and aged, talked zestfully about the operation. The Nips could hardly stand by idly while MacArthur recaptured the Philippines. They might well hit back with everything they had. That would be the chance to make a killing, to annihilate the Imperial Fleet once for all; the chance Ray Spruance had passed up at Saipan.

His pouchy eyes glinting, Halsey read aloud from Nimitz's directive. He was ordered to cover and support the forces under MacArthur " *in order to assist in the seizure and occupation of all objectives in the Central Philippines.*" That much he intoned in a level voice. Then giving the assembled admirals an amused yet menacing glare, he grated slow words: "*In case opportunity for destruction of major portion of the enemy fleet is offered or can be created, SUCH DESTRUCTION BECOMES THE PRIMARY TASK.*"

That was the sentence, he said, that had been missing from Ray Spruance's directive for Saipan. Getting it into his own orders for Leyte had been a job, but there it was. So everybody at the conference now knew what the Third Fleet was going to Leyte for; to destroy the Japanese navy, once the invasion forced it out of hiding.

At the eager exclamations of approval around the table, the old warrior grinned with tired happiness. The talk moved to routine details of the air strikes. The chief of staff mentioned that some newspapermen flown out by Cincpac to observe the Third Fleet in action would be berthed in the *Iowa* as guests of ComBatDiv Seven.

Amused glances all turned on Pug Henry, who blurted, "Oh, Christ, no! I'd rather have a bunch of women aboard."

Halsey wagged gray thick eyebrows. "Ha! Who wouldn't?"

Barks of laughter.

"Admiral, I mean old, bent, toothless women, with skin ailments."

"Of course, Pug. We can't be all that fussy out here."

The conference broke up in ribald merriment.

When Pug returned to the *Iowa* his chief of staff told him that the newspapermen were already aboard, berthed in wardroom country. "Just keep them away from me," Pug growled.

"The fact is," said the chief of staff, a pleasant and able captain of the class of '24, with thick prematurely white hair, "they've already asked for a press conference with you."

Pug used obscenity sparely, but he let fly at the chief of staff, who departed fast.

Mail lay on the desk in two baskets: official, stacked high as as usual, and a small personal pile. He always looked first for Pamela's letters. There was one, promisingly thick. Pulling it out, he saw a small pink envelope, with the address on the back that still jarred him:

MRS. HARRISON PETERS
1417 FOXHALL ROAD
WASHINGTON, D.C.

The letter was brisk. The longer Hack lived in the Foxhall Road house, Rhoda wrote, the better he liked it. In fact, he wanted to buy it. She knew Pug had never really been fond of the place. It was a messy thing, since the divorce settlement had given her rent-free occupancy, but left the house in his name until she felt like disposing of it. If Pug would just write to his lawyer and suggest a sale price, the "legal beagles" could get started. Rhoda reported that Janice was seeing a lot of a law school instructor, and that Vic was doing admirably in nursery school.

Madeline has been a great comfort, too. She actually writes every month or so, cheering me up. She seems to love New Mexico. I got one lovely letter from

Byron at last. I wondered and wondered how he would take it. Frankly I sort of *cringed*. He doesn't understand, any more than I do, exactly, but he wished me and Hack happiness. He said that to him I would always be just Mom, no matter what. Couldn't be sweeter. Sooner or later you'll see him out there. When you explain, don't be too hard on me. The whole thing's been hard enough. However, I am perfectly happy.

> Love,
> Rho

Pug rang for coffee, and told his Filipino steward that he would be dining in his quarters with one guest. He wrote a terse reply to Rhoda, sealed it up, and tossed it in his out-basket. The thickness of Pam's envelope, perhaps because of the pall of Rhoda's letter, now seemed ominous. He settled down with coffee in an armchair to read.

It was indeed a grave letter. It began, "Sorry, love, but I'm going to write about nothing but death." Three shocks had struck her in two weeks, the first by far the worst, the others hitting her hard because of her low state. Burne-Wilke had died, swept away by a fulminating pneumonia. She had left Stoneford months ago, and the family had not notified her, so she had first learned about it at the Air Ministry, and had missed the funeral. Guilt was gnawing at her. Would he have sickened if she had stayed on with him, cared for him, and said nothing about the future until the end of the war? Had the hurt and the loneliness weakened him? She could never know, but she was having an unhappy time over it.

There's something awful altogether about this September. It's a brown wet ugly fall. The buzz bombs were bad enough, but these new horrors, huge rockets that arrive and fall without a sound, have thrown us into a funk. After all the wretched years of war, after the great Normandy landing and the sweep through France, with victory apparently days away, we're back in the blitz! It's just too damned much — the sirens, the all-night fires, the frightful explosions, the roped-off streets, the acres of smoking rubble, the civilian death lists, all over again — ghastly, ghastly, ghastly!

And Montgomery has had an atrocious fiasco in Holland, with an enormous commitment of airborne troops. It's probably killed any chance of ending the war before mid-1945. The worst of it is that Monty keeps telling the papers it was a "partial victory." Ugh!

It was a rocket that killed Phil Rule, poor wretch. It blew to smithereens the newsmen's pub he haunted, leaving nothing but a crater for two blocks in all directions. Days went by before there even was a reliable death list. Phil has simply vanished. Of course he was killed. I had no feelings left about Philip Rule, as you well know, but too much of my youth was thrown away on him, and his death hurts.

As for Leslie, it's conceivable that he's still alive, but not likely. The French dentist who was in the team made his way to Bradley's army, and I've read his report. The team was betrayed by an informer in Saint-Nazaire. They got into the town hidden inside big wine casks, in a huge vanload of wine delivered to the German garrison. They managed to obtain and send out excellent intelligence about the defenses. In trying to organize an uprising, they got careless about the Frenchmen they took into their confidence, and the Germans trapped them. The dentist, before he escaped from the house where they were ambushed, saw Leslie fall, shot. Another pointless death! As you know the Brittany ports are no longer significant. Eisenhower is just letting the German garrisons wither there. Leslie's death, if he died, was sheer waste.

Leslie Slote, Phil Rule, and Natalie Jastrow! Pug, you dear good upright man of arms, you can't picture what it was like to be young in Paris with those three in the mid-thirties. What in God's name has become of poor Natalie? Is *she* dead, too?

What has this gruesome war all been for? Can you tell me? Poor Duncan believed — and I'm sure he was right — that as soon as the war ends and we pull out of India, the Hindus and Moslems will butcher each other in the millions. He predicted, too, that a Chinese civil war "will turn the Yellow River red." Certainly the Empire is finished. You saw Russia, a gutted slaughterhouse to the Volga. And what have we achieved? We have almost succeeded in murdering enough Germans and Japanese to convince them to quit trying to plunder the world. That's all. We haven't finished with that dirty business yet, after five long years.

Duncan said — it was on our last night together at Stoneford, actually, and he was of course melancholy, but unfailingly gentle and decent as always — that the worst part of this century would not be the war, but the aftermath. He said the young would be left with such utter contempt for their elders, after this stupid bath of world carnage, that there would be a general collapse of religion, morals, values, and politics. "Hitler will have his *Götterdämmerung*," Duncan said. "He's pulled it off. The West is done for. The Americans will seem all right for a while, but they'll go too, at last, in a spectacular and probably sudden racial blowup."

I wonder what you'd say to that! Duncan was rather down on Americans, for complicated reasons, not wholly excluding you and me. He saw the world going Buddhist in the end, after perhaps another half century of horror and impoverishment. I could never follow him into the *Bhagavad-Gita*, but he was morbidly persuasive that night, poor darling.

———————

Well, now it's a rainy morning.

Can you guess that I was pretty tipsy last night when I clattered out all those pages? I'm wondering whether to send such a depressing wail to you, out there in the Pacific, still with the job of fighting the war, and therefore still having to believe in it. Well, I'll send it. It's how I feel, and it's the news. In a day or two I'll write you another and more cheery one, I promise. I don't expect to be knocked on the head by a V-2, and if I should be, it's a quick painless exit from this crazed world. I only want to live to love you. Everything else is gone, but that's enough to build on, for me. I swear I'll be jolly in my next one, especially if my resignation from the WAAFs is accepted, and I can start planning to join you. It's in the works; very irregular, horridly unpatriotic, but I may just pull it off. I know people.

> All my love,
> Pamela

Pug took from a drawer and set on his desk the picture of Pamela, in the old silver frame from which Rhoda had smiled for almost thirty years, stowed away for the typhoon sortie. Pamela was in uniform, full-length, frowning. The picture was cropped from a news shot and blurrily blown up; far from flattering, but quite real, unlike Rhoda's old softly lit studio portrait, so many years out of date. He got at his official mail.

The gangway messenger of the *Barracuda* knocked at Byron's cabin door. "Captain, the admiral's barge is coming alongside."

"Thanks, Carson." In jockey shorts, his body shining with sweat, Byron was taking down from a bulkhead the Red Cross photograph of Natalie and Louis. "Ask Mr. Philby to meet me topside."

He came out on deck buttoning a faded gray shirt. The new exec was at the gangway; a foxy-faced Academy lieutenant who (Byron already surmised) did not much relish serving under a reserve skipper. The *Barracuda* was tied up port side to an ammunition ship. A working party aft was making a great profane noise around a torpedo swinging down on a crane.

"Tom, when all the fish are aboard, cast off, and take her alongside the *Bridge* for provisioning. I'll be back by 1900."

"Aye aye, sir."

ComBatDiv Seven's long barge, all gleaming white cordwork and white leather cushioning inside, purred away from the submarine. The luxury charmed Byron for what it said of his father's new status, but his mind was mainly on the divorce. Madeline had written that she had "seen it coming for a long time." Byron could not understand her. To him, until the arrival of the long sad sugary letter from Rhoda, his parents' marriage had been a monolithic fact, literally the Bible's "one flesh." No doubt his flighty mother was at fault, yet one passage in a letter his father had written from London still puzzled him: "I hope your mother will be happy. Things have been happening in my life, too, better discussed face to face, when the occasion offers, than written about."

Now they would come face to face. It would be awkward, possibly painful for his father, but at least the identity of the *Barracuda*'s captain should give him a nice surprise.

The watch book of the *Iowa*'s OOD noted, *At 1730 admiral's guest will arrive. JOOD escort to flag quarters.* But at 1720 the admiral himself appeared, squinting toward the south anchorage. In the glittering weather after the typhoon, the low sun blazed and the lagoon blindingly sparkled. The officer of the deck had seldom seen Rear Admiral Henry up close, this bloodless force called ComBatDiv Seven, a spruce squat grizzled man, a tongue-tying icy presence. The barge came alongside and a tall officer in dingy wrinkled grays leaped up the steps, jingling the guy chains.

"Request permission to come aboard."

"Permission granted."

"Good evening, Admiral." A sharp unsmiling salute by the officer in gray.

"Hello there." A casual return salute. ComBatDiv Seven said to the OOD, "Log my visitor aboard, please. Commanding officer of the *Barracuda*, SS 204. Lieutenant Commander Byron Henry, USNR."

The OOD, glancing from father to son, ventured a grin. A brief cool smile was the admiral's response.

"When did all this happen?" Pug asked as they left the quarterdeck.

"As a matter of fact, only three days ago."

The father's right hand momentarily gripped Byron's shoulder. They mounted the ladders inside the citadel at a run. "You're in pretty good condition," the son panted.

"I may drop dead doing that," said Pug, breathing hard. "But I'll be the healthiest man ever buried at sea. Come out on my bridge for a minute."

"Wow!" Byron shaded his eyes to look around.

"You don't get this view from a submarine."

"God, no. Doesn't it beat anything in history?"

"Eisenhower had a bigger fleet for the crossing to Normandy. But for striking power, you're right, the earth's never seen its like before."

"And the *size* of the *Iowa!*" Byron was looking aft. "What a beauty!"

"Ah, Briny, she's put together like a Swiss watch. Maybe later we'll mosey around."

Pug was still digesting the surprise. *Commander of a submarine!* Byron was growing into an eerie resemblance to the lost Warren; too pale, though, too tense in his movements.

"I'm pretty tight for time, Dad."

"Then let's go in to dinner."

"Snazzy setup," Byron said, as they entered the flag quarters. Sunlight streamed through the portholes, brightening the impressive outer cabin.

"Comes with the job. Beats a desk in Washington."

"I'll say —" Byron halted, his eyes widening at the silver-framed photograph on the desk. "Who's *that?*" Before Pug could answer he turned on his father. "Christ, isn't that Pamela Tudsbury?"

"Yes. It's a long story." Pug had not intended to break it this way, but the thing was done now. "I'll explain at dinner."

Byron's right hand shot up, palm and fingers stiff and flat. "It's your life." He yanked the snapshot of Natalie and Louis from a breast pocket. "I think I wrote you about this."

"Ah! The Red Cross picture." Pug scanned it avidly. "Why, Byron, they both look very well. How big the boy is!"

"It was taken in June. God knows what's happened since."

"They're in a playground, aren't they? Those children in the background look fine, too."

"Yes, it's encouraging, as far as it goes. But the Red Cross has ignored my letters ever since. The State Department remains a total zilch."

Pug handed back the picture. "Thanks. Seeing it does my heart good. Sit you down."

"Dad, maybe I'll just have a cup of coffee and run on back. We sortie at 0500. I've got a new exec, and —"

"Byron, dinner takes fifteen minutes." Pug gestured at his conference table, already set with two places at one end: white napery, silver and china, a vase of pink frangipani sprigs. "You've got to eat."

"Well, if it'll only take fifteen minutes."

"I'll see to that."

Pug strode out. Sinking into the chair at his desk, Byron peered incredulously at the photograph in the old silver frame that, as far back as he could remember, had held his mother's picture.

Sons find it uncomfortable to confront the reality of their fathers' sexual lives. Psychologists can analyze the reasons till the cows come home, and they tend to, but it is a clear fact of human nature. Had the picture of a woman his mother's age filled the frame, Byron could have absorbed the jolt. But *Pamela Tudsbury*, a girl who had helled around with Natalie in Paris! Byron had liked her well enough for the way she looked after her father. Even so, he had wondered, especially at Gibraltar, how such a hot dish — Pamela had been lightly clad on that Mediterranean midsummer day in a gauzy white sleeveless frock — could devote herself to following an old man about. She must have a lover, he had thought, if not several.

Her picture on his father's desk, in that frame, conjured up ugly visions of crude sex, mismatched sex, shacked-up sex, wartime London sex. There it stared, the proclamation of Pug Henry's weakness, the explanation of the divorce. To think that his idolized father — while he himself and Natalie were separated by the war — had groaned and thumped around on a bed in London with a girl Natalie's age! Byron resolved to keep utter silence, and at the first possible moment to get the hell off this battleship.

"Chow down," said his father.

They sat at the table, and the beaming Filipino steward served bowls of fragrant fish soup. Because this was such a rare moment for Pug — himself a flag officer, Byron a submarine captain, meeting for the first time in their new dignities — he put his head down and said a long heartfelt grace. Byron said, "*Amen,*" and not another word while he gulped soup.

There was nothing unusual about that. Pug had always had trouble conversing with Byron. His mere presence was satisfying enough. Pug did not realize that Pamela's picture had caused an earthquake in his son. He knew it was a surprise, a disconcerting one, and he intended to explain. To get talk going again he remarked, "Say, incidentally, aren't you the first reserve skipper in the whole submarine fleet?"

"No, three of the guys have S-boats by now, and Moose Holloway just got *Flounder*. He's the first one to get a fleet boat. Of course he's Yale NROTC from way back, and from an old Navy family. I guess being your son did me no harm."

"You had to have the record."

"Well, Carter Aster qualified me long ago, but I've not yet had a PCO cruise, and — what happened was, my skipper took sick out on station off Sibutu." Byron was glad to fill the time with talk that stayed off his father's personal life. "Woke up one morning in a fever and couldn't walk, not without terrible pain. Dragged himself around for a week, taking aspirin, but then he tried an attack on a freighter and botched it. By then he obviously was so damned sick we headed straight in here instead of returning to Saipan. They're still giving him blood tests on the *Solace*. He's half-paralyzed. I thought SubPac would fly out a CO, but they sent an exec instead, and I got the orders. Floored me."

"Talking of surprises," said Pug, by way of leading up to Pamela, "that fellow Leslie Slote is probably a goner. You remember him?"

"Slote? Of course. He's dead?"

"Well, that's Pam's information." Pug recounted his sketchy knowledge of the parachute mission on which Slote had been lost. "How about that? Would you have figured him as a volunteer for extra-hazardous duty?"

"Do you still have Mom's picture?" Byron said, looking at his wristwatch and pushing away his half-eaten food. "If you have, I'll take it."

"I have it, but not here. Let me tell you about Pamela."

"Not if it's a long story, Dad. I've got to go. What happened to you and Mom?"

"Well, son, the war."

"Did Mom ask for the divorce so as to marry Peters? Or did you want it because of *her?*" Byron jerked a thumb toward the picture.

"Byron, don't look for someone to blame."

Pug could not tell his son the truth. On the bald facts Byron would probably absolve him and despise his mother; this hard-faced young submariner was a black-or-white moralist such as he had himself been before the war. But Pug no longer condemned Rhoda for the Kirby business, he only felt sorry for her. These nuances went with being older, sadder, and more self-knowing than Byron could yet be. His son's silence and the rigid face made Pug very uneasy, and he added, "I know Pamela's young. That troubles me, and the whole thing may not come off."

"Dad, I don't know if I'm fit for command."

The sudden words hit Pug a hammer blow.

"ComSubPac thinks you are."

"ComSubPac can't look into my mind."

"What's your problem?"

"Possible instability under combat stress."

"You're cool by nature under the severest stress. That, I know."

"By nature, maybe. I'm in an unnatural state. Natalie and Louis haunt me. Warren's dead and I'm the one you've got left. Also, I'm a reserve skipper, one of the first, and that's a hot spot. I've been emulating you, Dad, or trying to. I came here today hoping for a shot in the arm. Instead —" again, the thumb pointing to Pamela's picture.

"I'm sorry that you're taking it that way, because —"

"There's always a shortage of aggressive COs," Byron rode over his father, something he never did. "I rate high for aggressiveness, I know that. The trouble is, my stomach for the whole thing is dropping out. This picture" — he touched his breast pocket —"is driving me crazy. If Natalie had listened to me and risked a few hours on a French train, she'd be back home now. It doesn't help to remember that. Nor does your divorce. I'm not in the best of shape, Dad. I can take the *Barracuda* back to Saipan and ask for a relief. Or I can go out on lifeguard station off Formosa as ordered, for the air strikes. What would you recommend?"

"Only you can make that decision."

"Why? You were willing to decide my whole life for me, weren't you? If you hadn't pushed me into submarine school — if you hadn't flown down to Miami the very day I proposed to Natalie, and forced the issue, with her sitting there and listening — she wouldn't have gone back to Europe. She and my kid wouldn't be over there now, if in fact they're even alive."

"I regret what I did. At the time it seemed right."

This answer caused Byron's eyes to redden. "Okay, okay. I'll tell you something, it's a bad symptom of my instability that I throw that up to you."

"Byron, when I was in bad shape myself, I requested the *Northampton*. I found that command at sea made life more bearable, because it was so all-absorbing."

"But I'm not a professional like you, and a submarine is a mortal responsibility."

"If you return to Saipan, some aviators may drown off Formosa that you might save."

After a silence Byron said, "Well, I'd better get back to my boat."

They did not speak again until they were out on the warm breezy quarterdeck in a magnificent sunset, leaning side by side on the rail. Byron said as though talking to himself, "There's something else. My exec's an Academy man. Taking orders from me grates on him."

"Judge him on performance at sea. Never mind how he feels."

Below from astern came the clanging of the barge. Byron straightened up and saluted. It hurt Pug to look into his son's remote eyes. "Good luck and good hunting, Byron." He returned the salute, they shook hands, and Byron went down the accommodation ladder.

The barge thrummed away. Pug returned to his quarters, and found the operation order for the Formosa strike on his desk, just delivered. Concentrating on the thick pile of inky-smelling mimeographed sheets was almost impossible. Pug kept thinking that he could not survive as a functioning man the loss of Byron.

And with this strained parting, father and son headed out into the biggest fleet battle in the history of the world.

PART SEVEN

Leyte Gulf

86

THE great sea fight turned on four elements: two strategic, one geographical, one human. The fate of Victor Henry and his son now rode on these four elements, so they should be borne in mind.

The geographical element was simply the conformation of the Philippines. Seven thousand islands straggle roughly north and south over a thousand miles of ocean between Japan and the East Indies. Capture of the Philippines meant cutting off Japan from oil, metal, and food. Luzon, the northernmost and largest island, was the key to the archipelago; and Lingayen Gulf, the classic landing area on Luzon for a drive to Manila, opens northwestward into the South China Sea.

Choosing as his stepping-stone to Luzon the smaller island of Leyte far to the southeast, MacArthur planned a landing in force on the shores of Leyte Gulf; a body of water hemmed in by island masses and small islets, opening eastward into the Philippine Sea. From the east, the American attackers could steam straight into the gulf, but from the west, the land masses and islets of the archipelago barred the way. Nearly all the water passages that threaded through the island maze were too shallow for fleet use.

Getting to Leyte from Japan itself, counterattacking Japanese units could steam down the eastern side of the archipelago and head straight in. Coming from the west or southwest, however — say from Singapore, or Borneo — there were but two usable ways through the archipelago to Leyte Gulf for warships: San Bernardino Strait, which would bring a task force past the big island of Samar for a turn down into the gulf from the north, or Surigao Strait, which enters the gulf from the south.

To be near fuel sources, the Main Striking Force of the Imperial Fleet was based off Singapore. It was scheduled to refuel in Borneo, if it had to do battle for the Philippines.

The human element was Admiral Halsey's frame of mind. This was dominated by an event five months in the past.

Back in June, the Pacific Fleet under Spruance had taken Saipan, an island in the Marianas chain, as a long hop toward Japan. The landing had provoked a major carrier duel, at once dubbed by American naval aviators as the "Marianas Turkey Shoot"; an aerial disaster for Japan, in which most of her surviving first-line pilots were shot down with small loss to Spruance. The Japanese carriers fled. The Americans in a short brutal land fight for Saipan gained an air base within bomber range of Tokyo. Spruance's opponent of Midway, Admiral Nagumo, the man who had bombed Pearl Harbor, committed suicide on Saipan; for with this breach of the Empire's inner defenses he deemed the war lost. So did many of Japan's leaders. The fall of Tojo, the militarist prime minister, was a world sensation, but the cause was not. The battle for Saipan was fought while Eisenhower's troops were grinding toward Cherbourg; so, like Imphal and Bagration, it was eclipsed in the newspapers.

Despite this historic if obscure victory, Spruance came in for savage insiders' criticism. His carrier commanders had yearned to steam out from Saipan to meet the oncoming Japanese for a head-on battle; they felt they could have annihilated the Imperial Fleet once for all. Spruance had reluctantly vetoed the idea. He would not be pulled away from the landing force he was there to shield, not knowing what other enemy forces might cut in behind him and wipe out the beachhead. So the Japanese aircraft had attacked in a cloud the Spruance forces hugging Saipan, and had fallen in the "Turkey Shoot," but their flattops and support forces had for the most part gotten away. King and Nimitz afterward praised Spruance's decision, but it remains in controversy. There were no other enemy forces at sea, critics still argue, and Spruance in his caution had passed up a chance for a big killing that might have shortened the war.

That was certainly Admiral Halsey's view. His character was eagerly aggressive, and at Leyte, he did not intend to repeat what he regarded as Spruance's great mistake.

As to strategy: on the American side two conflicting concepts for the Pacific war at last collided head-on — MacArthur's push northwest from Australia in land campaigns, the "South Pacific strategy"; and the Navy's island-to-island thrust across the broad watery wastes between Pearl Harbor and Tokyo, the "Central Pacific strategy."

The Navy planners wanted to bypass the Philippines altogether, land on Formosa or the China coast, and so "cork the bottle" of East Indies supplies. The bombing of shipping lanes, ports, and cities, they contended, with the submarine stranglehold, would in time force a surrender. MacArthur held the classic Army view that the enemy armed forces had to be defeated on land. New Guinea, the Philippines, then the home islands: that was his path to victory. King and Spruance, the chief Navy strategists, thought this would waste blood and time. Spruance even argued for a waterborne thrust straight to Iwo Jima and Okinawa. From these two small manageable objectives, he believed, air and submarine warfare could finish off Japan.

After Saipan, the Joint Chiefs of Staff got interested in the Navy strategy. MacArthur was outraged. In 1942 he had fled the Philippines by air on Roosevelt's orders. On arriving in Australia, he had publicly vowed, *I shall return*. He did not mean to return in a civilian airliner, after the Japanese had been beaten the Navy way. He demanded a personal meeting with the President, and he got it at Pearl Harbor in July.

Roosevelt had just been nominated for a fourth term. With the war going brilliantly in Europe, he undoubtedly wanted no trouble with Mac-Arthur, whom the political opposition was portraying as a neglected and mistreated military genius. Arriving at Pearl Harbor an ailing man, Roosevelt heard out MacArthur's impassioned appeal for recapturing the Philippines as a "requirement of the national honor"; also Nimitz's quiet professional argument for the Navy plan.

MacArthur won. The invasion of the Philippines was on. Yet the radical Army–Navy split persisted. Nimitz assigned to MacArthur for his amphibious operation the entire Seventh Fleet under Vice Admiral Thomas Kinkaid; a grand armada of old battleships, with cruisers, escort carriers, and a train of destroyers, minesweepers, and oilers. But Nimitz kept tight control of the new fleet carriers and fast battleships, his striking arm; called Fifth Fleet when Spruance was leading it, and Third Fleet during Halsey operations.

Thus Kinkaid was heading a large sea force under MacArthur; Halsey was heading another large sea force under Nimitz; *and there was no supreme commander of the Leyte invasion.*

As to the Japanese strategy: Halsey's Formosa strikes before the battle had led to a vast Japanese victory celebration. Imperial General Headquarters jubilantly announced that the rash Yankees had at last come to grief; Japanese army and navy planes had swarmed out over the Third Fleet and crushed it!

Eleven aircraft carriers sunk, eight damaged; two battleships sunk, two damaged; three cruisers sunk, four damaged; destroyers, light cruisers, and dozens of other unidentified ships destroyed or set afire.

So ran the official communiqué. With this stunning reversal of fortunes, Saipan was avenged! The threat of invasion to the Philippines was over! Mass demonstrations of joy broke out all over Japan. Hitler and Mussolini sent telegrams of congratulation. "Victory is within our grasp," the new premier announced, and the Emperor himself issued a rescript commemorating the triumph.

In rude fact, Halsey's Third Fleet had retired after the strikes without losing a single ship. The Japanese army air squadrons had been slaughtered, and their bases razed. The toll was about six hundred aircraft shot down, with two hundred more smashed and burned on the ground. The Japanese high command, taken in by overoptimism, had stripped the navy's carriers too, and flung their squadrons into the fight. Army and navy pilots alike were nearly all green recruits. Halsey's veteran aviators had made sport of them, but the few returning stragglers had brought back ridiculous victory reports. Splashing bombs, or their own comrades' aircraft exploding in the sea, had seemed to their excited innocent eyes flaming sinking battleships and carriers. The Japanese command had discounted the reports by fifty percent, but they were pure moonshine.

Then MacArthur's advance units landed on islands in Leyte Gulf, and reconnaissance reported a giant invasion expedition — Kinkaid's Seventh Fleet under MacArthur, seven hundred vessels or more — headed for the Philippines. Search planes from Luzon also found Halsey's Third Fleet afloat, intact, and on the prowl. The war-weary Japanese woke from the victory dream to the real nightmare. Word flashed out to the Imperial Fleet: *Execute Plan SHO-ONE*. The Japanese code name *Sho* meant "conquer." There were four versions of *Sho* to oppose a stab at four probable points of the Empire's shrinking perimeter. *Sho-One* was the Philippines plan.

Sho was a strategy of desperation. The whole Imperial Fleet would sail, covered by army air forces in the Philippines and Formosa, to blast through the American support forces, sink the troop transports, and wipe out the landing parties with gunfire. The plan assumed that the Japanese would be outnumbered about three to one; and that Halsey alone, with his carriers and fast battleships, would wield striking power the Imperial Fleet could not match.

The whole theme of *Sho* was therefore *deception*. To neutralize the lopsided advantage of the foe, Japan's remaining aircraft carriers would decoy Halsey's Third Fleet far away from the beachhead, in quest of a carrier duel. The Main Body would then shoot its way past the support ships of Kinkaid's Seventh Fleet, wreak its havoc on MacArthur's landing force, and depart.

But the Formosa "victory" had already crippled *Sho*. Land-based support from the decimated army air force would be scant; and the decoy carriers, stripped of their squadrons, could no longer fight. They could at best tantalize the Third Fleet into roaring far away from the beachhead to butcher them. This would suffice, the Japanese command bitterly decided. If only Halsey would take the bait and get out of the way, the Main Striking Force of battleships and cruisers might still penetrate Leyte Gulf and wipe out MacArthur's beachhead. The goal of all this sacrifice was only a tolerable peace settlement after a success. The operation was in essence a giant kamikaze attack. In itself the fleet advancing to the sacrifice was formidable, but it faced almost hopeless odds.

Was it wrong to sacrifice the remnant of a great navy at a blow? Hardly, in Japanese thinking. What was there to lose? With the Philippines gone, the oil supply would be cut off anyway. The warships would be like toys with broken springs. Surrender now? A logical course, but logic in war is for the strong. For the weak there is proud defiance, deemed laudable in most cultures, and noble in Japan.

The problem of oil further complicated *Sho*. So low had the nation's supply sunk from the submarine attrition that the fleet could not even fuel at home. That was why the Main Striking Force under Vice Admiral Kurita — two new monster battleships, the biggest and most powerful in the world, with three other battleships and many cruisers and destroyers — laid off Singapore, so as to have access to the oil of Java and Borneo. The decoy carriers were in the home waters of the Inland Sea.

So the gigantic *Sho* deception, which hinged on many precise interlocking moves, had to start with its forces far apart, in touch only by radio. Yet communication personnel, like pilots, were in low supply. The best technicians had mostly drowned in the Coral Sea, at Midway, around Guadalcanal, and at Saipan. The Imperial Fleet sallied forth to execute *Sho*, in short, scattered over thousands of miles by the oil shortage, and stuttering with communication failures; still powerful, however, and bent on victory or self-immolation.

On October 20, MacArthur's forces landed on Leyte. The general waded up on the beach to broadcast, *"People of the Philippines, I have returned! Rally to me! . . . For your homes and hearths, strike! For future generations of your sons and daughters, strike! . . . Let no heart be faint. Let every arm be steeled. . . . Follow in His name to the Holy Grail of righteous victory!"* etc. These glorious thoughts provoked much unseemly snickering and snorting in the Navy crews gathered at radios.

The Japanese hardly seemed to oppose the invasion at first. Their fleet did not visibly move. Admiral Halsey, panting for his great fleet killing, talked of cutting through the archipelago into the South China Sea to smoke out the enemy, leaving the beachhead for Kinkaid to defend. A severe dispatch from Nimitz cooled that notion. It did not, however, cool Halsey's itch to trounce the Japanese navy.

Here was the human element coming into play. Halsey's war record and his public reputation were curiously at odds. He was the only admiral the home front knew about. He radiated the he-man aura of a Western movie star. He had led many carrier strikes. In the South Pacific his pugnacious spirit had revived sagging American morale and rescued the Guadalcanal campaign. The newspapers and the nation loved this rough tough Pacific gunfighter with his quotable taunts like "The Japs are losing their grip, even with their tails." But with the war winding down, he had yet to get into an actual gunfight. He had missed them all, while Spruance, his junior and his old friend, had fought and won big sea victories.

Halsey's staff was not sure that the enemy would fight for Leyte by risking a transit from the west of either of the two narrow straits, San Bernardino or Surigao. The Japs might well wait until MacArthur landed on Luzon, it was thought, for there they had a powerful army and big air bases. There, moreover, the Imperial Fleet would have a clear run in to Lingayen Gulf, and MacArthur could be heavily blasted by land, sea, and air. On some such reasoning, once Nimitz vetoed the South China Sea dash, Halsey released the strongest of his four task groups, a group of five carriers — he had nineteen in all — for rest and replenishment at Ulithi, some eight hundred miles away. Another task group was ordered to sail for Ulithi October 23, removing four more carriers from the scene.

These releases deeply troubled Pug Henry. Remembering Halsey from destroyer days, he could well picture the old man chafing and fuming aboard the *New Jersey,* as his great Third Fleet slowly patrolled empty tropic seas a hundred miles off the Philippines, burning up oil. The idea of charging westward through the islands into the China Sea was Halsey all over. So were the impulsive last-minute shifts of plans and orders. So to Pug's mind was the airy release of half his carrier strength only three days after the landing. Halsey worked in two modes, casual or ferocious. True, the task force had been at sea for ten months, refueled and replenished by ComServPac's remarkable ship-to-ship system. Men were weary. Ships needed time in port. But wasn't the chance for battle paramount? Halsey was behaving as though the sea threat to Leyte had faded away, but in fact the whereabouts of the foe was still a mystery.

Pug also wished Halsey would leave management of the carriers to their commander, Marc Mitscher, the most skilled air admiral in the Navy. Halsey was directly ordering the flattops about, and their real boss had become a silent passenger on the *Lexington.* It was as though Pug had taken to running the *Iowa* himself. A very bad business! Spruance had let Mitscher fight his ships at Saipan, overriding him only on the idea of abandoning the beachhead.

Still, the fleet loved Halsey. The sailors liked to say they would follow the "Bull" to hell, and they had hardly been aware of Spruance. Pug himself was excited to be sailing under Halsey again. The electricity of Halsey had the whole Third Fleet hot for the fight. That was something. But cool good sense in the fog of battle was just as important. That was Spruance's demonstrated strong point, and whether Halsey possessed it, the Navy was now for the first time going to find out.

87

TO: COM THIRD FLEET
FROM: DARTER
MANY SHIPS SIGHTED INCLUDING THREE PROBABLE BB'S X AM CHASING X

"KICKOFF!" Pug thought. The dispatch came from a picket submarine far out to the west, in the Palawan Passage, about halfway from Borneo to Leyte; sent during the night, it gave the position, course, and speed of the heavy enemy force. At once Pug marked the information in orange ink on the chart in his office. It was just sunrise of the twenty-third of October.

So there would be a fight, after all. Those battleships were heading for the Sibuyan Sea and San Bernardino Strait. Halsey's prompt orders quickened Pug's pulse. He was cancelling the release to Ulithi of a carrier group. Good! The three flattop groups on hand were to space themselves along two hundred fifty miles of the eastern Philippine coast for air searches and strikes next morning, when the Jap battleships would be steaming within range. Halsey's own group, including Victor Henry's BatDiv Seven, would stand off San Bernardino Strait to meet the foe as he came.

The ships the submarine had sighted were in fact Vice Admiral Kurita's Main Striking Force, on its way from Borneo to storm into Leyte Gulf and wipe out MacArthur's beachhead. The two chief opponents in the vast melee, Halsey and Kurita, were thus touching gloves at a range of about six hundred miles. Admirals would be plentiful as blackberries around Leyte Gulf, but the battle would turn on what these two would do as they drew together.

Takeo Kurita was a hard-willed dried-up salt of fifty-five. His force — five battleships, ten heavy cruisers, with light cruisers and destroyers — made a mighty parade as it plowed the blue swells of the Palawan Passage. Two of his battleships were the seventy-thousand-ton monsters *Musashi* and *Yamato*, with secret eighteen-inch guns built in violation of arms limitation treaties, and never yet fired at a foe. Pug Henry's *Iowa* and *New Jersey* carried sixteen-inch guns. No United States ship packed bigger armament. The two-inch difference in bore meant that Kurita could stand off beyond Henry's range and smash at him with shells perhaps twice as destructive as any he could fire back. Conceived in 1934, built over fifteen years at a nation-straining cost of manpower and treasure, these were the strongest gunships on the globe. Reckoning only with BatDiv Seven types they might have been invincible, but warfare had moved past them. Submarines and carrier aircraft were menaces the great guns could not fight.

From Admiral Kurita's viewpoint, therefore, all depended on the decoy carriers. If they would but suck Halsey out of the way, he could perhaps bull through San Bernardino Strait and annihilate the MacArthur beachhead with his giant guns. Under the able Vice Admiral Ozawa, those decoy carriers were already at sea, heading down from Japan toward Luzon. That was about all Kurita knew, for thirty parallels of latitude separated the two forces when they sailed.

Kurita had one more major factor to bear in mind. The Tokyo strategists, with their obsessive taste for razzle-dazzle, had improvised a third force — battleships and cruisers with their destroyer screens — to run far south and come up into Leyte Gulf through the other access route, Surigao Strait. On the war game boards *Sho* must have looked very pretty indeed: Kurita with the powerhouse armada driving through the central Philippines to steam at Leyte Gulf from the north; the other force closing a pincer from the south; and Ozawa, in waters far north of Luzon, teasing the bellicose Halsey clear of the troops he was supposed to protect.

But in such a slow-moving ballet of great ships over thousands of miles, precise timing was critical. Kurita had to get to Leyte on the morning of the twenty-fifth, when the Surigao force would arrive. Well before that morning, the decoy flattops had to lure Halsey northward. None of this could come off, on the face of it, except at high cost. The question was whether early losses would stop *Sho* cold, or whether it would bloodily go through.

A hint of the answer came at sunrise of the twenty-third. Without warning, four torpedoes one after the other struck Kurita's flagship. The whole force had just begun its daylight zigzagging. As the flag bridge of the heavy cruiser *Atago* shuddered under Kurita's feet, he saw the next cruiser astern get hit too in smoke, flame, and great climbing showers of white water. Within minutes the *Atago* was wrapped in fire, shaking with explosions, and going down. Kurita's attention narrowed to saving himself. Destroyers approached the burning wreck to take him off, but there was no time. The admiral and his staff had to swim for their lives in heaving warm salt water.

A destroyer fished Kurita aboard. There another sad sight met his brine-stung eyes: a third heavy cruiser nearby, blowing apart like a firecracker in pale flame and dense black smoke, its pieces going down while he stood there dripping. This day was not half an hour old, and he had lost two heavy cruisers out of ten to submarine assault; a third was dead in the water and afire; and he was two full days' steaming from Leyte Gulf.

The picket submarines *Darter* and *Dace* had detected Kurita's force in the night, chased it on the surface, and submerged for this dawn attack. They escaped the cascade of destroyer depth charges that raised great geysers all over the sea, but tracking the crippled cruiser, the *Darter* ran up on a reef. The *Dace* rescued its crew. The *Darter* had sounded the alarm and drawn first blood, but its day was done.

Panicky false periscope sightings disarrayed Kurita's force most of that day until he managed to transfer with his staff to the *Yamato*. There, in the world's mightiest gunship, in spacious elegant flag quarters, he regained his grip on the situation. His grand armada was, after all, mainly intact. He had not expected to advance without losses. Night would soon fall and cover his movements. Tokyo radioed him that the decoy force had as yet made no contact with Halsey; so aircraft attacks, as well as the submarine menace, lay ahead for the morrow. The day after that, it now seemed, he would run straight into Halsey at the mouth of San Bernardino Strait. But Takeo Kurita had this command because he was a man who would push on through fire walls. As the sun set he went to full speed.

Night gave him twelve hours of a peaceful fast run. With the sunrise on October twenty-fourth the carrier attacks came, and never stopped coming. Five major strikes, hundreds of sorties, repeated and repeated assaults with bombs and torpedoes, kept the air buzzing over the Main Striking Force all day. Kurita had been promised air cover from Luzon and Formosa. There was none.

Still he steamed doughtily on, winding a course past beautiful mountainous islands, throwing up AA fire from hundreds of guns, in desperation shooting his main batteries at oncoming clusters of airplanes. In this greatest of all fights between aircraft and surface ships, on October twenty-fourth, called now the Battle of the Sibuyan Sea, Kurita did very well. Only the supergiant *Musashi*, hit early by a torpedo, attracted the full fury of the waspish Yank planes. Supposedly unsinkable, it absorbed in the five strikes nineteen torpedoes and uncounted bombs; sank lower and listed farther as it fell astern, the hours passed, and the punishment went on; and toward sundown it rolled over and sank with half its crew, never having fought except with tiny flying machines.

That was the worst. A tragic loss, but the Main Striking Force had weathered the storm with plenty of power to carry out its mission. However, no word had ever come from Ozawa's decoy force. Was there to be no relief, all the way to Leyte? Halsey obviously had not yet been tricked; this day's harsh pounding had come from carrier aircraft. Kurita's radioed pleas for air cover were going unheeded. The day's attrition so far — the *Musashi* in tragic death throes, the disabling of yet another cruiser, and much bomb damage to other ships — could be accepted; but how long could a force defenseless from the air survive against fifteen or twenty carriers?

About four o'clock Kurita turned his ships around and retreated west-ward, to increase the range from Halsey's flattops and stay in open water, where his captains could at least continue their successful squirming and dodging; for once in the straits, they would lose maneuverability and become easy targets. Again he beseeched Tokyo and Manila for air cover, citing the damage he was sustaining. Manila made no answer. The air commander there had decided to use his planes against enemy carriers, not in covering Kurita.

It seemed to Takeo Kurita at this juncture, as his ships milled about on a calm sea bounded by the ridges of green islands, and the blasted *Musashi* dropped out of sight trying to beach itself and "become a land battery," that the *Sho* plan was already collapsing. The air and submarine attacks had thrown off the timing. The air cover element was missing. The deception was not working. Still, having put off entering narrow waters until darkness was near, he reversed course once again, and made for San Bernardino Strait. As he went he notified the southern force to slow down and post-pone the pincer attack on the gulf by several hours. Tokyo headquarters in a helpful mood now sent this message: "*All forces will dash to the attack, counting on Divine assistance.*"

Night once more veiled the Main Striking Force. Yet even so, Kurita faced mounting perils. Ahead lay narrow heavily mined waters. In traversing San Bernardino Strait, he would have to take his force through in column. Halsey's battleships and cruisers would undoubtedly be patrolling the en-trance, waiting to cross the *T* and pick off his ships one by one as they came out. In precisely such a maneuver, during the great Battle of Tsushima Strait in 1905, the Japanese navy had crushed the czarist fleet and won a war. Now Kurita was cast in the Russian role of that battle he had studied all his life, with no way to escape; no alternative but to steam on to his fate, "counting on Divine assistance."

Astern, a yellow quarter-moon was setting over the dark Sibuyan Sea. Ahead, the Japanese command in Manila had turned on the navigation lights of San Bernardino Strait. The night was clear. Posting himself on the flag bridge of the giant *Yamato*, Takeo Kurita sent a blunt final dispatch to his crews: *Chancing annihilation, we are determined to break through to the an-chorage and destroy the enemy.* The force passed into the narrows, forming into column, and all ships went to battle stations. Despite the hellish day the haggard crews stood to their guns. They were good men, well trained in night action. Kurita could count on them to give the Americans up ahead a real fight, and die for the Emperor if they must.

At midnight the moon went down. Half an hour later, in starlit dark-ness, the Main Striking Force began to emerge, ship by ship, between the headlands of Luzon and Samar into the quiet open waters of the Philippine Sea. Admiral Kurita could see nothing ahead. Nor could the lookouts on any of his vessels. Radar sweeping the sea for fifty miles in all directions found nothing.

Nothing! Not so much as a single picket destroyer guarding the entrance to San Bernardino Strait!

Astounded, his hopes rebounding, Kurita formed up for battle and made full speed south along the coast of Samar for Leyte Gulf. He had to accept the evidence of his senses. By some fantastic chance of war Halsey was gone, and MacArthur lay at the mercy of the Emperor's biggest guns.

88

THE strange events on the American side which led to this incredible circumstance will remain in controversy as long as anybody cares about naval battles. The events are clear enough. The controversy lies in how and why they happened. Victor Henry lived through them in the *Iowa's* flag quarters.

• • •

He was up well before dawn of that October twenty-fourth, in flag plot, checking his staff's setup for following the situation, for joining battle, and even for taking command of the task group if necessary. Pug knew very well how junior he was in Halsey's force, yet misfortune might thrust extraordinary responsibility on him. He intended to stay as fully informed as though he were Halsey's chief of staff.

Flag plot was a large dimly lit room over his quarters, reached by a private ladder. Here radar scopes showed in phosphorescent green tracery movements of ships and aircraft, storm patterns, configuration of nearby land, and — especially in night action — a better picture of the foe than eyes could discern on the sea. Here large Plexiglas displays manned by telephone talkers gave at a glance in vivid orange or red grease hand-printing abstract summaries of what was happening. Here dispatches poured in to the watch officer for quick digest and display. Coffee, tobacco smoke, and ozone from the electronic gear stewed together in an unchanging flag-plot smell. Loudspeakers hoarsely spouted bursts of signal jargon: *"Baker Jig How Seven, Baker Jig How Seven, this is Courthouse Four. Request Able Mike Report Peter Slant Zed. Over,"* and the like.

But sometimes — as now at five in the morning, when the admiral looked in — flag plot was quiet. Shadowy sailors sat at the scopes, their faces ghastly in the glow, drinking coffee, smoking, or munching candy bars. Telephone talkers murmured into their receivers or wrote on the Plexiglas; stationed behind the display, they were adept at printing backward. Officers bent over charts, calculating and talking low. The chief of staff was already at the central chart desk. In the Formosa strikes Captain Bradford had satisfied Pug that he could run flag plot and sort out pertinent facts from the torrent of noise. Pug went below and alone in his quarters heartily ate canned peaches, cornflakes, ham and eggs, and fresh biscuits with honey. It might be a long time before he sat down to a meal again. He was drinking coffee when Bradford buzzed him.

"Preparing to launch air searches, Admiral."

"Very well, Ned."

Pug ran up the ladder, went out on the flag bridge in a clear warm violet dawn, and watched the dive-bomber squadrons soaring off under the morning stars from the *Intrepid,* the *Hancock,* and the *Independence.* A quiet pain stirred in his heart. (*Absalom, Absalom!*) When the last planes left he returned below to a small office off his sea cabin. Pug meant to keep his own command chart here. Only in combat would he post himself in flag plot near the radars, the TBS, and the flag bridge. For many hours yet, bald plotted facts would matter most: sightings, distances, courses, speeds, damage reports, and what these implied.

It was Blue versus Orange again, after all, the old clash of the War College game boards and the peacetime fleet exercises. The real thing was flaringly different, yet one factor would not change. Even in make-believe combat the hardest thing to do was to keep one's head; how much more so now! Let Bradford enjoy the excitement and the hot news in flag plot. Pug meant to weigh essentials here until the fight was on, and talk to his staff only when he had to.

In the peace of this office, as he plotted on his chart in orange and blue ink reports of the morning sightings and strikes, what struck him most was the steady Jap advance. This fellow heading for San Bernardino Strait meant business. The reported submarine sinkings the day before had failed to shake him. Unless the air strikes could turn him back, it looked like night battle off the strait, perhaps only sixteen to twenty hours hence.

An early sighting of a second surface force far to the south heading for Surigao Strait didn't surprise Pug. Diversionary end run, standard Jap tactics. This was exactly why Spruance had refused to leave the Saipan beachhead. The Japs were really throwing everything in! Davison's task group, to the south, would probably go after that force. No, wrong guess, Halsey was ordering him to concentrate off San Bernardino, too. Well, Kinkaid's fleet down in the gulf had six old battleships, five of them resurrected from the Pearl Harbor graveyard, including the good old *California* — also plenty of cruisers and escort carriers, to hit that diversionary force making for Surigao. The jeep flattops were converted merchantmen, slow as molasses, small and flimsy; but in the aggregate they could launch a fair air strike.

First damage to the Halsey fleet! Sherman's flattops, the northernmost group, under air attack at nine-thirty A.M.; *Princeton* bombed and on fire. Planes could be from Luzon or Jap carriers, according to Sherman. His aviators massacring the enemy pilots. Now a welcome intercept: Halsey calling back the fourth carrier group, until now bound for Ulithi. At last, and none too soon! The chart indicated that they would have to fuel at sea, and were a full day's run away. If the blow to the *Princeton* had jolted this decision out of Halsey, it might prove worth the cost.

More air strikes against the oncoming Japs in the center; more jubilant damage reports; battleships and cruisers bombed, torpedoed, on fire, turned turtle. On Pug's chart these reports looked thrilling. The symbols for sunk or damaged ships crowded the Sibuyan Sea. If the reports were true the Jap would never make it, he was a goner already. But why in that case was he continuing to advance? Strikes by thirty to seventy planes were hitting him at will, yet on he came.

Why did he have no air cover? *Where were the Jap carriers?* The question had been nagging at Victor Henry all day, and not only at him; it was troubling William Halsey and his staff, and his group commanders, and Admiral Nimitz in Pearl Harbor, where night had already fallen, and Admiral King in Washington. Those missing flattops weren't covering the oncoming San Bernardino force. They weren't with the end runners to the south. What then was their role in this supreme gamble of the Imperial Fleet? It was unthinkable that they could be idling in the Inland Sea. Pug saw two possibilities. He wrote them, for his own future smiles or groans, on a separate sheet of paper.

24 October, 1430, off Leyte.
    Q: Where are the enemy carriers?
    A: (1) Hanging back outside search range in the South China Sea. They'll run in toward us at high speed once the sun gets low, to strike at dawn tomorrow the cripples of the coming night action off San Bernardino Strait.
    (2) They're heading down from the north to decoy us away from San Bernardino Strait. If so, they'll make certain they're seen before dark, probably well north of Luzon.

There was nothing prescient in Pug's second guess. Several of Halsey's group commanders were making the same surmise. A captured Japanese tactical manual recently sent out by ONI had discussed sacrificing carriers as a diversion gambit. Somehow the carrier force had gotten out of the Inland Sea undetected by submarine pickets. They might just now be moving into air search range. The answer — so Pug felt as the last Halsey strike was heading home — would come before sundown.

Vice Admiral Ozawa's gambit carriers were in fact already to the north of Luzon, and Ozawa was doing everything to attract Halsey's attention except — so to say — stand on his head and wiggle his ears. But Halsey had assigned the northward search to Sherman, and in the confusion of the air attack and the *Princeton* fire the launch had stalled. So Ozawa had dispatched the motley aircraft in his flattops — only seventy-six in all — to attack Sherman's group, hoping to alert Halsey if nothing else. This flight had less luck than the land-based strike that had fired the *Princeton*. Many of the pilots were shot down; most of the rest were too green to land on a moving carrier, so they flew on to Luzon or else dropped in the sea. Halsey was not alerted; this straggling strike was evaluated as probably coming from Luzon.

Ozawa also broadcast copious radio signals, hoping to be detected. Late in the day, desperate to be seen and pursued, he sent southward two hermaphrodite battleships — bizarre gunships with flight decks grafted on — to engage Sherman's group in surface combat. Ozawa notified Kurita by radio of all these actions. The two forces were about a thousand miles apart, well within radio range. But Kurita received no messages from him, either directly or via Tokyo or Manila.

Halsey's battle plan for the night came through about three o'clock. It named four battleships, including the *Iowa* and the *New Jersey*, two heavy cruisers, three light cruisers, and fourteen destroyers.

THESE SHIPS WILL BE FORMED AS TASK FORCE 34 UNDER VICE ADMIRAL LEE COMMANDER BATTLE LINE X TASK FORCE 34 WILL ENGAGE DECISIVELY AT LONG RANGES X

Form Battle Line!
Pug Henry had studied battle-line tactics all his life. He knew the manual by heart. He had gamed, times beyond counting, Jutland and Tsushima Strait, and Nelson's classic actions at Trafalgar and Saint Vincent. The showdown between ships of the line was the supreme historical test of navies. So far in this war, the graceless weak floating barns called carriers had eclipsed the battleship. Well, by God, here was Japan sending its battle line through San Bernardino Strait to smash the Leyte invasion, and all Halsey's carriers were not stopping it from coming on.

Form Battle Line! It was the sounding of the charge. His blood racing as though he were twenty, Victor Henry pulled the telephone from its bracket and buzzed Captain Bradford. "Staff meeting in my quarters at sixteen hundred. Leave one watch officer in flag plot. You come down."

It did not escape Pug's notice that Halsey, in the *New Jersey*, would be OTC of the Battle Line. Willis Lee would form the task force, and he would do a superb job, but Halsey would take over and fight the engagement. What wild excitement must be fizzing over in the flag quarters of the *New Jersey*! If Pug Henry had been waiting thirty years for this, Bill Halsey had been waiting forty years. Of all admirals in history, not one had been more hungry or ready for an all-out fleet battle. The man and the moment had come together for the forging of a famous victory.

Pug ran up to the flag bridge to air out his lungs. He had gone through three packs of cigarettes. The scene on the sea could not be more tranquil: carriers, battleships, and their screening vessels spreading as far as the eye could see in afternoon sunshine, extending below the horizon north and south, gray familiar shapes of war steaming slowly in AA formation on the mildly foaming blue ocean. No land was in sight, no foe, no smoke, no fire. All the excitement was in the chatter of the flag plot loudspeakers, in the facts tumbling out of the coding machines in Navy abracadabra. Wireless communications, airplanes, and black oil had made for a new kind of sea warfare reaching out hundreds, thousands of miles for contact, encompassing millions of square miles as the field of battle. Yet the signal of signals was unchanged from Trafalgar, and no doubt from Salamis.

Form Battle Line!

Battle was the ultimate risk. The giant *Iowa* could go down like any other warship. The sinking of the *Northampton* was much on Pug's mind, and he was running over what he would say to the staff about torpedo attack. Yet he felt, as he stood there alone in rumpled khakis, taking deep breaths of the streaming tropic sea air, that this night would do much to justify his life. He was filled with exaltation that was half-guilty because the business was only slaughter, and many Americans might die, and yet he was so damned happy about it.

The staff conference was not fifteen minutes along when flag plot called him with a new position report on the Japs in the Sibuyan Sea. Noting the latitude and longitude on a scratch pad, Pug snapped, "Check the decoding, that's a mistake," and hung up. Soon the watch officer apologetically called again. The decode checked out. There was another sighting, a much more recent one. Pug wrote down the numbers, abruptly went off into his office, and presently called in the chief of staff.

"What do you make of that?"

On his chart the orange track of the Jap force now hooked around to westward. Retreat!

"Admiral, I didn't see how he could keep coming as long as he did." Running his fingers through his white hair, Bradford shook his head. "He was like a snowball rolling along on a hot stove. He'd have arrived with nothing."

"You think he's quit?"

"Yes, sir."

"I don't. Meeting's suspended. Get on up there, Ned. Sift the dispatches. Pick up what you can on TBS. Double the coding watch on command channel intercepts. Let's get the word on these position reports."

Soon Bradford telephoned down that the whole ·fleet was buzzing with the Jap turnaround. Pug stared at the chart, calculating the possibilities, as in a chess game after a surprise move. He began to write:

24 October, 1645. Central Force turns west.
                    Why?
    1. Beaten by air strike. Slinking home to Nippon.
    2. Ahead of schedule. Carriers not yet in search range. Rendezvous off Leyte fouled up. Killing time. Also confusing us.
    3. Avoiding a night action. Jap minor forces prefer night fighting, what with long-range torpedoes, etc. This fellow wants good visibility for his big guns.
    4. Preserving maneuverability in daylight hours.
    5. Made damage report to Tokyo and awaits further orders.
    6. Remember Spruance "retreating" at Midway? This is a tough individual, a strong force, and a resourceful mind at work. May be tantalizing Halsey to charge through San Bernardino Strait after him, whereupon he'll come about and cross our T.

As Pug sat mulling over these possibilities an excited knock came at his door. "Admiral, I thought I'd better bring you this." Eyes gleaming, Bradford laid a decode on his desk, strips of tape pasted on a blank form. It was from Halsey.

TO: ALL GROUP COMS AND DIV COMS THIRD FLEET
SHERMAN REPORTS X 3 CARRIERS 2 LIGHT CRUISERS 3 DESTROYERS 18–32 N
125–28 E X

Pug darted his orange pen to the chart. Northeast of Luzon, two hundred miles off shore; there was the answer on the Jap carriers.

"Hm! Any late word on that force in the Sibuyan Sea?"

"None, Admiral."

They looked at the chart, and at each other, wryly grinning. Pug said, "Okay, you're Halsey. What do you do?"

"Take off like a bat out of hell after those carriers."

"What about San Bernardino Strait? What about that fellow in the Sibuyan Sea?"

"He's still retreating. If he turns around and comes back, the Battle Line will fix him."

"So you go north with the carriers only, leaving the battleships behind? Isn't that risky?"

"The carriers can pick up Sherman's two battleships as they steam north. That's enough power to handle any carrier force the Japs have got."

"What about concentration of force?"

Bradford scratched his head. "Well, the Japs haven't done that, have they? They're coming at me from two directions. They're too far apart for me to hit one outfit and then the other with a concentrated force. I'd say the tactical situation prevails over the principle. I've got to divide my force to make sure I hit both his teams. My two sections are much stronger than his two, anyway." Pug gave him a horrible frown. Bradford added uncertainly, "Admiral, I get paid for saying what I think, however stupid, when asked."

"You've made Mahan turn over in his grave. However, I agree with you. Get back up there, Ned."

The steward knocked and offered to bring the admiral dinner on a tray. Pug felt he could not force an olive down his throat. He asked for more coffee, and sat smoking cigarette after cigarette, trying to think himself into Halsey's brain.

Here was an embarrassment of riches for the old gunfighter — *two* great engagements within his grasp! He could be the Lord Nelson of either one, but not of both; too far apart, as Bradford said. The *New Jersey* would have to be detached from the Battle Line, if he decided to run north with the carriers. In that case Willis Lee would fight the Battle Line night action, with one of Sherman's battlewagons replacing the *New Jersey*. Or Halsey could stay off San Bernardino with the battleships, and turn Mitscher's flattops loose to run north and get the carriers. That was what Ray Spruance had declined to do at Saipan.

The San Bernardino fight, Pug thought, would be the more decisive one. That was the big immediate menace to the beachhead. But suppose the Jap didn't reverse course and come on? In that case Bill Halsey would patrol at dead slow all night with silent guns, while Marc Mitscher sailed off to the biggest carrier victory since Midway.

Not a chance, Pug Henry thought. Not a chance. Bradford was right. In Halsey's place he, Pug, might well go north himself.

But he hoped Halsey would take only the *New Jersey* and not drag the *Iowa* along. Those Jap flattops would be meat for Mitscher's aviators. The battleship function in the north would be merely sinking cripples. At San Bernardino Strait there would be battle. That Jap had not quit; so a sixth sense told Pug.

Down from flag plot came an intercepted visual signal from Willis Lee to Halsey, sent just before dark. It was a situation analysis close to Pug's, which made him feel good. Lee was a shrewd veteran strategist. The Jap carriers were weak decoys, Lee said, low on aircraft; the Sibuyan turnaround was temporary; that force would return and come through the strait at night.

Division of opinion in Halsey's staff quarters must be deep and debate furious, Pug surmised. Time was slipping by. No orders were forthcoming, not even the "Execute" for the Battle Line plan, and Willis Lee needed time to organize and form up his force. Shortly after eight o'clock the orders did at last come through. Bradford did not deliver or telephone this crucial dispatch. He sent it down by messenger, a very odd thing to do. When Pug read the long battle order, he understood why.

Halsey was going north after the carriers, all right; but he was taking with him the entire Third Fleet, *leaving not one vessel behind to guard San Bernardino Strait.*

Pug was still digesting this sickening surprise when another dispatch came down, again by messenger. It was a sighting report of the Sibuyan Sea force by a night search plane. The longitude numbers made his hair prickle before he put his pen to the chart. The Jap had turned around and was heading for San Bernardino Strait at twenty-two knots.

The date-time of the dispatch was 2210; ten minutes past ten at night, October 24, 1944.

89

A Jew's Journey
(*from Aaron Jastrow's manuscript*)

OCTOBER 24, 1944.

Natalie and I have received our deportation notices. We leave in the eleventh transport on October 28. Appeal is quite useless. Nobody gets excused from these October transports.

Theresienstadt is a desolate and terrible scene. Perhaps twelve thousand people are left. In less than a month since the filming ended, the trains have taken away almost twenty thousand, all under sixty-five. Above that age one is still safe, unless, as in my case, one has offended. The young, the strong, the able, the good-looking, are gone. The aged remnants of a jammed and bustling ghetto creep about the nearly empty streets, freezing, frightened, and starving. The town's institutions and services have broken down. There is no hot food, not even the wretched slops of former days. No cooks are left. Garbage piles up, for there is nobody to remove it. In empty barracks abandoned clothes, books, carpets, and pictures are strewn around. There is nobody to clean up, and nobody is interested in looting. The hospitals are empty, for all the sick were transported. Everywhere there is the smell of decay, abandonment, and rot.

The gimcrackery of the Beautification — the quaint signposts, the shop fronts, the bandstand, the cafés, the children's pavilion — is falling apart in the harsh weather, the colors fading, the paint peeling. Despite dire posted penalties, the old people pilfer the planks of these Potemkin constructions for firewood. There is no music. Hardly a child is left, except for those of mixed couples, war veterans, municipal officials, and *Prominente*. But this eleventh transport, a big one of more than two thousand souls, is cutting like a scythe into the ranks of privilege. There will be plenty of children in it.

My offense was refusal to cooperate. The new High Elder, who replaced the pathetic, mysteriously vanished Eppstein at the end of September, is a certain Dr. Murmelstein of Vienna, a former rabbi and university lecturer. I am sure that the SS put him up to designating me as his chief deputy. The motive must have been window dressing again, in case of a sudden end to the war. It would look good for them, these twisted minds must calculate, if an American Jew would be on hand as a high official to greet the conquerors. Not that the war looks to be ending. East and west it appears to have bogged down for the winter, and the crimes of the Germans will go on for many more months unchecked, perhaps multiplying because this is their last chance to commit them.

Murmelstein worked on me for hours with a wearisome flood of flattery and argument. To cut it off, I said I would think about it. Natalie's reaction that night was the same as mine. I pointed out to her that if I were transported for refusing, she would probably share my fate. "Do as you please," she said, "but don't accept it on my account."

When I gave Murmelstein my answer next day, I had to endure the whole rigmarole again, ending in threats, grovelling, beseeching, and real tears. No doubt he feared the displeasure of his masters upon conveying my refusal. A sketch of this man and how he thinks is worth preserving in these last sheets. He is a type. There have surely been Murmelsteins all over Europe. His theme in brief is that the Germans as direct overseers are far more brutal and murderous than the Jewish officials who are willing to interpose themselves as buffers, carry out their orders, absorb their anger at delays, exemptions, and evasions, endure the hatred and contempt of the Jews, and work unceasingly at reducing hardships and saving lives.

I retorted that even if this had once been so in Theresienstadt, the officials now were doing nothing but organizing and sending off the transports, and that I would not be part of it. I refrained from pointing out that such officials are saving their skins, or at least postponing their fates, by designating fellow Jews for death. Epicurus said that everything in this world can be taken by two handles. I don't condemn Murmelstein. There may be a color of truth in his argument that things would be worse if Jews like him did not administer the orders of the Germans, and try to soften the impact. Nevertheless, I will not do it. I knew when I refused that I risked torture, but I was not going to yield.

Among his blandishments was an appeal to me as between fellow scholars. Our fields overlap, for he taught ancient Jewish history at Vienna University. I have heard him lecture here in the ghetto, and don't think much of his scholarship. He cited Flavius Josephus, a figure he clings to in his desperate self-justification; a man hated by the Jews as a collaborationist and a tool of the Romans, whose whole aim was to benefit his people. History's verdict on Josephus is equivocal at best. The Murmelsteins will not come out that well.

After warning me with popping eyes and a skull-like expression of the SS anger that hung over me, he broke down and wept. He was not acting, or else he is very good at it, for the tears really gushed. His burdens were overpowering, he wailed. He respected me more than almost anybody in the ghetto. As an American, at this stage of the war, I had unusual power to intercede with the Germans and do good. He was ready to go down on his knees to change my mind, save me from going to the Little Fortress, and get me to share his frightful responsibilities. He could no longer carry on alone.

I told him he would have to carry on without me, and that as to my own fate, I would risk anything my frail body could still endure. So I left him, shaking his head and drying his eyes. That was almost three weeks ago. I trembled with fear for days. I have not become any braver, but there are really things worse than pain, worse than dying; not to mention that, in the grip of the Germans, a Jew probably has no way in the long run of escaping pain or death, unless the outside world rescues him. He may as well do what is right.

I heard nothing further until the blow fell today. I feel sure that Murmelstein is not to blame. Of course he countersigned the orders, as he does for all the transportees. But I was simply on the SS list. Not being able to use me, or not interested in forcing me, as they were for the Red Cross visit, they are getting rid of me. Unless they can have me on their side, as a tool of theirs and therefore an accomplice of sorts, I am not one they want to have around when the Americans arrive. Or the Russians, either.

The notices came in the morning, just before Natalie went off to the mica factory. The thing has become commonplace, and we both half-expected it. I offered to go to Murmelstein and say I had reconsidered. I meant it. I pointed out that she has her son to live for, and that though we have had no word in months (all communication with the outside has long since broken down) she has every reason to hope that he is all right, and that when this long nightmare ends, if she can manage to survive, she will find him.

She said sombrely, her face drawn and somewhat scared — and I want to record this little exchange before I seal away these pages — "I don't want you to protect me by sending Jews off in trains."

"Natalie, that is how I talked to Murmelstein. But you and I know that the transports will go anyway."

"Not by your hand, though."

I was moved. I said, *"Ye-horeg v'al ya-harog."*

She has learned some Hebrew from me and from the Zionists, but not much. She looked puzzled. I explained, "It's from the Talmud. There are three things a Jew must die rather than do under compulsion, and that's one of them. *Let yourself be killed, but do not kill.*"

"I call that common decency."

"According to Hillel the whole Torah is only common decency."

"What are the other two things a Jew must die rather than do?"

"Worship of false gods, and forbidden sexual conduct."

She looked thoughtful, then smiled at me like the Mona Lisa, and went off to the mica factory.

I, Aaron Jastrow the Jew, began this record of a journey aboard a vessel docked in Naples harbor, in December 1941. It was bound for Palestine. My niece and I left that vessel before it sailed and were interned in Siena. We escaped from Fascist Italy through the help of the underground, intending to return to America via Portugal. Mischances and misjudgments brought us to Theresienstadt.

Here I have seen German barbarism and duplicity with my own eyes, and have tried to record the truth in bald hurried language. I have not recorded one one-thousandth of the daily agony, brutality, and degradation I have witnessed. Yet Theresienstadt is a "model ghetto." The accounts I have heard of what the Germans are doing in camps like Oswiecim exceed all human experience. Words break down as a means of describing them. So, in writing what I have heard, I have put down the plainest possible words that come to mind. The Thucydides who will tell this story so that the world can picture, believe, and remember may not be born for centuries. Or if he lives now, I am not he.

I am going to my death. I have heard that strong young people are spared to work in Oswiecim, so my niece may survive. I am in my sixty-eighth year, and will not lack much of the Biblical threescore-and-ten. Millions of Jews, I now believe, have already perished at German hands with half or less than half of their lives lived. A million or more of these must have been little children.

The world will be a long time fathoming this fact about human nature, this new fact, the thing the Germans have done. These scribbled sheets are a miserable fragment of testimony to the truth. Such records will be found all over Europe when the National Socialist curse passes.

I was a man of nimble Talmudic wit, insight quick rather than profound, with a literary gift graceful rather than powerful. I was at my best in my youth, a prodigy. My parents took me from Poland to America. I expended my gifts there in pleasing the Gentiles. I became an apostate. I dropped my Jewishness outside and inside, and strove only to be like other people, and to be accepted by them. In this I was successful. This period of my life stretched from my sixteenth year, when I arrived in New York, to my sixty-sixth year, when I arrived in Theresienstadt. Here under the Germans I resumed my Jewishness because they forced me to.

I have been in Theresienstadt about a year. I value this year more than all my fifty-one years of *hefkerut*, of being like others. Degraded, hungry, oppressed, beaten, frightened, I have found myself, my God, and my self-respect here. I am terribly afraid of dying. I am bowed to the ground by the tragedy of my people. But I have experienced a strange bitter happiness in Theresienstadt that I missed as an American professor and as a fashionable author living in a Tuscan·villa. I have been myself. I have taught bright-eyed, sharp-minded Jewish boys the Talmud. They are gone. I do not know whether one of them still lives. But the words of the Talmud lived on our lips and burned in our minds. I was born to carry that flame. The world has greatly changed, and the change was too much for me, until I came to Theresienstadt. Here I mastered the change, and returned to myself. Now I will return to Oswiecim, where I studied in the yeshiva and where I abandoned the Talmud, and there the Jew's Journey will end. I am ready.

There is such a world still to write about Theresienstadt! And ah, if a good angel would but give me a year to tell my story from my early days! But these scattered notes, much more than anything else I have written, must serve as the mark over the emptiness that will be my grave.

Earth, cover not their blood!

Aaron Jastrow
October 24, 1944
Theresienstadt

90

WHEN it is midnight in Leyte, the sun rides high over Washington. About halfway between them lies Pearl Harbor. From there, Chester Nimitz was transmitting to Ernest King in his Washington headquarters all the Leyte events as they broke. In Tokyo, of course, the naval HQ was following the battle step by step.

So far had the art of communication advanced, so powerful were the transmitters, so swift the coding, so deliberate the movements of fleets traversing long distances at twenty or twenty-five miles an hour, that the far-off high commands could watch this entire battle like Homeric gods hovering overhead, or like Napoleon on a hill at Austerlitz. The Battle of Leyte Gulf was not only the biggest sea fight of all time, it was unique in having all these distant spectators; unique, too, in the flood of on-the-spot facts pouring out of transmitters and cryptographic machines.

It is interesting, therefore, that nobody on the scene, or anywhere else in the world, really knew what the hell was going on. There never was a denser fog of war. All the sophisticated communication only spread and thickened it.

Halsey totally confused everybody. In a very terse dispatch he notified Kinkaid down in the gulf of his decision to leave San Bernardino Strait unguarded, making Nimitz and King information addressees:

CENTRAL FORCE HEAVILY DAMAGED ACCORDING TO STRIKE REPORTS X AM PROCEEDING NORTH WITH THREE GROUPS TO ATTACK CARRIER FORCE AT DAWN X

That was all. Kinkaid assumed this meant that Halsey was taking his three *carrier* groups north, leaving Task Force Thirty-four, the Battle Line, to guard the strait. That is what Nimitz assumed. That is what King assumed. That is what Mitscher assumed. To all of them the dispatch could mean nothing else, for leaving the strait open to the enemy was unthinkable. But to Halsey and his staff it was crystal clear that since he had not ordered the battle plan *executed*, there was no Battle Line. Therefore San Bernardino was unguarded. Therefore Kinkaid was duly warned. Therefore he would have to look out for himself and for the beachhead.

In Pearl Harbor Raymond Spruance, standing at Nimitz's side by the chart table when the dispatch came in, softly remarked, "If I were there, I would keep my forces right here," placing his hand off San Bernardino Strait. But he too was referring to the carriers; it did not even cross his mind that Halsey was pulling out the battleships.

Halsey confused the Japanese by waiting until after dark to sally northward. Kurita therefore thought his Main Striking Force was steaming head-on into the Third Fleet. Ozawa in the decoy carriers was doubly confused; he had received word of Kurita's turn west, but not of his reversal toward San Bernardino Strait, so he did not know whether *Sho* was off or on, and whether or not he had succeeded in luring Halsey. First he fled north, then getting the "Divine assistance" message, turned back south to resume his role of worm on a hook, then again went north. As for the Japanese commanders in Manila and Tokyo, they no longer had the dimmest idea of what to think.

However, the admirals Halsey was taking north with him did have ideas.

Pug Henry was haunting flag plot, hoping for new orders from Halsey. For long dragging hours, there was only dead silence in the transmitters, while the unguarded strait fell farther and farther astern. What was going on? Could Halsey *possibly* have failed to get the word that the Central Force was heading for Leyte again?

Suddenly the TBS began grating out tense harsh questions and answers between Admiral Bogan, the commander of Pug's task group, and the captain of the *Independence,* the carrier of the night search planes. Pug recognized the admiral's voice through the gargling wireless distortion. Were those position reports on the Sibuyan Sea force accurate? Had the captain closely questioned the pilots? Absolutely, the captain replied. Those Japs were coming on fast, no doubt of it. In fact, a snooper pilot out on search now had just reported the navigation lights in San Bernardino Strait brilliantly lit.

Pug heard the admiral exclaim in a most irregular and refreshing way, "Jesus Christ!" Within minutes Bogan was on the TBS again, calling "Blackjack personally," the inter-ship call sign for Admiral Halsey. This took some temerity, but it was fruitless. Not "Blackjack" but an unidentifiable voice responded. Bogan repeated the news of the illuminated strait, underlining its import with his urgent excited tones. The voice said in audible boredom, "Yes, yes, we have that information."

Again, long silence. Pug was working up his nerve to speak his own view over the TBS — for the little it was worth — that the San Bernardino situation was getting desperate, when Willis Lee beat him to it, calling Halsey to say he was sure the Central Force would be coming through San Bernardino Strait in the darkness. Pug heard the same bored voice say, "Roger," and no more. That decided Pug against inviting a similar squelching.

Long after the battle it turned out that both Bogan and Lee intended to urge Halsey to send the Battle Line back to the strait. The bland cold anonymous voice silenced both of them. It turned out, too, that talking to Halsey wouldn't have helped. The old man had made up his mind to get the Jap carriers. He had shut off all further debate in his staff, and gone to sleep. It also turned out that Marc Mitscher's chief of staff, a belligerent sort nicknamed "Thirty-one Knot" Burke, had awakened Mitscher at midnight, imploring him to tell Halsey to send back the Battle Line. Mitscher's answer is immortal: "If he wants my advice, he'll ask for it." With that he rolled over in his bunk.

So the mighty fleet went pottering north at varying moderate speeds — no faster, for Halsey did not want to run past the elusive Japs in the dark. Halsey's admirals, in varying states of disagreement, apprehension, and consternation, held their tongues. October twenty-fourth melted at midnight into October twenty-fifth, the day of reckoning at Leyte Gulf; also, as it happened, the ninetieth anniversary of the Charge of the Light Brigade.

On October twenty-fifth, three different battles broke out, touched off by the three-pronged *Sho* approach. The Sibuyan Sea battle of the twenty-fourth is merged with these three, when Leyte Gulf is called "a combat of four engagements."

Broad wastes of peaceful sea separated the three massive fights on the twenty-fifth. They had no tactical connection. No commander on either side coordinated them, or had any grasp of the whole picture. They started and ended at different times. Any one of the engagements might have gone down in history as the great Battle of Leyte Gulf, had the other two not occurred. In military records they have coalesced into one vast impenetrably tangled sea fight. Each of the three battles would need a long book to tell its violent smoky tale in full. A brief bare sorting out of the famous October twenty-fifth triple melee, which was spaced over six hundred sea miles, is this:

In the southern battle of Surigao Strait, the action took place in early morning darkness and lasted to the dawn, a smashing American victory.

In the northern battle off Luzon, Mitscher's air strikes went on all day against Ozawa's empty carriers and his supporting force; the carriers were sunk, but most of the supporting force escaped.

In the central battle off Samar, Seventh Fleet jeep carriers were surprised at sunrise by Kurita as he sped toward Leyte Gulf. In this chance encounter, the odds were totally reversed, in favor of the Japanese. The awesome Main Striking Force stumbled on a cheap victory to be had for the taking, in routine gunnery, on the way to the beachhead: six slow tubby little flattops and a few destroyers and DEs, not one armed with more than a five-inch gun.

Here took place the crucial battle for Leyte Gulf.

The most spectacular battle, however, was fought in the south, in the dark: a crossing of the *T*, the first on earth's waters since Jutland, no doubt the last the world will witness.

The Japanese diversionary force, ignoring Kurita's order to slow down, entered Surigao Strait — the southern entrance to Leyte Gulf — shortly after midnight. Every gunship of Kinkaid's Seventh Fleet lay in wait, in textbook Battle Line formation: in all, forty-two warships against eight, six battleships against two.

Advancing blindly and doughtily in column, the Japanese first ran a gauntlet of thirty-nine PT boats, which they drove off with searchlights and secondary battery fire. Next they butted into destroyer attacks; one column after another, steaming past neatly as in a fleet exercise, discharging volleys of torpedoes, which ran through four miles of black water and blew up one battleship, holed the other, which was the flagship, sank one destroyer and crippled two more. A pitiful little tail for the *T* limped up the strait to be crossed: one battleship, one cruiser, and one destroyer, all damaged. The Battle Line blasted them into oblivion. Pursuit of retreating cripples lasted well into daylight. Only one destroyer escaped to tell the grisly story of Surigao Strait back in Japan.

A second Japanese group of cruisers and destroyers, sailing down from Japan to join the southern attack, failed to arrive in time for this massacre. Coming on the scene before dawn, seeing the flaming hulks drifting on the sea, hearing the anguished radio exchanges among the doomed ships, the admiral turned and departed, after sustaining one PT boat torpedo hit on a cruiser. A cowardly or a prudent act? Judgments will vary on such discreetness in war.

By all accounts the Battle of Surigao Strait was ferocious fun for the Americans. They took many chances, absorbed some hits, and executed classic slaughter. Men wrote afterward of the beauty and the color of this last Battle Line fight: the long long wait for the enemy on the calm sea in the warm night under a setting moon, the tightening of nerves, the once-in-a-lifetime exaltation of destroyer run-ins against heavy ships in searchlight beams, under star shells, under the red blazing flying arches of tracers; the breathless wait for torpedoes to find their marks in the night; the ships blowing up and burning on the sea, the blue-white searchlights blindingly sweeping the black waters, the great guns erupting in salvo after salvo. The Japanese lost all their ships but one, and thousands of lives. The Americans lost thirty-nine lives and no ships.

So to the south Leyte Gulf was safe. But what of the north? At about four in the morning, with the battle going so well, Kinkaid decided to eliminate any farfetched concern by inquiring directly from Halsey whether Task Force Thirty-four was indeed guarding San Bernardino Strait. Off went the dispatch. By that time, the distance between Halsey and Kurita, who was well along toward the gulf, was widening to two hundred miles.

On the flag bridge of the *Iowa*, Victor Henry paced, sleepless. He knew he should be in his sea cabin, resting before the battle. But whenever he tried to lie down the miles kept clicking off in his mind as on a taxi meter, with the price in hours to get back to Leyte Gulf. Blocking San Bernardino Strait, crossing the *T* of the Central Force; blasted dreams! The Jap was certainly through the strait by now, going hell for leather for the beachhead. When would the first howl for help come? The sooner the better, Pug thought; a historic disgrace eclipsing Pearl Harbor was in the making, and the margin of time for averting it was melting away.

The fleet was moving with slow majesty on a smooth sea under thick-sown stars. Far below, the black swells sliding past the *Iowa*'s hull made a quiet slosh. Dead astern, high over the horizon, the Southern Cross blazed. Pug wanted to enjoy the sweet night air, the splendor of the stars, the religious awe of darkness on the ocean. He tried to force his thoughts away from the fleet's predicament. Why torture himself with this empty fretful masterminding? Who was he, anyway, to question his chief? Suppose Halsey had top-secret instructions to do exactly what he was doing? Suppose orders or information had come in on channels for which BatDiv Seven lacked the codes?

His watch officer spoke in the darkness. "Admiral? Urgent dispatch from Com Third Fleet."

Pug hurried into the smoky red-lit flag plot, where sailors slumped at the radars in tired mid-watch attitudes. On the chart desk lay the dispatch. His heart thumped painfully and joyously as his eye caught the words:

FORM BATTLE LINE.

Halsey was ordering Task Force Thirty-four into existence, after all! But, alas, not to speed south; on the contrary. The six fast battleships, with cruisers and destroyers, were to rush ahead, still farther *northward*, to engage the Jap carriers if they showed up by daylight within gunfire range. Otherwise Mitscher's carriers would hit them, and the Battle Line would hound down and destroy the cripples. Pug's hopes died as quickly as they had flared.

Maneuvering the six giant black shapes out of a formation of sixty-odd vessels by starlight was a tedious tricky business. Pug Henry, almost dropping with weariness but unable to rest, prowled flag quarters and the bridge, tried to eat and failed, smoked and drank coffee until his hammering pulse warned him to take it easy. He had nothing to do; it was the captain's job to handle the ship. Daylight found the Battle Line on station, ten miles north of the carriers, foaming along on the sunlit sea. Squadrons of aircraft were roaring by overhead to strike the quarry, discovered by search planes a hundred fifty miles away.

Pug had ordered his communications officer to intercept every message between Kinkaid and Halsey that could be decoded, for he was starting a separate file of dispatches bearing on the Central Force crisis, noting the time he read each one. So far the file held three sheets:

0650. KINKAID TO HALSEY. AM NOW ENGAGING ENEMY SURFACE FORCES SURIGAO STRAIT. QUESTION. IS TASK FORCE 34 GUARDING SAN BERNARDINO STRAIT.

0730. HALSEY TO KINKAID. NEGATIVE. IT IS WITH OUR CARRIERS NOW ENGAGING ENEMY CARRIERS.

Pug thought bitterly that the face of Admiral Kinkaid, far down there in Leyte Gulf, would be a memorable study in shock when he read *that* one.

0825. KINKAID TO HALSEY. ENEMY VESSELS RETIRING SURIGAO STRAIT. OUR LIGHT FORCES IN PURSUIT.

That was the last calm message. Now came the howl for help Pug was partly dreading, partly hoping for:

0837. KINKAID TO HALSEY. ENEMY BATTLESHIPS AND CRUISERS REPORTED FIRING ON TASK UNIT 77.4.3 FROM 15 MILES ASTERN.

The coding officer had noted "Sent in the clear." Plain English! Kinkaid's dropping of secrecy for the sake of fast communication, allowing the Jap to copy, spoke more stridently than his words.

Quickly Pug thumbed through the thick operation order to identify Task Unit 77.4.3. Ye gods! The jeep carrier outfit of Ziggy Sprague had run afoul of the whole damned Jap battle line. Clifton Sprague was an old friend, class of '18, one of the smart ones who had gone into aviation early and had beaten many seniors like Pug to flag rank. God help Ziggy now, and God help those matchbox ships of his!

Pug was at the flag plot desk, with Bradford facing him. Here the messages began to pile up in his file, while the business of flag plot swirled around him, having to do with the fighting up ahead.

0840. KINKAID TO HALSEY. URGENTLY NEED FAST BATTLESHIPS LEYTE GULF AT ONCE.

Muttering "At once, hey?" Pug measured off the Battle Line's distance to Leyte Gulf: two hundred twenty-five miles. At flank speed, a nine-hour run would get them there by sundown. Too late to save Ziggy Sprague's unit and the landing force from a holocaust; but providing that Halsey acted at once and sent the battleships back they might yet cut off and sink the marauders.

But the only word from Halsey went to the fourth carrier group, still plodding back from Ulithi:

0855. HALSEY TO MCCAIN. STRIKE ENEMY VICINITY 11–20 N 127 E AT BEST POSSIBLE SPEED.

Pug's plotted track of McCain's force showed him over three hundred miles from Leyte. Even if he started maneuvers at once to launch his planes, they could not reach the battle scene for hours, and what would be left of Ziggy's ships?

Meanwhile, pilots' reports were coming in from the air strikes to the north. Cheers rang through flag plot as sailors posted the score in bold grease-pencil strokes on the Plexiglas. Halsey was chalking up his victory early: one carrier sunk, two carriers and a cruiser "badly hit," only one carrier left undamaged; all in the first strike! *"Little or no opposition,"* went up in big orange letters. Not much for the Battle Line to do here, obviously. Mitscher's four hundred planes would mince up this weak wounded force. It would be a sweep like Midway for ships sunk, though of no comparable significance.

The ship's captain buzzed Pug from the bridge to exult over the news. Flag plot was bubbling with the excitement of victory. Only Victor Henry sat glum and isolated. Even as the reports of triumph were spreading over the Plexiglas, a coding room ensign brought him several Kinkaid messages. Coming thick and fast now!

0910. KINKAID TO HALSEY. OUR ESCORT CARRIERS BEING ATTACKED BY 4 BATTLESHIPS, 8 CRUISERS, PLUS OTHERS. REQUEST LEE COVER LEYTE AT TOP SPEED. REQUEST FAST CARRIERS MAKE IMMEDIATE STRIKE.

0914. KINKAID TO HALSEY. HELP NEEDED FROM HEAVY SHIPS IMMEDIATELY.

0925. KINKAID TO HALSEY. SITUATION CRITICAL, BATTLESHIPS AND FAST CARRIERS WANTED TO PREVENT ENEMY PENETRATING LEYTE GULF.

God in Heaven, how long would Halsey hold out? The messages were arriving in scrambled sequence. There seemed to be major foul-ups in transmission. Still, the import was clear. Surely Nimitz must be picking up these appalling messages from Com Seventh Fleet's powerful transmitter, and sending them on to King. At this point it seemed to Pug that Halsey's actual career was at stake; not only a defeat, but a court-martial was building up in these dispatches.

0930. KINKAID TO HALSEY. TASK UNIT 77.4.3 UNDER ATTACK BY CRUISERS AND BATTLESHIPS AT 0700. REQUEST IMMEDIATE AIR STRIKES. ALSO REQUEST SUPPORT BY HEAVY SHIPS. MY OLD BATTLESHIPS LOW ON AMMUNITION.

This message did at last provoke a response.

0940. HALSEY TO KINKAID. I AM STILL ENGAGING ENEMY CARRIERS. MCCAIN WITH 5 CARRIERS 4 HEAVY CRUISERS HAS BEEN ORDERED TO ASSIST YOU IMMEDIATELY.

Now for the first time Halsey gave his own latitude and longitude. So Kinkaid had the bad news, flat out, that the Battle Line was about ten hours from Leyte Gulf. What Kinkaid did not know was that it was still going the other way at full speed.

1005. KINKAID TO HALSEY. WHERE IS LEE? SEND LEE.

The coding officer again noted "Broadcast in the clear."
A true bellow of agony in plain English for the Japs to pick up!
Pug's telephone buzzed. The coding officer said in a trembling voice, "Admiral, we're breaking a message from Nimitz." Pug ran to the small top-secret room, and looked over the decoder's shoulder through dense cigarette smoke as he tapped the keys. The message came snaking out of the machine on paper tape:

1000. NIMITZ TO HALSEY. TURKEY TROTS TO WATER GG. WHERE REPEAT WHERE IS TASK FORCE 34 RR. THE WORLD WONDERS.

The nonsense padding set off by double letters was standard encoding procedure. Yet "The world wonders" from "The Charge of the Light Brigade" (though Pug had no idea that this day was an anniversary) was apt enough to the situation! Well, Pug thought, this does it; this unprecedented rebuke from Nimitz in mid-battle would penetrate the hide of a dinosaur; here we go at last. He strode out on the bridge, absolutely certain that within minutes he would see the *New Jersey* streaming the colored signal flags ordering the Battle Line to reverse course: *Turn one-eight*.
Ten minutes passed, a quarter hour, a half hour.
One hour.
The Battle Line continued to steam away from Leyte Gulf at twenty-five knots.

91

WHAT Admiral Kinkaid did not know, and what Pug Henry could not possibly imagine, was the course the combat off Samar was taking. Of all the long books to be written about the three battles on October 25, the tale of this fray is the one any chronicler would most enjoy writing, for its theme is one that will stir human hearts long after all the swords are plowshares: gallantry against high odds.

Sprague's unit of six jeep carriers had the shortwave call sign Taffy Three. When it was surprised, Taffy Three was eighty miles north of the entrance to Leyte Gulf, doing the donkeywork of amphibious warfare; small air strikes at enemy fields, combat air patrol over the beachhead, antisubmarine patrol, bombing of truck convoys, parachuting of supplies to Army units.

These mass-produced runt flattops were not built to fight. Nor was the screen of three destroyers and four smaller destroyer escorts expected to do battle, except against submarines. Most of the sailors and officers of Taffy Three were reserves. A goodly number were draftees. The prima donnas Halsey had taken north, the fleet carriers and fast battleships, were manned by the professional Navy; not the likes of Taffy Three. But Taffy Three, not Halsey, was in Kurita's way as he bore down on Leyte Gulf, and so Taffy Three had to fight him.

Two other jeep carrier units, Taffy Two and Taffy One, were patrolling farther to the south. The gap between each unit was thirty to fifty miles. A glorious harvest for Kurita! Merely continuing to sweep southward, he could pick off most of these slow thin-skinned ships and their little screen vessels one by one. The carriers could not escape him, for his powerful gunships were much faster, and could shoot fifteen miles or more; a heaven-sent opportunity, in short, to lay waste an entire flotilla of flattops on his way to his main job of annihilating the invasion.

But Kurita had not planned to catch the Taffys unawares. He was as surprised by this encounter as they were. Relaxed by the luck of finding the strait unguarded, worn down by the swim for his life on the twenty-third, the air strikes of the twenty-fourth, the loss of the mighty *Musashi,* and three sleepless nights culminating in the tense night passage through mine fields, Kurita was in no jolly mood for pursuing aircraft carriers. The first sight of the low flat shapes on the horizon in the sunrise confounded him. Who were they? Where had they come from? Was Halsey lying in wait here, instead of at the strait? Was the Main Striking Force in for another day of unopposed mayhem from the air?

The apparition met Kurita's eyes at a bad moment. His vessels were crisscrossing helter-skelter all around him, for he had ordered the force into AA formation for daylight steaming. To reshuffle his force into line of battle would take time. Yet the AA "ring formation" was no way to pursue a foe. As Kurita tried to think all this out, staring at the minute gray silhouettes to the south, frantic reports were pouring in from the *Yamato*'s lookouts and from other ships: *"Fleet carriers ahead! Cruisers! Battleships! Small carriers! Tankers! Destroyers!"*— a bedlam of agitated cries. Desperate for information, Kurita launched the *Yamato*'s two scout planes. They vanished and never reported in again. He had to make his decisions without knowing what force he had encountered, and he had to surmise the worst case: that this was Halsey.

Sprague, on the other hand, knew exactly what he faced. These vessels jutting up in a mass over the horizon were the Jap Central Force. Their foreign TBS gabble was coming in plainly. Sprague had assumed with everyone else that Halsey's Battle Line was guarding the strait, and that the Central Force would be none of his business. Now here it was. Most of his planes were already launched, flying CAP over the beachhead, or patrolling for submarines, or circling above his own outfit. The crews of his feeble ships were not even at General Quarters. It took them seconds to abandon their breakfasts and man battle stations, but this scarcely improved the ships' defense stance. Each had one five-inch gun; just one.

Kurita at last ordered "General Attack." The command let loose every ship in the Central Force to pick and chase its own target. They ran off in an uncoordinated pursuit, firing at will; some ships in column, some acting singly, all bearing down at flank speed on the Americans.

Sprague reacted like a War College student solving a battle problem. He went to full speed upwind, making smoke with his carriers. He ordered the escorts to lay a smoke screen. He launched all aircraft still on board his vessels. He notified Kinkaid of his danger, calling for battleship help. He put out an emergency combat call to all aircraft within range. Those things done, he headed for a rainsquall lying upwind, and his formation gradually disappeared into it, about a quarter of an hour after sighting the Japanese. Near-misses had jolted the force, but the ships were safe and whole. At the War College he would have received good marks for his solution, worked out while red, purple, green, and yellow splashes from the big guns sprang up all over the sea about him, and destruction seemed minutes away.

In the squall he was far from safe, of course. He was like a fugitive hiding from a cop behind a moving wagon. The rainsquall would not hold still. Nor could he. The enemy kept gaining on him, and could see him with radar. Sprague headed windward and southward through thick rain to keep sea room, and to close with whatever ships were coming to his aid. His tactic was to play for time and keep his carriers together and afloat until deliverance came from *some* quarter: Halsey, Kinkaid, the other Taffys, Army air, or a merciful God.

Through the drifting rain and smoke, he could see the battleships getting bigger astern, and cruisers drawing near on his quarters. He ordered his three destroyers to make a torpedo attack against the huge force. It was a hardhearted, cold-blooded delaying move. The three slim gray vessels pulled out of the rainsquall and steamed straight toward the battleships and cruisers, through a barrage of big shells. On opposing courses, the Main Striking Force and the little ships closed fast. Hit after hit smashed into the destroyers, but they shot off their torpedoes and limped away under fire. Two eventually sank. They got only a single hit on a cruiser.

Still, the pursuers had had to break off the chase to evade the torpedoes, giving Sprague a start on his escape dash. For Kurita the result was very bad. By his own orders the heavy *Yamato* wheeled north to evade while the fight ran southward. The super-battleship steamed seven miles northward before turning around again, for the destroyer attacks were not simultaneous and the torpedo tracks kept coming. Kurita lost contact with the engagement. His force was headless thereafter, committing itself piecemeal to no plan.

Meantime, aircraft were showing up: Sprague's planes, planes from Leyte, planes from Taffy One and Taffy Two; bombing, torpedoing, and strafing the Japanese. During the long fight the air attacks hit three cruisers; all three in the end went down. Yet the pursuers fought back hard, knocking down over a hundred aircraft while gaining on Sprague in a gun chase lasting two hours. As a last resort Sprague ordered his four destroyer escorts, equipped with torpedoes but untrained in their use, to make another delaying attack. These puny vessels too charged into the teeth of the big guns. They got no hits, took brutal damage, and one sank. They gained Sprague a little more time.

But after two hours his game was about played out. Heavy cruisers were pulling abeam to port and starboard, pumping shells into his carriers. Two battleships were rapidly coming up astern. He had no tricks left but violent zigzagging among the gruesomely beautiful shell splashes. American planes were smoking and burning all over the sea. None of his carriers was undamaged, and one was sinking. Impotently they kept firing their single five-inch guns.

At this point, Kurita on the distant *Yamato* ordered all his ships to cease fire and rejoin him.

The guns fell silent. The Japanese vessels turned away from their gasping prey and headed north. Taffy Three fled southward, its sailors — from the admiral down to the youngest seaman — incredulous at this mysterious deliverance. The Battle of Samar was over. It was about a quarter past nine.

Under sporadic air harassment, Takeo Kurita next gathered up his force for the thrust into Leyte Gulf. He steamed a slow circle off the entrance, reuniting the scattered units. It took three hours. Leyte Gulf now lay open before him. With Taffy Three distantly on the run, nothing any longer barred the way. Against unbelievable odds, despite mistakes, misfortunes, miscalculations, communication failures, and terrible punishment, the *Sho* plan had worked! Kinkaid's old battleships, trying to hurry back from their Surigao Strait pursuit, were far off and low on ammunition. The MacArthur invasion in the gulf, transports and troops alike, lay helpless before the Main Striking Force.

At half past twelve, Admiral Kurita, having regrouped his force, *decided on his own not to enter Leyte Gulf. Asking no permission from Tokyo, notifying nobody, he turned north to head home through San Bernardino Strait.*

The signal flags for reversing course ran up on the *New Jersey* halyards about a quarter past eleven.

TURN ONE-EIGHT

According to Pug's chart, the crippled carriers were only forty-five miles away, dodging and burning under the air strikes. Leyte Gulf was three hundred miles to the south. Now, less than an hour's steaming from the force he had run northward all night and half the day to destroy, Halsey was turning back.

The captain of the *Iowa* burst into flag plot. Could the admiral tell him what was happening? There was great hunting directly ahead. Why were they turning away?

"Looks like a bigger fight making up back at Leyte Gulf, Skipper."

"We can't get there until sunup tomorrow, Admiral. At best."

"I know," Pug said in a dry tone that guillotined the conversation, and the captain left.

Pug could not trust himself to talk to the captain. He was in the emotional turmoil of a mutinous ensign. Could Halsey really be throwing away one of the major battles of all time, covering the United States Navy with ignominy, endangering the Leyte landing force, fumbling the winning of the war? Or was he himself — deprived of the big chance of his life to fight a battle-line engagement — too upset to think straight?

Yet he could not stop his mind from working. Even on this turnaround, he judged Halsey was making serious mistakes. Why was he taking six battleships? Two could still press ahead to the Northern Force; surface fire was the right way to sink cripples. And why was he dragging along a mass of destroyers? They would all have to be fueled first.

Pug recalled how Churchill, coming to meet Roosevelt at Argentia aboard the *Prince of Wales*, had left the destroyer screen behind to speed through a gale faster than they could go. That was a man! Here was the redeeming moment, the very last chance to rush back and gun down the Central Force. Halsey had lost six hours by not turning back at Kinkaid's first bellow. Only desperate measures would answer now. The Central Force must be a weary battered outfit, perhaps with empty torpedo tubes, low fuel bunkers, possibly even low magazines. Surely it was a moment to pitch all on one throw; to forgo destroyer protection and destroyer torpedoes, and roar down there with the big guns.

But it was not to be. The "rescue run" became an exasperating leisurely saunter at ten knots in the hot humid afternoon. One by one, hour after hour, the destroyers pulled up alongside the battleships to fuel. The carriers went by the other way, at full speed in pursuit of the Northern Force. It was a bitter sight; bitter to be becalmed in this great Battle Line in the midst of vast engagements, not yet having fired a shot.

Bitterer yet was the stench of oil. Pug was observing the refueling from the flag bridge. It was a skillfully done business: each small ship nosing up alongside the giant *Iowa*, its young skipper on his bridge, far below Pug, matching speeds until relative movement was zero; then the touch-and-go passing of the swaying oil lines over the splashing blue swells between the ships, and the parallel steaming until the little nursing vessel dropped away sated. Pug was used to the sight, yet, like carrier flight operations, he usually enjoyed watching it.

But today, in his overwrought state, the smell of black oil brought back the night of the *Northampton*'s sinking. That remembrance twisted the knife of his present impotence. Division commander of two battleships, he was being robbed of vengeance for the men who had died in the *Northampton*, by the bellicose blundering of Bill Halsey.

A despairing vision came over Pug Henry as these dragging hours passed. It struck him that the whole war had been generated by this damned viscous black fluid. Hitler's tanks and planes, the Jap carriers that had hit Pearl Harbor, all the war machinery hurtling and clashing all over the earth, ran on this same stinking gunk. The Japs had gone to war to grab a supply of it. Not fifty years had passed since the first Texas oil field had come in, and the stuff had caused this world inferno. At Oak Ridge they were cooking up something even more potent than petroleum, racing to isolate it and use it for slaughter.

Pug felt on this October twenty-fifth, during this endless, nerve-wracking, refueling crawl toward Leyte Gulf at ten knots, that he belonged to a doomed species. God had weighed modern man in the balance with three gifts of buried treasure — coal, oil, uranium — and found him wanting. Coal had fueled Jutland and the German trains in the Great War, petroleum had turned loose air war and tank war, and the Oak Ridge stuff would probably end the whole horrible business. God had promised not to send another deluge; He had said nothing about preventing men from setting fire to their planet and themselves.

Pug's mood had reached this depth of dismalness when Captain Bradford came running out on the flying bridge. ComBatDiv Seven was being summoned on the TBS by "Blackjack."

"It's not a communicator, Admiral," said Bradford with some agitation, "it's Halsey."

Pug's apocalyptic vision vanished. He darted into flag plot and seized the TBS receiver.

"Blackjack, this is Buckeye Seven, over."

"Say, Pug," came Halsey's familiar voice, grainy and buoyant, using the informal style privileged to high flag officers, "we're about through refueling here, and time's a-wasting. Our division can sustain a long flank speed run. What say we mosey on ahead down there, and try to catch those monkeys? The others will follow. Bogan will back us up with his carriers."

The proposal knocked Pug's breath out. At that rate the *New Jersey* and the *Iowa* could reach San Bernardino Strait about one in the morning, Leyte Gulf at three or four. If they did encounter the enemy, it would mean a night action. The Japs were old hands at that, and BatDiv Seven had no night fighting experience at all. Two battleships would be fighting at least four battleships, including one with eighteen-inch guns.

But, by God, here was *Form Battle Line*, at long last; wrong, rash, tardy, but the thing itself! And Halsey would be right there. Pug could not keep out of his voice a flash of reluctant regard for the crazy old fighting son of a bitch.

"I'm for it."

"I thought you would be. Form Task Group Thirty-four point five, Pug. Designate *Biloxi, Vincennes, Miami*, and eight DDs for the screen. You've got tactical command. Let's get the hell down to Leyte Gulf."

"Aye aye, sir."

*   *   *

92

Japan's Last Gasp

(from *World Holocaust* by Armin von Roon)

TRANSLATOR'S NOTE: *When* World Holocaust *first appeared in German, a translation of this controversial chapter was published in the* U.S. Naval Institute Proceedings. *As a BatDiv commander at Leyte, I was invited to write a rejoinder. It is appended here. — V.H.*

Our Ardennes offensive in late 1944, the so-called Battle of the Bulge, and the Battle for Leyte Gulf were parallel operations. In each case a nation close to defeat staked all on one last throw of the dice. Hitler wanted to panic the Western allies into a settlement that would give him a breather to hold off the Russians; he even harbored grandiose delusions of getting the Anglo-Americans to fight on his side. The Japanese wanted to make the Americans sick of the distant war, and willing to negotiate a peace.

Our Ardennes offensive, discussed in my next section, gave Roosevelt and Churchill anxious weeks. The two aging warmongers thought Germany was done for, but we split their front in France and made good progress for a while, though Hitler's overambitious battle plan and tactical meddling, plus Allied air power, probably doomed us from the start.

The Japanese, however, almost brought off a world-shaking success. The chance for this success was created by the imbecility of the American fleet commander, Halsey. It was thrown away by the greater imbecility of the Japanese fleet commander, Kurita. The Battle for Leyte Gulf is a study in military folly on the vastest scale. Its lessons should be pondered by the armed forces of all countries.

Politics and War

War is politics implemented by the use of force. A military undertaking seldom rises above its political genesis; if that is unsound the guns will speak and the blood flow in vain. These Clausewitzian commonplaces will shed light on the grotesque fiasco at Leyte Gulf.

The political situation in the Pacific in late 1944 was this. On the one hand, the Japanese nation, in its gallant try for hegemony in its own geographical area, had already been ruthlessly beaten by the American imperialists; but its leaders wanted to fight on. Unconditional surrender was unthinkable to these Samurai idealists. Yet Franklin Roosevelt had laid down those terms to suit the mentality of his countrymen, on whose soil not one bomb had yet fallen, and who were fighting a Hollywood war.

This being the political deadlock in the Pacific — for on military grounds the Japanese should have been suing for peace once Tojo fell — a military *shock* was needed to break the stalemate. In long wars, peace parties develop: in democratic systems openly, in dictatorships within the ruling cadre. A shock strengthens the peace party of the shocked side. The Japanese planned to lie back until the Americans struck the Empire's inner perimeter, and then smash them. At the end of extended supply lines, near Japanese air and naval bases, the Yanks would be at a transient disadvantage, and might be shocked by a bloody setback into a reasonable peace.

The American concept behind the invasion of the Philippines was a mere empty gratification of General MacArthur's vanity, which would also palliate some home-front grumbling. It brought major Japanese land forces in the Philippines unnecessarily into action. These were already stymied by the horrible unrestricted U-boat warfare of the Americans, and should have been left to wither on the vine. But Douglas MacArthur wanted to return to the Philippines, and Roosevelt wanted such a theatrical reconquest right before the election.

The ostensible reason for taking Leyte, a large central island of the archipelago, was to establish supply depots and a large air base for the attack on Luzon. But Leyte is mountainous, and its one important flat valley is a mass of soggy rice paddies. MacArthur's own engineers protested at choosing Leyte for such purposes. The generalissimo, in his hunger for his great Return, ignored them. Leyte after its capture never became a significant operational base. The world's most massive sea battle was fought for a trivial and useless prize.

Following the Nimitz strategy of a Central Pacific drive, Admirals King and Spruance had offered better plans for ending the war. Both proposed to bypass the Philippines. King wanted to take Formosa. Spruance — who has an undeserved reputation for caution — suggested the audacious project of landing on Okinawa. Such a landing, virtually in Japan's home waters, might well have been the shock to topple the war cabinet and bring peace. The atomic bomb was then still more than half a year from becoming a reality. The barbaric deed of Hiroshima might never have been necessary. But nine months later when the Americans did take Okinawa, the Japanese were hardened in last-ditch resistance, and only nuclear slaughter could jolt them out of the war.

In short, the overweening ego of Generalissimo MacArthur and the cold-blooded politicking of Franklin Roosevelt gave the Japanese their chance. They seized it, and they should have won. The Americans stumbled, fumbled, and flopped into a sorry "victory," thanks to one Japanese admiral's unbelievable folly.

My operational analysis gives the Japanese *Sho* plan in detail, with daily charts of the four main engagements. This sketch will be limited to the outstanding Leyte controversies.

A pincer attack on MacArthur's landing force through Surigao Strait and San Bernardino Strait was a sound idea. The use of Ozawa's impotent carriers as a decoy force was brilliant. Unless Halsey's Third Fleet could be lured from the scene, the pincer attack could not succeed. The chief controversies center around the battle decisions of Halsey and Kurita.

Halsey

The American commander who botched the battle, William F. Halsey, rushed into print after the war to cover his tracks with a book that ran serially in a popular magazine while the nations were still burying their dead. The book opens with these words, purportedly written by his collaborator, a staff officer: *Fleet Admiral Halsey was attending a reception in 1946 when a woman broke through the crowd around him, grasped his hand, and cried, "I feel as if I were touching the hand of God!"*

This first sentence in *Admiral Halsey's Story* characterizes the man. He was a seagoing George Patton, a blustering war lover with a gift for publicity; but one finds in his combat record nothing to match Patton's advance in Sicily, his flank march during "the Bulge" to relieve Bastogne, or his dashing drive across Germany.

The critique of Halsey's actions at Leyte goes to these questions:

a. Did he make the correct decision in pursuing Ozawa's carriers, even if the force was a decoy?
b. Why did he leave San Bernardino Strait unguarded?
c. Who was to blame for the surprise of Sprague's "jeep" carriers off Samar?

Admiral Halsey wrote a defensive dispatch to Nimitz on these very points the evening after the battle, when he and his staff were still gloomy at the fearful mess they had made, and had not yet worked up their alibi. By the time he wrote his book, Halsey's defense had hardened into an explicit position.

a. He was right to go after the carriers. They were the main threat of the Pacific war. Had he not attacked them, they might have "shuttle-bombed" his fleet, the planes hopping from the carrier decks to fields in the Philippines and back again. As to Ozawa's being a decoy, Halsey suggested he lied under interrogation. *"The Japs had continuously lied during the war. . . . Why believe them implicitly as soon as the war ends?"*

b. Staying at San Bernardino Strait was a bad idea, since the Japanese might also "shuttle-bomb" the Third Fleet there. Leaving the Battle Line to guard the strait was also a bad idea. "Shuttle-bombing" would be even more effective against divided forces. He took all his ships north to "preserve his fleet's integrity and keep the initiative."

c. Kinkaid was to blame for the surprise off Samar. He had been notified that Halsey was abandoning the strait. Protecting the MacArthur landing and his own jeep carriers was Kinkaid's job. He was derelict in not sending air searches north that would have spotted Kurita's approach.

This flimsy apologia may do for magazine readers, but not for military historians.

As for "shuttle-bombing," Halsey himself had successfully urged the Joint Chiefs to advance the date of the Leyte invasion, because of the weak air resistance he had encountered from Philippine bases. He had himself crushed most of Japan's residual air strength in the Formosa operation. He had himself observed the pitiful calibre of the raw Japanese pilots still flying. He had himself struck the Luzon airfields almost with impunity. His own admirals did not think Ozawa's carriers could be strongly manned. The strategist Lee warned him in so many words that they were a decoy force. The "shuttle-bombing" story is a weak attempt to make the facts fit Halsey's fatuous action in swallowing the Japanese bait.

His reason for taking all ships north and abandoning the strait — "to preserve his fleet's integrity" — is bombast. He did not need sixty-four warships to fight seventeen, or ten carriers to fight four. Common sense required leaving a force to guard the strait. All the high commanders thought he had done that. Only his sloppy communications failed to undeceive them in time.

In blaming Kinkaid for the surprise off Samar, Halsey sinks to his nadir. Guarding San Bernardino Strait was Halsey's responsibility, and he was the senior naval officer present. If he really was shifting such a heavy responsibility to Kinkaid's shoulders, he should have done so in clear terms by dispatch, preferably after consulting Nimitz, for which there was plenty of time.

At Leyte Halsey made the essential mistake of Napoleon at Waterloo. He faced two forces, and dealt one a hard but not a decisive blow; then, in his obsessive desire to strike the second force, he chose to believe that the first force was done for, and closed his ears and his mind to all evidence to the contrary. Kurita's advance after his retreat in the Sibuyan Sea parallels Blücher's advance after his retreat at Ligny. (The reader may wish to glance at my *Waterloo: A Modern Analysis,* published in Hamburg in 1937.)

Halsey was obsessed with the carrier force because he wanted to outdo Spruance. The sickness that had taken him out of the Battle of Midway had been the disappointment of his life. He was wild for a great carrier victory. He intended to be there in person, and in command, when it happened. Since he was riding a battleship, he disposed his forces so that the battleships could have a glorious time sinking cripples, and he went steaming north with the lot of them.

Roosevelt's straddling between the MacArthur and the Nimitz strategies for defeating Japan — between the naval drive across the central Pacific, and the long plod of armies up the South Pacific archipelagoes — came to catastrophe at Leyte. Halsey was Nimitz's man. Kinkaid by his orders was MacArthur's man. The Leyte invasion was the triumph of the MacArthur strategy. Halsey with his simple-minded dash after the carriers thought he was implementing the Nimitz strategy. In swallowing the Japanese bait, he forgot what he was at Leyte for; that is, if he had ever understood it.

Halsey never admitted making any mistake at Leyte Gulf except turning back to help Kinkaid. That, he asserted, was an error made in anger, and due to a misunderstanding. Nimitz's inquiry at ten in the morning, WHERE IS TASK FORCE 34, was astounding, so Halsey insisted, since he had notified everybody that the Battle Line was going north with him. But the next phrase, THE WORLD WONDERS, seemed a deliberate insult, and threw him into a rage. Only much later did he learn that it was padding added by a coding officer.

This is such foolishness that the worst would be if it were true, and if Halsey had acted in pique. Morison, the American navy's fine historian, charitably ignores this excuse in his volume on Leyte. So Halsey regrets the only sensible thing he did in the Battle of Leyte Gulf, and blames his putative mistake on some anonymous little "squirt," to use his own word, at a coding machine.

Halsey was a newspaper tiger the American navy did not dare disown. In the inner circles, after Leyte, there was talk of retiring him. But he stayed on to run the fleet into two typhoons, incurring as much damage and loss of life as in a major defeat. He was promoted to five-star admiral, and he stood on the deck of the *Missouri* by Nimitz's side when the Japanese signed the instrument of surrender. Spruance was then in Manila. Spruance never received a fifth star. Hitler's treatment of our General Staff was senselessly unfair, but the American Congress and the navy have something to answer for in this matter.

Kurita

Kurita's role at Leyte had elements of the noble and the pathetic, before his collapse into imbecility. He set out on a suicidal mission. He bore on bravely through submarine and air blows that staggered and shrank his force. His reward was finding the exit of San Bernardino Strait unguarded. He should have gone on to penetrate Leyte Gulf and crush MacArthur's landing. That he did not was high tragedy for Japan; also, as I shall show, for Germany.

Kurita's disintegration on the morning of October twenty-fifth was due to the human limits of strain and fatigue, and the failure of Japanese communications. American communications were poor, considering their wealth of sophisticated equipment, but the only word for the Japanese performance is *lamentable.* Kurita also suffered from the absence of air support and air reconnaissance, as we did in the Ardennes. To an extent hard to imagine, he fought blind.

He made three major blunders, and the third is the crux of Leyte Gulf. One man's mental blackout ruined the last hopes of two great nations.

The first mistake was to order "General Attack" on sighting Sprague's escort carriers. He should have formed for battle, then speeded up and wiped Sprague out. He could then have proceeded into the gulf after a shining victory, while scarcely breaking stride. "General Attack," a lapse into Asiatic excitability, released his ships like a pack of hounds each chasing its own rabbit. In the ensuing confusion Sprague escaped.

The second mistake was breaking off the action when his disorganized forces had managed to overhaul Sprague. Because of the abominable communications Kurita did not realize what had happened in the smoke and rainsqualls far to the south. He thought that he had done very well: surprised Halsey's big carriers, routed them from his path to Leyte Gulf, and sunk several, as his excited subordinates reported. So he decided to get on into the gulf.

The puzzle at which military writers stand confounded is Kurita's fatal third mistake: his turnabout and departure without entering Leyte Gulf, when he had fought his way to the entrance and could no longer be stopped.

Under American interrogation, Kurita later explained that by midday of October twenty-fifth he could accomplish little in the gulf. The landing was "confirmed," and the question was, what could he do instead? He got word of a large carrier force about a hundred miles to the north (a false report) and he decided to head that way to attack it, perhaps in conjunction with

Ozawa. Northward was also the way to escape, but he always denied that intention.

One report Kurita certainly never received was that Ozawa was under attack by Halsey three hundred miles from Leyte Gulf. *Had Kurita received such a dispatch he would have entered the gulf and accomplished his mission. Kurita's ignorance of the fact that Halsey had been decoyed is the solution to the mystery of Leyte Gulf.*

This abysmal communication failure, so reminiscent — once again — of episodes at Waterloo, by no means absolves Kurita of imbecility. Like Halsey, he forgot what he was there for. Halsey was distracted by lust for a showy triumph. Kurita was distracted by bad information, fatigue, and the enemy's spate of plain-language messages. Kinkaid's cries for help, instead of reassuring Kurita, appear to have worried him with fears of enormous reinforcements on the way.

But none of these excuses will answer. It was not for Kurita to decide that MacArthur's landing was "confirmed." He was there to sail in, destroy that landing, and perish if he had to, like the wasp that stings and dies. This was the whole mission of *Sho.* Kurita had the prize in his grasp. He let it slip and fled the field. One short dispatch of less than ten words from Ozawa to Kurita — AM ENGAGING ENEMY FLEET NE OF LUZON — could have altered the outcome of the battle and the war.

For the American election was then less than two weeks away. There was growing disillusionment with the old hypocrite in the White House and his pseudo-royal family. There was also widespread suspicion that he was a dying man, as he was. His lead over his Republican opponent was fragile. Had Roosevelt fallen, and his relatively young and unknown Republican opponent, Dewey, taken office, the shape of the future might have been different. American antipathy for the Bolsheviks might have broken to the surface, in time to save Europe from the spectre of Soviet domination, which now rots our culture and our politics with the leprosy of communism.

Certainly a setback at Leyte would have called for a rethinking of American strategy, including "unconditional surrender." With a resurgent Japan at their backs, the Russians might have halted on the eastern front. Germany and Japan could no longer have won; but with less draconic peace terms, both nations would have recovered sooner from the war, and become more credible counterweights to Chinese and Russian communism.

As it was, thanks to his good luck at Leyte, the dying Roosevelt had his dear wish of crushing all competition to American capitalism in the short run. He may thereby have sold out Western Christian civilization to the Marxists in the long run. That seems not to have occurred to him or to have troubled him.

"Form Battle Line"

A Rejoinder
by Vice Admiral Victor Henry, USN (Ret.)

Not being equipped to discuss General von Roon's peculiar geopolitics, I will make one or two general comments and then get to the battle.

Roon's slurs on Roosevelt, our greatest President since Lincoln, are not worth discussing, coming as they do from a man imprisoned for faithfully abetting Adolf Hitler's crimes until the day that monster shot himself.

What he says about shock in the last stages of a war is interesting. The well-known Tet offensive in Viet Nam was such a shock; a last-gasp effort, and as an attack a costly failure. But President Johnson had assured the American people that the South Viet Nam communists were done for. The public was extremely shocked by Tet, the tepid support for the war evaporated, and the agitation for peace prevailed.

World War II was different. Annihilation of MacArthur's beachhead might have affected the peace terms, but Roon exaggerates its potential. The country was behind that war. The submarine throttling of Japan, the crushing of Germany between Eisenhower and the Russians, would have continued. Whether President Roosevelt would have lost the election is one of those "ifs" beyond determination.

Roon is a little shaky on some facts. Spruance's plan to take Okinawa depended on an unsolved logistical problem, the transfer of heavy ammunition at sea. Nimitz approved the advance on the Philippines, after study.

I find Roon's criticisms of Kurita and Halsey facile and trite. Insight into Leyte requires a detailed knowledge of what went on, and a sense of the geography, and what the sea and air distances meant in terms of hard-sweating time. I was there, and I can point out Roon's obvious sour notes.

Kurita's Mistakes

Taking Roon's criticisms of Kurita's actions on October twenty-fifth one by one:

a. The order, "General Attack"

Roon follows Morison in condemning this move.

Yet think about it. Kurita's surface force had surprised carriers. Carriers had given him a terrible pasting and had sunk the *Musashi*. Carriers needed time to maneuver into the wind for launching. If he could rush them and start gunning them down before they could get going, he stood his best chance with this target of opportunity. He hit out at once with everything he had. That was not "Asiatic excitability," it was desperate aggressiveness. Roon's racial phrasing is deplorable.

Kurita kept driving to windward to interfere with the carriers' launching and recovery operations during the running fight. He knew what he was about. In fact, his force did catch up at last with Sprague, and "the definite partiality of Almighty God," as Sprague put it in his action report, was all that saved Taffy Three.

b. Breaking off the fight with Sprague

Clearly a mistake, in 20/20 hindsight. But nothing was clear to Kurita at the time, far off to the north on the *Yamato*. He should have turned south into the torpedo tracks to comb them, rather than away. That would have kept him in the picture.

He got some very bum reports from his commanders. It was the Formosa business all over again. If he believed half of them, he had won the biggest victory since Midway. But the air attacks were stepping up, the day was wearing on, and three of his heavy cruisers were dead in the water and burning. His ships were scattered over forty square miles of ocean. He decided to rally them and proceed into the gulf. Considering his faulty information, it was a reasonable move.

c. Turning away from Leyte Gulf

Indefensible. Still, "imbecile" is hardly a professional term. Roon ignores the mitigating factors.

It took Kurita over three hours to round up his force. Air attacks slowed the process, and the buzzing planes and bursting bombs must have been driving him cuckoo. By the time he was ready to head into the gulf, it was getting on to one o'clock. His surprise was blown. He surmised — quite correctly — that wherever Halsey was, he was coming on fast. Ozawa was silent, and the Southern Force had evidently never made it into the gulf. To Kurita the gulf had become a death trap, a hornets' nest of land-based and carrier planes, where his whole force would be sunk in the remaining daylight hours without laying a glove on MacArthur.

Granted, he was in a funk. All of us like to think that in his place we would have plunged on into Leyte Gulf anyway. But if we are honest with ourselves we can understand, if not admire, what Kurita did.

The real "solution" of Leyte Gulf is that Ziggy Sprague, an able American few remember or honor, frustrated the *Sho* plan and saved Halsey's reputation and MacArthur's beachhead. He held up Kurita for six crucial hours: two and a half hours in the running fight, and three and a half hours in regrouping. After midday, proceeding into the gulf was a very iffy shot.

Kurita did not lose the Battle of Leyte Gulf because of one wrong decision or one missing dispatch. The U.S. Navy won it with some magnificent fighting. The long and the short of Leyte Gulf was that the Japanese navy was routed and broken, and never sailed again. For all our mistakes, Leyte was an honorable, not a "sorry" victory, and a very hard-fought one. We had superiority in Surigao Strait and in the north, but not off the gulf, where it mattered most.

The vision of Sprague's three destroyers — the *Johnston,* the *Hoel,* and the *Heermann* — charging out of the smoke and the rain straight toward the main batteries of Kurita's battleships and cruisers, can endure as a picture of the way Americans fight when they don't have superiority. Our schoolchildren should know about that incident, and our enemies should ponder it.

Halsey's Mistakes

I have never been madder at anybody in my life than I was at Halsey during Leyte Gulf. To this hour I can remember my rage and despair. I can get sick at heart all over again at the missed chance to fight the Battle Line action off San Bernardino Strait.

Nor am I about to defend either his swallowing the Ozawa lure, or his failure to leave a force to await Kurita. These were blunders. Roon's criticism of Halsey's published alibi is on target. His excessive eagerness for action, his lack of cool analytical powers — which I observed when I was an ensign on a destroyer he commanded — were his ruination. If he had stayed at San Bernardino Strait and sent Mitscher after Ozawa, or if he had simply left Lee and the Battle Line on guard, he would have creamed both Japanese forces, and William Halsey would stand in history with John Paul Jones. As it was, both partially escaped, and his name remains under a cloud.

And yet, I say Armin von Roon misses the truth about Admiral Halsey by a wide sea mile.

His concern about shuttle-bombing was not a mere weak excuse after the fact. October twenty-fifth was not two hours along when planes from Luzon knocked out the *Princeton.* Halsey was right to worry about more such attacks. If he gave that worry too much weight, that's another matter.

In Leo Tolstoy's *War and Peace,* which all military men have read (or should have), there are some pretty questionable historical and military theories; among them, the notion that strategic and tactical plans do not actually matter a damn in war. The variables are infinite, confusion reigns, and chance governs all. So says Tolstoy. Most of us have had that feeling in battle, one time or another. Still, it is not so. The battles of Grant and Spruance — to take American instances — show solid results from solid planning. However, the author makes one telling point: that victory turns on the individual brave spirit in the field, the man who snatches the flag, shouts

"Hurrah!" and rushes forward when the issue is in doubt. That is a truth we all know too.

In the Pacific war, William F. Halsey was that man.

After his botch at Leyte there was indeed thought of retiring him. The powers that be decided that he was a "national asset," and could not be spared. They were right. Nobody but the professional officers, and the high-ranking ones at that, knew who Spruance was. Scarcely any more knew of Nimitz and King. But every last draftee knew about "Bull" Halsey, and felt safe and proud sailing under him. In the dark days of Guadalcanal, he made our dispirited forces believe in themselves again with his "Hurrah!" and they came from behind to win that gory fight.

On the afternoon of October twenty-fifth, Halsey called me on the TBS. I commanded BatDiv Seven in the *Iowa,* and he was in the *New Jersey.* We were heading back with most of the fleet to help Kinkaid. With the gallant good humor of a star quarterback leading a team in trouble, he asked me — not ordered me, asked me — what I thought about making a high-speed run with BatDiv Seven, ahead of the fleet, to take on the Central Force. I agreed. He put me in tactical command, and off we roared at twenty-eight knots.

We missed Kurita. He had hightailed it through San Bernardino Strait a few hours earlier, thanks to his decision not to enter the gulf. We caught one lagging destroyer about two in the morning, and our screen vessels sank it. As Halsey writes in his book, that was the only gunfighting he ever saw, in his forty-three years at sea.

Furious as I was at Halsey, I forgave him that day as we talked on the TBS. Rushing two battleships into a night action against Kurita was fool-hardy, perhaps fully as bullheaded as his run after Ozawa. Yet I couldn't help shouting my "Hurrah!" to echo his. Spruance wouldn't have dashed ahead like that, perhaps; but then Spruance wouldn't have run six battle-ships three hundred miles north and then three hundred miles south during a great battle without firing a shot. That was Halsey, the good and the bad of him. I executed *Form Battle Line* with Halsey at Leyte Gulf, and went hunting the enemy through the tropical night with great trepidation against great odds. Nothing came of it, and I may be a fool, but that farewell "Hur-rah!" of my career remains a good memory.

"Form Battle Line"

This order will not be heard again on earth. The days of naval engage-ments are finished. Technology has overwhelmed this classic military con-cept. A very old sailor may perhaps be permitted to ramble a bit, in conclu-sion, on the real lessons of Leyte Gulf.

Leyte stands as a monument to the subhuman stupidity of warfare in our age of science and industry. War has always been violent blindman's buff, played with men's lives and nations' resources. But the time for it is over. As the race has outgrown human sacrifice, human slavery, and duelling, it has to outgrow war. The means now dwarf the results, and destructive machinery has become a senseless resort in politics. This was already the case at Leyte. It was truly "imbecile" to launch the colossal navies that clashed there, at a cost of manpower and treasure almost beyond imagining, and to pin the fate of nations on the decisions of a couple of agitated, ill-informed, fatigued old men, acting under impossible pressure. The silliness of it all would be slapstick if it were not so tragic.

Yet granting all that, *what alternative was there but to fight at Leyte Gulf?* That is the crack we were in, and still are.

Forty years ago, when I was a lieutenant commander and our pacifists were pointing out quite accurately the obsolete folly of industrialized war, Hitler and the Japanese militarists were arming to the teeth, with the most formidable weapons science and industry could give them, for a criminal attempt to loot the world. The English-speaking countries and the Russians fought a just war to stop the crime. At horrible cost, we succeeded. What would the world be like had we disarmed, and Nazi Germany prevailed and won world dominion?

Yet today, when every intelligent man is sick with unspoken fear of nuclear weapons, the benighted Marxist autocrats in the Kremlin, ruling the very great, very brave, very unlucky people who were our comrades-in-arms, are conducting foreign affairs as though Catherine the Great were still running the show there; only they call their grabby czarist policy the "struggle against colonialism."

I have no answer to this dilemma, and I will not live to see it resolved. I honor the young men in our armed forces who must man machinery of hideous potential, in a profession despised and feared by their fellow countrymen. I honor them to my very soul, and they have my sympathy. Their sacrifice is far greater than ours ever was. We could still believe in, and hope for, the great hour of *Form Battle Line.* We were looked up to for that by our country. We felt proud. That is no more. The world now loathes the very thought of industrialized war, after two big doses of it. Yet, while belligerent fools or villains anywhere on earth consider it an optional policy, what can free men do but confront them with what met the Japanese at Leyte Gulf, and Adolf Hitler in the skies over England in 1940 — daunting force, and self-sacrificing brave spirits ready to wield it?

If the hope is not the coming of the Prince of Peace, it has to be that in their hearts most people, even the most fanatical and boneheaded Marxists, even the craziest nationalists and revolutionaries, love their children, and don't want to see them burn up. There is no politician imbecile enough, surely, to want a nuclear Leyte Gulf. The future now seems to depend on that grim assumption. Either war is finished or we are.

93

AN officious Jew from the Transport Section stops Aaron Jastrow by bustling through the crowd and grabbing his arm, as he and Natalie are climbing the wooden ramp into the train.

"Dr. Jastrow, you'll ride up ahead in the passenger coach."

"I would rather stay with my niece."

"Don't argue or it will be the worse for you. Go where you're told, quick march."

All along the track SS men are bellowing obscenities and threats, and thrashing at the transportees with stout sticks. The Jews are panicking up the ramps into the cattle cars, dragging suitcases, bundles, sacks, and whimpering children. Natalie manages one hasty kiss on Aaron's bearded cheek. He says in Yiddish, which Natalie can barely hear over the German shouting, *"Zye mutig."* ("Keep up your spirit.") The shoving crowd thrusts them apart.

As the moving crush bears her inside the gloomy car, the cow-barn smell gives her an incongruous memory flash of childhood summers. Places to sit along the rough wooden walls are being fought over with exasperated yells and violent pushing and pulling. She makes her way as through a rush-hour subway mob to a corner under a barred window where two Viennese co-workers from the mica factory are sitting with husbands, children, and luggage crammed around them. They make a bit of room for her by moving their legs. Natalie sits down in a place which becomes hers for the next three days, as though she has bought a ticket for this one dung-caked spot on the slatted floor, where the wind whistles through a broad crack, the racket of the wheels sounds loud as the train rolls, and querulous people press against her from all sides.

They leave in rain, and they travel through rain. Though it is almost November the weather is not cold. When Natalie struggles to her feet and takes her turn at the high barred window to look out and breathe sweet air, she sees trees in autumn colors and peasants picking fruits. These moments at the window are delicious. They pass all too quickly and she must drop back into the fetor of the car. The barn odor and the smell of unwashed crowded people in old wet clothes is soon overwhelmed by a stink of broken toilets. The men, women, and children in the car, a hundred or more, must relieve themselves into two overflowing pails, one at each end, to which they must squirm and struggle through the crowd, and which are emptied only when the train stops and an SS man remembers to slide open the door a crack. Natalie has to face away from the pail not five feet from her; less to avoid the stench and the sounds, for that is futile, than to give the pitiful squatters some privacy.

This one breakdown of primitive human decency — more even than the hunger, the thirst, the crowding, the lack of sleep, the wailing of miserable children, the grating outbreaks of nerve-shattered squabbles, more even than the fear of what lies ahead — dominates the start of this journey; the stink and the humiliation of lacking a clean private way to dispose of one's droppings. Weak, old, sick people, helpless to get to the pails through the jam, even void where they sit, choking and disgusting those around them.

Yet there are brave spirits in the car. A strong gray-headed Czech Jewish nurse pushes around with one bucket of water, which the SS refills every few hours, doling out cupfuls to the sick and the children ahead of others. She recruits women to help tend the sick and clean up the unfortunates who foul themselves. A burly blond-bearded Polish Jew in a sort of military cap makes himself the car captain. He rigs blankets to screen the pails, puts a stop to the worst quarrels, and appoints distributors for the food scraps thrown into the car by the SS. Here and there in the lugubrious crush sour laughter can be heard, especially after a share-out of food; and when things have settled down, the car captain even leads some doleful singing.

Rumors keep rippling through the car about where they are going, and what will happen when they arrive. The announced destination is a "work camp outside Dresden," but the Czech Jews say that the line of stations they are going through points toward Poland. Each time the train passes a station the name is shouted around and fresh speculation starts up. Oswiecim is hardly mentioned. All eastern Europe lies ahead. Tracks branch off every few miles; if not toward Dresden, then to many other places. Why necessarily must they be travelling to Oswiecim? Most of these Theresienstadt Jews have heard of Oswiecim. Some have received cards from transportees who have landed there, though it is a long time since any postcards have come. The name evokes a shadowy terror laced with whispered details too gruesome to be believed. No, there is no reason to assume they are going to Oswiecim; or even if they are, that conditions there in any way resemble the frightful stories.

Such is the state of mind that Natalie discerns in the car. She knows better. She cannot rid herself of the information that Berel Jastrow imparted. Nor does she want to muffle her mind in fantasies. Her will to live, to see Louis again, demands that she think straight. She has plenty of time to think, sitting there over the drafty crack in the splintered floor hour after hour after hour, through long nights and long days, hungry, thirsty, sick from the stench, her teeth and bones jarring with the jolts of the train.

The abrupt separation from her uncle is clearing her mind and hardening her resolve. She is on her own, one more body in an anonymous rabble training eastward. The SS men who herded the Jews into the cattle cars took no roll calls, only head counts. Aaron Jastrow is still identified, still a name, still an Elder, still a *Prominent,* up front in the coach. She is a nameless nobody. He will probably survive in some clerkish job, wherever they are going, until the Allies smash through the failing German armies. Perhaps he will find her and protect her there, too; but instinct tells her that she has looked her last on Aaron.

Really believing that one is about to die is hard. Hospital patients rotted through with cancer, criminals walking to the electric chair or the gallows, sailors on a ship going down in a storm, cling to a secret hope that it is all a mistake, that some relieving word will come to lift the strangling nightmare; so why not Natalie Henry, young and healthy, riding a train through eastern Europe? She has her private hope, as no doubt each troubled Jew does all through the cattle cars.

She is an American. This sets her off from the others. By crazy circumstances and her own stupid mistakes she is trapped in this train, slowing and groaning up into the mountains on the second night, twisting through timbered valleys and rocky gorges, passing at dead slow through moonlit snowdrifts that spray glittering away from the wheels and whirl off on the wind. Looking out at this pretty scene, freezing and shivering, Natalie thinks of her Christmas vacation in Colorado when she was a college senior; so the moonlit snow sprayed from the train climbing up the Rockies to Denver. She is grasping for American memories. A moment lies ahead when she may live or die by her capacity to look a German official in the face and make him take pause with the words, "I am an American."

For, given the chance, she can prove it. Surprisingly, she still has her passport. Battered, creased, stamped *Ghetoisiert,* it lies in the breast pocket of her gray suit under the yellow star. With their peculiar respect for official paper, the Germans have not confiscated or destroyed it. In Baden-Baden they held it for weeks but returned it when she went to Paris. Arriving in Theresienstadt, she had to turn it in, but after many months she found it one day on her bed with Byron's picture still clipped inside. Perhaps German intelligence used it for forging spy documents; perhaps it merely moldered in an SS desk. Anyway, she has it. She knows it will not protect her. International law does not exist for her, or for any rider on this train. Still, in this crowd of unfortunates it is a unique identifying document; and to a German eye, the photograph of a husband in a United States naval uniform should also strike home.

Natalie pictures Oswiecim as a more dreadful Theresienstadt, larger, harsher, with gas chambers instead of a Little Fortress. Surely there will be work to do even there. The barracks may be as bad as this cattle car or worse, the weak, the old, the unskilled transportees may die, but the rest will be laborers. She intends to look her best, produce her passport, tell of her mica job, offer her language skills, flirt, prostitute herself if she is forced, but live till deliverance comes. That much, however short of the reality, is not entirely delusory. But her ultimate hope is a mirage: namely, that some farseeing SS officer will take her under his wing, so as to lean on her as a character witness after the German defeat. What she cannot conceive is that most Germans do not yet believe they will lose the war. Faith in Adolf Hitler keeps this maddened nation going strong.

Her surmise about the progress of the war is quite correct. German higher-ups know their game is almost played out. Little peace feelers like maggots are creeping out of the dying Nazi leviathan. Reichsführer SS Himmler is about to order the gassings halted. He is covering his tracks, preparing his alibi, stolidly setting about to refurbish his image. Natalie is riding the last train taking Jews to Oswiecim; bureaucratic delay in reversing policy has allowed it to roll. But to the SS staff waiting for it at the Birkenau ramp, with crematoriums fired up and Sonderkommandos on the alert, it is just one more routine job. Nobody is thinking of taking on a pet American Jewess as a shield in defeat. Natalie's passport may be a mental comfort, but it is just a scrap of paper.

Conditions in the car keep worsening. By the second day the sickest begin to die where they lie, stand, or sit. Shortly after dawn of the third day, a feverish small girl near Natalie goes into convulsions, writhes, beats her hands about, then becomes limp and still. There is no room to lay out bodies, so the moaning mother of the dead girl holds the corpse huddled to her as in life. The child's face is blue, the eyes shut and sunken, the jaw hanging loose. About an hour later an old woman whose feet touch Natalie dribbles blood, gasps, makes noisy rattling sounds, and topples from her wall space. The Czech nurse, who squirms tirelessly through the car trying to keep people alive, cannot revive her. Somebody else seizes the wall space.

The old woman lies under her own short coat in a heap. One skinny wool-stockinged leg with a green garter protrudes until Natalie pushes it under the coat, trying to suppress her horror with callous thinking of other days, other things. It is not easy. The smell of death comes through the excrement stink, more and more strongly as the train clacks, sways, and rolls on to the east. Farther down the car, where the SS crammed in the Theresienstadt sick, perhaps fifteen people are dead. The transportees, sunk in wretched apathy, doze or stare about in the asphyxiating miasma.

A halt.

Rough voices shout outside. Bells clang. The train moves jerkily backward and then forward again, changing locomotives. It stops. The car door opens to allow the emptying of the reeking slop pails. Sunshine and fresh air flood in like a burst of music. The Czech nurse gets her water bucket refilled. The car captain talks about the corpses to the SS guard bringing the water, who shouts, *"Na, die haben noch Glück!"* ("Well, they're lucky!") He slides the door shut, and turns a screeching bolt.

When the train moves again, the stations that glide by have Polish names. Now one hears "Oswiecim" spoken aloud in the car. A Polish couple near Natalie says they are heading straight for Oswiecim. It is as though Oswiecim is a giant magnet sucking in the train. Sometimes the route has seemed to turn in another direction and spirits have revived, but sooner or later it always bends back to Oswiecim — Auschwitz, the Viennese women call it.

Natalie has now been sitting up for seventy-two hours. The elbow she leans on is rubbed raw and staining her suit with blood. Her hunger is gone. Thirst is racking her, blotting out everything else. Since leaving Theresienstadt *she has had two cups of water*. Her mouth is as dry as if she has been eating dust. The Czech nurse gives water to people who need it more: the children, the sick, the old, the dying. Natalie keeps thinking of American drinks, of the times and the places where she drank them: ice-cream sodas in drugstores, Coca-Colas at high school dances, cold beer at college picnics, water from kitchen taps, water from office coolers, water from an icy brown mountain pool in the Adirondacks where she could see trout swimming, water in a cold shower after tennis that she caught in her hands and drank. But she has to shut off these visions. They are driving her crazy.

A halt.

Looking out, she sees farmlands, woods, a village, a wooden church. SS men in gray-green uniform pass outside, stretching their legs, smoking cigars she can smell, chatting amiably in German. From a farmhouse close to the railroad a whiskered man in boots and muddy clothes comes, carrying a large lumpy sack. He pulls off his cap to talk to an SS officer, who grins and makes a contemptuous gesture at the train. In a moment the door slides open, the sack is tossed through the aperture, and it closes.

"Apples! Apples!" The joyous unbelieving word sings through the car.

Who was this softhearted benefactor, this muddy bewhiskered man who knew there were Jews in the silent train and pitied them? Nobody can say. The transportees get to their feet, eyes gleaming, gaunt faces suffering and eager. Men move about putting fruit into snatching hands. The train starts. The jerk throws Natalie off her numb feet. She has to grab at the man bringing the apples. He glares at her, then laughs. He was the construction foreman at the children's pavilion. "Steady, Natalie!" He fishes in the sack and gives her a big greenish fruit.

The first squirt of apple juice in Natalie's mouth sets her stopped saliva flowing; it cools; it sweetens; it sends life stinging electrically through her. She eats the apple as slowly as she can. Around her everybody is crunching fruit. A fragrance of harvest time, the smell of apples, steals through the foul air. Natalie chews the apple down, bite by exquisite bite. She eats the core. She chews the bitter stem. She licks the streaks of sweet juice from her fingers and her palm. Then she gets as drowsy as though she has eaten a meal and drunk wine. Sitting cross-legged, her head leaned on her hand, her one raw elbow on the floor, she sleeps.

When she wakes moonlight makes a blue barred rectangle of the high window. It is warmer than before, when they were coming out of the mountains. Exhausted Jews slump or lean on each other in sleep all through the vile-smelling car. Almost too stiff to move, she pulls herself to the window for air. They are running through scrubby marshy wasteland. The moonlight glitters on patches of swampy water where cattails and leafy reeds grow thick. The train traverses a high barbed-wire fence, strung on concrete posts as far as the moon illumines, spaced with shadowy watchtowers. One tower is so close to the track that Natalie glimpses two guards silhouetted at their machine guns, under the cylinders of darkened searchlights.

Inside the fence, more wasteland. Up ahead, Natalie perceives a yellowish glow. The train is slowing down; the clacks of the wheels are lower in pitch and fewer. Straining her eyes she discerns in the distance rows of long huts. Now the train sharply turns. Some of the Jews rouse themselves at the screech of wheels and groan of the rickety car. Natalie sees up ahead, before the train straightens out, a wide heavy building with two arched entrances into which the moonlit railroad tracks disappear. Clearly this is the terminal, their destination, Oswiecim. Trembling and sickness seize her, though nothing frightening is in sight.

The train passes through a dark arch into a dazzling white glare. The train is gliding to a halt alongside a very long floodlit wooden platform. SS men line the track, some with large black dogs on leashes. Many strange-looking figures also await the train: bald-skulled men in ragged vertical-striped pajamas, dozens of them, all along the platform.

The train stops.

A terrifying din breaks out: clubs pounding at the wooden car walls, dogs barking, Germans roaring, *"Get out! Everybody out! Quick! Out! Out!"*

Though the Jews cannot know it, this reception is rather unusual. The SS prefers a quiet arrival that keeps up the hoax to the last: peaceable unloading, lectures about health examinations and work possibilities, reassurance of luggage delivery, and the rest of the standard game. But word has come that this transport may prove unruly, so the less common harsh procedure is on.

Doors slide open. Light glares in on the dazed crowded Jews. *"Down!*

Out! Jump! Leave your baggage! No baggage! You'll get it in your barracks! Out! Get down! Out!" The Jews begin to vanish out into the white glare. Big uniformed men jump into the car, brandishing clubs and snarling, *"Out! What are you waiting for? Move your shitty asses! Out! Drop that baggage! Get out!"* As fast as they can crowd forward, Jews are stampeding out of the car. Natalie, far from the door, is caught in a crush thrusting her toward the light. Her feet scarcely touch the floor. Sweating with fear, she finds herself in the full blinding glare of a floodlight. God, it is a long jump to the platform! Children are sprawling all over down there, old ladies lie on their faces and backs where they have tumbled, showing their pitiful white or pink drawers. The striped spooks are moving among them, lifting up the fallen. So much registers on Natalie's nearly paralyzed consciousness. She hesitates, not wanting to jump on a child. There is no clear space to land. The thought flashes through her mind, "At least I spared Louis this!" A heavy blow cracks her shoulder, and she leaps with a scream.

Her uncle has a different experience.

He knows from Berel's revelations the precise fate that awaits him. In his final entry in *A Jew's Journey*, Aaron has recorded an almost Socratic acceptance of death, but this serenity is hard to sustain on a three-day train trip toward extermination by poison gas. Socrates, it will be recalled, drank the hemlock and faded off after a short noble discourse to sorrowing and admiring disciples. Jastrow has no disciples, but *A Jew's Journey* — though he has secreted it behind the planks of the library wall in Theresienstadt, with no hope of living until it is found — is addressed to an audience too, its eventual readers; and Jastrow, a writer to the core, has left the noblest last words he could muster. Thereafter, however, he remains very much alive, and the trip is long.

Seventeen *Prominente* are crammed with him into two rear compartments of the coach in which the SS rides. It is very close quarters. They must take turns standing and sitting, dozing when they can. They are fed watery soup and stale bread at night, one cup of brown slop in the morning. For a half hour each morning they have access to a toilet, which they must then scrub and disinfect, ceiling to floor, for German use. It is not first-class travel. Still, compared with their fellows in the cattle cars they are well off, and they know it.

That is, in fact, Jastrow's torment. The privileged coach ride gnaws at his fatalistic serenity. Can there be any hope? Certainly the seventeen others think so. They talk of little else, day and night, but the positive aspects of their favored treatment. Those who have wives and children in other cars are optimistic even about them. True, the train evidently is not heading for Dresden. But wherever it is going, on this transport *Prominente* remain

Prominente. That's the main thing! Once at their destination, they will manage to look after their loved ones.

Common sense warns Aaron Jastrow that the coach ride can be more sadistic German foolery, or a bureaucratic mischance, or a calculated move to keep out of the cattle cars personages around whom a spark of resistance might flicker. But it is hard to hold out against the desperate ebullience of the others. He too yearns to live. These seventeen cultivated, highly superior men can argue persuasively: three Elders, two rabbis, a symphony conductor, a painter, a concert pianist, a newspaper publisher, three doctors, two army officers with war wounds, two half-Jewish industrialists, and the head of the Transport Section, a bitter-faced little Berlin lawyer, who alone does not talk to the others or even look at them. Nobody knows how he fell afoul of his bosses.

Except for one guard posted outside their compartments, the Germans pay no attention whatever to the Jews. Riding in the SS car, however great a privilege, is unnerving. Jews are usually quarantined from this elite like diseased animals. They can smell the hearty meals brought on board for the SS. At night jolly songs drunkenly roar out in the car, and loud arguments go on, sometimes sounding ugly. This Teutonic boisterousness close at hand makes the *Prominente* shudder, for at any time it can occur to the SS to work off their boredom by making sport with Jews.

Late on the second night, the SS men are beerily bellowing the *Horst Wessel* song, and Jastrow is remembering the first time he heard it, in Munich in the mid-thirties. Those early feelings flood over him. Ridiculous though he thought the Nazis were then, their song did embody a certain elemental German wistfulness; and now that he is probably about to die at their hands he can still hear that simple romantic *Heimweh* in this discordant chorus. The compartment door bursts open. The guard shouts, "The stinking Jew Jastrow! To compartment number four!" He is shocked into shivery alertness. With long faces the other Jews make way. He goes, the guard tramping behind him.

In compartment four, a gray-headed SS officer with a gross double chin, sitting with several other officers drinking schnapps, tells him to stand there and listen. This SS man is discoursing on a comparison of the Seven Years' War and World War II, pointing out the comforting analogies between Hitler and Frederick the Great. Both wars show, he argues, how a small disciplined nation under a great warlord can hold its own against a huge shaky coalition led by mediocrities. Frederick made brilliant use of diplomatic surprise just like the Führer; he always attacked first; time after time he reversed what looked like sure defeat by iron willpower; and in the end, the sudden death of Elizabeth of Russia gave him the break he needed for a favorable peace. Stalin, Roosevelt, and Churchill are all elderly ailing men of unhealthy habits. The death of any one of them could similarly explode the coalition overnight, says the grayhead. The other officers are most impressed, looking at each other and wisely nodding.

Abruptly he says to Jastrow, "They tell me you are a famous American historian. You must be familiar with all this."

The eighteenth century is not Jastrow's field, but he knows Carlyle's work on Frederick. "*Ach, ja! Carlyle!*" exclaims the gray-headed officer, encouraging him to proceed. Aaron says that the two wars are indeed amazingly similar; that Hitler seems an absolute reincarnation of Frederick the Great; and that the death of Elizabeth of Russia certainly was a providential break, such as could happen any day in this war. When he is dismissed, he returns to his compartment full of disgust with himself. But the guard brings him a roll and sausage which he gives to the others to share out, and that makes him feel better.

Next morning the gray-headed officer summons him again, this time for a private talk, just the two of them. He seems quite senior and quite sure of himself; he allows Jastrow to sit down, something unheard of for a Jew in an SS presence. He once taught history, he says, but a scheming Jew got a university professorship he was in line for, ruining his career. Puffing on heavy cigars, he treats Aaron to a three-hour pedantic harangue on the probable political structure of German Europe for the next three or four centuries, branching off into Germany's world leadership, quoting authors back to Plutarch and comparing Hitler to such great men as Lycurgus, Solon, Mohammed, Cromwell, and Darwin. Aaron has only to listen and nod. In a way this drivel is a diversion from the waves of fear and uncertainty about oncoming death which have been plaguing him like migraine. Dismissed, he receives another sausage and roll in the compartment, which he shares out again. He sees the grayhead no more. Once the train enters Poland, and the names of the towns they pass draw an arrow toward Auschwitz, Aaron finds himself wishing for some such distraction, even a rowdy SS songfest to kill the nerve-wracking hours. But this day the Germans have fallen silent.

Only when he descends on the Birkenau ramp does Aaron fully grasp what he has been spared so far. Standing huddled with the *Prominente* beyond the floodlights, he sees at a distance the detraining — the terrorized leaping, falling, and milling about of the Jews, the casual tossing out of bodies and luggage by bald-skulled prisoners in stripes, the long row the corpses make laid out along the platform; especially the far-stretching separate line of children's bodies, which the unloaders throw about like sawdust dolls. He looks for Natalie in the floodlight glare. Once or twice he thinks he sees her. But more than two thousand Jews have poured out of all those cattle cars. They crowd the long platform, lining up in fives under the shouts and club blows of the Germans, the men separately from the women and children. It is hard to be sure of anybody's identity in that confused mass of drooping heads.

After this first violent and noisy ejection of the Jews from the train, the scene on the ramp for a while looks tame and tedious, reminding Jastrow queerly of his own family's disembarkation at night from the steerage of a Polish ship at Ellis Island amid a throng of shabby Jewish immigrants. Uniformed officials strut about under floodlights now as then, shouting orders. The new arrivals, bewildered and helpless in a foreign place, stand and wait for something to happen. But at Ellis Island there were no dogs, no machine guns, and no rows of the dead.

In fact, something is happening. The living and the dead are being counted, to confirm that as many passengers arrived as departed. The SS pays a group fare to the Reichsbahn for every Jew transported to Oswiecim, and bookkeeping must be punctilious. Separated by sexes, the Jews stand quietly five abreast in two dark queues all the way down the track. The baldheads in stripes have time to empty the cars and stack all the belongings on the platform.

These make enormous mounds. The stuff looks like the rubbish of beggars, but Jastrow can guess what wealth may be hidden there. The Jews find desperate ways to carry a remnant of their lives' earnings with them, and it is all hidden in those shabby piles or concealed on their bodies. Knowing what lies in store for him, Aaron Jastrow has left his money belt behind the wall in Theresienstadt with the manuscript of *A Jew's Journey*. Let the finders have both, and may their hands not be German! Berel's description of the looting of the dead in Auschwitz gave Aaron Jastrow his first slippery grip on the crazy massacre. Murder for plunder is an ancient risk Jewry runs; the innovation of National Socialism is only to organize it as an industrial process. Well, the Germans may kill him but they will not plunder him.

The women's line at last begins to move. Now Jastrow sees before his eyes the process that Berel described. SS officers are separating the Jewesses into two lines. One tall thin officer seems to be making the final decision with a flick of a hand, left or right. It all goes in a quiet matter-of-fact official manner. The talk of the Germans, the rare yap of a dog, and hissing bursts of steam from the cooling locomotive are all one hears.

He stands in the shadows with the *Prominente*, watching. Evidently they are exempt from the selection process. Their baggage remains in the coach, so far. Can the optimists possibly have been right? One SS officer and one guard have been detailed to this special handful of Jews; average-looking young Germans who, except for their intimidating uniforms, are not menacing in aspect. The guard, rather short and in rimless glasses, looks as mild as he can with a submachine gun in his hands. Both seem bored with their routine chore. The officer has ordered the *Prominente* not to talk, that is all.

Shading his eyes from the floodlights, Aaron Jastrow keeps peering down the platform for a sight of Natalie. He means to take his life in his hands if he can spot her; point her out to the officer as his niece, and tell him she has an American passport. The utterance will take thirty seconds. If he gets beaten or shot, let it be so. Conceivably the Germans may want to know about her. But he cannot pick her out, though he knows she is there somewhere. She was too strong to sicken and die on the train. Certainly she is not in the thin straggle of women going to the left. Those are easy to tell apart. She could be in the thick crowd of women sent to the right, many of them leading or carrying children, or in the long line of the unselected.

The women sent to the right come shuffling past the *Prominente*, with scared stunned faces. Half-blinded by the floodlight glare, Jastrow cannot discern Natalie as they go by, if she is among them. The children walk docilely, holding on to their mothers' hands or skirts. Some of the children are being carried, sound asleep, for it is after all the middle of the night; the full moon rides in the zenith above the glare. The line passes by. Now two striped men board the SS coach and toss down the privileged Jews' luggage.

"Attention!" says the SS officer to the *Prominente*. "You will go along with those now, for disinfection." His tone is offhand, his gesture toward the departing women is forceful and unmistakable.

Dumbfounded, the seventeen look at each other, and at their tumbling luggage.

"Quick march!" The officer's voice hardens. "Follow them!"

The guard waves at the men with the submachine gun.

In a quavering, ingratiating voice, the Berlin lawyer exclaims, stepping forward, *"Herr Untersturmführer,* your honor, aren't you making a very serious mistake? We are all *Prominente,* and —"

The officer moves two stiff fingers. The guard drives the gun butt into the lawyer's face. He drops, bleeding and groaning.

"Pick him up," says the officer to the others, "and get along with you."

So Aaron has his answer. The uncertainty is finished, he is going to die. He will die very soon, probably within minutes. It is an exceedingly peculiar realization: awesome, agonizing, but at the same time sadly liberating. He is looking his last at the moon, at things like trains, at women, at children, at Germans in uniform. It is a surprise, but not such a great one. This was what he was ready for when he left Theresienstadt. He helps the others pick up the Transport Section head, whose mouth is a bloody mess, but whose frightened eyes are worse to see. In a last glance behind him, Jastrow observes the long lines still stretching down the floodlit platform, the selections still going on. Will he ever know what happened to Natalie?

A long trudge in cold air under the moon; a silent trudge, except for the crunch of footfalls on frozen muck, and the sleepy whimpering of children.

The line arrives at a beautifully kept lawn, bright green under tremendous floodlights, in front of a long low windowless building of dark red brick, with tall square chimneys which fitfully flare. It might be a bakery or a laundry. The baldheads lead the line down broad cement steps, along a dim corridor and into a big bare room brightly lit with naked electric lights, rather like a bathhouse at a beach, with benches and hooks for undressing along the walls, and around pillars down the middle. On the pillar facing the entrance a sign in several languages, with Yiddish at the top, reads:

UNDRESS HERE FOR DISINFECTANT BATHS.
FOLD CLOTHES NEATLY.
REMEMBER WHERE YOU LEAVE THEM.

It is disconcerting that men and women must undress in the same place. The striped prisoners herd the few *Prominente* off in one corner, and to Aaron's surprise, they help the women and children undress, chattering apologies all the time. It is the rules of the camp, they say. None of this takes long. The main thing is to hurry, fold clothes neatly, and obey orders. Soon Aaron Jastrow sits naked on a rough wooden bench, murmuring psalms, his bare feet on chilly cement. One must not pray naked or utter God's name bareheaded, but this is *shat hadhak*, an hour of emergency, when the law is lenient. He sees that some women are young and enchanting to look upon, their rounded naked flesh rosy as Rubens nudes under the bright lights. Of course most of the figures are spoiled: scrawny or drooping, with pendulous breasts and stomachs. The children all look thin as plucked fowl.

A second group of women comes crowding into the disrobing room, with many more men behind them. He cannot tell if Natalie is there, it is such a mob. Strange brief reunions occur between naked women and their clothed husbands: joyous cries of recognition, embraces, fathers hugging their bare children. But the baldheads cut these scenes short. There will be plenty of time later! Now people must get on with the undressing.

German voices soon call flat harsh orders outside: *"Attention! Men only! Proceed by twos to the showers!"*

The striped prisoners shepherd the men out of the disrobing room. This lot of naked males jostling along with exposed dangling genitals in bushy hair is very like a bathhouse scene, except for the strange stripe-clothed baldheads among them, and the crowd of nude women and children watching them go and calling out to them affectionately. Some women are crying. Some, Aaron can see, must be stifling screams, with hands clutched to their mouths. They fear being beaten, perhaps, or they do not want to alarm the children.

It is cold in the corridor; not for the armed SS men who line the walls, but certainly for the naked Aaron and the men marching with him. His mind remains clear enough to note that the fraud grows thin. Why this cordon of armed booted men in uniforms for a few Jews going to the showers? The faces of the SS men are ordinary German faces, mostly young, such as one might see on the Kurfürstendamm strolling on a Sunday with their girls, but they frown in an unpleasant way, like police facing a disorderly crowd and watching for violence. But the naked Jewish men, young and old, are not at all disorderly. There is no violence on this short walk.

They are led into a long narrow room of raw cement floors and walls, almost large enough to be a theatre, though the ceiling filled with hundreds of shower heads is too low for that, and the rows of pillars would be in the way. On the walls and the pillars — some of solid concrete, some of perforated sheet iron — are soap racks with bars of yellow soap. This chamber too is lit to almost uncomfortable brightness by bare bulbs in the ceiling.

So much registers on Aaron Jastrow's consciousness, as in his detached and fatalistic frame of mind he murmurs Hebrew psalms, until physical discomfort erases his tightly controlled religious composure. The prisoners in stripes keep pushing the men farther and farther inside. *"Make room! Make room! All men to the back!"* He is being jammed against the clammy skin of other men taller than he is, a miserable sensation for a fastidious person; he can feel their soft genitals crushing against him. The women are coming in now, though Aaron can only hear them. He can see nothing but the naked bodies pressing in around him. Some children are bawling, some women weeping, and there are random forlorn shrieks amid distant German shouts of command. Also many women's voices are soothing their children or greeting their men.

The crowding, ever tighter, throws panic into Jastrow. He cannot help it. He has always had a fear of crowds, a fear that he would die trampled or smothered. He absolutely cannot move, cannot see, can hardly breathe, packed in on all sides by naked strangers in a gymnasium reek, jammed against a chilly perforated iron pillar, directly under a light that shines in his face as an elbow jams under his chin and roughly forces his head up.

The light suddenly is extinguished. The whole place goes black. From far down the chamber comes a slam of heavy doors, a screech of iron bolts, turning and tightening. In the huge chamber a mournful general wail rises. Amid the wail there is terrific shrieking and yelling: *"The gas! The gas! They are killing us! Oh, God have mercy! The gas!"*

Aaron smells it, strong, chokingly strong, the disinfectant smell, but far more powerful. It is coming from the iron pillar. The first whiff burns, stabbing into his lungs like a red-hot sword, shooting alarm through his frame, racking him with cramps. He tries in vain to shrink away from the pillar. All is howling chaos and terror in the dark. He gasps out a deathbed confession, or tries to, with congesting lungs, swelling mouth tissues, in breath-stopping pain: *"The Lord is God. Blessed be His name for ever and ever. Hear O Israel, the Lord our God is One God."* He falls to the cement. Writhing bodies pile on top of him, for he is one of the first adults to go down. He falls on his back, striking his head hard. Naked flesh presses on his face and all over him, stilling his contortions. He cannot move. He does not die of the gas. Very little enters his system. He goes almost at once, the life smothered out of him by the weight of dying Jews. Call it a blessing, for death by the gas can take a long time. The Germans allow a half hour for the process.

When the men in stripes pull apart the tangled dead mass, the sea of stiff human nakedness, and uncover him, his face is less contorted than others, though nobody notices one old thin dead body among thousands. Jastrow is dragged by a rubber-gloved Sonderkommando to a table in a mortuary where his gold-filled teeth are ripped out with pliers and dropped in a pail. This process goes on wholesale all over the mortuary, with the search of orifices and the cutting off of the women's hair. He is then loaded on a hoist which is lifting bodies in assembly-line fashion to a hot room where a crowd of Sonderkommandos is busily at work at a row of furnaces. His body on an iron cradle, with two children's bodies piled on top of him because he is so small, goes into an oven. The iron door with a glass peephole slams shut. The bodies rapidly swell and burst, and the flames burn the fragments like coal. Not until the next day are his ashes carted to the Vistula in a big truck loaded with human ash and bone fragments, and dumped into the river.

So the dissolved atoms of Aaron Jastrow float past the river banks of Medzice where he played as a boy, and float all the way through Poland, past Warsaw to the Baltic Sea. The diamonds he swallowed on the walk to the crematorium may have burned up, for diamonds burn. Or they may lie on the river bed of the Vistula. They were the finest stones, saved for an ultimate extremity, and he had meant to slip them to Natalie on the train. Their sudden parting prevented that, but the Germans never got them.

94

THE turning earth brings the same bright moon over a low black vessel cutting through rough waters off Kyushu. Spray glitters up over the bridge as the *Barracuda* speeds toward a dawn attack on a Leyte Gulf cripple; a big fleet tanker screened by four escorts, crawling at nine knots and down hard by the bow. An Ultra dispatch has vectored the *Barracuda* to this limping ship, and the new captain's test of fire is on. Tankers have become prime targets. The Japs cannot fight on without oil, and it all comes in by sea. Hence four escorts. A tough shot! Byron has rescued downed airmen, helped a grounded submarine free itself from a reef, and patrolled all during the battle with no results. He has yet to conduct an attack.

He and his exec are getting soaked by the cold spray. Lieutenant Philby wears foul-weather gear, but Byron has come topside for a look around at midnight in his khakis. He does not mind; the salt shower is cheering. On the sharp moonlit horizon the tanker is a smudge. The escorts are invisible.

"How are we doing?"

"Okay. We'll be on station at 0500, if he doesn't change course."

The exec's tone is reserved. He wanted to try a stern chase and a night attack up-moon. Had they done that they would now be in the approach phase. Byron doesn't regret his decision for an end-around run; not yet. The enemy is holding course. If the sky had clouded over the night attack would have been chancy. Carter Aster always favored an approach on the bow with good visibility.

"Well, I'll turn in, then. Call me at 0430."

The skeptical squint on the exec's wet face all but shouts, *Who are you kidding? Sleep before your first attack?*

"Aye aye, sir." A faint note of disapproval.

Byron is unoffended. Philby is a good exec, he has found. He hardly sleeps, he is getting ashen as a dead man, and he has the ship up to the mark in all departments. On torpedo maintenance and readiness he is red-hot. How he performs in an attack and holds up under depth charging is the real question. That will probably soon be clear.

Shucking off the wet uniform, Byron lies down in his cabin facing pictures of Natalie and Louis taped on the bulkhead. Often he no longer notices them; they have been there too long. Now he sees them afresh: the snapshots from Rome and Theresienstadt, and a studio photograph of Natalie. The old aches throb. Are his wife and son still in the Czech town? Are they even alive? How beautiful she was; how he loved her! The memory of Louis is almost unbearable. Frustration has turned the love he felt for that boy to a festering grudge: at his father for driving Natalie to Europe, at her for her funk in Marseilles. And Dad's involvement with Pamela Tudsbury . . .

Profitless thoughts! Out goes the light. In the dark Byron whispers a prayer for Natalie and Louis, something he used to do every night, but has been forgetting lately. His father was right about that, at least; command has proven a distraction and an anodyne. He falls asleep almost at once. What was a joke about him as a junior officer is an asset in command.

The steward brings him coffee at 0430. He wakes nervily confident. He is no Carter Aster, never will be, and twenty things can foul up in an attack, but he is ready to go. That is one hell of a target out there. Rough weather; his second cup sloshes over the wardroom table. Topside, the tossing dark ocean is flecked with whitecaps in stormy dawn light; a strong wind blows. Visibility way down, the tanker not in sight. Philby still mans the bridge, his rubber clothes streaming. Radar has the target at fourteen thousand yards, he says, heading 310 as before, target angle zero. The *Barracuda* now lies ahead of its prey.

Submerging for his approach, Byron sees the screen vessels appear through a misty dawn, coming straight on: four frigate types, gray small ships like American DEs. The station-keeping is ragged; inexperienced reserve skippers, no doubt. On the zigzag a gap opens to port, and Byron heads through it, undetected by the pinging, toward the huge listing tanker. Attack phase: range closing to fifteen hundred . . . twelve hundred . . . nine hundred yards . . . "I like short ranges," Aster used to say; greater peril, but a surer shot. Byron and Philby work smoothly together, and the sailors and officers in the conning tower are all old hands. In the tension of the hunt and the technical torpedo problem, Byron loses all sense that this is a debut. Many a time he has manned the scope during Aster's attacks. It is old stuff, scary and thrilling as ever. He has the last word on firing; only that is new.

When he calls "Up scope!" for a final bearing, the tanker hull looms ahead like the side of a stadium, a pathetic gigantic victim. How can he miss? He is so close he sees swarms of Japs repairing bomb damage on the steeply slanting deck.

He shoots. The submarine ejects four torpedoes, the slower and more reliable electrics. At this short range only a minute elapses. Then, *"Up scope! HIT, by God!"* Three white splashes leap high at the tanker's side. Earthquake rumblings shake the *Barracuda*. Cheers break out in the conning tower. Byron whips the scope around and sees the two escorts he evaded turning toward him.

"Take her deep! Level at three hundred feet!"

The first depth charges fall astern, thunderous jolts that do no harm. At three hundred feet the submarine creeps away, running silent, but a sonar picks up the trail. The pinging grows louder, and shifts to short scale. Screw noises approach, pass overhead. The seasoned sailors in the conning tower wince, crouch, hold their ears.

A pattern of depth charges drops all around the *Barracuda:* a perfect shot, a barrage of explosions. The vessel takes a sharp down angle and sinks like a rock, the lights going out, clocks, gauges, other loose objects flying around, anguished voices jabbering confused damage reports in the sound-powered telephones. Emergency lights show depth increasing alarmingly: three fifty, four hundred, four hundred fifty feet. Four hundred is maximum test depth. Never down this deep before, the submarine still descends.

Philby goes staggering down the ladder to check on damage, while Byron fights to arrest the plunge. The exec shouts up from the control room that the stern planes are jammed on hard dive. The steering planes are jammed too. At *five hundred and seventy feet,* Byron is dripping sweat amid gray-faced sailors, in a conning tower half-lit by emergency lights and awash to his ankles. Philby has reported the hull dished in by sea pressure and leaking in several compartments, many hull fittings and valves spurting water, air and hydraulic systems out, electrical control panels shorting, and pumps not functioning. Byron blows the forward high-pressure group, his emergency reserve of compressed air, his very last resort, for an up-angle. That arrests the dive. Then he blows the after high-pressure group, and he has buoyancy.

Powering up to the surface, he orders all hands to battle stations as soon as they can crack the hatches. When the quartermaster opens the conning tower hatch, an astonishing waterspout rises through the hole, and for a long minute nobody can get up to the forward guns or the bridge. The diesels catch and roar, a welcome sound. When Byron does reach the bridge the enemy ship, about three miles off, is already firing, pale yellow flashes from guns that look like three-inch fifties, kicking up misses well astern of the partly disabled submarine. The other escorts are far off, rescuing survivors around the foundering tanker. The *Barracuda* fires back with its four-inch bow gun, and the escort stands off, peppering away. Its gunnery is poor. For fifteen minutes Byron avoids being hit, twisting here and there, while Philby roams the ship below, trying to restore diving condition. As things stand, one square hit on the thin old hull can probably finish the *Barracuda*.

The low-pressure blowers start up, and the submarine slowly rights a list to port. The jammed stern planes are freed. The steering planes are made to work by hand. The pumps begin to master the flooding. All this time, the gun duel goes on; and at last Philby comes up and tells Byron that the hull has been dangerously weakened. The submarine cannot dive again, probably not until major repairs are made in a Navy Yard. So the *Barracuda* is stripped of its chief defense, the safety of the deep.

All this time the frigate captain has not called for help; no doubt he wants sole credit for the kill. As Philby shouts his report between salvos of the bow gun, Byron keeps his eye on the Jap through the cloud of gunsmoke tumbling over the bridge, and sees him speed up and turn. Black smoke pours from the two stumpy stacks. He has surmised, it seems, the trouble the *Barracuda* is in, and has decided to ram. At about four thousand yards, closing at twenty knots or more, he will hit in a few minutes. A foaming bow-wave flies as his sharp antisubmarine prow cuts the sea. His outline swells.

The exec is at Byron's side. "What do we do, Captain?" he says, in a reasonably concerned tone, no note of hysteria.

A good question!

So far Byron has acted from experience. Aster too once had to blow his high-pressure group, on the third patrol, when depth charges jammed the controls and unseated a hatch, and the flooding *Moray* went down past five hundred feet. But that time they surfaced at night and Aster escaped into the darkness. Aster never faced a ramming.

Byron's best speed now is eighteen knots. Given time, the engineers can probably restore full power, but there is no time. Flight? A stern chase will gain time, but then the other frigates will pursue. The *Barracuda* will probably be outgunned and sunk.

Byron seizes the microphone. "Now engine rooms, this is the captain. Give me all the power you've got, we're about to be rammed . . . Helmsman, right standard rudder."

The helmsman turns startled eyes at him. "*Right*, Captain?"

The order will turn the submarine *toward* the charging gray frigate.

"Right, right full rudder! I want to clear and pass him."

"Aye aye, sir. Right full rudder . . . Rudder is hard right, sir."

The submarine surges forward and turns. Both ships, smashing toward each other through high green waves, are throwing up curtains of foam. Byron shouts to Philby, "We've got him outgunned with small calibre, Tom. I'm going to rake him broadside. Let's have continuous fire from the AA while we pass him. Tell the four-inch to aim for the bridge!"

"Aye aye, sir."

The enemy captain's reaction is slow. By the time he starts his counter-turn to port the submarine's stern is slipping past his prow. The *Barracuda* sails down the frigate's port side scarcely fifty feet away, the seas noisily splashing and spiring between them. The sailors over on the other deck are visibly Japanese. From the submarine there bursts a rattling din, a blaze of gun flashes, a cloud of smoke. Red tracer streams comb the frigate's deck.

The four-inch blasts away, *Crumpp! Crumpp! Crumpp!* The frigate's guns stammer in reply, but by the time the *Barracuda* has sailed past the stern they have fallen silent.

"Byron, he's dead in the water," says Philby, as Byron orders a hard turn away. He is now heading straight toward the settling tanker and the other escorts. The tanker is on its side, its red bottom scarcely visible above the swells. "Maybe you killed the captain."

"Maybe. We've got three other captains to worry about. They're turning this way. Lay below to the maneuvering room, Tom, and bend on every possible turn, for God's sake. This is it."

Philby produces a speed of twenty knots. After a twenty-minute chase the *Barracuda* disappears from its pursuers into a broad black rainsquall. Soon the three escorts drop from the radar screen.

A tour of the damaged compartments convinces Byron that the *Barracuda* is no longer seaworthy. The dents in the pressure hull from the deep-sea squeeze are serious; the malfunctions beyond repair by the crew are many; the pumps are working full-time to keep the water out. But there has been no loss of life, and only a few injuries.

"Let me have a course for Saipan, Tom," he tells the exec, on returning to the rainy bridge. "Set the regular watch. Post a one-in-three standby watch for damage control. Tell the chief of boat to draw up the bill."

"Yes, sir." The word *sir* resonates with new respect.

In his cabin, taking off wet clothes, Byron says aloud to the photograph of Natalie, "Well, I guess I can command a submarine, if that proves anything." In the aftermath of the battle, to his own puzzlement, he is deeply depressed. He dries himself with a towel, and sticky with salt tumbles into his bunk.

Late that night, he and Philby are compiling the action report in the wardroom. Philby scrawls the narrative; Byron draws neat charts of the sinking and the gunfight, in blue and orange ink. At one point Philby looks up, dropping his pen. "Captain, can I say something?"

"Sure."

"You were magnificent today."

"Well, the crew was magnificent. I had a pretty competent exec."

The long white face of Philby turns bright pink. "Captain, you're a cinch for a Navy Cross." Byron says nothing, bent over his chart. "How do you feel about it?"

"About what?"

"I mean your first sinking, and then that great fight?"

"How do you feel?"

"Goddamn proud I was part of it."

"Well, as for me, I hope we get sent all the way back to Mare Island. And that the war ends before our overhaul does." He laughs wryly at the disappointment in Philby's face. "Tom, I saw hundreds of Japs walking around and working on that tanker. Killing Japs always gave Carter Aster a big charge. It leaves me cold."

"It's the way to win the war." Philby's tone is injured, almost piously so.

"This war is won. The agony may drag on, but it's won. If I had my choice, I'd sleep the war out on dry land. I'm not a professional naval officer. I never was. Let's finish the report."

Byron got part of his wish. The *Barracuda* went back to San Francisco, and the overhaul took a long time. For a Navy Yard captain swamped by destroyers, carriers, even battleships crowding in with kamikaze damage, an old crippled submarine was a low-priority customer. Nor was ComSubPac screaming for the *Barracuda*'s return. New submarines were out on patrol in a flock. Targets were actually becoming scarce.

At the end of the overhaul an experimental undersea sonar called the FM was put aboard, and Byron was ordered to test it in dummy mine fields off California. A mine picked up by this fancy short-range sonar set off a gong in the ship; in theory, therefore, a submarine so equipped could gong its way in through the undersea dark through Japanese mine fields and into the Sea of Japan, where merchant traffic was still thick. ComSubPac was very high on the FM sonar; think of all those nice fat juicy targets still skulking in the Sea of Japan!

Byron had his doubts because the sonar was erratic; he bumped many a dummy mine on his runs. His crew, good submariners all, were appalled at the notion of nosing through rows of Jap mines with an electronic gadget. They knew Navy gadgets. Most of them had sweated through two years of dud torpedoes and BuOrd excuses. The chief of the boat warned Byron that he would lose a third of his crew by transfer requests or desertions if he sailed on an FM probe of the Sea of Japan.

But Byron was not sure he would ever leave the West Coast. In San Francisco the end-of-the-war feeling was marked. The blackout was over. Cars were crowding the streets and highways. The black market had made a farce of gasoline rationing. There were no food shortages. The headlines of Allied advances and Axis retreats were becoming boring. Only reverses made news: the kamikaze campaign, and the German last gasp dubbed the "Battle of the Bulge." Byron cared about Europe mainly because a German defeat might uncover news of Natalie. As for the Pacific, he hoped that the B-29 raids, the submarine blockade, and MacArthur's advance through the Philippines would bring a Jap surrender before he went gonging into their mine fields. How much longer could the agony really drag on?

His was a not uncommon American view of this peculiar phase of the war. Staggering events were being pureed by journalism into a pap of continuous victory. Surely the thing would end any day! But a war is easier to start than to stop. This one was now a worldwide way of life. Germany and Japan were resilient, desperate great nations under firm totalitarian control. They had no plans for quitting. The Allies had no way to make them quit but by more and more killing. Everything conspired to produce unprecedented military butcheries; while Byron (more or less oblivious to the horrors) pottered with the *Barracuda*'s machinery and the FM sonar.

Adolf Hitler, of course, had no way to quit. He could keep afloat only in blood. From the east, the west, the south, and from the air his end was closing in. His response at this time was the Ardennes offensive, the "Battle of the Bulge." Back in late August, with all his fronts crumbling, he had ordered a stand-fast on the Russian front and a giant surprise counterpunch in the west. The aim was vague: some kind of success, leading to a cease-fire that did not involve his extinction. The German army and people had rallied around him in fantastic preparations that took months, scraping together their remaining strength and concentrating it in the west.

But all this was essentially dreamy lunacy. In the east the Soviet Union was assembling five replenished army groups, more than two million men with mountains of supplies, for a drive to Berlin. Scarcely a German alive preferred a Russian to an Anglo-American occupation. Hitler was between a torrent and a trickle, so to say, of menace to Germany's future; and he was damming the trickle and neglecting the torrent, dreaming of a second 1940, another Ardennes breakthrough, a new march to the sea. When Guderian showed him accurate intelligence reports on the Soviet buildup he sneered, *"Why, it's the biggest fake since Genghis Khan! Who's responsible for this rubbish?"*

The Ardennes offensive lasted two weeks, from mid-December through Christmas. It lives on in American memory chiefly as the time a general said "Nuts!" to a German call for surrender. More prosaically, there were a hundred thousand German and seventy-five thousand Allied casualties, and on both sides, great loss of arms. The western Allies were briefly surprised but recovered. The end was German disaster. In his private circle Hitler was vocally very jolly about having "recovered the initiative in the west." He never spoke or showed himself publicly anymore.

As the Ardennes push collapsed, the Russians came roaring in from the Baltic to the Carpathians. In crossing Poland, the Red Army overran a vast industrial complex and prison camp at Oswiecim, abandoned except by a few dying scarecrows in striped rags, who pointed out some dynamited ruins as crematoriums where millions of people had been secretly murdered. Events on the Russian front got little play in California newspapers. If there was such a story Byron missed it.

Within four weeks the Russians stood everywhere deep in Germany on the Oder-Neisse River line, at some points only eighty miles from Berlin. Having run hundreds of miles, they paused for resupply. Now Hitler ordered the bulk of his forces pell-mell eastward, stripping the western front. At that time Eisenhower's armies, quite recovered from the Bulge, were preparing a Rhine crossing as big as the Russian attack. This frantic shuttling of dwindling armies across Germany from east to west and to the east again at a lunatic's whim may seem ludicrous today, but it unfolded early in 1945 as very serious military and railroading business inside the Reich. Certainly it prolonged the agony.

Of these tides of battle in Europe Byron had little grasp. He knew more about the Pacific. Even so, MacArthur's massive Philippines campaign came through to him mainly as a meteor shower of kamikazes on the naval forces. He knew that the British were driving the Japanese out of Burma, because of the dull daily stories about fighting along a river called the Irrawaddy; and that B-29 "Superfortresses" based in the Marianas were setting Japanese cities on fire. But to him the capture of Iwo Jima was the big event in the Pacific — some twenty-five thousand United States Marine casualties, a rock with airfields eight hundred miles from Yokohama! Surely the Japs would quit now.

It was in fact a time of peace feelers, German and Japanese; tenuous, unofficial, contrary to government public policy, and futile. Officially Germany and Japan bellowed defiance and the imminent collapse of their war-weary foes. But both nations were now helpless in the air, and plans took form to topple their intransigent governments with airborne massacres. Like Byron, the Allied leaders were getting impatient for the end.

In mid-February, British and American bombers killed more than a hundred thousand Germans with a single fire raid on Dresden.

In mid-March the Superfortresses killed more than a hundred thousand Japanese in a single fire raid on Tokyo.

These vast slaughters have since become notorious. They went by for Byron, and for nearly all Americans, as just undistinguished headlines of the day's far-off successes. More people died in these raids than at Hiroshima and Nagasaki, but there was no novelty in them. Albert Speer, Hitler's astute production chief, is reported to have chided an American Air Force general, after the war, for not laying on more raids like Dresden; it was the sovereign way to end the war, he said, but the Allies failed to follow through.

Nor did Byron make much of the Yalta Conference, which ended as the Dresden raid was taking off. It was hailed in the papers as a cordial triumph of Allied comradeship. Only gradually did a sour counterswell spread that Roosevelt had "sold out" to Stalin. Quite simply, he had traded Balkan, Polish, and Asian geography to Stalin for American lives. Stalin was glad of the trade, and pledged a lot more Russian deaths than he ever had to deliver. Given the facts, Byron Henry probably would have been for the trade. He just wanted to win the war, find his family, and go home.

At Yalta Roosevelt wanted and got from Stalin a renewed pledge to attack

Japan once Germany fell. He did not know that the atom bomb would work. An invasion of Japan, he had been advised, might cost half a million casualties or more. As for the Balkans and Poland, the Red Army already practically held them. No doubt Roosevelt sensed the general American sentiment typified in Byron Henry for being done with the mess, and the indifference to foreign geography. Perhaps he foresaw that modern warfare must soon cease of its own impractical horror, and that geography would then become of little consequence. Dying men sometimes have visions denied to the active and the cunning.

Thus, at any rate, the agony went on and on, and in mid-March the *Barracuda* was ordered back to Pearl Harbor. There it was assigned to a submarine pack that would penetrate the Sea of Japan with FM sonar.

95

Eighth Air Force Command
Army Air Corps
U.S. Army Post Office
San Francisco

15 March 1945

Pamela, my love,

Remember the Air Corps general who slugged down a bottle of vodka and danced at your Moscow wingding for the ballet people? He's here in the Marianas on LeMay's staff. I'm batting out this letter in his office. He's flying to the States tomorrow and he'll mail it there. Otherwise I'd probably have to cable you. I want you to meet me in Washington instead of San Diego, and there's much for you to do meantime. Captain Williams, our naval attaché in London, is a whiz at air priorities. Tell him you're my bride-to-be and he'll get you to Washington.

The news is that Rhoda's husband offered his vacant apartment to me for the run of the lease. That broke the lawyers' deadlock. I didn't calculate the financial quid pro quo, I just wrote my lawyer, Charlie Lyons, to drop the arguing. So the house goes to Peters at his price, and we now have a flat on Connecticut Avenue to land in. Charlie will see to the lease and get you moved in; and Peters has quite decently offered to refurnish as you desire.

I'll be relieved soon, I'm sure. BuPers is speeding up the rotation of sea billets. It's like the fourth quarter of a won football game, when the substitutes come streaming out on the field for a few plays. I'll request duty in Washington, and we can start living our lives.

All my movable possessions are in Foxhall Road. If I know Rhoda she's already crated and boxed them out of sight. Have the stuff delivered to the apartment. There won't be room for my books, Peters doesn't strike me as a reader. Leave those crated and I'll buy bookcases.

Incidentally, Pam, once you're in Washington, start drawing on Charlie Lyons for expenses. Don't argue, you're not to blow in your funds at Washington prices. Please buy yourself all the clothes you need. "Trousseau" may not be an appropriate word, but call it what you will, your wardrobe's important. You've been living for years in uniforms and travel clothes.

Well, there I go again. You've chided me before about filling my letters with money matters. I'm a poor hand at "the love stuff," which is what Warren and Byron, when they were boys, called the romantic scenes in cowboy movies. I admit it. I've really cheated you out of the love stuff, haven't I? The fact is, Pam, I can read the love poems of Keats or Shelley or Heine with deeply stirred emotions, even gooseflesh, but I can no more express such emotions than I can saw a woman in half. I don't know the trick. You and I can talk at length about the inarticulateness of American men as we lie naked in bed together. (How's that?)

I'm waiting around here for dinner time. LeMay has invited me to dine. My flag's in the *New Jersey* while the *Iowa*'s getting a Stateside overhaul, and we just put in here for replenishment. This island, Tinian, is a rock off the southern coast of Saipan, designed by nature as a bomber airfield. It's a staggeringly vast airport, biggest on earth, they say. The B-29s take off from here to drop their fire bombs on the Japs.

I'm developing a grudging respect for the Japanese. I commanded the bombardment group at Iwo Jima. It was Admiral Spruance's show, so he gave me something to do. I had battlewagons, heavy cruisers, destroyers pounding away for days at that little island. I don't believe we left one square yard unblasted. Carrier aircraft bombed it, too. When the landing craft hit the beaches, that island was silent as a tomb. Then, by God, if Japs didn't swarm up out of the ground and inflict twenty-five thousand casualties on our marines. It was the bloodiest fighting of the whole Pacific. My ships kept socking them, the carrier planes too, but they wouldn't quit. When Iwo was secured I don't think there were fifty Japs left alive on it.

Simultaneously their suicide pilots were damn near panicking our task force. Fleet morale is way down. The sailors thought they had the war won, and along comes this menace. Our newspapers are abusing the kamikazes as fanatics, madmen, drug addicts, and whatnot. It's balderdash. Those same papers spread a legend right after Pearl Harbor about an Air Corps flier, Colin Kelly, diving his plane into a battleship smokestack off Luzon. The press to-do about Colin Kelly at the time was tumultuous. Yet the thing never even happened, Kelly was shot down in a bombing mission. The Japs have thousands of real Colin Kellys. The kamikaze pilots may be ignorant and misled, and they can't win the war, but there's a sad magnificence about such willingness to die in young men, and I ruefully admire the culture that has produced them, while I deplore the wasteful, useless tactic.

Spruance is now taking flak about the need for the capture of Iwo Jima, but LeMay wanted an emergency landing field halfway to Tokyo. The B-29s go in vast numbers, and Fitzgerald tells me Iwo has already cut plane losses and picked up air crew morale. Whether it was worth it or not, the blood has been spilled.

I came ashore at Fitz's invitation to watch the biggest B-29 raid of the war take off and return. Pamela, it's an indescribable spectacle, these giant machines roaring off in succession for hours. My God, what the American factories have poured out, and what airmen the Army's trained! Fitzpatrick went along on the raid. It just about wiped out Tokyo, he says, set it on fire from end to end, all those square miles of matchbox houses burning away. He thinks maybe they left half a million dead.

Well, these airedales tend to overestimate their havoc, but I saw that armada take off. It must have created another "firestorm," like Hamburg and Dresden. An incendiary raid of that magnitude sucks all the oxygen out of the air, I'm told, and people suffocate even if they're not burned up. So far the Japs are saying nothing about it, but you'll see plenty of stories on this attack sooner or later.

Here in the officers' mess I've been reading in old papers and magazines about the Dresden raid. The Germans raised quite a howl. Evidently it was a honey. My tour of duty in the Soviet Union equips me to contemplate Dr. Goebbels's anguished tears over Dresden unmoved. if the Russians had our planes and pilots, they'd do a raid like that on a German city every week till this war ends. They'd do it with joy, and they still wouldn't half-repay the Germans for the devastation in the Soviet Union and the civilian deaths. I think the Germans hanged more Russian kids as partisans or in reprisals than have died in all the air raids on Germany put together. God knows I pity the Dresden women and children whose charred bodies are piled up in Goebbels's propaganda photographs, but nobody made the Germans follow Hitler. He wasn't a legitimate ruler. He was a man with a mouth, and they liked what he said. They got behind him, and they let loose a firestorm that's sucking all the decent instincts out of human society. My peerless son died fighting it. It's made savages of all of us. Hitler gloried in savagery, he proclaimed it as his battle cry, and the Germans shouted *Sieg Heil!* They still go on laying down their misguided lives for him, and the lives of their unfortunate families. I wish them joy of their Fuhrer while he lasts.

The Japs seem to take their punishment differently. They richly deserve what's happening to them, too, but they bear themselves as though they know it.

God in Heaven, I wish all this brutalizing would end.

Pamela, did you hear Roosevelt's Yalta report to the Congress on the radio? It scared me. He kept wandering and slurring as though he were sick or drunk. He apologized for speaking seated, and talked about "all this iron on my legs." I have never before heard him refer to his paralysis. The one thing that can go wrong in the war now is his death or disability — well, here's General Fitzgerald. Chow down. I didn't mean to get off on war and politics, and now there's no time for the love stuff, is there? You know that I adore you. I thought my life was finished after Midway. In a way it was, as you yourself saw. I was an ambulatory fighting corpse. I'm alive again, or I will be when we embrace as man and wife. See you in Washington!

> Much love stuff,
> Pug

H APPIER than she had ever believed she could be, but very edgy, Pamela kept looking out of the open window for the moving van. The blooming magnolia in front of the old apartment house perfumed the air clear up to the third floor. in a schoolyard across the windy sunny avenue, blossoming cherry trees were showering petals past the Stars and Stripes briskly flapping on a jonquil-bordered flagpole. Washington in springtime, again; but this time, what a difference!

She still felt half in a dream. To be back in this rich untouched beautiful city, among these well-dressed, well-fed bustling Americans; to be buying in shops crammed with fine clothes, feasting in restaurants on meats and fruits not seen in London for years; and not drifting in her poor father's wake, not fearing the collapse of England, not gnawed by guilt or grief or melancholy, but getting ready for marriage to Victor Henry! Colonel Peters's apartment, with its broad rooms and masculine furnishings (except for the frilly pink and gold boudoir, a tart's delight), still chilled her a bit. It was so big and so much a stranger's, with nothing in it of Pug. But today that would change.

The van came. Two sweating men grunted in with trunks, filing cabinets, packing boxes, suitcases, and cartons — more, and more, and more. The living room filled up. When Rhoda arrived, Pamela was relieved. She had been dreading handling Pug's things with his ex-wife; a sticky business, she had thought. But it had been damned sensible, after all, to accept Rhoda's offer of help with this jumble. Mrs. Harrison Peters was cheery as a robin in an Eastery sort of outfit, pastel colors, big silk hat with veil, matching gloves and shoes. She was on her way to a tea, she said, a church benefit. She had brought a typed list of Pug's belongings several pages long. Every container was numbered, and the list described what each held. "Don't bother to open numbers seven, eight, and nine, dear. Books. No matter how you arrange them, he'll GROWL. Then, let's see, numbers three and four are winter civilian stuff — suits, sweaters, overcoats, and such. They're mothballed. Air them in September and have them cleaned, and they'll be fine. Better stash all that stuff in the spare room for now. Where is it?"

Surprised, Pamela blurted, "Don't you know?"

"I've never been here before. Young man, we'll have some of these things moved, please."

Rhoda took charge, ordering the men to shift containers about and open those that were nailed or roped up. Once they left she produced keys to the trunks and suitcases, and pitched in on the unpacking of Pug's clothes, chattering about how he liked his shirts done, the dry cleaner he used, and so on. Her affectionate proprietary manner and tone about Pug, a bit like a mother packing off a grown-up son on a long trip, deeply disconcerted Pamela. Passing her hand fondly over his suits as she hung them up one by one, Rhoda told where they had been made, which he favored, which he seldom put on. Twice she mentioned that his waist measurement was the same as it had been on their wedding day. She lined up his shoes in Peters's shoe cupboard with care. "You'll ALWAYS have to put the shoe trees in, honey. He wants his shoes to look just so, but will he take five seconds to put in the trees? Never. Not him. Away from the Navy, dear, he's a bit of an absent-minded PROFESSOR, you'll find. Last thing you'd expect of Pug Henry, hey?"

"Rhoda, I really think I can do the rest of this. I'm frightfully grateful —"

"Oh? Well then, there's still number fifteen. Let's get at that. It's hard, you know, to split the herring down the BACKBONE, as you might say. There are some things Pug and I really share. One of us will have to end up without them. It can't be helped. Pictures, mementos, that sort of thing. I've made a selection. Pug can have anything I've kept back. I'll take anything he doesn't want. Can't be fairer than that, can I?" Rhoda gave her a bright smile.

"Certainly not," said Pamela, and to turn the conversation she added, "Look, something is bothering me. Did you say you'd never been here before?"

"No."

"Why not?"

"Well, dear, before I married Hack I wouldn't have DREAMED of coming to his bachelor lair. Caesar's wife, and all that. And afterward, well —" Rhoda's mouth twisted to one side, and she suddenly looked coarser, older, and very cynical — "I decided I really wanted no part of his memories here. Do I have to draw you a PICTURE?"

At the brief uncomfortable meeting in a lawyer's office for signing documents about the house and the apartment — which Pamela had attended at Pug's lawyer's request, and at which Rhoda had offered to help with this move — Rhoda's face had flashed that look just once; when Peters had overridden a remark of hers in an offhand contemptuous way.

"No, I guess not."

"All right. So let's just dig into number fifteen, shall we? Look here."

Rhoda pulled out and showed her photograph albums of the children, of houses the Henrys had lived in, of picnics, dances, banquets, of ships in which Pug had served, where Rhoda posed with him in sunlight at a gun mount, or on a bridge, or walking the deck, or with the commanding officer. There were framed pictures of the couple — young, not so young, middle-aged, but always close, familiar, happy; Pug's usual pose was a half-admiring, half-amused look at Rhoda, the look of a loving husband aware of his wife's foibles and crazy about her. Pamela felt as never before that she herself was a young interloper at the tail end of Victor Henry's life; that whomever he lived with and called his wife, his center of gravity was forever fixed in this woman.

"Now take this, for instance," Rhoda said, laying the leather-bound Warren album on top of a box and turning the pages. "I had a hard time deciding about THIS one, I can tell you. Naturally I never thought of making two of these. Maybe Pug finds it painful. I don't know. I love it. I made it for him, but he never uttered a single word about it." Rhoda glanced at Pamela with hard shiny eyes. "You'll find him tough to figure out sometimes. Or have you already?" She carefully closed the album. "Well, there it is, anyway. Pug can have it if he wants it."

"Rhoda," Pamela said with difficulty, "I don't think he'd want you to give up such things, and —"

"Oh, there's more, plenty more. I've got my share. You accumulate LOTS in thirty years. You don't have to tell me ANYTHING about what I've given up, honey. So let's have a look around at Hack's den of INIQUITY, shall we? And then I'll be on my merry way. Do you have a decent kitchen?"

"Immense," Pamela said hurriedly. "It's through here."

"I'll bet you found it FILTHY."

"Well, I did have to scrape and scrub some." Pamela nervously laughed. "Bachelors, you know."

"Men, dear. Still, there's a difference between Army and Navy. I've found that out." Showing Rhoda through the place, Pamela tried to slip past the closed door of the pink and gold room, but Rhoda opened it and walked in. "Oh, GAWD. Whorehouse modern."

"It is a bit giddy, isn't it?"

"It's ABOMINABLE. Why didn't you make Hack redecorate and refurnish it?"

"Oh, it's simpler just to close it off. I don't need it."

One entire wall consisted of sliding mirrors that covered a long closet. The two women stood side by side, looking into the mirror, and addressing each other's images: Rhoda smartly dressed for springtime, Pamela in a plain blouse and straight skirt. Pamela looked like her daughter.

I don't need it was a trivial remark, or Pamela meant it so. But Rhoda failed to answer. Their eyes met in the mirror. A silence lengthened. The words gained portentousness second by second, and tactlessness, too. In Pug's room there was only a double bed. The innocent statement swelled into something like this, and true enough: *I'll sleep with Pug, and live in that room with him. There are closets enough for both of us. I don't want a separate room. I love him too much. I want to stay near him.*

Rhoda's mouth twisted far to one side. The eyes of her image, cynical and sad, wandered from Pamela's face to the garish room. "I guess you don't. Hack and I are finding separate rooms pretty handy, but then I'm getting on, aren't I? Well, what else is on the tour?"

Back in the living room, she looked out of the window and said, "You face south. That's cheerful. What a fine magnolia tree! These older apartment houses are the best. Isn't that schoolyard noisy? Of course it's after hours now."

"I haven't noticed."

"Why is their flag at half-mast, do you suppose?"

"Is it? So it is. It wasn't half an hour ago."

"Are you sure of that?" Wrinkling her brows, Rhoda said, "Something about the war, maybe."

Pamela said, "I'll turn on the radio."

It warmed up gibbering a Lucky Strike commercial. Pamela turned the dial.

". . . and Chief Justice Stone is now on the way to the White House," said an announcer's smooth voice, in professional dramatic tones troubled with real emotion, "to administer the oath of office to Vice President Harry Truman. Mrs. Eleanor Roosevelt is flying to Warm Springs, Georgia —"

"God save us, it's the PRESIDENT," Rhoda exclaimed. She threw a hand to her forehead, knocking her hat askew.

The news was scanty. He had suddenly died of a stroke at his vacation home in Georgia. That was all. The announcer talked on and on about reactions in Washington. Rhoda gestured at Pamela to shut it off. She dropped in an armchair, staring. "Franklin Roosevelt DEAD! Why, it's like the end of the world." She spoke very hoarsely. "I knew him. I sat beside him at dinner at the White House. What an utter CHARMER he was! Do you know what he said to me? I'll never forget it as long as I live. He said, 'Not many men deserve a wife as beautiful as you, Rhoda, but Pug does.' Those were his words. Just being NICE, you know. But he certainly looked at me as though he MEANT it. Dead! Roosevelt! What about the war? Truman's a NOBODY. Oh, what a nightmare!"

"It's ghastly," Pamela said, her mind racing across world strategy to discern whether this might delay Pug's return to Washington.

"Hack said he left some booze here," Rhoda said.

"There's lots."

"Well, you know what? The hell with that tea. Give me a good drink of straight Scotch, will you, dear? Then I'll just go home."

Pamela was pouring the drink in the kitchen when she heard sobs. She hurried back into the living room. Rhoda sat amid the empty boxes and crates and trunks, streaming tears, her hat crooked, with the Warren album open on her lap. "It's the end of the world," she moaned. "It's the end."

* * *

96

The Bitter End

(from "Hitler as Military Leader" by Armin von Roon)

Brief Joy

On 12 April when the news of Roosevelt's death came, I was out inspecting Berlin's defenses, mainly to ascertain for Speer how far along the demolition preparations were. Returning to the bunker, I could hear the sounds of rejoicing echo up the long stairs. I walked in on a celebration complete with champagne, cakes, dancing, music, and happy toasts. Amidst all the joy and wassail Hitler sat smiling around in a dazed benign way, holding his left hand with his right to still the trembling. Goebbels himself deigned to greet me, hobbling up and waving a newspaper. "Only cheerful faces here tonight, my good General! It's the big turnabout at last. The mad dog has croaked."

That was the tenor of the party. Here was the break Germany was waiting for, the "miracle of the House of Brandenburg" all over again, the deliverance of Frederick the Great by the Russian empress's death, 1945 version. This was quite a success for the astrologers. They had been predicting a grand deliverance in mid-April.

Of course the Russians under Zhukov were massing along the Oder, at one point only thirty-five miles from the bunker; and Eisenhower was marching to the Elbe; and southward the Anglo-Americans were breaking apart our lines in Italy; and another great Russian force under Konev was grinding through the Balkans to race Zhukov and the Americans to Berlin; and the skies over the city were raining bombs day and night. Our war production had virtually ceased. Our forces everywhere were running out of ammunition and gasoline. Millions of refugees from east and west were clogging the roads, bringing Wehrmacht movements to a standstill. Trains were being shunted here and there by the SS, blocking up the railroad system. But in the atmosphere of the cement molehole under the Chancellery, what did all that matter? It had become a place of dreams and fantasies. Any excuse for optimism was inflated into a "big turnabout," though nothing ever equalled the brief glee over Roosevelt's death.

Next day the Red Army secured Vienna, and that let some gas out of the balloon. Yet on that very day as Speer and I sat discussing the grave demolition problem in Berlin, the Nazi labor administrator Ley came bubbling up to announce that some German back yard genius had just invented "the Death Ray!" It was as simple and cheap to manufacture as a machine gun. Ley had seen the plans himself, and prominent scientists had analyzed the apparatus for him. This was the big turnabout, if Speer would only start mass-producing the thing at once. With a straight face Speer appointed Ley on the spot "Commissioner of Death Rays," with full authority to commandeer all German industry in Speer's name for production of the wonder weapon. Ley went off drivelling happily, and we got back to our painful discussion.

This whole swindle of "wonder weapons" and "secret weapons" was a trial for Speer, and for me once I became his liaison to OKW. Generals, manufacturers, bigwig politicians, and ordinary people would approach me with a nudge and a wink. "Isn't it about time the Führer unleashed the secret weapon? When will it happen?" My own wife, the daughter of a general and an army wife to the core, pathetically asked me this herself. So far had Goebbels spread this cruel delusion through "leaks" and whispering campaigns, just to keep the bloodshed going and the Nazi cancer flourishing.

The Party Takes Over

By 1945 that cancer had metastasized all through the Fatherland. Party fools and plug-uglies like Ley permeated the state and military structures. The Waffen SS had become a rival army, absorbing the best new troops and equipment. In January Hitler actually appointed Heinrich Himmler to command Army Group Vistula, facing the brunt of the Red Army breakthrough in the north. Of course the result was disaster. Himmler's idea of generalship was to execute officers who failed to hold hopeless positions he had ordered held. Later he threatened to execute their families, too. The bridges and villages in his area were festooned with the hanging bodies of German soldiers, labelled cowards or deserters.

Naturally, all this National Socialist "inspiration" only reduced further the waning capability of our forces. The Russians quickly broke through Himmler's front to the Baltic, cutting off much of our German power in East Prussia and Latvia. Only Dönitz's splendid evacuation by sea, a forgotten rescue much greater than Dunkirk, saved those forces and much of the civilian population. Himmler meanwhile, as has been subsequently revealed, was secretly making his own peace feelers through Sweden, and simultaneously conducting fantastic negotiations to release surviving Jews for a big ransom.

At last, much too late, Hitler sent General Heinrici to relieve this incompetent brute. Meanwhile, however, Hitler too was showing his true Nazi colors. When the Americans in a brilliant dash captured the Remagen bridge, he flew into a tantrum and ordered four fine officers shot for failing to blow up the bridge in time. One of them, as it happened, was my own brother-in-law. In such circumstances one's oath of loyalty was quite a burden.

Speer versus Hitler

As staff liaison to Speer, I found my loyalty tested to the limit, for I was caught squarely between him and Hitler in the matter of demolition. The Führer was decreeing a "scorched-earth policy" in the face of the advancing enemy, east and west. In Berlin, essential services were to be totally demolished by our own explosives. Everywhere the Wehrmacht in retreat was to blow up bridges, railroads, waterways, highways, and leave a "transportation desert"; we were to flood the coal mines of the Ruhr, dynamite the steel plants, the electric and gas works, the dams, and in effect render Germany uninhabitable for a hundred years. When Speer ventured to object, Hitler simply shouted that the Germans had shown themselves unfit to survive anyway, or some such obdurate and merciless nonsense.

Speer was as dedicated a Nazi as any of them. There was something doglike about his squirming deference to Hitler that always disgusted me; nevertheless he was a master of modern technology, and responsibility for the nation's war production had forced him to keep his sanity. He knew that the war was lost, and he risked his neck for months to foil Hitler's demolition orders. Sometimes he wheedled his way out of them by arguing that we would soon need all those bridges and other facilities, to support the Führer's brilliant plans for counterattacking and regaining the lost territory. At other times he fudged his orders, authorizing a bridge or two blown up and leaving the rest of an area intact.

Unfortunately, this double-dealing backed up to me, because I had to handle the generals who received Hitler's orders. My job was to induce delays in carrying them out. After the execution of the four Remagen officers, these generals became harder to convince. Then at the situation conferences I had to exaggerate the demolition that had been done, and prevaricate about the rest. I was risking my head, as Speer was. The Führer was so far gone, however, in his dream world, that with luck one could wriggle through each conference by answering a perfunctory question or two.

Besides, I was not alone now in lying to him. These conferences in April had become war games on paper, with no relation to the frightening realities outside the bunker. Hitler pored over the maps, ordered phantom divisions moved about, commanded big counterattacks, argued over minor withdrawals, just as in the old days, but none of it was actually happening. We were all in a tacit conspiracy to humor him with soothing pretenses. Yet his person continued to command our unswerving loyalty. Jodl and Keitel issued streams of methodical realistic orders to deal with the collapsing situation into which German honor had led us. Of course it could not go on. Reality had to come crashing into the dreamland.

The Blowup

On the twentieth of April, during the lugubrious little birthday party for Hitler, Jodl told me that I was to leave at once and set up a skeleton OKW North in conjunction with Dönitz's staff. Our land communications were about to be cut in two by the juncture at the Elbe of the Americans and the Russians. Our military orientation therefore had to shift at a right angle; instead of facing west and east, we would now have a northern and a southern "front"! Words cannot convey the gloomy eeriness of all this at the time. So I missed the historic blowup at the situation conference on the twenty-second, which led to Hitler's decision to die in Berlin, instead of flying to Obersalzberg to carry on the war from the southern redoubt.

In my operational analysis of the battle for Berlin, I describe in detail the events of the twenty-second, turning on the phantom "Steiner attack." For once Hitler could not be put off with soothing lies, because Russian shells were falling on the Chancellery and shaking the bunker. He had ordered a big counterattack from the southern suburbs under SS General Steiner. The staff had assured him, with the usual wealth of mendacious detail, that the attack was on. Well, then, he demanded, where was Steiner? Why weren't the Russians being driven back?

When he was at last brought face to face with the truth that there was no Steiner attack, Hitler threw a fit of rage so horrible that nobody present could write or talk coherently about it thereafter. It seems to have been the last eruption of a dying volcano; a frightening explosion that left the man a dull burned-out shell, as I myself later saw; a three-hour screaming fit about the betrayal, treachery, and incompetence all around him that had frustrated his genius, lost the war, and destroyed Germany. Then and there he made his decision for suicide. Nothing could alter it. The result was a big exodus next day from the bunker. Jodl and Keitel went northwest to meet up with Dönitz, and most of the Nazi entourage scuttled off westward into one hole or another. *Sauve qui peut!*

My Last Talk with Hitler

I saw Hitler once more, on the twenty-fourth. Things were becoming very confused in this period. I received a peremptory summons by telex from Bormann, the repulsive toad who was Hitler's shadow and appointments secretary, to report to the Chancellery. The Russians had the city surrounded, the air was thick with their fighters, their artillery made rings of bright fire, but with luck one could still fly over their lines at night and land near the Chancellery on the East-West Axis boulevard, which had been marked with red lanterns. Not caring much what happened to me, I found a young Luftwaffe pilot who regarded the thing as a sporting challenge. He got hold of a small Stork reconnaissance plane, and flew me in there and out again. I will never forget coming in over the Brandenburg Tor in the green glare of Russian star shells. That pilot is now, incidentally, a well-known newspaper publisher in Munich.

Hitler received me in his private chambers. He questioned me closely about Dönitz's headquarters at Plön, the efficiency of his staff, the communications with the south, and the state of Dönitz's spirits. Perhaps he was making up his mind about the succession. It was after one in the morning, and I was desperately weary, but he was wound up, and he talked on and on. His eyes were glazed, his face doughy white with purple streaks. He hunched down in an armchair, rolling a stubby pencil in his left hand.

Glowering at me from under his eyebrows, he disclosed that Speer, that very day, had confessed to him the sabotage of his demolition orders in the past months. "You are implicated, and you deserve to be treated accordingly," he said, in a nasty snarling tone full of the old menace. For an unpleasant moment I thought I had been summoned to be shot, as had happened to many of my comrades-in-arms, and I wondered whether Speer was still alive. Hitler went on, "However, I've forgiven Speer because of his service to the Reich. I forgive you because, contrary to the nature of your whole damned breed, and despite the lapses that have not once escaped me, you have on the whole been a loyal general."

This led into the threadbare tirade on how the German General Staff had lost the war. Hitler could not converse at all. He had certain monologues which at a cue he would play out again and again, like phonograph records or an actor's repertoire. That is why, though he had a sharp mind and a certain coarse wit, all the memoirs quite truly describe his company as stupefyingly boring.

Beginning with the assertion that he had been betrayed, let down, and doublecrossed by us ever since 1939, this soliloquy reviewed the entire war in astonishing detail, rehashing his favorite grievances against the military, from Brauchitsch and Halder to Manstein and Guderian, the whole tragic procession that had taken the blame for his blunders. His grand strategy for the war, as he described it, could not possibly have failed except for the incompetence and treachery of our General Staff. In every disagreement he had been proved right and the generals wrong; the invasion of Poland, the attack on France, the hold-or-die order in Russia in December 1941, and all the smaller tactical disputes and disappointments he treasured in his unusual memory, right down to the Steiner attack.

That is my final impression of "Hitler as Military Leader" — a maundering paranoiac in an underground shelter in Berlin which shuddered under the blast of Russian shells, explaining for the thousandth time how our nation's catastrophe had been everybody else's fault but his; how he, its absolute ruler who had run the war first to last, had never made a mistake.

In the document that turned up after the war as his last Will and Testament, he blamed the Jews. In this tirade he blamed our General Staff. But to the last, one thing remained perfectly clear to him: Adolf Hitler himself had never made a mistake.

· · ·

My long labor draws to a close. I have, I believe, in the course of my operational analysis, given this strange historic figure due credit for his positive qualities. All writings about him tend to end in contradiction because the authors write of "Hitler" as though he were one person. But there was more than one Hitler.

The early Hitler, as I have written, was undeniably "the soul of Germany." He fully expressed our people's vigorous yearning for a place in the sun, and for a healthy German culture uncontaminated by the poisons of Asiatic communism, Western materialism, and the weak negative aspects of Judeo-Christian morality exposed by Friedrich Nietzsche. His domestic policies brought prosperity and tranquillity. His foreign policies brought diplomatic victories over the world's strongest nations, our recent conquerors. When he led us to war, against the forebodings of our General Staff because we were far from ready, our nation won magnificent military triumphs. I have acknowledged his flair for adventurist opportunities in military strategy. None of this can be denied.

But at Stalingrad the later Hitler was born. This was another person, an insane monster. He more and more revealed himself as such, as adversity stripped away the glamour of the early Hitler, the protean masks he devised fell off one by one, and he dwindled to the broken jabberer I last glimpsed in the bunker.

In passing my own final judgment on the man, I must suspend the military historian's critical detachment, and speak from a soldier's heart.

His manner of death laid bare his character. A general may fall on his sword when the battle ends, a captain may go down with his ship, but a head of state is different. Was this the act of a head of state in wartime — to desert his office in the hour of his nation's greatest agony; to leave his disasters and his crimes for others to liquidate; to shoot his dog, poison his mistress, and seek Lethe at the muzzle of a pistol? His apologists call it "a Roman death." It was the death of a hysterical coward.

Napoleon in defeat behaved like a proper head of state. For two decades he had made all Europe run red with blood. Yet he faced up to his conquerors, accepted his fate, and purged France of his personal guilt. He was a soldier. Hitler was not, though he talked endlessly about his service in the trenches.

The unconscionable Nuremberg trials proved nothing but our foes' frustrated rage at the escape of Hitler from their hands. This vengeful and unjust farce condemned a whole nation for the deeds of one vanished man, and hanged and imprisoned the generals who were honor bound to obey him. Had Hitler abdicated, let Dönitz surrender, and offered himself to the fury of the victors, such a show of dignified courage would have done much to redeem his failures. Had he done so, I would not now be writing from a prison cell; of that I am convinced. As a master demagogue Hitler tricked his way to absolute power in Germany; then, as our Supreme Warlord, he betrayed our trust.

Epitaph

We are too vigorous a nation not to recover in time. However badly we lost, the German spirit strides on. All modern military strategy, as well as the world's hopes for an adequate energy supply, now turn on nuclear fission, a discovery of German science. Americans have walked on the moon, propelled there by an improved German V-2 rocket, in a program administered by German brains. The Soviet Union dominates Europe with its German-organized Red Army, administered on the German model. Captive German science and engineering have equipped Russia to confront the U.S.A. with intercontinental missiles armed with atom bombs.

In world politics, Hitler's brew of nationalism plus socialism — with its revolutionary egalitarian propaganda, terror apparatus, and one-party dictatorship — is the worldwide political trend. It governs Russia, China, and most developing countries. Perhaps it is nothing to be proud of, but such is the fact. The ideas of the great German philosopher Hegel, popularized and twisted by the converted German Jew Karl Marx, are becoming a new Islam.

In the arts, the Western perverters of form and beauty only echo the avant-garde abstraction and corruption of the Weimar Republic in the 1930s. They are doing nothing now that our clever decadents did not do half a century ago, in the period of anarchy that brought on the Hitler regime.

We Germans have been the bellwether people of the twentieth century, with our triumphs and our tragedies. Though we lost our gallant bid for world empire, our great marches to the Atlantic, the Volga, and the Caucasus will shine forever in the chronicles of war.

But one historical fact we can never live down: that at the apogee of our national strength we gambled our destiny, and shot our bolt, for the sake of a common poltroon. Napoleon lies in the splendid tomb of the Invalides, a world shrine. Hitler ended as a mess of charred carrion in flaming gasoline. Only Shakespeare could write the appropriate epitaph for him:

Nothing in his life became him like the leaving it.

TRANSLATOR'S NOTE: *In Roon's view the early "Dr. Jekyll" Hitler made it to Stalingrad. There he turned into "Mr. Hyde." I am sure Roon meant this. Stalingrad occurred at the end of 1942. By then Hitler had led his people to commit virtually all the crimes for which the world execrates National Socialist Germany. However, he was still winning the war. He became "an insane monster," by Roon's lights, when he began to lose. — V.H.*

* * *

97

WHAT startled Pug Henry most was seeing the President stand up. To come on this small new man at Roosevelt's seat in the Oval Office was itself unsettling, but Truman's bouncy walk around a desk cleared of the familiar clutter gave Pug the queer sensation that the flow of history had left him stranded in the past; that reality was becoming dreamlike, and that this perky little "President" in a double-breasted suit and bright bow tie was some sort of imposter. Harry Truman shook hands briskly, told his secretary to buzz him the moment Mr. Byrnes arrived, and invited Pug to sit down.

"I need a naval aide, Admiral Henry." The voice was tart, high, businesslike, the tone flat, midwestern, abrasive; the other American pole from Roosevelt's creamy Harvard accent. "Now, Harry Hopkins and Admiral Leahy have both recommended you. Would you like the job?"

"Very much, Mr. President."

"You're hired. That does our business. Wish all the transactions in this office were that simple." President Truman uttered a short self-conscious laugh. "Now it's in the nature of things, Admiral, that the military and the President don't see eye to eye on lots of things. So let's get that straight right from the start. Who will you work for — me, or the Navy?"

"You're my Commander-in-Chief."

"Good enough."

"However, if I think you're wrong in a disagreement with the Navy, I'll tell you so."

"All right. That's what I want. Just remember that the military can be wrong, too. Very wrong!" Truman emphasized his words with short chops of both hands. "Why, the day after I was sworn in, the Joint Chiefs gave me a briefing on the war. Six more months to lick Germany, they said, and another year and a half to beat Japan. Well, here's old Hitler dead or disappeared, and surrender talks under way, and it's been all of three weeks. Hey? How about that? Will the Joint Chiefs be just as far off about the Pacific? You've just come from there."

"That sounds like an Army estimate."

"Now exactly what does that mean? And just remember I'm a field artillery man."

"General MacArthur projects long land campaigns, Mr. President. But the submarine blockade and the destruction from the air should make the Japs quit sooner than that."

"Why, they're fighting like devils on Okinawa."

"They do fight hard. But they'll run out of the wherewithal."

"Without our invading Honshu?"

"That's my judgment, Mr. President."

"Then we won't need the Russians' help to finish the war out there?"

"No. I don't think so."

Resting both hands on the desk before him, Truman stared through glittering glasses at the admiral. Pug's short assured answers were instinctive returns of the hard straight quizzing. He did not know how else to handle it. This man's style was not Roosevelt's at all. FDR would first have made or elicited some mild jokes, inquired about Pug's family, put him at ease, and made him feel that they might chat all day. Like a new ship's captain, Truman seemed not quite the real thing because of the change in look and manners. But no matter how long in office he would never acquire Roosevelt's lordly authority. That seemed plain.

"Well, I hope you're right," Truman said.

"I can be as wrong as the Joint Chiefs of Staff, Mr. President."

"What about that big Jap army on the Chinese mainland?"

"Well, sir, you cut off an octopus's head, and the arms go kind of limp."

A natural smile softened the President's stiff expression and relaxed the tight mouth. He sat back, clasping his hands behind his head. "Say, what's the matter with those Russians, anyway, Admiral? You've had duty there. Why don't they stick to their agreements?"

"Which agreements, sir?"

"Why, any agreements."

"In my experience they usually do."

"Is that so? Well, you're dead wrong, right there. Stalin agreed at Yalta to hold free elections in Poland, and that's a serious commitment. Now they're handpicking all the candidates, so as to force in that puppet Lublin government of theirs. Figure they can get away with it because their army's occupying Poland. Churchill's up in arms about that, and so am I. I told Molotov just how I felt about it last week. He said he'd never been talked to like that in his life. I said, 'Keep your agreements and you won't get talked to like that!' "

Truman looked and sounded comfortable now, and quite pleased with himself. As he talked, Pug Henry had flashing memories of the devastated landscape in the Soviet Union, the trips with General Yevlenko, the ruins of Stalingrad, the burned-out German and Russian tanks, the corpses; memories too of trying to deal with Russians, of drinking with them, of hearing their songs and watching them dance. Harry Truman was a straight-shooting fellow from Missouri. He expected everybody else to behave like prosperous, unbombed, uninvaded, straight-shooting fellows from Missouri. Quite a gap. Roosevelt had understood that gap, and had bridged it long enough to win the war. Maybe nothing more was possible with the Soviet Union.

"Mr. President, you've got Russian experts to advise you on that. I'm not one. I don't know the language of the Yalta agreements. With the Russians, if there's a single loophole in the language of an agreement, they'll drive a truck through it. That much you can count on."

A buzzer, and a voice: *"Mr. Byrnes is arriving, Mr. President."*

Truman stood up. Again it surprised Pug. This would take getting used to. "I'm told you've just been married."

"Yes, Mr. President."

"I suppose you'll want a few weeks for your honeymoon."

"Sir, I'm prepared to report for duty now."

Again the smile. Roosevelt's world-famous smile had been more spectacular, but Pug was beginning to like Truman's better. It was genuine, with no trace of condescension. Here was a simple smart man, and he was the President, after all; that showed in the confident natural smile. He was still somewhat ill at ease in the presidency, not an unlikable trait. "Well, very good. The sooner the better. Is your bride a Washington lady?"

"No, sir. An Englishwoman." Truman blinked. "Her father was the British war correspondent, Alistair Tudsbury."

"Oh, yes. The fat man. He interviewed me once. He stuck to the truth in that article. Didn't he get killed in North Africa?"

"Yes."

"I'll look forward to meeting her."

Playing with her gloves, Pamela was strolling along the sunny tulip beds near the old Dodge she had acquired. The uniformed White House guards were watching her swaying walk. When she waved the gloves at the admiral, they took their eyes off her. Her look was affectionate and subtly inquiring.

"Where to now?" he said. "That thing at your embassy?"

"If you're free, darling. And if you don't mind."

"Let's go."

She drove out of the gate and around toward the north in the old too-quick way, with jerky stops and fast starts at the lights of Connecticut Avenue. The traffic was heavy, the gasoline fumes choking through the open car windows. Again the feeling stole over Victor Henry of being stranded in the past. On Connecticut Avenue what was different from 1939? Franklin Roosevelt had kept the war from this untouched avenue, this untouched capital, this untouched land. Had he been too successful? Did these contented people swarming in automobiles up and down Connecticut Avenue have any idea of what war was? The Russians knew, and the future required the toughest realism about war.

"Penny for your thoughts," Pamela said to her silent husband, with a jackrabbit start away from a red light at Dupont Circle.

"I'd be overcharging you. Tell me again what this embassy shindig is about."

"Oh, just a little reception. Our press corps, the British purchase mission, and such."

"But what's the occasion?"

"Frankly, so that I can show you off." She gave him a sidewise glance. "Okay? Mostly my friends will be there. Lady Halifax is curious to meet you."

"Okay."

Pamela took his hand as she drove, and twined cool fingers in his. "It isn't every little British popsie, you see, who hooks herself an American admiral."

"And the naval aide to the President." Pug had held out long enough. By now Rhoda would have asked him.

The grip on his hand tightened. "That's what it was about then. Are you pleased?"

"Well, the alternative was BuOrd or BuShips again. You'll enjoy this more. So will I."

"How did he strike you?"

"He's no Roosevelt. But Roosevelt's dead, Pamela."

Victor Henry was clearly on display at the party. Pam walked around the embassy garden on his arm, introducing him. For all the British nonchalance with which he was greeted in the sparse little gathering, the studied avoidance of stares or questions, he felt himself measured by all eyes. Thirty years ago, Rhoda had dragged her Navy quarterback to a luncheon of her Sweetbriar classmates. Some things did not change much. Pamela in her flowered frock and cartwheel hat was enchanting to look at, and her proud glow was a little comical to Pug, and a little sad. He did not think himself much of a prize; though he cut a better figure than he perhaps realized, with his South Pacific tan and his banks of battle-starred campaign ribbons on dress whites.

Lord and Lady Halifax moved genially about among their guests. Pug kept watching this tall bald gloomy man who had spent so much time with Hitler during the Munich debacle, and right up to the outbreak of the war. There he stood, this man of history, holding a glass and making chitchat with ladies. Lord Halifax caught Pug's eye and walked straight up to him. "Admiral, I believe Sumner Welles told me about you, long ago. Didn't you see

Hitler in 1939, with the banker your President sent over on a peace mission?"

"Yes. I was naval attaché in Berlin then. I translated."

"He wasn't easy to deal with, was he?" Halifax said morosely. "Anyway, we've done for him at last."

"Could he have been stopped before the war, Mr. Ambassador?"

Halifax looked thoughtful, and spoke straightforwardly. "No. Churchill's wrong about that. We made mistakes, but given the mood of our people and the French there was no stopping him. They thought war was a thing of the past."

"A misimpression," Pug said.

"Rather. Pamela is a lovely woman. Congratulations, and good luck." Halifax shook hands, smiled a shade wearily, and walked off.

Driving back to the apartment, Pamela remarked, "Lady Halifax says you're rather a lamb."

"Is that good?"

"The accolade."

Back at Peters's apartment Pug showered, and with the smell of a broiling steak drifting through the open bedroom door, he put on old gray slacks that fitted loosely, much to his satisfaction; an open white shirt, a maroon pullover, and moccasins. It was his customary off-duty dress of peacetime days. He heard the tinkle of ice in a jug. In the living room Pamela, wearing a plain dress and apron, handed him a martini. "My God, I can't get used to the sight of you like this," she said. "You look thirty."

Pug growled, "I don't function like thirty," and sat down with his drink. It was a glancing comment on the bedchamber: exquisite joy for him, and he hoped for her, but nothing record-breaking in the newlywed line. Her reply was a throaty laugh and a caress on his neck.

Soon they sat facing each other in the breakfast nook; they ate all their meals there because the dining room was cavernous. They drank red wine, and ate with great gusto, and said many foolish and wise things, laughing almost all the time. Pug was quite reconciled in such moments to being out of the war, though at other times he had qualms about having hung up his arms too soon.

The telephone rang. Pamela went out to the living room to answer it, and came back looking very sober. "It's Rhoda."

The instant fear stabbed through Victor Henry's mind: *bad news about Byron.* He hurried out. Pamela heard him say, "Good God!" Then: "Wait a minute, let me get a pencil. Okay, go ahead. . . . Got it. No, no, Rhoda. I'll see to this myself. Of course, and I'll let you know."

Pamela stood in the doorway. He was picking up the telephone again and dialling. "Darling, what is it?"

Mutely he handed her the scrawl on the telephone pad. *Natalie Henry German internee hospitalized Army facility Erfurt condition critical malnutrition typhus American Red Cross Germany.*

Three days out from Guam, Byron received the message on the Fox schedule. Several submarines equipped with FM sonar were heading for some final training in Guam waters, and then for a wolf-pack penetration of the Sea of Japan. He could not break radio silence. Those were three long days for Byron. Coming into Guam, a mountainous gardenlike island breaking out in a rash of Navy construction and bulldozed roads, Byron paced the forecastle while Philby brought the vessel alongside. He leaped before the *Barracuda* tied up, and trotted across the decks and gangways of the submarine nest, and all the way to the communications office. No further messages for him; no quick way to get in touch with his father. "You can try a personal," said a sympathetic watch officer, "but we're loaded with urgent and operational priority traffic. The kamikazes are raising hell at Okinawa. A routine message won't hit the sked for maybe two weeks."

Still, Byron sent the dispatch:

FROM: CO BARRACUDA
TO: BUPERS
PERSONAL RADM VICTOR HENRY WHAT ABOUT LOUIS

The yeoman brought to his cabin the mail from the fleet post office. Amid all the official stuff lay a letter from Madeline. This was as rare an event as a total eclipse of the sun, and ordinarily Byron would have ripped it open on sight, but he went at the Navy correspondence instead, taking work like aspirin to dull his agitation.

What about Louis?

However worrisome the report on Natalie, she was alive, and in American hands. The silence about his son was doubly disturbing, since the boy was evidently not with her. German captivity had hospitalized her with "malnutrition and typhus." What had it done to a three-and-a-half-year-old child?

After dinner in the wardroom, at which he ate so little and looked so glum that his officers kept exchanging glances, he shut himself in his cabin with Madeline's letter.

Los Alamos, New Mexico
April 20, 1945

Dear Briny —

Sorry I threw you. I thought I'd get to San Francisco during your overhaul. Truly I did. I tried, but I lead a very strange and complicated life nowadays. Letters out of here are censored. I can't say much about it, but coming and going isn't all that simple. And Sime is working his fool head off day and night, and I guess I felt guilty about leaving him, and so I just let the whole thing slide. I'm fine, and all's well. No baby in sight, if you're curious; not while we're up on this weird hill cut off from the world, no thanks.

Now about Dad and Mom. The main reason I wanted to come to San Francisco was to have all that out with you. You're so misinformed and wrong-headed that it's pitiful. Dad's just come back to Washington and yes, he's going to marry Pam Tudsbury, just a quiet private ceremony. I thought of flying there to be with him, poor lonely man, but it isn't in the cards. I only hope she makes him happy. There's no reason she shouldn't, if she really loves him. The age difference doesn't matter. He's the best man alive.

Your resentment of that match is plain dumb. You don't know certain facts, and here they are. Remember Fred Kirby, the big tall engineer you all met in Berlin? Well, he got a job in Washington after that, *and he and Mom had a wild two-year affair.* Surprised? It's true. Mom wrote Dad and asked for a divorce. I don't know all the details, but after Warren died she took it back, and they patched things up. Then when he went to Russia she got into this big romance with Colonel Peters, and that was the end. Whether *they* had an affair, too, I don't know, and don't much care. Mom's all set now.

But Dad did not have an affair with Pamela Tudsbury, not that I'd condemn him if he had. Good God, what's the matter with you? It's *wartime.* I know he didn't, because Mama and I got very swozzled one night, when he was off in the Soviet Union and Colonel Peters was falling for her. Mom was all confused and upset, and just spilled everything. Said she'd hurt Dad so bad that the marriage was finished, even though he was sticking it out and had never reproached her, never even mentioned Kirby's name. Frankly I think Mom was choked by Dad's forbearance. Pamela told Mom in Hollywood that she and Dad had had an innocent romance, and that after Warren's death she was bowing out. She did, too.

You are an impossible fellow. Where did you get your fossilized morality from? Dad's from another generation, and it's understandable in him, but at that he's more tolerant than you. I confess you did me a favor in your quaint way, when you knocked out Hugh Cleveland's bridgework. God, was that ever hilarious. If you'd been any less stern I'd have dragged on and on with Hugh — he kept promising to get a divorce and marry me, you know, that was what *that* was all about — but a fat toothless man was just too much. And so, bless your neanderthal heart, I broke free in time to marry Sime Anderson, by the skin of my teeth.

Well, now *I'm* spilling more than I should, but when I do take up a pen once in seven years it just runs. I'll stop now because I have to cook dinner. Admiral ████, no less, is coming, and that's quite an honor around here. Let's hope the roast doesn't burn. I do have the crappiest stove. Everything here is tacky and make-do. Most of the scientists' wives here are older and smarter than little Madeline, but thanks to my home training I cook better than most, and my showbiz background goes for something, too. Some of these big brains even like Hugh Cleveland.

Oh, Briny, I hope Natalie and your boy are all right! That war in Europe is folding up. You'll hear something very soon, I'm sure. I have painful memories of a mean thing or two I said about Natalie. She intimidated me, she was so beautiful and seemed so dignified and brilliant. And you were being pretty mean about Cleveland then. There's a church here and I do go on Sunday, which is more than Sime does, and I pray for your wife and kid.

I hope I've straightened you out about Dad. Don't you know that he worships the ground you walk on? He'd have done ANYTHING to keep your good opinion, except say a word against Mom. He'll go to the grave without doing that. You and I have an incredible father, as we once had an incredible brother. Mom is — well, she's Mom. She's all right.

Good hunting, darling, and good luck.

Love,
Mad

The name of the admiral had been neatly cut from the letter, leaving a rectangular hole.

Byron went ashore that night to the officers' club and got very drunk. Next morning he was on the bridge as the flotilla put out to sea for a training exercise, then he went to his cabin and slept for twenty-four hours, while Philby accumulated experience maneuvering underwater by the sound of gongs.

Two weeks later, the admiral who was so hot on the FM sonar held a farewell luncheon for the skippers of the wolf pack. Some Navy nurses came, too; to add glamour, as he put it. The Guam nurses were a tired beaten-down lot, what with the casualties pouring in from Okinawa, and the sexual demands of hordes of young servicemen, fended off or yielded to; but they smirked and giggled dutifully with the submarine captains. "You fellows are sailing to finish the job we started," shouted the admiral in his little speech, "to sink everything that floats and flies a Jap flag!"

Byron knew that the admiral meant well, and had even asked Nimitz in vain for permission to go with the wolf pack. But the whole FM caper was unnecessary, in his view. He had penetrated the Sea of Japan two years ago with Carter Aster in the *Moray*, via La Pérouse Strait. They could enter the same way now, probably at less hazard than through the Tsushima Strait mines. They were planning to leave that way, after all. But the FM sonar had been developed with much trouble, expense, and scientific ingenuity; and the admiral was damned well going to use it. Nobody was asking Byron's opinion. He had convinced his crew that he would get them through the mines; few sailors had transferred, and none had deserted.

The wolf pack sailed, and reached Japan without incident, seeing no shipping whatever on the way. Transiting the mine field was a long tense misery. The FM sonar, dubbed by the sailors, none too affectionately,

"Hell's Bells," rang for fish, kelp beds, temperature gradients, and mine cables, with fine changes in tone. Byron bypassed the danger for the most part, by creeping along at maximum charted depth, below the antisubmarine mines that set off the bells at a hundred feet. The riskiest moment came when he surfaced, just once, to be sure where he was. He took quick bearings, satisfied himself that his submerged dead reckoning wasn't being thrown off by the current, and proceeded. On two occasions, mine cables grated slowly along the clearing wires, all the way down the hull. Nasty minutes, but that was the worst of it.

His patrol sector was in the southeast, so he had to wait while the rest of the wolf pack crawled north into station. The thick Jap traffic ran peaceably past his periscope, showing lights at night, moving unescorted by day, like shipping in New York harbor — small passenger vessels, coastal cargo carriers and tankers, assorted small craft, even pleasure sailboats. He saw no warships. When the slaughter began at a scheduled hour, Byron was holding a clumsy little freighter in his sights. He turned the periscope over to Philby, who neatly and exuberantly torpedoed the victim.

All in all, over the two weeks of the pack's assault, the *Barracuda* sank three ships. On the last two, in 1943, Aster would have scorned to expend torpedoes. All the torpedoes worked quite well now. The traffic dwindled after the first sinkings alarmed the Japs. Targets became scarce, and Byron crept here and there off the west coast of Honshu, admiring the pretty landscape.

At the rendezvous in La Pérouse Strait, eight of the nine submarines showed up. The wolf pack left in a welcome fog. Once clear of aircraft search range, they ran for Pearl Harbor on the surface, exchanging cheerful notes on their scores, and worried inquiries about the missing *Bonefish*. The *Barracuda* resumed copying Fox, but nothing came in for Byron. Entering port on July fourth, the flotilla encountered no jubilation, no ceremony. Byron went straight to the telephone office and put in a call to his mother, not knowing where his father was. It went through quickly, but there was no answer.

ComSubPac's operations officer jumped up to throw his arms around Byron when he came into the office. "Hey, Byron! Christ, what a sweep!"

"Bill, I request relief."

"*Relief!* Are you out of your mind? Why?"

The operations officer sat down and heard the story out, chewing his lips and looking hard at Byron. His comment was tentative and cool. "That's rough. But look here, your wife may be home by now. Maybe she's got your boy, too. Why don't you find out first? Don't go off half-cocked like this. You're on your way to a great record."

"I've made my record. I request relief, Bill."

"Sit down. Stop pounding my desk. That isn't necessary." Byron was in fact slamming his fist on the glass top.

"Sorry." Byron dropped in a chair.

The operations officer offered him a cigarette. Taking a confidential tone he began to reveal surprising secrets. Russia was coming into the war. Sub-Pac had the word. MacArthur was going to land in Japan; first on Kyushu, then Honshu. The Sea of Japan was going to be zoned off between U.S. forces and the Russians. So it would be a whole new ball game. The only fat pickings left were in the Sea of Japan, and ComSubPac wanted to pour on the Hell's Bells forays, and really clean up while he could. "The submarines have won this war, Byron, you know that. But no job's done until it's over. You're doing superbly. Lady Aster would have been proud of you. Don't walk away from a fight."

"Okay," Byron said. "Thanks."

He was not angry at the operations officer. The man's purpose in life was fat pickings. He went to the office of the admiral, the enthusiast for FM sonar, and got right in. Byron calmly described to the admiral his talk with the operations officer.

"Admiral, here it is," Byron said. "You may want to court-martial me for desertion, or you may not. I'm going to see my wife, and find my son if he's alive. Please give me orders to enable me to do this. I've tried to serve. If I find my family, and the war's still on, I'll fly back here and take an FM submarine into Tokyo Bay. I'll take one into Vladivostok, if you want me to."

The admiral, with an annoyed squint and a jutting jaw, said, "You have one hell of a nerve." He began looking through papers on his desk. "Whatever your personal hardship, I don't appreciate being told off like that."

"Sorry, Admiral."

"I have a letter here from CNO, as it happens — now where the devil is it? Here we are. CNO wants a team of experienced skippers to inspect captured U-boats over in Germany. Preliminary reports are that those boats look better than ours. Embarrassingly so. The only way to get the real dope is to go out with the skippers and operate them. Do you know any German?"

"Sir, I speak it well."

"Interested?"

"God, I'll be so grateful, Admiral!"

"Well, you have the operational background. You'll have to qualify your relief on the FM sonar first. Give him a week of runs in the dummy field off Molokai."

"Aye aye, sir. Thank you and God bless you, Admiral."

"Say, Byron, how did your FM sonar perform?"

"Magnificently, sir."

"Greatest thing since canned beer," said the admiral.

98

THE usual pile of mail after a patrol lay on Byron's bunk, including a heavy manila envelope from his father. Byron pounced on it. A handwritten letter was clipped to the bulky sheaf of papers inside.

14 June 1945

Dear Byron:

I know you're out on operations, so I've opened your mail from Europe. Here it is, as of now. In case this envelope goes astray, I've made facsimiles. Natalie's story fills Pamela and me with horror. Horror is too weak a word. We still can't grasp that an American girl went through these things, but it seems she just got caught in the mill.

Here in the U.S.A. the true facts are only now starting to sink in. General Eisenhower brought the press into Buchenwald, Dachau, Bergen-Belsen, and all those places. The papers have been full of the pictures and the accounts. Natalie's survival shows her stamina, and perhaps the effect of our prayers, too. But prayer didn't help the millions who got massacred. The decisive thing was that this man Rabinovitz's outfit was working in Thuringia. That I call miraculous intervention. I believe that's why she's alive. His letter gives the details.

For a long time Pamela's been asking me, "What's this filthy war all about? Why did your son have to die? What have we achieved?" Now it's clear. The political system that could perpetrate such foul deeds had to be wiped off the planet. It was damned powerful, too. The combined strength of the Russians, the British, and ourselves barely contained the thing. It could have overrun the earth. Because the Japs made league with it, we had to crush Japan too. Warren died in a right and great cause. I know that now, and I will never think otherwise.

Your little boy was well many months after he was taken out of Theresienstadt, since Natalie saw that snapshot of him on the farm outside Prague. Don't give up hope. The search may take a long time. If you want to telephone me, I'm at the White House, office of the Naval Aide. That's my new job. Evenings, Republic 4698 is our apartment number. Pam joins me in sending love,

Dad

Below this, on a single sheet of paper with an Army Medical Corps heading, Byron read these few typed words:

20 May 1945

Dear Byron:

I am a little better. Berel came to Theresienstadt and got Louis last July. Then later I received a picture of him on a farm outside Prague. He looked well. Avram says they will find him. I love you.

Natalie

(Dictated to Nurse Emily Denny, First Lieutenant USANC)

The shaky signature was in green ink.

Avram Rabinovitz's long typed letter on flimsy onionskin paper was signed with the same pen.

17th May 1945

Dear Byron:

I speak better than I write English, and I am also very busy. So I will make this short and give you what happened. The important thing is that she is over the typhus. Now she has to build up, she is in very poor condition. The interviewer from the War Refugee Board was a stupid woman so Natalie sounds stupid in the affidavit. Her mind is now clear and she talks nicely, but she cries a lot, and she does not like to talk about what happened. She ran a fever for three days after the interview. That is not being allowed any more. She has asked me to write to you. As you will see, her handwriting is unsteady and she is weak. Also she does not want to remember and write things down.

To make it short, I am based in Paris with a rescue organization, I won't go into too many details. We are cleaning up the Nazi wreckage, putting the Jews who are wandering homeless and starving into camps, in order to get their health back and go to Palestine. It is terrible work. When Germany was falling apart the SS didn't know what to do with the Jews they had not yet killed. It all happened too fast to kill them all and cover up the camps, although they tried. They marched them around or moved them sealed in trains, no orders, no destination, no food or water, and when the Americans or the Russians came the Germans just ran and left the Jews where they were, I don't know how many thousands of them like that, all over Europe. Our people found Natalie in a train that came from Ravensbrück which was a women's concentration camp, and was stalled in a forest outside Weimar, just standing there. Probably it was heading for Buchenwald. Natalie was under the train, lying on the railroad bed. She crawled out because women were dying all around her in the car. I was with a different unit, we talked on the telephone at night and they told me they had found a woman under a train who said she was an American. A lot of Jews claim they are Americans to get better treatment. These fellows couldn't talk English, so I drove over from Erfurt, never expecting to find your wife, God knows, but even stranger things have happened to me in this work. She was not very recognizable, skin and bones, and she was delirious, but I knew her and besides she kept talking about Louis and Byron. So I went to the American Army HQ and told them we had an American woman. This was in the middle of the night, and they sent a field ambulance for her right away. The treatment the army gave her is marvelous since she is an American.

They are trying to move her to Paris and I think they will succeed. There is a fine American hospital there in which Natalie worked for a while. The administrator remembers her and although it's crowded he is willing to take her in. However, the red tape is tremendous, for instance the army officials are still trying to get her a new passport, but all that will be all right. Now about your son there is really no news. You will read in the affidavit how they got separated and Natalie did the right thing. That was very brave. However, it is not easy in Prague, because the Russians are occupying it, and they are not cooperative. Still, our people have been checking around Prague with no results yet. Just before the Russians arrived there was a lot of disorder in Prague, an uprising, Germans killing communists and so forth, and when the Germans retreated they looted a lot of the farms around there and set fire to them, so there is no telling what happened. Chances are your boy is certainly alive, but finding him is "looking for a needle in a haystack." The homeless Jewish children are a problem in themselves, hundreds of thousands of them are roaming Europe, and some of them have become savages, wolves, their parents were killed and they learned to live by stealing. What the Germans did will never be repaired enough. Big card indexes are being assembled in Paris and Geneva by Red Cross, UNRRA, the Joint, and other organizations, but so far it is only a drop in the bucket. I have given the information on your son to our people who visit the files but they are swamped. It will take time. So that is the story, and I am sorry it is not a pleasanter one, but Natalie is alive at least, and she is beginning to look better. She has no appetite or she would recuperate faster. Letters from you would be a big help, and you had better send them to me, I'll see that she gets them. Be as cheerful as possible when you write, tell her you believe your son is alive and we will find him.

Yours truly,
Avram Rabinovitz

The affidavit was a smudged faint single-spaced carbon copy, so poorly written that Byron could hardly follow some of it. It sounded nothing like Natalie. The interviewer obviously had taken notes, then typed them up in a hurry. The story began in peacetime in Siena, describing her entrapment by the Pearl Harbor attack and everything that had followed. Up to their meeting in Marseilles Byron knew most of it. The long Theresienstadt narrative, especially the scene in the SS cellar, made him cringe (though she or the interviewer had omitted the sexual details). The heading of the affidavit said there had been three interview sessions, but from Theresienstadt onward the narrative became sparse. The last words about Aaron Jastrow were oddly flat.

When we were getting on the train, an official of the Transport Section separated us. I never saw my uncle again. I heard later that all the *Prominente* in the transport went to the gas. He was an old frail man. They only picked a few young strong ones to live, so I am sure he is dead.

That was all. Her Auschwitz narrative after that rambled: how it felt to have her head shaved and a number tattooed on her arm, the rags she was given to wear, the conditions in the women's brick blockhouse, the sanitary and feeding arrangements. A man called Udam, a friend from Theresienstadt, had obtained work for her in the warehouses of looted Jewish belongings. She had been assigned to the section of children's toys, taking apart dolls, teddy bears, and other stuffed toys in search of money and valuables, then restoring them for sale or distribution to children in Germany. The most vivid passage in the whole affidavit described a punishment at this job.

I got very good at disassembling and reassembling the toys. There were mountains of them, and every one meant a little child murdered by Germans. But we stopped thinking about that, we were numb. Many toys were identical, from the same manufacturers. Occasionally we found something; jewelry, gold coins, or currency. There was pilfering, of course. We risked our lives when we kept things, because we were searched every afternoon when we left Canada. The warehouse section was called "Canada" because Polish people think Canada is a land of gold. We had to steal, because we could trade loot for food. Whose property was it, after all? Not the Germans'! I was never caught, but once I was beaten almost to death for nothing at all. I took apart a worn-out, ragged teddy bear with nothing in it. There was just no way to repair it. It fell to pieces in my hands. The supervisor was a loathsome Greek Jewess who strutted around dressed like an SS woman guard. She hated me because I was an American, and she jumped on the chance to make an example of me. She reported me to the SS. I was sentenced to twenty strokes of the cane on my bare skin, "for criminal destruction of Reich property." The sentence was carried out at a roll call of all the workers in Canada. I had to bend over a wooden frame naked, and an SS man flogged me. I have never known such agony. I fainted before he was finished. Udam and some of my women friends carried me to the blockhouse, and Udam got me into the hospital. Otherwise I would have died from loss of blood. I couldn't walk for a week. I found out how strong my constitution is, however. I healed up and went back to the same job. The Greek woman acted as though nothing had happened.

The narrative passed into incoherent generalities about life in Auschwitz: the smell from the mass graves where the bodies were being dug up and burned, the black market, the exceptional steadfastness of Jehovah's Witnesses, a kindly SS man, having an affair with a woman in the blockhouse, who had brought them much good food. It described the rumors of the Russian approach, the distant sound of the guns, the three-day march of thousands of women in the snow to a railroad terminal, the train ride in open coal cars to Ravensbrück. She had gone to work in a clothing plant, living in terror of Ravensbrück medical experiments, of which she had heard rumors even in Auschwitz. Field whores for the Wehrmacht, also for SS brothels, were recruited from this camp; but about this her comment, even filtered through the interviewer's mind and style, was pitiful.

That was one threat that did not concern me. I had once been considered attractive, but a few months in Auschwitz had fixed that. Anyway, they only recruited the youngest, freshest Jewish girls. Some of the Hungarian Jewesses who came to Ravensbrück were really delicate beauties. Moreover, in Ravensbrück I had no way to get extra food, and I was shrinking to a skeleton, as I am now. Also, I would never have passed the physical examination because of the scars. The German men wouldn't have enjoyed the sight.

In April thousands of us were loaded onto trains. We had heard that the war was almost over, that the Russians and the Americans were about to join hands, and we were counting the days and praying to be liberated. But the Germans stuffed us into sealed cattle cars and sent us God knows where, with no provision whatever for food, water, or health. Typhus had already broken out in the camp. On the train it spread like wildfire. I remember very little after I left Ravensbrück. Just how horrible it was on that train, worse than anything yet. My car was a morgue, practically all the women were dead or dying. They tell me I was found under the train. I don't know how I got there, and I can't understand how it is that I'm still alive. If anything kept me going all these months it was the hope of one day seeing my son again. I think that was what gave me the strength to get out of that car. I can't tell you who opened the door or how I got out. I have told you all I know.

99

ASTRONG child can hold fifteen pounds or so in his two hands, if the stuff is not bulky: say, two lumps of the man-made heavy element, plutonium. If the child holds the lumps far apart nothing will happen. If he can clap his hands together very fast, and if he is a big-city child, he can make a "critical mass" and kill a million people; that is, in theory. Actually no child can move his arms that fast; at worst he would make a fizzle that would kill him and cause a bad mess. One needs a device that zips the little lumps together, for an atomic blast and a city-destroying blaze of light.

This fact of nature, so earthshaking in 1945, is an old story now. Still, it remains strange and frightening. We prefer not to think about it, as we prefer not to think much about the attempted murder of all the Jews in Europe by a modern government. But these are ruling realities of the way we live now. Our little earth contains traces of the primordial ash of creation, powerful enough in handful sizes to wipe us all out: and human nature contains traces of savagery, persisting in advanced society, which can use the stuff to wipe us out. These were the two fundamental developments of the Second World War. Obscured in the dustclouds of conventional history kicked up by the great battles, they emerge plain as the dust settles. Whether in consequence the human story, like this tale, is entering its last chapter, nobody yet knows.

●　●　●

To go on with the story: the first time plutonium lumps blazed out in the new light, Sime Anderson was there.

"What on earth?" Madeline muttered, as the alarm went off at midnight.

"Sorry," he said with a yawn. "Duty calls."

"Again? Gawd," she said, turning over.

Sime dressed, went out in the chilly drizzle, and boarded one of the crowded buses carrying selected Los Alamos scientists and engineers to the test ground. Sime had been a small fish in the vast effort, but he was going with Captain Parsons, a large fish. The weather was bad for the test. For a while postponement was in the air, and the hour of the shot was delayed. The spectators waited in the dark many miles from the test tower, drinking coffee, smoking, and making airy or somber conversation. Nobody knew exactly what was going to happen when the shot went off. There was some talk, not quite persiflage, about the possibility that the explosion would set fire to the atmosphere, or start a process that would disintegrate the earth. There was nervous talk too about a fizzle.

That was the point of the test. Laboratory tickling of uranium 235 had satisfied the scientists that it would certainly go off with a proper bang in a critical mass; and so it did over Hiroshima without a previous test. The trouble was that the mountainous Manhattan Project had labored and brought forth only one small lethal mouse of U-235, just enough for a single bomb. Plutonium had turned out to be relatively simpler to produce, and there was more of it. But it was touchier stuff. Nobody could be sure whether it would not pre-detonate — that is, fizzle — as the lumps came together. There had to be a test of a device, worked out by the world's best brains, to whisk the lumps into an explosive mass in an eyeblink. The rain and wind abated, and the test went on. It worked. Flying from San Francisco to Washington on a night plane held up by weather, Byron saw the vague flash in the sky to the south, but he thought it was lightning. There were many electrical storms in the American West that morning. His sister, like most Los Alamos wives, slept straight through the test.

It did not look like lightning to Sime Anderson, of course. Standing twenty-five miles away, he saw through dark glasses a glare never before viewed by men on the earth's surface, though they had always seen it burning in the sun and twinkling in the stars. Sime fell on his face. It was instinct. When he got up, the cloud of fire — which reminded Dr. Oppenheimer of the apparition of Vishnu in the *Bhagavad-Gita* — already towered many miles high. A brigadier general and a scientist stood near Sime, paper coffee cups in hand, staring through goggles.

"There's the end of the war," he heard the scientist say.

"Yes," he heard the general say, "once we drop a couple of those on the Japs."

At the Andrews airfield, Pug and Pamela met Byron. After the warm letter Byron had written from Guam, Pug expected a bearhug, but it was his son's embrace of Pamela that gave him the feeling of a won war. Byron hugged and kissed his new stepmother, held her by the shoulders, looked her up and down, and shouted over the roar of a MATS plane just taking off, "You know what? I'm damned if I'm going to call you mama."

She burst into a joyous laugh. "How about Pamela?"

"No change," said Byron. "Easy to remember. Dad, is there any news?"

"Since you called from San Francisco? None."

"When does she go into the convalescent home, did you say?"

"Day after tomorrow."

"I'd like to see Rabinovitz's letter."

"Here it is. There's another one from her."

Byron read his mail as Pamela drove wildly back to Washington. "She sounds better. Dad, I can't get on a plane to Europe. I was on the phone for hours in San Francisco, trying to wangle a priority."

"How much leave have you got?"

"Thirty days. Little enough."

"I'm flying there myself tomorrow."

"Where to?"

"Berlin. Potsdam."

"God, that would be perfect. I have to report to Swinemünde before my leave starts. Can I bum a ride?"

Pug's mouth wrinkled in a reluctant smile. "Let me find out."

Lunch with his mother at Foxhall Road was pleasanter than Byron had anticipated. Brigadier General Peters was not there. (He was, in fact, the general who had spoken at Los Alamos of dropping a couple on the Japs.) Janice showed up in a straight skirt, a plain brown blouse, and glasses, carrying a briefcase. She would not drink. She was working "on the hill" in a summer job, and did not want to get sleepy. She had put on weight, she wore little makeup, and her hair was pulled straight back. She was genially talkative about her plans after law school. When her eyes met Byron's he saw there only alert friendly intelligence. Her snapshots of little Victor, so much like Warren's kindergarten pictures, hurt Byron, but Rhoda made sweet grandmotherly noises over them.

"Mom's drinking too much," Byron said to his father that evening at the apartment.

"She has spells. What do you call too much?"

"Two Scotch-and-sodas before lunch, two bottles of white wine with the chicken salad. She polished off most of the wine herself."

"That's too much. I know she was tense about seeing you. She told me so."

"What about that plane ride?"

"Pack up in the morning and come with me. All they can do is bounce you."

"I haven't unpacked."

A courier in a special plane was rushing papers and pictures from Los Alamos to Secretary Stimson and President Truman in Potsdam, and Pug was going in that plane. This news was not being entrusted to the telephone or telegraph. It was still a secret of secrets. Only a short, enigmatic cable had been sent to the President, announcing the arrival of a healthy "baby," and he had informed Churchill. So these two knew. Most likely Stalin did too, since a leading scientist at Los Alamos was a faithful communist spy. Otherwise it was a secret of secrets. So Byron got rapid transportation to Europe on the courier plane, which turned out to make a great difference. As they say, it's an ill wind.

"There's no reason why he shouldn't be alive," Rabinovitz said. "She got him out of the Germans' hands. She took a hell of a chance, and I give her credit."

"How do I go about finding him?"

"That's another question. Very tough."

They sat drinking coffee at an outdoor café in Neuilly, waiting for Natalie to wake from her afternoon sleep. "Don't go into that with her," Rabinovitz said. "And don't stay too long, not this time. It'll be hard for her."

"We're bound to talk about Louis."

"Keep it vague. Just tell her that you're going to search for him. Twenty-five days isn't much time, but you can make an effort."

"Where's the best place to start?"

"Geneva. You'll find the big card files on kids there, the Red Cross, the Joint, the World Jewish Congress. They're starting a cross-index there, too. After Geneva, Paris. We have some files here. And I can give you a list of the D.P. camps that have a lot of children."

"Why don't I go straight to Prague? He ought to be around there somewhere."

"I went to Prague." Rabinovitz slumped over the coffee like an old man. He needed a shave, and his bloodshot eyes in sunken sockets were puffed almost shut. "I went to all four centers where they've got kids. I checked the card indexes and looked over the four-year-olds. I think I'd have recognized him, though they change a lot in a year and a half. Now as to the farmhouse, the name Natalie had, it's burned down and everything's overgrown and wild. Most of the neighbors are gone. Only one farmer would talk. He said he remembered a little boy, and he said the people weren't massacred, they got away. The Germans looted an empty house. Anyway, that was his story, and there you are. So it's tough. But kids can endure a lot, and Louis is a strong kid with plenty of spirit."

"I'll go to Geneva tomorrow."

Rabinovitz looked at the clock on the wall. "She's awake now. Do you want me to come with you?"

"I think so. Just to start with, you know."

"I can't stay long anyhow. Byron, she said more than once to me that if she ever finds Louis she'll take him to Palestine."

"Do you think she means that?"

Rabinovitz's shrug and look were skeptical. "She's not well yet. Don't get into an argument over it."

They gave their names at the reception desk, and waited in a flowery garden where patients sat about in the sunshine, some dressed, some in bathrobes. She came out and walked toward them with something of the old swing, in a dark dress, her hair cropped short. She was smiling uncertainly. Her legs were thin, her face gaunt.

"Well, Byron, so it's you," she said, holding out her arms. He embraced her and got a shock. Her body felt nothing like a woman's. The chest was almost flat. He was holding bones.

She leaned back in his arms, staring with strange eyes. "You look like a movie star," she said. Byron was wearing his dress whites and ribbons, because, as he had told Rabinovitz, the uniform helped him squelch fools behind desks. "And I look ghastly, don't I?"

"Not at all. Not to me, God knows."

"I should have gone with you in Marseilles." She recited the words dully, a rehearsed apology.

"None of that, Natalie."

She glanced at Rabinovitz, who stood stooped near them, smoking a cigarette. "Avram saved my life, you know."

Rabinovitz said, "You saved your own life. I'll go about my business, Byron."

Jumping at Rabinovitz, Natalie kissed him with much more feeling than she had shown Byron. She said something in Yiddish. Rabinovitz shrugged and walked out of the garden.

"Let's sit down," Natalie said to Byron with effortful politeness. "Your father has written me lovely letters. He's a fine man."

"Did you get any of mine?"

"No, Byron. Not that I remember. My memory is not too good, not yet." Natalie was speaking in a groping manner, almost as though trying to remember a foreign language. Her great dark eyes in shadowed hollows were scared and remote. They sat down on a stone bench by blooming rose bushes. "Not real letters. I dream, you know. I've dreamed a lot about you. I dreamed letters, too. But your father's letters, I know they were real. I'm sorry your parents broke up."

"My father's happy, and my mother's all right."

"Good. Of course, I knew Pamela in Paris. Strange, isn't it? And Slote, what about Slote? Do you know anything about Slote?"

For Byron, this conversation was starting very strangely. Her recent letters had been more affectionate and coherent. Now she seemed to be saying whatever came into her head, to cover fear or embarrassment; nothing that mattered, nothing about Louis, nothing about Aaron Jastrow, nothing intimate, mere forced chatter. He went along with it. He told her at length how Slote had ruined his career trying to get State Department action on the

Jews, and about his end as a Jedburgh agent, what he knew of that from Pamela and his father. Natalie's eyes became more normal as she listened. Some of the alarm faded. "My heavens. Poor Slote, a parachutist! He couldn't have been very good at it, could he? But you see, I wasn't wrong to like him. His heart was in the right place, for a Gentile. I sensed that." She did not know how she brought Byron up short with those words. She was smiling at him. "You really do look so imposing. Were you in much danger?"

"*You* ask *me* that?"

"Well, there's danger and danger."

"I had narrow scrapes, sure. Ninety-nine percent of it was boring dead time. At least when I got in danger I could fight."

"I tried to fight. Maybe it was foolish, but that was my nature." Her mouth quivered. "Well, tell me about your narrow escapes. Tell me about Lady Aster. Is he a big hero now?"

Byron talked of Aster's exploits and his death. She seemed interested, though her eyes sometimes wandered. Then a silence fell between them. They sat in shade, in the fragrance of blooming roses, looking at each other. Natalie said brightly, "Oh, I finally got my new passport. It came yesterday. Lord, that little book looked good, Byron!"

"I'll bet."

"You know, I managed to keep my old one for a long, long time. Right into Auschwitz. Would you believe it? But there they took all my clothes away. One of the girls in Canada must have found it. She probably traded it for a nice big chunk of gold." Natalie's voice began to shake, her hands to tremble, her eyes to brim.

Byron decided to break through all this. He clasped her in his arms. "Natalie, I love you."

She clutched him with bony fingers, sobbing. "Sorry, sorry. I'm not in good condition yet. The nightmares, the nightmares! Every single night, Byron. Every night. And all the drugs, I get needles night and day —"

"I'm going to Geneva tomorrow to start looking for Louis."

"Oh, are you? Thank God." She wiped her eyes. "How much time have you got?"

"About a month. I'll come to see you, too."

"Yes, yes, but the main thing is to look for him." She seized his arm with both thin hands, her dark eyes widened, and her voice became an intense hissing whisper. "*He's alive. I know he is. Find him.*"

"Darling, I'll give it the old college try."

She blinked, then laughed as she used to do. " 'The old college try.' How long since I've heard that!" She put her arms around his neck. "I love you, too. You're much, much older, Byron."

A nurse approached them, pointing at her wristwatch. Natalie looked surprised and rather relieved. "Oh, dear, already?" When she stood up, the nurse took her elbow. "But we haven't even talked about Aaron, have we? Byron, he was brave. The worse things got, the braver he was. I could tell you about him for hours. He wasn't the man we knew in Siena. He became very religious."

"I always thought he was, the way he wrote about Jesus."

Leaning on the nurse, Natalie frowned. At the entrance she again hugged him weakly. "I'm glad you're here. *Find him.* Forgive me, Byron, I'm in lousy shape. I'll do better next time." She kissed his mouth with dry rough lips, and went in.

"Lousy." The American slang word, ringing so naturally, slightly reassured Byron. He hunted up the chief doctor, a prissy old Frenchman with a Pétain-like white mustache. "Ah, but she is doing very well, Monsieur. You have no idea. After the liberation, I worked for a month in the camps. Wreckage! Wreckage! Dante's Inferno! She will get well."

"She wrote me about scars on her legs and back."

The doctor's face twitched. "Not pretty, but ah, Monsieur, she is a lovely woman, and she is alive. The scars, *eh bien,* plastic surgery, and so forth. It is more a question now of mental scars, of restoring her flesh, and her spiritual balance."

After two weeks of combing the Geneva cards, and visiting displaced persons' camps, broken by one trip to see Natalie, Byron despaired. He was swamped. In an index book of his own he had compiled the leads under three categories:

> *Possible.*
> *Remote.*
> *Worth a Try.*

There were over seventy "possibles" alone; four-year-olds scattered over Europe, who from hair and eye color and languages understood might be his son. He had gone through some ten thousand listings of homeless children. No card showed a Louis Henry — nor a "Henry Lewis," a brainstorm which had come to him during a sleepless night and sent him running around to all the card index centers again. Following up these leads might take months. Years! He had days. Rabinovitz was not expecting Byron when he showed up in the shabby office on the Rue des Capuchins over a very ill-smelling restaurant.

"I'm going to Prague," Byron said. "Maybe it's a long shot, but I'm starting over."

"Well, all right, but you'll butt up against stone walls. The Russians are tough and uninterested, and they're in complete control."

"My father's in Potsdam. He's President Truman's naval aide."

Rabinovitz straightened up with a squeak of his swivel chair. "You didn't mention that."

"I didn't think it was relevant. He's had duty in the Soviet Union, and he speaks Russian in a fashion."

"Well, that could help you get around Prague. If the Military Governor receives word from Potsdam about you, the wheels will turn. At least you'll satisfy yourself whether he's there or not."

"Why should he be anywhere else, if he's alive?"

"He wasn't there, Byron, when I searched, though God knows I could have missed something. Go ahead, but talk to your father first."

Rabinovitz worked with an organization taking Jews into Palestine in defiance of the British immigration laws. Briefly relaxed at the first exposure of the Nazi horrors, these laws had tightened up again. He was grindingly busy. Natalie Henry was not a main concern of his. He felt compassion for her, and a wistful trace of the old hopeless love; but compared with most Jews in Europe, she was now out of danger, a convalescing cossetted American. With the arrival of Byron he put her from his mind, and did not visit her again. When a couple of weeks later the telephone rang in his Paris flat at two in the morning, waking the three men he shared it with, and the operator said, "Hold for London, please," his sleepy mind ran through many dealings he was having with London, most of them illegal and risky. He did not think of the Henrys.

"Hello. This is Byron."

"Who?"

"Byron Henry." The postwar connection to London was not good. The voice wavered. ". . . him."

"What? What did you say, Byron?"

"I said I've got him."

"What? You mean your son?"

"He's sitting here in my hotel room."

"Goddamn! He was in England?"

"I'm bringing him to Paris day after tomorrow. There's a lot of red tape still, and —"

"Byron, what's his condition?"

"Not so hot, but I've got him. Now, will you tell Natalie, please? Let her get used to the idea that he's found. Then when she sees him it won't upset her too much. Or him. I don't want him upset. Will you do that?"

"With the greatest pleasure in my life! Listen, what's the story? What shall I tell her?"

"Well, it's complicated. The RAF flew a bunch of Czech pilots back to

Prague right after the war. A British rescue outfit got them to bring homeless kids back in the empty planes. I found this out last week in Prague. Pure luck. The records there are unbelievably rotten, Avram. I heard a guy in a restaurant talking about it, a Czech pilot, telling it to a British girl. It was luck. Luck or God. I followed it up and I've got him."

It was raining hard in the morning. Rabinovitz telephoned the convalescent home, and left a message for Natalie that he would come at eleven with important news. She stood waiting for him in the lobby when he arrived, shaking rain from his trench coat.

"I thought you must have gone to Palestine." Her face was taut. Her hands were clasped in front of her, the knuckles white. She was filling out; there were hints of curves under the dark dress.

"Well, I am going next week."

"What's your important news?"

"I heard from Byron."

"Yes?"

"Natalie." He held out his hands to her, and she seized them. "Natalie, he found him."

His grip on her hands was not firm enough. She grinned crazily and dropped to the floor.

The strong child brought the two little lumps together over Hiroshima that day. The new light seared more than sixty thousand people to cinders. The lone plane headed back to Tinian, radioing, *Mission successful.*

The controversy will go on while human life survives. Some of the arguments:

The Japanese would have surrendered anyway, without being bombed by radioactive lumps. They had sent out peace feelers. The American code-breakers knew from their diplomatic messages that they wanted peace.

Yet the Japanese rejected the Potsdam ultimatum.

Truman wanted to keep the Russians out of the Japanese war.

Yet at Potsdam he did not waive Stalin's commitment to attack Japan. He had Marshall's advice that the Russians could not be kept from attacking if they wanted to.

An invasion of Japan would have caused far more Japanese deaths, let alone American ones, than the Hiroshima casualties. The Japanese army leaders controlled the government, and their plan to fight invasion called for a bloody scorched-earth battle to the last like Hitler's. The bomb gave the Emperor leverage to force a decision for the peace party in his councils.

Yet the B-29 bombardments and the submarine blockade might have done so too, in time to scrub the invasion.

If not, and if the Soviet Union had materially aided an invasion, the

Red Army would have occupied part of the land. Japan might have ended partitioned like Germany.

Yet whether the Japanese think the deaths at Hiroshima were an acceptable price for warding off that possibility is far from certain.

This much is certain.

The uranium weapon had been perfected barely in time for use in the war. There were two bombs available; only two, one of U-235, one of plutonium. The President, the cabinet, the scientists, the military men, all wanted the bomb rushed into combat. Harry Truman later said, "It was a bigger piece of artillery, so we used it." There were worried dissenting voices: few, and futile. The momentum of all that expenditure of money, manpower, industrial plant, and scientific genius was irresistible.

War scares nations, by murdering their people, into changing their politics. Here was the ultimate expression of war, after all, a child's handfuls murdering a city. How could it not be used? It did scare a nation into changing its politics overnight. "Greatest thing in history!" said President Truman at the news of Hiroshima.

Greatest thing since canned beer.

Byron came through the plane gate leading by the hand a pale small boy in a neat gray suit, who walked docilely beside him. Rabinovitz recognized Louis, though he was taller and thinner.

"Hello, Louis." The boy looked solemnly at him. "Byron, she's fine today, and waiting. I'll drive you there. Did you hear about the atom bomb?"

"Yes. I guess that's the end, all right."

Walking to Rabinovitz's very decrepit Citroën, they made the common talk being repeated all over the world, about the terrific news.

"Natalie says she's ready to go home, now that you've got him," Rabinovitz said as they drove. "She thinks she'll recuperate better there."

"Yes, we talked about that last time I saw her. Also she has property. Aaron's publisher has been in touch with her. There's quite a lot of money. And that villa in Siena, if it's still standing. His lawyer has the deeds. It makes sense for her to go back right now."

"She won't go with you to Germany, that I can tell you."

"I don't expect her to."

"How will you feel there yourself?"

"Well, the U-boat men are just professionals. I've got a job to do with them."

"They're murderers."

"So am I," Byron said without rancor, stroking Louis's head. The boy sat on his lap, soberly looking out of the window at the sunny flat green fields outside Paris. "They're the conquered enemy. We study their equipment and methods as soon as possible after surrender. That's standard."

Silenced for a minute or so, Rabinovitz said abruptly, "I think she'll stay in America, once she goes there."

"She doesn't know what she'll do. First she has to get well."

"Would you come with her to Palestine?"

"That's a tough one. I know nothing about Zionism."

"We Jews need a state of our own to live in, where we won't get massacred. That's all there is to Zionism."

"She won't get massacred in America."

"Can the Jews all go there?"

"What about the Arabs?" Byron asked after a pause. "The ones that are there in Palestine already?"

Rabinovitz's face as he drove became grave, almost tragic. He looked straight ahead, and his reply came slowly. "The Arabs can be grim, and they can also be noble. Christian Europe has tried to kill us. What choice have we? Palestine is our traditional home. Islam has a tradition to let the Jews live. Not in a state of our own, not as yet, that's a new thing in their history. But it will work out." He glanced toward Louis, and caressed the quiet boy's cheek. "With a hell of a lot of trouble first. That's why we need him."

"Will you need a navy?"

Rabinovitz briefly sourly smiled. "Between you and me, we have one. I helped organize it. A goddamn small one, so far."

"Well, I'll never be separated from this kid, once I'm demobilized. That much I know."

"Isn't he very quiet?"

"He doesn't talk."

"What do you mean?"

"Just that. He doesn't smile, and he doesn't talk. He hasn't said a word to me yet. I had a time getting him released. They had him classified as psychologically disabled, some such fancy category. He's fine. He eats, he dresses and cleans himself, in fact he's very neat, and he understands anything you say. He obeys. He doesn't talk."

Rabinovitz said in Yiddish, "Louis, look at me." The boy turned and faced him. "Smile, little fellow." Louis's large eyes conveyed faint dislike and contempt, and he looked out of the window again.

"Let him be," Byron said. "I had to sign more damned papers and raise more hell before I could pry him loose. It's lucky I got there when I did. They're shipping about a hundred of these so-called psychologically disabled kids to Canada next week. God knows if we could ever have traced him there."

"What's the story on him?"

"Very sparse. I can't read Czech, naturally, and the translation of the card was pretty poor. I gather he was picked up in a woods near Prague, where the Germans took a lot of Jews and Czechs and shot them. The bodies were just lying around. That's where somebody found him, among the bodies."

As they walked into the sunny garden of the convalescent home, Byron said, "Look, Louis, there's Mama."

Natalie stood near the same stone bench, in a new white frock. Louis let go of his father's hand, walked toward Natalie, then broke into a run and leaped at her.

"Oh, my God! How *big* you are! How heavy you are! Oh, Louis!"

She sat down, embracing him. The child clung, his face buried on her shoulder, and she rocked him, saying through tears, "Louis, you came back. You came back!" She looked up at Byron. "He's glad to see me."

"Sort of."

"Byron, you can do anything, can't you?"

His face still hidden, the boy was gripping his mother hard. Rocking him back and forth, she began to sing slowly in Yiddish,

> *Under Louis's cradle,*
> *Lies a little white goat.*
> *The little goat went into business —*

Louis let go of her, sat up smiling on her lap, and tried to sing along in Yiddish, in a faltering hoarse voice, a word here and there,

> *"Dos vet zein dein baruf,*
> *Rozhinkes mit mandlen —"*

Almost at the same moment, Byron and Rabinovitz each put a hand over his eyes, as though dazzled by an unbearable sudden light.

In a shallow, hastily dug grave in the wood outside Prague, Berel Jastrow's bones lie unmarked, like so many bones all over Europe. And so this story ends.

It is only a story, of course. Berel Jastrow was never born and never existed. He was a parable. In truth his bones stretch from the French coast to the Urals, dry bones of a murdered giant. And in truth a marvelous thing happens; his story does not end there, for the bones stand up and take on flesh. God breathes spirit into the bones, and Berel Jastrow turns eastward and goes home. In the glare, the great and terrible light of this happening, God seems to signal that the story of the rest of us need not end, and that the new light can prove a troubled dawn.

For the rest of us, perhaps. Not for the dead, not for the more than fifty million real dead in the world's worst catastrophe: victors and vanquished, combatants and civilians, people of so many nations, men, women, and children, all cut down. For them there can be no new earthly dawn. Yet though their bones lie in the darkness of the grave, they will not have died in vain, if their remembrance can lead us from the long, long time of war to the time for peace.

Historical Notes

The history of the war in this romance, as in *The Winds of War*, is offered as accurate; the statistics, as reliable; the words and acts of the great personages, as either historical, or derived from accounts of their words and deeds in similar situations. Major figures of history do not appear in times and places not historically true.

World Holocaust, the military treatise by "Armin von Roon," is of course an invention from start to finish. Still, General von Roon's book is offered as a professional German view of the other side of the hill, reliable within the limits peculiar to that self-justifying literature. Except where directly challenged by Victor Henry, Roon's facts are accurate, however warped by nationalism his judgments may be.

The reliability of detail in the well-known battles, campaigns, and events of the war — Singapore, Midway, Leyte Gulf, the Tehran Conference, the sieges of Imphal and Leningrad, and the like — will, it is hoped, be evident to the informed reader. The notes that follow deal with little-known or unusual historical elements of the story, and with passages where fact and fiction are especially intertwined.

The exploits of the fictional submarines *Devilfish*, *Moray*, and *Barracuda* are improvisations on actual wartime submarine patrol reports. The death of Carter Aster is based on the famous self-sacrifice of Commander Howard W. Gilmore of U.S.S. *Growler*, for which he was posthumously awarded the Congressional Medal of Honor. Aster, however, is a different and fictional character.

All other Navy vessels in the novel are actual and their movements and actions follow the historical record. All admirals in the Pacific are real personages and are treated like the major political figures. The story of the heavy cruiser *Northampton*, except for the fictitious captains Hickman and Henry, follows its war diary from Pearl Harbor to its sinking at the Battle of Tassafaronga.

The names of the pilots and gunners in the three torpedo squadrons at Midway proved surprisingly difficult to recover and verify, so quickly is the record fading. The rosters printed in the novel are the result of a long search. Any reliable corrections will be welcomed for future editions.

The story of the *Izmir* is a fictionalization of actual illegal voyages of refugees from the Nazis, who reached Palestine in this way or died trying.

"The Wannsee Protocol" is a historical document, and as described in the story, only one copy out of thirty of this top-secret record was preserved, through an accident of bureaucratic overthoroughness. Disclosure of a smuggled photocopy to the American legation in Bern is fictional, as are the characters in the legation.

Americans caught in Italy by the war were interned in Siena, as narrated. Those caught in southern France were first interned in Lourdes, then moved to Baden-Baden, as in the story; and harshly bargained for by the Germans thereafter, for more than a year.

The Comte and Comtesse de Chambrun are real figures; the comte did administer the American Hospital in Paris. The German ambassador in Paris, Otto Abetz, is historical. Werner Beck is a fictional character.

The Joint Declaration of the United Nations in December 1942, which led to the Bermuda Conference, is history. Its text is given in full in the novel. Assistant Secretary of State Breckinridge Long is an actual person, whose conversation and actions are drawn largely from his own writings and his congressional testimony. Foxy Davis is fictitious.

The Bermuda Conference happened as described. The public reaction that gradually ensued, and the establishment of the War Refugee Board, are facts.

The main source for the furor in 1943 over Soviet suppression of Lend-Lease facts is Admiral William Standley's autobiography. This Soviet practice, incidentally, continues to the present day. General Yevlenko is fictional.

"The Declaration of the Three Powers Regarding Iran" (referred to in the text as "The Declaration of Iran") is a historical fact, as is the general outline of how it came about; though of course Victor Henry's conversation with the Minister of the Imperial Court, Hussein Ala — a real person — is invented. General Connolly of the Persian Gulf Command is an actual officer, and the description of Lend-Lease aid to the Soviet Union through that corridor is factual. The fictitious Granville Seaton describes true Persian history.

"The Paradise Ghetto" in Terezin, or Theresienstadt, Czechoslovakia, was known about during the war. Nothing is invented or exaggerated in this account, though the parts played by Natalie and Dr. Jastrow are fictitious. The SS officers are all real, as are the High Elders Eppstein and Murmelstein. The general history of the ghetto is true. The "Great Beautification" for the one visit of neutral Red Cross observers is a well-documented fact, in all its bizarre details, as is the visit itself. A fragment of the film "The Führer Grants the Jews a Town" survives in the Yad Vashem archive in Jerusalem. The making of the film took place as described, but the film was never exhibited.

The scenes in Oswiecim, or Auschwitz, are based on a study of the available documents and literature, as well as on consultations with survivors. These scenes have been meticulously reviewed for authenticity by eminent authorities on this terrible subject. Oswiecim may be forever beyond the grasp of the human mind, now that nothing is left of it but a dead museum. It is hoped that living survivors of Auschwitz, comparing their recollections with this fictional Remembrance, created by one who was not there, will see an honest effort to make the vanished horror live for all the world that was not there.

The march of Soviet prisoners from Lamsdorf to Oswiecim, the episodes of cannibalism, the experimental gassing of these Soviet prisoners of war with Zyklon B to test its efficacy for killing Jews en masse: all these are facts. An important source is the memoir of the Commandant himself, Rudolf Hoess, written while he was awaiting trial after the war. He was found guilty of the mass murders, which he freely admitted, and was hanged in Auschwitz.

The other SS officers are real people, except that Klinger is fictitious. The inspection visit of Himmler, and his viewing of the gassing process from beginning to end, took place as described; in July, however, not in June. The construction of the crematoriums, the general picture of the Auschwitz Interest Area with its industries and agricultural installations, the treatment of prisoners who attempted to escape, the roll calls, "Canada": all facts.

Kommando 1005, the roving German unit that exhumed and eradicated the mass graves, is a matter of history. SS Colonel Paul Blobel is an actual person. The mutiny of Mutterperl is fictitious. The mass escape of some prisoners is improvised out of accounts of such escapes from SS slave gangs.

Berel Jastrow's fictitious journey from Ternopol through the Carpathians to Prague is based on several such incredible journeys, made by Jews who escaped from the death camps with photographic and documentary evidence, and crossed all of Nazi-held Europe to bring the revelation to the outside world; only to encounter the almost universal "will not to believe." The fictitious partisan bands of Nikonov and Levine are derived from existing partisan literature. Reference is made in this passage to some actual partisan bands.

The treatment of the landing craft and atomic bomb programs is factual. There was a conflict over priorities involving a coupling. Victor Henry's part in it is of course fictitious; Dr. Oppenheimer's visit to Oak Ridge is a fictional scene; and Kirby, Peters, and Anderson are fictional characters. It is a fact that Dr. Oppenheimer recommended the very late introduction of the Navy's thermal diffusion system into Oak Ridge, to provide enriched feed for the electromagnetic separation process; and that this made possible the production of one U-235 bomb for use in the war, over Hiroshima. The Nagasaki bomb of plutonium was produced in the Hanford reactors. It is also a fact that no other bombs were available from the Manhattan Project when these two were dropped.

The account of the FM sonar, "Hell's Bells," and of its use late in the war, is factual.

To sum up: the purpose of the author in both *War and Remembrance* and *The Winds of War* was to bring the past to vivid life through the experiences, perceptions, and passions of a few people caught in the war's maelstrom. This purpose was best served by scrupulous accuracy of locale and historical fact, as the backdrop against which the invented drama would play. Such at least was the working ideal.

Herman Wouk

1962–1978